THE WORKS

OF

THOMAS REID, D. D.

NOW FULLY COLLECTED,

WITH SELECTIONS FROM HIS UNPUBLISHED LETTERS

PREFACE,
NOTES AND SUPPLEMENTARY DISSERTATIONS,
BY
WILLIAM HAMILTON

Volume 1

Elibron Classics
www.elibron.com

.

THE WORKS

OF

THOMAS REID, D.D.

NOW FULLY COLLECTED,

WITH SELECTIONS FROM HIS UNPUBLISHED LETTERS.

PREFACE,

NOTES AND SUPPLEMENTARY DISSERTATIONS,

BY

SIR WILLIAM HAMILTON, BART.,

ADVOCATE; A.M. (OXON.); ETC.; CORRESPONDING MEMBER OF THE INSTITUTE OF FRANCE ;
HONORARY MEMBER OF THE AMERICAN ACADEMY OF ARTS AND SCIENCES; OF THE
LATIN SOCIETY OF JENA; ETC.; PROFESSOR OF LOGIC AND METAPHYSICS
IN THE UNIVERSITY OF EDINBURGH.

PREFIXED,

STEWART'S ACCOUNT OF THE LIFE AND WRITINGS OF REID.

VOL. I.

SEVENTH EDITION.

EDINBURGH:

MACLACHLAN AND STEWART.

LONDON: LONGMAN, GREEN, LONGMAN, ROBERTS, AND GREEN.

MDCCCLXXII.

ON EARTH, THERE IS NOTHING GREAT BUT MAN;
IN MAN, THERE IS NOTHING GREAT BUT MIND.

TO
VICTOR COUSIN,
PEER OF FRANCE, LATE MINISTER OF PUBLIC INSTRUCTION,
MEMBER OF THE INSTITUTE, PROFESSOR OF PHILOSOPHY,
ETC., ETC.,
THIS EDITION OF THE WORKS OF REID
IS DEDICATED;
NOT ONLY,
IN TOKEN OF THE EDITOR'S ADMIRATION
OF
THE FIRST PHILOSOPHER OF FRANCE,
BUT,
AS A TRIBUTE, DUE APPROPRIATELY AND PRE-EMINENTLY
TO
THE STATESMAN,
THROUGH WHOM
SCOTLAND HAS BEEN AGAIN UNITED INTELLECTUALLY
TO HER OLD POLITICAL ALLY,
AND
THE AUTHOR'S WRITINGS,
(THE BEST RESULT OF SCOTTISH SPECULATION,)
MADE THE BASIS OF ACADEMICAL INSTRUCTION IN PHILOSOPHY
THROUGHOUT THE CENTRAL NATION OF EUROPE.

ADVERTISEMENT.

November 1846.—The present issue (ending with page 914) contains the whole Works of Reid, hitherto published, with many of his writings, printed or collected for the first time. The text has been collated, revised, and corrected; useful distinctions and supplements inserted; the leading words and propositions marked out; the allusions indicated; the quotations filled up. It contains also the Foot-Notes of the Editor on the texts of Reid and Stewart, and a large proportion (in length) of the Editor's Supplementary Dissertations. There remain the sequel of these Dissertations, the General Preface, and the Indices;—all of which are either prepared, or their materials collected. These (Deo volente) will be comprised in a concluding issue, and title-pages for *two* volumes then given. The Notes and Dissertations have insensibly increased to a size and importance far beyond what was ever anticipated; but the book having been always destined primarily for academical use, the price of the whole will not exceed thirty shillings. Being stereotyped, what additions may be made to any subsequent edition, will be published also apart.

It is proper to state :—that the Foot-notes were written, as the texts passed through the press, in 1837 and 1838; that the Supplementary Dissertations, to the end of D*, were written and stereotyped in 1841 and 1842; the rest being added recently.

[*October* 1863.—In the present edition the errata have been, for the most part, corrected on the stereotype plates; the Indices have been added; and the sequel of the Dissertations has been, so far as possible, completed from Sir W. Hamilton's MSS. For an account of what has been done in this last respect, the reader is referred to the Postscript at the end of the Supplementary Dissertations.]

CONTENTS.

CONTENTS. v

CHAPTER VII.—Conclusion.

B.—ESSAYS ON THE INTELLECTUAL POWERS OF MAN.

ESSAY I.—Preliminary.

ESSAY II.—Of the Powers we have by means of our External Senses.

b

PAGE

C.—ESSAYS ON THE ACTIVE POWERS OF THE HUMAN MIND.

CHAPTER V.—ACCOUNT OF THE REMAINING BOOKS OF THE ORGANON.

CHAPTER VI.—REFLECTIONS ON THE UTILITY OF LOGIC, AND THE MEANS OF ITS IMPROVEMENT.

E.—ESSAY ON QUANTITY.

F.—ACCOUNT OF THE UNIVERSITY OF GLASGOW.

EDITOR'S SUPPLEMENTARY DISSERTATIONS.

(A.)—ON THE PHILOSOPHY OF COMMON SENSE; OR, OUR PRIMARY BELIEFS CONSIDERED AS THE ULTIMATE CRITERION OF TRUTH.

MEMORANDA FOR PREFACE.

[FROM the Advertisement prefixed to this work, it appears that Sir William Hamilton's contributions as Editor were intended to include, in addition to the Foot-Notes and Supplementary Dissertations, a General Preface to the whole. This Preface was never written, and its plan can only be conjectured from a few memoranda marked as intended for it, and some fragments apparently designed to be incorporated with it. The principal of these have been printed below.—ED.]

[*Of the Scottish Philosophy in General.*]

Results of Locke's philosophy—Collins, &c., see Cousin in Vacherot, [Cours de 1819-20, partie 2, Leçon 1.*] Berkeley, Hume — adopted at first by Scottish school; Reid's reaction.

Hume's scepticism proceeds in two momenta.

1°, In shewing that the notions of Cause and Effect, Substance and Accident, which he wishes to make merely subjective, have no *genuine* necessity; (under and after this, but not developed, that even if the necessity be not a bastard one—from custom—it is at best only a legitimate *subjective* one, and without objective validity.)

2°, In shewing that the mind is not conscious of any *real* existence in perception ; that its representations are no guarantee for anything represented (*Idealism.*)

Now Kant and Reid both combated Hume. Kant applied himself to the causal nexus ; Reid to the idealism.

Shew how both were equally intent on shewing that causality is a real necessity of mind. Though both *only subjective,* Kant more articulate.

How, in regard to idealism, Kant confirmed Hume, giving his premises, whereas Reid's doctrine, though confused and vacillating, was a real refutation.

[These memoranda have been partly worked out in a paper printed in the Appendix to the *Lectures on Metaphysics,* vol. i., p. 392 sq. Another aspect of the Scottish Philosophy, in relation to that of Germany, is indicated in the following fragment, which is apparently related to the reference above, p. 793.—ED.]

---

* See also M. Cousin's own edition of these Lectures, Leçon 2.—ED.

It was Jacobi who first in Germany attacked the mediate and demonstrating philosophy of the Leibnitians, and shewed the necessity of immediate knowledge. This he took from Reid.—See Francke, p. 227 sq. Schulze, another great promoter of this.—Ibid., p. 230.

[The purport of this memorandum is explained by the following extracts, translated from Francke's work, Das selbststaendige und reine Leben des Gefuehls, als des Geistes urspruenglichen Urtheils, u.s.w. Leipzig, 1838 : —

"The union of the English and French empiricism with the German logical rationalism produced that maxim of the philosophy of reflection, which maintains that nothing can be admitted as truth which cannot be proved, or logically deduced, from the perceptions of sense ; a position which leads, as a natural consequence, to the scepticism of Hume. On the other hand, Reid, Beattie, and Oswald, advocating the hitherto obscured element of Feeling, maintained that the human mind possesses immediately in consciousness principles of knowledge independent of experience ; and a more cautious attempt was made by Richard Price to shew that the Understanding, or Faculty of Thought, as distinguished from the deductive faculty, is essentially different from the faculty of sense, and is a source of special representations distinct from those of the senses. Yet, on the whole, all these writers, as regards the scientific vindication of their teaching, were compelled to place the foundation of the immediate cognition of the higher truths of reason in a Common Sense ; and the assumption of this pretended source necessarily involved suspicion and doubt as regards the truth of the cognitions derived from it. And so also Jacobi, if

we except the negative, polemical side of
his teaching, wherein he certainly accomplished much, has advanced little or
nothing beyond his English predecessors
in laying a firm scientific foundation for
his own view; though he was the first
among ourselves who, in the controversy
with the disciples of Wolf and other cognate schools, by the employment of the
terms *feeling* and *belief*, directed attention
to the necessity of acknowledging the
importance of immediate cognition and
its consciousness. . . . .

"Although Jacobi's system, on account
of its vacillating language, and still more
on account of its intuitive narrowness and
subjective character, was not fitted to benefit philosophy immediately, it had, notwithstanding, a foundation of truth, which
could not long fail of producing its effect.
Many soon became clearly convinced that
the Kantian philosophy also was liable to
the charge of onesidedness, and failed to
satisfy the requirements of the entire man:
they acknowledged that Jacobi, notwithstanding the enthusiastic vehemence of his
decisions, had seized and brought to light
a principle of our mental life hitherto
marvellously overlooked, the discovery of
which would henceforth fill up a great
void in the culture of the age, and the
recognition of which was indispensable to
the preservation and progress of philosophy. Even men who could not directly
be classed as belonging to the school of
Jacobi, the clearest and most cautious
thinkers, acknowledged the importance of
the distinction between mediate and immediate knowledge, and between the
mediate and immediate consciousness of
it; and although they would not concede
to Feeling an independent significance,
and were unable to assign to it a sure
psychological position, they at least saw
clearly, and proved conclusively, that the
power and efficacy of this Feeling must
be a necessary condition of knowledge
antecedent to all determinate conceptions
and reasonings. Among these men may
be especially mentioned the so-called
sceptic, (who in his later writings is a
natural realist,) G. E. Schulze,[*] Bouter-
wek,[†] and Gerlach.[‡]

"Schulze, indeed, regards the Feelings as
the most obscure and variable phase of the

mental life: he holds them to be incapable
of establishing or proclaiming anything objective, and hence to be useless as principles for the demonstration of truth; but
he repeatedly asserts the existence in the
human consciousness of certain fundamental assumptions, of which, by the constitution of our nature, we are unable arbitrarily to divest ourselves, and which have
a place in all natural science and in moral
and religious convictions. It is true that
Schulze did not penetrate to a complete
insight into the nature of demonstrative
knowledge and transcendental idealism;
and hence, from the position of his natural
objective realism, he is unable to discover
that our ideal convictions can attain to an
equal certainty with the natural conviction
of knowledge based on intuition. Bouter-
wek, adhering more closely to Jacobi's
doctrine, speaks of the consciousness of
the original feeling of truth as the first
witness of certainty in all human conviction; but, like Jacobi, he seems to believe
in a perceptive power of the internal
sense, by which even demonstrative philosophical cognitions may be realised in
consciousness. . . . . Fries is the
first who, by opening a new path of
anthropologico-critical inquiry, has completely and fully succeeded in organi-
cally uniting the immediate products of
Jacobi's philosophy with the results of the
Kantian criticism, and thus in exhibiting
in a clear and scientific light, from the
laws of the theory of man's mental life,
the relation of Knowledge to Belief, of the
natural and ideal aspect of the world, as
well as the important relation between the
feeling and the *conception* of the truth. He
is the first philosopher in whose system
Feeling has won an independent and firmly
established position among the *philosophical* convictions of the reason." [*]—ED.]

Merits of the Scottish School.

Their proclaiming it as a rule, 1°, That
the province of a preliminary or general
Logic (Noology)—the ultimate laws, &c.,
of the human mind—should be sought
out and established; 2°, That once recognised and given, they should be accepted to govern philosophy, as all other
sciences.

With regard to the first, the Scottish
philosophers are not original. It is a
perennis philosophia, gravitated towards

* Psych. Anthropol. ed. 2, § 151, pp. 259, 260;
Encycl. der philos. Wissensch. §§ 39, 115; Kritik
der theor. Philos. i. p. 702-720; Ueber die
menschl. Erkenntniss, § 45-50, pp. 155-174.
† Lehrb. der philos. Wissensch. Apod. p.
15-86.
‡ Lehrb. der philos. Wissensch. i. § 48, p. 48.

* On the relation of the system of Fries to
that of Reid, see below, Note A, p. 798, No. 95;
and the references there given.—ED.

even by those who revolted against it. (See Note A.) The merit of the Scottish school is one only of degree,—that it *is* more consistent, more catholic, and embodies this *perennis philosophia* more purely. [Its writers, however,] are themselves peccant in details, and have not always followed out the spirit of their own doctrines.

[With regard to the second,] Dr Reid and Mr Stewart not only denounce as absurd the attempt to demonstrate that the original data of Consciousness are for us the rule of what *we* ought to believe, that is, the criteria of a relative—human—subjective truth; but interdict as unphilosophical all question in regard to their validity, as the vehicles of an absolute or objective truth.

M. Jouffroy,* of course, coincides with the Scottish philosophers in regard to the former; but, as to the latter, he maintains, with Kant, that the doubt is legitimate, and, though he admits it to be insoluble, he thinks it ought to be entertained. Nor, on the ground on which they and he consider the question, am I disposed to dissent from his conclusion. But on that on which I have now placed it, I cannot but view the inquiry as incompetent. For what is the question in plain terms? Simply,—Whether what our nature compels us to believe as true and real, be true and real, or only a consistent illusion? Now this question cannot be philosophically entertained, for two reasons. 1°, Because there exists a presumption in favour of the veracity of our nature, which either precludes or peremptorily repels a gratuitous supposition of its mendacity. 2°, Because we have no mean out of Consciousness of testing Consciousness. If its data are found concordant, they must be presumed trustworthy; if repugnant, they are already proved unworthy of credit. Unless, therefore, the mutual collation of the primary data of Consciousness be held such an inquiry, it is, I think, manifestly incompetent. It is only in the case of one or more of these original facts being rejected as false, that the question can emerge in regard to the truth of the others. But, in reality, on this hypothesis, the problem is already decided; their character for truth is gone; and all subsequent canvassing of their probability is profitless speculation.

Kant started, like the philosophers in general, with the non-acceptance of the deliverance of Consciousness,—that we are immediately cognisant of extended objects. This first step decided the destiny of his philosophy. The external world, as known, was, therefore, only a phænomenon of the internal; and our knowledge in general only of self; the objective only subjective; and truth only the harmony of thought with thought, not of thought with things; reality only a necessary illusion.

It was quite in order, that Kant should canvass the veracity of all our primary beliefs, having founded his philosophy on the presumed falsehood of one; and an inquiry followed out with such consistency and talent, could not, from such a commencement, terminate in a different result.*

Fichte evolved this explicit idealism—Nihilism.†

Following the phantom of the Absolute, Schelling rejected the law of Contradiction, as Hegel that of Excluded Middle; ‡ with the result that, as acknowledged by the former, the worlds of common sense and of philosophy are reciprocally the converse of each other. Did the author not see that this is a *reductio ad absurdum* of philosophy itself? For, *ex hypothesi*, philosophy, the detection of the illusion of our nature, shews the absurdity of nature; but its instruments are only those of this illusive nature. Why, then, is it not an illusion itself?

The philosophy which relies on the data of Consciousness may not fulfil the conditions of what men conceit that a philosophy should be: it makes no pretension to any knowledge of the absolute—the unconditioned—but it is the only philosophy which is conceded to man below; and if we neglect it, we must either renounce philosophy or pursue an *ignis fatuus* which will only lead us into quagmires. §

[Defects of the Scottish School.]

Scottish school too exclusive—intolerant, not in spirit and intention, for Reid

---

* Œuvres de Reid, Préface, p. clxxxv.—ED.

* Reprinted from *Lectures on Metaphysics*, vol. i. p. 399. From the reference below, p. 746 a, n. *, it appears that this question was intended to be discussed in the Preface.—ED.

† See below, p. 129, n. *, and 796 b.—ED.

‡ See *Lectures on Logic*, vol. i. p. 90.—ED.

§ In the MS. follow references to the two Scaligers, to Grotius, and to Cusa; the last being, through Bruno, the father of the modern Philosophy of the Absolute. All these references are given in full, *Discussions*, pp. 638-641.—ED.

and Stewart were liberal—but from not taking high enough ground, and studying opinions with sufficient accuracy, and from a sufficiently lofty point of view.

On the nature and domain of the philosophy of mind.

Reid and Stewart do not lay it out properly, though their practice is better than their precept. They do not take notice of the difference between mental and physical inquiry—that the latter is mere inductive classification, the former more speculative, secerning necessary from contingent. But an element of thought being *found necessary*, there remains a further process —to ascertain whether it be, 1°, by nature or by education; 2°, ultimately or derivatively necessary; 3°, positive or negative. . . . . A law of nature is only got by general induction; a law of mind is got by experiment—whether we can *not think it;* e. g. cause in objective and subjective philosophy. The progress of the two sciences not parallel—error of Stewart (Essays, p. xiii.*)

An experimental analysis, but of different kinds, is competent to physical and mental science, besides the observation common to both. To mental, the trying what parts of a concrete thought or cognition can be thought away, what cannot.

[*Further developments supplementary to the philosophy of the Scottish school, as represented by Reid and Stewart.*]

[A. *On the Principle of Common Sense.*]

I would, with Leibnitz,† distinguish truths or cognitions into those of *Fact*, or of *Perception*, (external and internal), and those of *Reason*. The truths or cognitions of both classes rest on an ultimate and common ground of a primary and inexplicable belief. This ground may be called by the names of *Common Sense*, of *Fundamental* or *Transcendental Consciousness*,

---

* Coll. Works, vol. v. p. 13. "The order established in the intellectual world seems to be regulated by laws perfectly analogous to those which we trace among the phænomena of the material system; and in all our philosophical inquiries, (to whatever subject they may relate,) the progress of the mind is liable to be affected by the same tendency to a premature generalisation." On this passage, there is the following marginal note in Sir W. Hamilton's copy: "Shew how this analogy is vitiated by the fact that the *most general* facts, being *necessities* of thought, are among the first established. Existence, the last in the order of induction, is the first in the order of ——."—ED.

† Nouveaux Essais, L. iv. ch. 2.—ED.

---

of *Feeling of Truth* or *Knowledge*, of *Natural* or *Instinctive Belief*. This, in itself, is simply a fact, simply an experience, and is purely subjective and purely negative. It supports the validity of a proposition, only on the fact that I find that it is impossible for me not to hold it for true, to suppose it therefore not true—without denying, in the one case, the veracity of consciousness; and, in the other, the possibility of thought; [without presuming] that I am necessitated to hold the false for the true, the unreal for the real, and therefore that my intelligent nature is radically mendacious. But this is not to be gratuitously presumed; therefore the proposition must be admitted. But to apply it to the two classes of truths.

I. Truths of Fact or of Perception (External and Internal.)

Am I asked, for example, how I know that the series of phænomena called the external world or the non-ego exists—I answer, that I know it by external Perception. But if further asked, how I know that this Perception is not an illusion — that what I perceive as the external world, is not merely a particular order of phænomena pertaining to the internal—that what I am conscious of as something different from me, is not merely self representing a not-self — I can only answer, that I know this solely inasmuch as I find that I cannot but feel, hold, or believe that what I perceive as not-self, is really presented in consciousness as not-self. I can, indeed, in this, as in the case of every other truth of Fact, imagine the possibility of the converse—imagine that what is given as a mode of not-self, may be in reality only a mode of self. But this only in imagining that my primary consciousness deceives me; which is not to be supposed without a ground. Now, the conviction here cannot in propriety be called Reason, because the truth avouched by it is one only of Fact, and because the conviction avouching it is itself only manifested as a Fact. It may, however, be well denominated Common Sense, Fundamental or Transcendental Consciousness. Other examples may be taken from Memory and its reality, Personal Identity, &c.

II. Truths of Reason.

Again, if I am asked, how I know that every change must have its cause, that every quality must have its substance, that there is no mean between two contradictories, &c., I answer, that I know it by Reason, νοῦς—Reason or νοῦς being a name for the mind considered as the source, or as the complement, of first principles, axioms, native notions, κοιναὶ or φυσικαὶ ἔννοιαι.

But if further asked, how I know that Reason is not illusive—that this, or that first principle may not be false—I can only answer, that I know it to be true, solely inasmuch as I am conscious that I cannot but feel, hold, believe it to be true, seeing that I cannot even realise in imagination the possibility of the converse. Now, this last ground of conviction, in the conscious impotence of conceiving the converse, is not, I think, so properly styled Reason, which is more of a positive character, as Common Sense, Fundamental Consciousness, &c. This is shewn in the quotations from Locke and Price. Note A, Testimonies, Nos. 51, 78.

[The substance of these remarks on the Principle of Common Sense, has been already printed, in an abbreviated form, in Note A, p. 754. The present fragment, which has the appearance of being an earlier sketch of the same note, has been inserted in this place, as containing a somewhat fuller statement of an important distinction, which is perhaps liable to be overlooked in the brief form in which it was previously published. Though not apparently designed for this Preface, it is sufficiently cognate in matter to the preceding fragments, to be entitled to a place with them. The following fragment, which is marked "Preface," may be regarded as a continuation of the same subject, being a step toward that further analysis of the Truths of Reason, in relation to the Philosophy of the Conditioned, which the Author regarded as his peculiar addition to the philosophy of his predecessors. This analysis will be found further pursued in Notes H and T, and especially in the Philosophical Appendix to the *Discussions.*—ED.]

[B. *Stages in the method of Mental Science.*]

Three degrees or stages in the method of mental science.

1°, When the mind is treated as matter, and the mere Baconian observation and induction applied.

2°, When the quality of Necessity is investigated, and the empirical and necessary elements thus discriminated. (Here Reid is honourably distinguished even from Stewart, not to say Brown and other British philosophers.)

3°, When the necessity is distinguished into two classes—the one being founded on a power or potency, the other upon an impotence of mind. Hence the Philosophy of the Conditioned.

*   *   *   *

[*Testimonies to the merits of the Scottish Philosophy, and of Reid as its founder.*]

1.—PORET.—Manuel de Philosophie par Auguste Henri Matthiæ, traduit de l'Allemand sur la troisième édition, par M. H. Poret, Professeur suppléant à la Faculté des Lettres, et Professeur de Philosophie au Collége Rollin. Paris, 1837.

Préface du Traducteur.—'Il suffit d'avoir une idée de l'état des études en France pour reconnaître que la philosophie écossaise y est aujourd'hui naturalisée. Nous la voyons défrayer à peu près seule l'enseignement de nos colléges; sa langue et ses doctrines ont passé dans la plupart des ouvrages élémentaires qui se publient sur les matières philosophiques; sa méthode sévère et circonspecte a satisfait les plus difficiles et rassuré les plus défiants, et en même temps son profond respect pour les croyances morales et religieuses lui a concilié ceux qui reconnaissent la vérité surtout à ses fruits. Les penseurs prévoyants qui se donnèrent tant de soins pour l'introduire parmi nous ont eu à se féliciter du succès de leur efforts. La seule apparition de cette philosophie si peu fastueuse suffit pour mettre à terre le sensualisme; une doctrine artificielle dut s'évanouir devant la simple exposition des faits; le sens intime fut rétabli dans sa prérogative; les éléments *a priori* de l'intelligence, si ridiculement honnis par Locke et son école, rentrèrent dans la science dont on avait prétendu les bannir, et y reprirent leur place légitime. Cette espèce de restauration philosophique devait avoir ses conséquences: des questions assoupies, mais non pas mortes, se réveillèrent; les limites arbitrairement posées à la connaissance disparurent; la philosophie retrouva son domaine, et de nouveau les esprits s'efforcèrent de le conquérir. En général, le bienfait des doctrines écossaises importées en France, ç'a été d'affranchir les intelligences de tout préjugé d'école et de les remettre en présence de la réalité. Nul doute que ce ne fut là l'indispensable condition de tout progrès ultérieur, et cette condition indispensable, elles l'ont remplie dans toute son étendue. Aujourd'hui même qu'elles ont porté ces premiers fruits, les bons effets de ces doctrines ne sont pas, nous le croyons, près de s'épuiser, et nous regarderions comme un échec à la prospérité des études philosophiques tout ce qui tendrait à en contrarier l'influence.'

2.—GARNIER.—Critique de la Philosophie de Thomas Reid, Paris, 1840.

P. 112.—'Demandez à ce philosophe une distribution méthodique des matériaux qu'il a recueillis, une adroite induction qui des phénomènes nous conduise à un petit nombre de causes, vous ne trouverez ni cette classification, ni cette analyse. Ce n'était pourtant pas la tâche la plus malaisée; et le dépit de lui voir négliger ce facile travail est ce qui nous a mis la plume à la main. Mais ces matériaux innombrables, ces milliers de phénomènes si patiemment décrits, faut-il les oublier? N'est-ce pas Reid qui nous a montré à ne plus confondre les perceptions des différents sens, et en particulier, celles de la vue et du toucher? Malgré quelques contradictions, n'est-ce pas chez lui seul qu'on peut recontrer une théorie raisonnable de la perception? Où trouver une plus savante exposition de la mémoire et des merveilles si variées qui présente la suite de nos conceptions? Ses essais sur l'abstraction, le jugement, et le raisonnement sont encore plus lumineux et plus instructifs que les mêmes chapitres dans l'admirable Logique de Port-Royal, et les savants solitaires ont partagé la faute de regarder ces opérations de l'esprit comme les actes d'autant de facultés distinctes. Enfin, avec quel profit et quel intérêt ne lit-on pas les chapitres sur le goût intellectuel, sur les affections si variées qui se partagent notre âme, sur le sens du devoir et sur la morale? Avec tous ses défauts, l'ouvrage de Reid offrira longtemps encore la lecture la plus instructive pour l'esprit, la plus délicieuse pour le cœur, et la plus profitable pour la philosophie.'

P. 118.—'En présence des constructions fantastiques de l'Allemagne, j'aime mieux les matériaux épars de l'Ecosse. Thomas Reid est l'ouvrier laborieux, qui a péniblement extrait les blocs de la carrière, qui a taillé les mâts et les charpentes : vienne l'architecte, il en construira des villes et des flottes. L'Allemand est l'entrepreneur audacieux qui dans la hâte de bâtir se contente de terre et de paille.'

3.—RÉMUSAT.—Essais de Philosophie, Paris 1842, t. i. p. 250.—'La philosophie de Reid nous paraît un des plus beaux résultats de la méthode psychologique. Plus approfondie, mieux ordonnée, elle peut devenir plus systématique et plus complète ; elle peut donner à l'observation une forme plus rationnelle. Sans doute elle n'est pas tout la vérité philosophique ; mais dans son ensemble elle est vraie, et nous croyons qu'elle doit être considérée par les écoles modernes comme la philosophie élémentaire de l'esprit humain.'

4.—THUROT.—Introduction à l'Étude de la Philosophie, Discours Préliminaire, t. i. p. LXIV. Speaking of Reid's Essays—

'L'érudition choisie et variée qu'il a su y répandre, l'amour sincère de la vérité qui s'y montre partout, et la dignité calme de l'expression en rendent la lecture extrêmement attachante.'

5.—COUSIN.—[Cours d'Histoire de la Philosophie Morale au dix-huitième Siécle, seconde partie, publiée par MM. Danton et Vacherot, Paris, 1840], p. 241 sq.*

'There is a final merit in the doctrine of the Scottish philosopher, which it is impossible too highly to extol. He has done better than ruin the hypotheses which had shaken all the bases of human belief ; in fixing with precision the limits of science, he has destroyed for ever the spirit itself which had inspired them. The philosophy which Reid combated had not understood that there were facts inexplicable, facts which carry with them their own light ; and had therefore gone, in quest of a principle of explanation, into a foreign sphere. It is thus that to explain the phænomena of perception, of memory, of imagination, recourse was had to images from the external world ; the phænomena of the soul were represented as the effects of sensible impressions, themselves resulting from a contact between the mind and the body. Reid has laid down the true criterium, in virtue of which we can always recognise the point at which an attempt at explanation ought to stop, when he says :—*Facts simple and primitive are inexplicable.* It is thus that he has cut short those hypotheses, those presumptuous theories, which history has consigned for ever to the romances of Metaphysic.

'In the meanwhile, it remains for me to consider, whether the remedy be not excessive, and whether the philosophy of Reid, in ruining the metaphysical hypotheses, has not proscribed the metaphysical spirit itself. But before entering upon the question, it is requisite to premise, that even if this be done by Reid, still there is nothing in the proceeding at which criticism ought to take offence. His mission was to proclaim the application of the experimental method to the philosophy of the human mind, on the ruins of the hypotheses which had issued from the Cartesian school ; this mission he has completely fulfilled, for he has purged philosophy, one after another, of the theory of ideas, of the desolating scepticism

---

* This passage is given in a translation found among Sir W. Hamilton's papers. The other testimonies have been added from his extracts and references.—ED.

of Hume, of the idealism of Berkeley, of the demonstrations of Descartes ; he has thus made a *tabula rasa.* Were it then the fact, that the abuse of the metaphysical spirit, and the spectacle of the aberrations into which this spirit has betrayed the human mind, had carried Reid to pronounce its banishment from science, for this we ought no more seriously to reproach him, than we should condemn Bacon for his proscription of the Syllogism, of which the Schoolmen had made so flagrant an abuse. My intention, therefore, in touching on this delicate point, is, far less to evince the too empirical character of the philosophy of Reid, than to relieve a great and noble science from the unjust contempt to which it has been exposed from the philosophers both of the school of Bacon and of the Scottish school.

'But let us first see, how far Reid's neglect of Metaphysic has extended.—According to him, to explain a fact is to carry it up into a fact more simple; so that the explanatory principle is of the same nature as the fact explained, nor, in our explanation of facts, is it ever necessary for us to transcend experience. I admit the truth of this definition for a certain number of the sciences which ought not to transgress the bounds of observation : thus in Physics, in Natural History, in Psychology even, the explanation of the fact can possess no other character, can propose no other aim. But I believe the human mind goes farther ; the explanation which consists in the connecting one fact to another more simple does not suffice for it, nor does it even recognise this as a veritable explanation. To explain, to explicate, in the strict propriety of language, is to reduce that which *is* to that which *ought to be,* in other words, to connect a fact to a principle. Reid, therefore, in the view he takes of the explanation of facts, has banished from science the research of principles, of the necessary causes and reasons of things,— that is, precisely, metaphysical speculation.

'On the other hand, to distinguish philosophy from the sciences which have nature for their object, he defines it—*the science of the human mind;* he thus considers philosophy as a science no less special than the others, which is only discriminated from them by the nature of its object, and which, moreover, has with them the same method and the same end. The same method : for, like the natural sciences, it observes ; only the facts which it observes are immaterial. The same end : for it proposes the discovery of laws, like the sciences of nature ; the only difference lying in the nature of these laws. As to that general and synthetic science, which applies itself to all, and to which no matter comes amiss, which is distinguished from other sciences, not by the character of its object but by the elevated point of view from which it contemplates the universe of things, which styles itself philosophy of Nature, philosophy of Mind, philosophy of History, according to the limitation of the object which for the moment it considers,—of such a science Reid does not appear to have even suspected the existence.

'In fine, we ought not to forget that Reid is a partisan of the Baconian method, which he has extended from the sciences of nature to the science of mind. Now, as is well known, Bacon had a proud contempt of Metaphysic, and names it only to deride it, or to shew that in retaining the word, he rejects the thing. Accordingly, in his classification of the sciences, he reduces Metaphysic to the mere science of the immutable and universal forms of nature, that is to say, to a transcendental physics; while subsequently, in his Novum Organum, there is no mention of it at all. Reid, who inherited from Bacon his method, inherited likewise from him his contempt of Metaphysic; and, with Reid, the whole Scottish school.

'Once more I repeat, the reaction of the experimental philosophy, so much and so long oppressed by speculation, is excusable in Reid as in Bacon, because on their part it was natural and almost necessary ; but in the present day, when this philosophy has everywhere triumphed over the obstacles which the spirit of system, the prejudices and the authority of the past, had accumulated in its path,—in the present day, when this philosophy in its turn oppresses Metaphysic, and would, if it could, exclude it from the domain of science, it may not be unimportant briefly to shew, that Metaphysic also has its titles, and its legitimate place in the cycle of human knowledge.

'In the first place, it is a very ancient science ; under definitions the most diverse, it has always appeared as the science of principles. Until the eighteenth century, it has never for a moment quitted the philosophic stage, and on that stage has never ceased to occupy the most distinguished part. The reason of this preeminence was very simple ; for to Metaphysic was confided the task of resolving the most extensive, arduous, and important problems : Metaphysic alone spoke of God and his attributes, of the universe considered in its totality and its laws, of the human soul and of its destiny; Metaphysic alone shewed to each faculty the end in view for its activity, to the imagination the ideal of the beautiful, to the will the ideal of the good, to the intelligence the ideal of the true. Since the empirism of the last century, dominant in France and England, has relegated Metaphysic to the region of chimæras, science rarely agitates those mighty problems, and if perchance it moots them, it does so with a timidity and weakness which make us regret that powerful impulse of the metaphysical genius which alone is competent to handle and resolve these formidable questions. Why then has it been repudiated by science? Is it only proper to generate magnificent romances? Is it that Metaphysic is without a basis?

'To judge of it by the objections of its adversaries and by the unreflective enthusiasm of its partisans, to judge of it especially by the strange forms in which imagination has been pleased to clothe it, it would seem that Metaphysic is a philosophy mysterious and almost superhuman, which descends from another world, and which has nothing in common with the positive and natural methods of science. There is nothing more false. Metaphysic, like the other sciences, has its roots in the nature of the mind. If the sciences of fact repose in observation, if the abstract sciences are founded upon reasoning, Metaphysic has for its basis the conceptions of reason, as well pure as in combination with the data of experience. I say the conceptions of reason, which I distinguish, and which every observer of the acts of intelligence may distinguish, from the fantastic or arbitrary creations of imagination. When on occasion of an existence finite, contingent, relative, individual, attested by experience, I conceive the infinite, the necessary, the absolute, the universal; when rising from the phænomena which the universe presents to my observation, I contemplate the great laws of this universe, those laws which constitute the harmony of its movements, the order and the beauty of its plan; when retiring within the limits of my proper nature, I connect the phænomena, so various and so mutable, in which it is manifested, to a principle, simple, identical, and immutable in essence,—I neither imagine, nor dream, nor fabricate; I conceive. My conception is an act of my mind, necessary and legitimate as the very simplest perception. No intelligent being has a right to contest the authority of any faculty whatever of intelligence, and it is lament-able to see the highest and divinest of its functions treated with contempt.'

6.—JOUFFROY.—Œuvres Complètes de Thomas Reid, Paris, 1836.

Préface, pp. cc. cci.—' S'il est un service et un service éminent que les Écossais aient rendu à la philosophie, c'est assurément d'avoir établi une fois pour toutes dans les esprits, et de manière à ce qu'elle ne puisse plus en sortir, l'idée qu'il y a une science d'observation, une science de faits, à la manière dont l'entendent les physiciens, qui a l'esprit humain pour objet et le sens intime pour instrument, et dont lo résultat doit être la détermination des lois de l'esprit, comme celui des sciences physiques doit être la détermination des lois de la matière. Les philosophes écossais ont-ils eu les premiers cette idée ? Non, sans doute, si par avoir une idée on entend simplement en émettre d'autres qui la contiennent; à le prendre ainsi plusieurs philosophes l'avaient eue avant eux, et, pour ne citer que les plus célèbres, on la trouve dans Locke et dans Descartes. Mais si par inventer une idée on entend non pas seulement en concevoir le germe, mais la saisir en elle-même dans toute sa vérité et son étendue, mais en voir la portée et les conséquences, mais y croire, mais la pratiquer, mais la prêcher, mais la mettre dans une telle lumière qu'elle pénètre dans tous les esprits et qu'elle soit désormais acquise d'une manière définitive à l'intelligence humaine, on peut dire avec vérité que, l'idée dont il s'agit, les Écossais l'ont eue les premiers et qu'ils en sont les véritables inventeurs.'

P. cciv.-ccvi.—' C'est là en effet le vrai titre, le titre éminent des philosophes écossais à l'estime de la postérité et le principal service qu'ils aient rendu à la philosophie. C'est un fait qu'avant eux, ni l'idée de cette science ainsi nettement démêlée, ni l'idée de la méthode vraie à y appliquer, ni l'exemple d'une application rigoureuse de cette méthode, n'existaient; c'en est un autre que depuis eux tout cela existe et que c'est à eux qu'on le doit. Qu'ils soient trop restés dans les limites de cette science, et, faute d'en être assez sortis, qu'ils n'en aient pas vu toute la portée, ni l'ensemble des liens qui, en y rattachant toutes les sciences philosophiques, en forment le point de départ et la racine de la moitié des connaissances humaines, cela est vrai, et nous l'avons montré; que les vues historiques qui les ont conduits à l'idée de cette science manquent souvent d'étendue et de justesse, et que dans la détermination de la méthode, des limites et des conditions de la science même, ils n'aient pas toujours ni bien vu, ni assez vu, c'est ce qui est encore vrai et ce que nous avons également montré; mais toujours est-il que l'honneur de l'avoir créée est à eux, et que, quand l'histoire voudra marquer l'époque où la science de l'esprit humain a véritablement été conçue telle qu'elle doit l'être, elle sera forcée d'indiquer celle où les philosophes écossais ont écrit.

'Une seconde idée qui reste gravée dans l'esprit quand on a lu les philosophes écossais, et dont on peut dire, comme de la précédente, qu'ils l'ont mise au monde, quoique plusieurs philosophes, et Locke en dernier lieu, l'eussent indiquée, c'est que la connaissance de l'esprit humain et de ses lois est la condition de solution de la plupart des questions dont la philosophie s'occupe, de manière que pour résoudre ces questions il faut avant tout acquérir cette connaissance, et qu'elles ne peuvent être résolues que par hypothèse tant qu'on ne la possède pas. Nous avons montré que cette idée n'était que le germe d'une idée plus grande que les Écossais n'ont saisie qu'à moitié, à savoir que toutes les sciences philosophiques dépendent de la psychologie, parce que toutes les questions qu'elles agitent viennent se résoudre dans la connaissance des phénomènes spirituels, et que c'est là le caractère commun qui unit toutes ces sciences entre elles, qui en constitue l'unité, et les distingue des sciences physiques. Nous avons ajouté que si les Écossais s'étaient élevés jusqu'à cette idée, à la gloire d'avoir fondé la science de l'esprit humain ils auraient ajouté celle d'avoir fixé l'idée de la philosophie et d'avoir organisé cette moitié de la connaissance humaine. Mais si cette conception est restée imparfaite dans leur esprit, il n'en est pas moins vrai qu'elle s'y est suffisamment développée pour imprimer à la philosophie écossaise une direction originale et qui est selon nous celle-là même que la philosophie doit suivre. Subordonner toute recherche philosophique à la psychologie, sur ce fondement que toute question philosophique a sa solution dans quelques lois de la nature spirituelle, comme toute question physique a la sienne dans quelques lois de la nature physique, voilà en réalité ce que les Écossais ont fait, et le principe qui plane sur toute leur philosophie, qui l'anime, qui la dirige, et dont on reste pénétré quand on l'a étudiée. La méthode philosophique des Écossais n'est autre chose qu'une conséquence de ce principe; et non-seulement ils ont prouvé la vérité de ce principe pour un grand nombre de questions philosophiques et pour les plus importantes, mais ils l'ont constamment pratiqué.'

Pp. ccvii., ccviii.—'Avant et depuis les Écossais aucun autre système n'offre cette construction de la science; elle leur appartient en propre. et c'est là le second service qu'ils ont rendu à la philosophie. Ils ont fondé la science de l'esprit humain, c'est le premier; après en avoir fixé l'idée, ils ont fait de cette science le point de départ de la philosophie et sont venus chercher dans ses données la solution scientifique de toute question, c'est là le second.

'Une troisième idée qui n'est moins importante ni moins propre aux Écossais que les précédentes, c'est l'assimilation complète des recherches philosophiques et des recherches physiques, fondée sur ce principe que les unes et les autres ont également pour objet la connaissance d'une partie des œuvres de Dieu, et qu'il n'y a pas deux manières de connaître les œuvres de Dieu, mais une seule, qui s'applique à la solution des questions philosophiques comme à celle des questions physiques.'

P. ccxiii.—'En prouvant cette similitude, ils dissipent la superstitieuse obscurité qui entoure les recherches philosophiques; ils les ramènent aux simples conditions, à la simple nature, à la simple méthode de toutes les recherches scientifiques; ils montrent l'erreur constante des philosophes qui ont méconnu cette vérité; ils expliquent par cette erreur la destinée malheureuse de ces recherches; ils rassurent ainsi les esprits que cette destinée éloignait de s'en occuper, et les rappellent à la philosophie en la mettant dans une voie nouvelle et cependant éprouvée, dans la grande voie qu'indiquent les lois de l'entendement, par où suit toutes les sciences, et par laquelle l'esprit humain est arrivé à toutes les vérités qui font sa puissance et sa gloire.'

ERRATA.

Page 10 a, l. 17, *for* 1763, *read* 1763 [1764].

„ 11 a, l. 61, *for* 1781, *read* 1781 [1780].

„ 33 b, l. 35, *for* fifteen, *read* sixteen.

„ 803, among the authorities, Omphalius should be entered as *German*,
not as *French*.

„ 861 b, l. 51, n, *for* L. ii. c., *read* L. i. c. 8.

ACCOUNT

OF

THE LIFE AND WRITINGS

OF

THOMAS REID, D.D., F.R.S.E.,

LATE PROFESSOR OF MORAL PHILOSOPHY IN THE UNIVERSITY OF GLASGOW.

BY

DUGALD STEWART, Esq., F.R.SS L. & E,

PROFESSOR OF MORAL PHILOSOPHY IN THE UNIVERSITY OF EDINBURGH.

READ AT DIFFERENT MEETINGS OF THE ROYAL SOCIETY OF EDINBURGH,

AND

PUBLISHED IN 1803.

ACCOUNT

OF

THE LIFE AND WRITINGS

OF

THOMAS REID D.D.

SECTION I.

FROM DR REID'S BIRTH TILL THE DATE OF
HIS LATEST PUBLICATION.

THE life of which I am now to present to the Royal Society a short account, although it fixes an era in the history of modern philosophy, was uncommonly barren of those incidents which furnish materials for biography—strenuously devoted to truth, to virtue, and to the best interests of mankind, but spent in the obscurity of a learned retirement, remote from the pursuits of ambition, and with little solicitude about literary fame. After the agitation, however, of the political convulsions which Europe has witnessed for a course of years, the simple record of such a life may derive an interest even from its uniformity ; and, when contrasted with the events of the passing scene, may lead the thoughts to some views of human nature on which it is not ungrateful to repose.

Thomas Reid, D.D., late Professor of Moral Philosophy in the University of Glasgow, was born, on the 26th of April 1710, at Strachan, in Kincardineshire, a country parish, situated about twenty miles from Aberdeen, on the north side of the Grampian mountains.

His father, the Rev. Lewis Reid, was minister of this parish for fifty years. He was a clergyman, according to his son's account of him, respected by all who knew him, for his piety, prudence, and benevolence ; inheriting from his ancestors (most of whom, from the time of the Protestant establishment, had been ministers of the Church of Scotland) that purity and simplicity of manners which became his station ;

and a love of letters, which, without attracting the notice of the world, amused his leisure and dignified his retirement.

For some generations before his time, a propensity to literature, and to the learned professions—a propensity which, when it has once become characteristical of a race, is peculiarly apt to be propagated by the influence of early associations and habits—may be traced in several individuals among his kindred. One of his ancestors, James Reid, was the first minister of Banchory-Ternan after the Reformation, and transmitted to four sons a predilection for those studious habits which formed his own happiness. He was himself a younger son of Mr Reid of Pitfoddels, a gentleman of a very ancient and respectable family in the county of Aberdeen.

James Reid was succeeded as minister of Banchory by his son Robert. Another son, Thomas, rose to considerable distinction, both as a philosopher and a poet ; and seems to have wanted neither ability nor inclination to turn his attainments to the best advantage. After travelling over Europe, and maintaining, as was the custom of his age, public disputations in several universities, he collected into a volume the theses and dissertations which had been the subjects of his literary contests ; and also published some Latin poems, which may be found in the collection entitled, " *Deliciæ Poëtarum Scotorum.*" On his return to his native country, he fixed his residence in London, where he was appointed secretary in the Greek and Latin tongues to King James I. of England,* and lived in habits of intimacy with some

* Whose English works he, along with the learned Patrick Young, translated into Latin.—H.

B 2

of the most distinguished characters of that period. Little more, I believe, is known of Thomas Reid's history, excepting that he bequeathed to the Marischal College of Aberdeen a curious collection of books and manuscripts, with a fund for establishing a salary to a librarian.

Alexander Reid, the third son, was physician to King Charles I., and published several books on surgery and medicine. The fortune he acquired in the course of his practice was considerable, and enabled him (beside many legacies to his relations and friends) to leave various lasting and honourable memorials, both of his benevolence and of his attachment to letters.

A fourth son, whose name was Adam, translated into English Buchanan's History of Scotland. Of this translation, which was never published, there is a manuscript copy in the possession of the University of Glasgow.

A grandson of Robert, the eldest of these sons, was the third minister of Banchory after the Reformation, and was great-grandfather of Thomas Reid, the subject of this memoir.*

The particulars hitherto mentioned, are stated on the authority of some short memorandums written by Dr Reid a few weeks before his death. In consequence of a suggestion of his friend, Dr Gregory, he had resolved to amuse himself with collecting such facts as his papers or memory could supply, with respect to his life, and the progress of his studies ; but, unfortunately, before he had fairly entered on the subject, his design was interrupted by his last illness. If he had lived to complete it, I might have entertained hopes of presenting to the public some details with respect to the history of his opinions and speculations on those important subjects to which he dedicated his talents—the most interesting of all articles in the biography of a philosopher, and of which it is to be lamented that so few authentic records are to be found in the annals of letters. All the information, however, which I have derived from these notes, is exhausted in the foregoing pages ; and I must content myself, in the continuation of my narrative, with those indirect aids which tradition, and the recollection of a few old acquaintance, afford ; added to what I myself have learned from Dr Reid's conversation, or collected from a careful perusal of his writings.

His mother, Margaret Gregory, was a daughter of David Gregory, Esq. of Kinnairdie, in Banffshire, elder brother of James Gregory, the inventor of the reflecting telescope, and the antagonist of Huyghens. She was one of twenty-nine children ;

the most remarkable of whom was David Gregory, Savilian Professor of Astronomy at Oxford, and an intimate friend of Sir Isaac Newton. Two of her younger brothers were at the same time Professors of Mathematics—the one at St Andrew's, the other at Edinburgh—and were the first persons who taught the Newtonian philosophy in our northern universities. The hereditary worth and genius which have so long distinguished, and which still distinguish, the descendants of this memorable family, are well known to all who have turned their attention to Scottish biography ; but it is not known so generally, that, through the female line, the same characteristical endowments have been conspicuous in various instances ; and that to the other monuments which illustrate the race of the Gregories, is to be added the Philosophy of Reid.

With respect to the earlier part of Dr Reid's life, all that I have been able to learn amounts to this :—That, after two years spent at the parish school of Kincardine, he was sent to Aberdeen, where he had the advantage of prosecuting his classical studies under an able and diligent teacher ; that, about the age of twelve or thirteen, he was entered as a student in Marischal College ; and that his master in philosophy for three years was Dr George Turnbull, who afterwards attracted some degree of notice as an author ; particularly by a book entitled, " Principles of Moral Philosophy ;" and by a voluminous treatise (long ago forgotten) on " Ancient Painting."* The sessions of the College were, at that time, very short, and the education (according to Dr Reid's own account) slight and superficial.

It does not appear, from the information which I have received, that he gave any early indications of future eminence. His industry, however, and modesty, were conspicuous from his childhood ; and it was foretold of him, by the parish schoolmaster, who initiated him in the first principles of learning, " That he would turn out to be a man of good and well-wearing parts ;" a prediction which touched, not unhappily, on that capacity of " patient thought" which so peculiarly characterised his philosophical genius.

His residence at the University was prolonged beyond the usual term, in consequence of his appointment to the office of librarian, which had been endowed by one of his ancestors about a century before. The situation was acceptable to him, as it afforded an opportunity of indulging his passion for study, and united the charms of a learned society with the quiet of an academical retreat.

During this period, he formed an intimacy with John Stewart, afterwards Professor of Mathematics in Marischal College, and author of "A Commentary on Newton's Quadrature of Curves." His predilection for mathematical pursuits was confirmed and strengthened by this connection. I have often heard him mention it with much pleasure, while he recollected the ardour with which they both prosecuted these fascinating studies, and the lights which they imparted mutually to each other, in their first perusal of the "*Principia*," at a time when a knowledge of the Newtonian discoveries was only to be acquired in the writings of their illustrious author. In 1736, Dr Reid resigned his office of librarian, and accompanied Mr Stewart on an excursion to England. They visited together London, Oxford, and Cambridge, and were introduced to the acquaintance of many persons of the first literary eminence. His relation to Dr David Gregory procured him a ready access to Martin Folkes, whose house concentrated the most interesting objects which the metropolis had to offer to his curiosity. At Cambridge he saw Dr Bentley, who delighted him with his learning, and amused him with his vanity; and enjoyed repeatedly the conversation of the blind mathematician, Saunderson—a phenomenon in the history of the human mind to which he has referred more than once in his philosophical speculations.

With the learned and amiable man who was his companion in this journey, he maintained an uninterrupted friendship till 1766, when Mr Stewart died of a malignant fever. His death was accompanied with circumstances deeply afflicting to Dr Reid's sensibility; the same disorder proving fatal to his wife and daughter, both of whom were buried with him in one grave.

In 1737, Dr Reid was presented, by the King's College of Aberdeen, to the living of New-Machar, in the same county; but the circumstances in which he entered on his preferment were far from auspicious. The intemperate zeal of one of his predecessors, and an aversion to the law of patronage, had so inflamed the minds of his parishioners against him, that, in the first discharge of his clerical functions, he had not only to encounter the most violent opposition, but was exposed to personal danger. His unwearied attention, however, to the duties of his office, the mildness and forbearance of his temper, and the active spirit of his humanity, soon overcame all these prejudices; and, not many years afterwards, when he was called to a different situation, the same persons who had suffered themselves to be so far misled as to take a share in the outrages against him, followed him, on his departure, with their blessings and tears.

Dr Reid's popularity at New-Machar (as I am informed by the respectable clergyman[*] who now holds that living) increased greatly after his marriage, in 1740, with Elizabeth, daughter of his uncle, Dr George Reid, physician in London. The accommodating manners of this excellent woman, and her good offices among the sick and necessitous, are still remembered with gratitude, and so endeared the family to the neighbourhood, that its removal was regarded as a general misfortune. The simple and affecting language in which some old men expressed themselves on this subject, in conversing with the present minister, deserves to be recorded:—"We fought *against* Dr Reid when he came, and would have fought *for* him when he went away."

In some notes relative to the earlier part of his history, which have been kindly communicated to me by the Rev. Mr Davidson, minister of Rayne, it is mentioned, as a proof of his uncommon modesty and diffidence, that, long after he became minister of New-Machar, he was accustomed, from a distrust in his own powers, to preach the sermons of Dr Tillotson and of Dr Evans. I have heard, also, through other channels, that he had neglected the practice of composition to a more than ordinary degree in the earlier part of his studies. The fact is curious, when contrasted with that ease, perspicuity, and purity of style, which he afterwards attained. From some information, however, which has been lately transmitted to me by one of his nearest relations, I have reason to believe that the number of original discourses which he wrote while a country clergyman, was not inconsiderable.

The satisfaction of his own mind was probably, at this period, a more powerful incentive to his philosophical researches, than the hope of being able to instruct the world as an author. But, whatever his views were, one thing is certain, that, during his residence at New-Machar, the greater part of his time was spent in the most intense study; more particularly in a careful examination of the laws of external perception, and of the other principles which form the groundwork of human knowledge. His chief relaxations were gardening and botany, to both of which pursuits he retained his attachment even in old age.

A paper which he published in the Philosophical Transactions of the Royal Society of London, for the year 1748, affords some light with respect to the progress of his speculations about this period. It is entitled, "An Essay on Quantity, occasioned by reading a Treatise in which Simple and Compound Ratios are applied to Virtue and

---

[*] The Rev. William Stronach.

Merit ;" and shews plainly, by its contents, that, although he had not yet entirely relinquished the favourite researches of his youth, he was beginning to direct his thoughts to other objects.

The treatise alluded to in the title of this paper, was manifestly the " Inquiry into the Origin of our Ideas of *Beauty* and *Virtue* ;" by Dr. Hutcheson of Glasgow. According to this very ingenious writer, the *moment* of public good produced by an individual, depending partly on his *benevolence*, and partly on his *ability*, the relation between these different moral ideas may be expressed in the technical form of algebraists, by saying that the first is in the compound proportion of the two others. Hence, Dr Hutcheson infers, that " *the benevolence* of an agent (which in this system is synonymous with his *mo al merit*) is proportional to a fraction, having the moment of good for the numerator, and the ability of the agent for the denominator." Various other examples of a similar nature occur in the same work ; and are stated with a gravity not altogether worthy of the author. It is probable that they were intended merely as *illustrations* of his general reasonings, not as *media* of investigation for the discovery of new conclusions ; but they appeared to Dr Reid to be an innovation which it was of importance to resist, on account of the tendency it might have (by confounding the evidence of different branches of science) to retard the progress of knowledge. The very high reputation which Dr Hutcheson then possessed in the universities of Scotland, added to the recent attempts of Pitcairn and Cheyne to apply mathematical reasoning to medicine, would bestow, it is likely, an interest on Dr Reid's Essay at the time of its publication, which it can scarcely be expected to possess at present. Many of the observations, however, which it contains, are acute and original ; and all of them are expressed with that clearness and precision so conspicuous in his subsequent compositions. The circumstance which renders a subject susceptible of mathematical consideration, is accurately stated ; and the proper province of that science defined in such a manner as sufficiently to expose the absurdity of those abuses of its technical phraseology which were at that time prevalent. From some passages in it, there is, I think, ground for concluding that the author's reading had not been very extensive previous to this period. The enumeration, in particular, which he has given of the different kinds of *proper quantity*, affords a proof that he was not acquainted with the refined yet sound disquisitions concerning the nature of *number* and of *proportion*, which had appeared, almost a century before, in the " Mathematical Lectures" of Dr Barrow ; nor with the remarks on the same subject introduced by Dr Clarke in one of his controversial letters addressed to Leibnitz.

In the same paper, Dr Reid takes occasion to offer some reflections on the dispute between the Newtonians and Leibnitzians, concerning the measure of forces. The fundamental idea on which these reflections proceed, is just and important ; and it leads to the correction of an error committed very generally by the partisans of both opinions — that of mistaking a question concerning the comparative advantages of two *definitions* for a difference of statement with respect to a *physical fact*. It must, I think, be acknowledged, at the same time, that the whole merits of the controversy are not here exhausted ; and that the honour of placing this very subtle and abstruse question in a point of view calculated to reconcile completely the contending parties, was reserved for M. D'Alembert. To have fallen short of the success which attended the inquiries of that eminent man, on a subject so congenial to his favourite habits of study, will not reflect any discredit on the powers of Dr Reid's mind, in the judgment of those who are at all acquainted with the history of this celebrated discussion.

In 1752, the professors of King's College elected Dr Reid Professor of Philosophy, in testimony of the high opinion they had formed of his learning and abilities. Of the particular plan, which he followed in his academical lectures, while he held this office, I have not been able to obtain any satisfactory account ; but the department of science which was assigned to him by the general system of education in that university, was abundantly extensive ; comprehending Mathematics and Physics as well as Logic and Ethics. A similar system was pursued formerly in the other universities of Scotland ; the same professor then conducting his pupil through all those branches of knowledge which are now appropriated to different teachers. And where he happened fortunately to possess those various accomplishments which distinguished Dr Reid in so remarkable a degree, it cannot be doubted that the unity and comprehensiveness of method of which such academical courses admitted, must necessarily have possessed important advantages over that more minute subdivision of literary labour which has since been introduced. But, as public establishments ought to adapt themselves to what is ordinary, rather than to what is possible, it is not surprising that experience should have gradually suggested an arrangement more suitable to the narrow limits which commonly circumscribe human genius.

Soon after Dr Reid's removal *to* Aberdeen, he projected (in conjunction with his friend Dr John Gregory) a literary society, which subsisted for many years, and which seems to have had the happiest effects in awakening and directing that spirit of philosophical research which has since reflected so much lustre on the north of Scotland. The meetings of this society were held weekly; and afforded the members (beside the advantages to be derived from a mutual communication of their sentiments on the common objects of their pursuit) an opportunity of subjecting their intended publications to the test of friendly criticism. The number of valuable works which issued, nearly about the same time, from individuals connected with this institution—more particularly the writings of Reid, Gregory, Campbell, Beattie, and Gerard—furnish the best panegyric on the enlightened views of those under whose direction it was originally formed.

Among these works, the most original and profound was unquestionably the "Inquiry into the Human Mind," published by Dr Reid in 1764. The plan appears to have been conceived, and the subject deeply meditated, by the author long before; but it is doubtful whether his modesty would have ever permitted him to present to the world the fruits of his solitary studies, without the encouragement which he received from the general acquiescence of his associates in the most important conclusions to which he had been led.

From a passage in the dedication, it would seem that the speculations which terminated in these conclusions, had commenced as early as the year 1739; at which period the publication of Mr Hume's "Treatise of Human Nature," induced him, for the first time, (as he himself informs us,) "to call in question the principles commonly received with regard to the human understanding." In his "Essays on the Intellectual Powers," he acknowledges that, in his youth, he had, without examination, admitted the established opinions on which Mr Hume's system of scepticism was raised; and that it was the consequences which these opinions seemed to involve, which roused his suspicions concerning their truth. "If I may presume," says he, "to speak my own sentiments, I once believed *the doctrine of Ideas* so firmly as to embrace the whole of Berkeley's system along with it; till, finding other consequences to follow from it, which gave me more uneasiness than the want of a material world, it came into my mind, more than forty years ago, to put the question, What evidence have I for this doctrine, that all the objects of my knowledge are ideas in my own mind? From that time to the present, I have been candidly and impartly,all as I think, seeking for the evidence of this

principle; but can find none, excepting tha authority of philosophers."

In following the train of Dr Reid's researches, this last extract merits attention, as it contains an explicit avowal, on his own part, that, at one period of his life, he had been led, by Berkeley's reasonings, to abandon the belief of the existence of *matter*. The avowal does honour to his candour, and the fact reflects no discredit on his sagacity. The truth is, that this article of the Berkleian system, however contrary to the conclusions of a sounder philosophy, was the error of no common mind. Considered in contrast with that theory of materialism which the excellent author was anxious to supplant, it possessed important advantages, not only in its tendency, but in its scientific consistency; and it afforded a proof, wherever it met with a favourable reception, of an understanding superior to those casual associations which, in the apprehensions of most men, blend indissolubly the phenomena of thought with the objects of external perception. It is recorded as a saying of M. Turgot, (whose philosophical opinions in some important points approached very nearly to those of Dr Reid,[*]) that "he who had never doubted of the existence of matter, might be assured he had no turn for metaphysical disquisitions."

As the refutation of Mr Hume's sceptical theory was the great and professed object of Dr Reid's "Inquiry," he was anxious, before taking the field as a controversial writer, to guard against the danger of misapprehending or misrepresenting the meaning of his adversary, by submitting his reasonings to Mr Hume's private examination. With this view, he availed himself of the good offices of Dr Blair, with whom both he and Mr Hume had long lived in habits of friendship. The communications which he at first transmitted, consisted only of detached parts of the work; and appear evidently, from a correspondence which I have perused, to have conveyed a very imperfect idea of his general system. In one of Mr Hume's letters to Dr Blair, he betrays some want of his usual good humour, in looking forward to his new antagonist. "I wish," says he, "that the parsons would confine themselves to their old occupation of worrying one another, and leave philosophers to argue with temper, moderation, and good manners." After Mr Hume, however, had read the manuscript, he addressed himself directly to the Author, in terms so candid and liberal, that it would be unjust to his memory to withhold from the public so pleasing a memorial of his character :—

"By Dr Blair's means I have been

---

* See, in particular, the article "Existence" in the "Encyclopedie."

favoured with the perusal of your performance, which I have read with great pleasure and attention. It is certainly very rare that a piece so deeply philosophical is wrote with so much spirit, and affords so much entertainment to the reader ; though I must still regret the disadvantages under which I read it, as I never had the whole performance at once before me, and could not be able fully to compare one part with another. To this reason, chiefly, I ascribe some obscurities, which, in spite of your short analysis or abstract, still seem to hang over your system ; for I must do you the justice to own that, when I enter into your ideas, no man appears to express himself with greater perspicuity than you do—a talent which, above all others, is requisite in that species of literature which you have cultivated. There are some objections which I would willingly propose to the chapter, ' Of Sight,' did I not suspect that they proceed from my not sufficiently understanding it ; and I am the more confirmed in this suspicion, as Dr Blair tells me that the former objections I made had been derived chiefly from that cause. I shall, therefore, forbear till the whole can be before me, and shall not at present propose any farther difficulties to your reasonings. I shall only say that, if you have been able to clear up these abstruse and important subjects, instead of being mortified, I shall be so vain as to pretend to a share of the praise ; and shall think that my errors, by having at least some coherence, had led you to make a more strict review of my principles, which were the common ones, and to perceive their futility.

" As I was desirous to be of some use to you, I kept a watchful eye all along over your style ; but it is really so correct, and so good English, that I found not anything worth the remarking. There is only one passage in this chapter, where you make use of the phrase *hinder to do*, instead of *hinder from doing*, which is the English one ; but I could not find the passage when I sought for it. You may judge how unexceptionable the whole appeared to me, when I could remark so small a blemish. I beg my compliments to my friendly adversaries, Dr Campbell and Dr Gerard ; and also to Dr Gregory, whom I suspect to be of the same disposition, though he has not openly declared himself such."

Of the particular doctrines contained in Dr Reid's "Inquiry," I do not think it necessary here to attempt any abstract ; nor, indeed, do his speculations (conducted, as they were, in strict conformity to the rules of inductive philosophizing) afford a subject for the same species of rapid outline which is so useful in facilitating the study of a merely hypothetical theory.

Their great object was to record and to classify the phenomena which the operations of the human mind present to those who reflect carefully on the subjects of their consciousness ; and of such a history, it is manifest that no abridgement could be offered with advantage. Some reflections on the peculiar plan adopted by the author, and on the general scope of his researches in this department of science, will afterwards find a more convenient place, when I shall have finished my account of his subsequent publications.

The idea of prosecuting the study of the human mind, on a plan analagous to that which had been so successfully adopted in physics by the followers of Lord Bacon, if not first conceived by Dr Reid, was, at least, first carried successfully into execution in his writings. An attempt had, long before, been announced by Mr Hume, in the title-page of his " Treatise of Human Nature," to introduce the experimental method of reasoning into moral subjects ; and some admirable remarks are made in the introduction to that work, on the errors into which his predecessors had been betrayed by the spirit of hypothesis ; and yet it is now very generally admitted, that the whole of his own system rests on a principle for which there is no evidence but the authority of philosophers ; and it is certain that, in no part of it has he aimed to investigate, by a systematical analysis, those general principles of our constitution which can alone afford a synthetical explanation of its complicated phenomena.

I have often been disposed to think that Mr Hume's inattention to those rules of philosophizing which it was his professed intention to exemplify, was owing, in part, to some indistinctness in his notions concerning their import. It does not appear that, in the earlier part of his studies, he had paid much attention to the models of investigation exhibited in the writings of Newton and of his successors ; and that he was by no means aware of the extraordinary merits of Bacon as a philosopher, nor of the influence which his writings have had on the subsequent progress of physical discovery, is demonstrated by the cold and qualified encomium which is bestowed on his genius in one of the most elaborate passages of the " History of England."

In these respects, Dr Reid possessed important advantages ; familiarized, from his early years, to those experimental inquiries which, in the course of the two last centuries, have exalted natural philosophy to the dignity of a science, and determined strongly, by the peculiar bent of his genius, to connect every step in the progress of discovery with the history of the human mind. The influence of the general views opened in the "Novum Organon" may be traced in almost every page of his writings; and, indeed, the circumstance by which these are so strongly and characteristically distinguished, is, that they exhibit the first systematical attempt to exemplify, in the study of human nature, the same plan of investigation which conducted Newton to the properties of light, and to the law of gravitation. It is from a steady adherence to this plan, and not from the superiority of his inventive powers, that he claims to himself any merit as a philosopher; and he seems even willing (with a modesty approaching to a fault) to abandon the praise of what is commonly called *genius*, to the authors of the systems which he was anxious to refute. "It is genius," he observes in one passage, "and not the want of it, that adulterates philosophy, and fills it with error and false theory. A creative imagination disdains the mean offices of digging for a foundation, of removing rubbish, and carrying materials: leaving these servile employments to the drudges in science, it plans a design, and raises a fabric. Invention supplies materials where they are wanting, and fancy adds colouring and every befitting ornament. The work pleases the eye, and wants nothing but solidity and a good foundation. It seems even to vie with the works of nature, till some succeeding architect blows it into ruins, and builds as goodly a fabric of his own in its place."

"Success in an inquiry of this kind," he observes farther, "it is not in human power to command; but perhaps it is possible, by caution and humility, to avoid error and delusion. The labyrinth may be too intricate, and the thread too fine, to be traced through all its windings; but, if we stop where we can trace it no farther, and secure the ground we have gained, there is no harm done; a quicker eye may in time trace it farther."

The unassuming language with which Dr Reid endeavours to remove the prejudices naturally excited by a new attempt to philosophize on so unpromising, and hitherto so ungrateful a subject, recalls to our recollection those passages in which Lord Bacon —filled as his own imagination was with the future grandeur of the fabric founded by his hand—bespeaks the indulgence of his readers, for an enterprise apparently so hopeless and presumptuous. The apology he offers for himself, when compared with the height to which the structure of physical knowledge has since attained, may perhaps have some effect in attracting a more general attention to pursuits still more immediately interesting to mankind; and, at any rate, it forms the best comment on the prophetic suggestions in which Dr Reid

occasionally indulges himself concerning the future progress of moral speculation:—

"Si homines per tanta annorum spatia viam veram inveniendi et colendi scientias tenuissent, nec tamen ulterius progredi potuissent, audax procul dubio et temeraria foret opinio, posse rem in ulterius provehi. Quod si in *via* ipsa erratum sit, atque hominum opera in iis consumpta in quibus minime oportebat, sequitur ex eo, non in rebus ipsis difficultatem oriri, quæ potestatis nostræ non sunt; sed in intellectu humáno, ejusque usu et applicatione, quæ res remedium et medicinam suscipit."[*]—"De nobis ipsis silemus: de re autem quæ agitur, petimus; Ut homines eam non opinionem, sed opus esse cogitent; ac pro certo habeant, non sectæ nos alicujus, aut placiti, sed utilitatis et amplitudinis humanæ fundamenta moliri. Præterea, ut bene sperent; neque Instaurationem nostram ut quiddam infinitum et ultra mortale fingant, et animo concipiant; quum revera sit infiniti erroris finis et terminus legitimus."[†]

The impression produced on the minds of speculative men, by the publication of Dr Reid's "Inquiry," was fully as great as could be expected from the nature of his undertaking. It was a work neither addressed to the multitude, nor level to their comprehension; and the freedom with which it canvassed opinions sanctioned by the highest authorities, was ill calculated to conciliate the favour of the learned. A few, however, habituated, like the author, to the analytical researches of the Newtonian school, soon perceived the extent of his views, and recognised in his pages the genuine spirit and language of inductive investigation. Among the members of this University, Mr Ferguson was the first to applaud Dr Reid's success; warmly recommending to his pupils a steady prosecution of the same plan, as the only effectual method of ascertaining the general principles of the human frame: and illustrating, happily, by his own profound and eloquent disquisitions, the application of such studies to the conduct of the understanding and to the great concerns of life. I recollect, too, when I attended (about the year 1771) the lectures of the late Mr Russell, to have heard high encomiums on the philosophy of Reid, in the course of those comprehensive discussions concerning the objects and the rules of experimental science, with which he so agreeably diversified the particular doctrines of physics. Nor must I omit this opportunity of paying a tribute to the memory of my old friend, Mr Stevenson, then Professor of Logic; whose candid mind, at the age of seventy, gave a welcome reception to a system subversive of the theories which he had taught for

---

[*] Nov. Org. 94.   [†] Instaur. Mag.—Præfat.

forty years; and whose zeal for the advancement of knowledge prompted him, when his career was almost finished, to undertake the laborious task of new-modelling that useful compilation of elementary instruction to which a singular diffidence of his own powers limited his literary exertions.

It is with no common feelings of respect and of gratitude, that I now recall the names of those to whom I owe my first attachment to these studies, and the happiness of a liberal occupation superior to the more aspiring aims of a servile ambition.

From the University of Glasgow, Dr Reid's "Inquiry" received a still more substantial testimony of approbation; tne author having been invited, in 1763, by that learned body, to the Professorship of Moral Philosophy, then vacant by the resignation of Mr Smith. The preferment was, in many respects, advantageous; affording an income considerably greater than he enjoyed at Aberdeen; and enabling him to concentrate to his favourite objects, that attention which had been hitherto distracted by the miscellaneous nature of his academical engagements. It was not, however, without reluctance, that he consented to tear himself from a spot where he had so long been fastening his roots; and, much as he loved the society in which he passed the remainder of his days, I am doubtful if, in his mind, it compensated the sacrifice of earlier habits and connections.

Abstracting from the charm of local attachment, the University of Glasgow, at the time when Dr Reid was adopted as one of its members, presented strong attractions to reconcile him to his change of situation. Robert Simson, the great restorer of ancient geometry, was still alive; and, although far advanced in years, preserved unimpaired his ardour in study, his relish for social relaxation, and his amusing singularities of humour. Dr Moor combined, with a gaiety and a levity foreign to this climate, the profound attainments of a scholar and of a mathematician. In Dr Black, to whose fortunate genius a new world of science had just opened, Reid acknowledged an instructor and a guide; and met a simplicity of manners congenial to his own. The Wilsons (both father and son) were formed to attach his heart by the similarity of their scientific pursuits, and an entire sympathy with his views and sentiments. Nor was he less delighted with the good-humoured opposition which his opinions never failed to encounter in the acuteness of Millar—then in the vigour of youthful genius, and warm from the lessons of a different school. Dr Leechman, the friend and biographer of Hutcheson, was the official head of the College; and added

the weight of a venerable name to the reputation of a community which he had once adorned in a more active station.*

Animated by the zeal of such associates, and by the busy scenes which his new residence presented in every department of useful industry, Dr Reid entered on his functions at Glasgow with an ardour not common at the period of life which he had now attained. His researches concerning the human mind, and the principles of morals, which had occupied but an inconsiderable space in the wide circle of science allotted to him by his former office, were extended and methodized in a course which employed five hours every week, during six months of the year; the example of his illustrious predecessor, and the prevailing topics of conversation around him, occasionally turned his thoughts to commercial politics, and produced some ingenious essays on different questions connected with trade, which were communicated to a private society of his academical friends; his early passion for the mathematical sciences was revived by the conversation of Simson, Moor, and the Wilsons; and, at the age of fifty-five, he attended the lectures of Black, with a juvenile curiosity and enthusiasm.

As the substance of Dr Reid's lectures at Glasgow (at least of that part of them which was most important and original) has been since given to the public in a more improved form, it is unnecessary for me to enlarge on the plan which he followed in the discharge of his official duties. I shall therefore only observe, that, beside his speculations on the intellectual and active powers of man, and a system of practical ethics, his course comprehended some general views with respect to natural jurisprudence, and the fundamental principles of politics. A few lectures on rhetoric, which were read, at a separate hour, to a more advanced class of students, formed a voluntary addition to the appropriate functions of his office, to which it is probable he was prompted, rather by a wish to supply what was then a deficiency in the established course of education, than by any predilection for a branch of study so foreign to his ordinary pursuits.

The merits of Dr Reid as a public teacher were derived chiefly from that rich fund of original and instructive philosophy which is to be found in his writings, and from his unwearied assiduity in inculcating principles which he conceived to be of essential importance to human happiness. In his elocution and mode of instruction, there was nothing peculiarly attractive. He seldom, if ever, indulged himself in the warmth of extempore discourse; nor was his manner of

---

* Note C.

reading calculated to increase the effect of what he had committed to writing. Such, however, was the simplicity and perspicuity of his style, such the gravity and authority of his character, and such the general interest of his young hearers in the doctrines which he taught, that, by the numerous audiences to which his instructions were addressed, he was heard uniformly with the most silent and respectful attention. On this subject, I speak from personal knowledge; having had the good fortune, during a considerable part of winter 1772, to be one of his pupils.

It does not appear to me, from what I am now able to recollect of the order which he observed in treating the different parts of his subject, that he had laid much stress on systematical arrangement. It is probable that he availed himself of whatever materials his private inquiries afforded, for his academical compositions, without aiming at the merit of combining them into *a whole*, by a comprehensive and regular design—an undertaking to which, if I am not mistaken, the established forms of his university, consecrated by long custom, would have presented some obstacles. One thing is certain, that neither he nor his immediate predecessor ever published any general *prospectus* of their respective plans, nor any *heads* or *outlines* to assist their students in tracing the trains of thought which suggested their various transitions.

The interest, however, excited by such details as these even if it were in my power to render them more full and satisfactory, must necessarily be temporary and local; and I, therefore, hasten to observations of a more general nature, on the distinguishing characteristics of Dr Reid's philosophical genius, and on the spirit and scope of those researches which he has bequeathed to posterity concerning the phenomena and laws of the human mind. In mentioning his first performance on this subject, I have already anticipated a few remarks which are equally applicable to his subsequent publications; but the hints then suggested were too slight to place in so strong a light as I could wish the peculiarities of that mode of investigation which it was the great object of his writings to recommend and to exemplify. His own anxiety to neglect nothing that might contribute to its farther illustration induced him, while his health and faculties were yet entire, to withdraw from his public labours, and to devote himself, with an undivided attention, to a task of more extensive and permanent utility. It was in the year 1781 that he carried this design into execution, at a period of life (for he was then upwards of seventy) when the infirmities of age might be supposed to account sufficiently for his

retreat; but when, in fact, neither the vigour of his mind nor of his body seemed to have suffered any injury from time. The works which he published not many years afterwards, afford a sufficient proof of the assiduity with which he had availed himself of his literary leisure—his "Essays on the Intellectual Powers of Man" appearing in 1785, and those on the "Active Powers" in 1788.

As these two performances are, both of them, parts of one great work, to which his "Inquiry into the Human Mind" may be regarded as the introduction, I have reserved for this place whatever critical reflections I have to offer on his merits as an author; conceiving that they would be more likely to produce their intended effect, when presented at once in a connected form, than if interspersed, according to a chronological order, with the details of a biographical narrative.

SECTION II.

OBSERVATIONS ON THE SPIRIT AND SCOPE OF DR REID'S PHILOSOPHY.

I HAVE already observed that the distinguishing feature of Dr Reid's philosophy, is the systematical steadiness with which he has adhered in his inquiries, to that plan of investigation which is delineated in the "Novum Organon," and which has been so happily exemplified in physics by Sir Isaac Newton and his followers. To recommend this plan as the only effectual method of enlarging our knowledge of nature, was the favourite aim of all his studies, and a topic on which he thought he could not enlarge too much, in conversing or corresponding with his younger friends. In a letter to Dr Gregory, which I have perused, he particularly congratulates him upon his acquaintance with Lord Bacon's works; adding, " I am very apt to measure a man's understanding by the opinion he entertains of that author."

It were perhaps to be wished that he had taken a little more pains to illustrate the fundamental rules of that logic the value of which he estimated so highly; more especially, to point out the modifications with which it is applicable to the science of mind. Many important hints, indeed, connected with this subject, may be collected from different parts of his writings; but I am inclined to think that a more ample discussion of it, in a preliminary dissertation, might have thrown light on the scope of many of his researches, and obviated some of the most plausible objections which have been stated to his conclusions.

It is not, however, my intention at present to attempt to supply a *desideratum* of so great a magnitude—an undertaking which, I trust, will find a more convenient place, in the farther prosecution of those speculations with respect to the intellectual powers which I have already submitted to the public. The detached remarks which follow, are offered merely as a supplement to what I have stated concerning the nature and object of this branch of study, in the Introduction to the "Philosophy of the Human Mind."

The influence of Bacon's genius on the subsequent progress of physical discovery, has been seldom fairly appreciated—by some writers almost entirely overlooked, and by others considered as the sole cause of the reformation in science which has since taken place. Of these two extremes, the latter certainly is the least wide of the truth; for, in the whole history of letters, no other individual can be mentioned, whose exertions have had so indisputable an effect in forwarding the intellectual progress of mankind. On the other hand, it must be acknowledged, that, before the era when Bacon appeared, various philosophers in different parts of Europe had struck into the right path; and it may perhaps be doubted whether any one important rule with respect to the true method of investigation be contained in his works, of which no hint can be traced in those of his predecessors. His great merit lay in concentrating their feeble and scattered lights; fixing the attention of philosophers on the distinguishing characteristics of true and of false science, by a felicity of illustration peculiar to himself, seconded by the commanding powers of a bold and figurative eloquence. The method of investigation which he recommended had been previously followed in every instance in which any solid discovery had been made with respect to the laws of nature; but it had been followed accidentally and without any regular, preconceived design; and it was reserved for him to reduce to rule and method what others had effected, either fortuitously, or from some momentary glimpse of the truth. It is justly observed by Dr Reid, that "the man who first discovered that cold freezes water, and that heat turns it into vapour, proceeded on the same general principle by which Newton discovered the law of gravitation and the properties of light. His 'Regulæ Philosophandi' are maxims of commonsense, and are practised every day in common life; and he who philosophizes by other rules, either concerning the material system or concerning the mind, mistakes his aim."

These remarks are not intended to detract from the just glory of Bacon; for they apply to all those, without exception, who have systematized the principles of any of the arts. Indeed, they apply less forcibly to him than to any other philosopher whose studies have been directed to objects analogous to his; inasmuch as we know of no art of which the rules have been reduced successfully into a didactic form, when the art itself was as much in infancy as experimental philosophy was when Bacon wrote. Nor must it be supposed that the utility was small of thus attempting to systematize the accidental processes of unenlightened ingenuity, and to give to the noblest exertions of human reason, the same advantages of scientific method which have contributed so much to insure the success of genius in pursuits of inferior importance. The very philosophical motto which Reynolds has so happily prefixed to his "Academical Discourses," admits, on this occasion, of a still more appropriate application:—" Omnia fere quæ præceptis continentur ab ingeniosis hominibus fiunt; sed casu quodam magis quam scientia. Ideoque doctrina et animadversio adhibenda est, ut ea quæ interdum sine ratione nobis occurrunt, semper in nostra protestate sint; et quoties res postulaverit, a nobis ex præparato adhibeantur."

But, although a few superior minds seem to have been, in some measure, predisposed for that revolution in science which Bacon contributed so powerfully to accomplish, the case was very different with the great majority of those who were then most distinguished for learning and talents. His views were plainly too advanced for the age in which he lived; and, that he was sensible of this himself, appears from those remarkable passages in which he styles himself "the servant of posterity," and "bequeaths his fame to future times." Hobbes, who, in his early youth, had enjoyed his friendship, speaks, a considerable time after Bacon's death, of experimental philosophy, in terms of contempt; influenced, probably, not a little by the tendency he perceived in the inductive method of inquiry, to undermine the foundations of that fabric of scepticism which it was the great object of his labours to rear. Nay, even during the course of the last century, it has been less from Bacon's own speculations, than from the examples of sound investigation exhibited by a few eminent men, who professed to follow him as their guide, that the practical spirit of his writings has been caught by the multitude of physical experimentalists over Europe; truth and good sense descending gradually, in this as in other instances, by the force of imitation and of early habit, from the higher orders of intellect to the lower. In some parts of the Continent, more especially, the circulation of Bacon's philosophical works has been surprisingly slow. It is doubtful whether Des Cartes himself ever perused them; and, as late as the year 1759, if we may credit Montucla, they were very little known in France. The introductory discourse prefixed by D'Alembert to the "Encyclopedie," first recommended them, in that country, to general attention.

The change which has taken place, during the two last centuries, in the plan of physical research, and the success which has so remarkably attended it, could not fail to suggest an idea, that something analogous might probably be accomplished at a future period, with respect to the phenomena of the intellectual world. And, accordingly, various hints of this kind may be traced in different authors, since the era of Newton's discoveries. A memorable instance occurs in the prediction with which that great man concludes his "Optics:"— "That, if natural philosophy, in all its parts, by pursuing the inductive method, shall at length be perfected, the bounds of moral philosophy will also be enlarged." Similar remarks may be found in other publications; particularly in Mr Hume's "Treatise of Human Nature," where the subject is enlarged on with much ingenuity. As far, however, as I am able to judge, Dr Reid was the first who conceived justly and clearly the analogy between these two different branches of human knowledge; defining, with precision, the distinct provinces of observation and reflection,† in furnishing the data of all our reasonings concerning matter and mind; and demonstrating the necessity of a careful separation between the phenomena which they respectively exhibit, while we adhere to the same mode of philosophizing in investigating the laws of both. That so many philosophers should have thus missed their aim, in prosecuting the study of the human mind, will appear the less surprising when we consider in how many difficulties, peculiar to itself, this

* This is a mistake, which it is the more requisite to correct, because Mr Stewart's authority in historical points is, in consequence of his habitual accuracy, deservedly high. It is repeated, if I recollect aright, in more articulate terms, in the "Dissertation on the Progress of Metaphysical Philosophy." Des Cartes, in three or four passages of his "Letters," makes honourable mention of Bacon and his method; his works he seems not only to have perused but studied There is, however, no reason to suppose that Des Cartes was acquainted with the writings of his great predecessor in the early part of his life; and his own views in philosophy were probably not affected by this influence. Mr Stewart, likewise, greatly underrates the influence of the Baconian writings in general, previous to the recommendation of D'Alembert. On this subject, the reader is referred to a valuable paper by Professor Napier on the "Scope and Influence of the Baconian Philosophy," in the Transactions of the Royal Society of Edinburgh.—H.

† See a note on Reid's sixth "Essay on the Intellectual Powers," chap. I., and of the original edition, p. 517.—H

science is involved. It is sufficient at present to mention those which arise from the metaphorical origin of all the words which express the intellectual phenomena; from the subtle and fugitive nature of the objects of our reasonings; from the habits of inattention we acquire, in early life, to the subjects of our consciousness; and from the prejudices which early impressions and associations create to warp our opinions. It must be remembered, too, that, in the science of mind, (so imperfectly are its logical rules as yet understood!) we have not the same checks on the abuses of our reasoning powers which serve to guard us against error in our other researches. In physics, a speculative mistake is abandoned when contradicted by facts which strike the senses. In mathematics, an absurd or inconsistent conclusion is admitted as a demonstrative proof of a faulty hypothesis. But, in those inquiries which relate to the principles of human nature, the absurdities and inconsistencies to which we are led by almost all the systems hitherto proposed, instead of suggesting corrections and improvements on these systems, have too frequently had the effect of producing scepticism with respect to all of them alike. How melancholy is the confession of Hume!—"The intense view of these manifold contradictions and imperfections in human reason, has so wrought upon me, and heated my brain, that I am ready to reject all belief and reasoning, and can look upon no opinion even as more probable or likely than another."

Under these discouragements to this branch of study, it affords us some comfort to reflect on the great number of important facts with respect to the mind, which are scattered in the writings of philosophers. As the subject of our inquiry here lies within our own breast, a considerable mixture of truth may be expected even in those systems which are most erroneous; not only because a number of men can scarcely be long imposed on by a hypothesis which is perfectly groundless, concerning the objects of their own consciousness, but because it is generally by an alliance with truth, and with the original principles of human nature, that prejudices and associations produce their effects. Perhaps it may even be affirmed, that our progress in this research depends less on the degree of our industry and invention, than on our sagacity and good sense in separating old discoveries from the errors which have been blended with them; and on that candid and dispassionate temper which may prevent us from being led astray by the love of novelty, or the affectation of singularity. In this respect, the science of mind possesses a very important advantage over that which relates to the laws of the material world. The former has been cultivated with more or less success in all ages and countries: the facts which serve as the basis of the latter have, with a very few exceptions, been collected during the course of the two last centuries. An observation similar to this is applied to systems of ethics by Mr Smith, in his account of the theory of Mandeville; and the illustration he gives of it may be extended with equal propriety to the science of mind in general: —" A system of natural philosophy," he remarks, " may appear very plausible, and be, for a long time, very generally received in the world, and yet have no foundation in nature, nor any sort of resemblance to the truth. But it is otherwise with systems of moral philosophy. When a traveller gives an account of some distant country, he may impose upon our credulity the most groundless and absurd fictions as the most certain matters of fact; but when a person pretends to inform us of what passes in our neighbourhood, and of the affairs of the very parish we live in—though here, too, if we are so careless as not to examine things with our own eyes, he may deceive us in many respects—yet the greatest falsehoods which he imposes on us must bear some resemblance to the truth, and must even have a considerable mixture of truth in them."

These considerations demonstrate the essential importance, in this branch of study, of forming, at the commencement of our inquiries, just notions of the *criteria* of true and false science, and of the rules of philosophical investigation. They demonstrate, at the same time, that an attention to the rules of philosophizing, as they are exemplified in the physical researches of Newton and his followers, although the best of all preparations for an examination of the mental phenomena, is but one of the steps necessary to insure our success. On an accurate comparison of the two subjects, it might probably appear, that, after this preliminary step has been gained, the most arduous part of the process still remains. One thing is certain, that it is not from any defect in the power of ratiocination or deduction, that our speculative errors chiefly arise — a fact of which we have a decisive proof in the facility with which most students may be taught the mathematical and physical sciences, when compared with the difficulty of leading their minds to the truth, on questions of morals and politics.

The logical rules which lay the foundation of sound and useful conclusions concerning the laws of this internal world, although not altogether overlooked by Lord Bacon, were plainly not the principal object of his work; and what he has written on the subject, consists chiefly of detached hints dropped

casually in the course of other speculations. A comprehensive view of the sciences and arts dependent on the philosophy of the human mind, exhibiting the relations which they bear to each other, and to the general system of human knowledge, would form a natural and useful introduction to the study of these logical principles; but such a view remains still a *desideratum*, after all the advances made towards it by Bacon and D'Alembert. Indeed, in the present improved state of things, much is wanting to complete and perfect that more simple part of their intellectual map which relates to the material universe. Of the inconsiderable progress hitherto made towards a just delineation of the method to be pursued in studying the mental phenomena, no other evidence is necessary than this, That the sources of error and false judgment, so peculiarly connected, in consequence of the association of ideas, with studies in which our best interests are immediately and deeply concerned, have never yet been investigated with such accuracy as to afford effectual aid to the student, in his attempts to counteract their influence. One of these sources alone—that which arises from the imperfections of language—furnishes an exception to the general remark. It attracted, fortunately, the particular notice of Locke, whose observations with respect to it, compose, perhaps, the most valuable part of his philosophical writings; and, since the time of Condillac, the subject has been still more deeply analyzed by others. Even on this article, much yet remains to be done; but enough has been already accomplished to justify the profound aphorism in which Bacon pointed it out to the attention of his followers:—" Credunt homines rationem suam verbis imperare; sed fit etiam ut verba vim suam super rationem retorqueant."[*]

Into these logical discussions concerning the means of advancing the philosophy of human nature, Dr Reid has seldom entered; and still more rarely has he indulged himself in tracing the numerous relations by which this philosophy is connected with the practical business of life. But he has done what was still more essential at the time he wrote: he has exemplified, with the happiest success, that method of investigation by which alone any solid progress can be made; directing his inquiries to a subject which forms a necessary groundwork for the labours of his successors—an analysis of the various powers and principles belonging to our constitution. Of the importance of this undertaking, it is sufficient to observe, that it

---

* This passage of Bacon forms the motto to a very ingenious and philosophical dissertation, (lately published by M. Prevost of Geneva,) entitled, "Des Signes envisagés relativement à leur Influence sur la Formation des Idées." Paris, an 8.

stands somewhat, although I confess not altogether, in the same relation to the different branches of intellectual and moral science, (such as grammar, rhetoric, logic, ethics, natural theology, and politics,) in which the anatomy of the human body stands to the different branches of physiology and pathology. And, as a course of medical education naturally, or rather necessarily, begins with a general survey of man's animal frame, so I apprehend that the proper, or rather the essential preparation for those studies which regard our nobler concerns, is an examination of the principles which belong to man as an intelligent, active, social, and moral being. Nor does the importance of such an analysis rest here ; it exerts an influence over all those sciences and arts which are connected with the material world ; and the philosophy of Bacon itself, while it points out the road to physical truth, is but a branch of the philosophy of the human mind.

The substance of these remarks is admirably expressed by Mr Hume in the following passage—allowances being made for a few trifling peculiarities of expression, borrowed from the theories which were prevalent at the time when he wrote :—" 'Tis evident that all the sciences have a relation, greater or less, to human nature; and that, however wide any of them may seem to run from it, they still return back by one passage or another. Even mathematics, natural philosophy, and natural religion, are in some measure dependent on the science of man ; since they lie under the cognizance of men, and are judged of by their powers and faculties. It is impossible to tell what changes and improvements we might make in these sciences, were we thoroughly acquainted with the extent and force of human understanding, and could explain the nature of the ideas we employ, and of the operations we perform in our reasonings.

" If, therefore, the sciences of mathematics, natural philosophy, and natural religion, have such a dependence on the knowledge of man, what may be expected in the other sciences, whose connection with human nature is more close and intimate ? The sole end of logic is to explain the principles and operations of our reasoning faculty, and the nature of our ideas ; morals and criticism regard our tastes and sentiments ; and politics consider men as united in society and dependent on each other. In these four sciences of logic, morals, criticism, and politics, is comprehended almost everything which it can any way import us to be acquainted with, or which can tend either to the improvement or ornament of the human mind.

" Here, then, is the only expedient from which we can hope for success in our philo-sophical researches : to leave the tedious, lingering method, which we have hitherto followed ; and, instead of taking, now and then, a castle or village on the frontier, to march up directly to the capital or centre of these sciences—to human nature itself; which being once masters of, we may everywhere else hope for an easy victory. From this station, we may extend our conquests over all those sciences which more intimately concern human life, and may afterwards proceed at leisure to discover more fully those which are the objects of pure curiosity. There is no question of importance whose decision is not comprised in the science of man ; and there is none which can be decided with any certainty before we become acquainted with that science."

To prepare the way for the accomplishment of the design so forcibly recommended in the foregoing quotation—by exemplifying, in an analysis of our most important intellectual and active principles, the only method of carrying it successfully into execution— was the great object of Dr Reid in all his various philosophical publications. In examining these principles, he had chiefly in view a vindication of those fundamental laws of belief which form the groundwork of human knowledge, against the attacks made on their authority in some modern systems of scepticism ; leaving to his successors the more agreeable task of applying the philosophy of the mind to its practical uses. On the *analysis* and classification of our powers, which he has proposed, much room for improvement must have been left in so vast an undertaking ; but imperfections of this kind do not necessarily affect the justness of his conclusions, even where they may suggest to future inquirers the advantages of a simpler arrangement, and a more definite phraseology. Nor must it be forgotten that, in consequence of the plan he has followed, the mistakes which may be detected in particular parts of his works imply no such weakness in the fabric he has reared as might have been justly apprehended, had he presented a connected system founded on gratuitous hypothesis, or on arbitrary definitions. The detections, on the contrary, of his occasional errors, may be expected, from the invariable consistency and harmony of truth, to throw new lights on those parts of his work where his inquiries have been more successful ; as the correction of a particular mistatement in an authentic history is often found, by completing an imperfect link, or reconciling a seeming contradiction, to dispel the doubts which hung over the most faithful and accurate details of the narrative.

In Dr Reid's first performance, he confined himself entirely to the five senses, and the principles of our nature necessarily connected with them ; reserving the further prosecution of the subject for a future period. At that time, indeed, he seems to have thought, that a more comprehensive examination of the mind was an enterprise too great for one individual. " The powers," he observes, " of memory, of imagination, of taste, of reasoning, of moral perception, the will, the passions, the affections, and all the active powers of the soul, present a boundless field of philosophical disquisition, which the author of this ' Inquiry' is far from thinking himself able to explore with accuracy. Many authors of ingenuity, ancient and modern, have made incursions into this vast territory, and have communicated useful observations ; but there is reason to believe that those who have pretended to give us a map of the whole, have satisfied themselves with a very inaccurate and incomplete survey. If Galileo had attempted a complete system of natural philosophy, he had probably done little service to mankind ; but, by confining himself to what was within his comprehension, he laid the foundation of a system of knowledge, which rises by degrees, and does honour to the human understanding. Newton, building upon this foundation, and in like manner, confining his inquiries to the law of gravitation, and the properties of light, performed wonders. If he had attempted a great deal more, he had done a great deal less, and perhaps nothing at all. Ambitious of following such great examples, with unequal steps, alas! and unequal force, we have attempted an inquiry into one little corner only of the human mind ; that corner which seems to be most exposed to vulgar observation, and to be most easily comprehended ; and yet, if we have delineated it justly, it must be acknowledged that the accounts heretofore given of it were very lame, and wide of the truth."

From these observations, when compared with the magnitude of the work which the author lived to execute, there is some ground for supposing, that, in the progress of his researches, he became more and more sensible of the mutual connection and dependence which exists among the conclusions we form concerning the various principles of human nature ; even concerning those which seem, on a superficial view, to have the most remote relation to each other : and it was fortunate for the world, that, in this respect, he was induced to extend his views so far beyond the limits of his original design. His examination, indeed, of the powers of external perception, and of the questions immediately connected with them, bears marks of a still more minute diligence and accuracy than appear in some of his speculations concerning the other parts of our frame ; and what he has

written on the former subject, in his " Inquiry into the Human Mind," is evidently more highly finished, both in matter and form, than the volumes which he published in his more advanced years. The value, however, of these is inestimable to future adventurers in the same arduous undertaking ; not only in consequence of the aids they furnish as a rough draught of the field to be examined, but by the example they exhibit of a method of investigation on such subjects, hitherto very imperfectly understood by philosophers. It is by the originality of this method, so systematically pursued in all his researches, still more than by the importance of his particular conclusions, that he stands so conspicuously distinguished among those who have hitherto prosecuted analytically the study of man.

I have heard it sometimes mentioned, as a subject of regret, that the writers who have applied themselves to this branch of knowledge have, in general, aimed at a great deal more than it was possible to accomplish ; extending their researches to all the different parts of our constitution, while a long life might be well employed in examining and describing the phenomena connected with any one particular faculty. Dr Reid, in a passage already quoted from his " Inquiry," might have been supposed to give some countenance to this opinion, if his own subsequent labours did not so strongly sanction the practice in question. The truth, I apprehend, is, that such detached researches concerning the human mind can seldom be attempted with much hope of success ; and that those who have recommended them, have not attended sufficiently to the circumstances which so remarkably distinguish this study from that which has for its object the philosophy of the material world. A few remarks in illustration of this proposition seem to me to be necessary, in order to justify the reasonableness of Dr Reid's undertaking ; and they will be found to apply with still greater force to the labours of such as may wish to avail themselves of a similar analysis in explaining the varieties of human genius and character, or in developing the latent capacities of the youthful mind.

One consideration of a more general nature is, in the first place, worthy of notice ; that, in the infancy of every science, the grand and fundamental *desideratum* is a bold and comprehensive outline ; somewhat for the same reason that, in the cultivation of an extensive country, forests must be cleared and wildernesses reclaimed, before the limits of private property are fixed with accuracy ; and long before the period when the divisions and subdivisions of separate possessions give rise to the details of a curious and refined husbandry.

The speculations of Lord Bacon embraced all the objects of human knowledge. Those of Newton and Boyle were confined to physics; but included an astonishing range of the material universe. The labours of their successors, in our own times, have been employed with no less zeal in pursuing those more particular, but equally abstruse investigations, in which they were unable to engage, for want of a sufficient stock both of facts and of general principles; and which did not perhaps interest their curiosity in any considerable degree.

If these observations are allowed to hold to a certain extent with respect to all the sciences, they apply in a more peculiar manner to the subjects treated of in Dr Reid's writings—subjects which are all so intimately connected, that it may be doubted if it be possible to investigate any one completely, without some general acquaintance, at least, with the rest. Even the theory of the understanding may receive important lights from an examination of the active and the moral powers; the state of which, in the mind of every individual, will be found to have a powerful influence on his intellectual character;—while, on the other hand, an accurate analysis of the faculties of the understanding, would probably go far to obviate the sceptical difficulties which have been started concerning the origin of our moral ideas. It appears to me, therefore, that, whatever be the department of mental science that we propose more particularly to cultivate, it is necessary to begin with a survey of human nature in all its various parts; studying these parts, however, not so much on their own account, as with a reference to the applications of which our conclusions are susceptible to our favourite purpose. The researches of Dr Reid, when considered carefully in the relation which they bear to each other, afford numberless illustrations of the truth of this remark. His leading design was evidently to overthrow the modern system of scepticism; and, at every successive step of his progress, new and unexpected lights break in on his fundamental principles.

It is, however, chiefly in their practical application to the conduct of the understanding, and the culture of the heart, that such partial views are likely to be dangerous; for here, they tend not only to mislead our theoretical conclusions, but to counteract our improvement and happiness. Of this I am so fully convinced, that the most faulty theories of human nature, provided only they embrace the whole of it, appear to me less mischievous in their probable effects than those more accurate and microscopical researches which are habitually confined to one particular corner of our constitution. It is easy to conceive that, where the attention is wholly engrossed with the intellectual powers, the moral principles will be in danger of running to waste; and it is no less certain, on the other hand, that, by confining our care to the moral constitution alone, we may suffer the understanding to remain under the influence of unhappy prejudices, and destitute of those just and enlightened views without which the worthiest dispositions are of little use, either to ourselves or to society. An exclusive attention to any one of the subordinate parts of our frame—to the culture of taste, for example, or of the argumentative powers, or even to the refinement of our moral sentiments and feelings—must be attended with a hazard proportionally greater.

"In forming the human character," says Bacon, in a passage which Lord Bolingbroke has pronounced to be one of the finest and deepest in his writings, "we must not proceed as a statuary does in forming a statue, who works sometimes on the face, sometimes on the limbs, sometimes on the folds of the drapery; but we must proceed (and it is in our power to proceed) as Nature does in forming a flower, or any other of her productions: she throws out altogether, and at once, the whole system of being, and the rudiments of all the parts. *Rudimenta partium simul parit et producit.*" *

Of this passage, so strongly marked with Bacon's capacious intellect, and so richly adorned with his "philosophical fancy," I will not weaken the impression by any comment; and, indeed, to those who do not intuitively perceive its evidence, no comment would be useful.

In what I have hitherto said of Dr Reid's speculations, I have confined myself to such general views of the scope of his researches, and of his mode of philosophizing, as seemed most likely to facilitate the perusal of his works to those readers who have not been much conversant with these abstract disquisitions. A slight review of some of the more important and fundamental objections which have been proposed to his doctrines, may, I hope, be useful as a farther preparation for the same course of study.

Of these objections, the four following appear to me to be chiefly entitled to attention:—

1. That he has assumed gratuitously, in all his reasonings, that theory concerning the human soul which the scheme of materialism calls in question.

2. That his views tend to damp the ardour of philosophical curiosity, by stating as ultimate facts, phenomena which

---

* In the foregoing paragraph, I have borrowed (with a very trifling alteration) Lord Bolingbroke's words, in a beautiful paraphrase on Bacon's remark —See his " Idea of a Patriot King."

C

may be resolved into principles more simple and general.

3. That, by an unnecessary multiplication of original or instinctive principles, he has brought the science of mind into a state more perplexed and unsatisfactory than that in which it was left by Locke and his successors.

4. That his philosophy, by sanctioning an appeal from the decisions of the learned to the voice of the multitude, is unfavourable to a spirit of free inquiry, and lends additional stability to popular errors.

1. With respect to Dr Reid's supposed assumption of a doubtful hypothesis concerning the nature of the thinking and sentient principle, it is almost sufficient for me to observe, that the charge is directed against that very point of his philosophy in which it is most completely invulnerable. The circumstance which peculiarly characterises the inductive science of mind is, that it professes to abstain from all speculations concerning its nature and essence ; confining the attention entirely to phenomena for which we have the evidence of consciousness, and to the laws by which these phenomena are regulated. In this respect, it differs equally, in its scope, from the pneumatological discussions of the schools, and from the no less visionary theories so loudly vaunted by the physiological metaphysicians of more modern times. Compared with the first, it differs as the inquiries of the mechanical philosophers concerning the laws of moving bodies differ from the discussions of the ancient sophists concerning the existence and the nature of motion. Compared with the other, the difference is analogous to what exists between the conclusions of Newton concerning the law of gravitation, and his query concerning the invisible ether of which he supposes it might possibly be the effect. The facts which this inductive science aims at ascertaining, rest on their own proper evidence ; an evidence unconnected with all these hypotheses, and which would not, in the smallest degree, be affected, although the truth of any one of them should be fully established. It is not, therefore, on account of its inconsistency with any favourite opinions of my own, that I would oppose the disquisitions either of scholastic pneumatology, or of physiological metaphysics ; but because I consider them as an idle waste of time and genius on questions where our conclusions can neither be verified nor overturned by an appeal to experiment or observation. Sir Isaac Newton's query concerning the cause of gravitation was certainly not *inconsistent* with his own discoveries concerning its laws ; but what would have been the consequences

to the world, if he had indulged himself in the prosecution of hypothetical theories with respect to the former, instead of directing his astonishing powers to an investigation of the latter ?

That the general spirit of Dr Reid's philosophy is hostile to the conclusions of the materialist, is indeed a fact. Not, however, because his system rests on the contrary hypothesis as a fundamental principle, but because his inquiries have a powerful tendency to wean the understanding gradually from those obstinate associations and prejudices to which the common mechanical theories of mind owe all their plausibility. It is, in truth, much more from such examples of sound research concerning the laws of thought, than from any direct metaphysical refutation, that a change is to be expected in the opinions of those who have been accustomed to confound together two classes of phenomena, so completely and essentially different. But this view of the subject does not belong to the present argument.

It has been recommended of late, by a medical author of great reputation, to those who wish to study the human mind, to begin with preparing themselves for the task by the study of anatomy. I must confess, I cannot perceive the advantages of this order of investigation ; as the anatomy of the body does not seem to me more likely to throw light on the philosophy of the mind, than an analysis of the mind to throw light on the physiology of the body. To ascertain, indeed, the general laws of their connection from facts established by observation or experiment, is a reasonable and most interesting object of philosophical curiosity ; and in this inquiry, (which was long ago proposed and recommended by Lord Bacon,) a knowledge of the constitution both of mind and body is indispensably requisite ; but even here, if we wish to proceed on firm ground, the two classes of facts must be kept completely distinct ; so that neither of them may be warped or distorted in consequence of theories suggested by their supposed relations or analogies.*
Thus, in many of the phenomena connected with custom and habit, there is ample scope for investigating general laws, both with respect to our mental and our corporeal frame ; but what light do we derive from such information concerning this part of our constitution as is contained in the following sentence of Locke ?—" Habits seem to be but trains of motion in the animal spirits, which, once set a-going, continue in the same steps they had been used to, which, by often treading, are worn into a

---

* " Elements of the Philosophy of the Human Mind," pp. 11, 12. 2d edit.

smooth path." In like manner, the laws which regulate the connection between the mind and our external organs, in the case of perception, have furnished a very fertile subject of examination to some of the best of our modern philosophers; but how impotent does the genius of Newton itself appear, when it attempts to shoot the gulf which separates the sensible world and the sentient principle! "Is not the sensorium of animals," he asks in one of his queries, "the place where the sentient substance is present, and to which the sensible species of things are brought through the nerves and brain, that they may be perceived by the mind present in that place?"

It ought to be remembered, also, that this inquiry, with respect to the laws regulating the connection between our bodily organization, and the phenomena subjected to our own consciousness, is but one particular department of the philosophy of the mind; and that there still remains a wide, and, indeed, boundless region, where all our *data* must be obtained from our own mental operations. In examining, for instance, the powers of judgment and reasoning, let any person of sound understanding, after perusing the observations of Bacon on the different classes of our prejudices, or those of Locke on the abuse of words, turn his attention to the speculations of some of our contemporary theorists, and he will at once perceive the distinction between the two modes of investigation which I wish at present to contrast. "Reasoning," says one of the most ingenious and original of these, "is that operation of the *sensorium* by which we excite two or many tribes of ideas, and then re-excite the ideas in which they differ or correspond. If we determine this difference, it is called Judgment; if we in vain endeavour to determine it, it is called Doubting; if we re-excite the ideas in which they differ, it is called Distinguishing; if we re-excite those in which they correspond, it is called Comparing."[*] In what acceptation the word *idea* is to be understood in the foregoing passage, may be learned from the following definition of the same author: —"The word *idea* has various meanings in the writers of metaphysic: it is here used simply for those notions of external things which our organs of sense bring us acquainted with originally; and is defined a contraction, or motion, or configuration, of the fibres which constitute the immediate organ of sense."[†] Mr Hume, who was less of a physiologist than Dr Darwin, has made use of a language by no means so theoretical and arbitrary, but still widely removed from the simplicity and precision essentially neces-

sary in studies where everything depends on the cautious use of terms. "Belief," according to him, is "a lively idea related to or associated with a present impression; Memory is the faculty by which we repeat our impressions, so as that they retain a considerable degree of their first vivacity, and are somewhat intermediate betwixt an idea and an impression."

According to the views of Dr Reid, the terms which express the simple powers of the mind, are considered as unsusceptible of definition or explanation; the words, Feeling, for example, Knowledge, Will, Doubt, Belief, being, in this respect, on the same footing with the words, Green or Scarlet, Sweet or Bitter. To the names of these mental operations, all men annex some notions, more or less distinct; and the only way of conveying to them notions more correct, is by teaching them to exercise their own powers of reflection. The definitions quoted from Hume and Darwin, even if they were more unexceptionable in point of phraseology, would, for these reasons, be unphilosophical, as attempts to simplify what is incapable of analysis; but, as they are actually stated, they not only envelope truth in mystery, but lay a foundation, at the very outset, for an erroneous theory. It is worth while to add, that, of the two theories in question, that of Darwin, how inferior soever, in the estimation of competent judges, as a philosophical work, is by far the best calculated to impose on a very wide circle of readers, by the mixture it exhibits of crude and visionary metaphysics, with those important facts and conclusions which might be expected from the talents and experience of such a writer, in the present advanced state of medical and physiological science. The questions which have been hitherto confined to a few, prepared for such discussions by habits of philosophical study, are thus submitted to the consideration, not only of the cultivated and enlightened minds which adorn the medical profession, but of the half-informed multitude who follow the medical trade: nor is it to be doubted, that many of these will give the author credit, upon subjects of which they feel themselves incompetent to judge, for the same ability which he display, within their own professional sphere. The hypothetical principles assumed by Hume are intelligible to those only who are familiarized to the language of the schools: and his ingenuity and elegance, captivating as they are to men of taste and refinement, possess slight attractions to the majority of such as are most likely to be misled by his conclusions.

After all, I do not apprehend that the physiological theories concerning the mind, which have made so much noise of late

---

[*] "Zoonomia," vol. i. p 181, 3d edit.
[†] Ibid., vol. i. pp. 11, 12.

will produce a very lasting impression. The splendour of Dr Darwin's accomplishments could not fail to bestow a temporary importance on whatever opinions were sanctioned by his name ; as the chemical discoveries which have immortalized that of Priestley, have, for a while, recalled from oblivion the reveries of Hartley. But, abstracting from these accidental instances, in which human reason seems to have held a retrograde course, there has certainly been, since the time of Des Cartes, a continual, and, on the whole, a very remarkable approach to the inductive plan of studying human nature. We may trace this in the writings even of those who profess to consider *thought* merely as *an agitation of the brain*—in the writings more particularly of Hume and of Helvetius ; both of whom, although they may have occasionally expressed themselves in an unguarded manner concerning the nature of mind, have, in their most useful and practical disquisitions, been prevented, by their own good sense, from blending any theory with respect to the *causes* of the intellectual phenomena with the history of facts, or the investigation of general laws. The authors who form the most conspicuous exceptions to this gradual progress, consist chiefly of men whose errors may be easily accounted for, by the prejudices connected with their circumscribed habits of observation and inquiry : of physiologists, accustomed to attend to that part alone of the human frame which the knife of the anatomist can lay open ; or of chemists, who enter on the analysis of thought, fresh from the decompositions of the laboratory—carrying into the theory of mind itself (what Bacon expressively calls) " the smoke and tarnish of the furnace." Of the value of such pursuits, none can think more highly than myself ; but I must be allowed to observe, that the most distinguished pre-eminence in them does not necessarily imply a capacity of collected and abstracted reflection, or an understanding superior to the prejudices of early association, and the illusions of popular language. I will not go so far as Cicero, when he ascribes to those who possess these advantages, a more than ordinary vigour of intellect :—" *Magni est ingenii revocare mentem a sensibus, et cogitationem a consuetudine abducere.*" I would only claim for them the merit of patient and cautious research ; and would exact from their antagonists the same qualifications.*

In offering these remarks, I have no wish to exalt any one branch of useful knowledge at the expense of another, but to combat prejudices equally fatal to the

progress of them all. With the same view, I cannot help taking notice of a prevailing, but very mistaken idea, that the formation of a hypothetical system is a stronger proof of inventive genius than the patient investigation of Nature in the way of induction. To form a system, appears to the young and inexperienced understanding a species of creation ; to ascend slowly to general conclusions, from the observation and comparison of particular facts, is to comment servilely on the works of another.

No opinion, surely, can be more groundless. To fix on a few principles, or even on a single principle, as the foundation of a theory ; and, by an artful statement of supposed facts, aided by a dexterous use of language, to give a plausible explanation, by means of it, of an immense number of phenomena, is within the reach of most men whose talents have been a little exercised among the subtilties of the schools : whereas, to follow Nature through all her varieties with a quick yet an exact eye—to record faithfully what she exhibits, and to record nothing more—to trace, amidst the diversity of her operations, the simple and comprehensive laws by which they are regulated, and sometimes to guess at the beneficent purposes to which they are subservient—may be safely pronounced to be the highest effort of a created intelligence. And, accordingly, the number of ingenious theorists has, in every age, been great ; that of sound philosophers has been wonderfully small ;—or, rather, they are only beginning now to have a glimpse of their way, in consequence of the combined lights furnished by their predecessors.

Des Cartes aimed at a complete system of physics, deduced *à priori* from the abstract suggestions of his own reason ; Newton aspired no higher than at a faithful " interpretation of Nature," in a few of the more general laws which she presents to our notice : and yet the intellectual power displayed in the voluminous writings of the former vanishes into nothing when compared with what we may trace in a single page of the latter. On this occasion, a remark of Lord Bacon appears singularly apposite—that " Alexander and Cæsar, though they acted without the aid of magic or prodigy, performed exploits that are truly greater than what fable reports of King Arthur or Amadis de Gaul."

I shall only add farther on this head, that the last observation holds more strictly with respect to the philosophy of the human mind, than any other branch of science ; for there is no subject whatever on which it is so easy to form theories calculated to impose on the multitude ; and none where the discovery of truth is attended with so many difficulties. One great cause of this

---

* Note D.

Is, the analogical or theoretical terms employed in ordinary language to express every thing relating either to our intellectual or active powers; in consequence of which, specious explanations of the most mysterious phenomena may be given to superficial inquirers; while, at the same time, the labour of just investigation is increased to an incalculable degree.

2. To allege that, in this circumscription of the field of our inquiries concerning the mind, there is any tendency to repress a reasonable and philosophical curiosity, is a charge no less unfounded than the former; inasmuch as every physical inquiry concerning the material world is circumscribed by limits precisely analogous. In all our investigations, whatever their subject may be, the business of philosophy is confined to a reference of particular facts to other facts more general; and our most successful researches must at length terminate in some law of nature, of which no explanation can be given. In its application to Dr Reid's writings, this objection has, I think, been more pointedly directed against his reasonings concerning the process of nature in perception; a part of his writings which (as it is of fundamental importance in his general system) he has laboured with peculiar care. The result is, indeed, by no means flattering to the pride of those theorists who profess to explain everything; for it amounts to an acknowledgment that, after all the lights which anatomy and physiology supply, the information we obtain by means of our senses, concerning the existence and the qualities of matter, is no less incomprehensible to our faculties than it appears to the most illiterate peasant; and that all we have gained, is a more precise and complete acquaintance with some particulars in our animal economy—highly interesting, indeed, when regarded in their proper light, as accessions to our physical knowledge, but, considered in connection with the philosophy of the mind, affording only a more accurate statement of the astonishing phenomena which we would vainly endeavour to explain. This language has been charged, but most unjustly and ignorantly, with *mysticism ;* for the same charge may be brought, with equal fairness, against all the most important discoveries in the sciences. It was, in truth, the very objection urged against Newton, when his adversaries contended, that *gravity* was to be ranked with the *occult qualities* of the schoolmen, till its mechanical cause should be assigned ; and the answer given to this objection, by Sir Isaac Newton's commentator, Mr Maclaurin, may be literally applied, in the instance before us. to the inductive philosophy of the human mind :—

" The opponents of Newton, finding no-

thing to object to his observations and reasonings, pretended to find a resemblance between his doctrines and the exploded tenets of the scholastic philosophy. They triumphed mightily in treating gravity as an occult quality, because he did not pretend to deduce this principle fully from its cause.

. . . I know not that ever it was made an objection to the circulation of the blood, that there is no small difficulty in accounting for it mechanically. They, too, who first extended gravity to air, vapour, and to all bodies round the earth, had their praise ; though the cause of gravity was as obscure as before ; or *rather appeared more mysterious,* after they had shewn that there was no body found near the earth, exempt from gravity, that might be supposed to be its cause. Why, then, were his admirable discoveries, by which this principle was extended over the universe, so ill relished by some philosophers ? The truth is, he had, with great evidence, overthrown the boasted schemes by which they pretended to unravel all the mysteries of nature ; and the philosophy he introduced in place of them, carrying with it a sincere confession of our being far from a complete and perfect knowledge of it, could not please those who had been accustomed to imagine themselves possessed of the eternal reasons and primary causes of all things.

" It was, however, no new thing that this philosophy should meet with opposition. All the useful discoveries that were made in former times, and particularly in the seventeenth century, had to struggle with the prejudices of those who had accustomed themselves, not so much as to think but in a certain systematic way ; who could not be prevailed on to abandon their favourite schemes, while they were able to imagine the least pretext for continuing the dispute. Every art and talent was displayed to support their falling cause ; no aid seemed foreign to them that could in any manner annoy their adversary ; and such often was their obstinacy, that truth was able to make little progress, till they were succeeded by younger persons, who had not so strongly imbibed their prejudices."

These excellent observations are not the less applicable to the subject now under consideration, that the part of Dr Reid's writings which suggested the quotation, leads only to the correction of an inveterate prejudice, not to any new general conclusion. It is probable, indeed, (now that the ideal theory has, in a great measure, disappeared from our late metaphysical systems,) that those who have a pleasure in detracting from the merits of their predecessors, may be disposed to represent it as an idle waste of labour and ingenuity to have entered into a serious refutation of a hypothesis at once gratuitous and inconceivable. A different judgment, however, will be formed by such as are acquainted with the extensive influence which, from the earliest accounts of science, this single prejudice has had in vitiating almost every branch of the philosophy of the mind; and who, at the same time, recollect the names of the illustrious men by whom, in more modern times, it has been adopted as an incontrovertible principle. It is sufficient for me to mention those of Berkeley, Hume, Locke, Clarke, and Newton. To the two first of these, it has served as the basis of their sceptical conclusions, which seem, indeed, to follow from it as necessary consequences; while the others repeatedly refer to it in their reasonings, as one of those facts concerning the mind of which it would be equally superfluous to attempt a proof or a refutation.

I have enlarged on this part of Dr Reid's writings the more fully, as he was himself disposed, on all occasions, to rest upon it his chief merit as an author. In proof of this, I shall transcribe a few sentences from a letter of his to Dr Gregory, dated 20th August 1790:—

"It would be want of candour not to own that I think there is some merit in what you are pleased to call *my Philosophy*; but I think it lies chiefly in having called in question the common theory of *Ideas, or Images of things in the mind* being the only objects of thought; a theory founded on natural prejudices, and so universally received as to be interwoven with the structure of language. Yet, were I to give you a detail of what led me to call in question this theory, after I had long held it as self-evident and unquestionable, you would think, as I do, that there was much of chance in the matter. The discovery was the birth of time, not of genius; and Berkeley and Hume did more to bring it to light than the man that hit upon it. I think there is hardly anything that can be called *mine* in the philosophy of the mind, which does not follow with ease from the detection of this prejudice.

"I must, therefore, beg of you most earnestly, to make no contrast in my favour to the disparagement of my predecessors in the same pursuit. I can truly say of them, and shall always avow, what you are pleased to say of me, that, but for the assistance I have received from their writings, I never could have wrote or thought what I have done."

3. Somewhat connected with the last objection, are the censures which have been so frequently bestowed on Dr Reid, for an unnecessary and unsystematical multiplication of original or instinctive principles. In reply to these censures, I have little

to add to what I have remarked on the same topic, in the " Philosophy of the Human Mind." That the fault which is thus ascribed to Dr Reid has been really committed by some ingenious writers in this part of the island, I most readily allow; nor will I take upon me to assert that he has, in no instance, fallen into it himself. Such instances, however, will be found, on an accurate examination of his works, to be comparatively few, and to bear a very trifling proportion to those in which he has most successfully and decisively displayed his acuteness in exposing the premature and flimsy generalizations of his predecessors.

A certain degree of leaning to that extreme to which Dr Reid seems to have inclined, was, at the time when he wrote, much safer than the opposite bias. From the earliest ages, the sciences in general, and more particularly the science of the human mind, have been vitiated by an undue love of simplicity; and, in the course of the last century, this disposition, after having been long displayed in subtle theories concerning the active powers, or the principles of human conduct, has been directed to similar refinements with respect to the faculties of the understanding, and the truths with which they are conversant. Mr Hume himself has coincided so far with the Hartleian school, as to represent the " principle of union and cohesion among our simple ideas as a kind of *attraction*, of as universal application in the mental world as in the natural;"[*] and Dr Hartley, with a still more sanguine imagination, looked forward to an era " when future generations shall put all kinds of evidences and inquiries into mathematical forms; reducing Aristotle's ten categories, and Bishop Wilkin's forty *summa genera*, to the head of quantity alone, so as to make mathematics and logic, natural history and civil history, natural philosophy and philosophy of all other kinds, coincide, *omni ex parte*."[†]

It is needless to remark the obvious tendency of such premature generalizations, to withdraw the attention from the study of particular phenomena; while the effect of Reid's mode of philosophizing, even in those instances where it is carried to an excess, is to detain us, in this preliminary step, a little longer than is absolutely necessary. The truth is, that, when the phenomena are once ascertained, generalization is here of comparatively little value, and a task of far less difficulty than to observe facts with precision, and to record them with fairness.

---

* " Treatise of Human Nature," vol. i. p. 30.
† Hartley " On Man," p. 207, 4to edit. London, 1791.

In no part of Dr Reid's writings, I am inclined to think, could more plausible criticisms be made on this ground, than in his classification of our active principles : but, even there, the facts are always placed fully and distinctly before the reader. That several of the benevolent affections which he has stated as ultimate facts in our constitution, might be analyzed into the same general principle differently modified, according to circumstances, there can, in my opinion, be little doubt. This, however, (as I have elsewhere observed,*) notwithstanding the stress which has been sometimes laid upon it, is chiefly a question of arrangement. Whether we suppose these affections to be all ultimate facts, or some of them to be resolvable into other facts more general, they are equally to be regarded as constituent parts of human nature ; and, upon either supposition, we have equal reason to admire the wisdom with which that nature is adapted to the situation in which it is placed. The laws which regulate the acquired perceptions of sight, are surely as much a part of our frame as those which regulate any of our original perceptions ; and, although they require, for their developement, a certain degree of experience and observation in the individual, the uniformity of the result shews that there is nothing arbitrary nor accidental in their origin. In this point of view, what can be more philosophical, as well as beautiful, than the words of Mr Ferguson, that "natural affection springs up in the soul of the mother, as the milk springs in her breast, to furnish nourishment to her child !" "The effect is here to the race," as the same author has excellently observed, "what the vital motion of the heart is to the individual ; too necessary to the preservation of nature's works, to be intrusted to the precarious will or intention of those most nearly concerned."†

The question, indeed, concerning the origin of our different affections, leads to some curious analytical disquisitions ; but is of very subordinate importance to those inquiries which relate to their laws, and uses, and mutual references. In many ethical systems, however, it seems to have been considered as the most interesting subject of disquisition which this wonderful part of our frame presents.

In Dr Reid's " Essays on the Intellectual Powers of Man," and in his " Inquiry into the Human Mind," I recollect little

that can justly incur a similar censure, notwithstanding the ridicule which Dr Priestley has attempted to throw on the last of these performances, in his " Table of Reid's Instinctive Principles."* To examine all the articles enumerated in that table, would require a greater latitude of disquisition than the limits of this memoir allow ; and, therefore, I shall confine my observations to a few instances, where the precipitancy of the general criticism seems to me to admit of little dispute. In this light I cannot help considering it, when applied to those dispositions or determinations of the mind to which Dr Reid has given the names of the " Principle of Credulity," and the " Principle of Veracity." How far these titles are happily chosen, is a question of little moment ; and on that point I am ready to make every concession. I contend only for what is essentially connected with the objection which has given rise to these remarks.

" That any man," says Dr Priestley, " should imagine that a peculiar instinctive principle was necessary to explain our giving credit to the relations of others, appears to me, who have been used to see things in a different light, very extraordinary ; and yet this doctrine is advanced by Dr Reid, and adopted by Dr Beattie. But really," he adds, " what the former says in favour of it, is hardly deserving of the slightest notice."†

The passage quoted by Dr Priestley, in justification of this very peremptory decision, is as follows :—" If credulity were the effect of reasoning and experience, it must grow up and gather strength in the same proportion as reason and experience do. But, if it is the gift of nature, it will be the strongest in childhood, and limited and restrained by experience ; and the most superficial view of human life shews that this last is the case, and not the first."

To my own judgment, this argument of Dr Reid's, when connected with the excellent illustrations which accompany it, carries complete conviction ; and I am confirmed in my opinion by finding, that Mr Smith (a writer inferior to none in acuteness, and strongly disposed, by the peculiar bent of his genius, to simplify, as far as possible, the philosophy of human nature) has, in the latest edition of his " Theory of Moral Sentiments," acquiesced in this very conclusion ; urging in support of it the same reasoning which Dr Priestley affects to estimate so lightly. " There seems to be in young children an instinctive

---

* " Outlines of Moral Philosophy," pp. 79, 80, 2d edit. Edinburgh, 1801.
† " Principles of Moral and Political Science," part I. chap. I. sect. 3. " Of the Principles of Society in Human Nature." The whole discussion unites, in a singular degree, the soundest philosophy with the most eloquent description.

* Examination of Reid's " Inquiry," &c. London 1774.
† Examination of Reid's " Inquiry," &c., p. 82

disposition to believe whatever they are told. Nature seems to have judged it necessary for their preservation that they should, for some time at least, put implicit confidence in those to whom the care of their childhood, and of the earliest and most necessary part of their education, is intrusted. Their credulity, accordingly, is excessive; and it requires long and much experience of the falsehood of mankind to reduce them to a reasonable degree of diffidence and distrust."[*] That Mr Smith's opinion also coincided with Dr Reid's, in what he has stated concerning the *principle of veracity*, appears evidently from the remarks which immediately follow the passage just quoted. But I must not add to the length of this memoir by unnecessary citations.

Another instinctive principle mentioned by Reid, is " our belief of the continuance of the present course of nature." "All our knowledge of nature," he observes, " beyond our original perceptions, is got by experience, and consists in the interpretation of natural signs. The appearance of the sign is followed by the belief of the thing signified. Upon this principle of our constitution, not only acquired perception, but also inductive reasoning, and all reasoning from analogy, is grounded; and, therefore, for want of a better name, we shall beg leave to call it the *inductive principle*. It is from the force of this principle that we immediately assent to that axiom upon which all our knowledge of nature is built, that effects of the same kind must have the same cause. Take away the light of this inductive principle, and experience is as blind as a mole. She may indeed feel what is present, and what immediately touches her, but she sees nothing that is either before or behind, upon the right hand or upon the left, future or past."

On this doctrine, likewise, the same critic has expressed himself with much severity; calling it " a mere quibble;" and adding, " every step that I take among this writer's sophisms, raises my astonishment higher than before." In this, however, as in many other instances, he has been led to censure Dr Reid, not because he was able to see farther than his antagonist, but because he did not see quite so far. Turgot, in an article inserted in the French " Encyclopédie," and Condorcet, in a discourse prefixed to one of his mathematical publications,[†] have, both of them, stated the fact with a true philosophical precision; and, after doing so, have deduced from it an inference, not only the same in substance with that of Dr Reid, but almost expressed in the same form of words.

In these references, as well as in that already made to Mr Smith's " Theory," I would not be understood to lay any undue stress on authority in a philosophical argument. I wish only—by contrasting the modesty and caution resulting from habits of profound thought, with that theoretical intrepidity which a blindness to insuperable difficulties has a tendency to inspire— to invite those whose prejudices against this part of Reid's system rest chiefly on the great names to which they conceive it to be hostile, to re-examine it with a little more attention, before they pronounce finally on its merits.

The prejudices which are apt to occur against a mode of philosophizing so mortifying to scholastic arrogance, are encouraged greatly by that natural disposition, to refer particular facts to general laws, which is the foundation of all scientific arrangement; a principle of the utmost importance to our intellectual constitution, but which requires the guidance of a sound and experienced understanding to accomplish the purposes for which it was destined. They are encouraged also, in no inconsiderable degree, by the acknowledged success of mathematicians, in raising, on the basis of a few simple *data*, the most magnificent, and, at the same time, the most solid fabric of science, of which human genius can boast. The absurd references which logicians are accustomed to make to Euclid's " Elements of Geometry," as a model which cannot be too studiously copied, both in physics and in morals, have contributed, in this as in a variety of other instances, to mislead philosophers from the study of facts, into the false refinements of hypothetical theory.

On these misapplications of mathematical method to sciences which rest ultimately on experiment and observation, I shall take another opportunity of offering some strictures. At present, it is sufficient to remark the peculiar nature of the truths about which pure or abstract mathematics are conversant. As these truths have all a necessary connection with each other, (all of them resting ultimately on those definitions or hypotheses which are the principles of our reasoning,) the beauty of the science cannot fail to increase in proportion to the simplicity of the *data*, compared with the incalculable variety of consequences which they involve: and to the simplifications and generalizations of theory on such a subject, it is perhaps impossible to conceive any limit. How different is the case in those inquiries where our first principles are not *definitions* but

---

* Smith's " Theory," last edit. part VII. sect 1.
† " Essai sur l'application de l'analyse à la probabilité des decisions rendues à la pluralité des voix." Paris, 1785.

facts, and wnere our business is not to trace necessary connections, but the laws which regulate the established order of the universe !

In various attempts which have been lately made, more especially on the Continent, towards a systematical exposition of the elements of physics, the effects of the mistake I am now censuring are extremely remarkable. The happy use of mathematical principles, exhibited in the writings of Newton and his followers, having rendered an extensive knowledge of them an indispensable preparation for the study of the mechanical philosophy, the early habits of thought acquired in the former pursuit are naturally transferred to the latter. Hence the illogical and obscure manner in which its elementary principles have frequently been stated; an attempt being made to deduce, from the smallest possible number of *data*, the whole system of truths which it comprehends. The analogy existing among some of the fundamental laws of mechanics, bestows, in the opinion of the multitude, an appearance of plausibility on such attempts; and their obvious tendency is to withdraw the attention from that unity of design which it is the noblest employment of philosophy to illustrate, by disguising it under the semblance of an eternal and necessary order, similar to what the mathematician delights to trace among the mutual relations of quantities and figures.

These slight hints may serve as a reply in part to what Dr Priestley has suggested with respect to the consequences likely to follow, if the spirit of Reid's philosophy should be introduced into physics.* One consequence would unquestionably be, a careful separation between the principles which we learn from experience alone, and those which are fairly resolvable, by mathematical or physical reasoning, into other facts still more general ; and, of course, a correction of that false logic which, while it throws an air of mystery over the plainest and most undeniable facts, levels the study of nature, in point of moral interest, with the investigations of the geometer or of the algebraist.

It must not, however, be supposed, that, in the present state of natural philosophy, a false logic threatens the same dangerous effects as in the philosophy of the mind. It may retard somewhat the progress of the student at his first outset ; or it may confound, in his apprehensions, the harmony of systematical order with the consistency and mutual dependency essential to a series of mathematical theorems : but the fundamental truths of physics are now too well

established, and the checks which it furnishes against sophistry are too numerous and palpable, to admit the possibility of any permanent error in our deductions. In the philosophy of the mind, so difficult is the acquisition of those habits of reflection which can alone lead to a correct knowledge of the intellectual *phænomena*, that a faulty hypothesis, if skilfully fortified by the imposing, though illusory strength of arbitrary definitions and a systematical phraseology, may maintain its ground for a succession of ages.

It will not, I trust, be inferred from anything I have here advanced, that I mean to offer an apology for those who, either in physics or morals, would presumptuously state their own opinions with respect to the laws of nature, as a bar against future attempts to simplify and generalize them still farther. To assert that none of the mechanical explanations yet given of gravitation are satisfactory, and even to hint that ingenuity might be more profitably employed than in the search of such a theory, is something different from a gratuitous assumption of ultimate facts in physics ; nor does it imply an obstinate determination to resist legitimate evidence, should some fortunate inquirer—contrary to what seems probable at present—succeed where the genius of Newton has failed. If Dr Reid has gone farther than this in his conclusions concerning the principles which he calls original or instinctive, he has departed from that guarded language in which he commonly expresses himself—for all that it was of importance for him to conclude was, that the theories of his predecessors were, in these instances, exceptionable ; and the doubts he may occasionally insinuate, concerning the success of future adventurers, so far from betraying any overweening confidence in his own understanding, are an indirect tribute to the talents of those from whose failure he draws an argument against the possibility of their undertaking.

The same eagerness to simplify and to generalize, which led Priestley to complain of the number of Reid's instinctive principles, has carried some later philosophers a step farther. According to them, the very word *instinct* is unphilosophical ; and everything, either in man or brute, which has been hitherto referred to this mysterious source, may be easily accounted for by experience or imitation. A few instances in which this doctrine appears to have been successfully verified, have been deemed sufficient to establish it without any limitation.

In a very original work, on which I have already hazarded some criticisms, much ingenuity has been employed in analyzing the wonderful efforts which the human infant

---

* "Examination of Reid's Inquiry, p 110.

is enabled to make for its own preservation the moment after its introduction to the light. Thus, it is observed that the *fœtus*, while still in the *uterus*, learns to perform the operation of swallowing; and also learns to relieve itself, by a change of posture, from the irksomeness of continued rest: and, therefore, (if we admit these propositions,) we must conclude that some of the actions which infants are vulgarly supposed to perform in consequence of instincts coeval with birth, are only a continuation of actions to which they were determined at an earlier period of their being. The remark is ingenious, and it may perhaps be just; but it does not prove that *instinct* is an unphilosophical term; nor does it render the operations of the infant less mysterious than they seem to be on the common supposition. How far soever the analysis, in such instances, may be carried, we must at last arrive at some *phænomenon* no less wonderful than that we mean to explain : in other words, we must still admit as an ultimate fact, the existence of an original determination to a particular mode of action salutary or necessary to the animal; and all we have accomplished is, to connect the origin of this instinct with an earlier period in the history of the human mind.

The same author has attempted to account, in a manner somewhat similar, for the different degrees in which the young of different animals are able, at the moment of birth, to exert their bodily powers. Thus, calves and chickens are able to walk almost immediately; while the human infant, even in the most favourable situations, is six or even twelve months old before he can stand alone. For this Dr Darwin assigns two causes. 1. That the young of some animals come into the world in a more complete state than that of others— the colt and lamb, for example, enjoying, in this respect, a striking advantage over the puppy and the rabbit. 2. That the mode of walking of some animals, coincides more perfectly than that of others, with the previous motions of the *fœtus in utero*. The struggles of all animals, he observes, in the womb, must resemble their manner of swimming, as by this kind of motion they can best change their attitude in water. But the swimming of the calf and of the chicken resembles their ordinary movements on the ground, which they have thus learned in part to execute while concealed from our observation; whereas, the swimming of the human infant differing totally from his manner of walking, he has no opportunity of acquiring the last of these arts till he is exposed to our view. The theory is extremely plausible, and does honour to the author's sagacity; but it only places in a new light that provident care which Nature

has taken of all her offspring in the infancy of their existence.

Another instance may contribute towards a more ample illustration of the same subject. A lamb, not many minutes after it is dropped, proceeds to search for its nourishment in that spot where alone it is to be found; applying both its limbs and its eyes to their respective offices. The peasant observes the fact, and gives the name of *instinct*, or some corresponding term, to the unknown principle by which the animal is guided. On a more accurate examination of circumstances, the philosopher finds reason to conclude that it is by the sense of smelling it is thus directed to its object. In proof of this, among other curious facts, the following has been quoted :—" On dissecting," says Galen, " a goat great with young, I found a brisk *embryon*, and having detached it from the *matrix*, and snatching it away before it saw its dam, I brought it into a room where there were many vessels; some filled with wine, others with oil, some with honey, others with milk, or some other liquor; and in others there were grains and fruits. We first observed the young animal get upon its feet and walk; then it shook itself, and afterwards scratched its side with one of its feet; then we saw it smelling to every one of those things that were set in the room; and, when it had smelt to them all, it drank up the milk."* Admitting this very beautiful story to be true, (and, for my own part, I am far from being disposed to question its probability,) it only enables us to state the fact with a little more precision, in consequence of our having ascertained, that it is to the sense of smelling the instinctive determination is attached. The conclusion of the peasant is not here at variance with that of the philosopher. It differs only in this, that he expresses himself in those general terms which are suited to his ignorance of the particular process by which Nature, in this case, accomplishes her end; and, if he did otherwise, he would be censurable for prejudging a question of which he is incompetent to form an accurate opinion.

The application of these illustrations to some of Dr Reid's conclusions concerning the instinctive principles of the human mind, is, I flatter myself, sufficiently manifest. They relate, indeed, to a subject which differs, in various respects, from that which has fallen under his more particular consideration; but the same rules of philosophizing will be found to apply equally to both.

4. The criticisms which have been made on what Dr Reid has written concerning

---

* Darwin, vol. i pp. 195, 196.

the intuitive truths which he distinguishes by the title of " Principles of Common Sense," would require a more ample discussion than I can now bestow on them; not that the importance of these criticisms (of such of them, at least, as I have happened to meet with) demands a long or elaborate refutation, but because the subject, according to the view I wish to take of it, involves some other questions of great moment and difficulty, relative to the foundations of human knowledge. Dr Priestley, the most formidable of Dr Reid's antagonists, has granted as much in favour of this doctrine as it is worth while to contend for on the present occasion. " Had these writers," he observes, with respect to Dr Reid and his followers, " assumed, as the elements of their Common Sense, certain truths which are so plain that no man could doubt of them, (without entering into the ground of our assent to them,) their conduct would have been liable to very little objection. All that could have been said would have been, that, without any necessity, they had made an innovation in the received use of a term; for no person ever denied that there are self-evident truths, and that these must be assumed as the foundation of all our reasoning. I never met with any person who did not acknowledge this, or heard of any argumentative treatise that did not go upon the supposition of it."[*] After such an acknowledgment, it is impossible to forbear asking, (with Dr Campbell,) " What is the great point which Dr Priestley would controvert? Is it, whether such self-evident truths shall be denominated Principles of Common Sense, or be distinguished by some other appellation ?"[†]

That the doctrine in question has been, in some publications, presented in a very exceptionable form, I most readily allow; nor would I be understood to subscribe to it implicitly, even as it appears in the works of Dr Reid. It is but an act of justice to him, however, to request that his opinions may be judged of from his own works alone, not from those of others who may have happened to coincide with him in certain tenets, or in certain modes of expression; and that, before any ridicule be attempted on his conclusions concerning the authority of Common Sense, his antagonists would take the trouble to examine in what acceptation he has employed that phrase. The truths which Dr Reid seems, in most instances, disposed to refer to the judgment of this tribunal, might, in my opinion, be denominated more unexceptionably, " fundamental laws of human belief." They

have been called by a very ingenious foreigner, (M. Trembley of Geneva,) but certainly with a singular infelicity of language, *Préjugés Légitimes.* Of this kind are the following propositions :—" I am the same person to-day that I was yesterday ;" " The material world has an existence independent of that of percipient beings ;" " There are other intelligent beings in the universe beside myself ;" " The future course of nature will resemble the past." Such truths no man but a philosopher ever thinks of stating to himself in words ; but all our conduct and all our reasonings proceed on the supposition that they are admitted. The belief of them is essential for the preservation of our animal existence ; and it is accordingly coeval with the first operations of the intellect.

One of the first writers who introduced the phrase Common Sense into the technical or appropriate language of logic, was Father Buffier, in a book entitled, " *Traité des Premières Verités.*" It has since been adopted by several authors of note in this country ; particularly by Dr Reid, Dr Oswald, and Dr Beattie; by all of whom, however, I am afraid, it must be confessed, it has been occasionally employed without a due attention to precision. The last of these writers uses it[*] to denote that power by which the mind perceives the truth of any intuitive proposition ; whether it be an axiom of abstract science ; or a statement of some fact resting on the immediate information of consciousness, of perception, or of memory ; or one of those fundamental laws of belief which are implied in the application of our faculties to the ordinary business of life. The same extensive use of the word may, I believe, be found in the other authors just mentioned. But no authority can justify such a laxity in the employment of language in philosophical discussions ; for, if mathematical axioms be (as they are, manifestly and indisputably) a class of propositions essentially distinct from the other kinds of intuitive truths now described, why refer them all indiscriminately to the same principle in our constitution ? If this phrase, therefore, be at all retained, precision requires that it should be employed in a more limited acceptation ; and, accordingly, in the works under our consideration, it is appropriated most frequently, though by no means uniformly, to that class of intuitive truths which I have already called " fundamental laws of belief."[†] When thus restricted, it conveys a notion, unambiguous, at least,

---

* " Examination of Dr Reid's Inquiry." &c p. 119.
† " Philosophy of Rhetoric," vol. i. p. 111.—See Note E.

* " Essay on Truth," edition second, p. 40, *et seq.* ; also p 166, *et s-q.*
† This seems to be nearly the meaning annexed to the phrase, by the learned and acute author of " The Philosophy of Rhetoric," vol i p 109, *et seq.*

and definite ; and, consequently, the question about its propriety or impropriety turns entirely on the coincidence of this definition with the meaning of the word as employed in ordinary discourse. Whatever objections, therefore, may be stated to the expression as now defined, will apply to it with additional force, when used with the latitude which has been already censured.

I have said that the question about the propriety of the phrase Common Sense as employed by philosophers, must be decided by an appeal to general practice ; for, although it be allowable, and even necessary, for a philosopher to limit the acceptation of words which are employed vaguely in common discourse, it is always dangerous to give to a word a scientific meaning essentially distinct from that in which it is usually understood. It has, at least, the effect of misleading those who do not enter deeply into the subject ; and of giving a paradoxical appearance to doctrines which, if expressed in more unexceptionable terms, would be readily admitted.

It appears to me that this has actually happened in the present instance. The phrase Common Sense, as it is generally understood, is nearly synonymous with *mother-wit;* denoting that degree of sagacity (depending partly on original capacity, and partly on personal experience and observation) which qualifies an individual for those simple and essential occupations which all men are called on to exercise habitually by their common nature. In this acceptation, it is opposed to those mental acquirements which are derived from a regular education, and from the study of books ; and refers, not to the speculative convictions of the understanding, but to that prudence and discretion which are the foundation of successful conduct. Such is the idea which Pope annexes to the word, when, speaking of good sense, (which means only a more than ordinary share of common sense,) he calls it—

" The gift of Heaven,
And, though no science, fairly worth the seven."

To speak, accordingly, of appealing from the conclusions of philosophy to common sense, had the appearance, to title-page readers, of appealing from the verdict of the learned to the voice of the multitude ; or of attempting to silence free discussion by a reference to some arbitrary and undefinable standard, distinct from any of the intellectual powers hitherto enumerated by logicians. Whatever countenance may be supposed to have been given by some writers to such an interpretation of this doctrine, I may venture to assert that none is afforded by the works of Dr Reid. The standard to which he appeals is neither the creed of a particular sect, nor the inward light of

enthusiastic presumption, but that constitution of human nature without which all the business of the world would immediately cease ; and the substance of his argument amounts merely to this, that those essential laws of belief to which sceptics have objected, when considered in connection with our scientific reasonings, are implied in every step we take as active beings ; and if called in question by any man in his practical concerns would expose him universally to the charge of insanity.

In stating this important doctrine, it were perhaps to be wished that the subject had been treated with somewhat more of analytical accuracy ; and it is certainly to be regretted that a phrase should have been employed, so well calculated by its ambiguity to furnish a convenient handle to misrepresentations ; but, in the judgment of those who have perused Dr Reid's writings with an intelligent and candid attention, these misrepresentations must recoil on their authors ; while they who are really interested in the progress of useful science, will be disposed rather to lend their aid in supplying what is defective in his views than to reject hastily a doctrine which aims, by the developement of some logical principles overlooked in the absurd systems which have been borrowed from the schools, to vindicate the authority of truths intimately and extensively connected with human happiness.

In the prosecution of my own speculations on the human mind, I shall have occasion to explain myself fully concerning this, as well as various other questions connected with the foundations of philosophical evidence. The new doctrines and new phraseology on that subject, which have lately become fashionable among some metaphysicians in Germany, and which, in my opinion, have contributed not a little to involve it in additional obscurity, are a sufficient proof that this essential and fundamental article of logic is not as yet completely exhausted.

In order to bring the foregoing remarks within some compass, I have found it necessary to confine myself to such objections as strike at the root of Dr Reid's philosophy, without touching on any of his opinions on particular topics, however important. I have been obliged also to compress what I have stated within narrower limits than were perhaps consistent with complete perspicuity ; and to reject many illustrations which crowded upon me at almost every step of my progress.

It may not, perhaps, be superfluous to add, that, supposing some of these objections to possess more force than I have ascribed to them in my reply, it will not therefore follow, that little advantage is to be derived from a careful perusal of the speculations against which they are directed. Even they who dissent the most widely from Dr Reid's conclusions, can scarcely fail to admit, that, as a writer, he exhibits a striking contrast to the most successful of his predecessors, in a logical precision and simplicity of language—his statement of facts being neither vitiated by physiological hypothesis, nor obscured by scholastic mystery. Whoever has reflected on the infinite importance, in such inquiries, of a skilful use of words as the essential instrument of thought, must be aware of the influence which his works are likely to have on the future progress of science, were they to produce no other effect than a general imitation of his mode of reasoning, and of his guarded phraseology.

It is not, indeed, every reader to whom these inquiries are accessible ; for habits of attention in general, and still more habits of attention to the *phænomena* of thought, require early and careful cultivation ; but those who are capable of the exertion will soon recognise, in Dr Reid's statements, the faithful history of their own minds, and will find their labours amply rewarded by that satisfaction which always accompanies the discovery of useful truth. They may expect, also, to be rewarded by some intellectual acquisitions not altogether useless in their other studies. An author well qualified to judge, from his own experience, of whatever conduces to invigorate or to embellish the understanding, has beautifully remarked, that " by turning the soul inward on itself, its forces are concentrated, and are fitted for stronger and bolder flights of science ; and that, in such pursuits, whether we take, or whether we lose the game, the chase is certainly of service."* In this respect, the philosophy of the mind (abstracting entirely from that pre-eminence which belongs to it in consequence of its practical applications) may claim a distinguished rank among those preparatory disciplines which another writer, of no less eminence, has happily compared to " the crops which are raised, not for the sake of the harvest, but to be ploughed in as a dressing to the land."†

SECTION III.

CONCLUSION OF THE NARRATIVE.

THE three works to which the foregoing remarks refer—together with the Essay on Quantity, published in the " Philosophical

Transactions of the Royal Society of London," and a short but masterly Analysis of Aristotle's Logic, which forms an appendix to the third volume of Lord Kames' " Sketches'—comprehend the whole of Dr Reid's publications.* The interval between the dates of the first and last of these amounts to no less than forty years, although he had attained to the age of thirty-eight before he ventured to appear as an author.

With the " Essays on the Active Powers of Man," he closed his literary career ; but he continued, notwithstanding, to prosecute his studies with unabated ardour and activity. The more modern improvements in chemistry attracted his particular notice ; and he applied himself, with his wonted diligence and success, to the study of its new doctrines and new nomenclature. He amused himself also, at times, in preparing, for a philosophical society of which he was a member, short essays on particular topics which happened to interest his curiosity, and on which he thought he might derive useful hints from friendly discussion. The most important of these were—"An Examination of Priestley's Opinions concerning Matter and Mind;" "Observations on the ' Utopia' of Sir Thomas More ;" and " Physiological Reflections on Muscular Motion." This last essay appears to have been written in the eighty-sixth year of his age, and was read by the author to his associates, a few months before his death. His " thoughts were led to the speculations it contains," (as he himself mentions in the conclusion,) " by the experience of some of the effects which old age produces on the muscular motions." " As they were occasioned, therefore," he adds, " by the infirmities of age, they will, I hope, be heard with the greater indulgence."

Among the various occupations with which he thus enlivened his retirement, the mathematical pursuits of his earlier years held a distinguished place. He delighted to converse about them with his friends ; and often exercised his skill in the investigation of particular problems. His knowledge of ancient geometry had not probably been, at any time, very extensive ; but he had cultivated diligently those parts of mathematical science which are subservient to the study of Sir Isaac Newton's works. He had a predilection, more particularly, for researches requiring the aid of arithmetical calculation, in the practice of which he possessed uncommon expertness and address. I think I have sometimes observed in him a slight and amiable vanity, connected with this accomplishment.

---

* Preface to Mr Burk 's " Essay on the Sublime and Beautiful."
† Bishop Berkeley's " Querist."

* Reid's " History of the University of Glasgow" was published, after his death, in the " Statistical Account of Scotland " It is now, for the first time, added to his other works.—H.

The revival, at this period, of Dr Reid's first scientific propensity, has often recalled to me a favourite remark of Mr Smith's —that of all the amusements of old age, the most grateful and soothing is a renewal of acquaintance with the favourite studies and favourite authors of our youth ; a remark which, in his own case, seemed to be more particularly exemplified, while he was re-perusing, with the enthusiasm of a student, the tragic poets of ancient Greece. I heard him, at least, repeat the observation more than once, while Sophocles or Euripides lay open on his table.

In the case of Dr Reid, other motives perhaps conspired with the influence of the agreeable associations to which Mr Smith probably alluded. His attention was always fixed on the state of his intellectual faculties ; and for counteracting the effects of time on these, mathematical studies seem to be fitted in a peculiar degree. They are fortunately, too, within the reach of many individuals, after a decay of memory disqualifies them for inquiries which involve a multiplicity of details. Such detached problems, more especially, as Dr Reid commonly selected for his consideration—problems where all the *data* are brought at once under the eye, and where a connected train of thinking is not to be carried on from day to day—will be found, (as I have witnessed with pleasure in several instances,) by those who are capable of such a recreation, a valuable addition to the scanty resources of a life protracted beyond the ordinary limit.

While he was thus enjoying an old age happy in some respects beyond the usual lot of humanity, his domestic comfort suffered a deep and incurable wound by the death of Mrs Reid. He had had the misfortune, too, of surviving, for many years, a numerous family of promising children ; four of whom (two sons and two daughters) died after they attained maturity. One daughter only was left to him when he lost his wife ; and of her affectionate good offices he could not always avail himself, in consequence of the attentions which her own husband's infirmities required. Of this lady, who is still alive, (the widow of Patrick Carmichael, M. D.,*) I shall have occasion again to introduce the name, before I conclude this narrative.

---

* A learned and worthy physician, who, after a long residence in Holland, where he practised medicine, retired to Glasgow. He was a younger son of Professor Gerschom Carmichael, who published, about the year 1720, an edition of Puffendorff, *De Officio H minis et Civis*, and who is pronounced by Dr Hutcheson, "by far the best commentator on that book." [Carmichael was Hutcheson's immediate predecessor in the chair of M·ral Philosophy in the University of Glasgow, and may be regarded, on good grounds, as the real founder of the Scottish school of philosophy.—H.]

A short extract from a letter addressed to myself by Dr Reid, not many weeks after his wife's death, will, I am persuaded, be acceptable to many, as an interesting relic of the writer.

" By the loss of my bosom friend, with whom I lived fifty-two years, I am brought into a kind of new world, at a time of life when old habits are not easily forgot, or new ones acquired. But every world is God's world, and I am thankful for the comforts he has left me. Mrs Carmichael has now the care of two old deaf men, and does every thing in her power to please them ; and both are very sensible of her goodness. I have more health than, at my time of life, I had any reason to expect. I walk about; entertain myself with reading what I soon forget ; can converse with one person, if he articulates distinctly, and is within ten inches of my left ear ; go to church, without hearing one word of what is said. You know I never had any pretensions to vivacity, but I am still free from languor and *ennui.*

" If you are weary of this detail, impute it to the anxiety you express to know the state of my health. I wish you may have no more uneasiness at my age,—being yours most affectionately."

About four years after this event, he was prevailed on, by his friend and relation, Dr Gregory, to pass a few weeks, during the summer of 1796, at Edinburgh. He was accompanied by Mrs Carmichael, who lived with him in Dr Gregory's house ; a situation which united under the same roof, every advantage of medical care, of tender attachment, and of philosophical intercourse. As Dr Gregory's professional engagements, however, necessarily interfered much with his attentions to his guest, I enjoyed more of Dr Reid's society than might otherwise have fallen to my share. I had the pleasure, accordingly, of spending some hours with him daily, and of attending him in his walking excursions, which frequently extended to the distance of three or four miles. His faculties (excepting his memory, which was considerably impaired) appeared as vigorous as ever ; and, although his deafness prevented him from taking any share in general conversation, he was still able to enjoy the company of a friend. Mr Playfair and myself were both witnesses of the acuteness which he displayed on one occasion, in detecting a mistake, by no means obvious, in a manuscript of his kinsman, David Gregory, on the subject of " Prime and Ultimate Ratios." Nor had his temper suffered from the hand of time, either in point of gentleness or of gaiety. " Instead of repining at the enjoyments of the young, he delighted in promoting them ; and, after all the losses he had sustained in his own family, he continued to treat children with such condescension and benignity, that some very young ones noticed the peculiar kindness of h s eye."* In apparent soundness and activity of body, he resembled more a man of sixty than of eighty-seven.

He returned to Glasgow in his usual health and spirits ; and continued, for some weeks, to devote, as formerly, a regular portion of his time to the exercise both of body and of mind. It appears, from a letter of Dr Cleghorn's to Dr Gregory, that he was still able to work with his own hands in his garden ; and he was found by Dr Brown, occupied in the solution of an algebraical problem of considerable difficulty, in which, after the labour of a day or two, he at last succeeded. It was in the course of the same short interval, that he committed to writing those particulars concerning his ancestors, which I have already mentioned.

This active and useful life was now, however, drawing to a conclusion. A violent disorder attacked him about the end of September ; but does not seem to have occasioned much alarm to those about him, till he was visited by Dr Cleghorn, who soon after communicated his apprehensions in a letter to Dr Gregory. Among other symptoms, he mentioned particularly "that alteration of voice and features which, though not easily described, is so well known to all who have opportunities of seeing life close." Dr Reid's own opinion of his case was probably the same with that of his physician ; as he expressed to him on his first visit his hope that he was "soon to get his dismission." After a severe struggle, attended with repeated strokes of palsy, he died on the 7th of October following. Dr Gregory had the melancholy satisfaction of visiting his venerable friend on his deathbed, and of paying him this unavailing mark of attachment before his powers of recollection were entirely gone.

The only surviving descendant of Dr Reid is Mrs Carmichael, a daughter worthy in every respect of such a father—long the chief comfort and support of his old age, and his anxious nurse in his last moments.†

In point of bodily constitution, few men have been more indebted to nature than Dr Reid. His form was vigorous and athletic ; and his muscular force (though he was somewhat under the middle size) uncommonly great ; advantages to which his habits of temperance and exercise, and the unclouded serenity of his temper, did ample

justice. His countenance was strongly expressive of deep and collected thought ; but, when brightened up by the face of a friend, what chiefly caught the attention was a look of good-will and of kindness. A picture of him, for which he consented, at the particular request of Dr Gregory, to sit to Mr Raeburn, during his last visit to Edinburgh, is generally and justly ranked among the happiest performances of that excellent artist. The medallion of Tassie, also, for which he sat in the eighty-first year of his age, presents a very perfect resemblance.

I have little to add to what the foregoing pages contain with respect to his character. Its most prominent features were, intrepid and inflexible rectitude, a pure and devoted attachment to truth, and an entire command (acquired by the unwearied exertions of a long life) over all his passions. Hence, in those parts of his writings where his subjectforces him to dispute the conclusions of others, a scrupulous rejection of every expression calculated to irritate those whom he was anxious to convince : and a spirit of liberality and good-humour towards his opponents, from which no asperity on their part could provoke him for a moment to deviate. The progress of useful knowledge, more especially in what relates to human nature and to human life, he believed to be retarded rather than advanced by the intemperance of controversy ; and to be secured most effectually when intrusted to the slow but irresistible influence of sober reasoning. That the argumentative talents of the disputants might be improved by such altercations, he was willing to allow ; but, considered in their connection with the great objects which all classes of writers profess equally to have in view, he was convinced "that they have done more harm to the practice, than they have done service to the theory, of morality.' *

In private life, no man ever maintained, more eminently or more uniformly, the dignity of philosophy ; combining with the most amiable modesty and gentleness, the noblest spirit of independence. The only preferments which he ever enjoyed he owed to the unsolicited favour of the two learned bodies who successively adopted him into their number ; and the respectable rank which he supported in society was the well-earned reward of his own academical labours. The studies in which he delighted were little calculated to draw on him the patronage of the great ; and he was unskilled in the art of courting advancement by "fashioning his doctrines to the varying hour."

As a philosopher, his genius was more

---

* I have borrowed this sentence from a just and elegant character of Dr Reid, which appeared, a few days after his death, in one of the Glasgow journals I had occasion frequently to verify the truth of the observation during his visit to Edinburgh.

† Note F

* Preface to Pope's " Essay on Man."

peculiarly characterised by a sound, cautious, distinguishing judgment, by a singular patience and perseverance of thought, and by habits of the most fixed and concentrated attention to his own mental operations; endowments which, although not the most splendid in the estimation of the multitude, would seem entitled, from the history of science, to rank among the rarest gifts of the mind.

With these habits and powers, he united (what does not always accompany them) the curiosity of a naturalist, and the eye of an observer; and, accordingly, his information about everything relating to physical science, and to the useful arts, was extensive and accurate. His memory for historical details was not so remarkable; and he used sometimes to regret the imperfect degree in which he possessed this faculty. I am inclined, however, to think, that, in doing so, he underrated his natural advantages; estimating the strength of memory, as men commonly do, rather by the recollection of particular facts, than by the possession of those general conclusions, from a subserviency to which such facts derive their principal value.

Towards the close of life, indeed, his memory was much less vigorous than the other powers of his intellect; in none of which could I ever perceive any symptom of decline. His ardour for knowledge, too, remained unextinguished to the last; and, when cherished by the society of the young and inquisitive, seemed even to increase with his years. What is still more remarkable, he retained, in extreme old age, all the sympathetic tenderness and all the moral sensibility of youth; the liveliness of his emotions, wherever the happiness of others was concerned, forming an affecting contrast to his own unconquerable firmness under the severest trials.

Nor was the sensibility which he retained the selfish and sterile offspring of taste and indolence. It was alive and active, wherever he could command the means of relieving the distresses or of adding to the comforts of others; and was often felt in its effects, where he was unseen and unknown. Among the various proofs of this which have happened to fall under my own knowledge, I cannot help mentioning particularly (upon the most unquestionable authority) the secrecy with which he conveyed his occasional benefactions to his former parishioners at New-Machar, long after his establishment at Glasgow. One donation, in particular, during the scarcity of 1782—a donation which, notwithstanding all his precautions, was distinctly traced to his beneficence—might perhaps have been thought disproportionate to his limited income, had not his own simple and moderate habits multiplied the resources of his humanity.

His opinions on the most important subjects are to be found in his works; and that spirit of piety which animated every part of his conduct forms the best comment on their practical tendency. In the state in which he found the philosophical world, he believed that his talents could not be so usefully employed as in combating the schemes of those who aimed at the complete subversion of religion, both natural and revealed; convinced, with Dr Clarke, that, "as Christianity presupposes the truth of Natural Religion, whatever tends to discredit the latter must have a proportionally greater effect in weakening the authority of the former."[*] In his views of both, he seems to have coincided nearly with Bishop Butler, an author whom he held in the highest estimation. A very careful abstract of the treatise entitled "Analogy," drawn up by Dr Reid, many years ago, for his own use, still exists among his manuscripts; and the short "Dissertation on Virtue" which Butler has annexed to that work, together with the "Discourses on Human Nature" published in his volume of Sermons, he used always to recommend as the most satisfactory account that has yet appeared of the fundamental principles of Morals: nor could he conceal his regret, that the profound philosophy which these Discourses contain should of late have been so generally supplanted in England by the speculations of some other moralists, who, while they profess to idolize the memory of Locke, "approve little or nothing in his writings, but his errors."[†]

Deeply impressed, however, as he was with his own principles, he possessed the most perfect liberality towards all whom he believed to be honestly and conscientiously devoted to the search of truth. With one very distinguished character, the late Lord Kames, he lived in the most cordial and affectionate friendship, notwithstanding the avowed opposition of their sentiments on some moral questions to which he attached the greatest importance. Both of them, however, were the friends of virtue and of mankind; and both were able to temper the warmth of free discussion with the forbearance and good humour founded on reciprocal esteem. No two men, certainly, ever exhibited a more striking contrast in their conversation, or in their constitutional tempers:—the one, slow and cautious in

* Collection of Papers which passed between Leibnitz and Clarke. See Dr Clarke's Dedication.
† I have adopted here, the words which Dr Clarke applied to some of Mr Locke's earlier followers. They are still more applicable to many writers of the present times. See Clarke's First Reply to Leibnitz.

his decisions, even on those topics which he had most diligently studied; reserved and silent in promiscuous society; and retaining, after all his literary eminence, the same simple and unassuming manners which he brought from his country residence: the other, lively, rapid, and communicative; accustomed, by his professional pursuits, to wield with address the weapons of controversy, and not averse to a trial of his powers on questions the most foreign to his ordinary habits of inquiry. But these characteristical differences, while to their common friends they lent an additional charm to the distinguishing merits of each, served only to enliven their social intercourse, and to cement their mutual attachment.

I recollect few, if any anecdotes of Dr Reid, which appear to me calculated to throw additional light on his character; and I suspect strongly, that many of those which are to be met with in biographical publications are more likely to mislead than to inform. A trifling incident, it is true, may sometimes paint a peculiar feature better than the most elaborate description; but a selection of incidents really characteristical, presupposes, in the observer, a rare capacity to discriminate and to generalize; and where this capacity is wanting, a biographer, with the most scrupulous attention to the veracity of his details, may yet convey a very false conception of the individual he would describe. As, in the present instance, my subject afforded no materials for such a choice, I have attempted, to the best of my abilities, (instead of retailing detached fragments of conversations, or recording insulated and unmeaning occurrences,) to communicate to others the general impressions which Dr Reid's character has left on my own mind. In this attempt I am far from being confident that I have succeeded; but, how barren soever I may have thus rendered my pages in the estimation of those who consider biography merely in the light of an amusing tale, I have, at least, the satisfaction to think, that my picture, though faint in the colouring, does not present a distorted resemblance of the original.

The confidential correspondence of an individual with his friends, affords to the student of human nature, materials of far greater authenticity and importance; more particularly, the correspondence of a man like Dr Reid, who will not be suspected by those who knew him, of accommodating his letters (as has been alleged of Cicero) to the humours and principles of those whom he addressed. I am far, at the same time, from thinking that the correspondence of Dr Reid would be generally interesting; or even that he excelled in this species of writing: but few men, I sincerely believe, who have written so much, have left behind them such unblemished memorials of their virtue.

At present, I shall only transcribe two letters, which I select from a considerable number now lying before me, as they seem to accord, more than the others, with the general design of this Memoir. The first (which is dated January 13, 1779) is addressed to the Rev. William Gregory, (now Rector of St Andrew's, Canterbury,) then an undergraduate in Balliol College, Oxford. It relates to a remarkable peculiarity in Dr Reid's physical temperament, connected with the subject of dreaming; and is farther interesting as a genuine record of some particulars in his early habits, in which it is easy to perceive the openings of a superior mind.

"The fact which your brother the Doctor desires to be informed of, was as you mention it. As far as I remember the circumstances, they were as follow:—

"About the age of fourteen, I was, almost every night, unhappy in my sleep, from frightful dreams: sometimes hanging over a dreadful precipice, and just ready to drop down; sometimes pursued for my life, and stopped by a wall, or by a sudden loss of all strength; sometimes ready to be devoured by a wild beast. How long I was plagued with such dreams, I do not now recollect. I believe it was for a year or two at least; and I think they had quite left me before I was fifteen. In those days, I was much given to what Mr Addison, in one of his "Spectators," calls castle-building; and, in my evening solitary walk, which was generally all the exercise I took, my thoughts would hurry me into some active scene, where I generally acquitted myself much to my own satisfaction; and in these scenes of imagination I performed many a gallant exploit. At the same time, in my dreams I found myself the most arrant coward that ever was. Not only my courage, but my strength failed me in every danger; and I often rose from my bed in the morning in such a panic that it took some time to get the better of it. I wished very much to get free of these uneasy dreams, which not only made me unhappy in sleep, but often left a disagreeable impression in my mind for some part of the following day. I thought it was worth trying whether it was possible to recollect that it was all a dream, and that I was in no real danger. I often went to sleep with my mind as strongly impressed as I could with this thought, that I never in my lifetime was in any real danger, and that every fright I had was a dream. After many fruitless endeavours to recollect this when the danger appeared I effected it at last, and have often, when I was sliding over a precipice into the abyss, recollected that it was all a dream, and boldly jumped down. The effect of this commonly was, that I immediately awoke. But I awoke calm and intrepid, which I thought a great acquisition. After this, my dreams were never very uneasy ; and, in a short time, I dreamed not at all.

" During all this time I was in perfect health ; but whether my ceasing to dream was the effect of the recollection above mentioned, or of any change in the habit of my body, which is usual about that period of life, I cannot tell. I think it may more probably be imputed to the last. However, the fact was, that, for at least forty years after, I dreamed none, to the best of my remembrance ; and finding, from the testimony of others, that this is somewhat uncommon, I have often, as soon as I awoke, endeavoured to recollect, without being able to recollect, anything that passed in my sleep. For some years past, I can sometimes recollect some kind of dreaming thoughts, but so incoherent that I can make nothing of them.

" The only distinct dream I ever had since I was about sixteen, as far as I remember, was about two years ago. I had got my head blistered for a fall. A plaster, which was put upon it after the blister, pained me excessively for a whole night. In the morning I slept a little, and dreamed, very distinctly, that I had fallen into the hands of a party of Indians, and was scalped.

" I am apt to think that, as there is a state of sleep, and a state wherein we are awake, so there is an intermediate state, which partakes of the other two. If a man peremptorily resolves to rise at an early hour for some interesting purpose, he will of himself awake at that hour. A sick-nurse gets the habit of sleeping in such a manner that she hears the least whisper of the sick person, and yet is refreshed by this kind of half sleep. The same is the case of a nurse who sleeps with a child in her arms. I have slept on horseback, but so as to preserve my balance ; and, if the horse stumbled, I could make the exertion necessary for saving me from a fall, as if I was awake.

" I hope the sciences are not in this state. Yet, from so many learned men, so much at their ease, one would expect something more than we hear of."

For the other letter, I am indebted to one of Dr Reid's most intimate friends, to whom it was addressed, in the year 1784, on occasion of the melancholy event to which it alludes.

" I sympathize with you very sincerely in the loss of a most amiable wife. I judge of your feelings by the impression she made upon my own heart, on a very short acquaintance. But all the blessings of this world are transient and uncertain ; and it would be but a melancholy scene if there were no prospect of another.

" I have often had occasion to admire the resignation and fortitude of young persons, even of the weaker sex, in the views of death, when their imagination is filled with all the gay prospects which the world presents at that period. I have been witness to instances of this kind, which I thought truly heroic, and I hear Mrs G—— gave a remarkable one.

" To see the soul increase in vigour and wisdom, and in every amiable quality, when health, and strength, and animal spirits decay—when it is to be torn by violence from all that filled the imagination and flattered hope—is a spectacle truly grand and instructive to the surviving. To think that the soul perishes in that fatal moment when it is purified by this fiery trial, and fitted for the noblest exertions in another state, is an opinion which I cannot help looking down upon with contempt and disdain.

" In old people, there is no more merit in leaving this world with perfect acquiescence than in rising from a feast after one is full. When I have before me the prospect of the infirmities, the distresses, and the peevishness of old age, and when I have already received more than my share of the good things of this life, it would be ridiculous indeed to be anxious about prolonging it ; but, when I was four-and-twenty, to have had no anxiety for its continuance, would, I think, have required a noble effort. Such efforts in those that are called to make them surely shall not lose their reward."

I have now finished all that the limits of my plan permit me to offer here as a tribute to the memory of this excellent person. In the details which I have stated, both with respect to his private life and his scientific pursuits, I have dwelt chiefly on such circumstances as appeared to me most likely to interest the readers of his works, by illustrating his character as a man, and his views as an author. Of his merits as an instructor of youth, I have said but little ; partly from a wish to avoid unnecessary diffuseness, but chiefly from my anxiety to enlarge on those still more important labours of which he has bequeathed the fruits to future ages. And yet, had he left no such monument to perpetuate his name, the fidelity and zeal with which he discharged, during so long a period, the obscure but momentous duties of his official station would, in the judgment of the wise and good, have ranked him in the first order of

useful citizens. "Nec enim is solus rei-
publicæ prodest, qui candidatos extrahit, et
tuetur reos, et de pace belloque censet ; sed
qui juventutem exhortatur ; qui, in tantâ
bonorum præceptorum inopiâ, virtute in-
struit animos ; qui, ad pecuniam luxuri-
amque cursu ruentes prensat ac retrahit, et,
si nihil aliud, certe moratur : in privato,
publicum negotium agit."[*]

In concluding this memoir, I trust I
shall be pardoned, if, for once, I give way
to a personal feeling, while I express the
satisfaction with which I now close, finally,
my attempts as a biographer. Those which
I have already made, were imposed on me
by the irresistible calls of duty and attachment ; and, feeble as they are, when compared with the magnitude of subjects so
splendid and so various, they have en-
croached deeply on that small portion of
literary leisure which indispensable engagements allow me to command. I cannot,
at the same time, be insensible to the grati-
fication of having endeavoured to associate,
in some degree, my name with three of the
greatest which have adorned this age—

happy, if, without deviating intentionally
from truth, I may have succeeded, however
imperfectly, in my wish to gratify at once
the curiosity of the public, and to soothe the
recollections of surviving friends.——But I,
too, have designs and enterprises of my
own ; and the execution of these (which,
alas ! swell in magnitude, as the time for
their accomplishment hastens to a period)
claims, at length, my undivided attention.
Yet I should not look back on the past
with regret, if I could indulge the hope,
that the facts which it has been my province
to record—by displaying those fair rewards
of extensive usefulness, and of permanent
fame, which talents and industry, when
worthily directed, cannot fail to secure—
may contribute, in one single instance, to
foster the proud and virtuous independence
of genius ; or, amidst the gloom of poverty
and solitude, to gild the distant prospect of
the unfriended scholar, whose laurels are
now slowly ripening in the unnoticed pri-
vacy of humble life.[*]

[*] Seneca," De Tranquill. An." cap. 3.

[*] On Reid's doctrines Mr Stewart has also some
valuable observations in his " Dissertation on the Progress of Metaphysical and Ethical Philosophy "—H.

NOTES.[*]

Note A.—Page 4.

In the account given in the text of Dr
Reid's ancestors, I have followed scrupu-
lously the information contained in his own
memorandums. I have some suspicion,
however, that he has committed a mistake
with respect to the name of the translator
of Buchanan's History ; which would appear, from the MS. in Glasgow College, to
have been, not Adam, but John. At the
same time, as this last statement rests on
an authority altogether unknown, (being
written in a hand different from the rest of
the MS.,[†]) there is a possibility that Dr

[*] If another edition of this Memoir should ever
be called for, I must request that the printer may
adhere to the plan which I myself have thought
advisable to adopt in the distribution of my notes.
A mistake which has been committed in a late edition of my Life of Dr Robertson, where a long
Appendix is broken down into *foot-notes*, will sufficiently account for this request to those who have
seen that publication.

[†] It is to the following purport :—" The Historie
of Scotland, first written in the Latin tungue by
that famous and learned man, George Buchanan,
and afterwards translated into the Scottishe tungue
by John Read, Esquyar, brother to James Read,
person of Banchory-Ternan, whyle he lived. They
both ly intered in the parish church of that towne,
seated not farre from the banke of the river of Dee,
expecting the general resurrection, and the glorious
appearing of Jesus Christ, there Redimer." The date

Reid's account may be correct ; and, therefore, I have thought it advisable, in a matter
of so very trifling consequence, to adhere to
it in preference to the other.

The following particulars with respect to
Thomas Reid may, perhaps, be acceptable
to some of my readers. They are copied
from Dempster, a contemporary writer ;
whose details concerning his countrymen, it
must, however, be confessed, are not always
to be implicitly relied on :—

" Thomas Reidus, Aberdonensis, pueri-
tiæ meæ et infantilis otii sub Thoma Car-
gillo collega, Lovanii literas in schola Lipsii[*]
seriò didicit, quas magno nomine in Germania docuit, carus Principibus. Londini
diu in comitatu humanissimi ac clarissimi
viri, Fulconis Grevilli, Regii Consiliarii
Interioris et Angliæ Proquæstoris, egit :
tum ad amicitiam Regis, eodem Fulcone
deducente, evectus, inter Palatinos admis-

of the transcript is 12th December 1694. According to Calderwood's MS. History of the Church of
Scotland, John Read was " servitor and writer to
Mr George Buchanan." But this is not likely.—H.
[*] This is doubtful ; for Sir Robert Aytoun, in the
account he gives of Reid's studies, makes no mention
of so remarkable a circumstance. Dempster possibly
confused Thomas Reid with Reid's friend, Sir Thomas
Seghet, another learned and wandering Scotchman,
and a favourite pupil of " the Prince of Latin Let
ters.'—H.

sus, à literis Latinis Regi fuit. Scripsit multa, ut est magnâ indole et variâ eruditione," &c. " Ex aula se, nemine conscio, nuper proripuit, dum illi omnia festinati honoris augmenta singuli ominarentur, nec quid deinde egerit aut quo locorum se contulerit quisquam indicare potuit. Multi suspicabantur, trædio aulæ affectum, monasticæ quieti seipsum tradidisse, sub annum 1618. Rumor postea fuit in aulam rediise, et meritissimis honoribus redditum, sed nunquam id consequetur quod virtus promeretur."—*Hist. Ecclesiastica Gentis Scotorum*, lib. xvi. p. 576.

What was the judgment of Thomas Reid's own times with respect to his genius, and what their hopes of his posthumous fame, may be collected from an elegy on his death by his learned countryman [Sir] Robert Aytoun. Already, before the lapse of two hundred years, some apology, alas! may be thought necessary for an attempt to rescue his name from total oblivion.

Aytoun's elegy on Reid is referred to in terms very flattering both to its author and to its subject, by the editor of the collection entitled, " Poëtarum Scotorum Musæ Sacræ." * " In obitum Thomæ Rheidi [Rhædi] epicedium extat elegantissimum Roberti Aytoni, viri literis ac dignitate clarissimi, in Delitiis Poëtarum Scotorum, ubi et ipsius quoque poëmata, paucula quidem illa, sed venusta, sed elegantia, comparent."†

---

* The well-known William Lauder.—H.

† I add the following brief notices, which I chance to have, in regard to this elegant scholar and acute philosopher. From Sir Robert Aytoun's Elegy, it appears, that, after finishing his studies in Scotland, Reid proceeded to France. There, however, he did no' tarry; for, as Scottish-philosophers-were then in high academical repute, he soon received a call to Germany:—

——" attraxit Germania philtro
Et precis et pretii."

In that country, he taught philosophy and humane letters for several years with distinguished reputation, in the universities of Leipsic and Rostoch.

" Palladis in castris multa hic cum laude merentem, Et victa de Barbarie sciolisque sophistis Ducentem insignes fama victrice triumphos Lipsia detinuit longum. Quis credidit illic Se rite admissum in Phœbi sacraria, Rhædo Non pandente fores? Quis per dumeta I.rcæi Ausus iter tentare, nisi duce et auspice Rhædo ? Nec tibi fama minor qua Balthica littora spectat Rostochium, paucis istic tibi plurimus annis Crevit hono^, nullo non admirante profundæ Doctrinæ aggestos tot in uno pectore acervos, Felicemque viam fandi, quocunque liberet Ore loqui, quocunque habitu producere partus Mentis, et exanimes scriptis animare papyros."

While in Germany, he wrote the following treatises. which display great philosophical talent :—
" Thomæ Rhædi, Scoti, De Objecto Metaphysicæ Dissertatio contra Henningum Arnisæum. Rostochii : 1613 ' 4to.
" Thomæ Rhædi, Scoti, Pervigilia Metaphysica desideratissima. Rostochii : 1613." 4to.
I have likewise seen referred to, a System of Logic by him, published at Rostoch; but in what year I know not. Though the date of the earliest of the preceding treatises be 1613, it appears that he was at Rostoch before 1611, and that he then had pub-

---

The only works of Alexander Reid of which I have heard are " Chirurgical Lectures on Tumors and Ulcers," London, 1635 ; and a " Treatise of the First Part of Chirurgerie," London, 1638. He appears to have been the physician and friend of the celebrated mathematician Thomas Harriot, of whose interesting history so little was known till the recent discovery of his manuscripts by Mr Zach of Saxe-Gotha.

A remarkable instance of the careless or capricious orthography formerly so common in writing proper names, occurs in the different individuals to whom this note refers. Sometimes the family name is written— Reid ; on other occasions, Riede, Read, Rhead, or Rhaid.

NOTE B.—Page 4.

Dr Turnbull's work on moral philosophy was published at London in 1740. As I have only turned over a few pages, I cannot say anything with respect to its merits. The mottoes on the title-page are curious, when considered in connection with those inquiries which his pupil afterwards prosecuted with so much success ; and may, perhaps, without his perceiving it, have had some effect in suggesting to him that plan of philosophizing which he so systematically and so happily pursued :—
" If natural philosophy, in all its parts,

---

lished a dissertation against Arnisæus; to which this philosopher in that year replied in his " Vindiciæ secundum veritatem pro Aristotele et sanioribus quibusque philosophis contra Thomæ Rhædi, Scoti, Dissertationem elenchticam de subjecto Metaphysices et natura Entis, assertæ ab Henningo Arnisæo, Halberstadiensi. Francofurti : 1611." 4to.

At what date Reid returned to England, or when he was appointed Latin Secretary to King James, does not appear. I find, however, from Smith's Life of Patrick Young, who was associated with him in the translation into Latin of James's English works, and who succeeded him as Secretary, that Reid died in 1624. There is also to be found in the same Life (see " Vitæ quorundam eruditissimorum virorum," &c.) the fragment of a Dissertation by Reid—" Quod Regibus et Licitum et Decorum sit Scribere." A considerable number of Reid's poems are to be found in the " Delitiæ Poëtarum Scotorum :" and his paraphrase of the 104th Psalm, which is not among these, was published during his life, with high encomium, by William Barclay in his " Judicium de Poetico duello Eglisemmii." The writings which he left were, however, only occasional and fugitive pieces—only indications of what he would have accomplished had an early death not frustrated his great designs.

" Et tu Rhæde jaces opera inter manca, minæque Scriptorum ingentes, queis si supremæ fuisset Cum lima porrecta manus, non ulla fuisset Calliopes toto Sophiæve illustrior alibi Quam quæ Rhædeum præferret pagina nomen, Paucula furtivas schediasmata fusa per horas, Qualiacunque tamen sunt hæc, hæc ipsa revincent Esse Caledoniis etiamnum lumen alumnis Et genium, quo vel Scoti Subtilis acumen, Vel operum dulces Buchanani æquare Camœnas."

Mr Stewart (p 3) is misinformed in stating that Reid published any collection of his Dissertations.— H.

by pursuing this method, shall, at length, be perfected, the bounds of moral philosophy will also be enlarged."

Newton's Optics.

" Account for moral as for natural things."

POPE.

For the opinion of a very competent judge, with respect to the merits of the " Treatise on Ancient Painting," *vide* Hogarth's Print, entitled "Beer-Lane."

NOTE C.—Page 10.

" Dr Moor combined," &c.—James Moor, LL.D., author of a very ingenious fragment on Greek grammar, and of other philological essays. He was also distinguished by a profound acquaintance with ancient geometry. Dr Simson, an excellent judge of his merits, both in literature and science, has somewhere honoured him with the following encomium :—" Tum in Mathesi, tum in Græcis Literis multum et feliciter versatus."

" The Wilsons," (both father and son,) &c.—Alexander Wilson, M.D., and Patrick Wilson, Esq., well known over Europe by their " Observations on the Solar Spots," and many other valuable memoirs.

NOTE D.—Page 20.

A writer of great talents (after having reproached Dr Reid with "a gross ignorance, disgraceful to the university of which he was a member") boasts of the trifling expense of time and thought which it had cost himself to overturn his philosophy. " Dr Oswald is pleased to pay me a compliment in saying, that 'I might employ myself to more advantage to the public, by pursuing other branches of science, than by deciding rashly on a subject which he sees I have not studied.' In return to this compliment, I shall not affront him, by telling him how very little of my time this business has hitherto taken up. If he alludes to my *experiments*, I can assure him that I have lost no time at all ; for, having been intent upon such as require the use of a burning lens, I believe I have not lost one hour of sunshine on this account. And the public may, perhaps, be informed, some time or other, of what I have been doing in the *sun*, as well as in the *shade*."—[Priestley's] " Examination of Reid's Inquiry," &c., p. 357. See also pp. 101, 102 of the same work.

NOTE E.—Page 27.

The following strictures on Dr Priestley's " Examination," &c., are copied from a very judicious note in Dr Campbell's " Philosophy of Rhetoric," vol i. p. 3.

——" I shall only subjoin two remarks on this book. The first is, that the author, through the whole, confounds two things totally distinct—certain associations of ideas, and certain judgments implying belief, which, though in *some*, are not in *all* cases, and, therefore not *necessarily* connected with association. And if so, merely to account for the association is in no case to account for the belief with which it is attended. Nay, admitting his plea, (p. 86,) that, by the principle of association, not only the ideas, but the concomitant belief may be accounted for, even this does not invalidate the doctrine he impugns; for, let it be observed, that it is one thing to assign a cause, which, from the mechanism of our nature, has given rise to a particular tenet of belief, and another thing to produce a reason by which the understanding has been convinced. Now, unless this be done as to the principles in question, they must be considered as primary truths in respect of the understanding, which never deduced them from other truths, and which is under a necessity, in all her moral reasonings, of founding upon them. In fact, to give any other account of our conviction of them, is to confirm, instead of confuting the doctrine, that, in all argumentation, they must be regarded as primary truths, or truths which reason never inferred through any medium, from other truths previously perceived. My second remark is, that, though this examiner has, from Dr Reid, given us a catalogue of first principles, which he deems unworthy of the honourable place assigned them, he has nowhere thought proper to give us a list of those self-evident truths which, by his own account, and in his own express words, ' must be assumed as the foundation of all our reasoning.' How much light might have been thrown upon the subject by the contrast ! Perhaps we should have been enabled, on the comparison, to discover some distinctive characters in his genuine axioms, which would have preserved us from the danger of confounding them with their spurious ones. Nothing is more evident than that, in whatever regards matter of fact, the mathematical axioms will not answer. These are purely fitted for evolving the abstract relations of quantity. This he in effect owns himself, (p. 39.) It would have been obliging, then, and would have greatly contributed to shorten the controversy, if he had given us, at least, a specimen of those self-evident princip'es which, in his estimation, are the *non plus ultra* of moral reasoning."

NOTE F.—Page 31.

Dr Reid's father, the Rev. Lewis Reid, married, for his second wife, Janet, daughter of Mr Fraser of Phopachy, in the county of Inverness. A daughter of this marriage is still alive ; the wife of the Rev. Alexander Leslie, and the mother of the Rev. James Leslie, ministers of Fordoun. To the latter of these gentlemen, I am indebted for the greater part of the information I have been able to collect with respect to Dr Reid, previous to his removal to Glasgow— Mr Leslie's regard for the memory of his uncle having prompted him, not only to transmit to me such particulars as had fallen under his own knowledge, but some valuable letters on the same subject, which he procured from his relations and friends in the north.

For all the members of this most respectable family, Dr Reid entertained the strongest sentiments of affection and regard. During several years before his death, a daughter of Mrs Leslie's was a constant inmate of his house, and added much to the happiness of his small domestic circle.

Another daughter of Mr Lewis Reid was married to the Reverend John Rose, minister of Udny.—She died in 1793.—In this connection Dr Reid was no less fortunate than in the former ; and to Mr Rose I am indebted for favours of the same kind with those which I have already acknowledged from Mr Leslie.

The widow of Mr Lewis Reid died in 1798, in the eighty-seventh year of her age; having survived her step-son, Dr Reid, more than a year.

The limits within which I was obliged to confine my biographical details, prevented me from availing myself of many interesting circumstances which were communicated to me through the authentic channels which I have now mentioned. But I cannot omit this opportunity of returning to my different correspondents, my warmest acknowledgments for the pleasure and instruction which I received from their letters.

Mr Jardine, also, the learned Professor of Logic in the University of Glasgow---a gentleman who, for many years, lived in habits of the most confidential intimacy with Dr Reid and his family---is entitled to my best thanks for his obliging attention to various queries which I took the liberty to propose to him, concerning the history of our common friend. *

* The preceding sheets were set before I was favoured with the following interesting notices in sup-

plement of Mr Stewart's account of Reid's Life, by Dr Knight, Professor of Natural Philosophy in Marischal College, Aberdeen ; and, in consequence, it has been found impossible to distribute them in the proper places.—H.

P. 3. It is probable that Thomas Reid had been educated at Marischal College, where the teaching of classes commenced immediately on its foundatio in 1593. In Wood's ' Fasti Oxon.' (third or Bliss's edition, I. 394,) is the following entry :—

" 1620, May 28, Thomas Reid, (Rhœdus,) M. A. of Aberdene in Scotland. Incorporated. He had before been a student of this Universitie, and published this year ' Paraphrasis Psalmi civ.' London : 1620. 8vo. And about the same time, ' Epist. ad Episcopum Rolfensem,' in 8vo."

Both Secretary Reid and his brother Alexander, the physician, seem to have died in rather early life from some expressions in their wills.

Secretary Reid's transcript of King James VI's. " Treatise on the Revelations," is preserved in Marischal College library. It is interleaved, has the royal arms on the cover, and on the margins several alterations in the well known hand writing of that monarch.

In his will, dated 19th May 1621, he designs himself " Secretary to his Majesty for the Latin Tongue." In Devon's " Issues of the Exchequer, being payments made in the reign of James I., from the original Records in the ancient Poll office," (published 1836,) is the following entry :—

" To Thomas Reed, Gentleman, the sum of £26 : 9 : 4, in reward for the travail, charges, and expenses of himself and others, employed in writing and translating the book of his Majesty's works out of English into Latin, by his Majesty's special commandment, and for other his Highness's services, in the month of October 1617," &c.

The original catalogue of his library, which he bequeathed to Marischal College, " for the love I bear to the town of New Aberdeen, and wishing the new college and schools thereof should flourish," is still extant amongst the town's records. He had purchased in his travels some of the best editions of the classics and commentators upon them, which were then to be obtained.

His brother Alexander, M D., (Stewart, p. 4,) died in London about 1631. In 1630, he intimated to the magistrates of Aberdeen his having bequeathed his books and MSS., and funds for bursaries to the college ; and, in a letter to them, (4th Oct. 1633,) he transmitted £110 sterling for the latter purpose.

From a paper, dated in 1736, in Dr Thomas Reid's hand.writing, it appears that he had an intention of being served heir to his direct progenitor, Robert, the brother and heir of Secretary Reid in 1624, in order to enable him to institute a suit with the magistrates of Aberdeen, about their management of the fund left by his ancestor for the librarian's salary, which fund had been greatly dilapidated by them since 1677. This was, however, rendered unnecessary by a decision of the Court of Session, which deprived them of the patronage of that office, and restored it to the persons in whom the Secretary's will had vested it.

Dr Reid appears from the College records, to have been in Dr G. Turnbull's class, (as Mr Stewart mentions p. 4,) studying under him three sessions, and becoming A. M. in 1726. He entered college in 1722, and was in the first Greek class taught by Dr Thomas Blackwell, afterwards Principal, and celebrated, at the time, for his strenuous attempts to revive the study of the Greek language in the northern parts of Scotland.

Dr Reid had entered into this plan with enthusiasm ; for his pupil and colleague, the late Professor William Ogilvie, used to relate that he had heard him recite to his class, demonstrations of Euclid in the original language

The sermon which was preached by Mr John Bisset, on the day of moderating a call for Dr Reid, (to the parish of New-Machar, near Aberdeen,) p. 5, attracted much attention, and continued to be long a favourite with the opponents of patronage.

P. 6. Immediately on Dr Reid's appointment to the place of one of the Regents of King's College, he prevailed on his colleagues to make great improvements in their system of University education. The session was extended from five to seven months.

CORRESPONDENCE OF DR REID.

THE following correspondence consists of three consecutive series.

The *first*, for which I am indebted to my friend, Alexander Thomson, Esq., of Banchory, extends from 1764 to 1770, and contains letters by Reid, during the first six years after his removal to Glasgow, to Dr Andrew Skene, and his son, Dr David Skene, physicians in Aberdeen. This correspondence was terminated, by the death of the father, in 1767, and of the son, in 1771. Both were highly eminent in their profession; but the latter, who hardly reached the age of forty, was one of the most zealous cultivators of the natural sciences in Scotland, and the valued correspondent of Linnæus, Pennant, Lord Kames, and other distinguished contemporaries. These letters afford what was perhaps wanting to Mr Stewart's portraiture of Reid—they shew us the philosopher in all the unaffected simplicity of his character, and as he appeared to his friends in the familiar intercourse of ordinary life.

The *second* series comprises the letters addressed to Lord Kames, as given in Lord Woodhouselee's Memoirs of the Life and Writings of that ingenious philosopher. They extend from 1772 to 1782, and are chiefly of scientific interest.

The *third* series contains a selection from Reid's letters to his kinsman, the late Dr James Gregory, Professor of the Practice of Medicine in the University of Edinburgh. Dr Gregory is known, not only as a distinguished physician, but as one of the most elegant scholars and vigorous thinkers of his time. He was indeed a remarkable member even of a family in which, for two centuries, talent would almost seem to have been entailed. To Dr Gregory and Mr Dugald Stewart, Reid appropriately dedicated his principal work—the "Essays on the Intellectual Powers." The correspondence, which is of varied interest, extends from 1783, and was only terminated by Reid's death in 1796.

I owe my best thanks to John Gregory, Esq., for the flattering manner in which he placed these valuable letters at my disposal; but my friend Dr Alison is not the only other member of the family for whose kindness I have also to express my obligation.—H.

A.—LETTERS TO DRS ANDREW AND DAVID SKENE.

I.

TO DR ANDREW SKENE.

Glasgow, Nov. 14th, 1764.

DEAR SIR,—I have been for a long time wishing for as much leisure as to write you, if it was only to revive the memory of the many happy hours which I have enjoyed in your company, when, tête-à-tête, we sat down to speak freely of men and things, without reserve and without malignity. The time slipt away so smoothly, that I could often have wished to have clipt its wings. I dare not now be guilty of any such agreeable irregularities; for I must launch forth in the morning, so as to be at the College (which is a walk of eight minutes) half an hour after seven, when I speak for an hour, without interruption, to an audience of about a hundred. At eleven I examine for an hour upon my morning prelection; but my audience is little more than a third part of what it was in the morning. In a week or two, I must, for three days in the week, have a second prelection at twelve, upon a different subject, where my audience will be made up of those who hear me in the morning, but do not attend at eleven. My hearers commonly attend my class two years at least. The first session they attend the morning prelection, and the hour of examination at eleven; the second and subsequent years they attend the two prelections, but not the hour of examination. They pay fees for the first two years, and then they are *cives*

humanity class was added, on a higher scale than had been taught previously; and the teaching of the elements of Latin, by the Professor of Humanity, discontinued; some of the small bursaries were united; and an account of these alterations was given to the public in a small tract, published in 1754. Dr Reid was in favour of one professor teaching the whole, or the greater part of the curriculum, and therefore did not follow the plan of confining the professors to separate branches, as had been done in Glasgow since 1727, and in Marischal College since 1753. The plan of a seven months' session, after a trial of five years, was abandoned.

of that class, and may attend gratis as many years as they please. Many attend the Moral Philosophy class four or five years ; so that I have many preachers and students of divinity and law of considerable standing, before whom I stand in awe to speak without more preparation than I have leisure for. I have a great inclination to attend some of the professors here—several of whom are very eminent in their way ; but I cannot find leisure. Much time is consumed in our college meetings about business, of which we have commonly four or five in the week. We have a literary society once a-week, consisting of the Masters and two or three more ; where each of the members has a discourse once in the session. The Professors of Humanity, Greek, Logic, and Natural Philosophy, have as many hours as I have, some of them more. All the other professors, except one, teach at least one hour a-day ; and we are no less than fourteen in number. The hours of the different professors are different so far as can be, that the same student may attend two or three, or perhaps more, at the same time. Near a third part of our students are Irish. Thirty came over lately in one ship, besides three that went to Edinburgh. · We have a good many English, and some foreigners. Many of the Irish, as well as Scotch, are poor, and come up late, to save money ; so that we are not yet fully convened, although I have been teaching ever since the 10th of October. Those who pretend to know, say that the number of students this year, when fully convened, will amount to 300.

The Masters live in good habits with one another, and manage their political differences with outward decency and good manners, although with a good deal of intrigue and secret caballing when there is an election. I have met with perfect civility from them all. By this time, I am sure you have enough of the College ; for you know as much as I can tell you of the fine houses of the Masters, of the Astronomical Observatory, of Robin Fowlis' collection of pictures and painting college, of the foundery for types and printing house ; therefore, I will carry you home to my own house, which lyes among the middle of the weavers, like the Back Wynd in Aberdeen. You go through a long, dark, abominably nasty entry, which leads you into a clean little close You walk up stairs to a neat little dining-room, and find as many other little rooms as just accommodate my family so scantily that my apartment is a closet of six feet by eight or nine off the dining-room. To balance these little inconveniences, the house is new and free of buggs ; it has the best air and the finest prospect in Glasgow ; the privilege of

a large garden, very airy, to walk in, which is not so nicely kept but one may use freedom with it. A five minutes' walk leads us up a rocky precipice into a large park, partly planted with firs and partly open, which overlooks the town and all the country round, and gives a view of the windings of the Clyde for a great way. The ancient cathedral stands at the foot of the rock, half of its height below you, and half above you ; and, indeed, it is a very magnificent pile.

When we came here, the street we live in (which is called the Drygate) was infested with the smallpox, which were very mortal. Two families in our neighbourhood lost all their children, being three each. Little David was seized with the infection, and had a very great eruption both in his face and over his whole body, which you will believe would discompose his mother. .

. . . .

Although my salary here be much the same as at Aberdeen, yet, if the class does not fall off, nor my health, so as to disable me from teaching, I believe I shall be able to live as easily as at Aberdeen, notwithstanding the difference of the expense of living at the two places. I have touched about £70 of fees, and may possibly make out the hundred this session.

And now, sir, after I have given you so full an account of my own state, spiritual and temporal, how goes it with you ? Are George and Molly minding their business ? I know Kate will mind hers. Is Dr David littering up your house more and more with all the birds of the air, the beasts of the field, and the clods of the valley ? Or has Walker, the botanist, been carrying him about to visit vegetable patients, while you are left to drudge among the animal ones ? Is your head steady, or is it sometimes [turning] round ? I have a thousand questions to ask about our [country] people, but I ought rather to put them to those who have more time to answer them. I was very sorry to hear, by a letter from Lady Forbes, of Hatton's misfortune, and am left in doubt whether the next account shall be of his death or recovery.

The common people here have a gloom in their countenance, which I am at a loss whether to ascribe to their religion or to the air and climate. There is certainly more of religion among the common people in this town than in Aberdeen ; and, although it has a gloomy, enthusiastical cast, yet I think it makes them tame and sober. I have not heard either of a house or of a head broke, of a pocket picked, or of any flagrant crime, since I came here. I have not heard any swearing in the streets, nor seen a man drunk, (excepting, inter nos, one Prof——r,) since I came here. If this scroll tire you, impute it to this, that to-morrow is to be employed in choosing a Rector, and I can sleep till ten o'clock, which I shall not do again for six weeks; and believe me to be, with sincere friendship and regard, dear Sir, yours,

THOMAS REID.

II.

DEAR SIR,—We had a Turin Professor of Medicine here lately, whom I wished you acquainted with : Count Carburi is his name; an Athenian born, but has been most of his time in Italy.* He seems to be a great connoisseur in natural history, and has seen all the best collections in Europe. The Emperor and King of France, as well as many persons in Italy, he says, have much more compleat collections of our Scotch fossils than any we have in Britain. I described to him our Bennachie porphyry; but he says all that they call porphyry in Italy, consists of small dark-coloured grains, in a grey ground, and has very much the same appearance as many of our granites, before it is polished. He wanted much to know whether we had any authentic evidence from Ireland, or anywhere else, of wood that had been seen in the state of wood, and afterwards petrified. He would have gone over to Ireland on purpose, if we could have given him ground to expect this. He says MM. Buffon and Daubenton are both positive that no such thing was ever known, and that all the petrified wood dug up on various parts of the earth—of which Carburi says he has two waggon-loads, found in Piedmont—has been petrified before our earth put on its present form; and that there is no evidence of any such petrification now going on. I have a strong inclination to attend the chymical lecture here next winter; but am afraid I shall not have time. I have had but very imperfect hints of Dr Black's theory of fire. He has a strong apprehension that the phlogistick principle is so far from adding to the weight of bodies, by being joyned to them, that it diminishes it; and, on the contrary, by taking the phlogistick from any body, you make it heavier. He brings many experiments to prove this : the calcination of metals, and the decomposition of sulphur, you will easily guess to be among the number; but he is very modest and cautious in his conclusions, and wants to have them amply confirmed before he asserts them positively. I am told that Black's theory is not known at Edinburgh. Chemistry

seems to be the only branch of philosophy that can be said to be in a progressive state here, although other branches are neither ill taught nor ill studied. As Black is got into a good deal of practice, it is to be feared that his chymical inquiries must go on slowly and heavily in time to come. I never considered Dollond's telescopes till I came here. I think they open a new field in opticks which may greatly enrich that part of philosophy. The laws of the refraction of light seem to be very different, in different kinds both of glass and of native chrystal. I have seen a prism of Brazil pebble, which forms two distinct speculums in Sir I. Newton's experiment, each of them containing all the primary colours. A German native chrystal seemed to me to form four or five. One composition of glass separates the different colours much more than another composition, even with the same degree of refraction. Dollond has made a fortune by his telescopes, nobody else having attempted to imitate them, and is now, I am told, grown lazy. Nor is the theory of them prosecuted as it ought. Dollond's micrometer is likewise a very fine instrument, although not built upon anything new in opticks. We have one of them here fitted to a reflecting telescope of about 18 inches, by which one may take the apparent diameter of the sun, or of any planet, within a second of a degree.

I find a variety of things here to amuse me in the literary world, and want nothing so much as my old friends, whose place I cannot expect, at my time of life, to supply. I think the common people here and in the neighbourhood greatly inferior to the common people with you. They are Bœotian in their understandings, fanatical in their religion, and clownish in their dress and manners. The clergy encourage this fanaticism too much, and find it the only way to popularity. I often hear a gospel here which you know nothing about; for you neither hear it from the pulpit, nor will you find it in the bible.

What is your Philosophical Society* doing? Still battling about D. Hume? or have you time to look in? I hope your papa holds out in his usual way. I beg to be remembered to him most affectionately, and to all the rest of your family. But I believe you do not like to be charged with compliments, otherwise I would desire of you likewise to remember me respectfully to Sir Archibald Grant, Sir Arthur and Lady Forbes, and others of my country

---

* This was Count *Marco*, not Count Marino, Carburi; born at *Cephalonia*, and, from 1759 to 1808, Professor of *Chemistry* in *Padua*.—H.

* The Philosophical Society to which Reid here alludes was founded by himself and his relative, Dr John Gregory. It was vulgarly styled the *Wise Club*. Dr David Skene, who is called by Sir W. Forbes "a physician of genius and taste," was one of its original members. See Forbes's "Life of Beattie," i. 35.—H.

acquaintance, when you have occasion to see them. I should be glad. too, to hear from you, when leisure, and opportunity, and the epistolary humour all meet together. My folks are all pretty well, and beg their compliments to you and all yours.—I am, dear Sir, most affectionately, yours,

THOMAS REID.

Glasgow, 13 *July* 1765, being the first warm day we have had since the month of May.

III.

TO DR DAVID SKENE.

Glasgow, 20 *Dec.* 1765.

DEAR SIR,—Your commissions have been lying by me some time, for want of a proper conveyance. An Aberdeen carrier promised to call for them, but disappointed me; I therefore sent the two thermometers wrapt up in paper, and directed for you by Mr. Menzies, merchant in the Narrow Wynd, who was to set out from hence yesterday morning. One has a circular bore in the small tube, the other an elliptical one, and is on that account much fitter for experiments. As there is a much greater quantity of quicksilver in the circular one, it may take four or five minutes to bring it to the temperature of a fluid in which it is immersed. For nice experiments, some of the elliptical ones are made by Dr Wilson with the bulb of the small tube naked. But these are so liable to accidents that few choose them. The perspective machine goes to Edinburgh to-morrow with Dr Trail, who will send it to my sisters by the first proper opportunity. . . . Mr Watt has made two small improvements of the steam-engine. The first is in the iron bars which support the fire. These have always been made of solid iron, and burn away so fast by the great heat, that the expense of repairing them comes to be very considerable. He uses hollow square bars of plate iron, always kept full of water, which communicates with a pretty large reservoir, so that the bars can never be heated above the degree of boyling water, and may be kept far below that degree of heat. The other improvement is to prevent the waste of heat by the chimney pipe of the furnace. It is evident that a very large proportion of the heat of the fire passes off in this way without being applied to the water in the boyler. To prevent this, he makes three small chimney pipes of iron, which are made to pass through the boyler. He is just now employed in setting up an engine for the Carron Company with these improvements.

Since I saw C. Carburi, I have it upon good authority that there are petrifying springs in England which petrify things put into them in a short time. And a gentleman here expects, in a short time, a petrified periwig from one of them.

Dr Black tells me that Cramer's furnaces, both for essaying and melting, as you have them described in his "*Ars Decimastica*," are the best he knows. His are of this kind, being made of plate iron, lined with a coat of a lute, which is composed of one-part clay and three-parts firesand, which, he says, never cracks. He has not examined the Fechel earth, but conjectures it to be a composition of the same kind with Prussian blue. He has seen a horse's head, which, by being long buried in a clay which had some mixture of iron, had in several places taken a fine blue tinge, or rather was covered with a fine blue dust.

I have attended Dr Black's lectures hitherto. His doctrine of latent heat is the only thing I have yet heard that is altogether new. And, indeed, I look upon it as a very important discovery. As Mr Ogilvie attended him and took notes, I believe he can give you a fuller account of it than I can. It gives a great deal of light to the phænomena of heat that appear in mixture, solution, and evaporation; but, as far as I see, it gives no light to those which appear in animal heat, inflammation, and friction. I wish this discovery may not reach any person who may be so ungenerous as to make it public before the Dr has time to publish it himself. If the account which Ogilvie can give you should suggest any doubts, I will be glad to clear them, so far as my knowledge of this doctrine reaches.—I am very glad to hear that Dr Hope has a prospect of raising the true rhubarb. I believe I forgot to tell you that I wrapped up a head of what I take to be the *daucus sylvestris*, in a piece of paper, and put it in the box with the drawing machine. It grows in great plenty in the fields here; but I never saw it with you. I have not met with any botanists here.

Our College is considerably more crowded than it was last session. My class, indeed, is much the same as last year; but all the rest are better. I believe the number of our students, of one kind or another, may be between four and five hundred. But the College of Edinburgh is increased this year much more than we are. The Moral Philosophy class there, is more than double ours. The Professor, Ferguson, is, indeed, as far as I can judge, a man of a noble spirit, of very elegant manners, and has a very uncommon flow of eloquence. I hear he is about to publish, I don't know under what title, a natural history of man: exhibiting a view of him in the savage state, and in the several successive states of pasturage, agriculture, and commerce.

Your friend, the Cte. de Lauraguais, was very full of you when he was here, and shewed an anxiety that your merit should be known. I am told that he has wrote many things in the Memoirs of the Academy; but I know nobody here that has read them. Our College Library is ten or twelve years behind in the Memoirs of the Royal Academy; and all that the Cte. has wrote must fall within that period. He seems to have attached himself so entirely to chemistry as to have neglected every other branch of knowledge. Carburi was more universal; he gave attention chiefly to the progress of manufactures and commerce, and to collect books and specimens of natural or artificial things.

Our society is not so harmonious as I wish. Schemes of interest, pushed by some and opposed by others, are like to divide us into parties, and, perhaps, engage us in law-suits.* When you see Mr W. Ogilvie, please make my compliments to him. I received his letter, and will write him when I can find leisure. I hope your papa is quite recovered of his cold, and that all the rest of the family are in good health. Pray, make my best compliments to him. Mrs Reid, Pegie, and I, have all had a severe cold and cough. I have been keeping the house these two days, in order to get the better of it.---I am, dear Sir,

Yours most affectionately,

THOMAS REID.

Ended, Dec. 30.

Wishing you many happy years.

IV.

TO DR ANDREW SKENE.

DEAR SIR,—I have been sometimes apt to impute it to laziness, and sometimes to hurry of business, that I have been so long without writing you. I am ashamed to plead the last of these excuses when I consider how many people there are of my acquaintance that have a great deal more to do than I have, and would think all my business but idleness. Yet, I assure you, I can rarely find an hour which I am at liberty to dispose of as I please. The most disagreeable thing in the teaching part is to have a great number of stupid Irish teagues who attend classes for two or three years to qualify them for teaching schools, or being dissenting teachers. I preach to these as St Francis did to the fishes.† I

don't know what pleasure he had in his audience; but I should have none in mine if there was not in it a mixture of reasonable creatures. I confess I think there is a smaller proportion of these in my class this year than was the last, although the number of the whole is not less. I have long been of the opinion, that, in a right constituted college, there ought to be two Professors for each class—one for the dunces, and another for those who have parts. The province of the former would not be the most agreeable, but, perhaps, it would require the greatest talents, and, therefore, ought to be accounted the post of honour. There is no part of my time more disagreeably spent than that which is spent in College meetings, of which we have often five or six in a week. And I should have been attending one this moment if a bad cold I have got had not furnished me with an excuse. These meetings are become more disagreeable by an evil spirit of party that seems to put us in a ferment, and, I am afraid, will produce bad consequences.

The temper of our northern colonies makes our mercantile people here look very grave. Several of them are going to London about this matter, to attend the proceedings of Parliament. It is said that the effects in those colonies belonging to this town amount to above £400,000 sterling. The mercantile people are for suspending the stamp-act, and redressing the grievances of the colonists. Others consider their conduct as an open rebellion, and an avowed claim to independence, which ought to be checked in the beginning. They say that, for all their boasting, the colonists are a dastardly, pusillanimous race, and that a British fleet and army would soon reduce them to such terms as would secure their future dependence upon the mother country; that this is the most proper time for doing so when we are at peace with all our neighbours. In what light the House of Commons will view this matter, I don't know, but it seems to be one of the most important matters that have come before them. I wish often an evening with you, such as we have enjoyed in the days of former times, to settle the important affairs of State and Church, of Colleges and Corporations. I have found this the best expedient to enable me to think of them without melancholy and chagrin. And I think all that a man has to do in the world is to keep his temper and to do his duty. Mrs Reid is tolerably well just now, but is often ailing. She desires to be remembered to you and all your family.— I am, dear Sir,

Yours most affectionately,

THOMAS REID.

Glasgow. Dec. 30, 1765.

---

* See above, p 40, A, below, pp. 46, A, and 47, B. All theory and all experience prove, that the worst and the most corrupt depositaries of academical patronage are a self-elective body of professors.—H.

† Not St Francis, but St Antony (of Padua.)—H.

V.

TO DR DAVID SKENE.

Glasgow, 23 March 1766.

DEAR SIR,—I had yours of the 14th, and this moment that of Thursday the 20, with the inclosed, a letter from your papa by Mr Duguid, with your circular thermometer. I returned the thermometer, repaired by Mr Annan, who left this two days ago, but was to be a week at Edinburgh in his return. I shall remember Sir Archibald Grant's commission, but must take some time to think of it. What would you think of Alex. Mearns in Gordon's Hospital? If you are not acquainted with him, you may learn his qualities. and tell me your sentiments. I shall likewise mind your elliptical thermometer. Mr Stewart's* death affects me deeply. A sincere friendship, begun at twelve years of age, and continued to my time of life without any interruption, cannot but give you some pangs. You know his worth, yet it was shaded ever since you knew him by too great abstraction from the world. The former part of his life was more amiable and more social, but the whole was of a piece in virtue, candour, and humanity. I have often regretted that the solicitude of providing for a numerous family, and the labour of managing an estate and a farm, should make a man in a great measure unknown, whose virtue, integrity, and judgment ought to have shone in a more extensive sphere. His scholars could not but observe and revere his virtues; and I have no doubt but great numbers of them have reaped great improvement by him in matters of higher importance than mathematical knowledge. I have always regarded him as my best tutor, though of the same age with me. If the giddy part of my life was in any degree spent innocently and virtuously, I owe it to him more than to any human creature; for I could not but be virtuous in his company, and I could not be so happy in any other. But I must leave this pleasing melancholy subject. He is happy; and I shall often be happy in the remembrance of our friendship; and I hope we shall meet again.

There is no such thing as chymical furnaces made here for sale. They are made of plate iron; and a white-iron-man manages that material better than a blacksmith. But you must direct them in everything, and be still over the work.

I can give but an imperfect account of

the doctrine of latent heat; but some hint I shall give, trusting entirely to your honour that you will be cautious not to make any use of it that may endanger the discoverer being defrauded of his property.

There is in every body a certain quantity of heat, which makes a part of its form or constitution, and which it never parts with without losing or changing its form. This is called the latent heat of that body. All or most bodies have three different forms—hardness, fluidity, and steam or vapour. Take water, for an example, in its hard state, that of ice: we have no means of knowing what latent heat it may contain; but in its fluid state it has about 140° of latent heat more than it had in the state of ice. This heat is latent while the water is fluid; it does not affect the thermometer, nor produce any other effect but that of making the body fluid. In the very act of melting from the state of ice to that of water, 140° of heat is absorbed from the circumambient bodies without making the water sensibly warmer than the ice; and in the act of passing from the state of water to that of ice, 140° of heat which was latent in the water becomes sensible, and must pass from the water to the ambient bodies before it can wholly be converted into ice. As there is no intermediate state between water and ice, a very small part of the water freezes at once; and the latent heat of that part being communicated to the remaining water, the freezing even in the coldest air goes on piecemeal, according as the latent heat goes off first into the water not yet frozen, and from that into the air or ambient bodies.

Spermaceti, in passing from a solid to a perfectly fluid form, requires about 150° of heat, which becomes latent; bees' wax about 160°. But there is this remarkable difference between these bodies—as well as iron and some other metals on the one hand, and water on the other—that the former soften by degrees, so that there are many intermediate degrees of softness between the hardest state which the body takes by cold, and the state of perfect fluidity; whereas in water there seems to be no intermediate degree between perfect ice and perfect water. Accordingly, in spermaceti, bees' wax, and iron, the latent heat is more or less, according to the degree of softness; but in water it is always the same. As water has about 140° of latent heat more than ice, so steam has about 800° of latent heat more than water; hence, an ounce of steam, though it have little more sensible heat than boyling water, will heat the cold water that condenses it almost as much as four ounces of boyling water would do. I can only at present give you an experiment or two of the many by which this theory is confirmed. But first, it is proper to observe, that equal quantities of the same fluid of different temperatures, being mixed, the temperature of the mixed fluid is always an arithmetical mean between the temperatures of the ingredients. Thus, if a pound of water of 40° be mixed with a pound of 100°, the mixed is found precisely 60°. This has been tried in an infinite variety of cases, and found to hold invariably, proper allowance being made for the heat communicated to the vessels, or drawn from them in the operation.

Experiment 1.—Two Florence flasks had six ounces of water put into each. In one it was made to freeze ; in the other brought as near as possible to the freezing point without freezing—that is, to about 33°. Both were set to warm in a large warm room. The unfrozen water soon came to the temperature of the room ; but the frozen water took eleven or twelve hours to dissolve, and for the greatest part of that time was not sensibly heated. A calculation was made upon the supposition that the frozen water had as much heat communicated to it every half hour as the unfrozen water had the first half hour. The result of this calculation was, that the frozen water had absorbed 136° or 140° of heat in melting, over and above that which affected the thermometer.

Exp. 2.—Six ounces of ice of the temperature of 32° had six ounces of boyling water poured upon it. The ice melted immediately, and the whole water was 52° temperature.

Exp. 3.—From Musschenbroek, with a little variation. When the air is ten degrees below the freezing point, set a deep, narrow beer-glass of water to freeze, and let it remain perfectly at rest, without the least motion. The water will cool regularly below 32° without freezing, even to 22° ; but, as soon as it is disturbed, a number of icy spiculæ are formed ; and in the same moment the sensible heat rises to 32°, and continues so till all is frozen.

I need not tell you, that by sensible heat is meant that which diffuses itself to the ambient bodies till all are brought to an equilibrium. Of this the thermometer is the measure. But latent heat adheres to the body without any tendency to diffuse itself to other bodies, unless they are able to change the form of the body from vapour to a fluid, or from a fluid to ice or hardness— then the latent heat goes off to other bodies, and becomes sensible. I hope you will understand me, though I have wrote in a great hurry. Yet I cannot find that Cullen or the Edinburgh people know anything of this matter. I may give you more of the experiments afterwards.

THOMAS REID.

VI.

TO DR DAVID SKENE.

Glasgow, 18th April [1766.]

DEAR SIR,---There is like to be a vacancy in one of the medical professions of this college, by the removal of Joseph Black to Edinburgh. I thought, when I heard of Dr White's death, that there was very little probability of our losing Dr Black by that event ; because the Chymical Profession in Edinburgh was that which was thought fittest for Dr Black ; and there was good reason to think that Cullen would not give up the Chemistry for the Theory of Medicine---though he would very willingly exchange it for the Practice of Medicine. But I was informed late yesternight, that Dr Black is willing to accept of the Theory of Medicine in Edinburgh, and that the Council are certainly to present him. I am very dubious whether his place here would be worth your acceptance ; but I am sure it would be so much the interest of this society to have such a man in it, (and I need not say how agreeable it would be to me,) that I beg leave to inform you of what I know of the state of the matter, that you may think of it, and let me know your thoughts. The salary of Dr Black's place, is £50 as Professor of the Theory and Practice of Medicine ; and the presentation is in the Crown. The recommendation of the College would probably have great weight, if unanimous ; but I think there is no probability of an unanimous recommendation ; so that the Court interest must probably determine it. Dr Black, and Dr Cullen before him, had £20 yearly from the College, for teaching chemistry ; and the College have, from time to time, allowed, I believe, above £500 for a laboratory. The chemical class this session might bring £50 or £60 of fees, and the medical class from £20 to £30 ; so that the whole salary and fees will be between £140 and £160. At the same time, the College can at any time withdraw the £20, and give that and the chemical laboratory to another ; and it is not improbable that this may be done if one be presented of whose abilities in chemistry the College is not satisfied. Dr Black, of late, had got a great deal of practice in the medical way, so as to leave him but little time for prosecuting his chemical discourses, and I think you might expect the same after some time ; for he had no natural connection here : it was his merit alone that brought him into it ; and he long resisted, instead of courting it ; so that it was in a manner forced upon him. The other medical Professor has anatomy and botany for his province ; he has a good anatomical class : but he does not teach botany at all, nor is, as I apprehend, qualified to teach it. All I have farther to say is, that there is a great spirit of inquiry here among the young people. Literary merit is much regarded; and I conceive the opportunities a man has of improving himself are much greater than at Aberdeen. The communication with Edinburgh is easy. One goes in the stage-coach to Edinburgh before dinner; has all the afternoon there; and returns to dinner at Glasgow next day: so that, if you have any ambition to get into the College of Edinburgh, (which, I think, you ought to have,) I conceive Glasgow would be a good step. Now, sir, if you incline this place, you must, without delay, try your interest at Court, and get the best recommendations you can to the members of this College. The Principal and Mr Clow are not engaged; they are the only persons to whom I have made known, or intend to make known, my writing to you. Lord Findlater's interest, I think, would have weight with Trail and Williamson. I am told of three candidates—Dr Stevenson, in Glasgow; Dr Smith Carmichael, a young doctor, presently at London; and one Dr Stork, who was educated here. Each of these, I apprehend, has interest with some of the members, and depend upon them; so that we will probably be divided, and, consequently, our recommendation, if any is given, will have little weight at Court. If, after due deliberation, you think it not worth your while to stir in this matter for yourself, will you be so good as communicate the state of the case to Dr George Skene?* He is the man—that is, next to you—I would be fond of for a colleague; and in this I think I am determined more by the public good than my private.

VII.

DEAR SIR,—I cannot presently lay my hand upon the last letter I had from you, and I beg you will impute it to that and to my bad memory if there was anything in it I ought to answer. I have sent by the bearer, Mr Duguid, merchant in Aberdeen, an elliptical thermometer for Dr David, which I could not find an opportunity of sending till now. Mrs Reid was, this day, at one in the afternoon, brought to bed of a daughter, whom we have named Elizabeth, and I hope is in a good way. . . . .
We have had great canvassing here about

* A third Aberdonian physician of distinction, of the name of Skene; but not a relation, at least not a near relation, of the other two. He was Professor of Philosophy, Marischal ollege; an eminent scholar; and father of the late Solicitor-General.—H.

a Professor of the Theory and Practice of Physic, to succeed Dr Jo. Black, although all that we do is to recommend one to the King, who has the presentation. Dr Stevenson, a son of the late Dr Stevenson in Edinburgh, who has by much the best practice in this town and neighbourhood, has obtained a recommendation from the majority of the College, not without much interest. The only objection to him was his great practice, which it was thought might tempt him to neglect regular teaching. And, I believe, the majority would have preferred to him any man of character who had not such a temptation to neglect the duties of his office. However, the strongest assurances that he would not neglect the class—nay, that he would think himself bound in honour to give up the Profession if he could not keep up a class, brought in a majority to sign a recommendation in his favour; and, as he has a strong interest at Court, and no rival, as far as we know, it is thought he will be the man. He declines teaching the chemistry class, which is in the gift of the College, and, I conceive, will be given to one of Dr Black's scholars. My class will be over in less than a month, and by that time I shall be glad to have some respite. I hope to have the pleasure of seeing my friends at Aberdeen in the month of August, if not sooner. We have had a thronger College this year than ever before. I had some reason to think that I should not have so good a class as last year, and was disappointed, for it was somewhat better. I expect a good one next winter, if I live so long. The Irish, on whom we depend much, have an ebb and flow, as many of them come but one year in two. We have been remarkably free from riots and disorders among the students, and I did not indeed expect that 350 young fellows could have been kept quiet, for so many months, with so little trouble. They commonly attend so many classes of different professors, from half-an-hour after seven in the morning till eight at night, that they have little time to do mischief.
You'll say to all this that cadgers are aye speaking of crooksaddles. I think so they ought; besides, I have nothing else to say to you, and I have had no time to think of anything but my crooksaddles for seven months past. When the session is over I must rub up my mathematicks against the month of August. There is one candidate for your Profession of Mathematicks to go from this College; and, if your College get a better man or a better mathematician, they will be very lucky. I am so sensible of the honour the magistrates have done me in naming me to be one of the examinators, that I will not decline it, though, I confess,

I like the honour better than the office.—
I am, dear Sir,
            Yours most affectionately,
                        THOMAS REID.
Glasgow, 8th May, 1766.
Half an hour after eleven at night.

VIII.

TO DR ANDREW SKENE.

. . . . When you are disposed to laugh you may look into the inclosed proposals from a physician here who
has been persecuting everybody with an
edition of Celsus, and now with an index to
him as large as the book. Another physician here is printing a History of Medicine,
and of all the arts and sciences from the
beginning to the present time, four vols.
8vo, price one guinea. He is not thought
mad, but whimsical. I have not the proposals to send you, and I suppose I have
sent enough of this kind. We authors had
rather be known for madmen or fools than
pass our lives in obscurity. Stevenson's
presentation to the Profession of Medicine
here is not yet come, but is expected as certain. The College have appointed a Lecturer in Chemistry, and one in Materia
Medica, for next session. I think we might
have a college of medicine here if we had
an infirmary. I think our surgeons eclipse
our M.D's. I do not hear much of the
last, if you except Black and Stevenson.
Our Professor of Anatomy is not an M.D.,
otherwise I would have excepted him also.
Have you ever tried the seeds of the *daucus sylvestris* in nephritick cases? It has
been much talked of of late. I never saw
it in the north, but it is pretty common in
the fields here.—I am, dear Sir,
            Yours most affectionately,
                        THOMAS REID.
Glasgow, 15*th July* 1766.

IX

TO DR ANDREW SKENE.

Glasgow College, Dec. 17, 1766.
. . . I live now in the College, and
have no distance to walk to my class in
dark mornings, as I had before. I enjoy
this ease, though I am not sure whether
the necessity of walking up and down a
steep hill three or four times a-day, was not
of use. I have of late had a little of your
distemper, finding a giddiness in my head
when I lie down or rise, or turn myself in
my bed.
Our College is very well peopled this
session; my public class is above three

score, besides the private class. Dr Smith
never had so many in one year. There is
nothing so uneasy to me here as our fac-
tions in the College, which seem to be
rather more inflamed than last session.
Will you take the trouble to ask of Dr
David, whether he knows of a bird called
a stankhen.* It is a water fowl, less than
a duck, with scolloped membranes at the
toes, but not close-footed, and has a crest
on the forehead of the same kind of substance with a cock's comb, but white and flat.
It has a very fishy taste, and is found here
in the lochs. If he has none of this kind,
I could send him one when I find a proper
occasion. I am, with entire affection and
regard, dear Sir, yours,
                        THOMAS REID.

X.

TO DR DAVID SKENE.

Glasgow College, 25*th Feby.* 1767.
DEAR SIR,—I intend to send your stankhen along with the furnace, which was
ready long ago, and I suppose would have
been sent before now, but that Dr Irvine
was confined a long time by a megrim, and
was like to lose one eye by it; but is now
pretty well recovered, and intends to send
your furnace this week.
Since the repeal of the stamp-act, trade,
which was languishing, has revived in this
place, and there is a great bustle and great
demand for money. We are now resolved
to have a canal from Carron to this place,
if the Parliament allows it. £40,000 was
subscribed last week by the merchants and
the Carron Company for this purpose; and
commissioners are immediately going up
to London to apply for an act of Parliament. The freight upon this canal is not
to exceed twopence per ton for every mile;
the land carriage is more than ten times as
much.
Our medical college has fallen off greatly
this session, most of the students of medicine having followed Dr Black; however,
our two medical professors and two lec-
turers have each of them a class, and Irvine
expects a great many to attend him for
botany in summer. The natural and moral
philosophy classes are more numerous than
they have ever been; but I expect a great
falling off, if I see another session. The
Lecturer in Chemistry has general approbation. He chiefly follows Dr Black and
Stahl. There is a book of Stahl's, called
" Three Hundred Experiments," which he
greatly admires, and very often quotes. I
was just now seeing your furnace along with

* The Gallinula Chloropus.—H.

Irvine ; I think it a very decent piece of furniture for a man of your profession, and that no limb of the faculty should be without one, accompanied with a proper apparatus of retorts, cucurbits, &c. For my part, if I could find a machine as proper for ana- lyzing ideas, moral sentiments, and other materials belonging to the fourth kingdom, I believe I should find in my heart to be- stow the money for it. I have the more use for a machine of this kind, because my alembick for performing these operations— I mean my cranium—has been a little out of order this winter, by a vertigo, which has made my studies go on heavily, though it has not hitherto interrupted my teaching. I have found air and exercise, and a clean stomach, the best remedies ; but I cannot command the two former as often as I could wish. I am sensible that the air of a crowded class is bad, and often thought of carrying my class to the common hall ; but I was afraid it might have been construed as a piece of ostentation. I hope you are carrying on your natural history, or something else, in the Club, with a view to make the world wiser. What is my Lord Linnæus doing ? Are we ever to expect his third volume upon the fossile kingdom or not ? We are here so busie reading lec- tures, that we have no time to write. . . .

XI.

TO DR DAVID SKENE.

Glasgow College, 14 *Sept.* 1767.

DEAR SIR,—It gives me much surprise, as well as affliction, to hear from my daughter Patty, of the death of my dear friend, your papa. Fifteen years ago it would have been no surprise ; but for some years back, I thought there was great probability that his life and usefulness might have had a longer period. I can never, while I remember anything, forget the many agreeable hours I have en- joyed with him in that entire confidence and friendship which give relish to life. I never had a friend that shewed a more hearty affection, or a more uniform dispo- sition to be obliging and useful to me and to my family. I had so many opportuni- ties of observing his disinterested concern to be useful in his profession to those from whom he could expect no return, his sym- pathy with the distressed, and his assiduity in giving them his best assistance, that, if I had had no personal friendship with him, I could not but lament his death as a very great and general loss to the place. It is very uncommon to find a man that at any time of life, much more at his, possessed the active, the contemplative, and the social disposition at once in so great vigour. I

sincerely sympathize with you ; and I beg you will assure each of your brothers and sisters of my sympathy ; and that, besides my personal regard to every one of them, I hold myself to be under the strongest obligation from gratitude and regard to the memory of my deceased friend, if I can ever be of the least use to any of them.

You are now, dear Sir, in the providence of God, called to be a father as well as a brother ; and I doubt not but you will ac- quit yourself in that character as you have done in the other. I need not say that Dr Skene's death gave very great affliction to Mrs Reid and to all my family ; they all desire that you and all your family may be assured of their respect and sympathy. . . .

Some days after I parted from you at Edinburgh, I was called home to do the last duty to my sweet little Bess, whom I had left in perfect health some days after her innoculation. Since that time I have not been three miles from Glasgow, but once at Hamilton with Mr Beattie. Hav- ing my time at command, I was tempted to fall to the tumbling over books, as we have a vast number here which I had not access to see at Aberdeen. But this is a *mare magnum,* wherein one is tempted, by hopes of discoveries, to make a tedious voy- age, which seldom rewards his labour. I have long ago found my memory to be like a vessel that is full ; if you pour in more, you lose as much as you gain ; and, on this account, have a thousand times resolved to give up all pretence to what is called learn- ing, being satisfied that it is more profitable to ruminate on the little I have laid up, than to add to the indigested heap. To pour learning into a leaky vessel is indeed a very childish and ridiculous imagination. Yet, when a man has leisure, and is placed among books that are new to him, it is difficult to resist the temptation. I have had little society, the college people being out of town, and have almost lost the faculty of speech by disuse. I blame my- self for having corresponded so little with my friends at Aberdeen.

I wished to try Linnæus's experiment, which you was so good as to communicate to me. I waited for the heat of summer, which never came till the first of August, and then lasted butia few days. Not hav- ing any of the fungus powder at hand, I put a piece of fresh fungus which grew on rot- ten wood in pure water. In a day or two I found many animalcules diverting them- selves in the water by diving and rising again to the top. But, after three or four days, the water turned muddy and stunk. And, from all I could then observe, I should rather have concluded that my animalcules died and putrified, than that they were transformed into young mushrooms. I see a letter in *The Edinburgh Courant* of Wednesday last on this subject. About twenty hours ago, I put some smutty oats in water: but have not seen any animals in it yet. A nasty custom I have of chewing tobacco has been the reason of my observing a species of as nasty little animals. On the above occasion, I spit in a bason of sawdust, which, when it comes to be drenched, produces a vast number of animals, three or four times as large as a louse, and not very different in shape; but armed with four or five rows of prickles like a hedgehog, which seem to serve it as feet. Its motion is very sluggish. It lies drenched in the foresaid mass, which swarms with these animals of all ages from top to bottom; whether they become winged at last I have not discovered.

Dr Irvine was taken up a great part of the summer with his botanical course; and, since that was over, has been in the country. I have gone over Sir James Stewart's great book of political œconomy, wherein I think there is a great deal of good materials, carelessly put together indeed; but I think it contains more sound principles concerning commerce and police than any book we have yet had. We had the favour of a visit from Sir Archibald Grant. It gave me much pleasure to see him retain his spirits and vigor. I beg when you see him you will make my best compliments to him. I beg to be remembered to the Club, which I hope goes on with spirit. I am, with great regard, dear Sir, yours most affectionately,

THOMAS REID.

Be so good as to put the inclosed into Sandie Leslie's shop.

XII.

TO DR DAVID SKENE.

DEAR SIR,—You will easily guess that my chief motive in writing you at this time, is, by the benefit of your frank, to save the postage of the two inclosed, of which I give you the trouble. Perhaps I would have dissembled this, if I had had anything to say. I long to hear how Linnæus' experiment has succeeded with you. For my own part, I have found nothing about it but what I wrote you before. The chymists here are hunting for something by which cambrick may be stamped as it comes from the loom, so that the stamps shall stand out all the operations of boyling, bleaching, &c. The only thing that is like to answer, I am told, is that solution of silver which is used to dye ivory black. The act of Parliament anent cambrick requires it to be stamped in the loom; and, if this stamp is not apparent after bleaching, it is contraband. But the wisdom of the nation has not thought fit to prescribe the material to be used for that purpose; if no such material is found, the act will be useless.

I passed eight days lately with Lord Kaims at Blair-Drummond. You were very honourably mentioned. My Lord has it much at heart to have a professor of practical mechanicks established at Edinburgh, and wants only a proper person. He is preparing a fourth edition of his "Elements." I have been labouring at *Barbara Celarent* for three weeks bygone;* and on Monday begin my own course. I do not expect such a crop of students as I had last year; but the College in general promises pretty well. My compliments to all your family; and believe me to be, with great affection, dear Sir,

Yours,

THOMAS REID.

Glasgow College, 31 *Oct.* 1767.

XIII.

TO DR DAVID SKENE.

[*July* 1770.]

DEAR SIR,—Having this opportunity, I could not forbear asking how you do, and what you are doing. I know you are giving feet to the lame, and eyes to the blind. and healing the sick. I know you are gathering heaps of fossils, vegetables, and animals, and I hope among other fossils you are gathering gold and silver; this is all very right. I know, likewise, that you have been, ever since you was in petticoats, most avariciously amassing knowledge. But is it all to die with you, and to be buried in your grave? This, my dear sir, ought not to be. You see we Scotch people will be blotting paper though you should hold your hand: *stultum est periturœ parcere chartœ.* Can you find no time, either when you are laid up in the gout, or when the rest of the world is in good health, to bequeath something to posterity? Think seriously of this, if you have not done so already. Permit me, sir, to offer you another counsell; for you know we moralists know better how to give good counsell than to take it. Is it not possible for you to order things so as to take a jaunt of six weeks or two months? I verily believe there are things worth knowing here, much more at Edinburgh, of which you cannot be fully informed while you keep be-north Tay. We have speculatists in medicine, in chemistry, in mechanics, in natural history, that are worth being acquainted with, and that

* This alludes to his "Analysis of Aristotle's Logic," which he was then preparing as an Appendix to one of Lord Kames's "Sketches of the History of Man."—H.

E

would be fond of your acquaintance. As to myself, the immaterial world has swallowed up all my thoughts since I came here; but I meet with few that have travelled far in that region, and am often left to pursue my dreary way in a more solitary manner than when we used to meet at the club. What is Linnæus doing? When you have leisure, indulge me with the pleasure of knowing that you have not forgot, dear Sir, your affectionate friend,

THOMAS REID.

B.—LETTERS TO LORD KAMES.

I.

ON THE DOCTRINE OF NECESSITY IN RELATION TO MORALS.

Glasgow College, 3d Dec. 1772.

MY LORD,—I was very glad to understand, by the letter you honoured me with of November 9, that you got safe home, after a long journey, in such dreadful rainy weather. I got to Mr C——'s on horseback soon after you left me, where I was in good warm quarters.

The case you state is very proper, to discover how far we differ with respect to the influence of the doctrine of necessity upon morals.

A man in a mad fit of passion stabs his best friend; immediately after, he condemns himself; and, at last, is condemned by a court of justice, although his passion was no less irresistible than if he had been pushed on by external violence.

My opinion of the case, my Lord, is this: if the passion was really as irresistible as you represent it, both in its beginning and progress, the man is innocent in the sight of God, who knows that he was driven as by a whirlwind, and that, the moment he was master of himself, he abhorred the action as much as a good man ought to do.

At the same time, he reasonably may condemn himself, and be condemned by a court of justice.

He condemns himself, because, from his very constitution, he has a conviction that his passion was not irresistible. Every man has this conviction as long as he believes himself not to be really mad, and incapable of self-government. Even if he is a fatalist in speculation, that will not hinder this natural conviction when his conscience smites him, any more than speculative scepticism will hinder a man from apprehension of danger when a cart runs against him.

The court of justice condemns him for the same reason, because they believe that his passion was not irresistible. It could not be proved that the man was really incapable of bridling his passion—that is, that he was really mad—then the court of justice

ought not to punish him as a criminal, but to confine him as a madman.

What is madness, my Lord? In my opinion, it is such weakness in the power of self-government, or such strength of passion, as deprives a man of the command of himself. The madman has will and intention, but he has no power to restrain them. If this madness continues so long as to be capable of proof from the tenor of a man's actions, he is no subject of criminal law, because he is not a free agent. If we suppose real madness to continue but for a moment, it makes a man incapable of a crime, while it lasts, as if it had continued for years. But a momentary madness can have no effect to acquit a man in a court of justice, because it cannot be proved. It would not even hinder him from condemning himself, because he cannot know that he was mad.

In a word, if, by a mad fit of passion, your Lordship means real madness, though temporary, and not permanent, the man is not criminal for what this fit of madness produced. A court of justice would not impute the action to him, if this could be proved to be the case. But if, by a mad fit of passion, you mean only a strong passion, which still leaves a man the power of self-government, then he is accountable for his conduct to God and man; for every good man—yea, every man that would avoid the most heinous crimes—must at some times do violence to very strong passions. But hard would be our case indeed, if we were required, either by God or man, to resist irresistible passions.

You think that will and intention is sufficient to make an action imputable, even though that will be irresistibly determined. I beg leave to dissent, for the following reasons:—

1. An invincible error of the understanding, of memory, of judgment, or of reasoning, is not imputable, for this very reason, that it is invincible: why, then, should an error of the will be imputable, when it is supposed equally invincible? God Almighty has given us various powers of understanding and of will. They are all equally his workmanship. Our

understandings may deviate from truth, as our wills may deviate from virtue. You will allow that it would be unjust and tyrannical to punish a man for unavoidable deviations from truth. Where, then, is the justice of condemning and punishing him for the deviations of another faculty, which are equally unavoidable?

You say we are not to judge of this matter by reasons, but by the moral sense. Will you forgive me, my Lord, to put you in mind of a saying of Mr Hobbes, *that when reason is against a man he will be against reason.* I hope reason and the moral sense are so good friends as not to differ upon any point. But, to be serious, I agree with your Lordship, that it is the moral sense that must judge of this point, whether it be just to punish a man for doing what it was not in his power not to do. The very ideas or notions of just and unjust are got by the moral sense; as the ideas of blue and red are got by the sense of seeing. And as by the sense of seeing we determine that this body is red, and that is blue; so, by the moral sense, we determine this action to be just, and that to be unjust. It is by the moral sense that I determine, in general, that it is unjust to require any duty of a man which it is not in his power to perform. By the same moral sense, in a particular case, I determine a man to be guilty, upon finding that he did the deed voluntarily and with intention, without making any inquiry about his power. The way to reconcile these two determinations I take to be this:—that, in the last case, I take for granted the man's power, because the common sense of mankind dictates, that what a man did voluntarily and with intention, he had power not to do.

2. A second reason of my dissent is, That the guilt of a bad action is diminished in proportion as it is more difficult to resist the motive. Suppose a man entrusted with a secret, the betraying of which to the enemy may ruin an army. If he discloses it for a bribe, however great, he is a villain and a traitor, and deserves a thousand deaths. But, if he falls into the enemy's hands, and the secret be wrested from him by the rack, our sentiments are greatly changed; we do not charge him with villany, but with weakness. We hardly at all blame a woman in such a case, because we conceive torture, or the fear of present death, to be a motive hardly resistible by the weaker sex. As it is, therefore, the uniform judgment of mankind, that, where the deed is the same, and the will and intention the same, the degree of guilt must depend upon the difficulty of resisting the motive, will it not follow, that, when the motive is absolutely irresistible, the guilt vanishes altogether?

3. That this is the common sense of mankind, appears further from the way in which we treat madmen. They have will and intention in what they do; and, therefore, if no more is necessary to constitute a crime, they ought to be found guilty of crimes. Yet no man conceives that they can be at all subjects of criminal law. For what reason? for this, in my opinion, that they have not that power of self-command which is necessary to make a man accountable for his conduct.

You suppose, my Lord, a physical power to forbear an action even when it is necessary. But this I cannot grant. Indeed, upon the system of free agency, I can easily conceive a power which is not exerted; but, upon the system of necessity, there can be no such thing—every power that acts by necessity must be exerted.

I do indeed think, that a man may act without a motive; and that, when the motives to action lie all on one side, he may act in contradiction to them. But I agree with your Lordship, that all such actions are capricious; and I apprehend that, if there were no actions of this kind, there could be no such thing as caprice, nor any word in language to signify it: for why should every language have a word to signify a thing which never did nor can exist?

I agree also with your Lordship, that there can be no merit in such an action, even if it is innocent. But if it is vicious, it has the highest degree of demerit; for it is sinning without any temptation, and serving the devil without any wages. It ought to be observed, however, that a virtuous action can never be capricious; because there is always a just and sufficient motive to it. For, if I have no other motive, I must at least have this, that is a worthy action, and is my duty; which, in reason, ought to weigh down all motives that can be put into the opposite scale. A capricious action may be innocent, and then it is folly; or it may be vicious, and then it is pure wickedness.

Liberty, like all other good gifts of God, may be abused. As civil liberty may be abused to licentiousness, so our natural liberty may be abused to caprice, folly, and vice. But the proper exercise of liberty is, after weighing duly the motives on both sides, to be determined, not by the strongest motive, but by that which has most authority.

It is of great importance in this matter, to distinguish between the authority of motives and their force. The part that is decent, that is manly, that is virtuous, that is noble, has always authority upon its side. Every man feels this authority in his own breast; and there are few men so wicked as not to yield to it when it has no antagonist.

But pleasure, interest, passion, sloth, often muster a great force on the other side, which, though it has no authority, has often the greater power; and a conflict arises between these opposite parties. Every man is conscious of this conflict in his own breast, and is too often carried down by the superior force of the party which he knows to have no authority.

This is the conflict which Plato describes between reason and appetite; this is the conflict which the New Testament describes between the spirit and the flesh. The opposite parties, like Israel and Amalek, dispute the victory in the plain. When the self-determining power, like Moses upon the mount, lifts up its hand and exerts itself, then Israel prevails, and virtue is triumphant; but when its hands hang down and its vigour flags, then Amalek prevails. I am, my dear Lord, most respectfully yours,

THO. REID.

II.

ON THE MATERIALISM OF PRIESTLEY AND THE EGOISM OF FRENCH PHILOSOPHERS.

———————— 1775.

. . . Dr Priestley, in his last book, thinks that the power of perception, as well as all the other powers that are termed mental, is the result of such an organical structure as that of the brain. Consequently, says he, the whole man becomes extinct at death, and we have no hope of surviving the grave, but what is derived from the light of Revelation. I would be glad to know your Lordship's opinion, whether, when my brain has lost its original structure, and when, some hundred years after, the same materials are again fabricated so curiously as to become an intelligent being, whether, I say, that being will be *me* ;[*] or, if two or three such beings should be formed out of my brain, whether they will all be *me*, and consequently all be one and the same intelligent being.

This seems to me a great mystery, but Priestley denies all mysteries. He thinks, and rejoices in thinking so, that plants have some degree of sensation. As to the lower animals, they differ from us in degree only, and not in kind. Only they have no promise of a resurrection. If this be true, why should not the King's advocate be ordered to prosecute criminal *brutes*, and

you criminal judges to try them? You are obliged to Dr Priestley for teaching you one-half of your duty, of which you knew nothing before. But I forgot that the fault lies in the legislature, which has not given you laws for this purpose. I hope, however, when any of them shall be brought to a trial, that he will be allowed a *jury of his peers*.

I am not much surprised that your Lordship has found little entertainment in a late French writer on human nature.[*] From what I learn, they are all become rank Epicureans. One would think that French politesse might consort very well with disinterested benevolence; but, if we believe themselves, it is all grimace. It is flattery, in order to be flattered; like that of the horse, who when his neck itches, scratches his neighbour, that he may be scratched by him again. I detest all systems that depreciate human nature. If it be a delusion, that there is something in the constitution of man that is venerable and worthy of its author, let me live and die in that delusion, rather than have my eyes opened to see my species in a humiliating and disgusting light. Every good man feels his indignation rise against those who disparage his *kindred* or his *country* ; why should it not rise against those who disparage his *kind?* Were it not that we sometimes see extremes meet, I should think it very strange to see atheists and high-shod divines contending as it were who should most blacken and degrade human nature. Yet I think the atheist acts the more consistent part of the two : for surely such views of human nature tend more to promote atheism, than to promote religion and virtue. . . . . .

III.

ON THE CONVERSION OF CLAY INTO VEGETABLE MOULD.

October 1, 1775.

. . . The theory of agriculture is a wide and deep ocean, wherein we soon go beyond our depth.

I believe a lump of dry clay has much the same degree of hardness, whether the weather be hot or cold. It seems to be more affected by moisture or drought : and to be harder in dry weather, and more easily broken when a little moistened. But there is a degree of wetness in clay which makes it not break at all when struck or pressed : it is compressed and changes its figure, but does not break.

Clay ground, I think, ought to be ploughed

---

[*] Our English *t* being of an ambiguous sound, it would be convenient in psychology, could we occasionally employ *me* for a nominative, as the French do their *moi*. But this not being the case, Reid is here, as elsewhere in his letters, grammatically at fault. —H.

[*] Helvetius, De l'Esprit.—LORD WOODHOUSELEE. Hardly ; this work being then nearly twenty year old Probably the work, "Sur I Homme."—H

in the middle state between wetness and dryness, for this reason : When too dry, the plough cannot enter, or cannot make handsome work. Those clods are torn up, which require great labour and expense to break them. And unless they are broken, the roots of vegetables cannot enter into them. When too wet, the furrow, in being raised and laid over by the plough, is very much compressed, but not broken. The compression makes it much harder when it dries, than it would have been without that compression. But when the ground is neither too wet nor too dry, the furrow, in being raised and laid over by the plough, breaks or cracks with innumerable crevices, which admit air and moisture, and the roots of vegetables.

Clay, when exposed in small parts to the air, and to alternate moisture and drought, mellows into mould. Thus a clod of clay, which is so hard in seed-time that you may stand upon it without breaking it, will be found in autumn of the colour of mould, and so softened, that when you press it with the foot it crumbles to pieces. On some clays this change is produced in a shorter time, in the same circumstances ; others are more refractory, and require more time.

If wet clay is put into the fire uncompressed, I am informed that it burns to ashes, which make no bad manure.

But if the clay be wrought and compressed when wet, and then dried, and then put into the fire, it burns into brick, and with a greater degree of heat, into a kind of glass.

These, my Lord, are facts ; but to deduce them from principles of attraction and repulsion, is beyond the reach of my philosophy : and I suspect there are many things in agriculture, and many things in chemistry, that cannot be reduced to such principles ; though Sir Isaac Newton seems to have thought otherwise.

Human knowledge is like the steps of a ladder. The first step consists of particular truths, discovered by observation or experiment: the second collects these into more general truths : the third into still more general. But there are many such steps before we come to the top ; that is, to the most general truths. Ambitious of knowledge, and unconscious of our own weakness, we would fain jump at once from the lowest step to the highest : but the consequence of this is, that we tumble down, and find that our labour must be begun anew. Is not this a good picture of a philosopher, my Lord ? I think so truly ; and I should be vain of it, if I were not afraid that I have stolen it from Lord Bacon. I am, &c.

THO. REID.

IV.

ON THE GENERATION OF PLANTS AND ANIMALS.

No date—but supposed 1775.

MY LORD,—I have some compunction for having been so tardy in answering the letter which your Lordship did me the honour to write me of the 6th November, especially as it suggests two very curious subjects of correspondence. But, indeed, my vacant time has been so much filled up with trifles of College business, and with the frequent calls of a more numerous class of students than I ever had before, that there was no room for anything that could admit of delay.

You have expressed with great elegance and strength the conjecture I hinted with regard to the generation of plants.

I am indeed apt to conjecture, that both plants and animals are at first organized atoms, having all the parts of the animal or plant, but so slender, and folded up in such a manner, as to be reduced to a particle far beyond the reach of our senses, and perhaps as small as the constituent parts of water.* The earth, the water, and the air may, for anything I know, be full of such organized atoms. They may be no more liable to hurt or injury, than the constituent elementary parts of water or air. They may serve the purposes of common matter until they are brought into that situation which nature has provided for their unfolding themselves. When brought into their proper matrix or womb, perhaps after some previous preparations, they are commonly surrounded with some fluid matter, in which they unfold and stretch themselves out to a length and breadth perhaps some thousand times greater than they had when folded up in the atom. They would now be visible to the naked eye, were it not that their limbs and vessels are so slender that they cannot be distinguished from the fluid in which they float. All is equally transparent, and therefore neither figure nor colour can be discerned, although the object has a considerable bulk. The fœtus now has a fluid circulating in its vessels ; all the animal functions go on ; it is nourished and grows ; and some parts, first the heart, then the head, then the

---

* This opinion is similar to that of M. Bonnet. See his " Considérations sur les Corps Organisés," and his " Contemplation de la Nature." LORD WOODHOUSELEE.—Reid's opinion has comparatively little resemblance to the *involution* theory of Bonnet : it bears, however, a strong analogy to the *Panspermia* of the Ionic philosophers, more especially as modified by some of the recent physiological speculatists of Germany. This conjecture is curious, as a solitary escapade of our cautious philosopher in the region of imagination.—H.

opine, by getting some colour, become visible.

It is to be observed, that, from the time that the heart first appears in the pellucid liquor, until the time of birth, the animal grows gradually and insensibly, as it does after birth. But, before it is visible, it must have increased in size many thousand times in a few days. This does not look like growth by nourishment, but like a sudden unfolding of parts, which before were wrapped up in a small atom.

I go along with your Lordship cordially, till you come to the first formation of an organized body. But there I hesitate. "May there," say you, " not be particles of a certain kind endowed with a power to form in conjunction an organized body?" Would your Lordship allow that certain letters might be endowed with the power of forming themselves into an " Iliad" or " Æneid," or even into a sensible discourse in prose?* I confess our faculties carry us but a very little way in determining what is possible and what is impossible, and therefore we ought to be modest. But I cannot help thinking that such a work as the " Iliad," and much more an animal or vegetable body, must have been made by express design and counsel employed for that end. And an author whom I very much respect has taught me, " That we form this conclusion, not by any process of reasoning, but by mere perception and feeling."† And I think that conclusions formed in this manner, are of all others most to be trusted. It seems to me as easy to contrive a machine that should compose a variety of epic poems and tragedies, as to contrive laws of motion, by which unthinking particles of matter should coalesce into a variety of organized bodies.

" But," says your Lordship, " certainly the Almighty has made none of his works so imperfect as to stand in need of perpetual miracles." Can we, my Lord, shew, by any good reason, that the Almighty finished his work at a stroke, and has continued ever since an unactive spectator? Can we prove that this method is the best; or that it is possible that the universe should be well governed in this way? I fear we cannot.

And, if his continued operation be necessary or proper, it is no miracle, while it is uniform, and according to fixed laws. Though we should suppose the gravitation of matter to be the immediate operation of the Deity, it would be no miracle, while it is constant and uniform ; but if in that case it should cease for a moment, only by his

withholding his hand, this would be a miracle.

That an animal or vegetable body is a work of art, and requires a skilful workman, I think we may conclude, without going beyond our sphere. But when we would determine how it is formed, we have no *data;* and our most rational conjectures are only reveries, and probably wide of the mark. We travel back to the first origin of things on the wings of fancy. We would discover Nature *in puris naturalibus,* and trace her first operations and gradual progress. But, alas ! we soon find ourselves unequal to the task : and perhaps this is an entertainment reserved for us in a future state.

As to what you say about earth or soil ; there seems, indeed, to be a repulsion of the parts, when it is enriched by the air, or by manure. And, in consequence of this, it swells and occupies more space. But, I conceive, it gets an additional quantity of matter, from the moisture and air which it imbibes, and thereby increases both in bulk and weight. I have been told that a dunghill made up of earth, dung, and lime, trenched over two or three times, at proper intervals, and then led out, will be found to make more cart-loads than it received : and I believe this to be true. If the earth taken out of a pit does not fill it again, I am apt to think there must have been vacuities in the earth at first, perhaps made by the roots of plants that have decayed, by moles, insects, or other causes.—I am, my Lord, &c.

THO. REID.

V.

ON THE LAWS OF MOTION.—NEWTON'S AXIOMS AND DEFINITIONS.

Glasgow College, May 19, 1780.

MY LORD,—In order to understand the preliminary part of Newton's *Principia,* it is necessary to attend to his general design, both in his axioms and definitions.

First, As to his axioms : he sets down the three laws of motion as axioms. But he does not mean by this, that they are to be held as self-evident truths ; nor does he intend to prove them in what he says upon them. They are incapable of demonstration, being matters of fact, which universally obtain in the material world, and which had before been observed by philosophers, and verified by thousands of experiments by Galileo, by Wren, Wallis, Huygens, and Mariotte, to whom he refers for the proof of them. Therefore, that he might not *actum agere,* he lays them down as established truths, saying some things upon them by

---

* This illustration is borrowed from Cicero. (" De Natura Deorum," l. ii c. 37.)—H ꝙ꜠ ꝋ꜠꜠꜠꜠ �eꝋ꜠
† Lord Kames himself. " Essays on Morality," &c., Chapter " On the Idea of Power."

way of illustration, and deducing some general corollaries from them.

That this was his view, he expressly says in the scholium following the axioms : *Hactenùs principia tradidi, a Mathematicis recepta, et multiplici experientiâ confirmata, &c.* The very same method he follows in his optics, laying down as axioms what had before been discovered in that science.

The axioms, or established principles in the *Principia*, are three :—1st, Every body perseveres in its present state, whether of motion or rest, until it is made to change that state by some force impressed upon it. 2d, The change of motion produced is always proportional to the force impressed, and in the direction of that force. 3d, All action of bodies upon each other is mutual or reciprocal, and in contrary directions ; that is, if the body *A* produces any motion or change of motion in *B* ; by the reaction of *B*, an equal change of motion, but in a contrary direction, will be produced in *A*. This holds in all action of bodies on each other, whether by a stroke, by pressure, by attraction, or by repulsion.

Perhaps, you will say these principles ought not to be taken for granted, but to be proved. True, my Lord, they ought to be proved by a very copious induction of experiments ; and, if they are not proved, the whole system of the *Principia* falls to the ground ; for it is all built upon them. But Sir Isaac thought they were already proved, and refers you to the authors by whom. He never intended to prove them, but to build upon them, as mathematicians do upon the *Elements of Euclid.*

Secondly, As to the definitions. They are intended to give accuracy and precision to the terms he uses, in reasoning from the laws of motion. The definitions are accommodated to the laws of motion, and fitted so as to express with precision all reasoning grounded upon the laws of motion. And, for this reason, even the definitions will appear obscure, if one has not a distinct conception of the laws of motion always before his eye.

Taking for granted the laws of motion, therefore, he gives the name of *vis insita*, or *vis inertiæ*, to that property of bodies, whereby, according to the first and second laws of motion, they persevere in their state, and resist any change, either from rest to motion, or from motion to rest, or from one degree or direction of motion to another.

This *vis insita* is exercised in every case wherein one body is made to change its state by the action of another body ; and the exertion of it may, in different respects, be called both resistance and impetus.

The reluctance which the body *A* has to change its state, which can be overcome only by a force proportioned to that reluctance, is resistance. The reaction of the body *A* upon *B*, which, according to the third law of motion, is equal to the action of *B* upon *A*, and in a contrary direction, is impetus.

Thus, in every change made in the state of one body by another, there is mutual resistance and mutual impetus. The one never exists without the other. A body at rest not only resists, but gives an impetus to the body that strikes it. And a body in motion coming against a body at rest, not only gives an impetus to the body that was at rest, but resists that change of its own motion which is produced by the stroke. Each gives an impetus to the other, and exerts a resistance to the impetus it receives from the other.

This is the notion which Newton affixes to the words—impetus and resistance ; and, I think, it corresponds perfectly with the third law of motion, but may appear dark if that is not kept in view.

But, because this notion of resistance and impetus differs somewhat from the vulgar application of those words, in order to point out the difference, he contrasts it with the vulgar meaning in the words which your Lordship quotes :—*Vulgus resistentiam quiescentibus et impetum moventibus tribuit: sed motus et quies, ut vulgò concipiuntur, respectu solo distinguuntur, neque semper verè quiescunt quæ vulgò tanquam quiescentia spectantur.* He considers both resistance and impetus as belonging to every body, in every case in which it is made to change its state, whether from rest to motion, or from motion to rest. It resists the change of its own state, and, by its reaction, gives an impetus to the body that acts upon it. The vulgar, having no notion, or no distinct notion, of this reaction established by the third law of motion, suit their language to their conceptions. He suits his to the laws of motion.

A post, you say, resists, but has no impetus. This is true in the vulgar sense of the word. But, in order to shew you that his sense differs somewhat from the vulgar, he would say, that the post has impetus in his sense. And by this he means only, that the post stops, or changes the motion of the body that strikes it ; and, in producing this change, exerts a force equal to that with which it was struck, but in a contrary direction. This is a necessary consequence of the third law of motion. The vulgar both speak and judge of motion and rest in a body, by its situation with respect to some other body, which, perhaps, from prejudice, they conceive to be at rest. This makes Newton say, " That motion and rest, as commonly conceived, are distinguished by relation ; nor are those bodies always really at rest which are commonly conceived to be at rest."

Rest, when we speak of bodies, is opposed, not to self-motion only, but to all change of place. Absolute, or real rest, is opposed to real motion; and relative rest---that is, rest with relation to such a body that is supposed at rest, is opposed to relative motion with respect to the same body. But a body may be relatively at rest, and, at the same time, really in motion. Thus, a house rests upon its foundation for ages; but this rest is relative with respect to the earth. For it has gone round the earth's axis every day, and round the sun every year.

The distinction your Lordship makes between moving and being moved, belongs not to physics, but to metaphysics. In physics, you may use the active or the passive verb as you like best. The reason is, that in physics we seek not the efficient causes of phenomena, but only the rules or laws by which they are regulated. We know, that a body once put in motion, continues to move, or, if you please, to be moved, until some force is applied to stop or retard it. But, whether this phenomenon is produced by some real activity in the body itself, or by the efficiency of some external cause; or whether it requires no efficiency at all to continue in the state into which it is put, is, perhaps, difficult to determine; and is a question that belongs not to physics, but to metaphysics.

Some divines and philosophers have maintained, that the preservation of a created being in existence, is a continued act of creation; and that annihilation is nothing but the suspending that exertion of the Creator by which the being was upheld in existence.

Analogous to this, I think, is the opinion, that the continuance of motion in a body requires a continued exertion of that active force which put it into the state of motion. I am rather inclined to the contrary of both these opinions, and disposed to think that continuance of existence, and continuance of motion in a body, requires no active cause; and that it is only a change of state, and not a continuance of the present state, that requires active power. But, I suspect, both questions are rather beyond the reach of the human faculties. However, they belong not to the province of physics, but to that of metaphysics.

I wish I may be intelligible, and that I do not oppress your Lordship with the garrulity of old age. I find myself, indeed, growing old, and have no right to plead exemption from the infirmities of that stage of life. For that reason, I have made choice of an assistant in my office. Yesterday, the college, at my desire, made choice of Mr Archibald Arthur, preacher, to be my assist-

ant and successor.[*] I think I have done good service to the college by this, and procured some leisure to myself, though with a reduction of my finances. May your Lordship live long and happy.—Yours,

THO. REID.

VI.

ON CONJECTURES AND HYPOTHESES IN PHILOSOPHY.—CAUSE WHAT IN RELATION TO PHYSICS.—DIFFERENT PROVINCES OF PHYSICAL AND OF METAPHYSICAL SCIENCE.

16th December 1780.

MY LORD,—1. I am now to answer the letter you honoured me with of 7th November. And, first, I disclaim what you seem to impute to me—to wit, "the valuing myself upon my ignorance of the cause of gravity." To confess ignorance when one is conscious of it, I take to be a sign, not of pride, but of humility, and of that candour which becomes a philosopher; and so I meant it.

2. Your Lordship thinks, "That never to trust to hypotheses and conjectures about the works of God, and being persuaded that they are more like to be false than true, is a discouraging doctrine, and damps the spirit of inquiry," &c. Now, my Lord, I have, ever since I was acquainted with Bacon and Newton, thought that this doctrine is the very key to natural philosophy, and the touchstone by which everything that is legitimate and solid in that science, is to be distinguished from what is spurious and hollow; and I can hardly think, that we can differ in so capital a point, if we understood each other's meaning.

3. I would discourage no man from conjecturing, only I wish him not to take his conjectures for knowledge, or to expect that others should do so. Conjecturing may be a useful step even in natural philosophy. Thus, attending to such a phenomenon, I conjecture that it may be owing to such a cause. This may lead me to make the experiments or observations proper for discovering whether that is really the cause or not: and if I can discover, either that it is or is not, my knowledge is improved; and my conjecture was a step to that im-

---

[*] Mr Arthur, a man of learning, abilities, and worth, filled the Chair of Moral Philosophy in the University of Glasgow for fifteen years, with a reputation which did not disappoint the hopes of his respectable predecessor. A volume of "Discourses on Theological and Literary Subjects," which give a very favourable idea of his talents, the justness of his taste, and the rectitude of His moral and religious principles, has been published, since his death, by Professor Richardson of the same college—a gentleman distinguished in the literary world, and who has done honour to the memory of his friend, by an interesting sketch of his life and character, subjoined to these discourses.—LORD WOODHOUSELEE.

provement. But, while I rest in my conjecture, my judgment remains in suspense, and all I can say is, it may be so, and it may be otherwise.

4. A cause that is conjectured ought to be such, that, if it really does exist, it will produce the effect. If it have not this quality, it hardly deserves the name of a conjecture. Supposing it to have this quality, the question remains—Whether does it exist or not? And this, being a question of fact, is to be tried by positive evidence. Thus, Des Cartes conjectured, that the planets are carried round the sun in a vortex of subtile matter. The cause here assigned is s fficient to produce the effect. It may, therefore, be entitled to the name of a conjecture. But where is the evidence of the existence of such a vortex? If there be no evidence for it, even though there were none against it, it is a conjecture only, and ought to have no admittance into chaste natural philosophy.

5. All investigation of what we call the causes of natural phenomena may be reduced to this syllogism—If such a cause exists, it will produce such a phenomenon : but that cause does exist : Therefore, &c. The first proposition is merely hypothetical. And a man in his closet, without consulting nature, may make a thousand such propositions, and connect them into a system ; but this is only a system of hypotheses, conjectures, or theories ; and there cannot be one conclusion in natural philosophy drawn from it, until he consults nature, and discovers whether the causes he has conjectured do really exist. As far as he can shew that they do, he makes a real progress in the knowledge of nature, and not a step further. I hope in all this your Lordship will agree with me. But it remains to be considered how the second proposition of the syllogism is to be proved—to wit, that such a cause does really exist. Will nothing satisfy here but demonstration?

6. I am so far from thinking so, my Lord, that I am persuaded we never can have demonstration in this case. All that we know of the material world, must be grounded on the testimony of our senses. Our senses testify particular facts only : from these we collect, by induction, general facts, which we call laws of nature, or natural causes. Thus, ascending by a just and cautious induction, from what is less to what is more general, we discover, as far as we are able, natural causes, or laws of nature. This is the analytical part of natural philosophy. The synthetical part takes for granted, as principles, the causes discovered by induction, and from these explains or accounts for the phenomena which result from them. This analysis and synthesis make up the whole theory of natural philosophy. The

practical part consists in applying the laws of nature to produce effects useful in life.

7. From this view of natural philosophy, which I have learned from Newton, your Lordship will perceive that no man who understands it will pretend to demonstrate any of its principles. Nay, the most certain and best established of them may, for anything we know, admit of exceptions. For instance, there is no principle in natural philosophy better established than the universal gravitation of matter. But, can this be demonstrated? By no means. What is the evidence of it, then? It is collected by induction, partly from our daily experience, and from the experience of all nations, in all ages, in all places of earth, sea, and air, which we can reach ; and partly from the observations and experiments of philosophers, which shew that even air and smoke, and every body upon which experiments have been made, gravitate precisely in proportion to the quantity of matter ; that the sea and earth gravitate towards the moon, and the moon towards them ; that the planets and comets gravitate towards the sun, and towards one another, and the sun towards them. This is the sum of evidence ; and it is as different from demonstration, on the one hand, as from conjecture on the other. It is the same kind of evidence which we have, that fire will burn and water drown, that bread will nourish and arsenic poison, which, I think, would not properly be called conjecture.

8. It is proper here to explain what is meant by the cause of a phenomenon, when that word is used in natural philosophy. The word cause is so ambiguous, that I fear many mistake its meaning, and take it to mean the efficient cause, which I think it never does in this science.

9. By the cause of a phenomenon, nothing is meant but the law of nature, of which that phenomenon is an instance, or a necessary consequence. The cause of a body's falling to the ground is its gravity. But gravity is not an efficient cause, but a general law, that obtains in nature, of which law the fall of this body is a particular instance. The cause why a body projected moves in a parabola, is, that this motion is the necessary consequence of the projectile force and gravity united. But these are not efficient causes ; they are only laws of nature. In natural philosophy, therefore, we seek only the general laws, according to which nature works, and these we call the causes of what is done according to them. But such laws cannot be the efficient cause of anything. They are only the rule according to which the efficient cause operates.

10. A natural philosopher may search after the cause of a law of nature ; but this means no more than searching for a

more general law, which includes that particular law, and perhaps many others under it. This was all that Newton aimed at by his *ether*. He thought it possible, that, if there was such an ether, the gravitation of bodies, the reflection and refraction of the rays of light, and many other laws of nature, might be the necessary consequences of the elasticity and repelling force of the ether. But, supposing this ether to exist, its elasticity and repelling force must be considered as a law of nature ; and the efficient cause of this elasticity would still have been latent

11. Efficient causes, properly so called, are not within the sphere of natural philosophy. Its business is, from particular facts in the material world, to collect, by just induction, the laws that are general, and from these the more general, as far as we can go. And when this is done, natural philosophy has no more to do. It exhibits to our view the grand machine of the material world, analysed, as it were, and taken to pieces, with the connexions and dependencies of its several parts, and the laws of its several movements. It belongs to another branch of philosophy to consider whether this machine is the work of chance or of design, and whether of good or of bad design ; whether there is not an intelligent first Mover who contrived the whole, and gives motion to the whole, according to the laws which the natural philosopher has discovered, or, perhaps, according to laws still more general, of which we can only discover some branches ; and whether he does these things by his own hand, so to speak, or employs subordinate efficient causes to execute his purposes. These are very noble and important inquiries, but they do not belong to natural philosophy ; nor can we proceed in them in the way of experiment and induction, the only instruments the natural philosopher uses in his researches.

12. Whether you call this branch of philosophy Natural Theology or Metaphysics, I care not ; but I think it ought not to be confounded with Natural Philosophy ; and neither of them with Mathematics. Let the mathematician demonstrate the relation of abstract quantity ; the natural philosopher investigate the laws of the material system by induction ; and the metaphysician, the final causes, and the efficient causes of what we see and what natural philosophy discovers in the world we live in.

13. As to final causes, they stare us in the face wherever we cast our eyes. I can no more doubt whether the eye was made for the purpose of seeing. and the ear of hearing, than I can doubt of a mathematical axiom ; yet the evidence is neither mathematical demonstration, nor is it in-duction. In a word, final causes, good final causes, are seen plainly everywhere : in the heavens and in the earth ; in the constitution of every animal, and in our own constitution of body and of mind ; and they are most worthy of observation, and have a charm in them that delights the soul.

14. As to Efficient Causes, I am afraid our faculties carry us but a very little way, and almost only to general conclusions. I hold it to be self-evident, that every production, and every change in nature, must have an efficient cause that has power to produce the effect ; and that an effect which has the most manifest marks of intelligence, wisdom, and goodness, must have an intelligent, wise, and good efficient cause. From these, and some such self-evident truths, we may discover the principles of natural theology, and that the Deity is the first efficient cause of all nature. But how far he operates in nature immediately, or how far by the ministry of subordinate efficient causes, to which he has given power adequate to the task committed to them, I am afraid our reason is not able to discover, and we can do little else than conjecture. We are led by nature to believe ourselves to be the efficient causes of our own voluntary actions ; and, from analogy, we judge the same of other intelligent beings. But with regard to the works of nature, I cannot recollect a single instance wherein I can say, with any degree of assurance, that such a thing is the efficient cause of such a phenomenon of nature.

15. Malebranche, and many of the Cartesians, ascribed all to the immediate operation of the Deity, except the determinations of the will of free agents. Leibnitz, and all his followers, maintain, that God finished his work at the creation, having endowed every creature and every individual particle of matter, with such internal powers as necessarily produce all its actions, motions, and changes, to the end of time. Others have held, that various intelligent beings, appointed by the Deity to their several departments, are the efficient causes of the various operations of nature. Others, that there are beings endowed with power without intelligence, which are the efficient causes in nature's operations ; and they have given them the name of Plastic Powers, or Plastic Natures. A late author of your Lordship's acquaintance,* has given it as ancient metaphysics, That every body in the universe is compounded of two substances united—to wit, an immaterial mind or soul, which, in the inanimate creation, has the power of motion without thought ; and of inert matter as the other part. The celebrated Dr Priestley maintains, that

---

* Lord Monboddo.—H.

matter, properly organized, has not only the power of motion, but of thought and intelligence ; and that a man is only a piece of matter properly organized.

16. Of all these systems about the efficient causes of the phenomena of nature, there is not one that, in my opinion, can be either proved or refuted from the principles of natural philosophy. They belong to metaphysics, and affect not natural philosophy, whether they be true or false. Some of them, I think, may be refuted upon metaphysical principles ; but, as to the others, I can neither see such evidence for them or against them as determines my belief. They seem to me to be conjectures only about matters where we have not evidence ; and, therefore, I must confess my ignorance.

17. As to the point which gave occasion to this long detail, Whether there is reason to think that matter gravitates by an inherent power, and is the efficient cause of its own gravitation, I say, first, This is a metaphysical question, which concerns not natural philosophy, and can neither be proved nor refuted by any principle in that science. Natural philosophy informs us, that matter gravitates according to a certain law ; and it says no more. Whether matter be active or passive in gravitation, cannot be determined by any experiment I can think of. If it should be said that we ought to conclude it to be active, because we perceive no external cause of its gravitation, this argument, I fear, will go too far. Besides it is very weak, amounting only to this : I do not perceive such a thing, therefore it does not exist.

18. I never could see good reason to believe that matter has any active power at all. And, indeed, if it were evident that it has *one*, I think there could be no good reason assigned for not allowing it *others*. Your Lordship speaks of the power of resisting motion, and some others, as acknowledged active powers inherent in matter. As to the resistance to motion, and the continuance in motion, I never could satisfy myself whether these are not the necessary consequences of matter being inactive. If they imply activity, that may lie in some other cause.

19. I am not able to form any distinct conception of active power but such as I find in myself. I can only exert my active power by will, which supposes thought. It seems to me, that, if I was not conscious of activity in myself, I could never, from things I see about me, have had the conception or idea of active power. I see a succession of changes, but I see not the power, that is, the efficient cause of them ; but, having got the notion of active power, from the consciousness of my own activity, and finding

it a first principle, that every production requires active power, I can reason about an active power of that kind I am acquainted with—that is, such as supposes thought and choice, and is exerted by will. But, if there is anything in an unthinking inanimate being that can be called active power, I know not what it is, and cannot reason about it.

20. If you conceive that the activity of matter is directed by thought and will in matter, every particle of matter must know the situation and distance of every other particle within the planetary system ; but this, I am apt to think, is not your Lordship's opinion.

21. I must therefore conclude, that this active power is guided in all its operations by some intelligent Being, who knows both the law of gravitation, and the distance and situation of every particle of matter with regard to every other particle, in all the changes that happen in the material world. I can only conceive two ways in which this particle of matter can be guided, in all the exertions of its active power, by an intelligent Being. Either it was formed, in its creation, upon a foreknowledge of all the situations it shall ever be in with respect to other particles, and had such an internal structure given it, as necessarily produces, in succession, all the motions, and tendencies to motion, it shall ever exert. This would make every particle of matter a machine or automaton, and every particle of a different structure from every other particle in the universe. This is indeed the opinion of Leibnitz ; but I am not prejudiced against it upon that account ; I only wished to know whether your Lordship adopted it or not. Another way, and the only other way, in which I can conceive the active power of a particle of matter, guided by an intelligent Being, is by a continual influence exerted according to its situation and the situation of other particles. In this case, the particle would be guided as a horse is by his rider ; and I think it would be improper to ascribe to it the power of gravitation. It has only the power of obeying its guide. Whether your Lordship chooses the first or the last in this alternative, I should be glad to know ; or whether you can think of a third way better than either.

22. I will not add to the length of so immoderately long a letter by criticising upon the passages you quote from Newton. I have a great regard for his judgment ; but where he differs from me, I think him wrong.

The idea of natural philosophy I have given in this letter, I think I had from him. If in scholia and queries he gives a range to his thoughts, and sometimes enters the regions of natural theology and metaphysics, this I think is very allowable, and is not to be considered a part of his physics, which are contained in his propositions and corollaries. Even his queries and conjectures are valuable ; but I think he never intended that they should be taken for granted, but made the subject of inquiry.

Tho. Reid.

VII.

LAWS OF MOTION—PRESSURE OF FLUIDS.

January 25, 1781.

My Lord,—To what cause is it owing that I differ so much from your Lordship in Physics, when we differ so little in Metaphysics ? I am at a loss to account for this phenomenon. Whether is it owing to our having different conceptions to the same words ?—or, as I rather think it is, to your being dissatisfied with the three general laws of motion ? Without them I know not indeed how to reason in physics. Archimedes reasoned from them both in mechanics and hydrostatics. Galileo, Huygens, Wren, Wallis, Mariotte, and many others, reasoned from them, without observing that they did so.

I have not indeed any scruples about the principles of hydrostatics. They seem to me to be the necessary consequences of the definition of a fluid, the three laws of motion, and the law of gravitation ; and, therefore, I cannot assent to your Lordship's reasoning, either about the pressure of fluids, or about the suspension of the mercury in the barometer.

As to the first, the experiments which shew that fluids do, in fact, press *undequaque*, are so numerous, and so well known to your Lordship, that I apprehend it is not the fact you question, but the cause. You think that gravity is not the cause. Why ? Because gravity gives to every part of the fluid a tendency downwards only ; and what is true of every part, is true of the whole : therefore, the whole has no other tendency but downward. This argument is specious, but there is a fallacy in it. If the parts did not act upon one another, and counteract one another, the argument would be good ; but the parts are so connected, that one cannot go down but another must go up, and, therefore, that very gravity which presses down one part presses up another : so that every part is pressed down by its own gravity, and pressed up, at the same time, by the gravity of other parts ; and the contrary pressures being equal, it remains at rest.

This may be illustrated by a balance equilibrating by equal weights in both scales. I say each arm of the balance is equally pressed upwards and downwards at the same time, and from that cause is at rest ; although the tendency of the weights, in each of the scales, is downwards only. I prove it *a posteriori ;* because the arm of a balance being moveable by the least force, if it was pressed in one *direction* only, it would move in that direction : but it does not move. I prove it *a priori ;* because the necessary effect of pressing one arm down, is the pressing the other up with the same force : therefore, each arm is pressed down by the weight in its own scale, and equally pressed up by the weight in the other scale ; and, being pressed with equal force in contrary directions, it remains at rest. Your Lordship will easily apply this reasoning to a fluid, every part of which is as moveable as the balance is about its *fulcrum ;* and no one part can move, but an equal part must be moved in a contrary direction. And I think it is impossible we should differ in this, but in words.

Next, as to the barometer. You say the mercury is kept up by the expansive power of the air : but you say further, that it is not kept up by the weight of the air. I agree to the first, but not to the last. The expansive power of the air is owing to its being compressed ; and it is compressed by the weight of the incumbent atmosphere. Its expansive force is exactly equal to the force that presses and condenses it ; and that force is the weight of the air above it, *to the top of the atmosphere*—so that the expansive force of the air is the *causa proxima*, the weight of the atmosphere the *causa remota* of the *suspension* of the mercury. Your Lordship knows the maxim, *Causa causæ est causa causati.* The barometer, therefore, while it measures the expansive force of the air which presses upon the lower end of the tube, at the same time measures the weight of the atmosphere, which is the cause of that expansive force, and exactly equal to it. If the air was not pressed by the incumbent weight, it would expand in boundless space, until it had no more expansive force.

As to the observation in the postscript, it is true, that the gravity of the air, while it rests upon an unyielding bottom, will give no motion to it ; but the mercury in the lower end of the tube yields to the pressure of the air upon it, until the weight of the mercury is balanced by the pressure of the air.

What your Lordship is pleased to call the *Opus Magnum*, goes on, but more slowly than I wish.—I am, most respectfully, my Lord, yours,

Tho. Reid.

VIII.

ON THE ACCELERATED MOTION OF FALLING
BODIES.

Glasgow College, Nov. 11, 1782.

My LORD,—My hope that your Lordship is in no worse state of health than when I left you, and that the rest of the good family are well, is confirmed by your continuing your favourite speculations. I promised to call upon you in the morning before I came away. I sent in Samuel to see if you was awake : he reported that you was sleeping sound ; and I could not find it in my heart to disturb your repose.

When we say, that, in falling bodies, the space gone through is as the square of the velocity, it must be carefully observed that the velocity meant in this proposition, is the last velocity, which the body acquires only the last moment of its fall : but the space meant is the whole space gone through, from the beginning of its fall to the end.

As this is the meaning of the proposition, your Lordship will easily perceive, that the velocity of the last moment must indeed correspond to the space gone through in that moment, but cannot correspond to the space gone through in any preceding moment, with a less velocity ; and, consequently, cannot correspond to the whole space gone through in the last and all preceding moments taken together. You say very justly, that, whether the motion be equable or accelerated, the space gone through in any instant of time corresponds to the velocity in that instant. But it does not follow from this, that, in accelerated motion, the space gone through in many succeeding instants will correspond to the velocity of the last instant.

If any writer in physics has pretended to demonstrate mathematically this proposition—that a body falling by gravity *in vacuo,* goes through a space which is as the square of its last velocity ; he must be one who writes without distinct conceptions, of which kind we have not a few.

The proposition is not mathematical, but physical. It admits not of demonstration, as your Lordship justly observes, but of proof by experiment, or reasoning grounded on experiment. There is, however, a mathematical proposition, which possibly an inaccurate writer might confound with the last mentioned. It is this—that a body uniformly accelerated from a state of rest, will go through a space which is as the square of the last velocity. ' This is an abstract proposition, and has been mathematically demonstrated ; and it may be made a step in the proof of the physical proposition. But the proof must be completed by shewing, that, in fact, bodies descending by gravitation are uniformly accelerated. This is sometimes shewn by a machine invented by S'Gravesande, to measure the velocities of falling bodies ; sometimes it is proved by the experiments upon pendulums ; and sometimes we deduce it by reasoning from the second law of motion, which we think is grounded on universal experience.· So that the proof of the physical proposition always rests ultimately upon experience, and not solely upon mathematical demonstration.—I am, my Lord, respectfully yours,

THO. REID.

IX.

EXTRACT OF A LETTER TO MRS DRUMMOND,
AFTER THE DEATH OF HER HUSBAND,
LORD KAMES, IN 1782.

I accept, dear madam, the present you sent me,* as a testimony of your regard, and as a precious relic of a man whose talents I admired and whose virtues I honoured ; a man who honoured me with a share of his conversation, and of his correspondence, which is my pride, and which gave me the best opportunity of knowing his real worth.

I have lost in him one of the greatest comforts of my life ; but his remembrance will always be dear to me, and demand my best wishes and prayers for those whom he has left behind him.

When time has abated your just grief for the loss of such a husband, the recollection of his eminent talents, and of his public and domestic virtues, will pour balm into the wound. Friends are not lost who leave such a character behind them, and such an example to those who come after them.

---

* A gold snuff box.

C.—LETTERS TO DR JAMES GREGORY.

I.

Glasgow College, April 7, 1783.

DEAR SIR,—By favour of Mr Patrick Wilson, our Assistant Professor of Astronomy, I send you two more numbers of my lucubrations.* I am not sure when I can send more, as I am not sure whether my scribe may soon leave the College.

I shall be much obliged to you if you will continue to favour me with your observations, though I have put off examining those you have sent until the MSS. be returned, which I expect about the end of this month, along with Dug. Stewart's observations. I have also sent the Genealogy of the Gregories, which your brother left with me : I suspected that it was more particular than the copy I had, but I find they agree perfectly.

You will please deliver it to him, with my compliments. The few days he was here he payed his respects to all the Professors and all his acquaintance, and they are all very much pleased with his appearance. If it please God to spare his life, I hope he will do honour to his *Alma Mater,* and to his friends.†

I know not upon what authority the Edinburgh and London news-writers have given contradictory accounts of Dr Hunter's settlements.‡ There is nothing certainly known here. I know that, six or seven years ago, he made a settlement very favourable to this College. But whether this is altered, or in what respect, I believe nobody here knows. But we shall probably know soon. He was surely a man that did great honour to his country, and I doubt not but his publick spirit, which I take to have been great, will have disposed him to leave his books, medals, and other literary furniture—which he had collected at vast expense, and with great industry—in such a way as that it may be useful to the publick.

I beg you to make my best respects to Mrs Gregory, and to all your family ; and I am, dear Sir,

Your most obedient Servant,
THO. REID.

* His "*Essays on the Intellectual Powers.*"—H.
† This was the Rev. William Gregory, A. M. of Balliol College, Oxford, afterwards Rector of St Mary's, Bentham, and one of the Preachers of Canterbury Cathedral. He had studied at Glasgow previously to entering at Oxford —H.
‡ The celebrated Dr Wm. Hunter. He bequeathed his anatomical preparations, library, and collection of medals, to the University of Glasgow, and a sum of money for the erection of a museum.—H.

II.

Glasgow College, June 8, 1783.

DEAR SIR,

.   .   .   .   I cannot get more copied of my papers till next winter, and indeed have not much more ready. This parcel goes to page 658. I believe what you have got before may be one-half or more of all I intend. The materials of what is not yet ready for the copyer are partly discourses read in our Literary Society, partly notes of my Lectures.

Your judgment of what you have seen flatters me very much, and adds greatly to my own opinion of it, though authors seldom are deficient in a good opinion of their own works.

I am at a loss to express my obligations to you for the pains you have taken, and propose to take again upon it. I have carefully laid up the observations you sent me, to be considered when the copy they refer to is returned, and I hope for the continuation of them. The analogy between memory and prescience is, I believe, a notion of my own. But I shall be open to conviction on this and every thing else we may differ about.

I have often thought of what you propose —to give the History of the Ideal System ; and what I have to say against it, by itself, and I am far from being positive that it stands in the most proper place. Perhaps it will be easier to judge of this when the work is concluded. I have endeavoured to put it in separate chapters, whose titles may direct those who have no taste for it to pass over them. But I hope to have your opinion upon this point at more length when we meet. I observe that Boyle and others, who, at the Reformation of Natural Philosophy, gave new light, found it necessary to contrast their discoveries with the Aristotelian notions which then prevailed. We could now wish their works purged of the controversial part ; but, perhaps, it was proper and necessary at the time they wrote, when men's minds were full of the old systems, and prepossessed in its favour. What I take to be the genuine philosophy of the human mind, is in so low a state, and has so many enemies, that, I apprehend those who would make any improvement in it must, for some time at least, build with one hand, and hold a weapon with the other.

I shall be very glad to see you here, and will take it as a favour if you acquaint me when you have fixed your time, that I may be sure to be at home. I beg you will make my best compliments to Mrs Gregory, whom I should be happy to see along with you in good health, and to Mr D. Gordon, if he is still with you, and to all your family ; and am, dear sir,

Yours most affectionately,
THO. REID.

III.

March 14, 1784.

DEAR SIR,—I send you now the remainder of what I propose to print with respect to the Intellectual Powers of the Mind. It may, perhaps, be a year before what relates to the Active Powers be ready, and, therefore, I think the former might be published by itself, as it is very uncertain whether I shall live to publish the latter.

I have enclosed, in the first of the three papers now sent, the contents of the whole, which you was so good as to write out as far as it was carried last year. I think the title may be, *Essays on the Intellectual Powers of the Human Mind.* It will easily divide into eight essays, as you will see by the contents ; but with regard to this, as well as whether the two parts may be published separately, I wish to have your advice and Mr Stuart's—(*Sic.*) Since you have been so good as to take a concern in it, I apprehend that the second Part—I mean what relates to the Active Powers—will not be near so large as the first. I wish to have the manuscript, with your remarks and Mr Stuart's, (*sic,*) about the end of April, if you can. Dr Rose at Chiswick—who, you know, has all along had a principal concern in *The Monthly Review*—has made me a very kind offer, that, if I please to send the MSS. to him, he will both give me his remarks, and treat with a bookseller about the sale of it. I think this is an offer that I ought not to refuse ; and I can have a good occasion of sending it about the beginning of the month of May, by his son, who is at this college. I long to hear how Mrs Gregory has stood this severe winter, and beg my most humble respects to her, and to the Rev. Mr William, when you write him.

I send you on the other page an anecdote respecting Sir I. Newton,[*] which I do not remember whether I ever happened to mention to you in conversation. If his descent be not clearly ascertained, (as I think it is not in the books I have seen,) might it not be worth while for the antiquarian branch of your R. Society, to inquire if they can find evidence to confirm the account which he is said to have given of himself. Sheriff Cross was very zealous about it,

[*] See Brewster's "Life of Newton," and, *infra,* Reid's letter to Mr Robison, at the end of his Correspondence.—H.

when death put a stop to his inquiries.—I am, dear Sir, yours most respectfully,

THO. REID.

When I lived in Old Aberdeen, above twenty years ago, I happened to be conversing over a pipe of tobacco, with a gentleman of that country, who had been lately at Edinburgh. He told me that he had been often in company with Mr Hepburn of Keith, with whom I had the honour of some acquaintance. He said that, speaking of Sir Isaac Newton, Mr Hepburn mentioned an anecdote, which he had from Mr James Gregory, Professor of Mathematics at Edinburgh, which was to this purpose :—Mr Gregory being at London for some time after he resigned the mathematical chair, was often with Sir I. Newton. One day Sir Isaac said to him, " Gregory, I believe you don't know that I am connected with Scotland." " Pray, how, Sir Isaac ?" said Gregory. Sir Isaac said—" He was told, that his grandfather was a gentleman of East Lothian ; that he came to London with King James at his accession to the Crown of England, and there spent his fortune, as many more did at that time, by which his son (Sir Isaac's father) was reduced to mean circumstances." To this Gregory bluntly replied—" Newton, a gentleman in East Lothian ?—I never heard of a gentleman of East Lothian of that name." Upon this Sir Isaac said, that, being very young when his father died, he had it only by tradition, and it might be a mistake ; and immediately turned the conversation to another subject.

I confess I suspected that the gentleman who was my author had given some colouring to this story ; and, therefore, I never mentioned it for a good many years.

After I removed to Glasgow, I came to be very intimately acquainted with Mr Cross, the Sheriff of Lanerick, and one day at his own house mentioned this story without naming my author, of whom I expressed some diffidence. The Sheriff immediately took it up as a matter worth being inquired into. He said he was well acquainted with Mr Hepburn of Keith, (who was then alive,) and that he would write him, to know whether he ever heard Mr Gregory say that he had such a conversation with Sir Isaac Newton. He said. he knew that Mr Keith, the ambassador, was also intimate with Mr Gregory, and that he would write him to the same purpose. Some time after, Mr Cross told me, that he had answers from both the gentlemen abovementioned, and that both remembered to have heard Mr Gregory mention the conversation between him and Sir Isaac Newton to the purpose above narrated ; and at the same time acknowledged that they had made no farther inquiry about the matter.

Mr Cross, however, continued in the inquiry; and, a short time before his death, told me, that all he had learned was, that there is, or was lately, a baronet's family of the name of Newton in West-Lothian, or Mid-Lothian, (I have forgot which;) that there is a tradition in that family that Sir Isaac Newton wrote a letter to the old knight that was, (I think Sir John Newton of Newton was his name,) desiring to know what children, and particularly what sons he had; their age, and what professions they intended. That the old baronet never deigned to return an answer to this letter, which his family was sorry for, as they thought Sir Isaac might have intended to do something for them.

IV.

DEAR SIR,—Happening to have gone into the country a little way, your letter of 5th June did not reach me in time to write you before you set out upon your journey, which I wish to be attended with much happiness to the parties, and comfort to their friends.*

I was so stupid at first as to misunderstand the direction you gave me how to write you. Now I see it is plain enough, and I hope have taken it right. I send you the enclosed to Dr Rose, as you desire.

I have by me our friend D. Stewart's "Discourse on the Ideas of Cause and Effect," &c.; and I have this day sent him my remarks upon it. I am happy to find his sentiments on that subject agree so much with my own. I think it well wrote, and hope it will be very useful.

Dr Rose will shew you the letter I wrote to him along with the MSS., and one from Mr Bell† to me, which I enclosed in it: these contain all the information I have to give, and all the instructions I thought necessary. I expect an answer from one quarter, at least, before the work be cold from the press. But the only answer that shall ever have any reply from me must be one who keeps good temper, and who observes good manners, in the first place; and next one who, in my opinion, gives new light to the subject.

I wish you happy success in your own affairs, and a safe return. If nothing happens of which you wish to acquaint me sooner, I shall be glad to hear from you on your return; being, dear sir,

Most affectionately yours,
THO. REID.

Glasgow Coll. 1784.

---

* This alludes to the marriage of Dr Gregory's eldest sister to the Rev. Archibald Alison.—H.
† The publisher.—H.

[*The letter quoted above by Mr Stewart, (p. 34) " to one of Dr Reid's most intimate friends," was addressed to Dr James Gregory on the death of his first wife, and should properly here find its place.*—H]

V.

ON THE MEANING OF NOTION.

Glasgow Col'ege, December 31, 1784.

DEAR SIR,—I had the favour of yours by Mr Tower, and take the opportunity of his return to wish you many happy returns of this season.

I believe you and I cannot differ about right or wrong *notions*, but in words.

The notions we have of real existences, may with good reason be said to be right or wrong, true or false; but I think every notion of this kind has a standard to which I believe my notion to agree; and as that belief is true or false, so my notion of the thing is true or false. For instance, if my notion of the Devil includes horns and cloven feet, I must believe these to be attributes of the Devil, otherwise they would not be included in my notion of him. If this belief be wrong, I have a wrong notion of him; and, as soon as I am convinced that this belief is wrong, I leave out these attributes in my notion of him.

I may have an abstract notion of a being with horns and cloven feet, without applying it to any individual—then it is a simple apprehension, and neither true nor false; but it cannot be my notion of any individual that exists, unless I believe that being to have these attributes. I am therefore still apt to think that true and false can only with propriety be applied to notions which include some belief; but whether my remark on your use of the word *notion* be just or not, I cannot presently say: you will judge for yourself.

I thought to have seen D. Stewart here about this time. When you see him, please acquaint him that I have made my remarks upon the performance he left with me. I am extremely obliged to you and him for correcting the sheets of my performance. You leave me very little to do.

By the slowness of printing, I conjecture that the book cannot be published next spring, and can only be ready for the spring 1786. I desired long ago to know of Mr Bell whether he proposed to publish it in one vol. or two; but I have not had an answer. I suspect it will be too thick for one vol. and too thin for two. Perhaps if the publication is delayed to 1786, I might have my Essays on the Active Powers ready, of which Mr Bell shall have the first offer; and I apprehend that, with this addition, there may be two sizeable 4tos in the whole.—I am, dear Sir,

Yours most affectionately,

Tho. Reid.

VI.

Dear Sir,—I send you enclosed what I propose as the title page of my essays, with an epistle, which, I hope, you and Mr Stewart will please to allow me to prefix to them.

Whether your name should go first, on account of your doctor's degree, or Mr Stewart's, on account of his seniority as a professor, I leave you to adjust between yourselves.[*]

As to the title-page, you and he may alter what you think fit,[†] and deliver it to Mr Bell without farther communication with me, as he intends immediately to advertise the book.

If you find anything in the epistle that you would have altered or corrected, you may please write me; but you need not send back the copy, as I have a copy by me.

I know not how to express my obligations to you and Mr Stewart for the aid you have given me.—I am, dear Sir, your most obliged servant,

Tho. Reid.

May 2d, 1785,
Glasgow College.

You will give the epistle to the printers when it is wanted. I send with this the last part of the MS.

VII.

MEANINGS OF CAUSE—MOTIVE—LAW OF NATURE.

June 14, 1785.

Dear Sir,—I am extremely obliged to you for your friendly consultation about my health. For two days past, I have had almost nothing of my ailment, which I ascribe to some exercise I have taken, and to a comfortable warmness in the air. I resolve to try some short excursions, which I can make either on foot or in a chaise. If that do not produce the effect, I shall fall to your prescriptions, which I think very rational. I very probably may be at home when you propose to be in Glasgow.

Your speculation to demonstrate, mathematically, the difference between the relation of motive and action, and the relation of cause and effect,[*] is, indeed, so new to me, that I cannot easily form a judgment about it. I shall offer some of my thoughts on the subject of those two relations. Whether they be favourable to your speculation, or unfavourable, I cannot immediately determine.

The word *cause*, is very ambiguous in all languages. I have wrote a chapter lately upon the causes of this ambiguity. The words *power, agent, effect*, have a like ambiguity ; each different meaning of the first mentioned word leading to a corresponding meaning of the three last. A reason, an end, an instrument, and even a motive, is often called a cause. You certainly exclude the last from what you call a cause. Whether you exclude all the other meanings which I think improper meanings, I am not so sure.

In the strict and proper sense, I take an efficient cause to be a being who had power to produce the effect, and exerted that power for that purpose.

Active power is a quality which can only be in a substance that really exists, and is endowed with that power. Power to produce an effect, supposes power not to produce it ; otherwise it is not power but necessity, which is incompatible with power taken in a strict sense. The exertion of that power, is agency, or efficiency. That every event must have a cause in this proper sense, I take to be self-evident.

I should have noticed that I am not able to form a conception how power, in the strict sense, can be exerted without will ; nor can there be will without some degree of understanding. Therefore, nothing can be an efficient cause, in the proper sense, but an intelligent being.

I believe we get the first conception of power, in the proper sense, from the consciousness of our own exertions ; and, as all our power is exerted by will, we cannot form a conception how power can be exerted without will. Hence the only notion we can form of Almighty power in the Deity, is that

---

[*] In the MS. dedication of the "Essays on the Intellectual Powers," Dr Gregory's name stands before that of Mr Stewart. This order was, probably by Dr Gregory himself, reversed. There are also some verbal improvements in the style of the dedication, as it stands printed, which, it is likely, were introduced by Dr Gregory or Mr Stewart.—H.

[†] The title sent was, " Essays on the Intellectual Powers of the Human Mind," or, " Essays on the Intellectual Powers of Man." The latter was preferred.—H.

[*] This refers to Dr Gregory's ingenious " Essay on the Difference between the Relation of Motive and Action, and that of Cause and Effect in Physics ; on physical and mathematical principles." This treatise, which was published in 1792, had been previously communicated to various philosophical friends, and in particular to every Necessitarian of the author's acquaintance, with the assurance that, if any error could be pointed out in the reasoning—which, as mathematical, could be examined with the utmost rigour—the objection should either be completely answered, or the essay itself suppressed. Only one Necessitarian, however, allowed his objections to be published ; and these, with Dr Gregory's answers, are to be found in the appendix to the essay. Dr Reid was among the first to whom Dr Gregory communicated this work ; and to Dr Reid, when published, the " Philosophical and Literary Essays" were inscribed.—H.

P

he can do whatever he wills A power to do what he does not will, is words without a meaning.

Matter cannot be the cause of anything; it can only be an instrument in the hands of a real cause. Thus, when a body has a certain force given it by impulse, it may communicate that force to another body, and that to a third, and so on. But, when we trace back this motion to its origin, it must have been given, not by matter, but by some being which had in itself the power of beginning motion—that is, by a proper efficient cause of motion.

It cannot be said that there is a constant conjunction between a proper cause and the effect ; for, though the effect cannot be, without power to produce it, yet that power may be, without being exerted, and power which is not exerted produces no effect.

You will see, by what is said above, what I take to be the strict and proper meaning of the word *cause*, and the related words, *power, agent, &c.* In this sense we use it in reasoning concerning the being and attributes of the Deity. In this sense we ought to use it in the question about liberty and necessity, and, I think, in all metaphysical reasoning about causes and effects; for when, in metaphysical reasoning, we depart from this sense, the word is so vague that there can be no clear reasoning about it.

Suppose, now, that you take the word cause in this strict sense ; its relation to its effect is so self-evidently different from the relation of a motive to an action, that I am jealous of a mathematical demonstration of a truth so self-evident. Nothing is more difficult than to demonstrate what is self-evident. A cause is a being which has a real existence ; a *motive* has no real existence, and, therefore, can have no active power. It is a thing conceived, and not a thing that exists; and, therefore, can neither be active nor even passive. To say that a motive really acts, is as absurd as to say that a motive drinks my health, or that a motive gives me a box on the ear.

In physics, the word *cause* has another meaning, which, though I think it an improper one, yet is distinct, and, therefore, may be reasoned upon. When a phenomenon is produced according to a certain law of nature, we call the law of nature the cause of that phenomenon ; and to the laws of nature we accordingly ascribe power, agency, efficiency. The whole business of physics is to discover, by observation and experiment, the laws of nature, and to apply them to the solution of the phenomena: this we call discovering the causes of things. But this, however common, is an improper sense of the word *cause*.

A *law of nature* can no more be an agent

than can a motive. It is a thing conceived, and not a thing that exists ; and, therefore, can neither act, nor be acted upon. A law of nature is a purpose or resolution of the author of nature, to act according to a certain rule—either immediately by himself or by instruments that are under his direction. There must be a real agent to produce the phenomenon *according* to the law. A malefactor is not hanged by the law, but according to the law, by the executioner.

I suspect you use the word cause in this sense for a law of nature, according to which a phenomenon is produced. If so, it should appear distinctly that you do so.

But is it not self-evident, that the relation between a law of nature and the event which is produced according to it, is very different from the relation between a motive and the action to which it is a motive ? Is there any need of demonstration for this? or does it admit of demonstration ?

There is, indeed, a supposition upon which the two relations would be very similar. The supposition is, that, by a law of nature, the influence of motives upon actions is as invariable as is the effect of impulse upon matter ; but to suppose this is to suppose fatality and not to prove it.

It is a question of fact, whether the influence of motives be fixed by laws of nature, so that they shall always have the same effect in the same circumstances. Upon this, indeed, the question about liberty and necessity hangs. But I have never seen any proof that there are such laws of nature, far less any proof that the strongest motive always prevails. However much our late fatalists have boasted of this principle as of a law of nature, without ever telling us what they mean by the strongest motive. I am persuaded that, whenever they shall be pleased to give us any measure of the strength of motives distinct from their prevalence, it will appear, from experience, that the strongest motive does not always prevail. If no other test or measure of the strength of motives can be found but their prevailing, then this boasted principle will be only an identical proposition, and signify only that the strongest motive is the strongest motive, and the motive that prevails is the motive that prevails—which proves nothing.

May it not be objected to your reasoning, that you apply the three laws of motion to motives ; but motives may be subject to other laws of nature, no less invariable than the laws of motion, though not the same. Different parts of nature have different laws, it may be said ; and to apply the laws of one part to another part, particularly to apply the laws of inert matter to the phenomena of mind, may lead into great fallacies. I think, indeed, that your reasoning proves, that, between the influence of motives upon a mind and the influence of impulse upon a body, there is but a very slight analogy, which fails in many instances.

I have wearied you and myself with a long detail, I fear, little to the purpose; but it was in my head, and so came out. I am just setting out on a jaunt to Paisley, with my wife, son-in-law, and daughter, to come home at night.

Yours most affectionately,
THO. REID.

VIII.

MEANING OF CAUSE.

DEAR SIR,—I believe I have never answered the letter you favoured me with of Aug. 9, by Capt. Gallie. First, I obeyed your commands in attending Mrs Siddons twice, in "Douglas," and in "Venice Preserved." I believe I should have had much more pleasure if, on account of deafness, I had not lost much of what she said, and had been better acquainted with the plays. But I believe she is really an admirable actress, and deserves the admiration you express of her.

You say, you fear we shall never agree with respect to the notion of cause and effect. I am at a loss to know wherein we differ. I think we agree in this, that a cause, in the proper and strict sense, (which, I think, we may call the metaphysical sense,) signifies a being or mind that has power and will to produce the effect. But there is another meaning of the word cause, which is so well authorized by custom, that we cannot always avoid using it, and I think we may call it the physical sense; as when we say that heat is the cause that turns water into vapour, and cold the cause that freezes it into ice. A cause, in this sense, means only something which, by the laws of nature, the effect always follows. I think natural philosophers, when they pretend to shew the *causes* of natural phenomena, always use the word in this last sense; and the vulgar in common discourse very often do the same.

The reason why I take no notice of neuter verbs is, that I conceive they are used to express an event, without any signification of its having a cause or not. But I shall be very glad to see your speculations upon this subject when they are ready.

I had a letter from Dr Price lately, thanking me for a copy of the Essays I ordered to be presented to him, which he has read, and calls it a work of the first value; commends me particularly for treat-

ing his friend Dr Priestly so gently, who, he says, had been unhappily led to use me ill. . . . .

As you are so kind as to ask about my distemper, I think it is almost quite gone, so as to give me no uneasiness. I abstain from fruit and malt liquor, and take a little port wine, morning, noon, and night, not above two bottles in a week when alone. The more I walk, or ride, or even talk or read audibly, I am the better.

When your time is fixed for coming here, I shall be glad to know it.—I am, dear Sir,
Most affectionately yours,
THO. REID.
Glasgow, 23d Sept. 1785.

IX.

ON CAUSE AND EFFECT—MOTIVE AND ACTION.

[*March* 1786.]

DEAR SIR,—I hope your essay, along with this, will come to your hand by the carrier, and within the time you mention. It would have been sent sooner if I had not had a discourse to deliver before our Literary Society last Friday.

You give me most agreeable intelligence—first, of Mrs Stewart's being so far recovered of a dangerous illness, and then of my friend William's promotion, who, I hope, will wear the robe with decency and dignity.

Your essay I have read several times with attention, and I think the reasoning perfectly conclusive to prove that the relation between motives and actions is totally of a different kind from that which physical causes bear to their effects.

I agree with you that the hypothesis you combat in this essay is more unreasonable than that of constant conjunction. Not because it is more reasonable to conceive a constant conjunction between motives and actions than an occasional one; but because the first agrees better than the last with the hypothesis of motives being physical causes of actions. Between a physical cause and its effect, the conjunction must be constant, unless in the case of a miracle, or suspension of the laws of nature. What D. Hume says of causes, in general, is very just when applied to physical causes, that a constant conjunction with the effect is essential to such causes, and implied in the very conception of them.

The style of this essay is more simple than that of the last, and, I think, on that account, more proper for a philosophical dissertation.

I am proud of the approbation you express of the essays:* I have made some

---

* On the Active Powers.—H.

corrections and additions, but such as I hope will not make it necessary to write it over again. But I wish, if I find health and leisure, in summer, to add some essays to go before that on liberty, in order to give some farther elucidation to the principles of morals, both theoretical and practical. I expect your remarks and D. Stewart's upon what is in hand. It will be no inconvenience to wait for them two or three, or even four months.—I am, dear Sir,

Yours most affectionately,
THO. REID.

X.

DEAR SIR,—In answer to your queries,*

* The following may serve to explain the allusions in these letters, and, in general, the connection of Reid with the family of Gregory :—

The Reverend *John* Gregory of Drumoak, in the county of Aberdeen, was the common ancestor of two lines, both greatly distinguished for mathematical and general ability. His wife was a daughter of David Anderson of Finzaugh, cousin-german of the celebrated analyst, Alexander Anderson, the friend and follower of Vieta. By her, he had two sons, David and James, progenitors of the several lines.

I. LINE.

The elder son, *David* Gregory of Kinairdy, in the county of Aberdeen, was bred a merchant, and lived the greater part of a long life in Holland He had the singular fortune of seeing three sons Professors of Mathematics at the same time in three British universities.

Of these sons, the eldest, *David*, (born 1666, died 1710,) though inferior to his uncle James in inventive genius, was one of the most illustrious geometers and geometrical authors of his time. In 1683, elected Professor of Mathematics in the University of Edinburgh, he was, in 1691, by the influence of Newton nominated Savilian Professor of Astronomy in Oxford. His son, *David*, who died 1767, was student, canon, and dean of Christ Church, and Regius Professor of Modern History in the same university.

The second of these sons, *James*, succeeded his brother David as Professor of Mathematics in Edinburgh, and retired in favour of the celebrated Maclaurin, in 1725.

The third son, *Charles*, was Professor of Mathematics in St Andrews from 1707 to 1739, when he resigned in favour of his son, David, who held the Chair until his death in 1764.

Dr *Reid's* mother was a daughter of David Gregory of Kinairdy, and sister of the three Mathematical Professors.

II. LINE.

James, the younger son of the Rev. John Gregory, was born in 1638, and died at the early age of thirty-seven. He was Professor of Mathematics at St Andrew's and Edinburgh ; inventor of the Reflecting or Gregorian Telescope ; author of several remarkable treatises on optics and geometry ; and, altogether, one of the most original mathematicians of his age.

His son, *James*, Professor of Medicine in King's College, Aberdeen, was father of a more celebrated son—

John, who was born 1724, and died 1773. He was successively Professor of Philosophy and of Medicine in King's College, Aberdeen, and of the Practice of Physic in the University of Edinburgh ; author of the "Comparative View of the State and Faculties of Man and Animals," of the "Lectures on the Duties and Qualifications of a Physician," of "Elements of the Practice of Physic," and of "A Father's Legacy to his Daughters" His eldest son (Dr Reid's correspondent)—

James, was born 1753, and died 1821. He was Professor of the Theory, afterwards of the Practice,

I know not precisely either the year of my grandfather's death or his age. But all that I have heard agrees very well with the account you mention. He served apprentice to a merchant in Rotterdam or Campvere, and, I believe, continued there till the murder of his elder brother. After he came home, he prosecuted the murderer, (son and heir to Viscount Frendritt, as I have heard, though I find not the title among the extinct or forfeited Peers,) who, being a Roman Catholic, was protected by all the interest of the Duke of York ; but was at last condemned, but pardoned by the crown, and soon after killed in a naval engagement.* Your g-grandfather was so much younger than Kinairdy, as to be educated by him. Kinairdy had no more sons professors than the three you mention, who were all professors before he died. David and James were of the first marriage, and Charles of the second. The two first were settled before the Revolution—David as Professor of Mathematics at Edinburgh, and, I suppose, immediately succeeded his uncle, and James as a Professor of Philosophy at St Andrews. I think I have a printed thesis of James, published at St Andrews before the Revolution, which is a compend of Newtonian philosophy, with some strictures against the scholastic philosophy. With regard to the ten categories in particular, he says there neither are nor can be more than two categories, viz. Data and Quæsita.† I believe he was the first professor of philosophy that taught the doctrines of Newton in a Scotch university ; for the Cartesian was

of Medicine, in the University of Edinburgh ; and author of "Conspectus Medicinæ Theoreticæ," of "Philosophical and Literary Essays," and of various other works, distinguished by a talent which promises still to be hereditary.

* The murder here alluded to was committed on Alexander Gregory of Netherdcel, eldest son and heir of the Rev. John Gregory, minister of Drumoak ; and the person indicted for the crime, was James (Crichton) Viscount Frendraught. The Books of Adjournal (records of the Scottish Criminal Court) detail the circumstances of the case. In 1664, Alexander Gregory, who held, in security, a part of the estate of Frendraught, was decoyed by Francis Crichton, the Viscount's uncle, to accompany him to the house of Bognie, where that nobleman then lodged. On the way he was assaulted by Crichton and his servant ; and, after he had surrendered his arms, was wounded by them with swords and pistols, and then carried a prisoner to Bognie. Here he was watched during the night, among others, by the Viscount, whose servants, next day, early in a cold morning, threw him across a horse, his wounds undressed and bleeding, and brought him to a lone cottage, where he was left till found by his friends, who conveyed him to Aberdeen, where, after languishing for a few days, he died. Mr Francis and his servant did not compear. The relevancy of the libel against Lord Frendraught was impugned, on the ground that the crimes libelled being only statutory, and the pannel a minor, they ought not to pass to an assize. But, though the libel was found relevant, the proof seems to have been defective ; the jury, at least, found a verdict of acquittal.—I am indebted for this information to Duncan Gregory and James Maidment, Esquires.—H.

† This illustrates a statement in "The Analysis of Aristotle's Logic," ch. ii. sec. 2.—H.

the orthodox system at that time, and continued to be so till 1715. I asked him once how he came to give up his place at St Andrew's on the change of government, and afterwards to take the mathematical chair at Edinburgh. "Faith, nephew," said he, "I never minded politicks much; but my dearest companions in the college were going out, and I did not like those that were to keep their places; and I thought it better to go out in good company, than to stay behind with ill." I believe Kinairdy's mathematical and medical knowledge was the effect of his own study and reading. He was much employed as a physician, not only by the poor, but by the nobility and gentry; but he took no fees; and, I conceive, his younger brother and his sons had their mathematical education chiefly from him. He had a barometer, and had a correspondence with some foreigners, particularly with Mariotte, on barometrical observations. As a barometer had never been heard of in his country before, he was once in danger of being brought to some trouble by the Presbytery on account of it. In Queen Ann's war, Kinairdy employed himself upon an invention for improving the effect of firearms, of which he at last completed a model, and sent it to his son David at Oxford, that he might take the opinion of Sir Isaac Newton about it. I have heard my mother say that he was so sanguine upon this project, that he intended to make a campaign in Flanders himself, and prepared for it. But it is said that Sir I. Newton persuaded the suppression of the invention as destructive of the human species, and that it was never brought to light. I knew a clockmaker in Aberdeen who made all the parts by Kinairdy's direction; but never saw them put together, and could give no account of the principles of it. Kinairdy carried his family over to Holland, about the year 1715, as I believe, and, after some time, returned to Aberdeen, and·died soon after. His widow was alive when I went first to Aberdeen in April 1722; but old and bedrid. I never saw a more ladylike woman; I was now and then called in to her room, when she sat up in her bed, and entertained with sweetmeats and grave advices. Her daughters, that assisted her often, as well as one who lived with her, treated her as if she had been of a superior rank; and, indeed, her appearance and manner commanded respect. I don't believe that she could ever descend so far from her dignity and magnanimity as to scold. And the reverence paid her by all her descendants to the last period of her life, seems inconsistent with that character. She and all her children were zealous Presbyterians. The first wife's children were rather Tories and Episcopalians. I believe she had much

ado to keep up her authority with them while they were in the family. David and James, when prosecuting their studies at Edinburgh, used to pass their vacations at Kinairdy; and very often Dr Pitcairn, or some other fellow-student came along with them; and, as the master of the family was very much from home, it was not easy for a stepmother to keep them to her rules. One of her stepdaughters married a Mr Cuthbert, of the family of Castlehill, a writer in Aberdeen, and was the mother of David Cuthbert, who saved millions to the nation in the war before last, by controling the accounts of the commissaries in Germany.

Another daughter of the first marriage, married a Mr Innes of Tilliefour. A grandson of hers, Alexander Innes, was a professor of philosophy in Marischal College, Aberdeen. He had a great turn to natural history and to medicine; but died young.

My mother, Margaret Gregory, was the oldest daughter of the second marriage. Besides Charles, there was a George of the second marriage, a merchant in Campvere, and the father of David Gregory at Dunkirk, and of John Gregory at Campvere. Your uncle, David Gregory, served an apprenticeship to this George Gregory, and married his widow after his death. Charles told me that his brother George fell to the study of mathematics in Holland, and wrote him an account of his discoveries. But Charles bid him mind his mercantile affairs; for these things had been discovered already by authors he was unacquainted with. The only daughter of the second marriage, besides my mother, who left issue, was Anne, the youngest daughter, grandmother to James Bartlet, banker in Edinburgh.

The story of the watch, to which, I suppose, you allude, I have heard very often. By the descendants of the first wife it was imputed to the second wife; but the descendants of the second wife imputed it to the first wife. The first time I was in Dean Gregory's house at Oxford, he told it very well to a large company of Oxonians. He prefaced it by saying that his grandfather had a termagant to his second wife; but turning to me and another Scotch gentleman that was with me, he said, "I beg your pardon, gentlemen, for I don't know but one of you may be come of her." I answered that I believed I had heard the story he was about to tell, and heard it imputed to the first wife, of whom he was come; but it was no matter which: I begged he would proceed. To this he agreed, and proceeded to the story of the watch.*

Another story, somewhat similar, is told of Kinairdy. On some occasion his wife, I know not which wife, insisted very per-

---

* Which is now forgotten in the family.—H.

emptorily that he should correct two of his sons, which, it seems, he was not accustomed to do; but the offence was such, that nothing less would satisfy the wife. He took them to a room where his saddle and bridle hung, and shut the door. What satisfaction he required for the fault I know not; but, after the matter was compromised, he took the bridle, and lashed the said saddle very unmercifully, and ordered the boys to cry, which they did most pitifully. The mother hearing the noise, thought her boys would be killed, and wanted to interpose, but the door was bolted. She was forced to stand behind the door, and felt every stroke more than either the saddle or the boys, resolving never again to trust her husband with the rod of correction.

I have found the printed thesis of James Gregory, above mentioned; it is printed at Edinburgh, 1690. It would seem that the reform of St Andrew's University, after the Revolution, was not overtaken at that time. The students' names who were to defend the thesis at Salvator College, in St Andrew's, on such a day of June, are all mentioned, to the number of twenty-one. Kinairdy was a Scotch Episcopalian. He wrote memoirs of his own times, which my father, who had read them, told me were unfavourable to the Covenant—the idol of the Presbyterians at that time. These Memoirs were in your father's possession, and I suppose are in yours. You see, my dear sir, that I have answered more than I was asked, because I like to dwell upon the subject; but you must not think nor say that my grandmother was a scold; she might have strong passions, but no scold ever had her dignity and magnanimity. She had a brother, whom I knew well, who was very like to her—Provost John Gordon. He was long at the head of the magistracy in Aberdeen; and had been a member of the Scotch Parliament, and was one of the most respected magistrates that ever was in that city.—I ever am, dear Sir, yours,

THO. REID.

Aug. 24, 1787.

XI.

ON THE ORIGIN, PROGRESS, AND THEORY OF LANGUAGE.

DEAR SIR,—I have read your theory of the moods of verbs* over and over, and shall give you a few trifling remarks when the MS. is returned, or sooner, if I see you sooner. It is not yet sent to Dr Cleghorn, but shall be this week. In the meantime,

having the opportunity of my good friend Mr John Duguid, I send you some reveries on the invention and progress of language.

The art of communicating our sentiments by articulate sounds, is certainly, of all human arts, the most ingenious, and that which has required most of thought, of abstraction, and nice metaphysical discrimination. This has led our friend L. M.* to think that it must have been, at first, the work of philosophers. I rather consider it as a huge and complicated machine, which was very imperfect at first, but gradually received improvements from the judgment and invention of all who used it in the course of many ages.

It is a machine which every man must use, and which he finds of such utility and importance, that, if he has any genius, he has sufficient inducement to employ it in making language more subservient to his purpose.

In the natural talents of genius and invention, there is no less difference among savages than among philosophers. One savage, in the use of natural signs, will shew great superiority to others in conveying his sentiments distinctly and intelligibly; and the same superiority he will shew in the use of a rude language of articulate sounds—sometimes by giving a more easy or more agreeable sound to words that are in use; sometimes by distinguishing, by some inflection or inversion, words or phrases that were before ambiguous; sometimes by a new metaphorical meaning; and sometimes by new words or new derivations, where they were wanted.

So fond are ingenious men to invent such improvements in language, and so prone the multitude to adopt them, when they please the public taste, that all languages are perpetually changing, according to the beautiful simile of Horace—*Ut silvæ foliis pronos mutantur in annos, &c.* In a rude language it is easy to make improvements; and changes that are found useful and important, though invented by one man, will soon be adopted by the multitude.

Thus the inventions of thousands of ingenious men, in a succession of ages, all employed upon this one machine, bring it by insensible degrees to its perfection; as knowledge grows, language grows along with it, till it arrive at that stately form which we contemplate with admiration.

The steam engine was invented not much more than a century ago; but it has received so many and so great improvements in that short period, that, if the inventor were to arise from the dead, and view it in its improved state, he would hardly be able to discern his own share of the invention.

---

* Subsequently printed in "The Transactions of the Royal Society of Edinburgh."—H.

* Lord Monboddo.—H.

Language is like a tree, which. from a small seed, grows imperceptibly, till the fowls of the air lodge in its branches, and the beasts of the earth rest under its shadow. The seed of language is the natural signs of our thoughts, which nature has taught all men to use, and all men to understand. But its growth is the effect of the united energy of all who do or ever did use it. One man pushes out a branch, another a leaf, one smooths a rough part, another lops off an excrescence. Grammarians have, without doubt, contributed much to its regularity and beauty; and philosophers, by increasing our knowledge, have added many a fair branch to it; but it would have been a tree without the aid of either.

The rudest tribes of men soon find language to express their confined wants and desires; and the natural love of analogy will produce much analogy even in the language of savages. We see that children of two or three years old, having got a few plurals, without being taught, form new ones analogically, and often, in the pursuit of analogy, break through the rules of grammar.

A man born deaf, who has no opportunity of conversing with other deaf men, has to invent a language for himself, along with the additional labour of teaching others to understand it. One who has had access to know to what degree of perfection some deaf men have carried their art of communicating their thoughts, will not think it incredible that a nation flourishing in arts and sciences should, in a course of ages, by their united efforts, bring language to all the perfection it has ever attained.

In speech, the true natural unit is a sentence. No man intends less when he speaks; what is less than a complete sentence is not speech, but a part or parts of speech; to divide a sentence into parts requires greater abstraction than to divide the unit into fractions of a unit. It is, therefore, extremely probable that men expressed sentences by one complex sound or word, before they thought of dividing them into parts, signified by different words. One word signified, *give me bread*; another, *take bread*; another, *eat bread*; another, *bake bread*. As all these sentences have something common in their meaning, the natural love of analogy would lead to something common in the word by which they were expressed; and in the progress·of language, that which was common in the sound of all these sentences might be separated from that which was proper to each; and, being thus separated, it becomes that part of speech which we call a substantive

noun, signifying *bread*, which substantive will be fit to make a part of many other sentences.

Thus the object, or accusative, may be, as it were, cut out of the sentence, so as to form a word by itself, though originally it was only a part of a word.

Another set of sentences—such as, *I love Martha, You love Mary, John loves Matilda*—might lead men to separate what is common in the word by which each of these three sentences is expressed, from what is proper to each, and by that means to have a word for the verb love.

To shew how all the parts of speech may be cut out of words that signify whole sentences, by separating that part of the sound which is common to many sentences, from that which is proper to each, would be more tedious than difficult, and may easily be conceived. By dividing the sound, the mental abstraction is made easy, even to rude men, who, without some aid of this kind, would find it above their reach. Such division facilitates greatly the use of language, and, therefore, when once begun, will go on.

That the parts of speech should be conceived before speech was in use, and that speech should at first be formed by putting together parts of speech, which before had got names, seems to me altogether incredible; no less incredible than if it should be said that before men had the conception of a body, they first formed the conception of matter, then the conception of form, and, putting these two together, they got the conception of body, which is made up of matter and form.

Perhaps, in the language of some savages, all the parts of speech have not yet been separated into different words. Charlevoix has given a very full account of some of the Canadian languages. I quote him from memory, having read his history of Canada, I think, about forty years ago; but, as it first led me into this speculation, I remember it the better.

He says, of one of their languages, (I think that of the Hurons,) that in each of their villages there is a public orator chosen, who makes it the whole study of his life to speak the language with propriety and force; that the people are very nice judges of the defects and excellencies of their orators; so that there are very few of them that can perfectly please the public ear; that their verbs have as many moods and tenses as the Greek verbs have, and, besides this, that the accusative or object always makes a part of the verb. Thus, one verb *signifies to drink wine*; another, *to drink water*; one, *to kill a brother*; another, *to kill an enemy*; so that the verb very often expresses the whole sentence.

---

* This is an important truth, the ignorance of which is seen in our perverted systems of Grammar, Logic, and Psychology.—H.

I believe, in all languages of nations which we account civilized, the several parts of speech have been separated from one another, and are often expressed by words proper to them. But in all of them, and in some more than in others, several parts of speech are often combined in one word, not from necessity, but for the sake of elegance and beauty.

Thus, in the Latin and Greek verbs, besides the radical signification of the verb, its voice, mood, tense, person, and number are all expressed in one word. In nouns, both substantive and adjective, we have the noun, together with its case, number, and gender, in one word. Nor is this owing to a want of words in those languages to express separately those accidents of verbs and nouns. It seems rather to be a matter of choice, to give greater beauty and strength to the language. By this expedient, much may be said in few words—and these, lofty and sonorous words, with a beautiful variety and harmony of termination, and great power of inversion ; which are qualities of great importance in poetry and eloquence.

In language, as in many other things, necessity, convenience, and long practice, have, without the rules of art, produced artifices, which the artist or the philosopher has reason to admire, which, sitting in his chair, he would never have been able to invent, and which, now that they are invented, he finds it very difficult to reduce to principles of art.

I believe the principles of the art of language are to be found in a just analysis of the various species of sentences. Aristotle and the logicians have analysed one species—to wit, *the proposition*. To enumerate and analyse the other species, must, I think, be the foundation of a just theory of language.

—I am, dear Sir, yours affectionately,

THO. REID.

Aug. 26, 1787.

XII.

[1788.]

DEAR SIR,—I received yours of Feb. 19, and last evening received, by the fly, the very acceptable present of the new edition of your father's works, for which I heartily thank you. I have read the Life, which I think well wrote. I am much obliged to the author* of it for the notice he has taken of me ; but I wish he had spared some epithets, which I could not read to myself without a blush ; I have exceptions to some things in the narrative, but they relate to unimportant circumstances. The quotation from " Whiston's Memoirs" delighted me, and does honour to Scotland.†

* Lord Woodhouselee.— H.
† It is of the following purport :—Speaking of Dr

Perhaps it might have been added, that James, the brother of David, was at that time teaching the same doctrine, as a Professor of Philosophy, in another Scotch university. I have by me a thesis he published in 1690, which is a compend of the conclusions of Newton's " Principia." I have always heard, by tradition, that D. Gregory, the astronomer, was chosen to be preceptor to the Duke of Gloucester, Queen Ann's son ; but whether his entering upon that office was prevented by his death, or by the death of the young prince, I know not. I have also heard that the Profession of Modern History in Oxford was erected in favour of his son, David, when he came home from his travels.*

. . . .

I am happy in the account you give me of our friend, William. I hope he will continue the race of the Gregories, if you do not—which, however, I do not yet despair of. Our University has sent a petition to the House of Commons, in favour of the African slaves. I hope yours will not be the last in this humane design ; and that the Clergy of Scotland will likewise join in it. I comfort my grey hairs with the thoughts that the world is growing better, having long resolved to resist the common sentiment of old age, that it is always growing worse. I am grown so deaf that I can only converse with one person, and that when he speaks into my left ear ; but I hope to resist that depression of spirits which commonly attends that disorder. I can see people conversing together without any uneasiness ; the only difficulty is, when a laugh is raised, whether to laugh at one does not know what,

David Gregory, when Professor of Mathematics at Edinburgh, Whiston says—" He had already caused several of his scholars to keep acts, as we call them, upon several branches of the Newtonian philosophy, while we at Cambridge, poor wretches! were ignominiously studying the fictitious hypotheses of the Cartesian."—*Whiston's Memoirs*, p. 32.—There is in this, however, no just ground of panegyric on Scotland. In the intrusive system of the English universities, where the tutor has illegally superseded the professor, all change from one set of doctrines to a better, must be the tardy and painful work of time and necessity. The evolutions of a university are prompt and easy where each department of its cyclopædia is separately taught by an able professor ; whereas a university which abandons instruction, in all branches, to any individual of a host of tutors—the majority of whom assume the office of instructor for their own convenience, though without the ability adequate to discharge its duties—such a university must be content, not only always to teach little, and that little ill, but to continue often for a long time to teach what is elsewhere obsolete or exploded. Accordingly, in Newton's own university, the Cartesian theories continued to be taught as the orthodox doctrine, after the Newtonian physics had, in other universities, superseded the Cartesian. And why? Simply because, in Cambridge, instruction was carried on by tutors ; and the majority of the Cambridge tutors, educated in the old system, were unable or unwilling to qualify themselves to become instructors in the new.—H.

* David Gregory, the son, was certainly *first* Professor in the chair of *Modern History and Languages*, founded by George I.—H.

or to be grave when other people laugh. I am very glad to hear that Dug. Stewart lectures in physicks so acceptably, but wish his health be not affected by his being overwrought.—I am, dear Sir, very affectionately yours,

THO. REID.

XIII.

ON USURY.

. . . . I am much pleased with the tract you sent me on usury.* I think the reasoning unanswerable, and have long been of the author's opinion, though I suspect that the general principle, that bargains ought to be left to the judgment of the parties, may admit of some exceptions, when the buyers are the many, the poor, and the simple—the sellers few, rich, and cunning; the former may need the aid of the magistrate to prevent their being oppressed by the latter. It seems to be upon this principle that portage, freight, the hire of chairs and coaches, and the price of bread, are regulated in most great towns. But with regard to the loan of money in a commercial state, the exception can have no place—the borrowers and lenders are upon an equal footing, and each may be left to take care of his own interest. Nor do I see any good reason for the interposition of law in bargains about the loan of money more than in bargains of any other kind. I am least pleased with the 10th letter, wherein he accounts for the infamy of usury. In one of the papers you mention, (which I give you liberty to use as you please,) I have attempted an account of that phenomenon, which satisfies me more than his account does.—I am, dear Sir,

Yours most affectionately,

THO. REID.

Glasgow, 5th Sep^t. 1788.

XIV.

CAUSE—PHYSICAL CAUSE—LAWS OF NATURE —AGENT—POWER AND ACTIVITY.

MY DEAR SIR,—On Monday evening I received your book,† with the letter inclosed. The book I shall peruse at leisure with the eye of a critick; but, as it is proper to acquaint you soon of my having received it safe, I shall now answer your letter, though perhaps in too much haste. Your

intention of inscribing the book, if published, to me, I account a very great honour done me; and, if you do not alter your mind, would not be so self-denying as to decline it; but, as a real friend, I think you ought to inscribe it to some man in power that may be of use to you, though I hate dedications stuffed with flattery to great men. Yet I know no reason why a man of your time of life may not court the notice of a great man by a dedication, as well as by a visit. When I inscribed a book to you, my situation was very different. I was past all hopes and fears with regard to this world; and, indeed, had Lord Kaimes been alive, intended to have addressed it to him. When he was dead, there was not a man of his eminence that I had so much acquaintance with as to justify such an address. I therefore seriously wish you to spend a second thought upon this subject; and not to suffer your friendship, of which I need no new proof, to lead you to do an imprudent thing, and what the world would think such, or even perhaps construe as a contempt put upon your *great* friends.*

As to the two points wherein you and I differ, after what you have said of them in this letter, I am really uncertain whether we differ about things or only about words. You deny that of every change there must be an efficient cause, in my sense—that is, an intelligent agent, who by his power and will effected the change. But I think you grant that, when the change is not effected by such an agent, it must have a physical cause—that is, it must be the necessary consequence of the nature and previous state of things unintelligent and inactive.

I admit that, for anything I know to the contrary, there may be such a nature and state of things which have no proper activity, as that certain events or changes must necessarily follow. I admit that, in such a case, that which is antecedent may be called the physical cause, and what is necessarily consequent, may be called the effect of that cause.

I likewise admit, laws of nature may be called (as they commonly are called) physical causes—in a sense indeed somewhat different from the former—because laws of nature effect nothing, but as far as they are put to execution, either by some agent, or by some physical cause; they being, however, our *ne plus ultra* in natural philosophy, which professes to shew us the causes of natural things, and being, both in ancient and modern times, called *causes*, they have by prescription acquired a right to that name.

I think also, and I believe you agree with

---

* " Letters On Usury," by Mr Jeremy Bentham, addressed to George Wilson, Esq., (Dr Gregory's friend,) and published, by Mr Wilson in 1787.—H.

† The " Philosophical and Literary Essays," or rather their introduction, which was in great part printed several years before publication.—H.

* It is needless to say that Dr Gregory did not comply with this prudent advice. The " Essays" are dedicated to Reid.—H.

me, that every physical cause must be the work of some agent or efficient cause. Thus, that a body put in motion continues to move till it be stopped, is an effect which, for what I know, may be owing to an inherent property in matter; if this be so, this property of matter is the physical cause of the continuance of the motion; but the ultimate efficient cause is the Being who gave this property to matter.

If we suppose this continuance of motion to be an arbitrary appointment of the Deity, and call that appointment a law of nature and a physical cause; such a law of nature requires a Being who has not only enacted the law, but provided the means of its being executed, either by some physical cause, or by some agent acting by his order. If we agree in these things, I see not wherein we differ, but in words.

I agree with you that to confound the notion of agent or efficient cause with that of physical cause, has been a common error of philosophers, from the days of Plato to our own. I could wish that the same general name of *cause* had not been given to both, as if they were two *species* belonging to the same *genus*. They differ *toto genere*. For a physical cause is not an agent. It does not act, but is acted upon, and is as passive as its effect. You accordingly give them different generical names, calling the one the *agent*, and not the cause—the other the *cause*, but not the agent.

I approve of your view in this; but think it too bold an innovation in language. In all writing, preaching, and speaking, men have been so much accustomed to call the Deity the first cause of all things, that to maintain that he is no cause at all, would be too shocking. To say that the world exists without a cause, would be accounted Atheism, in spite of all explications that could be given of it. Agency, efficiency, operation, are so conjoyned in our conceptions with a cause, that an age would not be sufficient to disjoyn them.

The words *agent* and *action* are not less ambiguous than *cause* and *causation;* they are applied, by the most accurate thinkers and speakers, to what you call physical causes. So we say, one body acts upon another, by a stroke, by pressure, by attraction or repulsion; and in vain would one attempt to abolish this language. We must bear with the imperfections of language in some degree; we are not able to make it so philosophical as we wish.

To remedy the ambiguity of *cause* and *agent* as far as possible, without too bold an innovation, I say that each of these words has two meanings—a lax and popular meaning, and a philosophical. In the popular meaning, both are applied to what you call a physical cause. In the strict or philo-

sophical meaning, both are applied only to what you call an agent—I, an efficient cause. I choose to distinguish the philosophical meaning of *cause*, by calling it an efficient cause; and to distinguish the philosophical meaning of agent, by calling it an agent in the strict and proper sense.

You distinguish the philosophical meaning of these two ambiguous words from the popular, by appropriating one to the philosophical meaning, and the other to the popular. Is not this the difference between you and me?

It is remarkable that the philosophical meaning of those two words, and of the others that depend upon them, must have been the first, and the popular meaning a corruption of the philosophical, introduced by time, but so deeply rooted in the structure of all languages, that it is impossible to eradicate it; for nothing external to us could introduce into the human mind the general notion of priority and constant conjunction, but nothing farther.

Power and activity are first conceived from being conscious of them in ourselves. Conceiving of other beings from what we know of ourselves, we first ascribe to them such powers as we are conscious of in ourselves. Experience, at least, informs us that the things about us have not the same powers that we have; but language was formed on a contrary supposition before this discovery was made, and we must give a new, and perhaps a very indistinct, meaning to words which before had a clear and distinct one.

As to the other difference you mention between you and me, I have quite forgot it. But I think one can hardly be too cautious of denying the *bona fides* of an antagonist in a philosophical dispute. It is so bitter a pill, that it cannot be swallowed without being very well gilded and aromatized. I cannot but agree with you that assent or belief is not a voluntary act. Neither is seeing when the eyes are open. One may voluntarily shut his bodily eyes, and perhaps the eye of his understanding. I confess this is *mala fides*. But as light may be so offensive that the bodily eye is shut involuntarily, may not something similar happen to the eye of the understanding, when brought to a light too offensive to some favourite prejudice or passion, to be endured?[*]

As soon as I have done with your book, I shall execute your commission to Mr Arthur.—I am, dear Sir, yours very sincerely,

THO. REID.

Thursday, July 30, 1789.

---

[*] This passage ("But I think"—"be endured?") is quoted in the Introduction to Dr Gregory's Essays, p. 316.—H.

XV.

ARISTOTELIC SPECIES OF CAUSES—ORIGIN OF NOTIONS OF CAUSE AND POWER—WHAT ESSENTIAL TO THE NATURE OF CAUSE—DISTINCTION OF PHYSICAL AND METAPHYSICAL CAUSES.

*Remarks on the Introduction.**

l. I humbly think you are too severe against Aristotle and Plato, especially the former.† Two hundred years ago, it was proper to pull him down from the high seat he held; but now he is sufficiently humbled, and I would not have him trampled upon. I confess that his distinction of causes into four kinds is not a division of a *genus* into its *species*, but of an ambiguous word into its different meanings, and that this is the case with many of his divisions. But, in the infancy of philosophy, this ought to be corrected without severity. It was more inexcusable in many philosophers and divines of the scholastick ages to handle every subject in one method, namely, by shewing its four causes—Efficient, Material, Formal, and Final. A very learned divine, whose compend was the text-book in the school where I was taught, treating of the creation, when he comes to the material cause, pronounces it to be *nihil.* If Aristotle had treated of his *materia prima* in this method, he must have made the material cause to be the thing itself, and all the three other causes to be *nihil;* for it had no form, no efficient, consequently no end. But the absurdity of making everything to have four causes, cannot, I believe, be imputed to Aristotle.

2. You challenge him with a violation of propriety in the Greek language.‡ I am disposed to take it upon the authority of Aristotle, as a man who understood Greek better than any modern, that the word ἄιτιον was sometimes used to signify the form, sometimes the matter of a thing. If these were not popular meanings of the word, might they not be philosophical, and perhaps to be found only in the writings of philosophers, which are now lost? But I cannot think that Aristotle would have given these meanings without authority; and I think it bold in any modern to impute this to him.

3. You are likewise severe upon the τὸ ἐξ ὖ.‖ May it not be said that it is very like *the supposed principle of change,* which, in page xvii., you make the general meaning of the word *cause* ?

4. You seem to think (end of page xxi.) that there are different kinds of causes, each having something specifick in its relation to the effect.

I know not what the kinds are which you have in your eye, and therefore speak in the dark upon this point. I mean onely to put you upon your guard that they be really *species* of the same *genus,* that you may not fall under the censure you have passed upon Aristotle.

You will forgive my offering this caution, because I apprehend that there is one original notion of *cause* grounded in human nature, and that this is the notion on which the maxim is grounded—that every change or event must have a cause. This maxim is so universally held, and forces itself upon the judgment so strongly, that I think it must be a first principle, or what you call a law of human thought. And I think the only distinct and true meaning of this maxim is, that there must be something that had power to produce the event, and did produce it. We are early conscious of some power in ourselves to produce some events; and our nature leads us to think that every event is produced by a power similar to that which we find in ourselves—that is, by will and exertion: when a weight falls and hurts a child, he is angry with it—he attributes power and will to everything that seems to act. Language is formed upon these early sentiments, and attributes action and power to things that are afterwards discovered to have neither will nor power. By this means, the notion of action and causation is gradually changed; what was essential to it at first is left out, while the name remains : and the term cause is applied to things which we believe to be inanimate and passive.

I conceive that, from the original notion or sentiment above described, all the different notions of *cause* have been derived, by some kind of analogy, or perhaps abuse; and I know not but the τὸ ἐξ ὖ may comprehend them all, as well as any other general name, as they are so heterogeneous.

A law plea is the *cause* of a litigation. The motive that induces a great body of men to act in concert, is the cause of a revolution in politicks. A law of nature is the *cause* of a phenomenon in physicks, or, perhaps, the *cause* is another phenomenon which always goes before it. The *cause* of the universe has been by some thought to be necessity, by others chance, by others a powerful intelligent being.

I think it is a good division in Aristotle, that the same word may be applied to different things in three ways—univocally, analogically, and equivocally. Univocally, when the things are *species* of the same *genus;* analogically, when the things are related by some similitude or analogy; equivocally, when they have no relation but a common name. When a word is analogi-

---

* "Introduction to the Essay," &c. printed in part.—H.
† *Vide* "Essays," Introduction, p. xvi. sq.—H.
‡ *Ibidem,* p. xvii.—H.   ‖ *Ibidem,* p. xvii.—H.

cally applied to different things, as, I believe, the word cause is, there must be an original meaning from which the things related to it have borrowed the name; and it happens not unfrequently that the original notion loses the name by disuse, while the relatives monopolize it; as in the English words, *deliberate, suspense, project,* and many others.

The vulgar, in their notion even of the physical cause of a phænomenon, include some conception of efficiency or productive influence. So all the ancient philosophers did. *Itaque non sic causa intelligi debet, ut quod cuique antecedat, id ei causa sit, sed quod efficienter antecedit.*—CICERO.

Modern philosophers know that we have no ground to ascribe efficiency to natural causes, or even necessary connection with the effect. But we still call them causes, including nothing under the name but priority and constant conjunction. Thus the giving the name of causation to the relation of connected events in physicks, is, in modern philosophers, a kind of abuse of the name, because we know that the thing most essential to causation in its proper meaning—to wit, efficiency—is wanting. Yet this does not hinder our notion of a physical cause from being distinct and determinate, though, I think, it cannot be said to be of the same *genus* with an efficient cause or agent. Even the great Bacon seems to have thought that there is a *latens processus,* as he calls it, *by which* natural causes really produce their effects; and that, in the progress of philosophy, this might be discovered. But Newton, more enlightened on this point, has taught us to acquiesce in *a law of nature, according to which* the effect is produced, as the utmost that natural philosophy can reach, leaving what can be known of the agent or efficient cause to metaphysicks or natural theology. This I look upon as one of the great discoveries of Newton; for I know of none that went before him in it. It has newmodelled our notion of physical causes, but, at the same time, carried it farther from what I take to be the original notion of cause or agent.

If you have found, as you seem to say, (page xxii.,) that the different relations of things, which we call cause and effect, differ only as species of the same genus, and have found the general notion which comprehends them all under it—this, indeed, is more than I am able to do. Supposing it to be done, I should think that the genus, being an abstract notion, would be capable of a just definition. Yet I do not find fault with your declining to set out by giving the definition; for I conceive you may, with great propriety, pave the way to it by a preliminary induction.

XVI.

ON CAUSE—OBJECTS OF GEOMETRY—POWER
—AGENCY, &c.

[*No date.*]

MY DEAR SIR,—I must thank you, in the first place, for your attention to my interest in writing to Dr Rose what you informed me of in your answer to my last.

I received your three volumes* on Wednesday evening, with the letter and plan of the Essay. . . . .

Volume First.

In the induction made to prove that men have a notion of the relation of cause and effect, this case ought to be particularly in the view of the author, (as I take it to be the case that really exists)—to wit, that cause and effect, from the imperfection of language, signifie many different relations, and yet, by those who write and think distinctly, will be used without ambiguity; the things of which they are predicated explaining sufficiently what relation is meant. This is the case of many words that have various meanings really different, though, perhaps, somewhat similar or analogous. It is remarkably the case of prepositions. Yet such words as prepositions are used without ambiguity by those who think distinctly. How many relations are expressed by the preposition *of?*—and yet, when it is put between two words, we are never at a loss for its meaning. In Aristotle's days, a cause meant four things—to wit, the Efficient, the Form, the Matter, and the End. Yet, when it was used by a good writer, it was easy to see in which of these senses it was meant. With us the word cause has lost some of these four meanings, and has got others to supply their places, and, perhaps, has not, in one language, all the meanings which it has in another. Perhaps, therefore, it may be said, that all men have many notions of cause and effect, and some men more than others; the same observation may, I think, be applied to the words Power, Agent, and Activity.

To give you a hint of my notion of the word cause, I think it has one strict and philosophical meaning which is a single relation, and it has a lax and popular meaning which includes many relations. The popular meaning I think I can express by a definition. *Causa est id, quo posito ponitur*

---

* The MS. of the *Essay* itself. The Essay was probably considerably modified before publication; and I have been unable to attempt the task of discovering how far, and to what pages of the published book, the following remarks apply.—H.

Effectus, quo sublato tollitur. This, you will easily see, includes many relations, and, I believe, includes all that in any language are expressed by cause, though, in some languages some of the relations included under the definition may not be called causes, on account, perhaps, of their having some other word appropriated to signify such relations.

In the strict philosophical sense, I take a cause to be that which has the relation to the effect which I have to my voluntary and deliberate actions; for I take this notion of a cause to be derived from the power I feel in myself to produce certain effects. In this sense, we say that the Deity is the cause of the universe.

I think there is some ambiguity in your use of the words *The notion of a cause.* Through a considerable part of Vol. I. it means barely a conception of the meaning of the word *cause;* then suddenly it means some opinion or judgment about the word *cause,* or the thing meant by that word. The last must be the meaning when you speak of the notion of a cause being true or false, being condemned or justified. The bare conception of a cause, without any opinion about it, can neither be true nor false. It is true that notion often signifies opinion; but when, in a train of discourse, it has been put for simple conception, and then immediately for opinion, the reader is apt to overlook the change of signification, or to think that the author means to impute truth or falsehood to a bare conception, without opinion.

The same thing I observe when you speak of the notion of power, vol. II. p. 19.

. . . .

Page 40, &c.—What is said about the non-existence of the objects of geometry, I think, is rather too strongly expressed. I grant that they are things conceived without regard to their existence; but they are possible modifications of things which we dayly perceive by our senses. We perceive length, breadth, and thickness: these attributes do really exist. The objects of geometry are modifications of one or more of these, accurately conceived and defined.

Nor do I think it can be said, without great exceptions, that the notions of the objects of geometry are not common among mankind. The notions of a straight and a curve line, of an angle, of a plain surface, and others, are common; though, perhaps, in the minds of the vulgar, not so accurately defined as in those of geometers. The more complex geometrical conceptions of cycloids and other curves, are only artificial compositions of more simple notions which are common to the vulgar. Hence, a man of ordinary capacity finds no difficulty in understanding the definitions of Euclid. All the difficulty lies in forming the habit by which

the name, and an accurate conception of its meaning, are so associated, that the one readily suggests the other. To form this habit requires time, and in some persons much more than in others.

Page 68.—You may use freedom with Aristotle, because he won't feel it. But I would not have you laugh at the restorer of ancient metaphysicks* in publick while he is alive. Why hurt a man who is not hurting you?

Page 70.—I thought the *animal implume bipes* was Plato's definition, and I think I quoted it as his; but you may examine. I think it is Diog. Laertius that says so; but I am not sure, nor have I the book here.†

What you say of definitions in natural history, chemistry, and medicine, may perhaps be taken by some persons as a disapprobation of definitions in those sciences. Would it not be proper to guard against this misconstruction? I think them very useful to the present age, and that they may be still more useful to future ages, though you observe, very justly, that we cannot reason from them as we do from mathematical definitions. The most common words may flow with the flux of time, and have their meaning contracted, enlarged, or altered. Definition seems to be the only mean of fixing them to one meaning, or, at least, of shewing what was the meaning when that definition had authority.

Volume Second.

After what I have already said, you will not be surprized to find me one of those who think that the notions of Power and of Agency or Activity, have a share in the relation of Cause and Effect. I take all the three words to have a lax and popular meaning, in which they are nearly related; and a strict and philosophical meaning, in which also they have the same affinity.

In the strict sense, I agree with you that power and agency are attributes of mind onely; and I think that mind onely can be a cause in the strict sense. This power, indeed, may be where it is not exerted, and so may be without agency or causation; but there can be no agency or causation without power to act, and to produce the effect. As far as I can judge, to everything we call a cause we ascribe power to produce the effect. In intelligent causes, the power may be without being exerted; so I have power to run, when I sit still or walk. But in inanimate causes, we conceive no power but what is exerted; and, therefore, measure the power of the cause by the effect

---

* Lord Monboddo.—H.
† See Laertius, L. vi. Seg. 40. The definition is Plato's.—H.

which it actually produces. The power of an acid to dissolve iron is measured by what it actually dissolves.

We get the notion of active power, as well as of cause and effect, as I think, from what we feel in ourselves. We feel in ourselves a power to move our limbs, and to produce certain effects when we choose. Hence, we get the notion of power, agency, and causation, in the strict and philosophical sense ; and this I take to be our first notion of these three things.

If this be so, it is a curious problem in human nature, how, in the progress of life, we come by the lax notion of power, agency, cause, and effect, and to ascribe them to things that have no will nor intelligence. I am apt to think, with the Abbé Raynal, " that savages," (I add children as in the same predicament,) " wherever they see motion which they cannot account for, there they suppose a soul." Hence they ascribe active power and causation to sun, moon, and stars, rivers, fountains, sea, air, and earth ; these are 'conceived to be causes in the strict sense. In this period of society, language is formed, its fundamental rules and forms established. Active verbs are applied onely to things that are believed to have power and activity in the proper sense. Every part of nature which moves, without our seeing any external cause of its motion, is conceived to be a cause in the strict sense, and, therefore, is called so. At length, the more acute and speculative few discover that some of those things which the vulgar believe to be animated like themselves, are inanimate, and have neither will nor understanding. These discoveries grow and spread slowly in a course of ages. In this slow progress, what use must the wise men make of their discoveries ? Will they affirm that the sun does not shine nor give heat, that the sea never rages, nor do the winds blow, nor the earth bring forth grass and corn ? If any bold spirit should maintain such paradoxes, he would probably repent his temerity. The wiser part will speak the common language, and suit it to their new notions as well as they can ; just as philosophers say with the vulgar, that the sun rises and sets, and the moon changes. The philosopher must put a meaning upon vulgar language that suits his peculiar tenets as well as he can. And, even if all men should become philosophers, their language would still retain strong marks of the opinions that prevailed when it was first made. If we allow that active verbs were made to express action, it seems to be a necessary consequence, that all the languages we know were made by men who believed almost every part of nature to be active, and to have inherent power.

Volume Third.

The philological discussion is new to me ; and it would require more time in my slow way to make up my mind about it, than you allow me. But the general principle—that every distinction which is found in the structure of a common language, is a real distinction, and is perceivable by the common sense of mankind—this I hold for certain, and have made frequent use of it. I wish it were more used than it has been ; for I believe the whole system of metaphysicks, or the far greater part, may be brought out of it ; and, next to accurate reflexion upon the operations of our own minds, I know nothing that can give so much light to the human faculties as a due consideration of the structure of language.

From this principle, you prove to my satisfaction that there is a real distinction between the relation which a living agent has to his action, and the relation between an inanimate and the effect of which it is the cause, mean, or instrument.

But I know no language in which the word cause is confined to inanimate things, though, perhaps, it may be more frequently applied to them than to things that have life and intelligence.

If I were convinced that it cannot be said, in a plain, literal sense, that I am the cause of my own actions, or that the Deity is the cause of the universe—if I were convinced that my actions, or the production of the universe, are not effects, or that there must be a cause of these effects distinct from the agent, I should in this case agree to your reasoning.

The rule of Latin syntax from which you reason, seems, indeed, to suppose that all causes are inanimate things, like means and instruments ; but I desiderate better authority. I am not sure but power and agency are as often ascribed to inanimate things as causation. Thus we speak of the powers of gravity, magnetism, mechanical powers, and a hundred more. Yet there is a kind of power and agency which you acknowledge to belong only to mind.

Your system, if I comprehend it, (which, indeed, I am dubious about,) seems to go upon the supposition that power and agency belong onely to mind. and that in language causation never belongs to mind. If this be so, you and I may, after all, differ only about the meaning of words. What you call an agent, and a being that has power, that I call a cause with regard to every exertion of his power.

That which alone you call a cause, I think is no cause at all in the strict sense of the word ; but I acknowledge it is so in the lax and popular sense.   .   .   .

In these remarks I thought friendship obliged me to lay aside all regard to friendship, and even to indulge a spirit of severity that seems opposite to it. I hope you will make allowance for this. For, in reality, I have such an opinion of your judgment and taste, that I cannot help suspecting my own where they differ.

XVII.

AN AMBIGUITY OF HUME—MEANINGS OF WILL AND VOLITION—POWER.

Motive—Sect 1.

27. [Page 21, published work.]—It does not appear to me, that the long passage quoted from Mr Hume's reconciling project, is so full of ambiguous expressions and hypothetical doctrine, as it is said to be ; though I think it is very clearly shewn to be full of weak reasoning. I think he does not confound a *constant conjunction* with a *necessary connection,* but plainly distinguishes them ; affirming, that the first is all the relation which, upon accurate reflection, we are able to perceive between *cause and effect ;* but that mankind, by some prejudice, are led to think that cause and effect have moreover a necessary connection; when at the same time they acknowledge onely a constant conjunction between motive and action ; so far I see no obscurity or ambiguity. The words *constant conjunction* and *necessary connection,* I think, are the best that can be used to express the meaning of each, and the difference between them. At the same time, to suppose, without assigning any reason for the supposition, that the constant conjunction of *cause* and *effect* leads men to believe a necessary connection between them, but that the constant conjunction between *motive* and *action* has no such effect, appears to me very weak and unphilosophical ; and this account of the phenomenon of men's putting a difference between the relation of motive and action, and the relation of cause and effect, does not appear to me to deserve the epithet you give it, of *very ingenious.*
The last part of the quotation, beginning with—" *Let any one define a cause without comprehending,*"&c.,* I think has a distinct

meaning ; but that meaning is so impertinent to his purpose, and so contrary to his principles, that I cannot help thinking that he meant to say the very contrary of what he says ; and that the word *without* has slipt into the sentence by an oversight of the author or printer. For, does not he himself define a cause without comprehending, as a part of the definition, a necessary connection between the cause and the effect ? Does he not maintain that we have no idea of necessary connection ? He certainly meant to say, that he would give up the whole controversy, if any one could shew that we have such an idea, and not to say that he would give up the controversy, if any one could give a definition of cause without comprehending that idea. Were I to comment upon this passage in the Bentleian style, I would say dele *without, meo periculo.* After all, how he should think that the bulk of mankind have, without reason, joyned the idea of necessary connection to that of constant conjunction, in the relation of cause and effect, when mankind have no such idea, I cannot account for.

Of the Notion of Instrument.

. . . .

66, &c.—I am not pleased with the three different meanings you put upon the word *volition,* nor do I think it ambiguous. *Will* is indeed an ambiguous word, being sometimes put for the faculty of willing ; sometimes for the act of that faculty, besides other.meanings. But volition always signifies the act of willing, and nothing else. Willingness, I think, is opposed to unwillingness or aversion. A man is willing to do what he has no aversion to do, or what he has some desire to do, though perhaps he has not the opportunity ; and I think this is never called volition.
Choice or preference, in the proper sense, is an act of the understanding ; but sometimes it is improperly put for volition, or the determination of the will in things where there is no judgment or preference ; thus, a man who owes me a shilling, lays down three or four equally good, and bids me take which I choose. I take one without any judgment or belief that there is any ground of preference—this is merely an act of will that is a volition.
An effort greater or less, I think, always accompanies volition, but is not called volition. There may be a determination of will to do something to-morrow or next week. This, though it be properly an act

---

* The whole sentence is as follows:—It is from Hume's " Inquiry concerning the Human Understanding," sect. viii. part l. *prope finem.* " Let any one *define* a cause, without comprehending, as a part of the definition, a *necessary connection* with its effect ; and let him shew distinctly the origin of the idea, expressed by the definition, and I shall readily give up the whole controversy."—Dr Reid, in his remarks on this passage, would be right, did Hume mean by *necessary connection,* a *really* necessary connection, and not merely a feeling of necessity *in us,* and that not *a priori,* but *a po teriori*—not the

offspring of knowledge, but of blind habit. It is he e the part of the sceptic, not to disprove the subjective phenomenon of necessity, but to shew that it is illegitimate and objectively barren.—H.

of will, is not called volition, because it has a proper name of its own—we call it a resolution or purpose; and here the effort is suspended till the purpose is to be executed.

I apprehend that, in dreaming, the effort accompanies volition, as well as when we are awake; but in most persons the effort in dreaming produces little or no motion in the body, as is the case in palsy. When a hound dreams, we see a feeble attempt to move his limbs and to bark, as if he had the palsy. And a man dreaming that he cries desperately for help, is often heard to make a feeble attempt to cry.

Power.

16, &c.—I humbly think that my power to ride or to walk, and the king's power to call or to dissolve a parliament, are different kinds, or rather different meanings of the word power. In the former meaning, everything depending upon my will is in my power, and consequently my will itself; for, if I had not power to will, I could have no power to do what depends upon my will. In the second meaning, power signifies a right by the law or by the constitution, according to that maxim of law, *Nihil possum quod jure non possum.*

In another law sense, we say—It is part of the king's prerogative that he can do no wrong. The meaning of this is not that he has no legal right to do wrong, for this may be said of the meanest of his subjects; but it means that he cannot be accused or tried for any wrong before any criminal judicature. It is his prerogative, that he cannot be called to account for any wrong.

71, &c.—The doctrine delivered from page 71 to 76, I suspect very much not to be just. If it be true, it is surely important, and would make many difficulties instantly to vanish, which the bulk of philosophers have laboured in vain to resolve, and the wiser part have reckoned to be insolvable. It is so new and so contrary to all that philosophers have taught and believed since the days of Aristotle, that it ought to be proposed and supported with great modesty; but, indeed, I cannot yet assent to it.

I have, for instance, the power of moving my hand; all the activity I am conscious of exerting, is volition and effort to move the hand; the motion must begin somewhere. Suppose it begins at the nerves, and that its being continued till the hand be moved, is all mechanism. The first motion, however, cannot be mechanism. It follows immediately upon my volition and effort.

Nor do I know how my volition and effort to move my hand, produces a certain motion in the nerves. I am conscious that in this there is something which I do not comprehend, though I believe He that made me comprehends it perfectly. If I be struck with a palsy, that volition and effort which before moved my hand, is now unable to do it. Is this owing to an inability to produce the first motion? or is it owing to some derangement of the machine of the body? I know not. Nay, I am uncertain whether I be truly and properly the agent in the first motion; for I can suppose, that, whenever I will to move my hand, the Deity, or some other agent, produces the first motion in my body—which was the opinion of Malebranche. This hypothesis agrees with all that I am conscious of in the matter. I am like a child turning the handle of a hand organ —the turning of the handle answers to my volition and effort. The music immediately follows; but how it follows, the child knows not. Were two or three ingenious children to speculate upon the subject, who had never seen nor heard of such a machine before, perhaps one who had seen strange effects of mechanism, might conjecture that the handle, by means of machinery, produced the music: another, like Malebranche, might conjecture that a musician, concealed in the machine, always played when the handle was turned.

We know as little how our intellectual operations are performed as how we move our own body. I remember many things past; but how I remember them I know not. Some have attempted to account for memory by a repository of ideas, or by traces left in the brain of the ideas we had before. Such accounts would appear ridiculous at first sight, if we knew how the operation of memory is performed. But, as we are totally ignorant how we remember, such weak hypotheses have been embraced by sensible men.

In these, and in innumerable cases that might be mentioned, it seems to me to be one thing to know that such a thing is, and another to know how it is.

Perhaps you may have been led into the mistake, if it be a mistake, by what you say about definition in the note, p. 76. An operation, or any other thing that is perfectly simple, cannot be defined—this is true. Nor can it be explained by words to a man who had not the conception of it before; for words can give us no new simple conceptions, but such only as we had before, and had annexed to such words.

Thus, if a man born blind asks me what a scarlet colour is, the question, I think, is not impertinent, or nugatory, or absurd; but I can only answer him, that, though I know perfectly what a scarlet colour is, it is impossible to give him a distinct conception of it unless he saw. But, if he asks me how my volition and effort moves my hand, I not onely cannot satisfy him, but am conscious that I am ignorant myself. We both know that there is a constant conjunction between the volition and the motion, when I am in health, but how they are connected I know not, but should think myself much wiser than I am, if I did know. For anything I know, some other being may move my hand as often as I will to move it. The volition, I am conscious, is my act; but I am not conscious that the motion is so. I onely learn from experience that it always follows the volition, when I am in sound health.

Activity.—Sect. 1.

P. 24, &c.—The distinction between the two kinds of active verbs here marked, appears no less clearly when they are used in the passive voice. *To be known, to be believed*, &c., imply nothing done to the things known or believed. But *to be wounded, to be healed*, implies something done to the wounded or healed. A scholastick philosopher would say that *to be wounded*, belongs to the category of passion; but *to be known*. belongs to none of the categories—being only an *external denomination*. Indeed, however grammarians might confound these two kinds of active verbs, the scholastick philosophers very properly distinguished the acts expressed by them. They called the acts expressed by the first kind *immanent acts*, and those expressed by the second kind, *transitive acts*. Immanent acts of mind are such as produce no change in the object. Such are all acts of understanding, and even some that may be called voluntary—such as attention, deliberation, purpose.

Activity—Sect. 2.

P. 43.—If my memory does not deceive me, Charlevoix, in his history of Canada, says, that, in the Huron language, or in some language of that country, there is but one word for both the sexes of the human species, which word has two genders, not a masculine and feminine—for there is no such distinction of genders in the language—but a a noble and an ignoble gender: the ignoble gender signifies not a woman, though we improperly translate it so. It signifies a coward, or a good-for-nothing creature of either sex. A woman of distinguished talents that create respect, is always of the noble gender. I know not whether it be owing to something of this kind in the Gaelic language, that a Highlander, who has got onely a little broken English, modestly

takes the feminine gender to himself, and, in place of saying *I did so*, says, *her own self did so*. . . . .
As to the mathematical reasoning on *motive*, Section 2, to prove that the relation of motive and agent is very different from that of a physical cause to its effect, I think it just and conclusive; and that it is a good argument *ad hominem*, against the scheme of Necessity held by Hume, Priestley, and other modern advocates for Necessity, who plainly make these two relations the same. Mr Hume holds it for a maxim no less applicable to intelligent beings and their actions, than to physical causes and their effects, that the cause is to be measured by the effect. And from this maxim he infers, or makes an Epicurean to infer, that we have reason to ascribe to the Deity just as much of wisdom, power, and goodness, as appears in the constitution of things, and no more.

The reasoning in the papers on activity, to shew that the relation between an agent and his action is, in the structure of language, distinguished from the relation between a cause and its effect, is, I think, perfectly just when cause is taken in a certain sense; but I am not so clear that the word *cause* is never, except metaphorically or figuratively, taken in any other sense. You will see my sentiments about that word in two chapters of my "Essay on the Liberty of Moral Agents," now in your hands. If I had seen your papers before I wrote those two chapters, perhaps I would have been more explicit. However, they will save you and me the trouble of repeating here what is there said.

I think, after all, the difference between you and me is merely about the use of a word; and that it amounts to this—whether the word *cause*, and the corresponding words in other languages, has, or has not, from the beginning, been used to express, without a figure, a being that produces the effect by his will and power.

I see not how mankind could ever have acquired the conception of a cause, or of any relation, beyond a mere conjunction in time and place between it and its effect, if they were not conscious of active exertions in themselves, by which effects are produced. This seems to me to be the origin of the idea or conception of production.

In the grammar rule, *causa, modus et instrumentum*, &c., the word cause is taken in a limited sense, which is explained by the words conjoyned with it. Nor do I see that any part of the rule would be lost if the word *causa* had been altogether left out. Is not everything which you would call a cause a mean or an instrument? May not everything to which the rule applies be called a mean or an instrument? But surely many things are called *causes* that are

G

neither means nor instruments, and to which the rule does not apply.

You know that Aristotle, who surely understood Greek, makes four kinds of causes—the efficient, the matter, the form, and the end. I think the grammar rule applies to none of these; for they are not in Latin expressed by an oblative without a preposition.

That nothing can happen without a cause, is a maxim found in Plato, in Cicero, and, I believe, never brought into doubt till the time of D. Hume. If this be not understood of an efficient cause, it is not true of any other kind of cause; nor can any reason be given why it should have been universally received as an axiom. All other causes suppose an efficient cause ; but it supposes no other ; and, therefore, in every enumeration of causes, it is made the first ; and the word cause, without any addition, is put to signify an efficient cause ; as in that of Cicero, (which I quote only from memory,) "*Itaque non est causa quod cuique antecedit, sed quod cuique efficienter antecedit.*"

XVIII.

ON THE TERMS, PHILOSOPHICAL NECESSITY, AND NECESSARIAN—ON DETERMINATION BY STRONGEST MOTIVE—REPROACH OF MALA FIDES—CONSCIOUSNESS OF LIBERTY —ARGUMENTUM PIGRUM, &c.—IN A PAPER ENTITLED—

Remarks. [*]

PAGE 2.—"*Philosophical Necessity.*"— This, I think, is an epithet given to the doctrine of Necessity by Dr Priestley only ; and I do not see that he deserves to be followed in it. The vulgar have, from the beginning of the world, had the conception of it as well as philosophers. Whether they ground it upon the influence of the stars, or the decrees of fate, or of the gods, or upon the influence of motives, it is necessity still. I have often found the illiterate vulgar have recourse to it to exculpate their own faults, or those of their friends, when no other excuse could be found. It lurks in their minds as a last shift to alleviate the pangs of guilt, or to soften their indignation against those whom they love.[†] But it is not admitted on other occasions. Dr Priestley by this epithet no doubt wished it to pass for a profound discovery of philosophy ; but

I know no claim it has to be called philosophical.

In other places, you use another of Dr Priestley's words—*the Necessarians.* I see no reason for adding this word to our language, when *Fatalists* might do as well. Sometimes I think you call them the *Philosophers* indefinitely. I don't like this neither. Fatalism was never so general among philosophers, nor so peculiar to them, as to justify it.

.   .   .   .   .

P. 27.—In my "Essay on Liberty" I have censured the defenders of Necessity for grounding one of their chief arguments upon this as a self-evident axiom, *That the strongest motive always determines the agent,* while no one of them, as far as I know, has offered to explain what is meant by the *strongest* motive, or given any test by which we may know which of two contrary motives is the strongest ; without which the axiom is an identical proposition, or has no meaning at all. I have offered two tests of the strength of motives—according as they operate upon the will immediately, or upon the understanding—and endeavoured to shew that the maxim is not true according to either.

.   .   .   .   .

P. 72.—The want of sincerity or *bona fides,* in a large body of men, respected and respectable, is a very tender place, and cannot be touched with too much delicacy. Though you were sure of being able to demonstrate it, I am afraid it may be taken as an insult, which even demonstration cannot justify. Your not making the conclusion general, for want of a sufficiently extensive information, will not satisfy, because it seems to extend the conclusion as far as your observation has extended, and because the reasons on which you ground your conclusion seem to extend it to all fatalists who can draw a conclusion from premises. If David Hume, or any other person, has charged those who profess to believe men to be free agents with insincerity, I think he did wrong, and that I should do wrong in following the example.

But, setting apart the consideration of *bienseance,* I doubt of the truth of your conclusion. If human reason were perfect, I think you would be better founded ; but we are such imperfect creatures, that I fear we are not exempted from the possibility of swallowing contradictions. Could you not prove with equal strength that all bad men are infidels ? Yet I believe this not to be true.

In page 76, you speak of our having a consciousness of independent activity. I think this cannot be said with strict propriety. It is only the operations of our own mind that we are conscious of. Activity is not an operation of mind ; it is a

---

[*] On the "Essay" Some pages correspond to the published work, others do not. The "Essay" was, therefore, probably printed but in proof.—H.

[†] Thus Agamemnon :—'Εγὼ δ' οὐκ αἴτιός εἰμι, Ἀλλὰ Ζεὺς καὶ Μοῖρα καὶ ἠεροφοῖτις Ἐριννύς.—H.

power to act. We are conscious of our volitions, but not of the cause of them.

I think, indeed, that we have an early and a natural conviction that we have power to will this or that; that this conviction precedes the exercise of reasoning ; that it is implyed in all our deliberations, purposes, promises, and voluntary actions: and I have used this as an argument for liberty. But I think this conviction is not properly called consciousness.

I truly think that a fatalist who acted agreeably to his belief, would sit still, like a passenger in a ship, and suffer himself to be carried on by the tide of fate ; and that, when he deliberates, resolves, promises, or chuses, he acts inconsistently with his belief. But such inconsistencies, I fear, are to be found in life ; and, if men be ever convinced of them, it must be by soothing words and soft arguments, which *ludunt circum præcordia ;* for the force of prejudice, joyned with that of provocation, will shut the door against all conviction.

I humbly think, therefore, that it will be prudent and becoming to express less confidence in your mathematical reasonings, though I really believe them to be just upon the hypothesis you combat. Fatalists will think that, when you put the issue of the controversy solely upon the experiments, you treat them like children. No fatalist will contend with you upon that footing, nor take it well to be challenged to do so ; and I think you have a good plea with any man who disputes the strength of your mathematical reasoning, to prove that the relation between motives and actions is altogether of a different kind, and subject to different laws from that between physical causes and their effects.

XIX.

ON VULGAR NOTION OF NECESSARY CONNECTION—INADVERTENCY OF HUME—REID'S REPUTATION OF IDEAS—REID'S USE OF THE WORD CAUSE—INERTIA, PASSIVITY, STATE, OF MIND—AND SUNDRY OBSERVATIONS ON THE NECESSITARIAN CONTROVERSY—IN A PAPER ENTITLED

Remarks on the Essay.

Page 23.—I am apt to think even the vulgar have the notion of necessary connection, and that they perceive it in arithmetical and mathematical axioms, though they do not speculate about it ; nor do they perceive it between physical causes and their effects. Does not every man of common sense perceive the ridiculousness of

that complaint to the gods, which one of the heroes of the "Dunciad" makes—

——" And am I now fourscore ?
Ah! why, ye gods, should two and two make four ?"

But is it not remarkable that Mr Hume, after taking so much pains to prove that we have no idea of necessary connection, should impute to the bulk of mankind the opinion of a necessary connection between physical causes and their effects ? Can they have this opinion without an idea of necessary connection ?

33.—The passage here quoted from Mr Hume is, indeed, so extraordinary, that I suspect an error in printing, and that the word *without* has been put in against his intention, though I find it in my copy of his essays, as well as in your quotation. For how could a man who denies that we have any idea of necessary connection, defy any one to define a cause without comprehending necessary connection ? He might, consistently with himself, have defied any one to define a cause, comprehending in the definition necessary connection ; and at the same time to shew distinctly the origin of the idea expressed by the definition. How could he pledge himself to give up the controversy on the condition of getting such a definition, when, as you observe, he had given two such definitions himself ? If there be no error of the press, we must say, *Aliquando bonus dormitat Humius.* [*]

34 and 35.—You observe justly and pertinently, that "the intelligible and consistent use of a word shews that the speaker had some thought, notion, or idea, corresponding to it." Idea is here put for the meaning of a word, which can neither be true nor false, because it implies neither affirmation nor negation. But in the same paragraph it is supposed that this idea may be improper, groundless, and to be given up. This can onely be applied to *idea*, taken in another sense—to wit, when it implies some affirmation or negation. I know this ambiguity may be found in Locke and Hume ; but I think it ought to be avoided.

36.—" Or the philosophical doctrine of ideas." If, an hundred years after this, the philosophical doctrine of ideas be as little regarded as the Vortices of Des Cartes are at this day, they may then be coupled in the manner you here do. But at present, though I am proud of your opinion, that that doctrine must be given up, I think it is expressed in a way too assuming with regard to the publick.

40.—I know of no philosopher who makes the word *cause* extend solely to the giving of existence.

44. Dr Reid agrees with the author of the Essay, that the word *cause* ought to be

---

* As published.—H.

* See note at page 79.—H.

G 2

used in the most common sense.* But one sense may be the most common in one science, and another in others. He thinks that, in theology and in metaphysicks, the most common sense is that of agent or efficient cause; and for this he thinks he has the authority of Des Cartes, Locke, Dr Clarke, Bishop Butler, and many others. In physics, and in all its branches, medicine, chymistry, agriculture, the mechanical arts, &c., he thinks the most common meaning of *cause* is Hume's notion of it—to wit, something which goes before the effect, and is conjoyned with it in the course of nature. As this notion is vague and popular, philosophers, when they would speak more precisely of a cause in physicks, mean by it some law of nature, of which the phænomenon called the effect is a necessary consequence. Therefore, in writings of the former kind, he would think himself warranted to use the word cause, without addition in the first of these senses; and, if he had occasion to use it in the last sense, he would call it *physical* cause. In writings of the last kind, he thinks it may, with propriety, be used without addition in the last sense; and if, in such writings, it be used in the first sense, he would have it called the *efficient* cause. But the additions of *efficient* and *physical*, he does [not] conceive as denoting two *species* of the same *genus*,

but as distinguishing two different meanings of the same ambiguous word.

You have good reason to dispute the maxim about causes, as laid down by Mr Hume, in whatever sense he takes the word *cause*. It is a maxim in natural theology, universally admitted, that everything that *begins* to exist must have a cause, meaning an efficient cause; and from this maxim we easily deduce the existance of a Being who neither had a cause nor a beginning of existance, but exists necessarily. Physicks, in all its branches, is conversant about the phenomena of nature, and their physical causes; and I think it may be admitted as a maxim that every phenomenon of nature has a physical cause. But the actions of men, or of other rational beings, are not phenomena of nature, nor do they come within the sphere of physicks. As little is a beginning of existance a phenomenon of nature.

.   .   .   .

Page 154.—" *Expressly excluding from the meaning of the phrase,*" &c., to the end of the paragraph.* My remark upon this paragraph I think more important than any other I have made on the Essay; and, therefore, I beg your attention to it.

Inertia of mind seems to be a very proper name for a quality which, upon every system of Necessity, must belong to the mind. It is likewise very proper to explain the meaning of that term when applied to the mind.

But when you " expressly exclude from the meaning of the phrase, the circumstance of mind remaining or persevering in any state into which it once gets," I wish you to consider very seriously whether this concession be not more generous than just; and, if it be not just, whether by making it, you

---

* This is in reference to what Dr Gregory says of the meaning attached by Reid himself to the word cause. The passage is as follows:—" As little could he (Hume) have in view the meaning expressed in the third query, in which meaning Dr Reid (I own I think with too little regard to the common use and application of the word cause) hath employed it in arguing this question; (' Essays on the Active Powers,' *passim*;) as where he says, after admitting that everything must have a cause, that, in the case of voluntary actions, it is not the motive, but the person, that is the cause of them. This meaning of the term cause—to wit, a being having power (and optional or discretionary power) to produce or not to produce a certain change—is not only evidently different from Mr Hume's, but completely repugnant to his whole system. We may therefore set it aside too."

It is necessary to quote the queries to which reference is made in the preceding passage. They are these:—" It might reasonably be asked—(1°) Is the word *cause* employed in that general fourfold sense mentioned by Aristotle, and applied equally to the essence or form of a being, to the matter of it, to the efficient or agent, and to the motive, or purpose, or final cause? Or (2°) is it employed in its more common and limited acceptation, as generally used in physics, and, indeed, in popular discourse, as when we say, ' Heat is the cause of expansion,' excluding all the other meanings of it, and particularly that of the agent? Or (3·) is it employed in that more limited sense in which it hath been defined and used by several philosophers, to denote exclusively the agent, in contradistinction to the physical cause? Or (4ᵇ) is it used to express the vague notion insinuated by Aristotle's τὸ τί ἦν εἶν, comprehending all these already mentioned, and many more? For example—what the parts are to the whole, what a right angle in a triangle is to the proportion between the squares of the sides of it, what the absence of a pilot is to a shipwreck, what the seed is to a plant, what a father is to his son, what the removal of an opposing cause is to any event or effect, &c. &c."—H.

* The whole passage referred to is as follows:— " I have occasion often to consider the supposed want of any such attribute of mind [viz., Power] as this is the fundamental principle of the doctrine of necessity. And, for the sake of brevity, and the opposition to what has been often termed *Activity* and *Force of Mind*, I call it the *Inertia of Mind*; limiting, however, the signification of the phrase, to denote merely the incapacity of acting optionally or discretionally without motives, or in opposition to all motives, or in any other way but just according to the motives applied, and expressly excluding from the meaning of the phrase the circumstance of *mind* remaining or persevering in any state into which it once gets, as *body* does in a state, either of rest or of uniform progressive rectilinear motion, into which it is once put. Such permanency of state does not appear to be any part of the constitution of the human mind, with respect to any of its operations. Sensation of every kind—memory, imagination, judgment, emotion, or passion, volition, and involuntary effort—all appear to be transient conditions, or attributes of mind; which, of their own nature, independently of any cause applied, pass away or come to an end. And this I conceive to be one of the most general circumstances of distinction between mere sta e or condition, which is predicable of mind as well as body, (as, for example, madness, idiotism, vivacity, dulness, peculiar genius, wisdom knowledge, virtue, vice,) and those things which are termed acts or operations of mind or though ."—H.

do not much weaken the force of a great part of your subsequent reasoning.

The justice of the concession is not evident to me. To be *merely passive*, and to *remain in the state into which it is put*, seem to signify the same thing; as, on the other hand, to be *active*, and to *have power to change its own state*, have the same meaning. If the mind be passive onely, all its changes are phenomena of nature, and therefore belong to the science of physicks, and require a physical cause, no less than does the change of direction or of velocity in a moving body.

Of all things that belong to the mind, its acts and operations are the onely things which have any analogy to motion in a body. The same analogy there is between the ceasing of any act or operation and the ceasing of motion. If, therefore, from mere inactivity, the body, once put in the state of motion, continues or perseveres in that state, why should not a mind, which is equally inactive, being once put in the state of action or operation, continue in that state? You say, "Such permanency of state does not appear to be the constitution of the mind in any of its operations." I grant this. But the question is not, "What really is its constitution?" but "What would be its constitution if it were as inert and inactive as body is?" To admit this want of permanency is to admit that the mind is active in some degree, which is contrary to the supposition.

The reason why madness, idiotism, &c., are called states of mind, while its acts and operations are not,* is because mankind have always conceived the mind to be passive in the former and active in the later. But on the system of Necessity, this distinction has no place. Both are equally states, onely the first are not so frequently changed as the last.

If the concession be just and consistent with necessity, it must be granted, whatever be its consequences; but I apprehend the consequences will deeply affect your essay. For, first, it contradicts what you have said, page 336, and, perhaps, in several other places, that, "according to Mr Hume's doctrine, a living person, in relation to motives and actions, is *precisely* in the situation of an inanimate body in relation to projection and gravity." If an inanimate body had not the quality of persevering in its state of motion, the effect of projection and gravity upon it would be very different from what it is with that quality.

Secondly, by this concession, your reasoning from the laws of motion and their corollaries, is much weakened; for those laws

* The term *State* has, more especially of late years, and principally by Necessitarian philosophers, been applied to all modifications of mind indifferently.—H.

and corollaries are founded on the supposition that bodies persevere in the state of motion as well as of rest; and, therefore, are not properly applied to a being which has not that quality. Indeed, perseverance in its state is so essential to inertia, that it will be thought unjustifiable to apply that name to what you acknowledge does not persevere in its state. And you will, perhaps, be charged with giving an invidious epithet to the mind, which, by your own acknowledgment, is not due, and then reasoning from that epithet as if it were due.

226.—In the style of physicks, to carry a letter in *the direction* A B, and to carry a letter from A to the point B, are different things. Any line parallel to A B, is said to be in the direction A B, though it cannot lead to the point B.

The case, therefore, here put, is, that the porter is offered a guinea a-mile to carry a letter from A to the point B, and half-a-guinea a-mile to carry a letter, at the same time, from A to the point C. And both motives must necessarely operate according to their strength. I truely think it impossible to say how the porter would act upon these suppositions. He would be in an inextricable puzzle between contrary actions and contrary wills.

One should think that the two motives mentioned, would conjoyn their force in the diagonal. But, by going in the diagonal, he loses both the guineas and the half-guineas; this is implied in the offer, and is a motive not to go in the diagonal, as strong as the two motives for going in it. By the force of the two motives, he must *will* to go in the diagonal; by the force of the third, he must *will* not to go in the diagonal.

You pretend to demonstrate that he must go in the diagonal willingly. I think it may be demonstrated, with equal force, that he must will not to go in the diagonal. I perceive no error in either demonstration; and, if both demonstrations be good, what must be the conclusion? The conclusion must be, that the supposition on which both demonstrations are grounded must be false— I mean the supposition that motives are the physical causes of actions; for it is possible, and often happens, that, from a false supposition, two contradictory conclusions may be drawn; but, from a true supposition, it is impossible.

I think it were better to omit the case stated toward the end of this page,* because I think it hardly possible to conceive two motives, which, being conjoyned, shall have an analogy to a projectile and centripetal force conjoyned; and your concession, that

* This has been done.—H.

the effect of a motive is not permanent, adds to the difficulty. A projectile force requires a cause to begin it, but it requires no continuance of the cause—it continues by the inertia of matter. A centripetal force is the effect of a cause acting constantly; and the effect of that cause must bear some proportion to the time it acts. Diminish the time, *in infinitum*, and the effect of a centripetal force is diminished, *in infinitum*; so that, in any one instant of time, it bears no proportion to a projectile force ; and, what makes the effect of a centripetal, in a given time, to be capable of comparison with a projectile force, is, that the effects of the centripetal force, during every instant of the time, are accumulated by the inertia of matter, and all, as it were, brought into one sum. Now, how can you conceive two motives, which have a difference and a relation to each other, corresponding to the difference and the relation of these two kinds of force ? Both kinds of force suppose the permanency of motion once acquired, and, I think, cannot be distinctly conceived, or their effects ascertained, without that supposition.

337.—Upon the scheme of Necessity, considered in this section, it must be maintained, that there is some unknown cause or causes of human actions, besides motives, which sometimes oppose motives with greater force, sometimes produce actions without motives ; and, as there are no causes but physical causes, all actions must be necessary, whether produced by motives or by other physical causes. This scheme of Necessity appears, indeed, to me more tenable than that of Hume and Priestley ; and I wonder that Mr Hume, who thought that he had proved, beyond doubt, that we have no conception of any cause but a physical cause, did not rest the doctrine of Necessity upon that principle solely. Unknown causes would have afforded him a retreat in all attacks upon his system. That motives are the sole causes of action, is onely an outwork in the system of Necessity, and may be given up, while it is maintained that every action must have a physical cause ; for physical causes of all human actions, whether they be known or unknown, are equally inconsistent with liberty.

342.—A physical cause, from its nature, must be constant in its effects, when it exists, and is applied to its proper object. But of unknown causes, the existence and the application may depend upon a concurrence of accidents, which is not subject to calculation, or even to rational conjecture. So that, I apprehend, the existance of such causes can never be demonstrated to be contrary to matter of fact. Unknown causes, like occult qualities, suit every occasion, and can never be contradicted by phænomena ; for,

as we cannot, *a priori*, determine what shall be the effects of causes absolutely unknown ; so it is impossible to prove, of any effect whatsoever, that it cannot be produced by some unknown physical cause or causes.

The defects of this system of Necessity, I think, are these two :—first, it is a mere arbitrary hypothesis, brought to prop a weak side in the hypothesis of Necessity ; and, secondly, it is grounded on the supposition that every event must have a physical cause, a supposition which demonstrably terminates in an infinite series of physical causes, every one of which is the effect of a physical cause.

If the doctrine opposed in this 16th section be as it is expressed, page 338—that, though the connection of motive and action is but occasional, the volitions and actions of men are absolutely produced by motives as physical causes—this doctrine I take to be a contradiction in terms, and unworthy of confutation. It maintains that men are absolutely determined by motives, and yet onely occasionally determined by motives— which, if I understand it right, is a contradiction.

351. The case supposed in this page seems perfectly similar to that of page 226 ; the same reasoning is applied to both   Should not the conclusion be the same in both ?

431.—Is there not some inaccuracy in the reasoning in this and the next page ? I take X and Y to represent equal motives to action, and V a motive to inaction, which equally opposes both. If this be so, the motives to the opposite action stand thus : X—V + Z on one side, and Y—V on the other. Then there will be a preponderancy on the side of X as long as X and its equal Y is greater than V ; and if X be withdrawn on one side, and Y on the other, we shall have —V + Z opposed to —V. In this case, if Z be equal to V, the motives to act and not to act on the side of Z will be equal ; if Z be less than V, the strongest motive will be for inaction ; and if Z be greater than V, there will be a preponderating motive to act on the side of Z.

As to the style in general, the only fault I find is, that it abounds too much in long and complex sentences, which have so many clauses, and so much meaning, that it is difficult to carry it all from the beginning to the end of the sentence. The reader's understanding should have gentle exercise, but not hard labour, to comprehend the author's meaning. I dislike a style that is cut down into what the ancients called commas of a line or half a line. This, like water falling drop by drop, disposes one to sleep. But I think you rather go into the contrary extreme. Your friend, Lord Bacon, says, " *A fluent and luxuriant speech becomes youth well, but not age.*" I believe he had in his view a rhetorical speech, and not the *lene et temperatum dicendi genus*, which, in Cicero's judgment, best suits philosophy.

XX.

ON A NOVEL USE OF THE WORD MOTIVE—CAUSALITY OF MOTIVES, &c.

1793.

DEAR SIR —I received Mr Crombie's Essay* on Friday the 11th, at night, and have read it twice, though interrupted by the removal of my family to the college. If this be Mr Crombie's first essay in controversy, I think he shews no mean talent, and may in time become an able champion.

He has done me particular honour in directing so great a part of the book against me ; yet, though I read the work without prejudice, my opinion is not changed in any point of the controversy.

He has strengthened his defensive armour by extending the meaning of the word *motive*. I understood a motive, when applied to a human being, to be that for the sake of which† he acts, and, therefore, that what he never was conscious of, can no more be a motive to determine his will, than it can be an argument to convince his judgment.

Now, I learn that any circumstance arising from habit, or some mechanical instinctive cause, may be a motive, though it never entered into the thought of the agent.

From this reinforcement of motives, of which we are unconscious, every volition may be supplied with a motive, and even a predominant one, when it is wanted.

Yet this addition to his defensive force takes just as much from his offensive.

The chief argument for Necessity used by D. Hume and Lord Kames is, that, from experience, it appears that men are always determined by the strongest motive. This argument admits of much embellishment by a large and pleasant induction.

* Dr Crombie, the well-known author of the "Gymnasium," and other able works, published an "Essay on Philosophical Necessity," London, 1793, in which Dr Gregory's reasoning is assailed with much acrimony and considerable acuteness. It is to this treatise that Reid's remarks apply. There subsequently appeared, "Letters from Dr James Gregory of Edinburgh, in Defence of his Essay on the Difference of the relation between Motive and Action, and that of Cause and Effect in Physics; with Replies by the Rev. Alexander Crombie, LL.D.;" London, 1819. It is much to be regretted, that Dr Gregory did not find leisure to complete his " Answer to Messrs Crombie, Priestley, and Co.;" of which 512 pages have been printed, but are still unpublished.

† This is Aristotle's definition (τὸ ἕνεκα οὗ) of *end* or *final cause*; and, as a synonyme for end or final cause, the term *motive* had been long exclusively employed. There are two schemes of Necessity—the Necessitation by efficient—the Necessitation by final causes. The former is brute or blind Fate ; the latter rational Determinism. Though their practical results be the same, they ought to be carefully distinguished in theory.—H.

After these two authors had exhausted their eloquence upon it, Mr Crombie adds his, from page 27 to 39. Now, if motives we are unconscious of be the cause of many actions, it will be impossible to prove from experience, that they are all caused by motives. For no experiment can be made upon motives we are unconscious of. If, on the contrary, all our actions are found by experience to proceed from motives known or felt, there is no work left for the unknown, nor any evidence of their existance. I apprehend, therefore, Mr Crombie must either keep by the old meaning of *motive*, or give up this argument for Necessity taken from experience.

But he lays the main stress, as Dr Priestley likewise has done, upon another argument. It is, that a volition not determined by motives, is an uncaused effect, and therefore an absurdity, a contradiction, and the greatest of all absurdities.

I think, indeed, it is in vain to reason upon the subject of Necessity *pro* or *con*, till this point be determined ; for, on the one side, to what purpose is[it] to disprove by argument a proposition that is absurd ? On the other side, demonstration itself cannot prove that to be true which is absurd.

If this be really an absurdity, Liberty must be given up. And if the appearance of absurdity be owing to false colouring, I think every argument this author has used, when weighed in the balance of reason, will be found light.

I would, therefore, think it a prudent saving of time and labour, that controvertists on both sides should lay aside every other weapon, till the force of this be fairly tried. Mr Crombie triumphs in it almost in every page ; and I think Dr Priestley urged it as an apology for neglecting your essay, that you pretended to demonstrate an absurdity. It must, indeed, be granted, that even the Deity cannot give a power to man, which involves an absurdity. But if this absurdity vanish, when seen in a just light, then it will be time to examine the fact, whether such a power is given to man or not.

Is a volition, undetermined by motives, an uncaused effect, and therefore an absurdity and a contradiction ?

I grant that an uncaused effect is a contradiction in terms ; for an effect is something effected, and what is effected implies an efficient, as an action implies an agent. To say an *effect* must have a cause, is really an identical proposition, which carries no information but of the meaning of a word. To say that an *event*—that is, a thing which began to exist—must have a cause, is not an identical proposition, and might have been as easily said. I know [no] reason why Mr Crombie should stick by this impropriety, after it was censured in Dr Priestley, but that impropriety in the use of terms is an expedient either to cover an absurdity where it really is, or to make that appear absurd which is not so in reality.

I grant, then, that an effect uncaused is a contradiction, and that an event uncaused is an absurdity. The question that remains is whether a volition, undetermined by motives, is an event uncaused. This I deny. The cause of the volition is the man that willed it. This Mr Crombie grants in several places of his Essay—that the man is the efficient cause of all his volitions. Is it not strange, then, that, almost in every page, he should affirm that a volition, undetermined by motives, is an effect uncaused? Is an efficient cause no cause? or are two causes necessary to every event?[*] Motives, he thinks, are not the efficient but the physical cause of volitions, as gravity is of the descent of a stone. Then, fair dealing would have made him qualify the absurdity, and, say that it is absurd that a volition should be without a physical cause; but to have pleaded the absurdity thus qualified, would have been a manifest *petitio principii.*

I can see nothing in a physical cause but a constant conjunction with the effect. Mr Crombie calls it a necessary connection; but this no man sees in physical causes; and, if every event must have a physical cause, then every event must have been repeated in conjunction with its cause from eternity, for it could have no constant conjunction when first produced.

The most shocking consequences of the system of necessity are avowed by this author without shame. Moral evil is nothing but as it tends to produce natural evil. A man truly enlightened, ought to have no remorse for the blackest crimes. I think he might have added that the villain has reason to glory in his crimes, as he suffers for them without his fault, and for the common good. Among the arts of this author, the following are often put in practice:—1. To supply the defect of argument by abuse. 2. What he thinks a consequence of the system of Liberty he imputes to his adversaries as their opinion, though they deny it. 3. What is urged as a consequence of Necessity, he considers as imputing an opinion to those who hold Necessity, and thinks it answer that they hold no such opinion. 4. What is said to invalidate an argument for Necessity, he considers as an

argument against Necessity; and thinks it sufficient to shew that it does not answer a purpose for which it never was intended, as if what is a sufficient answer to an argument for Necessity must be a conclusive argument against Necessity. I believe, however, he may claim the merit of adding the word *Libertarian* to the English language, as Priestley added that of Necessarian.—Yours,

THO. REID.[*]

XXI.

[*The following Letter to Dr Gregory is quoted by Mr Stewart in his "Dissertation on the Progress of Metaphysical and Moral Science." The date is not given; and the original is not now extant among the letters of Reid in the hands of Dr Gregory's family.*—H.]

The merit of what you are pleased to call *my philosophy,* lies, I think, chiefly, in having called in question the common theory of ideas, or images of things in the mind, being the only objects of thought; a theory founded on natural prejudices, and so universally received as to be interwoven with the structure of the language. Yet, were I to give you a detail of what led me to call in question this theory, after I had long held it as self-evident and unquestionable, you would think, as I do, that there was much of chance in the matter. The discovery was the birth of time, not of genius; and Berkeley and Hume did more to bring it to light than the man that hit upon it. I think there is hardly anything that can be called *mine* in the philosophy of the mind, which does not follow with ease from the detection of this prejudice. I must, therefore, beg of you most earnestly to make no contrast in my favour to the disparagement of my predecessors in the same pursuits. I can truly say of them, and shall always avow, what you are pleased to say of me, that, but for the assistance I have received from their writings, I never could have wrote or thought what I have done.

---

[*] This is no removal of the difficulty. Is the *man* determined to volition, and to a certain kind of volition, or is he not? If the former, necessitation is not avoided; if the latter, the admitted absurdity emerges. The schemes of Liberty and of Necessity are contradictory of each other: they consequently exclude any intermediate theory; and one or other must be true. Yet the possibility of neither can be conceived; for each equally involves what is incomprehensible, if not what is absurd. But of this again.—H.

[*] Besides the preceding papers on the question of Liberty and Necessity, there are extant, *Remarks* at considerable length by Reid, on three sets of *Objections* made by a distinguished natural philosopher to Dr Gregory's Essay, in the years 1786, 1789, and 1790. These Remarks, though of much interest, have been omitted: for they could not adequately be understood apart from the relative Objections; and these it was deemed improper to publish posthumously, after their author had expressly refused to allow them to be printed during his life.—There are also omitted, as of minor importance, two other papers on the same question; the one containing, "Remarks on the Objections to Dr Gregory's Essay," which were printed in the appendix to that Essay; the other, "Remarks" on a pamphlet entitled "Illustrations of Liberty and Necessity, in Answer to Dr Gregory," published in 1795.—H.

D.—LETTER TO THE REV. ARCHIBALD ALISON.

The following letter was addressed, by Dr Reid, to the Rev. Archibald Alison, (LL.B., Prebendary of Sarum, &c.,) on receiving a copy of his " Essays on the Nature and Principles of Taste"—a work of great ingenuity and elegance, and the first systematic attempt to explain the emotions of sublimity and beauty on the principles of association. It was originally published in 1790.   It is, perhaps, needless to remind the reader that Mr Alison was brother-in-law of Dr Gregory.—H.

ON THE PHILOSOPHY OF TASTE.

DEAR SIR,—I received your very obliging letter of Jan. 10, with two copies of your book, about the middle of last week.   I expected a meeting of Faculty, to which I might present the book, and return you the thanks of the society along with my own ; but we have had no meeting since I received it. In the meantime, I have read it with avidity and with much pleasure ; and cannot longer forbear to return you my cordial thanks for this mark of your regard, and for the handsome compliment you make me in the book.

I think your principles are just, and that you have sufficiently justified them by a great variety of illustrations, of which many appear new to me, and important in themselves, as well as pertinent to the purpose for which they are adduced.

That your doctrine concerning the sublime and beautiful in objects of sense coincides, in a great degree, with that of the Platonic school, and with Shaftesbury and Akenside among the moderns, I think may justly be said.   They believed intellectual beauties to be the highest order, compared with which the terrestrial hardly deserve the name.   They taught beauty and good to be one and the same thing.   But both Plato and those two, his admirers, handle the subject of beauty rather with the enthusiasm of poets or lovers, than with the cool temper of philosophers.   And it is difficult to determine what allowance is to be made, in what they have said, for the hyperbolical language of enthusiasm.

The other two you mention, Dr Hutcheson and Mr Spence, though both admirers of Plato, do not appear to me either to have perceived this doctrine in him, or to have discovered it themselves.   The first places beauty in uniformity and variety, which, when they are perceived, immediately affect that internal sense which he calls the sense of beauty.   The other makes colour, form, expression, and grace to be the four ingredients of beauty in the female part of our species, without being aware that the beauty of colour, form, and grace is nothing but expression, as well as what he calls by that name.

On these grounds, I am proud to think that I first, in clear and explicit terms, and in the cool blood of a philosopher, maintained that all the beauty and sublimity of objects of sense is derived from the expression they exhibit of things intellectual, which alone have original beauty.   But in this I may deceive myself, and cannot claim to be held an impartial judge.

Though I don't expect to live to see the second part of your work, I have no hesitation in advising you to prosecute it ; being persuaded that criticism is reducible to principles of philosophy, which may be more fully unfolded than they have been, and which will always be found friendly to the best interests of mankind, as well as to manly and rational entertainment.

Mrs Reid desires to present her best respects to Mrs Alison, to which I beg you to add mine, and to believe me to be your much obliged and faithful servant,

THO. REID.

Glasgow College,
3d Feb. 1790.

E.—LETTER TO PROFESSOR ROBISON.

There has been given above, (p. 63,) a letter by Dr Reid, in 1784, recording a remarkable conversation between Sir Isaac Newton and Professor James Gregory, relative to Sir Isaac's descent from the family of Newton of Newton, in the county of East Lothian.   Some years thereafter, Mr Barron, a relation of Sir Isaac, seems to have instituted inquiries in regard to the Scottish genealogy of the philosopher; in consequence of which, the late Professor Robison of Edinburgh, aware, probably, of the letter to Dr Gregory, was induced to apply to Dr Reid for a more particular account of the conversation in question. The following is Reid's answer, as published in Sir David Brewster's " Life of Sir Isaac Newton."—H.

DEAR SIR,—I am very glad to learn, by yours of April 4, that a Mr Barron, a near relation of Sir Isaac Newton, is anxious to inquire into the descent of that great man, as the family cannot trace it farther, with any certainty, than his grandfather. I therefore, as you desire, send you a precise account of all I know ; and am glad to have this opportunity, before I die, of putting this information in hands that will make the proper use of it, if it shall be found of any use.

Several years before I left Aberdeen, (which I did in 1764,) Mr Douglas of Fechel, the father of Sylvester Douglas, now a barrister at London, told me, that, having been lately at Edinburgh, he was often in company of Mr Hepburn of Keith, a gentleman with whom I had some acquaintance, by his lodging a night at my house at New Machar, when he was in the rebel army in 1745. That Mr Hepburn told him, that he had heard Mr James Gregory, Professor of Mathematics, Edinburgh, say, that, being one day in familiar conversation with Sir Isaac Newton at London, Sir Isaac said— " Gregory, I believe you don't know that I am a Scotchman."—" Pray, how is that?" said Gregory. Sir Isaac said, he was informed that his grandfather (or great-grandfather) was a gentleman of East (or West) Lothian ; that he went to London with King James I at his accession to the crown of England ; and that he attended the court, in expectation, as many others did, until he spent his fortune, by which means his family was reduced to low circumstances. At the time this was told me, Mr Gregory was dead, otherwise I should have had his own testimony ; for he was my mother's brother. I likewise thought at that time, that it had been certainly known that Sir Isaac had been descended from an old English family, as I think is said in his *eloge* before the Academy of Sciences at Paris ; and therefore I never mentioned what I had heard for many years, believing that there must be some mistake in it.

Some years after I came to Glasgow, I mentioned, (I believe for the first time,) what I had heard to have been said by Mr Hepburn, to Mr Cross, late sheriff of this county, whom you will remember. Mr Cross was moved by this account, and immediately said—" I know Mr Hepburn very well, and I know he was intimate with Mr Gregory. I shall write him this same night, to know whether he heard Mr Gregory say so or not." After some reflection, he added

—" I know that Mr Keith, the ambassador, was also an intimate acquaintance of Mr Gregory, and, as he is at present in Edinburgh, I shall likewise write to him this night."

The next time I waited on Mr Cross, he told me that he had wrote both to Mr Hepburn and Mr Keith, and had an answer from both ; and that both of them testified that they had several times heard Mr James Gregory say, that Sir Isaac Newton told him what is above expressed, but that neither they nor Mr Gregory, as far as they knew, ever made any farther inquiry into the matter. This appeared very strange both to Mr Cross and me ; and he said he would reproach them for their indifference, and would make inquiry as soon as he was able.

He lived but a short time after this ; and, in the last conversation I had with him upon the subject, he said, that all he had yet learned was, that there was a Sir John Newton of Newton in one of the counties of Lothian, (but I have forgot which,) some of whose children are yet alive ; that they reported that their father, Sir John, had a letter from Sir Isaac Newton, desiring to know the state of his family ; what children he had, particularly what sons ; and in what way they were. The old knight never returned an answer to this letter, thinking, probably, that Sir Isaac was some upstart, who wanted to claim a relation to his worshipful house. This omission the children regretted, conceiving that Sir Isaac might have had a view of doing something for their benefit.

After this, I mentioned occasionally in conversation what I knew, hoping that these facts might lead to some more certain discovery ; but I found more coldness about the matter than I thought it deserved. I wrote an account of it to Dr Gregory, your colleague, that he might impart it to any member of the Antiquarian Society who he judged might have had the curiosity to trace the matter farther.

In the year 1787, my colleague, Mr Patrick Wilson, Professor of Astronomy, having been in London, told me, on his return, that he had met accidentally with a James Hutton, Esq. of Pimlico, Westminster, a near relation of Sir Isaac Newton, to whom he mentioned what he had heard from me with respect to Sir Isaac's descent, and that I wished much to know something decisive on the subject. Mr Hutton said, if I pleased to write to him, he would give me all the information he could give. I wrote him, accordingly, and had a very polite answer, dated at Bath, 25th December 1787, which is now before me. He says, " I shall be glad, when I return to London, if I can find, in some old notes of my mother, any thing that may fix the certainty of Sir Isaac's descent. If he spoke so to Mr James Gregory, it is most certain he spoke truth. But Sir Isaac's grandfather, not his great-grandfather, must be the person who came from Scotland with King James I. If I find any thing to the purpose, I will take care it shall reach you."

This is all I know of the matter; and for the facts above mentioned, I pledge my veracity. I am much obliged to you,

dear Sir ,for the kind expressions. of your affection and esteem, which, I assure you, are mutual on my part; and I sincerely sympathise with you on your afflicting state of health, which makes you consider yourself as out of the world, and despair of seeing me any more.

I have been long out of the world by deafness and extreme old age. I hope, however, if we should not meet again in this world, that we shall meet and renew our acquaintance in another. In the meantime, I am, with great esteem, dear Sir, yours affectionately,

THO. REID.

Glasgow College,
12th April 1792.

F.—LETTER TO DAVID HUME.

The following is in answer to the letter of Hume, given by Mr Stewart in his Account of Reid, (*supra*, p. 7, sq.) It is recently published, from the Hume papers, by Mr Burton, in his very able life of the philosopher; and, though out of chronological order, (by the reprinting of a leaf,) it is here inserted.—H.

IN REFERENCE TO HIS OWN INQUIRY, PRIOR TO ITS PUBLICATION.

King's College, [Aberdeen,]
18th March 1763.

SIR,—On Monday last, Mr John Farquhar brought me your letter of February 25th, enclosed in one from Dr Blair. I thought myself very happy in having the means of obtaining at second hand, through the friendship of Dr Blair, your opinion of my performance: and you have been pleased to communicate it directly in so polite and friendly a manner, as merits great acknowledgments on my part. Your keeping a watchful eye over my style, with a view to be of use to me, is an instance of candour and generosity to an antagonist, which would affect me very sensibly, although I had no personal concern in it, and I shall always be proud to show so amiable an example. Your judgment of the style, indeed, gives me great consolation, as I was very diffident of myself in regard to English, and have been indebted to Drs Campbell and Gerard for many corrections of that kind.

In attempting to throw some new light

upon those abstruse subjects, I wish to preserve the due mean betwixt confidence and despair. But whether I have any success in this attempt or not, I shall always avow myself your disciple in metaphysics. I have learned more from your writings in this kind, than from all others put together. Your system appears to me not only coherent in all its parts, but likewise justly deduced from principles commonly received among philosophers; principles which I never thought of calling in question, until the conclusions you draw from them in the Treatise of Human Nature made me suspect them. If these principles are solid, your system must stand; and whether they are or not, can better be judged after you have brought to light the whole system that grows out of them, than when the greater part of it was wrapped up in clouds and darkness. I agree with you, therefore, that if this system shall ever be demolished, you have a just claim to a great share of the praise, both because you have made it a distinct and determined mark to be aimed at, and have furnished proper artillery for the purpose.[*]

---

[*] Kant makes a similar acknowledgment. " By Hume," he says, " I was first startled out of my dogmatic slumber." Thus Hume (as elsewhere stated) is author, in a sort, of all our subsequent philosophy. For out of Reid and Kant, mediately or immediately, all our subsequent philosophy is evolved; and the doctrines of Kant and Reid are both avowedly recoils from the annihilating scepticism of Hume—both attempts to find for philosophy deeper foundations than those which he had so thoroughly subverted.—H.

92 CORRESPONDENCE OF DR REID.

When you have seen the whole of my performance, I shall take it as a very great favour to have your opinion upon it, from which I make no doubt of receiving light, whether I receive correction or no. Your friendly adversaries Drs Campbell and Gerard, as well as Dr Gregory, return their compliments to you respectfully. A little philosophical society here, of which all the three are members, is much indebted to you for its entertainment. Your company would, although we are all good Christians, be more acceptable than that of St Athanasius; and since we cannot have you upon the bench, you are brought oftener than any other man to the bar, accused and defended with great zeal, but without bitterness. If you write no more in morals, politics, or metaphysics, I am afraid we shall be at a loss for subjects. I am, respectfully, Sir, your most obliged, humble servant,

THOMAS REID.

The following should have been inserted in the correspondence with Kames. Kames's objection to Dr Adam Smith's theory of Sympathy as the sole foundation of our moral judgments, which appeared in the third edition of the " Essays on Morality," were, previously to publication, communicated to Dr Reid, who thus expresses his opinion on the subject :—

" I have always thought Dr S——'s system of sympathy wrong. It is indeed only a refinement of the selfish system ; and I think your arguments against it are solid. But you have smitten with a friendly hand, which does not break the head ; and your compliment to the author I highly approve of."—*From Letter of 30th October* 1778.

In this judgment of Smith, Reid and Kant are at one. The latter condemns the Ethic of Sympathy as a Eudæmonism, or rather Hedonism.—H.

In Hutton's Mathematical Dictionary, 1795, in the article, David Gregory, there are given, " Some farther particulars of the families of Gregory and Anderson, communicated by Dr Thomas Reid," &c., probably written in the year of publication, or the preceding. As these notices contain nothing of any moment which does not appear in the foregoing correspondence, it has been deemed unnecessary to reprint them.—H.

AN

INQUIRY

INTO

THE HUMAN MIND,

ON THE PRINCIPLES OF

COMMON SENSE.

By THOMAS REID, D.D.,

PROFESSOR OF MORAL PHILOSOPHY IN THE UNIVERSITY OF GLASGOW.

" The inspiration of the Almighty giveth them understanding."—Job.

☞ This *Inquiry* was first published in 1764, when Dr Reid was Professor of Philosophy, in King's College, Aberdeen. Three subsequent editions were printed during the author's lifetime—in 1765, 1769, and 1785. The text of the present impression is taken from the last authentic edition—the fourth, or that of 1785, which professes to be " corrected ;" collated, however, with the first, and any variations of importance noticed.—H.

DEDICATION.

THE RIGHT HONOURABLE

JAMES, EARL OF FINDLATER AND SEAFIELD,*

CHANCELLOR OF THE UNIVERSITY OF OLD ABERDEEN.

My Lord,—Though I apprehend that there are things new and of some importance, in the following Inquiry, it is not without timidity that I have consented to the publication of it. The subject has been canvassed by men of very great penetration and genius: for who does not acknowledge DesCartes, Malebranche, Locke, Berkeley, and Hume, to be such? A view of the human understanding, so different from that which they have exhibited, will, no doubt, be condemned by many, without examination, as proceeding from temerity and vanity.

But I hope the candid and discerning Few, who are capable of attending to the operations of their own minds, will weigh deliberately what is here advanced, before they pass sentence upon it. To such I appeal, as the only competent judges. If they disapprove, I am probably in the wrong, and shall be ready to change my opinion upon conviction. If they approve, the Many will at last yield to their authority, as they always do.

However contrary my notions are to those of the writers I have mentioned, their speculations have been of great use to me, and seem even to point out the road which I have taken: and your Lordship knows, that the merit of useful discoveries is sometimes not more justly due to those that have hit upon them, than to others that have ripened them, and brought them to the birth.

I acknowledge, my Lord, that I never thought of calling in question the principles commonly received with regard to the human understanding, until the "Treatise of Human Nature" was published in the year 1739. The ingenious author of that treatise upon the principles of Locke—who was no

sceptic—hath built a system of scepticism, which leaves no ground to believe any one thing rather than its contrary. His reasoning appeared to me to be just; there was, therefore, a necessity to call in question the principles upon which it was founded, or to admit the conclusion *

But can any ingenuous mind admit this sceptical system without reluctance? I truly could not, my Lord; for I am persuaded, that absolute scepticism is not more destructive of the faith of a Christian than of the science of a philosopher, and of the prudence of a man of common understanding. I am persuaded, that the unjust *live by faith*† as well as the *just;* that, if all belief could be laid aside, piety, patriotism, friendship, parental affection, and private virtue, would appear as ridiculous as knight-errantry; and that the pursuits of pleasure, of ambition, and of avarice, must be grounded upon belief, as well as those that are honourable or virtuous.

The day-labourer toils at his work, in the belief that he shall receive his wages at night; and, if he had not this belief, he would not toil. We may venture to say, that even the author of this sceptical system wrote it in the belief that it

---

* "In the first edition. "James Lord Deskfoord"—his father being still alive.—H.

* "This doctrine of Ideas,"(says Dr'Reid, in a subsequent work,) "I once believed so firmly as to embrace the whole of Berkeley's system in consequence of it; till, finding other consequences to follow from it, which gave me more uneasiness than the want of a material world, it came into my mind, more than forty years ago, to put the question, What evidence have I for this doctrine, that all the objects of my knowledge are ideas in my own mind?"—*Essays on the Intellectual Powers, Ess. II. ch. x. p.* 162.

In like manner, Kant informs us, that it was by Hume's sceptical inferences, in regard to the causal nexus, that he also "was first roused from his dogmatic slumber." See the "Prolegomena," p. 13.—H.

† See Note A at the end of the volume, in illustration of the principle, that the root of Knowledge is Belief.—H.

should be read and regarded. I hope he
wrote it in the belief also that it would be
useful to mankind; and, perhaps, it may
prove so at last. For I conceive the sceptical writers to be a set of men whose business it is to pick holes in the fabric of
knowledge wherever it is weak and faulty;
and, when these places are properly repaired,
the whole building becomes more firm and
solid than it was formerly.

For my own satisfaction, I entered into
a serious examination of the principles upon
which this sceptical system is built; and
was not a little surprised to find, that it
leans with its whole weight upon a hypothesis, which is ancient indeed, and hath
been very generally received by philosophers, but of which I could find no solid
proof. The hypothesis I mean, is, That
nothing is perceived but what is in the
mind which perceives it: That we do not
really perceive things that are external, but
only certain images and pictures of them
imprinted upon the mind, which are called
impressions and ideas.

If this be true, supposing certain impressions and ideas to exist in my mind,[*] I
cannot, from their existence, infer the existence of anything else: my impressions and
ideas are the only existences of which I can
have any knowledge or conception; and
they are such fleeting and transitory beings,
that they can have no existence at all, any
longer than I am conscious of them. So
that, upon this hypothesis, the whole universe about me, bodies and spirits, sun,
moon, stars, and earth, friends and rela
tions, all things without exception, which
I imagined to have a permanent existence,
whether I thought of them or not, vanish
at once;

"And, like the baseless fabric of a vision,
Leave not a track behind."

I thought it unreasonable, my Lord, upon
the authority of philosophers, to admit a
hypothesis which, in my opinion, overturns
all philosophy, all religion and virtue, and
all common sense[†]—and, finding that all the
systems concerning the human understanding which I was acquainted with, were built
upon this hypothesis, I resolved to inquire
into this subject anew, without regard to any
hypothesis.

What I now humbly present to your
Lordship, is the fruit of this inquiry, so far
only as it regards the five senses: in which
I claim no other merit than that of having

given great attention to the operations of my
own mind, and of having expressed, with all
the perspicuity I was able, what I conceive
every man, who gives the same attention,
will feel and perceive. The productions of
imagination require a genius which soars
above the common rank; but the treasures
of knowledge are commonly buried deep,
and may be reached by those drudges who
can dig with labour and patience, though
they have not wings to fly. The experiments that were to be made in this investigation suited me, as they required no other
expense but that of time and attention,
which I could bestow. The leisure of an
academical life, disengaged from the pursuits of interest and ambition; the duty of
my profession, which obliged me to give
prelections on these subjects to the youth;
and an early inclination to speculations of
this kind, have enabled me, as I flatter myself, to give a more minute attention to the
subject of this inquiry, than has been given
before.

My thoughts upon this subject were, a
good many years ago, put together in another form, for the use of my pupils, and
afterwards were submitted to the judgment
of a private philosophical society,[*] of which
I have the honour to be a member. A
great part of this Inquiry was honoured
even by your Lordship's perusal. And
the encouragement which you, my Lord,
and others, whose friendship is my boast,
and whose judgment I reverence, were
pleased to give me, counterbalance my timidity and diffidence, and determined me to
offer it to the public.

If it appears to your Lordship to justify
the common sense and reason of mankind,
against the sceptical subtilties which, in
this age, have endeavoured to put them out
of countenance—if it appears to throw any
new light upon one of the noblest parts of
the divine workmanship—your Lordship's
respect for the arts and sciences, and your
attention to everything which tends to the
improvement of them, as well as to everything else that contributes to the felicity of
your country, leave me no room to doubt
of your favourable acceptance of this essay,
as the fruit of my industry in a profession[†]
wherein I was[‡] accountable to your Lordship; and as a testimony of the great esteem
and respect wherewith I have the honour
to be,

My Lord,
Your Lordship's most obliged
And most devoted Servant,
THO. REID.[§]

---

[*] In first edition, "to exist presently in my
mind." I may here, once for all, notice that *presently*, (in its original and proper sense, and as it is
frequently employed by Reid,) for *now* or *at present*,
has waxed obsolete in English. For above a century
and a half, it is only to be found in good English
writers in the secondary meaning of *in a little while*
—*without delay.*—H.

[†] See Note A at the end of the volume, in defence
and illustration of the term *Common Sense.*—H.

[*] See above, p. 41, b.—H.

[†] Reid, here and elsewhere, uses *profession* for *chair*
or *professorship.*—H.

[‡] "Am"—first edition —H.

[§] In first edition this dedication is dated—"King's
College, Nov. 9, 1763."—H.

INQUIRY INTO THE HUMAN MIND.

CHAPTER I.

INTRODUCTION.

Section I.

THE IMPORTANCE OF THE SUBJECT, AND THE MEANS OF PROSECUTING IT.

THE fabric of the human mind is curious and wonderful, as well as that of the human body. The faculties of the one are with no less wisdom adapted to their several ends than the organs of the other. Nay, it is reasonable to think, that, as the mind is a nobler work and of a higher order than the body, even more of the wisdom and skill o. the divine Architect hath been employed in its structure. It is, therefore, a subject highly worthy of inquiry on its own account, but still more worthy on account of the extensive influence which the knowledge of it hath over every other branch of science.

In the arts and sciences which have least connection with the mind, its faculties are the engines which we must employ; and the better we understand their nature and use, their defects and disorders, the more skilfully we shall apply them, and with the greater success. But in the noblest arts, the mind is also the subject* upon which we operate. The painter, the poet, the actor, the orator, the moralist, and the statesman, attempt to operate upon the mind in different ways, and for different ends; and they succeed according as they touch properly the strings of the human frame. Nor can

their several arts ever stand on a solid foundation, or rise to the dignity of science, until they are built on the principles of the human constitution.

Wise men now agree, or ought to agree, in this, that there is but one way to the knowledge of nature's works—the way of observation and experiment. By our constitution, we have a strong propensity to trace particular facts and observations to general rules, and to apply such general rules to account for other effects, or to direct us in the production of them. This procedure of the understanding is familiar to every human creature in the common affairs of life, and it is the only one by which any real discovery in philosophy can be made.

The man who first discovered that cold freezes water, and that heat turns it into vapour, proceeded on the same general principles, and in the same method by which Newton discovered the law of gravitation and the properties of light. His *regulæ philosophandi* are maxims of common sense, and are practised every day in common life; and he who philosophizes by other rules, either concerning the material system or concerning the mind, mistakes his aim.

Conjectures and theories* are the creatures of men, and will always be found very unlike the creatures of God. If we would know the works of God, we must consult themselves with attention and humility, without daring to add anything of ours to what they declare. A just interpretation of nature is the only sound and orthodox philosophy: whatever we add of our own, is apocryphal, and of no authority.

All our curious theories of the formation of the earth, of the generation of animals, of the origin of natural and moral evil, so far as they go beyond a just induction from

---

* In philosophical language, it were to be wished that the word *subject* should be reserved for the *subject of inhesion*—the *materia in qua*; and the term *object* exclusively applied to the *subject of operation*—the *materia circa quam*. If this be not done, the grand distinction of *subjective* and *objective*, in philosophy, is confounded. But if the employment of Subject for Object is to be deprecated, the employment of Object for purpose or final cause, (in the French and English languages,) is to be absolutely condemned, as a recent and irrational confusion of notions which should be carefully distinguished.—H.

* Reid uses the terms, *Theory, Hypothesis,* and *Conjecture,* as convertible, and always in an unfavourable acceptation. Herein there is a double inaccuracy. But of this again.—H.

facts, are vanity and folly, no less than the Vortices of Des Cartes," or the Archæus of Paracelsus. Perhaps the philosophy of the mind hath been no less adulterated by theories, than that of the material system. The theory of Ideas is indeed very ancient, and hath been very universally received; but, as neither of these titles can give it authenticity, they ought not to screen it from a free and candid examination; especially in this age, when it hath produced a system of scepticism that seems to triumph over all science, and even over the dictates of common sense.

All that we know of the body, is owing to anatomical dissection and observation, and it must be by an anatomy of the mind that we can discover its powers and principles.

Section II.

THE IMPEDIMENTS TO OUR KNOWLEDGE OF THE MIND.

But it must be acknowledged, that this kind of anatomy is much more difficult than the other; and, therefore, it needs not seem strange that mankind have made less progress in it. To attend accurately to the operations of our minds, and make them an object of thought, is no easy matter even to the contemplative, and to the bulk of mankind is next to impossible.

An anatomist who hath happy opportunities, may have access to examine with his own eyes, and with equal accuracy, bodies of all different ages, sexes, and conditions; so that what is defective, obscure, or preternatural in one, may be discerned clearly and in its most perfect state in another. But the anatomist of the mind cannot have the same advantage. It is his own mind only that he can examine with any degree of accuracy and distinctness. This is the only subject he can look into. He may, from outward signs, collect the operations of other minds; but these signs are for the most part ambiguous, and must be interpreted by what he perceives within himself.

So that, if a philosopher could delineate to us, distinctly and methodically, all the operations of the thinking principle within him, which no man was ever able to do, this would be only the anatomy of one particular subject; which would be both deficient and erroneous, if applied to human nature in general. For a little reflection

may satisfy us, that the difference of minds is greater than that of any other beings which we consider as of the same species.

Of the various powers and faculties we possess, there are some which nature seems both to have planted and reared, so as to have left nothing to human industry. Such are the powers which we have in common with the brutes, and which are necessary to the preservation of the individual, or the continuance of the kind. There are other powers, of which nature hath only planted the seeds in our minds, but hath left the rearing of them to human culture. It is by the proper culture of these that we are capable of all those improvements in intellectuals, in taste, and in morals, which exalt and dignify human nature; while, on the other hand, the neglect or perversion of them makes its degeneracy and corruption.

The two-legged animal that eats of nature's dainties, what his taste or appetite craves, and satisfies his thirst at the crystal fountain, who propagates his kind as occasion and lust prompt, repels injuries, and takes alternate labour and repose, is, like a tree in the forest, purely of nature's growth. But this same savage hath within him the seeds of the logician, the man of taste and breeding, the orator, the statesman, the man of virtue, and the saint; which seeds, though planted in his mind by nature, yet, through want of culture and exercise, must lie for ever buried, and be hardly perceivable by himself or by others.

The lowest degree of social life will bring to light some of those principles which lay hid in the savage state; and, according to his training, and company, and manner of life, some of them, either by their native vigour, or by the force of culture, will thrive and grow up to great perfection, others will be strangely perverted from their natural form, and others checked, or perhaps quite eradicated.

This makes human nature so various and multiform in the individuals that partake of it, that, in point of morals and intellectual endowments, it fills up all that gap which we conceive to be between brutes and devils below, and the celestial orders above; and such a prodigious diversity of minds must make it extremely difficult to discover the common principles of the species.

The language of philosophers, with regard to the original faculties of the mind, is so adapted to the prevailing system, that it cannot fit any other; like a coat that fits the man for whom it was made, and shews him to advantage, which yet will sit very awkward upon one of a different make, although perhaps as handsome and as well proportioned. It is hardly possible to make any innovation in our philosophy concerning the mind and its operations, without

---

* No one deemed more lightly of his hypotheses than Des Cartes himself He called them "philosophical romances;" and thus anticipated Father Daniel, who again anticipated Voltaire, in the saying—*The Philosophy of Des Cartes is the Romance of Nature.*—H.

using new words and phrases, or giving a different meaning to those that are received —a liberty which, even when necessary, creates prejudice and misconstruction, and which must wait the sanction of time to authorize it; for innovations in language, like those in religion and government, are always suspected and disliked by the many, till use hath made them familiar, and prescription hath given them a title.

If the original perceptions and notions of the mind were to make their appearance single and unmixed, as we first received them from the hand of nature, one accustomed to reflection would have less difficulty in tracing them; but before we are capable of reflection, they are so mixed, compounded, and decompounded, by habits, associations, and abstractions, that it is hard to know what they were originally. The mind may, in this respect, be compared to an apothecary or a chemist, whose materials indeed are furnished by nature; but, for the purposes of his art, he mixes, compounds, dissolves, evaporates, and sublimes them, till they put on a quite different appearance; so that it is very difficult to know what they were at first, and much more to bring them back to their original and natural form. And this work of the mind is not carried on by deliberate acts of mature reason, which we might recollect, but by means of instincts, habits, associations, and other principles, which operate before we come to the use of reason; so that it is extremely difficult for the mind to return upon its own footsteps, and trace back those operations which have employed it since it first began to think and to act.

Could we obtain a distinct and full history of all that hath past in the mind of a child, from the beginning of life and sensation, till it grows up to the use of reason— how its infant faculties began to work, and how they brought forth and ripened all the various notions, opinions, and sentiments which we find in ourselves when we come to be capable of reflection—this would be a treasure of natural history, which would probably give more light into the human faculties, than all the systems of philosophers about them since the beginning of the world. But it is in vain to wish for what nature has not put within the reach of our power. Reflection, the only instrument by which we can discern the powers of the mind, comes too late to observe the progress of nature, in raising them from their infancy to perfection.

It must therefore require great caution, and great application of mind, for a man that is grown up in all the prejudices of education, fashion, and philosophy, to unravel his notions and opinions, till he find out the simple and original principles of his constitution, of which no account can be given but the will of our Maker. This may be truly called an *analysis* of the human faculties; and, till this is performed, it is in vain we expect any just *system* of the mind—that is, an enumeration of the original powers and laws of our constitution, and an explication from them of the various phænomena of human nature.

Success in an inquiry of this kind, it is not in human power to command; but, perhaps, it is possible, by caution and humility, to avoid error and delusion. The labyrinth may be too intricate, and the thread too fine, to be traced through all its windings; but, if we stop where we can trace it no farther, and secure the ground we have gained, there is no harm done; a quicker eye may in time trace it farther.

It is genius, and not the want of it, that adulterates philosophy, and fills it with error and false theory. A creative imagination disdains the mean offices of digging for a foundation, of removing rubbish, and carrying materials; leaving these servile employments to the drudges in science, it plans a design, and raises a fabric. Invention supplies materials where they are wanting, and fancy adds colouring and every befitting ornament. The work pleases the eye, and wants nothing but solidity and a good foundation. It seems even to vie with the works of nature, till some succeeding architect blows it into rubbish, and builds as goodly a fabric of his own in its place. Happily for the present age, the castle-builders employ themselves more in romance than in philosophy. That is undoubtedly their province, and in those regions the offspring of fancy is legitimate, but in philosophy it is all spurious. *

Section III.

THE PRESENT STATE OF THIS PART OF PHILOSOPHY—OF DES CARTES, MALEBRANCHE, AND LOCKE.

That our philosophy concerning the mind and its faculties is but in a very low state, may be reasonably conjectured even by those who never have narrowly examined it. Are there any principles, with regard to the mind, settled with that perspicuity and evidence which attends the principles of mechanics; astronomy, and optics? These are really sciences built upon laws of nature which universally obtain. What is

* The same doctrine of the incompatibility of creative imagination and philosophical talent, is held by Hume and Kant. There is required, however, for the metaphysician, not less imagination than for the poet, though of a different kind; it may, in fact, be doubted whether Homer or Aristotle possessed this faculty in greater vigour.—H.

H 2

discovered in them is no longer matter of dispute : future ages may add to it ; but, till the course of nature be changed, what is already established can never be overturned. But when we turn our attention inward, and consider the phænomena of human thoughts, opinions, and perceptions, and endeavour to trace them to the general laws and the first principles of our constitution, we are immediately involved in darkness and perplexity ; and, if common sense, or the principles of education, happen not to be stubborn, it is odds but we end in absolute scepticism.

Des Cartes, finding nothing established in this part of philosophy, in order to lay the foundation of it deep, resolved not to believe his own existence till he should be able to give a good reason for it. He was, perhaps, the first that took up such a resolution ; but, if he could indeed have effected his purpose, and really become diffident of his existence, his case would have been deplorable, and without any remedy from reason or philosophy. A man that disbelieves his own existence, is surely as unfit to be reasoned with as a man that believes he is made of glass. There may be disorders in the human frame that may produce such extravagancies, but they will never be cured by reasoning. Des Cartes, in deed, would make us believe that he got out of this delirium by this logical argument, *Cogito, ergo sum* ; but it is evident he was in his senses all the time, and never seriously doubted of his existence ; for he takes it for granted in this argument, and proves nothing at all. I am thinking, says he—therefore, I am. And is it not as good reasoning to say, I am sleeping—therefore, I am ? or, I am doing nothing—therefore, I am ? If a body moves, it must exist, no doubt ; but, if it is at rest, it must exist likewise.[*]

Perhaps Des Cartes meant not to assume his own existence in this enthymeme, but the existence of thought ; and to infer from that the existence of a mind, or subject of thought. But why did he not prove the existence of his thought ? Consciousness, it may be said, vouches that. But who is voucher for consciousness ? Can any man prove that his consciousness may not deceive him ? No man can ; nor can we give a better reason for trusting to it, than that every man, while his mind is sound, is determined, by the constitution of his nature, to give implicit belief to it, and to laugh at or pity the man who doubts its testimony. And is not every man, in his wits, as much determined to take his existence upon trust as his consciousness ?

The other proposition assumed in this argument, That thought cannot be without a mind or subject, is liable to the same objection : not that it wants evidence, but that its evidence is no clearer, nor more immediate, than that of the proposition to be proved by it. And, taking all these pro positions together—I think ; I am conscious ; Everything that thinks, exists ; I exist—would not every sober man form the same opinion of the man who seriously doubted any one of them ? And if he was his friend, would he not hope for his cure from physic and good regimen, rather than from metaphysic and logic ?

But supposing it proved, that my thought and my consciousness must have a subject, and consequently that I exist, how do I know that all that train and succession of thoughts which I remember belong to one subject, and that the I[*] of this moment is the very individual I of yesterday and of times past ?

Des Cartes did not think proper to start this doubt ; but Locke has done it ; and, in order to resolve it, gravely determines that personal identity consists in consciousness— that is, if you are conscious that you did such a thing a twelvemonth ago, this consciousness makes you to be the very person that did it. Now, consciousness of what is past can signify nothing else but the remembrance that I did it ; so that Locke's principle must be, That identity consists in remembrance ; and, consequently, a man must lose his personal identity with regard to everything he forgets.

Nor are these the only instances whereby our philosophy concerning the mind appears to be very fruitful in creating doubts, but very unhappy in resolving them.

Des Cartes, Malebranche, and Locke, have all employed their genius and skill to prove the existence of a material world : and with very bad success. Poor untaught mortals believe undoubtedly that there is a sun, moon, and stars ; an earth, which we inhabit ; country, friends, and relations, which we enjoy ; land, houses, and moveables, which we possess. But philosophers, pitying the credulity of the vulgar, resolve to have no faith but what is founded upon reason.[†] They apply to philosophy to fur-

---

[*] The nature of the Cartesian Doubt and its solution is here misapprehended—how, will be shewn in a note upon the eighth chapter of the second " Essay on the Intellectual Powers."—H.

[*] In English, we cannot say *the I*, and *the Not.I* so happily as the French *le Moi*, and *le Non.Moi*, or even the Germans *das Ich*, and *das Nicht.Ich*. The ambiguity arising from the identity of sound between *the I* and *the eye*, would of itself preclude the ordinary employment of the former. *The Ego* and the *Non.Ego* are the best terms *we* can use ; and, as the expressions are scientific, it is perhaps no loss that their technical precision is guarded by their non.vernacularity.—H.

[†] Reason is here employed, by Reid, not as a synonyme for Common Sense, (νους, locus principiorum,) and as he himself more correctly employs it in his latter works, but as equivalent to Reasoning, (διανοια, discursus mentalis.) See Note A.—H.

nish them with reasons for the belief of those things which all mankind have believed, without being able to give any reason for it. And surely one would expect, that, in matters of such importance, the proof would not be difficult: but it is the most difficult thing in the world. For these three great men, with the best good will, have not been able, from all the treasures of philosophy, to draw one argument that is fit to convince a man that can reason, of the existence of any one thing without him. Admired Philosophy! daughter of light! parent of wisdom and knowledge! if thou art she, surely thou hast not yet arisen upon the human mind, nor blessed us with more of thy rays than are sufficient to shed a darkness visible upon the human faculties. and to disturb that repose and security which happier mortals enjoy, who never approached thine altar, nor felt thine influence! But if, indeed, thou hast not power to dispel those clouds and phantoms which thou hast discovered or created, withdraw this penurious and malignant ray: I despise Philosophy, and renounce its guidance—let my soul dwell with Common Sense.*

Section IV.

APOLOGY FOR THOSE PHILOSOPHERS.

But, instead of despising the dawn of light, we ought rather to hope for its increase: instead of blaming the philosophers I have mentioned for the defects and blemishes of their system, we ought rather to honour their memories, as the first discoverers of a region in philosophy formerly unknown; and, however lame and imperfect the system may be, they have opened the way to future discoveries, and are justly entitled to a great share in the merit of them. They have removed an infinite deal of dust and rubbish, collected in the ages of scholastic sophistry, which had obstructed the way. They have put us in the right road—that of experience and accurate reflection. They have taught us to avoid the snares of ambiguous and ill-defined words, and have spoken and thought upon this subject with a distinctness and perspicuity formerly unknown. They have made many openings that may lead to the discovery of truths which they did not reach, or to the detection of errors in which they were involuntarily entangled.

It may be observed, that the defects and blemishes in the received philosophy concerning the mind, which have most exposed

*Mr Stewart very justly censures the vagueness and ambiguity of this passage. *Elem.* vol. ii., ch. i., § 3, p. 92, 8vo editions.—H.

it to the contempt and ridicule of sensible men, have chiefly been owing to this—that the votaries of this Philosophy, from a natural prejudice in her favour, have endeavoured to extend her jurisdiction beyond its just limits, and to call to her bar the dictates of Common Sense. But these decline this jurisdiction; they disdain the trial of reasoning, and disown its authority; they neither claim its aid, nor dread its attacks.

In this unequal contest betwixt Common Sense and Philosophy, the latter will always come off both with dishonour and loss; nor can she ever thrive till this rivalship is dropt, these encroachments given up, and a cordial friendship restored: for, in reality, Common Sense holds nothing of Philosophy, nor needs her aid. But, on the other hand, Philosophy (if I may be permitted to change the metaphor) has no other root but the principles of Common Sense; it grows out of them, and draws its nourishment from them. Severed from this root, its honours wither, its sap is dried up, it dies and rots.

The philosophers of the last age, whom I have mentioned, did not attend to the preserving this union and subordination so carefully as the honour and interest of philosophy required: but those of the present have waged open war with Common Sense, and hope to make a complete conquest of it by the subtilties of Philosophy—an attempt no less audacious and vain than that of the giants to dethrone almighty Jove.

Section V.

OF BISHOP BERKELEY—THE "TREATISE OF HUMAN NATURE"—AND OF SCEPTICISM.

The present age, I apprehend, has not produced two more acute or more practised in this part of philosophy, than the Bishop of Cloyne, and the author of the "Treatise of Human Nature." The first was no friend to scepticism, but had that warm concern for religious and moral principles which became his order: yet the result of his inquiry was a serious conviction that there is no such thing as a material world—nothing in nature but spirits and ideas; and that the belief of material substances, and of abstract ideas, are the chief causes of all our errors in philosophy, and of all infidelity and heresy in religion. His arguments are founded upon the principles which were formerly laid down by Des Cartes, Malebranche, and Locke, and which have been very generally received.

And the opinion of the ablest judges seems to be, that they neither have been, nor can be confuted; and that he hath proved by unanswerable arguments what no man in his senses can believe.

The second proceeds upon the same principles, but carries them to their full length ; and, as the Bishop undid the whole material world, this author, upon the same grounds, undoes the world of spirits, and leaves nothing in nature but ideas and impressions, without any subject on which they may be impressed.

It seems to be a peculiar strain of humour in this author, to set out in his introduction by promising, with a grave face, no less than a complete system of the sciences, upon a foundation entirely new—to wit, that of human nature—when the intention of the whole work is to shew, that there is neither human nature nor science in the world. It may perhaps be unreasonable to complain of this conduct in an author who neither believes his own existence nor that of his reader ; and therefore could not mean to disappoint him, or to laugh at his credulity. Yet I cannot imagine that the author of the " Treatise of Human Nature" is so sceptical as to plead this apology. He believed, against his principles, that he should be read, and that he should retain his personal identity, till he reaped the honour and reputation justly due to his metaphysical *acumen.* Indeed, he ingeniously acknowledges, that it was only in solitude and retirement that he could yield any assent to his own philosophy ; society, like day-light, dispelled the darkness and fogs of scepticism, and made him yield to the dominion of common sense. Nor did I ever hear him charged with doing anything, even in solitude, that argued such a degree of scepticism as his principles maintain. Surely if his friends apprehended this, they would have the charity never to leave him alone.

Pyrrho the Elean, the father of this philosophy, seems to have carried it to greater perfection than any of his successors : for, if we may believe Antigonus the Carystian, quoted by Diogenes Laertius, his life corresponded to his doctrine. And, therefore, if a cart run against him, or a dog attacked him, or if he came upon a precipice, he would not stir a foot to avoid the danger, giving no credit to his senses. But his attendants, who, happily for him, were not so great sceptics, took care to keep him out of harm's way ; so that he lived till he was ninety years of age. Nor is it to be doubted but this author's friends would have been equally careful to keep him from harm, if ever his principles had taken too strong a hold of him.

It is probable the " Treatise of Human Nature" was not written in company ; yet it contains manifest indications that the author every now and then relapsed into the faith of the vulgar, and could hardly, for half a dozen pages, keep up the sceptical character.

In like manner, the great Pyrrho himself forgot his principles on some occasions ; and is said once to have been in such a passion with his cook, who probably had not roasted his dinner to his mind, that with the spit in his hand, and the meat upon it, he pursued him even into the market-place. [*]

It is a bold philosophy that rejects, without ceremony, principles which irresistibly govern the belief and the conduct of all mankind in the common concerns of life ; and to which the philosopher himself must yield, after he imagines he hath confuted them. Such principles are older, and of more authority, than Philosophy : she rests upon them as her basis, not they upon her. If she could overturn them, she must be buried in their ruins ; but all the engines of philosophical subtilty are too weak for this purpose ; and the attempt is no less ridiculous than if a mechanic should contrive an *axis in peritrochio* to remove the earth out of its place ; or if a mathematician should pretend to demonstrate that things equal to the same thing are not equal to one another.

Zeno[†] endeavoured to demonstrate the impossibility of motion ;[‡] Hobbes, that there was no difference between right and wrong ; and this author, that no credit is to be given to our senses, to our memory, or even to demonstration. Such philosophy is justly ridiculous, even to those who cannot detect the fallacy of it. It can have no other tendency, than to shew the acuteness of the sophist, at the expense of disgracing reason and human nature, and making mankind Yahoos.

Section VI.

OF THE " TREATISE OF HUMAN NATURE."

There are other prejudices against this system of human nature, which, even upon a general view, may make one diffident of it.

Des Cartes, Hobbes, and this author. have each of them given us a system of human nature ; an undertaking too vast for any one man, how great soever his genius and abilities may be. There must surely be reason to apprehend, that many parts of human nature never came under their observation ; and that others have been stretched and distorted, to fill up blanks, and complete the system. Christopher

* Laertius, L. ix. Seg 68.—H.
† Zeno of *Elea*   There are fifteen Zenos known in the history of Philosophy ; of these, Laertius signalizes eight.—H.
‡ The *fallacy* of Zeno's exposition of the contradictions involved in our notion of motion, has not yet been *detected.*—H.

Columbus, or Sebastian Cabot, might almost as reasonably have undertaken to give us a complete map of America.

There is a certain character and style in Nature's works, which is never attained in the most perfect imitation of them. This seems to be wanting in the systems of human nature I have mentioned, and particularly in the last. One may see a puppet make variety of motions and gesticulations, which strike much at first view; but when it is accurately observed, and taken to pieces, our admiration ceases: we comprehend the whole art of the maker. How unlike is it to that which it represents! What a poor piece of work compared with the body of a man, whose structure the more we know, the more wonders we discover in it, and the more sensible we are of our ignorance! Is the mechanism of the mind so easily comprehended, when that of the body is so difficult? Yet, by this system, three laws of association, joined to a few original feelings, explain the whole mechanism of sense, imagination, memory, belief, and of all the actions and passions of the mind. Is this the man that Nature made? I suspect it is not so easy to look behind the scenes in Nature's work. This is a puppet, surely, contrived by too bold an apprentice of Nature, to mimic her work. It shews tolerably by candle light; but, brought into clear day, and taken to pieces, it will appear to be a man made with mortar and a trowel. The more we know of other parts of nature, the more we like and approve them. The little I know of the planetary system; of the earth which we inhabit; of minerals, vegetables, and animals; of my own body; and of the laws which obtain in these parts of nature—opens to my mind grand and beautiful scenes, and contributes equally to my happiness and power. But, when I look within, and consider the mind itself, which makes me capable of all these prospects and enjoyments—if it is, indeed, what the "Treatise of Human Nature" makes it—I find I have been only in an enchanted castle, imposed upon by spectres and apparitions. I blush inwardly to think how I have been deluded; I am ashamed of my frame, and can hardly forbear expostulating with my destiny. Is this thy pastime, O Nature, to put such tricks upon a silly creature, and then to take off the mask, and shew him how he hath been befooled? If this is the philosophy of human nature, my soul enter thou not into her secrets! It is surely the forbidden tree of knowledge; I no sooner taste of it, than I perceive myself naked, and stript of all things—yea, even of my very self. I see myself, and the whole frame of nature, shrink into fleeting ideas, which, like Epicurus's atoms, dance about in emptiness.

Section VII.

THE SYSTEM OF ALL THESE AUTHORS IS THE SAME, AND LEADS TO SCEPTICISM.

But what if these profound disquisitions into the first principles of human nature, do naturally and necessarily plunge a man into this abyss of scepticism? May we not reasonably judge so from what hath happened? Des Cartes no sooner began to dig in this mine, than scepticism was ready to break in upon him. He did what he could to shut it out. Malebranche and Locke, who dug deeper, found the difficulty of keeping out this enemy still to increase; but they laboured honestly in the design. Then Berkeley, who carried on the work, despairing of securing all, bethought himself of an expedient:—By giving up the material world, which he thought might be spared without loss, and even with advantage, he hoped, by an impregnable partition, to secure the world of spirits. But, alas! the "Treatise of Human Nature" wantonly sapped the foundation of this partition, and drowned all in one universal deluge.

These facts, which are undeniable, do, indeed, give reason to apprehend that Des Cartes' system of the human understanding, which I shall beg leave to call the ideal system, and which, with some improvements made by later writers, is now generally received, hath some original defect; that this scepticism is inlaid in it, and reared along with it; and, therefore, that we must lay it open to the foundation, and examine the materials, before we can expect to raise any solid and useful fabric of knowledge on this subject.

Section VIII.

WE OUGHT NOT TO DESPAIR OF A BETTER.

But is this to be despaired of, because Des Cartes and his followers have failed? By no means. This pusillanimity would be injurious to ourselves and injurious to truth. Useful discoveries are sometimes indeed the effect of superior genius; but more frequently they are the birth of time and of accidents. A traveller of good judgment may mistake his way, and be unawares led into a wrong track; and, while the road is fair before him, he may go on without suspicion and be followed by others; but, when it ends in a coal-pit, it requires no great judgment to know that he hath gone wrong, nor perhaps to find out what misled him.

In the meantime, the unprosperous state of this part of philosophy hath produced an effect, somewhat discouraging indeed to any attempt of this nature, but an effect which might be expected, and which time only and better success can remedy. Sensible men, who never will be sceptics in matters of common life, are apt to treat with sovereign contempt everything that hath been said, or is to be said, upon this subject. It is metaphysic, say they: who minds it? Let scholastic sophisters entangle themselves in their own cobwebs; I am resolved to take my own existence, and the existence of other things, upon trust; and to believe that snow is cold, and honey sweet, whatever they may say to the contrary. He must either be a fool, or want to make a fool of me, that would reason me out of my reason and senses.

I confess I know not what a sceptic can answer to this, nor by what good argument he can plead even for a hearing; for either his reasoning is sophistry, and so deserves contempt; or there is no truth in human faculties—and then why should we reason?

If, therefore, a man find himself intangled in these metaphysical toils, and can find no other way to escape, let him bravely cut the knot which he cannot loose, curse metaphysic, and dissuade every man from meddling with it; for, if I have been led into bogs and quagmires by following an *ignis fatuus*, what can I do better than to warn others to beware of it? If philosophy contradicts herself, befools her votaries, and deprives them of every object worthy to be pursued or enjoyed, let her be sent back to the infernal regions from which she must have had her original.

But is it absolutely certain that this fair lady is of the party? Is it not possible she may have been misrepresented? Have not men of genius in former ages often made their own dreams to pass for her oracles? Ought she then to be condemned without any further hearing? This would be unreasonable. I have found her in all other matters an agreeable companion, a faithful counsellor, a friend to common sense, and to the happiness of mankind. This justly entitles her to my correspondence and confidence, till I find infallible proofs of her infidelity.

CHAPTER II.

OF SMELLING.

Section I.

THE ORDER OF PROCEEDING—OF THE MEDIUM AND ORGAN OF SMELL.

IT is so difficult to unravel the operations of the human understanding, and to reduce them to their first principles, that we cannot expect to succeed in the attempt, but by beginning with the simplest, and proceeding by very cautious steps to the more complex. The five external senses may, for this reason, claim to be first considered in an analysis of the human faculties. And the same reason ought to determine us to make a choice even among the senses, and to give the precedence, not to the noblest or most useful, but to the simplest, and that whose objects are least in danger of being mistaken for other things.

In this view, an analysis of our sensations may be carried on, perhaps with most ease and distinctness, by taking them in this order: Smelling, Tasting, Hearing, Touch, and, last of all, Seeing.

Natural philosophy informs us, that all animal and vegetable bodies, and probably all or most other bodies, while exposed to the air, are continually sending forth effluvia of vast subtilty, not only in their state of life and growth, but in the states of fermentation and putrefaction. These volatile particles do probably repel each other, and so scatter themselves in the air, until they meet with other bodies to which they have some chemical affinity, and with which they unite, and form new concretes. All the smell of plants, and of other bodies, is caused by these volatile parts, and is smelled wherever they are scattered in the air: and the acuteness of smell in some animals, shews us, that these effluvia spread far, and must be inconceivably subtile.

Whether, as some chemists conceive, every species of bodies hath a *spiritus rector*, a kind of soul, which causes the smell and all the specific virtues of that body, and which, being extremely volatile, flies about in the air in quest of a proper receptacle, I do not inquire. This, like most other theories, is perhaps rather the product of imagination than of just induction. But that all bodies are smelled by means of effluvia* which they emit, and which are drawn into the nostrils along with the air, there is no reason to doubt. So that there is manifest appearance of design in placing the organ of smell in the inside of that canal, through which the air is continually passing in inspiration and expiration.

Anatomy informs us, that the *membrana pituitaria*, and the olfactory nerves, which are distributed to the villous parts of this membrane, are the organs destined by the

---

* It is wrong to say that "*a body is smelled by m ans of effluvia.*" Nothing is smelt but the effluvia themselves. They constitute the total object of *perception* in smell; and in all the senses the only object perceived. is that in immediate contact with the organ. There is, in reality, no medium in any sense; and, as Democritus long ago shrewdly observed, all the senses are only modifications of touch.—H.

wisdom of nature to this sense; so that when a body emits no effluvia, or when they do not enter into the nose, or when the pituitary membrane or olfactory nerves are rendered unfit to perform their office, it cannot be smelled.

Yet, notwithstanding this, it is evident that neither the organ of smell, nor the medium, nor any motions we can conceive excited in the membrane above mentioned or in the nerve or animal spirits, do in the least resemble the sensation of smelling: nor could that sensation of itself ever have led us to think of nerves animal spirits, or effluvia.

Section II.

THE SENSATION CONSIDERED ABSTRACTLY.

Having premised these things with regard to the medium and organ of this sense, let us now attend carefully to what the mind is conscious of when we smell a rose or a lily; and, since our language affords no other name for this sensation, we shall call it a *smell* or *odour*, carefully excluding from the meaning of those names everything but the sensation itself, at least till we have examined it.

Suppose a person who never had this sense before, to receive it all at once, and to smell a rose—can he perceive any similitude or agreement between the smell and the rose? or indeed between it and any other object whatsoever? Certainly he cannot. He finds himself affected in a new way, he knows not why or from what cause. Like a man that feels some pain or pleasure formerly unknown to him, he is conscious that he is not the cause of it himself; but cannot, from the nature of the thing, determine whether it is caused by body or spirit, by something near, or by something at a distance. It has no similitude to anything else, so as to admit of a comparison ; and, therefore, he can conclude nothing from it, unless, perhaps, that there must be some unknown cause of it.

It is evidently ridiculous to ascribe to it figure, colour, extension, or any other quality of bodies. He cannot give it a place, any more than he can give a place to melancholy or joy : nor can he conceive it to have any existence, but when it is smelled. So that it appears to be a simple and original affection or feeling of the mind, altogether inexplicable and unaccountable. It is, indeed, impossible that it can be in any body : it is a sensation, and a sensation can only be in a sentient thing.

The various odours have each their different degrees of strength or weakness. Most of them are agreeable or disagreeable; and frequently those that are agreeable when weak, are disagreeable when stronger. When we compare different smells together, we can perceive very few resemblances or contrarieties, or, indeed, relations of any kind between them. They are all so simple in themselves, and so different from each other, that it is hardly possible to divide them into *genera* and *species*. Most of the names we give them are particular ; as the smell of a *rose*, of a *jessamine*, and the like. Yet there are some general names—as *sweet, stinking, musty, putrid, cadaverous, aromatic.* Some of them seem to refresh and animate the mind, others to deaden and depress it.

Section III.

SENSATION AND REMEMBRANCE, NATURAL PRINCIPLES OF BELIEF.

So far we have considered this sensation abstractly. Let us next compare it with other things to which it bears some relation. And first I shall compare this sensation with the remembrance, and the imagination of it.

I can think of the smell of a rose when I do not smell it; and it is possible that when I think of it, there is neither rose nor smell anywhere existing. But when I smell it, I am necessarily determined to believe that the sensation really exists. This is common to all sensations, that, as they cannot exist but in being perceived, so they cannot be perceived but they must exist. I could as easily doubt of my own existence, as of the existence of my sensations. Even those profound philosophers who have endeavoured to disprove their own existence, have yet left their sensations to stand upon their own bottom, stript of a subject, rather than call in question the reality of their existence.

Here, then, a sensation, a smell for instance, may be presented to the mind three different ways: it may be smelled, it may be remembered, it may be imagined or thought of. In the first case, it is necessarily accompanied with a belief of its present existence ; in the second, it is necessarily accompanied with a belief of its past existence ; and in the last, it is not accompanied with belief at all,* but is what the logicians call a *simple apprehension.*

Why sensation should compel our belief of the present existence of the thing, memory a belief of its past existence, and

---

* This is not strictly correct. The *imagination* of an object is necessarily accompanied with a belief of the existence of the mental representation. Reid uses the term existence for *objective existenc* only, and takes no account of the possibility of a *subjective existence*

imagination no belief at all, I believe no philosopher can give a shadow of reason, but that such is the nature of these operations : they are all simple and original, and therefore inexplicable acts of the mind.

Suppose that once, and only once, I smelled a tuberose in a certain room, where it grew in a pot, and gave a very grateful perfume. Next day I relate what I saw and smelled. When I attend as carefully as I can to what passes in my mind in this case, it appears evident that the very thing I saw yesterday, and the fragrance I smelled, are now the immediate objects of my mind, when I remember it. Further, I can imagine this pot and flower transported to the room where I now sit, and yielding the same perfume. Here likewise it appears, that the individual thing which I saw and smelled, is the object of my imagination.*

Philosophers indeed tell me, that the immediate object of my memory and imagination* in this case, is not the past sensation, but an idea of it, an image, phantasm, or species,† of the odour I smelled : that this idea now exists in my mind, or in my sensorium ; and the mind, contemplating this present idea, finds it a representation of what is past, or of what may exist ; and accordingly calls it memory, or imagination. This is the doctrine of the ideal philosophy ; which we shall not now examine, that we may not interrupt the thread of the present investigation. Upon the strictest attention, memory appears to me to have things that are past, and not present ideas, for its object. We shall afterwards examine this system of ideas and endeavour to make it appear, that no solid proof has ever been advanced of the existence of ideas ; that they are a mere fiction and hypothesis, contrived to solve the phænomena of the human understanding ; that they do not at all answer this end ; and that this hypothesis of ideas or images of things in the mind, or in the sensorium, is the parent of those many paradoxes so shocking to common sense, and of that scepticism which disgrace our philosophy of the mind, and have brought upon it the ridicule and contempt of sensible men.

In the meantime, I beg leave to think, with the vulgar, that, when I remember the smell of the tuberose, that very sensation which I had yesterday, and which has now

no more any existence, is the immediate object of my memory ; and when I imagine it present, the sensation itself, and not any idea of it, is the object of my imagination. But, though the object of my sensation, memory, and imagination, be in this case the same, yet these acts or operations of the mind are as different, and as easily distinguishable, as smell, taste, and sound. I am conscious of a difference in kind between sensation and memory, and between both and imagination. I find this also, that the sensation compels my belief of the present existence of the smell, and memory my belief of its past existence. There is a smell, is the immediate testimony of sense ; there was a smell, is the immediate testimony of memory. If you ask me, why I believe that the smell exists, I can give no other reason, nor shall ever be able to give any other, than that I smell it. If you ask, why I believe that it existed yesterday, I can give no other reason but that I remember it.

Sensation and memory, therefore, are simple, original, and perfectly distinct operations of the mind, and both of them are original principles of belief. Imagination is distinct from both, but is no principle of belief. Sensation implies the present existence of its object, memory its past existence, but imagination views its object naked, and without any belief of its existence or nonexistence, and is therefore what the schools call *Simple Apprehension.* *

Section IV.

JUDGMENT AND BELIEF IN SOME CASES PRE-
CEDE SIMPLE APPREHENSION.

But here, again, the ideal system comes in our way : it teaches us that the first operation of the mind about its ideas, is simple apprehension—that is, the bare conception of a thing without any belief about it : and that, after we have got simple apprehensions, by comparing them together, we perceive agreements or disagreements between them ; and that this perception of the agreement or disagreement of ideas, is all that we call belief, judgment, or knowledge. Now, this appears to me to be all fiction, without any foundation in nature ; for it is acknowledged by all, that sensation must go before memory and imagination ; and hence it necessarily follows, that apprehension, accompanied with belief and knowledge, must go before simple apprehension, at least in the matters we are now speaking of. So that here, instead of

---

* For an exposition of Reid's error in regard to the *immediate* object of Memory and Imagination, see Note B at the end of the volume.—H.

† It will be observed, that Reid understands by *Idea, Image, Phantasm. Species, &c,* always a *ter- tium quid* numerically different both from the Object existing and from the Subject knowing. He had formed no conception of a doctrine in which a representative object is allowed, but only as a modification of the mind itself. On the evil consequences of this error, both on his own philosophy and on his criticism of other opinions, see Note C at the end of the volume. —H.

* *Simple Apprehension,* in the language of the Schools, has no reference to any exclusion of belief. It was merely given to the conception of simple, in contrast to the cognition of complex, terms.—H.

saying that the belief or knowledge is got by putting together and comparing the simple apprehensions, we ought rather to say that the simple apprehension is performed by resolving and analysing a natural and original judgment. And it is with the operations of the mind, in this case, as with natural bodies, which are, indeed, compounded of simple principles or elements. Nature does not exhibit these elements separate, to be compounded by us; she exhibits them mixed and compounded in concrete bodies, and it is only by art and chemical analysis that they can be separated.

Section V.

TWO THEORIES OF THE NATURE OF BELIEF REFUTED — CONCLUSIONS FROM WHAT HATH BEEN SAID.

But what is this belief or knowledge which accompanies sensation and memory? Every man knows what it is, but no man can define it. Does any man pretend to define sensation, or to define consciousness? It is·happy, indeed, that no man does. And if no philosopher had endeavoured to define and explain belief, some paradoxes in philosophy, more incredible than ever were brought forth by the most abject superstition or the most frantic enthusiasm, had never seen the light. Of this kind surely is that modern discovery of the ideal philosophy, that sensation, memory, belief, and imagination, when they have the same object, are only different degrees of strength and vivacity in the idea.* Suppose the idea to be that of a future state after death : one man believes it firmly—this means no more than that he hath a strong and lively idea of it ; another neither believes nor disbelieves—that is, he has a weak and faint idea. Suppose, now, a third person believes firmly that there is no such thing ; I am at a loss to know whether his idea be faint or lively : if it is faint, then there may be a firm belief where the idea is faint ; if the idea is lively, then the belief of a future state and the belief of no future state·must be one and the same. The same arguments that are used to prove that belief implies only a stronger idea of the object than simple apprehension, might as well be used to prove that love implies only a stronger idea of the object than indifference. And then what shall we say of hatred, which must upon this hypothesis be a degree of love, or a degree of indifference? If it should be said, that in love there is something more than an idea—to wit, an affection of the mind—may it not be said

* He refers to Hume.—H.

with equal reason, that in belief there is something more than an idea—to wit, an assent or persuasion of the mind ?

But perhaps it may be thought as ridiculous to argue against this strange opinion, as to maintain it. Indeed, if a man should maintain that a circle, a square, and a triangle differ only in magnitude, and not in figure, I believe he would find nobody disposed either to believe him or to argue against him ; and yet I do not think it less shocking to common sense, to maintain that sensation, memory, and imagination differ only in degree, and not in kind. I know it is said, that, in a delirium, or in dreaming, men are apt to mistake one for the other. But does it follow from this, that men who are neither dreaming nor in a delirium cannot distinguish them ? But how does a man know that he is not in a delirium ? I cannot tell : neither can I tell how a man knows that he exists. But, if any man seriously doubts whether he is in a delirium, I think it highly probable that he is, and that it is time to seek for a cure, which I am persuaded he will not find in the whole system of logic.

I mentioned before Locke's notion of belief or knowledge ; he holds that it consists in a perception of the agreement or disagreement of ideas ; and this he values himself upon as a very important discovery.

We shall have occasion afterwards to examine more particularly this grand principle of Locke's philosophy, and to shew that it is one of the main pillars of modern scepticism, although he had no intention to make that use of it. At present let us only consider how it agrees with the instances of belief now under consideration ; and whether it gives any light to them. I believe that the sensation I have exists ; and that the sensation I remember does not now exist, but did exist yesterday. Here, according to Locke's system, I compare the idea of a sensation with the ideas of past and present existence : at one time I perceive that this idea agrees with that of present existence, but disagrees with that of past existence ; but, at another time, it agrees with the idea of past existence, and disagrees with that of present existence. Truly these ideas seem to be very capricious in their agreements and disagreements. Besides, I cannot, for my heart, conceive what is meant by either. I say a sensation exists, and I think I understand clearly what I mean. But you want to make the thing clearer, and for that end tell me, that there is an agreement between the idea of that sensation and the idea of existence. To speak freely, this conveys to me no light, but darkness ; I can conceive no otherwise of it, than as an odd and obscure circumlocution. I conclude, then, that the belief which accompanies sensation and memory, is a simple act of the mind, which cannot be defined. It is, in this respect, like seeing and hearing, which can never be so defined as to be understood by those who have not these faculties ; and to such as have them, no definition can make these operations more clear than they are already. In like manner, every man that has any belief—and he must be a curiosity that has none—knows perfectly what belief is, but can never define or explain it. I conclude, also, that sensation, memory, and imagination, even where they have the same object, are operations of a quite different nature, and perfectly distinguishable by those who are sound and sober. A man that is in danger of confounding them, is indeed to be pitied ; but whatever relief he may find from another art, he can find none from logic or metaphysic. I conclude further, that it is no less a part of the human constitution, to believe the present existence of our sensations, and to believe the past existence of what we remember, than it is to believe that twice two make four. The evidence of sense, the evidence of memory, and the evidence of the necessary relations of things, are all distinct and original kinds of evidence, equally grounded on our constitution : none of them depends upon, or can be resolved into another. To reason against any of these kinds of evidence, is absurd ; nay, to reason for them is absurd. They are first principles ; and such fall not within the province of reason,* but of common sense.

Section VI.

APOLOGY FOR METAPHYSICAL ABSURDITIES— SENSATION WITHOUT A SENTIENT, A CONSEQUENCE OF THE THEORY OF IDEAS— CONSEQUENCES OF THIS STRANGE OPINION.

Having considered the relation which the sensation of smelling bears to the remembrance and imagination of it, I proceed to consider what relation it bears to a mind, or sentient principle. It is certain, no man can conceive or believe smelling to exist of itself, without a mind, or something that has the power of smelling, of which it is called a sensation, an operation, or feeling. Yet, if any man should demand a proof, that sensation cannot be without a mind or sentient being, I confess that I can give none ; and that to pretend to prove it, seems to me almost as absurd as to deny it.

This might have been said without any apology before the " Treatise of Human Nature" appeared in the world. For till

that time, no man, as far as I know, ever thought either of calling in question that principle, or of giving a reason for his belief of it. Whether thinking beings were of an ethereal or igneous nature, whether material or immaterial, was variously disputed ; but that thinking is an operation of some kind of being or other, was always taken for granted, as a principle that could not possibly admit of doubt.

However, since the author above mentioned, who is undoubtedly one of the most acute metaphysicians that this or any age hath produced, hath treated it as a vulgar prejudice, and maintained that the mind is only a succession of ideas and impressions without any subject ; his opinion, however contrary to the common apprehensions of mankind, deserves respect. I beg therefore, once for all, that no offence may be taken at charging this or other metaphysical notions with absurdity, or with being contrary to the common sense of mankind. No disparagement is meant to the understandings of the authors or maintainers of such opinions. Indeed, they commonly proceed, not from defect of understanding, but from an excess of refinement ; the reasoning that leads to them often gives new light to the subject, and shews real genius and deep penetration in the author ; and the premises do more than atone for the conclusion.

If there are certain principles, as I think there are, which the constitution of our nature leads us to believe, and which we are under a necessity to take for granted in the common concerns of life, without being able to give a reason for them—these are what we call the principles of common sense ; and what is manifestly contrary to them, is what we call absurd.

Indeed, if it is true, and to be received as a principle of philosophy, that sensation and thought may be without a thinking being, it must be acknowledged to be the most wonderful discovery that this or any other age hath produced. The received doctrine of ideas is the principle from which it is deduced, and of which indeed it seems to be a just and natural consequence. And it is probable, that it would not have been so late a discovery, but that it is so shocking and repugnant to the common apprehensions of mankind, that it required an uncommon degree of philosophical intrepidity to usher it into the world. It is a fundamental principle of the ideal system, that every object of thought must be an impression or an idea—that is, a faint copy of some preceding impression. This is a principle so commonly received, that the author above mentioned, although his whole system is built upon it, never offers the least proof of it. It is upon this principle,

---

* See Note † at p. 100, b.—H.

as a fixed point, that he erects his metaphysical engines, to overturn heaven and earth, body and spirit. And, indeed, in my apprehension, it is altogether sufficient for the purpose. For, if impressions and ideas are the only objects of thought, then heaven and earth, and body and spirit, and everything you please, must signify only impressions and ideas, or they must be words without any meaning. It seems, therefore, that this notion, however strange, is closely connected with the received doctrine of ideas, and we must either admit the conclusion, or call in question the premises.

Ideas seem to have something in their nature unfriendly to other existences. They were first introduced into philosophy, in the humble character of images or representatives of things; and in this character they seemed not only to be inoffensive, but to serve admirably well for explaining the operations of the human understanding. But, since men began to reason clearly and distinctly about them, they have by degrees supplanted their constituents, and undermined the existence of everything but themselves. First, they discarded all secondary qualities of bodies; and it was found out by their means, that fire is not hot, nor snow cold, nor honey sweet; and, in a word, that heat and cold, sound, colour, taste, and smell, are nothing but ideas or impressions. Bishop Berkeley advanced them a step higher, and found out, by just reasoning from the same principles, that extension, solidity, space, figure, and body, are ideas, and that there is nothing in nature but ideas and spirits. But the triumph of ideas was completed by the "Treatise of Human Nature," which discards spirits also, and leaves ideas and impressions as the sole existences in the universe. What if, at last, having nothing else to contend with, they should fall foul of one another, and leave no existence in nature at all? This would surely bring philosophy into danger; for what should we have left to talk or to dispute about?

However, hitherto these philosophers acknowledge the existence of impressions and ideas; they acknowledge certain laws of attraction, or rules of precedence, according to which, ideas and impressions range themselves in various forms, and succeed one another: but that they should belong to a mind, as its proper goods and chattels, this they have found to be a vulgar error. These ideas are as free and independent as the birds of the air, or as Epicurus's atoms when they pursued their journey in the vast inane. Shall we conceive them like the films of things in the Epicurean system?

Principio hoc dico, rerum simulacra vagari,
Multa modis multis, in cunctas undique parteis
Tenuia, quæ facile inter se junguntur in auris,
Obvia cum veniunt.- Lucr.

Or do they rather resemble Aristotle's intelligible species, after they are shot forth from the object, and before they have yet struck upon the passive intellect? But why should we seek to compare them with anything, since there is nothing in nature but themselves? They make the whole furniture of the universe; starting into existence, or out of it, without any cause; combining into parcels, which the vulgar call *minds*; and succeeding one another by fixed laws, without time, place, or author of those laws.

Yet, after all, these self-existent and independent ideas look pitifully naked and destitute, when left thus alone in the universe, and seem, upon the whole, to be in a worse condition than they were before. Des Cartes, Malebranche, and Locke, as they made much use of ideas, treated them handsomely, and provided them in decent accommodation; lodging them either in the pineal gland, or in the pure intellect, or even in the divine mind. They moreover clothed them with a commission, and made them representatives of things, which gave them some dignity and character. But the "Treatise of Human Nature," though no less indebted to them, seems to have made but a bad return, by bestowing upon them this independent existence; since thereby they are turned out of house and home, and set adrift in the world, without friend or connection, without a rag to cover their nakedness; and who knows but the whole system of ideas may perish by the indiscreet zeal of their friends to exalt them?

However this may be, it is certainly a most amazing discovery that thought and ideas may be without any thinking being —a discovery big with consequences which cannot easily be traced by those deluded mortals who think and reason in the common track. We were always apt to imagine, that thought supposed a thinker, and love a lover, and treason a traitor: but this, it seems, was all a mistake; and it is found out, that there may be treason without a traitor, and love without a lover, laws without a legislator, and punishment without a sufferer, succession without time, and motion without anything moved, or space in which it may move: or if, in these cases, ideas are the lover, the sufferer, the traitor, it were to be wished that the author of this discovery had farther condescended to acquaint us whether ideas can converse together, and be under obligations of duty or gratitude to each other; whether they can make promises and enter into leagues and covenants, and fulfil or break them, and be punished for the breach. If one set of ideas makes a covenant, another breaks it, and a third is punished for it, there is reason to think that justice is no natural virtue in this system.

It seemed very natural to think, that the "Treatise of Human Nature" required an author, and a very ingenious one too ; but now we learn that it is only a set of ideas which came together and arranged themselves by certain associations and attractions. After all, this curious system appears not to be fitted to the present state of human nature. How far it may suit some choice spirits, who are refined from the dregs of common sense, I cannot say. It is acknowledged, I think, that even these can enter into this system only in their most speculative hours, when they soar so high in pursuit of those self-existent ideas as to lose sight of all other things. But when they condescend to mingle again with the human race, and to converse with a friend, a companion, or a fellow-citizen, the ideal system vanishes ; common sense, like an irresistible torrent, carries them along ; and, in spite of all their reasoning and philosophy, they believe their own existence, and the existence of other things.

Indeed, it is happy they do so ; for, if they should carry their closet belief into the world, the rest of mankind would consider them as diseased, and send them to an infirmary. Therefore, as Plato required certain previous qualifications of those who entered his school, I think it would be prudent for the doctors of this ideal philosophy to do the same, and to refuse admittance to every man who is so weak as to imagine that he ought to have the same belief in solitude and in company, or that his principles ought to have any influence upon his practice ; for this philosophy is like a hobby-horse, which a man in bad health may ride in his closet, without hurting his reputation ; but, if he should take him abroad with him to church, or to the exchange, or to the play-house, his heir would immediately call a jury, and seize his estate.

Section VII.

THE CONCEPTION AND BELIEF OF A SENTIENT BEING OR MIND IS SUGGESTED BY OUR CONSTITUTION—THE NOTION OF RELATIONS NOT ALWAYS GOT BY COMPARING THE RELATED IDEAS.

Leaving this philosophy, therefore, to those who have occasion for it, and can use it discreetly as a chamber exercise, we may still inquire how the rest of mankind, and even the adepts themselves, except in some solitary moments, have got so strong and irresistible a belief, that thought must have a subject, and be the act of some thinking being ; how every man believes himself to be something distinct from his ideas and impressions—something which continues the same identical self when all his ideas and impressions are changed. It is impossible to trace the origin of this opinion in history ; for all languages have it interwoven in their original construction. All nations have always believed it. The constitution of all laws and governments, as well as the common transactions of life, suppose it.

It is no less impossible for any man to recollect when he himself came by this notion ; for, as far back as we can remember, we were already in possession of it, and as fully persuaded of our own existence, and the existence of other things, as that one and one make two. It seems, therefore, that this opinion preceded all reasoning, and experience, and instruction ; and this is the more probable, because we could not get it by any of these means. It appears, then, to be an undeniable fact, that, from thought or sensation, all mankind, constantly and invariably, from the first dawning of reflection, do infer a power or faculty of thinking, and a permanent being or mind to which that faculty belongs ; and that we as invariably ascribe all the various kinds of sensation and thought we are conscious of, to one individual mind or self.

But by what rules of logic we make these inferences, it is impossible to shew ; nay, it is impossible to shew how our sensations and thoughts can give us the very notion and conception either of a mind or of a faculty. The faculty of smelling is something very different from the actual sensation of smelling ; for the faculty may remain when we have no sensation. And the mind is no less different from the faculty ; for it continues the same individual being when that faculty is lost. Yet this sensation suggests to us both a faculty and a mind ; and not only suggests the notion of them, but creates a belief of their existence ; although it is impossible to discover, by reason, any tie or connection between one and the other.

What shall we say, then ? Either those inferences which we draw from our sensations—namely, the existence of a mind, and of powers or faculties belonging to it—are prejudices of philosophy or education, mere fictions of the mind, which a wise man should throw off as he does the belief of fairies ; or they are judgments of nature—judgments not got by comparing ideas, and perceiving agreements and disagreements, but immediately inspired by our constitution.

If this last is the case, as I apprehend it is, it will be impossible to shake off those opinions, and we must yield to them at last, though we struggle hard to get rid of them. And if we could, by a determined obstinacy, shake off the principles of our nature, this is not to act the philosopher, but the fool or the madman. It is incumbent upon those who think that these are not natural principles, to shew, in the first place, how we can otherwise get the notion of a mind and its faculties; and then to shew how we come to deceive ourselves into the opinion that sensation cannot be without a sentient being.

It is the received doctrine of philosophers, that our notions of relations can only be got by comparing the related ideas: but, in the present case, there seems to be an instance to the contrary. It is not by having first the notions of mind and sensation, and then comparing them together, that we perceive the one to have the relation of a subject or substratum, and the other that of an act or operation: on the contrary, one of the related things—to wit, sensation—suggests to us both the correlate and the relation.

I beg leave to make use of the word *suggestion*, because I know not one more proper, to express a power of the mind, which seems entirely to have escaped the notice of philosophers, and to which we owe many of our simple notions which are neither impressions nor ideas, as well as many original principles of belief. I shall endeavour to illustrate, by an example, what I understand by this word. We all know, that a certain kind of sound suggests immediately to the mind, a coach passing in the street; and not only produces the imagination, but the belief, that a coach is passing. Yet there is here no comparing of ideas, no perception of agreements or disagreements, to produce this belief: nor is there the least similitude between the sound we hear and the coach we imagine and believe to be passing.*

It is true that this suggestion is not natural and original; it is the result of experience and habit. But I think it appears, from what hath been said, that there are natural suggestions: particularly, that sensation suggests the notion of present existence, and the belief that what we perceive or feel does now exist; that memory suggests the notion of past existence, and the belief that what we remember did exist in time past; and that our sensations and thoughts do also suggest the notion of a mind, and the belief of its existence, and of its relation to our thoughts. By a like natural principle it is, that a beginning of existence, or any change in nature, suggests to us the notion of a cause, and compels our belief of its existence. And, in like manner, as shall be shewn when we come to the sense of touch, certain sensations of touch, by the constitution of our nature, suggest to us extension, solidity, and motion, which are nowise like to sensations, although they have been hitherto confounded with them.*

* " The word *suggest* " (says Mr Stewart, in reference to the preceding passage) "is much used by Berkeley, in this appropriate and technical sense, not only in his ' Theory of Vision,' but in his ' Principles of Human Knowledge,' and in his ' Minute Philosopher.' It expresses, indeed, the cardinal principle on which his ' Theory of Vision' hinges, and is now so incorporated with some of our best metaphysical speculations, that one cannot easily conceive how the use of it was so long dispensed with. Locke uses the word *excite* for the same purpose; but it seems to imply an hypothesis concerning the *mechanism* of the mind, and by no means expresses the fact in question, with the same force and precision.

"It is remarkable, that Dr Reid should have thought it incumbent on him to apologise for introducing into philosophy a word so familiar to every person conversant with Berkeley's works. ' I beg leave to make use of the word *suggestion*, because,' &c.

" So far Dr Reid's use of the word coincides exactly with that of Berkeley; but the former will be found to annex to it a meaning more extensive than the latter, by employing it to comprehend, not only those *intima ions* which are the result of experience and habit; but another class of *intimations*, (quite overlooked by Berkeley,) those which result from the original frame of the human mind."—*Disserta-*

tion on the History of Metaphysical and Ethical Science. P. 167. Second edition

Mr Stewart might have adduced, perhaps, a higher and, certainly, a more proximate authority, in favour, not merely of the term in general, but of Reid's restricted employment of it, as an intimation of what he and others have designated the Common Sense of mankind. The following sentence of Tertullian contains a singular anticipation, both of the philosophy and of the philosophical phraseology of our author. Speaking of the universal belief of the soul's immortality:—" Natura pleraque *suggeruntur*, quasi de *publico sensu* quo animam Deus ditare dignatus est."—DE ANIMA, c. 2.

Some strictures on Reid's employment of the term *suggestion* may be seen in the " Versuche" of Tetens, I., p. 508, sqq.—H.

* This last statement is not historically correct. But, waving this, there may be adduced, in illustration of the two last paragraphs, the following remarkable passage from St Augustine:—" AU. Recte fortasse existimas. Sed responde obsecro, utrum omne quod per visum cognoscimus, videamus. EV. Ita credo. AU. Credis etiam omne quod videndo cognoscimus, per visum nos cognoscere ? EV. Et hoc credo. AU. Cur ergo plerumque fumum solum videndo, ignem subter latere cognoscimus quem non videmus ? EV. Verum dicis. Et jam non puto nos videre quicquid per visum cognoscimus : possumus enim, ut docuisti, aliud videndo aliud cognoscere quod visus non attigerit. AU. Quid, illud quod per visum sentimus, possumusne non videre ? EV. Nullo modo. AU. Aliud est ergo sentire, aliud cognoscere. V. Omnino aliud, nam sentimus fumum quem videmus, et ex eo ignem quem non videmus, subesse cognoscimus. YAE. Bene intelligis. Sed vides certe cum hoc accidit, corpus nostrum, id est oculos, nihil pati ex igne, sed ex fumo quem solum vident. Etenim videre sentire, et sentire pati esse, jam supra concensimus. EV. Teneo, & assentior. AU. Cum ergo per passionem corporis non latet aliquid animam, non continuo sensus vocatur unus de quinque memoratis, sed cum ipsa passio non latet : namque ille ignis non visus, nec auditus, nec olfactus, nec gustatus, nec tactus a nobis, non tamen latet animam fumo vbo Et cum hoc non latere non vocatur *sensus*, quia ex igne corpus nihil est passum, vocatur tamen *cognitio per sensum*, quia ex passione corporis quamvis alia, id est ex alterius rei visione, conjectatum est atque compertum. EV. Intelligo, et optime video is*t*ud congruere ac favere illi definitioni tuæ, quam ut meam mihi defendendam dedisti: nam ita memini esse abs te sensum definitum, cum animam non latet quod patitur corpus. Itaque illud quod *fumus videretur*,

Section VIII.

THERE IS A QUALITY OR VIRTUE IN BODIES,
WHICH WE CALL THEIR SMELL—HOW
THIS IS CONNECTED IN THE IMAGINATION
WITH THE SENSATION.

We have considered smell as signifying
a sensation, feeling, or impression upon the
mind; and in this sense, it can only be in
a mind, or sentient being: but it is evident
that mankind give the name of *smell* much
more frequently to something which they
conceive to be external, and to be a quality
of body: they understand something by it
which does not at all infer a mind; and
have not the least difficulty in conceiving
the air perfumed with aromatic odours in
the deserts of Arabia, or in some uninhab-
ited island, where the human foot never
trod. Every sensible day-labourer hath as
clear a notion of this, and as full a conviction of the possibility of it, as he hath of
his own existence; and can no more doubt
of the one than of the other.

Suppose that such a man meets with a
modern philosopher, and wants to be informed what smell in plants is. The philosopher tells him, that there is no smell in
plants, nor in anything but in the mind;
that it is impossible there can be smell but
in a mind; and that all this hath been
demonstrated by modern philosohy. The
plain man will, no doubt, be apt to think
him merry: but, if he finds that he is
serious, his next conclusion will be that he
is mad; or that philosophy, like magic,
puts men into a new world, and gives them
different faculties from common men. And
thus philosophy and common sense are set
at variance. But who is to blame for it?
In my opinion the philosopher is to blame.
For if he means by smell, what the rest of
mankind most commonly mean, he is certainly mad. But if he puts a different
meaning upon the word, without observing
it himself, or giving warning to others,
he abuses language and disgraces philosophy, without doing any service to truth:
as if a man should exchange the meaning
of the words *daughter* and *cow*, and then
endeavour to prove to his plain neighbour,
that his cow is his daughter, and his
daughter his cow.

I believe there is not much more wisdom
in many of those paradoxes of the ideal
philosophy, which to plain sensible men
appear to be palpable absurdities, but with
the adepts pass for profound discoveries. I

resolve, for my own part, always to pay a
great regard to the dictates of common
sense, and not to depart from them without
absolute necessity: and, therefore, I am
apt to think that there is really something
in the rose or lily, which is by the vulgar
called *smell*, and which continues to exist
when it is not smelled: and shall proceed
to inquire what this is; how we come by
the notion of it; and what relation this
quality or virtue of smell hath to the sensation which we have been obliged to call
by the same name, for want of another.

Let us therefore suppose, as before, a
person beginning to exercise the sense of
smelling; a little experience will discover
to him, that the nose is the organ of this
sense, and that the air, or something in the
air, is a medium of it. And finding, by
farther experience, that, when a rose is near,
he has a certain sensation, when it is
removed, the sensation is gone, he finds a
connection in nature betwixt the rose and
and this sensation. The rose is considered
as a cause, occasion, or antecedent of the
sensation; the sensation as an effect or
consequence of the presence of the rose;
they are associated in the mind, and constantly found conjoined in the imagination.

But here it deserves our notice, that,
although the sensation may seem more
closely related to the mind its subject, or
to the nose its organ, yet neither of these
connections operate so powerfully upon the
imagination as its connection with the rose
its concomitant. The reason of this seems
to be, that its connection with the mind is
more general, and noway distinguisheth it
from other smells, or even from tastes,
sounds, and other kinds of sensations. The
relation it hath to the organ is likewise
general, and doth not distinguish it from
other smells; but the connection it hath
with the rose is special and constant; by
which means they become almost inseparable in the imagination, in like manner as
thunder and lightning, freezing and cold.

Section IX.

THAT THERE IS A PRINCIPLE IN HUMAN
NATURE, FROM WHICH THE NOTION OF
THIS, AS WELL AS ALL OTHER NATURAL
VIRTUES OR CAUSES, IS DERIVED.

In order to illustrate further how we
come to conceive a quality or virtue in the
rose which we call *smell*, and what this
smell is, it is proper to observe, that the
mind begins very early to thirst after principles which may direct it in the exertion
of its powers. The smell of a rose is a
certain affection or feeling of the mind:
and, as it is not constant, but comes and

---

*sensum vocamus; passi sunt enim eum oculi videndo
qui sunt corporis partes et corpora; ignem autem ex
quo nihil corpus est passum, quamvis cognitus fuerit,
sensum non vocamus.*—DE QUANTITATE ANIMÆ, c.
xxiv. § 45.—H.

goes, we want to know when and where we may expect it; and are uneasy till we find something which, being present, brings this feeling along with it, and, being removed, removes it. This, when found, we call the cause of it; not in a strict and philosophical sense, as if the feeling were really effected or produced by that cause, but in a popular sense; for the mind is satisfied if there is a constant conjunction between them; and such causes are in reality nothing else but laws of nature. Having found the smell thus constant'y conjoined with the rose, the mind is at rest, without inquiring whether this conjunction is owing to a real efficiency or not; that being a philosophical inquiry, which does not concern human life. But every discovery of such a constant conjunction is of real importance in life, and makes a strong impression upon the mind.

So ardently do we desire to find everything that happens within our observation thus connected with something else as its cause or occasion, that we are apt to fancy connections upon the slightest grounds; and this weakness is most remarkable in the ignorant, who know least of the real connections established in nature. A man meets with an unlucky accident on a certain day of the year, and, knowing no other cause of his misfortune, he is apt to conceive something unlucky in that day of the calendar; and, if he finds the same connection hold a second time, is strongly confirmed in his superstition. I remember, many years ago, a white ox was brought into this country, of so enormous a size that people came many miles to see him. There happened, some months after, an uncommon fatality among women in child-bearing. Two such uncommon events, following one another, gave a suspicion of their connection, and occasioned a common opinion among the country-people that the white ox was the cause of this fatality.

However silly and ridiculous this opinion was, it sprung from the same root in human nature on which all natural philosophy grows—namely, an eager desire to find out connections in things, and a natural, original, and unaccountable propensity to believe that the connections which we have observed in time past will continue in time to come. Omens, portents, good and bad luck, palmistry, astrology, all the numerous arts of divination and of interpreting dreams, false hypotheses and systems, and true principles in the philosophy of nature, are all built upon the same foundation in the human constitution, and are distinguished only according as we conclude rashly from too few instances, or cautiously from a sufficient induction.

As it is experience only that discovers these connections between natural causes and their effects; without inquiring further, we attribute to the cause some vague and indistinct notion of power or virtue to produce the effect. And, in many cases, the purposes of life do not make it necessary to give distinct names to the cause and the effect. Whence it happens, that, being closely connected in the imagination, although very unlike to each other, one name serves for both; and, in common discourse, is most frequently applied to that which, of the two, is most the object of our attention. This occasions an ambiguity in many words, which, having the same causes in all languages, is common to all, and is apt to be overlooked even by philosophers. Some instances will serve both to illustrate and confirm what we have said.

Magnetism signifies both the tendency of the iron towards the magnet, and the power of the magnet to produce that tendency; and, if it was asked, whether it is a quality of the iron or of the magnet, one would perhaps be puzzled at first; but a little attention would discover, that we conceive a power or virtue in the magnet as the cause, and a motion in the iron as the effect; and, although these are things quite unlike, they are so united in the imagination, that we give the common name of *magnetism* to both. The same thing may be said of *gravitation*, which sometimes signifies the tendency of bodies towards the earth, sometimes the attractive power of the earth, which we conceive as the cause of that tendency. We may observe the same ambiguity in some of Sir Isaac Newton's definitions; and that even in words of his own making. In three of his definitions, he explains very distinctly what he understands by the *absolute* quantity, what by the *accelerative* quantity, and what by the *motive* quantity, of a centripetal force. In the first of these three definitions, centripetal force is put for the cause, which we conceive to be some power or virtue in the centre or central body; in the two last, the same word is put for the effect of this cause, in producing velocity, or in producing motion towards that centre.

Heat signifies a sensation, and *cold* a contrary one; but *heat* likewise signifies a quality or state of bodies, which hath no contrary, but different degrees. When a man feels the same water hot to one hand and cold to the other, this gives him occasion to distinguish between the feeling and the heat of the body; and, although he knows that the sensations are contrary, he does not imagine that the body can have contrary qualities at the same time. And when he finds a different taste in the same body in sickness and in health, he is easily convinced, that the quality in the body called *taste* is the same as before, although

I

the sensations he has from it are perhaps opposite.

The vulgar are commonly charged by philosophers, with the absurdity of imagining the smell in the rose to be something like to the sensation of smelling; but I think unjustly; for they neither give the same epithets to both, nor do they reason in the same manner from them. What is smell in the rose? It is a quality or virtue of the rose, or of something proceeding from it, which we perceive by the sense of smelling; and this is all we know of the matter. But what is smelling? It is an act of the mind, but is never imagined to be a quality of the mind. * Again, the sensation of smelling is conceived to infer necessarily a mind or sentient being; but smell in the rose infers no such thing. We say, this body smells sweet, that stinks; but we do not say, this mind smells sweet and that stinks. Therefore, smell in the rose, and the sensation which it causes, are not conceived, even by the vulgar, to be things of the same kind, although they have the same name.

From what hath been said, we may learn that the smell of a rose signifies two things: *First*, a sensation, which can have no existence but when it is perceived, and can only be in a sentient being or mind; *Secondly*, it signifies some power, quality, or virtue, in the rose, or in effluvia proceeding from it, which hath a permanent existence, independent of the mind, and which, by the constitution of nature, produces the sensation in us. By the original constitution of our nature, we are both led to believe that there is a permanent cause of the sensation, and prompted to seek after it; and experience determines us to place it in the rose. The names of all smells, tastes, sounds, as well as heat and cold, have a like ambiguity in all languages; but it deserves our attention, that these names are but rarely, in common language, used to signify the sensations; for the most part, they signify the external qualities which are indicated by the sensations—the cause of which phænomenon I † take to be this. † Our sensations have very different degrees of strength. Some of them are so quick and lively as to give us a great deal either of pleasure or of uneasiness. When this is the case, we are compelled to attend to the sensation itself, and to make it an object of thought and discourse‡; we give it a name, which signifies nothing but the sensation; and in this case we readily acknowledge, that the thing meant by that name is in the mind only, and not in anything external. Such are the various kinds of pain, sickness, and the sensations of hunger and other appetites. / But, where the sensation is not so interesting as to require to be made an object of thought, our constitution leads us to consider it as a sign of something external, which hath a constant conjunction with it; and, having found what it indicates, we give a name to that: the sensation, having no proper name, falls in as an accessory to the thing signified by it, and is confounded under the same name. / So that the name may, indeed, be applied to the sensation, but most properly and commonly is applied to the thing indicated by that sensation. The sensations of smell, taste, sound, and colour, are of infinitely more importance as signs or indications, than they are upon their own account; like the words of a language, wherein we do not attend to the sound but to the sense.

Section X.

WHETHER IN SENSATION THE MIND IS ACTIVE OR PASSIVE?

There is one inquiry remains, Whether, in smelling, and in other sensations, the mind is active or passive? This possibly may seem to be a question about words, or, at least, of very small importance; however, if it leads us to attend more accurately to the operations of our minds than we are accustomed to do, it is, upon that very account, not altogether unprofitable. I think the opinion of modern philosophers is, that in sensation the mind is altogether passive.* And this undoubtedly is so far true, that we cannot raise any sensation in our minds by willing it; and, on the other hand, it seems hardly possible to avoid having the sensation when the object is presented. Yet it seems likewise to be true, that, in proportion as the attention is more or less turned to a sensation or diverted from it, that sensation is more or less perceived and remembered. Every one knows that very intense pain may be diverted by a surprise, or by anything that entirely occupies the mind. When we are engaged in earnest conversation, the clock may strike by us without being heard; at least, we remember not, the next moment, that we did hear it. The noise and tumult of a great trading city is not heard by them who have lived in it all their days; but it stuns those strangers who have lived in the peaceful retirement of the country. Whether, therefore, there can be any sensation where the mind is purely passive, I will not say; but I think we are conscious of having given some attention to every sensation which we remember, though ever so recent.

* This is far too absolutely stated.—H.

No doubt, where the impulse is strong and uncommon, it is as difficult to withhold attention as it is to forbear crying out in racking pain, or starting in a sudden fright. But how far both might be attained by strong resolution and practice, is not easy to determine. So that, although the Peripatetics had no good reason to suppose an active and a passive intellect, since attention may be well enough accounted an act of the will, yet I think they came nearer to the truth, in holding the mind to be in sensation partly passive and partly active, than the moderns, in affirming it to be purely passive. Sensation, imagination, memory, and judgment, have, by the vulgar in all ages, been considered as acts of the mind. The manner in which they are expressed in all languages, shews this. When the mind is much employed in them, we say it is very active; whereas, if they were impressions only, as the ideal philosophy would lead us to conceive, we ought, in such a case, rather to say, that the mind is very passive; for, I suppose, no man would attribute great activity to the paper I write upon, because it receives variety of characters.

The relation which the sensation of smell bears to the memory and imagination of it, and to a mind or subject, is common to all our sensations, and, indeed, to all the operations of the mind: the relation it bears to the will is common to it with all the powers of understanding; and the relation it bears to that quality or virtue of bodies which it indicates, is common to it with the sensations of taste, hearing, colour, heat, and cold—so that what hath been said of this sense, may easily be applied to several of our senses, and to other operations of the mind; and this, I hope, will apologize for our insisting so long upon it.

CHAPTER III.

OF TASTING.

A GREAT part of what hath been said of the sense of smelling, is so easily applied to those of tasting and hearing, that we shall leave the application entirely to the reader's judgment, and save ourselves the trouble of a tedious repetition.

It is probable that everything that affects the taste is, in some degree, soluble in the *saliva*. It is not conceivable how anything should enter readily, and of its own accord, as it were, into the pores of the tongue, palate, and *fauces*, unless it had some chemical affinity to that liquor with which these pores are always replete. It is, therefore, an admirable contrivance of nature, that the organs of taste should always be moist with a liquor which is so universal a menstruum, and which deserves to be examined more than it hath been hitherto, both in that capacity, and as a medical unguent. Nature teaches dogs, and other animals, to use it in this last way; and its subserviency both to taste and digestion shews its efficacy in the former.

It is with manifest design and propriety, that the organ of this sense guards the entrance of the alimentary canal, as that of smell the entrance of the canal for respiration. And from these organs being placed in such manner that everything that enters into the stomach must undergo the scrutiny of both senses, it is plain that they were intended by nature to distinguish wholesome food from that which is noxious. The brutes have no other means of choosing their food; nor would mankind, in the savage state. And it is very probable that the smell and taste, noway vitiated by luxury or bad habits, would rarely, if ever, lead us to a wrong choice of food among the productions of nature; although the artificial compositions of a refined and luxurious cookery, or of chemistry and pharmacy, may often impose upon both, and produce things agreeable to the taste and smell, which are noxious to health. And it is probable that both smell and taste are vitiated, and rendered less fit to perform their natural offices, by the unnatural kind of life men commonly lead in society.

These senses are likewise of great use to distinguish bodies that cannot be distinguished by our other senses, and to discern the changes which the same body undergoes, which, in many cases, are sooner perceived by taste and smell than by any other means. How many things are there in the market, the eating-house, and the tavern, as well as in the apothecary and chemist's shops, which are known to be what they are given out to be, and are perceived to be good or bad in their kind, only by taste or smell? And how far our judgment of things, by means of our senses, might be improved by accurate attention to the small differences of taste and smell, and other sensible qualities, is not easy to determine. Sir Isaac Newton, by a noble effort of his great genius, attempted, from the colour of opaque bodies, to discover the magnitude of the minute pellucid parts of which they are compounded: and who knows what new lights natural philosophy may yet receive from other secondary qualities duly examined?

Some tastes and smells stimulate the nerves and raise the spirits: but such an artificial elevation of the spirits is, by the laws of nature, followed by a depression, which can only be relieved by time, or by the repeated use of the like *stimulus*. By the use of such things we create an appetite for them, which very much resembles, and hath all the force of a natural one. It is in this manner that men acquire an appetite for snuff, tobacco, strong liquors, laudanum, and the like.

Nature, indeed, seems studiously to have set bounds to the pleasures and pains we have by these two senses, and to have confined them within very narrow limits, that we might not place any part of our happiness in them; there being hardly any smell or taste so disagreeable that use will not make it tolerable, and at last perhaps agreeable, nor any so agreeable as not to lose its relish by constant use. Neither is there any pleasure or pain of these senses which is not introduced or followed by some degree of its contrary, which nearly balances it; so that we may here apply the beautiful allegory of the divine Socrates—that, although pleasure and pain are contrary in their nature, and their faces look different ways, yet Jupiter hath tied them so together that he that lays hold of the one draws the other along with it.

As there is a great variety of smells, seemingly simple and uncompounded, not only altogether unlike, but some of them contrary to others, and as the same thing may be said of tastes, it would seem that one taste is not less different from another than it is from a smell: and therefore it may be a question, how all smells come to be considered as one *genus*, and all tastes as another ? What is the generical distinction ? Is it only that the nose is the organ of the one and the palate of the other ? or, abstracting from the organ, is there not in the sensations themselves something common to smells, and something else common to tastes, whereby the one is distinguished from the other ? It seems most probable that the latter is the case; and that, under the appearance of the greatest simplicity, there is still in these sensations something of composition.

If one considers the matter abstractly, it would seem that a number of sensations, or, indeed, of any other individual things, which are perfectly simple and uncompounded, are incapable of being reduced into *genera* and *species ;* because individuals which belong to a species must have something peculiar to each, by which they are distinguished, and something common to the whole species. And the same may be said of *species* which belong to one *genus*. And, whether this does not imply some kind of composition, we shall leave to metaphysicians to determine.

The sensations both of smell and taste do undoubtedly admit of an immense variety of modifications, which no language can express. If a man was to examine five

hundred different wines, he would hardly find two of them that had precisely the same taste. The same thing holds in cheese, and in many other things. Yet, of five hundred different tastes in cheese or wine, we can hardly describe twenty, so as to give a distinct notion of them to one who had not tasted them.

Dr Nehemiah Grew, a most judicious and laborious naturalist, in a discourse read before the Royal Society, *anno* 1675, hath endeavoured to shew that there are at least sixteen different simple tastes, which he enumerates.* How many compounded ones may be made out of all the various combinations of two, three, four, or more of these simple ones, they who are acquainted with the theory of combinations will easily perceive. All these have various degrees of intenseness and weakness. Many of them have other varieties ; in some the taste is more quickly perceived upon the application of the sapid body, in others more slowly—in some the sensation is more permanent, in others more transient—in some it seems to undulate or return after certain intervals, in others it is constant ; the various parts of the organ—as the lips, the tip of the tongue, the root of the tongue, the *fauces*, the *uvula*, and the throat—are some of them chiefly affected by one sapid body, and others by another. All these, and other varieties of tastes, that accurate writer illustrates by a number of examples. Nor is it to be doubted, but smells, if examined with the same accuracy, would appear to have as great variety.

CHAPTER IV.

OF HEARING.

Section I.

VARIETY OF SOUNDS—THEIR PLACE AND DISTANCE LEARNED BY CUSTOM, WITHOUT REASONING.

SOUNDS have probably no less variety of modifications, than either tastes or odours. For, first, sounds differ in tone. The ear is capable of perceiving four or five hundred variations of tone in sound, and probably as many different degrees of strength ; by combining these, we have above twenty thousand simple sounds that differ either in tone or strength, supposing every tone to be perfect. But it is to be observed, that to make a perfect tone, a great many

---

* Plato and Galen reckon *seven*, Aristotle and Theophrastus *eight* species of simple tastes. Among the moderns, (as I recollect,) these are estimated at *ten*, by Boerhaave and Linnaeus ; by Haller, at *twelve.*—H.

undulations of elastic air are required, which must all be of equal duration and extent, and follow one another with perfect regularity ; and each undulation must be made up of the advance and recoil of innumerable particles of elastic air, whose motions are all uniform in direction, force, and time. Hence we may easily conceive a prodigious variety in the same tone, arising from irregularities of it, occasioned by the constitution, figure, situation, or manner of striking the sonorous body ; from the constitution of the elastic medium, or its being disturbed by other motions ; and from the constitution of the ear itself, upon which the impression is made.

A flute, a violin, a hautboy, and a French horn, may all sound the same tone, and be easily distinguishable. Nay, if twenty human voices sound the same note, and with equal strength, there will still be some difference. The same voice, while it retains its proper distinctions, may yet be varied many ways,·by sickness or health, youth or age, leanness or fatness, good or bad humour. The same words spoken by foreigners and natives—nay, by persons of different provinces of the same nation—may be distinguished.

Such an immense variety of sensations of smell, taste, and sound, surely was not given us in vain. They are signs by which we know and distinguish things without us ; and it was fit that the variety of the signs should, in some degree, correspond with the variety of the things signified by them.

It seems to be by custom that we learn to distinguish both the place of things, and their nature, by means of their sound. That such a noise is in the street, such another in the room above me ; that this is a knock at my door, that a person walking up stairs—is probably learnt by experience. I remember, that once lying a-bed, and having been put into a fright, I heard my own heart beat ; but I took it to be one knocking at the door, and arose and opened the door oftener than once, before I discovered that the sound was in my own breast. It is probable, that, previous to all experience, we should as little know whether a sound came from the right or left, from above or below, from a great or a small distance, as we should know whether it was the sound of a drum, or a bell, or a cart. Nature is frugal in her operations, and will not be at the expense of a particular instinct, to give us that knowledge which experience will soon produce, by means of a general principle of human nature.

For a little experience, by the constitution of human nature, ties together, not only in our imagination, but in our belief, those things which were in their nature unconnected. When I hear a certain sound, I conclude immediately, without reasoning, that a coach passes by. There are no premises from which this conclusion is inferred by any rules of logic. It is the effect of a principle of our nature, common to us with the brutes.

Although it is by hearing that we are capable of the perceptions of harmony and melody, and of all the charms of music, yet it would seem that these require a higher faculty, which we call *a musical ear.* This seems to be in very different degrees, in those who have the bare faculty of hearing equally perfect ; and, therefore, ought not to be classed with the external senses, but in a higher order.

Section II.

OF NATURAL LANGUAGE.

One of the noblest purposes of sound undoubtedly is language, without which mankind would hardly be able to attain any degree of improvement above the brutes. Language is commonly considered as purely an invention of men, who by nature are no less mute than the brutes ; but, having a superior degree of invention and reason, have been able to contrive artificial signs of their thoughts and purposes, and to establish them by common consent. But the origin of language deserves to be more carefully inquired into, not only as this inquiry may be of importance for the improvement of language, but as it is related to the present subject, and tends to lay open some of the first principles of human nature. I shall, therefore, offer some thoughts upon this subject.

By language I understand all those signs which mankind use in order to communicate to others their thoughts and intentions, their purposes and desires. And such signs may be conceived to be of two kinds : First, such as have no meaning but what is affixed to them by compact or agreement among those who use them—these are artificial signs ; Secondly, such as, previous to all compact or agreement, have a meaning which every man understands by the principles of his nature. Language, so far as it consists of artificial signs, may be called *artificial ;* so far as it consists of natural signs, I call it *natural.*

Having premised these definitions, I think it is demonstrable, that, if mankind had not a natural language, they could never have invented an artificial one by their reason and ingenuity. For all artificial language supposes some compact or agreement to affix a certain meaning to certain signs; therefore, there must be compacts or agreements before the use of artificial signs; but there can be no compact or agreement without signs, nor without language; and, therefore, there must be a natural language before any artificial language can be invented: which was to be demonstrated.

Had language in general been a human invention, as much as writing or printing, we should find whole nations as mute as the brutes. Indeed, even the brutes have some natural signs by which they express their own thoughts, affections, and desires, and understand those of others. A chick, as soon as hatched, understands the different sounds whereby its dam calls it to food, or gives the alarm of danger. A dog or a horse understands, by nature, when the human voice caresses, and when it threatens him. But brutes, as far as we know, have no notion of contracts or covenants, or of moral obligation to perform them. If nature had given them these notions, she would probably have given them natural signs to express them. And where nature has denied these notions, it is as impossible to acquire them by art, as it is for a blind man to acquire the notion of colours. Some brutes are sensible of honour or disgrace; they have resentment and gratitude; but none of them, as far as we know, can make a promise or plight their faith, having no such notions from their constitution. And if mankind had not these notions by nature, and natural signs to express them by, with all their wit and ingenuity they could never have invented language.

The elements of this natural language of mankind, or the signs that are naturally expressive of our thoughts, may, I think, be reduced to these three kinds: modulations of the voice, gestures, and features. By means of these, two savages who have no common artificial language, can converse together; can communicate their thoughts in some tolerable manner; can ask and refuse, affirm and deny, threaten and supplicate; can traffic, enter into covenants, and plight their faith. This might be confirmed by historical facts of undoubted credit, if it were necessary.

Mankind having thus a common language by nature, though a scanty one, adapted only to the necessities of nature, there is no great ingenuity required in improving it by the addition of artificial signs, to supply the deficiency of the natural. These artificial signs must multiply with the arts of life, and the improvements of knowledge. The articulations of the voice seem to be, of all signs, the most proper for artificial language; and as mankind have universally used them for that purpose, we may reasonably judge that nature intended them for it.

But nature probably does not intend that we should lay aside the use of the natural signs; it is enough that we supply their defects by artificial ones. A man that rides always in a chariot, by degrees loses the use of his legs; and one who uses artificial signs only, loses both the knowledge and use of the natural. Dumb people retain much more of the natural language than others, because necessity obliges them to use it. And for the same reason, savages have much more of it than civilized nations. It is by natural signs chiefly that we give force and energy to language; and the less language has of them, it is the less expressive and persuasive. Thus, writing is less expressive than reading, and reading less expressive than speaking without book; speaking without the proper and natural modulations, force, and variations of the voice, is a frigid and dead language, compared with that which is attended with them; it is still more expressive when we add the language of the eyes and features; and is then only in its perfect and natural state, and attended with its proper energy, when to all these we superadd the force of action.

Where speech is natural, it will be an exercise, not of the voice and lungs only, but of all the muscles of the body: like that of dumb people and savages, whose language, as it has more of nature, is more expressive, and is more easily learned.

Is it not pity that the refinements of a civilized life, instead of supplying the defects of natural language, should root it out and plant in its stead dull and lifeless articulations of unmeaning sounds, or the scrawling of insignificant characters? The perfection of language is commonly thought to be, to express human thoughts and sentiments distinctly by these dull signs; but if this is the perfection of artificial language, it is surely the corruption of the natural.

Artificial signs signify, but they do not express; they speak to the understanding, as algebraical characters may do, but the passions, the affections, and the will, hear them not: these continue dormant and inactive, till we speak to them in the language of nature, to which they are all attention and obedience.

It were easy to shew, that the fine arts of the musician, the painter, the actor, and the orator, so far as they are expressive—although the knowledge of them requires in us a delicate taste, a nice judgment, and much study and practice—yet they are nothing else but the language of nature, which we brought into the world with us, but have unlearned by disuse, and so find the greatest difficulty in recovering it.

Abolish the use of articulate sounds and writing among mankind for a century, and every man would be a painter, an actor, and an orator. We mean not to affirm that such an expedient is practicable; or, if it were, that the advantage would counterbalance the loss; but that, as men are led by nature and necessity to converse together, they will use every mean in their power to make themselves understood; and where they cannot do this by artificial signs, they will do it, as far as possible, by natural ones: and he that understands perfectly the use of natural signs, must be the best judge in all the expressive arts.

CHAPTER V.

OF TOUCH.

Section I.

OF HEAT AND COLD.

THE senses which we have hitherto considered, are very simple and uniform, each of them exhibiting only one kind of sensation, and thereby indicating only one quality of bodies. By the ear we perceive sounds, and nothing else; by the palate, tastes; and by the nose, odours. These qualities are all likewise of one order, being all secondary qualities; whereas, by touch we perceive not one quality only, but many, and those of very different kinds.* The chief of them are heat and cold, hardness and softness, roughness and smoothness, figure, solidity, motion, and extension. We shall consider these in order.

As to heat and cold, it will easily be allowed that they are secondary qualities, of the same order with smell, taste, and sound. And, therefore, what hath been already said of smell, is easily applicable to them; that is, that the words *heat* and *cold* have each of them two significations; they sometimes signify certain sensations of the mind, which can have no existence but when when they are not felt, nor can exist anywhere but in a mind or sentient being; but more frequently they signify a quality in bodies, which, by the laws of nature, occasions the sensations of heat and cold in us— a quality which, though connected by custom so closely with the sensation, that we cannot, without difficulty, separate them, yet hath not the least resemblance to it,

and may continue to exist when there is no sensation at all.

The sensations of heat and cold are perfectly known; for they neither are, nor can be, anything else than what we feel them to be; but the qualities in bodies which we call *heat* and *cold*, are unknown. They are only conceived by us, as unknown causes or occasions of the sensations to which we give the same names. But, though common sense says nothing of the nature of these qualities, it plainly dictates the existence of them; and to deny that there can be heat and cold when they are not felt, is an absurdity too gross to merit confutation. For what could be more absurd, than to say, that the thermometer cannot rise or fall, unless some person be present, or that the coast of Guinea would be as cold as Nova Zembla, if it had no inhabitants?

It is the business of philosophers to investigate, by proper experiments and induction, what heat and cold are in bodies. And whether they make heat a particular element diffused through nature, and accumulated in the heated body, or whether they make it a certain vibration of the parts of the heated body; whether they determine that heat and cold are contrary qualities, as the sensations undoubtedly are contrary, or that heat only is a quality, and cold its privation: these questions are within the province of philosophy; for common sense says nothing on the one side or the other.

But, whatever be the nature of that quality in bodies which we call *heat*, we certainly know this, that it cannot in the least resemble the sensation of heat. It is no less absurd to suppose a likeness between the sensation and the quality, than it would be to suppose that the pain of the gout resembles a square or a triangle. The simplest man that hath common sense, does not imagine the sensation of heat, or anything that resembles that sensation, to be in the fire. He only imagines that there is something in the fire which makes him and other sentient beings feel heat. Yet, as the name of *heat*, in common language, more frequently and more properly signifies this unknown something in the fire, than the sensation occasioned by it, he justly laughs at the philosopher who denies that there is any heat in the fire, and thinks that he speaks contrary to common sense.

Section II

OF HARDNESS AND SOFTNESS.

Let us next consider hardness and softness; by which words we always under-

---

* It has been very commonly held by philosophers, both in ancient and modern times, that the division of the senses into five, is altogether inadequate; and psychologists, though not at one in regard to the distribution, are now generally agreed, that under *Touch* —or *Feeling*, in the strictest signification of the term —are comprised perceptions which are, at least, as well entitled to be opposed in species, as those of Taste and Smell.—H.

stand real properties or qualities of bodies of which we have a distinct conception.

When the parts of a body adhere so firmly that it cannot easily be made to change its figure, we call it *hard*; when its parts are easily displaced, we call it *soft*. This is the notion which all mankind have of hardness and softness; they are neither sensations, nor like any sensation; they were real qualities before they were perceived by touch, and continue to be so when they are not perceived; for if any man will affirm that diamonds were not hard till they were handled, who would reason with him?

There is, no doubt, a sensation by which we perceive a body to be hard or soft. This sensation of hardness may easily be had, by pressing one's hand against the table, and attending to the feeling that ensues, setting aside, as much as possible, all thought of the table and its qualities, or of any external thing. But it is one thing to have the sensation, and another to attend to it, and make it a distinct object of reflection. The first is very easy; the last, in most cases, extremely difficult.

We are so accustomed to use the sensation as a sign, and to pass immediately to the hardness signified, that, as far as appears, it was never made an object of thought, either by the vulgar or by philosophers; nor has it a name in any language. There is no sensation more distinct, or more frequent; yet it is never attended to, but passes through the mind instantaneously, and serves only to introduce that quality in bodies, which, by a law of our constitution, it suggests.

There are, indeed, some cases, wherein it is no difficult matter to attend to the sensation occasioned by the hardness of a body; for instance, when it is so violent as to occasion considerable pain: then nature calls upon us to attend to it, and then we acknowledge that it is a mere sensation, and can only be in a sentient being. If a man runs his head with violence against a pillar, I appeal to him whether the pain he feels resembles the hardness of the stone, or if he can conceive anything like what he feels to be in an inanimate piece of matter.

The attention of the mind is here entirely turned towards the painful feeling; and, to speak in the common language of mankind, he feels nothing in the stone, but feels a violent pain in his head. It is quite otherwise when he leans his head gently against the pillar; for then he will tell you that he feels nothing in his head, but feels hardness in the stone. Hath he not a sensation in this case as well as in the other? Undoubtedly he hath; but it is a sensation which nature intended only as a sign of something in the stone; and, accordingly, he instantly fixes his attention upon the thing signified; and cannot, without great difficulty, attend so much to the sensation as to be persuaded that there is any such thing distinct from the hardness it signifies.

But, however difficult it may be to attend to this fugitive sensation, to stop its rapid progress, and to disjoin it from the external quality of hardness, in whose shadow it is apt immediately to hide itself; this is what a philosopher by pains and practice must attain, otherwise it will be impossible for him to reason justly upon this subject, or even to understand what is here advanced. For the last appeal, in subjects of this nature, must be to what a man feels and perceives in his own mind.

It is indeed strange that a sensation which we have every time we feel a body hard, and which, consequently, we can command as often and continue as long as we please, a sensation as distinct and determinate as any other, should yet be so much unknown as never to have been made an object of thought and reflection, nor to have been honoured with a name in any language; that philosophers, as well as the vulgar, should have entirely overlooked it, or confounded it with that quality of bodies which we call *hardness*, to which it hath not the least similitude. May we not hence conclude, that the knowledge of the human faculties is but in its infancy?—that we have not yet learned to attend to those operations of the mind, of which we are conscious every hour of our lives?—that there are habits of inattention acquired very early, which are as hard to be overcome as other habits? For I think it is probable, that the novelty of this sensation will procure some attention to it in children at first; but, being in nowise interesting in itself, as soon as it becomes familiar, it is overlooked, and the attention turned solely to that which it signifies. Thus, when one is learning a language, he attends to the sounds; but when he is master of it, he attends only to the sense of what he would express. If this is the case, we must become as little children again, if we will be philosophers; we must overcome this habit of inattention which has been gathering strength ever since we began to think—a habit, the usefulness of which, in common life, atones for the difficulty it creates to the philosopher in discovering the first principles of the human mind.

The firm cohesion of the parts of a body, is no more like that sensation by which I perceive it to be hard, than the vibration of a sonorous body is like the sound I hear: nor can I possibly perceive, by my reason, any connection between the one and the other. No man can give a reason, why the vibration of a body might not have given the sensation of smelling, and the effluvia of bodies affected our hearing, if it had so pleased our Maker. In like manner, no man can give a reason why the sensations of smell, or taste, or sound, might not have indicated hardness, as well as that sensation which, by our constitution, does indicate it. Indeed, no man can conceive any sensation to resemble any known quality of bodies. Nor can any man shew, by any good argument, that all our sensations might not have been as they are, though no body, nor quality of body, had ever existed.

Here, then, is a phænomenon of human nature, which comes to be resolved. Hardness of bodies is a thing that we conceive as distinctly, and believe as firmly, as anything in nature. We have no way of coming at this conception and belief, but by means of a certain sensation of touch, to which hardness hath not the least similitude; nor can we, by any rules of reasoning, infer the one from the other. The question is, How we come by this conception and belief?

First, as to the conception: Shall we call it an idea of sensation, or of reflection? The last will not be affirmed; and as little can the first, unless we will call that an idea of sensation which hath no resemblance to any sensation. So that the origin of this idea of sensation, one of the most common and most distinct we have, is not to be found in all our systems of the mind: not even in those which have so copiously endeavoured to deduce all our notions from sensation and reflection.

But, secondly, supposing we have got the conception of hardness, how come we by the belief of it? Is it self-evident, from comparing the ideas, that such a sensation could not be felt, unless such a quality of bodies existed? No. Can it be proved by probable or certain arguments? No; it cannot. Have we got this belief, then, by tradition, by education, or by experience? No; it is not got in any of these ways. Shall we then throw off this belief as having no foundation in reason? Alas! it is not in our power; it triumphs over reason, and laughs at all the arguments of a philosopher. Even the author of the "Treatise of Human Nature," though he saw no reason for this belief, but many against it, could hardly conquer it in his speculative and solitary moments; at other times, he fairly yielded to it, and confesses that he found himself under a necessity to do so.

What shall we say, then, of this conception, and this belief, which are so unaccountable and untractable? I see nothing left, but to conclude, that, by an original principle of our constitution, a certain sensation of touch both suggests to the mind the conception of hardness, and creates the belief of it: or, in other words, that this sens-

ation is a natural sign of hardness. And this I shall endeavour more fully to explain.

Section III.

OF NATURAL SIGNS.

As in artificial signs there is often neither similitude between the sign and thing signified, nor any connection that arises necessarily from the nature of the things, so it is also in natural signs. The word *gold* has no similitude to the substance signified by it; nor is it in its own nature more fit to signify this than any other substance; yet, by habit and custom, it suggests this and no other. In like manner, a sensation of touch suggests hardness, although it hath neither similitude to hardness, nor, as far as we can perceive, any necessary connection with it. The difference betwixt these two signs lies only in this—that, in the first, the suggestion is the effect of habit and custom; in the second, it is not the effect of habit, but of the original constitution of our minds.

It appears evident from what hath been said on the subject of language, that there are natural signs as well as artificial; and particularly, that the thoughts, purposes, and dispositions of the mind, have their natural signs in the features of the face, the modulation of the voice, and the motion and attitude of the body: that, without a natural knowledge of the connection between these signs and the things signified by them, language could never have been invented and established among men: and, that the fine arts are all founded upon this connection, which we may call *the natural language of mankind.* It is now proper to observe, that there are different orders of natural signs, and to point out the different classes into which they may be distinguished, that we may more distinctly conceive the relation between our sensations and the things they suggest, and what we mean by calling sensations signs of external things.

The first class of natural signs comprehends those whose connection with the thing signified is established by nature, but discovered only by experience. The whole of genuine philosophy consists in discovering such connections, and reducing them to general rules. The great Lord Verulam had a perfect comprehension of this, when he called it *an interpretation of nature.* No man ever more distinctly understood or happily expressed the nature and foundation of the philosophic art. What is all we know of mechanics, astronomy, and optics, but connections established by nature, and discovered by experience or observation, and consequences deduced from them?

All the knowledge we have in agriculture, gardening, chemistry, and medicine, is built upon the same foundation. And if ever our philosophy concerning the human mind is carried so far as to deserve the name of science, which ought never to be despaired of, it must be by observing facts, reducing them to general rules, and drawing just conclusions from them. What we commonly call natural *causes* might, with more propriety, be called natural *signs*, and what we call *effects*, the things signified. The causes have no proper efficiency or casuality, as far as we know ; and all we can certainly affirm is, that nature hath established a constant conjunction between them and the things called their effects ; and hath given to mankind a disposition to observe those connections, to confide in their continuance, and to make use of them for the improvement of our knowledge, and increase of our power.

A second class is that wherein the connection between the sign and thing signified, is not only established by nature, but discovered to us by a natural principle, without reasoning or experience. Of this kind are the natural signs of human thoughts, purposes, and desires, which have been already mentioned as the natural language of mankind. An infant may be put into a fright by an angry countenance, and soothed again by smiles and blandishments. A child that has a good musical ear, may be put to sleep or to dance, may be made merry or sorrowful, by the modulation of musical sounds. The principles of all the fine arts, and of what we call *a fine taste*, may be resolved into connections of this kind. A fine taste may be improved by reasoning and experience ; but if the first principles of it were not planted in our minds by nature, it could never be acquired. Nay, we have already made it appear, that a great part of this knowledge which we have by nature, is lost by the disuse of natural signs, and the substitution of artificial in their place.

A third class of natural signs comprehends those which, though we never before had any notion or conception of the thing signified, do suggest it, or conjure it up, as it were, by a natural kind of magic, and at once give us a conception and create a belief of it. I shewed formerly, that our sensations suggest to us a sentient being or mind to which they belong—a being which hath a permanent existence, although the sensations are transient and of short duration—a being which is still the same, while its sensations and other operations are varied ten thousand ways—a being which hath the same relation to all that infinite variety of thoughts, purposes, actions, affections, enjoyments, and sufferings, which we are conscious of, or can remember. The

conception of a mind is neither an idea of sensation nor of reflection ; for it is neither like any of our sensations, nor like anything we are conscious of. The first conception of it, as well as the belief of it, and of the common relation it bears to all that we are conscious of, or remember, is suggested to every thinking being, we do not know how.

The notion of hardness in bodies, as well as the belief of it, are got in a similar manner ; being, by an original principle of our nature, annexed to that sensation which we have when we feel a hard body. And so naturally and necessarily does the sensation convey the notion and belief of hardness, that hitherto they have been confounded by the most acute inquirers into the principles of human nature, although they appear, upon accurate reflection, not only to be different things, but as unlike as pain is to the point of a sword.

It may be observed, that, as the first class of natural signs I have mentioned is the foundation of true philosophy, and the second the foundation of the fine arts, or of taste—so the last is the foundation of common sense—a part of human nature which hath never been explained. *

I take it for granted, that the notion of hardness, and the belief of it, is first got by means of that particular sensation which, as far back as we can remember, does invariably suggest it ; and that, if we had never had such a feeling, we should never have had any notion of hardness. I think it is evident, that we cannot, by reasoning from our sensations, collect the existence of bodies at all, far less any of their qualities. This hath been proved by unanswerable arguments by the Bishop of Cloyne, and by the author of the "Treatise of Human Nature." It appears as evident that this connection between our sensations and the conception and belief of external existences cannot be produced by habit, experience, education, or any principle of human nature that hath been admitted by philosophers. At the same time, it is a fact that such sensations are invariably connected with the conception and belief of external existences. Hence, by all rules of just reasoning, we must conclude, that this connection is the effect of our constitution, and ought to be considered as an original principle of human nature, till we find some more general principle into which it may be resolved.†

* See Stewart's "Elements of the Philosophy of the Human Mind." Vol. II.; chap. i., § 3, last note.—H.

† This whole doctrine of *natural signs*, on which his philosophy is in a great measure established, was borrowed by Reid, in principle, and even in expression, from Berkeley. Compare "Minute Philosopher," Dial. IV., §§ 7, 11, 12 ; "New Theory of Vision," §§ 144, 147; "Theory of Vision Vindicated," §§ 32 —13.—H.

Section IV.

OF HARDNESS, AND OTHER PRIMARY QUALITIES.

Further, I observe that hardness is a quality, of which we have as clear and distinct a conception as of anything whatsoever. The cohesion of the parts of a body with more or less force, is perfectly understood, though its cause is not; we know what it is, as well as how it affects the touch. It is, therefore, a quality of a quite different order from those secondary qualities we have already taken notice of, whereof we know no more naturally than that they are adapted to raise certain sensations in us. If hardness were a quality of the same kind, it would be a proper inquiry for philosophers, what hardness in bodies is? and we should have had various hypotheses about it, as well as about colour and heat. But it is evident that any such hypothesis would be ridiculous. If any man should say, that hardness in bodies is a certain vibration of their parts, or that it is certain effluvia emitted by them which affect our touch in the manner we feel—such hypotheses would shock common sense; because we all know that, if the parts of a body adhere strongly, it is hard, although it should neither emit effluvia nor vibrate. Yet, at the same time, no man can say, but that effluvia or the vibration of the parts of a body, might have affected our touch, in the same manner that hardness now does, if it had so pleased the Author of our nature; and, if either of these hypotheses is applied to explain a secondary quality—such as smell, or taste, or sound, or colour, or heat—there appears no manifest absurdity in the supposition.

The distinction betwixt primary and secondary qualities hath had several revolutions. Democritus and Epicurus, and their followers, maintained it. Aristotle and the Peripatetics abolished it. Des Cartes, Malebranche, and Locke, revived it, and were thought to have put it in a very clear light. But Bishop Berkeley again discarded this distinction, by such proofs as must be convincing to those that hold the received doctrine of ideas.[*] Yet, after all, there appears to be a real foundation for it in the principles of our nature.

What hath been said of hardness, is so easily applicable, not only to its opposite, softness, but likewise to roughness and smoothness, to figure and motion, that we may be excused from making the application, which would only be a repetition of what hath been said. All these, by means of certain corresponding sensations of touch, are presented to the mind as real external qualities; the conception and the belief of them are invariably connected with the corresponding sensations, by an original principle of human nature. Their sensations have no name in any language; they have not only been overlooked by the vulgar, but by philosophers; or, if they have been at all taken notice of, they have been confounded with the external qualities which they suggest.

Section V.

OF EXTENSION.

It is further to be observed, that hardness and softness, roughness and smoothness, figure and motion, do all suppose extension, and cannot be conceived without it; yet, I think it must, on the other hand, be allowed that, if we had never felt any thing hard or soft, rough or smooth, figured or moved, we should never have had a conception of extension;[*] so that, as there is good ground to believe that the notion of extension could not be prior to that of other primary qualities, so it is certain that it could not be posterior to the notion of any of them, being necessarily implied in them all.[†]

Extension, therefore, seems to be a quality *suggested* to us, by the very same sensations which suggest the other qualities above mentioned. When I grasp a ball in my hand, I perceive it at once hard, figured, and extended. The feeling is very simple, and hath not the least resemblance to any quality of body. Yet it suggests to us three primary qualities perfectly distinct from one another, as well as from the sensation which indicates them. When I move my hand along the table, the feeling is so simple that I find it difficult to distinguish it into things of different natures; yet, it immediately suggests hardness, smoothness, extension, and motion—things

---

[*] On this distinction of *Primary* and *Secondary* Qualities, see "Essays on the Intellectual Powers," Essay II., chap. 17, and Note D, at the end of the volume.—H.

[*] According to Reid, Extension (Space) is a notion *a posteriori*, the result of experience. According to Kant, it is *a priori*; experience only affording the occasions required by the mind to exert the acts, of which the intuition of space is a condition. To the former it is thus a *contingent*: to the latter, a *necessary* mental possession.—H.

[†] In this paragraph, to say nothing of others in the "Inquiry," Reid evidently excludes *sight* as a sense, through which the notion of *extension* or space, enters into the mind. In his later work, the "Essays on the Intellectual Powers," he, however, expressly allows that function to *sight and touch*, and to those senses alone. See Essay II., chap. 19, p. 262, quarto edition.—H.

of very different natures, and all of them as distinctly understood as the feeling which suggests them.

We are commonly told by philosophers, that we get the idea of extension by feeling along the extremities of a body, as if there was no manner of difficulty in the matter. I have sought, with great pains, I confess, to find out how this idea can be got by feeling ; but I have sought in vain. Yet it is one of the clearest and most distinct notions we have; nor is there anything whatsoever about which the human understanding can carry on so many long and demonstrative trains of reasoning.*

The notion of extension is so familiar to us from infancy, and so constantly obtruded by everything we see and feel, that we are apt to think it obvious how it comes into the mind ; but upon a narrower examination we shall find it utterly inexplicable. It is true we have feelings of touch, which every moment present extension to the mind ; but how they come to do so, is the question ; for those feelings do no more resemble extension, than they resemble justice or courage—nor can the existence of extended things be inferred from those feelings by any rules of reasoning ; so that the feelings we have by touch, can neither explain how we get the notion, nor how we come by the belief of extended things.

What hath imposed upon philosophers in this matter is, that the feelings of touch, which suggest primary qualities, have no names, nor are they ever reflected upon. They pass through the mind instantaneously, and serve only to introduce the notion and belief of external things, which, by our constitution, are connected with them. They are natural signs, and the mind immediately passes to the thing signified, without making the least reflection upon the sign, or observing that there was any such thing. Hence it hath always been taken for granted, that the ideas of extension, figure, and motion, are ideas of sensation, which enter into the mind by the sense of touch, in the same manner as the sensations of sound and smell do by the ear and nose.† The sensations of touch are so con-

nected, by our constitution, with the notions of extension, figure, and motion, that philosophers have mistaken the one for the

strictly relative to the assertion in the text :—" It is not easy to divide distinctly our several *senta ions* into cla-ses. The division of our External Senses into the five common classes, seems very imperfect. Some sensations, received without any previous idea, can either be reduced to none of them—such as the sensations of Hunger, Thirst, Weariness, Sickness ; or if we reduce th..m to the sense of Feeling, they are perceptions as different from the other ideas of Touch —such as Cold, Heat, Hardness, Softness—as the ideas of taste or smell. Others have hinted at an external sense, different from all of the-e." [This allusion has puzzled our Scotti-h p-ychologists. Hutcheson evidently refers to the sixth sense, or sense of venereal titillation, proposed by the elder Scaliger, and approved of by Bacon, Buffon, Voltaire, &c.] ' The following general account may possibly be useful. (1°)—That certain motions raised in our bodies are, by a general law, constituted the *occasiun of perceptions in the mind.* (2°) These perceptions never come entirely alone, but have some other perception joined with them Thus *every sensation is accompanied with the idea of Duration, and yet duration is not a sensible idea, since it also accompanies ideas of internal consciousness or reflection :* so the idea of *Number* may accompany any sensible ideas, and yet may also accompany any other ideas, as well as external sensations. Brutes, when several objects are before them, have probably all the proper ideas of sight which we have, without the idea of number. (3°) Some ideas are found *accompanying* the most different sensations, which yet are not to be perceived s..parately from some.sensible quality. Such are *Extension, Figure, Motion,* and *Rest,* which accompany the ideas of Sight or Colours, and yet may be perceived without them, as in the idea- of Touch, at least if we move our organs along the parts of the body touched. *Extension, Figure, Motion, or Rest, seem therefore to be more properly called ideas accompanying the sensations of Sight and Touch, than the sensations of either of these senses ;* since they can be received sometimes without the ideas of Colour, and sometimes without those of Touching, though never without the one or the other. The *perceptions which are purely sensible,* received each by its proper sense, are Tastes, Smells, Colours, Sound, Cold, Heat, &c. The *universal concomitant ideas* which may attend any idea whatsoever, are Duration and Number. The ideas which accompany the most different sensations, are Extension, Figure, Motion, and Rest. *These all arise without any previous ideas assembled or compared—the concomitant ideas are reputed images of something external*"— ect 1, Art. 1. The reader may likewise consult the same author's "Synopsis Metaphysicæ," Part. 11., cap. i., § 3. See below, p. 829, b, note.

But here I may observe, in the first place, that the statement made in the preceding quotation, (and still more articulately in the " Synopsis,") that *Duration* or *Time* is the inseparable concomitant both of sense and reflection, had been also made by Aristotle and many other philosophers ; and it is indeed curious how long philosophers were on the verge of enunciating the great doctrine first proclaimed by Kant —that Time is a fundamental condition, form, or category of thought. In the second place, I may notice that Hutcheson is not entitled to the praise accorded him by Stewart and Royer Collard for his originality in " the fine and important observation that *Extension, Figure, Motion,* and *Rest,* are rather ideas accompanying the perceptions of touch and vision, than perceptions of these sense, properly so called." In this, he seems only to have, with others, repeated Aristotle, who, in his treatise on the Soul, (Book 11., Ch. 6, Text 64, and Book III. Ch. l, Text 135,) calls *Motion* and *Rest, Magnitude,* (*Extension,*) *Figure,* and *Number,* (Hutcheson's very list,) the common concomitants (ἀκολουθοῦντα καὶ κοινα) of sight and touch, and expressly denies them to be impressions of sense—the sense having no passive affection from these qualities. To these five common concomitants, some of the schoolmen added also, (but out of Aristotle,) *Place, Distance, Position,* and *Continuity.*—H.

---

* All the attempts that have, subsequently to Reid, been made, to analyse the notion of Space into the experience of sense, have failed, equally as those before him.—H.

† It has not " always been taken for granted, that the ideas of Extension, Figure, and Motion, are ideas of sensation." Even a distinguished predecessor of Reid, in his Chair at Glasgow, denied this doctrine of the sensual school, to which he generally adhered. I would not be supposed to suspect Reid of the slightest disingenuousness, but he has certainly here and elsewhere been anticipated by Hutcheson, in some of the most important principles, no less than in some of the weaker positions of his philosophy. I quote, without retrenchment, the following note from Hutcheson's " Essay on the Passions," though only part of it is

other, and never have been able to discern that they were not only distinct things, but altogether unlike. However, if we will reason distinctly upon this subject, we ought to give names to those feelings of touch ; we must accustom ourselves to attend to them, and to reflect upon them, that we may be able to disjoin them from, and to compare them with, the qualities signified or suggested by them.

The habit of doing this is not to be attained without pains and practice ; and till a man hath acquired this habit, it will be impossible for him to think distinctly, or to judge right, upon this subject.

Let a man press his hand against the table—*he feels it hard*. But what is the meaning of this?—The meaning undoubtedly is, that he hath a certain feeling of touch, from which he concludes, without any reasoning, or comparing ideas, that there is something external really existing, whose parts stick so firmly together, that they cannot be displaced without considerable force. There is here a feeling, and a conclusion drawn from it, or some way suggested by it. In order to compare these, we must view them separately, and then consider by what tie they are connected, and wherein they resemble one another. The hardness of the table is the conclusion, the feeling is the medium by which we are led to that conclusion. Let a man attend distinctly to this medium, and to the conclusion, and he will perceive them to be as unlike as any two things in nature. The one is a sensation of the mind, which can have no existence but in a sentient being : nor can it exist one moment longer than it is felt ; the other is in the table, and we conclude, without any difficulty, that it was in the table before it was felt, and continues after the feeling is over. The one implies no kind of extension, nor parts, nor cohesion ; the other implies all these. Both, indeed, admit of degrees, and the feeling, beyond a certain degree, is a species of pain ; but adamantine hardness does not imply the least pain.

And as the feeling hath no similitude to hardness, so neither can our reason perceive the least tie or connection between them ; nor will the logician ever be able to shew a reason why we should conclude hardness from this feeling, rather than softness, or any other quality whatsoever. But, in reality, all mankind are led by their constitution to conclude hardness from this feeling.

The sensation of heat, and the sensation we have by pressing a hard body, are equally feelings ; nor can we, by reasoning, draw any conclusion from the one but what may be drawn from the other : but, by our constitution, we conclude from the first an ob-

scure or occult quality, of which we have only this relative conception, that it is something adapted to raise in us the sensation of heat ; from the second, we conclude a quality of which we have a clear and distinct conception—to wit, the hardness of the body.

Section VI.

OF EXTENSION.

To put this matter in another light, it may be proper to try, whether from sensation alone we can collect any notion of extension, figure, motion, and space.* I take it for granted, that a blind man hath the same notions of extension, figure, and motion, as a man that sees ; that Dr Saunderson had the same notion of a cone, a cylinder, and a sphere, and of the motions and distances of the heavenly bodies, as Sir Isaac Newton.†

As sight, therefore, is not necessary for our acquiring those notions, we shall leave it out altogether in our inquiry into the first origin of them ; and shall suppose a blind man, by some strange distemper, to have lost all the experience, and habits, and notions he had got by touch ; not to have the least conception of the existence, figure, dimensions, or extension, either of his own body, or of any other ; but to have all his knowledge of external things to acquire anew, by means of sensation, and the power of reason, which we suppose to remain entire.

We shall, first, suppose his body fixed immovably in one place, and that he can only have the feelings of touch, by the application of other bodies to it. Suppose him first to be pricked with a pin—this will, no doubt, give a smart sensation : he feels pain ; but what can he infer from it ? Nothing, surely, with regard to the existence or figure of a pin. He can infer nothing from this species of pain, which he may not as well infer from the gout or sciatica. Common sense may lead him to think that this pain has a cause ; but whether this cause is body or spirit, extended or unextended, figured or not figured, he cannot possibly, from any principles he is supposed to have, form the least conjecture. Having had formerly no notion of body or of extension, the prick of a pin can give him none.

Suppose, next, a body not pointed, but

* Why are *Extension* and *Spa e* distinguished as co-ordinate, and thus oddly sundered?—H.

† The observations of Platner, on a person born blind, would prove, however, that *sight*, not *touch*, is the sense by which we principally obtain our knowledge of Figure, and our *empirical* knowledge of Space. Saunderson, at any rate, was not born blind.—H.

blunt, is applied to his body with a force gradually increased until it bruises him. What has he got by this, but another sensation or train of sensations, from which he is able to conclude as little as from the former ? A scirrhous tumour in any inward part of the body, by pressing upon the adjacent parts, may give the same kind of sensation as the pressure of an external body, without conveying any notion but that of pain, which, surely, hath no resemblance to extension.

Suppose, thirdly, that the body applied to him touches a larger or a lesser part of his body. Can this give him any notion of its extension or dimensions ? To me it seems impossible that it should, unless he had some previous notion of the dimensions and figure of his own body, to serve him as a measure.* When my two hands touch the extremities of a body, if I know them to be a foot asunder, I easily collect that the body is a foot long ; and, if I know them to be five feet asunder, that it is five feet long ; but, if I know not what the distance of my hands is, I cannot know the length of the object they grasp ; and, if I have no previous notion of hands at all, or of distance between them, I can never get that notion by their being touched.

Suppose, again, that a body is drawn along his hands or face, while they are at rest. Can this give him any notion of space or motion ? It no doubt gives a new feeling ; but how it should convey a notion of space or motion to one who had none before, I cannot conceive. The blood moves along the arteries and veins, and this motion, when violent, is felt: but I imagine no man, by this feeling, could get the conception of space or motion, if he had it not before. Such a motion may give a certain succession of feelings, as the colic may do ; but no feelings, nor any combination of feelings, can ever resemble space or motion.

Let us next suppose, that he makes some instinctive effort to move his head or his hand ; but that no motion follows, either on account of external resistance, or of palsy. Can this effort convey the notion of space and motion to one who never had it before ? Surely it cannot.

Last of all, let us suppose that he moves a limb by instinct, without having had any previous notion of space or motion. He has here a new sensation, which accompanies the flexure of joints, and the swelling of muscles. But how this sensation can convey into his mind the idea of space and motion, is still altogether mysterious and unintelligible. The motions of the heart

and lungs are all performed by the contraction of muscles, yet give no conception of space or motion. An embryo in the womb has many such motions, and probably the feelings that accompany them, without any idea of space or motion.

Upon the whole, it appears that our philosophers have imposed upon themselves and upon us, in pretending to deduce from sensation the first origin of our notions of external existences, of space, motion, and extension,* and all the primary qualities of body—that is, the qualities whereof we have the most clear and distinct conception. These qualities do not at all tally with any system of the human faculties that hath been advanced. They have no resemblance to any sensation, or to any operation of our minds ; and, therefore, they cannot be ideas either of sensation or of reflection. The very conception of them is irreconcilable to the principles of all our philosophic systems of the understanding. The belief of them is no less so.

Section VII.

OF THE EXISTENCE OF A MATERIAL WORLD.

It is beyond our power to say when, or in what order, we came by our notions of these qualities. When we trace the operations of our minds as far back as memory and reflection can carry us, we find them already in possession of our imagination and belief, and quite familiar to the mind : but how they came first into its acquaintance, or what has given them so strong a hold of our belief, and what regard they deserve, are, no doubt, very important questions in the philosophy of human nature.

Shall we, with the Bishop of Cloyne, serve them with a *quo warranto*, and have them tried at the bar of philosophy, upon the statute of the ideal system ? Indeed, in this trial they seem to have come off very pitifully ; for, although they had very able counsel, learned in the law—viz., Des Cartes, Malebranche, and Locke, who said everything they could for their clients—the

---

* Nay, the recent observations of Weber establish the curious fact, that the same extent will not appear the same to the touch at different parts of the body. —H.

* That the notion of Space is a necessary condition of thought, and that, *as such,* it is impossible to derive it from experience, has been cogently demonstrated by Kant. But that we may not, through sense. have empirically an immediate perception of something *extended,* I have yet seen no valid reason to doubt. The *a priori* Conception does not exclude the *a posteriori* Perception ; and this latter cannot be rejected without belying the evidence of consciousness, which assures us that we are immediately cognizant, not only of a *Self* but of a *Not-Self,* not only of *mind* but of *matter* : and matter cannot be immediately known—that is, known as existing—except as *something extended*. In this, however, I venture a step beyond Reid and Stewart, no less than beyond Kant ; though I am convinced that the philosophy of the two former tended to his conclusion, which is, in fact, that of the common sense of mankind.—H.

Bishop of Cloyne, believing them to be aiders and abetters of heresy and schism, prosecuted them with great vigour, fully answered all that had been pleaded in their defence, and silenced their ablest advocates, who seem, for half a century past, to decline the argument, and to trust to the favour of the jury rather than to the strength of their pleadings.

Thus, the wisdom of *philosophy* is set in opposition to the *common sense* of mankind. The first pretends to demonstrate, *a priori*, that there can be no such thing as a material world; that sun, moon, stars, and earth, vegetable and animal bodies, are, and can be nothing else, but sensations in the mind, or images of those sensations in the memory and imagination; that, like pain and joy, they can have no existence when they are not thought of. The last can conceive no otherwise of this opinion, than as a kind of metaphysical lunacy, and concludes that too much learning is apt to make men mad; and that the man who seriously entertains this belief, though in other respects he may be a very good man, as a man may be who believes that he is made of glass; yet, surely he hath a soft place in his understanding, and hath been hurt by much thinking.

This opposition betwixt philosophy and common sense, is apt to have a very unhappy influence upon the philosopher himself. He sees human nature in an odd, unamiable, and mortifying light. He considers himself, and the rest of his species, as born under a necessity of believing ten thousand absurdities and contradictions, and endowed with such a pittance of reason as is just sufficient to make this unhappy discovery: and this is all the fruit of his profound speculations. Such notions of human nature tend to slacken every nerve of the soul, to put every noble purpose and sentiment out of countenance, and spread a melancholy gloom over the whole face of things.

If this is wisdom, let me be deluded with the vulgar. I find something within me that recoils against it, and inspires more reverent sentiments of the human kind, and of the universal administration. Common Sense and Reason[*] have both one author; that Almighty Author in all whose other works we observe a consistency, uniformity, and beauty which charm and delight the understanding: there must, therefore, be some order and consistency in the human faculties, as well as in other parts of his workmanship. A man that thinks reverently of his own kind, and esteems true wisdom and philosophy, will not be fond, nay, will be very suspicious, of such strange

[*] The reader will again notice this and the other instances which follow, of the inaccuracy of Reid's language in his earlier work, constituting, as different, *Reason* and *Common Sense.*—H.

and paradoxical opinions. If they are false, they disgrace philosophy; and, if they are true, they degrade the human species, and make us justly ashamed of our frame.

To what purpose is it for philosophy to decide against common sense in this or any other matter? The belief of a material world is older, and of more authority, than any principles of philosophy. It declines the tribunal of reason,[*] and laughs at all the artillery of the logician. It retains its sovereign authority in spite of all the edicts of philosophy, and reason itself must stoop to its orders. Even those philosophers who have disowned the authority of our notions of an external material world, confess that they find themselves under a necessity of submitting to their power.

Methinks, therefore, it were better to make a virtue of necessity; and, since we cannot get rid of the vulgar notion and belief of an external world, to reconcile our reason to it as well as we can; for, if Reason[*] should stomach and fret ever so much at this yoke, she cannot throw it off; if she will not be the servant of Common Sense, she must be her slave.

In order, therefore, to reconcile Reason to Common Sense[*] in this matter, I beg leave to offer to the consideration of philosophers these two observations. First, That, in all this debate about the existence of a material world, it hath been taken for granted on both sides, that this same material world, if any such there be, must be the express image of our sensations; that we can have no conception of any material thing which is not like some sensation in our minds; and particularly that the sensations of touch are images of extension, hardness, figure, and motion. Every argument brought against the existence of a material world, either by the Bishop of Cloyne, or by the author of the "Treatise of Human Nature," supposeth this. If this is true, their arguments are conclusive and unanswerable; but, on the other hand, if it is not true, there is no shadow of argument left. Have those philosophers, then, given any solid proof of this hypothesis, upon which the whole weight of so strange a system rests. No. They have not so much as attempted to do it. But, because ancient and modern philosophers have agreed in this opinion, we have taken it for granted. But let us, as becomes philosophers, lay aside authority; we need not, surely, consult Aristotle or Locke, to know whether pain be like the point of a sword. I have as clear a conception of extension, hardness, and motion, as I have of the point of a sword: and, with some pains and practice, I can form as clear a notion of the other sensa-

[*] See last note.—H.

tions of touch as I have of pain. When I do so, and compare them together, it appears to me clear as daylight, that the former are not of kin to the latter, nor resemble them in any one feature. They are as unlike, yea as certainly and manifestly unlike, as pain is to the point of a sword. It may be true, that those sensations first introduced the material world to our acquaintance; it may be true. that it seldom or never appears without their company; but, for all that, they are as unlike as the passion of anger is to those features of the countenance which attend it.

So that, in the sentence those philosophers have passed against the material world, there is an error persona. Their proof touches not matter, or any of its qualities ; but strikes directly against an idol of their own imagination, a material world made of ideas and sensations, which never had, nor can have an existence.

Secondly, The very existence of our conceptions of extension, figure, and motion, since they are neither ideas of sensation nor reflection, overturns the whole ideal system, by which the material world hath been tried and condemned ;* so that there hath been likewise in this sentence an error juris.

It is a very fine and a just observation of Locke, that, as no human art can create a single particle of matter, and the whole extent of our power over the material world consists in compounding, combining, and disjoining the matter made to our hands ; so, in the world of thought, the materials are all made by nature, and can only be variously combined and disjoined by us So that it is impossible for reason or prejudice, true or false philosophy, to produce one simple notion or conception, which is not the work of nature, and the result of our constitution. The conception of extension, motion, and the other attributes of matter, cannot be the effect of error or prejudice ; it must be the work of nature. And the power or faculty by which we acquire those conceptions, must be something different from any power of the human mind that hath been explained, since it is neither sensation nor reflection.

This I would, therefore, humbly propose as an experimentum crucis, by which the ideal system must stand or fall ; and it brings the matter to a short issue : Extension, figure, motion, may, any one, or all of them, be taken for the subject of this experiment. Either they are ideas of sens-

ation, or they are not. If any one of them can be shewn to be an idea of sensation, or to have the least resemblance to any sensation, I lay my hand upon my mouth, and give up all pretence to reconcile reason to common sense in this matter, and must suffer the ideal scepticism to triumph. But if, on the other hand, they are not ideas of sensation, nor like to any sensation, then the ideal system is a rope of sand, and all the laboured arguments of the sceptical philosophy against a material world, and against the existence of every thing but impressions and ideas, proceed upon a false hypothesis.*

* Nothing is easier than to shew, that, so far from refuting Idealism, this doctrine affords it the best of all possible foundations. If Idealism, indeed, supposed the existence of ideas as tertia quædam, distinct at once from the material object and the immaterial subject, these intermediate entities being likewise held to originate immediately or mediately in sense—if this hypothesis, I say, were requisite to Idealism, then would Reid's criticism of that doctrine be a complete and final confutation. But as this criticism did not contemplate, so it does not confute that simpler and more refined Idealism, which views in ideas only modifications of the mind itself; and which, in place of sensualizing intellect, intellectualizes sense. On the contrary, Reid, (and herein he is followed by Mr Stewart,) in the doctrine now maintained, asserts the very positions on which this scheme of Idealism establishes its conclusions. An Egoistical Idealism is established, on the doctrine, that all our knowledge is merely subjective, or of the mind itself; that the Ego has no immediate cognizance of a Non-Ego as existing, but that the Non-Ego is only represented to us in a modification of the self-conscious Ego. This doctrine being admitted, the Idealist has only to shew that the supposition of a Non-Ego, or external world really existent, is a groundless and unnecessary assumption; for, while the law of parcimony 'prohibits the multiplication of substances or causes beyond what the phænomena require, we have manifestly no right to postulate for the Non-Ego the dignity of an independent substance beyond the Ego, seeing that this Non-Ego is, ex hypothesi, known to us, consequently exists for us, only as a phænomenon of the Ego.—Now, the doctrine of our Scottish philosophers is, in fact, the very groundwork on which the Egoistical Idealism reposes. That doctrine not only maintains our sensations of the secondary qualities to be the mere effects of certain unknown causes, of which we are consequently entitled to affirm nothing, but that we have no direct and immediate perception of extension and the other primary qualities of matter. To limit ourselves to extension, (or space,) which figure and motion (the two other qualities proposed by Reid for the experiment) suppose, it is evident that if extension be not immediately perceived as externally existing, extended objects cannot be immediately perceived as realities out, and independent, of the percipient subject ; for, if we were capable of such a perception of such objects, we should necessarily be also capable of a perception of this, the one essential attribute of their existence. But, on the doctrine of our Scottish philosophers, Extension is a notion suggested on occasion of sensations supposed to be determined by certain unknown causes ; which unknown causes are again supposed to be existences independent of the mind, and extended—their complement, in fact, constituting the external world All our knowledge of the Non-Ego is thus merely ideal and mediate; we have no knowledge of any really objective reality, except through a subjective representation or notion ; in other words. we are only immediately cognizant of certain modes of our own minds, and, in and through them, mediately warned of the phænomena of the material universe. In all essential respects, this doctrine of Reid and Stewart is identical with Kant's ; except that the German philosopher, in holding space

* It only overturns that Idealism founded on the clumsy hypothesis of ideas being something different, both from the reality they represent, and from the mind contemplating their representation, and which, also, derives all such ideas from without. This doctrine may subvert the Idealism of Berkeley, but it even supplies a basis for an Idealism like that of Fichte. See the following note.—H.

If our philosophy concerning the mind be so lame with regard to the origin of our notions of the clearest, most simple, and most familiar objects of thought, and the powers from which they are derived, can we expect that it should be more perfect in the account it gives of the origin of our opinions and belief? We have seen already some instances of its imperfection in this respect: and, perhaps, that same nature which hath given us the power to conceive things altogether unlike to any of our sensations, or to any operation of our minds, hath likewise provided for our belief of them, by some part of our constitution hitherto not explained.

Bishop Berkeley hath proved, beyond the possibility of reply, that we cannot by reasoning infer the existence of matter from our sensations; and the author of the "Treatise of Human Nature" hath proved no less clearly, that we cannot by reasoning infer the existence of our own or other minds from our sensations. But are we to admit nothing but what can be proved by reasoning? Then we must be sceptics indeed, and believe nothing at all. The author of the "Treatise of Human Nature" appears to me to be but a half-sceptic. He hath not followed his principles so far as they lead him; but, after having, with unparalleled intrepidity and success, combated vulgar prejudices, when he had but one blow to strike, his courage fails him, he fairly lays down his arms, and yields himself a captive to the most common of all vulgar prejudices—I mean the belief of the existence of his own impressions and ideas. *

I beg, therefore, to have the honour of making an addition to the sceptical system, without which I conceive it cannot hang together. I affirm, that the belief of the existence of impressions and ideas, is as little supported by reason, as that of the existence of minds and bodies. No man ever did or could offer any reason for this belief.

ness are real, in so far as we are cons-ious of them. I cannot doubt, for example, that I am actually conscious of a certain feeling of fragrance, and of certain perceptions of colour, figure, &c. when I see and smell a rose. Of the reality of these, as experienced, I cannot doubt, because they are facts of consciousness; and of consciousness I cannot doubt, because such doubt being itself an act of consciousness, would contradict. and, consequently, annihilate itself. But of all beyond the mere phænomena of which we are conscious, we may—without fear of self-contradiction at least—doubt. I may, for instance, doubt whether the rose I see and smell has any existence beyond a phænomenal existence in my consciousness. I cannot doubt that I am conscious of it *as* something different from self, but whether it have, indeed, any reality beyond my mind—whether the *not-self* be not in truth only *self*—that I may philosophically question. In like manner, I am conscious of the memory of a certain past event. Of the contents of this memory, as a phænomenon given in consciousness, scepticism is impossible. But I may by possibility demur to the reality of all beyond these contents and the sphere of present consciousness.

In Reid's strictures upon Hume, he confounds two opposite things. He reproaches that philosopher with inconsequence, in holding to " the belief of the existence of his own impressions and ideas." Now, if, by *the existence of impressions and ideas*, Reid meant their existence as mere phænomena of consciousness, his criticism is inept; for a disbelief of their existence, as such phænomena, would have been a suicidal act in the sceptic. If, again, he meant by *impressions* and *ideas* the hypothesis of representative entities different from the mind and its modifications; in that case the objection is equally invalid. Hume was a sceptic; that is, he accepted the premises afforded him by the dogmatist, and carried these premises to their legitimate consequences. To blame Hume, therefore, for not having doubted of his borrowed principles, is to blame the sceptic for not performing a part altogether inconsistent with his vocation. But, in point of fact, the hypothesis of such entities is of no value to the idealist or sceptic. *Impressions* and *ideas*, viewed as mental modes, would have answered Hume's purpose not a whit worse than *impressions* and *ideas* viewed as objects, but not as affections of mind. The most consistent scheme of idealism known in the history of philosophy is that of Fichte; and Fichte's idealism is founded on a basis which excludes that crude hypothesis of ideas on which alone Reid imagined any doctrine of Idealism could possibly be established. And is the acknowledged result of the Fichtean dogmatism less a nihilism than the scepticism of Hume? "The sum to al," says Fichte, " is this :—There is absolutely nothing permanent either without me or within me, but only an unceasing change. I know absolutely nothing of any existence, not even of my own. I myself know nothing, and am nothing. Images (Bilder) there are: they constitute all that apparently exists, and what they know of themselves is after the manner of images; images that pass and vanish without there being aught to witness their transition; that consist in fact of the images of images, without significance and without an aim. I myself am one of these images; nay, I am not even thus much, but only a confused image of images All reality is converted into a marvellous dream, without a life to dream of, and without a mind to dream; into a dream made up only of a dream of itself. Perception is a dream; thought—the source of all the existence and all the reality which I imagine to myself of *my* existence, of my power, of my destination— is the dream of that dream."—H.

to be a necessary form of our conceptions of external things, prudently declined asserting that these unknown things are, *in themselves*, extended.

Now, the doctrine of Kant has been rigorously proved by Jacobi and Fichte to be, in its legitimate issue, a doctrine of absolute Idealism; and the demonstrations which the philosopher of Koenigsberg has given of the existence of an external world, have been long admitted, even by his disciples them elves, to be inconclusive. But our Scottish philosophers appeal to an argument which the German philosopher overtly rejected—the argument, as it is called, from common sense. In their hands however, this argument is unavailing; for, if it be good against the conclusions of the Idealist, it is good against the premises which they afford him. The common sense of mankind only assures us of the existence of an external and extended world, in assuring us that we are conscious, not merely of the phænomena of mind in relation to matter, but of the phænomena of matter in relation to mind—in other words, that we are immediately percipient of extended things.

Reid himself seems to have become obscurely aware of this condition; and, though he never retracted his doctrine concerning the mere *representation of extern-i* n, we find, in his " Essays on the Intellectual Powers," assertions in regard to the immediate perception of external things, which would tend to shew that his later views were more in unison with the necessary convictions of mankind. But of this again.
—H.

* There is in this and the two following paragraphs a confusion and inaccuracy which it is requisite to notice—There is no scepticism possible touching the facts of consciousness in themselves. We cannot doubt that the phænomena of conscious-

K

Des Cartes took it for granted; that he thought, and had sensations and ideas; so have all his followers done. Even the hero of scepticism hath yielded this point, I crave leave to say, weakly and imprudently. I say so, because I am persuaded that there is no principle of his philosophy that obliged him to make this concession. And what is there in impressions and ideas so formidable that this all-conquering philosophy, after triumphing over every other existence, should pay homage to them? Besides, the concession is dangerous: for belief is of such a nature, that, if you leave any root, it will spread; and you may more easily pull it up altogether, than say, Hitherto shalt thou go and no further: the existence of impressions and ideas I give up to thee; but see thou pretend to nothing more. A thorough and consistent sceptic will never, therefore, yield this point; and while he holds it, you can never oblige him to yield anything else.

To such a sceptic I have nothing to say; but of the semi-sceptics, I should beg to know, why they believe the existence of their impressions and ideas. The true reason I take to be, because they cannot help it; and the same reason will lead them to believe many other things.

All reasoning must be from first principles; and for first principles no other reason can be given but this, that, by the constitution of our nature, we are under a necessity of assenting to them. Such principles are parts of our constitution, no less than the power of thinking: reason can neither make nor destroy them; nor can it do anything without them: it is like a telescope, which may help a man to see farther, who hath eyes; but, without eyes, a telescope shews nothing at all. A mathematician cannot prove the truth of his axioms, nor can he prove anything, unless he takes them for granted. We cannot prove the existence of our minds, nor even of our thoughts and sensations. A historian, or a witness, can prove nothing, unless it is taken for granted that the memory and senses may be trusted. A natural philosopher can prove nothing, unless it is taken for granted that the course of nature is steady and uniform.

How or when I got such first principles, upon which I build all my reasoning, I know not; for I had them before I can remember: but I am sure they are parts of my constitution, and that I cannot throw them off. That our thoughts and sensations must have a subject, which we call *ourself*, is not therefore an opinion got by reasoning, but a natural principle. That our sensations of touch indicate something external, extended, figured, hard or soft, is not a deduction of reason, but a natural

principle. The belief of it, and the very conception of it, are equally parts of our constitution. If we are deceived in it, we are deceived by Him that made us, and there is no remedy.[*]

I do not mean to affirm, that the sensations of touch do, from the very first, suggest the same notions of body and its qualities which they do when we are grown up. Perhaps Nature is frugal in this, as in her other operations. The passion of love, with all its concomitant sentiments and desires, is naturally suggested by the perception of beauty in the other sex; yet the same perception does not suggest the tender passion till a certain period of life. A blow given to an infant, raises grief and lamentation; but when he grows up, it as naturally stirs resentment, and prompts him to resistance. Perhaps a child in the womb, or for some short period of its existence, is merely a sentient being; the faculties by which it perceives an external world, by which it reflects on its own thoughts, and existence, and relation to other things, as well as its reasoning and moral faculties, unfold themselves by degrees; so that it is inspired with the various principles of common sense, as with the passions of love and resentment, when it has occasion for them.

Section VIII.

OF THE SYSTEMS OF PHILOSOPHERS CONCERNING THE SENSES.[†]

All the systems of philosophers about our senses and their objects have split upon this rock, of not distinguishing properly

---

* The philosophers who have most loudly appealed to the veracity of God, and the natural conviction of mankind, in refutation of certain obnoxious conclusions, have too often silently contradicted that veracity and those convictions, when opposed to certain favourite opinions. But it is evident that such authority is either good for all, or good for nothing. Our natural consciousness assures us (and the *fact* of that *assurance* is admitted by philosophers of all opinions) that we have an immediate knowledge of the very things themselves of an external and extended world; and, on the ground of this knowledge alone, is the belief or mankind founded, that such a world really exists. Reid ought, therefore, either to have given up his doctrine of the mere *suggestion* of extension, &c., as subjective notions, on the occasion of sensation, or not to appeal to the Divine veracity, and the common sense of mankind, in favour of conclusions of which that doctrine subverts the foundation. In this inconsistency, Reid has, however, besides Des Cartes, many distinguished copartners.—H.

† On this subject, see " Essays on the Intellectual Powers," Essay II., chap. 7-15, and the notes thereon. It is perhaps proper to recall to the reader's attention, that, by the Ideal Theory, Reid always understands the ruder form of the doctrine, which holds that ideas are entities, different both from the external object and from the percipient mind, and that he had no conception of the finer form of that doctrine, which holds that all that we are conscious of in perception, (of course also in imagination,) is only a modification of the mind itself.—See Note C.—H.

sensations which can have no existence but when they are felt, from the things suggested by them. Aristotle—with as distinguishing a head as ever applied to philosophical disquisitions—confounds these two; and makes every sensation to be the form, without the matter, of the thing perceived by it. As the impression of a seal upon wax has the form of the seal but nothing of the matter of it, so he conceived our sensations to be impressions upon the mind, which bear the image, likeness, or form of the external thing perceived, without the matter of it. Colour, sound, and smell, as well as extension, figure, and hardness, are, according to him, various forms of matter : our sensations are the same forms imprinted on the mind, and perceived in its own intellect. It is evident from this, that Aristotle made no distinction between primary and secondary qualities of bodies, although that distinction was made by Democritus, Epicurus, and others of the ancients. *

Des Cartes, Malebranche, and Locke, revived the distinction between primary and secondary qualities; but they made the secondary qualities mere sensations, and the primary ones resemblances of our sensations. They maintained that colour, sound, and heat, are not anything in bodies, but sensations of the mind ; at the same time, they acknowledged some particular texture or modification of the body to be the cause or occasion of those sensations ; but to this modification they gave no name. Whereas, by the vulgar, the names of colour, heat, and sound, are but rarely applied to the sensations, and most commonly to those unknown causes of them, as hath been already explained. The constitution of our nature leads us rather to attend to the things signified by the sensation than to the sensation itself, and to give a name to the former rather than to the latter. Thus we see, that, with regard to secondary qualities, these philosophers thought with the vulgar, and with common sense. Their paradoxes were only an abuse of words; for when they maintain, as an important modern discovery, that there is no heat in the fire, they mean no more, than that the fire does not feel heat, which every one knew before. With regard to primary qualities, these philosophers erred more grossly. They indeed believed the existence of those qualities ; but they did not at all attend to the sensations that suggest them, which, having no names, have been as little considered as if they had no existence. They were aware that figure, extension, and

hardness, are perceived by means of sensations of touch ; whence they rashly concluded, that these sensations must be images and resemblances of figure, extension, and hardness.

The received hypothesis of ideas naturally led them to this conclusion : and indeed cannot consist with any other ; for, according to that hypothesis, external things must be perceived by means of images of them in the mind ; and what can those images of external things in the mind be, but the sensations by which we perceive them ?

This, however, was to draw a conclusion from a hypothesis against fact. We need not have recourse to any hypothesis to know what our sensations are, or what they are like. By a proper degree of reflection and attention we may understand them perfectly, and be as certain that they are not like any quality of body, as we can be, that the toothache is not like a triangle. How a sensation should instantly make us conceive and believe the existence of an external thing altogether unlike to it, I do not pretend to know ; and when I say that the one suggests the other, I mean not to explain the manner of their connection, but to express a fact, which every one may be conscious of—namely, that, by a law of our nature, such a conception and belief constantly and immediately follow the sensation.

Bishop Berkeley gave new light to this subject, by shewing, that the qualities of an inanimate thing, such as matter is conceived to be, cannot resemble any sensation ; that it is impossible to conceive anything like the sensations of our minds, but the sensations of other minds. Every one that attends properly to his sensations must assent to this ; yet it had escaped all the philosophers that came before Berkeley ; it had escaped even the ingenious Locke, who had so much practised reflection on the operations of his own mind. So difficult it is to attend properly even to our own feelings. They are so accustomed to pass through the mind unobserved, and instantly to make way for that which nature intended them to signify, that it is extremely difficult to stop, and survey them ; and when we think we have acquired this power, perhaps the mind still fluctuates between the sensation and its associated quality, so that they mix together, and present something to the imagination that is compounded of both. Thus, in a globe or cylinder, whose opposite sides are quite unlike in colour, if you turn it slowly, the colours are perfectly distinguishable, and their dissimilitude is manifest ; but if it is turned fast, they lose their distinction, and seem to be of one and the same colour.

---

* On this last, see Aristotle. *De Anima*, L. III., c. 1, and *Metaph*. L. III. c. 5.—The Aristotelic distinction of *first* and *second* qualities was of another kind.—H. See Note D, p. 829 b.

No succession can be more quick than that of tangible qualities to the sensations with which nature has associated them: but when one has once acquired the art of making them separate and distinct objects of thought, he will then clearly perceive that the maxim of Bishop Berkeley, above-mentioned, is self-evident; and that the features of the face are not more unlike to a passion of the mind which they indicate, than the sensations of touch are to the primary qualities of body.

But let us observe what use the Bishop makes of this important discovery. Why, he concludes, that we can have no conception of an inanimate substance, such as matter is conceived to be, or of any of its qualities; and that there is the strongest ground to believe that there is no existence in nature but minds, sensations, and ideas: if there is any other kind of existence, it must be what we neither have nor can have any conception of. But how does this follow? Why, thus: We can have no conception of anything but what resembles some sensation or idea in our minds; but the sensations and ideas in our minds can resemble nothing but the sensations and ideas in other minds; therefore, the conclusion is evident. This argument, we see, leans upon two propositions. The last of them the ingenious author hath, indeed, made evident to all that understand his reasoning, and can attend to their own sensations: but the first proposition he never attempts to prove; it is taken from the doctrine of ideas, which hath been so universally received by philosophers, that it was thought to need no proof.

We may here again observe, that this acute writer argues from a hypothesis against fact, and against the common sense of mankind. That we can have no conception of anything, unless there is some impression, sensation, or idea, in our minds which resembles it, is indeed an opinion which hath been very generally received among philosophers; but it is neither self-evident, nor hath it been clearly proved; and therefore it hath been more reasonable to call in question this doctrine of philosophers, than to discard the material world, and by that means expose philosophy to the ridicule of all men who will not offer up common sense as a sacrifice to metaphysics.

We ought, however, to do this justice both to the Bishop of Cloyne and to the author of the "Treatise of Human Nature," to acknowledge, that their conclusions are justly drawn from the doctrine of ideas, which has been so universally received. On the other hand, from the character of Bishop Berkeley, and of his predecessors, Des Cartes, Locke, and Malebranche, we may venture to say, that, if they had seen all the consequences of this doctrine, as clearly as the author before mentioned did, they would have suspected it vehemently, and examined it more carefully than they appear to have done.

The theory of ideas, like the Trojan horse, had a specious appearance both of innocence and beauty; but if those philosophers had known that it carried in its belly death and destruction to all science and common sense, they would not have broken down their walls to give it admittance.

That we have clear and distinct conceptions of extension, figure, motion, and other attributes of body, which are neither sensations, nor like any sensation, is a fact of which we may be as certain as that we have sensations. And that all mankind have a fixed belief of an external material world—a belief which is neither got by reasoning nor education, and a belief which we cannot shake off, even when we seem to have strong arguments against it and no shadow of argument for it—is likewise a fact, for which we have all the evidence that the nature of the thing admits. These facts are phœnomena of human nature, from which we may justly argue against any hypothesis, however generally received. But to argue from a hypothesis against facts, is contrary to the rules of true philosophy.

CHAPTER VI.

OF SEEING.

Section I;

THE EXCELLENCE AND DIGNITY OF THIS FACULTY.

THE advances made in the knowledge of optics in the last age and in the present, and chiefly the discoveries of Sir Isaac Newton, do honour, not to philosophy only, but to human nature. Such discoveries ought for ever to put to shame the ignoble attempts of our modern sceptics to depreciate the human understanding, and to dispirit men in the search of truth, by representing the human faculties as fit for nothing but to lead us into absurdities and contradictions.

Of the faculties called *the five senses,* sight is without doubt the noblest. The rays of light, which minister to this sense, and of which, without it, we could never have had the least conception, are the most wonderful and astonishing part of the inanimate creation. We must be satisfied of this, if we consider their extreme minuteness; their inconceivable velocity;

the regular variety of colours which they exhibit; the invariable laws according to which they are acted upon by other bodies, in their reflections, inflections, and refractions, without the least change of their original properties; and the facility with which they pervade bodies of great density and of the closest texture, without resistance, without crowding or disturbing one another, without giving the least sensible impulse to the lightest bodies.

The structure of the eye, and of all its appurtenances, the admirable contrivances of nature for performing all its various external and internal motions, and the variety in the eyes of different animals, suited to their several natures and ways of life, clearly demonstrate this organ to be a masterpiece of Nature's work. And he must be very ignorant of what hath been discovered about it, or have a very strange cast of understanding, who can seriously doubt whether or not the rays of light and the eye were made for one another, with consummate wisdom, and perfect skill in optics.

If we shall suppose an order of beings, endued with every human faculty but that of sight, how incredible would it appear to such beings, accustomed only to the slow informations of touch, that, by the addition of an organ, consisting of a ball and socket of an inch diameter, they might be enabled, in an instant of time, without changing their place, to perceive the disposition of a whole army or the order of a battle, the figure of a magnificent palace or all the variety of a landscape! If a man were by feeling to find out the figure of the peak of Teneriffe, or even of St Peter's Church at Rome, it would be the work of a lifetime.[*]

It would appear still more incredible to such beings as we have supposed, if they were informed of the discoveries which may be made by this little organ in things far beyond the reach of any other sense : that by means of it we can find our way in the pathless ocean ; that we can traverse the globe of the earth, determine its figure and dimensions, and delineate every region of it ;—yea, that we can measure the planetary orbs, and make discoveries in the sphere of the fixed stars.

Would it not appear still more astonishing to such beings, if they should be farther informed, that, by means of this same organ, we can perceive the tempers and dispositions, the passions and affections, of our fellow-creatures, even when they want most to conceal them ?—that, when the tongue

is taught most artfully to lie and dissemble, the hypocrisy should appear in the countenance to a discerning eye ?—and that, by this organ, we can often perceive what is straight and what is crooked in the mind as well as in the body ? How many mysterious things must a blind man believe, if he will give credit to the relations of those that see ? Surely he needs as strong a faith as is required of a good Christian.

It is not therefore without reason that the faculty of seeing is looked upon, not only as more noble than the other senses, but as having something in it of a nature superior to sensation. The evidence of reason is called *seeing*, not *feeling*, *smelling*, or *tasting*. Yea, we are wont to express the manner of the Divine knowledge by *seeing*, as that kind of knowledge which is most perfect in us.

Section II.

SIGHT DISCOVERS ALMOST NOTHING WHICH THE BLIND MAY NOT COMPREHEND—THE REASON OF THIS.

Notwithstanding what hath been said of the dignity and superior nature of this faculty, it is worthy of our observation, that there is very little of the knowledge acquired by sight, that may not be communicated to a man born blind. One who never saw the light, may be learned and knowing in every science, even in optics ; and may make discoveries in every branch of philosophy. He may understand as much as another man, not only of the order, distances, and motions of the heavenly bodies ; but of the nature of light, and of the laws of the reflection and refraction of its rays. He may understand distinctly how those laws produce the phænomena of the rainbow, the prism, the camera obscura, and the magic lanthorn, and all the powers of the microscope and telescope. This is a fact sufficiently attested by experience.

In order to perceive the reason of it, we must distinguish the appearance that objects make to the eye, from the things suggested by that appearance : and again, in the visible appearance of objects, we must distinguish the appearance of colour from the appearance of extension, figure, and motion. First, then, as to the visible appearance of the figure, and motion, and extension of bodies, I conceive that a man born blind may have a distinct notion, if not of the very things, at least of something extremely like to them. May not a blind man be made to conceive that a body moving directly from the eye, or directly towards it, may appear to be at rest ? and that the same motion may appear quicker

---

[*] The thing would be impossible. Let any one try by touch to ascertain the figure of a room, with which he is previously unacquainted, and not altogether of the usual shape, and he will find that 'ouch will afford him but slender aid.—H.

or slower, according as it is nearer to the eye or farther off, more direct or more oblique? May he not be made to conceive, that a plain surface, in a certain position, may appear as a straight line, and vary its visible figure, as its position, or the position of the eye, is varied?—that a circle seen obliquely will appear an ellipse; and a square, a rhombus, or an oblong rectangle? Dr Saunderson understood the projection of the sphere, and the common rules of perspective; and if he did, he must have understood all that I have mentioned. If there were any doubt of Dr Saunderson's understanding these things, I could mention my having heard him say in conversation, that he found great difficulty in understanding Dr Halley's demonstration of that proposition, that the angles made by the circles of the sphere, are equal to the angles made by their representatives in the stereographic projection; but, said he, when I laid aside that demonstration, and considered the proposition in my own way, I saw clearly that it must be true. Another gentleman, of undoubted credit and judgment in these matters, who had part in this conversation, remembers it distinctly.

As to the appearance of colour, a blind man must be more at a loss; because he hath no perception that resembles it. Yet he may, by a kind of analogy, in part supply this defect. To those who see, a scarlet colour signifies an unknown quality in bodies, that makes to the eye an appearance which they are well acquainted with and have often observed—to a blind man, it signifies an unknown quality, that makes to the eye an appearance which he is unacquainted with. But he can conceive the eye to be variously affected by different colours, as the nose is by different smells, or the ear by different sounds. Thus he can conceive scarlet to differ from blue, as the sound of a trumpet does from that of a drum; or as the smell of an orange differs from that of an apple. It is impossible to know whether a scarlet colour has the same appearance to me which it hath to another man; and, if the appearances of it to different persons differed as much as colour does from sound, they might never be able to discover this difference. Hence, it appears obvious, that a blind man might talk long about colours distinctly and pertinently; and, if you were to examine him in the dark about the nature, composition, and beauty of them, he might be able to answer, so as not to betray his defect.

We have seen how far a blind man may go in the knowledge of the appearances which things make to the eye. As to the things which are suggested by them or

inferred from them, although he could never discover them of himself, yet he may understand them perfectly by the information of others. And everything of this kind that enters into our minds by the eye, may enter into his by the ear. Thus, for instance, he could never, if left to the direction of his own faculties, have dreamed of any such thing as light; but he can be informed of everything we know about it. He can conceive, as distinctly as we, the minuteness and velocity of its rays, their various degrees of refrangibility and reflexibility, and all the magical powers and virtues of that wonderful element. He could never of himself have found out, that there are such bodies as the sun, moon, and stars; but he may be informed of all the noble discoveries of astronomers about their motions, and the laws of nature by which they are regulated. Thus, it appears, that there is very little knowledge got by the eye, which may not be communicated by language to those who have no eyes.

If we should suppose that it were as uncommon for men to see as it is to be born blind, would not the few who had this rare gift appear as prophets and inspired teachers to the many? We conceive inspiration to give a man no new faculty, but to communicate to him, in a new way, and by extraordinary means, what the faculties common to mankind can apprehend, and what he can communicate to others by ordinary means. On the supposition we have made, sight would appear to the blind very similar to this; for the few who had this gift, could communicate the knowledge acquired by it to those who had it not. They could not, indeed, convey to the blind any distinct notion of the manner in which they acquired this knowledge. A ball and socket would seem, to a blind man, in this case, as improper an instrument for acquiring such a variety and extent of knowledge, as a dream or a vision. The manner in which a man who sees, discerns so many things by means of the eye, is as unintelligible to the blind, as the manner in which a man may be inspired with knowledge by the Almighty, is to us. Ought the blind man, therefore, without examination, to treat all pretences to the gift of seeing as imposture? Might he not, if he were candid and tractable, find reasonable evidence of the reality of this gift in others, and draw great advantages from it to himself?

The distinction we have made between the visible appearances of the objects of sight, and things suggested by them, is necessary to give us a just notion of the intention of nature in giving us eyes. If we attend duly to the operation of our mind in the use of this faculty, we shall perceive that the visible, appearance of objects is hardly ever regarded by us. It is not at all made an object of thought or reflection, but serves only as a sign to introduce to the mind something else, which may be distinctly conceived by those who never saw.

Thus, the visible appearance of things in my room varies almost every hour, according as the day is clear or cloudy, as the sun is in the east, or south, or west, and as my eye is in one part of the room or in another; but I never think of these variations, otherwise than as signs of morning, noon, or night, of a clear or cloudy sky. A book or a chair has a different appearance to the eye, in every different distance and position; yet we conceive it to be still the same; and, overlooking the appearance, we immediately conceive the real figure, distance, and position of the body, of which its visible or perspective appearance is a sign and indication.

When I see a man at the distance of ten yards, and afterwards see him at the distance of a hundred yards, his visible appearance, in its length, breadth, and all its linear proportions, is ten times less in the last case than it is in the first; yet I do not conceive him one inch diminished by this diminution of his visible figure. Nay, I do not in the least attend to this diminution, even when I draw from it the conclusion of his being at a greater distance. For such is the subtilty of the mind's operation in this case, that we draw the conclusion, without perceiving that ever the premises entered into the mind. A thousand such instances might be produced, in order to shew that the visible appearances of objects are intended by nature only as signs or indications; and that the mind passes instantly to the things signified, without making the least reflection upon the sign, or even perceiving that there is any such thing. It is in a way somewhat similar, that the sounds of a language, after it is become familiar, are overlooked, and we attend only to the things signified by them.

It is therefore a just and important observation of the Bishop of Cloyne, That the visible appearance of objects is a kind of language used by nature, to inform us of their distance, magnitude, and figure. And this observation hath been very happily applied by that ingenious writer, to the solution of some phænomena in optics, which had before perplexed the greatest masters in that science. The same observation is further improved by the judicious Dr Smith, in his Optics, for explaining the apparent figure of the heavens, and the apparent distances and magnitudes of objects seen with glasses, or by the naked eye.

Avoiding as much as possible the repe-

tition of what hath been said by these excellent writers, we shall avail ourselves of the distinction between the signs that nature useth in this visual language, and the things signified by them: and in what remains to be said of sight, shall first make some observations upon the signs.

Section III.

OF THE VISIBLE APPEARANCES OF OBJECTS.

In this section we must speak of things which are never made the object of reflection, though almost every moment presented to the mind. Nature intended them only for signs; and in the whole course of life they are put to no other use. The mind has acquired a confirmed and inveterate habit of inattention to them; for they no sooner appear, than quick as lightning the thing signified succeeds, and engrosses all our regard. They have no name in language; and, although we are conscious of them when they pass through the mind, yet their passage is so quick and so familiar, that it is absolutely unheeded; nor do they leave any footsteps of themselves, either in the memory or imagination. That this is the case with regard to the sensations of touch, hath been shewn in the last chapter; and it holds no less with regard to the visible appearances of objects.

I cannot therefore entertain the hope of being intelligible to those readers who have not, by pains and practice, acquired the habit of distinguishing the appearance of objects to the eye, from the judgment which we form by sight of their colour, distance, magnitude, and figure. The only profession in life wherein it is necessary to make this distinction, is that of painting. The painter hath occasion for an abstraction, with regard to visible objects, somewhat similar to that which we here require: and this indeed is the most difficult part of his art. For it is evident, that, if he could fix in his imagination the visible appearance of objects, without confounding it with the things signified by that appearance, it would be as easy for him to paint from the life, and to give every figure its proper shading and relief, and its perspective proportions, as it is to paint from a copy. Perspective, shading, giving relief, and colouring, are nothing else but copying the appearance which things make to the eye. We may therefore borrow some light on the subject of visible appearance from this art.

Let one look upon any familiar object, such as a book, at different distances and in different positions: is he not able to affirm, upon the testimony of his sight, that it is the same book, the same object, whether seen at the distance of one foot or of ten, whether in one position or another ; that the colour is the same, the dimensions the same, and the figure the same, as far as the eye can judge ? This surely must be acknowledged. The same individual object is presented to the mind, only placed at different distances and in different positions. Let me ask, in the next place, Whether this object has the same appearance to the eye in these different distances ? Infallibly it hath not. For,

First, However certain our judgment may be that the colour is the same, it is as certain that it hath not the same appearance at different distances. There is a certain degradation of the colour, and a certain confusion and indistinctness of the minute parts, which is the natural consequence of the removal of the object to a greater distance. Those that are not painters, or critics in painting, overlook this; and cannot easily be persuaded, that the colour of the same object hath a different appearance at the distance of one foot and of ten, in the shade and in the light. But the masters in painting know how, by the degradation of the colour and the confusion of the minute parts, figures which are upon the same canvass, and at the same distance from the eye, may be made to represent objects which are at the most unequal distances. They know how to make the objects appear to be of the same colour, by making their pictures really of different colours, according to their distances or shades.

Secondly, Every one who is acquainted with the rules of perspective, knows that the appearance of the figure of the book must vary in every different position : yet if you ask a man that has no notion of perspective, whether the figure of it does not appear to his eye to be the same in all its different positions ? he can with a good conscience affirm that it does. He hath learned to make allowance for the variety of visible figure arising from the difference of position, and to draw the proper conclusions from it. But he draws these conclusions so readily and habitually, as to lose sight of the premises : and therefore where he hath made the same conclusion, he conceives the visible appearance must have been the same.

Thirdly, Let us consider the apparent magnitude or dimensions of the book. Whether I view it at the distance of one foot or of ten feet, it seems to be about seven inches long, five broad, and one thick. I can judge of these dimensions very nearly by the eye, and I judge them to be the same at both distances. But yet it is certain, that, at the distance of one foot, its visible length and breadth is about ten times as great as at the distance of ten feet ; and consequently its surface is about a hundred times as great. This great change of apparent magnitude is altogether overlooked, and every man is apt to imagine, that it appears to the eye of the same size at both distances. Further, when I look at the book, it seems plainly to have three dimensions, of length, breadth, and thickness : but it is certain that the visible appearance hath no more than two, and can be exactly represented upon a canvass which hath only length and breadth.

In the last place, does not every man, by sight, perceive the distance of the book from his eye ? Can he not affirm with certainty, that in one case it is not above one foot distant, that in another it is ten ? Nevertheless, it appears certain, that distance from the eye is no immediate object of sight. There are certain things in the visible appearance, which are signs of distance from the eye, and from which, as we shall afterwards shew, we learn by experience to judge of that distance within certain limits ; but it seems beyond doubt, that a man born blind, and suddenly made to see, could form no judgment at first of the distance of the objects which he saw. The young man couched by Cheselden thought, at first, that everything he saw touched his eye,* and learned only by experience to judge of the distance of visible objects.

I have entered into this long detail, in order to shew that the visible appearance of an object is extremely different from the notion of it which experience teaches us to form by sight ; and to enable the reader to attend to the visible appearance of colour, figure, and extension, in visible things, which is no common object of thought, but must be carefully attended to by those who would enter into the philosophy of this sense, or would comprehend what shall be said upon it. To a man newly made to see, the visible appearance of objects would be the same as to us ; but he would see nothing at all of their real dimensions, as we do. He could form no conjecture, by means of his sight only, how many inches or feet they were in length, breadth, or thickness. He could perceive little or nothing of their real figure ; nor could he discern that this was a cube, that a sphere ; that this was a cone, and that a cylinder.†

---

* Still they appeared external to the eye.—H.

† This is a misinterpretation of Cheselden, on whose authority this statement is made ; though it must be confessed that the mode in which the case of the young man, couched by that distinguished surgeon, is reported, does not merit all the eulogia that have been lavished on it. It is at once imperfect and indistinct. Thus, on the point in question Cheselden says:—"He (the patient) knew not the shape of anything, nor any one thing from another,

His eye could not inform him that this object was near, and that more remote. The habit of a man or of a woman, which appeared to us of one uniform colour, variously folded and shaded, would present to his eye neither fold or shade, but variety of colour. In a word, his eyes, though ever so perfect, would at first give him almost no information of things without him. They would indeed present the same appearances to him as they do to us, and speak the same language; but to him it is an unknown language; and, therefore, he would attend only to the signs, without knowing the signification of them, whereas to us it is a language perfectly familiar; and, therefore, we take no notice of the signs, but attend only to the thing signified by them.

Section IV.

THAT COLOUR IS A QUALITY OF BODIES, NOT
A SENSATION OF THE MIND.

By colour, all men, who have not been tutored by modern philosophy, understand, not a sensation of the mind, which can have no existence when it is not perceived, but a quality or modification of bodies, which continues to be the same whether it is seen or not. The scarlet-rose which is before me, is still a scarlet-rose when I shut my

however different in shape or magnitude; but, upon being told what things were, whose form he before knew from feeling, he would carefully observe, that he might know them again; but, having too many objects to learn at once, he forgot many of them, and (as he said) at first he learned to know, and again forgot a thousand things in a day. One particular only, though it may appear trifling, I will relate: Having often forgot which was the cat and which the dog, he was ashamed to ask; but, catching the cat, which he knew by feeling, he was observed to look at her steadfastly, and then, setting her down, said, ' So, puss! I shall know you another time.' "
Here, when Cheselden says, "that his patient, when recently couched, knew not the shape of any thing, nor any one thing from another," &c, this cannot mean that he saw no difference between objects of different shapes and sizes; for, if this interpretation were adopted, the rest of the statement becomes nonsense. If he had been altogether incapable of apprehending differences, it could not be said that, "being told what things were whose form he before knew from feeling, he would carefully observe, that he might know them again;" for observation supposes the power of discrimination; and, in particular, the anecdote of the dog and cat would be inconceivable on that hypothesis. It is plain that Cheselden only meant to say, that the things which the patient could previously distinguish and denominate by touch, he could not now identify and refer to their appellations by sight. And this is what we might, a priori, be assured of. A sphere and a cube would certainly make different impressions on him; but it is probable that he could not assign to each its name, though, in this particular case, there is good ground for holding that the slightest consideration would enable a person, previously acquainted with these figures, and aware that the one was a cube and the other a sphere, to connect them with his anterior experience, and to discriminate them by name.—See *Philos. Trans.*, 1728, nn. 402.—H.

eyes, and was so at midnight when no eye saw it. The colour remains when the appearance ceases; it remains the same when the appearance changes. For when I view this scarlet-rose through a pair of green spectacles, the appearance is changed; but I do not conceive the colour of the rose changed. To a person in the jaundice, it has still another appearance; but he is easily convinced that the change is in his eye, and not in the colour of the object. Every different degree of light makes it have a different appearance, and total darkness takes away all appearance, but makes not the least change in the colour of the body. We may, by a variety of optical experiments, change the appearance of figure and magnitude in a body, as well as that of colour; we may make one body appear to be ten. But all men believe, that, as a multiplying glass does not really produce ten guineas out of one, nor a microscope turn a guinea into a ten-pound piece, so neither does a coloured glass change the real colour of the object seen through it, when it changes the appearance of that colour.

The common language of mankind shews evidently, that we ought to distinguish between the colour of a body, which is conceived to be a fixed and permanent quality in the body, and the appearance of that colour to the eye, which may be varied a thousand ways, by a variation of the light, of the medium, or of the eye itself. The permanent colour of the body is the cause which, by the mediation of various kinds or degrees of light, and of various transparent bodies interposed, produces all this variety of appearances. When a coloured body is presented, there is a certain apparition to the eye, or to the mind, which we have called *the appearance of colour*. Mr Locke calls it *an idea*; and, indeed, it may be called so with the greatest propriety. This idea can have no existence but when it is perceived. It is a kind of thought, and can only be the act of a percipient or thinking being. By the constitution of our nature, we are led to conceive this idea as a sign of something external, and are impatient till we learn its meaning. A thousand experiments for this purpose are made every day by children, even before they come to the use of reason. They look at things, they handle them, they put them in various positions, at different distances, and in different lights. The ideas of sight, by these means, come to be associated with, and readily to suggest, things external, and altogether unlike them. In particular, that idea which we have called *the appearance of colour*, suggests the conception and belief of some unknown quality in the body which occasions the idea; and it is to this quality, and not to the idea, that we give the name of *colour.** The various colours, although in their nature equally unknown, are easily distinguished when we think or speak of them, by being associated with the ideas which they excite. In like manner, gravity, magnetism, and electricity, although all unknown qualities, are distinguished by their different effects. As we grow up, the mind acquires a habit of passing so rapidly from the ideas of sight to the external things suggested by them, that the ideas are not in the least attended to, nor have they names given them in common language.

When we think or speak of any particular colour, however simple the notion may seem to be which is presented to the imagination, it is really in some sort compounded. It involves an unknown cause and a known effect. The name of *colour* belongs indeed to the cause only, and not to the effect. But, as the cause is unknown, we can form no distinct conception of it but by its relation to the known effect; and, therefore, both go together in the imagination, and are so closely united, that they are mistaken for one simple object of thought.† When I would conceive those colours of bodies which we call *scarlet* and *blue*—if I conceived them only as unknown qualities, I could perceive no distinction between the one and the other. I must, therefore, for the sake of distinction, join to each of them, in my imagination, some effect or some relation that is peculiar; and the most obvious distinction is, the appearance which one and the other makes to the eye. Hence the appearance is, in the imagination, so closely united with the quality called *a scarlet-colour*, that they are apt to be mistaken for one and the same thing, although they are in reality so different and so unlike, that one is an idea in the mind, the other is a quality of body.

I conclude, then, that colour is not a sensation, but a secondary quality of bodies, in the sense we have already explained; that it is a certain power or virtue in bodies, that in fair daylight exhibits to the eye an appearance which is very familiar to us, although it hath no name. Colour differs from other secondary qualities in this, that, whereas the name of the quality is sometimes given to the sensation which indicates it, and is occasioned by it, we never, as far as I can judge, give the name of *colour* to the sensation, but to the quality only.‡ Perhaps

the reason of this may be, that the appearances of the same colour are so various and changeable, according to the different modifications of the light, of the medium, and of the eye, that language could not afford names for them. And indeed, they are so little interesting, that they are never attended to, but serve only as signs to introduce the things signified by them. Nor ought it to appear incredible, that appearances so frequent and so familiar should have no names, nor be made objects of thought; since we have before shewn that this is true of many sensations of touch, which are no less frequent nor less familiar.

Section V.

From what hath been said about colour, we may infer two things. The first is, that one of the most remarkable paradoxes of modern philosophy, which hath been universally esteemed as a great discovery, is, in reality, when examined to the bottom, nothing else but an abuse of words. The paradox I mean is, That colour is not a quality of bodies, but only an idea in the mind. We have shewn, that the word *colour*, as used by the vulgar, cannot signify an idea in the mind, but a permanent quality of body. We have shewn, that there is really a permanent quality of body, to which the common use of this word exactly agrees. Can any stronger proof be desired, that this quality is that to which the vulgar give the name of *colour*? If it should be said, that this quality, to which we give the name of *colour*, is unknown to the vulgar, and, therefore, can have no name among them, I answer, it is, indeed, known only by its effects—that is, by its exciting a certain idea in us; but are there not numberless qualities of bodies which are known only by their effects, to which, notwithstanding, we find it necessary to give names? Medicine alone might furnish us with a hundred instances of this kind. Do not the words *astringent, narcotic, epispastic, caustic,* and innumerable others, signify qualities of bodies, which are known only by their effects upon animal bodies? Why, then, should not the vulgar give a name to a quality, whose effects are every moment perceived by their eyes? We have all the reason, therefore, that the nature of the thing admits, to think that the vulgar apply the name of *colour* to that quality of bodies which excites in us what

---

*†‡ It is justly observed by Mr Stewart, that these passages seem inconsistent with each other. It is in the perception of colour, the sensation and the quality "be so closely united as to be mistaken for one simple object of thought," does it not obviously follow, that it is to this compounded notion the name of *colour* must in general be given? On the other hand, when it is said *that the name of colour is never given to the sensation, but to the quality only,* does not this imply, that every time the word is pronounced, the quality is separated from

the sensation, even in the imagination of the vulgar?—H.

the philosophers call the *idea of colour*. And that that there is such a quality in bodies, all philosophers allow, who allow that there is any such thing as body. Philosophers have thought fit to leave that quality of bodies which the vulgar call *colour*, without a name, and to give the name of *colour* to the idea or appearance, to which, as we have shewn, the vulgar give no name, because they never make it an object of thought or reflection. Hence it appears, that, when philosophers affirm that colour is not in bodies, but in the mind, and the vulgar affirm that colour is not in the mind, but is a quality of bodies, there is no difference between them about things, but only about the meaning of a word.

The vulgar have undoubted right to give names to things which they are daily conversant about; and philosophers seem justly chargeable with an abuse of language, when they change the meaning of a common word, without giving warning.

If it is a good rule, to think with philosophers and speak with the vulgar, it must be right to speak with the vulgar when we think with them, and not to shock them by philosophical paradoxes, which, when put into common language, express only the common sense of mankind.

If you ask a man that is no philosopher, what colour is, or what makes one body appear white, another scarlet, he cannot tell. He leaves that inquiry to philosophers, and can embrace any hypothesis about it, except that of our modern philosophers, who affirm that colour is not in body, but only in the mind.

Nothing appears more shocking to his apprehension, than that visible objects should have no colour, and that colour should be in that which he conceives to be invisible. Yet this strange paradox is not only universally received, but considered as one of the noblest discoveries of modern philosophy. The ingenious Addison, in the *Spectator*, No. 413, speaks thus of it :—

" I have here supposed that my reader is acquainted with that great modern discovery, which is at present universally acknowledged by all the inquirers into natural philosophy—namely, that light and colours, as apprehended by the imagination, are only ideas in the mind, and not qualities that have any existence in matter. As this is a truth which has been proved incontestably by many modern philosophers, and is, indeed, one of the finest speculations in that science, if the English reader would see the notion explained at large, he may find it in the eighth chapter of the second book of Locke's 'Essay on Human Understanding.'"

Mr Locke and Mr Addison are writers who have deserved so well of mankind, that one must feel some uneasiness in differing from them, and would wish to ascribe all the merit that is due to a discovery upon which they put so high a value. And, indeed, it is just to acknowledge that Locke, and other modern philosophers, on the subject of secondary qualities, have the merit of distinguishing more accurately than those that went before them, between the sensation in the mind, and that constitution or quality of bodies which gives occasion to the sensation. They have shewn clearly that these two things are not only distinct, but altogether unlike : that there is no similitude between the effluvia of an odorous body and the sensation of smell, or between the vibrations of a sounding body and the sensation of sound : that there can be no resemblance between the feeling of heat, and the constitution of the heated body which occasions it; or between the appearance which a coloured body makes to the eye, and the texture of the body which causes that appearance.

Nor was the merit small of distinguishing these things accurately ; because, however different and unlike in their nature, they have been always so associated in the imagination, as to coalesce, as it were, into one two-faced form, which, from its amphibious nature, could not justly be appropriated either to body or mind ; and, until it was properly distinguished into its different constituent parts, it was impossible to assign to either their just shares in it. None of the ancient philosophers had made this distinction.* The followers of Democritus and Epicurus conceived the forms of heat, and sound, and colour, to be in the mind only ; but that our senses fallaciously represented them as being in bodies. The Peripatetics imagined that those forms are really in bodies ; and that the images of them are conveyed to the mind by our senses.†

The one system made the senses naturally fallacious and deceitful ; the other made the qualities of body to resemble the sensations of the mind. Nor was it possible to find a third, without making the distinction we have mentioned ; by which, indeed, the errors of both these ancient systems are avoided, and we are not left under the hard necessity of believing, either, on the one hand, that our sensations are like to the qualities of body, or, on the other, that God hath given us one faculty to deceive us, and another to detect the cheat.

* This is inaccurate. The distinction was known to the ancient philosophers ; and Democritus was generally allowed to be its author. This Reid himself elsewhere indeed admits.—(See above, p. 123, a ; and p. 131, a.)—H.
† These statements concerning both classes of philosophers are vague and incorrect. The latter, in general, only allowed *species* for two senses, Sight and Hearing; few admitted them in Feeling ; and some rejected them altogether.—H.

We desire, therefore, with pleasure, to do justice to the doctrine of Locke, and other modern philosophers, with regard to colour and other secondary qualities, and to ascribe to it its due merit, while we beg leave to censure the language in which they have expressed their doctrine. When they had explained and established the distinction between the appearance which colour makes to the eye, and the modification of the coloured body which, by the laws of nature, causes that appearance, the question was, whether to give the name of *colour* to the cause or to the effect? By giving it, as they have done, to the effect, they set philosophy apparently in opposition to common sense, and expose it to the ridicule of the vulgar. But had they given the name of *colour* to the cause, as they ought to have done, they must then have affirmed, with the vulgar, that colour is a quality of bodies ; and that there is neither colour nor anything like it in the mind. Their language, as well as their sentiments, would have been perfectly agreeable to the common apprehensions of mankind, and true Philosophy would have joined hands with Common Sense. As Locke was no enemy to common sense, it may be presumed, that, in this instance, as in some others, he was seduced by some received hypothesis ; and that this was actually the case, will appear in the following section.

Section VI.

THAT NONE OF OUR SENSATIONS ARE RESEMBLANCES OF ANY OF THE QUALITIES OF BODIES.

A second inference is, that, although colour is really a quality of body, yet it is not represented to the mind by an idea or sensation that resembles it ; on the contrary, it is suggested by an idea which does not in the least resemble it. And this inference is applicable, not to colour only, but to all the qualities of body which we have examined.

It deserves to be remarked, that, in the analysis we have hitherto given of the operations of the five senses, and of the qualities of bodies discovered by them, no instance hath occurred, either of any sensation which resembles any quality of body, or of any quality of body whose image or resemblance is conveyed to the mind by means of the senses.

There is no phænomenon in nature more unaccountable than the intercourse that is carried on between the mind and the external world—there is no phænomenon which philosophical spirits have shewn greater avidity to pry into, and to resolve. It is agreed by all, that this intercourse is carried on by means of the senses ; and this satisfies the vulgar curiosity, but not the philosophic. Philosophers must have some system, some hypothesis, that shews the manner in which our senses make us acquainted with external things. All the fertility of human invention seems to have produced only one hypothesis for this purpose, which, therefore, hath been universally received ; and that is, that the mind, like a mirror, receives the images of things from without, by means of the senses ; so that their use must be to convey these images into the mind.*

Whether to these images of external things in the mind, we give the name of *sensible forms*, or *sensible species*, with the Peripatetics, or the name *of ideas of sensation*, with Locke ; or whether, with later philosophers, we distinguish *sensations*, which are immediately conveyed by the senses, from *ideas of sensation*, which are faint copies of our sensations retained in the memory and imagination ;† these are only differences about words. The hypothesis I have mentioned is common to all these different systems.

The necessary and allowed consequence of this hypothesis is, *that no material thing, nor any quality of material things, can be conceived by us, or made an object of thought, until its image is conveyed to the mind by means of the senses.* We shall examine this hypothesis particularly afterwards, and at this time only observe, that, in consequence of it, one would naturally expect, that to every quality and attribute of body we know or can conceive, there should be a sensation corresponding, which is the image and resemblance of that quality ; and that the sensations which have no similitude or resemblance to body, or to any of its qualities, should give us no conception of a material world, or of anything belonging to it. These things might be expected as the natural consequences of the hypothesis we have mentioned.

Now, we have considered, in this and the preceding chapters, Extension, Figure, Solidity, Motion, Hardness, Roughness, as well as Colour, Heat, and Cold, Sound, Taste, and Smell. We have endeavoured to shew that our nature and constitution lead us to conceive these as qualities of body, as all mankind have always con-

---

* This is incorrect, especially as it asserts that the *one universal* hypothesis of philosophy was, that "the mind receives the images of things from without," meaning by these images, immediate or representative objects, different from the modifications of the thinking subject itself.—H.
† He refers to Hume ; Aristotle, however, and Hobbes, had previously called Imagination a *decaying sense.*—H.

ceived them to be. We have likewise examined with great attention the various sensations we have by means of the five senses, and are not able to find among them all one single[*] image of body, or of any of its qualities. From whence, then, come those images of body and of its qualities into the mind? Let philosophers resolve this question. All I can say is, that they come not by the senses. I am sure that, by proper attention and care, I may know my sensations, and be able to affirm with certainty what they resemble, and what they do not resemble. I have examined them one by one, and compared them with matter and its qualities; and I cannot find one of them that confesses a resembling feature.

A truth so evident as this—that our sensations are not images of matter, or of any of its qualities—ought not to yield to a hypothesis such as that above-mentioned, however ancient, or however universally received by philosophers; nor can there be any amicable union between the two. This will appear by some reflections upon the spirit of the ancient and modern philosophy concerning sensation.

During the reign of the Peripatetic philosophy, our sensations were not minutely or accurately examined. The attention of philosophers, as well as of the vulgar, was turned to the things signified by them: therefore, in consequence of the common hypothesis, it was taken for granted, that all the sensations we have from external things, are the forms or images of these external things. And thus the truth we have mentioned yielded entirely to the hypothesis, and was altogether suppressed by it.

Des Cartes gave a noble example of turning our attention inward, and scrutinizing our sensations; and this example hath been very worthily followed by modern philosophers, particularly by Malebranche, Locke, Berkeley, and Hume. The effect of this scrutiny hath been, a gradual discovery of the truth above-mentioned—to wit, the dissimilitude between the sensations of our minds, and the qualities or attributes of an insentient inert substance, such as we conceive matter to be. But this valuable and useful discovery, in its different stages, hath still been unhappily united to the ancient hypothesis—and from this inauspicious match of opinions, so unfriendly and discordant in their natures, have arisen those monsters of paradox and scepticism with which the modern philosophy is too justly chargeable.

Locke saw clearly, and proved incontestably, that the sensations we have by taste, smell, and hearing, as well as the sensations of colour, heat, and cold, are not resemblances of anything in bodies; and in this he agrees with Des Cartes and Malebranche. Joining this opinion with the hypothesis, it follows necessarily, that three senses of the five are cut off from giving us any intelligence of the material world, as being altogether inept for that office. Smell, and taste, and sound, as well as colour and heat, can have no more relation to body, than anger or gratitude; nor ought the former to be called qualities of body, whether primary or secondary, any more than the latter. For it was natural and obvious to argue thus from that hypothesis: If heat, and colour, and sound are real qualities of body, the sensations by which we perceive them must be resemblances of those qualities; but these sensations are not resemblances; therefore, those are not real qualities of body.

We see, then, that Locke, having found that the ideas of secondary qualities are no resemblances, was compelled, by a hypothesis common to all philosophers, to deny that they are real qualities of body. It is more difficult to assign a reason why, after this, he should call them *secondary qualities;* for this name, if I mistake not, was of his invention.[*] Surely he did not mean that they were secondary qualities of the mind; and I do not see with what propriety, or even by what tolerable license, he could call them secondary qualities of body, after finding that they were no qualities of body at all. In this, he seems to have sacrificed to Common Sense, and to have been led by her authority even in opposition to his hypothesis. The same sovereign mistress of our opinions that led this philosopher to call those things secondary qualities of body, which, according to his principles and reasonings, were no qualities of body at all, hath led, not the vulgar of all ages only, but philosophers also, and even the disciples of Locke, to believe them to be real qualities of body—she hath led them to investigate, by experiments, the nature of colour, and sound, and heat, in bodies. Nor hath this investigation been fruitless, as it must have been if there had been no such thing in bodies; on the contrary, it hath produced very noble and useful discoveries, which make a very considerable part of natural philosophy. If, then, natural philosophy be not a dream, there is something in bodies which we call *colour,* and *heat,* and *sound.* And if this be so, the hypothesis from which the con-

---

[*] *One single*—a common but faulty pleonasm.—H.

[*] The terms *First* and *Second,* or *Primary* and *Secondary qualities,* were no more an invention of Locke than the distinction which he applied them to denote. The terms First and Second Qualities, as I have noticed, in the Aristotelian philosophy, marked out, however, a different distribution of qualities than that in question.—H.

trary is concluded, must be false: for the argument, leading to a false conclusion, recoils against the hypothesis from which it was drawn, and thus directs its force backward. If the qualities of body were known to us only by sensations that resemble them, then colour, and sound, and heat could be no qualities of body; but these are real qualities of body; and, therefore, the qualities of bo   are not known only by means of sensations that resemble them.

But to proceed. What Locke had proved with regard to the sensations we have by smell taste, and hearing, Bishop Berkeley proved no less unanswerably with regard to all our other sensations;* to wit, that none of them can in the least resemble the qualities of a lifeless and insentient being, such as matter is conceived to be. Mr Hume hath confirmed this by his authority and reasoning. This opinion surely looks with a very malign aspect upon the old hypothesis; yet that hypothesis hath still been retained, and conjoined with it. And what a brood of monsters hath this produced!

The first-born of this union, and, perhaps, the most harmless, was, That the secondary qualities of body were mere sensations of the mind. To pass by Malebranche's notion of seeing all things in the ideas of the divine mind,† as a foreigner, never naturalized in this island; the next was Berkeley's system, That extension, and figure, and hardness, and motion—that land, and sea, and houses, and our own bodies, as well as those of our wives, and children, and friends—are nothing but ideas of the mind: and that there is nothing existing in nature, but minds and ideas.

The progeny that followed, is still more frightful; so that it is surprising, that one could be found who had the courage to act the midwife, to rear it up, and to usher it into the world. No causes nor effects; no substances, material or spiritual; no evidence, even in mathematical demonstration; no liberty nor active power; nothing existing in nature, but impressions and ideas following each other, without time, place, or subject. Surely no age ever produced such a system of opinions, justly deduced with great acuteness, perspicuity, and elegance, from a principle universally received.

* Bayle, *before Berkeley*, shewed that the reasoning of Malebranche against the external reality of the secondary qualities, when carried to its legitimate issue, subverted also that of the primary.—H.

† Malebranche, it should be observed, distinguished more precisely than Des Cartes, or any previous philosopher, *primary* from *secondary* qualities; and *perception* (*idée*) from *sensation* (*sentiment*.) He regarded the sensation of the secondary qualities as the mere subjective feeling which the human mind had of its own affections; but the perception of the primary he considered as an objective intuition it obtained of these, as represented in the divine mind.—H.

The hypothesis we have mentioned is the father of them all. The dissimilitude of our sensations and feelings to external things, is the innocent mother of most of them.

As it happens sometimes, in an arithmetical operation, that two errors balance one another, so that the conclusion is little or nothing affected by them; but when one of them is corrected, and the other left, we are led farther from the truth than by both together: so it seems to have happened in the Peripatetic philosophy of sensation, compared with the modern. The Peripatetics adopted two errors; but the last served as a corrective to the first, and rendered it mild and gentle; so that their system had no tendency to scepticism. The moderns have retained the first of those errors, but have gradually detected and corrected the last. The consequence hath been, that the light we have struck out hath created darkness, and scepticism hath advanced hand in hand with knowledge, spreading its melancholy gloom, first over the material world, and at last over the whole face of nature. Such a phænomenon as this, is apt to stagger even the lovers of light and knowledge, while its cause is latent; but, when that is detected, it may give hopes that this darkness shall not be everlasting, but that it shall be succeeded by a more permanent light.

Section VII.

OF VISIBLE FIGURE AND EXTENSION.

Although there is no resemblance, nor, as far as we know, any necessary connection. between that quality in a body which we call its *colour*, and the appearance which that colour makes to the eye, it is quite otherwise with regard to its *figure* and *magnitude*. There is certainly a resemblance, and a necessary connection, between the visible figure and magnitude of a body, and its real figure and magnitude; no man can give a reason why a scarlet colour affects the eye in the manner it does; no man can be sure that it affects his eye in the same manner as it affects the eye of another, and that it has the same appearance to him as it has to another man;—but we can assign a reason why a circle placed obliquely to the eye, should appear in the form of an ellipse. The visible figure, magnitude, and position may, by mathematical reasoning, be deduced from the real; and it may be demonstrated, that every eye that sees distinctly and perfectly, must, in the same situation, see it under this form, and no other. Nay, we may venture to affirm, that a man born blind, if he were instructed in mathematics would be able to determine the visible figure of a body, when its real figure, distance, and position, are given. Dr Saunderson understood the projection of the sphere, and perspective. Now, I require no more knowledge in a blind man, in order to his being able to determine the visible figure of bodies, than that he can project the outline of a given body, upon the surface of a hollow sphere, whose centre is in the eye. This projection is the visible figure he wants : for it is the same figure with that which is projected upon the *tunica retina* in vision.

A blind man can conceive lines drawn from every point of the object to the centre of the eye, making angles. He can conceive that the length of the object will appear greater or less, in proportion to the angle which it subtends at the eye; and that, in like manner, the breadth, and in general the distance, of any one point of the object from any other point, will appear greater or less, in proportion to the angles which those distances subtend. He can easily be made to conceive, that the visible appearance has no thickness, any more than a projection of the sphere, or a perspective draught. He may be informed, that the eye, until it is aided by experience, does not represent one object as nearer or more remote than another. Indeed, he would probably conjecture this of himself, and be apt to think that the rays of light must make the same impression upon the eye, whether they come from a greater or a less distance.

These are all the principles which we suppose our blind mathematician to have ; and these he may certainly acquire by information and reflection. It is no less certain, that, from these principles, having given the real figure and magnitude of a body, and its position and distance with regard to the eye, he can find out its visible figure and magnitude. He can demonstrate in general, from these principles, that the visible figure of all bodies will be the same with that of their projection upon the surface of a hollow sphere, when the eye is placed in the centre. And he can demonstrate that their visible magnitude will be greater or less, according as their projection occupies a greater or less part of the surface of this sphere.

To set this matter in another light, let us distinguish betwixt the *position* of objects with regard to the eye, and their *distance* from it. Objects that lie in the same right line drawn from the centre of the eye, have the same position, however different their distances from the eye may be: but objects which lie in different right lines drawn from the eye's centre, have a different position ; and this difference of position is greater or less in proportion to the angle made at the

eye by the right lines mentioned. Having thus defined what we mean by the position of objects with regard to the eye, it is evident that, as the real figure of a body consists in the situation of its several parts with regard to one another, so its visible figure consists in the position of its several parts with regard to the eye ; and, as he that hath a distinct conception of the situation of the parts of the body with regard to one another, must have a distinct conception of its real figure ; so he that conceives distinctly the position of its several parts with regard to the eye, must have a distinct conception of its visible figure. Now, there is nothing, surely, to hinder a blind man from conceiving· the position of the several parts of a body with regard to the eye, any more than from conceiving their situation with regard to one another ; and, therefore, I conclude, that a blind man may attain a distinct conception of the visible figure of bodies. [*]

Although we think the arguments that have been offered are sufficient to prove that a blind man may conceive the visible extension and figure of bodies; yet, in order to remove some prejudices against this truth, it will be of use to compare the notion which a blind mathematician might form to himself of visible figure, with that which is presented to the eye in vision, and to observe wherein they differ.

First, Visible figure is never presented to the eye but in conjunction with colour: and, although there be no connection between them from the nature of the things, yet, having so invariably kept company together, we are hardly able to disjoin them even in our imagination.[†] What mightily increases this difficulty is, that we have never been accustomed to make visible figure an object of thought. It is only used as a sign, and, having served this purpose, passes away, without leaving a trace behind. The drawer or designer, whose business it is to hunt this fugitive form, and to take a copy of it, finds how difficult his task is, after many years' labour and practice. Happy ! if at last he can acquire the art of arresting it in his imagination, until he can delineate it. For then it is evident that he must be able to draw as accurately from the life as from a copy. But how few of the professed masters of designing are ever able to arrive at this degree of perfection ! It is no wonder, then, that we should find so great difficulty in conceiving this form apart from its constant associate,

---

[*] The most accurate observations of the blind from birth evince, however, that their conceptions of figure are extremely limited.—H.

[†] In other words, that *unextended* colour can be perceived—*can* be imagined. (Of this paradox (which is also adopted by Mr Stewart) in the sequel.—H.

when it is so difficult to conceive it at all. But our blind man's notion of visible figure will not be associated with colour, of which he hath no conception, but it will, perhaps, be associated with hardness or smoothness, with which he is acquainted by touch. These different associations are apt to impose upon us, and to make things seem different, which, in reality, are the same.

Secondly, The blind man forms the notion of visible figure to himself, by thought, and by mathematical reasoning from principles; whereas, the man that sees, has it presented to his eye at once, without any labour, without any reasoning, by a kind of inspiration. A man may form to himself the notion of a parabola, or a cycloid, from the mathematical definition of those figures, although he had never seen them drawn or delineated. Another, who knows nothing of the mathematical definition of the figures, may see them delineated on paper, or feel them cut out in wood. Each may have a distinct conception of the figures, one by mathematical reasoning, the other by sense. Now, the blind man forms his notion of visible figure in the same manner as the first of these formed his notion of a parabola or a cycloid, which he never saw.

Thirdly, Visible figure leads the man that sees, directly to the conception of the real figure, of which it is a sign. But the blind man's thoughts move in a contrary direction. For he must first know the real figure, distance, and situation of the body, and from thence he slowly traces out the visible figure by mathematical reasoning. Nor does his nature lead him to conceive this visible figure as a sign; it is a creature of his own reason and imagination.

Section VIII.

SOME QUERIES CONCERNING VISIBLE FIGURE ANSWERED.

It may be asked, What kind of thing is this visible figure? Is it a Sensation, or an Idea? If it is an idea, from what sensation is it copied? These questions may seem trivial or impertinent to one who does not know that there is a tribunal of inquisition erected by certain modern philosophers, before which everything in nature must answer. The articles of inquisition are few indeed, but very dreadful in their consequences. They are only these: Is the prisoner an Impression or an Idea? If an idea, from what impression copied? Now, if it appears that the prisoner is neither an impression, nor an idea copied from some impression, immediately, without being allowed to offer anything in

arrest of judgment, he is sentenced to pass out of existence, and to be, in all time to come, an empty unmeaning sound, or the ghost of a departed entity.*

Before this dreadful tribunal, cause and effect, time and place, matter and spirit, have been tried and cast: how then shall such a poor flimsy form as visible figure stand before it? It must even plead guilty, and confess that it is neither an impression nor an idea. For, alas! it is notorious, that it is extended in length and breadth; it may be long or short, broad or narrow, triangular, quadrangular, or circular; and, therefore, unless ideas and impressions are extended and figured, it cannot belong to that category.

If it should still be asked, To what category of beings does visible figure then belong? I can only, in answer, give some tokens, by which those who are better acquainted with the categories, may chance to find its place. It is, as we have said, the position of the several parts of a figured body with regard to the eye. The different positions of the several parts of the body with regard to the eye, when put together, make a real figure, which is truly extended in length and breadth, and which represents a figure that is extended in length, breadth, and thickness. In like manner, a projection of the sphere is a real figure, and hath length and breadth, but represents the sphere, which hath three dimensions. A projection of the sphere, or a perspective view of a palace, is a representative in the very same sense as visible figure is: and wherever they have their lodgings in the categories, this will be found to dwell next door to them.

It may farther be asked, Whether there be any sensation proper to visible figure, by which it is suggested in vision?—or by what means it is presented to the mind?†

* " Where Entity and Quiddity,
    The ghosts of defunct bodies, fly."
                                    Hudibras.—H.

† " In Dr Reid's ' Inquiry,' " (says Mr Stewart, in one of his last works, in reference to the following reasoning,) " he has introduced a discussion concerning the perception of *visible figure*, which has puzzled me since the first time (more than forty years ago) that I read his work. The discussion relates to the question, ' Whether there be any sensation proper to visible figure, by which it is suggested in vision?' The result of the argument is, that ' our eye *might* have been so framed as to suggest the figure of the object, without suggesting colour or any other quality; and, of consequence, there seems to be *no sensation* appropriated to visible figure; this quality being suggested *immediately* by the material impression upon the organ, of which impression we are not conscious.—*Inquiry*, &c. chap. vi. § 8. To my apprehension, nothing can appear more manifest than this, that, if there had been no *variety* in our sensations of colour, and, still more, if we had had no sensation of colour whatsoever, the organ of sight could have given us no information, either with respect to *figures* or to *distances*: and, of consequence, would have been as useless to us, as if we had been afflicted, from the moment of our birth, with a *gutta serena.*"—*Dissertation*, &c., p. 66, note; 2d ed.

This is a question of some importance, in order to our having a distinct notion of the faculty of seeing: and to give all the light to it we can, it is necessary to compare this sense with other senses, and to make some suppositions, by which we may be enabled to distinguish things that are apt to be confounded, although they are totally different.

There are three of our senses which give us intelligence of things at a distance:* smell, hearing, and sight. In smelling and in hearing, we have a sensation or impression upon the mind, which, by our constitution, we conceive to be a sign of something external: but the position of this external thing, with regard to the organ of sense, is not presented to the mind along with the sensation. When I hear the sound of a coach, I could not, previous to experience, determine whether the sounding body was above or below, to the right hand or to the left. So that the sensation.suggests to me some external object as the cause or occasion of it; but it suggests not the position of that object, whether it lies in this direction or in that. The same thing may be said with regard to smelling. But the case is quite different with regard to seeing. When I see an object, the appearance which the colour of it makes, may be called *the sensation*, which suggests to me some external thing as its cause; but it suggests likewise the individual direction and position of this cause with regard to the eye. I know it is precisely in such a a direction, and in no other. At the same time, I am not conscious of anything that can be called *sensation*, but the sensation of colour. The position of the coloured thing is no sensation; but it is by the laws of my constitution presented to the mind along with the colour, without any additional sensation.

Let us suppose that the eye were so constituted that the rays coming from any one point of the object were not, as they are in our eyes, collected in one point of the *retina*, but diffused over the whole: it is evident to those who understand the structure of the eye, that such an eye as we have supposed, would shew the colour of a body as our eyes do, but that it would neither shew figure nor position. The operation of such an eye would be precisely similar to that of hearing and smell; it would give

no perception of figure or extension, but merely of colour. Nor is the supposition we have made altogether imaginary: for it is nearly the case of most people who have cataracts, whose crystalline, as Mr Cheselden observes, does not altogether exclude the rays of light, but diffuses them over the *retina*, so that such persons see things as one does through a glass of broken gelly: they perceive the colour, but nothing of the figure or magnitude of objects.*

Again, if we should suppose that smell and sound were conveyed in right lines from the objects, and that every sensation of hearing and smell suggested the precise direction or position of its object; in this case, the operations of hearing and smelling would be similar to that of seeing: we should smell and hear the figure of objects, in the same sense as now we see it; and every smell and sound would be associated with some figure in the imagination, as colour is in our present state.†

The questions concerning the mutual dependence of colour on extension, and of extension and figure on colour, in perception and imagination, cannot be dismissed in a foot-note. I shall endeavour, in Note E, to shew that we can neither see nor imagine colour apart from extension, nor extension and figure apart from colour.—H.

* Properly speaking, no *sense* gives us a knowledge of aught but what is in *immediate* contact with its organ. All else is something over and above perception.—H.

* Reid, as remarked by Mr Fearn, misinterprets Cheselden in founding on the expressions of this report, a proof of his own paradox, that-colour can possibly be an object of vision, apart from extension. There is no ground in that report for such an inference; for it contains absolutely nothing to invalidate, and much to support the doctrine—that, though sensations of colour may be experienced through the medium of an imperfect cataract, while the figures of external objects are intercepted or broken down; yet that, in these sensations, colour being diffused over the retina, must appear to us extended. and of an extension limited by the boundaries of that sensitive membrane itself. The relative passage of Cheselden is as follows:—" Though we say of the gentleman couched between thirteen and fourteen years of age, that he was blind, as we do of all people who have ripe cataracts, yet they are never so blind from that cause, but they can discern day from night, and for the most part in a strong light distinguish black, white, and scarlet; but the light by which these perceptions are made, being let in obliquely through the aqueous humour, or the anterior surface of the crystalline, by which the rays cannot be brought into a focus upon the retina, they can discern in no other manner than a sound eye can through a glass of broken jelly, where a great variety of surfaces so differently refract the light, that the several distinct pencils of rays cannot be collected by the eye into their proper foci, wherefore the shape of an object in such a case cannot be at all discerned, though the colour may. And thus it was with this young gentleman, who, though he knew these colours asunder in a good light, yet, when he saw them after he was couched, the faint ideas he had of them before, were not sufficient for him to know them by afterwards, and therefore he did not think them the same which he had before known by those names."— There are also several statements in the report which shew that the patient was, on the recovery of distinct vision, perfectly familiar with differences of visible magnitude. See Note E.—H.

† To render this supposition possible, we must not only change the *objective*, but also the *subjective* conditions of smell and hearing; for, with our organs of these senses, and our nervous system in general, constituted as they are at present, the result would not be as assumed, even were the olfactory effluvia and audible vibrations conveyed in right lines, from bodies to the nose and ear. But to suppose both subjective and objective conditions changed is to suppose new qualities and new senses altogether; an hypothesis which would hardly serve the purpose of an illustration, *a notiori*.

A similar hypothesis and illustration is to be found in Condillac's " Traité des Sensations;" but,

L

We have reason to believe, that the rays of light make some impression upon the *retina;* but we are not conscious of this impression; nor have anatomists or philosophers been able to discover the nature and effects of it; whether it produces a vibration in the nerve, or the motion of some subtile fluid contained in the nerve, or something different from either, to which we cannot give a name. Whatever it is, we shall call it the *material impression;* remembering carefully, that it is not an impression upon the mind, but upon the body; and that it is no sensation, nor can resemble sensation, any more than figure or motion can resemble thought. Now, this material impression, made upon a particular point of the *retina,* by the laws of our constitution, suggests two things to the mind—namely, the colour and the position of some external object. No man can give a reason why the same material impression might not have suggested sound, or smell, or either of these, along with the position of the object. That it should suggest colour and position, and nothing else, we can resolve only into our constitution, or the will of our Maker. And since there is no necessary connection between these two things suggested by this material impression, it might, if it had so pleased our Creator, have suggested one of them without the other. Let us suppose, therefore, since it plainly appears to be possible, that our eyes had been so framed as to suggest to us the position of the object, without suggesting colour, or any other quality : What is the consequence of this supposition ? It is evidently this, that the person endued with such an eye, would perceive the visible figure of bodies, without having any sensation or impression made upon his mind. The figure he perceives is altogether external ; and therefore cannot be called an impression upon the mind, without the grossest abuse of language. If it should be said, that it is impossible to perceive a figure, unless there be some impression of it upon the mind, I beg leave not to admit the impossibility of this without some proof : and I can find none. Neither can I conceive what is meant by an impression of figure upon the mind. I can conceive an impression of figure upon wax, or upon any body that is fit to receive it ; but an impression of it upon the mind, is to me quite unintelligible ; and, although I form the most distinct conception of the figure, I cannot, upon the strictest examination, find any impression of it upon my mind.

If we suppose, last of all, that the eye hath the power restored of perceiving colour,

I apprehend that it will be allowed, that now it perceives figure in the very same manner as before, with this difference only, that colour is always joined with it.

In answer, therefore, to the question proposed, there seems to be no sensation that is appropriated to visible figure, or whose office it is to suggest it. It seems to be suggested immediately by the material impression upon the organ, of which we are not conscious : and why may not a material impression upon the *retina* suggest visible figure, as well as the material impression made upon the hand, when we grasp a ball, suggests real figure ? In the one case, one and the same material impression, suggests both colour and visible figure ; and in the other case, one and the same material impression suggests hardness, heat, or cold, and real figure, all at the same time.

We shall conclude this section with another question upon this subject. Since the visible figure of bodies is a real and external object to the eye, as their tangible figure is to the touch, it may be asked, Whence arises the difficulty of attending to the first, and the facility of attending to the last ? It is certain that the first is more frequently presented to the eye, than the last is to the touch ; the first is as distinct and determinate an object as the last, and seems in its own nature as proper for speculation. Yet so little hath it been attended to, that it never had a name in any language, until Bishop Berkeley gave it that which we have used after his example, to distinguish it from the figure which is the object of touch.

The difficulty of attending to the visible figure of bodies, and making it an object of thought, appears so similar to that which we find in attending to our sensations, that both have probably like causes. Nature intended the visible figure as a sign of the tangible figure and situation of bodies, and hath taught us, by a kind of instinct, to put it always to this use. Hence it happens, that the mind passes over it with a rapid motion, to attend to the things signified by it. It is as unnatural to the mind to stop at the visible figure, and attend to it, as it is to a spherical body to stop upon an inclined plane. There is an inward principle, which constantly carries it forward, and which cannot be overcome but by a contrary force.

There are other external things which nature intended for signs ; and we find this common to them all, that the mind is disposed to overlook them, and to attend only to the things signified by them. Thus there are certain modifications of the human face, which are natural signs of the present disposition of the mind. Every man understands the meaning of these signs, but not one of a hundred ever attended to

---

the signs themselves, or knows anything about them. Hence you may find many an excellent practical physiognomist who knows nothing of the proportions of a face, nor can delineate or describe the expression of any one passion.

An excellent painter or statuary can tell, not only what are the proportions of a good face, but what changes every passion makes in it. This, however, is one of the chief mysteries of his art, to the acquisition of which infinite labour and attention, as well as a happy genius, are required: but when he puts his art in practice, and happily expresses a passion by its proper signs, every one understands the meaning of these signs, without art, and without reflection.

What has been said of painting, might easily be applied to all the fine arts. The difficulty in them all consists in knowing and attending to those natural signs whereof every man understands the meaning.

We pass from the sign to the thing signified, with ease, and by natural impulse; but to go backward from the thing signified to the sign, is a work of labour and difficulty. Visible figure, therefore, being intended by nature to be a sign, we pass on immediately to the thing signified, and cannot easily return to give any attention to the sign.

Nothing shews more clearly our indisposition to attend to visible figure and visible extension than this—that, although mathematical reasoning is no less applicable to them, than to tangible figure and extension, yet they have entirely escaped the notice of mathematicians. While that figure and that extension which are objects of touch, have been tortured ten thousand ways for twenty centuries, and a very noble system of science has been drawn out of them, not a single proposition do we find with regard to the figure and extension which are the immediate objects of sight!

When the geometrician draws a diagram with the most perfect accuracy—when he keeps his eye fixed upon it, while he goes through a long process of reasoning, and demonstrates the relations of the several parts of his figure—he does not consider that the visible figure presented to his eye, is only the representative of a tangible figure, upon which all his attention is fixed; he does not consider that these two figures have really different properties; and that, what he demonstrates to be true of the one, is not true of the other.

This, perhaps, will seem so great a paradox, even to mathematicians, as to require demonstration before it can be believed. Nor is the demonstration at all difficult, if the reader will have patience to enter but a little into the mathematical consideration of visible figure, which we shall call *the geometry of visibles.*

Section IX.

OF THE GEOMETRY OF VISIBLES.*

In this geometry, the definitions of a point; of a line, whether straight or curve; of an angle, whether acute, or right, or obtuse; and of a circle—are the same as in common geometry. The mathematical reader will easily enter into the whole mystery of this geometry, if he attends duly to these few evident principles.

1. Supposing the eye placed in the centre of a sphere, every great circle of the sphere will have the same appearance to the eye as if it was a straight line; for the curvature of the circle being turned directly toward the eye, is not perceived by it. And, for the same reason, any line which is drawn in the plane of a great circle of the sphere, whether it be in reality straight or curve, will appear straight to the eye.

2. Every visible right line will appear to coincide with some great circle of the sphere; and the circumference of that great circle, even when it is produced until it returns into itself, will appear to be a continuation of the same visible right line, all the parts of it being visibly *in directum.* For the eye, perceiving only the position of objects with regard to itself, and not their distance, will see those points in the same visible place which have the same position with regard to the eye, how different soever their distances from it may be. Now, since a plane passing through the eye and a given visible right line, will be the plane of some great circle of the sphere, every point of the visible right line will have the same position as some point of the great circle; therefore, they will both have the same visible place, and coincide to the eye; and the whole circumference of the great circle, continued even until it returns into itself, will appear to be a continuation of the same visible right line.

Hence it follows—

3. That every visible right line, when it is continued in *directum,* as far as it may be continued, will be represented by a great circle of a sphere, in whose centre the eye is placed. It follows—

4. That the visible angle comprehended under two visible right lines, is equal to the spherical angle comprehended under the two great circles which are the representatives of these visible lines. For, since the visible lines appear to coincide with the

---

* How does this differ from a doctrine of Perspective?—At any rate, the notion is Berkeley's. Compare " New Theory of Vision," §§ 153–159.—H.

L 2

great circles, the visible angle comprehended under the former must be equal to the visible angle comprehended under the latter. But the visible angle comprehended under the two great circles, when seen from the centre, is of the same magnitude with the spherical angle which they really comprehend, as mathematicians know ; therefore, the visible angle made by any two visible lines is equal to the spherical angle made by the two great circles of the sphere which are their representatives.

5. Hence it is evident, that every visible right-lined triangle will coincide in all its parts with some spherical triangle. The sides of the one will appear equal to the sides of the other, and the angles of the one to the angles of the other, each to each ; and, therefore, the whole of the one triangle will appear equal to the whole of the other. In a word, to the eye they will be one and the same, and have the same mathematical properties. The properties, therefore, of visible right-lined triangles are not the same with the properties of plain triangles, but are the same with those of spherical triangles.

6. Every lesser circle of the sphere will appear a circle to the eye, placed, as we have supposed all along, in the centre of the sphere ; and, on the other hand, every visible circle will appear to coincide with some lesser circle of the sphere.

7. Moreover, the whole surface of the sphere will represent the whole of visible space ; for, since every visible point coincides with some point of the surface of the sphere, and has the same visible place, it follows, that all the parts of the spherical surface taken together, will represent all possible visible places—that is, the whole of visible space. And from this it follows, in the last place—

8. That every visible figure will be represented by that part of the surface of the sphere on which it might be projected, the eye being in the centre. And every such visible figure will bear the same *ratio* to the whole of visible space, as the part of the spherical surface which represents it, bears to the whole spherical surface.

The mathematical reader, I hope, will enter into these principles with perfect facility, and will as easily perceive that the following propositions with regard to visible figure and space, which we offer only as a specimen, may be mathematically demonstrated from them, and are not less true nor less evident than the propositions of Euclid, with regard to tangible figures.

Prop. 1. Every right line being produced, will at last return into itself.

2. A right line, returning into itself, is the longest possible right line ; and all other right lines bear a finite *ratio* to it.

3. A right line returning into itself, divides the whole of visible space into two equal parts, which will both be comprehended under this right line.

4. The whole of visible space bears a finite *ratio* to any part of it.

5. Any two right lines being produced, will meet in two points, and mutually bisect each other

6. If two lines be parallel—that is, every where equally distant from each other—they cannot both be straight.

7. Any right line being given, a point may be found, which is at the same distance from all the points of the given right line.

8. A circle may be parallel to a right line—that is, may be equally distant from it in all its parts.

9. Right-lined triangles that are similar, are also equal.

10. Of every right-lined triangle, the three angles taken together, are greater than two right angles.

11. The angles of a right-lined triangle, may all be right angles, or all obtuse angles.

12. Unequal circles are not as the squares of their diameters, nor are their circumferences in the *ratio* of their diameters.

This small specimen of the geometry of visibles, is intended to lead the reader to a clear and distinct conception of the figure and extension which is presented to the mind by. vision ; and to demonstrate the truth of what we have affirmed above—namely, that those figures and that extension which are the immediate objects of sight, are not the figures and the extension about which common geometry is employed ; that the geometrician, while he looks at his diagram, and demonstrates a proposition, hath a figure presented to his eye, which is only a sign and representative of a tangible figure ; that he gives not the least attention to the first, but attends only to the last ; and that these two figures have different properties, so that what he demonstrates of the one, is not true of the other.

It deserves, however, to be remarked, that, as a small part of a spherical surface differs not sensibly from a plain surface, so a small part of visible extension differs very little from that extension in length and breadth, which is the object of touch. And it is likewise to be observed, that the human eye is so formed, that an object which is seen distinctly and at one view can occupy but a small part of visible space ; for we never see distinctly what is at a considerable distance from the axis of the eye ; and, therefore, when we would see a large object at one view, the eye must be at so great a distance, that the object occupies but a small part of visible space. From these two observations, it follows, that plain figures which are seen at one view, when their planes are not oblique, but direct to the eye, differ little from the visible figures which they present to the eye. The several lines in the tangible figure, have very nearly the same proportion to each other as in the visible; and the angles of the one are very nearly, although not strictly and mathematically, equal to those of the other. Although, therefore, we have found many instances of natural signs which have no similitude to the things signified, this is not the case with regard to visible figure. It hath, in all cases, such a similitude to the thing signified by it, as a plan or profile hath to that which it represents; and, in some cases, the sign and thing signified have to all sense the same figure and the same proportions. If we could find a being endued with sight only, without any other external sense, and capable of reflecting and reasoning upon what he sees, the notions and philosophical speculations of such a being, might assist us in the difficult task of distinguishing the perceptions which we have purely by sight, from those which derive their origin from other senses. Let us suppose such a being, and conceive, as well as we can, what notion he would have of visible objects, and what conclusions he would deduce from them. We must not conceive him disposed by his constitution, as we are, to consider the visible appearance as a sign of something else: it is no sign to him, because there is nothing signified by it; and, therefore, we must suppose him as much disposed to attend to the visible figure and extension of bodies, as we are disposed to attend to their tangible figure and extension.

If various figures were presented to his sense, he might, without doubt, as they grow familiar, compare them together, and perceive wherein they agree, and wherein they differ. He might perceive visible objects to have length and breadth, but could have no notion of a third dimension, any more than we can have of a fourth.[*] All visible objects would appear to be terminated by lines, straight or curve; and objects terminated by the same visible lines, would occupy the same place, and fill the same part of visible space. It would not be possible for him to conceive one object to be behind another, or one to be nearer, another more distant.

To us, who conceive three dimensions, a line may be conceived straight; or it may be conceived incurvated in one dimension,

and straight in another; or, lastly, it may be incurvated in two dimensions. Suppose a line to be drawn upwards and downwards, its length makes one dimension, which we shall call *upwards and downwards*; and there are two dimensions remaining, according to which it may be straight or curve. It may be bent to the right or to the left; and, if it has no bending either to right or left, it is straight in this dimension. But supposing it straight in this dimension of right and left, there is still another dimension remaining, in which it may be curve; for it may be bent backwards or forwards. When we conceive a tangible straight line, we exclude curvature in either of these two dimensions: and as what is conceived to be excluded, must be conceived, as well as what is conceived to be included, it follows that all the three dimensions enter into our conception of a straight line. Its length is one dimension, its straightness in two other dimensions is included, or curvature in these two dimensions excluded, in the conception of it.

The being we have supposed, having no conception of more than two dimensions, of which the length of a line is one, cannot possibly conceive it either straight or curve in more than one dimension; so that, in his conception of a right line, curvature to the right hand or left is excluded: but curvature backwards or forwards cannot be excluded, because he neither hath, nor can have any conception of such curvature. Hence we see the reason that a line, which is straight to the eye, may return into itself; for its being straight to the eye, implies only straightness in one dimension; and a line which is straight in one dimension may, notwithstanding, be curve in another dimension, and so may return into itself.

To us, who conceive three dimensions, a surface is that which hath length and breadth, excluding thickness; and a surface may be either plain in this third dimension, or it may be incurvated: so that the notion of a third dimension enters into our conception of a surface; for it is only by means of this third dimension that we can distinguish surfaces into plain and curve surfaces; and neither one nor the other can be conceived without conceiving a third dimension.

The being we have supposed, having no conception of a third dimension, his visible figures have length and breadth indeed; but thickness is neither included nor excluded, being a thing of which he has no conception. And, therefore, visible figures, although they have length and breadth, as surfaces have, yet they are neither plain surfaces nor curve surfaces. For a curve surface implies curvature in a third dimension, and a plain surface implies the want

---

[*] This proceeds upon the supposition that our notion of space is merely empirical.—H.

of curvature in a third dimension; and such a being can conceive neither of these, because he has no conception of a third dimension. Moreover, although he hath a distinct conception of the inclination of two lines which make an angle, yet he can neither conceive a plain angle nor a spherical angle. Even his notion of a point is somewhat less determined than ours. In the notion of a point, we exclude length, breadth, and thickness; he excludes length and breadth, but cannot either exclude or include thickness, because he hath no conception of it.

Having thus settled the notions which such a being as we have supposed might form of mathematical points, lines, angles, and figures, it is easy to see, that, by comparing these together, and reasoning about them, he might discover their relations, and form geometrical conclusions built upon self-evident principles. He might likewise, without doubt, have the same notions of numbers as we have, and form a system of arithmetic. It is not material to say in what order he might proceed in such discoveries, or how much time and pains he might employ about them, but what such a being, by reason and ingenuity, without any materials of sensation but those of sight only, might discover.

As it is more difficult to attend to a detail of possibilities than of facts, even of slender authority, I shall beg leave to give an extract from the travels of Johannes Rudolphus Anepigraphus, a Rosicrucian philosopher, who having, by deep study of the occult sciences, acquired the art of transporting himself to various sublunary regions, and of conversing with various orders of intelligences, in the course of his adventures became acquainted with an order of beings exactly such as I have supposed.

How they communicate their sentiments to one another, and by what means he became acquainted with their language, and was initiated into their philosophy, as well as of many other particulars, which might have gratified the curiosity of his readers, and, perhaps, added credibility to his relation, he hath not thought fit to inform us; these being matters proper for adepts only to know.

His account of their philosophy is as follows : –

"The Idomenians," saith he, "are many of them very ingenious, and much given to contemplation. In arithmetic, geometry, metaphysics, and physics, they have most elaborate systems. In the two latter, indeed, they have had many disputes carried on with great subtilty, and are divided into various sects; yet in the two former there hath been no less unanimity than among the human species. Their principles relating to numbers and arithmetic, making allowance for their notation, differ in nothing from ours—but their geometry differs very considerably."

As our author's account of the geometry of the Idomenians agrees in everything with the geometry of visibles, of which we have already given a specimen, we shall pass over it. He goes on thus :—" Colour, extension, and figure, are conceived to be the essential properties of body. A very considerable sect maintains, that colour is the essence of body. If there had been no colour, there had been no perception or sensation. Colour is all that we perceive, or can conceive, that is peculiar to body; extension and figure being modes common to body and to empty space. And if we should suppose a body to be annihilated, colour is the only thing in it that can be annihilated; for its place, and consequently the figure and extension of that place, must remain, and cannot be imagined not to exist. These philosophers hold space to be the place of all bodies, immoveable and indestructible, without figure, and similar in all its parts, incapable of increase or diminution, yet not unmeasurable; for every the least part of space bears a finite ratio to the whole. So that with them the whole extent of space is the common and natural measure of everything that hath length and breadth; and the magnitude of every body and of every figure is expressed by its being such a part of the universe. In like manner, the common and natural measure of length is an infinite right line, which, as hath been before observed, returns into itself, and hath no limits, but bears a finite ratio to every other line.

"As to their natural philosophy, it is now acknowledged by the wisest of them to have been for many ages in a very low state. The philosophers observing, that body can differ from another only in colour, figure, or magnitude, it was taken for granted, that all their particular qualities must arise from the various combinations of these their essential attributes; and, therefore, it was looked upon as the end of natural philosophy, to shew how the various combinations of these three qualities in different bodies produced all the phænomena of nature. It were endless to enumerate the various systems that were invented with this view, and the disputes that were carried on for ages; the followers of every system exposing the weak sides of other systems, and palliating those of their own, with great art.

" At last, some free and facetious spirits, wearied with eternal disputation, and the labour of patching and propping weak systems, began to complain of the subtilty of nature; of the infinite changes that bodies undergo in figure, colour, and magnitude; and of the difficulty of accounting for these appearances—making this a pretence for giving up all inquiries into the causes of things, as vain and fruitless.

"These wits had ample matter of mirth and ridicule in the systems of philosophers; and, finding it an easier task to pull down than to build or support, and that every sect furnished them with arms and auxiliaries to destroy another, they began to spread mightily, and went on with great success. Thus philosophy gave way to scepticism and irony, and those systems which had been the work of ages, and the admiration of the learned, became the jest of the vulgar: for even the vulgar readily took part in the triumph over a kind of learning which they had long suspected, because it produced nothing but wrangling and altercation. The wits, having now acquired great reputation, and being flushed with success, began to think their triumph incomplete, until every pretence to knowledge was overturned; and accordingly began their attacks upon arithmetic, geometry, and even upon the common notions of untaught Idomenians. So difficult it hath always been," says our author, "for great conquerors to know where to stop.

"In the meantime, natural philosophy began to rise from its ashes, under the direction of a person of great genius, who is looked upon as having had something in him above Idomenian nature. He observed, that the Idomenian faculties were certainly intended for contemplation, and that the works of nature were a nobler subject to exercise them upon, than the follies of systems, or the errors of the learned; and being sensible of the difficulty of finding out the causes of natural things, he proposed, by accurate observation of the phœnomena of nature, to find out the rules according to which they happen, without inquiring into the causes of those rules. In this he made considerable progress himself, and planned out much work for his followers, who call themselves *inductive philosophers*. The sceptics look with envy upon this rising sect as eclipsing their reputation, and threatening to limit their empire; but they are at a loss on what hand to attack it. The vulgar begin to reverence it as producing useful discoveries.

"It is to be observed, that every Idomenian firmly believes, that two or more bodies may exist in the same place. For this they have the testimony of sense, and they can no more doubt of it, than they can doubt whether they have any perception at all. They often see two bodies meet and coincide in the same place, and separate again, without having undergone any change in their sensible qualities by this

penetration. When two bodies meet, and occupy the same place, commonly one only appears in that place, and the other disappears. That which continues to appear is said to overcome, the other to be overcome."

To this quality of bodies they gave a name, which our author tells us hath no word answering to it in any human language. And, therefore, after making a long apology, which I omit, he begs leave to call it *the overcoming quality of bodies*. He assures us, that "the speculations which had been raised about this single quality of bodies, and the hypotheses contrived to account for it, were sufficient to fill many volumes. Nor have there been fewer hypotheses invented by their philosophers, to account for the changes of magnitude and figure; which, in most bodies that move, they perceive to be in a continual fluctuation. The founder of the inductive sect, believing it to be above the reach of Idomenian faculties, to discover the real causes of these phænomena, applied himself to find from observation, by what laws they are connected together; and discovered many mathematical ratios and relations concerning the motions, magnitudes, figures, and overcoming quality of bodies, which constant experience confirms. But the opposers of this sect choose rather to content themselves with feigned causes of these phænomena, than to acknowledge the real laws whereby they are governed, which humble their pride, by being confessedly unaccountable."

Thus far Johannes Rudolphus Anepigraphus. Whether this Anepigraphus be the same who is recorded among the Greek alchemistical writers not yet published, by Borrichius, Fabricius, and others,[*] I do not pretend to determine. The identity of their name, and the similitude of their studies, although no slight arguments, yet are not absolutely conclusive. Nor will I take upon me to judge of the narrative of this learned traveller, by the *external* marks of his credibility; I shall confine myself to those which the critics call *internal*. It would even be of small importance to inquire, whether the Idomenians have a real, or only an ideal existence; since this is disputed among the learned with regard to things with which we are more nearly connected. The important question is, whether the account above given, is a just account of their geometry and philosophy? We have all the faculties which they

---

* This is true; the *name* is not imaginary "Anepigraphus the Philosopher" is the reputed author of several chemical treatises in Greek, which have not as yet been deemed worthy of publication. See Du Cange, "Gloss. med. et inf. Græcitatis," voce Ἀνεπίγραφος, and Reinesii, "Var. Lectt" L. II. c. 5. —H.

have, with the addition of others which they have not ; we may, therefore, form some judgment of their philosophy and geometry, by separating from all others, the perceptions we have by sight and reasoning upon them. As far as I am able to judge in this way, after a careful examination, their geometry must be such as Anepigraphus hath described. Nor does his account of their philosophy appear to contain any evident marks of imposture ; although here, no doubt, proper allowance is to be made for liberties which travellers take, as well as for involuntary mistakes which they are apt to fall into.

Section X.

OF THE PARALLEL MOTION OF THE EYES.

Having explained, as distinctly as we can, visible figure, and shewn its connection with the things signified by it, it will be proper next to consider some phænomena of the eyes, and of vision, which have commonly been referred to custom, to anatomical or to mechanical causes ; but which, as I conceive, must be resolved into original powers and principles of the human mind; and, therefore, belong properly to the subject of this inquiry.

The first is the parallel motion of the eyes ; by which, when one eye is turned to the right or to the left, upwards or downwards, or straight forwards, the other always goes along with it in the same direction. We see plainly, when both eyes are open, that they are always turned the same way, as if both were acted upon by the same motive force ; and if one eye is shut, and the hand laid upon it, while the other turns various ways, we feel the eye that is shut turn at the same time, and that whether we will or not. What makes this phænomenon surprising is, that it is acknowledged, by all anatomists, that the muscles which move the two eyes, and the nerves which serve these muscles, are entirely distinct and unconnected. It would be thought very surprising and unaccountable to see a man, who, from his birth, never moved one arm, without moving the other precisely in the same manner, so as to keep them always parallel—yet it would not be more difficult to find the physical cause of such motion of the arms, than it is to find the cause of the parallel motion of the eyes, which is perfectly similar.

The only cause that hath been assigned of this parallel motion of the eyes, is custom. We find by experience, it is said, when we begin to look at objects, that, in order to have distinct vision, it is necessary to turn both eyes the same way ; therefore,

we soon acquire the habit of doing it constantly, and by degrees lose the power of doing otherwise.

This account of the matter seems to be insufficient ; because habits are not got at once ; it takes time to acquire and to confirm them ; and if this motion of the eyes were got by habit, we should see children, when they are born, turn their eyes different ways, and move one without the other, as they do their hands or legs. I know some have affirmed that they are apt to do so. But I have never found it true from my own observation, although I have taken pains to make observations of this kind, and have had good opportunities. I have likewise consulted experienced midwives, mothers, and nurses, and found them agree, that they had never observed distortions of this kind in the eyes of children, but when they had reason to suspect convulsions, or some preternatural cause.

It seems, therefore, to be extremely probable, that, previous to custom, there is something in the constitution, some natural instinct, which directs us to move both eyes always the same way.[*]

We know not how the mind acts upon the body, nor by what power the muscles are contracted and relaxed—but we see that, in some of the voluntary, as well as in some of the involuntary motions, this power is so directed, that many muscles which have no material tie or connection,[†] act in concert, each of them being taught to play its part in exact time and measure. Nor doth a company of expert players in a theatrical performance, or of excellent musicians in a concert, or of good dancers in a country dance, with more regularity and order, conspire and contribute their several parts, to produce one uniform effect, than a number of muscles do, in many of the animal functions, and in many voluntary actions. Yet we see such actions no less skilfully and regularly performed in children, and in those who know not that they have such muscles, than in the most skilful anatomist and physiologist.

Who taught all the muscles that are concerned in sucking, in swallowing our food, in breathing, and in the several natural expulsions, to act their part in such regular order and exact measure ? It was not custom surely. It was that same powerful and wise Being who made the fabric of the human body, and fixed the laws by which the mind operates upon every part

* The parallel movement, like other reciprocities of the two eyes, can be explained *physiologically*, by the mutual relation of their nerves, without recurring to any higher or more mysterious principle.—H.

† This is not correct. Muscles which have correlative motions are now either known or admitted to have correlative nerves.—H.

of it, so that they may answer the purposes intended by them. And when we see, in so many other instances, a system of unconnected muscles* conspiring so wonderfully in their several functions, without the aid of habit, it needs not be thought strange, that the muscles of the eyes should, without this aid, conspire to give that direction to the eyes, without which they could not answer their end.

We see a like conspiring action in the muscles which contract the pupils of the two eyes; and in those muscles, whatever they be, by which the conformation of the eyes is varied according to the distance of objects.

It ought, however, to be observed, that, although it appears to be by natural instinct that both eyes are always turned the same way, there is still some latitude left for custom.

What we have said of the parallel motion of the eyes, is not to be understood so strictly as if nature directed us to keep their axes always precisely and mathematically parallel to each other. Indeed, although they are always nearly parallel, they hardly ever are exactly so. When we look at an object, the axes of the eyes meet in that object: and, therefore, make an angle, which is always small, but will be greater or less, according as the object is nearer or more remote. Nature hath very wisely left us the power of varying the parallelism of our eyes a little, so that we can direct them to the same point, whether remote or near. This, no doubt, is learned by custom; and accordingly we see, that it is a long time before children get this habit in perfection.

This power of varying the parallelism of the eyes is naturally no more than is sufficient for the purpose intended by it; but by much practice and straining, it may be increased. Accordingly, we see, that some have acquired the power of distorting their eyes into unnatural directions, as others have acquired the power of distorting their bodies into unnatural postures.

Those who have lost the sight of an eye, commonly lose what they had got by custom, in the direction of their eyes, but retain what they had by nature; that is, although their eyes turn and move always together, yet, when they look upon an object, the blind eye will often have a very small deviation from it; which is not perceived by a slight observer, but may be discerned by one accustomed to make exact observations in these matters.

* See the preceding note.

Section XI.

OF OUR SEEING OBJECTS ERECT BY INVERTED IMAGES.

Another phænomenon which hath perplexed philosophers, is, our seeing objects erect, when it is well known that their images or pictures upon the *tunica retina* of the eye are inverted.

The sagacious Kepler first made the noble discovery, that distinct but inverted pictures of visible objects are formed upon the *retina* by the rays of light coming from the object. The same great philosopher demonstrated, from the principles of optics, how these pictures are formed—to wit, That the rays coming from any one point of the object, and falling upon the various parts of the pupil, are, by the *cornea* and crystalline, refracted so as to meet again in one point of the *retina*, and there paint the colour of that point of the object from which they come. As the rays from different points of the object cross each other before they come to the *retina*, the picture they form must be inverted; the upper part of the object being painted upon the lower part of the *retina*, the right side of the object upon the left of the *retina*, and so of the other parts.*

This philosopher thought that we see objects erect by means of these inverted pictures, for this reason, that, as the rays from different points of the object cross each other before they fall upon the *retina*, we conclude that the impulse which we feel upon the lower part of the *retina* comes from above, and that the impulse which we feel upon the higher part comes from below.

Des Cartes afterwards gave the same solution of this phænomenon, and illustrated it by the judgment which we form of the position of objects which we feel with our arms crossed, or with two-sticks that cross each other.

But we cannot acquiesce in this solution. First, Because it supposes our seeing things erect, to be a deduction of reason, drawn from certain premises: whereas it seems to be an immediate perception. And, secondly, Because the premises from which all mankind are supposed to draw this conclusion, never entered into the minds of the far greater part, but are absolutely unknown to them. We have no feeling or perception of the pictures upon the *retina*, and as little surely

* This inverted picture is seen if we take the eye of an ox, for example, and cut away the posterior part of the sclerotica and choroid; but, without this preparation, it is apparent in the eyes of albino animals, of the owl, &c., in which the *hard coat* and *choroid* are semi-diaphanous.—H.

of the position of them. In order to see objects erect, according to the principles of Kepler or Des Cartes, we must previously know that the rays of light come from the object to the eye in straight lines ; we must know that the rays from different points of the object cross one another before they form the pictures upon the *retina*; and, lastly, we must know that these pictures are really inverted. Now, although all these things are true, and known to philosophers, yet they are absolutely unknown to the far greatest part of mankind : nor is it possible that they who are absolutely ignorant of them, should reason from them, and build conclusions upon them. Since, therefore, visible objects appear erect to the ignorant as well as to the learned, this cannot be a conclusion drawn from premises which never entered into the minds of the ignorant. We have indeed had occasion to observe many instances of conclusions drawn, either by means of original principles, or by habit, from premises which pass through the mind very quickly, and which are never made the objects of reflection ; but surely no man will conceive it possible to draw conclusions from premises which never entered into the mind at all.

Bishop Berkeley having justly rejected this solution, gives one founded upon his own principles ; wherein he is followed by the judicious Dr Smith, in his " Optics ;" and this we shall next explain and examine.

That ingenious writer conceives the ideas of sight to be altogether unlike those of touch. And, since the notions we have of an object by these different senses have no similitude, we can learn only by experience how one sense will be affected, by what, in a certain manner, affects the other. Figure, position, and even number, in tangible objects, are ideas of touch ; and, although there is no similitude between these and the ideas of sight, yet we learn by experience, that a triangle affects the sight in such a manner, and that a square affects it in such another manner—hence we judge that which affects it in the first manner, to be a triangle, and that which affects it in the second, to be a square. In the same way, finding, from experience, that an object in an erect position affects the eye in one manner, and the same object in an inverted position affects it in another, we learn to judge, by the manner in which the eye is affected, whether the object is erect or inverted. In a word, visible ideas, according to this author, are signs of the tangible ; and the mind passeth from the sign to the thing signified, not by means of any similitude between the one and other, nor by any natural principle, but by having found them constantly conjoined in experience as the sounds of a language are with the things they signify : so that, if the images upon the *retina* had been always erect, they would have shewn the objects erect, in the manner as they do now that they are inverted—nay, if the visible idea which we now have from an inverted object, had been associated from the beginning with the erect position of that object, it would have signified an erect position, as readily as it now signifies an inverted one. And, if the visible appearance of two shillings had been found connected from the beginning with the tangible idea of one shilling, that appearance would as naturally and readily have signified the unity of the object as now it signifies its duplicity.

This opinion is, undoubtedly, very ingenious ; and, if it is just, serves to resolve not only the phænomenon now under consideration, but likewise that which we shall next consider—our seeing objects single with two eyes.

It is evident that, in this solution, it is supposed that we do not originally, and previous to acquired habits, see things either erect or inverted, of one figure or another, single or double ; but learn, from experience, to judge of their tangible position, figure, and number, by certain visible signs.

Indeed, it must be acknowledged to be extremely difficult to distinguish the immediate and natural objects of sight, from the conclusions which we have been accustomed from infancy to draw from them. Bishop Berkeley was the first that attempted to distinguish the one from the other, and to trace out the boundary that divides them. And if, in doing so, he hath gone a little to the right hand or to the left, this might be expected in a subject altogether new, and of the greatest subtilty. The nature of vision hath received great light from this distinction ; and many phænomena in optics, which before appeared altogether unaccountable, have been clearly and distinctly resolved by it. It is natural, and almost unavoidable, to one who hath made an important discovery in philosophy, to carry it a little beyond its sphere, and to apply it to the resolution of phænomena which do not fall within its province. Even the great Newton, when he had discovered the universal law of gravitation, and observed how many of the phænomena of nature depend upon this, and other laws of attraction and repulsion, could not help expressing his conjecture, that all the phænomena of the material world depend upon attracting and repelling forces in the particles of matter. And I suspect that the ingenious Bishop of Cloyne, having found so many phænomena of vision reducible to the constant association of the ideas of sight and touch, carried this principle a little beyond its just limits.

In order to judge as well as we can whether it is so, let us suppose such a blind man as Dr Saunderson, having all the knowledge and abilities which a blind man may have, suddenly made to see perfectly. Let us suppose him kept from all opportunities of associating his ideas of sight with those of touch, until the former become a little familiar ; and the first surprise, occasioned by objects so new, being abated, he has time to canvass them, and to compare them, in his mind, with the notions which he formerly had by touch ; and, in particular, to compare, in his mind, that visible extension which his eyes present, with the extension in length and breadth with which he was before acquainted.

We have endeavoured to prove, that a blind man may form a notion of the visible extension and figure of bodies, from the relation which it bears to their tangible extension and figure. Much more, when this visible extension and figure are presented to his eye, will he be able to compare them with tangible extension and figure, and to perceive that the one has length and breadth as well as the other ; that the one may be bounded by lines, either straight or curve, as well as the other. And, therefore, he will perceive that there may be visible as well as tangible circles, triangles, quadrilateral and multilateral figures. And, although the visible figure is coloured, and the tangible is not, they may, notwithstanding, have the same figure ; as two objects of touch may have the same figure, although one is hot and the other cold.

We have demonstrated, that the properties of visible figures differ from those of the plain figures which they represent ; but it was observed, at the same time, that when the object is so small as to be seen distinctly at one view, and is placed directly before the eye, the difference between the visible and the tangible figure is too small to be perceived by the senses. Thus, it is true, that, of every visible triangle, the three angles are greater than two right angles ; whereas, in a plain triangle, the three angles are equal to two right angles ; but when the visible triangle is small, its three angles will be so nearly equal to two right angles, that the sense cannot discern the difference. In like manner, the circumferences of unequal visible circles are not, but those of plain circles are, in the *ratio* of their diameters ; yet, in small visible circles, the circumferences are very nearly in the *ratio* of their diameters ; and the diameter bears the same *ratio* to the circumference, as in a plain circle, very nearly.

Hence it appears, that small visible figures (and such only can be seen distinctly at one view) have not only a resemblance to the plain tangible figures which have the same name, but are to all sense the same : so that, if Dr Saunderson had been made to see, and had attentively viewed the figures of the first book of Euclid, he might, by thought and consideration, without touching them, have found out that they were the very figures he was before so well acquainted with by touch.

When plain figures are seen obliquely, their visible figure differs more from the tangible ; and the representation which is made to the eye, of solid figures, is still more imperfect ; because visible extension hath not three, but two dimensions only. Yet, as it cannot be said that an exact picture of a man hath no resemblance of the man, or that a perspective view of a house hath no resemblance of the house, so it cannot be said, with any propriety, that the visible figure of a man or of a house hath no resemblance of the objects which they represent.

Bishop Berkeley therefore proceeds upon a capital mistake, in supposing that there is no resemblance betwixt the extension, figure, and position which we see, and that which we perceive by touch.

We may further observe, that Bishop Berkeley's system, with regard to material things, must have made him see this question, of the erect appearance of objects, in a very different light from that in which it appears to those who do not adopt his system.

In his theory of vision, he seems indeed to allow, that there is an external material world : but he believed that this external world is tangible only, and not visible ; and that the visible world, the proper object of sight, is not external, but in the mind. If this is supposed, he that affirms that he sees things erect and not inverted, affirms that there is a top and a bottom, a right and a left in the mind. Now, I confess I am not so well acquainted with the topography of the mind, as to be able to affix a meaning to these words when applied to it.

We shall therefore allow, that, if visible objects were not external, but existed only in the mind, they could have no figure, or position, or extension ; and that it would be absurd to affirm, that they are seen either erect or inverted, or that there is any resemblance between them and the objects of touch. But when we propose the question, why objects are seen erect and not inverted, we take it for granted, that we are not in Bishop Berkeley's ideal world, but in that world which men who yield to the dictates of common sense, believe themselves to inhabit. We take it for granted, that the objects both of sight and touch, are external, and have a certain figure, and a certain position with regard to one another, and with regard to our bodies, whether we perceive it or not.

When I hold my walking-cane upright in my hand, and look at it, I take it for granted that I see and handle the same individual object. When I say that I feel it erect, my meaning is, that I feel the head directed from the horizon, and the point directed towards it ; and when I say that I see it erect, I mean that I see it with the head directed from the horizon, and the point towards it. I conceive the horizon as a fixed object both of sight and touch, with relation to which, objects are said to be high or low, erect or inverted ; and when the question is asked, why I see the object erect, and not inverted, it is the same as if you should ask, why I see it in that position which it really hath, or why the eye shews the real position of objects, and doth not shew them in an inverted position, as they are seen by a common astronomical telescope, or as their pictures are seen upon the *retina* of an eye when it is dissected.

Section XII.

THE SAME SUBJECT CONTINUED.

It is impossible to give a satisfactory answer to this question, otherwise than by pointing out the laws of nature which take place in vision; for by these the phænomena of vision must be regulated.

Therefore, I answer, First, That, by a law of nature, the rays of light proceed from every point of the object to the pupil of the eye, in straight lines ; Secondly, That, by the laws of nature, the rays coming from any one point of the object to the various parts of the pupil, are so refracted as to meet again in one point of the *retina ;* and the rays from different points of the object, first crossing each other,* and then proceeding to as many different points of the *retina,* form an inverted picture of the object.

So far the principles of optics carry us ; and experience further assures us, that, if there is no such picture upon the *retina,* there is no vision ; and that such as the picture on the *retina* is, such is the appear-

ance of the object, in colour and figure, distinctness or indistinctness, brightness or faintness.

It is evident, therefore, that the pictures upon the *retina* are, by the laws of nature, a mean of vision ; but in what way they accomplish their end, we are totally ignorant. Philosophers conceive, that the impression made on the *retina* by the rays of light, is communicated to the optic nerve, and by the optic nerve conveyed to some part of the brain, by them called the *sensorium ;* and that the impression thus conveyed to the *sensorium* is immediately perceived by the mind, which is supposed to reside there. But we know nothing of the seat of the soul : and we are so far from perceiving immediately what is transacted in the brain, that of all parts of the human body we know least about it. It is indeed very probable, that the optic nerve is an instrument of vision no less necessary than the *retina ;* and that some impression is made upon it, by means of the pictures on the *retina.* But of what kind this impression is, we know nothing.

There is not the least probability that there is any picture or image of the object either in the optic nerve or brain. The pictures on the *retina* are formed by the rays of light ; and, whether we suppose, with some, that their impulse upon the *retina* causes some vibration of the fibres of the optic nerve, or, with others, that it gives motion to some subtile fluid contained in the nerve, neither that vibration nor this motion can resemble the visible object which is presented to the mind. Nor is there any probability that the mind perceives the pictures upon the *retina.* These pictures are no more objects of our perception, than the brain is, or the optic nerve. No man ever saw the pictures in his own eye, nor indeed the pictures in the eye of another, until it was taken out of the head and duly prepared.

It is very strange, that philosophers, of all ages, should have agreed in this notion, that the images of external objects are conveyed by the organs of sense to the brain, and are there perceived by the mind.* Nothing can be more unphilosophical. For, First, This notion hath no foundation in fact and observation. Of all the organs of sense, the eye only, as far as we can discover, forms any kind of image of its object ; and the images formed by the eye are not in the brain, but only in the bottom of the eye ; nor are they at all perceived or felt by the mind.† Secondly, It is as difficult

---

* It is marvellous how widely both natural philosophers and physiologists are at variance with regard to the point of the eye at which the rays cross each other. Some place this point in the cornea—some in the region of the pupil—some in the centre of the crystalline—and some in the vitreous humour. Recent experiments, instituted for the purpose of determining its locality, and still unknown in this country, place it behind the crystalline lens. This is found to be at once the crossing point, both of the rays of light and of the line of visible direction, and the turning point on which the eye rolls.—H.

---

* This statement in its unqualified universality is altogether erroneous.—H.
† This would require a second eye behind the *retina*; which eye would also see the images bent.

to conceive how the mind perceives images in the brain, as how it perceives things more distant., If any man will shew how the mind may perceive images in the brain, I will undertake to shew how it may perceive the most distant objects ; for, if we give eyes to the mind, to perceive what is transacted at home in its dark chamber, why may we not make these eyes a little longer-sighted ? and then we shall have no occasion for that unphilosophical fiction of images in the brain. (In a word, the manner and mechanism of the mind's perception is quite beyond our comprehension ; and this way of explaining it, by images in the brain, seems to be founded upon very gross notions of the mind and its operations ; as if the supposed images in the brain, by a kind of contact, formed similar impressions or images of objects upon the mind, of which impressions it is supposed to be conscious.

We have endeavoured to shew, throughout the course of this inquiry, that the impressions made upon the mind by means of the five senses, have not the least resemblance to the objects of sense ; and, therefore, as we see no shadow of evidence that there are any such images in the brain, so we see no purpose, in philosophy, that the supposition of them can answer. Since the picture upon the *retina*, therefore, is neither itself seen by the mind, nor produces any impression upon the brain or *sensorium*, which is seen by the mind, nor makes any impression upon the mind that resembles the object, it may still be asked, How this picture upon the *retina* causes vision ?

Before we answer this question, it is proper to observe, that, in the operations of the mind, as well as in those of bodies, we must often be satisfied with knowing that certain things are connected, and invariably follow one another, without being able to discover the chain that goes between them. It is to such connections that we give the name of *laws of nature ;* and when we say that one thing produces another by a law of nature, this signifies no more, but that one thing, which we call in popular language *the cause*, is constantly and invariably followed by another, which we call *the effect ;* and that we know not how they are connected. Thus, we see it is a fact, that bodies gravitate towards bodies ; and that this gravitation is regulated by certain mathematical proportions, according to the distances of the bodies from each other, and their quantities of matter. Being unable to discover the cause of this gravitation, and presuming that it is the immediate operation, either of the Author of nature,

or of some subordinate cause, which we have not hitherto been able to reach, we call it *a law of nature*. If any philosopher should hereafter be so happy as to discover the cause of gravitation, this can only be done by discovering some more general law of nature, of which the gravitation of bodies is a necessary consequence. In every chain of natural causes, the highest link is a primary law of nature, and the highest link which we can trace, by just induction, is either this primary law of nature, or a necessary consequence of it. To trace out the laws of nature, by induction from the phænomena of nature, is all that true philosophy aims at, and all that it can ever reach.

There are laws of nature by which the operations of the mind are regulated, there are also laws of nature that govern the material system ; and, as the latter are the ultimate conclusions which the human faculties can reach in the philosophy of bodies, so the former are the ultimate conclusions we can reach in the philosophy of minds.

To return, therefore, to the question above proposed, we may see, from what hath been just now observed, that it amounts to this—By what law of nature is a picture upon the *retina* the mean or occasion of my seeing an external object of the same figure and colour in a contrary position, and in a certain direction from the eye ?

It will, without doubt, be allowed that I see the whole object in the same manner and by the same law by which I see any one point of it. Now, I know it to be a fact, that, in direct vision, I see every point of the object in the direction of the right line that passeth from the centre of the eye to that point of the object. And I know, likewise, from optics, that the ray of light that comes to the centre of my eye, passes on to the *retina* in the same direction. Hence, it appears to be a fact, *that every point of the object is seen in the direction of a right line passing from the picture of that point on the retina, through the centre of the eye*. As this is a fact that holds universally and invariably, it must either be a law of nature, or the necessary consequence of some more general law of nature ; and, according to the just rules of philosophising, we may hold it for a law of nature, until some more general law be discovered, whereof it is a necessary consequence—which, I suspect, can never be done.[*]

---

as they are pictured on the concavity of that membrane.—H.

[*] A confirmation of this doctrine is drawn from the cases of Cheselden and others, in which no mental inversion of the objects is noticed, and which had it occurred, is too remarkable a phænomenon to have been overlooked It is, indeed, generally asserted that

Thus, we see that the phænomena of vision lead us by the hand to a law of nature, or a law of our constitution, of which law, our seeing objects erect by inverted images, is a necessary consequence. For it necessarily follows, from the law we have mentioned, that the object whose picture is lowest on the *retina* must be seen in the highest direction from the eye ; and that the object whose picture is on the right of the *retina* must be seen on the left ; so that, if the pictures had been erect in the *retina*, we should have seen the object inverted. My chief intention in handling this question, was to point out this law of nature, which, as it is a part of the constitution of the human mind, belongs properly to the subject of this inquiry. For this reason, I shall make some farther remarks upon it, after doing justice to the ingenious Dr Porterfield, who, long ago, in the " Medical Essays," or, more lately, in his

such inversion has never been observed in any patient, surgically restored to sight. I am aware, however, of one case of an opposite purport. It is mentioned, on his own observation, by a very intelligent philosopher and physician, Professor Leidenfrost of Duisburg ; and, as his rare work—" Confessio quid putet per Experientiam diiilicisse de Mente Humana," 1793—is altogether unknown in this country, I shall extract from it the whole passage :—
" Hae imagines formantur in organo, non in cerebro.—Mutantur et pervertuntur ab organo laeso, etiamsi illaesum maneat cerebrum. Non eas connatas habemus, sed exercitio continuato eas formare discimus. Elegans exemplum habemus in evangelio Marc. 8. cf. Ioh. 9. Vir adultus a nativitate coecus, et potentia miraculosa sancti servatoris subito curatus primo actu visionis utens distinguere non poterat, utrumne staturae, quas videbat, homines essent, an arbores. Sine dubio jam ante curationem sciverat ex relatione aliorum, et ex manuum suarum experientia, tam hominis quam stipitis arboreae staturas esse erectas, at ulteriori exercitio tuerit opus ad utrumque distinguendum. Aliquid simile aliquando in juvene propter cataractam congenitam coeco mihi observare licuit. Hic ex paupercula familia rustica ortus, statim post partum utramque pupillam habuit obscuratam ; probabiliter membrana pupillaris crassa et opaca erat. Pro incurabili habitus nullam curationem habuit. Sanus excrevit, sed plane coecus, omni lumine orbus, in scholas missus lepidi ingenii signa dedit. Anno aetatis circiter decimo septimo, nescio ex qua causa gravissima ophthalmia corripitur cum tumore palpebrarum et acerbo dolore. In hoc statu aliqualis medicatio adhibita est. Observarunt parentes lucem ab eo fugi, a luce dolores crescere Post aliquot hebdomades foetus et ophthalmia decrescunt ; cum summo ejus stupore aliqualem luminis usuram nanciscitur. Coepit scribere plures memorabiles hujus visionis conditiones, nam ab eo tempore frequenter, et semper admirans, eum conspexi Hoc unum, quod ad rem facit, addo ; imagines in oculo orsas penitus ei novas fuisse. Ab initio non pariebatur sibi persuaderi, reliquos homines erectos incedere, putabat hominum capita sui ipsius pedibus esse obversa. Similiter arbores et objecta omnia ratione sui inversa esse. Colorum diversitate vehementer delectabatur, quorum nullum conceptum habuerat Nam quamdiu coecus erat, si quid de rubro aut alio colore audiverat, id comparaverat cum sensationibus aurium. Rubrum sibi praesentaverat esse aliquid quasi dulce, nigrum cum amarore comparaverat Successive sibi imagines has formabat, et dijudicabat, ut reliqui homines. In hoc homine nullae imagines visivae prae extiterunt, neque in organo, neque in cerebro, cujus nulla passio aut mutatio facta erat. Aliquot annis post, hic juvenis, non sine meo dolore, phthisicus moriebatur."—P. 54.

" Treatise of the Eye," pointed out,* as a primary law of our nature. That a visible object appears in the direction of a right line perpendicular to the *retina* at that point where its image is painted. If lines drawn from the centre of the eye to all parts of the *retina* be perpendicular to it, as they must be very nearly, this coincides with the law we have mentioned, and is the same in other words. In order, therefore, that we may have a more distinct notion of this law of our constitution, we may observe—

1. That we can give no reason why the *retina* is, of all parts of the body, the only one on which pictures made by the rays of light cause vision ; and, therefore, we must resolve this solely into a law of our constitution. We may form such pictures by means of optical glasses, upon the hand, or upon any other part of the body ; but they are not felt, nor do they produce anything like vision. A picture upon the *retina* is as little felt as one upon the hand ; but it produces vision, for no other reason that we know, but because it is destined by the wisdom of nature to this purpose. The vibrations of the air strike upon the eye, the palate, and the olfactory membrane, with the same force as upon the *membrani tympani* of the ear. The impression they make upon the last produces the sensation of sound ; but their impression upon any of the former produces no sensation at all. This may be extended to all the senses, whereof each hath its peculiar laws, according to which the impressions made upon the organ of that sense, produce sensations or perceptions in the mind, that cannot be produced by impressions made upon any other organ.

2. We may observe, that the laws of perception, by the different senses, are very different, not only in respect of the nature of the objects perceived by them, but likewise in respect of the notices they give us of the distance and situation of the object. In all of them the object is conceived† to be external, and to have real existence, independent of our perception : but in one, the distance, figure, and situation of the object, are all presented to the mind ; in another, the figure and situation, but not the distance ; and in others, neither figure, situation, nor distance. In vain do we attempt to account for these varieties in the manner of perception by the different

* Porterfield did not first point this out ; on the contrary, it was a common, if not *the* common doctrine at the time he wrote. See below, the first note of § xviii.—H.
† The common sense of mankind assures us that the object of sense, is not merely *conceived* to be external, but *perceived* in its externality ; that we know the Non-Ego, not merely mediately, by a representation in the Ego, but immediately, as existing through only as existing in relation to our organs.—H.

senses, from principles of anatomy or natural philosophy. They must at last be resolved into the will of our Maker, who intended that our powers of perception should have certain limits, and adapted the organs of perception, and the laws of nature by which they operate, to his wise purposes.

When we hear an unusual sound, the sensation indeed is in the mind, but we know that there is something external that produced this sound. At the same time, our hearing does not inform us whether the sounding body is near or at a distance, in this direction or that; and therefore we look round to discover it.

If any new phænomenon appears in the heavens, we see exactly its colour, its apparent place, magnitude, and figure; but we see not its distance. It may be in the atmosphere, it may be among the planets, or it may be in the sphere of the fixed stars, for anything the eye can determine.

The testimony of the sense of touch reaches only to objects that are contiguous to the organ, but, with regard to them, is more precise and determinate. When we feel a body with our hand, we know the figure, distance, and position of it, as well as whether it is rough or smooth, hard or soft, hot or cold.

The sensations of touch, of seeing, and hearing, are all in the mind, and can have no existence but when they are perceived. How do they all constantly and invariably suggest the conception and belief of external objects, which exist whether they are perceived or not? No philosopher can give any other answer to this, but that such is the constitution of our nature. How do we know that the object of touch is at the finger's end, and nowhere else?—that the object of sight is in such a direction from the eye, and in no other, but may be at any distance?*—and that the object of hearing may be at any distance,* and in any direction? Not by custom surely—not by reasoning, or comparing ideas—but by the constitution of our nature. How do we perceive visible objects in the direction of right lines perpendicular to that part of the *retina* on which the rays strike, while we do not perceive the objects of hearing in lines perpendicular to the *membrana tympani* upon which the vibrations of the air strike? Because such are the laws of our nature. How do we know the parts of our bodies affected by particular pains? Not by experience or by reasoning, but by the constitution of nature. The sensation of pain is, no doubt, in the mind, and cannot be said to have any relation, from its own nature, to any part

of the body; but this sensation, by our constitution, gives a perception of some particular part of the body, whose disorder causes the uneasy sensation. If it were not so, a man who never before felt either the gout or the toothache, when he is first seized with the gout in his toe, might mistake it for the toothache.

Every sense, therefore, hath its peculiar laws and limits, by the constitution of our nature; and one of the laws of sight is, that we always see an object in the direction of a right line, passing from its image on the *retina* through the centre of the eye.

3. Perhaps some readers will imagine that it is easier, and will answer the purpose as well, to conceive a law of nature, by which we shall always see objects in the place in which they are, and in their true position, without having recourse to images on the *retina*, or to the optical centre of the eye.

To this I answer, that nothing can be a law of nature which is contrary to fact. The laws of nature are the most general facts we can discover in the operations of nature. Like other facts, they are not to be hit upon by a happy conjecture, but justly deduced from observation; like other general facts, they are not to be drawn from a few particulars, but from a copious, patient, and cautious induction. That we see things always in their true place and position, is not fact; and therefore it can be no law of nature. In a plain mirror, I see myself, and other things, in places very different from those they really occupy.* And so it happens in every instance wherein the rays coming from the object are either reflected or refracted before falling upon the eye. Those who know anything of optics, know that, in all such cases, the object is seen in the direction of a line passing from the centre of the eye, to the point where the rays were last reflected or refracted; and that upon this all the powers of the telescope and microscope depend.

Shall we say, then, that it is a law of nature, that the object is seen in the direction which the rays have when they fall on the eye, or rather in the direction contrary to that of the rays when they fall upon the eye? No. This is not true; and therefore it is no law of nature. For the rays, from any one point of the object, come to all parts of the pupil; and therefore must have different directions: but we see the object only in one of these directions—to wit, in the direction of the rays that come to the centre of the eye. And this holds true, even when the rays that should pass through the centre are stopped,

---

* It has been previously noticed, that in no *sense* does the mind *perceive* any di tant or inediate object.—H.

* This is a very inaccurate statement. In a mirror I do not see *myself*, &c.—H.

and the object is seen by rays that pass at a distance from the centre.*

Perhaps it may still be imagined, that, although we are not made so as to see objects always in their true place, nor so as to see them precisely in the direction of the rays when they fall upon the *cornea ;* yet we may be so made as to see the object in the direction which the rays have when they fall upon the *retina,* after they have undergone all their refractions in the eye—that is, in the direction in which the rays pass from the crystalline to the *retina.* But neither is this true ; and consequently it is no law of our constitution. In order to see that it is not true we must conceive all the rays that pass from the crystalline to one point of the *retina,* as forming a small cone, whose base is upon the back of the crystalline, and whose vertex is a point of the *retina.* It is evident that the rays which form the picture in this point, have various directions, even after they pass the crystalline : yet the object is seen only in one of these directions—to wit, in the direction of the rays that come from the centre of the eye. Nor is this owing to any particular virtue in the central rays, or in the centre itself; for the central rays may be stopped. When they are stopped, the image will be formed upon the same point of the *retina* as before, by rays that are not central, nor have the same direction which the central rays had : and in this case the object is seen in the same direction as before, although there are now no rays coming in that direction.*

From this induction we conclude, That our seeing an object in that particular direction in which we do see it, is not owing to any law of nature by which we are made to see it in the direction of the rays, either before their refractions in the eye, or after, but to a law of our nature, by which we see the object in the direction of the right line that passeth from the picture of the object upon the *retina* to the centre of the eye.†

The facts upon which I ground this induction, are taken from some curious experiments of Scheiner, in his "Fundamentum Opticum," quoted by Dr Porterfield, and confirmed by his experience. I have also repeated these experiments, and found them to answer. As they are easily made, and tend to illustrate and confirm the law of nature I have mentioned, I shall recite them as briefly and distinctly as I can.

Experiment 1. Let a very small object, such as the head of a pin, well illuminated, be fixed at such a distance from the eye as to be beyond the nearest limit and within the farthest limit of distinct vision. For a young eye, not near-sighted, the object may be placed at the distance of eighteen inches. Let the eye be kept steadily in one place, and take a distinct view of the object. We know, from the principles of optics, that the rays from any one point of this object, whether they pass through the centre of the eye, or at any distance from the centre which the breadth of the pupil will permit, do all unite again in one point of the *retina.* We know, also, that these rays have different directions, both before they fall upon the eye, and after they pass through the crystalline.

Now, we can see the object by any one small parcel of these rays, excluding the rest, by looking through a small pin-hole in a card. Moving this pin-hole over the various parts of the pupil, we can see the object, first by the rays that pass above the centre of the eye, then by the central rays, then by the rays that pass below the centre, and in like manner by the rays that pass on the right and left of the centre. Thus, we view this object, successively, by rays that are central, and by rays that are not central ; by rays that have different directions, and are variously inclined to each other, both when they fall upon the *cornea,* and when they fall upon the *retina ;* but always by rays which fall upon the same point of the *retina.* And what is the event ? It is this—that the object is seen in the same individual direction, whether seen by all these rays together, or by any one parcel of them.

Experiment 2. Let the object above mentioned be now placed within the nearest limit of distinct vision—that is, for an eye that is not near-sighted, at the distance of four or five inches. We know that, in this case, the rays coming from one point of the object do not meet in one point of the *retina*, but spread over a small circular spot of it; the central rays occupying the centre of this circle, the rays that pass above the centre occupying the upper part of the circular spot, and so of the rest. And we know that the object is, in this case, seen confused; every point of it being seen, not in one, but in various directions. To remedy this confusion, we look at the object through the pin-hole, and, while we move the pin-hole over the various parts of the pupil, the object does not keep its place, but seems to move in a contrary direction.

It is here to be observed, that, when the pin-hole is carried upwards over the pupil, the picture of the object is carried upwards upon the *retina*, and the object, at the same time, seems to move downwards, so as to be always in the right line, passing from the picture through the centre of the eye. It is likewise to be observed, that the rays which form the upper and the lower pictures upon the *retina* do not cross each other, as in ordinary vision; yet, still, the higher picture shews the object lower, and the lower picture shews the object higher, in the same manner as when the rays cross each other. Whence we may observe, by the way, that this phænomenon of our seeing objects in a position contrary to that of their pictures upon the *retina*, does not depend upon the crossing of the rays, as Kepler and Des Cartes conceived.

Experiment 3. Other things remaining as in the last experiment, make three pin-holes in a straight line, so near that the rays coming from the object through all the holes may enter the pupil at the same time. In this case, we have a very curious phænomenon; for the object is seen triple with one eye. And if you make more holes within the breadth of the pupil, you will see as many objects as there are holes. However, we shall suppose them only three—one on the right, one in the middle, and one on the left; in which case you see three objects standing in a line from right to left.

It is here to be observed, that there are three pictures on the *retina*; that on the left being formed by the rays which pass on the left of the eye's centre, the middle picture being formed by the central rays, and the right-hand picture by the rays which pass on the right of the eye's centre. It is farther to be observed, that the object which appears on the right, is not that which is seen through the hole on the right, but that which is seen through the hole on the left; and, in like manner, the left-hand object is seen through the hole on the right, as is easily proved by covering the holes successively: so that, whatever

is the direction of the rays which form the right-hand and left-hand pictures, still the right-hand picture shews a left-hand object, and the left-hand picture shews a right-hand object.

Experiment 4. It is easy to see how the two last experiments may be varied, by placing the object beyond the farthest limit of distinct vision. In order to make this experiment, I looked at a candle at the distance of ten feet, and put the eye of my spectacles behind the card, that the rays from the same point of the object might meet and cross each other, before they reached the *retina*. In this case, as in the former, the candle was seen triple through the three pin-holes; but the candle on the right was seen through the hole on the right; and, on the contrary, the left-hand candle was seen through the hole on the left. In this experiment it is evident, from the principles of optics, that the rays forming the several pictures on the *retina* cross each other a little before they reach the *retina;* and, therefore, the left-hand picture is formed by the rays which pass through the hole on the right: so that the position of the pictures is contrary to that of the holes by which they are formed; and, therefore, is also contrary to that of their objects—as we have found it to be in the former experiments.

These experiments exhibit several uncommon phænomena, that regard the apparent place, and the direction of visible objects from the eye; phænomena that seem to be most contrary to the common rules of vision. When we look at the same time through three holes that are in a right line, and at certain distances from each other, we expect that the objects seen through them should really be, and should appear to be, at a distance from each other. Yet, by the first experiment, we may, through three such holes, see the same object, and the same point of that object; and through all the three it appears in the same individual place and direction.

When the rays of light come from the object in right lines to the eye, without any reflection, inflection, or refraction, we expect that the object should appear in its real and proper direction from the eye; and so it commonly does. But in the second, third, and fourth experiments, we see the object in a direction which is not its true and real direction from the eye, although the rays come from the object to the eye, without any inflection, reflection, or refraction.

When both the object and the eye are fixed without the least motion, and the medium unchanged, we expect that the object should appear to rest, and keep the same place. Yet, in the second and fourth

M

experiments, when both the eye and the object are at rest, and the medium unchanged, we make the object appear to move upwards or downwards, or in any direction we please.

When we look, at the same time and with the same eye, through holes that stand in a line from right to left, we expect that the object seen through the left-hand hole should appear on the left, and the object seen through the right-hand hole should appear on the right. Yet, in the third experiment, we find the direct contrary.

Although many instances occur in seeing the same object double with two eyes, we always expect that it should appear single when seen only by one eye. Yet, in the second and fourth experiments, we have instances wherein the same object may appear double, triple, or quadruple to one eye, without the help of a polyhedron or multiplying glass.

All these extraordinary phænomena, regarding the direction of visible objects from the eye, as well as those that are common and ordinary, lead us to that law of nature which I have mentioned, and are the necessary consequences of it. And, as there is no probability that we shall ever be able to give a reason why pictures upon the *retina* make us see external objects, any more than pictures upon the hand or upon the cheek; or, that we shall ever be able to give a reason, why we see the object in the direction of a line passing from its picture through the centre of the eye, rather than in any other direction—I am, therefore, apt to look upon this law as a primary law of our constitution.

To prevent being misunderstood, I beg the reader to observe, that I do not mean to affirm that the picture upon the *retina* will make us see an object in the direction mentioned, or in any direction, unless the optic nerve, and the other more immediate instruments of vision, be sound, and perform their function. We know not well what is the office of the optic nerve, nor in what manner it performs that office ; but that it hath some part in the faculty of seeing, seems to be certain ; because, in an *amaurosis*, which is believed to be a disorder of the optic nerve, the pictures on the *retina* are clear and distinct, and yet there is no vision.

We know still less of the use and function of the choroid membrane : but it seems likewise to be necessary to vision : for it is well known, that pictures upon that part of the *retina* where it is not covered by the choroid—I mean at the entrance of the optic nerve—produce no vision any more than a picture upon the hand. * We ac-

knowledge, therefore, that the *retina* is not the last and most immediate instrument of the mind in vision. There are other material organs, whose operation is necessary to seeing, even after the pictures upon the *retina* are formed. If ever we come to know the structure and use of the choroid membrane, the optic nerve, and the brain, and what impressions are made upon them by means of the pictures on the *retina*, some more links of the chain may be brought within our view, and a more general law of vision discovered ; but, while we know so little of the nature and office of these more immediate instruments of vision, it seems to be impossible to trace its laws beyond the pictures upon the *retina*.

Neither do I pretend to say, that there may not be diseases of the eye, or accidents, which may occasion our seeing objects in a direction somewhat different from that mentioned above. I shall beg leave to mention one instance of this kind that concerns myself.

In May 1761, being occupied in making an exact meridian, in order to observe the transit of Venus, I rashly directed to the sun, by my right eye, the cross hairs of a small telescope. I had often done the like in my younger days with impunity ; but I suffered by it at last, which I mention as a warning to others.

I soon observed a remarkable dimness in that eye ; and for many weeks, when I was in the dark, or shut my eyes, there appeared before the right eye a lucid spot, which trembled much like the image of the sun seen by reflection from water. This appearance grew fainter, and less frequent, by degrees ; so that now there are seldom any remains of it. But some other very sensible effects of this hurt still remain. For, First, The sight of the right eye continues to be more dim than that of the left. Secondly, The nearest limit of distinct vision is more remote in the right eye than in the other ; although, before the time mentioned, they were equal in both these respects, as I had found by many trials. But, thirdly, what I chiefly intended to mention is, That a straight line, in some circumstances, appears to the right eye to have a curvature in it. Thus, when I look upon a music book, and, shutting my left eye, direct the right to a point of the mid-

---

* Reid here adopts the theory of Mariotte, who first discovered the curious fact of this local insensibility,

and who ingeniously employed it in support of his opinion, that the choroid, not the retina, is the proximate organ in vision. But not only is the absence of the choroid not to be viewed as the cause of this phænomenon ; it is not even to be attributed to the entrance of the optic nerve. For it is proved that the impassive portion of the retina does not occupy above a third part of the disc, corresponding to the circumference of that nerve ; and the conjecture of Rudolphi seems probable, that the insensibility is limited to the spot where the *arteria centralis* enters.—H.

dle line of the five which compose the staff of music the middle line appears dim, indeed, at the point to which the eye is directed, but straight ; at the same time, the two lines above it, and the two below it, appear to be bent outwards, and to be more distant from each other and from the middle line, than at other parts of the staff, to which the eye is not directed. Fourthly, Although I have repeated this experiment times innumerable, within these sixteen months, I do not find that custom and experience takes away this appearance of curvature in straight lines. Lastly, This appearance of curvature is perceptible when I look with the right eye only, but not when I look with both eyes ; yet I see better with both eyes together, than even with the left eye alone.

I have related this fact minutely as it is, without regard to any hypothesis ; because I think such uncommon facts deserve to be recorded. I shall leave it to others to conjecture the cause of this appearance. To me it seems most probable, that a small part of the *retina* towards the centre is shrunk, and that thereby the contiguous parts are drawn nearer to the centre, and to one another, than they were before ; and that objects, whose images fall on these parts, appear at that distance from each other which corresponds, not to the interval of the parts in their present preternatural contraction, but to their interval in their natural and sound state.

Section XIII.

OF SEEING OBJECTS SINGLE WITH TWO EYES.

Another phænomenon of vision which deserves attention, is our seeing objects single with two eyes.* There are two pic-

tures of the object, one on each *retina* , and each picture by itself makes us see an object in a certain direction from the eye ; yet both together commonly make us see only one object. All the accounts or solutions of this phænomenon given by anatomists and philosophers seem to be unsatisfactory. I shall pass over the opinions of Galen, of Gassendus, of Baptista Porta, and of Rohault. The reader may see these examined and refuted by Dr Porterfield. I shall examine Dr Porterfield's own opinion, Bishop Berkeley's, and some others. But it will be necessary first to ascertain the facts : for, if we mistake the phænomena of single and double vision, it is ten to one but this mistake will lead us wrong in assigning the causes. This likewise we ought carefully to attend to, which is acknowledged in theory by all who have any true judgment or just taste in inquiries of this nature, but is very often overlooked in practice—namely, that, in the solution of natural phænomena, all the length that the human faculties can carry us, is only this, that, from particular phænomena, we may, by induction, trace out general phænomena, of which all the particular ones are necessary consequences. And when we have arrived at the most general phænomena we can reach, there we must stop. If it is asked, Why such a body gravitates towards the earth ? all the answer that can be given is, Because all bodies gravitate towards the earth. This is resolving a particular phænomenon into a general one. If it should again be asked, Why do all bodies gravitate towards the earth ? we can give no other solution of this phænomenon, but that all bodies whatsoever gravitate towards each other. This is resolving a general phænomenon into a more general one. If it should be asked, Why all bodies gravitate to one another ? we cannot tell ; but, if we could tell, it could only be by resolving this universal gravitation of bodies into some other phænomenon still more general, and of which the gravitation of all bodies is a particular instance. The most general phænomena we can reach, are what we call *laws of nature* ; so that the laws of nature are nothing else but the most general facts relating to the operations of nature, which include a great many particular facts under them. And if, in any case, we should give the name of a law of nature to a general phænomenon, which human industry shall afterwards trace to one more general, there is no great harm done. The most general assumes the name of a law of nature when it is discovered, and the less general is contained and comprehended in it. Having premised these things, we proceed to consider the phænomena of single

---

* The opinions relative to single vision with two eyes, may, I think, be reduced to *two supreme classes* The one attempts to shew that there is no difficulty to be solved ; the other attempts to solve the difficulty which is admitted.—Under the *former* class, there are, as I recollect, *three* hypotheses. The *first* supposes that we see only with one eye—that man is in reality a Cyclops ; the *second* supposes that the two impressions are not, in fact, made at the same instant in both eyes, and, consequently, that two simultaneous impressions are not conveyed to the brain and mind ; the *third* supposes that, although a separate impression be made on each retina, yet that these several impressions are, as it were, fused into one before they reach the common sensory, in consequence of a union of the optic nerves.—The hypotheses of the *latter* class which, I think, may also be reduced to *three*, all admit that there are simultaneous impressions on the two *retinæ*, and that these impressions are separately conveyed to the termination of the organic apparatus ; but still hold that, in the mind, there is determined only a single perception. One opinion allows the perception to have been originally twofold, and saves the phænomenon, by supposing that it became single through the influence of custom and association. Another explains it more subjectively, by an ultimate and inexplicable law of our constitution ; and the last, more objectively, on some intelligible principle of optics.—H.

M 2

and double vision, in order to discover some general principle to which they all lead, and of which they are the necessary consequences. If we can discover any such general principle, it must either be a law of nature, or the necessary consequence of some law of nature ; and its authority will be equal whether it is the first or the last.

1. We find that, when the eyes are sound and perfect, and the axes of both directed to one point, an object placed in that point is seen single—and here we observe, that in this case the two pictures which shew the object single, are in the centres of the *retina*. When two pictures of a small object are formed upon points of the *retina*, if they shew the object single, we shall, for the sake of perspicuity, call such two points of the *retina*, *corresponding points ;* and where the object is seen double, we shall call the points of the *retina* on which the pictures are formed, *points that do not correspond.**** Now, in this first phænomenon, it is evident, that the two centres of the *retina* are corresponding points.

2. Supposing the same things as in the last phænomenon, other objects at the same distance from the eyes as that to which their axes are directed, do also appear single. Thus if I direct my eyes to a candle placed at the distance of ten feet, and, while I look at this candle, another stands at the same distance from my eyes, within the field of vision, I can, while I look at the first candle, attend to the appearance which the second makes to the eye ; and I find that in this case it always appears single. 'It is here to be observed, that the pictures of the second candle do not fall upon the centres of the *retinæ*, but they both fall upon the same side of the centres—that is, both to the right, or both to the left ; and both are at the same distance from the centres. This might easily be demonstrated from the principles of optics. Hence it appears, that in this second phænomenon of single vision, the corresponding points are points of the two *retinæ*, which are similarly situate with respect to the two centres, being both upon the same side of the centre, and at the same distance from it. It appears likewise, from this phænomenon, that every point in one *retina* corresponds with that which is similarly situate in the other.

3. Supposing still the same things, objects which are much nearer to the eyes, or much more distant from them, than that to which the two eyes are directed, appear double. Thus, if the candle is placed at the distance of ten feet, and I hold my finger at arms-length between my eyes and the candle—when I look at the candle, I see my finger double ; and when I look at my finger, I see the candle double ; and the same thing happens with regard to all other objects at like distances which fall within the sphere of vision. In this phænomenon, it is evident to those who understand the principles of optics, that the pictures of the objects which are seen double, do not fall upon points of the *retinæ* which are similarly situate, but that the pictures of the objects seen single do fall upon points similarly situate. Whence we infer, that, as the points of the two *retinæ*, which are similarly situate with regard to the centres, do correspond, so those which are dissimilarly situate do not correspond.

4. It is to be observed, that, although, in such cases as are mentioned in the last phænomenon, we have been accustomed from infancy to see objects double which we know to be single ; yet custom, and experience of the unity of the object, never take away this appearance of duplicity.

5. It may, however, be remarked that the custom of attending to visible appearances has a considerable effect, and makes the phænomenon of double vision to be more or less observed and remembered. Thus you may find a man that can say, with a good conscience, that he never saw things double all his life ; yet this very man, put in the situation above mentioned, with his finger between him and the candle, and desired to attend to the appearance of the object which he does not look at, will, upon the first trial, see the candle double, when he looks at his finger ; and his finger double, when he looks at the candle. Does he now see otherwise than he saw before ? No, surely ; but he now attends to what he never attended to before. The same double appearance of an object hath been a thousand times presented to his eye before now, but he did not attend to it ; and so it is as little an object of his reflection and memory, as if it had never happened.

When we look at an object, the circumjacent objects may be seen at the same time, although more obscurely and indistinctly : for the eye hath a considerable field of vision, which it takes in at once. But we attend only to the object we look at. The other objects which fall within the field of vision, are not attended to ; and therefore are as if they were not seen. If any of them draws our attention, it naturally draws the eyes at the same time : for, in the com-

* It is to be noticed that Reid uses the terms, *corresponding points* in a sense opposite to that of Smith, and some optical writers ; they use it *anatomically*, he *physiologically*. Two points are anatomically correspondent, when on opposite sides of the body they severally hold the same relation to the centre. J. Mueller, and other recent physiologists, employ these terms in the same signification as Reid An argument *a priori* has been employed against the doctrine here maintained, on the ground that the congruent points in the opposite *eyes* are not anatomically corresponding points.—H.

OF SEEING.

65

mon course of life, the eyes always follow the attention : or if at any time, in a revery, they are separated from it, we hardly at that time see what is directly before us. Hence we may see the reason why the man we are speaking of thinks that he never before saw an object double. When he looks at any object, he sees it single, and takes no notice of other visible objects at that time, whether they appear single or double. If any of them draws his attention, it draws his eyes at the same time ; and, as soon as the eyes are turned towards it, it appears single. But, in order to see things double—at least, in order to have any reflection or remembrance that he did so—it is necessary that he should look at one object, and at the same time attend to the faint appearance of other objects which are within the field of vision. This is a practice which perhaps he never used, nor attempted ; and therefore he does not recollect that ever he saw an object double. But when he is put upon giving this attention, he immediately sees objects double, in the same manner, and with the very same circumstances, as they who have been accustomed, for the greatest part of their lives, to give this attention.

There are many phænomena of a similar nature, which shew that the mind may not attend to, and thereby, in some sort, not perceive objects that strike the senses. I had occasion to mention several instances of this in the second chapter ; and I have been assured, by persons of the best skill in music, that, in hearing a tune upon the harpsichord, when they give attention to the treble, they do not hear the bass ; and when they attend to the bass, they do not perceive the air of the treble. Some persons are so near-sighted, that, in reading, they hold the book to one eye, while the other is directed to other objects. Such persons acquire the habit of attending, in this case, to the objects of one eye, while they give no attention to those of the other.

6. It is observable, that, in all cases wherein we see an object double, the two appearances have a certain position with regard to one another, and a certain apparent or angular distance. This apparent distance is greater or less in different circumstances; but, in the same circumstances, it is always the same, not only to the same, but to different persons.

Thus, in the experiment above mentioned, if twenty different persons, who see perfectly with both eyes, shall place their finger and the candle at the distances above expressed, and hold their heads upright, looking at the finger, they will see two candles, one on the right, another on the left. That which is seen on the right, is seen by the right eye, and that which is seen on the left, by the left eye : and they will see them at the same

apparent distance from each other. If, again, they look at the candle, they will see two fingers, one on the right, and the other on the left ; and all will see them at the same apparent distance ; the finger towards the left being seen by the right eye, and the other by the left. If the head is laid horizontally to one side, other circumstances remaining the same, one appearance of the object seen double, will be directly above the other. In a word, vary the circumstances as you please, and the appearances are varied to all the spectators in one and the same manner.

7. Having made many experiments in order to ascertain the apparent distance of the two appearances of an object seen double, I have found that in all cases this apparent distance is proportioned to the distance between the point of the *retina*, where the picture is made in one eye, and the point which is situated similarly to that on which the picture is made on the other eye; so that, as the apparent distance of two objects seen with one eye, is proportioned to the arch of the *retina*, which lies between their pictures, in like manner, when an object is seen double with the two eyes, the apparent distance of the two appearances is proportioned to the arch of either *retina*, which lies between the picture in that *retina*, and the point corresponding to that of the picture in the other *retina*.

8. As, in certain circumstances, we invariably see one object appear double, so, in others, we as invariably see two objects unite into one, and, in appearance, lose their duplicity. This is evident in the appearance of the binocular telescope. And the same thing happens when any two similar tubes are applied to the two eyes in a parallel direction ; for, in this case, we see only one tube. And if two shillings are placed at the extremities of the two tubes, one exactly in the axis of one eye, and the other in the axis of the other eye, we shall see but one shilling. If two pieces of coin, or other bodies, of different colour, and of different figure be properly placed in the two axes of the eyes, and at the extremities of the tubes, we shall see both the bodies in one and the same place, each as it were spread over the other, without hiding it ; and the colour will be that which is compounded of the two colours.*

* This last statement is incorrect ; it misrepresents, if it does not reverse, the observation of Du Tour. But, though Reid's assertion be inaccurate, there is great difference (proba ly from the different constitution of their organs) in the phænomeno , as reported by various observers. None, seemingly, (the reverse of what Reid says,) in looking, e. g., with one eye through a blue, and with t e other through a yellow glass, experience a complementary sensation of green. But some see both colours at once ; some only one colour—a colour, however, wh ch corresponds neither to yellow nor to blue, and, at the same time, is not green. In my

9. From these phænomena, and from all the trials I have been able to make, it appears evidently, that, in perfect human eyes, the centres of the two *retinæ* correspond and harmonize wth one another, and that every other point in one *retina* doth correspond and harmonize with the point which is similarly situate in the other; in such manner, that pictures falling on the corresponding points of the two *retinæ*, shew only one object, even when there are really two; and pictures falling upon points of the *retinæ* which do not correspond, shew us two visible appearances, although there be but one object: so that pictures, upon corresponding points of the two *retinæ*, present the same appearance to the mind as if they had both fallen upon the same point of one *retina*; and pictures upon points of the two *retinæ*, which do not correspond, present to the mind the same apparent distance and position of two objects, as if one of those pictures was carried to the point corresponding to it in the other *retina*. This relation and sympathy between corresponding points of the two *retinæ*, I do not advance as an hypothesis, but as a general fact or phænomenon of vision. All the phænomena before mentioned, of single or double vision, lead to it, and are necessary consequences of it. It holds true invariably in all perfect human eyes, as far as I am able to collect from innumerable trials of various kinds made upon my own eyes, and many made by others at my desire. Most of the hypotheses that have been contrived to resolve the phænomena of single and double vision, suppose this general fact, while their authors were not aware of it. Sir Isaac Newton, who was too judicious a philosopher, and too accurate an observer, to have offered even a conjecture which did not tally with the facts that had fallen under his observation, proposes a query with respect to the cause of it—"Optics," Query, 15. The judicious Dr Smith, in his "Optics," Book 1, § 137, hath confirmed the truth of this general phænomenon from his own experience, not only as to the apparent unity of objects whose pictures fall upon the corresponding points of the *retinæ*, but also as to the apparent distance of the two appearances of the same object when seen double. *

This general phænomenon appears, therefore, to be founded upon a very full induction, which is all the evidence we can have for a fact of this nature. Before we make an end of this subject, it will be proper to inquire, First, Whether those animals whose eyes have an adverse position in their heads, and look contrary ways, have such corresponding points in their *retinæ*? Secondly, What is the position of the corresponding points in imperfect human eyes—I mean in those that squint? And, in the last place, Whether this harmony of the corresponding points in the *retinæ*, be natural and original, or the effect of custom? And, if it is original, Whether it can be accounted for by any of the laws of nature already discovered? or whether it is itself to be looked upon as a law of nature, and a part of the human constitution?

Section XIV.

OF THE LAWS OF VISION IN BRUTE ANIMALS.

It is the intention of nature, in giving eyes to animals, that they may perceive the situation of visible objects, or the direction in which they are placed—it is probable, therefore, that, in ordinary cases, every animal, whether it has many eyes or few, whether of one structure or of another, sees objects single, and in their true and proper direction. And, since there is a prodigious variety in the structure, the motions, and the number of eyes in different animals and insects, it is probable that the laws by which vision is regulated, are not the same in all, but various, adapted to the eyes which nature hath given them.

Mankind naturally turn their eyes always the same way, so that the axes of the two eyes meet in one point. They naturally attend to or look at that object only which is placed in the point where the axes meet. And whether the object be more or less distant, the configuration of the eye is adapted to the distance of the object, so as to form a distinct picture of it.

When we use our eyes in this natural way, the two pictures of the object we look at are formed upon the centres of the two *retinæ*; and the two pictures of any contiguous object are formed upon the points of the *retinæ* which are similarly situate with regard to the centres. Therefore, in order to our seeing objects single, and in their proper direction, with two eyes, it is

own eye, I can see either of these phænomena, under certain conditions, at will. Johannes Mueller, Weber, Volkmann, and Heermann, are the most recent observers. I may also notice, that the congruence between the corresponding points (in Reid's sense) of the two retinæ, is admitted for the perception of *figure*, but not for the sensations of *light* and *colour* —H.

* It might be proper here to say something of the strictures of Dr Wells on Reid's doctrine of single vision; but, as the matter is, after all, of no high psychological importance, while the whole theory of the form of the Horopter is, in consequence of Mueller's observations, anew under discussion, I shall

only refer the reader who is curious in such points, to the following recent publications:—J. Mueller, " Zur Vergleichenden Physiologie des Gesichtssinnes," &c., 1826.—Volkmann, " Neue Beytraege zur Physiologie des Gesichtsinnes," 1836.—Heermann, " Ueber die Bildung der Gesichtsvorstellungen," &c., 1835 —H.

sufficient that we be so constituted, that objects whose pictures are formed upon the centres of the two *retinæ*, or upon points similarly situate with regard to these centres, shall be seen in the same visible place. And this is the constitution which nature hath actually given to human eyes.

When we distort our eyes from their parallel direction, which is an unnatural motion, but may be learned by practice ; or when we direct the axes of the two eyes to one point, and at the same time direct our attention to some visible object much nearer or much more distant than that point, which is also unnatural, yet may be learned : in these cases, and in these only, we see one object double, or two objects confounded in one. In these cases, the two pictures of the same object are formed upon points of the *retinæ* which are not similarly situate, and so the object is seen double ; or the two pictures of different objects are formed upon points of the *retinæ* which are similarly situate, and so the two objects are seen confounded in one place.

Thus it appears, that the laws of vision in the human constitution are wisely adapted to the natural use of human eyes, but not to that use of them which is unnatural. We see objects truly when we use our eyes in the natural way ; but have false appearances presented to us when we use them in a way that is unnatural. We may reasonably think that the case is the same with other animals. But is it not unreasonable to think, that those animals which naturally turn one eye towards one object, and another eye towards another object, must thereby have such false appearances presented to them, as we have when we do so against nature ?

Many animals have their eyes by nature placed adverse and immoveable, the axes of the two eyes being always directed to opposite points. Do objects painted on the centres of the two *retinæ* appear to such animals as they do to human eyes, in one and the same visible place ? I think it is highly probable that they do not ; and that they appear, as they really are, in opposite places.

If we judge from analogy in this case, it will lead us to think that there is a certain correspondence between points of the two *retinæ* in such animals, but of a different kind from that which we have found in human eyes. The centre of one *retina* will correspond with the centre of the other, in such manner that the objects whose pictures are formed upon these corresponding points, shall appear not to be in the same place, as in human eyes, but in opposite places. And in the same manner will the superior part of one *retina* corre-

spond with the inferior part of the other, and the anterior part of one with the posterior part of the other.

Some animals, by nature, turn their eyes with equal facility, either the same way or different ways, as we turn our hands and arms. Have such animals corresponding points in their *retinæ*, and points which do not correspond, as the human kind has ? I think it is probable that they have not ; because such a constitution in them could serve no other purpose but to exhibit false appearances.

If we judge from analogy, it will lead us to think, that, as such animals move their eyes in a manner similar to that in which we move our arms, they have an immediate and natural perception of the direction they give to their eyes, as we have of the direction we give to our arms ; and perceive the situation of visible objects by their eyes, in a manner similar to that in which we perceive the situation of tangible objects with our hands.

We cannot teach brute animals to use their eyes in any other way than in that which nature hath taught them ; nor can we teach them to communicate to us the appearances which visible objects make to them, either in ordinary or in extraordinary cases. We have not, therefore, the same means of discovering the laws of vision in them, as in our own kind, but must satisfy ourselves with probable conjectures ; and what we have said upon this subject, is chiefly intended to shew, that animals to which nature hath given eyes differing in their number, in their position, and in their natural motions, may very probably be subjected to different laws of vision, adapted to the peculiarities of their organs of vision.

Section XV.

SQUINTING CONSIDERED HYPOTHETICALLY.

Whether there be corresponding points in the *retinæ* of those who have an involuntary squint ? and, if there are, Whether they be situate in the same manner as in those who have no squint ? are not questions of mere curiosity. They are of real importance to the physician who attempts the cure of a squint, and to the patient who submits to the cure. After so much has been said of the *strabismus*, or squint, both by medical and by optical writers, one might expect to find abundance of facts for determining these questions. Yet, I confess, I have been disappointed in this expectation, after taking some pains both to make observations, and to collect those which have been made by others.

Nor will this appear very strange, if we consider, that to make the observations which are necessary for determining these questions, knowledge of the principles of optics, and of the laws of vision, must concur with opportunities rarely to be met with.

Of those who squint, the far greater part have no distinct vision with one eye.* When this is the case, it is impossible, and indeed of no importance, to determine the situation of the corresponding points. When both eyes are good, they commonly differ so much in their direction, that the same object cannot be seen by both at the same time ; and, in this case, it will be very difficult to determine the situation of the corresponding points; for such persons will probably attend only to the objects of one eye, and the objects of the other will be as little regarded as if they were not seen.

We have before observed, that, when we look at a near object, and attend to it, we do not perceive the double appearances of more distant objects, even when they are in the same direction, and are presented to the eye at the same time. It is probable that a squinting person, when he attends to the objects of one eye, will, in like manner, have his attention totally diverted from the objects of the other ; and that he will perceive them as little as we perceive the double appearances of objects when we use our eyes in the natural way. Such a person, therefore, unless he is so much a philosopher as to have acquired the habit of attending very accurately to the visible appearances of objects, and even of objects which he does not look at, will not be able to give any light to the questions now under consideration.

It is very probable that hares, rabbits, birds, and fishes, whose eyes are fixed in an adverse position, have the natural faculty of attending at the same time to visible objects placed in different, and even in contrary directions ; because, without this faculty, they could not have those advantages from the contrary direction of their eyes, which nature seems to have intended. But it is not probable that those who squint have any such natural faculty ; because we find no such faculty in the rest of the species. We naturally attend to objects placed in the point where the axes of the two eyes meet, and to them only. To give attention to an object in a different direction is unnatural, and not to be learned without pains and practice.

* On this imperfection of vision is rested the theory of Squinting, proposed by Buffon, and now generally adopted. The defective eye is turned aside, because, if it were directed to the object, together with the perfect one, a confused impression would be produced.—H.

A very convincing proof of this may be drawn from a fact now well known to philosophers : when one eye is shut, there is a certain space within the field of vision, where we can see nothing at all—the space which is directly opposed to that part of the bottom of the eye where the optic nerve enters. This defect of sight, in one part of the eye, is common to all human eyes, and hath been so from the beginning of the world ; yet it was never known, until the sagacity of the Abbé Mariotte discovered it in the last century. And now when it is known, it cannot be perceived, but by means of some particular experiments, which require care and attention to make them succeed.

What is the reason that so remarkable a defect of sight, common to all mankind, was so long unknown, and is now perceived with so much difficulty ? It is surely this— That the defect is at some distance from the axis of the eye, and consequently in a part of the field of vision to which we never attend naturally, and to which we cannot attend at all, without the aid of some particular circumstances.

From what we have said, it appears, that, to determine the situation of the corresponding points in the eyes of those who squint, is impossible, if they do not see distinctly with both eyes ; and that it will be very difficult, unless the two eyes differ so little in their direction, that the same object may be seen with both at the same time. Such patients I apprehend are rare ; at least there are very few of them with whom I have had the fortune to meet : and therefore, for the assistance of those who may have happier opportunities, and inclination to make the proper use of them, we shall consider the case of squinting, hypothetically, pointing out the proper articles of inquiry, the observations that are wanted, and the conclusions that may be drawn from them.

1. It ought to be inquired, Whether the squinting person sees equally well with both eyes ? and, if there be a defect in one, the nature and degree of that defect ought to be remarked. The experiments by which this may be done, are so obvious, that I need not mention them. But I would advise the observer to make the proper experiments, and not to rely upon the testimony of the patient ; because I have found many instances, both of persons that squinted, and others who were found, upon trial, to have a great defect in the sight of one eye, although they were never aware of it before. In all the following articles, it is supposed that the patient sees with both eyes so well as to be able to read with either, when the other is covered.

2. It ought to be inquired, Whether, when one eye is covered, the other is turned

directly to the object? This ought to be tried in both eyes successively. By this observation, as a touchstone, we may try the hypothesis concerning squinting, invented by M. de la Hire, and adopted by Boerhaave, and many others of the medical faculty.

The hypothesis is, That, in one eye of a squinting person, the greatest sensibility and the most distinct vision is not, as in other men, in the centre of the *retina*, but upon one side of the centre; and that he turns the axis of this eye aside from the object, in order that the picture of the object may fall upon the most sensible part of the *retina*, and thereby give the most distinct vision. If this is the cause of squinting, the squinting eye will be turned aside from the object, when the other eye is covered, as well as when it is not.

A trial so easy to be made, never was made for more than forty years; but the hypothesis was very generally received— so prone are men to invent hypotheses, and so backward to examine them by facts. At last, Dr Jurin having made the trial, found that persons who squint turn the axis of the squinting eye directly to the object, when the other eye is covered. This fact is confirmed by Dr Porterfield; and I have found it verified in all the instances that have fallen under my observation.

3. It ought to be inquired, Whether the axes of the two eyes follow one another, so as to have always the same inclination, or make the same angle, when the person looks to the right or to the left, upward or downward, or straight forward. By this observation we may judge whether a squint is owing to any defect in the muscles which move the eye, as some have supposed. In the following articles, we suppose that the inclination of the axes of the eyes is found to be always the same.

4. It ought to be inquired, Whether the person that squints sees an object single or double?

If he sees the object double, and if the two appearances have an angular distance, equal to the angle which the axes of his eyes make with each other, it may be concluded that he hath corresponding points in the *retinæ* of his eyes, and that they have the same situation as in those who have no squint. If the two appearances should have an angular distance which is always the same, but manifestly greater or less than the angle contained under the optic axes, this would indicate corresponding points in the *retinæ*, whose situation is not the same as in those who have no squint; but it is difficult to judge accurately of the angle which the optic axes make.

A squint too small to be perceived, may occasion double vision of objects: for, if we speak strictly, every person squints more or less, whose optic axes do not meet exactly in the object which he looks at. Thus, if a man can only bring the axes of his eyes to be parallel, but cannot make them converge in the least, he must have a small squint in looking at near objects, and will see them double, while he sees very distant objects single. Again, if the optic axes always converge, so as to meet eight or ten feet before the face at farthest, such a person will see near objects single; but when he looks at very distant objects, he will squint a little, and see them double.

An instance of this kind is related by Aguilonius in his " Optics," who says, that he had seen a young man to whom near objects appeared single, but distant objects appeared double.

Dr Briggs, in his " Nova Visionis Theoria," having collected from authors several instances of double vision, quotes this from Aguilonius, as the most wonderful and unaccountable of all, insomuch that he suspects some imposition on the part of the young man : but to those who understand the laws by which single and double vision are regulated, it appears to be the natural effect of a very small squint.*

Double vision may always be owing to a small squint, when the two appearances are seen at a small angular distance, although no squint was observed : and I do not remember any instances of double vision recorded by authors, wherein any account is given of the angular distance of the appearances.

In almost all the instances of double vision, there is reason to suspect a squint or distortion of the eyes, from the concomitant circumstances, which we find to be one or other of the following—the approach of death or of a *deliquium*, excessive drinking or other intemperance, violent headache, blistering the head, smoking tobacco, blows or wounds in the head. In all these cases, it is reasonable to suspect a distortion of the eyes, either from spasm, or paralysis in the muscles that move them. But, although it be probable that there is always a squint greater or less where there is double vision, yet it is certain that there is not double vision always where there is a squint. I know no instance of double vision that continued for life, or even for a great number of years. We shall therefore suppose, in the following articles, that the squinting person sees objects single.

5. The next inquiry, then, ought to be, Whether the object is seen with both eyes at the same time, or only with the eye

---

* It is observed by Purkinje and Volkmann, that short-sighted persons, under certain conditions, see distant objects double. Is the case of Aguilonius more than an example of this ? -H

whose axis is directed to it ? It hath been taken for granted, by the writers upon the *strabismus*, before Dr Jurin, that those who squint commonly see objects single with both eyes at the same time ; but I know not one fact advanced by any writer which proves it. Dr Jurin is of a contrary opinion ; and, as it is of consequence, so it is very easy, to determine this point, in particular instances, by this obvious experiment. While the person that squints looks steadily at an object, let the observer carefully remark the direction of both his eyes, and observe their motions ; and let an opaque body be interposed between the object and the two eyes successively. If the patient, notwithstanding this interposition, and without changing the direction of his eyes, continues to see the object all the time, it may be concluded that he saw it with both eyes at once. But, if the interposition of the body between one eye and the object makes it disappear, then we may be certain that it was seen by that eye only. In the two following articles, we shall suppose the first to happen, according to the common hypothesis.

6. Upon this supposition, it ought to be inquired, Whether the patient sees an object double in those circumstances wherein it appears double to them who have no squint ? Let him, for instance, place a candle at the distance of ten feet ; and holding his finger at arm's-length between him and the candle, let him observe, when he looks at the candle, whether he sees his finger with both eyes, and whether he sees it single or double ; and when he looks at his finger, let him observe whether he sees the candle with both eyes, and whether single or double.

By this observation, it may be determined, whether to this patient, the phænomena of double as well as of single vision are the same as to them who have no squint. If they are not the same—if he sees objects single with two eyes, not only in the cases wherein they appear single, but in those also wherein they appear double to other men—the conclusion to be drawn from this supposition is, that his single vision does not arise from corresponding points in the *retinæ* of his eyes ; and that the laws of vision are not the same in him as in the rest of mankind.

7. If, on the other hand, he sees objects double in those cases wherein they appear double to others, the conclusion must be, that he hath corresponding points in the *retinæ* of his eyes, but unnaturally situate. And their situation may be thus determined.

When he looks at an object, having the axis of one eye directed to it, and the axis of the other turned aside from it, let us suppose a right line to pass from the object

through the centre of the diverging eye. We shall, for the sake of perspicuity, call this right line, *the natural axis of the eye ;* and it will make an angle with the real axis, greater or less, according as his squint is greater or less. We shall also call that point of the *retina* in which the natural axis cuts it, *the natural centre of the retina ;* which will be more or less distant from the real centre, according as the squint is greater or less.

Having premised these definitions, it will be evident to those who understand the principles of optics, that in this person the natural centre of one *retina* corresponds with the real centre of the other, in the very same manner as the two real centres correspond in perfect eyes ; and that the points similarly situate with regard to the real centre in one *retina*, and the natural centre in the other, do likewise correspond, in the very same manner as the points similarly situate with regard to the two real centres correspond in perfect eyes.

If it is true, as has been commonly affirmed, that one who squints sees an object with both eyes at the same time, and yet sees it single, the squint will most probably be such as we have described in this article. And we may further conclude, that, if a person affected with such a squint as we have supposed, could be brought to the habit of looking straight, his sight would thereby be greatly hurt : for he would then see everything double which he saw with both eyes at the same time : and objects distant from one another would appear to be confounded together. His eyes are made for squinting, as much as those of other men are made for looking straight ; and his sight would be no less injured by looking straight, than that of another man by squinting. He can never see perfectly when he does not squint, unless the corresponding points of his eyes should by custom change their place ; but how small the probability of this is will appear in the 17th section.

Those of the medical faculty who attempt the cure of a squint, would do well to consider whether it is attended with such symptoms as are above described. If it is, the cure would be worse than the malady : for, every one will readily acknowledge that it is better to put up with the deformity of a squint, than to purchase the cure by the loss of perfect and distinct vision.

8. We shall now return to Dr Jurin's hypothesis, and suppose that our patient, when he saw objects single notwithstanding his squint, was found, upon trial, to have seen them only with one eye.

We would advise such a patient to endeavour, by repeated efforts, to lessen his squint, and to bring the axes of his eyes

nearer to a parallel direction. We have
naturally the power of making small variations in the inclination of the optic axes;
and this power may be greatly increased by
exercise.

In the ordinary and natural use of our
eyes, we can direct their axes to a fixed
star; in this case they must be parallel:
we can direct them also to an object six
inches distant from the eye; and in this
case the axes must make an angle of fifteen or twenty degrees. We see young
people in their frolics learn to squint, making their eyes either converge or diverge,
when they will, to a very considerable degree. Why should it be more difficult for
a squinting person to learn to look straight
when he pleases? If once, by an effort of
his will, he can but lessen his squint, frequent practice will make it easy to lessen
it, and will daily increase his power. So
that, if he begins this practice in youth, and
perseveres in it, he may probably, after
some time, learn to direct both his eyes to
one object.

When he hath acquired this power, it
will be no difficult matter to determine, by
proper observations, whether the centres of
the *retinæ*, and other points similarly situate
with regard to the centres, correspond, as
in other men.

9. Let us now suppose that he finds this
to be the case; and that he sees an object
single with both eyes, when the axes of
both are directed to it. It will then concern
him to acquire the habit of looking straight,
as he hath got the power, because he will
thereby not only remove a deformity, but
improve his sight; and I conceive this habit, like all others, may be got by frequent
exercise. He may practise before a mirror
when alone, and in company he ought to have
those about him who will observe and ad-
monish him when he squints.

10. What is supposed in the 9th article
is not merely imaginary; it is really the
case of some squinting persons, as will
appear in the next section. Therefore, it
ought further to be inquired, How it comes
to pass that such a person sees an object
which he looks at, only with one eye, when
both are open? In order to answer this
question, it may be observed, first, Whether,
when he looks at an object, the diverging
eye is not drawn so close to the nose, that it
can have no distinct images? Or, secondly,
whether the pupil of the diverging eye is not
covered wholly, or in part, by the upper eyelid? Dr Jurin observed instances of these
cases in persons that squinted, and assigns
them as causes of their seeing the object
only with one eye. Thirdly, it may be
observed, whether the diverging eye is not
so directed, that the picture of the object
falls upon that part of the *retina* where the

optic nerve enters, and where there is no
vision? This will probably happen in a
squint wherein the axes of the eyes converge
so as to meet about six inches before the
nose.

11. In the last place, it ought to be
inquired, Whether such a person hath any
distinct vision at all with the diverging
eye, at the time he is looking at an object
with the other?

It may seem very improbable that he
should be able to read with the diverging
eye when the other is covered, and yet, when
both are open, have no distinct vision with
it at all. But this, perhaps, will not appear
so improbable if the following considerations
are duly attended to.

Let us suppose that one who saw perfectly, gets, by a blow on the head, or some
other accident, a permanent and involuntary squint. According to the laws of vision, he will see objects double, and will see
objects distant from one another confounded
together; but, such vision being very disagreeable, as well as inconvenient, he will
do everything in his power to remedy it.
For alleviating such distresses, nature often
teaches men wonderful expedients, which
the sagacity of a philosopher would be unable to discover. Every accidental motion,
every direction or conformation of his eyes,
which lessens the evil, will be agreeable;
it will be repeated until it be learned to
perfection, and become habitual, even without thought or design. Now, in this case,
what disturbs the sight of one eye is the
sight of the other; and all the disagreeable
appearances in vision would cease if the
light of one eye was extinct. The sight of
one eye will become more distinct and
more agreeable, in the same proportion as
that of the other becomes faint and indistinct. It may, therefore, be expected,
that every habit will, by degrees, be acquired which tends to destroy distinct vision in one eye while it is preserved in the
other. These habits will be greatly facili-
tated if one eye was at first better than the
other; for, in that case, the best eye will
always be directed to the object which he
intends to look at, and every habit will be
acquired which tends to hinder his seeing
it at all, or seeing it distinctly by the other
at the same time.

I shall mention one or two habits that
may probably be acquired in such a case;
perhaps there are others which we cannot
so easily conjecture. First, By a small increase or diminution of his squint, he may
bring it to correspond with one or other of
the cases mentioned in the last article.
Secondly, The diverging eye may be brought
to such a conformation as to be extremely
short-sighted, and consequently to have no
distinct vision of objects at a distance. I

knew this to be the case of one person that squinted; but cannot say whether the short-sightedness of the diverging eye was original, or acquired by habit.

We see, therefore, that one who squints, and originally saw objects double by reason of that squint, may acquire such habits that, when he looks at an object, he shall see it only with one eye; nay, he may acquire such habits that, when he looks at an object with his best eye, he shall have no distinct vision with the other at all. Whether this is really the case—being unable to determine in the instances that have fallen under my observation—I shall leave to future inquiry.

I have endeavoured, in the foregoing articles, to delineate such a process as is proper in observing the phænomena of squinting. I know well by experience, that this process appears more easy in theory, than it will be found to be in practice; and that, in order to carry it on with success, some qualifications of mind are necessary in the patient, which are not always to be met with. But, if those who have proper opportunities and inclination to observe such phænomena, attend duly to this process, they may be able to furnish facts less vague and uninstructive than those we meet with, even in authors of reputation. By such facts, vain theories may be exploded, and our knowledge of the laws of nature, which regard the noblest of our senses, enlarged.

Section XVI.

FACTS RELATING TO SQUINTING.

Having considered the phænomena of squinting, hypothetically, and their connection with corresponding points in the retinæ. I shall now mention the facts I have had occasion to observe myself, or have met with in authors, that can give any light to this subject.

Having examined above twenty persons that squinted, I found in all of them a defect in the sight of one eye. Four only had so much of distinct vision in the weak eye, as to be able to read with it, when the other was covered. The rest saw nothing at all distinctly with one eye.

Dr Porterfield says, that this is generally the case of people that squint: and I suspect it is so more generally than is commonly imagined. Dr Jurin, in a very judicious dissertation upon squinting, printed in Dr Smith's "Optics," observes, that those who squint, and see with both eyes, never see the same object with both at the same time; that, when one eye is directed straight forward to an object the other is drawn so close to the nose that the object cannot at all be seen by it, the images being too oblique and too indistinct to affect the eye. In some squinting persons, he observed the diverging eye drawn under the upper eyelid, while the other was directed to the object. From these observations, he concludes that "the eye is thus distorted, not for the sake of seeing better with it, but rather to avoid seeing at all with it as much as possible." From all the observations he had made, he was satisfied that there is nothing peculiar in the structure of a squinting eye; that the fault is only in its wrong direction; and that this wrong direction is got by habit. Therefore, he proposes that method of cure which we have described in the eighth and ninth articles of the last section. He tells us, that he had attempted a cure, after this method, upon a young gentleman, with promising hopes of success; but was interrupted by his falling ill of the small-pox, of which he died.

It were to be wished that Dr Jurin had acquainted us whether he ever brought the young man to direct the axes of both eyes to the same object, and whether, in that case, he saw the object single, and saw it with both eyes; and that he had likewise acquainted us, whether he saw objects double when his squint was diminished. But as to these facts he is silent.

I wished long for an opportunity of trying Dr Jurin's method of curing a squint, without finding one; having always, upon examination, discovered so great a defect in the sight of one eye of the patient as discouraged the attempt.

But I have lately found three young gentlemen, with whom I am hopeful this method may have success, if they have patience and perseverance in using it. Two of them are brothers, and, before I had access to examine them, had been practising this method by the direction of their tutor, with such success that the elder looks straight when he is upon his guard: the younger can direct both his eyes to one object; but they soon return to their usual squint.

A third young gentleman, who had never heard of this method before, by a few days practice, was able to direct both his eyes to one object, but could not keep them long in that direction. All the three agree in this, that, when both eyes are directed to one object, they see it and the adjacent objects single; but, when they squint, they see objects sometimes single and sometimes double. I observed of all the three, that when they squinted most—that is, in the way they had been accustomed to—the axes of their eyes converged so as to meet five or six inches before the nose. It is probable that, in this case, the picture of the object in the diverging eye, must fall upon that part of the *retina* where the optic nerve enters; and, therefore, the object could not be seen by that eye.

All the three have some defect in the sight of one eye, which none of them knew until I put them upon making trials; and when they squint, the best eye is always directed to the object, and the weak eye is that which diverges from it. But when the best eye is covered, the weak eye is turned directly to the object. Whether this defect of sight in one eye, be the effect of its having been long disused, as it must have been when they squinted; or whether some original defect in one eye might be the occasion of their squinting, time may discover. The two brothers have found the sight of the weak eye improved by using to read with it while the other is covered. The elder can read an ordinary print with the weak eye; the other, as well as the third gentleman, can only read a large print with the weak eye. I have met with one other person only who squinted, and yet could read a large print with the weak eye. He is a young man, whose eyes are both tender and weak-sighted, but the left much weaker than the right. When he looks at any object, he always directs the right eye to it, and then the left is turned towards the nose so much that it is impossible for him to see the same object with both eyes at the same time. When the right eye is covered, he turns the left directly to the object; but he sees it indistinctly, and as if it had a mist about it.

I made several experiments, some of them in the company and with the assistance of an ingenious physician, in order to discover whether objects that were in the axes of the two eyes, were seen in one place confounded together, as in those who have no involuntary squint. The object placed in the axis of the weak eye was a lighted candle, at the distance of eight or ten feet. Before the other eye was placed a printed book, at such a distance as that he could read upon it. He said, that while he read upon the book, he saw the candle but very faintly. And from what we could learn, these two objects did not appear in one place, but had all that angular distance in appearance which they had in reality.[*]

If this was really the case, the conclusion to be drawn from it is, that the corresponding points in his eyes are not situate in the same manner as in other men; and that, if he could be brought to direct both eyes to one object, he would see it double. But, considering that the young man had never been accustomed to observations of this

kind, and that the sight of one eye was so imperfect, I do not pretend to draw this conclusion with certainty from this single instance.

All that can be inferred from these facts is, that, of four persons who squint, three appear to have nothing preternatural in the structure of their eyes. The centres of their *retinæ*, and the points similarly situate with regard to the centres, do certainly correspond in the same manner as in other men— so that, if they can be brought to the habit of directing their eyes right to an object, they will not only remove a deformity, but improve their sight. With regard to the fourth, the case is dubious, with some probability of a deviation from the usual course of nature in the situation of the corresponding points of his eyes.

Section XVII.

OF THE EFFECT OF CUSTOM IN SEEING OBJECTS SINGLE.

It appears from the phænomena of single and double vision, recited in § 13, that our seeing an object single with two eyes, depends upon these two things:—First, Upon that mutual correspondence of certain points of the *retina* which we have often described; Secondly, Upon the two eyes being directed to the object so accurately that the two images of it fall upon corresponding points. These two things must concur in order to our seeing an object single with two eyes; and, as far as they depend upon custom, so far only can single vision depend upon custom

With regard to the second—that is, the accurate direction of both eyes to the object—I think it must be acknowledged that this is only learned by custom. Nature hath wisely ordained the eyes to move in such manner that their axes shall always be nearly parallel; but hath left it in our power to vary their inclination a little, according to the distance of the object we look at. Without this power, objects would appear single at one particular distance only; and, at distances much less or much greater, would always appear double. The wisdom of nature is conspicuous in giving us this power, and no less conspicuous in making the extent of it exactly adequate to the end.

The parallelism of the eyes, in general, is therefore the work of nature; but that precise and accurate direction, which must be varied according to the distance of the object, is the effect of custom. The power which nature hath left us of varying the inclination of the optic axes a little, is turned into a habit of giving them always

---

[*] See Wells—("Two Essays," &c., p. 26.)—H.

that inclination which is adapted to the distance of the object.

But it may be asked, What gives rise to this habit ? The only answer that can be given to this question is, that it is found necessary to perfect and distinct vision. A man who hath lost the sight of one eye, very often loses the habit of directing it exactly to the object he looks at, because that habit is no longer of use to him. And if he should recover the sight of his eye, he would recover this habit, by finding it useful. No part of the human constitution is more admirable than that whereby we acquire habits which are found useful, without any design or intention. Children must see imperfectly at first ; but, by using their eyes, they learn to use them in the best manner, and acquire, without intending it, the habits necessary for that purpose. Every man becomes most expert in that kind of vision which is most useful to him in his particular profession and manner of life. A miniature painter, or an engraver, sees very near objects better than a sailor ; but the sailor sees very distant objects much better than they. A person that is short-sighted, in looking at distant objects, gets the habit of contracting the aperture of his eyes, by almost closing his eyelids. Why ? For no other reason, but because this makes him see the object more distinct. In like manner, the reason why every man acquires the habit of directing both eyes accurately to the object, must be, because thereby he sees it more perfectly and distinctly.

It remains to be considered, whether that correspondence between certain points of the *retinæ*, which is likewise necessary to single vision, be the effect of custom, or an original property of human eyes.

A strong argument for its being an original property, may be drawn from the habit, just now mentioned, of directing the eyes accurately to an object. This habit is got by our finding it necessary to perfect and distinct vision. But why is it necessary ? For no other reason but this, because thereby the two images of the object falling upon corresponding points, the eyes assist each other in vision, and the object is seen better by both together, than it could be by one ; but when the eyes are not accurately directed, the two images of an object fall upon points that do not correspond, whereby the sight of one eye disturbs the sight of the other, and the object is seen more indistinctly with both eyes than it would be with one. Whence it is reasonable to conclude, that this correspondence of certain points of the *retinæ*, is prior to the habits we acquire in vision, and consequently is natural and original. We have all acquired the habit of directing our eyes

always in a particular manner, which causes single vision. Now, if nature hath ordained that we should have single vision only, when our eyes are thus directed, there is an obvious reason why all mankind should agree in the habit of directing them in this manner. But, if single vision is the effect of custom, any other habit of directing the eyes would have answered the purpose ; and no account can be given why this particular habit should be so universal ; and it must appear very strange, that no one instance hath been found of a person who had acquired the habit of seeing objects single with both eyes, while they were directed in any other manner.*

The judicious Dr Smith, in his excellent system of optics, maintains the contrary opinion, and offers some reasonings and facts in proof of it. He agrees with Bishop Berkeley† in attributing it entirely to custom, that we see objects single with two eyes, as well as that we see objects erect by inverted images. Having considered Bishop Berkeley's reasonings in the 11th section, we shall now beg leave to make some remarks on what Dr Smith hath said upon this subject, with the respect due to an author to whom the world owes, not only many valuable discoveries of his own, but those of the brightest mathematical genius of this age, which, with great labour, he generously redeemed from oblivion.

He observes, that the question, Why we see objects single with two eyes ? is of the same sort with this, Why we hear sounds single with two ears ?—and that the same answer must serve both. The inference intended to be drawn from this observation is, that, as the second of these phænomena is the effect of custom, so likewise is the first.

Now, I humbly conceive that the questions are not so much of the same sort, that the same answer must serve for both ; and, moreover, that our hearing single with two ears, is not the effect of custom.

---

* This objection did not escape Dr Smith himself ; but it id seems to have overlooked his answer. " When we view," he says, " an object steadily, we have acquired a habit of directing the optic axes to the point in view ; because its pictures, falling upon the middle points of the retinas, are then distincer than if they fell upon any other places ; and, since the pictures of the whole object are equal to one another, and are both inverted with respect to the optic axes, it follows that the pictures of any collateral point are painted upon corresponding points of the retinas."

This answer is rendered more plausible from the subsequent anatomical discovery of Soemmering He found that, in that part of the retina which lies at the axis of the eye, there is, in man, and in other animals of acute vision, an opening, real or apparent, (*foramen centrale*,) the dimensions of which are such that the images of distincter vision would seem to be enclosed within it.—H.

† This is an inadvertency. Berkeley hazards no such opinion in any of his works.—H.

Two or more visible objects, although perfectly similar, and seen at the very same time, may be distinguished by their visible places; but two sounds perfectly similar, and heard at the same time, cannot be distinguished; for, from the nature of sound, the sensations they occasion must coalesce into one, and lose all distinction. If, therefore, it is asked, Why we hear sounds single with two ears? I answer, Not from custom; but because two sounds which are perfectly like and synchronous, have nothing by which they can be distinguished. But will this answer fit the other question? I think not.

The object makes an appearance to each eye, as the sound makes an impression upon each ear: so far the two senses agree. But the visible appearances may be distinguished by place, when perfectly like in other respects; the sounds cannot be thus distinguished: and herein the two senses differ. Indeed, if the two appearances have the same visible place, they are, in that case, as incapable of distinction as the sounds were, and we see the object single. But when they have not the same visible place, they are perfectly distinguishable, and we see the object double. We see the object single only, when the eyes are directed in one particular manner; while there are many other ways of directing them within the sphere of our power, by which we see the object double.

Dr Smith justly attributes to custom that well-known fallacy in feeling, whereby a button pressed with two opposite sides of two contiguous fingers laid across, is felt double. I agree with him, that the cause of this appearance is, that those opposite sides of the fingers have never been used to feel the same object, but two different objects, at the same time. And I beg leave to add, that, as custom produces this phœnomenon, so a contrary custom destroys it; for, if a man frequently accustoms himself to feel the button with his fingers across, it will at last be felt single; as I have found by experience.

It may be taken for a general rule, that things which are produced by custom, may be undone or changed by disuse, or by a contrary custom. On the other hand, it is a strong argument, that an effect is not owing to custom, but to the constitution of nature, when a contrary custom, long continued, is found neither to change nor weaken it. I take this to be the best rule by which we can determine the question presently* under consideration. I shall, therefore, mention two facts brought by Dr Smith, to prove that the corresponding points of the *retinæ* have been changed by

custom; and then I shall mention some facts tending to prove, that there are corresponding points of the *retinæ* of the eyes originally, and that custom produces no change in them.

"One fact is related upon the authority of Martin Folkes, Esq., who was informed by Dr Hepburn of Lynn, that the Rev. Mr Foster of Clinchwharton, in that neighbourhood, having been blind for some years of a *gutta serena*, was restored to sight by salivation; and that, upon his first beginning to see, all objects appeared to him double; but afterwards, the two appearances approaching by degrees, he came at last to see single, and as distinctly as he did before he was blind."

Upon this case, I observe, First, That it does not prove any change of the corresponding points of the eyes, unless we suppose, what is not affirmed, that Mr Foster directed his eyes to the object at first, when he saw double, with the same accuracy, and in the same manner, that he did afterwards, when he saw single. Secondly, If we should suppose this, no account can be given, why at first the two appearances should be seen at one certain angular distance rather than another; or why this angular distance should gradually decrease, until at last the appearances coincided. How could this effect be produced by custom? But, Thirdly, Every circumstance of this case may be accounted for on the supposition that Mr Foster had corresponding points in the *retinæ* of his eyes from the time he began to see, and that custom made no change with regard to them. We need only further suppose, what is common in such cases, that, by some years' blindness, he had lost the habit of directing his eyes accurately to an object, and that he gradually recovered this habit when he came to see.

The second fact mentioned by Dr Smith, is taken from Mr Cheselden's "Anatomy," and is this:—"A gentleman who, from a blow on the head, had one eye distorted, found every object appear double; but, by degrees, the most familiar ones became single; and, in time, all objects became so, without any amendment of the distortion."

I observe here, that it is not said that the two appearances gradually approached, and at last united, without any amendment of the distortion. This would indeed have been a decisive proof of a change in the corresponding points of the *retinæ*, and yet of such a change as could not be accounted for from custom. But this is not said; and, if it had been observed, a circumstance so remarkable would have been mentioned by Mr Cheselden, as it was in the other case by Dr Hepburn. We may, therefore, take it for granted, that one of the appearances vanished by degrees, without approaching to

* See note * at p. 96, x.—H.

the other. And this I conceive might happen several ways. First, The sight of the distorted eye might gradually decay by the hurt ; so the appearances presented by that eye would gradually vanish. Secondly, A small and unperceived change in the manner of directing the eyes, might occasion his not seeing the object with the distorted eye, as appears from § 15, Art. 10. Thirdly, By acquiring the habit of directing one and the same eye always to the object, the faint and oblique appearance presented by the other eye, might be so little attended to when it became familiar, as not to be perceived. One of these causes, or more of them concurring, might produce the effect mentioned, without any change of the corresponding points of the eyes.

For these reasons, the facts mentioned by Dr Smith, although curious, seem not to be decisive.

The following facts ought to be put in the opposite scale. First, in the famous case of the young gentleman couched by Mr Cheselden, after having had cataracts on both eyes until he was [above] thirteen years of age, it appears that he saw objects single from the time he began to see with both eyes. Mr Cheselden's words are, "And now, being lately couched of his other eye, he says, that objects, at first, appeared large to this eye, but not so large as they did at first to the other ; and, looking upon the same object with both eyes, he thought it looked about twice as large as with the first couched eye only, but not double, that we can anywise discover."

Secondly, The three young gentlemen mentioned in the last section, who had squinted, as far as I know, from infancy, as soon as they learned to direct both eyes to an object, saw it single. In these four cases, it appears evident that the centres of the *retinæ* corresponded originally, and before custom could produce any such effect ; for Mr Cheselden's young gentleman had never been accustomed to see at all before he was couched ; and the other three had never been accustomed to direct the axes of both eyes to the object.

Thirdly, from the facts recited in § 13, it appears, that, from the time we are capable of observing the phænomena of single and double vision, custom makes no change in them.

I have amused myself with such observations for more than thirty years ; and in every case wherein I saw the object double at first, I see it so to this day, notwithstanding the constant experience of its being single. In other cases, where I know there are two objects, there appears only one, after thousands of experiments.

Let a man look at a familiar object through a polyhedron, or multiplying-glass,

every hour of his life, the number of visible appearances will be the same at last as at first ; nor does any number of experiments, or length of time, make the least change.

Effects produced by habit, must vary according as the acts by which the habit is acquired are more or less frequent ; but the phænomena of single and double vision are so invariable and uniform in all men, are so exactly regulated by mathematical rules, that I think we have good reason to conclude that they are not the effect of custom, but of fixed and immutable laws of nature.

Section XVIII.

OF DR PORTERFIELD'S ACCOUNT OF SINGLE AND DOUBLE VISION.

Bishop Berkeley and Dr Smith seem to attribute too much to custom in vision, Dr Porterfield too little.

This ingenious writer thinks, that, by an original law of our nature, antecedent to custom and experience, we perceive visible objects in their true place, not only as to their direction, but likewise as to their distance from the eye ; and, therefore, he accounts for our seeing objects single, with two eyes, in this manner. Having the faculty of perceiving the object with each eye in its true place, we must perceive it with both eyes in the same place ; and, consequently, must perceive it single.

He is aware that this principle, although it accounts for our seeing objects single with two eyes, yet does not at all account for our seeing objects double ; and, whereas other writers on this subject take it to be a sufficient cause for double vision that we have two eyes, and only find it difficult to assign a cause for single vision, on the contrary, Dr Porterfield's principle throws all the difficulty on the other side.

Therefore, in order to account for the phænomena of double vision, he advances another principle, without signifying whether he conceives it to be an original law of our nature, or the effect of custom. It is, That our natural perception of the distance of objects from the eye, is not extended to all the objects that fall within the field of vision, but limited to that which we directly look at ; and that the circumjacent objects, whatever be their real distance, are seen at the same distance with the object we look at ; as if they were all in the surface of a sphere, whereof the eye is the centre.

Thus, single vision is accounted for by our seeing the true distance of an object which we look at ; and double vision, by a false appearance of distance in objects which we do not directly look at.

We agree with this earned and ingenious author, that it is by a natural and original principle that we see visible objects in a certain direction from the eye, and honour him as the author of this discovery :* but we cannot assent to either of those principles by which he explains single and double vision – for the following reasons :—

1. Our having a natural and original perception of the distance of objects from the eye, appears contrary to a well-attested fact : for the young gentleman couched by Mr Cheselden imagined, at first, that whatever he saw touched his eye, as what he felt touched his hand.†

2. The perception we have of the distance of objects from the eye, whether it be from nature or custom, is not so accurate and determinate as is necessary to produce single vision. A mistake of the twentieth or thirtieth part of the distance of a small object, such as a pin, ought, according to Dr Porterfield's hypothesis, to make it appear double. Very few can judge of the distance of a visible object with such accuracy. Yet we never find double vision produced by mistaking the distance of the object. There are many cases in vision, even with the naked eye, wherein we mistake the distance of an object by one half or more : why do we see such objects single ? When I move my spectacles from my eyes toward a small object, two or three feet distant, the object seems to approach, so as to be seen at last at about half its real distance ; but it is seen single at that apparent distance,

as well as when we see it with the naked eye at its real distance. And when we look at an object with a binocular telescope, properly fitted to the eyes, we see it single, while it appears fifteen or twenty times nearer than it is. There are then few cases wherein the distance of an object from the eye is seen so accurately as is necessary for single vision, upon this hypothesis : this seems to be a conclusive argument against the account given of single vision. We find, likewise, that false judgments or fallacious appearances of the distance of an object, do not produce double vision : this seems to be a conclusive argument against the account given of double vision.

3. The perception we have of the linear distance of objects seems to be wholly the effect of experience. This, I think, hath been proved by Bishop Berkeley and by Dr Smith ; and when we come to point out the means of judging of distance by sight, it will appear that they are all furnished by experience.

4. Supposing that, by a law of our nature, the distance of objects from the eye were perceived most accurately, as well as their direction, it will not follow that we must see the object single. Let us consider what means such a law of nature would furnish for resolving the question, Whether the objects of the two eyes are in one and the same place, and consequently are not two, but one ?

Suppose, then, two right lines, one drawn from the centre of one eye to its object, the other drawn, in like manner, from the centre of the other eye to its object. This law of nature gives us the direction or position of each of these right lines, and the length of each ; and this is all that it gives. These are geometrical *data*, and we may learn from geometry what is determined by their means. Is it, then, determined by these *data*, Whether the two right lines terminate in one and the same point, or not ? No, truly. In order to determine this, we must have three other *data*. We must know whether the two right lines are in one plane ; we must know what angle they make ; and we must know the distance between the centres of the eyes. And when these things are known, we must apply the rules of trigonometry, before we can resolve the question, Whether the objects of the two eyes are in one and the same place ; and, consequently, whether they are two or one ?

5. That false appearance of distance into which double vision is resolved, cannot be the effect of custom, for constant experience contradicts it. Neither hath it the features of a law of nature, because it does not answer any good purpose, nor, indeed, any purpose at all, but to deceive us. But why should we seek for arguments, in a question

---

* To this honour Porterfie'd has no title. The law of *the line of visible airection*, was a common theory long before the publication of his writings ; for it was maintained by Kepler, Gassendi, Scheiner, Rohault, Regis, Du Hamel, Mariotte, De Chales, Musschenbroek, Molyneux, &c. &c., and *many* of these maintained that this law was an *original principle or institution of our nature*.—H

† We must be careful not, like Reid and philosophers in general, to confound the perceptions of mere *externality* or *outness*, and the knowledge we have of *distance*, through the eye. The former may be, and probably is, natural ; while the latter, in a great but unappretiable measure, is acquired. In the case of Cheselden—that in which the blindness previous to the recovery of sight was most perfect, and therefore, the most instructive upon record—the patient, though he had little or no perception of distance, *i. e* of the *degree of externality*, had still a perception of that externality absolutely. The object, he said, seemed to "touch his eyes, as what he felt did his skin ;" but they did not appear to him as if in his eyes, far less as a mere affection of the organ. This, however, is erroneously assumed by Mr Fearn. This natural perception of Outness, which is the foundation of our acquired knowledge of distance, seems given us in the natural perception we have of the direction of the rays of light.

In like manner, we must not confound, as is commonly done, the fact of the eye affording us a perception of *extension* and *plain figure*, or outline, in the perception of colours, and the fact of its being the vehicle of intimations in regard to the comparative magnitude and cubical forms of the objects from which these rays proceed. The one is a knowledge by sense—natural, immediate, and infallible ; the other like that of distance, is, by inference, acquired, mediate, and at best always insecure.—H.

concerning what appears to us, or does not appear? The question is, At what distance do the objects now in my eye appear? Do they all appear at one distance, as if placed in the concave surface of a sphere, the eye being in the centre? Every man, surely, may know this with certainty; and, if he will but give attention to the testimony of his eyes, needs not ask a philosopher how visible objects appear to him. Now, it is very true, that, if I look up to a star in the heavens, the other stars that appear at the same time, do appear in this manner: yet this phænomenon does not favour Dr Porterfield's hypothesis; for the stars and heavenly bodies do not appear at their true distances when we look directly to them, any more than when they are seen obliquely: and if this phænomenon be an argument for Dr Porterfield's second principle, it must destroy the first.

The true cause of this phænomenon will be given afterwards; therefore, setting it aside for the present, let us put another case. I sit in my room, and direct my eyes to the door, which appears to be about sixteen feet distant: at the same time, I see many other objects faintly and obliquely—the floor, floor-cloth, the table which I write upon, papers, standish, candle, &c. Now, do all these objects appear at the same distance of sixteen feet? Upon the closest attention, I find they do not.

Section XIX.

OF DR BRIGGS'S THEORY, AND SIR ISAAC NEWTON'S CONJECTURE ON THIS SUBJECT.

I am afraid the reader, as well as the writer, is already tired of the subject of single and double vision. The multitude of theories advanced by authors of great name, and the multitude of facts, observed without sufficient skill in optics, or related without attention to the most material and decisive circumstances, have equally contributed to perplex it.

In order to bring it to some issue, I have, in the 13th section, given a more full and regular deduction than had been given heretofore, of the phænomena of single and double vision, in those whose sight is perfect; and have traced them up to one general principle, which appears to be a law of vision in human eyes that are perfect and in their natural state.

In the 14th section, I have made it appear, that this law of vision, although excellently adapted to the fabric of human eyes, cannot answer the purposes of vision in some other animals; and therefore, very

probably, is not common to all animals. The purpose of the 15th and 16th sections is, to inquire, Whether there be any deviation from this law of vision in those who squint?—a question which is of real importance in the medical art, as well as in the philosophy of vision; but which, after all that hath been observed and written on the subject, seems not to be ripe for a determination, for want of proper observations. Those who have had skill to make proper observations, have wanted opportunities; and those who have had opportunities, have wanted skill or attention. I have therefore thought it worth while to give a distinct account of the observations necessary for the determination of this question, and what conclusions may be drawn from the facts observed. I have likewise collected, and set in one view, the most conclusive facts that have occurred in authors, or have fallen under my own observation.

It must be confessed that these facts, when applied to the question in hand, make a very poor figure; and the gentlemen of the medical faculty are called upon, for the honour of their profession, and for the benefit of mankind, to add to them.

All the medical, and all the optical writers upon the *strabismus* that I have met with, except Dr Jurin, either affirm, or take it for granted, that squinting persons see the object with both eyes, and yet see it single. Dr Jurin affirms that squinting persons never see the object with both eyes; and that, if they did, they would see it double. If the common opinion be true, the cure of a squint would be as pernicious to the sight of the patient, as the causing of a permanent squint would be to one who naturally had no squint; and, therefore, no physician ought to attempt such a cure, no patient ought to submit to it. But, if Dr Jurin's opinion be true, most young people that squint may cure themselves, by taking some pains; and may not only remove the deformity, but, at the same time, improve their sight. If the common opinion be true, the centres, and other points of the two *retinæ*, in squinting persons, do not correspond, as in other men, and Nature, in them, deviates from her common rule. But, if Dr Jurin's opinion be true, there is reason to think that the same general law of vision which we have found in perfect human eyes, extends also to those which squint.

It is impossible to determine, by reasoning, which of these opinions is true; or whether one may not be found true in some patients, and the other in others. Here, experience and observation are our only guides; and a deduction of instances is the only rational argument. It might, therefore, have been expected, that the patrons of the contrary opinions should have given instances in support of them that are clear and indisputable ; but I have not found one such instance on either side of the question, in all the authors I have met with. I have given three instances from my own observation, in confirmation of Dr Jurin's opinion, which admit of no doubt ; and one which leans rather to the other opinion, but is dubious. And here I must leave the matter to further observation.

In the 17th section, I have endeavoured to shew that the correspondence and [or] sympathy of certain points of the two *retinæ*, into which we have resolved all the phænomena of single and double vision, is not, as Dr Smith conceived, the effect of custom, nor can [it] be changed by custom, but is a natural and original property of human eyes ; and, in the last section, that it is not owing to an original and natural perception of the true distance of objects from the eye, as Dr Porterfield imagined. After this recapitulation, which is intended to relieve the attention of the reader, shall we enter into more theories upon this subject ?

That of Dr Briggs—first published in English, in the "Philosophical Transactions," afterwards in Latin, under the title of "Nova Visionis Theoria," with a prefatory epistle of Sir Isaac Newton to the author—amounts to this, That the fibres of the optic nerves, passing from corresponding points of the *retinæ* to the *thalami nervorum opticorum*, having the same length, the same tension, and a similar situation, will have the same tone ; and, therefore, their vibrations, excited by the impression of the rays of light, will be like unisons in music, and will present one and the same image to the mind: but the fibres passing from parts of the *r tinæ* which do not correspond, having different tensions and tones, will have discordant vibrations ; and, therefore, present different images to the mind.

I shall not enter upon a particular examination of this theory. It is enough to observe, in general, that it is a system of conjectures concerning things of which we are entirely ignorant ; and that all such theories in philosophy deserve rather to be laughed at, than to be seriously refuted.

From the first dawn of philosophy to this day, it hath been believed that the optic nerves are intended to carry the images of visible objects from the bottom of the eye to the mind ; and that the nerves belonging to the organs of the other senses have a like office.* But how do we know this ? We conjecture it ; and, taking this conjecture for a truth, we consider how the nerves may best answer this purpose. The system of the nerves, for many ages, was taken to be a

hydraulic engine, consisting of a bundle of pipes, which carried to and fro a liquor calle l *animal spirits*. About the time of Dr Briggs, it was thought rather to be a stringed instrument, composed of vibrating chords, each of which had its proper tension and tone. But some, with as great probability, conceived it to be a wind instrument, which played its part by the vibrations of an elastic æther in the nervous fibrils.

These, I think, are all the engines into which the nervous system hath been moulded by philosophers, for conveying the images of sensible things from the organ to the *sensorium*. And, for all that we know of the matter, every man may freely choose which he thinks fittest for the purpose ; for, from fact and experiment, no one of them can claim preference to another. Indeed, they all seem so unhandy engines for carrying images, that a man would be tempted to invent a new one.

Since, therefore, a blind man may guess as well in the dark as one that sees, I beg leave to offer another conjecture touching the nervous system, which, I hope, will answer the purpose as well as those we have mentioned, and which recommends itself by its simplicity. Why may not the optic nerves, for instance, be made up of empty tubes, opening their mouths wide enough to receive the rays of light which form the image upon the *retinæ*, and gently conveying them safe, and in their proper order, to the very seat of the soul, until they flash in her face? It is easy for an ingenious philosopher to fit the caliber of these empty tubes to the diameter of the particles of light, so as they shall receive no grosser kind of matter ; and, if these rays should be in danger of mistaking their way, an expedient may also be found to prevent this ; for it requires no more than to bestow upon the tubes of the nervous system a peristaltic motion, like that of the alimentary tube.

It is a peculiar advantage of this hypothesis, that, although all philosophers believe that the species or images of things are conveyed by the nerves to the soul, yet none of their hypotheses shew how this may be done. For how can the images of sound, taste, smell, colour, figure, and all sensible qualities, be made out of the vibrations of musical chords, or the undulations of animal spirits, or of æther ? We ought not to suppose means inadequate to the end. / Is it not as philosophical, and more intelligible, to conceive, that, as the stomach receives its food, so the soul receives her images by a kind of nervous deglutition ? I might ad t, that we need only continue this peristaltic motion of the nervous tubes from the *sensorium* to the extremities of the nerves that serve the muscles, in order to account for muscular motion.

---

* This statement is far too unqualified.—H.

Thus Nature will be consonant to herself; and, as sensation will be the conveyance of the ideal aliment to the mind, so muscular motion will be the expulsion of the recrementitious part of it. For who can deny, that the images of things conveyed by sensation, may, after due concoction, become fit to be thrown off by muscular motion? I only give hints of these things to the ingenious, hoping that in time this hypothesis may be wrought up into a system as truly philosophical as that of animal spirits, or the vibration of nervous fibres.

To be serious: In the operations of nature, I hold the theories of a philosopher, which are unsupported by fact, in the same estimation with the dreams of a man asleep, or the ravings of a madman. We laugh at the Indian philosopher, who, to account for the support of the earth, contrived the hypothesis of a huge elephant, and, to support the elephant, a huge tortoise. If we will candidly confess the truth, we know as little of the operation of the nerves, as he did of the manner in which the earth is supported; and our hypotheses about animal spirits, or about the tension and vibrations of the nerves, are as like to be true, as his about the support of the earth. His elephant was a hypothesis, and our hypotheses are elephants. Every theory in philosophy, which is built on pure conjecture, is an elephant; and every theory that is supported partly by fact, and partly by conjecture, is like Nebuchadnezzar's image, whose feet were partly of iron and partly of clay.

The great Newton first gave an example to philosophers, which always ought to be, but rarely hath been followed, by distinguishing his conjectures from his conclusions, and putting the former by themselves, in the modest form of queries. This is fair and legal; but all other philosophical traffic in conjecture ought to be held contraband and illicit. Indeed, his conjectures have commonly more foundation in fact, and more verisimilitude, than the dogmatical theories of most other philosophers; and, therefore, we ought not to omit that which he hath offered concerning the cause of our seeing objects single with two eyes, in the 15th query annexed to his "Optics."

"Are not the species of objects seen with both eyes, united where the optic nerves meet before they come into the brain, the fibres on the right side of both nerves uniting there, and after union going thence into the brain in the nerve which is on the right side of the head, and the fibres on the left side of both nerves uniting in the same place, and after union going into the brain in the nerve which is on the left side of the head, and these two nerves meeting in the brain in such a manner that their fibres make but one entire species or picture, half of which on the right side of the *sensorium* comes from the right side of both eyes through the right side of both optic nerves, to the place where the nerves meet, and from thence on the right side of the head into the brain, and the other half on the left side of the *sensorium* comes, in like manner, from the left side of both eyes? For the optic nerves of such animals as look the same way with both eyes (as men, dogs, sheep, oxen, &c.) meet before they come into the brain; but the optic nerves of such animals as do not look the same way with both eyes (as of fishes, and of the chameleon) do not meet, if I am rightly informed."

I beg leave to distinguish this query into two, which are of very different natures; one being purely anatomical, the other relating to the carrying species or pictures of visible objects to the *sensorium*.

The first question is, Whether the fibres coming from corresponding points of the two *retinæ* do not unite at the place where the optic nerves meet, and continue united from thence to the brain; so that the right optic nerve, after the meeting of the two nerves, is composed of the fibres coming from the right side of both *retinæ*, and the left, of the fibres coming from the left side of both *retinæ*?

This is undoubtedly a curious and rational question; because, if we could find ground from anatomy to answer it in the affirmative, it would lead us a step forward in discovering the cause of the correspondence and sympathy which there is between certain points of the two *retinæ*. For, although we know not what is the particular function of the optic nerves, yet it is probable that some impression made upon them, and communicated along their fibres, is necessary to vision; and, whatever be the nature of this impression, if two fibres are united into one, an impression made upon one of them, or upon both, may probably produce the same effect. Anatomists think it a sufficient account of a sympathy between two parts of the body, when they are served by branches of the same nerve; we should, therefore, look upon it as an important discovery in anatomy, if it were found that the same nerve sent branches to the corresponding points of the *retinæ*.

But hath any such discovery been made? No, not so much as in one subject, as far as I can learn; but, in several subjects, the contrary seems to have been discovered. Dr Porterfield hath given us two cases at length from Vesalius, and one from Cæsalpinus, wherein the optic nerves, after touching one another as usual, appeared to be reflected back to the same side whence they came, without any mixture of their fibres. Each of these persons had lost an eye some time before his death, and the optic nerve belonging to that eye was shrunk, so that it could be distinguished from the other at the place where they met. Another case, which the same author gives from Vesalius, is still more remarkable; for in it the optic nerves did not touch at all ; and yet, upon inquiry, those who were most familiar with the person in his life-time, declared that he never complained of any defect of sight, or of his seeing objects double. Diemerbroeck tells us, that Aquapendens [ab Aquapendente] and Valverda likewise affirm, that they have met with subjects wherein the optic nerves did not touch.[*]

As these observations were made before Sir Isaac Newton put this query, it is uncertain whether he was ignorant of them, or whether he suspected some inaccuracy in them, and desired that the matter might be more carefully examined. But, f om the following passage of the most accurate Winslow, it does not appear that later observations have been more favourable to his conjecture. " The union of these (optic) nerves, by the small curvatures of their *cornua*, is very difficult to be unfolded in human bodies. This union is commonly found to be very close ; but, in some subjects, it seems to be no more than a strong adhesion—in others, to be partly made by an intersection or crossing of fibres. They have been found quite separate ; and, in other subjects, one of them has been found to be very much altered both in size and colour through its whole passage, the other remaining in its natural state."

When we consider this conjecture of Sir Isaac Newton by itself, it appears more ingenious, and to have more verisimilitude, than anything that has been offered upon the subject ; and we admire the caution and modesty of the author, in proposing it only as a subject of inquiry : but when we compare it with the observations of anatomists which contradict it,[†] we are naturally

led to this reflection, That, if we trust to the conjectures of men of the greatest genius in the operations of nature, we have only the chance of going wrong in an ingenious manner.

The second part of the query is, Whether the two species of objects from the two eyes are not, at the place where the optic nerves meet, united into one species or picture, half of which is carried thence to the *sensorium* in the right optic nerve, and the other half in the left ? and whether these two halves are not so put together again at the *sensorium*, as to make one species or picture ?

Here it seems natural to put the previous question, What reason have we to believe that pictures of objects are at all carried to the *sensorium*, either by the optic nerves, or by any other nerves ? Is it not possible that this great philosopher, as well as many of a lower form, having been led into this opinion at first by education, may have continued in it, because he never thought of calling it in question ? I confess this was my own case for a considerable part of my life. But since I was led by accident to think seriously what reason I had to believe it, I could find none at all. It seems to be a mere hypothesis, as much as the Indian philosopher's elephant. I am not conscious of any pictures of external objects in my *sensorium*, any more than in my stomach : the things which I perceive by my senses, appear to be external, and not in any part of the brain ; and my sensations, properly so called, have no resemblance of external objects.

The conclusion from all that hath been said, in no less than seven sections, upon our seeing objects single with two eyes, is this—That, by an original property of human eyes, objects painted upon the centres of the two *retinæ*, or upon points similarly situate with regard to the centres, appear in the same visible place ; that the most plausible attempts to account for this property of the eyes, have been unsuccessful ; and, therefore, that it must be either a primary law of our constitution, or the consequence of some more general law, which is not yet discovered.

We have now finished what we intended to say, both of the visible appearances of things to the eye, and of the laws of our constitution by which those appearances

---

[*] See Meckel's " Pathologi-che Anatomie," L., p. 399.—H.

[†] Anatomists are now nearly agreed, that, in the normal state, there is a partial decussation of the human optic nerve. Soemmering, Treviranus, Rudolphi, Johannes Mueller, Langenbeck, Magendie, Mayo, &c., are paramount authority for the fact. I do not know whether the observations has been made, that the degree of decussation on in different animals is exactly in the 'inverse ratio of what we might have been led, at first sight, theoretically to anticipate. In proportion as the convergence is complete—*i. e.*, where the axis of the field of vision of the several eyes coincides with the axis of the field of vision common to both, as in men and apes—there we find the decussation most partial and obscure ; whereas, in the lower animals, in proportion as we find the fields of the two eyes exclusive of each other, and where, consequently, the necessity of bringing the two organs into unison might seem abolished, there, however, we find the crossing of the optic fibres complete. In fishes, accordingly, it is distinct and isolated ; in birds, it takes

m re the appearance of an interlacement ; in the mammalia, that of a fusion of substance. A second consideration, however, reconciles theory and observation. Some, however, as Woolaston, make the parallel motion of the eyes to be dependent on the connection of the optic nerves ; and, besides experiments, there are various pathological cases in favour of Magendie's opinion, that the *fifth* pair are the nerves on, which the energies of *sight, hearing, smell,* and *taste* are proximately and principally dependent.—H.

are exhibited. But it was observed, in the beginning of this chapter, that the visible appearances of objects serve only as signs of their distance, magnitude, figure, and other tangible qualities. The visible appearance is that which is presented to the mind by nature, according to those laws of our constitution which have been explained. But the thing signified by that appearance, is that which is presented to the mind by custom.

When one speaks to us in a language that is familiar, we hear certain sounds, and this is all the effect that his discourse has upon us by nature ; but by custom we understand the meaning of these sounds ; and, therefore, we fix our attention, not upon the sounds, but upon the things signified by them. In like manner, we see only the visible appearance of objects by nature ; but we learn by custom to interpret these appearances, and to understand their meaning. And when this visual language is learned, and becomes familiar, we attend only to the things signified ; and cannot, without great difficulty, attend to the signs by which they are presented. The mind passes from one to the other so rapidly and so familiarly, that no trace of the sign is left in the memory, and we seem immediately, and without the intervention of any sign, to perceive the thing signified.

When I look at the apple-tree which stands before my window, I perceive, at the first glance, its distance and magnitude, the roughness of its trunk, the disposition of its branches, the figure of its leaves and fruit. I seem to perceive all these things immediately. The visible appearance which presented them all to the mind, has entirely escaped me ; I cannot, without great difficulty, and painful abstraction, attend to it, even when it stands before me. Yet it is certain that this visible appearance only is presented to my eye by nature, and that I learned by custom to collect all the rest from it. If I had never seen before now, I should not perceive either the distance or tangible figure of the tree ; and it would have required the practice of seeing for many months, to change that original perception which nature gave me by my eyes, into that which I now have by custom.

The objects which we see naturally and originally, as hath been before observed, have length and breadth, but no thickness nor distance from the eye. Custom, by a kind of legerdemain, withdraws gradually these original and proper objects of sight, and substitutes in their place objects of touch, which have length, breadth, and thickness, and a determinate distance from the eye. By what means this change is brought about, and what principles of the

human mind concur in it, we are next to inquire.

Section XX.

OF PERCEPTION IN GENERAL.

Sensation, and the perception[†] of external objects by the senses, though very different in their nature, have commonly been considered as one and the same thing.[‡] The purposes of common life do not make it necessary to distinguish them, and the received opinions of philosophers tend rather to confound them ; but, without attending carefully to this distinction, it is impossible to have any just conception of the operations of our senses. The most simple operations of the mind, admit not of a logical definition : all we can do is to describe them, so as to lead those who are conscious of them in themselves, to attend to them, and reflect upon them ; and it is often very difficult to describe them so as to answer this intention.

The same mode of expression is used to denote sensation and perception ; and, therefore, we are apt to look upon them as things of the same nature. Thus, *I feel a pain ; I see a tree :* the first denoteth a sensation, the last a perception. The grammatical analysis of both expressions is the same :

* Nothing in the compass of inductive reasoning appears more satisfactory than Berkeley's demonstration of the necessity and manner of our learning, by a slow process of observation and comparison alone, the connection between the perceptions of vision and touch, and, in general, all that relates to the distance and real magnitude of external things. But, although the same necessity seems in theory equally incumbent on the lower animals as on man, yet this theory is provokingly—and that by the most manifest experience—found totally at fault with regard to them ; for we find that all the animals who possess at birth the power of regulated motion (and these are those only through whom the truth of the theory can be brought to the test of a decisive experiment) possess also from birth the whole apprehension of distance, &c., which they are ever known to exhibit. The solution of this difference, by a resort to instinct, is unsatisfactory ; for instinct is, in fact, an occult principle—a kind of natural revelation—and the hypothesis of instinct, therefore, only a confession of our ignorance ; and, at the same time, if instinct be allowed in the lower animals, how can we determine whether and how far instinct may not in like manner operate to the same result in man ?—I have discovered, and, by a wide induction, established, that the power of *regulated* motion at birth is, in all animals, governed by the development, at that period, of the cerebellum, in proportion to the brain proper. Is this law to be extended to the faculty of determining distances, &c., by sight ?—H.

† On the distinction of *Sensation proper*, from *Perception proper*, see "Essays on the Intellectual Powers," Essay II., chap. 16, and Note D.* Reid himself, especially in th s work, has not been always rigid in observing their discrimination.—H.

‡ Not only are they different, but—what has escaped our philosophers—the law of their manifestation is, that, while both are co-existent, each is always in the inverse ratio of the other. Perception is the objective, Sensation the subjective, element. This by the way.—H.

for both consist of an active verb and an object. But, if we attend to the things signified by these expressions, we shall find that, in the first, the distinction between the act and the object is not real but grammatical ; in the second, the distinction is not only grammatical but real.

The form of the expression, *I feel pain*, might seem to imply that the feeling is something distinct from the pain felt ; yet, in reality, there is no distinction. As *thinking a thought* is an expression which could signify no more than *thinking*, so *feeling a pain* signifies no more than *being pained*. What we have said of pain is applicable to every other mere sensation. It is difficult to give instances, very few of our sensations having names ; and, where they have, the name being common to the sensation, and to something else which is associated with it. But, when we attend to the sensation by itself, and separate it from other things which are conjoined with it in the imagination, it appears to be something which can have no existence but in a sentient mind, no distinction from the act of the mind by which it is felt.

Perception, as we here understand it, hath always an object distinct from the act by which it is perceived ; an object which may exist whether it be perceived or not. I perceive a tree that grows before my window ; there is here an object which is perceived, and an act of the mind by which it is perceived ; and these two are not only distinguishable, but they are extremely unlike in their natures. The object is made up of a trunk, branches, and leaves ; but the act of the mind by which it is perceived hath neither trunk, branches, nor leaves. I am conscious of this act of my mind, and I can reflect upon it ; but it is too simple to admit of an analysis, and I cannot find proper words to describe it. I find nothing that resembles it so much as the remembrance of the tree, or the imagination of it. Yet both these differ essentially from perception ; they differ likewise one from another. It is in vain that a philosopher assures me, that the imagination of the tree, the remembrance of it, and the perception of it, are all one, and differ only in degree of vivacity. I know the contrary ; for I am as well acquainted with all the three as I am with the apartments of my own house. I know this also, that the perception of an object implies both a conception of its form, and a belief of its present existence.* I know, moreover, that

* It is to be observed that Reid himself does not discriminate *perception* and *imagination* by any essential difference. According to him, perception is only the conception (imagination) of an object, accompanied with a belief of its present existence ; and even this last distinction, a mere " faith without

this belief is not the effect of argumentation and reasoning ; it is the immediate effect of my constitution.

I am aware that this belief which I have in perception stands exposed to the strongest batteries of scepticism. But they make no great impression upon it. The sceptic asks me, Why do you believe the existence of the external object which you perceive ? This belief, sir, is none of my manufacture ; it came from the mint of Nature ; it bears her image and superscription ; and, if it is not right, the fault is not mine : I even took it upon trust, and without suspicion. Reason, says the sceptic, is the only judge of truth, and you ought to throw off every opinion and every belief that is not grounded on reason. Why, sir, should I believe the faculty of reason more than that of perception ?—they came both out of the same shop, and were made by the same artist ; and if he puts one piece of false ware into my hands, what should hinder him from putting another ?"

Perhaps the sceptic will agree to distrust reason, rather than give any credit to perception. For, says he, since, by your own concession, the object which you perceive, and that act of your mind by which you perceive it, are quite different things, the one may exist without the other ; and, as the object may exist without being perceived, so the perception may exist without an object. There is nothing so shameful in a philosopher as to be deceived and deluded ; and, therefore, you ought to resolve firmly to withhold assent, and to throw off this belief of external objects, which may be all delusion. For my part, I will never attempt to throw it off ; and, although the sober part of mankind will not be very anxious to know my reasons, yet, if they can be of use to any sceptic, they are these :—

First, because it is not in my power : why, then, should I make a vain attempt ? It would be agreeable to fly to the moon, and to make a visit to Jupiter and Saturn ; but, when I know that Nature has bound me down by the law of gravitation to this planet which I inhabit, I rest contented, and quietly

knowledge," is surrendered by Mr Stewart. Now, as conception (imagination) is only immediately cognisant of the *ego*, so must perception on this doctrine be a knowledge purely *subjective*. Perception must be wholly different in kind from Conception, if we are to possess a faculty informing us of the existence and qualities of an external world ; and, unless we are possessed of such a faculty, we shall never be competent to vindicate more than an ideal reality to the objects of our cognitions.—H.

* This argument would be good in favour of our belief, that we are really percipient of a *non-ego* : it is not good in favour of our belief that a *non-ego* really exists, our perception of its re l existence being abandoned. Mankind have the latter belief only as they have the former ; and, if we are deceived by our Nature touching the one, it is absurd to appeal to her veracity in proof of the other.—H.

suffer myself to be carried along in its orbit. My belief is carried along by perception, as irresistibly as my body by the earth. And the greatest sceptic will find himself to be in the same condition. He may struggle hard to disbelieve the informations of his senses, as a man does to swim against a torrent; but, ah! it is in vain. It is in vain that he strains every nerve, and wrestles with nature, and with every object that strikes upon his senses. For, after all, when his strength is spent in the fruitless attempt, he will be carried down the torrent with the common herd of believers.

Secondly, I think it would not be prudent to throw off this belief, if it were in my power. If Nature intended to deceive me, and impose upon me by false appearances, and I, by my great cunning and profound logic, have discovered the imposture, prudence would dictate to me, in this case, even to put up [with] this indignity done me, as quietly as I could, and not to call her an impostor to her face, lest she should be even with me in another way. For what do I gain by resenting this injury? You ought at least not to believe what she says. This indeed seems reasonable, if she intends to impose upon me. But what is the consequence? I resolve not to believe my senses. I break my nose against a post that comes in my way; I step into a dirty kennel; and, after twenty such wise and rational actions, I am taken up and clapped into a mad-house. Now, I confess I would rather make one of the credulous fools whom Nature imposes upon, than of those wise and rational philosophers who resolve to withhold assent at all this expense. If a man pretends to be a sceptic with regard to the informations of sense, and yet prudently keeps out of harm's way as other men do, he must excuse my suspicion, that he either acts the hypocrite, or imposes upon himself. For, if the scale of his belief were so evenly poised as to lean no more to one side than to the contrary, it is impossible that his actions could be directed by any rules of common prudence.*

Thirdly, Although the two reasons already mentioned are perhaps two more than enough, I shall offer a third. I gave implicit belief to the informations of Nature by my senses, for a considerable part of my life, before I had learned so much logic as to be able to start a doubt concerning them. And now, when I reflect upon what is past, I do not find that I have been imposed upon by this belief. I find that without it I must have perished by a thousand accidents. I find that without it I should have been no wiser now than when I was born. I should

not even have been able to acquire that logic which suggests these sceptical doubts with regard to my senses. Therefore, I consider this instinctive belief as one of the best gifts of Nature. I thank the Author of my being, who bestowed it upon me before the eyes of my reason were opened, and still bestows it upon me, to be my guide where reason leaves me in the dark. And now I yield to the direction of my senses, not from instinct only, but from confidence and trust in a faithful and beneficent Monitor, grounded upon the experience of his paternal care and goodness.

In all this, I deal with the Author of my being, no otherwise than I thought it reasonable to deal with my parents and tutors. I believed by instinct whatever they told me, long before I had the idea of a lie, or thought of the possibility of their deceiving me. Afterwards, upon reflection, I found they had acted like fair and honest people, who wished me well. I found that, if I had not believed what they told me, before I could give a reason of my belief, I had to this day been little better than a changeling. And although this natural credulity hath sometimes occasioned my being imposed upon by deceivers, yet it hath been of infinite advantage to me upon the whole; therefore, I consider it as another good gift of Nature. And I continue to give that credit, from reflection, to those of whose integrity and veracity I have had experience, which before I gave from instinct.

There is a much greater similitude than is commonly imagined, between the testimony of nature given by our senses, and the testimony of men given by language. The credit we give to both is at first the effect of instinct* only. When we grow up, and begin to reason about them, the credit given to human testimony is restrained and weakened, by the experience we have of deceit. But the credit given to the testimony of our senses, is established and confirmed by the uniformity and constancy of the laws of nature.

Our perceptions are of two kinds: some are natural and original; others acquired, and the fruit of experience. When I perceive that this is the taste of cyder, that of brandy; that this is the smell of an apple, that of an orange; that this is the noise of thunder, that the ringing of bells; this the sound of a coach passing, that the voice of such a friend: these perceptions, and others of the same kind, are not original—they are acquired. But the perception which I have, by touch, of the hardness and softness of bodies, of their extension, figure, and motion, is not acquired—it is original.

---

* This is not a fair consequence of Idealism; therefore, it is not a *reductio ad absurdum*.—H.

* On the propriety of the term "instinct," see in Note A.—H.

In all our senses, the acquired perceptions are many more than the original, especially in sight. By this sense we perceive originally the visible figure and colour of bodies only, and their visible place : but we learn to perceive by the eye, almost everything which we can perceive by touch. The original perceptions of this sense serve only as sigus to introduce the acquired.

The signs by which objects are presented to us in perception, are the language of Nature to man ; and as, in many respects, it hath great affinity with the language of man to man, so particularly in this, that both are partly natural and original, partly acquired by custom. Our original or natural perceptions are analogous to the natural language of man to man, of which we took notice in the fourth chapter ; and our acquired perceptions are analogous to artificial language, which, in our mother-tongue, is got very much in the same manner with our acquired perceptions—as we shall afterwards more fully explain.

Not only men, but children, idiots, and brutes, acquire by habit many perceptions which they had not originally. Almost every employment in life hath perceptions of this kind that are peculiar to it. The shepherd knows every sheep of his flock, as we do our acquaintance, and can pick them out of another flock one by one. The butcher knows by sight the weight and quality of his beeves and sheep before they are killed. The farmer perceives by his eye, very nearly, the quantity of hay in a rick, or of corn in a heap. The sailor sees the burthen, the built, and the distance of a ship at sea, while she is a great way off. Every man accustomed to writing, distinguishes his acquaintance by their hand-writing, as he does by their faces. And the painter distinguishes, in the works of his art, the style of all the great masters. In a word, acquired perception is very different in different persons, according to the diversity of objects about which they are employed, and the application they bestow in observing them.

Perception ought not only to be distinguished from sensation, but likewise from that knowledge of the objects of sense which is got by reasoning. There is no reasoning in perception, as hath been observed. The belief which is implied in it, is the effect of instinct. But there are many things, with regard to sensible objects, which we can infer from what we perceive ; and such conclusions of reason ought to be distinguished from what is merely perceived. When I look at the

moon, I perceive her to be sometimes circular, sometimes horned, and sometimes gibbous. This is simple perception, and is the same in the philosopher and in the clown : but from these various appearances of her enlightened part, I infer that she is really of a spherical figure. This conclusion is not obtained by simple perception, but by reasoning. Simple perception has the same relation to the conclusions of reason drawn from our perceptions, as the axioms in mathematics have to the propositions. I cannot demonstrate that two quantities which are equal to the same quantity, are equal to each other ; neither can I demonstrate that the tree which I perceive, exists. But, by the constitution of my nature, my belief is irresistibly carried along by my apprehension of the axiom ; and, by the constitution of my nature, my belief is no less irresistibly carried along by my perception of the tree. All reasoning is from principles. The first principles of mathematical reasoning are mathematical axioms and definitions ; and the first principles of all our reasoning about existences, are our perceptions. The first principles of every kind of reasoning are given us by Nature, and are of equal authority with the faculty of reason itself, which is also the gift of Nature. The conclusions of reason are all built upon first principles, and can have no other foundation. Most justly, therefore, do such principles disdain to be tried by reason, and laugh at all the artillery of the logician, when it is directed against them.

When a long train of reasoning is necessary in demonstrating a mathematical proposition, it is easily distinguished from an axiom ; and they seem to be things of a very different nature. But there are some propositions which lie so near to axioms, that it is difficult to say whether they ought to be held as axioms, or demonstrated as propositions. The same thing holds with regard to perception, and the conclusions drawn from it. Some of these conclusions follow our perceptions so easily, and are so immediately connected with them, that it is difficult to fix the limit which divides the one from the other.

Perception, whether original or acquired, implies no exercise of reason ; and is common to men, children, idiots, and brutes. The more obvious conclusions drawn from our perceptions, make what we call *common understanding ;* by which men conduct themselves in the common affairs of life, and by which they are distinguished from idiots. The more remote conclusions which are drawn from our perceptions, by reason, make what we commonly call *science* in the various parts of nature, whether in agriculture, medicine, mechanics, or in any

* In this passage Reid admits Figure and Place (consequently, Extension) to be *original* perceptions of vision. See above, p. 123, b . note †.—H.

part of natural philosophy. When I see a garden in good order, containing a great variety of things of the best kinds, and in the most flourishing condition, I immediately conclude from these signs the skill and industry of the gardener. A farmer, when he rises in the morning, and perceives that the neighbouring brook overflows his field, concludes that a great deal of rain hath fallen in the night. Perceiving his fence broken, and his corn trodden down, he concludes that some of his own or his neighbours' cattle have broke loose. Perceiving that his stable-door is broke open, and some of his horses gone, he concludes that a thief has carried them off. He traces the prints of his horses' feet in the soft ground, and by them discovers which road the thief hath taken. These are instances of common understanding, which dwells so near to perception that it is difficult to trace the line which divides the one from the other. In like manner, the science of nature dwells so near to common understanding that we cannot discern where the latter ends and the former begins. I perceive that bodies lighter than water swim in water, and that those which are heavier sink. Hence I conclude, that, if a body remains wherever it is put under water, whether at the top or bottom, it is precisely of the same weight with water. If it will rest only when part of it is above water, it is lighter than water. And the greater the part above water is, compared with the whole, the lighter is the body. If it had no gravity at all, it would make no impression upon the water, but stand wholly above it. Thus, every man, by common understanding, has a rule by which he judges of the specific gravity of bodies which swim in water: and a step or two more leads him into the science of hydrostatics.

All that we know of nature, or of existences, may be compared to a tree, which hath its root, trunk, and branches. In this tree of knowledge, perception is the root, common understanding is the trunk, and the sciences are the branches.

Section XXI.

OF THE PROCESS OF NATURE IN PERCEPTION.

Although there is no reasoning in perception, yet there are certain means and instruments, which, by the appointment of nature, must intervene between the object and our perception of it; and, by these, our perceptions are limited and regulated. First, If the object is not in contact with the organ of sense, there must be some medium which passes between them. Thus, in vision, the rays of light; in hearing, the vibrations of elastic air; in smelling, the effluvia of the body smelled—must pass from the object to the organ; otherwise we have no perception.* Secondly, There must be some action or impression upon the organ of sense, either by the immediate application of the object, or by the medium that goes between them. Thirdly, The nerves which go from the brain to the organ must receive some impression by means of that which was made upon the organ; and, probably, by means of the nerves, some impression must be made upon the brain. Fourthly, The impression made upon the organ, nerves, and brain, is followed by a sensation. And, last of all, This sensation is followed by the perception of the object.†

Thus, our perception of objects is the result of a train of operations; some of which affect the body only, others affect the mind. We know very little of the nature of some of these operations; we know not at all how they are connected together, or in what way they contribute to that perception which is the result of the whole; but, by the laws of our constitution, we perceive objects in this, and in no other way.

There may be other beings who can perceive external objects without rays of light, or vibrations of air, or effluvia of bodies—without impressions on bodily organs, or even without sensations; but we are so framed by the Author of Nature, that, even when we are surrounded by external objects, we may perceive none of them. Our faculty of perceiving an object lies dormant, until it is roused and stimulated by a certain corresponding sensation. Nor is this sensation always at hand to perform its office; for it enters into the mind only in consequence of a certain corresponding impression made on the organ of sense by the object.

Let us trace this correspondence of impressions, sensations, and perceptions, as far as we can—beginning with that which is first in order, the impression made upon the bodily organ. But, alas! we know not of what nature these impressions are, far less how they excite sensations in the mind.

We know that one body may act upon another by pressure, by percussion, by attraction, by repulsion, and, probably, in many other ways which we neither know nor have names to express. But in which of these ways objects, when perceived by us, act upon the organs of sense, these organs upon the nerves, and the nerves

---

* The only object of *perception* is the *immediate* object. The distant reality—the mediate object, or object simply of Reid and other philosophers—is unknown to the perception of sense, and only reached by reasoning.—H.

† That *sensation* proper precedes *perception* proper is a false assumption. They are simultaneous elements of the same indivisible energy.—H.

upon the brain, we know not. Can any man tell me how, in vision, the rays of light act upon the *retina*, how the *retina* acts upon the optic nerve, and how the optic nerve acts upon the brain? No man can. When I feel the pain of the gout in my toe, I know that there is some unusual impression made upon that part of my body. But of what kind is it? Are the small vessels distended with some redundant elastic, or unelastic fluid? Are the fibres unusually stretched? Are they torn asunder by force, or gnawed and corroded by some acrid humour? I can answer none of these questions. All that I feel is pain, which is not an impression upon the body, but upon the mind; and all that I perceive by this sensation is, that some distemper in my toe occasions this pain. But, as I know not the natural temper and texture of my toe when it is at ease, I know as little what change or disorder of its parts occasions this uneasy sensation. In like manner, in every other sensation, there is, without doubt, some impression made upon the organ of sense; but an impression of which we know not the nature. It is too subtile to be discovered by our senses, and we may make a thousand conjectures without coming near the truth. If we understood the structure of our organs of sense so minutely as to discover what effects are produced upon them by external objects, this knowledge would contribute nothing to our perception of the object; for they perceive as distinctly who know least about the manner of perception, as the greatest adepts. It is necessary that the impression be made upon our organs, but not that it be known. Nature carries on this part of the process of perception, without our consciousness or concurrence.

But we cannot be unconscious of the next step in this process—the sensation of the mind, which always immediately follows the impression made upon the body. It is essential to a sensation to be felt, and it can be nothing more than we feel it to be. If we can only acquire the habit of attending to our sensations, we may know them perfectly. But how are the sensations of the mind produced by impressions upon the body? Of this we are absolutely ignorant, having no means of knowing how the body acts upon the mind, or the mind upon the body. When we consider the nature and attributes of both, they seem to be so different, and so unlike, that we can find no handle by which the one may lay hold of the other. There is a deep and a dark gulf between them, which our understanding cannot pass; and the manner of their correspondence and intercourse is absolutely unknown.

Experience teaches us, that certain impressions upon the body are constantly followed by certain sensations of the mind and that, on the other hand, certain determinations of the mind are constantly followed by certain motions in the body; but we see not the chain that ties these things together. Who knows but their connection may be arbitrary, and owing to the will of our Maker? Perhaps the same sensations might have been connected with other impressions, or other bodily organs. Perhaps we might have been so made as to taste with our fingers, to smell with our ears, and to hear by the nose. Perhaps we might have been so made as to have all the sensations and perceptions which we have, without any impression made upon our bodily organs at all.

However these things may be, if Nature had given us nothing more than impressions made upon the body and sensations in our minds corresponding to them, we should, in that case, have been merely sentient, but not percipient beings. We should never have been able to form a conception of any external object, far less a belief of its existence. Our sensations have no resemblance to external objects; nor can we discover, by our reason, any necessary connection between the existence of the former, and that of the latter.

We might, perhaps, have been made of such a constitution as to have our present perceptions connected with other sensations. We might, perhaps, have had the perception of external objects, without either impressions upon the organs of sense, or sensations. Or, lastly, The perceptions we have, might have been immediately connected with the impressions upon our organs, without any intervention of sensations. This last seems really to be the case in one instance—to wit, in our perception of the visible figure of bodies, as was observed in the eighth section of this chapter.

The process of Nature, in perception by the senses, may, therefore, be conceived as a kind of drama, wherein some things are performed behind the scenes, others are represented to the mind in different scenes, one succeeding another. The impression made by the object upon the organ, either by immediate contact or by some intervening medium, as well as the impression made upon the nerves and brain, is performed behind the scenes, and the mind sees nothing of it. But every such impression, by the laws of the drama, is followed by a sensation, which is the first scene exhibited to the mind; and this scene is quickly succeeded* by another, which is the perception of the object.

In this drama, Nature is the actor, we are the spectators. We know nothing of

* See the preceding note.—H.

the machinery by means of which every different impression upon the organ, nerves, and brain, exhibits its corresponding sensation; or of the machinery by means of which each sensation exhibits its corresponding perception. We are inspired with the sensation, and we are inspired with the corresponding perception, by means unknown.[*] And, because the mind passes immediately from the sensation to that conception and belief of the object which we have in perception, in the same manner as it passes from signs to the things signified by them, we have, therefore, called our sensations *signs of external objects;* finding no word more proper to express the function which Nature hath assigned them in perception, and the relation which they bear to their corresponding objects.

There is no necessity of a resemblance between the sign and the thing signified; and indeed no sensation can resemble any external object. But there are two things necessary to our knowing things by means of signs. First, That a real connection between the sign and thing signified be established, either by the course of nature, or by the will and appointment of men. When they are connected by the course of nature, it is a natural sign; when by human appointment, it is an artificial sign. Thus, smoke is a natural sign of fire; certain features are natural signs of anger: but our words, whether expressed by articulate sounds or by writing, are artificial signs of our thoughts and purposes.

Another requisite to our knowing things by signs is, that the appearance of the sign to the mind, be followed by the conception and belief of the thing signified. Without this, the sign is not understood or interpreted; and, therefore, is no sign to us, however fit in its own nature for that purpose.

Now, there are three ways in which the mind passes from the appearance of a natural sign to the conception and belief of the thing signified—by *original principles of our constitution,* by *custom,* and by *reasoning.*

Our original perceptions are got in the first of these ways, our acquired perceptions in the second, and all that reason discovers of the course of nature, in the third. In the first of these ways, Nature, by means of the sensations of touch, informs us of the hardness and softness of bodies; of their extension, figure, and motion; and of that space in which they move and are placed—as hath been already explained in the fifth chapter of this inquiry. And, in the second of these ways, she informs us, by means of our eyes, of almost all the same things

which originally we could perceive only by touch.

In order, therefore, to understand more particularly how we learn to perceive so many things by the eye, which originally could be perceived only by touch, it will be proper, First, To point out the signs by which those things are exhibited to the eye, and their connection with the things signified by them; and, Secondly, To consider how the experience of this connection produces that habit by which the mind, without any reasoning or reflection, passes from the sign to the conception and belief of the thing signified.

Of all the acquired perceptions which we have by sight, the most remarkable is the perception of the distance of objects from the eye; we shall, therefore, particularly consider the signs by which this perception is exhibited, and only make some general remarks with regard to the signs which are used in other acquired perceptions.

Section XXII.

OF THE SIGNS BY WHICH WE LEARN TO PERCEIVE DISTANCE FROM THE EYE.

It was before observed in general, that the original perceptions of sight are signs which serve to introduce those that are acquired; but this is not to be understood as if no other signs were employed for that purpose. There are several motions of the eyes, which, in order to distinct vision, must be varied, according as the object is more or less distant; and such motions being by habit connected with the corresponding distances of the object, become signs of those distances.[*] These motions were at first voluntary and unconfined; but, as the intention of nature was to produce perfect and distinct vision by their means, we soon learn by experience to regulate them according to that intention only, without the least reflection.

A ship requires a different trim for every variation of the direction and strength of the wind; and, if we may be allowed to borrow that word, the eyes require a different trim for every degree of light, and for every variation of the distance of the object, while it is within certain limits. The eyes are trimmed for a particular object, by contracting certain muscles and relaxing others; as the ship is trimmed for a particular wind by drawing certain ropes and slackening others. The sailor learns the trim of his ship, as we learn the trim of our eyes, by experience. A ship, although the noblest machine that human art can boast, is far

* On perception as a revelation—"a miraculous revelation"—see Jacobi's "'David Hume."—H.

* See above, p. 182, note *.—H.

inferior to the eye in this respect, that it requires art and ingenuity to navigate her ; and a sailor must know what ropes he must pull, and what he must slacken, to fit her to a particular wind ; but with such superior wisdom is the fabric of the eye, and the principles of its motion contrived, that it requires no art nor ingenuity to see by it. Even that part of vision which is got by experience, is attained by idiots. We need not know what muscles we are to contract, and what we are to relax, in order to fit the eye to a particular distance of the object.

But, although we are not conscious of the motions we perform, in order to fit the eyes to the distance of the object, we are conscious of the effort employed in producing these motions ; and probably have some sensation which accompanies them, to which we give as little attention as to other sensations. And thus, an effort consciously exerted, or a sensation consequent upon that effort, comes to be conjoined with the distance of the object which gave occasion to it, and by this conjunction becomes a sign of that distance. Some instances of this will appear in considering the means or signs by which we learn to see the distance of objects from the eye. In the enumeration of these, we agree with Dr Porterfield, notwithstanding that distance from the eye, in his opinion, is perceived originally, but, in our opinion, by experience only.

In general, when a near object affects the eye in one manner, and the same object, placed at a greater distance, affects it in a different manner, these various affections of the eye become signs of the corresponding distances. The means of perceiving distance by the eye will therefore be explained by shewing in what various ways objects affect the eye differently, according to their proximity or distance.

1. It is well known, that, to see objects distinctly at various distances, the form of the eye must undergo some change : and nature hath given us the power of adapting it to near objects, by the contraction of certain muscles, and to distant objects by the contraction of other muscles. As to the manner in which this is done, and the muscular parts employed, anatomists do not altogether agree. The ingenious Dr Jurin, in his excellent essay on distinct and indistinct vision, seems to have given the most probable account of this matter ; and to him I refer the reader.*

But, whatever be the manner in which this change of the form of the eye is effected, it is certain that young people have commonly the power of adapting their eyes

to all distances of the object, from six or seven inches, to fifteen or sixteen feet ; so as to have perfect and distinct vision at any distance within these limits. From this it follows, that the effort we consciously employ to adapt the eye to any particular distance of objects within these limits, will be connected and associated with that distance, and will become a sign of it. When the object is removed beyond the farthest limit of distinct vision, it will be seen indistinctly ; but, more or less so, according as its distance is greater or less ; so that the degrees of indistinctness of the object may become the signs of distances considerably beyond the farthest limit of distinct vision.

If we had no other mean but this, of perceiving distance of visible objects, the most distant would not appear to be above twenty or thirty feet from the eye, and the tops of houses and trees would seem to touch the clouds ; for, in that case, the signs of all greater distances being the same, they have the same signification, and give the same perception of distance.

But it is of more importance to observe, that, because the nearest limit of distinct vision in the time of youth, when we learn to perceive distance by the eye, is about six or seven inches, no object seen distinctly ever appears to be nearer than six or seven inches from the eye. We can, by art, make a small object appear distinct, when it is in reality not above half an inch from the eye ; either by using a single microscope, or by looking through a small pin-hole in a card. When, by either of these means, an object is made to appear distinct, however small its distance is in reality, it seems to be removed at least to the distance of six or seven inches— that is, within the limits of distinct vision.

This observation is the more important, because it affords the only reason we can give why an object is magnified either by a single microscope, or by being seen through a pin-hole ; and the only mean by which we can ascertain the degree in which the object will be magnified by either. Thus, if the object is really half an inch distant from the eye, and appears to be seven inches distant, its diameter will seem to be enlarged in the same proportion as its distance—that is, fourteen times.

2. In order to direct both eyes to an object, the optic axes must have a greater or less inclination, according as the object is nearer or more distant. And, although we are not conscious of this inclination, yet we are conscious of the effort employed in it. By this mean we perceive small distances more accurately than we could do by the conformation of the eye only

And, therefore, we find, that those who have lost the sight of one eye are apt, even within arm's-length, to make mistakes in the distance of objects, which are easily avoided by those who see with both eyes. Such mistakes are often discovered in snuffing a candle, in threading a needle, or in filling a tea-cup.*

When a picture is seen with both eyes, and at no great distance, the representation appears not so natural as when it is seen only with one. The intention of painting being to deceive the eye, and to make things appear at different distances which in reality are upon the same piece of canvass, this deception is not so easily put upon both eyes as upon one ; because we perceive the distance of visible objects more exactly and determinately with two eyes than with one. If the shading and relief be executed in the best manner, the picture may have almost the same appearance to one eye as the objects themselves would have; but it cannot have the same appearance to both. This is not the fault of the artist, but an unavoidable imperfection in the art. And it is owing to what we just now observed, that the perception we have of the distance of objects by one eye is more uncertain, and more liable to deception, than that which we have by both.

The great impediment, and I think the only invincible impediment, to that agreeable deception of the eye which the painter aims at, is the perception which we have of the distance of visible objects from the eye, partly by means of the conformation of the eye, but chiefly by means of the inclination of the optic axes. If this perception could be removed, I see no reason why a picture might not be made so perfect as to deceive the eye in reality, and to be mistaken for the original object. Therefore, in order to judge of the merit of a picture, we ought, as much as possible, to exclude these two means of perceiving the distance of the several parts of it.

In order to remove this perception of distance, the connoisseurs in painting use a method which is very proper. They look at the picture with one eye, through a tube which excludes the view of all other objects. By this method, the principal mean whereby we perceive the distance of the object—to wit, the inclination of the optic axes—is entirely excluded. I would humbly propose, as an improvement of this method of viewing pictures, that the aperture of the tube next to the eye should be very small. If it is as small as a pin-hole, so much the better, providing there be light enough to see the picture clearly. The reason of this proposal

The same remark is made by many optical writers, old and new.—H.

is, that, when we look at an object through a small aperture, it will be seen distinctly, whether the conformation of the eye be adapted to its distance or not ; and we have no mean left to judge of the distance, but the light and colouring, which are in the painter's power. If, therefore, the artist performs his part properly, the picture will by this method affect the eye in the same manner that the object represented would do ; which is the perfection of this art.

Although this second mean of perceiving the distance of visible objects be more determinate and exact than the first, yet it hath its limits, beyond which it can be of no use. For when the optic axes directed to an object are so nearly parallel that, in directing them to an object yet more distant, we are not conscious of any new effort, nor have any different sensation, there our perception of distance stops ; and, as all more distant objects affect the eye in the same manner, we perceive them to be at the same distance. This is the reason why the sun, moon, planets, and fixed stars, when seen not near the horizon, appear to be all at the same distance, as if they touched the concave surface of a great sphere. The surface of this celestial sphere is at that distance beyond which all objects affect the eye in the same manner. Why this celestial vault appears more distant towards the horizon, than towards the zenith, will afterwards appear.

3. The colours of objects, according as they are more distant, become more faint and languid, and are tinged more with the azure of the intervening atmosphere : to this we may add, that their minute parts become more indistinct, and their outline less accurately defined. It is by these means chiefly, that painters can represent objects at very different distances, upon the same canvass. And the diminution of the magnitude of an object would not have the effect of making it appear to be at a great distance, without this degradation of colour, and indistinctness of the outline, and of the minute parts. If a painter should make a human figure ten times less than other human figures that are in the same piece, having the colours as bright, and the outline and minute parts as accurately defined, it would not have the appearance of a man at a great distance, but of a pigmy or Lilliputian.

When an object hath a known variety of colours, its distance is more clearly indicated by the gradual dilution of the colours into one another, than when it is of one uniform colour. In the steeple which stands before me at a small distance, the joinings of the stones are clearly perceptible ; the grey colour of the stone, and the white cement are distinctly limited : when

I see it at a greater distance, the joinings of the stones are less distinct, and the colours of the stone and of the cement begin to dilute into one another: at a distance still greater, the joinings disappear altogether, and the variety of colour vanishes.

In an apple-tree which stands at the distance of about twelve feet, covered with flowers, I can perceive the figure and the colour of the leaves and petals; pieces of branches, some larger, others smaller, peeping through the intervals of the leaves—some of them enlightened by the sun's rays, others shaded; and some openings of the sky are perceived through the whole. When I gradually remove from this tree, the appearance, even as to colour, changes every minute. First, the smaller parts, then the larger, are gradually confounded and mixed. The colours of leaves, petals, branches, and sky, are gradually diluted into each other, and the colour of the whole becomes more and more uniform. This change of appearance, corresponding to the several distances, marks the distance more exactly than if the whole object had been of one colour.

Dr Smith, in his "Optics," gives us a very curious observation made by Bishop Berkeley, in his travels through Italy and Sicily. He observed, That, in those countries, cities and palaces seen at a great distance appeared nearer to him by several miles than they really were: and he very judiciously imputed it to this cause, That the purity of the Italian and Sicilian air, gave to very distant objects that degree of brightness and distinctness which, in the grosser air of his own country, was to be seen only in those that are near. The purity of the Italian air hath been assigned as the reason why the Italian painters commonly give a more lively colour to the sky than the Flemish. Ought they not, for the same reason, to give less degradation of the colours, and less indistinctness of the minute parts, in the representation of very distant objects?

It is very certain that, as in air uncommonly pure, we are apt to think visible objects nearer and less than they really are, so, in air uncommonly foggy, we are apt to think them more distant and larger than the truth. Walking by the sea-side in a thick fog, I see an object which seems to me to be a man on horseback, and at the distance of about half a mile. My companion, who has better eyes, or is more accustomed to see such objects in such circumstances, assures me that it is a sea-gull, and not a man on horseback. Upon a second view, I immediately assent to his opinion; and now it appears to me to be a sea-gull, and at the distance only of seventy or eighty yards. The mistake made on this occasion, and the correction of it, are both

so sudden, that we are at a loss whether to call them by the name of *judgment*, or by that of *simple perception*.

It is not worth while to dispute about names; but it is evident that my belief, both first and last, was produced rather by signs than by arguments, and that the mind proceeded to the conclusion in both cases by habit, and not by ratiocination. And the process of the mind seems to have been this—First, Not knowing, or not minding, the effect of a foggy air on the visible appearance of objects, the object seems to me to have that degradation of colour, and that indistinctness of the outline, which objects have at the distance of half a mile; therefore, from the visible appearance as a sign, I immediately proceed to the belief that the object is half a mile distant. Then, this distance, together with the visible magnitude, signify to me the real magnitude, which, supposing the distance to be half a mile, must be equal to that of a man on horseback; and the figure, considering the indistinctness of the outline, agrees with that of a man on horseback. Thus the deception is brought about. But when I am assured that it is a sea-gull, the real magnitude of a sea-gull, together with the visible magnitude presented to the eye, immediately suggest the distance, which, in this case, cannot be above seventy or eighty yards: the indistinctness of the figure likewise suggests the fogginess of the air as its cause; and now the whole chain of signs, and things signified, seems stronger and better connected than it was before; the half mile vanishes to eighty yards; the man on horseback dwindles to a sea-gull; I get a new perception, and wonder how I got the former, or what is become of it; for it is now so entirely gone, that I cannot recover it.

It ought to be observed that, in order to produce such deceptions from the clearness or fogginess of the air, it must be uncommonly clear or uncommonly foggy; for we learn, from experience, to make allowance for that variety of constitutions of the air which we have been accustomed to observe, and of which we are aware. Bishop Berkeley therefore committed a mistake, when he attributed the large appearance of the horizontal moon to the faintness of her light, occasioned by its passing through a larger tract of atmosphere:* for we are so much accustomed to see the moon in all degrees of faintness and brightness, from the greatest to the least, that we learn to make allowance for it; and do not imagine her magnitude increased by the faintness of her appearance. Besides, it is certain that the horizontal moon seen through a tube

---

* This explanation was not original to Berkeley.—H.

which cuts off the view of the interjacent ground, and of all terrestrial objects, loses all that unusual appearance of magnitude.

4. We frequently perceive the distance of objects, by means of intervening or contiguous objects, whose distance or magnitude is otherwise known. When I perceive certain fields or tracts of ground to lie between me and an object, it is evident that these may become signs of its distance. And although we have no particular information of the dimensions of such fields or tracts, yet their similitude to others which we know, suggests their dimensions.

We are so much accustomed to measure with our eye the ground which we travel, and to compare the judgments of distances formed by sight, with our experience or information, that we learn by degrees, in this way, to form a more accurate judgment of the distance of terrestrial objects, than we could do by any of the means before mentioned. An object placed upon the top of a high building, appears much less than when placed upon the ground, at the same distance. When it stands upon the ground, the intervening tract of ground serves as a sign of its distance ; and the distance, together with the visible magnitude, serves as a sign of its real magnitude. But when the object is placed on high, this sign of its distance is taken away: the remaining signs lead us to place it at a less distance ; and this less distance, together with the visible magnitude, becomes a sign of a less real magnitude.

The two first means we have mentioned, would never of themselves make a visible object appear above a hundred and fifty, or two hundred feet, distant ; because, beyond that there is no sensible change, either of the conformation of the eyes, or of the inclination of their axes. The third mean is but a vague and undeterminate sign, when applied to distances above two or three hundred feet, unless we know the real colour and figure of the object ; and the fifth mean, to be afterwards mentioned, can only be applied to objects which are familiar, or whose real magnitude is known. Hence it follows, that, when unknown objects, upon or near the surface of the earth, are perceived to be at the distance of some miles, it is always by this fourth mean that we are led to that conclusion.

Dr Smith hath observed, very justly, that the known distance of the terrestrial objects which terminate our view, makes that part of the sky which is towards the horizon appear more distant than that which is towards the zenith. Hence it comes to pass, that the apparent figure of the sky is not that of a hemisphere, but rather a less segment of a sphere. And, hence, likewise, it comes to pass, that the diameter of the sun or moon, or the distance between two fixed stars, seen contiguous to a hill, or to any distant terrestrial object, appears much greater than when no such object strikes the eye at the same time.

These observations have been sufficiently explained and confirmed by Dr Smith. I beg leave to add, that, when the visible horizon is terminated by very distant objects, the celestial vault seems to be enlarged in all its dimensions. When I view it from a confined street or lane, it bears some proportion to the buildings that surround me ; but, when I view it from a large plain, terminated on all hands by hills which rise one above another to the distance of twenty miles from the eye, methinks I see a new heaven, whose magnificence declares the greatness of its Author, and puts every human edifice out of countenance ; for now the lofty spires and the gorgeous palaces shrink into nothing before it, and bear no more proportion to the celestial dome than their makers bear to its Maker.

5. There remains another mean by which we perceive the distance of visible objects— and that is, the diminution of their visible or apparent magnitude. By experience, I know what figure a man, or any other known object, makes to my eye at the distance of ten feet—I perceive the gradual and proportional diminution of this visible figure, as the distance of twenty, forty, a hundred feet, and at greater distances, until it vanish altogether. Hence a certain visible magnitude of a known object becomes the sign of a certain determinate distance, and carries along with it the conception and belief of that distance.

In this process of the mind, the sign is not a sensation ; it is an original perception. We perceive the visible figure and visible magnitude of the object, by the original powers of vision ; but the visible figure is used only as a sign of the real figure, and the visible magnitude is used only as a sign either of the distance, or of the real magnitude, of the object ; and, therefore, these original perceptions, like other mere signs, pass through the mind without any attention or reflection.

This last mean of perceiving the distance of known objects, serves to explain some very remarkable phænomena in optics, which would otherwise appear very mysterious. When we view objects of known dimensions through optical glasses, there is no other mean left of determining their distance, but this fifth. Hence it follows, that known objects seen through glasses, must seem to be brought nearer, in proportion to the magnifying power of the glass, or to be removed to a greater distance, in proportion to the diminishing power of the glass.

If a man who had never before seen objects through a telescope, were told that the telescope, which he is about to use, magnifies the diameter of the object ten times ; when he looks through this telescope at a man six feet high, what would he expect to see? Surely he would very naturally expect to see a giant sixty feet high. But he sees no such thing. The man appears no more than six feet high, and consequently no bigger than he really is ; but he appears ten times nearer than he is. The telescope indeed magnifies the image of this man upon the *retina* ten times in diameter, and must, therefore, magnify his visible figure in the same proportion ; and, as we have been accustomed to see him of this visible magnitude when he was ten times nearer than he is presently,* and in no other case, this visible magnitude, therefore, suggests the conception and belief of that distance of the object with which it hath been always connected. We have been accustomed to conceive this amplification of the visible figure of a known object, only as the effect or sign of its being brought nearer : and we have annexed a certain determinate distance to every degree of visible magnitude of the object ; and, therefore, any particular degree of visible magnitude, whether seen by the naked eye or by glasses, brings along with it the conception and belief of the distance which corresponds to it. This is the reason why a telescope seems not to magnify known objects, but to bring them nearer to the eye.

When we look through a pin-hole, or a single microscope, at an object which is half an inch from the eye, the picture of the object upon the *retina* is not enlarged, but only rendered distinct ; neither is the visible figure enlarged : yet the object appears to the eye twelve or fourteen times more distant, and as many times larger in diameter, than it really is. Such a telescope as we have mentioned amplifies the image on the *retina*, and the visible figure of the object, ten times in diameter, and yet makes it seem no bigger, but only ten times nearer. These appearances had been long observed by the writers on optics ; they tortured their invention to find the causes of them from optical principles ; but in vain : they must be resolved into habits of perception, which are acquired by custom, but are apt to be mistaken for original perceptions. The Bishop of Cloyne first furnished the world with the proper key for opening up these mysterious appearances ; but he made considerable mistakes in the application of it. Dr Smith, in his elaborate and judicious treatise of "Optics," hath applied it

* See note * p. 96, a.—H.

to the apparent distance of objects seen with glasses, and to the apparent figure of the heavens, with such happy success, that there can be no more doubt about the causes of these phænomena.

Section XXIII.

The distance of objects from the eye is the most important lesson in vision. Many others are easily learned in consequence of it. The distance of the object, joined with its visible magnitude, is a sign of its real magnitude : and the distance of the several parts of an object, joined with its visible figure, becomes a sign of its real figure. Thus, when I look at a globe which stands before me, by the original powers of sight I perceive only something of a circular form, variously coloured. The visible figure hath no distance from the eye, no convexity, nor hath it three dimensions ; even its length and breadth are incapable of being measured by inches, feet, or other linear measures. But, when I have learned to perceive the distance of every part of this object from the eye, this perception gives it convexity, and a spherical figure ; and adds a third dimension to that which had but two before. The distance of the whole object makes me likewise perceive the real magnitude ; for, being accustomed to observe how an inch or a foot of length affects the eye at that distance, I plainly perceive by my eye the linear dimensions of the globe, and can affirm with certainty that its diameter is about one foot and three inches.

It was shewn in the 7th section of this chapter that the visible figure of a body may, by mathematical reasoning, be inferred from its real figure, distance, and position, with regard to the eye : in like manner, we may, by mathematical reasoning, from the visible figure, together with the distance of the several parts of it from the eye, infer the real figure and position. But this last inference is not commonly made by mathematical reasoning, nor, indeed, by reasoning of any kind, but by custom.

The original appearance which the colour of an object makes to the eye, is a sensation for which we have no name, because it is used merely as a sign, and is never made an object of attention in common life : but this appearance, according to the different circumstances, signifies various things. If a piece of cloth, of one uniform colour, is laid so that part of it is in the sun, and part in the shade, the appearance of colour, in

o

these different parts, is very different: yet we perceive the colour to be the same; we interpret the variety of appearance as a sign of light and shade, and not as a sign of real difference in colour. But, if the eye could be so far deceived as not to perceive the difference of light in the two parts of the cloth, we should, in that case, interpret the variety of appearance to signify a variety of colour in the parts of the cloth.

Again, if we suppose a piece of cloth placed as before, but having the shaded part so much brighter in the colour that it gives the same appearance to the eye as the more enlightened part, the sameness of appearance will here be interpreted to signify a variety of colour, because we shall make allowance for the effect of light and shade.

When the real colour of an object is known, the appearance of it indicates, in some circumstances, the degree of light or shade; in others, the colour of the circumambient bodies, whose rays are reflected by it; and, in other circumstances, it indicates the distance or proximity of the object—as was observed in the last section; and by means of these, many other things are suggested to the mind. Thus, an unusual appearance in the colour of familiar objects may be the diagnostic of a disease in the spectator. The appearance of things in my room may indicate sunshine or cloudy weather, the earth covered with snow or blackened with rain. It hath been observed, that the colour of the sky, in a piece of painting, may indicate the country of the painter, because the Italian sky is really of a different colour from the Flemish.

It was already observed, that the original and acquired perceptions which we have by our senses, are the language of nature to man, which, in many respects, hath a great affinity to human languages. The instances which we have given of acquired perceptions, suggest this affinity—that, as, in human languages, ambiguities are often found, so this language of nature in our acquired perceptions is not exempted from them. We have seen, in vision particularly, that the same appearance to the eye, may, in different circumstances, indicate different things. Therefore, when the circumstances are unknown upon which the interpretation of the signs depends, their meaning must be ambiguous; and when the circumstances are mistaken, the meaning of the signs must also be mistaken.

This is the case in all the phænomena which we call *fallacies of the senses*; and particularly in those which are called *fallacies in vision*. The appearance of things to the eye always corresponds to the fixed laws of Nature; therefore, if we speak properly, there is no fallacy in the senses. Nature always speaketh the same language,

and useth the same signs in the same circumstances: but we sometimes mistake the meaning of the signs, either through ignorance of the laws of Nature, or through ignorance of the circumstances which attend the signs.*

To a man unacquainted with the principles of optics, almost every experiment that is made with the prism, with the magic lanthorn, with the telescope, with the microscope, seems to produce some fallacy in vision. Even the appearance of a common mirror, to one altogether unacquainted with the effects of it, would seem most remarkably fallacious. For how can a man be more imposed upon, than in seeing that before him which is really behind him? How can he be more imposed upon, than in being made to see himself several yards removed from himself? Yet children, even before they can speak their mother-tongue, learn not to be deceived by these appearances. These, as well as all the other surprising appearances produced by optical glasses, are a part of the visual language, and, to those who understand the laws of Nature concerning light and colours, are in nowise fallacious, but have a distinct and true meaning.

Section XXIV.

The objects of human knowledge are innumerable; but the channels by which it is conveyed to the mind are few. Among these, the perception of external things by our senses, and the informations which we receive upon human testimony, are not the least considerable; and so remarkable is the analogy between these two, and the analogy between the principles of the mind which are subservient to the one and those which are subservient to the other, that, without further apology, we shall consider them together.

In the testimony of Nature given by the senses, as well as in human testimony given by language, things are signified to us by signs: and in one as well as the other, the mind, either by original principles or by custom, passes from the sign to the conception and belief of the things signified.

We have distinguished our perceptions

---

* This is the doctrine of Aristotle; who holds that the senses never deceive us in relation to their proper objects.—H.

† Compare Mr Stewart's "Elements," vol I, ch ii, § 4, p. 217. Second edition. Campbell "On Miracles," Part I., § 1. Smith's "Theory of Moral Sentiment," vol. II., p. 382. Sixth edition.—H.

into original and acquired ; and language, into natural and artificial. Between acquired perception and artificial language, there is a great analogy ; but still a greater between original perception and natural language.

The signs in original perception are sensations, of which Nature hath given us a great variety, suited to the variety of the things signified by them. Nature hath established a real connection between the signs and the things signified; and Nature hath also taught us the interpretation of the signs—so that, previous to experience, the sign suggests the thing signified, and create the belief of it.

The signs in natural language are features of the face, gestures of the body, and modulations of the voice ; the variety of which is suited to the variety of the things signified by them. Nature hath established a real connection between these signs, and the thoughts and dispositions of the mind which are signified by them ; and Nature hath taught us the interpretation of these signs; so that, previous to experience, the signs suggest the thing signified, and create the belief of it.

A man in company, without doing good or evil, without uttering an articulate sound, may behave himself gracefully, civilly, politely ; or, on the contrary, meanly, rudely, and impertinently. We see the dispositions of his mind by their natural signs in his countenance and behaviour, in the same manner as we perceive the figure and other qualities of bodies by the sensations which nature hath connected with them.

The signs in the natural language of the human countenance and behaviour, as well as the signs in our original perceptions, have the same signification in all climates and in all nations ; and the skill of interpreting them is not acquired, but innate.

In acquired perception, the signs are either sensations, or things which we perceive by means of sensations. The connection between the sign and the thing signified, is established by nature ; and we discover this connection by experience ; but not without the aid of our original perceptions, or of those which we have already acquired. After this connection is discovered, the sign, in like manner as in original perception, always suggests the things signified, and creates the belief of it.

In artificial language, the signs are articulate sounds, whose connection with the things signified by them, is established by the will of men; and, in learning our mother tongue, we discover this connection by experience ; but not without the aid of natural language, or of what we had before attained of artificial language. And, after this connection is discovered, the sign, as in natural language, always suggests the thing signified, and creates the belief of it.

Our original perceptions are few, compared with the acquired ; but, without the former, we could not possibly attain the latter. In like manner, natural language is scanty, compared with artificial ; but, without the former, we could not possibly attain the latter.

Our original perceptions, as well as the natural language of human features and gestures, must be resolved into particular princip es of the human constitution. Thus, it is by one particular principle of our constitution that certain features express anger ; and, by another particular principle, that certain features express benevolence. It is, in like manner, by one particular principle of our constitution that a certain sensation signifies hardness in the body which I handle ; and it is by another particular principle that a certain sensation signifies motion in that body.

But our acquired perceptions, and the information we receive by means of artificial language, must be resolved into general principles of the human constitution. When a painter perceives that this picture is the work of Raphael, that the work of Titian ; a jeweller, that this is a true diamond, that a counterfeit ; a sailor, that this is a ship of five hundred ton, that of four hundred ; these different acquired perceptions are produced by the same general principles of the human mind, which have a different operation in the same person according as they are variously applied, and in different persons according to the diversity of their education and manner of life. In like manner, when certain articulate sounds convey to my mind the knowledge of the battle of Pharsalia, and others, the knowledge of the battle of Poltowa—when a Frenchman and an Englishman receive the same information by different articulate sounds—the signs used in these different cases, produce the knowledge and belief of the things signified, by means of the same general principles of the human constitution.

Now, if we compare the general principles of our constitution, which fit us for receiving information from our fellow-creatures by language, with the general principles which fit us for acquiring the perception of things by our senses, we shall find them to be very similar in their nature and manner of operation.

When we begin to learn our mother-tongue, we perceive, by the help of natural language, that they who speak to us use certain sounds to express certain things ; we imitate the same sounds when we would

o 2

express the same things; and find that we are understood.

But here a difficulty occurs which merits our attention, because the solution of it leads to some original principles of the human mind, which are of great importance, and of very extensive influence. We know by experience that men *have* used such words to express such things; but all experience is of the *past*, and can, of itself, give no notion or belief of what is *future*. How come we, then, to believe, and to rely upon it with assurance, that men, who have it in their power to do otherwise, will continue to use the same words when they think the same things? Whence comes this knowledge and belief—this foresight, we ought rather to call it—of the future and voluntary actions of our fellow-creatures? Have they promised that they will never impose upon us by equivocation or falsehood? No, they have not. And, if they had, this would not solve the difficulty; for such promise must be expressed by words or by other signs; and, before we can rely upon it, we must be assured that they put the usual meaning upon the signs which express that promise. No man of common sense ever thought of taking a man's own word for his honesty; and it is evident that we take his veracity for granted when we lay any stress upon his word or promise. I might add, that this reliance upon the declarations and testimony of men is found in children long before they know what a promise is.

There is, therefore, in the human mind an early anticipation, neither derived from experience, nor from reason, nor from any compact or promise, that our fellow-creatures will use the same signs in language, when they have the same sentiments.

This is, in reality, a kind of prescience of human actions; and it seems to me to be an original principle of the human constitution, without which we should be incapable of language, and consequently incapable of instruction.

The wise and beneficent Author of Nature, who intended that we should be social creatures, and that we should receive the greatest and most important part of our knowledge by the information of others, hath, for these purposes, implanted in our natures two principles that tally with each other.

The first of these principles is, a propensity to speak truth, and to use the signs of language so as to convey our real sentiments. This principle has a powerful operation, even in the greatest liars; for where they lie once, they speak truth a hundred times. Truth is always uppermost, and is the natural issue of the mind. It requires no art or training, no inducement

or temptation, but only that we yield to a natural impulse. Lying, on the contrary, is doing violence to our nature; and is never practised, even by the worst men, without some temptation. Speaking truth is like using our natural food, which we would do from appetite, although it answered no end; but lying is like taking physic, which is nauseous to the taste, and which no man takes but for some end which he cannot otherwise attain.

If it should be objected, That men may be influenced by moral or political considerations to speak truth, and, therefore, that their doing so is no proof of such an original principle as we have mentioned—I answer, First, That moral or political considerations can have no influence until we arrive at years of understanding and reflection; and it is certain, from experience, that children keep to truth invariably, before they are capable of being influenced by such considerations. Secondly, When we are influenced by moral or political considerations, we must be conscious of that influence, and capable of perceiving it upon reflection. Now, when I reflect upon my actions most attentively, I am not conscious that, in speaking truth, I am influenced on ordinary occasions by any motive, moral or political. I find that truth is always at the door of my lips, and goes forth spontaneously, if not held back. It requires neither good nor bad intention to bring it forth, but only that I be artless and undesigning. There may indeed be temptations to falsehood, which would be too strong for the natural principle of veracity, unaided by principles of honour or virtue; but where there is no such temptation, we speak truth by instinct—and this instinct is the principle I have been explaining.

By this instinct, a real connection is formed between our words and our thoughts, and thereby the former become fit to be signs of the latter, which they could not otherwise be. And although this connection is broken in every instance of lying and equivocation, yet these instances being comparatively few, the authority of human testimony is only weakened by them, but not destroyed.

Another original principle implanted in us by the Supreme Being, is a disposition to confide in the veracity of others, and to believe what they tell us. This is the counterpart to the former; and, as that may be called *the principle of veracity*, we shall, for want of a more proper name, call this *the principle of credulity*. It is unlimited in children, until they meet with instances of deceit and falsehood; and it retains a very considerable degree of strength through life.

If Nature had left the mind of the speaker

in *æquilibrio*, without any inclination to the side of truth more than to that of falsehood, children would lie as often as they speak truth, until reason was so far ripened as to suggest the imprudence of lying, or conscience, as to suggest its immorality. And if Nature had left the mind of the hearer *in æquilibrio*, without any inclination to the side of belief more than to that of disbelief, we should take no man's word until we had positive evidence that he spoke truth. His testimony would, in this case, have no more authority than his dreams; which may be true or false, but no man is disposed to believe them, on this account, that they were dreamed. It is evident that, in the matter of testimony, the balance of human judgment is by nature inclined to the side of belief; and turns to that side of itself, when there is nothing put into the opposite scale. If it was not so, no proposition that is uttered in discourse would be believed, until it was examined and tried by reason; and most men would be unable to find reasons for believing the thousandth part of what is told them. Such distrust and incredulity would deprive us of the greatest benefits of society, and place us in a worse condition than that of savages.

Children, on this supposition, would be absolutely incredulous, and, therefore, absolutely incapable of instruction: those who had little knowledge of human life, and of the manners and characters of men, would be in the next degree incredulous: and the most credulous men would be those of greatest experience, and of the deepest penetration; because, in many cases, they would be able to find good reasons for believing testimony, which the weak and the ignorant could not discover.

In a word, if credulity were the effect of reasoning and experience, it must grow up and gather strength, in the same proportion as reason and experience do. But, if it is the gift of Nature, it will be strongest in childhood, and limited and restrained by experience; and the most superficial view of human life shews, that the last is really the case, and not the first.[*]

It is the intention of Nature, that we should be carried in arms before we are able to walk upon our legs; and it is likewise the intention of Nature, that our belief should be guided by the authority and reason of others, before it can be guided by our own reason. The weakness of the infant, and the natural affection of the mother, plainly indicate the former; and the natural credulity of youth, and authority of age, as plainly indicate the latter. The infant, by

proper nursing and care, acquires strength to walk without support. Reason hath likewise her infancy, when she must be carried in arms: then she leans entirely upon authority, by natural instinct, as if she was conscious of her own weakness; and, without this support, she becomes vertiginous. When brought to maturity by proper culture, she begins to feel her own strength, and leans less upon the reason of others; she learns to suspect testimony in some cases, and to disbelieve it in others; and sets bounds to that authority to which she was at first entirely subject. But still to the end of life, she finds a necessity of borrowing light from testimony, where she has none within herself, and of leaning, in some degree, upon the reason of others, where she is conscious of her own imbecility.

And as, in many instances, Reason, even in her maturity, borrows aid from testimony, so in others she mutually gives aid to it, and strengthens its authority. For, as we find good reason to reject testimony in some cases, so in others we find good reason to rely upon it with perfect security, in our most important concerns. The character, the number, and the disinterestedness of witnesses, the impossibility of collusion, and the incredibility of their concurring in their testimony without collusion, may give an irresistible strength to testimony, compared to which its native and intrinsic authority is very inconsiderable.

Having now considered the general principles of the human mind which fit us for receiving information from our fellow-creatures, by the means of language, let us next consider the general principles which fit us for receiving the information of Nature by our acquired perceptions.

It is undeniable, and indeed is acknowledged by all, that when we have found two things to have been constantly conjoined in the course of nature, the appearance of one of them is immediately followed by the conception and belief of the other. The former becomes a natural sign of the latter; and the knowledge of their constant conjunction in time past, whether got by experience or otherwise, is sufficient to make us rely with assurance upon the continuance of that conjunction.

This process of the human mind is so familiar that we never think of inquiring into the principles upon which it is founded. We are apt to conceive it as a self-evident truth, that what is to come must be similar to what is past. Thus, if a certain degree of cold freezes water to-day, and has been known to do so in all time past, we have no doubt but the same degree of cold will freeze water to-morrow, or a year hence. That this is a truth which all men believe as

---

[*] See, *contra*, Priestley's "Examination," p. 85. "Brown's Lect." lect. lxxxiv.—H.

soon as they understand it, I readily admit; but the question is, Whence does its evidence arise? Not from comparing the ideas, surely. For, when I compare the idea of cold with that of water hardened into a transparent solid body, I can perceive no connection between them: no man can shew the one to be the necessary effect of the other; no man can give a shadow of reason why Nature hath conjoined them. But do we not learn their conjunction from experience? True; experience informs us that they have been conjoined in time *past*; but no man ever had any experience of what is *future*: and this is the very question to be resolved, How we come to believe that the *future* will be like the *past*? Hath the Author of nature promised this? Or were we admitted to his council, when he established the present laws of nature, and determined the time of their continuance. No, surely. Indeed, if we believe that there is a wise and good Author of nature, we may see a good reason why he should continue the same laws of nature, and the same connections of things, for a long time: because, if he did otherwise, we could learn nothing from what is past, and all our experience would be of no use to us. But, though this consideration, when we come to the use of reason, may confirm our belief of the continuance of the present course of nature, is certain that it did not give rise to this belief; for children and idiots have this belief as soon as they know that fire will burn them. It must, therefore, be the effect of instinct, not of reason.[*]

The wise Author of our nature intended, that a great and necessary part of our knowledge should be derived from experience, before we are capable of reasoning, and he hath provided means perfectly adequate to this intention. For, First, He governs nature by fixed laws, so that we find innumerable connections of things which continue from age to age. Without this stability of the course of nature, there could be no experience; or, it would be a false guide, and lead us into error and mischief. If there were not a principle of veracity in the human mind, men's words would not be signs of their thoughts: and if there were no regularity in the course of nature, no one thing could be a natural sign of another. Secondly, He hath implanted in human minds an original principle by which we believe and expect the continuance of the course of nature, and the continuance of those connec-

tions which we have observed in time past. It is by this general principle of our nature, that, when two things have been found connected in time past, the appearance of the one produces the belief of the other.

I think the ingenious author of the "Treatise of Human Nature" first observed, That our belief of the continuance of the laws of nature cannot be founded either upon knowledge or probability: but, far from conceiving it to be an original principle of the mind, he endeavours to account for it from his favourite hypothesis, That belief is nothing but a certain degree of vivacity in the idea of the thing believed. I made a remark upon this curious hypothesis in the second chapter and shall now make another.

The belief which we have in perception, is a belief of the present existence of the object; that which we have in memory, is a belief of its past existence; the belief of which we are now speaking is a belief of its future existence; and in imagination there is no belief at all. Now, I would gladly know of this author, how one degree of vivacity fixes the existence of the object to the present moment; another carries it back to time past; a third, taking a contrary direction, carries it into futurity; and a fourth carries it out of existence altogether. Suppose, for instance, that I see the sun rising out of the sea: I remember to have seen him rise yesterday; I believe he will rise to-morrow near the same place; I can likewise imagine him rising in that place, without any belief at all. Now, according to this sceptical hypothesis, this perception, this memory, this foreknowledge, and this imagination, are all the same idea, diversified only by different degrees of vivacity. The perception of the sun rising is the most lively idea; the memory of his rising yesterday is the same idea a little more faint; the belief of his rising to-morrow is the same idea yet fainter; and the imagination of his rising is still the same idea, but faintest of all. One is apt to think, that this idea might gradually pass through all possible degrees of vivacity without stirring out of its place. But, if we think so, we deceive ourselves; for no sooner does it begin to grow languid than it moves backward into time past. Supposing this to be granted, we expect, at least, that, as it moves backward by the decay of its vivacity, the more that vivacity decays it will go back the farther, until it remove quite out of sight. But here we are deceived again; for there is a certain period of this declining vivacity, when, as if it had met an elastic obstacle in its motion backward, it suddenly rebounds from the past to the future, without taking the present in its way. And now, having got

---

[*] Compare Stewart's "Elements," vol. I., chap. iv., § 5, p. 205, sixth edition; "Philosophical Essays," p 74, sqq., fourth edition; Royer Collard, in Jouffroy's "Oeuvres de Reid," t. IV., p. 270, sqq.; with Priestley's "Examination," p. 86, sqq. I merely refer to works relative to *Reid's* doctrine.—H.

into the regions of futurity, we are apt to think that it has room enough to spend all its remaining vigour: but still we are deceived; for, by another sprightly bound, it mounts up into the airy region of imagination. So that ideas, in the gradual declension of their vivacity, seem to imitate the inflection of verbs in grammar. They begin with the present, and proceed in order to the preterite, the future, and the indefinite. This article of the sceptical creed is indeed so full of mystery, on whatever side we view it, that they who hold that creed are very injuriously charged with incredulity; for, to me, it appears to require as much faith as that of St Athanasius.

However, we agree with the author of the "Treatise of Human Nature," in this, That our belief of the continuance of nature's laws is not derived from reason. It is an instinctive prescience of the operations of nature, very like to that prescience of human actions which makes us rely upon the testimony of our fellow-creatures; and as, without the latter, we should be incapable of receiving information from men by language, so, without the former, we should be incapable of receiving the information of nature by means of experience.

All our knowledge of nature beyond our original perceptions, is got by experience, and consists in the interpretation of natural signs. The constancy of nature's laws connects the sign with the thing signified; and, by the natural principle just now explained, we rely upon the continuance of the connections which experience hath discovered; and thus the appearance of the sign is followed by the belief of the thing signified.

Upon this principle of our constitution, not only acquired perception, but all inductive reasoning, and all our reasoning from analogy, is grounded; and, therefore, for want of another name, we shall beg leave to call it *the inductive principle*. It is from the force of this principle that we immediately assent to that axiom upon which all our knowledge of nature is built, That effects of the same kind must have the same cause; for *effects* and *causes*, in the operations of nature, mean nothing but signs and the things signified by them. We perceive no proper causality or efficiency in any natural cause; but only a connection established by the course of nature between it and what is called its effect. Antecedently to all reasoning, we have, by our constitution, an anticipation that there is a fixed and steady course of nature: and we have an eager desire to discover this course of nature. We attend to every conjunction of things which presents itself, and expect the continuance of that conjunction. And, when such a conjunction has been often

observed, we conceive the things to be naturally connected, and the appearance of one, without any reasoning or reflection, carries along with it the belief of the other.

If any reader should imagine that the inductive principle may be resolved into what philosophers usually call the *association of ideas*, let him observe, that, by this principle, natural signs are not associated with the idea only, but with the belief of the things signified. Now, this can with no propriety be called an association of ideas, unless ideas and belief be one and the same thing. A child has found the prick of a pin conjoined with pain; hence he believes, and knows, that these things are naturally connected; he knows that the one will always follow the other. If any man will call this only an association of ideas, I dispute not about words, but I think he speaks very improperly. For, if we express it in plain English, it is a prescience that things which he hath found conjoined in time past, will be conjoined in time to come. And this prescience is not the effect of reasoning, but of an original principle of human nature, which I have called *the inductive principle*.*

This principle, like that of credulity, is unlimited in infancy, and gradually restrained and regulated as we grow up. It leads us often into mistakes; but is of infinite advantage upon the whole. By it, the child once burnt shuns the fire; by it, he likewise runs away from the surgeon by whom he was inoculated. It is better that he should do the last, than that he should not do the first.

But the mistakes we are led into by these two natural principles, are of a different kind. Men sometimes lead us into mistakes, when we perfectly understand their language, by speaking lies. But Nature never misleads us in this way: her language is always true; and it is only by misinterpreting it that we fall into error. There must be many accidental conjunctions of things, as well as natural connections; and the former are apt to be mistaken for the latter. Thus, in the instance above mentioned, the child connected the pain of inoculation with the surgeon; whereas it was really connected with the incision only. Philosophers, and men of science, are not exempted from such mistakes; indeed, all false reasoning in philosophy is owing to them; it is drawn from experience and analogy, as well as just reasoning, otherwise it could have no verisimilitude; but the one is an unskilful and rash,

* This objection to the solution, on the ground of *association*, is unsound. It is generally admitted that the term "Association of Ideas" is inadequate; the law of association extending not only to Ideas, but to all our mental modifications.—H

the other a just and legitimate interpretation of natural signs. If a child, or a man of common understanding, were put to interpret a book of science, written in his mother-tongue, how many blunders and mistakes would he be apt to fall into? Yet he knows as much of this language as is necessary for his manner of life.

The language of Nature is the universal study; and the students are of different classes. Brutes, idiots, and children employ themselves in this study, and owe to it all their acquired perceptions. Men of common understanding make a greater progress, and learn, by a small degree of reflection, many things of which children are ignorant.

Philosophers fill up the highest form in this school, and are critics in the language of nature. All these different classes have one teacher—Experience, enlightened by the inductive principle. Take away the light of this inductive principle, and Experience is as blind as a mole: she may, indeed, feel what is present, and what immediately touches her; but she sees nothing that is either before or behind, upon the right hand or upon the left, future or past.

The rules of inductive reasoning, or of a just interpretation of Nature, as well as the fallacies by which we are apt to misinterpret her language, have been, with wonderful sagacity, delineated by the great genius of Lord Bacon: so that his "*Novum Organum*" may justly be called "A Grammar of the Language of Nature." It adds greatly to the merit of this work, and atones for its defects, that, at the time it was written, the world had not seen any tolerable model of inductive reasoning,* from which the rules of it might be copied. The arts of poetry and eloquence were grown up to perfection when Aristotle described them; but the art of interpreting Nature was yet *in embryo* when Bacon delineated its manly features and proportions. Aristotle drew his rules from the best models of those arts that have yet appeared; but the best models of inductive reasoning that have yet appeared, which I take to be the third book of the "Principia," and the "Optics," of Newton, were drawn from Bacon's rules. The purpose of all those rules, is to teach us to distinguish seeming or apparent connections of things, in the course of nature, from such as are real.

They that are unskilful in inductive reasoning, are more apt to fall into error in their *reasonings* from the phænomena of nature than in their *acquired perceptions;* because we often reason from a few instances, and thereby are apt to mistake accidental conjunctions of things for natural

connections: but that habit of passing, without reasoning, from the sign to the thing signified, which constitutes acquired perception, must be learned by many instances or experiments; and the number of experiments serves to disjoin those things which have been accidentally conjoined, as well as to confirm our belief of natural connections.

From the time that children begin to use their hands, Nature directs them to handle everything over and over, to look at it while they handle it, and to put it in various positions, and at various distances from the eye. We are apt to excuse this as a childish diversion, because they must be doing something, and have not reason to entertain themselves in a more manly way. But, if we think more justly, we shall find, that they are engaged in the most serious and important study; and, if they had all the reason of a philosopher, they could not be more properly employed. For it is this childish employment that enables them to make the proper use of their eyes. They are thereby every day acquiring habits of perception, which are of greater importance than anything we can teach them. The original perceptions which Nature gave them are few, and insufficient for the purposes of life; and, therefore, she made them capable of acquiring many more perceptions by habit. And, to complete her work, she hath given them an unwearied assiduity in applying to the exercises by which those perceptions are acquired.

This is the education which Nature gives to her children. And, since we have fallen upon this subject, we may add, that another part of Nature's education is, That, by the course of things, children must often exert all their muscular force, and employ all their ingenuity, in order to gratify their curiosity, and satisfy their little appetites. What they desire is only to be obtained at the expense of labour and patience, and many disappointments. By the exercise of body and mind necessary for satisfying their desires, they acquire agility, strength, and dexterity in their motions, as well as health and vigour to their constitutions; they learn patience and perseverance; they learn to bear pain without dejection, and disappointment without despondence. The education of Nature is most perfect in savages, who have no other tutor; and we see that, in the quickness of all their senses, in the agility of their motions, in the hardiness of their constitutions, and in the strength of their minds to bear hunger, thirst, pain, and disappointment, they commonly far exceed the civilized. A most ingenious writer, on this account, seems to prefer the savage life to that of society.

---

* Yet Galileo was anterior to Bacon.—H.

But the education of Nature could never of itself produce a Rousseau. It is the intention of Nature that human education should be joined to her institution, in order to form the man. And she hath fitted us for human education, by the natural principles of imitation and credulity, which discover themselves almost in infancy, as well as by others which are of later growth.

When the education which we receive from men, does not give scope to the education of Nature, it is wrong directed ; it tends to hurt our faculties of perception, and to enervate both the body and mind. Nature hath her way of rearing men, as she hath of curing their diseases. The art of medicine is to follow Nature, to imitate and to assist her in the cure of diseases ; and the art of education is to follow Nature, to assist and to imitate her in her way of rearing men. The ancient inhabitants of the Baleares followed Nature in the manner of teaching their children to be good archers, when they hung their dinner aloft by a thread, and left the younkers to bring it down by their skill in archery.

The education of Nature, without any more human care than is necessary to preserve life, makes a perfect savage. Human education, joined to that of Nature, may make a good citizen, a skilful artisan, or a well-bred man ; but reason and reflection must superadd their tutory, in order to produce a Rousseau, a Bacon, or a Newton.

Notwithstanding the innumerable errors committed in human education, there is hardly any education so bad as to be worse than none. And I apprehend that, if even Rousseau were to choose whether to educate a son among the French, the Italians, the Chinese, or among the Eskimaux, he would not give the preference to the last.

When Reason is properly employed, she will confirm the documents of Nature, which are always true and wholesome ; she will distinguish, in the documents of human education, the good from the bad, rejecting the last with modesty, and adhering to the first with reverence.

Most men continue all their days to be just what Nature and human education made them. Their manners, their opinions, their virtues, and their vices, are all got by habit, imitation, and instruction ; and reason has little or no share in forming them.

CHAPTER VII.

Conclusion.

CONTAINING REFLECTIONS UPON THE OPINIONS OF PHILOSOPHERS ON THIS SUBJECT.

THERE are two ways in which men may

form their notions and opinions concerning the mind, and concerning its powers and operations. The first is the only way that leads to truth ; but it is narrow and rugged, and few have entered upon it. The second is broad and smooth, and hath been much beaten, not only by the vulgar, but even by philosophers ; it is sufficient for common life, and is well adapted to the purposes of the poet and orator : but, in philosophical disquisitions concerning the mind, it leads to error and delusion.

We may call the first of these ways, *the way of reflection.* When the operations of the mind are exerted, we are conscious of them ; and it is in our power to attend to them, and to reflect upon them, until they become familiar objects of thought. This is the only way in which we can form just and accurate notions of those operations. But this attention and reflection is so difficult to man, surrounded on all hands by external objects which constantly solicit his attention, that it has been very little practised, even by philosophers. In the course of this inquiry, we have had many occasions to shew how little attention hath been given to the most familiar operations of the senses.

The second, and the most common way, in which men form their opinions concerning the mind and its operations, we may call *the way of analogy.* There is nothing in the course of nature so singular, but we can find some resemblance, or at least some analogy, between it and other things with which we are acquainted. The mind naturally delights in hunting after such analogies, and attends to them with pleasure. From them, poetry and wit derive a great part of their charms ; and eloquence, not a little of its persuasive force.

Besides the pleasure we receive from analogies, they are of very considerable use, both to facilitate the conception of things, when they are not easily apprehended without such a handle, and to lead us to probable conjectures about their nature and qualities, when we want the means of more direct and immediate knowledge. When I consider that the planet Jupiter, in like manner as the earth, rolls round his own axis, and revolves round the sun, and that he is enlightened by several secondary planets, as the earth is enlightened by the moon, I am apt to conjecture, from analogy, that, as the earth by these means is fitted to be the habitation of various orders of animals, so the planet Jupiter is, by the like means, fitted for the same purpose : and, having no argument more direct and conclusive to determine me in this point, I yield, to this analogical reasoning, a degree of assent proportioned to its strength. When I observe that the potato plant very much resembles the *solanum* in its flower and fructification, and am informed that the last is poisonous, I am apt from analogy to have some suspicion of the former : but, in this case, I have access to more direct and certain evidence ; and, therefore, ought not to trust to analogy, which would lead me into an error.

Arguments from analogy are always at hand, and grow up spontaneously in a fruitful imagination ; while arguments that are more direct and more conclusive often require painful attention and application : and therefore mankind in general have been very much disposed to trust to the former. If one attentively examines the systems of the ancient philosophers, either concerning the material world, or concerning the mind, he will find them to be built solely upon the foundation of analogy. Lord Bacon first delineated the strict and severe method of induction ; since his time, it has been applied with very happy success in some parts of natural philosophy— and hardly in anything else. But there is no subject in which mankind are so much disposed to trust to the analogical way of thinking and reasoning, as in what concerns the mind and its operations ; because, to form clear and distinct notions of those operations in the direct and proper way, and to reason about them, requires a habit of attentive reflection, of which few are capable, and which, even by those few, cannot be attained without much pains and labour.

Every man is apt to form his notions of things difficult to be apprehended, or less familiar, from their analogy to things which are more familiar. Thus, if a man bred to the seafaring life, and accustomed to think and talk only of matters relating to navigation, enters into discourse upon any other subject, it is well known that the language and the notions proper to his own profession are infused into every subject, and all things are measured by the rules of navigation ; and, if he should take it into his head to philosophize concerning the faculties of the mind, it cannot be doubted but he would draw his notions from the fabric of his ship, and would find in the mind, sails, masts, rudder, and compass.*

Sensible objects, of one kind or other, do no less occupy and engross the rest of mankind, than things relating to navigation the seafaring man. For a considerable part of life, we can think of nothing but the objects of sense ; and, to attend to objects of another nature, so as to form clear and distinct notions of them, is no easy matter, even after we come to years of reflection.

The condition of mankind, therefore, affords good reason to apprehend that their language, and their common notions concerning the mind and its operations, will be analogical, and derived from the objects of sense ; and that these analogies will be apt to impose upon philosophers, as well as upon the vulgar, and to lead them to materialize the mind and its faculties : and experience abundantly confirms the truth of this.

How generally men of all nations, and in all ages of the world, have conceived the soul, or thinking principle in man, to be some subtile matter, like breath or wind, the names given to it almost in all languages sufficiently testify.* We have words which are proper, and not analogical, to express the various ways in which we perceive external objects by the senses—such as *feeling, sight, taste ;* but we are often obliged to use these words analogically, to express other powers of the mind which are of a very different nature. And the powers which imply some degree of reflection, have generally no names but such as are analogical. The objects of thought are said to be *in the mind*—to be *apprehended, comprehended, conceived, imagined, retained, weighed, ruminated.*

It does not appear that the notions of the ancient philosophers, with regard to the nature of the soul, were much more refined than those of the vulgar, or that they were formed in any other way. We shall distinguish the philosophy that regards our subject into the *old* and the *new.* The old reached down to Des Cartes, who gave it a fatal blow, of which it has been gradually expiring ever since, and is now almost extinct. Des Cartes is the father of the new philosophy that relates to this subject ; but it hath been gradually improving since his time, upon the principles laid down by him. The old philosophy seems to have been purely analogical ; the new is more derived from reflection, but still with a very considerable mixture of the old analogical notions.

Because the objects of sense consist of *matter* and *form,* the ancient philosophers conceived everything to belong to one of these, or to be made up of both. Some, therefore, thought that the soul is a particular kind of subtile matter, separable from our gross bodies ; others thought that it is only a particular form of the body, and inseparable from it.† For there seem to have

* See " Essays on the Intellectual Powers," Ess. VI., ch. viii., Nos. 2 and 6.—H.

† It would, however, be a very erroneous assumption to hold, that those who viewed the *soul* as a form inseparable from the body, denied the existence, and the independent existence, of any mental principle after the dissolution of the material organism. Thus, Aristotle defines the soul, the Form or Entelechy of an

been some among the ancients, as well as among the moderns, who conceived that a certain structure or organization of the body, is all that is necessary to render it sensible and intelligent.* The different powers of the mind ware, accordingly, by the last sect of philosophers, conceived to belong to different parts of the body—as the heart, the brain, the liver, the stomach, the blood.†

They who thought that the soul is a subtile matter, separable from the body, disputed to which of the four elements it belongs—whether to earth, water, air, or fire. Of the three last, each had its particular advocates.‡ But some were of opinion, that it partakes of all the elements; that it must have something in its composition similar to everything we perceive; and that we perceive earth by the earthly part; water, by the watery part; and fire, by the fiery part of the soul.§ Some philosophers, not satisfied with determining of what kind of matter the soul is made, inquired likewise into its figure, which they determined to be spherical, that it might be the more fit for motion.‖ The most spiritual and sublime notion concerning the nature of the soul, to be met with among the ancient philosophers, I conceive to be that of the Platonists, who held that it is made of that celestial and incorruptible matter of which the fixed stars were made, and, therefore, has a natural tendency to rejoin its proper element.¶ I am at a loss

to say, in which of these classes of philosophers Aristotle ought to be placed.* He defines the soul to be, *The first ἐντελέχεια of a natural body which has potential life.* I beg to be excused from translating the Greek word, because I know not the meaning of it.†‡

The notions of the ancient philosophers with regard to the operations of the mind, particularly with regard to perception and ideas, seem likewise to have been formed by the same kind of analogy.

Plato, of the writers that are extant, first introduced the word *idea* into philosophy; but his doctrine upon this subject had somewhat peculiar. He agreed with the rest of the ancient philosophers in this— that all things consist of matter and form; and that the matter of which all things were made, existed from eternity, without

---

organized body; and yet he, hypothetically at least, admits that Νῦς, or Intelligence, is adventitious to this animated organism, and, therefore, possibly, and even probably, separable from it, and immortal. The term *soul* in this instance is not adequate to the Intellectual Ego.—H.

* Thus Parmenides:—

'Ὡς γὰρ ἑκάστῳ ἔχει κρᾶσις μελίων πολυπλάγκτων,

Τὼς νόος ἀνθρώποισι παρίστηκιν· τὸ γὰρ αὐτὸ

Ἐστὶν ὅπερ φρονέι μελίων φύσις ἀνθρώποισι.

So likewise Dicæarchus, Galen, and others.—H.

† This is altogether erroneous. Those philosophers who assigned different seats or organs for different parts or functions of the soul, did not therefore admit the absolute dependence of the soul upon the body. For instance, the Pythagoreans and the Platonists.—H.

‡ Aristotle observes that *earth* was the only element which had found no advocate. This he means only of earth *by itself*—for, in combination with one or more of the others, it was by many philosophers allowed to be a constituent of soul. Of these last, *water* had its champion in Hippo; air, in Anaximenes and Diogenes, with whom are sometimes enumerated Anaximander, Anaxagoras, Archelaus, Ænesidemus, &c.; *fire*, in Democritus and Leucippus, perhaps in Hipparchus and Heraclitus.—H.

§ Empedocles; and Plato, as interpreted by Aristotle.—H.

‖ Democritus and Leucippus held the soul, as an igneous principle, to consist of spherical atoms.—H.

¶ See the "Timæus" of Plato. Plotinus, and the lower Platonists in general, held the human soul to be an emanation from the *Anima Mundi*. Aristotle seems to have favoured an opinion correspondent to Plato's. Even the sentient or animal soul, inseparable as it is from body, he maintained to be

higher than any sublunary element, and supposed it to be "analogous to the element of the stars."—*De Generatione Animalium,* L. II., c. 2.—H.

* This is the former of the two definitions which Aristotle gives of the human soul, in the second book of his treatise, "Πιρὶ ψυχῆς." In the latter, by *which we live, feel or perceive,* [*will,*] *move, and understand :*—a definition which has been generally adopted by philosophers, and, though more complete, is in substance that of Reid himself. "*By the mind of a man,*" (says Reid,) "*we understand that in him which thinks, remembers, reasons, wills.*"—ESSAYS ON THE INTELLECTUAL POWERS, Essay I., chap. i. —H.

† Though Cicero misapprehended, and Hermolaus Barbarus raised the Devil to expound it, this Aristotelic term is by no means of a very arduous interpretation. It is not, however, here the place to explain the contents of this celebrated definition.—H.

‡ "For her [the soul's] true form how can my spark discern,
Which, dim by nature, art did never clear?
When the great wits, of whom all skill we learn,
Are ignorant both what she is, and where.

"One thinks the soul is air; another, fire;
Another, blood, diffus'd about the heart;
Another saith, the elements conspire,
And to her essence each doth lend a part.

"Musicians think our souls are harmonies;
Physicians hold that they complexions be;
Epicures make them swarms of atomies,
Which do by chance into our bodies flee.

"Some think one gen'ral soul fills every brain,
As the bright sun sheds light in every star;
While others think the name of soul is vain,
And that we only well-mixt bodies are.

"In judgment of her substance as they vary,
So vary they in judgment of her seat;
For some her chair up to the brain do carry,
Some thrust it down into the stomach's heat;

"Some place it in the root of life, the heart;
Some in the liver fountain of the veins;
Some say, she's all in all, and all in ev'ry part;
Some that she's not contain'd, but all contains.

"Thus these great clerks but little wisdom shew,
While with their do trines they at hazard play;
Tossing their light opinions to and fro,
To mock the lewd, as learn'd in this as they.

"For no cra 'd brain could ever yet profound,
Touching the soul, so vain and fond a thought,
But some among these masters have been found,
Which, in their schools, the self-same thing have taught."

SIR JOHN DAVIES.- H

form : but he likewise believed that there are eternal forms of all possible things which exist, without matter; and to these eternal and immaterial forms he gave the name of *ideas;* maintaining that they are the only object of true knowledge. It is of no great moment to us, whether he borrowed these notions from Parmenides, or whether they were the issue of his own creative imagination. The latter Platonists seem to have improved upon them, in conceiving those ideas, or eternal forms of things, to exist, not of themselves, but in the divine mind,* and to be the models and patterns according to which all things were made :—

"Then liv'd the Eternal One; then, deep retir'd
In his unfathom'd essence, view'd at large
The uncreated images of things."

To these Platonic notions, that of Malebranche is very nearly allied. This author seems, more than any other, to have been aware of the difficulties attending the common hypothesis concerning ideas†—to wit, That ideas of all objects of thought are in the human mind : and, therefore, in order to avoid those difficulties, makes the ideas which are the immediate objects of human thought, to be the ideas of things in the Divine mind, who, being intimately present to every human mind, may discover his ideas to it, as far as pleaseth him.

The Platonists and Malebranche excepted,‡ all other philosophers, as far as I know, have conceived that there are ideas or images of every object of thought in the human mind, or, at least, in some part of the brain, where the mind is supposed to have its residence.

Aristotle had no good affection to the word *idea*, and seldom or never uses it but

* Whether Plato viewed Ideas as existences independent of the divine mind, is a contested point; though, upon the whole, it appears more probable that he did not. It is, however, admitted, on all hands, to be his doctrine, that Ideas were the patterns according to which the Deity fashioned the phænomenal or ectypal world.—H.

† It should be carefully observed that the term *Idea*, previous to the time of Des Cartes, was used exclusively, or all but exclusively, in its Platonic signification. By Des Cartes, and other contemporary philosophers, it was first extended to denote our representations in general. Many curious blunders have arisen in consequence of an ignorance of this. I may notice, by the way, that a confusion of ideas in the Platonic with ideas in the Cartesian sense has here led Reid into the error of assimilating the hypothesis of Plato and the hypothesis of Malebranche in regard to our vision in the divine mind. The Platonic theory of *Perception*, in fact, bears a closer analogy to the Cartesian and Leibnitzian doctrines than to that of Malebranche. See notes on the "Essays on the Intellectual Powers." Ess. II., ch. iv. or vii., and Note G.—H.

‡ The Platonists are no exception ; for they allowed the human mind to have potentially within it the forms or representations for all possible objects of perception ; each representation being, by the spontaneity of mind itself, elicited into consciousness on occasion of its corresponding object coming within the sphere of sense. But of this again.—H.

in refuting Plato's notions about ideas. He thought that matter may exist without form; but that forms cannot exist without matter. But, at the same time, he taught, That there can be no sensation, no imagination, nor intellection, without forms, phantasms, or species in the mind ; and that things sensible are perceived by sensible species, and things intelligible by intelligible species.* His followers taught, more explicitly, that those sensible and intelligible species are sent forth by the objects, and make their impressions upon the passive intellect; and that the active intellect perceives them in the passive intellect. And this seems to have been the common opinion while the Peripatetic philosophy retained its authority.

The Epicurean doctrine, as explained by Lucretius, though widely different from the Peripatetic in many things, is almost the same in this. He affirms, that slender films or ghosts (*tenuia rerum simulacra*) are still going off from all things, and flying about ; and that these, being extremely subtile, easily penetrate our gross bodies, and, striking upon the mind, cause thought and imagination.†

After the Peripatetic system had reigned above a thousand years in the schools of Europe, almost without a rival, it sunk before that of Des Cartes ; the perspicuity of whose writings and reasoning, contrasted with the obscurity of Aristotle and his commentators, created a strong prejudice in favour of this new philosophy. The characteristic of Plato's genius was sublimity, that of Aristotle's, subtilty ; but Des Cartes far excelled both in perspicuity, and bequeathed this spirit to his successors. The system which is now generally received, with regard to the mind and its operations, derives not only its spirit from Des Cartes, but its fundamental principles; and, after all the improvements made by Malebranche, Locke, Berkeley, and Hume, may still be called *the Cartesian system :* we shall, therefore, make some remarks upon its spirit and tendency in general, and upon its doctrine concerning ideas in particular.

1. It may be observed, That the method which Des Cartes pursued, naturally led him to attend more to the operations of the mind by accurate reflection, and to trust less to analogical reasoning upon this sub-

* The doctrine of Aristotle on this subject, admits of an interpretation far more philosophical than that given to it by most of his followers. But of this again.—H.

† The ἀπόῤῥοιαι, Εἴδωλα τύποι, &c. of Democritus and Epicurus differed from the Εἴδη, or *species* of the later Peripatetics, in this—that the former were confessedly substantive and corporeal, while the latter, as mere accidents, shrewdly puzzled their advocates, to say how they were separable from a subject, and whether they were material, immaterial, or somehow intermediate between body and spirit —H.

ject, than any philosopher had done before him. Intending to build a system upon a new foundation, he began with a resolution to admit nothing but what was absolutely certain and evident. He supposed that his senses, his memory, his reason, and every other faculty to which we trust in common life, might be fallacious; and resolved to disbelieve everything, until he was compelled by irresistible evidence to yield assent.

In this method of proceeding, what appeared to him, first of all, certain and evident, was, That he thought—that he doubted—that he deliberated. In a word, the operations of his own mind, of which he was conscious, must be real, and no delusion; and, though all his other faculties should deceive him, his consciousness could not.* This, therefore, he looked upon as the first of all truths. This was the first firm ground upon which he set his foot, after being tossed in the ocean of scepticism; and he resolved to build all knowledge upon it, without seeking after any more first principles.

As every other truth, therefore, and particularly the existence of the objects of sense, was to be deduced by a train of strict argumentation from what he knew by consciousness, he was naturally led to give attention to the operations of which he was conscious, without borrowing his notions of them from external things.

It was not in the way of analogy, but of attentive reflection, that he was led to observe, That thought, volition, remembrance, and the other attributes of the mind, are altogether unlike to extension, to figure, and to all the attributes of body; that we have no reason, therefore, to conceive thinking substances to have any resemblance to extended substances; and that, as the attributes of the thinking substance are things of which we are conscious, we may have a more certain and immediate knowledge of them by reflection, than we can have of external objects by our senses.

These observations, as far as I know, were first made by Des Cartes; and they are of more importance, and throw more light upon the subject, than all that had been said upon it before. They ought to make us diffident and jealous of every notion concerning the mind and its operations, which is drawn from sensible objects in the way of analogy, and to make us rely only upon accurate reflection, as the source of all real knowledge upon this subject.

2. I observe that, as the Peripatetic

system has a tendency to materialize the mind and its operations, so the Cartesian has a tendency to spiritualize body and its qualities. One error, common to both systems, leads to the first of these extremes in the way of analogy, and to the last in the way of reflection. The error I mean is, That we can know nothing about body, or its qualities, but as far as we have sensations which resemble those qualities. Both systems agreed in this: but, according to their different methods of reasoning, they drew very different conclusions from it; the Peripatetic drawing his notions of sensation from the qualities of body; the Cartesian, on the contrary, drawing his notions of the qualities of body from his sensations.

The Peripatetic, taking it for granted that bodies and their qualities do really exist, and are such as we commonly take them to be, inferred from them the nature of his sensations, and reasoned in this manner:—Our sensations are the impressions which sensible objects make upon the mind, and may be compared to the impression of a seal upon wax: the impression is the image or form of the seal, without the matter of it; in like manner, every sensation is the image or form of some sensible quality of the object. This is the reasoning of Aristotle: and it has an evident tendency to materialize the mind and its sensations.

The Cartesian, on the contrary, thinks that the existence of body, or of any of its qualities, is not to be taken as a first principle; and that we ought to admit nothing concerning it, but what, by just reasoning, can be deduced from our sensations; and he knows that, by reflection, we can form clear and distinct notions of our sensations, without borrowing our notions of them by analogy from the objects of sense. The Cartesians, therefore, beginning to give attention to their sensations, first discovered that the sensations corresponding to secondary qualities, cannot resemble any quality of body. Hence, Des Cartes and Locke inferred, that sound, taste, smell, colour, heat, and cold, which the vulgar took to be qualities of body, were not qualities of body, but mere sensations of the mind.*

* Des Cartes did not commit Reid's error of making consciousness a co-ordinate and special faculty. —H.

* Des Cartes and Locke made no such inference. They only maintained as Reid himself states) that sound, taste, &c., as sensations in us, have no resemblance to any quality in bodies. If the names, therefore, of sound, taste, &c., were to be employed univocally—i. e., to denote always things the same or similar—in that case they argued that these terms, if properly applied to the relative qualities of the sensations, could not be properly applied to the relative qualities in external things. This is distinctly stated both by I es Cartes and Locke. But Des Cartes and the Cartesians observe that the terms in question are equivocally used; being commonly applied both to that in things which occasions the sensation in us, and to that sensation itself. Nay, the Cartesians, to avoid the ambiguity, distinguished the two relatives by differ-

Afterwards, the ingenious Berkeley, considering more attentively the nature of sensation in general, discovered and demonstrated, that no sensation whatever could possibly resemble any quality of an insentient being, such as body is supposed to be; and hence he inferred, very justly, that there is the same reason to hold extension, figure, and all the primary qualities, to be mere sensations, as there is to hold the secondary qualities to be mere sensations. Thus, by just reasoning upon the Cartesian principles, matter was stripped of all its qualities ; the new system, by a kind of metaphysical sublimation, converted all the qualities of matter into sensations, and spiritualized body, as the old had materialized spirit.

The way to avoid both these extremes, is to admit the existence of what we see and feel as a first principle, as well as the existence of things whereof we are conscious; and to take our notions of the qualities of body, from the testimony of our senses, with the Peripatetics ; and our notions of our sensations, from the testimony of consciousness, with the Cartesians.

3. I observe, That the modern scepticism is the natural issue of the new system ; and that, although it did not bring forth this monster until the year 1739,* it may be said to have carried it in its womb from the beginning.

The old system admitted all the principles of common sense as first principles, without requiring any proof of them ; and, therefore, though its reasoning was commonly vague, analogical, and dark, yet it was built upon a broad foundation, and had no tendency to scepticism. We do not find that any Peripatetic thought it incumbent upon him to prove the existence of a material world ;† but every writer upon the Cartesian system attempted this, until Berkeley clearly demonstrated the futility of their arguments ; and thence concluded

that there was no such thing as a material world ; and that the belief of it ought to be rejected as a vulgar error.

The new system admits only one of the principles of common sense as a first principle ; and pretends, by strict argumentation, to deduce all the rest from it. That our thoughts, our sensations, and every thing of which we are conscious, hath a real existence, is admitted in this system as a first principle ; but everything else must be made evident by the light of reason. Reason must rear the whole fabric of knowledge upon this single principle of consciousness.

There is a disposition in human nature to reduce things to as few principles as possible ;* and this, without doubt, adds to the beauty of a system, if the principles are able to support what rests upon them. The mathematicians glory, very justly, in having raised so noble and magnificent a system of science, upon the foundation of a few axioms and definitions. This love of simplicity, and of reducing things to few principles, hath produced many a false system ; but there never was any system in which it appears so remarkably as that of Des Cartes.† His whole system concerning matter and spirit is built upon one axiom, expressed in one word, *cogito*. Upon the foundation of conscious thought, with ideas for his materials, he builds his system of the human understanding, and attempts to account for all its phænomena : and having, as he imagined, from his consciousness, proved the existence of matter ; upon the existence of matter, and of a certain quantity of motion originally impressed upon it, he builds his system of the material world, and attempts to account for all its phænomena.

These principles, with regard to the material system, have been found insufficient ; and it has been made evident that, besides matter and motion, we must admit gravitation, cohesion, corpuscular attraction, magnetism, and other centripetal and centrifugal forces, by which the particles of matter attract and repel each other. Newton, having discovered this, and demonstrated that these principles cannot be resolved into matter and motion, was led, by analogy and the love of simplicity, to conjecture, but with a modesty and caution peculiar to him, that all the phænomena of the material world depended upon attracting and repelling forces in the particles of matter. But we may now venture to say, that this conjecture fell short of the mark. For, even in the unorganized kingdom, the

---

ent names. To take colour, for example: they called colour, *as* a sens tion in the mind, *formal* colour ; colour, *as* a quality in bodies capable of producing the sensation, *primitive* or *radical* colour. They had likewise another distinction of less importance—that of *seconda y* or *derivative* colour ; meaning thereby that which the coloured bodies impress upon the external medium Thus, again, *primitive* or *radical* sound was the property of a body to determine a certain agitation in the air or other medium ; *seco dary* or *derivative* sound, that agitation in the medium itself ; *formal* sound, the sensation occasioned by the impression made by the radical sound mediately, and by the derivative immediately, upon the organ of hearing. There is thus no difference between Reid and the Cartesians, except that the doctrine which he censures is in fact more precise and explicit than his own.— H.

* When Hume's " Treatise of Human Nature" appeared.—H.

† This is not correct ; but the reason why Idealism did not prevail in the schools of the middle ages is one, as it appears to me, merely theological. But on this curious question I cannot now touch.—H.

* See " Essays on the Intellectual Powers," p. 636, 4to edition.—H.

† We must except, however, before Reid, among others, the system of Spinoza, and, since Reid, those of Fichte, Schelling, Hegel, &c.—H.

powers by which salts, crystals, spars, and many other bodies, concrete into regular forms, can never be accounted for by attracting and repelling forces in the particles of matter. And in the vegetable and animal kingdoms, there are strong indications of powers of a different nature from all the powers of unorganized bodies. We see, then, that, although, in the structure of the material world, there is, without doubt, all the beautiful simplicity consistent with the purposes for which it was made, it is not so simple as the great Des Cartes determined it to be; nay, it is not so simple as the greater Newton modestly conjectured it to be. Both were misled by analogy, and the love of simplicity. One had been much conversant about extension, figure, and motion; the other had enlarged his views to attracting and repelling forces; and both formed their notions of the unknown parts of nature, from those with which they were acquainted, as the shepherd Tityrus formed his notion of the city of Rome from his country village :—

"Urbem quam dicunt Romam, Melibœe, putavi
Stultus ego, huic nostræ similem, quo sæpe solemus
Pastores ovium teneros depellere fœtus.
Sic canibus catulos similes, sic matribus hædos
Nôram : sic parvis componere magna solebam."

This is a just picture of the analogical way of thinking.

But to come to the system of Des Cartes, concerning the human understanding. It was built, as we have observed, upon consciousness as its sole foundation, and with ideas* as its materials; and all his followers have built upon the same foundation and with the same materials. They acknowledge that Nature hath given us various simple ideas. These are analogous to the matter of Des Cartes's physical system. They acknowledge, likewise, a natural power, by which ideas are compounded, disjoined, associated, compared. This is analogous to the original quantity of motion in Des Cartes's physical system. From these principles, they attempt to explain the phænomena of the human understanding, just as in the physical system the phænomena of nature were to be explained by matter and motion. It must, indeed, be acknowledged, that there is great simplicity in this system, as well as in the other. There is such a similitude between the two, as may be expected between children of the same father ; but, as the one has been found to be the child of Des Cartes, and not of Nature, there is ground to think that the other is so likewise.

That the natural issue of this system is

* There is no valid ground for supposing that Des Cartes meant by ideas aught but modifications of the mind itself. That the majority of the Cartesians did not, is certain. The case is, however, different with regard to Malebranche and Berkeley. But of this again.—H.

scepticism with regard to everything except the existence of our ideas, and of their necessary relations, which appear upon comparing them, is evident ; for ideas, being the only objects of thought, and having no existence but when we are conscious of them, it necessarily follows that there is no object of our thought which can have a continued and permanent existence. Body and spirit, cause and effect, time and space, to which we were wont to ascribe an existence independent of our thought, are all turned out of existence by this short dilemma. Either these things are ideas of sensation or reflection, or they are not : if they are ideas of sensation or reflection, they can have no existence but when we are conscious of them ; if they are not ideas of sensation or reflection, they are words without any meaning.*

Neither Des Cartes nor Locke perceived this consequence of their system concerning ideas. Bishop Berkeley was the first who discovered it. And what followed upon this discovery ? Why, with regard to the material world, and with regard to space and time, he admits the consequence, That these things are mere ideas, and have no existence but in our minds ; but with regard to the existence of spirits or minds, he does not admit the consequence ; and, if he had admitted it, he must have been an absolute sceptic. But how does he evade this consequence with regard to the existence of spirits ? The expedient which the good Bishop uses on this occasion is very remarkable, and shews his great aversion to scepticism. He maintains that we have no ideas of spirits ; and that we can think, and speak, and reason about them, and about their attributes, without having any ideas of them. If this is so, my Lord, what should hinder us from thinking and reasoning about bodies, and their qualities, without having ideas of them ? The Bishop either did not think of this question, or did not think fit to give any answer to it. However, we may observe, that, in order to avoid scepticism, he fairly starts out of the Cartesian system, without giving any reason why he did so in this instance, and in no other. This, indeed, is the only instance of a deviation from Cartesian principles which I have met with in the successors of Des Cartes ; and it seems to have been only a sudden start, occasioned by the terror of scepticism ; for, in all other things, Berkeley's system is founded upon Cartesian principles.

Thus we see that Des Cartes and Locke take the road that leads to scepticism, without knowing the end of it ; but they stop

* This dilemma applies to the *sensualism* of Locke, but not to the *rationalism* of Des Cartes.—H.

short for want of light to carry them farther. Berkeley, frighted at the appearance of the dreadful abyss, starts aside, and avoids it. But the author of the "Treatise of Human Nature," more daring and intrepid, without turning aside to the right hand or to the left, like Virgil's Alecto, shoots directly into the gulf:

"Hic specus horrendum, et sævi spiracula Ditis Monstrantur: ruptoque ingens Acheronte vorago Pestiferas aperit fauces."

4. We may observe, That the account given by the new system, of that furniture of the human understanding which is the gift of Nature, and not the acquisition of our own reasoning faculty, is extremely lame and imperfect.*

The natural furniture of the human understanding is of two kinds: First, The *notions* or simple apprehensions which we have of things; and, secondly, The *judgments* or the belief which we have concerning them. As to our notions, the new system reduces them to two classes—*ideas of sensation*, and *ideas of reflection:* the first are conceived to be copies of our sensations, retained in the memory or imagination; the second, to be copies of the operations of our minds whereof we are conscious, in like manner retained in the memory or imagination: and we are taught that these two comprehend all the materials about which the human understanding is, or can be employed. As to our judgment of things, or the belief which we have concerning them, the new system allows no part of it to be the gift of nature, but holds it to be the acquisition of reason, and to be got by comparing our ideas, and perceiving their agreements or disagreements. Now I take this account, both of our notions, and of our judgments or belief, to be extremely imperfect; and I shall briefly point out some of its capital defects.

The division of our notions into ideas of sensation,† and ideas of reflection, is contrary to all rules of logic: because the second member of the division includes the first. For, can we form clear and just notions of our sensations any other way than by reflection? Surely we cannot. Sensation is an operation of the mind of which we are conscious; and we get the notion of sensation by reflecting upon that which we are conscious of. In like manner, doubting and believing are operations of the mind whereof we are conscious; and we get the notion of them by reflecting upon what we are conscious of. The ideas of sensation, therefore, are ideas of reflection,

as much as the ideas of doubting, or believing, or any other ideas whatsoever.*

But, to pass over the inaccuracy of this division, it is extremely incomplete. For, since sensation is an operation of the mind, as well as all the other things of which we form our notions by reflection, when it is asserted that all our notions are either ideas of sensation or ideas of reflection, the plain English of this is, That mankind neither do nor can think of anything but of the operations of their own minds. Nothing can be more contrary to truth, or more contrary to the experience of mankind. I know that Locke, while he maintained this doctrine, believed the notions which we have of body and of its qualities, and the notions which we have of motion and of space, to be ideas of sensation. But why did he believe this? Because he believed those notions to be nothing else but images of our sensations. If, therefore, the notions of body and its qualities, of motion and space, be not images of our sensations, will it not follow that these notions are not ideas of sensation? Most certainly.†

* The following summary refers principally to Locke.—H.
† It must be remembered that under *Sensation* Locke and others included *Perception proper* and *Sensation proper.*—H.

* I do not see how this criticism on Locke's division can be defended, or even excused. It is perfectly evident that Reid here confounds *the proper ideas of sensation*—that is, the ideas of the qualities of matter, about which sensation (perception) is conversant—with the *idea of sensation* itself—that is, the idea of this faculty as an attribute of mind, and which is the object of a reflex consciousness. Nor would it be competent to maintain that Locke, allowing no immediate knowledge of aught but of mind and its contents, consequently reduces all our faculties to self-consciousness, and thus abolishes the distinction of sensation (perception) and reflection, as separate faculties, the one conversant with the qualities of the external world, the other with the qualities of the internal. For, in the *first* place, it would still be logically competent, on the hypothesis that all our knowledge is exclusively of self, to divide the ideas we possessed, into classes, according as these were given as representations of the *non-ego* by the *ego*, or as phænomena of the *ego* itself. In the *second* place, Reid's criticism does not admit of this excuse. But, in the *third*, if the defence were valid in itself, and here available, the philosophy of Reid himself would be obnoxious to a similar criticism. For he makes perception (consequently the object known in perception) an object of consciousness; but consciousness, in his view, is only of the phænomena of mind itself—all consciousness is to him *self-consciousness.* Thus, *his* perception, as contained under *his* consciousness, is only cognisant of the *ego.*† With all this, however, Reid distinguishes perception and consciousness as special and co-ordinate faculties; perception being conversant about the qualities of matter, as suggested—that is, as represented in the percipient subject—consciousness as conversant about perception and the other attributes of mind itself.—With the preceding observations, the reader may compare Priestley's "Examination," p 58, and Stewart's "Philosophical Essays," Note N—H.

† I may here notice—what I shall hereafter more fully advert to—that Reid's criticism of Locke, here and elsewhere, proceeds upon the implication that the English philosopher attached the same restricted meaning to the term Sensation that he did himself. But this is not the case. Locke employed *Sensation* to denote both the *idea* and the *sentiment* of the Cartesians—both the *perception* and the *sensation* of Reid. To confound this distinction was, indeed, wrong; but this is a separate and special ground of censure, and, in a general criticism of Locke's doc-

There is no doctrine in the new system which more directly leads to scepticism than this. And the author of the "Treatise of Human Nature" knew very well how to use it for that purpose; for, if you maintain that there is any such existence as body or spirit, time or place, cause or effect, he immediately catches you between the horns of this dilemma; your notions of these existences are either ideas of sensation, or ideas of reflection: if of sensation, from what sensation are they copied? if of reflection, from what operation of the mind are they copied?

It is indeed to be wished that those who have written much about sensation, and about the other operations of the mind, had likewise thought and reflected much, and with great care, upon those operations; but is it not very strange that they will not allow it to be possible for mankind to think of anything else?

The account which this system gives of our judgment and belief concerning things, is as far from the truth as the account it gives of our notions or simple apprehensions. It represents our senses as having no other office but that of furnishing the mind with notions or simple apprehensions of things; and makes our judgment and belief concerning those things to be acquired by comparing our notions together, and perceiving their agreements or disagreements.

We have shewn, on the contrary, that every operation of the senses, in its very nature, implies judgment or belief, as well as simple apprehension. Thus, when I feel the pain of the gout in my toe, I have not only a notion of pain, but a belief of its existence, and a belief of some disorder in my toe which occasions it; and this belief is not produced by comparing ideas, and perceiving their agreements and disagreements; it is included in the very nature of the sensation. When I perceive a tree before me, my faculty of seeing gives me not only a notion or simple apprehension of the tree, but a belief of its existence, and of its figure, distance, and magnitude; and this judgment or belief is not got by comparing ideas, it is included in the very nature of the perception. We have taken notice of several original principles of belief in the course of this inquiry; and

when other faculties of the mind are examined, we shall find more, which have not occurred in the examination of the five senses.

Such original and natural judgments are, therefore, a part of that furniture which Nature hath given to the human understanding. They are the inspiration of the Almighty, no less than our notions or simple apprehensions. They serve to direct us in the common affairs of life, where our reasoning faculty would leave us in the dark. They are a part of our constitution; and all the discoveries of our reason are grounded upon them. They make up what is called *the common sense of mankind;*[*] and, what is manifestly contrary to any of those first principles, is what we call *absurd.* The strength of them is *good sense,* which is often found in those who are not acute in reasoning. A remarkable deviation from them, arising from a disorder in the constitution, is what we call *lunacy;* as when a man believes that he is made of glass. When a man suffers himself to be reasoned out of the principles of common sense, by metaphysical arguments, we may call this *metaphysical lunacy;* which differs from the other species of the distemper in this, that it is not continued, but intermittent: it is apt to seize the patient in solitary and speculative moments; but, when he enters into society, Common Sense recovers her authority.[†] A clear explication and enumeration of the principles of common sense, is one of the chief *desiderata* in logic. We have only considered such of them as occurred in the examination of the five senses.

5. The last observation that I shall make upon the new system, is, that, although it professes to set out in the way of reflection, and not of analogy, it hath retained some of the old analogical notions concerning the

___

trine, the fact that he did so confound perception proper and sensation proper, should always be taken into account. But, waving this, what is gained by the distinction in Reid's hands? In his doctrine, space, motion, &c., as perceived, are only conceptions, only modifications of self, suggested, in some unknown way, on occasion of the impression made on the sense: consequently, in the one doctrine as in the other, what is known is nothing beyond the affections of the thinking subject itself; and this is the only basis required by the idealist and sceptic for the foundation of their systems.—H.

* See Note A.—H.
† No one admits this more promptly than the sceptic himself. See Hume's "Treatise of Human Nature," Book I., Part iv., § 7. and "Enquiry Concerning Human Understanding," § 12, Part II. "Nature," says he in the latter, "is always too strong for principle; and, though a Pyrrhonian may throw himself or others into a momentary amazement and confusion by his profound reasonings, the first and most trivial event in life will put to flight all his doubts and scruples, and leave him the same in every point of action and speculation with the philosophers of every other sect, or with those who never concerned themselves in any philosophical researches. When he awakes from his dream, he will be the first to join in the laugh against himself, and to confess that all his objections are mere amusement, and can have no other tendency than to shew the whimsical condition of mankind, who must act, and reason, and believe, though they are not able, by their most diligent enquiry, to satisfy themselves concerning the foundation of the operations, or to remove the objections which may be raised against them."
"La Nature confond les Pyrrhoniens," (says Pascal,) "et la Raison confond les Dogmatistes." How can philosophy be realised? is thus the grand question.—H.

P

operations of the mind ; particularly, that things which do not now exist in the mind itself, can only be perceived, remembered, or imagined, by means of ideas or images* of them in the mind, which are the immediate objects of perception, remembrance, and imagination. This doctrine appears evidently to be borrowed from the old system ; which taught that external things make impressions upon the mind, like the impressions of a seal upon wax ; that it is by means of those impressions that we perceive, remember, or imagine them ; and that those impressions must resemble the things from which they are taken. When we form our notions of the operations of the mind by analogy, this way of conceiving them seems to be very natural, and offers itself to our thoughts ; for, as everything which is felt must make some impression upon the body, we are apt to think that everything which is understood must make some impression upon the mind.

From such analogical reasoning, this opinion of the existence of ideas or images of things in the mind, seems to have taken its rise, and to have been so universally received among philosophers. It was observed already, that Berkeley, in one instance, apostatizes from this principle of the new system, by affirming that we have no ideas of spirits, and that we can think of them immediately, without ideas. But I know not whether in this he has had any followers. There is some difference, likewise, among modern philosophers with regard to the ideas or images by which we perceive, remember, or imagine sensible things. For, though all agree in the existence of such images,† they differ about their place ; some placing them in a particular part of the brain, where the soul is thought to have her residence, and others placing them in the mind itself. Des Cartes held the first of these opinions ;‡ to which Newton seems likewise to have inclined ; for he proposes this query in his " Optics :"—"Annon sensorium animalium est locus cui substantia sentiens adest, et in quem sensibiles rerum species per nervos et cerebrum deferuntur, ut ibi præsentes a præsente sentiri pos-

sint ?" But Locke seems to place the ideas of sensible things in the mind ;* and that Berkeley, and the author of the " Treatise of Human Nature," were of the same opinion, is evident. The last makes a very curious application of this doctrine, by endeavouring to prove from it, That the mind either is no substance, or that it is an extended and divisible substance ; because the ideas of extension cannot be in a subject which is indivisible and unextended.

I confess I think his reasoning in this, as in most cases, is clear and strong. For whether the idea of extension be only another name for extension itself, as Berkeley and this author assert ; or whether the idea of extension be an image and resemblance of extension, as Locke conceived ; I appeal to any man of common sense, whether extension, or any image of extension, can be in an unextended and indivisible subject.† But while I agree with him in his reasoning, I would make a different application of it. He takes it for granted, that there are ideas of extension in the mind ; and thence infers, that, if it is at all a substance, it must be an extended and divisible substance. On the contrary, I take it for granted, upon the testimony of common sense, that my mind is a substance —that is, a permanent subject of thought ; and my reason convinces me that it is an unextended and indivisible substance ; and hence I infer that there cannot be in it anything that resembles extension. If this reasoning had occurred to Berkeley, it would probably have led him to acknowledge that we may think and reason concerning bodies, without having ideas of them in the mind, as well as concerning spirits.

I intended to have examined more particularly and fully this doctrine of the existence of ideas or images of things in the mind ; and likewise another doctrine, which is founded upon it—to wit, That judgment or belief is nothing but a perception of the agreement or disagreement of our ideas ; but, having already shewn, through the course of this inquiry, that the operations of the mind which we have examined, give no countenance to either of these doctrines, and in many things contradict them, I have thought it proper to drop this part of my design. It may be executed with more advantage, if it is at all necessary, after inquiring into some other powers of the human understanding.

---

* That is, by *representative entities different from the modes of the mind itself.* This doctrine, I have already noticed, is attributed by Reid too universally to philosoph rs ; and is also a comparatively unimportant circumstance in reference to the Idealist and Sceptic. See Note C.—H.

† See last note. Berkeley did hold the hypothesis of Ideas as understood by Reid.—H.

‡ An unqualified error, arising from not understanding the ambiguous *language* of Des Cartes ; who calls, by the common name of *Ideas*, both the organic motions in the brain, of which the mind, in his doctrine, necessarily knows nothing, and the representations in the mind itself, hyperphysically determined on occasion of those motions, and of which alone the mind is cognizant. But of this under the " Essays on the Intellectual Powers."—H.

---

* Locke's opinion on this point is as obscure and doubtful as that of Des Cartes is clear and certain. But Reid is probably right.—H

† I do not recollect seeing any argument raised in favour of materialism, from the fact, that, *space* or *extension* is a notion necessary to the mind ; and yet it might, with some show of plausibility, be maintained, that extension is a necessary form of thought, because the thinking principle is itself extended —H

Although we have examined only the five senses, and the principles of the human mind which are employed about them, or such as have fallen in our way in the course of this examination, we shall leave the further prosecution of this inquiry to future deliberation. The powers of memory, of imagination, of taste, of reasoning, of moral perception, the will, the passions, the affections, and all the active powers of the soul, present a vast and boundless field of philosophical disquisition, which the author of this inquiry is far, from thinking himself able to survey with accuracy. Many authors of ingenuity, ancient and modern, have made excursions into this vast territory, and have communicated useful observations: but there is reason to believe that those who have pretended to give us a map of the whole, have satisfied themselves with a very inaccurate and incomplete survey. If Galileo had attempted a complete system of natural philosophy, he had, probably, done little service to mankind: but by confining himself to what was within his comprehension, he laid the foundation of a system of knowledge, which rises by degrees, and does honour to the human understanding. Newton, building upon this foundation, and, in like manner, confining his inquiries to the law of gravitation and the properties of light, performed wonders. If he had attempted a great deal more, he had done a great deal less, and perhaps nothing at all. Ambitious of following such great examples, with unequal steps, alas! and unequal force, we have attempted an inquiry only into one little corner of the human mind— that corner which seems to be most exposed to vulgar observation, and to be most easily comprehended; and yet, if we have delineated it justly, it must be acknowledged that the accounts heretofore given of it were very lame, and wide of the truth.

ESSAYS

ON THE

INTELLECTUAL POWERS OF MAN.

By THOMAS REID, D.D., F.R.S.E.,

PROFESSOR OF MORAL PHILOSOPHY IN THE UNIVERSITY OF GLASGOW.

" Who hath put wisdom in the inward parts? "—Job

☞ This impression of the " Essays on the Intellectual Powers," is made from the only authentic edition—that of 1785, in 4to. For the convenience of reference the pages of that edition are distinguished in the present ; and by these pages I shall always, in the notes, *prospectively*, quote. They will be found marked both in the text and on the lower margin.—H.

DEDICATION.

MR DUGALD STEWART,

LATELY PROFESSOR OF MATHEMATICS, NOW PROFESSOR OF MORAL PHILOSOPHY,

AND

DR JAMES GREGORY,

PROFESSOR OF THE THEORY OF PHYSIC IN THE UNIVERSITY OF EDINBURGH.*

My Dear Friends,—I know not to whom I can address these Essays with more propriety than to you; not only on account of a friendship begun in early life on your part, though an old age on mine, and in one of you I may say hereditary; nor yet on account of that correspondence in our literary pursuits and amusements, which has always given me so great pleasure; but because, if these Essays have any merit, you have a considerable share in it, having not only encouraged me to hope that [iv.] they may be useful, but favoured me with your observations on every part of them, both before they were sent to the press, and while they were under it.

I have availed myself of your observations, so as to correct many faults that might otherwise have escaped me; and I have a very grateful sense of your friendship, in giving this aid to one who stood much in need of it; having no shame, but much pleasure, in being instructed by those who formerly were my pupils, as one of you was.

It would be ingratitude to a man whose memory I most highly respect, not to mention my obligations to the late Lord Kames, for the concern he was pleased to take in this Work. Having seen a small part of it, he urged me to carry it on; took account of my progress from time to time; revised it more than once, as far as it was carried, before his death; and gave me his observations on it, both with respect to the matter and the expression. On some points we differed in opinion, and debated them keenly, both in conversation and by many letters, without any abatement of his affection, or of his zeal for the work's being carried on and published: for he had too much liberality of mind not to allow to [v.] others the same liberty in judging which he claimed to himself.

It is difficult to say whether that worthy man was more eminent in active life or in speculation. Very rare, surely, have been the instances where the talents for both were united in so eminent a degree.

His genius and industry, in many different branches of literature, will, by his works, be known to posterity: his private virtues and public spirit, his assiduity, through a long and laborious life, in many honourable public offices with which he was entrusted, and his zeal to encourage and promote everything that tended to the improvement of his country in laws, literature, commerce, manufactures, and agriculture, are best known to his friends and contemporaries.

The favourable opinion which he, and you my friends, were pleased to express of this work, has been my chief encouragement to lay it before the public; and perhaps, without that encouragement, it had never seen the light: for I have always found, that, without social intercourse, even a favourite speculation languishes; and that we cannot help thinking the better of our own opinions [vi.] when they are approved by those whom we esteem good judges.

You know that the substance of these Essays was delivered annually, for more

* See above, in " Correspondence," p. 65, a.—H.
[iii.–vi.]

than twenty years, in Lectures to a large body of the more advanced students in this University, and for several years before, in another University. Those who heard me with attention, of whom I presume there are some hundreds alive, will recognise the doctrine which they heard, some of them thirty years ago, delivered to them more diffusely, and with the repetitions and illustrations proper for such audiences.

I am afraid, indeed, that the more intelligent reader, who is conversant in such abstract subjects, may think that there are repetitions still left, which might be spared. Such, I hope, will consider, that what to one reader is a superfluous repetition, to the greater ·part, less conversant in such subjects, may be very useful. If this apology be deemed insufficient, and be thought to be the dictate of laziness, I claim some indulgence even for that laziness, at my period of life. [vii.]

You who are in the prime of life, with the vigour which it inspires, will, I hope, make more happy advances in this or in any other branch of science to which your talents may be applied.

THO. REID.

Glasgow College, June 1, 1785.

PREFACE.

HUMAN knowledge may be reduced to two general heads, according as it relates to body or to mind ; to things material or to things intellectual. *

The whole system of bodies in the universe, of which we know but a very small part, may be called the Material World ; the whole system of minds, from the infinite Creator to the meanest creature endowed with thought, may be called the Intellectual World. These are the two great kingdoms of nature† that fall within our notice ; and about the one, or the other, or things pertaining to them, every art, every science, and every human thought is employed ; nor can the boldest flight of imagination carry us beyond their limits.

Many things there are, indeed, regarding the nature and the structure both of body and of mind, which our faculties cannot reach ; many difficulties which the ablest philosopher cannot resolve : but of other natures, if any other there be, we have no knowledge, no conception at all.

That everything that exists must be either corporeal or incorporeal is evident. But it is not so evident that everything [2] that exists must either be corporeal or endowed with thought. Whether there be in the universe beings which are neither extended, solid, and inert, like body, nor active and intelligent, like mind, seems to be beyond the reach of our knowledge. There appears to be a vast interval between body and mind ; and whether there be any intermediate nature that connects them together, we know not.

We have no reason to ascribe intelligence, or even sensation, to plants ; yet there appears in them an active force and energy, which cannot be the result of any arrangement or combination of inert matter. The same thing may be said of those powers by which animals are nourished and grow, by which matter gravitates, by which magnetical and electrical bodies attract and repel each other, and by which the parts of solid bodies cohere.

Some have conjectured that the phænomena of the material world which require active force, are produced by the continual operation of intelligent beings : others have conjectured that there may be in the universe, beings that are active, without intelligence, which, as a kind of incorporeal machinery, contrived by the supreme wisdom, perform their destined task without any knowledge or intention.* But, laying aside conjecture, and all pretences to determine in things beyond our reach, we must

---

* See Stewart's " Life and Writings of Reid," *supra*, p. 14 ; and his " Elements," vol. I., introduction ; Jouffroy, in the preface to his " Oeuvres de Reid," t. i., pp. 23-53. This important Preface will soon be made generally accessible.to the British public by a highly competent translator.—H.

† The term *Nature* is used sometimes in a wider, sometimes in a narrower extension. When employed in its most extensive meaning, it embraces the two worlds of mind and matter. When employed in its more restricted signification, it is a synonyme for the latter only, and is then used in contradistinction to the former. In the Greek philosophy, the word φύσις was general in its meaning ; and the great branch of philosophy styled " *physical* or *physiological,*" included under it not only the sciences of matter, but also those of mind. With us, the term *Nature* is more vaguely extensive than the terms, *physics,* **physical,** *physiology, physiological,* or even than the adjective *natural* ; whereas, in the philosophy of Germany, *Natur,* and its correlatives, whether of Greek or Latin derivation, are, in general, expressive of the world of matter in contrast to the world of intelligence.—H.

[vii -2]

* Like the tripods of Vulcan—
Ὄφρα οἱ αὐτόμαται θεῖον δυσαίατ' ἀγῶνα.—H

rest in this, that body and mind are the only kinds of being of which we can have any knowledge, or can form any conception. If there are other kinds, they are not discoverable by the faculties which God hath given us; and, with regard to us, are as if they were not. [3]

As, therefore, all our knowledge is confined to body and mind, or things belonging to them, there are two great branches of philosophy, one relating to body, the other to mind. The properties of body, and the laws that obtain in the material system, are the objects of natural philosophy, as that word is now used. The branch which treats of the nature and operations of minds has, by some, been called Pneumatology.* And to the one or the other of these branches, the principles of all the sciences belong.

What variety there may be of minds or thinking beings, throughout this vast universe, we cannot pretend to say. We dwell in a little corner of God's dominion, disjoined from the rest of it. The globe which we inhabit is but one of seven planets that encircle our sun. What various orders of beings may inhabit the other six, their secondaries, and the comets belonging to our system, and how many other suns may be encircled with like systems, are things altogether hid from us. Although human reason and industry have discovered, with great accuracy, the order and distances of the planets, and the laws of their motion, we have no means of corresponding with them That they may be the habitation of animated beings, is very probable; but of the nature or powers of their inhabitants, we are perfectly ignorant. Every man is conscious of a thinking principle, or mind, in himself; and we have sufficient evidence of a like principle in other men. The actions of brute animals shew that they have some thinking principle, though of a nature far inferior to the human mind. And everything about us may convince us of the existence of a supreme mind, the Maker and Governor of the universe. These are all the minds of which reason can give us any certain knowledge. [4]

The mind of man is the noblest work of God which reason discovers to us, and, therefore, on account of its dignity, deserves our study.† It must, indeed, be acknowledged, that, although it is of all objects the nearest to us, and seems the most within our reach, it is very difficult to attend to its operations so as to form a distinct notion of them; and on that account there is no branch of knowledge in which the ingenious and speculative have fallen into so great errors, and even absurdities. These errors and absurdities have given rise to a general prejudice against all inquiries of this nature. Because ingenious men have, for many ages, given different and contradictory accounts of the powers of the mind, it is concluded that all speculations concerning them are chimerical and visionary.

But whatever effect this prejudice may have with superficial thinkers, the judicious will not be apt to be carried away with it. About two hundred years ago, the opinions of men in natural philosophy were as various and as contradictory as they are now concerning the powers of the mind. Galileo, Torricelli, Kepler, Bacon, and Newton, had the same discouragement in their attempts to throw light upon the material system, as we have with regard to the intellectual. If they had been deterred by such prejudices, we should never have reaped the benefit of their discoveries, which do honour to human nature, and will make their names immortal. The motto which Lord Bacon prefixed to some of his writings was worthy of his genius, *Inveniam viam aut faciam.*

There is a natural order in the progress of the sciences, and good reasons may be assigned why the philosophy of body should [5] be *elder sister* to that of mind, and of a quicker growth; but the last hath the principle of life no less than the first, and will grow up, though slowly, to maturity. The remains of ancient philosophy upon this subject, are venerable ruins, carrying the marks of genius and industry, sufficient to inflame, but not to satisfy our curiosity. In later ages, Des Cartes was the first that pointed out the road we ought to take in those dark regions. Malebranche, Arnauld, Locke, Berkeley, Buffier, Hutcheson, Butler, Hume, Price, Lord Kames, have laboured to make discoveries—nor have they laboured in vain; for, however different and contrary their conclusions are, however sceptical some of them, they have all given new light, and cleared the way to those who shall come after them.

We ought never to despair of human genius, but rather to hope that, in time, it may produce a system of the powers and operations of the human mind, no less certain than those of optics or astronomy.

This is the more devoutly to be wished, that a distinct knowledge of the powers of the mind would undoubtedly give great light to many other branches of science. Mr Hume hath justly observed, that " all the

---

* Now properly superseded by the term *Psychology*; to which no competent objection can be made, and which affords us—what the various clumsy periphrases in use do not—a convenient adjective, *psychological.*—H.

† " On earth," says a forgotten philosopher, " there is nothing great but Man; in man there is nothing great but Mind."—H.

[3—5]

* See Mr Stewart's " Philosophical Essays," Preliminary Dissertation, ch. ii

sciences have a relation to human nature; and, however wide any of them may seem to run from it, they still return back by one passage or another. This is the centre and capital of the sciences,* which, being once masters of, we may easily extend our conquests everywhere."

The faculties of our minds are the tools and engines we must use in every disquisition; and the better we understand their [6] nature and force, the more successfully we shall be able to apply them. Mr Locke gives this account of the occasion of his entering upon his essay concerning human understanding:—" Five or six friends," says he, " meeting at my chamber, and discoursing on a subject very remote from this, found themselves quickly at a stand by the difficulties that rose on every side. After we had for a while puzzled ourselves, without coming any nearer to a resolution of those doubts that perplexed us, it came into my thoughts that we took a wrong course; and that, before we set ourselves upon inquiries of that nature, it was necessary to examine our own abilities, and see what objects our understandings were fitted or not fitted to deal with. This I proposed to the company, who all readily assented; and thereupon it was agreed that this should be our first enquiry." If this be commonly the cause of perplexity in those disquisitions which have least relation to the mind, it must be so much more in those that have an immediate connection with it.

The sciences may be distinguished into two classes, according as they pertain to the material or to the intellectual world. The various parts of natural philosophy, the mechanical arts, chemistry, medicine, and agriculture, belong to the first; but, to the last, belong grammar, logic, rhetoric, na-

tural theology, morals, jurisprudence, law, politics, and the fine arts. The knowledge of the human mind is the root from which these grow, and draw their nourishment.* Whether, therefore, we consider the dignity of this subject, or its subserviency to science in general, and to the noblest branches of science in particular, it highly deserves to be cultivated. [7]

A very elegant writer, on the *sublime and beautiful*,† concludes his account of the passions thus:—" The variety of the passions is great, and worthy, in every branch of that variety, of the most diligent investigation. The more accurately we search into the human mind, the stronger traces we everywhere find of His wisdom who made it. If a discourse on the use of the parts of the body may be considered as a hymn to the Creator,‡ the use of the passions, which are the organs of the mind, cannot be barren of praise to Him, nor unproductive to ourselves of that noble and uncommon union of science and admiration, which a contemplation of the works of infinite Wisdom alone can afford to a rational mind; whilst referring to Him whatever we find of right, or good, or fair, in ourselves, discovering His strength and wisdom even in our own weakness and imperfection, honouring them where we discover them clearly, and adoring their profundity where we are lost in our search, we may be inquisitive without impertinence, and elevated without pride; we may be admitted, if I may dare to say so, into the counsels of the Almighty, by a consideration of his works. This elevation of the mind ought to be the principal end of all our studies, which, if they do not in some measure effect, they are of very little service to us."

---

* Hume probably had the saying of Polybius in his eye, who calls History the mother city (μητρόπολις) of Philosophy.—IL
[6. 7]

* It is justly observed by M. Jouffroy, that the division here enounced is not in principle identical with that previously propounded.—H.
† Burke.—H.
‡ Galen is referred to.—H.

ESSAYS

INTELLECTUAL POWERS OF MAN.

ESSAY I.

PRELIMINARY.

CHAPTER I.

THERE is no greater impediment to the advancement of knowledge than the ambiguity of words. To this chiefly it is owing that we find sects and parties in most branches of science; and disputes which are carried on from age to age, without being brought to an issue.

Sophistry has been more effectually excluded from mathematics and natural philosophy than from other sciences. In mathematics it had no place from the beginning; mathematicians having had the wisdom to define accurately the terms they use, and to lay down, as axioms, the first principles on which their reasoning is grounded. Accordingly, we find no parties among mathematicians, and hardly any disputes.* [10]

In natural philosophy, there was no less sophistry, no less dispute and uncertainty, than in other sciences, until, about a century and a half ago, this science began to be built upon the foundation of clear definitions and self-evident axioms. Since that time, the science, as if watered with the dew of Heaven, hath grown apace; disputes have ceased, truth hath prevailed, and the science hath received greater increase in two centuries than in two thousand years before.

It were to be wished that this method, which hath been so successful in those branches of science, were attempted in others; for definitions and axioms are the foundations of all science. But that definitions may not be sought where no definition can be given, nor logical definitions be attempted where the subject does not admit of them, it may be proper to lay down some general principles concerning definition, for the sake of those who are less conversant in this branch of logic.

When one undertakes to explain any art or science, he will have occasion to use many words that are common to all who use the same language, and some that are peculiar to that art or science. Words of the last kind are called *terms of the art*, and ought to be distinctly explained, that their meaning may be understood.

A definition* is nothing else but an explication of the meaning of a word, by words whose meaning is already known. Hence it is evident that every word cannot be defined; for the definition must consist of words; and there could be no definition, if there were not words previously understood without definition. Common words, therefore, ought to be used in their common acceptation; and, when they have different acceptations in common language, these, when it is necessary, ought to be distinguished. But they require no definition. It is sufficient to define words that are uncommon, or that are used in an uncommon meaning.

It may farther be observed, that there are many words, which, though they may need explication, cannot be logically defined. A [11] logical definition—that is, a strict and proper definition—must express the kind [genus] of the thing defined, and the specific difference by which the species defined is distinguished from every other species belonging to that kind. It is natural to the mind of man to class things under various kinds, and again to subdivide every kind into its various species. A species may often be subdivided into subordinate species, and then it is considered as a kind.

From what has been said of logical definition, it is evident, that no word can be logically defined which does not denote a

---

* It was not the superior wisdom of mathematicians, but the simple and palpable character of their object-matter, which determined the difference.—H.

* In what follows, there is a confusion of definitions verbal and real, which should have been carefully distinguished.—H.

species; because such things only can have a specific difference; and a specific difference is essential to a logical definition. On this account there can be no logical definition of individual things, such as London or Paris. Individuals are distinguished either by proper names, or by accidental circumstances of time or place; but they have no specific difference; and, therefore, though they may be known by proper names, or may be described by circumstances or relations, they cannot be defined.* It is no less evident that the most general words cannot be logically defined, because there is not a more general term, of which they are a species.

Nay, we cannot define every species of things, because it happens sometimes that we have not words to express the specific difference. Thus, a scarlet colour is, no doubt, a species of colour; but how shall we express the specific difference by which scarlet is distinguished from green or blue? The difference of them is immediately perceived by the eye; but we have not words to express it. These things we are taught by logic.

Without having recourse to the principles of logic, we may easily be satisfied that words cannot be defined, which signify things perfectly simple, and void of all composition. This observation, I think, was first made by Des Cartes, and afterwards more fully illustrated by Locke.† And, however obvious it appears to be, many instances may be given of great philosophers who have perplexed [12] and darkened the subjects they have treated, by not knowing, or not attending to it.

When men attempt to define things which cannot be defined, their definitions will always be either obscure or false. It was one of the capital defects of Aristotle's philosophy, that he pretended to define the simplest things, which neither can be, nor need to be defined—such as *time* and *motion*.‡ Among modern philosophers, I

know none that has abused definition so much as Carolus [Christianus] Wolfius, the famous German philosopher, who, in a work on the human mind, called "Psychologia Empirica," consisting of many hundred propositions, fortified by demonstrations, with a proportional accompaniment of definitions, corollaries, and scholia, has given so many definitions of things which cannot be defined, and so many demonstrations of things self-evident, that the greatest part of the work consists of tautology, and ringing changes upon words.*

There is no subject in which there is more frequent occasion to use words that cannot be logically defined, than in treating of the powers and operations of the mind. The simplest operations of our minds must all be expressed by words of this kind. No man can explain, by a logical definition, what it is to *think*, to *apprehend*, to *believe*, to *will*, to *desire*. Every man who understands the language, has some notion of the meaning of those words; and every man who is capable of reflection may, by attending to the operations of his own mind, which are signified by them, form a clear and distinct notion of them; but they cannot be logically defined.

Since, therefore, it is often impossible to define words which we must use on this subject, we must as much as possible use common words, in their common acceptation, pointing out their various senses where they are ambiguous; and, when we are obliged to use words less common, we must endeavour to explain them [13] as well as we can, without affecting to give logical definitions, when the nature of the thing does not allow it.

The following observations on the meaning of certain words are intended to supply, as far as we can, the want of definitions, by preventing ambiguity or obscurity in the use of them.

1. By the *mind* of a man, we understand that in him which thinks, remembers, reasons, wills.† The essence both of body and of mind is unknown to us. We know certain properties of the first, and certain operations of the last, and by these only we can define or describe them. We define body to be that which is extended, solid, moveable, divisible. In like manner, we define mind to be that which thinks. We are conscious that we think, and that we have a variety of thoughts of different kinds—such as seeing, hearing, remembering, deliberating, resolving, loving, hating, and many

* It is well said by the old logicians, *Omnis intuitiva notitia est definitio;*—that is, *a view of the thing itself is its best definition.* And this is true, both of the objects of sense, and of the objects of self-consciousness.—H.

† This is incorrect. Des Cartes has little, and Locke no title to praise for this observation. It had been made by Aristotle, and after him by many others; while, subsequent to Des Cartes, and *previous to Locke,* Pascal and the Port-Royal Logicians, to say nothing of a paper of Leibnitz, in 1684, had reduced it to a matter of commonplace. In this instance, Locke can, indeed, be *proved* a borrower. Mr Stewart ("Philosophical Essays," Note A) is wrong in thinking that, after Des Cartes, Lord Stair is the earliest philosopher who this logical principle was enounced; for Stair, as a writer, is subsequent to the authors adduced.—H.

‡ There is not a little, however, to be said in vindication of Aristotle's definitions. Leibnitz is not the only modern philosopher who has applauded that of *Motion,* which requires, however, some illustration of the special significance of its terms—H.

* This judgment is not false; but it is exaggerated —H.

† This corresponds to Aristotle's second definition of the soul, or that *a posteriori.* Vide *supra,* p. 203, b, note .—H.

other kinds of thought—all which we are taught by nature to attribute to one internal principle ; and this principle of thought we call the *mind* or *soul* of a man.

2. By the *operations*＊ of the mind, we understand every mode of thinking of which we are conscious.

It deserves our notice, that the various modes of thinking have always, and in all languages, as far as we know, been called by the name of operations of the mind, or by names of the same import. . To body we ascribe various properties, but not operations, properly so called : it is extended, divisible, moveable, inert ; it continues in any state in which it is put ; every change of its state is the effect of some force impressed upon it, and is exactly proportional to the force impressed, and in the precise direction of that force. These are the general properties of matter, and these are not operations ; on the contrary, they all imply its being a dead, inactive thing, which moves only as it is moved, and acts only by being acted upon.† [14]

But the mind is, from its very nature, a living and active being. Everything we know of it implies life and active energy ; and the reason why all its modes of thinking are called its operations, is, that in all, or in most of them, it is not merely passive, as body is, but is really and properly active.

In all ages, and in all languages, ancient and modern, the various modes of thinking have been expressed by words of active signification, such as *seeing, hearing, reasoning, willing*, and the like. It seems, therefore, to be the natural judgment of mankind, that the mind is active in its various ways of thinking : and, for this reason, they are called its operations, and are expressed by active verbs.

It may be made a question, What regard is to be paid to this natural judgment ? May it not be a vulgar error ? Philosophers who think so have, no doubt, a right to be heard. But, until it is proved that the mind is not active in thinking, but merely passive, the common language with regard to its operations ought to be used, and ought not to give place to a phraseology invented by philosophers, which implies its being merely passive.

3. The words *power* and *faculty*, which are often used in speaking of the mind, need little explication. Every operation supposes a power in the being that operates ; for to suppose anything to operate, which has no power to operate, is manifestly absurd. But, on the other hand,

there is no absurdity in supposing a being to have power to operate, when it does not operate. Thus I may have power to walk, when I sit ; or to speak, when I am silent. Every operation, therefore, implies power ; but the power does not imply the operation.

The *faculties* of the mind, and its *powers*, are often used as synonymous expressions. But, as most synonymes have some minute distinction that deserves notice, I apprehend that the word *faculty* [15] is most properly applied to those powers of the mind which are original and natural, and which make a part of the constitution of the mind. There are other powers, which are acquired by use, exercise, or study, which are not called faculties, but *habits*. There must be something in the constitution of the mind necessary to our being able to acquire habits—and this is commonly called *capacity*.＊

4. We frequently meet with a distinction in writers upon this subject, between things *in the mind*, and things *external* to the mind. The powers, faculties, and operations of the mind, are things in the mind. Everything is said to be in the mind, of which the mind is the *subject*. It is self-evident that there are some things which cannot exist without a subject to which they belong, and of which they are attributes. Thus, colour must be in something coloured ; figure in something figured ; thought can only be in something that thinks ; wisdom and virtue cannot exist but in some being that is wise and virtuous. When, therefore, we speak of things in the mind, we understand by this, things of which the mind is the subject. Excepting the mind itself, and things in the mind, all other things are said to be external. It ought therefore to be remembered, that this distinction between things in the mind and things external, is not meant to signify the place of the things we speak of, but their subject.†

There is a figurative sense in which things are said to be in the mind, which it is sufficient barely to mention. We say such a thing was not in my mind ; meaning no more than that I had not the least thought of it. By a figure, we put the thing for the thought

---

＊ *Operation, Act, Energy*, are nearly convertible terms ; and are opposed to *Faculty*, (of which anon,) as the *actual* to the *potential* —H.

† " Materiae datum est cogi, sed cogere Menti." MANILIUS.—H.

＊ These terms properly stand in the following relations :—*Powers* are *active* and *passive, natural* and *acquired*. Powers, natural and active, are called *Faculties* : Powers, natural and passive, *Capacities* or *Receptivities* : Powers acquired are *Habits*, and habit is used both in an active and in a passive sense : the Power, again, of acquiring a habit, is called a *Disposition*.—On the meaning of the term Power, see further, under the first Essay on the Active Powers, chap. iii, p 23.—H

† *Subject* and *Object* are correlative terms. The former is properly *id in quo* : the latter, *id circa quod*. Hence, in psychological language, the *subject*, absolutely, is the mind that knows or thinks—*i e.*, the mind considered as the subject of knowledge or thought ; the *object*, that wh'ich is known, or thought about. The adjectives *subjective* and *objective* are convenient, if not indispensable, expressions.—H.

of it. In this sense external things are in the mind as often as they are the objects of our thought.

5. *Thinking* is a very general word, which includes all the operations of our minds, and is so well understood as to need no definition.* [16]

To *perceive*, to *remember*, to be *conscious*, and to *conceive* or *imagine*, are words common to philosophers and to the vulgar. They signify different operations of the mind, which are distinguished in all languages, and by all men that think. I shall endeavour to use them in their most common and proper acceptation, and I think they are hardly capable of strict definition. But, as some philosophers, in treating of the mind, have taken the liberty to use them very improperly, so as to corrupt the English language, and to confound things which the common understanding of mankind hath always led them to distinguish, I shall make some observations on the meaning of them, that may prevent ambiguity or confusion in the use of them.

6. *First*, We are never said to *perceive* things, of the existence of which we have not a full conviction. I may *conceive* or *imagine* a mountain of gold, or a winged horse; but no man says that he perceives such a creature of imagination. Thus *perception* is distinguished from *conception* or imagination. *Secondly*, Perception is applied only to external objects, not to those that are in the mind itself. When I am pained, I do not say that I perceive pain, but that I feel it, or that I am conscious of it. Thus, *perception* is distinguished from *consciousness*. *Thirdly*, The immediate object of perception must be something present, and not what is past. We may remember what is past, but do not perceive it. I may say, I perceive such a person has had the small-pox; but this phrase is figurative, although the figure is so familiar that it is not observed. The meaning of it is, that I perceive the pits in his face, which are certain signs of his having had the small pox. We say we perceive the thing signified, when we only perceive the sign. But when the word *perception* is used properly, and without any figure, it is never applied to things past. And thus it is distinguished from *remembrance*. ‡

In a word, perception is most properly applied to the evidence which we have of external objects by our senses. But, as this is a [17] very clear and cogent kind of evidence, the word is often applied by analogy to the evidence of reason or of testimony, when it is clear and cogent. The perception of external objects by our senses, is an operation of the mind of a peculiar nature, and ought to have a name appropriated to it. It has so in all languages. And, in English, I know no word more proper to express this act of the mind than perception. Seeing, hearing, smelling, tasting, and touching or feeling, are words that express the operations proper to each sense; perceiving expresses that which is common to them all.

The observations made on this word would have been unnecessary, if it had not been so much abused in philosophical writings upon the mind; for, in other writings, it has no obscurity. Although this abuse is not chargeable on Mr Hume only, yet I think he has carried it to the highest pitch. The first sentence of his "Treatise of Human Nature" runs thus :—"All the perceptions of the human mind resolve themselves into two distinct heads, which I shall call impressions and ideas." He adds, a little after, that, under the name of impressions, he comprehends all our sensations, passions, and emotions. Here we learn that our passions and emotions are perceptions. I believe, no English writer before him ever gave the name of a perception to any passion or emotion. When a man is angry, we must say that he has the perception of anger. When he is in love, that he has the perception of love. He speaks often of the perceptions of memory, and of the perceptions of imagination; and he might as well speak of the hearing of sight, or of the smelling of touch; for, surely, hearing is not more different from sight, or smelling from touch, than perceiving is from remembering or imagining.*

7. *Consciousness* is a word used by philosophers, to signify that immediate knowledge which we have of our present thoughts and purposes, and, in general, of all the present operations of our minds. Whence we may observe, that consciousness is only of things present. To apply consciousness to things past, which sometimes [18] is done in popular discourse, is to confound consciousness with memory; and all such confusion of words ought to be avoided in philosophical discourse. It is likewise to be observed, that consciousness

---

* *Thought* and *thinking* are used in a more, and in a less, restricted signification. In the former meaning they are limited to the *discursive* energies alone; in the latter, they are co-extensive with consciousness.—H.

[16–18]

* In the Cartesian and Lockian philosophies, the term Perception was used almost convertibly with Consciousness : whatever we could be said to be conscious of, that we could be said to perceive. And there is nothing in the etymology of the word, or in its use by ancient writers, that renders this unexclusive application of it abusive. In the Leibnitzian philosophy, *perception* and *apperception* were distinguished in a peculiar manner—of which again. Reid is right in his own restriction of the term; but he is not warranted in blaming Hume for having used it in the wider signification of his predecessors.—H.

is only of things in the mind, and not of external things. It is improper to say, I am conscious of the table which is before me. I perceive it, I see it; but do not say I am conscious of it. As that consciousness by which we have a knowledge of the operations of our own minds, is a different power from that by which we perceive external objects, and as these different powers have different names in our language, and, I believe, in all languages, a philosopher ought carefully to preserve this distinction, and never to confound things so different in their nature.*

8. *Conceiving, imagining,* and *apprehending,* are commonly used as synonymous in our language, and signify the same thing which the logicians call simple apprehension. This is an operation of the mind different from all those we have mentioned. Whatever we perceive, whatever we remember, whatever we are conscious of, we have a full persuasion or conviction of its existence. But we may conceive or imagine what has no existence, and what we firmly believe to have no existence. What never had an existence cannot be remembered; what has no existence *at present* cannot be the object of perception or of consciousness; but what never had, nor has any existence, may be conceived. Every man knows that it is as easy to conceive a winged horse, or a centaur, as it is to conceive a horse or a man. Let it be observed, therefore, that to *conceive,* to *imagine,* to *apprehend,* when taken in the proper sense, signify an act of the mind which implies no belief or judgment at all.† It is an act of the mind by which nothing is affirmed or denied, and which, therefore, can neither be true nor false.

But there is another and a very different meaning of those words, so common and so well authorized in language that it cannot easily be avoided; and on that account we ought to be the more on our guard, that we be not misled by the ambiguity. Politeness and [19] good-breeding lead men, on most occasions, to express their opinions with modesty, especially when they differ from others whom they ought to respect. Therefore, when we would express our opinion modestly, instead of saying, "This is my opinion," or, "This is my judgment," which has the air of dogmaticalness, we say, "I conceive it to be thus—I imagine, or apprehend it to be thus;" which is understood as a modest declaration of our judgment. In like manner, when anything is said which we take to be impossible, we say, "We can-

not conceive it;" meaning that we cannot believe it.

Thus we see that the words *conceive, imagine, apprehend,* have two meanings, and are used to express two operations of the mind, which ought never to be confounded. Sometimes they express simple apprehension, which implies no judgment at all; sometimes they express judgment or opinion. This ambiguity ought to be attended to, that we may not impose upon ourselves or others in the use of them. The ambiguity is indeed remedied, in a great measure, by their construction. When they are used to express simple apprehension, they are followed by a noun in the *accusative case,* which signifies the object conceived; but, when they are used to express opinion or judgment, they are commonly followed by a verb, in the *infinitive mood.* "I conceive an Egyptian pyramid." This implies no judgment. "I conceive the Egyptian pyramids to be the most ancient monuments of human art." This implies judgment. When the words are used in the last sense, the thing conceived must be a proposition, because judgment cannot be expressed but by a proposition. When they are used in the first sense, the thing conceived may be no proposition, but a simple term only—as a pyramid, an obelisk. Yet it may be observed, that even a proposition may be simply apprehended, without forming any judgment of its truth or falsehood: for it is one thing to conceive the meaning of a proposition; it is another thing to judge it to be true or false. [20]

Although the distinction between simple apprehension, and every degree of assent or judgment, be perfectly evident to every man who reflects attentively on what passes in his own mind—although it is very necessary, in treating of the powers of the mind, to attend carefully to this distinction—yet, in the affairs of common life, it is seldom necessary to observe it accurately. On this account we shall find, in all common languages, the words which express one of those operations frequently applied to the other. To think, to suppose, to imagine, to conceive, to apprehend, are the words we use to express simple apprehension; but they are all frequently used to express judgment. Their ambiguity seldom occasions any inconvenience in the common affairs of life, for which language is framed. But it has perplexed philosophers, in treating of the operations of the mind, and will always perplex them, if they do not attend accurately to the different meanings which are put upon those words on different occasions.

9. Most of the operations of the mind, from their very nature, must have objects to which they are directed, and about which

---

* Reid's degradation of Consciousness into a special faculty, (in which he seems to follow Hutcheson, in opposition to other philosophers,) is, in every point of view, obnoxious to every possible objection. See note H —H

† Except of its own ideal reality.—H.

they are employed. He that perceives, must perceive something; and that which he perceives is called the object of his perception. To perceive, without having any object of perception, is impossible. The mind that perceives, the object perceived, and the *operation* of perceiving that object, are distinct things, and are distinguished in the structure of all languages. In this sentence, " I see, or perceive the moon," *I* is the person or *mind*, the active verb *see* denotes the operation of that mind, and the *moon* denotes the object. What we have said of perceiving, is equally applicable to most operations of the mind. Such operations are, in all languages, expressed by active transitive verbs; and we know that, in all languages, such verbs require a thing or person, which is the agent and a noun following in an oblique case, which is the object. Whence it is evident, that all mankind, both those who have contrived language, and those who use it with understanding, have distinguished these three things as different—to wit, the operations of the mind, which [21] are expressed by active verbs ; the mind itself, which is the nominative to those verbs; and the object, which is, in the oblique case, governed by them.

It would have been unnecessary to explain so obvious a distinction, if some systems of philosophy had not confounded it. Mr Hume's system, in particular, confounds all distinction between the operations of the mind and their objects. When he speaks of the ideas of memory, the ideas of imagination, and the ideas of sense, it is often impossible, from the tenor of his discourse, to know whether, by those ideas, he means the operations of the mind, or the objects about which they are employed. And, indeed, according to his system, there is no distinction between the one and the other.

A philosopher is, no doubt, entitled to examine even those distinctions that are to be found in the structure of all languages ; and, if he is able to shew that there is no foundation for them in the nature of the things distinguished—if he can point out some prejudice common to mankind which has led them to distinguish things that are not really different—in that case, such a distinction may be imputed to a vulgar error, which ought to be corrected in philosophy. But when, in his first setting out, he takes it for granted, without proof, that distinctions found in the structure of all languages, have no foundation in nature, this, surely, is too fastidious a way of treating the common sense of mankind. When we come to be instructed by philosophers, we must bring the old light of common sense along with us, and by it judge of the new light which the philosopher communicates to us. But when we are required to put out the old light altogether, that we may follow the new, we have reason to be on our guard. There may be distinctions that have a real foundation, and which may be necessary in philosophy, which are not made in common language, because not necessary in the common business of life. But I believe [22] no instance will be found of a distinction made in all languages, which has not a just foundation in nature.

10. The word *idea*[*] occurs so frequently in modern philosophical writings upon the mind, and is so ambiguous in its meaning, that it is necessary to make some observations upon it. There are chiefly two meanings of this word in modern authors—a popular and a philosophical.

First, In popular language, *idea* signifies the same thing as conception, apprehension, notion. To have an idea of any thing, is to conceive it. To have a distinct idea, is to conceive it distinctly. To have no idea of it, is not to conceive it at all. It was before observed, that conceiving or apprehending has always been considered by all men as an act or operation of the mind, and, on that account, has been expressed in all languages by an active verb. When, therefore, we use the phrase of having ideas, in the popular sense, we ought to attend to this, that it signifies precisely the same thing which we commonly express by the active verbs, conceiving or apprehending.

When the word idea is taken in this popular sense, no man can possibly doubt whether he has ideas. For he that doubts must think, and to think is to have ideas.

Sometimes, in popular language, a man's ideas signify his opinions. The ideas of Aristotle, or of Epicurus, signify the opinions of these philosophers. What was formerly said of the words *imagine, conceive, apprehend,* that they are sometimes used to express judgment, is no less true of the word idea. This signification of the word seems indeed more common in the French language than in English. But it is found in this sense in good English authors, and even in Mr Locke. Thus we see, that having *ideas*, taken in the popular sense, has precisely the same meaning with conceiving, imagining, apprehending, and has likewise [23] the same ambiguity. It may, therefore, be doubted, whether the introduction of this word into popular discourse, to signify the operation of conceiving or apprehending, was at all necessary. For, *first*, We have, as has been shewn, several words which are either originally English, or have been long naturalized, that express the same thing ;

---

* On the history of the term *Idea*, see Note G.—H.

why, therefore, should we adopt a Greek word in place of these, any more than a French or a German word? Besides, the words of our own language are less ambiguous. For the word idea has, for many ages, been used by philosophers as a term of art; and in the different systems of philosophers means very different things.

Secondly, According to the philosophical meaning of the word idea, it does not signify that act of the mind which we call thought or conception, but some object of thought. Ideas, according to Mr Locke, (whose very frequent use of this word has probably been the occasion of its being adopted into common language,) "are nothing but the immediate objects of the mind in thinking." But of those objects of thought called ideas, different sects of philosophers have given a very different account. Bruckerus, a learned German, wrote a whole book, giving the history of ideas.

The most ancient system we have concerning ideas, is that which is explained in several dialogues of Plato, and which many ancient, as well as modern writers, have ascribed to Plato, as the inventor. But it is certain that Plato had his doctrine upon this subject, as well as the name *idea,* from the school of Pythagoras. We have still extant, a tract of Timæus, the Locrian, a Pythagorean philosopher, concerning the soul of the world, in which we find the substance of Plato's doctrine concerning ideas.* They were held to be eternal, uncreated, and immutable forms, or models, according to which the Deity made every species of things that exists, of an eternal matter. Those philosophers held, that there are three first principles of all things: *First,* An eternal matter, of which all things were made; *Secondly,* Eternal and immaterial forms, or ideas, according to which they were made; and, [24] *Thirdly,* An efficient cause, the Deity who made them.† The mind of man, in order to its being fitted for the contemplation of these eternal ideas, must undergo a certain purification, and be weaned from sensible things. The eternal ideas are the only object of science; because the objects of sense, being in a perpetual flux, there can be no knowledge with regard to them.

The philosophers of the Alexandrian school, commonly called *the latter Platonists,* made some change upon the system of the ancient Platonists with respect to the eternal ideas. They held them not to be a principle distinct from the Deity, but to be the conceptions of things in the divine understanding; the natures and essences of all things being perfectly known to him from eternity.

It ought to be observed that the Pythagoreans, and the Platonists, whether elder or latter, made the eternal ideas to be objects of science only, and of abstract contemplation, not the objects of sense.* And in this, the ancient system of eternal ideas differs from the modern one of Father Malebranche. He held, in common with other modern philosophers, that no external thing is perceived by us immediately, but only by ideas. But he thought that the ideas, by which we perceive an external world, are the ideas of the Deity himself, in whose mind the ideas of all things, past, present, and future, must have been from eternity; for the Deity being intimately present to our minds at all times, may discover to us as much of his ideas as he sees proper, according to certain established laws of nature; and in his ideas, as in a mirror, we perceive whatever we do perceive of the external world.

Thus we have three systems, which maintain that the ideas which are the immediate objects of human knowledge, are eternal and immutable, and existed before the things which they represent. There are other systems, according to which the ideas which are the immediate objects of all our thoughts, are posterior to the things which they represent, and derived from them. We shall [25] give some account of these; but, as they have gradually sprung out of the ancient Peripatetic system, it is necessary to begin with some account of it.

Aristotle taught that all the objects of our thought enter at first by the senses; and, since the sense cannot receive external material objects themselves, it receives their species—that is, their images or forms, without the matter; as wax receives the form of the seal without any of the matter of it. These images or forms, impressed upon the senses, are called *sensible species,* and are the objects only of the sensitive part of the mind; but, by various internal powers, they are retained, refined, and spiritualized, so as to become objects of memory and imagination, and, at last, of pure intellection. When they are objects of memory and of imagination, they get the name of *phantasms.* When, by farther refinement, they become stripped of their particularities, they become objects of science, they are called *intelligible species:* so that every immediate

---

* The whole series of Pythagorean treatises and fragments in the Doric dialect, in which the doctrines and phraseology of Plato and Aristotle are so marvellously anticipated, are now proved to be comparatively recent forgeries. Of these, the treatise under the name of Timæus, is one.—H.

† See above, p. 204, a, note *—H.

* Reid, in common with our philosophers in general, had no knowledge of the Platonic theory of *sensible perception;* and yet the *gnostic forms,* the *cognitive reasons* of the Platonists, held a far more proximate relation to ideas in the modern acceptation, than the Platonic ideas themselves. These, in fact, as to all that relates to the doctrine of perception and imagination, may be thrown wholly out of account. See below, under p. 116.—H.

Q

object, whether of sense, of memory, of imagination, or of reasoning, must be some phantasm or species in the mind itself.*

The followers of Aristotle, especially the schoolmen, made great additions to this theory, which the author himself mentions very briefly, and with an appearance of reserve. They entered into large disquisitions with regard to the sensible species: what kind of things they are; how they are sent forth by the object, and enter by the organs of the senses; how they are preserved and refined by various agents, called internal senses, concerning the number and offices of which they had many controversies. But we shall not enter into a detail of these matters.

The reason of giving this brief account of the theory of the Peripatetics, with regard to the immediate objects of our thoughts, is, because the doctrine of modern philosophers concerning ideas is built upon it. Mr Locke, who uses this word so very frequently, tells us, that he means the same thing by it as is commonly [26] meant by *species* or *phantasm*. Gassendi, from whom Locke borrowed more than from any other author, says the same. The words *species* and *phantasm*, are terms of art in the Peripatetic system, and the meaning of them is to be learned from it.†

The theory of Democritus and Epicurus, on this subject, was not very unlike to that of the Peripatetics. They held that all bodies continually send forth slender films or spectres from their surface, of such extreme subtilty that they easily penetrate our gross bodies, or enter by the organs of sense, and stamp their image upon the mind. The sensible species of Aristotle were mere forms without matter. The spectres of Epicurus were composed of a very subtile matter.

Modern philosophers, as well as the Peripatetics and Epicureans of old, have conceived that external objects cannot be the immediate objects of our thought; that there must be some image of them in the mind itself, in which, as in a mirror, they are seen. And the name *idea*, in the philosophical sense of it, is given to those internal and immediate objects of our thoughts. The external thing is the remote or mediate object; but the idea, or image of that object in the mind, is the immediate object, without

which we could have no perception, no remembrance, no conception of the mediate object.*

When, therefore, in common language, we speak of having an idea of anything, we mean no more by that expression, but thinking of it. The vulgar allow that this expression implies a mind that thinks, an act of that mind which we call thinking, and an object about which we think. But, besides these three, the philosopher conceives that there is a fourth—to wit, the *idea*, which is the immediate object. The idea is in the mind itself, and can have no existence but in a mind that thinks; but the remote or mediate object may be something external, as the sun or moon; it may be something past or future; it may be something which never existed. [27] This is the philosophical meaning of the word *idea*; and we may observe that this meaning of that word is built upon a philosophical opinion: for, if philosophers had not believed that there are such immediate objects of all our thoughts in the mind, they would never have used the word idea to express them.

I shall only add, on this article, that, although I may have occasion to use the word idea in this philosophical sense in explaining the opinions of others, I shall have no occasion to use it in expressing my own, because I believe *ideas*, taken in this sense, to be a mere fiction of philosophers. And, in the popular meaning of the word, there is the less occasion to use it, because the English words *thought*, *notion*, *apprehension*, answer the purpose as well as the Greek word *idea*; with this advantage, that they are less ambiguous. There is, indeed, a meaning of the word idea, which I think most agreeable to its use in ancient philosophy, and which I would willingly adopt, if use, the arbiter of language, did permit. But this will come to be explained afterwards.

II. The word *impression* is used by Mr Hume, in speaking of the operations of the mind, almost as often as the word *idea* is by Mr Locke. What the latter calls ideas, the former divides into two classes; one of which he calls impressions, the other ideas. I shall make some observations upon Mr Hume's explication of *that* word, and then consider the proper meaning of it in the English language.

"We may divide," (says Mr Hume, "Essays," vol. II., p. 18,†) "all the perceptions of the human mind into two classes or species, which are distinguished by their

---

* This is a tolerable account of the doctrine *vulgarly* attributed to Aristotle.—H.
† If by this it be meant that the terms of *species* and *phantasm*, as occasionally employed by Gassendi and Locke, are used by them in the common meaning attached to them in the Schools, Reid is wrong. Gassendi, no more than Des Cartes, in adopting these terms of the Peripatetics, adopted them in their Peripatetic signification. Both these philosophers are explicit in declaring the contrary; and what these terms as employed by them denote, they have clearly stated. Locke is less precise.—H.

* On Reid's ambiguous employment of the expressions *mediate* and *immediate object*, see Note B; and, on his confusion of the two hypotheses of representation, Note C—H.
† "Enquiry concerning Human Understanding," § 2. The quotation has been filled up by the original.—H.

different degrees of force and vivacity. The less lively and forcible are commonly denominated THOUGHTS or IDEAS. The other species want a name in our language, and in most others ; [I suppose because it was not requisite for any but philosophical purposes to rank them under a general term or appellation.] Let us, therefore, use a little freedom, and call them IMPRESSIONS; [employing that word in a sense somewhat different from the usual.] By the term *impression*, then, I mean all our more lively perceptions, when we hear, or see, or feel, or love, or hate, or desire, or will. [And impressions are distinguished from] ideas [which] are the [28] less lively perceptions, of which we are conscious, when we reflect on any of those sensations or movements above mentioned."

This is the explication Mr Hume hath given in his "Essays" of the term *impressions*, when applied to the mind: and his explication of it, in his "Treatise of Human Nature," is to the same purpose. [Vol. I. p. 11.]

Disputes about words belong rather to grammarians than to philosophers ; but philosophers ought not to escape censure when they corrupt a language, by using words in a way which the purity of the language will not admit. I find fault with Mr Hume's phraseology in the words I have quoted—

First, Because he gives the name of perceptions to every operation of the mind. Love is a perception, hatred a perception ; desire is a perception, will is a perception ; and, by the same rule, a doubt, a question, a command, is a perception. This is an intolerable abuse of language, which no philosopher has authority to introduce.*

Secondly, When Mr Hume says, *that we may divide all the perceptions of the human mind into two classes or species, which are distinguished by their degrees of force and vivacity*, the manner of expression is loose and unphilosophical. To differ in species is one thing ; to differ in degree is another. Things which differ in degree only must be of the same species. It is a maxim of common sense, admitted by all men, that *greater* and *less* do not make a change of species.† The same man may differ in the degree of his force and vivacity, in the morning and at night, in health and in sickness ; but this is so far from making him a different species, that it does not so much as make him a different individual. To say, therefore, that two different classes, or species of percep-

tions, are distinguished by the degrees of their force and vivacity, is to confound a difference of *degree* with a difference of *species*, which every man of understanding knows how to distinguish.* [29]

Thirdly, We may observe, that this author, having given the general name of perception to all the operations of the mind,† and distinguished them into two classes or species, which differ only in degree of force and vivacity, tells us, that he gives the name of impressions to all our more lively perceptions—to wit, when we hear, or see, or feel, or love, or hate, or desire, or will. There is great confusion in this account of the meaning of the word *impression*. When I see, this is an *impression*. But why has not the author told us whether he gives the name of *impression* to the object seen, or to that act of my mind by which I see it ? When I see the full moon, the full moon is one thing, my perceiving it is another thing. Which of these two things does he call an impression ? We are left to guess this ; nor does all that this author writes about impressions clear this point. Everything he says tends to darken it, and to lead us to think that the full moon which I see, and my seeing it, are not two things, but one and the same thing.‡

The same observation may be applied to every other instance the author gives to illustrate the meaning of the word *impression*. "When we hear, when we feel, when we love, when we hate, when we desire, when we will." In all these acts of the mind there must be an *object*, which is heard, or felt, or loved, or hated, or desired, or willed. Thus, for instance, I love my country. This, says Mr Hume, is an *impression*. But what is the *impression* ? Is it my country, or is it the affection I bear to it ? I ask the philosopher this question ; but I find no answer to it. And when I read all

---

* Hume did not introduce it The term Perception was so used by Des Cartes and many others ; and, as desires, feelings, &c. exist only as known, so are they all, in a certain sense, cognitions (perceptions).—H.

† "Magis et minus non variant speciem."—H.

[28, 29]

---

* This objection reaches far more extensively than to Hume ; in fact, to all who do not allow an immediate knowledge or consciousness of the *non-ego* in perception. Where are the philosophers who so ?—Aristotle and Hobbes call imagination a dying sense; and Des Cartes is equally explicit.—H.

† As others previously had done.—H.

‡ This objection is easily answered. The thing, (Hume would say,) as *unknown*, as *unperceived*, as *beyond the sphere of my consciousness*, is to me as zero ; to that, therefore, I could not refer. As *perceived*, as known, it must be *within the sphere of my consciousness* ; but, as philosophers concur in maintaining that I can only be conscious of my mind and its contents, the object, as perceived, must be either a mode of, or something contained within my mind, and to that *internal object*, as *perceived*, I give the name of *impression*.—Nor can the act of perception (he would add) be really distinguished from the object perceived. Both are only relatives, mutually constituent of the same indivisible relation of knowledge ; and to that relation and these relatives I give the name of *impression*, precisely as, in different points of view, the term perception is applied to the mind perceiving, to the object perceived, and to the act of which these are the inseparable constituents. This likewise has reference to what follows.—H.

that he has *written* on this subject, I find this word *impression* sometimes used to signify an operation of the mind, sometimes the object of the operation; but, for the most part, it is a vague and indetermined word that signifies both.

I know not whether it may be considered as an apology for such abuse of words, in an author who understood the language so well, and used it with so great propriety in writing on other subjects, [30] that Mr Hume's system, with regard to the mind, required a language of a different structure from the common: or, if expressed in plain English, would have been too shocking to the common sense of mankind. To give an instance or two of this. If a man receives a present on which he puts a high value, if he see and handle it, and put it in his pocket, this, says Mr Hume, is an *impression.* If the man only dream that he received such a present, this is an *idea.* Wherein lies the difference between this impression and this idea—between the dream and the reality? They are different classes or species, says Mr Hume: so far all men will agree with him. But he adds, that they are distinguished only by different degrees of force and vivacity. Here he insinuates a tenet of his own, in contradiction to the commonsense of mankind. Common sense convinces every man, that a lively dream is no nearer to a reality than a faint one; and that, if a man should dream that he had all the wealth of Crœsus, it would not put one farthing in his pocket. It is impossible to fabricate arguments against such undeniable principles, without confounding the meaning of words.

In like manner, if a man would persuade me that the moon which I see, and my seeing it, are not two things, but one and the same thing, he will answer his purpose less by arguing this point in plain English, than by confounding the two under one name—such as that of an *impression.* For such is the power of words, that, if we can be brought to the habit of calling two things that are connected *by the same name,* we are the more easily led to believe them to be one and the same thing.

Let us next consider the proper meaning of the word *impression*[*] in English, that we may see how far it is fit to express either the operations of the mind or their objects.

When a figure is stamped upon a body by pressure, that figure is called an *impression,* as the impression of a seal on wax, of [31] printing-types, or of a copperplate on paper. This seems now to be the literal sense of the word; the effect borrowing its name from the cause. But, by metaphor or analogy, like most other words, its meaning is extended, so as to signify any change produced in a body by the operation of some external cause. A blow of the hand makes no impression on a stone wall; but a battery of cannon may. The moon raises a tide in the ocean, but makes no impression on rivers and lakes.

When we speak of making an impression on the mind, the word is carried still farther from its literal meaning; use, however, which is the arbiter of language, authorizes this application of it—as when we say that admonition and reproof make little impression on those who are confirmed in bad habits. The same discourse delivered in one way makes a strong impression on the hearers; delivered in another way, it makes no impression at all.

It may be observed that, in such examples, an impression made on the mind always implies some change of purpose or will; some new habit produced, or some former habit weakened; some passion raised or allayed. When such changes are produced by persuasion, example, or any external cause, we say that such causes make an impression upon the mind; but, when things are seen, or heard, or apprehended, without producing any passion or emotion, we say that they make no impression.

In the most extensive sense, an impression is a change produced in some passive subject by the operation of an external cause. If we suppose an active being to produce any change in itself by its own active power, this is never called an impression. It is the act or operation of the being itself, not an impression upon it. From this it appears, that to give the name of an impression to any effect produced in the mind, is to suppose that the mind does not act at all in the production of that effect. If seeing, hearing, desiring, willing, be operations of the mind, they cannot be impressions. If [32] they be impressions, they cannot be operations of the mind. In the structure of all languages, they are considered as acts or operations of the mind itself, and the names given them imply this. To call them impressions, therefore, is to trespass against the structure, not of a particular language only, but of all languages.[*]

If the word *impression* be an improper word to signify the operations of the mind, it is at least as improper to signify their objects; for would any man be thought to speak with propriety, who should say that the sun is an impression, that the earth and the sea are impressions?

It is commonly believed, and taken for granted, that every language, if it be sufficiently copious in words, is equally fit to express all opinions, whether they be true

---

or false. I apprehend, however, that there is an exception to this general rule, which deserves our notice. There are certain common opinions of mankind, upon which the structure and grammar of all languages are founded. While these opinions are common to all men, there will be a great similarity in all languages that are to be found on the face of the earth. Such a similarity there really is; for we find in all languages the same parts of speech, the distinction of nouns and verbs, the distinction of nouns into adjective and substantive, of verbs into active and passive. In verbs we find like tenses, moods, persons, and numbers. There are general rules of grammar, the same in all languages. This similarity of structure in all languages, shews an uniformity among men in those opinions upon which the structure of language is founded.

If, for instance, we should suppose that there was a nation who believed that the things which we call attributes might exist without a subject, there would be in their language no distinction between adjectives and substantives, nor would it be a rule with them that an adjective has no meaning, unless when joined to a substantive. If there was any nation who did not distinguish between [33] acting and being acted upon, there would in their language be no distinction between active and passive verbs; nor would it be a rule that the active verb must have an agent in the nominative case, but that, in the passive verb, the agent must be in an oblique case.

The structure of all languages is grounded upon common notions, which Mr Hume's philosophy opposes, and endeavours to overturn. This, no doubt, led him to warp the common language into a conformity with his principles; but we ought not to imitate him in this, until we are satisfied that his principles are built on a solid foundation.

12. *Sensation* is a name given by philosophers to an act of mind, which may be distinguished from all others by this, that it hath no object distinct from the act itself.* Pain of every kind is an uneasy sensation. When I am pained, I cannot say that the pain I feel is one thing, and that my feeling it is another thing. They are one and the same thing, and cannot be disjoined, even in imagination. Pain, when it is not felt, has no existence. It can be neither greater nor less in degree or duration, nor anything else in kind than it is felt to be. It cannot exist by itself, nor in any subject but in a sentient being. No quality of an inanimate

insentient being can have the least resemblance to it.

What we have said of pain may be applied to every other sensation. Some of them are agreeable, others uneasy, in various degrees. These being objects of desire or aversion, have some attention given to them; but many are indifferent, and so little attended to that they have no name in any language.

Most operations of the mind that have names in common language, are complex in their nature, and made up of various ingredients, or more simple acts; which, though conjoined in our constitution, must be disjoined by abstraction, in order to our having a distinct and scientific notion of the complex operation. [34] In such operations, sensation, for the most part, makes an ingredient. Those who do not attend to the complex nature of such operations, are apt to resolve them into some one of the simple acts of which they are compounded, overlooking the others. And from this cause many disputes have been raised, and many errors have been occasioned with regard to the nature of such operations.

The perception of external objects is accompanied with some sensation corresponding to the object perceived, and such sensations have, in many cases, in all languages, the same name with the external object which they always accompany. The difficulty of disjoining, by abstraction, things thus constantly conjoined in the course of nature, and things which have one and the same name in all languages, has likewise been frequently an occasion of errors in the philosophy of the mind. To avoid such errors, nothing is of more importance than to have a distinct notion of that simple act of the mind which we call *sensation*, and which we have endeavoured to describe. By this means, we shall find it more easy to distinguish it from every external object that it accompanies, and from every other act of the mind that may be conjoined with it. For this purpose, it is likewise of importance that the name of *sensation* should, in philosophical writings, be appropriated to signify this simple act of the mind, without including anything more in its signification, or being applied to other purposes.

I shall add an observation concerning the word *feeling*. This word has two meanings. *First*, it signifies the perceptions we have of external objects, by the sense of touch. When we speak of feeling a body to be hard or soft, rough or smooth, hot or cold, to feel these things is to perceive them by touch. They are external things, and that act of the mind by which we feel them is easily distinguished from the objects felt. *Secondly*, the word *feeling* is used to signify the same thing as *sensation*, which we have

---

* But sensation, in the language of philosophers, has been generally employed to denote the whole process of sensitive cognition, including both *perception proper* and *sensation proper*. On this distinction, see below, Essay II., ch. xvi., and Note D.*—H.

just now explained ; and, in this sense, it has no object ; the feeling and the thing felt are one and the same. [35]

Perhaps betwixt feeling, taken in this last sense, and sensation, there may be this small difference, that sensation is most commonly used to signify those feelings which we have by our external senses and bodily appetites, and all our bodily pains and pleasures.   But there are *feelings* of a nobler nature accompanying our affections, our moral judgments, and our determinations in matters of taste, to which the word *sensation* is less properly applied.

I have premised these observations on the meaning of certain words that frequently occur in treating of this subject, for two reasons : *First,* That I may be the better understood when I use them ; and, *Secondly,* That those who would make any progress in this branch of science, may accustom themselves to attend very carefully to the meaning of words that are used in it. They may be assured of this, that the ambiguity of words, and the vague and improper application of them, have thrown more darkness upon this subject than the subtilty and intricacy of things.

When we use common words, we ought to use them in the sense in which they are most commonly used by the best and purest writers in the language ; and, when we have occasion to enlarge or restrict the meaning of a common word, or give it more precision than it has in common language, the reader ought to have warning of this, otherwise we shall impose upon ourselves and upon him.

A very respectable writer has given a good example of this kind, by explaining, in an Appendix to his " Elements of Criticism," the terms he has occasion to use. In that Appendix, most of the words are explained on which I have been making observations ; and the explication I have given, I think, agrees, for the most part, with his.

Other words that need explication, shall be explained as they occur. [36]

CHAPTER II.

PRINCIPLES TAKEN FOR GRANTED.

As there are words common to philosophers and to the vulgar, which need no explication, so there are principles common to both, which need no proof, and which do not admit of direct proof.

One who applies to any branch of science, must be come to years of understanding, and, consequently, must have exercised his reason, and the other powers of his mind, in various ways. He must have formed various opinions and principles, by which he conducts himself in the affairs of life. Of those principles, some are common to all men, being evident in themselves, and so necessary in the conduct of life that a man cannot live and act according to the rules of common prudence without them.

All men that have common understanding, agree in such principles ; and consider a man as lunatic or destitute of common sense, who denies or calls them in question. Thus, if any man were found of so strange a turn as not to believe his own eyes, to put no trust in his senses, nor have the least regard to their testimony, would any man think it worth while to reason gravely with such a person, and, by argument, to convince him of his error ?   Surely no wise man would.   For, before men can reason together, they must agree in first principles ; and it is impossible to reason with a man who has no principles in common with you.

There are, therefore, common principles, which are the foundation of all reasoning and of all science. Such common principles seldom admit of direct proof, nor do they need it. Men need not to be taught them ; for they are such as all men of [37] common understanding know ; or such, at least, as they give a ready assent to, as soon as they are proposed and understood.

Such principles, when we have occasion to use them in science, are called *axioms.* And, although it be not absolutely necessary, yet it may be of great use, to point out the principles or axioms on which a science is grounded.

Thus, mathematicians, before they prove any of the propositions of mathematics, lay down certain axioms, or common principles, upon which they build their reasonings. And although those axioms be truths which every man knew before—such as, That the whole is greater than a part, That equal quantities added to equal quantities make equal sums ; yet, when we see nothing assumed in the proof of mathematical propositions, but such self-evident axioms, the propositions appear more certain, and leave no room for doubt or dispute.

In all other sciences, as well as in mathematics, it will be found that there are a few common principles, upon which all the reasonings in that science are grounded, and into which they may be resolved. If these were pointed out and considered, we should be better able to judge what stress may be laid upon the conclusions in that science. If the principles be certain, the conclusions justly drawn from them must be certain. If the principles be only probable, the conclusions can only be probable. If the principles be false, dubious, or obscure, the superstructure that is built upon them must partake of the weakness of the foundation.

[35-37]

Sir Isaac Newton, the greatest of natural philosophers, has given an example well worthy of imitation, by laying down the common principles or axioms, on which the reasonings in natural philosophy are built. Before this was done, the reasonings of philosophers in that science were as vague and uncertain as they are in most others. Nothing was fixed; all was dispute and controversy; [38] but, by this happy expedient, a solid foundation is laid in that science, and a noble superstructure is raised upon it, about which there is now no more dispute or controversy among men of knowledge, than there is about the conclusions of mathematics.

It may, however, be observed, that the first principles of natural philosophy are of a quite different nature from mathematical axioms: they have not the same kind of evidence, nor are they necessary truths, as mathematical axioms are. They are such as these: That similar effects proceed from the same or similar causes; That we ought to admit of no other causes of natural effects, but such as are true, and sufficient to account for the effects. These are principles which, though they have not the same kind of evidence that mathematical axioms have; yet have such evidence that every man of common understanding readily assents to them, and finds it absolutely necessary to conduct his actions and opinions by them, in the ordinary affairs of life.

Though it has not been usual, yet I conceive it may be useful, to point out some of those things which I shall take for granted, as first principles, in treating of the mind and its faculties. There is the more occasion for this: because very ingenious men, such as Des Cartes, Malebranche, Arnauld, Locke, and many others, have lost much labour, by not distinguishing things which require proof, from things which, though they may admit of illustration, yet, being self-evident, do not admit of proof. When men attempt to deduce such self-evident principles from others more evident, they always fall into inconclusive reasoning: and the consequence of this has been, that others, such as Berkeley and Hume, finding the arguments brought to prove such first principles to be weak and inconclusive, have been tempted first to doubt of them, and afterwards to deny them.

It is so irksome to reason with those who deny first principles, that wise men commonly decline it. Yet it is not impossible, that [39] what is only a vulgar prejudice may be mistaken for a first principle. Nor is it impossible that what is really a first principle may, by the enchantment of words, have such a mist thrown about it, as to

[38·40]

hide its evidence, and to make a man of candour doubt of it. Such cases happen more frequently, perhaps, in this science than in any other; but they are not altogether without remedy. There are ways by which the evidence of first principles may be made more apparent when they are brought into dispute; but they require to be handled in a way peculiar to themselves. Their evidence is not demonstrative, but intuitive. They require not proof, but to be placed in a proper point of view. This will be shewn more fully in its proper place, and applied to those very principles which we now assume. In the meantime, when they are proposed as first principles, the reader is put on his guard, and warned to consider whether they have a just claim to that character.

1. *First*, then, I shall take it for granted, that I *think*, that I *remember* that I *reason*, and, in general, that I really perform all those operations of mind of which I am conscious.

The operations of our minds are attended with consciousness; and this consciousness is the evidence, the only evidence, which we have or can have of their existence. If a man should take it into his head to think or to say that his consciousness may deceive him, and to require proof that it cannot, I know of no proof that can be given him; he must be left to himself, as a man that denies first principles, without which there can be no reasoning. Every man finds himself under a necessity of believing what consciousness testifies, and everything that hath this testimony is to be taken as a first principle. *

2. As by consciousness we know certainly the existence of our present thoughts and passions; so we know the past by remembrance.† And, when they are recent, and the remembrance of them fresh, [40] the knowledge of them, from such distinct remembrance, is, in its certainty and evidence, next to that of consciousness.

3. But it is to be observed that we are conscious of many things to which we give little or no *attention*. We can hardly attend to several things at the same time; and our attention is commonly employed about that which is the object of our thought, and rarely about the thought itself. Thus, when a man is angry, his

---

* To doubt that we are conscious of this or that, is impossible. For the doubt must at least postulate itself; but the doubt is only a datum of consciousness; therefore, in postulating its own reality, it admits the truth of consciousness, and consequently annihilates itself. See below, p. 579. On Consciousness, in the history of psychology, see Note H.—H.

† Remembrance cannot be taken out of Consciousness. See Note H.—H

attention is turned to the injury done him, or the injurious person ; and he gives very little attention to the passion of anger, although he is conscious of it. It is in our power, however, when we come to the years of understanding, to give attention to our own thoughts and passions, and the various operations of our minds. And, when we make these the objects of our attention, either while they are present or when they are recent and fresh in our memory, this act of the mind is called *reflection*.

We take it for granted, therefore, that, by attentive reflection, a man may have a clear and certain knowledge of the operations of his own mind ; a knowledge no less clear and certain than that which he has of an external object when it is set before his eyes.

This reflection is a kind of intuition, it gives a like conviction with regard to internal objects, or things in the mind, as the faculty of seeing gives with regard to objects of sight. A man must, therefore, be convinced beyond possibility of doubt, of everything with regard to the operations of his own mind, which he clearly and distinctly discerns by attentive reflection. *

4. I take it for granted that all the thoughts I am conscious of, or remember, are the thoughts of one and the same thinking principle, which I call *myself*, or my *mind*. Every man has an immediate and irresistible conviction, not only of his present existence, but of his continued existence and identity, as far back as he can remember. If any man should think fit to demand [41] a proof that the thoughts he is successively conscious of, belong to one and the same thinking principle—if he should demand a proof that he is the same person to-day as he was yesterday, or a year ago—I know no proof that can be given him : he must be left to himself, either as a man that is lunatic, or as one who denies first principles, and is not to be reasoned with.

Every man of a sound mind, finds himself under a necessity of believing his own identity, and continued existence. The conviction of this is immediate and irresistible ; and, if he should lose this conviction, it would be a certain proof of insanity, which is not to be remedied by reasoning.

5. I take it for granted, that there are some things which cannot exist by themselves, but must be in something else to which they belong, as qualities, or attributes.

Thus, motion cannot exist, but in some-thing that is moved. And to suppose that there can be motion while everything is at rest, is a gross and palpable absurdity. In like manner, hardness and softness, sweetness and bitterness, are things which cannot exist by themselves ; they are qualities of something which is hard or soft, sweet or bitter. That thing, whatever it be, of which they are qualities, is called their subject ; and such qualities necessarily suppose a subject.

Things which may exist by themselves, and do not necessarily suppose the existence of anything else, are called substances : and, with relation to the qualities or attributes that belong to them, they are called the subjects of such qualities or attributes.

All the things which we immediately perceive by our senses, and all the things we are conscious of, are things which must be in something else, as their subject. Thus, by my senses, I perceive figure, colour, hardness, softness, motion, resistance, and such [42] like things. But these are qualities, and must necessarily be in something that is figured, coloured, hard or soft, that moves, or resists. It is not to these qualities, but to that which is the subject of them, that we give the name of body. If any man should think fit to deny that these things are qualities, or that they require any subject, I leave him to enjoy his opinion as a man who denies first principles, and is not fit to be reasoned with. If he has common understanding, he will find that he cannot converse half an hour without saying things which imply the contrary of what he professes to believe.

In like manner, the things I am conscious of, such as thought, reasoning, desire, necessarily suppose something that thinks, that reasons, that desires. We do not give the name of mind to thought, reason, or desire ; but to that being which thinks, which reasons, and which desires.

That every act or operation, therefore, supposes an agent, that every quality supposes a subject, are things which I do not attempt to prove, but take for granted. Every man of common understanding discerns this immediately, and cannot entertain the least doubt of it. In all languages, we find certain words which, by grammarians, are called adjectives. Such words denote attributes, and every adjective must have a substantive to which it belongs—that is, every attribute must have a subject. In all languages, we find active verbs which denote some action or operation ; and it is a fundamental rule in the grammar of all languages, that such a verb supposes a person—that is, in other words, that every action must have an agent. We take it, therefore, as a first principle, that goodness, wisdom, and virtue, can only be in some

---

* See *infra*, pp. 60, 105, 581, where a *similar*, and pp. 324, 516, where a *different* extension is given to *Reflection.* On Attention and Reflection, in the history of psychology, see Note I.—H.

being that is good, wise, and virtuous; that thinking supposes a being that thinks; and that every operation we are conscious of supposes an agent that operates, which we call mind.

6. I take it for granted, that, in most operations of the mind, there [43] must be an object distinct from the operation itself. I cannot see, without seeing something. To see without having any object of sight is absurd. I cannot remember, without remembering something. The thing remembered is past, while the remembrance of it is present; and, therefore, the operation and the object of it must be distinct things. The operations of our mind are denoted, in all languages, by active transitive verbs, which, from their construction in grammar, require not only a person or agent, but likewise an object of the operation. Thus, the verb know, denotes an operation of mind. From the general structure of language, this verb requires a person—I know, you know, or he knows; but it requires no less a noun in the accusative case, denoting the thing known; for he that knows must know something; and, to know, without having any object of knowledge, is an absurdity too gross to admit of reasoning *

7. We ought likewise to take for granted, as first principles, things wherein we find an universal agreement, among the learned and unlearned, in the different nations and ages of the world.† A consent of ages and nations, of the learned and vulgar, ought, at least, to have great authority, unless we can shew some prejudice as universal as that consent is, which might be the cause of it. Truth is one, but error is infinite. There are many truths so obvious to the human faculties, that it may be expected that men should universally agree in them. And this is actually found to be the case with regard to many truths, against which we find no dissent, unless perhaps that of a few sceptical philosophers, who may justly be suspected, in such cases, to differ from the rest of mankind, through pride, obstinacy, or some favourite passion. Where there is such universal consent in things not deep nor intricate, but which lie, as it were, on the surface, there is the greatest presumption that can be, that it is the natural result of the human faculties; and it must have great authority with every sober [44] mind that loves truth. *Major enim pars eo fere deferri solet quo a natura deducitur.*—Cic. de Off. I. 41.

Perhaps it may be thought that it is impossible to collect the opinions of all men upon any point whatsoever; and, therefore, that this maxim can be of no use. But there are many cases wherein it is

otherwise. Who can doubt, for instance, whether mankind have, in all ages, believed the existence of a material world, and that those things which they see and handle are real, and not mere illusions and apparitions? Who can doubt whether mankind have universally believed that everything that begins to exist, and every change that happens in nature, must have a cause? Who can doubt whether mankind have been universally persuaded that there is a right and a wrong in human conduct?— some things which, in certain circumstances, they ought to do, and other things which they ought not to do? The universality of these opinions, and of many such that might be named, is sufficiently evident, from the whole tenor of men's conduct, as far as our acquaintance reaches, and from the records of history, in all ages and nations, that are transmitted to us.

There are other opinions that appear to be universal, from what is common in the structure of all languages, ancient and modern, polished and barbarous. Language is the express image and picture of human thoughts; and, from the picture, we may often draw very certain conclusions with regard to the original. We find in all languages the same parts of speech—nouns substantive and adjective, verbs active and passive, varied according to the tenses of past, present, and future; we find adverbs, prepositions, and conjunctions. There are general rules of syntax common to all languages. This uniformity in the structure of language shews a certain degree of uniformity in those notions upon which the structure of language is grounded.

We find, in the structure of all languages, the distinction of [45] acting and being acted upon, the distinction of action and agent, of quality and subject, and many others of the like kind; which shews that these distinctions are founded in the universal sense of mankind. We shall have frequent occasion to argue from the sense of mankind expressed in the structure of language; and therefore it was proper here to take notice of the force of arguments drawn from this topic.

8. I need hardly say that I shall also take for granted such facts as are attested to the conviction of all sober and reasonable men, either by our senses, by memory, or by human testimony. Although some writers on this subject have disputed the authority of the senses, of memory, and of every human faculty, yet we find that such persons, in the conduct of life, in pursuing their ends, or in avoiding dangers, pay the same regard to the authority of their senses and other faculties, as the rest of mankind. By this they give us just ground to doubt of

---

* See Note B.—H.   † See Note A.—H.

[43-45]

their candour in their professions of scepticism.

This, indeed, has always been the fate of the few that have professed scepticism, that, when they have done what they can to discredit their senses, they find themselves, after all, under a necessity of trusting to them. Mr Hume has been so candid as to acknowledge this; and it is no less true of those who have not shewn the same candour; for I never heard that any sceptic run his head against a post, or stepped into a kennel, because he did not believe his eyes.

Upon the whole, I acknowledge that we ought to be cautious that we do not adopt opinions as first principles which are not entitled to that character. But there is surely the least danger of men's being imposed upon in this way, when such principles openly lay claim to the character, and are thereby fairly exposed to the examination of those who may dispute their authority. We do not pretend that those things that are laid down as first principles may not be examined, and that we ought not to [46] have our ears open to what may be pleaded against their being admitted as such. Let us deal with them as an upright judge does with a witness who has a fair character. He pays a regard to the testimony of such a witness while his character is unimpeached; but, if it can be shewn that he is suborned, or that he is influenced by malice or partial favour, his testimony loses all its credit, and is justly rejected.

CHAPTER III.

OF HYPOTHESES.

EVERY branch of human knowledge hath its proper principles, its proper foundation and method of reasoning; and, if we endeavour to build it upon any other foundation, it will never stand firm and stable. Thus, the historian builds upon testimony, and rarely indulges conjecture; the antiquarian mixes conjecture with testimony, and the former often makes the larger ingredient; the mathematician pays not the least regard either to testimony or conjecture, but deduces everything, by demonstrative reasoning, from his definitions and axioms. Indeed, whatever is built upon conjecture, is improperly called science; for conjecture may beget opinion, but cannot produce knowledge. Natural philosophy must be built upon the phænomena of the material system, discovered by observation and experiment.

When men first began to philosophize--that is, to carry their thoughts beyond the objects of sense, and to inquire into the causes of things, and the secret operations of nature—it was very natural for them to indulge conjecture; nor was it to be expected that, in many ages, they should discover the proper and scientific way of proceeding in philosophical disquisitions. Accordingly, we find that the most ancient systems in every branch of philosophy were nothing but the conjectures of men famous for their wisdom, whose fame gave authority to their opinions. Thus, in early ages, [47] wise men conjectured that this earth is a vast plain, surrounded on all hands by a boundless ocean; that, from this ocean, the sun, moon, and stars emerge at their rising, and plunge into it again at their setting.

With regard to the mind, men in their rudest state are apt to conjecture that the principle of life in a man is his breath; because the most obvious distinction between a living and a dead man is, that the one breathes, and the other does not. To this it is owing that, in ancient languages, the word which denotes the soul, is that which properly signifies breath or air.

As men advance in knowledge, their first conjectures appear silly and childish, and give place to others, which tally better with later observations and discoveries. Thus one system of philosophy succeeds another, without any claim to superior merit, but this—that it is a more ingenious system of conjectures, and accounts better for common appearances.

To omit many ancient systems of this kind, Des Cartes, about the middle of the last century, dissatisfied with the *materia prima*, the *substantial forms*, and the *occult qualities* of the Peripatetics, conjectured boldly, that the heavenly bodies of our system are carried round by a vortex or whirlpool of subtile matter, just as straws and chaff are carried round in a tub of water. He conjectured, that the soul is seated in a small gland in the brain, called the pineal gland; that there, as in her chamber of presence, she receives intelligence of everything that affects the senses, by means of a subtile fluid contained in the nerves, called the animal spirits; and that she dispatches these animal spirits, as her messengers, to put in motion the several muscles of the body, as there is occasion.* By such con-

* It is not, however, to be supposed that Des Cartes allowed the soul to be seated by local presence in any part of the body; for the smallest point of body is still extended, and mind is absolutely simple and incapable of occupying place. The pineal gland, in the Cartesian doctrine, is only analogically called the seat of the soul, inasmuch as this is viewed as the central point of the corporeal organism; but while through this point the mind and body are mutually connected, that connection is not one of a mere physical dependence, as they do not operate on each by direct and natural causation.—H.

jectures as these, Des Cartes could account for every phænomenon in nature, in such a plausible manner as gave satisfaction to a great part of the learned world for more than half a century. [48] Such conjectures in philosophical matters have commonly got the name of *hypotheses*, or *theories*.* And the invention of a hypothesis, founded on some slight probabilities, which accounts for many appearances of nature, has been considered as the highest attainment of a philosopher. If the hypothesis hangs well together, is embellished by a lively imagination, and serves to account for common appearances, it is considered by many as having all the qualities that should recommend it to our belief, and all that ought to be required in a philosophical system.

There is such proneness in men of genius to invent hypotheses, and in others to acquiesce in them, as the utmost which the human faculties can attain in philosophy, that it is of the last consequence to the progress of real knowledge, that men should have a clear and distinct understanding of the nature of hypotheses in philosophy, and of the regard that is due to them.

Although some conjectures may have a considerable degree of probability, yet it is evidently in the nature of conjecture to be uncertain. In every case the assent ought to be proportioned to the evidence; for to believe firmly what has but a small degree of probability, is a manifest abuse of our understanding. Now, though we may, in many cases, form very probable conjectures concerning the works of men, every conjecture we can form with regard to the works of God has as little probability as the conjectures of a child with regard to the works of a man.

The wisdom of God exceeds that of the wisest man, more than his wisdom exceeds that of a child. If a child were to conjecture how an army is to be formed in the day of battle—how a city is to be fortified, or a state governed—what chance has he to guess right? As little chance has the wisest man when he pretends to conjecture how the planets move in their courses, how the sea ebbs and flows, and how our minds act upon our bodies. [49]

If a thousand of the greatest wits that ever the world produced were, without any previous knowledge in anatomy, to sit down and contrive how, and by what internal organs, the various functions of the human body are carried on, how the blood is made to circulate and the limbs to move, they would not, in a thousand years, hit upon anything like the truth.

Of all the discoveries that have been made concerning the inward structure of the human body, never one was made by conjecture. Accurate observations of anatomists have brought to light innumerable artifices of Nature in the contrivance of this machine of the human body, which we cannot but admire as excellently adapted to their several purposes. But the most sagacious physiologist never dreamed of them till they were discovered. On the other hand, innumerable conjectures, formed in different ages, with regard to the structure of the body, have been confuted by observation, and none ever confirmed.

What we have said of the internal structure of the human body, may be said, with justice, of every other part of the works of God, wherein any real discovery has been made. Such discoveries have always been made by patient observation, by accurate experiments, or by conclusions drawn from strict reasoning from observations and experiments; and such discoveries have always tended to refute, but not to confirm, the theories and hypotheses which ingenious men have invented.

As this is a fact confirmed by the history of philosophy in all past ages, it ought to have taught men, long ago, to treat with just contempt hypotheses in every branch of philosophy, and to despair of ever advancing real knowledge in that way. The Indian philosopher, being at a loss to know how the earth was supported, invented the hypothesis of a huge elephant; and this elephant he supposed to stand upon the back of a huge tortoise. This hypothesis, however ridiculous it appears to us, might seem very reasonable [50] to other Indians, who knew no more than the inventor of it; and the same will be the fate of all hypotheses invented by men to account for the works of God. They may have a decent and plausible appearance to those who are not more knowing than the inventor; but, when men come to be more enlightened, they will always appear ridiculous and childish.

This has been the case with regard to hypotheses that have been revered by the most enlightened part of mankind for hundreds of years; and it will always be the case to the end of the world. For, until the wisdom of men bear some proportion to the wisdom of God, their attempts to find out the structure of his works, by the force of their wit and genius, will be vain.

The finest productions of human art are immensely short of the meanest works of Nature. The nicest artist cannot make a feather or the leaf of a tree. Human workmanship will never bear a comparison with divine. Conjectures and hypotheses are the invention and the workmanship of men, and must bear proportion to the capacity and skill of the inventor; and, therefore, will always be very unlike to the works of God, which it is the business of philosophy to discover.

The world has been so long befooled by hypotheses in all parts of philosophy, that it is of the utmost consequence to every man who would make any progress in real knowledge, to treat them with just contempt, as the reveries of vain and fanciful men, whose pride makes them conceive themselves able to unfold the mysteries of nature by the force of their genius. A learned man, in an epistle to Des Cartes, has the following observation, which very much deserved the attention of that philosopher, and of all that come after him :—" When men, sitting in their closet, and consulting only their books, attempt disquisitions into nature, they may, indeed, tell how they would have made the world, if God had given them that in commission ; that is, they may describe [51] chimeras, which correspond with the imbecility of their own minds, no less than the admirable beauty of the universe corresponds with the infinite perfection of its Creator ; but without an understanding truly divine, they can never form such an idea to themselves as the Deity had in creating things."

Let us, therefore, lay down this as a fundamental principle in our inquiries into the structure of the mind and its operations—that no regard is due to the conjectures or hypotheses of philosophers, however ancient, however generally received. Let us accustom ourselves to try every opinion by the touchstone of fact and experience. What can fairly be deduced from facts duly observed or sufficiently attested, is genuine and pure ; it is the voice of God, and no fiction of human imagination.

The first rule of philosophising laid down by the great Newton, is this :—*Causas rerum naturalium, non plures admitti debere, quam quæ et veræ sint, et earum phæno menis explicandis sufficiant.* " No more causes, nor any other causes of natural effects, ought to be admitted, but such as are both true, and are sufficient for explaining their appearances." This is a golden rule ; it is the true and proper test, by which what is sound and solid in philosophy may be distinguished from what is hollow and vain.[*]

If a philosopher, therefore, pretends to shew us the cause of any natural effect, whether relating to matter or to mind, let us first consider whether there is sufficient

evidence that the cause he assigns does really exist. If there is not, reject it with disdain, as a fiction which ought to have no place in genuine philosophy. If the cause assigned really exists, consider, in the next place, whether the effect it is brought to explain necessarily follows from it. Unless it has these two conditions, it is good for nothing.

When Newton had shewn the admirable effects of gravitation in our planetary system, he must have felt a strong desire to know [52] its cause. He could have invented a hypothesis for this purpose, as many had done before him. But his philosophy was of another complexion. Let us hear what he says : *Rationem harum gravitatis proprietatum ex phænomenis non potui deducere, et hypotheses non fingo. Quicquid enim ex phænomenis non deducitur hypothesis vocanda est. Et hypotheses, seu metaphysicæ, seu physicæ, seu qualitatum occultarum, seu mechanicæ, in philosophia experimentali locum non habent.*

CHAPTER IV.

OF ANALOGY.

It is natural to men to judge of things less known, by some similitude they observe, or think they observe, between them and things more familiar or better known. In many cases, we have no better way of judging. And, where the things compared have really a great similitude in their nature, when there is reason to think that they are subject to the same laws, there may be a considerable degree of probability in conclusions drawn from analogy.

Thus, we may observe a very great similitude between this earth which we inhabit, and the other planets, Saturn, Jupiter, Mars, Venus, and Mercury. They all revolve round the sun, as the earth does, although at different distances and in different periods. They borrow all their light from the sun, as the earth does. Several of them are known to revolve round their axis like the earth, and, by that means, must have a like succession of day and night. Some of them have moons, that serve to give them light in the absence of the sun, as our moon does to us. They are all, in their motions, subject to the same law of gravitation, as the earth is. From all this similitude, it is not unreasonable to think, that those planets may, like our earth, be the habitation of various [53] orders of living creatures. There is some probability in this conclusion from analogy.

In medicine, physicians must, for the most part, be directed in their prescriptions

---

[*] For this rule we are not indebted to Newton. It is only the old law of parcimony, and that ambiguously expressed. For, in their plain meaning, the words " *et veræ sint* " are redundant ; or what follows is redundant, and the whole rule a barren truism.—H.

by analogy. The constitution of one human body is so like to that of another that it is reasonable to think that what is the cause of health or sickness to one, may have the same effect upon another. And this generally is found true, though not without some exceptions.

In politics we reason, for the most part, from analogy. The constitution of human nature is so similar in different societies or commonwealths, that the causes of peace and war, of tranquillity and sedition, of riches and poverty, of improvement and degeneracy, are much the same in all.

Analogical reasoning, therefore, is not, in all cases, to be rejected. It may afford a greater or a less degree of probability, according as the things compared are more or less similar in their nature. But it ought to be observed, that, as this kind of reasoning can afford only probable evidence at best; so, unless great caution be used, we are apt to be led into error by it. For men are naturally disposed to conceive a greater similitude in things than there really is.

To give an instance of this: Anatomists, in ancient ages, seldom dissected human bodies; but very often the bodies of those quadrupeds whose internal structure was thought to approach nearest to that of the human body. Modern anatomists have discovered many mistakes the ancients were led into, by their conceiving a greater similitude between the structure of men and of some beasts than there is in reality. By this, and many other instances that might be given, it appears that conclusions built on analogy stand on a slippery foundation; and that we ought never to rest upon evidence of this kind, when we can have more direct evidence. [54]

I know no author who has made a more just and a more happy use of this mode of reasoning than Bishop Butler, in his " Analogy of Religion, Natural and Revealed, to the Constitution and Course of Nature." In that excellent work the author does not ground any of the truths of religion upon analogy, as their proper evidence. He only makes use of analogy to answer objections against them. When objections are made against the truths of religion, which may be made with equal strength against what we know to be true in the course of nature, such objections can have no weight.

Analogical reasoning, therefore, may be of excellent use in answering objections against truths which have other evidence. It may likewise give a greater or a less degree of probability in cases where we can find no other evidence. But all arguments, drawn from analogy, are still the weaker, the greater disparity there is between the

[54. 55]

things compared; and, therefore, must be weakest of all when we compare body with mind, because there are no two things in nature more unlike.

There is no subject in which men have always been so prone to form their notions by analogies of this kind, as in what relates to the mind. We form an early acquaintance with material things by means of our senses, and are bred up in a constant familiarity with them. Hence we are apt to measure all things by them; and to ascribe to things most remote from matter, the qualities that belong to material things. It is for this reason, that mankind have, in all ages, been so prone to conceive the mind itself to be some subtile kind of matter: that they have been disposed to ascribe human figure and human organs, not only to angels, but even to the Deity. Though we are conscious of the operations of our own minds when they are exerted, and are capable of attending to them, so as to form a distinct notion of them, this is so difficult a work to men whose attention is constantly solicited by external objects, that we give them names from things that are familiar, and which [55] are conceived to have some similitude to them; and the notions we form of them are no less analogical than the names we give them. Almost all the words by which we express the operations of the mind, are borrowed from material objects. To understand, to conceive, to imagine, to comprehend, to deliberate, to infer, and many others, are words of this kind; so that the very language of mankind, with regard to the operations of our minds, is analogical. Because bodies are affected only by contact and pressure, we are apt to conceive that what is an immediate object of thought, and affects the mind, must be in contact with it, and make some impression upon it. When we imagine anything, the very word leads us to think that there must be some image in the mind of the thing conceived. It is evident that these notions are drawn from some similitude conceived between body and mind, and between the properties of body and the operations of mind.

To illustrate more fully that analogical reasoning from a supposed similitude of mind to body, which I conceive to be the most fruitful source of error with regard to the operations of our minds, I shall give an instance of it.

When a man is urged by contrary motives those on one hand inciting him to do some action, those on the other to forbear it—he deliberates about it, and at last resolves to do it, or not to do it. The contrary motives are here compared to the weights in the opposite scales of a balance; and there is not, perhaps, any instance that can be named of a more striking analogy between body and mind. Hence the phrases of weighing motives, of deliberating upon actions, are common to all languages.

From this analogy, some philosophers draw very important conclusions. They say, that, as the balance cannot incline to one side more than the other when the opposite weights are equal, so a man cannot possibly determine himself if the motives on both hands are equal ; and, as the balance must necessarily turn to that side [56] which has most weight, so the man must necessarily be determined to that hand where the motive is strongest. And on this foundation some of the schoolmen* maintained that, if a hungry ass were placed between two bundles of hay equally inviting, the beast must stand still and starve to death, being unable to turn to either, because there are equal motives to both. This is an instance of that analogical reasoning which I conceive ought never to be trusted ; for the analogy between a balance and a man deliberating, though one of the strongest that can be found between matter and mind, is too weak to support any argument. A piece of dead inactive matter, and an active intelligent being, are things very unlike ; and, because the one would remain at rest in a certain case, it does not follow that the other would be inactive in a case somewhat similar. The argument is no better than this—That, because a dead animal moves only as it is pushed, and, if pushed with equal force in contrary directions, must remain at rest ; therefore, the same thing must happen to a living animal : for, surely, the similitude between a dead animal and a living, is as great as that between a balance and a man.

The conclusion I would draw from all that has been said on analogy, is, that, in our inquiries concerning the mind and its operations, we ought never to trust to reasonings drawn from some supposed similitude of body to mind ; and that we ought to be very much upon our guard that we be not imposed upon by those analogical terms and phrases, by which the operations of the mind are expressed in all languages. [57]

* This illustration is specially associated with Joannes Buridanus, a celebrated Nominalis. of the 14th century, and one of the acutest reasoners on the great question of moral liberty. The supposition of the ass, &c., is not, however, as I have ascertained, to be found in his writings. Perhaps it was orally advanced in disputation, or in lecturing, as an example in illustration of his Determinism ; perhaps it was employed by his opponents as an instance to reduce that doctrine to absurdity. With this latter view, a similar refutation of the principles of our modern Fatalists was, as we have seen, ingeniously essayed by Reid's friend and kinsman, Dr James Gregory.—H.

CHAPTER V.

OF THE PROPER MEANS OF KNOWING THE OPERATIONS OF THE MIND.

SINCE we ought to pay no regard to hypotheses, and to be very suspicious of analogical reasoning, it may be asked, From what source must the knowledge of the mind and its faculties be drawn ?

I answer, the chief and proper source of this branch of knowledge is accurate reflection upon the operations of our own minds. Of this source we shall speak more fully, after making some remarks upon two others that may be subservient to it. The first of them is attention to the structure of language.

The language of mankind is expressive of their thoughts, and of the various operations of their minds. The various operations of the understanding, will, and passions, which are common to mankind, have various forms of speech corresponding to them in all languages, which are the signs of them, and by which they are expressed : And a due attention to the signs may, in many cases, give considerable light to the things signified by them.

There are in all languages modes of speech, by which men signify their judgment, or give their testimony ; by which they accept or refuse ; by which they ask information or advice ; by which they command, or threaten, or supplicate ; by which they plight their faith in promises or contracts. If such operations were not common to mankind, we should not find in all languages forms of speech, by which they are expressed.

All languages, indeed, have their imperfections—they can never be adequate to all the varieties of human thought ; and therefore things may be really distinct in their nature, and capable of being distinguished by the human mind, which are not distinguished [58] in common language. We can only expect, in the structure of languages, those distinctions which all mankind in the common business of life have occasion to make.

There may be peculiarities in a particular language, of the causes of which we are ignorant, and from which, therefore, we can draw no conclusion. But whatever we find common to all languages, must have a common cause ; must be owing to some common notion or sentiment of the human mind.

We gave some examples of this before, and shall here add another. All languages have a plural number in many of their nouns ; from which we may infer that all men have notions, not of individual things only, but of attributes, or things which are common to many individuals; for no individual can have a plural number.

Another source of information in this subject, is a due attention to the course of human actions and conduct. The actions of men are effects; their sentiments, their passions, and their affections, are the causes of those effects; and we may, in many cases, form a judgment of the cause from the effect.

The behaviour of parents towards their children gives sufficient evidence even to those who never had children, that the parental affection is common to mankind. It is easy to see, from the general conduct of men, what are the natural objects of their esteem, their admiration, their love, their approbation, their resentment, and of all their other original dispositions. It is obvious, from the conduct of men in all ages, that man is by his nature a social animal; that he delights to associate with his species; to converse, and to exchange good offices with them.

Not only the actions, but even the opinions of men may sometimes give light into the frame of the human mind. The opinions of men may be considered as the effects of their intellectual powers, [59] as their actions are the effects of their active principles. Even the prejudices and errors of mankind, when they are general, must have some cause no less general; the discovery of which will throw some light upon the frame of the human understanding.

I conceive this to be the principal use of the history of philosophy. When we trace the history of the various philosophical opinions that have sprung up among thinking men, we are led into a labyrinth of fanciful opinions, contradictions, and absurdities, intermixed with some truths; yet we may sometimes find a clue to lead us through the several windings of this labyrinth. We may find that point of view which presented things to the author of the system, in the light in which they appeared to him. This will often give a consistency to things seemingly contradictory, and some degree of probability to those that appeared most fanciful. *

The history of philosophy, considered as a map of the intellectual operations of men of genius, must always be entertaining, and may sometimes give us views of the human understanding, which could not easily be had any other way.

I return to what I mentioned as the main source of information on this subject—attentive reflection upon the operations of our own minds.

All the notions we have of mind and of its operations, are, by Mr Locke, called *ideas of reflection.* * A man may have as distinct notions of remembrance, of judgment, of will, of desire, as he has of any object whatever. Such notions, as Mr Locke justly observes, are got by the power of reflection. But what is this power of reflection? "It is," says the same author, "that power by which the mind turns its view inward, and observes its own actions and operations." He observes elsewhere, "That the understanding, like the eye, whilst it makes us see and perceive all [60] other things, takes no notice of itself; and that it requires art and pains to set it at a distance, and make it its own object." Cicero hath expressed this sentiment most beautifully. Tusc. I. 28.

This power of the understanding to make its own operations its object, to attend to them, and examine them on all sides, is the power of reflection, by which alone we can have any distinct notion of the powers of our own or of other minds.

This reflection ought to be distinguished from consciousness, with which it is too often confounded even by Mr Locke. All men are conscious of the operations of their own minds, at all times, while they are awake; but there are few who reflect upon them, or make them objects of thought.

From infancy, till we come to the years of understanding, we are employed solely about external objects. And, although the mind is conscious of its operations, it does not attend to them; its attention is turned solely to the external objects, about which those operations are employed. Thus, when a man is angry, he is conscious of his passion; but his attention is turned to the person who offended him, and the circumstances of the offence, while the passion of anger is not in the least the object of his attention.

I conceive this is sufficient to shew the difference between consciousness of the operations of our minds, and reflection upon them; and to shew that we may have the former without any degree of the latter. The difference between consciousness and reflection, is like to the difference between a superficial view of an object which presents itself to the eye while we are engaged about something else, and that attentive examination which we give to an object when we are wholly employed in surveying it. Attention is a voluntary act; it requires an active exertion to begin and to continue it, and it may be continued as long as we will; but consciousness [61] is

* "Every error," says Bossuet, "is a truth abused."—H.

[59—61]

* Locke is not (as Reid seems to think, and as Mr. Stewart expressly says) the first who introduced Reflection either as a psychological term, or as a psychological principle. See Note I.—H.

involuntary and of no continuance, changing with every thought.

The power of reflection upon the operations of their own minds, does not appear at all in children. Men must be come to some ripeness of understanding before they are capable of it. Of all the powers of the human mind, it seems to be the last that unfolds itself. Most men seem incapable of acquiring it in any considerable degree. Like all our other powers, it is greatly improved by exercise; and until a man has got the habit of attending to the operations of his own mind, he can never have clear and distinct notions of them, nor form any steady judgment concerning them. His opinions must be borrowed from others, his notions confused and indistinct, and he may easily be led to swallow very gross absurdities. To acquire this habit, is a work of time and labour, even in those who begin it early, and whose natural talents are tolerably fitted for it; but the difficulty will be daily diminishing, and the advantage of it is great. They will, thereby, be enabled to think with precision and accuracy on every subject, especially on those subjects that are more abstract. They will be able to judge for themselves in many important points, wherein others must blindly follow a leader.

CHAPTER VI.

OF THE DIFFICULTY OF ATTENDING TO THE OPERATIONS OF OUR OWN MINDS.

THE difficulty of attending to our mental operations, ought to be well understood, and justly estimated, by those who would make any progress in this science; that they may neither, on the one hand, expect success without pains and application of thought; nor, on the other, be discouraged, by conceiving that the obstacles that lie in the way are insuperable, and that there is no certainty to be attained in it. I shall, therefore, endeavour to point [62] out the causes of this difficulty, and the effects that have arisen from it, that we may be able to form a true judgment of both.

1. The number and quick succession of the operations of the mind, make it difficult to give due attention to them. It is well known that, if a great number of objects be presented in quick succession, even to the eye, they are confounded in the memory and imagination. We retain a confused notion of the whole, and a more confused one of the several parts, especially if they are objects to which we have never before given particular attention. No succession can be more quick than that of thought. The mind is busy while we are awake, con-

tinually passing from one thought and one operation to another. The scene is constantly shifting. Every man will be sensible of this, who tries but for one minute to keep the same thought in his imagination without addition or variation. He will find it impossible to keep the scene of his imagination fixed. Other objects will intrude, without being called, and all he can do is to reject these intruders as quickly as possible, and return to his principal object.

2. In this exercise, we go contrary to habits which have been early acquired, and confirmed by long unvaried practice. From infancy, we are accustomed to attend to objects of sense, and to them only; and, when sensible objects have got such strong hold of the attention by confirmed habit, it is not easy to dispossess them. When we grow up, a variety of external objects solicits our attention, excites our curiosity, engages our affections, or touches our passions; and the constant round of employment, about external objects, draws off the mind from attending to itself; so that nothing is more just than the observation of Mr Locke, before mentioned, "That the understanding, like the eye, while it surveys all the objects around it, commonly takes no notice of itself."

3. The operations of the mind, from their very nature, lead the mind to give its attention to some other object. Our sensations, [63] as will be shewn afterwards, are natural signs, and turn our attention to the things signified by them; so much that most of them, and those the most frequent and familiar, have no name in any language. ! In perception, memory, judgment, imagination, and reasoning, there is an object distinct from the operation itself; and, while we are led by a strong impulse to attend to the object, the operation escapes our notice. Our passions, affections, and all our active powers, have, in like manner, their objects which engross our attention, and divert it from the passion itself.

4. To this we may add a just observation made by Mr Hume, That, when the mind is agitated by any passion, as soon as we turn our attention from the object to the passion itself, the passion subsides or vanishes, and, by that means, escapes our inquiry. This, indeed, is common to almost every operation of the mind. When it is exerted, we are conscious of it; but then we do not attend to the operation, but to its object. When the mind is drawn off from the object to attend to its own operation, that operation ceases, and escapes our notice.

5. As it is not sufficient to the discovery of mathematical truths, that a man be able to attend to mathematical figures, as it is necessary that he should have the ability to

listinguish accurately things that differ, and to discern clearly the various relations of the quantities he compares—an ability which, though much greater in those who have the force of genius than in others, yet, even in them, requires exercise and habit to bring it to maturity—so, in order to discover the truth in what relates to the operations of the mind, it is not enough that a man be able to give attention to them : he must have the ability to distinguish accurately their minute differences ; to resolve and analyse complex operations into their simple ingredients ; to unfold the ambiguity of words, which in this science is greater than in any other, and to give them the same accuracy and precision that mathematical terms have ; for, indeed, the same precision in the use of words, the same cool attention to [64] the minute differences of things, the same talent for abstraction and analysing, which fit a man for the study of mathematics, are no less necessary in this. But there is this great difference between the two sciences—that the objects of mathematics being things external to the mind, it is much more easy to attend to them, and fix them steadily in the imagination.

The difficulty attending our inquiries into the powers of the mind, serves to account for some events respecting this branch of philosophy, which deserve to be mentioned.

While most branches of science have, either in ancient or in modern times, been highly cultivated, and brought to a considerable degree of perfection, this remains, to this day, in a very low state, and, as it were, in its infancy.

Every science invented by men must have its beginning and its progress ; and, from various causes, it may happen that one science shall be brought to a great degree of maturity, while another is yet in its infancy. The maturity of a science may be judged of by this—When it contains a system of principles, and conclusions drawn from them, which are so firmly established that, among thinking and intelligent men, there remains no doubt or dispute about them ; so that those who come after may raise the superstructure higher, but shall never be able to overturn what is already built, in order to begin on a new foundation.

Geometry seems to have been in its infancy about the time of Thales and Pythagoras ; because many of the elementary propositions, on which the whole science is built, are ascribed to them as the inventors. Euclid's " Elements," which were written some ages after Pythagoras, exhibit a system of geometry which deserves the name of a science ; and, though great additions have been made by Apollonius, Archi-

[64—66]

medes, Pappus, and others among the ancients, and still greater by the moderns ; yet what [65] was laid down in Euclid's " Elements" was never set aside. It remains as the firm foundation of all future superstructures in that science.

Natural philosophy remained in its infant state near two thousand years after geometry had attained to its manly form : for natural philosophy seems not to have been built on a stable foundation, nor carried to any degree of maturity, till the last century. The system of Des Cartes, which was all hypothesis, prevailed in the most enlightened part of Europe till towards the end of last century. Sir Isaac Newton has the merit of giving the form of a science to this branch of philosophy ; and it need not appear surprising, if the philosophy of the human mind should be a century or two later in being brought to maturity.

It has received great accessions from the labours of several modern authors ; and perhaps wants little more to entitle it to the name of a science, but to be purged of certain hypotheses, which have imposed on some of the most acute writers on this subject, and led them into downright scepticism.

What the ancients have delivered to us concerning the mind and its operations, is almost entirely drawn, not from accurate reflection, but from some conceived analogy between body and mind. And, although the modern authors I formerly named have given more attention to the operations of their own minds, and by that means have made important discoveries, yet, by retaining some of the ancient analogical notions, their discoveries have been less useful than they might have been, and have led to scepticism.

It may happen in science, as in building, that an error in the foundation shall weaken the whole ; and the farther the building is carried on, this weakness shall become the more apparent and the more threatening. Something of this kind seems to have happened in our systems concerning the mind. The accession they [66] have received by modern discoveries, though very important in itself, has thrown darkness and obscurity upon the whole, and has led men rather to scepticism than to knowledge. This must be owing to some fundamental errors that have not been observed ; and when these are corrected, it is to be hoped that the improvements that have been made will have their due effect.

The last effect I observe of the difficulty of inquiries into the powers of the mind, is, that there is no other part of human knowledge in which ingenious authors have been so apt to run into strange paradoxes, and even into gross absurdities.

When we find philosophers maintaining

that there is no heat in the fire, nor colour in the rainbow ;* when we find the gravest philosophers, from Des Cartes down to Bishop Berkeley, mustering up arguments to prove the existence of a material world, and unable to find any that will bear examination : when we find Bishop Berkeley and Mr Hume, the acutest metaphysicians of the age, maintaining that there is no such thing as matter in the universe—that sun, moon, and stars, the earth which we inhabit, our own bodies, and those of our friends, are only ideas in our minds, and have no existence but in thought ; when we find the last maintaining that there is neither body nor mind—nothing in nature but ideas and impressions, without any substance on which they are impressed—that there is no certainty, nor indeed probability, even in mathematical axioms : I say, when we consider such extravagancies of many of the most acute writers on this subject, we may be apt to think the whole to be only a dream of fanciful men, who have entangled themselves in cobwebs spun out of their own brain. But we ought to consider that the more closely and ingeniously men reason from false principles, the more absurdities they will be led into ; and when such absurdities help to bring to light the false principles from which they are drawn, they may be the more easily forgiven. [67]

CHAPTER VII.

DIVISION OF THE POWERS OF THE MIND.

THE powers of the mind are so many, so various, and so connected and complicated in most of its operations, that there never has been any division of them proposed which is not liable to considerable objections. We shall, therefore, take that general division which is the most common, into the powers of *understanding* and those of *will.*† Under the will we comprehend our active powers, and all that lead to action, or influence the mind to act—such as appetites, passions, affections. The understanding comprehends our contemplative powers ; by which we perceive objects ; by which we conceive or remember them ; by which we analyse or compound them ; and by which we judge and reason concerning them.

* A merely verbal dispute. See before, p. 2 5, b, note.—H.
† It would be out of place to enter on the extensive field of history and discussion relative to the distribution of our mental powers. It is sufficient to say, that the vulgar division of the faculties, adopted by Reid, into those of the *Understanding* and those of the *Will* is to be traced to the classification, taken in the Aristotelic school, of the powers into *gnostic*, or cognitive, and *orectic*, or appetent On this the reader may consult the admirable introduction of Philoponus—or rather of Ammonius Hermiæ—to the books of Aristotle upon the Soul.—H.

Although this general division may be of use in order to our proceeding more methodically in our subject, we are not to understand it as if, in those operations which are ascribed to the understanding, there were no exertion of will or activity, or as if the understanding were not employed in the operations ascribed to the will ; for I conceive there is no operation of the understanding wherein the mind is not active in some degree. We have some command over our thoughts, and can attend to this or to that, of many objects which present themselves to our senses, to our memory, or to our imagination. We can survey an object on this side or that, superficially or accurately, for a longer or a shorter time ; so that our contemplative powers are under the guidance and direction of the active ; and the former never pursue their object without being led and directed, urged or restrained by the latter : and because the understanding is always more or less directed by the will, mankind have ascribed some degree of activity to [68] the mind in its intellectual operations, as well as in those which belong to the will, and have expressed them by active verbs, such as seeing, hearing, judging, reasoning, and the like.

And as the mind exerts some degree of activity even in the operations of understanding, so it is certain that there can be no act of will which is not accompanied with some act of understanding. The will must have an object, and that object must be apprehended or conceived in the understanding. It is, therefore, to be remembered, that, in most, if not all operations of the mind, both faculties concur ; and we range the operation under that faculty which hath the largest share in it.*

The intellectual powers are commonly divided into simple apprehension, judgment, and reasoning.† As this division has in its favour the authority of antiquity, and of a very general reception, it would be improper to set it aside without giving any reason : I shall, therefore, explain it briefly, and give the reasons why I choose to follow another.

* It should be always remembered hat the various mental energies are all only possible in and through each other ; and that our psychological analyses do not suppose any real distinction of the operations which we discriminate by different names. Thought and volition can no more be exerted apart, than the sides and angles of a square can exist separately from each other.—H.
† This is a singular misapprehension. The division in question, I make bold to say, never was proposed by any philosopher as a *psychological* distribution of the cognitive faculties *in general*; on the contrary, it is only a *logical* distribution of that section of the cognitive faculties which we, denominate *discursive*, as those alone which are proximately concerned in the process of reasoning—or thought, in its strictest signification.—H.

It may be observed that, without apprehension of the objects concerning which we judge, there can be no judgment; as little can there be reasoning without both apprehension and judgment: these three operations, therefore, are not independent of each other. The second includes the first, and the third includes both the first and second; but the first may be exercised without either of the other two.* It is on that account called *simple apprehension ;* that is, apprehension unaccompanied with any judgment about the object apprehended. This simple apprehension of an object is, in common language, called *having a notion, or having a conception* of the object, and by late authors is called *having an idea of it.* In speaking, it is expressed by a word, or by a part of a proposition, without that composition and structure which makes a complete sentence ; as *a man, a man of fortune:* Such words, taken by themselves, signify simple apprehensions. They neither affirm nor [69] deny ; they imply no judgment or opinion of the thing signified by them ; and, therefore, cannot be said to be either true or false. The second operation in this division is *judgment ;* in which, say the philosophers, there must be two objects of thought compared, and some agreement or disagreement, or, in general, some relation discerned between them ; in consequence of which, there is an opinion or belief of that relation which we discern. This operation is expressed in speech by a proposition, in which some relation between the things compared is affirmed or denied ; as when we say, *All men are fallible.* Truth and falsehood are qualities which belong to judgment only ; or to propositions by which judgment is expressed. Every judgment, every opinion, and every proposition, is either true or false. But words which neither affirm nor deny anything, can have neither of those qualities ; and the same may be said of simple apprehensions, which are signified by such words. The third operation is *reasoning ;* in which, from two or more judgments, we draw a conclusion. This division of our intellectual powers corresponds perfectly with the account commonly given by philosophers, of the successive steps by which the mind proceeds in the acquisition of its knowledge ; which are these three : *First,* By the senses, or by other means, it is furnished with various

simple apprehensions, notions, or ideas. These are the materials which nature gives it to work upon ; and from the simple ideas it is furnished with by nature, it forms various others more complex. *Secondly,* By comparing its ideas, and by perceiving their agreements and disagreements, it forms its judgments. And, *Lastly,* From two or more judgments, it deduces conclusions of reasoning.

Now, if all our knowledge is got by a procedure of this kind, [70] certainly the threefold division of the powers of understanding, into simple apprehension, judgment, and reasoning, is the most natural and the most proper that can be devised. This theory and that division are so closely connected that it is difficult to judge which of them has given rise to the other ; and they must stand or fall together. But, if all our knowledge is not got by a process of this kind—if there are other avenues of knowledge besides the comparing our ideas, and perceiving their agreements and disagreements—it is probable that there may be operations of the understanding which cannot be properly reduced under any of the three that have been explained.

Let us consider some of the most familiar operations of our minds, and see to which of the three they belong. I begin with consciousness. I know that I think, and this of all knowledge is the most certain. Is that operation of my mind which gives me this certain knowledge, to be called simple apprehension? No, surely. Simple apprehension neither affirms nor denies. It will not be said that it is by reasoning that I know that I think. It remains, therefore, that it must be by judgment—that is, according to the account given of judgment, by comparing two ideas, and perceiving the agreement between them. But what are the ideas compared? They must be the idea of myself, and the idea of thought, for they are the terms of the proposition *I think.* According to this account, then, first, I have the idea of myself and the idea of thought ; then, by comparing these two ideas, I perceive that I think.

Let any man who is capable of reflection judge for himself, whether it is by an operation of this kind that he comes to be convinced that he thinks ? To me it appears evident, that the conviction I have that I think, is not got in this way ; and, therefore, I conclude, either that consciousness is not judgment, or that judgment is not rightly defined to be the perception of some agreement or disagreement between two ideas.

The perception of an object by my senses is another operation of [71] the understanding. I would know whether it be simple apprehension, or judgment, or

---

* This is not correct. Apprehension is as impossible without judgment, as judgment is impossible without apprehension . The apprehension of a thing or notion, is only realized in the mental affirmation that the *concept* ideally exists, and this affirmation is a judgment. In fact, all consciousness supposes a judgment, as all consciousness supposes a discrimination.—H

R 2

reasoning. It is not simple apprehension, because I am persuaded of the existence of the object as much as I could be by demonstration. It is not judgment, if by judgment be meant the comparing ideas, and perceiving their agreements or disagreements. It is not reasoning, because those who cannot reason can perceive.

I find the same difficulty in classing memory under any of the operations mentioned.

There is not a more fruitful source of error in this branch of philosophy, than divisions of things which are taken to be complete when they are not really so. To make a perfect division of any class of things, a man ought to have the whole under his view at once. But the greatest capacity very often is not sufficient for this. Something is left out which did not come under the philosopher's view when he made his division : and to suit this to the division, it must be made what nature never made it. This has been so common a fault of philosophers, that one who would avoid error ought to be suspicious of divisions, though long received, and of great authority, especially when they are grounded on a theory that may be called in question. In a subject imperfectly known, we ought not to pretend to perfect divisions, but to leave room for such additions or alterations as a more perfect view of the subject may afterwards suggest.

I shall not, therefore, attempt a complete enumeration of the powers of the human understanding. I shall only mention those which I propose to explain ; and they are the following :—

1st, The powers we have by means of our external senses. 2dly, Memory. 3dly, Conception. 4thly, The powers of resolving and analysing complex objects, and compounding those that are more simple. 5thly, Judging. 6thly, Reasoning. 7thly, Taste. 8thly, Moral Perception ;* and, last of all, Consciousness.† [72]

CHAPTER VIII.

OF SOCIAL OPERATIONS OF MIND.

THERE is another division of the powers of the mind, which, though it has been, ought not to be overlooked by writers on this subject, because it has a real foundation in nature. Some operations of our minds, from their very nature, are *social,* others are *solitary.*

By the first, I understand such operations as necessarily suppose an intercourse with some other intelligent being. A man may understand and will ; he may apprehend, and judge, and reason, though he should know of no intelligent being in the universe besides himself. But, when he asks information, or receives it ; when he bears testimony, or receives the testimony of another ; when he asks a favour, or accepts one ; when he gives a command to his servant, or receives one from a superior ; when he plights his faith in a promise or contract—these are acts of social intercourse between intelligent beings, and can have no place in solitude. They suppose understanding and will ; but they suppose something more, which is neither understanding nor will ; that is, society with other intelligent beings. They may be called intellectual, because they can only be in intellectual beings ; but they are neither simple apprehension, nor judgment, nor reasoning, nor are they any combination of these operations.

To ask a question, is as simple an operation as to judge or to reason ; yet it is neither judgment nor reasoning, nor simple apprehension, nor is it any composition of these. Testimony is neither simple apprehension, nor judgment, nor reasoning. The same may be said of a promise, or of a contract. These acts of mind are perfectly understood by every man of common understanding ; but, when philosophers attempt to bring them within the pale of their divisions, by analysing them, they find inexplicable mysteries, [73] and even contradictions, in them. One may see an instance of this, of many that might be mentioned, in Mr Hume's " Enquiry concerning the Principles of Morals," § 3, part 2, note, near the end.

The attempts of philosophers to reduce the social operations under the common philosophical divisions, resemble very much the attempts of some philosophers to reduce all our social affections to certain modifications of self-love. The Author of our being intended us to be social beings, and has, for that end, given us social intellectual powers, as well as social affections.* Both are original parts of our constitution, and the exertions of both no less natural than the exertions of those powers that are solitary and selfish.

Our social intellectual operations, as well as our social affections, appear very early in life, before we are capable of reasoning ; yet both suppose a conviction of the existence of other intelligent beings. When a child asks a question of his nurse, this act

---

* Moral Perception is treated under the Active Powers, in Essay V.—H.
† Consciousness obtains only an incidental consideration, under Judgment, in the Fifth Chapter of the Sixth Essay.—H.

* " Man," says Aristotle, " is, by nature, more political than any bee or ant." And, in another work, " Man is the sweetest thing to man"—ἀνθρώπω τῷ ἥδιστον ἄνθρωπος—H.

of his mind supposes not only a desire to know what he asks; it supposes, likewise, a conviction that the nurse is an intelligent being, to whom he can communicate his thoughts, and who can communicate her thoughts to him. How he came by this conviction so early, is a question of some importance in the knowledge of the human mind, and, therefore, worthy of the consideration of philosophers. But they seem to have given no attention, either to this early conviction, or to those operations of mind which suppose it. Of this we shall have occasion to treat afterwards.

All languages are fitted to express the social as well as the solitary operations of the mind. It may indeed be affirmed, that, to express the former, is the primary and direct intention of language. A man who had no intercourse with any other intelligent being, would never think of language. He would be as mute as the beasts of the field; even more so, because they have some degree of social intercourse with one another, and some of them [74] with man. When language is once learned, it may be useful even in our solitary meditations; and by clothing our thoughts with words, we may have a firmer hold of them. But this was not its first intention; and the structure of every language shews that it is not intended solely for this purpose.

In every language, a question, a command, a promise, which are social acts, can be expressed as easily and as properly as judgment, which is a solitary act. The expression of the last has been honoured with a particular name; it is called a proposition: it has been an object of great attention to philosophers; it has been analysed into its very elements of subject predicate, and copula. All the various modifications of these, and of propositions which are compounded of them, have been anxiously examined in many voluminous tracts. The expression of a question, of a command, or of a promise, is as capable of being analysed as a proposition is; but we do not find that this has been attempted; we have not so much as given them a name different from the operations which they express.

Why have speculative men laboured so anxiously to analyse our solitary operations, and given so little attention to the social? I know no other reason but this, that, in the divisions that have been made of the mind's operations, the social have been omitted, and thereby thrown behind the curtain.

In all languages, the second person of verbs, the pronoun of the second person, and the vocative case in nouns, are appropriated to the expression of social operations of mind, and could never have had place in language but for this purpose: nor is it a good argument against this observation, that, by a rhetorical figure, we sometimes address persons that are absent, or even inanimate beings, in the second person. For it ought to be remembered, that all figurative ways of using words or phrases suppose a natural and literal meaning of them.* [75]

* What, throughout this chapter, is implied, ought to have been explicitly stated—that *language* is natural to man; and consequently the faculty of speech ought to have been enumerated among the mental powers.—H.

ESSAY II.

OF THE POWERS WE HAVE BY MEANS OF OUR EXTERNAL SENSES.

CHAPTER I.

OF THE ORGANS OF SENSE.

Of all the operations of our minds, the perception of external objects is the most familiar. The senses come to maturity even in infancy, when other powers have not yet sprung up. They are common to us with brute animals, and furnish us with the objects about which our other powers are the most frequently employed. We find it easy to attend to their operations; and, because they are familiar, the names which properly belong to them are applied

[74, 75]

to other powers which are thought to resemble them. For these reasons, they claim to be first considered.

The perception of external objects is one main link of that mysterious chain which connects the material world with the intellectual. We shall find many things in this operation unaccountable; sufficient to convince us that we know but little of our own frame; and that a perfect comprehension of our mental powers, and of the manner of their operation, is beyond the reach of our understanding.

In perception, there are impressions upon the organs of sense, the nerves, and brain, which, by the laws of our nature, are followed by certain operations of mind. These two things are apt to be confounded ; but ought most carefully to be distinguished. Some philosophers, without good reason, have concluded, that the [76] impressions made on the body are the proper efficient cause of perception. Others, with as little reason, have concluded that impressions are made on the mind similar to those made on the body. From these mistakes many others have arisen. The wrong notions men have rashly taken up with regard to the senses, have led to wrong notions with regard to other powers which are conceived to resemble them. Many important powers of mind have, especially of late, been called internal senses, from a supposed resemblance to the external—such as, the sense of beauty, the sense of harmony, the moral sense.* And it is to be apprehended that errors, with regard to the external, have, from analogy, led to similar errors with regard to the internal ; it is, therefore, of some consequence, even with regard to other branches of our subject, to have just notions concerning the external senses.

In order to this, we shall begin with some observations on the organs of sense, and on the impressions which in perception are made upon them, and upon the nerves and brain.

We perceive no external object but by means of certain bodily organs which God has given us for that purpose. The Supreme Being who made us, and placed us in this world, hath given us such powers of mind as he saw to be suited to our state and rank in his creation. He has given us the power of perceiving many objects around us—the sun, moon, and stars, the earth and sea, and a variety of animals, vegetables, and inanimate bodies. But our power of perceiving these objects is limited in various ways, and particularly in this—that, without the organs of the several senses, we perceive no external object. We cannot see without eyes, nor hear without ears ; it is not only necessary that we should have these organs, but that they should be in a sound and natural state. There are many disorders of the eye that cause total blindness ; others that impair the powers of vision, without destroying it altogether : and the same may be said of the organs of all the other senses. [77]

All this is so well known from experience, that it needs no proof ; but it ought to be observed, that we know it from experience only. We can give no reason for it, but that such is the will of our Maker. No man can shew it to be impossible to the Supreme Being to have given us the power of

perceiving external objects without such organs.* We have reason to believe that, when we put off these bodies and all the organs belonging to them, our perceptive powers shall rather be improved than destroyed or impaired. We have reason to believe that the Supreme Being perceives everything in a much more perfect manner than we do, without bodily organs. We have reason to believe that there are other created beings endowed with powers of perception more perfect and more extensive than ours, without any such organs as we find necessary.

We ought not, therefore, to conclude, that such bodily organs are, in their own nature, necessary to perception ; but rather that, by the will of God, our power of perceiving external objects is limited and circumscribed by our organs of sense ; so that we perceive objects in a certain manner, and in certain circumstances, and in no other.†

If a man was shut up in a dark room, so that he could see nothing but through one small hole in the shutter of a window, would he conclude that the hole was the cause of his seeing, and that it is impossible to see any other way ? Perhaps, if he had never in his life seen but in this way, he might be apt to think so ; but the conclusion is rash and groundless. He sees, because God has given him the power of seeing ; and he sees only through this small hole, because his power of seeing is circumscribed by impediments on all other hands.

Another necessary caution in this matter is, that we ought not to confound the organs of perception with the being that perceives. Perception must be the act of some being that perceives. The eye [78] is not that which sees ; it is only the organ by which we see.‡ The ear is not that which hears, but the organ by which we hear ; and so of the rest.§

A man cannot see the satellites of Jupiter but by a telescope. Does he conclude from this, that it is the telescope that sees those stars ? By no means—such a conclusion would be absurd. It is no less absurd to

* He refers to Hutcheson.—H.

* However astonishing, it is now proved beyond all rational doubt, that, in certain abnormal states of the nervous organism, perceptions are possible, through other than the ordinary channels of the senses.—H

† The doctrine of Plato and of many other philosophers. Reid ought, however, to have said, *limited to,* instead of "*by our organs of sense:*" for, if the body be viewed as the prison of the soul, the senses must be viewed at least as partial outlets.—H.

‡ Δἱ ὀφθαλμῶν, οὐκ ὀφθαλμοῖς says Plato, followed by a host of philosophers, comparing the senses to windows of the mind.—H.

§ "The mind *sees,*" says Epicharmus—"the mind hears, all else is deaf and blind"—a saying alluded to as proverbial by Aristotle, in a passage to the same effect, which cannot adequately be translated :— Χωρισθεῖσα αἴσθησις διανοίας, καθάπερ ἀναίσθητον τοὖτον ἴσχει ὥστις τέχνεται τὸ, Νοῦς ὁρᾷ, καὶ νοῦς ἀκούει. This has escaped the commentators.—H. See p. 878, n.

conclude that it is the eye that sees, or the ear that hears. The telescope is an artificial organ of sight, but it sees not. The eye is a natural organ of sight, by which we see; but the natural organ sees as little as the artificial.

The eye is a machine most admirably contrived for refracting the rays of light, and forming a distinct picture of objects upon the retina; but it sees neither the object nor the picture. It can form the picture after it is taken out of the head; but no vision ensues. Even when it is in its proper place, and perfectly sound, it is well known that an obstruction in the optic nerve takes away vision, though the eye has performed all that belongs to it.

If anything more were necessary to be said on a point so evident, we might observe that, if the faculty of seeing were in the eye, that of hearing in the ear, and so of the other senses, the necessary consequence of this would be, that the thinking principle, which I call myself, is not one, but many. But this is contrary to the irresistible conviction of every man. When I say I see, I hear, I feel, I remember, this implies that it is one and the same self that performs all these operations; and, as it would be absurd to say that my memory, another man's imagination, and a third man's reason, may make one individual intelligent being, it would be equally absurd to say that one piece of matter seeing, another hearing, and a third feeling, may make one and the same percipient being.

These sentiments are not new; they have occurred to thinking men from early ages. Cicero, in his "Tusculan Questions," Book I., chap. 20, has expressed them very distinctly. Those who choose may consult the passage.* [79]

CHAPTER II.

OF THE IMPRESSIONS ON THE ORGANS, NERVES, AND BRAINS.

A SECOND law of our nature regarding perception is, *that we perceive no object, unless some impression is made upon the organ of sense, either by the immediate application of the object, or by some medium which passes between the object and the organ.*

In two of our senses—to wit, *touch* and *taste* there must be an immediate application of the object to the organ. In the other three, the object is perceived at a distance, but still by means of a medium, by

which some impression is made upon the organ.*

The effluvia of bodies drawn into the nostrils with the breath, are the medium of smell; the undulations of the air are the medium of hearing; and the rays of light passing from visible objects to the eye, are the medium of sight. We see no object unless rays of light come from it to the eye. We hear not the sound of any body, unless the vibrations of some elastic medium, occasioned by the tremulous motion of the sounding body, reach our ear. We perceive no smell, unless the effluvia of the smelling body enter into the nostrils. We perceive no taste, unless the sapid body be applied to the tongue, or some part of the organ of taste. Nor do we perceive any tangible quality of a body, unless it touch the hands, or some part of our bodies.

These are facts known from experience to hold universally and invariably, both in men and brutes. By this law of our nature, our powers of perceiving external objects, are farther limited and circumscribed. Nor can we give any other reason for this, than [80] that it is the will of our Maker, who knows best what powers, and what degrees of them, are suited to our state. We were once in a state, I mean in the womb, wherein our powers of perception were more limited than in the present, and, in a future state, they may be more enlarged.

It is likewise a law of our nature, that, in order to our perceiving objects, the impressions made upon the organs of sense must be communicated to the nerves, and by them to the brain. This is perfectly known to those who know anything of anatomy.

The nerves are fine cords, which pass from the brain, or from the spinal marrow, which is a production of the brain, to all parts of the body, dividing into smaller branches as they proceed, until at last they escape our eyesight: and it is found by experience, that all the voluntary and, involuntary motions of the body are performed by their means. When the nerves that serve any limb, are cut, or tied hard, we have then no more power to move that limb than if it was no part of the body.

As there are nerves that serve the muscular motions, so there are others that serve the several senses; and as without the former we cannot move a limb, so without the latter we can have no perception.

---

* This distinction of a mediate and immediate object, or of an object and a medium, in perception, is inaccurate, and a source of sad confusion. We perceive, and can perceive, nothing but what is in relation to the organ, and nothing is in relation to the organ that is not present to it. All the senses are, in fact, modifications of touch, as Democritus of old taught. We reach the distant reality, not by sense, not by perception, but by inference. Reid, however, in this only follows his predecessors.—H.

---

* Cicero says nothing on this head that had not been said before him by the Greek philosophers.—H.

[79, 80]

This train of machinery the wisdom of God has made necessary to our perceiving objects. Various parts of the body concur to it, and each has its own function. *First,* The object, either immediately, or by some medium, must make an impression on the organ. The organ serves only as a medium by which an impression is made on the nerve; and the nerve serves as a medium to make an impression upon the brain. Here the material part ends; at least we can trace it no farther; the rest is all intellectual.*

The proof of these impressions upon the nerves and brain in [81] perception is this, that, from many observations and experiments, it is found that, when the organ of any sense is perfectly sound, and has the impression made upon it by the object ever so strongly, yet, if the nerve which serves that organ be cut or tied hard, there is no perception; and it is well known that disorders in the brain deprive us of the power of perception when both the organ and its nerve are sound.

There is, therefore, sufficient reason to conclude that in perception, the object produces some change in the organ; that the organ produces some change upon the nerve; and that the nerve produces some change in the brain. And we give the name of an *impression* to those changes, because we have not a name more proper to express, in a general manner, any change produced in a body, by an external cause, without specifying the nature of that change. Whether it be pressure, or attraction, or repulsion, or vibration, or something unknown, for which we have no name, still it may be called an impression. But, with regard to the particular kind of this change or impression, philosophers have never been able to discover anything at all.

But, whatever be the nature of those impressions upon the organs, nerves, and brain, we perceive nothing without them. Experience informs that it is so; but we cannot give a reason why it is so. In the constitution of man, perception, by fixed laws of nature, is connected with those impressions; but we can discover no necessary connection. The Supreme Being has seen fit to limit our power of perception; so that we perceive not without such impressions; and this is all we know of the matter.

This, however, we have reason to conclude in general—that, as the impressions on the organs, nerves, and brain, correspond exactly to the nature and conditions of the objects by which they are made, so our perceptions and sensations correspond to those impressions, and vary in kind, and in degree, as they vary. [82] Without this exact correspondence, the information we receive by our senses would not only be imperfect, as it undoubtedly is, but would be fallacious, which we have no reason to think it is.

CHAPTER III.

HYPOTHESES CONCERNING THE NERVES AND BRAIN.

WE are informed by anatomists, that, although the two coats which inclose a nerve, and which it derives from the coats of the brain, are tough and elastic, yet the nerve itself has a very small degree of consistence, being almost like marrow. It has, however, a fibrous texture, and may be divided and subdivided, till its fibres escape our senses; and, as we know so very little about the texture of the nerves, there is great room left for those who choose to indulge themselves in conjecture.

The ancients conjectured that the nervous fibres are fine tubes, filled with a very subtile spirit, or vapour, which they called *animal spirits;* that the brain is a gland, by which the animal spirits are secreted from the finer part of the blood, and their continual waste repaired; and that it is by these animal spirits that the nerves perform their functions. Des Cartes has shewn how, by these animal spirits, going and returning in the nerves, muscular motion, perception, memory, and imagination, are effected. All this he has described as distinctly as if he had been an eye-witness of all those operations. But it happens that the tubular structure of the nerves was never perceived by the human eye, nor shewn by the nicest injections; and all that has been said about animal spirits, through more than fifteen centuries, is mere conjecture.

Dr Briggs, who was Sir Isaac Newton's master in anatomy, was the first, as far as I know, who advanced a new system concerning [83] the nerves.* He conceived them to be solid filaments of prodigious

---

* There can be no doubt that the whole organism of the sense, from periphery to centre, must co-operate simultaneously in perception; but there is no reason to place the mind at the central extremity alone, and to hold that not only a certain series of organic changes, but a sensation, must precede the mental cognition. This is mere hypothesis, and opposed to the testimony of consciousness.—E.

---

* Briggs was not the first. The Jesuit, Honoratus Fabry, had before him denied the old hypothesis of *spirits*; and the new hypothesis of cerebral fibres, and fibrils, by which he explains the phaenomena of sense, imagination and memory, is not only the first, but perhaps the most ingenious of the class that has been proposed. Yet the very name of Fabry is wholly unnoticed by those historians of philosophy who do not deem it superfluous to dwell on the tiresome reveries of Briggs, Hartley, and Bonnet.—H.

tenuity; and this opinion, as it accords better with observation, seems to have been more generally received since his time. As to the manner of performing their office, Dr Briggs thought that, like musical cords, they have vibrations differing according to their length and tension. They seem, however, very unfit for this purpose, on account of their want of tenacity, their moisture, and being through their whole length in contact with moist substances; so that, although Dr Briggs wrote a book upon this system, called *Nova Visionis Theoria*, it seems not to have been much followed.

Sir Isaac Newton, in all his philosophical writings, took great care to distinguish his doctrines, which he pretended to prove by just induction, from his conjectures, which were to stand or fall according as future experiments and observations should establish or refute them. His conjectures he has put in the form of queries, that they might not be received as truths, but be inquired into, and determined according to the evidence to be found for or against them. Those who mistake his queries for a part of his doctrine, do him great injustice, and degrade him to the rank of the common herd of philosophers, who have in all ages adulterated philosophy, by mixing conjecture with truth, and their own fancies with the oracles of Nature. Among other queries, this truly great philosopher proposed this, Whether there may not be an elastic medium, or æther, immensely more rare than air, which pervades all bodies, and which is the cause of gravitation; of the refraction and reflection of the rays of light; of the transmission of heat, through spaces void of air; and of many other phænomena? In the 23d query subjoined to his "Optics," he puts this question with regard to the impressions made on the nerves and brain in perception, Whether vision is effected chiefly by the vibrations of this medium, excited in the bottom of the eye by the rays of light, and propagated along the solid, pellucid, and uniform capillaments of the optic nerve? And whether hearing is effected [84] by the vibrations of this or some other medium, excited by the tremor of the air in the auditory nerves, and propagated along the solid, pellucid, and uniform capillaments of those nerves? And so with regard to the other senses.

What Newton only proposed as a matter to be inquired into, Dr Hartley conceived to have such evidence, that, in his "Observations on Man," he has deduced, in a mathematical form, a very ample system concerning the faculties of the mind, from the doctrine of vibrations, joined with that of association.

His notion of the vibrations excited in the nerves, is expressed in Propositions 4 [84, 85]

and 5 of the first part of his "Observations on Man." "Prop. 4. External objects impressed on the senses occasion, first in the nerves on which they are impressed, and then in the brain, vibrations of the small, and, as one may say, infinitesimal medullary particles. Prop. 5. The vibrations mentioned in the last proposition are excited, propagated, and kept up, partly by the æther—that is, by a very subtile elastic fluid; partly by the uniformity, continuity, softness, and active powers of the medullary substance of the brain, spinal marrow, and nerves."

The modesty and diffidence with which Dr Hartley offers his system to the world—by desiring his reader "to expect nothing but hints and conjectures in difficult and obscure matters, and a short detail of the principal reasons and evidences in those that are clear; by acknowledging, that he shall not be able to execute, with any accuracy, the proper method of philosophising, recommended and followed by Sir Isaac Newton; and that he will attempt a sketch only for the benefit of future enquirers"—seem to forbid any criticism upon it. One cannot, without reluctance, criticise what is proposed in such a manner, and with so good intention; yet, as the tendency of this system of vibrations is to make all the operations of the mind mere mechanism, dependent [85] on the laws of matter and motion, and, as it has been held forth by its votaries, *as in a manner demonstrated*, I shall make some remarks on that part of the system which relates to the impressions made on the nerves and brain in perception.

It may be observed, in general, that Dr Hartley's work consists of a chain of propositions, with their proofs and corollaries, digested in good order, and in a scientific form. A great part of them, however, are, as he candidly acknowledges, conjectures and hints only; yet these are mixed with the propositions legitimately proved, without any distinction. Corollaries are drawn from them, and other propositions grounded upon them, which, all taken together, make up a system. A system of this kind resembles a chain, of which some links are abundantly strong, others very weak. The strength of the chain is determined by that of the weakest links; for, if they give way, the whole falls to pieces, and the weight supported by it falls to the ground.

Philosophy has been, in all ages, adulterated by hypotheses; that is, by systems built partly on facts, and much upon conjecture. It is pity that a man of Dr Hartley's knowledge and candour should have followed the multitude in this fallacious tract, after expressing his approbation of the proper method of philosophising, pointed out by Bacon and Newton. The last considered it as a reproach when his system was called his hypothesis; and says, with disdain of such imputation, *Hypotheses non fingo.* And it is very strange that Dr Hartley should not only follow such a method of philosophising himself, but that he should direct others in their inquiries to follow it. So he does in Proposition 87, Part I., where he deduces rules for the ascertainment of truth, from the rule of false, in arithmetic, and from the art of decyphering; and in other places.

As to the vibrations and vibratiuncles, whether of an elastic æther, or of the infinitesimal particles of the brain and nerves, there [86] may be such things for what we know; and men may rationally inquire whether they can find any evidence of their existence; but, while we have no proof of their existence, to apply them to the solution of phænomena, and to build a system upon them, is what I conceive we call building a castle in the air.

When men pretend to account for any of the operations of Nature, the causes assigned by them ought, as Sir Isaac Newton has taught us, to have two conditions, otherwise they are good for nothing. *First,* They ought to be true, to have a real existence, and not to be barely conjectured to exist, without proof. *Secondly,* They ought to be sufficient to produce the effect.

As to the existence of vibratory motions in the medullary substance of the nerves and brain, the evidence produced is this: *First,* It is observed that the sensations of seeing and hearing, and some sensations of touch, have some short duration and continuance. *Secondly,* Though there be no direct evidence that the sensations of taste and smell, and the greater part of these of touch, have the like continuance, yet, says the author, analogy would incline one to believe that they must resemble the sensations of sight and hearing in this particular. *Thirdly,* The continuance of all our sensations being thus established it follows, that external objects impress vibratory motions on the medullary substance of the nerves and brain; because no motion, besides a vibratory one, can reside in any part for a moment of time.

This is the chain of proof, in which the first link is strong, being confirmed by experience; the second is very weak; and the third still weaker. For other kinds of motion, besides that of vibration, may have some continuance such as rotation, bending or unbending of a spring, and perhaps others which we are unacquainted with; nor do we know whether it is motion that is produced in the nerves—it may be pressure, attraction, repulsion, or something we do not know. This, indeed, is the common refuge of all hypotheses, [87] that we know

no other way in which the phænomena may be produced, and, therefore, they must be produced in this way. There is, therefore, no proof of vibrations in the infinitesimal particles of the brain and nerves.

It may be thought that the existence of an elastic vibrating æther stands on a firmer foundation, having the authority of Sir Isaac Newton. But it ought to be observed that, although this great man had formed conjectures about this æther near fifty years before he died, and had it in his eye during that long space as a subject of inquiry, yet it does not appear that he ever found any convincing proof of its existence, but considered it to the last as a question whether there be such an æther or not. In the premonition to the reader, prefixed to the second edition of his "Optics," *anno* 1717, he expresses himself thus with regard to it:—"Lest any one should think that I place gravity among the essential properties of bodies, I have subjoined one question concerning its cause; a question, I say, for I do not hold it as a thing established." If, therefore, we regard the authority of Sir Isaac Newton, we ought to hold the existence of such an æther as a matter not established by proof, but to be examined into by experiments; and I have never heard that, since his time, any new evidence has been found of its existence.

"But," says Dr Hartley, "supposing the existence of the æther, and of its properties, to be destitute of all direct evidence, still, if it serves to account for a great variety of phænomena, it will have an indirect evidence in its favour by this means." There never was an hypothesis invented by an ingenious man which has not this evidence in its favour. The vortices of Des Cartes, the sylphs and gnomes of Mr Pope, serve to account for a great variety of phænomena.

When a man has, with labour and ingenuity, wrought up an hypothesis into a system, he contracts a fondness for it, which is apt [88] to warp the best judgment. This, I humbly think, appears remarkably in Dr Hartley. In his preface, he declares his approbation of the method of philosophising recommended and followed by Sir Isaac Newton; but, having first deviated from this method in his practice, he is brought at last to justify this deviation in theory, and to bring arguments in defence of a method diametrically opposite to it. "We admit," says he, "the key of a cypher to be a true one when it explains the cypher completely." I answer, To find the key requires an understanding equal or superior to that which made the cypher. This instance, therefore, will then be in point, when he who attempts to decypher the works of Nature by an hypothesis, has an

[86–88]

understanding equal or superior to that which made them. The votaries of hypotheses have often been challenged to shew one useful discovery in the works of Nature that was ever made in that way. If instances of this kind could be produced, we ought to conclude that Lord Bacon and Sir Isaac Newton have done great disservice to philosophy by what they have said against hypotheses. But, if no such instance can be produced, we must conclude, with those great men, that every system which pretends to account for the phænomena of Nature by hypotheses or conjecture, is spurious and illegitimate, and serves only to flatter the pride of man with a vain conceit of knowledge which he has not attained.

The author tells us, "that any hypothesis that has so much plausibility as to explain a considerable number of facts, helps us to digest these facts in proper order, to bring new ones to light, and to make *experimenta crucis* for the sake of future inquirers."

Let hypotheses be put to any of these uses as far as they can serve. Let them suggest experiments, or direct our inquiries; but let just induction alone govern our belief.

"The rule of false affords an obvious and strong instance of the possibility of being led, with precision and certainty, to a [89] true conclusion from a false position. And it is of the very essence of algebra to proceed in the way of supposition."

This is true; but, when brought to justify the accounting for natural phænomena by hypotheses, is foreign to the purpose. When an unknown number, or any unknown quantity, is sought, which must have certain conditions, it may be found in a scientific manner by the rule of false, or by an algebraical analysis; and, when found, may be synthetically demonstrated to be the number or the quantity sought, by its answering all the conditions required. But it is one thing to find a quantity which shall have certain conditions; it is a very different thing to find out the laws by which it pleases God to govern the world and produce the phænomena which fall under our observation. And we can then only allow some weight to this argument in favour of hypotheses, when it can be shewn that the cause of any one phænomenon in nature has been, or can be found, as an unknown quantity is, by the rule of false, or by algebraical analysis. This, I apprehend, will never be, till the æra arrives, which Dr Hartley seems to foretell, "When future generations shall put all kinds of evidences and enquiries into mathematical forms; and, as it were, reduce Aristotle's ten Categories, and Bishop Wilkin's forty *Summa Genera* to the head of quantity alone, so as

[89, 90]

to make mathematics and logic, natural history and civil history, natural philosophy and philosophy of all other kinds, coincide *omni ex parte.*"

Since Sir Isaac Newton laid down the rules of philosophising in our inquiries into the works of Nature, many philosophers have deviated from them in practice; perhaps few have paid that regard to them which they deserve. But they have met with very general approbation, as being founded in reason, and pointing out the only path to the knowledge of Nature's works. Dr Hartley is the only author I have met with who reasons against them, and has taken pains to find out arguments in defence of the exploded method of hypothesis. [90]

Another condition which Sir Isaac Newton requires in the causes of natural things assigned by philosophers, is, that they be sufficient to account for the phænomena. Vibrations, and vibratiuncles of the medullary substance of the nerves and brain, are assigned by Dr Hartley to account for all our sensations and ideas, and, in a word, for all the operations of our minds. Let us consider very briefly how far they are sufficient for that purpose.

It would be injustice to this author to conceive him a materialist. He proposes his sentiments with great candour, and they ought not to be carried beyond what his words express. He thinks it a consequence of his theory, that matter, if it can be endued with the most simple kinds of sensation, might arrive at all that intelligence of which the human mind is possessed. He thinks that his theory overturns all the arguments that are usually brought for the immateriality of the soul, from the subtilty of the internal senses, and of the rational faculty; but he does not take upon him to determine whether matter can be endued with sensation or no. He even acknowledges that matter and motion, however subtilly divided and reasoned upon, yield nothing more than matter and motion still; and therefore he would not be any way interpreted so as to oppose the immateriality of the soul.

It would, therefore, be unreasonable to require that his theory of vibrations should, in the proper sense, account for our sensations. It would, indeed, be ridiculous in any man to pretend that thought of any kind must necessarily result from motion, or that vibrations in the nerves must necessarily produce thought, any more than the vibrations of a pendulum. Dr Hartley disclaims this way of thinking, and therefore it ought not to be imputed to him. All that he pretends is, that, in the human constitution, there is a certain connection between vibrations in the medullary substance of the nerves and brain, and the thoughts of the mind ; so that the last depend entirely upon the first, and every kind of thought [91] in the mind arises in consequence of a corresponding vibration, or vibratiuncle in the nerves and brain. Our sensations arise from vibrations, and our ideas from vibratiuncles, or miniature vibrations; and he comprehends, under these two words of *sensations* and *ideas*, all the operations of the mind.

But how can we expect any proof of the connection between vibrations and thought, when the existence of such vibrations was never proved ? The proof of their connection cannot be stronger than the proof of their existence ; for, as the author acknowledges that we cannot infer the existence of the thoughts from the existence of the vibrations, it is no less evident that we cannot infer the existence of vibrations from the existence of our thoughts. The existence of both must be known before we can know their connection. As to the existence of our thoughts, we have the evidence of consciousness, a kind of evidence that never was called in question. But as to the existence of vibrations in the medullary substance of the nerves and brain, no proof has yet been brought.

All, therefore, we have to expect from this hypothesis, is, that in vibrations, considered abstractly, there should be a variety in kind and degree, which tallies so exactly with the varieties of the thoughts they are to account for, as may lead us to suspect some connection between the one and the other. If the divisions and subdivisions of thought be found to run parallel with the divisions and subdivisions of vibrations, this would give that kind of plausibility to the hypothesis of their connection, which we commonly expect even in a mere hypothesis ; but we do not find even this.

For, to omit all those thoughts and operations which the author comprehends under the name of *ideas*, and which he thinks are connected with vibratiuncles ; to omit the perception of external objects, which he comprehends under the name of *sensations* ; to omit the sensations, properly so called, which accompany our passions [92] and affections, and to confine ourselves to the sensations which we have by means of our external senses, we can perceive no correspondence between the variety we find in their kinds and degrees, and that which may be supposed in vibrations.

We have five senses, whose sensations differ totally in kind. By each of these, excepting perhaps that of hearing, we have a variety of sensations, which differ specifically, and not in degree only. How many tastes and smells are there which are specifically different, each of them capable of all

degrees of strength and weakness ? Heat and cold, roughness and smoothness, hardness and softness, pain and pleasure, are sensations of touch that differ in kind, and each has an endless variety of degrees. Sounds have the qualities of acute and grave, loud and low, with all different degrees of each. The varieties of colour are many more than we have names to express. How shall we find varieties in vibrations corresponding to all this variety of sensations which we have by our five senses only ?

I know two qualities of vibrations in an uniform elastic medium, and I know no more. They may be quick or slow in various degrees, and they may be strong or weak in various degrees ; but I cannot find any division of our sensations that will make them tally with those divisions of vibrations. If we had no other sensations but those of hearing, the theory would answer well ; for sounds are either acute or grave, which may answer to quick or slow vibrations ; or they are loud or low, which answer to strong or weak vibrations. But then we have no variety of vibrations corresponding to the immense variety of sensations which we have by sight, smell, taste, and touch.

Dr Hartley has endeavoured to find out other two qualities of vibrations ; to wit, that they may primarily affect one part of the brain or another, and that they may vary in their direction according as they enter by different external nerves ; but these [93] seem to be added to make a number ; for, as far as we know, vibrations in an uniform elastic substance spread over the whole, and in all directions. However, that we may be liberal, we shall grant him four different kinds of vibrations, each of them having as many degrees as he pleases. Can he, or any man, reduce all our sensations to four kinds ? We have five senses, and by each of them a variety of sensations, more than sufficient to exhaust all the varieties we are able to conceive in vibrations.

Dr Hartley, indeed, was sensible of the difficulty of finding vibrations to suit all the variety of our sensations. His extensive knowledge of physiology and pathology could yield him but a feeble aid ; and, therefore, he is often reduced to the necessity of heaping supposition upon supposition, conjecture upon conjecture, to give some credibility to his hypothesis ; and, in seeking out vibrations which may correspond with the sensations of one sense, he seems to forget that those must be omitted which have been appropriated to another.

Philosophers have accounted in some degree for our various sensations of sound by the vibrations of elastic air ; but it is to be observed, *first*, That we know that such vibrations do really exist; and, *secondly*, That they tally exactly with the most remarkable phænomena of sound. We cannot, indeed, shew how any vibration should produce the sensation of sound. This must be resolved into the will of God, or into some cause altogether unknown. But we know that, as the vibration is strong or weak, the sound is loud or low; we know that, as the vibration is quick or slow, the sound is acute or grave. We can point out that relation of synchronous vibrations which produces harmony or discord, and that relation of successive vibrations which produces melody; and all this is not conjectured, but proved by a sufficient induction. This account of sounds, therefore, is philosophical: although, perhaps, there may be many things relating to sound that we cannot account for, and of which the causes remain latent. The connections described [94] in this branch of philosophy are the work of God, and not the fancy of men.

If anything similar to this could be shewn in accounting for all our sensations by vibrations in the medullary substance of the nerves and brain, it would deserve a place in sound philosophy: but, when we are told of vibrations in a substance which no man could ever prove to have vibrations, or to be capable of them; when such imaginary vibrations are brought to account for all our sensations, though we can perceive no correspondence in their variety of kind and degree to the variety of sensations—the connections described in such a system are the creatures of human imagination, not the work of God.

The rays of light make an impression upon the optic nerves; but they make none upon the auditory or olfactory. The vibrations of the air make an impression upon the auditory nerves; but none upon the optic or the olfactory. The effluvia of bodies make an impression upon the olfactory nerves; but make none upon the optic or auditory. No man has been able to give a shadow of reason for this. While this is the case, is it not better to confess our ignorance of the nature of those impressions made upon the nerves and brain in perception, than to flatter our pride with the conceit of knowledge which we have not, and to adulterate philosophy with the spurious brood of hypotheses?[*]

---

[*] Reid appears to have been unacquainted with the works and theory of Bonnet.—With our author's strictures on the physiological hypotheses, the reader may compare those of Tetens, in his "Versuche." and of Stewart in his "Philosophical Essays."—H.

CHAPTER IV.

FALSE CONCLUSIONS DRAWN FROM THE IMPRESSIONS BEFORE MENTIONED.

SOME philosophers among the ancients, as well as among the moderns, imagined that man is nothing but a piece of matter, so curiously organized that the impressions of external objects produce in it sensation, perception, remembrance, and all the other operations [95] we are conscious of.[*] This foolish opinion could only take its rise from observing the constant connection which the Author of Nature hath established between certain impressions made upon our senses and our perception of the objects by which the impression is made; from which they weakly inferred that those impressions were the proper efficient causes of the corresponding perception.

But no reasoning is m re fallacious than this—that, because two things are always conjoined, therefore one must be the cause of the other. Day and night have been joined in a constant succession since the beginning of the world; but who is so foolish as to conclude from this that day is the cause of night, or night the cause of the following day? There is indeed nothing more ridiculous than to imagine that any motion or modification of matter should produce thought.

If one should tell of a telescope so exactly made as to have the power of seeing; of a whispering gallery that had the power of hearing; of a cabinet so nicely framed as to have the power of memory; or of a machine so delicate as to feel pain when it was touched—such absurdities are so shocking to common sense that they would not find belief even among savages; yet it is the same absurdity to think that the impressions of external objects upon the machine of our bodies can be the real efficient cause of thought and perception.

Passing this, therefore, as a notion too absurd to admit of reasoning, another conclusion very generally made by philosophers is, that, in perception, an impression is made upon the mind as well as upon the organ, nerves, and brain. Aristotle, as was before observed, thought that the form or image of the object perceived, enters by

---

[*] The Stoics are reprehended for such a doctrine by Boethius:—
"Quondam porticus attulit
Obscuros nimium senes,
Qui sensus et imagines
E corporibus extimis
Credaut mentibus imprini,
Ut quondam celeri stylo
Mos est æquore paginæ
Quae nullas habeat notas,
Pressas figere literas " &c
The *tabula rasa* remounts, however, to Aristotle—indeed to Plato—as an illustration.—H.

the organ of sense, and strikes upon the mind.* Mr Hume gives the name of impressions to all our perceptions, to all our sensations, and even to the objects which we perceive. Mr Locke affirms very positively, that the ideas of external objects are produced [96] in our minds by impulse, "that being the only way we can conceive bodies to operate in." It ought, however, to be observed, in justice to Mr Locke, that he retracted this notion in his first letter to the Bishop of Worcester, and promised, in the next edition of his Essay, to have that passage rectified; but, either from forgetfulness in the author, or negligence in the printer, the passage remains in all the subsequent editions I have seen.

There is no prejudice more natural to man than to conceive of the mind as having some similitude to body in its operations. Hence men have been prone to imagine that, as bodies are put in motion by some impulse or impression made upon them by contiguous bodies, so the mind is made to think and to perceive by some impression made upon it, or some impulse given to it by contiguous objects. If we have such a notion of the mind as Homer had of his gods—who might be bruised or wounded with swords and spears—we may then understand what is meant by impressions made upon it by a body; but, if we conceive the mind to be immaterial—of which I think we have very strong proofs—we shall find it difficult to affix a meaning to *impressions made upon it.*

There is a figurative meaning of impressions on the mind which is well authorized, and of which we took notice in the observations made on that word; but this meaning applies only to objects that are interesting. To say that an object which I see with perfect indifference makes an impression upon my mind, is not, as I apprehend, good English. If philosophers mean no more but that I see the object, why should they invent an improper phrase to express what every man knows how to express in plain English?

But it is evident, from the manner in which this phrase is used by modern philosophers, that they mean, not barely to express by it my perceiving an object, but to explain the manner of perception. They think that the object perceived acts upon the mind in some way similar to that in which one body acts upon another, by making [97] an impression upon it. The impression upon the mind is conceived to be something wherein the mind is altogether passive, and has some effect produced in it by the object. But this is a hypothesis which contradicts the common sense of mankind, and which ought not to be admitted without proof.

When I look upon the wall of my room, the wall does not act at all, nor is capable of acting; the perceiving it is an act or operation in me. That this is the common apprehension of mankind with regard to perception, is evident from the manner of expressing it in all languages.

The vulgar give themselves no trouble how they perceive objects—they express what they are conscious of, and they express it with propriety; but philosophers have an avidity to know how we perceive objects; and, conceiving some similitude between a body that is put in motion, and a mind that is made to perceive, they are led to think that, as the body must receive some impulse to make it move, so the mind must receive some impulse or impression to make it perceive. This analogy seems to be confirmed, by observing that we perceive objects only when they make some impression upon the organs of sense, and upon the nerves and brain; but it ought to be observed, that such is the nature of body that it cannot change its state, but by some force impressed upon it. This is not the nature of mind. All that we know about it shews it to be in its nature living and active, and to have the power of perception in its constitution, but still within those limits to which it is confined by the laws of Nature.

It appears, therefore, that this phrase of the mind's having impressions made upon it by corporeal objects in perception, is either a phrase without any distinct meaning, and contrary to the propriety of the English language, or it is grounded upon an hypothesis which is destitute of proof. On that account, though we grant that in perception there is an impression made upon the organ of [98] sense, and upon the nerves and brain, we do not admit that the object makes any impression upon the mind.

There is another conclusion drawn from the impressions made upon the brain in perception, which I conceive to have no solid foundation, though it has been adopted very generally by philosophers. It is, that, by the impressions made on the brain, images are formed of the object perceived; and that the mind, being seated in the brain as its chamber of presence, immediately perceives those images only, and has no perception of the external object but by them. This notion of our perceiving external objects, not immediately, but in certain images or species of them conveyed by the senses, seems to be the most ancient philosophical hypothesis we have on the subject of perception, and to have with

---

* A mere metaphor in Aristotle. (See Notes K and M.) At any rate, the impression was supposed to be made on the animated sensory, and not on the intellect.—H.

small variations retained its authority to this day.

Aristotle, as was before observed, maintained, that the species, images, or forms of external objects, coming from the object, are impressed on the mind. The followers of Democritus and Epicurus held the same thing, with regard to slender films of subtile matter coming from the object, that Aristotle did with regard to his immaterial species or forms.

Aristotle thought every object of human understanding enters at first by the senses;* and that the notions got by them are by the powers of the mind refined and spiritualized, so as at last to become objects of the most sublime and abstracted sciences. Plato, on the other hand, had a very mean opinion of all the knowledge we get by the senses. He thought it did not deserve the name of knowledge, and could not be the foundation of science; because the objects of sense are individuals only, and are in a constant fluctuation. All science, according to him, must be employed about those eternal and immutable ideas which existed before the objects of sense, and are not liable to any change. In this there was an essential difference between the systems of these two philosophers. [99] The notion of eternal and immutable ideas, which Plato borrowed from the Pythagorean school, was totally rejected by Aristotle, who held it as a maxim, that there is nothing in the intellect, which was not at first in the senses.

But, notwithstanding this great difference in those two ancient systems, they might both agree as to the manner in which we perceive objects by our senses: and that they did so, I think, is probable; because Aristotle, as far as I know, neither takes notice of any difference between himself and his master upon this point, nor lays claim to his theory of the manner of our perceiving objects as his own invention. It is still more probable, from the hints which Plato gives in the seventh book of his Republic, concerning the manner in which we perceive the objects of sense; which he compares to persons in a deep and dark cave, who see not external objects themselves but only their shadows, by a light let into the cave through a small opening.†

It seems, therefore, probable that the Pythagoreans and Platonists agreed with the Peripatetics in this general theory of perception—to wit, that the objects of sense are perceived only by certain images, or shadows of them, let into the mind, as into a *camera obscura.*

The notions of the ancients were very various with regard to the seat of the soul Since it has been discovered, by the improvements in anatomy, that the nerves are the instruments of perception, and of the sensations accompanying it, and that the nerves ultimately terminate in the brain,† it has been the general opinion of philosophers that the brain is the seat of the soul; and that she perceives the images that are brought there, and external things, only by means of them.

Des Cartes, observing that the pineal gland is the only part of the brain that is single, all the other parts being double,‡ and thinking that the soul must have one seat, was determined by this [100] to make that gland the soul's habitation, to which, by means of the animal spirits, intelligence is brought of all objects that affect the senses.§

Others have not thought proper to confine the habitation of the soul to the pineal gland, but to the brain in general, or to some part of it, which they call the *sensorium.* Even the great Newton favoured this opinion, though he proposes it only as a query, with that modesty which distinguished him no less than his great genius. "Is not," says he, "the sensorium of animals the place where the sentient substance is present, and to which the sensible species of things are brought through the nerves and brain, that there they may be perceived by the mind present in that place? And is there not an incorporeal, living, intelligent, and omnipresent Being, who, in infinite space, as if it were in his sensorium, intimately perceives things themselves, and comprehends them perfectly, as being present to them; of which things, that principle in us, which perceives and thinks, discerns only, in its little sensorium, the images brought to it through the organs of the senses?"‖

His great friend Dr Samuel Clarke adopted the same sentiment with more confidence. In his papers to Leibnitz, we find the following passages: "Without being present to the images of the things perceived, it (the soul) could not possibly perceive them. A living substance can only there perceive where it is present, either to the things themselves, (as the omnipresent God is to the whole universe,)

---

* This is a very doubtful point, and has accordingly divided his followers. Texts can be quoted to prove, on the one side, that Aristotle derived all our notions, *a posteriori*, from the experience of sense; and, on the other, that he viewed sense only as affording to intellect the condition requisite for it to become actually conscious of the native and necessary notions it, *a priori*, virtually possessed.—H.

† Reid wholly mistakes the meaning of Plato's simile of the cave. See below, under p 116.—H.

* An error. See below, under p. 116.—H.

† That is, since the time of Erasistratus and Galen.—H.

‡ Which is not the case. The Hypophysis, the Vermiform process, &c., are not less single than the Conarium.—H.

§ See above, p. 214, b, note *.—H.

‖ Before Reid, these crude conjectures of Newton were justly censured by Genovesi, and other.—H.

or to the images of things, (as the soul of man is in its proper sensory.) Nothing can any more act, or be acted upon, where it is not present, than it can be where it is not. We are sure the soul cannot perceive what it is not present to, because nothing can act, or be acted upon, where it is not."

Mr Locke expresses himself so upon this point, that, for the [101] most part, one would imagine that he thought that the ideas, or images of things, which he believed to be the immediate objects of perception, are impressions upon the mind itself; yet, in some passages, he rather places them in the brain, and makes them to be perceived by the mind there present. " There are some ideas," says he, " which have admittance only through one sense; and, if the organs or the nerves, which are the conduits to convey them from without to their audience in the brain, the mind's presence room, if I may so call it, are so disordered as not to perform their function, they have no postern to be admitted by.

" There seems to be a constant decay of all our ideas, even of those that are struck deepest. The pictures drawn in our minds are laid in fading colours. Whether the temper of the brain makes this difference, that in some it retains the characters drawn on it like marble, in others like freestone, and in others little better than sand, I shall not enquire."‡

From these passages of Mr Locke, and others of a like nature, it is plain that he thought that there are images of external objects conveyed to the brain. But whether he thought with Des Cartes† and Newton, that the images in the brain are perceived by the mind there present, or that they are imprinted on the mind itself, is not so evident.

Now, with regard to this hypothesis, there are three things that deserve to be considered, because the hypothesis leans upon them; and, if any one of them fail, it must fall to the ground. The *first* is, That the soul has its seat, or, as Mr Locke calls it, its presence room in the brain. The *second*, That there are images formed in the brain of all the objects of sense. The *third*, That the mind or soul perceives these images in the brain; and that it perceives not external objects immediately, but only perceives them by means of those images. [102]

As to the *first* point—that the soul has its

seat in the brain—this, surely, is not so well established as that we can safely build other principles upon it. There have been various opinions and much disputation about the place of spirits: whether they have a place? and, if they have, how they occupy that place? After men had fought in the dark about those points for ages, the wiser part seem to have left off disputing about them, as matters beyond the reach of the human faculties.

As to the *second* point—that images of all the objects of sense are formed in the brain—we may venture to affirm that there is no proof nor probability of this, with regard to any of the objects of sense; and that, with regard to the greater part of them, it is words without any meaning.*

We have not the least evidence that the image of any external object is formed in the brain. The brain has been dissected times innumerable by the nicest anatomists; every part of it examined by the naked eye, and with the help of microscopes; but no vestige of an image of any external object was ever found. The brain seems to be the most improper substance that can be imagined for receiving or retaining images, being a soft, moist, medullary substance.

But how are these images formed? or whence do they come? Says Mr Locke, the organs of sense and nerves convey them from without. This is just the Aristotelian hypothesis of sensible species, which modern philosophers have been at great pains to refute, and which must be acknowledged to be one of the most unintelligible parts of the Peripatetic system. Those who consider species of colour, figure, sound, and smell, coming from the object, and entering by the organs of sense, as a part of the scholastic jargon long ago discarded from sound philosophy, ought to have discarded images in the brain along with them. There never was a shadow of argument brought by any author, to shew that an [103] image of any external object ever entered by any of the organs of sense.

That external objects make some impression on the organs of sense, and by them on the nerves and brain, is granted; but that those impressions resemble the objects they are made by, so as that they may be called images of the objects, is most improbable. Every hypothesis that has been contrived, shews that there can be no such resemblance; for neither the motions of animal spirits, nor the vibrations of elastic chords, or of elastic æther, or of the infinites-

---

* No great stress should be laid on such figurative passages as indications of the real opinion of Locke, which, on this point, it is not easy to discover. See Note O.—H.

† *Des Cartes* is perhaps an erratum for *Dr Clarke.* If not, the opinion of Des Cartes is misrepresented: for he denied to the mind all consciousness or immediate knowledge of matter and its modifications. But of this again. See Note N.—H.

* It would be rash to assume that, because a philosopher uses the term *image*, or *impression*, or *idea*, and places what it denotes in the brain, that he therefore means that the mind was cognizant of such corporeal affection, as of its object, either in perception or imagination. See Note K.—H.

imal particles of the nerves, can be supposed to resemble the objects by which they are excited.

We know that, in vision, an image of the visible object is formed in the bottom of the eye by the rays of light. But we know, also, that this image cannot be conveyed to the brain, because the optic nerve, and all the parts that surround it, are opaque and impervious to the rays of light; and there is no other organ of sense in which any image of the object is formed.

It is farther to be observed, that, with regard to some objects of sense, we may understand what is meant by an image of them imprinted on the brain; but, with regard to most objects of sense, the phrase is absolutely unintelligible, and conveys no meaning at all. As to objects of sight, I understand what is meant by an image of their figure in the brain. But how shall we conceive an image of their colour where there is absolute darkness? And as to all other objects of sense, except figure and colour, I am unable to conceive what is meant by an image of them. Let any man say what he means by an image of heat and cold, an image of hardness or softness, an image of sound, or smell, or taste. The word *image*, when applied to these objects of sense, has absolutely no meaning. Upon what a weak foundation, then, does this hypothesis stand, when it supposes that images of all the objects of sense are imprinted on the brain, being conveyed thither by the conduits of the organs and nerves!* [104]

The *third* point in this hypothesis is, That the mind perceives the images in the brain, and external objects only by means of them. This is as improbable as that there are such images to be perceived. If our powers of perception be not altogether fallacious, the objects we perceive are not in our brain, but without us.† We are so far from perceiving images in the brain, that we do not·perceive our brain at all; nor would any man ever have known that he had a brain, if anatomy had not discovered, by dissection, that the brain is a constituent part of the human body.

To sum up what has been said with regard to the organs of perception, and the impressions made upon our nerves and brain. It is a law of our nature, established by the will of the Supreme Being, that we perceive no external object but by

means of the organs given us for that purpose. But these organs do not perceive. The eye is the organ of sight, but it sees not. A telescope is an artificial organ of sight. The eye is a natural organ of sight, but it sees as little as the telescope. We know how the eye forms a picture of the visible object upon the retina; but how this picture makes us see the object we know not; and if experience had not informed us that such a picture is necessary to vision, we should never have known it. We can give no reason why the picture on the retina should be followed by vision, while a like picture on any other part of the body produces nothing like vision.

It is likewise a law of our nature, that we perceive not external objects, unless certain impressions be made by the object upon the organ, and by means of the organ upon the nerves and brain. But of the nature of those impressions we are perfectly ignorant; and though they are conjoined with perception by the will of our Maker, yet it does not appear that they have any necessary connection with it in their own nature, far less that they can be the proper efficient cause of it. [105] We perceive, because God has given us the power of perceiving, and not because we have impressions from objects. We perceive nothing without those impressions, because our Maker has limited and circumscribed our powers of perception, by such laws of Nature as to his wisdom seemed meet, and such as suited our rank in his creation.*

---

* These objections to the hypothesis in question, have been frequently urged both in ancient and in modern times. See Note K.—H.

† If this be taken literally and by itself, then, according to Reid, perception is not an immanent cognition; extension and figure are, in that act, not merely suggested conceptions; and, as we are percipient of the non-ego, and, conscious of the perception, we are therefore conscious of the non-ego. But see Note C.—H.

[104. 105]

* The doctrine of Reid and Stewart, in regard to our perception of external things, bears a close analogy to the Cartesian scheme of *divine assistance*, or of *occasional causes* It seems, however, to coincide most completely with the opinion of Ruardus Andala, a Dutch Cartesian, who attempted to reconcile the theory of *assistance* with that of *physical influence* "statuo," he says, "nos clarissimam et distinctissimam hujus *operationis et unionis* posse habere *ideam*, si modo, quod omnino facere oportet, ad Deum, causam ejus primam et liberam ascendamus, et ab ejus beneplacito admirandum hunc effectum derivemus. Nos possumus huic vel illi motui e. gr. campanæ, sic et hederæ suspensæ literis scriptis, verbis quibuscunque pronunciatis, aliisque signis, varias ideas alligare, ita, ut per visum, vel auditum in mente excitentur variæ ideæ, perceptiones et sensationes· annon hinc clare et facile intelligimus, Deum creatorem m·ntis et corporis potuisse instituere et or i. i are, ut per va ios in corpore motus variæ in mente excitentur ideæ et perceptiones; et vicissim, ut per varias mentis volitiones, varii in corpore excitentur et producantur motus? H nc et pro varia alterutrius partis dispositione altera pars variis modis affici potest. Hoc autem a Deo ita ordinatum et effectum esse, a posteriori, continua, certissima et clarissima experientia docet Testes irrefragabiles omnique exceptione majores reciproci hujus commercii, operationis men·is in corpus, et corporis in mentem, nec non commun·onis status, sunt *sensus* omnes tum *externi*, tum *interni*; ut et omnes et singulæ et continuæ actiones mentis in corp·s, de quibus modo fuit actum. Si quis vero a *proprietatibus* mentis ad *proprietates* corporis progredi velit, aut ex *natura* diversissimarum harum substantiarum deducere motum in corpore, & perceptiones in mente, aut hos effectus ut necessario connexos spectare; uæ is frustra erit, nihil intelliget, perversissime phi-

CHAPTER V.

OF PERCEPTION.

In speaking of the impressions made on our organs in perception, we build upon facts borrowed from anatomy and physiology, for which we have the testimony of our senses. But, being now to speak of perception itself, which is solely an act of the mind, we must appeal to another authority. The operations of our minds are known, not by sense, but by consciousness, the authority of which is as certain and as irresistible as that of sense.

In order, however, to our having a distinct notion of any of the operations of our own minds, it is not enough that we be conscious of them; for all men have this consciousness. It is farther necessary that we attend to them while they are exerted, and reflect upon them with care, while they are recent and fresh in our memory. It is necessary that, by employing ourselves frequently in this way, we get the habit of this attention and reflection; and, therefore, for the proof of facts which I shall have occasion to mention upon this subject, I can only appeal to the reader's own thoughts, whether such facts are not agreeable to what he is conscious of in his own mind. [106]

If, therefore, we attend to that act of our mind which we call the perception of an external object of sense, we shall find in it these three things:—*First*, Some conception or notion of the object perceived; *Secondly*, A strong and irresistible conviction and belief of its present existence; and, *Thirdly*, That this conviction and belief are immediate, and not the effect of reasoning.[*]

First, It is impossible to perceive an object without having some notion or conception of that which we perceive. We may, indeed, conceive an object which we do not perceive; but, when we perceive the object, we must have some conception of it at the same time; and we have commonly a more clear and steady notion of the object while we perceive it, than we have from memory or imagination when it is not perceived. Yet, even in perception, the notion which our senses give of the object may be more or less clear, more or less distinct, in all possible degrees.

Thus we see more distinctly an object at a small than at a great distance. An object at a great distance is seen more distinctly in a clear than in a foggy day. An object seen indistinctly with the naked eye, on account of its smallness, may be seen distinctly with a microscope. The objects in this room will be seen by a person in the room less and less distinctly as the light of the day fails; they pass through all the various degrees of distinctness according to the degrees of the light, and, at last, in total darkness they are not seen at all. What has been said of the objects of sight is so easily applied to the objects of the other senses, that the application may be left to the reader.

In a matter so obvious to every person capable of reflection, it is necessary only farther to observe, that the notion which we get of an object, merely by our external sense, ought not to be confounded with that more scientific notion which a man, come to the years of understanding, may have of the same object, by attending to its various attributes, or to its various parts, and their relation to each other, and to the whole. [107] Thus, the notion which a child has of a jack for roasting meat, will be acknowledged to be very different from that of a man who understands its construction, and perceives the relation of the parts to one another, and to the whole. The child sees the jack and every part of it as well as the man. The child, therefore, has all the notion of it which sight gives; whatever there is more in the notion which the man forms of it, must be derived from other powers of the mind, which may afterwards be explained. This observation is made here only that we may not confound the operations of different powers of the mind, which by being always conjoined after we grow up to understanding, are apt to pass for one and the same.

Secondly, In perception we not only have a notion more or less distinct of the object perceived, but also an irresistible conviction and belief of its existence. This is always the case when we are certain that we perceive it. There may be a perception so faint and indistinct as to leave us in doubt whether we perceive the object or not. Thus, when a star begins to twinkle as the light of the sun withdraws, one may, for a short time, think he sees it without being certain, until the perception acquire some strength and steadiness. When a ship just begins to appear in the utmost verge of the horizon, we may at first be dubious whether we perceive it or not; but when the perception is in any degree clear and steady, there remains no doubt of its reality; and when the reality of the perception is ascertained, the existence of the object perceived can no longer be doubted.[*]

losophabitur nullamque hujus rei ideam habere poterit. Si vero ad Deum Creatorem adscendamus, eumque vere agnoscamus, nihil hic erit obscuri, hunc effectum clarissime intelligemus, et quidem per caussam ejus primam; quæ perfectissima demum est scientia."—H.

[*] See above, p. 183, a, note [*]; p. 188, b, note [*]; and Note C.—H.

[*] In this paragraph there is a confusion of that which is *perceived* and that which is *inferred* from the perception.—H.

By the laws of all nations, in the most solemn judicial trials, wherein men's fortunes and lives are at stake, the sentence passes according to the testimony of eye or ear witnesses of good credit. An upright judge will give a fair hearing to every objection that can be made to the integrity of a witness, and allow it to be possible that he may be corrupted; but no judge will ever suppose that witnesses may be imposed upon by trusting to their eyes and ears. And if a sceptical counsel should plead against the testimony of the witnesses, that they had no other evidence for what they [108] declared but the testimony of their eyes and ears, and that we ought not to put so much faith in our senses as to deprive men of life or fortune upon their testimony, surely no upright judge would admit a plea of this kind. I believe no counsel, however sceptical, ever dared to offer such an argument; and, if it was offered, it would be rejected with disdain.

Can any stronger proof be given that it is the universal judgment of mankind that the evidence of sense is a kind of evidence which we may securely rest upon in the most momentous concerns of mankind; that it is a kind of evidence against which we ought not to admit any reasoning; and, therefore, that to reason either for or against it is an insult to common sense?

The whole conduct of mankind in the daily occurrences of life, as well as the solemn procedure of judicatories in the trial of causes civil and criminal, demonstrates this. I know only of two exceptions that may be offered against this being the universal belief of mankind.

The first exception is that of some lunatics who have been persuaded of things that seem to contradict the clear testimony of their senses. It is said there have been lunatics and hypochondriacal persons, who seriously believed themselves to be made of glass; and, in consequence of this, lived in continual terror of having their brittle frame shivered into pieces.

All I have to say to this is, that our minds, in our present state, are, as well as our bodies, liable to strange disorders; and, as we do not judge of the natural constitution of the body from the disorders or diseases to which it is subject from accidents, so neither ought we to judge of the natural powers of the mind from its disorders, but from its sound state. It is natural to man, and common to the species, to have two hands and two feet; yet I have seen a man, and a very ingenious one, who was born without either hands or feet. [109] It is natural to man to have faculties superior to those of brutes; yet we see some individuals whose faculties are not equal to those of many brutes; and the wisest man may,

by various accidents, be reduced to this state. General rules that regard those whose intellects are sound are not overthrown by instances of men whose intellects are hurt by any constitutional or accidental disorder.

The other exception that may be made to the principle we have laid down is that of some philosophers who have maintained that the testimony of sense is fallacious, and therefore ought never to be trusted. Perhaps it might be a sufficient answer to this to say, that there is nothing so absurd which some philosophers have not maintained.* It is one thing to profess a doctrine of this kind, another seriously to believe it, and to be governed by it in the conduct of life. It is evident that a man who did not believe his senses could not keep out of harm's way an hour of his life; yet, in all the history of philosophy, we never read of any sceptic that ever stepped into fire or water because he did not believe his senses, or that shewed in the conduct of life less trust in his senses than other men have.† This gives us just ground to apprehend that philosophy was never able to conquer that natural belief which men have in their senses; and that all their subtile reasonings against this belief were never able to persuade themselves.

It appears, therefore, that the clear and distinct testimony of our senses carries irresistible conviction along with it to every man in his right judgment.

I observed, *Thirdly,* That this conviction is not only irresistible, but it is immediate that is, it is not by a train of reasoning and argumentation that we come to be convinced of the existence of what we perceive; we ask no argument for the existence of the object, but that we perceive it; perception commands our belief upon its own authority, and disdains to rest its authority upon any reasoning whatsoever.‡ [110]

The conviction of a truth may be irresistible, and yet not immediate. Thus, my conviction that the three angles of every plain triangle are equal to two right angles, is irresistible, but it is not immediate; I am convinced of it by demonstrative reasoning. There are other truths in mathematics of which we have not only an irresistible but an immediate conviction. Such are the axioms. Our belief of the axioms in mathematics is not grounded upon argu-

---

* A saying of Varro.—H.
† All this we read, however, in Laërtius, of Pyrrho; and on the authority of Antigonus Carystius, the great sceptic's contemporary. Whether we are to believe the narrative is another question.—H.
‡ If Reid holds that in perception we have only a *conception* of the *Non-Ego* in the *Ego*, this belief is either not the reflex of a cognition, but a blind faith, or it is mediate, as held by Stewart.—*Phil. o., Ess. ii. c. 2.*—H.

s 2

ment—arguments are grounded upon them; but their evidence is discerned immediately by the human understanding.

It is, no doubt, one thing to have an immediate conviction of a self-evident axiom ; it is another thing to have an immediate conviction of the existence of what we see ; but the conviction is equally immediate and equally irresistible in both cases. No man thinks of seeking a reason to believe what he sees ; and, before we are capable of reasoning, we put no less confidence in our senses than after. The rudest savage is as fully convinced of what he sees, and hears, and feels, as the most expert logician. The constitution of our understanding determines us to hold the truth of a mathematical axiom as a first principle, from which other truths may be deduced, but it is deduced from none ; and the constitution of our power of perception determines us to hold the existence of what we distinctly perceive as a first principle, from which other truths may be deduced ; but it is deduced from none. What has been said of the irresistible and immediate belief of the existence of objects distinctly perceived, I mean only to affirm with regard to persons so far advanced in understanding as to distinguish objects of mere imagination from things which have a real existence. Every man knows that he may have a notion of Don Quixote, or of Garagantua, without any belief that such persons ever existed ; and that of Julius Cæsar and Oliver Cromwell, he has not only a notion, but a belief that they did really exist. [111] But whether children, from the time that they begin to use their senses, make a distinction between things which are only conceived or imagined, and things which really exist, may be doubted. Until we are able to make this distinction, we cannot properly be said to believe or to disbelieve the existence of anything. The belief of the existence of anything seems to suppose a notion of existence—a notion too abstract, perhaps, to enter into the mind of an infant. I speak of the power of perception in those that are adult and of a sound mind, who believe that there are some things which do really exist; and that there are many things conceived by themselves, and by others, which have no existence. That such persons do invariably ascribe existence to everything which they distinctly perceive, without seeking reasons or arguments for doing so, is perfectly evident from the whole tenor of human life.

The account I have given of our perception of external objects, is intended as a faithful delineation of what every man, come to years of understanding, and capable of giving attention to what passes in his own mind, may feel in himself. In what man-

ner the notion of external objects, and the immediate belief of their existence, is produced by means of our senses, I am not able to shew, and I do not pretend to shew. If the power of perceiving external objects in certain circumstances, be a part of the original constitution of the human mind, all attempts to account for it will be vain. No other account can be given of the constitution of things, but the will of Him that made them. As we can give no reason why matter is extended and inert, why the mind thinks and is conscious of its thoughts, but the will of Him who made both ; so I suspect we can give no other reason why, in certain circumstances, we perceive external objects, and in others do not.[*]

The Supreme Being intended that we should have such knowledge of the material objects that surround us, as is necessary in order to our supplying the wants of nature, and avoiding the dangers to which we are constantly exposed ; and he has admirably fitted our powers of perception to this purpose. [112] If the intelligence we have of external objects were to be got by reasoning only, the greatest part of men would be destitute of it ; for the greatest part of men hardly ever learn to reason ; and in infancy and childhood no man can reason : Therefore, as this intelligence of the objects that surround us, and from which we may receive so much benefit or harm, is equally necessary to children and to men, to the ignorant and to the learned, God in his wisdom conveys it to us in a way that puts all upon a level. The information of the senses is as perfect, and gives as full conviction to the most ignorant as to the most learned.

CHAPTER VI.

WHAT IT IS TO ACCOUNT FOR A PHÆNOMENON IN NATURE.

An object placed at a proper distance, and in a good light, while the eyes are shut, is not perceived at all ; but no sooner do we open our eyes upon it than we have, as it were by inspiration, a certain knowledge of its existence, of its colour, figure, and distance. This is a fact which every one knows. The vulgar are satisfied with knowing the fact, and give themselves no trouble about the cause of it : but a philosopher is impatient to know how this event is produced, to account for it, or assign its cause.

This avidity to know the causes of things is the parent of all philosophy, true and false. Men of speculation place a great part of their happiness in such knowledge.

---

[*] See above, p. 128, b, note ＊, and p. 130, b, note ＊; also Note A.—H.

Felix qui potuit rerum cognoscere causas, has always been a sentiment of human nature. But, as in the pursuit of other kinds of happiness men often mistake the road, so in none have they more frequently done it than in the philosophical pursuit of the causes of things. [113]

It is a dictate of common sense, that the causes we assign of appearances ought to be real, and not fictions of human imagination. It is likewise self-evident, that such causes ought to be adequate to the effects that are conceived to be produced by them.

That those who are less accustomed to inquiries into the causes of natural appearances, may the better understand what it is to shew the cause of such appearances, or to account for them, I shall borrow a plain instance of a phænomenon or appearance, of which a full and satisfactory account has been given. The phænomenon is this : That a stone, or any heavy body, falling from a height, continually increases its velocity as it descends ; so that, if it acquire a certain velocity in one second of time, it will have twice that velocity at the end of two seconds, thrice at the end of three seconds, and so on in proportion to the time. This accelerated velocity in a stone falling must have been observed from the beginning of the world ; but the first person, as far as we know, who accounted for it in a proper and philosophical manner, was the famous Galileo, after innumerable false and fictitious accounts had been given of it.

He observed, that bodies once put in motion continue that motion with the same velocity, and in the same direction, until they be stopped or retarded, or have the direction of their motion altered, by some force impressed upon them. This property of bodies is called their *inertia*, or inactivity ; for it implies no more than that bodies cannot of themselves change their state from rest to motion, or from motion to rest. He observed also, that gravity acts constantly and equally upon a body, and therefore will give equal degrees of velocity to a body in equal times. From these principles, which are known from experience to be fixed laws of nature, Galileo shewed that heavy bodies must descend with a velocity uniformly accelerated, as by experience they are found to do. [114]

For if the body by its gravitation acquire a certain velocity at the end of one second, it would, though its gravitation should cease that moment, continue to go on with that velocity ; but its gravitation continues, and will in another second give it an additional velocity, equal to that which it gave in the first ; so that the whole velocity at the end of two seconds, will be twice as great as at the end of one. In like manner, this

velocity being continued through the third second, and having the same addition by gravitation as in any of the preceding, the whole velocity at the end of the third second will be thrice as great as at the end of the first, and so on continually.

We may here observe, that the causes assigned of this phænomenon are two : *First,* That bodies once put in motion retain their velocity and their direction, until it is changed by some force impressed upon them. *Secondly,* That the weight or gravitation of a body is always the same. These are laws of Nature, confirmed by universal experience, and therefore are not feigned but true causes. Then, they are precisely adequate to the effect ascribed to them ; they must necessarily produce that very motion in descending bodies which we find to take place ; and neither more nor less. The account, therefore, given of this phænomenon, is just and philosophical ; no other will ever be required or admitted by those who understand this.

It ought likewise to be observed, that the causes assigned of this phænomenon, are things of which we can assign no cause. Why bodies once put in motion continue to move—why bodies constantly gravitate towards the earth with the same force—no man has been able to shew : these are facts confirmed by universal experience, and they must no doubt have a cause ; but their cause is unknown, and we call them laws of Nature, because we know no cause of them, but the will of the Supreme Being.

But may we not attempt to find the cause of gravitation, and of other phænomena, which we call laws of Nature ? No doubt we may. [115] We know not the limit which has been set to human knowledge, and our knowledge of the works of God can never be carried too far. But, supposing gravitation to be accounted for, by an æthereal elastic medium, for instance, this can only be done, *first,* by proving the existence and the elasticity of this medium ; and, *secondly,* by shewing that this medium must necessarily produce that gravitation which bodies are known to have. Until this be done, gravitation is not accounted for, nor is its cause known ; and when this is done, the elasticity of this medium will be considered as a law of nature whose cause is unknown. The chain of natural causes has, not unfitly, been compared to a chain hanging down from heaven : a link that is discovered supports the links below it, but it must itself be supported ; and that which supports it must be supported, until we come to the first link, which is supported by the throne of the Almighty. Every natural cause must have a cause, until we ascend to the first cause, which is uncaused, and operates not by necessity but by will.

By what has been said in this chapter, those who are but little acquainted with philosophical inquiries, may see what is meant by accounting for a phænomenon, or shewing its cause, which ought to be well understood, in order to judge of the theories by which philosophers have attempted to account for our perception of external objects by the senses.

CHAPTER VII.

SENTIMENTS[*] OF PHILOSOPHERS ABOUT THE PERCEPTION OF EXTERNAL OBJECTS ; AND, FIRST, OF THE THEORY OF FATHER MALEBRANCHE.†

How the correspondence is carried on between the thinking principle within us, and the material world without us, has always been found a very difficult problem to those philosophers who think themselves obliged to account for every phænomenon in nature. [116] Many philosophers, ancient and modern, have employed their invention to discover how we are made to perceive external objects by our senses ; and there appears to be a very great uniformity in their sentiments in the main, notwithstanding their variations in particular points.

Plato illustrates our manner of perceiving the objects of sense, in this manner. He supposes a dark subterraneous cave, in which men lie bound in such a manner that they can direct their eyes only to one part of the cave : far behind, there is a light, some rays of which come over a wall to that part of the cave which is before the eyes of our prisoners. A number of persons, variously employed, pass between them and the light, whose shadows are seen by the prisoners, but not the persons themselves.

In this manner, that philosopher conceived that, by our senses, we perceive the shadows of things only, and not things themselves. He seems to have borrowed his notions on this subject, from the Pythagoreans, and they very probably from Pythagoras himself. If we make allowance for Plato's allegorical genius, his sentiments on this subject, correspond very well with those of his scholar, Aristotle, and of the Peripatetics. The shadows of Plato may very well represent the species and phantasms of the Peripatetic school, and the ideas and impressions of modern philosophers.[*]

* This interpretation of the meaning of Plato's comparison of the cave exhibits a curious mistake, in which Reid is followed by Mr Stewart and many others, and which, it is remarkable, has never yet been detected. In the similitude in question, (which will be found in the seventh book of the Republic,) Plato is supposed to intend an illustration of the mode in which the shadows or vicarious images of external things are admitted into the mind—to typify, in short, an hypothesis of sensitive perception. On this supposition, the identity of the Platonic, Pythagorean, and Peripatetic theories of this process is inferred. Nothing can, however, be more groundless than the inference ; nothing more erroneous than the inference. By his *cave, images,* and *shadows,* Plato meant simply to illustrate the grand principle of his philosophy—that the Sensible or Ectypal world, (phænomenal, transitory, γιγνόμενον, ὂν καὶ μὴ ὂν,) stands to the Noetic or Archetypal, (substantial, permanent, ὄντως ὂν,) in the same relation of comparative unreality, in which the *shadows of the images* of sensible existences themselves, stand to the things of which they are the dim and distant adumbrations. In the language of an illustrious poet—
" An nescis, quæcunque heic sunt, quæ hæc nocte teguntur,
Omnia res prorsus veras non esse, sed umbras,
Aut specula, unde ad nos aliena elucet imago ?
Terra quidem, et maria alta, atque his circumfluus aer,
Et quæ consistunt ex iis, hæc omnia tenuis
Sunt umbræ, humanos quæ tanquam somnia quæ. dam
Pertingunt animos, fallaci et imagine ludunt,
Nunquam eadem, fluxu semper variata perenni.
Sol autem, Lunæque globus, fulgentiaque astra
Cætera, sint quamvis meliori prædita vita,
Et donata ævo immortali, hæc ipsa tamen sunt
Æterni specula, in quæ animus, qui est inde profectus,
Inspiciens, patriæ quodam quasi tactus amore,
Ardescit. Verum quoniam heic non perstat et ultra
Nescio quid sequitur secum, tacitusque requirit,
Nosse licet circum hæc ipsum consistere verum,
Non finem : sed enim esse aliud quid, cujus imago
Splendet in iis, quod per se ipsum est, et principium esse
Omnibus æternum, ante omnem numerumque diemque ;
In quo alium Solem atque aliam splendescere Lunam
Adspicias, aliosque orbes, alia astra manere,
Terramque, fluviosque alios, atque acra, et ignem,
Et nemora, atque aliis errare animalia silvis."
And as the comparison is misunderstood, so nothing can be conceived more adverse to the doctrine of Plato than the theory it is supposed to elucidate. Plotinus, indeed, formally refutes, as contrary to the Platonic, the very hypothesis thus attributed to his master. (Enn. IV., l. vi., cc. 1., 3.) The doctrine of the Platonists on this point has been almost wholly neglected ; and the author among them whose work contains its most articulate developement has been so completely overlooked, both by scholars and philosophers, that his work is of the rarest, while even his name is mentioned in no history of philosophy. It is here sufficient to state, that the ιδωλα, the λόγοι γνωστικοί, the forms representative of external things, and corresponding to the *species sensiles expressæ* of the schoolmen, were *not held by the Platonists to be derived from without.* Prior to the act of perception, they have a latent but real existence in the soul ; and, by the impassive energy of the mind itself, are elicited into consciousness, on occasion of the *impression* (κίνησις, πάθος, ἐμφασεις) made on the external organ, and of the *vital form* (ζωτικὸν ιδος,) in consequence thereof, sublimated in the animal life. The verses of Boethius, which have been so frequently misunderstood, contain an accurate statement of the Platonic theory of perception. After refuting the

* *Sentiment,* as here and elsewhere employed by Reid, in the meaning of opinion, (*sententia,*) is not to be imitated. There are, undoubtedly, precedents to be found for such usage in English writers ; and, in the French and Italian languages, this is one of the ordinary significations of the word —H.

† It is not easy to conceive by what principle the order of the history of opinions touching Perception, contained in the nine following chapters, is determined. It is not chronological, and it is not systematic. Of these theories, there is a very able survey, by M. Royer Collard, among the fragments of his lectures, in the third volume of Jouffroy's " Oeuvres de Reid." That distinguished philosopher has, however, placed too great a reliance upon the accuracy of Reid —H.

Two thousand years after Plato, Mr Locke, who studied the operations of the human mind so much, and with so great success, represents our manner of perceiving external objects, by a similitude very much resembling that of the cave. "Methinks," says he, "the understanding is not much unlike a closet wholly shut from light, with only some little opening left, to let in external visible resemblances or ideas of things without. Would the pictures coming into such a dark room but stay there, and lie so orderly as to be found upon occasion, it would very much resemble the understanding of a man, in reference to all objects of sight, and the ideas of them." [117]

Plato's subterranean cave, and Mr Locke's dark closet, may be applied with ease to all the systems of perception that have been invented : for they all suppose that we perceive not external objects immediately, and that the immediate objects of perception are only certain shadows of the external objects. Those shadows or images, which we immediately perceive, were by the ancients called *species, forms, phantasms.* Since the time of Des Cartes, they have commonly been called *ideas,* and by Mr Hume, *impressions.* But all philosophers, from Plato to Mr Hume, agree in this, That we do not perceive external objects immediately, and that the immediate object of perception must be some image present to the mind.* So far there ap-

pears an unanimity, rarely to be found among philosophers on such abstruse points.*

If it should be asked, Whether, according to the opinion of philosophers, we perceive the images or ideas only, and infer the existence and qualities of the external object from what we perceive in the image ; or, whether we really perceive the external object as well as its image ?—the answer to this question is not quite obvious.†

On the one hand, philosophers, if we except Berkeley and Hume, believe the existence of external objects of sense, and call them objects of perception, though not immediate objects. But what they mean by a mediate object of perception I do not find clearly explained : whether they suit their language to popular opinion, and mean that we perceive external objects in that figurative sense in which we say that we perceive an absent friend when we look on his picture ; or whether they mean that, really, and without a figure, we perceive both the external object and its idea in the mind. If the last be their meaning, it would follow that, in every instance of perception, there is a double object perceived : [118] that I perceive, for instance, one sun in the heavens, and another in my own mind.‡ But I do not find that they affirm this ; and, as it contradicts the experience of all mankind, I will not impute it to them.

It seems, therefore, that their opinion is, That we do not really perceive the external object, but the internal only ; and that, when they speak of perceiving external objects, they mean it only in a popular or in a figurative sense, as above explained. Several reasons lead me to think this to be the opinion of philosophers, beside what is mentioned above. *First,* If we do really perceive the external object itself, there seems to be no necessity, no use, for an image of it. *Secondly,* Since the time of Des Cartes, philosophers have very generally thought that the existence of external objects of sense requires proof, and can only be proved from the existence of their ideas. *Thirdly,* The way in which philosophers speak of ideas, seems to imply that they are the only objects of perception.

Stoical doctrine of the passivity of mind in this process, he proceeds :—

> " Mens est efficiens magis
> Longe causa potentior,
> Quam quæ materiæ modo
> Impressas patitur notas.
> *Præcedit tamen excitans*
> Ac vires animi movens
> *Vivo in corpore passio,*
> Cum vel lux oculos ferit,
> Vel vox auribus instrepit ;
> Tum *mentis vigor excitus*
> *Quas intus species tenet,*
> Ad motus similes vocans,
> Notis applicat exteris,
> *Introrsumque reconditis*
> *Formis* miscet imagines."

I cannot now do more than *indicate* the contrast of this doctrine to the Peripatetic (I do not say *Aristotelian*) theory, and its approximation to the Cartesian and Leibnitzian hypotheses ; which, however, both attempt to explain, what the Platonic did not—how the mind, *ex hypothesi,* above all *physical influence,* is determined, on the presence of the unknown reality within the sphere of *sense,* to call into consciousness the representation through which that reality is made known to us. I may add, that not merely the Platonists, but some of the older Peripatetics held that the soul virtually contained within itself representative forms, which were only excited by the external reality ; as Theophrastus and Themistius, to say nothing of the Platonizing Porphyry, Simplicius and Ammonius Hermiæ ; and the same opinion, adopted probably from the latter, by his pupil, the Arabian Adelandus, subsequently became even the common doctrine of the Moorish Aristotelians.

I shall afterwards have occasion to notice that Bacon has also wrested Plato's similitude of the cave from its genuine signification —H.

* This is not correct. There were philosophers

[117, 118]

who held a purer and preciser doctrine of immediate perception than Reid himself contemplated.—H.

* Reid himself, like the philosophers in general, really holds, that we do not perceive external things immediately, if he does not allow us a consciousness of the *non-ego.* It matters not whether the external reality be represented in a *tertium quid,* or in a modification of the mind itself ; in either case, it is not known in itself, but in something numerically different.—H.

† Nothing can be clearer than would be this answer. —In perception, the external reality, (the mediate object,) is only known to us in and through the immediate object, i. e., the representation of which we are conscious. As *existing,* and beyond the sphere of consciousness, the external reality is unknown.—H.

‡ " Et solem geminum et duplices se ostendere Thebas!"—H.

Having endeavoured to explain what is common to philosophers in accounting for our perception of external objects, we shall give some detail of their differences.

The ideas by which we perceive external objects, are said by some to be the ideas of the Deity; but it has been more generally thought, that every man's ideas are proper to himself, and are either in his mind, or in his *sensorium*, where the mind is immediately present. The *first* is the theory of Malebranche; the *second* we shall call the common theory.

With regard to that of Malebranche, it seems to have some affinity with the Platonic notion of ideas,* but is not the same. Plato believed that there are three eternal first principles, from which all things have their origin—matter, ideas, and an efficient cause. Matter is that of which all things are made, which, by all the ancient philosophers, was conceived to be eternal. [119] Ideas are forms without matter of every kind of things which can exist; which forms were also conceived by Plato to be eternal and immutable, and to be the models or patterns by which the efficient cause—that is, the Deity—formed every part of this universe. These ideas were conceived to be the sole objects of science, and indeed of all true knowledge. While we are imprisoned in the body, we are prone to give attention to the objects of sense only; but these being individual things, and in a constant fluctuation, being indeed shadows rather than realities, cannot be the object of real knowledge. All science is employed not about individual things, but about things universal and abstract from matter. Truth is eternal and immutable, and therefore must have for its object eternal and immutable ideas; these we are capable of contemplating in some degree even in our present state, but not without a certain purification of mind, and abstraction from the objects of sense. Such, as far as I am able to comprehend, were the sublime notions of Plato, and probably of Pythagoras.

The philosophers of the Alexandrian school, commonly called the latter Platonists, seem to have adopted the same system; but with this difference, that they made the eternal ideas not to be a principle distinct from the Deity, but to be in the divine intellect, as the objects of those conceptions which the divine mind must, from all eternity, have had, not only of every-

thing which he has made, but of every possible existence, and of all the relations of things.* By a proper purification and abstraction from the objects of sense, we may be in some measure united to the Deity, and, in the eternal light, be enabled to discern the most sublime intellectual truths.

These Platonic notions, grafted upon Christianity, probably gave rise to the sect called *Mystics*, which, though in its spirit and principles extremely opposite to the Peripatetic, yet was never extinguished, but subsists to this day. [120]

Many of the Fathers of the Christian church have a tincture of the tenets of the Alexandrian school; among others, St Augustine. But it does not appear, as far as I know, that either Plato, or the latter Platonists, or St Augustine, or the Mystics, thought that we perceive the objects of sense in the divine ideas. They had too mean a notion of our perception of sensible objects to ascribe to it so high an origin. This theory, therefore, of our perceiving the objects of sense in the ideas of the Deity, I take to be the invention of Father Malebranche himself. He, indeed, brings many passages of St Augustine to countenance it, and seems very desirous to have that Father of his party. But in those passages, though the Father speaks in a very high strain of God's being the light of our minds, of our being illuminated immediately by the eternal light, and uses other similar expressions; yet he seems to apply those expressions only to our illumination in moral and divine things, and not to the perception of objects by the senses. Mr Bayle imagines that some traces of this opinion of Malebranche are to be found in Amelius the Platonist, and even in Democritus; but his authorities seem to be strained.†

Malebranche, with a very penetrating genius, entered into a more minute examination of the powers of the human mind, than any one before him. He had the advantage of the discoveries made by Des Cartes, whom he followed without slavish attachment.

He lays it down as a principle admitted by all philosophers, and which could not be called in question, that we do not perceive external objects immediately, but by means of images or ideas of them present to the mind. "I suppose," says he, " that

---

* The Platonic theory of *Ideas* has nothing to do with a doctrine of sensitive perception; and its introduction into the question is only pregnant with confusion; while, in regard to sensitive perception, the peculiar hypothesis of Malebranche, is in fact not only not similar to, but much farther removed from, the Platonic than the common Cartesian theory, and the Leibnitzian.—H.

* And this, though Aristotle asserts the contrary, was perhaps also the doctrine of Plato.—H.
† The theory of Malebranche has been vainly sought for in the Bible, the Platonists, and the Fathers. It is, in fact, more clearly enounced in Homer than in any of these graver sources.
Τοίος γὰρ νόος ἐςὶν ἐπιχθονίων ἀνθρώπων,
Οἶον ἐπ᾽ ἦμαρ ἄγησι πατὴρ ἀνδρῶν τι θεῶν τι.
But for anticipations, see Note P.—H.

every one will grant that we perceive not the objects that are without us immediately, and of themselves.* We see the sun, the stars, and an infinity of objects without us; and it is not at all likely that the soul sallies out of the body, and, as it were, takes a walk through the heavens, to contemplate all those objects. [121] She sees them not, therefore, by themselves; and the immediate object of the mind, when it sees the sun, for example, is not the sun, but something which is intimately united to the soul; and it is that which I call an idea. So that by the word *idea*, I understand nothing else here but that which is the immediate object, or nearest to the mind, when we perceive† any object.‡ It ought to be carefully observed, that, in order to the mind's perceiving any object, it is absolutely necessary that the idea of that object be actually present to it. Of this it is not possible to doubt. . . . . . . The things which the soul perceives are of two kinds. They are either in the soul, or they are without the soul. Those that are in the soul are its own thoughts—that is to say, all its different modifications. [For by these words—*thought, manner of thinking*, or *modification of the soul*, I understand in general whatever cannot be in the mind without the mind perceiving it, as its proper sensations, its imaginations, its pure intellections, or simply its conceptions, its passions even, and its natural inclinations.]§ The soul has no need of ideas for perceiving these things.‖ But with regard to things without the soul, we cannot perceive them but by means of ideas."¶

Having laid this foundation, as a principle common to all philosophers, and which admits of no doubt, he proceeds to enumerate all the possible ways by which the ideas of sensible objects may be presented to the mind: Either, *first*, they come from the bodies which we perceive;** or, *secondly*, the soul has the power of producing them in itself;†† or, *thirdly*, they are produced by the

Deity, either in our creation, or occasionally, as there is use for them;* or, *fourthly*, the soul has in itself virtually and eminently, as the schools speak, all the perfections which it perceives in bodies;† or, *fifthly*, the soul is united with a Being possessed of all perfection, who has in himself the ideas of all created things.

This he takes to be a complete enumerations of all the possible ways in which the ideas of external objects may be presented to our minds. He employs a whole chapter upon each; refuting the four first, and confirming the last by various arguments. The Deity, being always present to our minds in a more intimate manner than any other being, may, upon occasion of the impressions made on our bodies, discover to us, as far as he thinks proper, and according to fixed laws, his own ideas of the object; and thus we see all things in God, or in the divine ideas.‡ [122]

However visionary this system may appear on a superficial view, yet, when we consider that he agreed with the whole tribe of philosophers in conceiving ideas to be the immediate objects of perception, and that he found insuperable difficulties, and even absurdities, in every other hypothesis concerning them, it will not appear so wonderful that a man of very great genius should fall into this; and, probably, it pleased so devout a man the more, that it sets, in the most striking light, our dependence upon God, and his continual presence with us.

He distinguished, more accurately than any philosopher had done before, the objects which we perceive from the sensations in our own minds, which, by the laws of Nature, always accompany the perception of the object. As in many things, so particularly in this, he has great merit. For this, I apprehend, is a key that opens the way to a right understanding, both of our external senses and of other powers of the mind. The vulgar confound sensation with other powers of the mind, and with their objects, because the purposes of life do not make a distinction necessary. The confounding of these in common language, has led philosophers, in one period, to make those things external which really are sensations in our own minds; and, in another period, running, as is usual, into the con-

---

* Rather *in* or *by themselves (par eux mêmes.)* —H.
† That is, in the language of philosophers before Reid, " where we have the apprehensive cognition or consciousness of any object."—H.
‡ In this definition, all philosophers concur. Des Cartes, Locke, &c., give it in almost the same terms. —H.
§ I have inserted this sentence, omitted by Reid, from the original, in order to shew in how extensive a meaning the term *thought* was used in the Cartesian school See Cartesii Princ., P. I., § 9.—H.
‖ Hence the distinction precisely taken by Malebranche of Idea (*idée*) and Feeling, (*sentiment*,) corresponding in principle to our Perception of the primary, and our Sensation of the secondary qualities —H.
¶ *De la Recherche de la Verité.* Liv. III., Partie ii., ch. 1.—H.
** The common Peripatetic doctrine, &c —H.
†† Malebranche refers, I presume, to the opinions of certain Cartesians. See Gassendi Opera, iii. p 321. —H.

[121, 122]

* Opinions analogous to the *second* or *third*, were held by the Platonists, by some of the Greek, and by many of the Arabian Aristotelians. See above, p. 262, note * —H.
† Something similar to this is hazarded by Des Cartes in his Third " Meditation," which it is likely that Malebranche had in his eye.—H.
‡ It should have been noticed that the Malebranchian philosophy is fundamentally Cartesian, and that, after De la Forge and Geulinx, the doctrine of *Divine Assistance*, implicitly maintained by Des Cartes, was most ably developed by Malebranche, to whom it owes, indeed, a principal share of its celebrity.—H.

trary extreme, to make everything almost to be a sensation or feeling in our minds.

It is obvious that the system of Malebranche leaves no evidence of the existence of a material world, from what we perceive by our senses; for the divine ideas, which are the objects immediately perceived, were the same before the world was created. Malebranche was too acute not to discern this consequence of his system, and too candid not to acknowledge it. [123] He fairly owns it, and endeavours to make advantage of it, resting the complete evidence we have of the existence of matter upon the authority of revelation. He shews that the arguments brought by Des Cartes to prove the existence of a material world, though as good as any that reason could furnish, are not perfectly conclusive; and, though he acknowledges with Des Cartes that we feel a strong propensity to believe the existence of a material world, yet he thinks this is not sufficient; and that to yield to such propensities without evidence, is to expose ourselves to perpetual delusion. He thinks, therefore, that the only convincing evidence we have of the existence of a material world *is*, that we are assured by revelation that God created the heavens and the earth, and that the Word was made flesh. He is sensible of the ridicule to which so strange an opinion may expose him among those who are guided by prejudice; but, for the sake of truth, he is willing to bear it. But no author, not even Bishop Berkeley, hath shewn more clearly, that, either upon his own system, or upon the common principles of philosophers with regard to ideas, we have no evidence left, either from reason or from our senses, of the existence of a material world. It is no more than justice to Father Malebranche, to acknowledge that Bishop Berkeley's arguments are to be found in him in their whole force.

Mr Norris, an English divine, espoused the system of Malebranche, in his " Essay towards the Theory of the Ideal or Intellectual World," published in two volumes 8°, *anno* 1701. This author has made a feeble effort to supply a defect which is to be found not in Malebranche only, but in almost all the authors who have treated of ideas—I mean, to prove their existence.* He has employed a whole chapter to prove that material things cannot be an immediate object of perception. His arguments are these: 1*st*, They are without the mind, and, therefore there can be no union between the object and the perception. 2*dly*, They are disproportioned to the mind, and removed

from it by the whole diameter of being. 3*dly*, Because, if material objects were immediate objects of perception, there could be no physical science; things necessary and immutable being the only objects of science. [124] 4*thly*, If material things were perceived by themselves, they would be a true light to our minds, as being the intelligible form of our understandings, and consequently perfective of them, and, indeed, superior to them.

Malebranche's system was adopted by many devout people in France of both sexes; but it seems to have had no great currency in other countries. Mr Locke wrote a small tract against it, which is found among his posthumous works:* but, whether it was written in haste, or after the vigour of his understanding was impaired by age, there is less of strength and solidity in it than in most of his writings. The most formidable antagonist Malebranche met with was in his own country— Antony Arnauld, doctor of the Sorbonne, and one of the acutest writers the Jansenists have to boast of, though that sect has produced many. Malebranche was a Jesuit, and the antipathy between the Jesuits and Jansenists left him no room to expect quarter from his learned antagonist.† Those who choose to see this system attacked on the one hand, and defended on the other, with subtilty of argument and elegance of expression,‡ and on the part of Arnauld with much wit and humour, may find satisfaction by reading Malebranche's " Enquiry after Truth;" Arnauld's book "Of True and False Ideas;" Malebranche's "Defence;" and some subsequent replies and defences. In controversies of this kind, the assailant commonly has the advantage, if they are not unequally matched; for it is easier to overturn all the theories of philosophers upon this subject, than to defend any one of them. Mr Bayle makes a very just remark upon this controversy—that the arguments of Mr Arnauld against the system of Malebranche, were often unanswerable, but

---

* This is incorrect. In almost every system of the Aristotelico-scholastic philosophy, the attempt is made to prove the existence of Species; nor is Reid's assertion true even of ideas in the Cartesian philosophy. In fact, Norris's arguments are all old and commonplace.—H.

* In answer to Locke's " Examination of P. Malebranche's Opinion," Leibnitz wrote " Remarks," which are to be found among his posthumous works, published by Raspe.—H.

† Malebranche was not a Jesuit, but a Priest of the Oratory; and so little was he either a favourer or favourite of the Jesuits, that, by the Pere de Valois, he was accused of heresy, by the Pere Hardouin, of Atheism. The endeavours of the Jesuits in France to prohibit the introduction of every form of the Cartesian doctrine into the public seminaries of education, are well known. Malebranche and Arnauld were therefore not opposed as Jesuit and Jansenist, and it should likewise be remembered that they were both Cartesians.—H.

‡ Independently of his principal hypothesis altogether, the works of Malebranche deserve the most attentive study, both on account of the many admirable thoughts and observations with which they abound, and because they are among the few consummate models of philosophical eloquence.—H.

they were capable of being retorted against his own system ; and his ingenious antagonist knew well how to use this defence. [125]

CHAPTER VIII.

OF THE COMMON THEORY OF PERCEPTION, AND OF THE SENTIMENTS OF THE PERIPATETICS, AND OF DES CARTES.

THIS theory, in general, is, that we perceive external objects only by certain images which are in our minds, or in the sensorium to which the mind is immediately present. Philosophers in different ages have differed both in the names they have given to those images, and in their notions concerning them. It would be a laborious task to enumerate all their variations, and perhaps would not requite the labour. I shall only give a sketch of the principal differences with regard to their names and their nature.

By Aristotle and the Peripatetics, the images presented to our senses were called *sensible species or forms ;* those presented to the memory or imagination were called *phantasms ;* and those presented to the intellect were called *intelligible species ;* and they thought that there can be no perception, no imagination, no intellection, without species or phantasms.* What the ancient philosophers called species, sensible and intelligible, and phantasms, in later times, and especially since the time of Des Cartes, came to be called by the common name of *ideas.*† The Cartesians divided our ideas into three classes—those of *sensation,* of *imagination,* and of *pure intellection.* Of the objects of sensation and imagination, they thought the images are in the brain ;‡ but of objects that are incorporeal the images are in the understanding or pure intellect.

Mr Locke, taking the word *idea* in the same sense as Des Cartes had done before him, to signify whatever is meant by phantasm, notion, or species, divides ideas into those of *sensation,* and those of *reflection ;* meaning by the first, the ideas of all corporeal objects, whether perceived, remembered, or imagined ; by the second, the ideas of the powers and operations of our minds. [126] What Mr Locke calls ideas, Mr Hume divides into two distinct kinds, *impressions* and *ideas.* The difference betwixt these, he says, consists in the degrees of force and liveliness with which they strike upon the mind. Under *impressions* he comprehends all our sensations, passions, and

emotions, as they make their first appearance in the soul. By *ideas,* he means the faint images of these in thinking and reasoning.

Dr Hartley gives the same meaning to ideas as Mr Hume does, and what Mr Hume calls impressions he calls sensations ; conceiving our sensations to be occasioned by vibrations of the infinitesimal particles of the brain, and ideas by miniature vibrations or vibratiuncles. Such differences we find among philosophers, with regard to the name of those internal images of objects of sense which they hold to be the immediate objects of perception.*

We shall next give a short detail of the sentiments of the Peripatetics and Cartesians, of Locke, Berkeley, and Hume, concerning them.

Aristotle seems to have thought that the soul consists of two parts, or rather that we have two souls—the animal and the rational ; or, as he calls them, the soul and the intellect.† To the *first,* belong the senses, memory, and imagination ; to the *last,* judgment, opinion, belief, and reasoning. The first we have in common with brute animals ; the last is peculiar to man. The animal soul he held to be a certain form of the body, which is inseparable from it, and perishes at death. To this soul the senses belong ; and he defines a sense to be that which is capable of receiving the sensible forms or species of objects, without any of the matter of them ; as wax receives the form of the seal without any of the matter of it. The forms of sound, of colour, of

---

* See Note M.—H.
† Not merely *especially,* but *only* since the time of Des Cartes. See Note G.—H.
‡ Incorrect. See Note N.—H.

[125, 126]

---

* Reid, I may observe in general, does not distinguish, as it especially behoved him to do, between what were held by philosophers to be the proximate *causes* of our mental representations, and these representations themselves as the *objects* of cognition —i. e, between what are known in the schools as the *species impressæ,* and the *species expressæ.* The former, to which the name of *species, image, idea,* was often given, in common with the latter, was held on all hands to be unknown to consciousness, and generally supposed to be merely certain occult motions in the organism. The latter, the result determined by the former, is the mental representation, and the immediate or proper object in perception. Great confusion, to those who do not bear this distinction in mind, is, however, the consequence of the verbal ambiguity ; and Reid's misrepresentations of the doctrine of the philosophers is, in a great measure, to be traced to this source.—H.
† This not correct. Instead of *two,* the *animal* and *rational,* Aristotle gave to the soul *three* generic functions, the *vegetable,* the *animal* or *sensual,* and the *rational ;* but whether he supposes these to constitute three concentric potences, three separate parts, or three distinct souls, has divided his disciples. He also defines the *soul in general,* and not, as Reid supposes, the mere ' *animal soul,*' to be the form or ἐντελέχεια of the body.—(De Anima l. ii. c. 1.) Intellect (νῦς) he however thought was inorganic ; but there is some ground for believing that he did not view this as personal, but harboured an opinion which, under various modifications, many of his followers also held, that the *active intellect* was common to all men, immortal and divine. Κινῦ γὰρ τωι πάντα τὸ ἐν ἡμῖν θεῖον· λόγου δ' ἀρχὴ ἐν λόγος ἀλλά τι κρεῖττον, τί οὖν ἄν κρεῖττον καὶ ἐπιστήμης ἐστι, πλὴν θεὸς ;—H.

taste, and of other sensible qualities, are, in manner, received by the senses.* [127]

It seems to be a necessary consequence of Aristotle's doctrine, that bodies are constantly sending forth, in all directions, as many different kinds of forms without matter as they have different sensible qualities; for the forms of colour must enter by the eye, the forms of sound by the ear, and so of the other senses. This, accordingly, was maintained by the followers of Aristotle, though not, as far as I know, expressly mentioned by himself.† They disputed concerning the nature of those forms of species, whether they were real beings or nonentities;‡ and some held them to be of an intermediate nature between the two. The whole doctrine of the Peripatetics and schoolmen concerning forms, substantial and accidental, and concerning the transmission of sensible species from objects of sense to the mind, if it be at all intelligible, is so far above my comprehension that I should perhaps do it injustice, by entering into it more minutely. Malebranche, in his "Recherche de la Verité," has employed a chapter to shew that material objects do not send forth sensible species of their several sensible qualities.

The great revolution which Des Cartes produced in philosophy, was the effect of a superiority of genius, aided by the circumstances of the times. Men had, for more than a thousand years, looked up to Aristotle as an oracle in philosophy. His authority was the test of truth. The small remains of the Platonic system were confined to a few mystics, whose principles and manner of life drew little attention. The feeble attempts of Ramus, and of some others, to make improvements in the system, had little effect. The Peripatetic doctrines were so interwoven with the whole system of scholastic theology, that to dissent from Aristotle was to alarm the Church. The most useful and intelligible parts, even of Aristotle's writings, were neglected, and philosophy was become an art of speaking learnedly, and disputing subtilely, without producing any invention of use in human life. It was fruitful of words, but barren of works, and admirably contrived for drawing a veil over human ignorance, and

putting a stop to the progress of knowledge, by filling men with a conceit that they knew everything. [128] It was very fruitful also in controversies; but, for the most part, they were controversies about words, or about things of no moment, or things above the reach of the human faculties. And the issue of them was what might be expected— that the contending parties fought, without gaining or losing an inch of ground, till they were weary of the dispute, or their attention was called off to some other subject.*

Such was the philosophy of the schools of Europe, during many ages of darkness and barbarism that succeeded the decline of the Roman empire; so that there was great need of a reformation in philosophy as well as in religion. The light began to dawn at last; a spirit of inquiry sprang up, and men got the courage to doubt of the dogmas of Aristotle, as well as of the decrees of Popes. The most important step in the reformation of religion, was to destroy the claim of infallibility, which hindered men from using their judgment in matters of religion; and the most important step in the reformation of philosophy, was to destroy the authority of which Aristotle had so long had peaceable possession. The last had been attempted by Lord Bacon and others, with no less zeal than the first by Luther and Calvin.

Des Cartes knew well the defects of the prevailing system, which had begun to lose its authority. His genius enabled him, and his spirit prompted him, to attempt a new one. He had applied much to the mathematical sciences, and had made considerable improvement in them. He wished to introduce that perspicuity and evidence into other branches of philosophy which he found in them.

Being sensible how apt we are to be led astray by prejudices of education, he thought the only way to avoid error was to resolve to doubt of everything, and hold everything to be uncertain, even those things which he had been taught to hold as most certain, until he had such clear and cogent evidence as compelled his assent. [129]

In this state of universal doubt, that which first appeared to him to be clear and certain, was his own existence. Of this he was certain, because he was conscious that he thought, that he reasoned, and that he doubted. He used this argument, therefore, to prove his own existence, *Cogito, ergo sum.* This he conceived to be the first of all truths, the foundation-stone upon which the whole fabric of human knowledge

---

* See Note M.—H.
† Nor is there valid ground for supposing that such an opinion was even implicitly held by the Stagirite. It was also explicitly repudiated by many of his followers. See Note M.—H.
‡ The question in the schools, between those who admitted species, was not, whether species, *in general,* were *real* beings or *nonentities* (which would have been, did they exist or not,) but whether *sensible* species were *material, immaterial,* or of a nature *between* body and spirit—a problem, it must be allowed, sufficiently futile, but not, like the other, self-contradictory.—H.

* This is the vulgar opinion in regard to the scholastic philosophy. The few are, however, now aware that the human mind, though partially, was never more powerfully developed than during the middle ages.—H.

is built, and on which it must rest.* And, as Archimedes thought that, if he had one fixed point to rest his engines upon, he could move the earth; so Des Cartes, charmed with the discovery of one certain principle, by which he emerged from the state of universal doubt, believed that this principle alone would be a sufficient foundation on which he might build the whole system of science. He seems, therefore, to have taken no great trouble to examine whether there might not be other first principles, which, on account of their own light and evidence, ought to be admitted by every man of sound judgment.† The love of simplicity so natural to the mind of man, led him to apply the whole force of his mind to raise the fabric of knowledge upon this one principle, rather than seek a broader foundation.

Accordingly, he does not admit the evidence of sense to be a first principle, as he does that of consciousness. The arguments of the ancient sceptics here occurred to him, that our senses often deceive us, and therefore ought never to be trusted on their own authority: that, in sleep, we often seem to see and hear things which we are convinced to have had no existence. But that which chiefly led Des Cartes to think that he ought not to trust to his senses, without proof of their veracity, was, that he took it for granted, as all philosophers had done before him, that he did not perceive external objects themselves, but certain images of them in his own mind, called *ideas.* He was certain, by consciousness, that he had the ideas of sun and moon, earth and sea; but how could he be assured that there really existed external objects like to these ideas?‡   [130]

Hitherto he was uncertain of everything but of his own existence, and the existence of the operations and ideas of his own mind. Some of his disciples, it is said, remained at this stage of his system, and got the name of Egoists.§ They could not find evidence in the subsequent stages of his progress. But Des Cartes resolved not to stop here; he endeavoured to prove, by a new argument, drawn from his idea of a Deity, the existence of an infinitely perfect Being, who made him and all his faculties. From the perfection of this Being, he inferred that he could be no deceiver; and therefore concluded that his senses, and the other faculties he found in himself, are not fallacious,

but may be trusted, when a proper use is made of them.

The system of Des Cartes is, with great perspicuity and acuteness, explained by himself in his writings, which ought to be consulted by those who would understand it.

The merit of Des Cartes cannot be easily conceived by those who have not some notion of the Peripatetic system, in which he was educated. To throw off the prejudices of education, and to create a system of nature, totally different from that which had subdued the understanding of mankind, and kept it in subjection for so many centuries, required an uncommon force of mind. The world which Des Cartes exhibits to our view, is not only in its structure very different from that of the Peripatetics, but is, as we may say, composed of different materials.

In the old system, everything was, by a kind of metaphysical sublimation, resolved into principles so mysterious that it may be a question whether they were words without meaning, or were notions too refined for human understanding.

All that we observe in nature is, according to Aristotle, a constant succession of the operations of generation and corruption. [131] The principles of generation are matter and form. The principle of corruption is privation. All natural things are produced or generated by the union of matter and form; matter being, as it were, the mother, and form the father. As to matter, or the first matter, as it is called, it is neither substance nor accident; it has no quality or property; it is nothing actually, but everything potentially. It has so strong an appetite for form, that it is no sooner divested of one form than it is clothed with another, and is equally susceptible of all forms successively. It has no nature, but only the capacity of having any one.

This is the account which the Peripatetics give of the first matter. The other principle of generation is *form, act, perfection;* for these three words signify the same thing. But we must not conceive form to consist in the figure, size, arrangement, or motion of the parts of matter. These, indeed, are accidental forms, by which things

---

* On the Cartesian doubt, see Note R.—H.
† This cannot justly be affirmed of Des Cartes —H
‡ On this point it is probable that Des Cartes and Reid are at one. See Notes C and N.—H.
§ I am doubtful about the existence of this supposed sect of Egoists. The Chevalier Ramsay, above a century ago, incidentally speaks of this doctrine as an offshoot of Spinozism, and under the

name of *Egomisme.* But Father Buffier, about the same time, and, be it noted, in a work published some ten years before Hume's " Treatise of Human Nature," talks of it, on hearsay, as the speculation of a Scotch philosopher:—" Un écrivain Écossois a publié, dit on, un ouvrage pour prouver qu'il n'avoit aucune évidence de l'existence d'aucun être que de lui; et encore de lui, en tant qu' *esprit;* n'aiant aucune demonstration véritable de l'existence d'aucun corps." —*Elemens de Metaphysique,* § 61. Now, we know that there is no such work. I am aware, however, that there is some discussion on this point in the " Memoirs de Trevoux," anno 1713, p. 922; to which however, I must refer the reader, as I have not that journal at hand.—But more of this below, under p 137.—H.

artificial are formed : but every production of Nature has a substantial form, which, joined to matter, makes it to be what it is. The substantial form is a kind of informing soul, which gives the thing its specific nature, and all its qualities, powers, and activity. Thus the substantial form of heavy bodies, is that which makes them descend ; of light bodies, that which makes them ascend. The substantial form of gold, is that which gives it its ductility, its fusibility, its weight, its colour, and all its qualities; and the same is to be understood of every natural production. A change in the accidental form of any body, is alteration only ; but a change in the substantial form is generation and corruption : it is corruption with respect to the substantial form, of which the body is deprived; it is generation with respect to the substantial form that succeeds. Thus, when a horse dies and turns to dust, the philosophical account of the phænomenon is this :—A certain portion of the *materia prima*, which was joined to the substantial form of a horse, is deprived of it by privation, and in the same instant is invested with the substantial form of earth. [132] As every substance must have a substantial form, there are some of those forms inanimate, some vegetable, some animal, and some rational. The three former kinds can only subsist in matter ; but the last, according to the schoolmen, is immediately created by God, and infused into the body, making one substance with it, while they are united; yet capable of being disjoined from the body, and of subsisting by itself.

Such are the principles of natural things in the Peripatetic system. It retains so much of the ancient Pythagorean doctrine, that we cannot ascribe the invention of it solely to Aristotle, although he, no doubt, made considerable alterations in it. The first matter was probably the same in both systems, and was in both held to be eternal. They differed more about form. The Pythagoreans and Platonists held forms or ideas, as they called them, to be eternal, immutable, and self-existent. Aristotle maintained that they were not eternal, nor self-existent. On the other hand, he did not allow them to be produced, but educed from matter ; yet he held them not to be actually in the matter from which they are educed, but potentially only. But these two systems differed less from one another, than that of Des Cartes did from both.

In the world of Des Cartes we meet with two kinds of beings only—to wit, body and mind; the first the object of our senses,

the other of consciousness ; both of them things of which we have a distinct apprehension, if the human mind be capable of distinct apprehension at all. To the first, no qualities are ascribed but extension, figure, and motion ; to the last, nothing but thought, and its various modifications, of which we are conscious. He could observe no common attribute, no resembling feature, in the attributes of body and mind, and therefore concluded them to be distinct* substances, and totally of a different nature ; and that body, from its very nature, is inanimate and inert, incapable of any kind of thought or sensation, or of producing any change or alteration in itself. [133]

Des Cartes must be allowed the honour of being the first who drew a distinct line between the material and intellectual world, which, in all the old systems, were so blended together that it was impossible to say where the one ends and the other begins.† How much this distinction hath contributed to the improvements of modern times, in the philosophy both of body and of mind, is not easy to say.

One obvious consequence of this distinction was, that accurate reflection on the operations of our own mind is the only way to make any progress in the knowledge of it. Malebranche, Locke, Berkeley, and Hume, were taught this lesson by Des Cartes ; and to it we owe their most valuable discoveries in this branch of philosophy. The analogical way of reasoning concerning the powers of the mind from the properties of body, which is the source of almost all the errors on this subject, and which is so natural to the bulk of mankind, was as contrary to the principles of Des Cartes, as it was agreeable to the principles of the old philosophy. We may therefore truly say, that, in that part of philosophy which relates to the mind, Des Cartes laid the foundation, and put us into that tract which all wise men now acknowledge to be the only one in which we can expect success.

With regard to physics, or the philosophy of body, if Des Cartes had not the merit of leading men into the right tract, we must allow him that of bringing them out of a wrong one. The Peripatetics, by assigning to every species of body a particular substantial form, which produces, in an unknown manner, all the effects we observe in it, put a stop to all improvement in this branch of philosophy. Gravity and levity, fluidity and hardness, heat and cold, were qualities arising from the substantial form of the bodies to which they belonged. Gen-

---

* It is not, however, to be supposed that the scholastic doctrine of *Substantial Forms* receives any countenance from the authority of Aristotle, if we lay aside his language touching the soul.—H.

* In the Cartesian language, the term *thought* included all of which we are conscious.—H.
† This assertion *is* true in general ; but some individual exceptions might be taken.—H.

eration and corruption, substantial forms and occult qualities, were always at hand, to resolve every phænomenon. This philosophy, therefore, instead of accounting for any of the phænomena of Nature, contrived only to give learned names to their unknown causes, and fed men with the husks of barbarous terms, instead of the fruit of real knowledge. [134]

By the spreading of the Cartesian system, *materia prima*, substantial forms, and occult qualities, with all the jargon of the Aristotelian physics, fell into utter disgrace, and were never mentioned by the followers of the new system, but as a subject of ridicule. Men became sensible that their understanding had been hoodwinked by those hard terms. They were now accustomed to explain the phænomena of nature, by the figure, size, and motion of the particles of matter, things perfectly level to human understanding, and could relish nothing in philosophy that was dark and unintelligible. Aristotle, after a reign of more than a thousand years, was now exposed as an object of derision even to the vulgar, arrayed in the mock majesty of his substantial forms and occult qualities. The ladies became fond of a philosophy which was easily learned, and required no words too harsh for their delicate organs. Queens and princesses, the most distinguished personages of the age, courted the conversation of Des Cartes, and became adepts in his philosophy. Witness Christina, Queen of Sweden, and Elizabeth, daughter of Frederick, King of Bohemia, the mother of our Royal Family. The last, though very young when Des Cartes wrote his " Principia," he declares to be the only person he knew, who perfectly understood not only all his philosophical writings, but the most abstruse of his mathematical works.

That men should rush with violence from one extreme, without going more or less into the contrary extreme, is not to be expected from the weakness of human nature. Des Cartes and his followers were not exempted from this weakness; they thought that extension, figure, and motion, were sufficient to resolve all the phænomena of the material system. To admit other qualities, whose cause is unknown, was to return to Egypt, from which they had been so happily delivered. [135]

When Sir Isaac Newton's doctrine of gravitation was published, the great objection to it, which hindered its general reception in Europe for half a century, was, that gravitation seemed to be an occult quality, as it could not be accounted for by extension, figure, and motion, the known attributes of body. They who defended him found it difficult to answer this objection to the satisfaction of those who had been [134–136]

initiated in the principles of the Cartesian system. But, by degrees, men came to be sensible that, in revolting from Aristotle, the Cartesians had gone into the opposite extreme ; experience convinced them that there are qualities in the material world, whose existence is certain though their cause be occult. To acknowledge this, is only a candid confession of human ignorance, than which there is nothing more becoming a philosopher.

As all that we can know of the mind must be derived from a careful observation of its operations in ourselves ; so all that we can know of the material system must be derived from what can be discovered by our senses. Des Cartes was not ignorant of this; nor was his system so unfriendly to observation and experiment as the old system was.* He made many experiments, and called earnestly upon all lovers of truth to aid him in this way; but, believing that all the phænomena of the material world are the result of extension, figure, and motion, and that the Deity always combines these, so as to produce the phænomena in the simplest manner possible, he thought that, from a few experiments, he might be able to discover the simplest way in which the obvious phænomena of nature can be produced by matter and motion only ; and that this must be the way in which they are actually produced. His conjectures were ingenious, upon the principles he had adopted ; but they are found to be so far from the truth, that they ought for ever to discourage philosophers from trusting to conjecture in the operations of nature. [136]

The vortices or whirlpools of subtile matter by which Des Cartes endeavoured to account for the phænomena of the material world, are now found to be fictions, no less than the sensible species of Aristotle.†

It was reserved for Sir Isaac Newton to point out clearly the road to the knowledge of nature's works. Taught by Lord Bacon to despise hypotheses as the fictions of human fancy, he laid it down as a rule of philosophising, that no causes of natural things ought to be assigned but such as can be proved to have a real existence. He saw that all the length men can go in accounting for phænomena, is to discover the laws of nature according to which they are produced; and, therefore, that the true method of philosophising is this : From real facts, ascertained by observation and experiment, to collect by just induction the

* That is, the Aristotelic. But Aristotle himself was as declared an advocate of experiment as any philosopher ; and it is not to be imputed to him that his authority had subsequently the effect of impeding, by being held to supersede, observation.—H.
† Read " the sensible species of the schoolmen." See Note M.—H.

laws of Nature, and to apply the laws so discovered, to account for the phænomena of Nature.

Thus, the natural philosopher has the rules of his art fixed with no less precision than the mathematician, and may be no less certain when he keeps within them, and when he deviates from them. And, though the evidence of a law of nature from induction is not demonstrative, it is the only kind of evidence on which all the most important affairs of human life must rest.

Pursuing this road without deviation, Newton discovered the laws of our planetary system, and of the rays of light; and gave the first and the noblest examples of that chaste induction which Lord Bacon could only delineate in theory.

How strange is it that the human mind should have wandered for so many ages, without falling into this tract! How much more strange, that, after it has been clearly discovered, and a happy progress made in it, many choose rather to wander in the fairy regions of hypothesis! [137]

To return to Des Cartes's notions of the manner of our perceiving external objects, from which a concern to do justice to the merit of that great reformer in philosophy has led me to digress, he took it for granted, as the old philosophers had done, that what we immediately perceive must be either in the mind itself, or in the brain, to which the mind is immediately present. The impressions made upon our organs, nerves, and brain could be nothing, according to his philosophy, but various modifications of extension, figure, and motion. There could be nothing in the brain like sound or colour, taste or smell, heat or cold; these are sensations in the mind, which, by the laws of the union of soul and body, are raised on occasion of certain traces in the brain; and although he gives the name of ideas to those traces in the brain, he does not think it necessary that they should be perfectly like to the things which they represent, any more than that words or signs should resemble the things they signify. But, says he, that we may follow the received opinion as far as is possible, we may allow a slight resemblance. Thus we know that a print in a book may represent houses, temples, and groves; and so far is it from being necessary that the print should be perfectly like the thing it represents, that its perfection often requires the contrary: for a circle must often be represented by an ellipse, a square by a rhombus, and so of other things.*

The perceptions of sense, he thought, are to be referred solely to the union of soul and body. They commonly exhibit to us only what may hurt or profit our bodies; and rarely, and by accident only, exhibit things as they are in themselves. It is by observing this, that we must learn to throw off the prejudices of sense, and to attend with our intellect to the ideas which are by nature implanted in it. By this means we shall understand that the nature of matter does not consist in those things that affect our senses, such as colour, or smell, or taste; but only in this, that it is something extended in length, breadth, and depth. [138]

The writings of Des Cartes have, in general, a remarkable degree of perspicuity; and he undoubtedly intended that, in this particular, his philosophy should be a perfect contrast to that of Aristotle; yet, in what he has said, in different parts of his writings, of our perceptions of external objects, there seems to be some obscurity, and even inconsistency; whether owing to his having had different opinions on the subject at different times, or to the difficulty he found in it, I will not pretend to say.

There are two points, in particular, wherein I cannot reconcile him to himself: the *first*, regarding the place of the ideas or images of external objects, which are the immediate objects of perception; the *second*, with regard to the veracity of our external senses.

As to the *first*, he sometimes places the ideas of material objects in the brain, not only when they are perceived, but when they are remembered or imagined; and this has always been held to be the Cartesian doctrine;* yet he sometimes says, that we are not to conceive the images or traces in the brain to be perceived, as if there were eyes in the brain; these traces are only occasions on which, by the laws of the union of soul and body, ideas are excited in the mind; and, therefore, it is not necessary that there should be an exact resemblance between the traces and the things represented by them, any more than that words or signs should be exactly like the things signified by them.†

These two opinions, I think, cannot be reconciled. For, if the images or traces in the brain are perceived,‡ they must be the

---

* But be it observed that Des Cartes did not allow, far less hold, that the mind had any cognizance of these organic motions—of these material ideas. They were merely the antecedents, established by the law of union, of the mental idea; which mental idea was no-

thing more than a modification of the mind itself.—H.

* But not in Reid's exclusive sense of the word *Idea*.—H.

† The non-negation, in this instance, of *all* resemblance between the material Ideas, or organic motions in the brain, and the external reality, is one of the occasional instances of Des Cartes's reticence of his subordinate doctrines, in order to avoid all useless tilting against prevalent opinions. Another is his sometimes giving to these motions the name of *Species*.—H.

‡ Which, in Des Cartes' doctrine, they are not.—H

objects of perception, and not the occasions of it only. On the other hand, if they are only the occasions of our perceiving, they are not perceived at all. Des Cartes seems to have hesitated between the two opinions, or to have passed from the one to the other.* Mr Locke seems, in like manner, to have wavered between the two ; sometimes representing the ideas of material things as being in the brain, but more frequently as in the mind itself.† [139] Neither Des Cartes nor Mr Locke could, consistently with themselves, attribute any other qualities to images in the brain but -extension, figure, and motion ; for as to those qualities which Mr Locke distinguished by the name of secondary qualities, both philosophers believed them not to belong to body at all,‡ and, therefore, could not ascribe them to images in the brain.§

Sir Isaac Newton and Dr Samuel Clarke uniformly speak of the species or images of material things as being in that part of the brain called the *sensorium*, and perceived by the mind there present ; but the former speaks of this point only incidentally, and with his usual modesty, in the form of a query.‖ Malebranche is perfectly clear and unambiguous in this matter. According to his system, the images or traces in the brain are not perceived at all—they are only occasions upon which, by the laws of Nature, certain sensations are felt by us, and certain of the divine ideas discovered to our minds.

The *second* point on which Des Cartes seems to waver, is with regard to the credit that is due to the testimony of our senses.

Sometimes, from the perfection of the Deity, and his being no deceiver, he infers that our senses and our other faculties cannot be fallacious ; and since we seem clearly to perceive that the idea of matter comes to us from things external, which it perfectly resembles, therefore we must conclude that there really exists something extended in length, breadth, and depth, having all the properties which we clearly perceive to belong to an extended thing.

At other times, we find Des Cartes and his followers making frequent complaints,

as all the ancient philosophers did, of the fallacies of sense. He warns us to throw off its prejudices, and to attend only with our intellect, to the ideas implanted there. By this means we may perceive, that the nature of matter does not consist in hardness, colour, weight, or any of those things that affect our senses, but in this only, that it is something extended in length, breadth, and depth. [140] The senses, he says, are only relative to our present state ; they exhibit things only as they tend to profit or to hurt us, and rarely, and by accident only, as they are in themselves.*

It was probably owing to an aversion to admit anything into philosophy, of which we have not a clear and distinct conception, that Des Cartes was led to deny that there is any substance of matter distinct from those qualities of it which we.perceive.† We say that matter is something extended, figured, moveable. Extension, figure, mobility, therefore, are not matter, but qualities, belonging to this something, which we call *matter*. Des Cartes could not relish this obscure *something*, which is supposed to be the subject or *substratum* of those qualities ; and, therefore, maintained that extension is the very essence of matter. But, as we must ascribe extension to space as well as to matter, he found himself under a necessity of holding that space and matter are the same thing, and differ only in our way of conceiving them ; so that, wherever there is space there is matter, and no void left in the universe. The necessary consequence of this is, that the material world has no bounds nor limits. He did not, however, choose to call it infinite, but indefinite.

It was probably owing to the same cause that Des Cartes made the essence of the soul to consist in thought. He would not allow it to be an unknown something that has the power of thinking ; it cannot, therefore, be without thought ; and, as he conceived that there can be no thought-without ideas, the soul must have had ideas in its first formation, which, of consequence, are innate.‡

The sentiments of those who came after Des Cartes, with regard to the nature of body and mind, have been various. Many have maintained that body is only a collection of qualities to which we give one

---

* Des Cartes had only one opinion on the point. The difficulty which perplexes Reid arose from his want of a systematic comprehension of the Cartesian philosophy, and his being unaware that, by Ideas, Des Cartes designated two very different things—viz., the proximate bodily antecedent, and the mental consequent.—H.

† Locke's opinion, if he had a precise one on the matter, it is impossible to ascertain. See Note O.—H.

‡ See above, p. 205, note * —H.

§ Yet Locke expressly denies them to be modifications of mind. See Note O.—H.

‖ Reid is correct in all he here says of Newton and Clarke; it is indeed virtually admitted by Clarke himself, in his controversy with Leibnitz. Compare Leibnitii Opera, II., p. 161, and p. 182.—H.

* But see " Principia," § 66, sqq.—H.
† See Stewart's " Elements," I., Note A ; Royer Collard's Fragment, VIII.—H.
‡ The doctrine of Des Cartes, in relation to *Innate Ideas*, has been very generally misunderstood ; and by no one more than by Locke. What it really amounted to, is clearly stated in his strictures on the Program of Regius. Justice has latterly been done him, among others, by Mr Stewart, in his " Dissertation, and by M. Laromiguiere, in his " Cours." See also the old controversy of De Vries with Röell on this point.—H.

name; and that the notion of a subject of inhesion, to which those qualities belong, is only a fiction of the mind.* [141] Some have even maintained that the soul is only a succession of related ideas, without any subject of inhesion.† It appears, by what has been said, how far these notions are allied to the Cartesian system.

The triumph of the Cartesian system over that of Aristotle, is one of the most remarkable revolutions in the history of philosophy, and has led me to dwell longer upon it than the present subject perhaps required. The authority of Aristotle was now no more. That reverence for hard words and dark notions, by which men's understanding had been strangled in early years, was turned into contempt, and everything suspected which was not clearly and distinctly understood. This is the spirit of the Cartesian philosophy, and is a more important acquisition to mankind than any of its particular tenets; and for exerting this spirit so zealously, and spreading it so successfully, Des Cartes deserves immortal honour.

It is to be observed, however, that Des Cartes rejected a part only of the ancient theory, concerning the perception of external objects by the senses, and that he adopted the other part. That theory may be divided into two parts: The *first*, that images, species, or forms of external objects, come from the object, and enter by the avenues of the senses to the mind; the *second* part is, That the external object itself is not perceived, but only the species or image of it in the mind. The first part Des Cartes and his followers rejected, and refuted by solid arguments; but the second part, neither he nor his followers have thought of calling in question; being persuaded that it is only a representative image in the mind of the external object that we perceive, and not the object itself. And this image, which the Peripatetics called a species, he calls an idea, changing the name only, while he admits the thing.‡ [142]

It seems strange that the great pains which this philosopher took to throw off the prejudices of education, to dismiss all his former opinions, and to assent to nothing, till he found evidence that compelled his assent, should not have led him to doubt of this opinion of the ancient philosophy. It is evidently a philosophical opinion; for the vulgar undoubtedly believe that it is the external object which we immediately perceive, and not a representative image of it only. It is for this reason that they look upon it as perfect lunacy to call in question the existence of external objects.*

It seems to be admitted as a first principle, by the learned and the unlearned, that what is really perceived must exist, and that to perceive what does not exist is impossible. So far the unlearned man and the philosopher agree. The unlearned man says—I perceive the external object, and I perceive it to exist. Nothing can be more absurd than to doubt of it. The Peripatetic says— What I perceive is the very identical form of the object. which came immediately from the object, and makes an impression upon my mind, as a seal does upon wax; and, therefore, I can have no doubt of the existence of an object whose form I perceive.† But what says the Cartesian? I perceive not, says he, the external object itself. So far he agrees with the Peripatetic, and differs from the unlearned man. But I perceive an image, or form, or idea, in my own mind, or in my brain. I am certain of the existence of the idea, because I immediately perceive it.† But how this idea is formed, or what it represents, is not self-evident; and therefore I must find arguments by which, from the existence of the idea which I perceive, I can infer the existence of an external object which it represents.

As I take this to be a just view of the principles of the unlearned man, of the Peripatetic, and of the Cartesian, so I think they all reason consequentially from their several principles: that the Cartesian has strong grounds to doubt of the existence of external objects; the Peripatetic very little ground of doubt; and the unlearned [143] man none at all: and that the difference of their situation arises from this—that the unlearned man has no hypothesis; the Peripatetic leans upon an hypothesis; and the Cartesian upon one half of that hypothesis.

Des Cartes, according to the spirit of his own philosophy, ought to have doubted of both parts of the Peripatetic hypothesis, or to have given his reasons why he adopted one part, as well as why he rejected the other

---

* As Locke, (but he is not consistent,) Law, Green, Watts, and others. See Cousin, "Cours de Philosophie." Tome II., Leçon xviii.—H.
† Hume—H
‡ Des Cartes and Reid coincide in doctrine, if Reid holds that we know the extended and external object only, by a conception or subjective modification of the percipient mind. See Notes N and C.—H.

* This is one of the passages which favour the opinion that Reid did suppose the *non-ego* to be known in itself as existing, and not only in and through the *ego*; for mankind in general believe that the extended reality, as perceived, is something more than a mere internal representation by the mind, suggested in consequence of the impression made by an unknown something on the sense. See Note C.—H.
† The Peripatetic and the Cartesian held that the *species* or *idea* was an object of consciousness. If Reid understood the language he uses, he must hold that the external and extended reality is an object of consciousness. But this does not quadrate with his doctrine, that we only know extension and figure by a suggested conception in the mind. See Note C.—H.

part; especially, since the unlearned, who have the faculty of perceiving objects by their senses in no less perfection than philosophers, and should, therefore, know, as well as they, what it is they perceive, have been unanimous in this, that the objects they perceive are not ideas in their own minds, but things external. It might have been expected that a philosopher who was so cautious as not to take his own existence for granted without proof, would not have taken it for granted without proof, that everything he perceived was only ideas in his own mind.

But, if Des Cartes made a rash step in this, as I apprehend he did, he ought not to bear the blame alone. His successors have still continued in the same track, and, after his example, have adopted one part of the ancient theory—to wit, that the objects we immediately perceive are ideas only. All their systems are built on this foundation.

CHAPTER IX.

OF THE SENTIMENTS OF MR LOCKE.

THE reputation which Locke's "Essay on Human Understanding" had at home from the beginning, and which it has gradually acquired abroad, is a sufficient testimony of its merit. [144] There is, perhaps, no book of the metaphysical kind that has been so generally read by those who understand the language, or that is more adapted to teach men to think with precision,* and to inspire them with that candour and love of truth which is the genuine spirit of philosophy. He gave, I believe, the first example in the English language of writing on such abstract subjects, with a remarkable degree of simplicity and perspicuity; and in this he has been happily imitated by others that came after him. No author hath more successfully pointed out the danger of ambiguous words, and the importance of having distinct and determinate notions in judging and reasoning. His observations on the various powers of the human understanding, on the use and abuse of words, and on the extent and limits of human knowledge, are drawn from attentive reflection on the operations of his own mind, the true source of all real knowledge on these subjects; and shew an uncommon degree of penetration and judgment. But he needs no panegyric of mine, and I mention these things, only that, when I have occasion to differ from him, I may not be thought insensible of the merit of an author whom I highly respect, and to whom I owe

my first lights in those studies, as well as my attachment to them.

He sets out in his essay with a full conviction, common to him with other philosophers, that ideas in the mind are the objects of all our thoughts in every operation of the understanding. This leads him to use the word *idea** so very frequently, beyond what was usual in the English language, that he thought it necessary, in his introduction, to make this apology:— "It being that term," says he, "which, I think, serves best to stand for whatsoever is the object of understanding when a man thinks, I have used it to express whatever is meant by phantasm, notion, species, or whatever it is which the mind can be employed about in thinking; and I could not avoid frequently using it. I presume it will be granted me, that there are such ideas in men's minds; every man is conscious of them in himself, and men's words and actions will satisfy him that they are in others." [145]

Speaking of the reality of our knowledge, he says, "It is evident the mind knows not things immediately, but only by the intervention of the ideas it has of them. Our knowledge, therefore, is real, only so far as there is a conformity between our ideas and the reality of things. But what shall be here the criterion? How shall the mind, when it perceives nothing but its own ideas, know that they agree with things themselves? This, though it seems not to want difficulty, yet, I think, there be two sorts of ideas that we may be assured agree with things."

We see that Mr Locke was aware, no less than Des Cartes, that the doctrine of ideas made it necessary, and at the same time difficult, to prove the existence of a material world without us; because the mind, according to that doctrine, perceives nothing but a world of ideas in itself. Not only Des Cartes, but Malebranche, Arnauld, and Norris, had perceived this difficulty, and attempted to remove it with little success. Mr Locke attempts the same thing; but his arguments are feeble. He even seems to be conscious of this; for he concludes his reasoning with this observation —"That we have evidence sufficient to direct us in attaining the good and avoiding the evil, caused by external objects, and that this is the important concern we have in being made acquainted with them." This, indeed, is saying no more than will be granted by those who deny the existence of a material world.

As there is no material difference between

---

* To praise Locke for *precision*, is rather too much.—H.

[144, 145]

* Locke may be said to have first naturalized the word in English philosophical language, in its Cartesian extension.—H.

Locke and Des Cartes with regard to the perception of objects by the senses, there is the less occasion, in this place, to take notice of all their differences in other points. They differed about the origin of our ideas. Des Cartes thought some of them were innate; the other maintained that there are no innate ideas, and that they are all derived from two sources—to wit, *sensation* and *reflection ;* meaning, by sensation, the operations of our external senses ; and, by reflection, that attention which we are capable of giving to the operations of our own minds. [146]

They differed with regard to the essence both of matter and of mind : the British philosopher holding that the real essence of both is beyond the reach of human knowledge ; the other conceiving that the very essence of mind consists in thought, and that of matter in extension, by which he made matter and space not to differ in reality, and no part of space to be void of matter.

Mr Locke explained, more distinctly than had been done before, the operations of the mind in classing the various objects of thought, and reducing them to genera and species. He was the first, I think, who distinguished in substances what he calls the nominal essence—which is only the notion we form of a genus or species, and which we express by a definition—from the real essence or internal constitution of the thing, which makes it to be what it is.*

Without this distinction, the subtile disputes which tortured the schoolmen for so many ages, in the controversy between the nominalists and realists, could never be brought to an issue. He shews distinctly how we form abstract and general notions, and the use and necessity of them in reasoning. And as (according to the received principles of philosophers) every notion of our mind must have for its object an idea in the mind itself,† he thinks that we form abstract ideas by leaving out of the idea of an individual everything wherein it differs from other individuals of the same species or genus ; and that this power of forming abstract ideas, is that which chiefly distinguishes us from brute animals, in whom he could see no evidence of any abstract ideas.

Since the time of Des Cartes, philosophers have differed much with regard to the share they ascribe to the mind itself, in the fabrication of those representative beings called *ideas*, and the manner in which this work is carried on.

Of the authors I have met with, Dr Robert Hook is the most explicit. He was one of the most ingenious and active members of the Royal Society of London at its first institution ; and frequently read lectures to the Society, which were published among his posthumous works. [147] In his "Lectures upon Light," § 7, he makes ideas to be material substances ; and thinks that the brain is furnished with a proper kind of matter for fabricating the ideas of each sense. The ideas of sight, he thinks, are formed of a kind of matter resembling the Bononian stone, or some kind of phosphorus ; that the ideas of sound are formed of some matter resembling the chords or glasses which take a sound from the vibrations of the air ; and so of the rest.

The soul, he thinks, may fabricate some hundreds of those ideas in a day ; and that, as they are formed, they are pushed farther off from the centre of the brain where the soul resides. By this means they make a continued chain of ideas, coyled up in the brain ; the first end of which is farthest removed from the centre or seat of the soul, and the other end is always at the centre, being the last idea formed, which is always present the moment when considered ; and, therefore, according as there is a greater number of ideas between the present sensation or thought in the centre and any other, the soul is apprehensive of a larger portion of time interposed.

Mr Locke has not entered into so minute a detail of this manufacture of ideas ; but he ascribes to the mind a very considerable hand in forming its own ideas. With regard to our sensations, the mind is passive, " they being produced in us, only by different degrees and modes of motion in our animal spirits, variously agitated by external objects." These, however, cease to be as soon as they cease to be perceived ; but, by the faculties of memory and imagination, " the mind has an ability, when it wills, to revive them again, and, as it were, to paint them anew upon itself, though some with more, some with less difficulty."

As to the ideas of reflection, he ascribes them to no other cause but to that attention which the mind is capable of giving to its own operations. These, therefore, are formed by the mind itself. [148] He ascribes likewise to the mind the power of compounding its simple ideas into complex ones of various forms ; of repeating them, and adding the repetitions together ; of dividing and classing them ; of comparing them, and, from that comparison, of forming the ideas of their relation ; nay, of forming a general idea of a species or genus, by taking from the idea of an individual everything by which it is distinguished from other individuals of the kind, till at last it becomes

[146–148]

---

* Locke has no originality in this respect.—H.
† Notion is here used for the apprehension of the idea, or representative reality, which Reid supposed that all philosophers viewed as something more than the mere act of knowledge, considered in relation to what was, through it, known or represented.—H.

an abstract general idea, common to all the individuals of the kind.

These, I think, are the powers which Mr Locke ascribes to the mind itself in the fabrication of its ideas. Bishop Berkeley, as we shall see afterwards, abridged them considerably, and Mr Hume much more.

The ideas we have of the various qualities of bodies are not all, as Mr Locke thinks, of the same kind. Some of them are images or resemblances of what is really in the body; others are not. There are certain qualities inseparable from matter; such as extension, solidity, figure, mobility. Our ideas of these are real resemblances of the qualities in the body: and these he calls primary qualities. But colour, sound, taste, smell, heat, and cold, he calls secondary qualities, and thinks that they are only powers in bodies of producing certain sensations in us; which sensations have nothing resembling them, though they are commonly thought to be exact resemblances of something in the body. "Thus," says he, " the idea of heat or light, which we receive, by our eye or touch, from the sun, are commonly thought real qualities existing in the sun, and something more than mere powers in it."

The names of primary and secondary qualities were, I believe, first used by Mr Locke; but the distinction which they express, was well understood by Des Cartes, and is explained by him in his " Principia," Part I., § 69, 70, 71. [149]

Although no author has more merit than Mr Locke, in pointing out the ambiguity of words, and resolving, by that means, many knotty questions, which had tortured the wits of the schoolmen, yet, I apprehend, he has been sometimes misled by the ambiguity of the word *idea*, which he uses so often almost in every page of his essay.

In the explication given of this word, we took notice of two meanings given to it—a popular and a philosophical. In the popular meaning, to have an idea of anything, signifies nothing more than to think of it.

Although the operations of the mind are most properly and naturally, and indeed most commonly in all vulgar languages, expressed by active verbs, there is another way of expressing them, less common, but equally well understood. To think of a thing, and to have a thought of it; to believe a thing, and to have a belief of it; to see a thing, and have a sight of it; to conceive a thing, and to have a conception, notion, or idea of it—are phrases perfectly synonymous. In these phrases, the thought means nothing but the act of thinking; the belief, the act of believing; and the conception, notion, or idea, the act of conceiving. To have a clear and distinct idea is, in this sense, nothing else but to conceive ⌈149, 150⌉

the thing clearly and distinctly. When the word *idea* is taken in this popular sense, there can be no doubt of our having ideas in our minds. To think without ideas would be to think without thought, which is a manifest contradiction.

But there is another meaning of the word *idea* peculiar to philosophers, and grounded upon a philosophical theory, which the vulgar never think of. Philosophers, ancient and modern, have maintained that the operations of the mind, like the tools of an artificer, can only be employed upon objects that are present in the mind, or in the brain, where the mind is supposed to reside. [150] Therefore, objects that are distant in time or place must have a representative in the mind, or in the brain—some image or picture of them, which is the object that the mind contemplates. This representative image was, in the old philosophy, called a *species* or *phantasm*. Since the time of Des Cartes, it has more commonly been called an *idea*; and every thought is conceived to have an idea of its object. As this has been a common opinion among philosophers, as far back as we can trace philosophy, it is the less to be wondered at that they should be apt to confound the operation of the mind in thinking with the idea or object of thought, which is supposed to be its inseparable concomitant.*

If we pay any regard to the common sense of mankind, thought and the object of thought are different things, and ought to be distinguished. It is true, thought cannot be without an object—for every man who thinks must think of something: but the object he thinks of is one thing, his thought of that object is another thing. They are distinguished in all languages, even by the vulgar; and many things may be affirmed of thought—that is, of the operation of the mind in thinking—which cannot, without error, and even absurdity, be affirmed of the object of that operation.*

From this, I think, it is evident that, if the word *idea*, in a work where it occurs in every paragraph, is used without any intimation of the ambiguity of the word, sometimes to signify thought, or the operation of the mind in thinking, sometimes to signify those internal objects of thought which philosophers suppose, this must occasion confusion in the thoughts both of the author and of the readers. I take this to be the greatest blemish in the " Essay on Human Understanding." I apprehend this is the true source of several paradoxical opinions in that excellent work, which I shall have occasion to take notice of.

Here it is very natural to ask, Whether it was Mr Locke's opinion, that ideas are

---

* See Note C.—II.

the only objects of thought? or, Whether it is not possible for men to think of things which are not ideas in the mind?* [151]

To this question it is not easy to give a direct answer. On the one hand, he says often, in distinct and studied expressions, that the term *idea* stands for whatever is the object of the understanding when a man thinks, or whatever it is which the mind can be employed about in thinking: that the mind perceives nothing but its own ideas: that all knowledge consists in the perception of the agreement or disagreement of our ideas: that we can have no knowledge farther than we have ideas. These, and many other expressions of the like import, evidently imply that every object of thought must be an idea, and can be nothing else.

On the other hand, I am persuaded that Mr Locke would have acknowledged that we may think of Alexander the Great, or of the planet Jupiter, and of numberless things which he would have owned are not ideas in the mind, but objects which exist independent of the mind that thinks of them.†

How shall we reconcile the two parts of this apparent contradiction? All I am able to say, upon Mr Locke's principles, to reconcile them, is this, That we cannot think of Alexander, or of the planet Jupiter, unless we have in our minds an idea—that is, an image or picture of those objects. The idea of Alexander is an image, or picture, or representation of that hero in my mind;

---

* It is to be remembered that Reid means, by *Ideas*, representative entities different from the cognitive modifications of the mind itself.—H.

† On the confusion of this and the four subsequent paragraphs, see Note C.— Whatever is the immediate object of thought, of that we are necessarily conscious. But of Alexander, for example, as existing, we are necessarily not conscious. Alexander, as existing, cannot, therefore, possibly be an immediate object of thought; consequently, if we can be said to think of Alexander at all, we can only be said to think of him mediately, in and through a representation of which we are conscious; and that representation is the immediate object of thought. It makes no difference whether this immediate object be viewed as a *tertium quid*, distinct from the existing reality and from the conscious mind; or whether as a mere modality of the conscious mind itself—as the mere act of thought considered in its relation to something beyond the sphere of consciousness. In neither case, can we be said (be it in the *imagination* of a possible or the *recollection* of a past existence) to know a thing as *existing*—that is, immediately; and, therefore, if in these operations we be said to know aught out the mind at all, we can only be said to know it mediately—in other words, as a mediate object. The whole perplexity arises from the ambiguity of the term object, that term being used both for the external reality of which we are here not conscious, and cannot therefore know in itself, and for the mental representation which we know in itself, but which is known only as relative to the other. Reid chooses to abolish the former signification, on the supposition that it only applies to a representative entity different from the act of thought. In this supposition, however, he is wrong; nor does he obtain an immediate knowledge, even in *perception*, by merely denying the *crude* hypothesis of representation.—H.

---

and this idea is the immediate object of my thought when I think of Alexander. That this was Locke's opinion, and that it has been generally the opinion of philosophers, there can be no doubt.

But, instead of giving light to the question proposed, it seems to involve it in greater darkness.

When I think of Alexander, I am told there is an image or idea of Alexander in my mind, which is the immediate object of this thought. The necessary consequence of this seems to be, that there are two objects of this thought—the idea, which is in the mind, and the person represented by that idea; the first, the immediate object of the thought, the last, the object of the same thought, but not the immediate object. [152] This is a hard saying; for it makes every thought of things external to have a double object. Every man is conscious of his thoughts, and yet, upon attentive reflection, he perceives no such duplicity in the object he thinks about. Sometimes men see objects double, but they always know when they do so: and I know of no philosopher who has expressly owned this duplicity in the object of thought, though it follows necessarily from maintaining that, in the same thought, there is one object that is immediate and in the mind itself, and another object which is not immediate, and which is not in the mind.*

Besides this, it seems very hard, or rather impossible, to understand what is meant by an object of thought that is not an immediate object of thought. A body in motion may move another that was at rest, by the medium of a third body that is interposed. This is easily understood; but we are unable to conceive any medium interposed between a mind and the thought of that mind; and, to think of any object by a medium, seems to be words without any meaning. There is a sense in which a thing may be said to be perceived by a medium. Thus any kind of sign may be said to be the medium by which I perceive or understand the thing signified. The sign by custom, or compact, or perhaps by nature, introduces the thought of the thing signified. But here the thing signified, when it is introduced to the thought, is an object of thought no less immediate than the sign was before. And there are here two objects of thought, one succeeding another, which we have shewn is not the case with respect to an idea, and the object it represents.

---

* That is, if by object was meant the same thing, when the term is applied to the external reality, and to its mental representation. Even under the Scholastic theory of representation, it was generally maintained that the *species* itself is not an object of perception, but the external reality through it; a mode of speaking justly reprehended by the acuter schoolmen. But in this respect Reid is equally to blame. See Note C.—H.

I apprehend, therefore, that, if philosophers will maintain that ideas in the mind are the only immediate objects of thought, they will be forced to grant that they are the sole objects of thought, and that it is impossible for men to think of anything else.

[153] Yet, surely, Mr Locke believed that we can think of many things that are not ideas in the mind ; but he seems not to have perceived, that the maintaining that ideas in the mind are the only immediate objects of thought, must necessarily draw this consequence along with it.

The consequence, however, was seen by Bishop Berkeley and Mr Hume, who rather chose to admit the consequence than to give up the principle from which it follows.

Perhaps it was unfortunate for Mr Locke that he used the word idea so very frequently as to make it very difficult to give the attention necessary to put it always to the same meaning. And it appears evident that, in many places, he means nothing more by it but the notion or conception we have of any object of thought ; that is, the act of the mind in conceiving it, and not the object conceived.*

In explaining this word, he says that he uses it for whatever is meant by phantasm, notion, species. Here are three synonymes to the word idea. The first and last are very proper to express the philosophical meaning of the word, being terms of art in the Peripatetic philosophy, and signifying images of external things in the mind, which, according to that philosophy, are objects of thought. But the word notion is a word in common language, whose meaning agrees exactly with the popular meaning of

the word idea, but not with the philosophical.

When these two different meanings of the word idea are confounded in a studied explication of it, there is little reason to expect that they should be carefully distinguished in the frequent use of it. There are many passages in the Essay in which, to make them intelligible, the word idea must be taken in one of those senses, and many others in which it must be taken in the other. It seems probable that the author, not attending to this ambiguity of the word, used it in the one sense or the other, as the subject-matter required ; and the far greater part of his readers have done the same. [154]

There is a third sense, in which he uses the word not unfrequently, to signify objects of thought that are not in the mind, but external. Of this he seems to be sensible, and somewhere makes an apology for it. When he affirms, as he does in innumerable places, that all human knowledge consists in the perception of the agreement or disagreement of our ideas, it is impossible to put a meaning upon this, consistent with his principles, unless he means by ideas every object of human thought, whether mediate or immediate ; everything, in a word, that can be signified by the subject, or predicate of a proposition.

Thus, we see that the word idea has three different meanings in the essay ; and the author seems to have used it sometimes in one, sometimes in another, without being aware of any change in the meaning. The reader slides easily into the same fallacy, that meaning occurring most readily to his mind which gives the best sense to what he reads. I have met with persons professing no slight acquaintance with the " Essay on Human Understanding," who maintained that the word idea, wherever it occurs, means nothing more than thought ; and that, where he speaks of ideas as images in the mind, and as objects of thought, he is not to be understood as speaking properly, but figuratively or analogically. And, indeed, I apprehend that it would be no small advantage to many passages in the book, if they could admit of this interpretation.

It is not the fault of this philosopher alone to have given too little attention to the distinction between the operations of the mind and the objects of those operations. Although this distinction be familiar to the vulgar, and found in the structure of all languages, philosophers, when they speak of ideas, often confound [155] the two together ; and their theory concerning ideas has led them to do so ; for ideas, being supposed to be a shadowy kind of beings, intermediate between the thought and the object of thought, sometimes seem to con-

---

* When we contemplate a triangle, we may consider it either as a complement of three sides or of three angles ; not that the three sides and the three angles are possible except through each other, but because we may in thought view the figure—qua triangle, in reality one and indivisible—in different relations. In like manner, we may consider a representative act of knowledge in two relations—1°, as an act representative of something, and, 2° as an act cognitive of that representation, although, in truth, these are both only one indivisible energy—the representation only existing as known, the cognition being only possible in a representation. Thus, e. g., in the imagination of a Centaur—the Centaur represented is the Centaur known, the Centaur known is the Centaur represented. It is one act under two relations—a relation to the subject knowing—a relation to the object represented. But to a cognitive act considered in these several relations we may give either different names, or we may confound them under one, or we may do both ; and this is actually done ; some words expressing only one relation, others both or either, and others properly the one but abusively also the other. Thus Idea properly denotes an act of thought considered in relation to an external something beyond the sphere of consciousness—a representation ; but some philosophers, as Locke, abuse it to comprehend the thought also, viewed as cognitive of this representation. Again, perception, notion, conception, &c. (concept is, unfortunately, obsolete) comprehend both, or may be used to denote either of the relations ; and it is only by the context that we can ever vaguely discover in which application they are intended. This is unfortunate ; but so it is.—H.

[153–155]

lesce with the thought, sometimes with the object of thought, and sometimes to have a distinct existence of their own.

The same philosophical theory of ideas has led philosophers to confound the different operations of the understanding, and to call them all by the name of perception.* Mr Locke, though not free from this fault, is not so often chargeable with it as some who came after him. The vulgar give the name of perception to that immediate knowledge of external objects which we have by our external senses.† This is its proper meaning in our language, though sometimes it may be applied to other things metaphorically or analogically.‡ When I think of anything that does not exist, as of the republic of Oceana, I do not perceive it—I only conceive or imagine it.§ When I think of what happened to me yesterday, I do not perceive but remember it.|| When I am pained with the gout, it is not proper to say I perceive it—I feel it, or am conscious of it: it is not an object of perception, but of sensation and of consciousness.¶ So far, the vulgar distinguish very properly the different operations of the mind, and never confound the names of things so different in their nature. But the theory of ideas leads philosophers to conceive all those operations to be of one nature, and to give them one name. They are all, according to that theory, the perception of ideas in the mind. Perceiving, remembering, imagining, being conscious, are all perceiving ideas in the mind, and are called *perceptions.* Hence it is that philosophers speak of the perceptions of memory, and the perceptions of imagina-

tion. They make sensation to be a perception; and everything we perceive by our senses to be an idea of sensation. Sometimes they say that they are conscious of the ideas in their own minds, sometimes that they perceive them.* [156]

However improbable it may appear that philosophers who have taken pains to study the operations of their own minds, should express them less properly and less distinctly than the vulgar, it seems really to be the case; and the only account that can be given of this strange phænomenon, I take to be this: that the vulgar seek no theory to account for the operations of their minds; they know that they see, and hear, and remember, and imagine; and those who think distinctly will express these operations distinctly, as their consciousness represents them to the mind; but philosophers think they ought to know not only that there are such operations, but how they are performed; how they see, and hear, and remember, and imagine; and, having invented a theory to explain these operations, by ideas or images in the mind, they suit their expressions to their theory; and, as a false comment throws a cloud upon the text, so a false theory darkens the phænomena which it attempts to explain.

We shall examine this theory afterwards. Here I would only observe that, if it is not true, it may be expected that it should lead ingenious men who adopt it to confound the operations of the mind with their objects, and with one another, even where the common language of the unlearned clearly distinguishes them. One that trusts to a false guide is in greater danger of being led astray, than he who trusts his own eyes, though he should be but indifferently acquainted with the road.

---

* No more than by calling them all by the name of *Cognitions*, or *Acts of Consciousness.* There was no reason, either from etymology or usage, why *perception* should not signify the energy of immediately apprehending, in general; and until Reid limited the word to our apprehension of an external world, it was, in fact, employed by philosophers, as tantamount to an act of apprehension. We were in need of a word to express our *sensitive cognitions* as distinct from our *sensitive feelings,* (for the term *sensation* involved both,) and, therefore, Reid's restriction, though contrary to all precedent, may be admitted; but his criticism of other philosophers for their employment of the term, in a wider meaning, is wholly groundless.—H

† But not exclusively.— H.

‡ This is not correct —H.

§ And why ? Simply because we do not, by such an act, *know,* or *apprehend* such an object to exist ; we merely represent it. But perception was only used for such an apprehension. We could say, however, that we perceived (as we could say that we were conscious of) the republic of Oceana, as imagined by us, after Harrington.— H.

|| And this, for the same reason. What is remembered is not and can not be immediately known ; nought but the present mental representation is so known ; and this we could properly say that we perceived.—H.

¶ Because the feeling of pain, though only possible through consciousness, is not an *act* of knowledge. But it could be properly said, *I perceive a feeling of pain.* At any rate, the expression *I perceive a pain,* is as correct as *I am conscious of a pain* —H.

CHAPTER X.

OF THE SENTIMENTS OF BISHOP BERKELEY.

GEORGE BERKELEY, afterwards Bishop of Cloyne, published his "New Theory of Vision," in 1709 ; his "Treatise concerning the Principles of Human Knowledge," in 1710 ; and his "Dialogues between Hylas and Philonous," in 1713 ; being then a Fellow of Trinity College, Dublin. [157] He is acknowledged universally to have great merit, as an excellent writer, and a very acute and clear reasoner on the most abstract subjects, not to speak of his virtues as a man, which were very conspicuous : yet the doctrine chiefly held forth in the treatises above mentioned, especially in the

---

* The connection of the wider signification of the term perception, with the more complex theory of representation, has no foundation—H.

two last, has generally been thought so very absurd, that few can be brought to think that he either believed it himself, or that he seriously meant to persuade others of its truth.

He maintains, and thinks he has demonstrated, by a variety of arguments, grounded on principles of philosophy universally received, that there is no such thing as matter in the universe; that sun and moon, earth and sea, our own bodies, and those of our friends, are nothing but ideas in the minds of those who think of them, and that they have no existence when they are not the objects of thought; that all that is in the universe may be reduced to two categories—to wit, *minds*, and *ideas in the mind*.

But, however absurd this doctrine might appear to the unlearned, who consider the existence of the objects of sense as the most evident of all truths, and what no man in his senses can doubt, the philosophers who had been accustomed to consider ideas as the immediate objects of all thought, had no title to view this doctrine of Berkeley in so unfavourable a light.

They were taught by Des Cartes, and by all that came after him, that the existence of the objects of sense is not self-evident, but requires to be proved by arguments; and, although Des Cartes, and many others, had laboured to find arguments for this purpose, there did not appear to be that force and clearness in them which might have been expected in a matter of such importance. Mr Norris had declared that, after all the arguments that had been offered, the existence of an external world is only probable, but by no means certain. [158] Malebranche thought it rested upon the authority of revelation, and that the arguments drawn from reason were not perfectly conclusive. Others thought that the argument from revelation was a mere sophism, because revelation comes to us by our senses, and must rest upon their authority.

Thus we see that the new philosophy had been making gradual approaches towards Berkeley's opinion; and, whatever others might do, the philosophers had no title to look upon it as absurd, or unworthy of a fair examination. Several authors attempted to answer his arguments, but with little success, and others acknowledged that they could neither answer them nor assent to them. It is probable the Bishop made but few converts to his doctrine; but it is certain he made some; and that he himself continued, to the end of his life, firmly persuaded, not only of its truth,[*] but of its

great importance for the improvement of human knowledge, and especially for the defence of religion. Dial. Pref. "If the principles which I here endeavour to propagate, are admitted for true, the consequences which I think evidently flow from thence are, that atheism and scepticism will be utterly destroyed, many intricate points made plain, great difficulties solved, several useless parts of science retrenched, speculation referred to practice, and men reduced from paradoxes to common sense."

In the "Theory of Vision," he goes no farther than to assert that the objects of sight are nothing but ideas in the mind, granting, or at least not denying, that there is a tangible world, which is really external, and which exists whether we perceive it or not. Whether the reason of this was, that his system had not, at that time, wholly opened to his own mind, or whether he thought it prudent to let it enter into the minds of his readers by degrees, I cannot say. I think he insinuates the last as the reason, in the "Principles of Human Knowledge." [159]

The "Theory of Vision," however, taken by itself, and without relation to the main branch of his system, contains very important discoveries, and marks of great genius. He distinguishes more accurately than any that went before him, between the immediate objects of sight, and those of the other senses which are early associated with them. He shews that distance, of itself and immediately, is not seen; but that we learn to judge of it by certain sensations and perceptions which are connected with it. This is a very important observation; and, I believe, was first made by this author.[*] It gives much new light to the operations of our senses, and serves to account for many phænomena in optics, of which the greatest adepts in that science had always either given a false account, or acknowledged that they could give none at all.

We may observe, by the way, that the ingenious author seems not to have attended to a distinction by which his general assertion ought to have been limited. It is true that the distance of an object from the eye is not immediately seen; but there is a certain kind of distance of one object from another which we see immediately. The author acknowledges that there is a visible extension, and visible figures, which are proper objects of sight; there must therefore be a visible distance. Astronomers call it angular distance; and, although they measure

---

○ Berkeley's confidence in his idealism was, however, nothing to Fichte's. This philosopher, in one of his controversial treatises, imprecates everlasting damnation on himself not only should he retract, but

should he even waver in regard to any one principle of his doctrine; a doctrine, the speculative result of which left him, as he confesses, without even a certainty of his own existence. (See above, p. 129, note *.) It is Varro who speaks of the *credula philosophorum natio*; but this is to be credulous even in incredulity.—H.

* This last statement is inaccurate.—H.

it by the angle, which is made by two lines drawn from the eye to the two distant objects, yet it is immediately perceived by sight, even by those who never thought of that angle.

He led the way in shewing how we learn to perceive the distance of an object from the eye, though this speculation was carried farther by others who came after him. He made the distinction between that extension and figure which we perceive by sight only, and that which we perceive by touch; calling the first, visible, the last, tangible extension and figure. He shewed, likewise, that tangible extension, and not visible, is the object of geometry, although mathematicians commonly use visible diagrams in their demonstrations.* [160]

The notion of extension and figure which we get from sight only, and that which we get from touch, have been so constantly conjoined from our infancy in all the judgments we form of the objects of sense, that it required great abilities to distinguish them accurately, and to assign to each sense what truly belongs to it; "so difficult a thing it is," as Berkeley justly observes, "to dissolve an union so early begun, and confirmed by so long a habit." This point he has laboured, through the whole of the essay on vision, with that uncommon penetration and judgment which he possessed, and with as great success as could be expected in a first attempt upon so abstruse a subject.

He concludes this essay, by shewing, in no less than seven sections, the notions which an intelligent being, endowed with sight, without the sense of touch, might form of the objects of sense. This speculation, to shallow thinkers, may appear to be egregious trifling.† To Bishop Berkeley it appeared in another light, and will do so to those who are capable of entering into it, and who know the importance of it, in solving many of the phænomena of vision. He seems, indeed, to have exerted more force of genius in this than in the main branch of his system.

In the new philosophy, the pillars by which the existence of a material world was supported, were so feeble that it did not require the force of a Samson to bring them

down; and in this we have not so much reason to admire the strength of Berkeley's genius, as his boldness in publishing to the world an opinion which the unlearned would be apt to interpret as the sign of a crazy intellect. A man who was firmly persuaded of the doctrine universally received by philosophers concerning ideas, if he could but take courage to call in question the existence of a material world, would easily find unanswerable arguments in that doctrine. [161] "Some truths there are," says Berkeley, "so near and obvious to the mind, that a man need only open his eyes to see them. Such," he adds, "I take this important one to be, that all the choir of heaven, and furniture of the earth—in a word, all those bodies which compose the mighty frame of the world—have not any subsistence without a mind." Princ. § 6.

The principle from which this important conclusion is obviously deduced, is laid down in the first sentence of his principles of knowledge, as evident; and, indeed, it has always been acknowledged by philosophers. "It is evident," says he, "to any one who takes a survey of the objects of human knowledge, that they are either ideas actually imprinted on the senses, or else such as are perceived, by attending to the passions and operations of the mind; or, lastly, ideas formed by help of memory and imagination, either compounding, dividing, or barely representing those originally perceived in the foresaid ways."

This is the foundation on which the whole system rests. If this be true, then, indeed, the existence of a material world must be a dream that has imposed upon all mankind from the beginning of the world.

The foundation on which such a fabric rests ought to be very solid and well established; yet Berkeley says nothing more for it than that it is evident. If he means that it is self-evident, this indeed might be a good reason for not offering any direct argument in proof of it. But I apprehend this cannot justly be said. Self-evident propositions are those which appear evident to every man of sound understanding who apprehends the meaning of them distinctly, and attends to them without prejudice. Can this be said of this proposition, That all the objects of our knowledge are ideas in our own minds?* I believe that, to any man

---

* Properly speaking, it is neither tangible nor visible extension which is the object of geometry, but intelligible, pure, or *a priori* extension.—H.

† This, I have no doubt, is in allusion to Priestley. That writer had, not very courteously, said, in his "Examination of Reid's Inquiry" " : do not remember to have seen a more *egregious piece of solemn trifling* than the chapter which our author calls the ' Geometry of Visibles,' and his account of the ' Idomenians,' as he terms the imaginary beings who had no ideas of substance but from sight."—In a note upon that chapter of "The Inquiry," I stated that the thought of a Geometry of Visibles was original to Berkeley, and I had then no recollection of Reid's acknowledgment in the present paragraph.—H.

* To the Idealist, it is of perfect indifference whether this proposition, in Reid's sense of the expression Ideas, be admitted, or whether it be held that we are conscious of nothing but of the modifications of our own minds. For, on the supposition that we can know the *non-ego* only in and through the *ego*, it follows, (since we can know nothing immediately of which we are not conscious, and it being allowed that we are conscious only of mind,) that it is contradictory to suppose aught, as known, (*i.e.*, any object of knowledge,) to be known otherwise than as a phænomenon of mind.—H.

uninstructed in philosophy, this proposition will appear very improbable, if not absurd. [162] However scanty his knowledge may be, he considers the sun and moon, the earth and sea, as objects of it; and it will be difficult to persuade him that those objects of his knowledge are ideas in his own mind, and have no existence when he does not think of them. If I may presume to speak my own sentiments, I once believed this doctrine of ideas so firmly as to embrace the whole of Berkeley's system in consequence of it; till, finding other consequences to follow from it, which gave me more uneasiness than the want of a material world, it came into my mind, more than forty years ago, to put the question, What evidence have I for this doctrine, that all the objects of my knowledge are ideas in my own mind? From that time to the present I have been candidly and impartially, as I think, seeking for the evidence of this principle, but can find none, excepting the authority of philosophers.

We shall have occasion to examine its evidence afterwards. I would at present only observe, that all the arguments brought by Berkeley against the existence of a material world are grounded upon it; and that he has not attempted to give any evidence for it, but takes it for granted, as other philosophers had done before him.

But, supposing this principle to be true, Berkeley's system is impregnable. No demonstration can be more evident than his reasoning from it. Whatever is perceived is an idea, and an idea can only exist in a mind. It has no existence when it is not perceived; nor can there be anything like an idea, but an idea.

So sensible he was that it required no laborious reasoning to deduce his system from the principle laid down, that he was afraid of being thought needlessly prolix in handling the subject, and makes an apology for it. Princ. § 22. "To what purpose is it," says he, "to dilate upon that which may be demonstrated, with the utmost evidence, in a line or two, to any one who is capable of the least reflection?" [163] But, though his demonstration might have been comprehended in a line or two, he very prudently thought that an opinion which the world would be apt to look upon as a monster of absurdity, would not be able to make its way at once, even by the force of a naked demonstration. He observes, justly, Dial. 2, "That, though a demonstration be never so well grounded and fairly proposed, yet if there is, withal, a strain of prejudice, or a wrong bias on the understanding, can it be expected to perceive clearly, and adhere firmly to the truth? No; there is need of time and pains; the attention must be awakened and detained, by a frequent re-

petition of the same thing, placed often in the same, often in different lights."

It was, therefore, necessary to dwell upon it, and turn it on all sides, till it became familiar; to consider all its consequences, and to obviate every prejudice and prepossession that might hinder its admittance. It was even a matter of some difficulty to fit it to common language, so far as to enable men to speak and reason about it intelligibly. Those who have entered seriously into Berkeley's system, have found, after all the assistance which his writings give, that time and practice are necessary to acquire the habit of speaking and thinking distinctly upon it.

Berkeley foresaw the opposition that would be made to his system, from two different quarters: *first*, from the philosophers; and, *secondly*, from the vulgar, who are led by the plain dictates of nature. The first he had the courage to oppose openly and avowedly; the second, he dreaded much more, and, therefore, takes a great deal of pains, and, I think, uses some art, to court into his party. This is particularly observable in his "Dialogues." He sets out with a declaration, Dial. 1, "That, of late, he had quitted several of the sublime notions he had got in the schools of the philosophers, for vulgar opinions," and assures Hylas, his fellow-dialogist, "That, since this revolt from metaphysical notions to the plain dictates of nature and common sense, he found his understanding strangely enlightened; so that he could now easily comprehend a great many things, which before were all mystery and riddle." [164] Pref. to Dial. "If his principles are admitted for true, men will be reduced from paradoxes to common sense." At the same time, he acknowledges, "That they carry with them a great opposition to the prejudices of philosophers, which have so far prevailed against the common sense and natural notions of mankind."

When Hylas objects to him, Dial. 3, "You can never persuade me, Philonous, that the denying of matter or corporeal substance is not repugnant to the universal sense of mankind"—he answers, "I wish both our opinions were fairly stated, and submitted to the judgment of men who had plain common sense, without the prejudices of a learned education. Let me be represented as one who trusts his senses, who thinks he knows the things he sees and feels, and entertains no doubt of their existence.—If by material substance is meant only sensible body, that which is seen and felt, (and the unphilosophical part of the world, I dare say, mean no more,) then I am more certain of matter's existence than you or any other philosopher pretend to be. If there be anything which makes the generality of mankind averse from the notions I espouse, it is a misapprehension that I deny the reality of sensible things: but, as it is you who are guilty of that, and not I, it follows, that, in truth, their aversion is against your notions, and not mine. I am content to appeal to the common sense of the world for the truth of my notion. I am of a vulgar cast, simple enough to believe my senses, and to leave things as I find them. I cannot, for my life, help thinking that snow is white and fire hot."

When Hylas is at last entirely converted, he observes to Philonous, "After all, the controversy about matter, in the strict acceptation of it, lies altogether between you and the philosophers, whose principles, I acknowledge, are not near so natural, or so agreeable to the common sense of mankind, and Holy Scripture, as yours." [165] Philonous observes, in the end, "That he does not pretend to be a setter up of new notions; his endeavours tend only to unite, and to place in a clearer light, that truth which was before shared between the vulgar and the philosophers; the former being of opinion, that those things they immediately perceive are the real things; and the latter, that the things immediately perceived, are ideas which exist only in the mind; which two things put together do, in effect, constitute the substance of what he advances." And he concludes by observing, "That those principles which at first view lead to scepticism, pursued to a certain point, bring men back to common sense."

These passages shew sufficiently the author's concern to reconcile his system to the plain dictates of nature and common sense, while he expresses no concern to reconcile it to the received doctrines of philosophers. He is fond to take part with the vulgar against the philosophers, and to vindicate common sense against their innovations. What pity is it that he did not carry this suspicion of the doctrine of philosophers so far as to doubt of that philosophical tenet on which his whole system is built—to wit, that the things immediately perceived by the senses are ideas which exist only in the mind!

After all, it seems no easy matter to make the vulgar opinion and that of Berkeley to meet. And, to accomplish this, he seems to me to draw each out of its line towards the other, not without some straining. The vulgar opinion he reduces to this, that the very things which we perceive by our senses do really exist. This he grants;* for these things, says he, are ideas in our minds, or complexions of ideas, to which

we give one name, and consider as one thing; these are the immediate objects of sense, and these do really exist. As to the notion that those things have an absolute external existence, independent of being perceived by any mind, he thinks [166] that this is no notion of the vulgar, but a refinement of philosophers; and that the notion of material substance, as a *substratum*, or support of that collection of sensible qualities to which we give the name of an apple or a melon, is likewise an invention of philosophers, and is not found with the vulgar till they are instructed by philosophers. The substance not being an object of sense, the vulgar never think of it; or, if they are taught the use of the word, they mean no more by it but that collection of sensible qualities which they, from finding them conjoined in nature, have been accustomed to call by one name, and to consider as one thing.

Thus he draws the vulgar opinion near to his own; and, that he may meet it half way, he acknowledges that material things have a real existence out of the mind of this or that person; but the question, says he, between the materialist and me, is, Whether they have an absolute existence distinct from their being perceived by God, and exterior to all minds? This, indeed, he says, some heathens and philosophers have affirmed; but whoever entertains notions of the Deity, suitable to the Holy Scripture, will be of another opinion.

But here an objection occurs, which it required all his ingenuity to answer. It is this: The ideas in my mind cannot be the same with the ideas of any other mind; therefore, if the objects I perceive be only ideas, it is impossible that the objects I perceive can exist anywhere, when I do not perceive them; and it is impossible that two or more minds can perceive the same object.

To this Berkeley answers, that this objection presses no less the opinion of the materialist philosopher than his. But the difficulty is to make his opinion coincide with the notions of the vulgar, who are firmly persuaded that the very identical objects which they perceive, continue to exist when they do not perceive them; and who are no less firmly persuaded that, when ten men look at the sun or the moon, they all see the same individual object.* [167]

To reconcile this repugnancy, he observes, Dial. 3—"That, if the term *same* be taken in the vulgar acceptation, it is certain (and not at all repugnant to the principles he maintains) that different persons may perceive the same thing; or the same thing or idea exist in different minds. Words are

* This is one of the passages that may be brought to prove that Reid did allow to the *ego* an immediate and real knowledge of the non-*ego*.—H.

* See the last note.—H.

of arbitrary imposition; and, since men are used to apply the word *same*, where no distinction or variety is perceived, and he does not pretend to alter their perceptions, it follows that, as men have said before, *several saw the same thing*, so they may, upon like occasions, still continue to use the same phrase, without any deviation, either from propriety of language, or the truth of things; but, if the term *same* be used in the acceptation of philosophers, who pretend to an abstracted notion of identity, then, according to their sundry definitions of this term, (for it is not yet agreed wherein that philosophic identity consists,) it may or may not be possible for divers persons to perceive the same thing; but whether philosophers shall think fit to call a thing the *same* or no is, I conceive, of small importance. Men may dispute about identity and diversity, without any real difference in their thoughts and opinions, abstracted from names."

Upon the whole, I apprehend that Berkeley has carried this attempt to reconcile his system to the vulgar opinion farther than reason supports him; and he was no doubt tempted to do so, from a just apprehension that, in a controversy of this kind, the common sense of mankind is the most formidable antagonist.

Berkeley has employed much pains and ingenuity to shew that his system, if received and believed, would not be attended with those bad consequences in the conduct of life, which superficial thinkers may be apt to impute to it. His system does not take away or make any alteration upon our pleasures or our pains: our sensations, whether agreeable or disagreeable, are the same upon his system as upon any other. These are real things, and the only things that interest us. [168] They are produced in us according to certain laws of nature, by which our conduct will be directed in attaining the one, and avoiding the other; and it is of no moment to us, whether they are produced immediately by the operation of some powerful intelligent being upon our minds; or by the mediation of some inanimate being which we call *matter*.

The evidence of an all-governing mind, so far from being weakened, seems to appear even in a more striking light upon his hypothesis, than upon the common one. The powers which inanimate matter is supposed to possess, have always been the stronghold of atheists, to which they had recourse in defence of their system. This fortress of atheism must be most effectually overturned, if there is no such thing as matter in the universe. In all this the Bishop reasons justly and acutely. But there is one uncomfortable consequence of his system, which he seems not to have attended to, and from which it will be found difficult, if at all possible, to guard it.

The consequence I mean is this—that, although it leaves us sufficient evidence of a supreme intelligent mind, it seems to take away all the evidence we have of other intelligent beings like ourselves. What I call a father, a brother, or a friend, is only a parcel of ideas in my own mind; and, being ideas in my mind, they cannot possibly have that relation to another mind which they have to mine, any more than the pain felt by me can be the individual pain felt by another. –I can find no principle in Berkeley's system, which affords me even probable ground to conclude that there are other intelligent beings, like myself, in the relations of father, brother, friend, or fellow-citizen. I am left alone, as the only creature of God in the universe, in that forlorn state of *egoism* into which it is said some of the disciples of Des Cartes were brought by his philosophy.* [169]

Of all the opinions that have ever been advanced by philosophers, this of Bishop Berkeley, that there is no material world, seems the strangest, and the most apt to bring philosophy into ridicule with plain men who are guided by the dictates of nature and common sense. And, it will not, I apprehend, be improper to trace this progeny of the doctrine of ideas from its origin, and to observe its gradual progress, till it acquired such strength that a pious and learned bishop had the boldness to usher it into the world, as demonstrable from the principles of philosophy universally received, and as an admirable expedient for the advancement of knowledge and for the defence of religion.

During the reign of the Peripatetic philosophy, men were little disposed to doubt, and much to dogmatize. The existence of the objects of sense was held as a first principle; and the received doctrine was, that the sensible species or idea is the very form of the external object, just separated from the matter of it, and sent into the mind that perceives it; so that we find no appearance of scepticism about the existence of matter under that philosophy.†

Des Cartes taught men to doubt even of those things that had been taken for first principles. He rejected‡ the doctrine of

* In which the soul, like the unhappy Dido—
———— " semperque relinqui
Sola sibi, semper longam in. omitata videtur
Ire viam."—H.
† This is not the case. It could easily be shewn that, in the schools of the middle ages, the arguments in favour of Idealism were fully understood; and they would certainly have obtained numerous partisans, had it not been seen that such a philosophical opinion involved a theological heresy touching the eucharist. This was even recognised by St Augustine.—H
‡ After many of the Peripatetics themselves.—H.

species or ideas coming from objects; but still maintained, that what we immediately perceive, is not the external object, but an idea or image of it in our mind. This led some of his disciples into Egoism, and to disbelieve the existence of every creature in the universe but themselves and their own ideas.*

But Des Cartes himself—either from dread of the censure of the church, which he took great care not to provoke; or to shun the ridicule of the world, which might have crushed his system at once, as it did that of the Egoists;* or, perhaps, from inward conviction—was resolved to support the existence of matter. To do this consistently with his principles, he found himself obliged to have recourse to arguments that are far-fetched, and not very cogent. Sometimes he argues that our senses are given us by God, who is no deceiver; and, therefore, we ought to believe their testimony. [170] But this argument is weak ; because, according to his principles, our senses testify no more but that we have certain ideas : and, if we draw conclusions from this testimony, which the premises will not support, we deceive ourselves. To give more force to this weak argument, he sometimes adds that we have by nature a strong propensity to believe that there is an external world corresponding to our ideas.†

Malebranche thought that this strong propensity is not a sufficient reason for believing the existence of matter; and that it is to be received as an article of faith, not certainly discoverable by reason. He is aware that faith comes by hearing ; and that it may be said that prophets, apostles, and miracles are only ideas in our minds. But to this he answers, that, though these things are only ideas, yet faith turns them into realities ; and this answer, he hopes, will satisfy those who are not too morose.

It may perhaps seem strange that Locke, who wrote so much about ideas, should not see those consequences which Berkeley thought so obviously deducible from that doctrine. Mr Locke surely was not willing that the doctrine of ideas should be thought to be loaded with such consequences. He acknowledges that the existence of a material world is not to be received as a first principle—nor is it demonstrable; but he offers the best arguments for it he can; and supplies the weakness of his arguments by this observation—that we have such evidence as is sufficient to direct us in pursuing the good and avoiding the ill we may receive from external things, beyond which we have no concern.

There is, indeed, a single passage in Locke's essay, which may lead one to conjecture that he had a glimpse of that system which Berkeley afterwards advanced, but thought proper to suppress it within his own breast. [171] The passage is in Book 4, c. 10, where, having proved the existence of an eternal intelligent mind, he comes to answer those who conceive that matter also must be eternal, because we cannot conceive how it could be made out of nothing ; and having observed that the creation of mind requires no less power than the creation of matter, he adds what follows :—"Nay, possibly, if we could emancipate ourselves from vulgar notions, and raise our thoughts, as far as they would reach, to a closer contemplation of things, we might be able to aim at some dim and seeming conception, how matter might at first be made and begin to exist, by the power of that eternal first Being; but to give beginning and being to a spirit, would be found a more inconceivable effect of omnipotent power. But this being what would perhaps lead us too far from the notions on which the philosophy now in the world is built, it would not be pardonable to deviate so far from them, or to inquire, so far as grammar itself would authorize, if the common settled opinion opposes it ; especially in this place, where the received doctrine serves well enough to our present purpose.*

It appears from this passage—First, That Mr Locke had some system in his mind, perhaps not fully digested, to which we might be led, by raising our thoughts to a closer contemplation of things, and emancipating them from vulgar notions ; Secondly, That this system would lead so far from the notions on which the philosophy now in the world is built, that he thought proper to keep it within his own breast ; Thirdly, That it might be doubted whether this system differed so far from the common settled opinion in reality, as it seemed to do in words ; Fourthly, By this system, we might possibly be enabled to aim at some dim and seeming conception how matter might at first be made and begin to exist ; but it would give no aid in conceiving how a spirit might be made. These are the characteristics of that system which Mr Locke had in his mind, and thought it prudent to suppress. May they not lead to a probable conjecture, that it was the same, or something similar to that of Bishop Berkeley ?

---

* See above, p. 269, note § ; and below, under p. 197.—H.

† We are only by nature led to believe in the existence of an *outer* world, *because* we are by nature led to believe that we have an immediate knowledge of it as existing. Now, *Des Cartes* and the philosophers in general (is Reid an exception ?) hold that we are deluded in the latter belief; and yet they argue, on the authority of the former, that an external world exists.—H.

---

* Mr Stewart plausibly supposes that this passage contains rather an anticipation of Boscovich's Theory of Matter, than of Berke'ey's Theory of Idealism *Philosophical Essays*, p. 64. But see note F.—H.

According to Berkeley's system, God's creating the material world at such a time, means no more but that he decreed from that time, to produce ideas in the minds of finite spirits, in that order and according to those rules which we call the laws of Nature. [172] This, indeed, removes all difficulty, in conceiving how matter was created; and Berkeley does not fail to take notice of the advantage of his system on that account. But his system gives no aid in conceiving how a spirit may be made. It appears, therefore, that every particular Mr Locke has hinted, with regard to that system which he had in his mind, but thought it prudent to suppress, tallies exactly with the system of Berkeley. , If we add to this, that Berkeley's system follows from Mr Locke's, by very obvious consequence, it seems reasonable to conjecture, from the passage now quoted, that he was not unaware of that consequence, but left it to those who should come after him to carry his principles their full length, when they should by time be better established, and able to bear the shock of their opposition to vulgar notions. Mr Norris, in his "Essay towards the Theory of the Ideal or Intelligible World," published in 1701, observes, that the material world is not an object of sense; because sensation is within us, and has no object. Its existence, therefore, he says, is a collection of reason, and not a very evident one.

From this detail we may learn that the doctrine of ideas, as it was new-modelled by Des Cartes, looked with an unfriendly aspect upon the material world; and, although philosophers were very unwilling to give up either, they found it a very difficult task to reconcile them to each other. In this state of things, Berkeley, I think, is reputed the first who had the daring resolution to give up the material world altogether, as a sacrifice to the received philosophy of ideas.

But we ought not, in this historical sketch, to omit an author of far inferior name, Arthur Collier, Rector of Langford Magna, near Sarum. He published a book in 1713, which he calls "Clavis Universalis; or, a New Inquiry after Truth; being a demonstration of the non-existence or impossibility of an external world." His arguments are the same in substance with Berkeley's; and he appears to understand the whole strength of his cause. [173] Though he is not deficient in metaphysical acuteness, his style is disagreeable, being full of conceits, of new-coined words, scholastic terms, and perplexed sentences. He appears to be well acquainted with Des Cartes, Malebranche, and Norris, as well as with Aristotle and the schoolmen. But, what is very strange, it does not appear that he had ever heard of Locke's Essay, which had been published twenty-four years, or of Berkeley's "Principles of Knowledge," which had been published three years.

He says he had been ten years firmly convinced of the non-existence of an external world, before he ventured to publish his book. He is far from thinking, as Berkeley does, that the vulgar are of his opinion. If his book should make any converts to his system, (of which he expresses little hope, though he has supported it by nine demonstrations,) he takes pains to shew that his disciples, notwithstanding their opinion, may, with the unenlightened, speak of material things in the common style. He himself had scruples of conscience about this for some time; and, if he had not got over them, he must have shut his lips for ever; but he considered that God himself has used this style in speaking to men in the Holy Scripture, and has thereby sanctified it to all the faithful; and that to the pure all things are pure. He thinks his opinion may be of great use, especially in religion: and applies it, in particular, to put an end to the controversy about Christ's presence in the sacrament.

I have taken the liberty to give this short account of Collier's book, because I believe it is rare, and little known. I have only seen one copy of it, which is in the University library of Glasgow.* [174]

CHAPTER XI

BISHOP BERKELEY'S SENTIMENTS OF THE NATURE OF IDEAS.

I PASS over the sentiments of Bishop Berkeley, with respect to abstract ideas, and with respect to space and time, as things which may more properly be considered in another place. But I must take notice of one part of his system, wherein he

* This work, though of extreme rarity, and long absolutely unknown to the philosophers of this country, had excited, from the first, the attention of the German metaphysicians. A long analysis of it was given in the "Acta Eruditorum;" it is found quoted by Bilfinger, and other Leibnitzians; and was subsequently translated into German, with controversial notes by Professor Eschenbach of Rostock, in his "Collection of the principal writers who deny the Reality of their own Body and of the whole Corporeal World," 1756. The late learned Dr.Parr had long the intention of publishing the work of Collier along with some other rare metaphysical treatises. He did not, however, accomplish his purpose; which involved, likewise, an introductory disquisition by himself; but a complete impression of the "Clavis Universalis" and four other tracts, was found, after his death; and this having been purchased by Mr Lumley, has by him, been recently published, under the title—"Metaphysical Tracts, by English Philosophers of the Eighteenth Century," &c. London: 1837. A very small edition of the "Clavis" had been printed in Edinbur. h, by private subscription, in the previous year. A Life of Collier has likewise recently appeared.—H.

[172–174]

seems to have deviated from the common opinion about ideas.

Though he sets out in his principles of knowledge, by telling us that it is evident the objects of human knowledge are ideas, and builds his whole system upon this principle; yet, in the progress of it, he finds that there are certain objects of human knowledge that are not ideas, but things which have a permanent existence. The objects of knowledge, of which we have no ideas, are our own minds, and their various operations, other finite minds, and the Supreme Mind. The reason why there can be no ideas of spirits and their operations, the author informs us is this, That ideas are passive, inert, unthinking beings;* they cannot, therefore, be the image or likeness of things that have thought, and will, and active power; we have notions of minds, and of their operations, but not ideas. We know what we mean by thinking, willing, and perceiving; we can reason about beings endowed with those powers, but we have no ideas of them. A spirit or mind is the only substance or support wherein the unthinking beings or ideas can exist; but that this substance which supports or perceives ideas, should itself be an idea, or like an idea, is evidently absurd.

He observes, farther, Princip. sect. 142, that "all relations, including an act of the mind, we cannot properly be said to have an idea, but rather a notion of the relations or habitudes between things. [175] But if, in the modern way, the word idea is extended to spirits, and relations, and acts, this is, after all, an affair of verbal concern; yet it conduces to clearness and propriety, that we distinguish things very different by different names."

This is an important part of Berkeley's system, and deserves attention. We are led by it to divide the objects of human knowledge into two kinds. The first is ideas, which we have by our five senses; they have no existence when they are not perceived, and exist only in the minds of those who perceive them. The second kind of objects comprehends spirits, their acts, and the relations and habitudes of things. Of these we have notions, but no ideas. No idea can represent them, or have any similitude to them: yet we understand what they mean, and we can speak with understanding, and reason about them, without ideas.

This account of ideas is very different from that which Locke has given. In his system, we have no knowledge where we have no ideas. Every thought must have

an idea for its immediate object. In Berkeley's, the most important objects are known without ideas. In Locke's system, there are two sources of our ideas, sensation and reflection. In Berkeley's, sensation is the only source, because of the objects of reflection there can be no ideas. We know them without ideas. Locke divides our ideas into those of substances, modes, and relations. In Berkeley's system, there are no ideas of substances, or of relations; but notions only. And even in the class of modes, the operations of our own minds are things of which we have distinct notions; but no ideas.

We ought to do the justice to Malebranche to acknowledge that, in this point, as well as in many others, his system comes nearer to Berkeley's than the latter seems willing to own. That author tells us that there are four different ways in which we come to the knowledge of things. To know things by their ideas, is only one of the four. [176] He affirms that we have no idea of our own mind, or any of its modifications: that we know these things by consciousness, without ideas. Whether these two acute philosophers foresaw the consequences that may be drawn from the system of ideas, taken in its full extent, and which were afterwards drawn by Mr Hume, I cannot pretend to say. If they did, their regard to religion was too great to permit them to admit those consequences, or the principles with which they were necessarily connected.

However this may be, if there be so many things that may be apprehended and known without ideas, this very naturally suggests a scruple with regard to those that are left: for it may be said, If we can apprehend and reason about the world of spirits, without ideas, Is it not possible that we may apprehend and reason about a material world, without ideas? If consciousness and reflection furnish us with notions of spirits and of their attributes, without ideas, may not our senses furnish us with notions of bodies and their attributes, without ideas?

Berkeley foresaw this objection to his system, and puts it in the mouth of Hylas, in the following words:—Dial. 3, Hylas. "If you can conceive the mind of God, without having an idea of it, why may not I be allowed to conceive the existence of matter, notwithstanding that I have no idea of it?" The answer of Philonous is—"You neither perceive matter objectively, as you do an inactive being or idea, nor know it, as you do yourself, by a reflex act, neither do you immediately apprehend it by similitude of the one or the other, nor yet collect it by reasoning from that which you know immediately; all which makes the case of matter widely different from that of the Deity."

* Berkeley is one of the philosophers who really held the doctrine of ideas, erroneously, by Reid, attributed to all.—H.

Though Hylas declares himself satisfied with this answer, I confess I am not : because, if I may trust the faculties that God has given me, I do perceive matter objectively—that is, something which is extended and solid, which may be measured and weighed, is the immediate object of my touch and sight.* [177] And this object I take to be matter, and not an idea. And, though I have been taught by philosophers, that what I immediately touch is an idea, and not matter ; yet I have never been able to discover this by the most accurate attention to my own perceptions.

It were to be wished that this ingenious author had explained what he means by ideas, as distinguished from notions. The word notion, being a word in common language, is well understood. All men mean by it, the conception, the apprehension, or thought which we have of any object of thought. A notion, therefore, is an act of the mind conceiving or thinking of some object. The object of thought may be either something that is in the mind, or something that is not in the mind. It may be something that has no existence, or something that did, or does, or shall exist. But the notion which I have of that object, is an act of my mind which really exists while I think of the object ; but has no existence when I do not think of it. The word idea, in popular language, has precisely the same meaning as the word notion. But philosophers have another meaning to the word idea ; and what that meaning is, I think, is very difficult to say.

The whole of Bishop Berkeley's system depends upon the distinction between notions and ideas ; and, therefore, it is worth while to find, if we are able, what those things are which he calls ideas, as distinguished from notions.

For this purpose, we may observe, that he takes notice of two kinds of ideas—the ideas of sense, and the ideas of imagination. "The ideas imprinted on the senses by the Author of Nature," he says, " are called real things ; and those excited in the imagination, being less regular, vivid, and constant, are more properly termed ideas, or images of things, which they copy and represent. [178] But then our sensations, be they never so vivid and distinct, are nevertheless ideas ; that is, they exist in the mind, or are perceived by it as truly as the ideas of its own framing. The ideas of sense are allowed to have more reality in them—that is, to be more strong, orderly, and coherent—than the creatures of

the mind. They are also less dependent on the spirit, or thinking substance which perceives them, in that they are excited by the will of another and more powerful spirit ; yet still they are ideas ; and certainly no idea, whether faint or strong, can exist, otherwise than in a mind perceiving it." Principles, § 33.

From this passage we see that, by the ideas of sense, the author means sensations ;* and this, indeed, is evident from many other passages, of which I shall mention a few.—Principles, § 5. " Light and colours, heat and cold, extension and figure—in a word, the things we see and feel—what are they but so many sensations, notions, ideas, or impressions on the sense ?—and is it possible to separate, even in thought, any of these from perception ? For my part, I might as easily divide a thing from itself." § 18. "As for our senses, by them we have the knowledge only of our sensations, ideas, or those things that are immediately perceived by sense, call them what you will ;—but they do not inform us that things exist without the mind, or unperceived, like to those which are perceived." § 25. " All our ideas, sensations, or the things which we perceive, by whatever names they may be distinguished, are visibly inactive ; there is nothing of power or agency included in them."

This, therefore, appears certain—that, by the ideas of sense, the author meant the sensations we have by means of our senses. I have endeavoured to explain the meaning of the word sensation, Essay I., chap. 1, [p. 229,] and refer to the explication there given of it, which appears to me to be perfectly agreeable to the sense in which Bishop Berkeley uses it.*

As there can be no notion or thought but in a thinking being ; so there can be no sensation but in a sentient being. [179] It is the act or feeling of a sentient being ; its very essence consists in its being felt. Nothing can resemble a sensation, but a similar sensation in the same or in some other mind. To think that any quality in a thing that is inanimate can resemble a sensation, is a great absurdity. In all this, I cannot but agree perfectly with Bishop Berkeley ; and I think his notions of sensa-

* Does Reid mean to surrender his doctrine, that perception is a conception—that extension and figure are not known by sense, but are notions suggested on the occasion of sensation ? If he does not, his language in the text is inaccurate.—H.

* How it can be asserted that by ideas of sense Berkeley meant only what Reid did by sensations, I cannot comprehend. That the former used ideas of sense and sensations as convertible expressions, is true. But then Berkeley's sensation was equivalent to Reid's sensation plus his perception. This is manifest even by the passages adduced in the text. In that from § v. of the " Principles," Berkeley expressly calls extension and figure sensations. But it is a fundamental principle of Reid's philosophy, not only that neither extension nor figure, but that none of the primary qualities, are sensations. To make a single quotation—"'The primary qualities," he says, " are neither sensations, nor are they the resemblances of sensations"—Infra, p. 288.—H.

tion much more distinct and accurate than Locke's, who thought that the primary qualities of body are resemblances of our sensations,* but that the secondary are not.

That we have many sensations by means of our external senses, there can be no doubt; and, if he is pleased to call those ideas, there ought to be no dispute about the meaning of a word. But, says Bishop Berkeley, by our senses, we have the knowledge *only* of our sensations or ideas, call them which you will. I allow him to call them which he will; but I would have the word *only* in this sentence to be well weighed, because a great deal depends upon it.

For, if it be true that, by our senses, we have the knowledge of our sensations only, then his system must be admitted, and the existence of a material world must be given up as a dream. No demonstration can be more invincible than this. If we have any knowledge of a material world, it must be by the senses : but, by the senses, we have no knowledge but of our sensations only ; and our sensations have no resemblance of anything that can be in a material world.† The only proposition in this demonstration which admits of doubt is, that, by our senses, we have the knowledge of our sensations only, and of nothing else. If there are objects of the senses which are not sensations, his arguments do not touch them : they may be things which do not exist in the mind, as all sensations do; they may be things of which, by our senses, we have notions, though no ideas; just as, by consciousness and reflection, we have notions of spirits and of their operations, without ideas or sensations.‡ [180]

Shall we say, then, that, by our senses, we have the knowledge of our sensations only ; and that they give us no notion of anything but of our sensations ? Perhaps this has been the doctrine of philosophers, and not of Bishop Berkeley alone, otherwise he would have supported it by arguments. Mr Locke calls all the notions we have by our senses, ideas of sensation ; and in this has been very generally followed. Hence it seems a very natural inference, that ideas

of sensation are sensations. But philosophers may err : let us hear the dictates of common sense upon this point.

Suppose I am pricked with a pin, I ask, Is the pain I feel, a sensation ? Undoubtedly it is. There can be nothing that resembles pain in any inanimate being. But I ask again, Is the pin a sensation ? To this question I find myself under a necessity of answering, that the pin is not a sensation, nor can have the least resemblance to any sensation. The pin has length and thickness, and figure and weight. A sensation can have none of those qualities. I am not more certain that the pain I feel is a sensation, than that the pin is not a sensation ; yet the pin is an object of sense ; and I am as certain that I perceive its figure and hardness by my senses, as that I feel pain when pricked by it.*

Having said so much of the ideas of sense in Berkeley's system, we are next to consider the account he gives of the ideas of imagination. Of these he says, Principles, § 28—" I find I can excite ideas in my mind at pleasure, and vary and shift the scene as oft as I think fit. It is no more than willing ; and straightway this or that idea arises in my fancy ; and by the same power it is obliterated, and makes way for another. This making and unmaking of ideas, doth very properly denominate the mind active. Thus much is certain, and grounded on experience. Our sensations," he says, " are called real things ; the ideas of imagination are more properly termed ideas, or images of things ;"† that is, as I apprehend, they are the images of our sensations. [181] It might surely be expected that we should be well acquainted with the ideas of imagination, as they are of our making ; yet, after all the Bishop has said about them, I am at a loss to know what they are.

I would observe, in the *first* place, with regard to these ideas of imagination—that they are not sensations ; for surely sensation is the work of the senses, and not of imagination ; and, though pain be a sensation, the thought of pain, when I am not pained, is no sensation.

I observe, in the *second* place—that I can find no distinction between ideas of imagination and notions, which the author says are not ideas. I can easily distinguish be-

---

* Here again we have a criticism which proceeds on the erroneous implication, that Locke meant by *sensation* what Reid himself did. If for sensation we substitute *perception*, (and by sensation Locke denoted both sensation proper and perception proper,) there remains nothing to censure ; for Reid maintains that " our senses give us a direct and a distinct notion of the *primary* qualities, and inform us *what they are in themselves* " (*infra*, p. 237 ;) which is only Locke's meaning in other words. The same observation applies to many of the following passages.—H.

† See the last note.—H.

‡ But, unless that be admitted, which the natural conviction of mankind certifies, that we have an immediate perception—a consciousness—of external and extended existences, it makes no difference, in regard to the conclusion of the Idealist, whether what we are conscious of in perception be supposed an entity *in* the mind, (an idea in Reid's meaning,) or a modification *of* the mind, (a notion or conception.) See above, p. 128, notes *.—H.

* This illustration is taken from Des Cartes. In this paragraph, the term sensation is again not used in the extension given to it by the philosophers in question.—H.

† Berkeley's real words are—" The ideas imprinted on the Senses by the Author of Nature are called *real things*, and those excited in the Imagination being less regular, vivid and constant, are more properly termed *ideas or images of things*, which they copy and represent. But then our Sensations, be they never so vivid and distinct, are nevertheless ideas—that is, they exist in the mind, or are perceived by it, as truly as the ideas of its own framing." Sect. xxxiii.—H.

tween a notion and a sensation. It is one thing. to say, I have the sensation of pain. It is another thing to say, I have a notion of pain. The last expression signifies no more than that I understand what is meant by the word *pain*. The first signifies that I really feel pain. But I can find no distinction between the notion of pain and the imagination of it, or indeed between the notion of anything else, and the imagination of it. I can, therefore, give no account of the distinction which Berkeley makes between ideas of imagination and notions, which, he says, are not ideas. They seem to me perfectly to coincide.*

He seems, indeed, to say, that the ideas of imagination differ not in kind from those of the senses, but only in the degree of their regularity, vivacity, and constancy. "They are," says he, "less regular, vivid, and constant." This doctrine was afterwards greedily embraced by Mr Hume, and makes a main pillar of his system ; but it cannot be reconciled to common sense, to which Bishop Berkeley professes a great regard. For, according to this doctrine, if we compare the state of a man racked with the gout, with his state when, being at perfect ease, he relates what he has suffered, the difference of these two states is only this—that, in the last, the pain is less regular, vivid, and constant, than in the first. [182] We cannot possibly assent to this. . Every man knows that he can relate the pain he suffered, not only without pain, but with pleasure ; and that to suffer pain, and to think of it, are things which totally differ in kind, and not in degree only.†

We see, therefore, upon the whole, that, according to this system, of the most important objects of knowledge—that is, of

* Yet the distinction of *ideas*, strictly so called, and *notions*, is one of the most common and important in the philosophy of mind. Nor do we owe it, as has been asserted, to Berkeley. It was virtually taken by Des Cartes and the Cartesians, in their discrimination of ideas of imagination and ide s-of intelligence; it was in terms vindicated against Locke, by Serjeant, Stillingfleet, Norris, Z. Mayne, Bishop Brown, and others; Bonnet signalized it; and, under the contrast of *Anschauungen* and *Begriffe*, it has long been an established and classical discrimination with the philosophers of Germany. Nay, Reid himself suggests it in the distinction he requires between *imagination* and *conception*, a distinction which he unfortunately did not carry out, and which Mr Stewart still more unhappily again perverted. See below, p. 371. The terms *notion* and *conception*, (or more correctly *concept* in this sense,) should be reserved to express what we comprehend but cannot picture in imagination, such as a relation, a general term, &c. The word *idea*, as one prostituted to all meanings, it were perhaps better altogether to discard. As for the representations of imagination or phantasy, I would employ the terms *image* or *phantasm*, it being distinctly understood that these terms are applied to denote the *re-presentations*, not of our visible perceptions merely, as the terms taken literally would indicate, but of our sensible perceptions in general.—H.

† There is here a confusion between pain considered as a *feeling*, and as the *cognition of a feeling*, to which the philosophers would object.—H.

[182, 183]

spirits, of their operations, and of the relations of things—we have no ideas at all ; we have notions of them, but not ideas ; the ideas we have are those of sense, and those of imagination. The first are the sensations we have by means of our senses, whose existence no man can deny, because he is conscious of them ; and whose nature hath been explained by this author with great accuracy. As to the ideas of imagination, he hath left us much in the dark. He makes them images of our sensations ; though, according to his own doctrine, nothing can resemble a sensation but a sensation.† He seems to think that they differ from sensations only in the degree of their regularity, vivacity, and constancy. But this cannot be reconciled to the experience of mankind ; and, besides this mark, which cannot be admitted, he hath given us no other mark by which they may be distinguished from notions. Nay, it may be observed, that the very reason he gives why we can have no ideas of the acts of the mind about its ideas, nor of the relations of things, is applicable to what he calls ideas of imagination. Principles, § 142. "We may not, I think, strictly be said to have an idea of an active being, or of an action, although we may be said to have a notion of them. I have some knowledge or notion of my mind, and its acts about ideas, in as much as I know or understand what is meant by these words. [I will not say that the terms *Idea* and *Notion* may not be used convertibly, if the world will have it so. But yet it conduces to clearness and propriety that we distinguish things very different by different names.] It is also to be remarked, that all relations including an act of the mind, we cannot so properly be said to have an idea, but rather a notion of the relations and habitudes between things." From this it follows, that our imaginations are not properly ideas, but notions, because they include an act of the mind. [183] For he tells us, in a passage already quoted, that they are creatures of the mind, of its own framing, and that it makes and unmakes them as it thinks fit, and from this is properly denominated active. If it be a good reason why we have not ideas, but notions only of relations, because they include an act of the mind, the same reason must lead us to conclude, that our imaginations are notions and not ideas, since they are made and unmade by the mind as it thinks fit : and, from this, it is properly denominated active.‡

* That is, no *images* of them in the phantasy. Reid himself would not say that such could be *imagined.*—H.

† Berkeley does not say so in the meaning supposed.—H.

‡ Imagination is an ambiguous word; it means either the *act* of imagining, or the *product—i.e.*, the image imagined. Of the form r, Berkeley held, we can form a *notion*, but not an *idea*, in the sense he

U 2

When so much has been written, and so many disputes raised about ideas, it were desirable that we knew what they are, and to what category or class of beings they belong. In this we might expect satisfaction in the writings of Bishop Berkeley, if anywhere, considering his known accuracy and precision in the use of words; and it is for this reason that I have taken so much pains to find out what he took them to be.

After all, if I understand what he calls the ideas of sense, they are the sensations which we have by means of our five senses; but they are, he says, less properly termed ideas.

I understand, likewise, what he calls notions; but they, says he, are very different from ideas, though, in the modern way, often called by that name.

The ideas of imagination remain, which are most properly termed ideas, as he says; and, with regard to these, I am still very much in the dark. When I imagine a lion or an elephant, the lion or elephant is the object imagined. The act of the mind, in conceiving that object, is the notion, the conception, or imagination of the object. If besides the object, and the act of the mind about it, there be something called the idea of the object, I know not what it is.*

If we consult other authors who have treated of ideas, we shall find as little satisfaction with regard to the meaning of this philosophical term. [184] The vulgar have adopted it; but they only mean by it the notion or conception we have of any object, especially our more abstract or general notions. When it is thus put to signify the operation of the mind about objects, whether in conceiving, remembering, or perceiving, it is well understood. But philosophers will have ideas to be the objects of the mind's operations, and not the operations themselves. There is, indeed, great variety of objects of thought. We can think of minds, and of their operations; of bodies, and of their qualities and relations. If ideas are not comprehended under any of these classes, I am at a loss to comprehend what they are.

In ancient philosophy, ideas were said to be immaterial forms, which, according to one system, existed from all eternity; and, according to another, are sent forth from the objects whose form they are.† In modern philosophy, they are things in the mind, which are the immediate objects of all our thoughts, and which have no existence when we do not think of them. They are called the images, the resemblances, the

representatives of external objects of sense; yet they have neither colour, nor smell, nor figure, nor motion, nor any sensible quality. I revere the authority of philosophers, especially where they are so unanimous; but until I can comprehend what they mean by ideas, I must think and speak with the vulgar.

In sensation, properly so called, I can distinguish two things—the mind, or sentient being, and the sensation. Whether the last is to be called a feeling or an operation, I dispute not; but it has no object distinct from the sensation itself. If in sensation there be a third thing, called an idea, I know not what it is.

In perception, in remembrance, and in conception, or imagination, I distinguish three things—the mind that operates, the operation of the mind, and the object of that operation.* [185] That the object perceived is one thing, and the perception of that object another, I am as certain as I can be of anything. The same may be said of conception, of remembrance, of love and hatred, of desire and aversion. In all these, the act of the mind about its object is one thing, the object is another thing. There must be an object, real or imaginary, distinct from the operation of the mind about it.† †Now, if in these operations the idea be a fourth thing different from the three I have mentioned, I know not what it is, nor have been able to learn from all that has been written about ideas. And if the doctrine of philosophers about ideas confounds any two of these things which I have mentioned as distinct—if, for example, it confounds the object perceived with the perception of that object, and represents them as one and the same thing—such doctrine is altogether repugnant to all that I am able to discover of the operations of my own mind; and it is repugnant to the common sense of mankind, expressed in the structure of all languages.

CHAPTER XII.

OF THE SENTIMENTS OF MR HUME.

Two volumes of the "Treatise of Human Nature" were published in 1739, and the third in 1740. The doctrine contained in this Treatise was published anew in a more popular form in Mr Hume's "Philosophical Essays," of which there have been various editions. What other authors, from the

---

uses the term; whereas, of the latter, we can form an *idea* by merely repeating the imaginary act.—H.

* On Reid's misconception on this point, see Note B.—H.

† Nothing by the *name* of *idea* was sent off from objects in the ancient philosophy.—H.

* See Note B.—H.

† If there be an *imaginary object* distinct from the act of imagination, where does it exist? It cannot be external to the mind—for, *ex hypothesi*, it is imaginary; and, if in the mind itself, distinct from the act of imagination—why, what is this but the very crudest doctrine of *species?* For Reid's puzzle, see Note B.—H.

time of Des Cartes, had called *ideas*, this author distinguishes into two kinds—to wit, *impressions* and *ideas*; comprehending under the first, all our sensations, passions, and emotions; and under the last, the faint images of these, when we remember or imagine them. [186]

He sets out with this, as a principle that needed no proof, and of which therefore he offers none—that all the perceptions of the human mind resolve themselves into these two kinds, *impressions* and *ideas*.

As this proposition is the foundation upon which the whole of Mr Hume's system rests, and from which it is raised with great acuteness indeed, and ingenuity, it were to be wished that he had told us upon what authority this fundamental proposition rests. But we are left to guess, whether it is held forth as a first principle, which has its evidence in itself; or whether it is to be received upon the authority of philosophers.

Mr Locke had taught us, that all the immediate objects of human knowledge are ideas in the mind. Bishop Berkeley, proceeding upon this foundation, demonstrated, very easily, that there is no material world. And he thought that, for the purposes both of philosophy and religion, we should find no loss, but great benefit, in the want of it. But the Bishop, as became his order, was unwilling to give up the world of spirits. He saw very well, that ideas are as unfit to represent spirits as they are to represent bodies. Perhaps he saw that, if we perceive only the ideas of spirits, we shall find the same difficulty in inferring their real existence from the existence of their ideas, as we find in inferring the existence of matter from the idea of it; and, therefore, while he gives up the material world in favour of the system of ideas, he gives up one-half of that system in favour of the world of spirits; and maintains that we can, without ideas, think, and speak, and reason, intelligibly about spirits, and what belongs to them.

Mr Hume shews no such partiality in favour of the world of spirits. He adopts the theory of ideas in its full extent; and, in consequence, shews that there is neither matter nor mind in the universe; nothing but impressions and ideas. What we call a *body*, is only a bundle of sensations; and what we call the *mind* is only a bundle of thoughts, passions, and emotions, without any subject. [187]

Some ages hence, it will perhaps be looked upon as a curious anecdote, that two philosophers of the eighteenth century, of very distinguished rank, were led, by a philosophical hypothesis, one, to disbelieve the existence of matter, and the other, to disbelieve the existence both of matter and of mind. Such an anecdote may not be uninstructive, if it prove a warning to [186—188]

philosophers to beware of hypotheses, especially when they lead to conclusions which contradict the principles upon which all men of common sense must act in common life.

The Egoists,* whom we mentioned before, were left far behind by Mr Hume; for they believed their own existence, and perhaps also the existence of a Deity. But Mr Hume's system does not even leave him a *self* to claim the property of his impressions and ideas.

A system of consequences, however absurd, acutely and justly drawn from a few principles, in very abstract matters, is of real utility in science, and may be made subservient to real knowledge. This merit Mr Hume's metaphysical writings have in a great degree.

We had occasion before to observe, that, since the time of Des Cartes, philosophers, in treating of the powers of the mind, have, in many instances, confounded things which the common sense of mankind has always led them to distinguish, and which have different names in all languages. Thus, in the perception of an external object, all languages distinguish three things— the *mind* that perceives, the operation of that mind, which is called *perception*, and the *object* perceived.† Nothing appears more evident to a mind untutored by philosophy, than that these three are distinct things, which, though related, ought never to be confounded. [188] The structure of all languages supposes this distinction, and is built upon it. Philosophers have introduced a fourth thing in this process, which they call the *idea* of the object, which is supposed to be an image, or representative of the object, and is said to be the immediate object. The vulgar know nothing about this idea; it is a creature of philosophy, introduced to account for and explain the manner of our perceiving external objects.

* In supplement to note § at p 289, *supra*, in regard to the pretended sect of Egoists, there is to be added the following notices, which I did not recollect till after that note was set:—

Wolf, (*Psychologia Rationalis*, § 39,) after dividing Idealists into *Egoists* and *Pluralists*, says, *inter alia*, of the former :—"Fuit paucis æthinc annis asseclâ quidam *Malebranchii*, Parisiis, qui Egoismum professus est (quod mirum mihi videtur) asseclas et ipse nactus est." In his *Vernünftige Gedanken von Gott*, &c., c. 1, § 2, he also mentions this *allerseltsamste Secte.* There is also an oration by Christopher Matthaeus Pfaff, the Chancellor of Tuebingen— "*De Egoismo, nova philosophica haeresi*," in 1722—which I have not seen.—Thus, what I formerly hazarded, is still farther confirmed. All is vague and contradictory hearsay in regard to the Egoists. The French place them in Scotland; the Scotch in Holland; the Germans in France; and they are variously stated as the immediate disciples of Des Cartes, Malebranche, Spinoza. There is certainly no reason why an Egoistical Idealism should not have been explicitly promulgated before Fichte, (whose doctrine, however, is not the same;) but I have, as yet, seen no satisfactory grounds on which it can be shewn that this had actually been done.—H.

† See Notes B and C.—H.

It is pleasant to observe that, while philosophers, for more than a century, have been labouring, by means of ideas, to explain perception and the other operations of the mind, those ideas have by degrees usurped the place of perception, object, and even of the mind itself, and have supplanted those very things they were brought to explain. Des Cartes reduced all the operations of the understanding to perception ; and what can be more natural to those who believe that they are only different modes of perceiving ideas in our own minds ?   Locke confounds ideas sometimes with the perception of an external object, sometimes with the external object itself. In Berkeley's system, the idea is the only object, and yet is often confounded with the perception of it. But, in Hume's, the idea or the impression, which is only a more lively idea, is mind, perception, and object, all in one : so that, by the term perception, in Mr Hume's system, we must understand the mind itself, all its operations, both of understanding and will, and all the objects of these operations. Perception taken in this sense he divides into our more lively perceptions, which he calls *impressions*,* and the less lively, which he calls *ideas*.   To prevent repetition, I must here refer the reader to some remarks made upon this division, Essay I. chap. 1, in the explication there given of the words, *perceive*, *object*, *impression*. [pp. 222, 223, 226.]

Philosophers have differed very much with regard to the origin of our ideas, or the sources whence they are derived. The Peripatetics held that all knowledge is derived originally from the senses ;† and this ancient doctrine seems to be revived by some late French philosophers, and by Dr Hartley and Dr Priestley among the British. [189] Des Cartes maintained, that many of our ideas are innate. Locke opposed the doctrine of innate ideas with much zeal, and employs the whole first book of his Essay against it. But he admits two different sources of ideas . the operations of our external senses, which he calls *sensation*, by which we get all our ideas of body, and its attributes ; and *reflection* upon the operations of our minds, by which we get the ideas of everything belonging to the mind. The main design of the second book of Locke's " Essay," is to shew, that all our simple ideas, without exception, are derived from the one or the other, or both of these sources. In doing this, the author is led into some paradoxes, although, in general, he is not fond of paradoxes : And had he foreseen all the consequences that may be drawn from his account of the origin of our ideas, he would probably have examined it more carefully.*

Mr Hume adopts Locke's account of the origin of our ideas ; and from that principle infers, that we have no idea of substance, corporeal or spiritual, no idea of power, no other idea of a cause, but that it is something antecedent, and constantly conjoined to that which we call its effect ; and, in a word, that we can have no idea of anything but our sensations, and the operations of mind we are conscious of.

This author leaves no power to the mind in framing its ideas and impressions ; and, no wonder, since he holds that we have no idea of power ; and the mind is nothing but that succession of impressions and ideas of which we are intimately conscious.

He thinks, therefore, that our impressions arise from unknown causes, and that the impressions are the causes of their corresponding ideas. By this he means no more but that they always go before the ideas ; for this is all that is necessary to constitute the relation of cause and effect. [190]

As to the order and succession of our ideas, he holds it to be determined by three laws of attraction or association, which he takes to be original properties of the ideas, by which they attract, as it were, or associate themselves with other ideas which either resemble them, or which have been contiguous to them in time and place, or to which they have the relations of cause and effect.

We may here observe, by the way, that the last of these three laws seems to be included in the second, since causation, according to him, implies no more than contiguity in time and place.†

* Mr Stewart (*Elem.* III. *Addenda* to vol I. p. 43) seems to think that the word *impression* was first introduced as a *technical* term, into the philosophy of mind, by Hume. This is not altogether correct. For, besides the instances which Mr Stewart himself adduces, of the illustration attempted, of the phænomena of memory from the analogy of an *impress* and a *trace*, words corresponding to *impression* were among the ancients familiarly applied to the processes of external perception, imagination, &c., in the Atomistic, the Platonic, the Aristotelian, and the Stoical philosophies ; while, among modern psychologists, (as Des Cartes and Gassendi,) the term was likewise in common use.—H.

† This is an incorrect, at least a too unqualified, statement.—H.

* At any rate, according to Locke, all our knowledge is a derivation from *experience*.—H.

† Mr Hume says—" I do not find that any philosopher has attempted to enumerate or class all the principles of Association ; a subject, however, that seems to me very worthy of curiosity. To me there appears to be only three principles of connection among ideas : Resemblance—Contiguity in time or place—Cause and Effect."—*Essays*, vol. ii., p. 24.—Aristotle, and, after him, many other philosophers, had, however, done this, and with even greater success than Hume himself. Aristotle's reduction is to the four following heads :—Proximity in time—Contiguity in place—Resemblance—Contrast. This is more correct than Hume's ; for Hume's second head ought to be divided into two ; while our contiguity in place, and contiguity in time, are, in fact, distinct. any *particular* events in the relation of cause and effect, is itself the result of their observed proximity in time and contiguity in place ; nay, to custom and this empirical connection, (as observed by Reid) does

[189, 190]

It is not my design at present to shew how Mr Hume, upon the principles he has borrowed from Locke and Berkeley, has, with great acuteness, reared a system of absolute scepticism, which leaves no rational ground to believe any one proposition, rather than its contrary : my intention in this place being only to give a detail of the sentiments of philosophers concerning ideas since they became an object of speculation, and concerning the manner of our perceiving external objects by their means.

CHAPTER XIII.

OF THE SENTIMENTS OF ANTHONY ARNAULD.

IN this sketch of the opinions of philosophers concerning ideas, we must not omit Anthony Arnauld, doctor of the Sorbonne, who, in the year 1683, published his book "Of True and False Ideas," in opposition to the system of Malebranche before mentioned. It is only about ten years since I could find this book, and I believe it is rare.* [191]

Though Arnauld wrote before Locke, Berkeley, and Hume, I have reserved to the last place some account of his sentiments, because it seems difficult to determine whether he adopted the common theory of ideas, or whether he is singular in rejecting it altogether as a fiction of philosophers.

The controversy between Malebranche and Arnauld necessarily led them to consider what kind of things ideas are—a point upon which other philosophers had very generally been silent. Both of them professed the doctrine universally received : that we perceive not material things immediately—that it is their ideas that are the immediate objects of our thought—and that it is in the idea of everything that we perceive its properties.

It is necessary to premise that both these authors use the word *perception*, as Des Cartes had done before them, to signify every operation of the understanding.† "To think, to know, to perceive, are the same thing," says Mr Arnauld, chap. v. def. 2. It is likewise to be observed, that the various operations of the mind are by both called *modifications* of the mind. Perhaps they were led into this phrase by the Cartesian doctrine, that the essence of the mind consists in thinking, as that of body consists in extension. I apprehend,

therefore, that, when they make sensation, perception, memory, and imagination, to be various modifications of the mind, they mean no more but that these are things which can only exist in the mind as their subject. We express the same thing, by calling them various modes of thinking, or various operations of the mind.*

The things which the mind perceives, says Malebranche, are of two kinds. They are either in the mind itself, or they are external to it. The things in the mind, are all its different modifications, its sensations, its imaginations, its pure intellections, its passions and affections. These are immediately perceived; we are conscious of them, and have no need of ideas to represent them to us. [192]

Things external to the mind, are either corporeal or spiritual. With regard to the last, he thinks it possible that, in another state, spirits may be an immediate object of our understandings, and so be perceived without ideas ; that there may be such an union of spirits as that they may immediately perceive each other, and communicate their thoughts mutually, without signs and without ideas.

But, leaving this as a problematical point, he holds it to be undeniable, that material things cannot be perceived immediately, but only by the mediation of ideas. He thought it likewise undeniable, that the idea must be immediately present to the mind, that it must touch the soul as it were, and modify its perception of the object.

From these principles we must necessarily conclude, either that the idea is some modification of the human mind, or that it must be an idea in the Divine Mind, which is always intimately present with our minds. The matter being brought to this alternative, Malebranche considers first all the possible ways such a modification may be produced in our mind as that we call an idea of a material object, taking it for granted always, that it must be an object perceived, and something different from the act of the mind in perceiving it. He finds insuperable objections against every hypothesis of such ideas being produced in our minds; and therefore concludes, that the immediate objects of perception are the ideas of the Divine Mind.

Against this system Arnauld wrote his book "Of True and False Ideas." He does not object to the alternative mentioned by Malebranche ; but he maintains, that ideas are modifications of our minds. And, finding no other modification of the

* *Modes*, or *modifications of mind*, in the Cartesian school, mean merely what some recent philosophers express by *states of mind* and include .both the *active* and *passive* phænomena of the conscious subject. The terms were used by Des Cartes as well as by his disciples.—H.

human mind which can be called the idea of an external object, he says it is only another word for perception. Chap. v., def. 3. [193] " I take the *idea* of an object, and the *perception* of an object, to be the same thing. I do not say whether there may be other things to which the name of idea may be given. But it is certain that there are ideas taken in this sense, and that these ideas are either attributes or modifications of our minds."*

This, I think, indeed, was to attack the system of Malebranche upon its weak side, and where, at the same time, an attack was least expected. Philosophers had been so unanimous in maintaining that we do not perceive external objects immediately,† but by certain representative images of them called *ideas*,‡ that Malebranche might well think his system secure upon that quarter, and that the only question to be determined was, in what subject those ideas are placed, whether in the human or in the divine mind?

But, says Mr Arnauld, those ideas are mere chimeras—fictions of philosophers; there are no such beings in nature; and, therefore, it is to no purpose to inquire whether they are in the divine or in the human mind. The only true and real ideas are our perceptions, which§ are acknowledged by all philosophers, and by Malebranche himself, to be acts or modifications of our own minds. He does not say that the fictitious ideas were a fiction of Malebranche. He acknowledges that they had been very generally maintained by the scholastic philosophers,‖ and points out, very judiciously, the prejudices that had led them into the belief of such ideas.

Of all the powers of our mind, the external senses are thought to be the best understood, and their objects are the most familiar. Hence we measure other powers by them, and transfer to other powers the language which properly belongs to them. The objects of sense must be present to the sense, or within its sphere, in order to their being perceived. Hence, by analogy, we are led to say of everything when we think of it, that it is present to the mind, or in the mind. [194] But this presence is metaphorical, or analogical only; and Arnauld calls it objective presence, to distinguish it from that local presence which is required in objects that are perceived by sense. But both being called by the same name, they are confounded together, and those things that belong only to real or local presence, are attributed to the metaphorical.

We are likewise accustomed to see objects by their images in a mirror, or in water; and hence are led, by analogy, to think that objects may be presented to the memory or imagination in some similar manner, by images, which philosopher have called *ideas*.

By such prejudices and analogies, Arnauld conceives, men have been led to believe that the objects of memory and imagination must be presented to the mind by images or ideas; and the philosophers have been more carried away by these prejudices than even the vulgar, because the use made of this theory was to explain and account for the various operations of the mind—a matter in which the vulgar take no concern.

He thinks, however, that Des Cartes had got the better of these prejudices, and that he uses the word idea as signifying the same thing with perception,* and is, therefore, surprised that a disciple of Des Cartes, and one who was so great an admirer of him as Malebranche was, should be carried away by them. It is strange, indeed, that the two most eminent disciples of Des Cartes and his contemporaries should differ so essentially with regard to his doctrine concerning ideas.†

I shall not attempt to give the reader an account of the continuation of this controversy between those two acute philosophers, in the subsequent defences and replies; because I have not access to see them. After much reasoning, and some animosity, each

---

* Arnauld did not allow that perceptions and ideas are *really* or *numerically* distinguished—*i.e.*, as one thing from another thing; not even that they are *modally* distinguished—*i.e.*, as a thing from its mode. He maintained that they are *really* identical, and only *rationally* discriminated as viewed in different relations; the indivisible mental modification being called a *perception*, by reference to the mind or thinking subject—an *idea*, by reference to the mediate object of this thought. Arnauld everywhere avows that he denies ideas only as existences distinct from the act itself of perception.—See *Oeuvres*, t. xxxviii pp. 187, 198, 199, 389.—H.

† Arnauld does not assert against Malebranche, "that we perceive external objects immediately"—that is, in themselves, and as existing. He was too accurate for this. By an *immediate* cognition, Reid means merely the negation of the intermediation of any third thing between the reality perceived and the percipient mind.—H.

‡ *Idea* was not the word by which representative images, distinct from the percipient act, had been commonly called; nor were philosophers at all unanimous in the admission of such vicarious objects.—See Notes G, L, M, N, O, &c.—H.

§ That is, *Perceptions*, (the cognitive acts,) but not *Ideas*, (the immediate objects of those acts.) The latter were not acknowledged by Malebranche and all philosophers to be mere acts or modifications of our own minds.—H.

‖ But by a different name.—H

* I am convinced that in this interpretation of Des Cartes' doctrine, Arnauld is right; for Des Cartes defines mental ideas—those, to wit, *of which we are conscious*—to be " *Cogitationes prout sunt tanquam imagines*—that is, thoughts considered in their representative capacity; nor is there any passage to be found in the writings of this philosopher, which, if properly understood, warrants the conclusion, that, by ideas *in the mind*, he meant aught distinct from the cognitive act. The double use of the term *idea* by Des Cartes has, however, led Reid and others into a misconception on this point. See Note N.—H.

† Reid's own doctrine is far more ambiguous.—H.

continued in his own opinion, and left his antagonist where he found him. [195] Malebranche's opinion of our seeing all things in God, soon died away of itself; and Arnauld's notion of ideas seems to have been less regarded than it deserved, by the philosophers that came after him ;* perhaps for this reason, among others, that it seemed to be, in some sort, given up by himself, in his attempting to reconcile it to the common doctrine concerning ideas.

From the account I have given, one would be apt to conclude that Arnauld totally denied the existence of ideas, in the philosophical sense of that word, and that he adopted the notion of the vulgar, who acknowledge no object of perception but the external object. But he seems very unwilling to deviate so far from the common track, and, what he had given up with one hand, he takes back with the other.

For, *first,* Having defined ideas to be the same thing with perceptions, he adds this qualification to his definition :—"I do not here consider whether there are other things that may be called ideas ; but it is certain there are ideas taken in this sense.† I believe, indeed, there is no philosopher who does not, on some occasions, use the word idea in this popular sense.

Secondly, He supports this popular sense of the word by the authority of Des Cartes, who, in his demonstration of the existence of God, from the idea of him in our minds, defines an idea thus :—" By the word *idea,* I understand that form of any thought, by the immediate perception of which I am conscious of that thought ; so that I can express nothing by words, with understanding, without being certain that there is in my mind the idea of that which is expressed by the words." This definition seems, indeed, to be of the same import with that which is given by Arnauld. But Des Cartes adds a qualification to it, which Arnauld, in quoting it, omits ; and which shews that Des Cartes meant to limit his definition to the idea then treated of—that is, to the idea of the Deity ; and that there are other ideas to which this definition does not apply. [196] For he adds :—" And thus I give the name of idea, not solely to the images painted in the phantasy ; nay, in this place, I do not at all give the name of ideas to those images, in so far as they are painted in the corporeal phantasy that is in some part of the brain, but only in so far as they inform the mind, turning its attention to that part of the brain."*

Thirdly, Arnauld has employed the whole of his sixth chapter, to shew that these ways of speaking, common among philosophers—to wit, *that we perceive not things immediately ; that it is their ideas that are the immediate objects of our thoughts; that it is in the idea of everything that we perceive its properties*—are not to be rejected, but are true when rightly understood. He labours to reconcile these expressions to his own definition of ideas, by observing, that every perception and every thought is necessarily conscious of itself, and reflects upon itself ; and that, by this consciousness and reflection, it is its own immediate object. Whence he infers, that the idea—that is, the perception—is the immediate object of perception. This looks like a weak attempt to reconcile two inconsistent doctrines by one who wishes to hold both.† It is true, that consciousness always goes along with perception ; but they are different operations of the mind, and they have their different objects. Consciousness is not perception, nor is the object of consciousness the object of perception.‡ The same may be said of

---

* The opinion of Arnauld in regard to the nature of ideas was by no means overlooked by subsequent philosophers. It is found fully detailed in almost every systematic course or compend of philosophy, which appeared for a long time after its first promulgation, and in many of these it is the doctrine recommended as the true. Arnauld's was indeed the opinion which latterly prevailed in the Cartesian school. From this it passed into other schools. Leibnitz, like Arnauld, regarded Ideas, Notions, Representations, as mere modifications of the mind, (what by his disciples, were called *material* ideas, like the cerebral ideas of Des Cartes, are out of the question,) and no cruder opinion than this has ever subsequently found a footing in any of the German systems.

" I don't know," says Mr Stewart, " of any author who, prior to Dr Reid, has expressed himself on this subject with so much justness and precision as Father Buffier, in the following passage of his Treatise on ' First Truths :'—

" ' If we confine ourselves to what is intelligible in our observations on *ideas,* we will say, they are nothing, but mere modifications of the mind as a thinking being. They are called *ideas* with regard to the object represented ; and *perceptions* with regard to the faculty representing. In this attempt he is, however, singularly unfortunate ; for, with the exception of Crousaz, all the examples he adduces to evince the prevalence of Arnauld's doctrine are only so many mistakes, so many instances, in fact, which might be alleged in confirmation of the very opposite conclusion. See *Edinburgh Review,* vol. iii., p. 181-198.—H.

† See following note.—H.

[195. 196]

* Des Cartes here refers to the other meaning which he gives to the term idea—that is, to denote the material motion, the organic affection of the brain, of which the mind is not conscious. On Reid's misapprehension of the Cartesian doctrine touching this matter, see Note N.—H.

† Arnauld's attempt is neither weak nor inconsistent. He had, in fact, a clearer view of the conditions of the problem than Reid himself, who has, in fact, confounded two opposite doctrines. See Note C.—H.

‡ On Reid's error in reducing consciousness to a special faculty, see Note H.—H.

every operation of mind that has an object. Thus, injury is the object of resentment. When I resent an injury, I am conscious of my resentment—that is, my resentment is the immediate and the only object of my consciousness; but it would be absurd to infer from this, that my resentment is the immediate object of my resentment. [197]

Upon the whole, if Arnauld—in consequence of his doctrine, that ideas, taken for representative images of external objects, are a mere fiction of the philosophers—had rejected boldly the doctrine of Des Cartes, as well as of the other philosophers, concerning those fictitious beings, and all the ways of speaking that imply their existence, I should have thought him more consistent with himself, and his doctrine concerning ideas more rational and more intelligible than that of any other author of my acquaintance who has treated of the subject.*

CHAPTER XIV.

REFLECTIONS ON THE COMMON THEORY OF IDEAS.

AFTER so long a detail of the sentiments of philosophers, ancient and modern, concerning ideas, it may seem presumptuous to call in question their existence. But no philosophical opinion, however ancient, however generally received, ought to rest upon authority. There is no presumption in requiring evidence for it, or in regulating our belief by the evidence we can find.

To prevent mistakes, the reader must again be reminded, that if by ideas are meant only the acts or operations of our minds in perceiving, remembering, or imagining objects, I am far from calling in question the existence of those acts; we are conscious of them every day and every hour of life; and I believe no man of a sound mind ever doubted of the real existence of the operations of mind, of which he is conscious. Nor is it to be doubted that, by the faculties which God has given us, we can conceive things that are absent, as well as perceive those that are within the reach of our senses; and that such conceptions may be more or less distinct, and

more or less lively and strong. We have reason to ascribe to the all-knowing and all-perfect Being distinct conceptions of all things existent and possible, and of all their relations; and if these conceptions are called his eternal ideas, there ought to be no dispute among philosophers about a word. [198] The ideas, of whose existence I require the proof, are not the operations of any mind, but supposed objects of those operations. They are not perception, remembrance, or conception, but things that are said to be perceived, or remembered, or imagined.

Nor do I dispute the existence of what the vulgar call the objects of perception. These, by all who acknowledge their existence, are called real things, not ideas. But philosophers maintain that, besides these, there are immediate objects of perception in the mind itself: that, for instance, we do not see the sun immediately, but an idea; or, as Mr Hume calls it, an impression in our own minds. This idea is said to be the image, the resemblance, the representative of the sun, if there be a sun. It is from the existence of the idea that we must infer the existence of the sun. But the idea, being immediately perceived, there can be no doubt, as philosophers think, of its existence.

In like manner, when I remember, or when I imagine anything, all men acknowledge that there must be something that is remembered, or that is imagined; that is, some object of those operations. The object remembered must be something that did exist in time past: the object imagined may be something that never existed.* But, say the philosophers, besides these objects which all men acknowledge, there is a more immediate object which really exists in the mind at the same time we remember or imagine. This object is an idea or image of the thing remembered or imagined.

The *first* reflection I would make on this philosophical opinion is, that it is directly contrary to the universal sense of men who have not been instructed in philosophy. When we see the sun or moon, we have no doubt that the very objects which we immediately see are very far distant from us, and from one another. We have not the least doubt that this is the sun and moon which God created some thousands of years ago, and which have continued to perform their revolutions in the heavens ever since. [199] But how are we astonished when the philosopher informs us that we are mistaken in all this; that the sun and moon which we see are not, as we imagine, many miles distant from us, and from each other,

---

* Reid's discontent with Arnauld's opinion—an opinion which is stated with great perspicuity by its author—may be used as an argument to shew that his own doctrine is, however ambiguous, that of intuitive or immediate perception. (See Note C.) Arnauld's theory is identical with the finer form of representative or mediate perception, and the difficulties of that doctrine were not overlooked by his great antagonist. Arnauld well objected that, when we see a horse, according to Malebranche, what we see is in reality God himself; but Malebranche well rejoined, that, when we see a horse, according to Arnauld, what we see is, in reality, only a modification of ourselves.—H.

* See Note B.—H

but that they are in our own mind; that they had no existence before we saw them, and will have none when we cease to perceive and to think of them; because the objects we perceive are only ideas in our own minds, which can have no existence a moment longer than we think of them!*

If a plain man, uninstructed in philosophy, has faith to receive these mysteries, how great must be his astonishment! He is brought into a new world, where everything he sees, tastes, or touches, is an idea —a fleeting kind of being which he can conjure into existence, or can annihilate in the twinkling of an eye.

After his mind is somewhat composed, it will be natural for him to ask his philosophical instructor, Pray, sir, are there then no substantial and permanent beings called the sun and moon, which continue to exist whether we think of them or not?

Here the philosophers differ. Mr Locke, and those that were before him, will answer to this question, that it is very true there are substantial and permanent beings called the sun and moon; but they never appear to us in their own person, but by their representatives, the ideas in our own minds, and we know nothing of them but what we can gather from those ideas.

Bishop Berkeley and Mr Hume would give a different answer to the question proposed. They would assure the querist that it is a vulgar error, a mere prejudice of the ignorant and unlearned, to think that there are any permanent and substantial beings called the sun and moon; that the heavenly bodies, our own bodies, and all bodies whatsoever, are nothing but ideas in our minds; and that there can be nothing like the ideas of one mind, but the ideas of another mind. [200] There is nothing in nature but minds and ideas, says the Bishop;—nay, says Mr Hume, there is nothing in nature but ideas only; for what we call a mind is nothing but a train of ideas connected by certain relations between themselves.

In this representation of the theory of ideas, there is nothing exaggerated or misrepresented, as far as I am able to judge; and surely nothing farther is necessary to shew that, to the uninstructed in philosophy, it must appear extravagant and visionary, and most contrary to the dictates of common understanding.

There is the less need of any farther proof of this, that it is very amply acknow-

ledged by Mr Hume in his Essay on the Academical or Sceptical Philosophy. "It seems evident," says he, "that men are carried, by a natural instinct or prepossession, to repose faith in their senses; and that, without any reasoning, or even almost before the use of reason, we always suppose an external universe, which depends not on our perception, but would exist though we and every sensible creature were absent or annihilated. Even the animal creation are governed by a like opinion, and preserve this belief of external objects in all their thoughts, designs, and actions."

"It seems also evident that, when men follow this blind and powerful instinct of nature, they always suppose the very images presented by the senses to be the external objects, and never entertain any suspicion that the one are nothing but representations of the other. This very table which we see white, and feel hard, is believed to exist independent of our perception, and to be something external to the mind which perceives it; our presence bestows not being upon it; our absence annihilates it not: it preserves its existence uniform and entire, independent of the situation of intelligent beings who perceive or contemplate it. [201]

" But this universal and primary notion of all men is soon destroyed by the slightest philosophy, which teaches us that nothing can ever be present to the mind, but an image or perception; and that the senses are only the inlets through which these images are received, without being ever able to produce any immediate intercourse between the mind and the object."

It is therefore acknowledged by this philosopher, to be a natural instinct or prepossession, an universal and primary opinion of all men, a primary instinct of nature, that the objects which we immediately perceive by our senses, are not images in our minds, but external objects, and that their existence is independent of us and our perception.

In this acknowledgment, Mr Hume indeed seems to me more generous, and even more ingenuous than Bishop Berkeley, who would persuade us that his opinion does not oppose the vulgar opinion, but only that of the philosophers; and that the external existence of a material world is a philosophical hypothesis, and not the natural dictate of our perceptive powers. The Bishop shews a timidity of engaging such an adversary, as a primary and universal opinion of all men. He is rather fond to court its patronage. But the philosopher intrepidly gives a defiance to this antagonist, and seems to glory in a conflict that was worthy of his arm. *Optat aprum aut fulvum descendere monte leonem.* After all, I suspect that a philo-

---

* Whether Reid himself do not virtually hold this last opinion, see Note C. At any rate, it is very incorrect to say that the *sun, moon,* &c., are, or can be, perceived by us as existent, and in their real distance in the heavens; all that we can be cognisant of (supposing that we are *immediately* percipient of the *non-ego*) is the rays of light emanating from them, and in contact and relation with our organ of sight. —H.

sopher who wages war with this adversary, will find himself in the same condition as a mathematician who should undertake to demonstrate that there is no truth in the axioms of mathematics.

A *second* reflection upon this subject is—that the authors who have treated of ideas, have generally taken their existence for granted, as a thing that could not be called in question ; and such arguments as they have mentioned incidentally, in order to prove it, seem too weak to support the conclusion. [202]

Mr Locke, in the introduction to his Essay, tells us, that he uses the word idea to signify whatever is the immediate object of thought ; and then adds, " I presume it will be easily granted me that there are such ideas in men's minds ; every one is conscious of them in himself ; and men's words and actions will satisfy him that they are in others." I am indeed conscious of perceiving, remembering, imagining; but that the objects of these operations are images in my mind, I am not conscious. I am satisfied, by men's words and actions, that they often perceive the same objects which I perceive, which could not be, if those objects were ideas in their own minds.

Mr Norris is the only author I have met with, who professedly puts the question, Whether material things can be perceived by us immediately ? He has offered four arguments to shew that they cannot. *First,* " Material objects are without the mind, and therefore there can be no union between the object and the percipient." *Answer,* This argument is lame, until it is shewn to be necessary that in perception there should be a union between the object and the percipient. *Second,* " Material objects are disproportioned to the mind, and removed from it by the whole diameter of Being." This argument I cannot answer, because I do not understand it.* *Third,* " Because,

if material objects were immediate objects of perception, there could be no physical science—things necessary and immutable being the only object of science." *Answer,* Although things necessary and immutable be not the immediate objects of perception, they may be immediate objects of other powers of the mind. *Fourth,* " If material things were perceived by themselves, they would be a true light to our minds, as being the intelligible form of our understandings, and consequently perfective of them, and indeed superior to them." If I comprehend anything of this mysterious argument, it follows from it, that the Deity perceives nothing at all, because nothing can be superior to his understanding, or perfective of it. [203]

There is an argument which is hinted at by Malebranche, and by several other authors, which deserves to be more seriously considered. As I find it most clearly expressed and most fully urged by Dr Samuel Clarke, I shall give it in his words, in his second reply to Leibnitz, § 4. " The soul, without being present to the images of the things perceived, could not possibly perceive them. A living substance can only there perceive, where it is present, either to the

* This confession would, of itself, prove how superficially Reid was versed in the literature of philosophy. Norris's second argument is only the statement of a principle generally assumed by philosophers —that the relation of knowledge infers a correspondence of nature between the subject knowing, and the object known. This principle has, perhaps, exerted a more extensive influence on speculation than any other ; and yet it has not been proved, and is incapable of proof—nay, is contradicted by the evidence of consciousness itself. To trace the influence of this assumption would be, in fact, in a certain sort, to write the history of philosophy ; for, though this influence has never yet been historically devel ped, it would be easy to shew that the belief, explicit or implicit, that what knows and what is immediately known must be of an analogous nature, lies at the root of almost every theory of cognition, from the very earliest to the very latest speculations. In the more ancient philosophy of Greece, three philosophers (Anaxagoras, Heraclitus, and Alcmæon) are found, who professed the opposite doctrine—that the condition of knowledge lies in the contrariety, in the natural antithesis, of subject and object. Aristotle, likewise, in his treatise *On the Soul,* expressly condemns the prevalent opinion, that the similar is only

cognisable by the similar ; but, in his *Nicomachian Ethics,* he reverts to the doctrine which, in the former work, he had rejected. With these exceptions, no principle, since the time of Empedocles, by whom it seems first to have been explicitly announced, has been more universally received, than this—that the *relation of knowledge* infers an *analogy of existence.* This analogy may be of two degrees. *What knows,* and *what is known,* may be either *similar* or the *same ;* and, i the principle itself be admitted, the latter alternative is the more philosophical. Without entering on details, I may here notice some of the more remarkable results of this principle, in both its degrees. The general principle, not, indeed, exclusively, but mainly, determined the admission of a representative perception, by disallowing the possibility of any consciousness, or immediate knowledge of matter, by a nature so different from it as mind ; and, in its two degrees, it determined the various hypotheses, by which it was attempted to explain the possibility of a representative or mediate perception of the external world. To this principle, in its lower potence—that what knows must be *similar* in nature to what is immediately known—we owe the *intentional species* of the Aristotelians, and the *ideas* of Malebranche and Berkeley. From this principle, in its higher potence—that what knows must be *identical* in nature with what is immediately known —there flow the *gnostic reasons* of the Platonists, the *pre-existing forms* or *species* of Theophrastus and Themistius, of Adelandus and Avicenna, the (mental) *ideas* of Des Cartes and Arnauld, the *representations, sensual ideas, &c.* of Leibnitz and Wolf, the *phænomena* of Kant, the *states* of Brown, and (shall we say ?) the vacillating doctrine of perception held by Reid himself. Mediately, this principle was the origin of many other famous theories :—of the hierarchical gradation of souls or faculties of the Aristotelians ; of the vehicular media of the Platonists ; of the hypotheses of a common intellect of Alexander, Themistius, Averroes, Cajetanus, and Zabarella ; of the vision in the deity of Malebranche ; and of the Cartesian and Leibnitzian doctrines of assistance and pre-established harmony. Finally, to this principle is to be ascribed the refusal of the evidence of consciousness to the primary fact, the duality of its perception ; and the unitarian schemes of Absolute Identity, Materialism, and Idealism, are the results.—H.

things themselves, (as the omnipresent God is to the whole universe,) or to the images of things, as the soul is in its proper *senso-rium.*"

Sir Isaac Newton expresses the same sentiment, but with his usual reserve, in a query only.

The ingenious Dr Porterfield, in his Essay concerning the motions of our eyes, adopts this opinion with more confidence. His words are: "How body acts upon mind, or mind upon body, I know not; but this I am very certain of, that nothing can act, or be acted upon, where it is not; and there-fore our mind can never perceive anything but its own proper modifications, and the various states of the sensorium, to which it is present: so that it is not the external sun and moon which are in the heavens, which our mind perceives, but only their image or representation impressed upon the sensorium. How the soul of a seeing man sees these images, or how it receives those ideas, from such agitations in the sensorium, I know not; but I am sure it can never perceive the external bodies themselves, to which it is not present."

These, indeed, are great authorities: but, in matters of philosophy, we must not be guided by authority, but by reason. Dr Clarke, in the place cited, mentions slightly, as the reason of his opinion, that "nothing can any more act, or be acted upon when it is not present, than it can be where it is not." [204] And again, in his third reply to Leibnitz, § 11—" We are sure the soul cannot perceive what it is not present to, because nothing can act, or be acted upon, where it is not." The same reason we see is urged by Dr Porterfield.

That nothing can act immediately where it is not, I think must be admitted: for I agree with Sir Isaac Newton, that power without substance is inconceivable. It is a consequence of this, that nothing can be acted upon immediately where the agent is not present: let this, therefore be granted. To make the reasoning conclusive, it is farther necessary, that, when we perceive objects, either they act upon us, or we act upon them. This does not appear self-evi-dent, nor have I ever met with any proof of it. I shall briefly offer the reasons why I think it ought not to be admitted.

When we say that one being acts upon another, we mean that some power or force is exerted by the agent, which produces, or has a tendency to produce, a change in the thing acted upon. If this be the meaning of the phrase, as I conceive it is, there appears no reason for asserting that, in perception, either the object acts upon the mind, or the mind upon the object.

An object, in being perceived, does not act at all. I perceive the walls of the room

[204, 205]

where I sit; but they are perfectly inactive, and therefore act not upon the mind. To be perceived, is what logicians call an ex-ternal denomination, which implies neither action nor quality in the object perceived.[*] Nor could men ever have gone into this notion, that perception is owing to some action of the object upon the mind, were it not that we are so prone to form our notions of the mind from some similitude we conceive between it and body. Thought in the mind is conceived to have some analogy to motion in a body : and, as a body is put in motion, by being acted upon by some other body ; so we are apt to think the mind is made to perceive, by some impulse it receives from the object. But reasonings, drawn from such analogies, ought never to be trusted. [205] They are, indeed, the cause of most of our errors with regard to the mind. And we might as well conclude, that minds may be measured by feet and inches, or weighed by ounces and drachms, because bodies have those properties.[+]

I see as little reason, in the second place, to believe that in perception the mind acts upon the object. To perceive an object is one thing, to act upon it is another; nor is the last at all included in the first. To say that I act upon the wall by looking at it, is an abuse of language, and has no meaning. Logicians distinguish two kinds of opera-tions of mind : the first kind produces no effect without the mind ; the last does. The first they call *immanent acts*, the se-cond *transitive*. All intellectual operations belong to the first class ; they produce no effect upon any external object. But, with-out having recourse to logical distinctions, every man of common sense knows, that to

---

[*] This passage, among others that follow, afford the foundation of an argument, to prove that Reid is not original in his doctrine of Perception ; but that it was borrowed from the speculations of cert in older philosophers, of which he was aware. See Note S.—H.

[+] This reasoning, which is not original to Reid, (see Note S,) is not clearly or precisely expressed. In asserting that " an object, in being perceived, does not act at all," our author cannot mean that it does not act upon the organ of sense ; for this would not only be absurd in itself, but in contradiction to his own doctrine—" it being," he says, " a law of our nature that we perceive not external objects un-less certain *impressions be made on the nerves and brain."* The assertion—" I perceive the walls of the room where I sit,-but they are perfectly inactive, and, therefore, act not on the mind," is equally in-correct in statement. *The walls of the room,* strictly so called, assuredly do not act on the mind or on the eye ; but the walls of the room, in this sense, are, in fact, no object of (visual) perception, at all. What we see in this instance, and what we loosely call the walls of the room, is only the light reflected from their surface in its relation to the organ of sight—i.e., colour ; but it cannot be affirmed that the rays of light do not act on and affect the retina, optic nerve, and brain. What Aristotle distinguished as the concomitants of sensation—as *extension, motion, position,* &c.—are, indeed, perceived without any relative passion of the sense. But, whatever may be Reid's meaning, it is, at best, vague and inexpli-cit.—H.

think of an object, and to act upon it, are very different things.

As we have, therefore, no evidence that, in perception, the mind acts upon the object, or the object upon the mind, but strong reasons to the contrary, Dr Clarke's argument against our perceiving external objects immediately falls to the ground.

This notion, that, in perception, the object must be contiguous to the percipient, seems, with many other prejudices, to be borrowed from analogy. In all the external senses, there must, as has been before observed, be some impression made upon the organ of sense by the object, or by something coming from the object. An impression supposes contiguity. Hence we are led by analogy to conceive something similar in the operations of the mind. Many philosophers resolve almost every operation of mind into impressions and feelings, words manifestly borrowed from the sense of touch. And it is very natural to conceive contiguity necessary between that which makes the impression, and that which receives it; between that which feels, and that which is felt. [206] And though no philosopher will now pretend to justify such analogical reasoning as this, yet it has a powerful influence upon the judgment, while we contemplate the operations of our minds, only as they appear through the deceitful medium of such analogical notions and expressions. *

When we lay aside those analogies, and reflect attentively upon our perception of the objects of sense, we must acknowledge that, though we are conscious of perceiving objects, we are altogether ignorant how it is brought about; and know as little how we perceive objects as how we were made. And, if we should admit an image in the mind, or contiguous to it, we know as little how perception may be produced by this image as by the most distant object. Why, therefore, should we be led, by a theory which is neither grounded on evidence, nor, if admitted, can explain any one phenomenon of perception, to reject the natural and immediate dictates of those perceptive powers, to which, in the conduct of life, we find a necessity of yielding implicit submission?

There remains only one other argument that I have been able to find urged against our perceiving external objects immediately. It is proposed by Mr Hume, who, in the essay already quoted, after acknowledging that it is an universal and primary opinion of all men, that we perceive external objects immediately, subjoins what follows:—

" But this universal and primary opinion of all men is soon destroyed by the slightest philosophy, which teaches us that nothing can ever be present to the mind but an image or perception ; and that the senses are only the inlets through which these images are received, without being ever able to produce any immediate intercourse between the mind and the object. The table, which we see, seems to diminish as we remove farther from it : but the real table, which exists independent of us, suffers no alteration. [207] It was, therefore, nothing but its image which was present to the mind. These are the obvious dictates of reason ; and no man who reflects ever doubted that the existences which we consider, when we say *this house*, and *that tree*, are nothing but perceptions in the mind, and fleeting copies and representations of other existences, which remain uniform and independent. So far, then, we are necessitated, by reasoning, to depart from the primary instincts of nature, and to embrace a new system with regard to the evidence of our senses."

We have here a remarkable conflict between two contradictory opinions, wherein all mankind are engaged. On the one side stand all the vulgar, who are unpractised in philosophical reseaches, and guided by the uncorrupted primary instincts of nature. On the other side stand all the philosophers, ancient and modern; every man, without exception, who reflects. In this division, to my great humiliation, I find myself classed with the vulgar.

The passage now quoted is all I have found in Mr Hume's writings upon this point: and, indeed, there is more reasoning in it than I have found in any other author; I shall, therefore, examine it minutely.

First, He tells us, that " this universal and primary opinion of all men is soon destroyed by the slightest philosophy, which teaches us that nothing can ever be present to the mind but an image or perception."

The phrase of being present to the mind has some obscurity; but I conceive he means being an immediate object of thought; an immediate object, for instance, of perception, of memory, or of imagination. If this be the meaning, (and it is the only pertinent one I can think of,) there is no more in this passage but an assertion of the proposition to be proved, and an assertion that philosophy teaches it. If this be so, I beg leave to dissent from philosophy till she gives me reason for what she teaches. [208] For, though common sense and my external senses demand my assent to their

---

* It is self-evident that, if a thing is to be an object *immediately* known, it must be known as it exists. Now, a body must exist in some definite part of space—in a certain *place*; it cannot, therefore, be immediately known *as existing*, except it be known *in its place*. But this supposes the mind to be immediately present to it in space.—H.

dictates upon their own authority, yet philosophy is not entitled to this privilege. But, that I may not dissent from so grave a personage without giving a reason, I give this as the reason of my dissent :—I see the sun when he shines ; I remember the battle of Culloden ;* and neither of these objects is an image or perception.

He tells us, in the next place, "That the senses are only the inlets through which these images are received."

I know that Aristotle and the schoolmen taught that images or species flow from objects, and are let in by the senses, and strike upon the mind ; but this has been so effectually refuted by Des Cartes, by Malebranche, and many others, that nobody now pretends to defend it. Reasonable men consider it as one of the most unintelligible and unmeaning parts of the ancient system. To what cause is it owing that modern philosophers are so prone to fall back into this hypothesis, as if they really believed it ? For, of this proneness I could give many instances besides this of Mr Hume ; and I take the cause to be, that images in the mind, and images let in by the senses, are so nearly allied, and so strictly connected, that they must stand or fall together. The old system consistently maintained both : but the new system has rejected the doctrine of images let in by the senses, holding, nevertheless, that there are images in the mind ; and, having made this unnatural divorce of two doctrines which ought not to be put asunder, that which they have retained often leads them back involuntarily to that which they have rejected.

Mr Hume surely did not seriously believe that an image of sound is let in by the ear, an image of smell by the nose, an image of hardness and softness, of solidity and resistance, by the touch. For, besides the absurdity of the thing, which has often been shewn, Mr Hume, and all modern philosophers, maintain that the images which are the immediate objects of perception have no existence when they are not perceived ; whereas, if they were let in by the senses, they must be, before they are perceived, and have a separate existence. [209]

He tell us, farther, that philosophy teaches that the senses are unable to produce any immediate intercourse between the mind and the object. Here, I still require the reasons that philosophy gives for this ; for, to my apprehension, I immediately perceive external objects, and this, I conceive is the immediate intercourse here meant.

Hitherto I see nothing that can be called

an argument. Perhaps it was intended only for illustration. The argument, the only argument, follows :—

The table which we see, seems to diminish as we remove farther from it ; but the real table, which exists independent of us suffers no alteration. It was, therefore, nothing but its image which was presented to the mind. These are the obvious dictates of reason.

To judge of the strength of this argument, it is necessary to attend to a distinction which is familiar to those who are conversant in the mathematical sciences.—I mean the distinction between real and apparent magnitude. The real magnitude of a line is measured by some known measure of length—as inches, feet, or miles : the real magnitude of a surface or solid, by known measures of surface or of capacity. This magnitude is an object of touch only, and not of sight ; nor could we even have had any conception of it, without the sense of touch ; and Bishop Berkeley, on that account, calls it *tangible magnitude.**

Apparent magnitude is measured by the angle which an object subtends at the eye. Supposing two right lines drawn from the eye to the extremities of the object making an angle, of which the object is the subtense, the apparent magnitude is measured by this angle. [210] This apparent magnitude is an object of sight, and not of touch. Bishop Berkeley calls it *visible magnitude.*

If it is asked what is the apparent magnitude of the sun's diameter, the answer is, that it is about thirty-one minutes of a degree. But, if it is asked what is the real magnitude of the sun's diameter, the answer must be, so many thousand miles, or so many diameters of the earth. From which it is evident that real magnitude, and apparent magnitude, are things of a different nature, though the name of magnitude is given to both. The first has three dimensions, the last only two ; the first is measured by a line, the last by an angle.

From what has been said, it is evident that the real magnitude of a body must continue unchanged, while the body is unchanged. This we grant. But is it likewise evident, that the apparent mag-

---

* The sun can be no immediate object of consciousness in perception, but only certain rays in connection with the eye. The battle of Culloden can be no immediate object of consciousness in recollection, but only a certain representation by the mind itself.—H.

* The doctrine of Reid—that *real* magnitude or extension is the object of touch, and of touch alone—is altogether untenable. For, in the *first* place, magnitude appears greater or less in proportion to the different size of the tactile organ in different subjects ; thus, an apple is larger to the hand of a child than to the hand of an adult. Touch, therefore, can, at best, afford a knowledge of the relation of magnitudes, in proportion to the organ of this or that individual. But, in the *second* place, even in the same individual, the same object appears greater or less, according as it is touched by one part of the body or by another. On this subject, see Weber's "Annotationes de Pulsu, Resorptione, Auditu et Tactu ;" Leipsic, 1834.—H

nitude must continue the same while the body is unchanged? So far otherwise, that every man who knows anything of mathematics can easily demonstrate, that the same individual object, remaining in the same place, and unchanged, must necessarily vary in its apparent magnitude, according as the point from which it is seen is more or less distant; and that its apparent length or breadth will be nearly in a reciprocal proportion to the distance of the spectator. This is as certain as the principles of geometry.*

We must likewise attend to this—that, though the real magnitude of a body is not originally an object of sight, but of touch, yet we learn by experience to judge of the real magnitude in many cases by sight. We learn by experience to judge of the distance of a body from the eye within certain limits; and, from its distance and apparent magnitude taken together, we learn to judge of its real magnitude. [211]

And this kind of judgment, by being repeated every hour and almost every minute of our lives, becomes, when we are grown up, so ready and so habitual, that it very much resembles the original perceptions of our senses, and may not improperly be called *acquired.perception.*

Whether we call it judgment or acquired perception is a verbal difference. But it is evident that, by means of it, we often discover by one sense things which are properly and naturally the objects of another. Thus I can say, without impropriety, I hear a drum, I hear a great bell, or I hear a small bell; though it is certain that the figure or size of the sounding body is not originally an object of hearing. In like manner, we learn by experience how a body of such a real magnitude and at such a distance appears to the eye. But neither its real magnitude, nor its distance from the eye, are properly objects of sight, any more than the form of a drum or the size of a bell, are properly objects of hearing.

If these things be considered, it will appear that Mr Hume's argument hath no force to support his conclusion—nay, that it leads to a contrary conclusion. The argument is this: the table we see seems to diminish as we remove farther from it; that is, its apparent magnitude is diminished; but the real table suffers no alteration—to wit, in its real magnitude: therefore, it is

not the real table we see. I admit both the premises in this syllogism, but I deny the conclusion. The syllogism has what the logicians call two middle terms: apparent magnitude is the middle term in the first premise; real magnitude in the second. Therefore, according to the rules of logic, the conclusion is not justly drawn from the premises; but, laying aside the rules of logic, let us examine it by the light of common sense.

Let us suppose, for a moment, that it is the real table we. see: Must not this real table seem to diminish as we remove farther from it? It is demonstrable that it must. How then can this apparent diminution be an argument that it is not the real table? [212] When that which must happen to the real table, as we remove farther from it, does actually happen to the table we see, it is absurd to conclude from this, that it is not the real table we see.* It is evident, therefore, that this ingenious author has imposed upon himself by confounding real magnitude with apparent magnitude, and that his argument is a mere sophism.

I observed that Mr Hume's argument not only has no strength to support his conclusion, but that it leads to the contrary conclusion—to wit, that it is the real table we see;* for this plain reason, that the table we see has precisely that apparent magnitude which it is demonstrable the real table must have when placed at that distance.

This argument is made much stronger by considering that the real table may be placed successively at a thousand different distances, and, in every distance, in a thousand different positions; and it can be determined demonstratively, by the rules of geometry and perspective, what must be its apparent magnitude and apparent figure, in each of those distances and positions. Let the table be placed successively in as many of those different distances and different positions as you will, or in them all; open your eyes and you shall see a table precisely of that apparent magnitude, and that apparent figure, which the real table must have in that distance and in that position. Is not this a strong argument that it is the real table you see?*

In a word, the appearance of a visible object is infinitely diversified, according to its distance and position. The visible appearances are innumerable, when we confine ourselves to one object, and they are multiplied according to the variety of objects. Those appearances have been matter of speculation to ingenious men, at least since the time of Euclid. They have accounted for all this variety, on the supposition that the objects we see are external,

* The whole confusion and difficulty in this matter arises from not determining what is the *true object* in visual perception. This is not any distant thing, but merely the rays of light in immediate relation to the organ. We therefore, see a *different object* at every movement, by which a different complement of rays is reflected to the eye. The things from which these rays are reflected are not, in truth, perceived at all; and to conceive them as objects of perception is therefore erroneous, and productive of error.—H.

* See last note.—H.

and not in the mind itself. [213] The rules they have demonstrated about the various projections of the sphere, about the appearances of the planets in their progressions, stations, and retrogradations, and all the rules of perspective, are built on the supposition that the objects of sight are external. They can each of them be tried in thousands of instances. In many arts and professions, innumerable trials are daily made; nor were they ever found to fail in a single instance. Shall we say that a false supposition, invented by the rude vulgar, has been so lucky in solving an infinite number of phænomena of nature? This, surely, would be a greater prodigy than philosophy ever exhibited : add to this, that, upon the contrary hypothesis—to wit, that the objects of sight are internal—no account can be given of any one of those appearances, nor any physical cause assigned why a visible object should, in any one case, have one apparent figure and magnitude rather than another.

Thus, I have considered every argument I have found advanced to prove the existence of ideas, or images of external things, in the mind; and, if no better arguments can be found, I cannot help thinking that the whole history of philosophy has never furnished an instance of an opinion so unanimously entertained by philosophers upon so slight grounds.

A *third* reflection I would make upon this subject is, that philosophers, notwithstanding their unanimity as to the existence of ideas,* hardly agree in any one thing else concerning them. If ideas be not a mere fiction, they must be, of all objects of human knowledge, the things we have best access to know, and to be acquainted with; yet there is nothing about which men differ so much.

Some have held them to be self-existent, others to be in the Divine mind, others in our own minds, and others in the brain or *sensorium.* I considered the hypothesis of images in the brain, in the fourth chapter of this essay. As to images in the mind, if anything more is meant by the image of an object in the mind than the thought of that object, I know not what it means. [214] The distinct conception of an object may, in a metaphorical or analogical sense, be called an *image* of it in the mind. But this image is only the conception of the object, and not the object conceived. It is an act of the mind, and not the object of that act.†

Some philosophers will have our ideas, or a part of them, to be innate; others will have them all to be adventitious : some derive them all from the senses alone; others from sensation and reflection : some think

they are fabricated by the mind itself; others that they are produced by external objects; others that they are the immediate operation of the Deity; others say, that impressions are the causes of ideas, and that the causes of impressions are unknown : some think that we have ideas only of material objects, but none of minds, of their operations, or of the relations of things; others will have the immediate object of every thought to be 'an idea : some think we have abstract ideas, and that by this chiefly we are distinguished from the brutes; others maintain an abstract idea to be an absurdity, and that there can be no such thing : with some they are the immediate objects of thought, with others the only objects.

A *fourth* reflection is, that ideas do not make any of the operations of the mind to be better understood, although it was probably with that view that they have been first invented, and afterwards so generally received.

We are at a loss to know how we perceive distant objects; how we remember things past; how we imagine things that have no existence. Ideas in the mind seem to account for all these operations : they are all by the means of ideas reduced to one operation—to a kind of feeling, or immediate perception of things present and in contact with the percipient; and feeling is an operation so familiar that we think it needs no explication, but may serve to explain other operations. [215]

But this feeling, or immediate perception, is as difficult to be comprehended as the things which we pretend to explain by it. Two things may be in contact without any feeling or perception; there must therefore be in the percipient a power to feel or to perceive. How this power is produced, and how it operates, is quite beyond the reach of our knowledge. As little can we know whether this power must be limited to things present, and in contact with us. Nor can any man pretend to prove that the Being who gave us the power to perceive things present, may not give us the power to perceive things that are distant,* to remember things past, and to conceive things that never existed.

Some philosophers have endeavoured to make all our senses to be only different modifications of touch;† a theory which serves only to confound things that are different, and to perplex and darken things that are clear. The theory of ideas resembles this, by reducing all the operations of the

* An *immediate* perception of things distant, is a contradiction in terms.—H.
† If an *immediate* perception be supposed, it can only be rationally supposed of objects as in contact with the organs of sense. But, in this case, all the senses would, as Democritus held, be, in a certain sort, only modifications of touch.—H.

x

human understanding to the perception of ideas in our own minds. This power of perceiving ideas is as inexplicable as any of the powers explained by it: and the contiguity of the object contributes nothing at all to make it better understood; because there appears no connection between contiguity and perception, but what is grounded on prejudices drawn from some imagined similitude between mind and body, and from the supposition that, in perception, the object acts upon the mind, or the mind upon the object. We have seen how this theory has led philosophers to confound those operations of mind, which experience teaches all men to be different, and teaches them to distinguish in common language; and that it has led them to invent a language inconsistent with the principles upon which all language is grounded.

The *last* reflection I shall make upon this theory, is—that the natural and necessary consequences of it furnish a just prejudice against it to every man who pays a due regard to the common sense of mankind. [216] Not to mention that it led the Pythagoreans and Plato to imagine that we see only the shadows of external things, and not the things themselves,* and that it gave rise to the Peripatetic doctrine of sensible *species*, one of the greatest absurdities of that ancient system, let us only consider the fruits it has produced since it was newmodelled by Des Cartes. That great reformer in philosophy saw the absurdity of the doctrine of ideas coming from external objects, and refuted it effectually, after it had been received by philosophers for thousands of years; but he still retained ideas in the brain and in the mind.† Upon this foundation all our modern systems of the powers of the mind are built. And the tottering state of those fabrics, though built by skilful hands, may give a strong suspicion of the unsoundness of the foundation.

It was this theory of ideas that led Des Cartes, and those that followed him, to think it necessary to prove, by philosophical arguments, the existence of material objects. And who does not see that philosophy must make a very ridiculous figure in the eyes of sensible men, while it is employed in mustering up metaphysical arguments, to prove that there is a sun and a moon, an earth and a sea? Yet we find these truly great men, Des Cartes, Malebranche, Arnauld, and Locke, seriously employing themselves in this argument.‡

Surely their principles led them to think

* See above, p. 262 col. b, note *—.H
† See Note N.— H.
‡ If Reid do not allow that we are immediately cognitive or conscious of the *non-ego*, his own doctrine of perception differs not from that of other philosophers in the necessity for this proof. H

that all men, from the beginning of the world, believed the existence of these things upon insufficient grounds, and to think that they would be able to place upon a more rational foundation this universal belief of mankind. But the misfortune is, that all the laboured arguments they have advanced, to prove the existence of those things we see and feel, are mere sophisms: Not one of them will bear examination.

I might mention several paradoxes, which Mr Locke, though by no means fond of paradoxes, was led into by this theory of ideas. [217] Such as, that the secondary qualities of body are no qualities of body at all, but sensations of the mind: That the primary qualities of body are resemblances of our sensations: That we have no notion of duration, but from the succession of ideas in our minds: That personal identity consists in consciousness; so that the same individual thinking being may make two or three different persons, and several different thinking beings make one person: That judgment is nothing but a perception of the agreement or disagreement of our ideas. Most of these paradoxes I shall have occasion to examine.

However, all these consequences of the doctrine of ideas were tolerable, compared with those which came afterwards to be discovered by Berkeley and Hume:—That there is no material world: No abstract ideas or notions: That the mind is only a train of related impressions and ideas, without any subject on which they may be impressed: That there is neither space nor time, body nor mind, but impressions and ideas only: And, to sum up all, That there is no probability, even in demonstration itself, nor any one proposition more probable than its contrary.

These are the noble fruits which have grown upon this theory of ideas, since it began to be cultivated by skilful hands. It is no wonder that sensible men should be disgusted at philosophy, when such wild and shocking paradoxes pass under its name. However, as these paradoxes have, with great acuteness and ingenuity, been deduced by just reasoning from the theory of ideas, they must at last bring this advantage, that positions so shocking to the common sense of mankind, and so contrary to the decisions of all our intellectual powers, will open men's eyes, and break the force of the prejudice which hath held them entangled in that theory. [218]

CHAPTER XV.

ACCOUNT OF THE SYSTEM OF LEIBNITZ.

THERE is yet another system concerning perception, of which I shall give some account.

count, because of the fame of its author. It is the invention of the famous German philosopher Leibnitz, who, while he lived, held the first rank among the Germans in all parts of philosophy, as well as in mathematics, in jurisprudence, in the knowledge of antiquities, and in every branch both of science and of literature. He was highly respected by emperors, and by many kings and princes, who bestowed upon him singular marks of their esteem. He was a particular favourite of our Queen Caroline, consort of George II., with whom he continued his correspondence by letters, after she came to the crown of Britain, till his death.

The famous controversy between him and the British mathematicians, whether he or Sir Isaac Newton was the inventor of that noble improvement in mathematics, called by Newton, *the method of fluxions*, and by Leibnitz *the differential method*, engaged the attention of the mathematicians in Europe for several years. He had likewise a controversy with the learned and judicious Dr Samuel Clarke, about several points of the Newtonian philosophy which he disapproved. The papers which gave occasion to this controversy, with all the replies and rejoinders, had the honour to be transmitted from the one party to the other, through the hands of Queen Caroline, and were afterwards published.

His authority, in all matters of philosophy, is still so great in most parts of Germany, that they are considered as bold spirits, and a kind of heretics, who dissent from him in anything. [219] Carolus* Wolfius, the most voluminous writer in philosophy of this age, is considered as the great interpreter and advocate of the Leibnitzian system, and reveres as an oracle whatever has dropped from the pen of Leibnitz. This author proposed two great works upon the mind. The first, which I have seen, he published with the title of " Psychologia Empirica, seu Experimentalis."† The other was to have the title of " Psychologia Rationalis ;" and to it he refers for his explication of the theory of Leibnitz with regard to the mind. But whether it was published I have not learned.‡

I must, therefore, take the short account I am to give of this system from the writings of Leibnitz himself, without the light which his interpreter Wolfius may have thrown upon it.

Leibnitz conceived the whole universe,

bodies as well as minds, to be made up of monads—that is, simple substances, each of which is, by the Creator, in the beginning of its existence, endowed with certain active and perceptive powers. A monad, therefore, is an active substance, simple, without parts or figure, which has within itself the power to produce all the changes it undergoes from the beginning of its existence to eternity. The changes which the monad undergoes, of what kind soever, though they may seem to us the effect of causes operating from without, yet they are only the gradual and successive evolutions of its own internal powers, which would have produced all the same changes and motions, although there had been no other being in the universe.

Every human soul is a monad joined to an organized body, which organized body consists of an infinite number of monads, each having some degree of active and of perceptive power in itself. But the whole machine of the body has a relation to that monad which we call the soul, which is, as it were, the centre of the whole. [220]

As the universe is completely filled with monads, without any chasm or void, and thereby every body acts upon every other body, according to its vicinity or distance, and is mutually reacted upon by every other body, it follows, says Leibnitz, that every monad is a kind of living mirror, which reflects the whole universe, according to its point of view, and represents the whole more or less distinctly.

I cannot undertake to reconcile this part of the system with what was before mentioned—to wit, that every change in a monad is the evolution of its own original powers, and would have happened though no other substance had been created. But, to proceed.

There are different orders of monads, some higher and others lower. The higher orders he calls dominant ; such is the human soul. The monads that compose organized bodies of men, animals, and plants, are of a lower order, and subservient to the dominant monads. But every monad, of whatever order, is a complete substance in itself—indivisible, having no parts ; indestructible, because, having no parts, it cannot perish by any kind of decomposition ; it can only perish by annihilation, and we have no reason to believe that God will ever annihilate any of the beings which he has made.

The monads of a lower order may, by a regular evolution of their powers, rise to a higher order. They may successively be joined to organized bodies, of various forms and different degrees of perception ; but they never die, nor cease to be in some degree active and percipient.

* His name was *Christian.*—H.
† This title is incorrect. It is "Psychologia Empirica methodo scientifica pertractata," &c. The work appeared in 1732.—H.
‡ It was published in 1734. Such careless ignorance of the most distinguished works on the subject of an author's speculations, is peculiarly British.—H.

⌈219, 220⌉

x 2

This philosopher makes a distinction between perception and what he calls *apperception.* The first is common to all monads, the last proper to the higher orders, among which are human souls. [221]

By apperception he understands that degree of perception which reflects, as it were, upon itself; by which we are conscious of our own existence, and conscious of our perceptions; by which we can reflect upon the operations of our own minds, and can comprehend abstract truths. The mind, in many operations, he thinks, particularly in sleep, and in many actions common to us with the brutes, has not this apperception, although it is still filled with a multitude of obscure and indistinct perceptions, of which we are not conscious.

He conceives that our bodies and minds are united in such a manner that neither has any physical influence upon the other. Each performs all its operations by its own internal springs and powers; yet the operations of one correspond exactly with those of the other, by a pre-established harmony; just as one clock may be so adjusted as to keep time with another, although each has its own moving power, and neither receives any part of its motion from the other.

So that, according to this system, all our perceptions of external objects would be the same, though external things had never existed; our perception of them would continue, although, by the power of God, they should this moment be annihilated. We do not perceive external things because they exist, but because the soul was originally so constituted as to produce in itself all its successive changes, and all its successive perceptions, independently of the external objects.

Every perception or apperception, every operation, in a word, of the soul, is a necessary consequence of the state of it immediately preceding that operation; and this state is the necessary consequence of the state preceding it; and so backwards, until you come to its first formation and constitution, which produces, successively and by necessary consequence, all its successive states to the end of its existence; [222] so that, in this respect, the soul, and every monad, may be compared to a watch wound up, which, having the spring of its motion in itself, by the gradual evolution of its own spring, produces all the successive motions we observe in it.

In this account of Leibnitz's system concerning monads and the pre-established harmony, I have kept, as nearly as I could, to his own expressions, in his " New System of the Nature and Communication of Substances, and of the Union of Soul and Body;" and in the several illustrations of that new system which he afterwards published; and in his " Principles of Nature and Grace founded in Reason." I shall now make a few remarks upon this system.

1. To pass over the irresistible necessity of all human actions, which makes a part of this system, that will be considered in another place, I observe, *first,* that the distinction made between perception and apperception is obscure and unphilosophical. As far as we can discover, every operation of our mind is attended with consciousness, and particularly that which we call the perception of external objects; and to speak of a perception of which we are not conscious, is to speak without any meaning.

As consciousness is the only power by which we discern the operations of our own minds, or can form any notion of them, an operation of mind of which we are not conscious, is, we know not what; and to call such an operation by the name of perception, is an abuse of language. No man can perceive an object without being conscious that he perceives it. No man can think without being conscious that he thinks. What men are not conscious of, cannot therefore, without impropriety, be called either perception or thought of any kind. And, if we will suppose operations of mind of which we are not conscious, and give a name to such creatures of our imagination, that name must signify what we know nothing about.* [223]

2. To suppose bodies organized or unorganized, to be made up of indivisible monads which have no parts, is contrary to all that we know of body. It is essential to a body to have parts; and every part of a body is a body, and has parts also. No number of parts, without extension or figure, not even an infinite number, if we may use that expression, can, by being put together, make a whole that has extension and figure, which all bodies have.

3. It is contrary to all that we know of bodies, to ascribe to the monads, of which they are supposed to be compounded, perception and active force. If a philosopher thinks proper to say, that a clod of earth both perceives and has active force, let him bring his proofs. But he ought not to expect that men who have understanding will so far give it up as to receive without proof whatever his imagination may suggest.

4. This system overturns all authority of our senses, and leaves not the least ground to believe the existence of the objects of

* The language in which Leibnitz expresses his doctrine of latent modifications of mind, which, though out of consciousness, manifest their existence in their effects, is objectionable; the doctrine itself is not only true but of the very highest importance in psychology, although it has never yet been appreciated or even understood by any writer on philosophy in this island.—H.

sense, or the existence of anything which depends upon the authority of our senses; for our perception of objects, according to this system, has no dependence upon anything external, and would be the same as it is, supposing external objects had never existed, or that they were from this moment annihilated.

It is remarkable that Leibnitz's system, that of Malebranche, and the common system of ideas or images of external objects in the mind, do all agree in overturning all the authority of our senses; and this one thing, as long as men retain their senses, will always make all these systems truly ridiculous.

5. The last observation I shall make upon this system, which, indeed, is equally applicable to all the systems of Perception I have mentioned, is, that it is all hypothesis, made up of conjectures and suppositions, without proof. The Peripatetics supposed sensible *species* to be sent forth by the objects of sense. The moderns suppose ideas in the brain or in the mind. [224] Malebranche supposed that we perceive the ideas of the Divine mind. Leibnitz supposed monads and a pre-established harmony; and these monads being creatures of his own making, he is at liberty to give them what properties and powers his fancy may suggest. In like manner, the Indian philosopher supposed that the earth is supported by a huge elephant, and that the elephant stands on the back of a huge tortoise.[*]

Such suppositions, while there is no proof of them offered, are nothing but the fictions of human fancy; and we ought no more to believe them, than we believe Homer's fictions of Apollo's silver bow, or Minerva's shield, or Venus's girdle. Such fictions in poetry are agreeable to the rules of art: they are intended to please, not to convince. But the philosophers would have us to believe their fictions, though the account they give of the phenomena of nature has commonly no more probability than the account that Homer gives of the plague in the Grecian camp, from Apollo taking his station on a neighbouring mountain, and from his silver bow letting fly his swift arrows into the camp.

Men then only begin to have a true taste in philosophy, when they have learned to hold hypotheses in just contempt; and to consider them as the reveries of speculative men, which will never have any similitude to the works of God.

The Supreme Being has given us some intelligence of his works, by what our senses inform us of external things, and by what our consciousness and reflection inform us concerning the operations of our own minds. Whatever can be inferred from these common informations, by just and sound reasoning, is true and legitimate philosophy: but what we add to this from conjecture is all spurious and illegitimate. [225]

After this long account of the theories advanced by philosophers, to account for our perception of external objects, I hope it will appear, that neither Aristotle's theory of sensible species, nor Malebranche's of our seeing things in God, nor the common theory of our perceiving ideas in our own minds, nor Leibnitz's theory of monads and a pre-established harmony, give any satisfying account of this power of the mind, or make it more intelligible than it is without their aid. They are conjectures, and, if they were true, would solve no difficulty, but raise many new ones. It is, therefore, more agreeable to good sense and to sound philosophy, to rest satisfied with what our consciousness and attentive reflection discover to us of the nature of perception, than, by inventing hypotheses, to attempt to explain things which are above the reach of human understanding. I believe no man is able to explain how we perceive external objects, any more than how we are conscious of those that are internal. Perception, consciousness, memory, and imagination, are all original and simple powers of the mind, and parts of its constitution. For this reason, though I have endeavoured to shew that the theories of philosophers on this subject are ill grounded and insufficient, I do not attempt to substitute any other theory in their place.

Every man feels that perception gives him an invincible belief of the existence of that which he perceives; and that this belief is not the effect of reasoning, but the immediate consequence of perception.[*] When philosophers have wearied themselves and their readers with their speculations upon this subject, they can neither strengthen this belief, nor weaken it; nor can they shew how it is produced. It puts the philosopher and the peasant upon a level; and neither of them can give any other reason for believing his senses, than that he finds it impossible for him to do otherwise. [226]

---

[*] It is a disputed point whether Leibnitz were serious in his monadology and pre-established harmony.—H.

[224-226]

[*] In an *immediate* perception of external things, the belief of their existence would not be a consequence of the perception, but be involved in the perception itself.—H.

CHAPTER XVI.

OF SENSATION.

HAVING finished what I intend, with regard to that act of mind which we call the perception of an external object, I proceed to consider another, which, by our constitution, is conjoined with perception, and not with perception only, but with many other acts of our minds; and that is sensation. To prevent repetition, I must refer the reader to the explication of this word given in Essay I., chap. i.

Almost all our perceptions have corresponding sensations which constantly accompany them, and, on that account, are very apt to be confounded with them. Neither ought we to expect that the sensation, and its corresponding perception, should be distinguished in common language, because the purposes of common life do not require it. Language is made to serve the purposes of ordinary conversation; and we have no reason to expect that it should make distinctions that are not of common use. Hence it happens, that a quality perceived, and the sensation corresponding to that perception, often go under the same name.

This makes the names of most of our sensations ambiguous, and this ambiguity hath very much perplexed philosophers. It will be necessary to give some instances, to illustrate the distinction between our sensations and the objects of perception.

When I smell a rose, there is in this operation both sensation and perception. The agreeable odour I feel, considered by itself, without relation to any external object, is merely a sensation. [227] It affects the mind in a certain way; and this affection of the mind may be conceived, without a thought of the rose, or any other object. This sensation can be nothing else than it is felt to be. Its very essence consists in being felt; and, when it is not felt, it is not. There is no difference between the sensation and the feeling of it—they are one and the same thing. It is for this reason that we before observed that, in sensation, there is no object distinct from that act of the mind by which it is felt—and this holds true with regard to all sensations.

Let us next attend to the perception which we have in smelling a rose. Perception has always an external object; and the object of my perception, in this case, is that quality in the rose which I discern by the sense of smell. Observing that the agreeable sensation is raised when the rose is near, and ceases when it is removed, I am led, by my nature, to conclude some quality to be in the rose, which is the cause of this sensation. This quality in the rose is the object perceived; and that act of my mind by which I have the conviction and belief of this quality, is what in this case I call perception.[*]

But it is here to be observed, that the sensation I feel, and the quality in the rose which I perceive, are both called by the same name. The smell of a rose is the name given to both: so that this name hath two meanings; and the distinguishing its different meanings removes all perplexity, and enables us to give clear and distinct answers to questions about which philosophers have held much dispute.[†]

Thus, if it is asked, whether the smell be in the rose, or in the mind that feels it, the answer is obvious: That there are two different things signified by the smell of a rose; one of which is in the mind, and can be in nothing but in a sentient being; the other is truly and properly in the rose. The sensation which I feel is in my mind. The mind is the sentient being; and, as the rose is insentient, there can be no sensation, nor anything resembling sensation in it. [228] But this sensation in my mind is occasioned by a certain quality in the rose, which is called by the same name with the sensation, not on account of any similitude, but because of their constant concomitancy.

All the names we have for smells, tastes, sounds, and for the various degrees of heat and cold, have a like ambiguity; and what has been said of the smell of a rose may be applied to them. They signify both a sensation, and a quality perceived by means of that sensation. The first is the sign, the last the thing signified. As both are conjoined by nature, and as the purposes of common life do not require them to be disjoined in our thoughts, they are both expressed by the same name: and this ambiguity is to be found in all languages, because the reason of it extends to all.

The same ambiguity is found in the names of such diseases as are indicated by a particular painful sensation: such as the toothache, the headache. The toothache

---

* This paragraph appears to be an explicit disavowal of the doctrine of an intuitive or immediate perception. If, from a certain sensible feeling, or sensation, (which is itself cognitive of no object,) I am only determined by my nature to *conclude* that there is some external quality which is the *cause* of this sensation, and if this quality, thus only known as an inference from its effect, be the *object perceived;* then is perception not an act immediately cognitive of any existing object, and the object perceived is, in fact, *except as an imaginary something, unknown.* —H.

† In reference to this and the following paragraphs. I may observe that the distinction of subjective and objective qualities here vaguely attempted, had been already precisely accomplished by Aristotle, in his discrimination of παθητικαὶ ποιότητες (qualitates patibiles,) and πάθη (passiones). In regard to the Cartesian distinction, which is equally precise, but of which likewise Reid is unaware, see above, p. 205. col. b, note *.—H

[227, 228]

signifies a painful sensation, which can only
be in a sentient being ; but it signifies also
a disorder in the body, which has no similitude to a sensation, but is naturally connected with it.

Pressing my hand with force against the
table, I feel pain, and I feel the table to be
hard. The pain is a sensation of the mind,
and there is nothing that resembles it in
the table. The hardness is in the table,
nor is there anything resembling it in the
mind. Feeling is applied to both ; but in
a different sense ; being a word common to
the act of sensation, and to that of perceiving by the sense of touch.

I touch the table gently with my hand,
and I feel it to be smooth, hard, and cold.
These are qualities of the table perceived by
touch ; but I perceive them by means of a
sensation which indicates them. This sensation not being painful, I commonly give no
attention to it. [229] It carries my thought
immediately to the thing signified by it, and
is itself forgot, as if it had never been. But,
by repeating it, and turning my attention
to it, and abstracting my thought from the
thing signified by it, I find it to be merely
a sensation, and that it has no similitude to
the hardness, smoothness, or coldness of
the table, which are signified by it.

It is indeed difficult, at first, to disjoin
things in our attention which have always
been conjoined, and to make that an object
of reflection which never was so before ;
but some pains and practice will overcome
this difficulty in those who have got the
habit of reflecting on the operations of their
own minds.

Although the present subject leads us
only to consider the sensations which we
have by means of our external senses, yet
it will serve to illustrate what has been said,
and, I apprehend, is of importance in itself,
to observe, that many operations of mind,
to which we give one name, and which we
always consider as one thing, are complex
in their nature, and made up of several
more simple ingredients; and of these ingredients sensation very often makes one. Of
this we shall give some instances.

The appetite of hunger includes an uneasy sensation, and a desire of food. Sensation and desire are different acts of mind.
The last, from its nature, must have an
object ; the first has no object. These two
ingredients may always be separated in
thought—perhaps they sometimes are, in
reality ; but hunger includes both.

Benevolence towards our fellow-creatures
includes an agreeable feeling; but it includes
also a desire of the happiness of others.
The ancients commonly called it desire.
Many moderns chuse rather to call it a feeling. Both are right: and they only err who
exclude either of the ingredients. [230]
⌈229–231⌉

Whether these two ingredients are necessarily connected, is, perhaps, difficult for us
to determine, there being many necessary
connections which we do not perceive to be
necessary ; but we can disjoin them in
thought. They are different acts of the
mind.

An uneasy feeling, and a desire, are, in
like manner, the ingredients of malevolent
affections; such as malice. envy, revenge.
The passion of fear includes an uneasy
sensation or feeling, and an opinion of
danger ; and hope is made up of the contrary ingredients. When we hear of a
heroic action, the sentiment which it raises
in our mind, is made up of various ingredients. There is in it an agreeable feeling,
a benevolent affection to the person, and a
judgment or opinion of his merit.

If we thus analyse the various operations
of our minds, we shall find that many of
them which we consider as perfectly simple,
because we have been accustomed to call
them by one name, are compounded of more
simple ingredients; and that sensation, or
feeling, which is only a more refined kind
of sensation, makes one ingredient, not
only in the perception of external objects,
but in most operations of the mind.

A small degree of reflection may satisfy
us that the number and variety of our sensations and feelings is prodigious; for, to
omit all those which accompany our appetites. passions, and affections, our moral
sentiments and sentiments of taste, even
our external senses, furnish a great variety
of sensations, differing in kind, and almost
in every kind an endless variety of degrees.
Every variety we discern, with regard to
taste, smell, sound, colour, heat, and cold,
and in the tangible qualities of bodies, is
indicated by a sensation corresponding to
it.

The most general and the most important division of our sensations and feelings,
is into the agreeable, the disagreeable, and
the indifferent Everything we call pleasure, happiness, or enjoyment, on the one
hand ; and, on the other, everything we
call misery, pain, or uneasiness, is sensation or feeling ; for no man can for the present be more happy or more miserable than
he feels himself to be. [231] He cannot
be deceived with regard to the enjoyment
or suffering of the present moment.

But I apprehend that, besides the sensations that are either agreeable or disagreeable, there is still a greater number that
are indifferent.* To these we give so little
attention, that they have no name, and are
immediately forgot, as if they had never
been ; and it requires attention to the ope-

---

* This is a point in dispute among philosophers.
—H.

rations of our minds to be convinced of their existence.

For this end we may observe, that, to a good ear, every human voice is distinguishable from all others. Some voices are pleasant, some disagreeable ; but the far greater part can neither be said to be one nor the other. The same thing may be said of other sounds, and no less of tastes, smells, and colours ; and, if we consider that our senses are in continual exercise while we are awake, that some sensation attends every object they present to us, and that familiar objects seldom raise any emotion, pleasant or painful, we shall see reason, besides the agreeable and disagreeable, to admit a third class of sensations that may be called indifferent.

The sensations that are indifferent, are far from being useless. They serve as signs to distinguish things that differ ; and the information we have concerning things external, comes by their means. Thus, if a man had no ear to receive pleasure from the harmony or melody of sounds, he would still find the sense of hearing of great utility. Though sounds give him neither pleasure nor pain of themselves, they would give him much useful information ; and the like may be said of the sensations we have by all the other senses. [232]

As to the sensations and feelings that are agreeable or disagreeable, they differ much not only in degree, but in kind and in dignity. Some belong to the animal part of our nature, and are common to us with the brutes ; others belong to the rational and moral part. The first are more properly called *sensations ;* the last, *feelings.* The French word *sentiment* is common to both.[*]

The intention of nature in them is for the most part obvious, and well deserving our notice. It has been beautifully illustrated by a very elegant French writer,[*] in his "*Theorie des Sentiments Agreables.*"

The Author of Nature, in the distribution of agreeable and painful feelings, hath wisely and benevolently consulted the good of the human species, and hath even shewn us, by the same means, what tenor of conduct we ought to hold. For, *first,* The painful sensations of the animal kind are admonitions to avoid what would hurt us ; and the agreeable sensations of this kind invite us to those actions that are necessary to the preservation of the individual or of the kind. *Secondly,* By the same means, nature invites us to moderate bodily exercise, and admonishes us to avoid idleness and inactivity on the one hand, and excessive labour and fatigue on the other.

Thirdly, The moderate exercise of all our rational powers gives pleasure. *Fourthly,* Every species of beauty is beheld with pleasure, and every species of deformity with disgust ; and we shall find all that we call beautiful, to be something estimable or useful in itself, or a sign of something that is estimable or useful. *Fifthly,* The benevolent affections are all accompanied with an agreeable feeling, the malevolent with the contrary. And, *sixthly,* The highest, the noblest, and most durable pleasure is that of doing well, and acting the part that becomes us ; and the most bitter and painful sentiment, the anguish and remorse of a guilty conscience. These observations, with regard to the economy of nature in the distribution of our painful and agreeable sensations and feelings, are illustrated by the author last mentioned, so elegantly and judiciously, that I shall not attempt to say anything upon them after him. [233]

I shall conclude this chapter by observing that, as the confounding our sensations with that perception of external objects which is constantly conjoined with them, has been the occasion of most of the errors and false theories of philosophers with regard to the senses ; so the distinguishing these operations seems to me to be the key that leads to a right understanding of both.

Sensation, taken by itself, implies neither the conception nor belief of any external object. It supposes a sentient being, and a certain manner in which that being is affected ; but it supposes no more. Perception implies an immediate conviction and belief of something external—something different both from the mind that perceives, and from the act of perception. Things so different in their nature ought to be distinguished ; but, by our constitution, they are always united. Every different perception is conjoined with a sensation that is proper to it. The one is the sign, the other the thing signified. They coalesce in our imagination. They are signified by one name, and are considered as one simple operation. The purposes of life do not require them to be distinguished.

It is the philosopher alone who has occasion to distinguish them, when he would analyse the operation compounded of them. But he has no suspicion that there is any composition in it ; and to discover this requires a degree of reflection which has been too little practised even by philosophers.

In the old philosophy, sensation and perception were perfectly confounded. The sensible species coming from the object, and impressed upon the mind, was the whole ; and you might call it sensation or perception as you pleased.[*]

---

[*] Some French philosophers, since Reid, have attempted the distinction of *sentiment* and *sensation.*—H

[†] Levesque de Poullly.—H.

[*] This is not correct ; for, in the distinction of the

Des Cartes and Locke, attending more to the operations of their own minds, say, that the sensations by which we have notice of secondary qualities have no resemblance to anything that pertains to body; but they did not see that this might, with equal justice, be applied to the primary qualities. [234] Mr Locke maintains, that the sensations we have from primary qualities are resemblances of those qualities. This shews how grossly the most ingenious men may err with regard to the operations of their minds. It must, indeed, be acknowledged, that it is much easier to have a distinct notion of the sensations that belong to secondary than of those that belong to the primary qualities.* The reason of this will appear in the next chapter.

But, had Mr Locke attended with sufficient accuracy to the sensations† which he was every day and every hour receiving from primary qualities, he would have seen that they can as little resemble any quality of an inanimated being as pain can resemble a cube or a circle.

What had escaped this ingenious philosopher, was clearly discerned by Bishop Berkeley. He had a just notion of sensations, and saw that it was impossible that anything in an insentient being could resemble them; a thing so evident in itself, that it seems wonderful that it should have been so long unknown.

But let us attend to the consequence of this discovery. Philosophers, as well as the vulgar, had been accustomed to comprehend both sensation and perception under one name, and to consider them as one uncompounded operation. Philosophers, even more than the vulgar, gave the name of sensation to the whole operation of the senses; and all the notions we have of material things were called ideas of sensation. This led Bishop Berkeley to take one ingredient of a complex operation for the whole; and, having clearly discovered the nature of sensation, taking it for granted that all that the senses present to the mind is sensation, which can have no resemblance to anything material, he concluded that there is no material world. [235]

If the senses furnished us with no materials of thought but sensations, his conclusion must be just; for no sensation can give us the conception of material things, far less

any argument to prove their existence. But, if it is true that by our senses we have not only a variety of sensations, but likewise a conception and an immediate natural conviction of external objects, he reasons from a false supposition, and his arguments fall to the ground.*

CHAPTER XVII.

OF THE OBJECTS OF PERCEPTION; AND, FIRST, OF PRIMARY AND SECONDARY QUALITIES.

The objects of perception are the various qualities of bodies. Intending to treat of these only in general, and chiefly with a view to explain the notions which our senses give us of them, I begin with the distinction between primary and secondary qualities. These were distinguished very early. The Peripatetic system confounded them, and left no difference. The distinction was again revived by Des Cartes and Locke, and a second time abolished by Berkeley and Hume. If the real foundation of this distinction can be pointed out, it will enable us to account for the various revolutions in the sentiments of philosophers concerning it.

Every one knows that extension, divisibility, figure, motion, solidity, hardness, softness, and fluidity, were by Mr Locke called *primary qualities of body;* and that sound, colour, taste, smell, and heat or cold, were called *secondary qualities.* Is there a just foundation for this distinction? Is there anything common to the primary which belongs not to the secondary? And what is it?

I answer, That there appears to me to be a real foundation for the distinction; and it is this—that our senses give us a direct and a distinct notion of the primary qualities, and inform us what they are in themselves.† But of the secondary qualities, our senses give us only a relative and obscure notion. [236] They inform us only, that they are qualities that affect us in a certain manner —that is, produce in us a certain sensation; but as to what they are in themselves, our senses leave us in the dark.‡

---

* On this whole distinction, see Note D. *. —H.
† By the expression, *" what they are in themselves,"* In reference to the primary qualities, and of "*relative notion,"* in reference to the secondary, Reid cannot mean that the former are known to us *absolutely and in themselves*—that is, *out of relation* to our cognitive faculties ; for he elsewhere admits that all our knowledge is relative. Farther, if *"* our senses give us a *direct and distinct notion* of the primary qualities, and *inform us what they are in themselves,"* these qualities, as known, must *resemble,* or be identical with, these qualities as existing.—H.
‡ The distinctions of perception and sensation, and of primary and secondary qualities, may be reduced to one higher princ ple. Knowledge is partly *objective,* partly *subjective ;* both these elements are essential to every cognition, but in every cognition they are always in the inverse ratio of each other. Now

species impressa and *species expressa,* the distinction of *sensation* and *perception* could be perceived ; but, in point of fact, many even of the Aristotelians, who admitted species at all, allowed them only in one or two of the senses. See Notes D * and M.—H.
* The reader will observe that Reid says, *"* distinct *notion of the sensations* that belong to the secondary qualities,*"* and not distinct notion of the secondary qualities themselves.—H.
† Here again the reader will observe that the term is *sensations,* and not *notions,* of the primary qualities.—H.

Every man capable of reflection may easily satisfy himself that he has a perfectly clear and distinct notion of extension, divisibility, figure, and motion. The solidity of a body means no more but that it excludes other bodies from occupying the same place at the same time Hardness, softness, and fluidity are different degrees of cohesion in the parts of a body. It is fluid when it has no sensible cohesion ; soft, when the cohesion is weak ; and hard, when it is strong. Of the cause of this cohesion we are ignorant, but the thing itself we understand perfectly, being immediately informed of it by the sense of touch. It is evident, therefore, that of the primary qualities we have a clear and distinct notion ; we know what they are, though we may be ignorant of their causes.

I observed, farther, that the notion we have of primary qualities is direct, and not relative only. A relative notion of a thing, is, strictly speaking, no notion of the thing at all, but only of some relation which it bears to something else.

Thus, gravity sometimes signifies the tendency of bodies towards the earth ; sometimes it signifies the cause of that tendency. When it means the first, I have a direct and distinct notion of gravity ; I see it, and feel it. and know perfectly what it is ; but this tendency must have a cause. We give the same name to the cause ; and that cause has been an object of thought and of speculation. Now, what notion have we of this cause when we think and reason about it ? It is evident we think of it as an unknown cause, of a known effect. This is a relative notion ; and it must be obscure, because it gives us no conception of what the thing is, but of what relation it bears to something else. Every relation which a thing unknown bears to something that is known, may give a relative notion of it ; and there are many objects of thought and of discourse of which our faculties can give no better than a relative notion. [237]

Having premised these things to explain what is meant by a relative notion, it is evident that our notion of primary qualities is not of this kind ; we know what they are, and not barely what relation they bear to something else.

It is otherwise with secondary qualities. If you ask me, what is that quality or modification in a rose which I call its smell, I am at a loss to answer directly. Upon reflection, I find, that I have a distinct notion of the sensation which it produces in my mind. But there can be nothing like to this sensation in the rose, because it is in-

sentient. The quality in the rose is something which occasions the sensation in me ; but what that something is, I know not. My senses give me no information upon this point. The only notion, therefore, my senses give is this—that smell in the rose is an unknown quality or modification, which is the cause or occasion of a sensation which I know well. The relation which this unknown quality bears to the sensation with which nature hath connected it, is all I learn from the sense of smelling ; but this is evidently a relative notion. The same reasoning will apply to every secondary quality.

Thus, I think it appears that there is a real foundation for the distinction of primary from secondary qualities ; and that they are distinguished by this—that of the primary we have by our senses a direct and distinct notion ; but of the secondary only a relative notion, which must, because it is only relative, be obscure ; they are conceived only as the unknown causes or occasions of certain sensations with which we are well acquainted.

The account I have given of this distinction is founded upon no hypothesis. [238] Whether our notions of primary qualities are direct and distinct, those of the secondary relative and obscure, is a matter of fact, of which every man may have certain knowledge by attentive reflection upon them. To this reflection I appeal, as the proper test of what has been advanced, and proceed to make some reflections on this subject.

1. The primary qualities are neither sensations, nor are they resemblances of sensations. This appears to me self-evident. I have a clear and distinct notion of each of the primary qualities. I have a clear and distinct notion of sensation. I can compare the one with the other ; and, when I do so, I am not able to discern a resembling feature. Sensation is the act or the feeling (I dispute not which) of a sentient being. Figure, divisibility, solidity, are neither acts nor feelings. Sensation supposes a sentient being as its subject ; for a sensation that is not felt by some sentient being, is an absurdity. Figure and divisibility supposes a subject that is figured and divisible, but not a subject that is sentient.

2. We have no reason to think that any of the secondary qualities resemble any sensation. The absurdity of this notion has been clearly shewn by Des Cartes, Locke, and many modern philosophers. It was a tenet of the ancient philosophy, and is still by many imputed to the vulgar, but only as a vulgar error. It is too evident to need proof, that the vibrations of a sounding body do not resemble the sensation of sound, nor the effluvia of an odorous body the sensation of smell.

In *perception* and the *primary* qualities, the objective element preponderates, whereas the subjective element preponderates in sensation and the secondary qualities. See Notes D and D * .—H.

3. The distinctness of our notions of primary qualities prevents all questions and disputes about their nature. There are no different opinions about the nature of extension, figure, or motion, or the nature of any primary quality. Their nature is manifest to our senses, and cannot be unknown to any man, or mistaken by him, though their causes may admit of dispute. [239]

The primary qualities are the object of the mathematical sciences; and the distinctness of our notions of them enables us to reason demonstratively about them to a great extent. Their various modifications are precisely defined in the imagination, and thereby capable of being compared, and their relations determined with precision and certainty.

It is not so with secondary qualities. Their nature not being manifest to the sense, may be a subject of dispute. Our feeling informs us that the fire is hot; but it does not inform us what that heat of the fire is. But does it not appear a contradiction, to say we know that the fire is hot, but we know not what that heat is? I answer, there is the same appearance of contradiction in many things that must be granted. We know that wine has an inebriating quality; but we know not what that quality is. It is true, indeed, that, if we had not some notion of what is meant by the heat of fire, and by an inebriating quality, we could affirm nothing of either with understanding. We have a notion of both; but it is only a relative notion. We know that they are the causes of certain known effects.

4. The nature of secondary qualities is a proper subject of philosophical disquisition; and in this philosophy has made some progress. It has been discovered, that the sensation of smell is occasioned by the effluvia of bodies; that of sound by their vibration. The disposition of bodies to reflect a particular kind of light, occasions the sensation of colour. Very curious discoveries have been made of the nature of heat, and an ample field of discovery in these subjects remains.

5. We may see why the sensations belonging to secondary qualities are an object of our attention, while those which belong to the primary are not.

The first are not only signs of the object perceived, but they bear a capital part in the notion we form of it. [240] We conceive it only as that which occasions such a sensation, and therefore cannot reflect upon it without thinking of the sensation which it occasions: we have no other mark whereby to distinguish it. The thought of a secondary quality, therefore, always carries us back to the sensation which it produces. We give the same name to both, and are apt to confound them together.

[239-241]

But, having a clear and distinct conception of primary qualities, we have no need, when we think of them, to recall their sensations. When a primary quality is perceived, the sensation immediately leads our thought to the quality signified by it, and is itself forgot. We have no occasion afterwards to reflect upon it; and so we come to be as little acquainted with it as if we had never felt it. This is the case with the sensations of all primary qualities, when they are not so painful or pleasant as to draw our attention.

When a man moves his hand rudely against a pointed hard body, he feels pain, and may easily be persuaded that this pain is a sensation, and that there is nothing resembling it in the hard body; at the same time, he perceives the body to be hard and pointed, and he knows that these qualities belong to the body only. In this case, it is easy to distinguish what he feels from what he perceives.

Let him again touch the pointed body gently, so as to give him no pain; and now you can hardly persuade him that he feels anything but the figure and hardness of the body: so difficult it is to attend to the sensations belonging to primary qualities, when they are neither pleasant nor painful. They carry the thought to the external object, and immediately disappear and are forgot. Nature intended them only as signs; and when they have served that purpose they vanish.

We are now to consider the opinions both of the vulgar and of philosophers upon this subject. [241] As to the former, it is not to be expected that they should make distinctions which have no connection with the common affairs of life; they do not, therefore, distinguish the primary from the secondary qualities, but speak of both as being equally qualities of the external object. Of the primary qualities they have a distinct notion, as they are immediately and distinctly, perceived by the senses; of the secondary, their notions, as I apprehend, are confused and indistinct, rather than erroneous. A secondary quality is the unknown cause or occasion of a well-known effect; and the same name is common to the cause and the effect. Now, to distinguish clearly the different ingredients of a complex notion, and, at the same time, the different meanings of an ambiguous word, is the work of a philosopher; and is not to be expected of the vulgar, when their occasions do not require it.

I grant, therefore, that the notion which the vulgar have of secondary qualities, is indistinct and inaccurate. But there seems to be a contradiction between the vulgar and the philosopher upon this subject, and each charges the other with a gross absurdity. The vulgar say, that fire is hot, and snow cold, and sugar sweet; and that to deny this is a gross absurdity, and contradicts the testimony of our senses. The philosopher says, that heat, and cold, and sweetness, are nothing but sensations in our minds; and it is absurd to conceive that these sensations are in the fire, or in the snow, or in the sugar.

I believe this contradiction, between the vulgar and the philosopher, is more apparent than real; and that it is owing to an abuse of language on the part of the philosopher, and to indistinct notions on the part of the vulgar. The philosopher says, there is no heat in the fire, meaning that the fire has not the sensation of heat. His meaning is just; and the vulgar will agree with him, as soon as they understand his meaning: But his language is improper; for there is really a quality in the fire, of which the proper name is heat; and the name of heat is given to this quality, both by philosophers and by the vulgar, much more frequently than to the sensation of heat. [242] This speech of the philosopher, therefore, is meant by him in one sense; it is taken by the vulgar in another sense. In the sense in which they take it, it is indeed absurd, and so they hold it to be. In the sense in which he means it, it is true; and the vulgar, as soon as they are made to understand that sense, will acknowledge it to be true. They know, as well as the philosopher, that the fire does not feel heat: and this is all that he means by saying there is no heat in the fire.*

In the opinions of philosophers about primary and secondary qualities, there have been, as was before observed, several revolutions.† They were distinguished, long before the days of Aristotle, by the sect called Atomists: among whom Democritus made a capital figure. In those times, the name of *quality* was applied only to those we call secondary qualities; the primary, being considered as essential to matter, were not called qualities.‡ That the atoms, which they held to be the first principles of things, were extended, solid, figured, and movable, there was no doubt; but the question was, whether they had smell, taste, and colour? or, as it was commonly expressed, whether they had qualities? The Atomists maintained, that they had not; that the qualities were not in bodies, but were something resulting from the operation of bodies upon our senses.§

It would seem that, when men began to speculate upon this subject, the primary qualities appeared so clear and manifest that they could entertain no doubt of their existence wherever matter existed; but the secondary so obscure that they were at a loss where to place them. They used this comparison: as fire, which is neither in the flint nor in the steel, is produced by their collision, so those qualities, though not in bodies, are produced by their impulse upon our senses. [243]

This doctrine was opposed by Aristotle.* He believed taste and colour to be substantial forms of bodies, and that their species, as well as those of figure and motion, are received by the senses.†

In believing that what we commonly call *taste* and *colour*, is something really inherent in body, and does not depend upon its being tasted and seen, he followed nature. But, in believing that our sensations of taste and colour are the forms or species of those qualities received by the senses, he followed his own theory, which was an absurd fiction.† Des Cartes not only shewed the absurdity of sensible species received by the senses, but gave a more just and more intelligible account of secondary qualities than had been given before. Mr Locke followed him, and bestowed much pains upon this subject. He was the first, I think, that gave them the name of secondary qualities,‡ which has been very generally adopted. He distinguished the sensation from the quality in the body, which is the cause or occasion of that sensation, and shewed that there neither is nor can be any similitude between them.§

By this account, the senses are acquitted of putting any fallacy upon us; the sensation is real, and no fallacy; the quality in the body, which is the cause or occasion of this sensation, is likewise real, though the nature of it is not manifest to our senses. If we impose upon ourselves, by confounding the sensation with the quality that occasions it, this is owing to rash judgment or weak understanding, but not to any false testimony of our senses.

This account of secondary qualities I take

---

* All this ambiguity was understood and articulately explained by former philosophers. See above, notes at pp 205 and 310, and Note D.—H.

† See Note D.—H.

‡ The Atomists derived the *qualitative* attributes of things from the *quantitative*.—H.

§ Still Democritus supposed certain real or objective causes for the subjective differences of our

sensations. Thus, in the different forms, positions, and relations of atoms, he sought the ground of difference of tastes, colours, heat and cold, &c. See Theophrastus *De Sensu*, § 65—Aristotle *De Anima*, iii. 2.—Galen *De Elementis*—Simplicius *in Phys. Auscult. libros*, f. 119, b.—H.

* Aristotle admitted that the doctrine in question was true, of colour, taste, &c, as κατ' ἐνέργειαν, but not true of them as κατὰ δύναμιν. See *De Anima* iii. 2.—H.

† This is not really Aristotle's doctrine.—H.

‡ Locke only gave a new meaning to old terms. The *first* and *second* or the *primary* and *secondary* qualities of Aristotle, denoted a distinction similar to, but not identical with, that in question—H.

§ He distinguished nothing which had not been more precisely discriminated by Aristotle and the Cartesians.—H.

to be very just; and if Mr Locke had stopped here, he would have left the matter very clear. But he thought it necessary to introduce the theory of ideas, to explain the distinction between primary and secondary qualities, and by that means, as I think, perplexed and darkened it.

When philosophers speak about ideas, we are often at a loss to know what they mean by them, and may be apt to suspect that they are mere fictions, that have no existence. [244] They have told us, that, by the ideas which we have immediately from our senses, they mean our sensations.* These, indeed, are real things, and not fictions. We may, by accurate attention to them, know perfectly their nature; and, if philosophers would keep by this meaning of the word *idea*, when applied to the objects of sense, they would at least be more intelligible. Let us hear how Mr Locke explains the nature of those ideas, when applied to primary and secondary qualities, Book 2, chap 8, § 7, tenth edition. " To discover the nature of our ideas the better, and to discourse of them intelligibly, it will be convenient to distinguish them, as they are ideas, or perceptions in our minds, and as they are modifications of matter in the bodies that cause such perceptions in us, that so we may not think (as perhaps usually is done) that they are exactly the images and resemblances of something inherent in the subject; most of those of sensation being, in the mind, no more the likeness of something existing without us, than the names that stand for them are the likeness of our ideas, which yet, upon hearing, they are apt to excite in us."

This way of distinguishing a thing, *first*, as what it is; and, *secondly*, as what it is not, is, I apprehend, a very extraordinary way of discovering its nature.† And if ideas are ideas or perceptions in our minds, and, at the same time, the modifications of matter in the bodies that cause such perceptions in us, it will be no easy matter to discourse of them intelligibly.

The discovery of the nature of ideas is carried on in the next section, in a manner no less extraordinary. " Whatsoever the mind perceives in itself. or is the immediate object of perception, thought, or understanding, that I call *idea ;* and the power to produce any idea in our mind, I call *quality* of the subject wherein that power is. Thus, a snowball having the power to produce in us the ideas of white, cold, and round—the powers to produce those ideas

in us, as they are in the snowball, I call *qualities ;* and, as they are sensations, or perceptions in our understandings, I call them *ideas ;* which ideas, if I speak of them sometimes as in the things themselves, I would be understood to mean those qualities in the objects which produce them in us." [245]

These are the distinctions which Mr Locke thought convenient, in order to discover the nature of our ideas of the qualities of matter the better, and to discourse of them intelligibly. I believe it will be difficult to find two other paragraphs in the essay so unintelligible. Whether this is to be imputed to the intractable nature of ideas, or to an oscitancy of the author, with which he is very rarely chargeable, I leave the reader to judge. There are, indeed, several other passages in the same chapter, in which a like obscurity appears; but I do not chuse to dwell upon them. The conclusion drawn by him from the whole is, that primary and secondary qualities are distinguished by this, that the ideas of the former are resemblances or copies of them, but the ideas of the other are not resemblances of them. Upon this doctrine, I beg leave to make two observations.

First, Taking it for granted that, by the ideas of primary and secondary qualities, he means the sensations* they excite in us, I observe that it appears strange, that a sensation should be the idea of a quality in body, to which it is acknowledged to bear no resemblance. If the sensation of sound be the idea of that vibration of the sounding body which occasions it, a surfeit may, for the same reason, be the idea of a feast.

A *second* observation is, that, when Mr Locke affirms, that the ideas of primary qualities—that is, the sensations* they raise in us—are resemblances of those qualities, he seems neither to have given due attention to those sensations, nor to the nature of sensation in general. [246]

Let a man press his hand against a hard body, and let him attend to the sensation he feels, excluding from his thought every thing external, even the body that is the cause of his feeling. This abstraction, indeed, is difficult, and seems to have been little, if at all practised. But it is not impossible, and it is evidently the only way to understand the nature of the sensation. A due attention to this sensation will satisfy

---

* The Cartesians, particularly Malebranche, distinguished the *Idea* and the *Feeling (sentiment, sensatio.)* Of the *primary* qualities in their doctrine we have Ideas; of the *secondary*, only Feelings.—H.

† This and some of the following strictures on Locke are rather hypercritical.—H.

* Here, as formerly, (*vide supra*, notes at pp 208, 290, &c.,) Reid will insist on giving a more limited meaning to the term *Sensation* than Locke did, and on criticising him by that imposed meaning. The *Sensation* of Locke was equivalent to the *Sensation* and *Perception* of Reid. It is to be observed that Locke did not, like the Cartesians, distinguish the Idea (corresponding to Reid's Perception) from the Feeling (sentiment, sens tio) corresponding to Reid's Sensation.—H.

him tnat it is no more like hardness in a body than the sensation of sound is like vibration in the sounding body.

I know of no ideas but my conceptions; and my idea of hardness in a body, is the conception of such a cohesion of its parts as requires great force to displace them. I have both the conception and belief of this quality in the body, at the same time that I have the sensation of pain, by pressing my hand against it. The sensation and perception are closely conjoined by my constitution; but I am sure they have no similitude; I know no reason why the one should be called the idea of the other, which does not lead us to call every natural effect the idea of its cause.

Neither did Mr Locke give due attention to the nature of sensation in general, when he affirmed that the ideas of primary qualities—that is, the sensations* excited by them—are resemblances of those qualities.

That there can be nothing like sensation in an insentient being, or like thought in an unthinking being, is self-evident, and has been shewn, to the conviction of all men that think, by Bishop Berkeley; yet this was unknown to Mr Locke. It is an humbling consideration, that, in subjects of this kind, self-evident truths may be hid from the eyes of the most ingenious men. But we have, withal, this consolation, that, when once discovered, they shine by their own light : and that light can no more be put out. [247]

Upon the whole, Mr Locke, in making secondary qualities to be powers in bodies to excite certain sensations in us, has given a just and distinct analysis of what our senses discover concerning them; but, in applying the theory of ideas to them and to the primary qualities, he has been led to say things that darken the subject, and that will not bear examination. †

Bishop Berkeley having adopted the sentiments common to philosophers, concerning the ideas we have by our senses—to wit, that they are all sensations—saw more clearly the necessary consequence of this doctrine; which is, that there is no material world—no qualities primary or secondary — and, consequently, no foundation for any distinction between them.‡ He exposed the absurdity of a resemblance between our sensations and any quality, primary or secondary, of a substance that is supposed to be insentient. Indeed, if it is granted that the senses have no other office but to furnish us with sensations, it will be found impossible to make any distinction between primary and secondary qualities, or even to maintain the existence of a material world.

From the account I have given of the various revolutions in the opinions of philosophers about primary and secondary qualities, I think it appears that all the darkness and intricacy that thinking men have found in this subject, and the errors they have fallen into, have been owing to the difficulty of distinguishing clearly sensation from perception—what we feel from what we perceive.

The external senses have a double province—to make us feel, and to make us perceive. They furnish us with a variety of sensations, some pleasant, others painful, and others indifferent ; at the same time, they give us a conception and an invincible belief of the existence of external objects. This conception of external objects is the work of nature. The belief of their existence, which our senses give, is the work of nature; so likewise is the sensation that accompanies it. This conception and belief which nature produces by means of the senses, we call *perception.** [248] The feeling which goes along with the perception, we call *sensation.* The perception and its corresponding sensation are produced at the same time. In our experience we never find them disjoined. Hence, we are led to consider them as one thing, to give them one name, and to confound their different attributes. It becomes very difficult to separate them in thought, to attend to each by itself, and to attribute nothing to it which belongs to the other.

To do this, requires a degree of attention to what passes in our own minds, and a talent of distinguishing things that differ, which is not to be expected in the vulgar, and is even rarely found in philosophers; so that the progress made in a just analysis of the operations of our senses has been very slow. The hypothesis of ideas, so generally adopted, hath, as I apprehend, greatly retarded this progress, and we might hope for a quicker advance, if philosophers could so far humble themselves as to believe that, in every branch of the philosophy of nature, the productions of human fancy and conjecture will be found to be dross; and that the only pure metal that will endure the test, is what is discovered by patient observation and chaste induction.

---

* No; not Sensations in Reid's meaning ; but *Percepts*—the immediate objects we are conscious of in the cognitions of sense.—H.

† The Cartesians did not apply the term *ideas* to our sensations of the secondary qualities.—H

‡ See above, p. 142, note *. The mere distinction of primary and secondary qualities, of perception and sensation, is of no importance against Idealism, if the primary qualities as immediately perceived. (i. e. as known to consciousness,) be only *conceptions, notions,* or modifications of mind itself. See following Note.—H.

** If the *conception,* like the *belief,* be subjective in perception, we have no refuge from Idealism in this doctrine. See above, the notes at pp. 128-130, 183, &c., and Note C.—H.

CHAPTER XVIII.

OF OTHER OBJECTS OF PERCEPTION.

BESIDES primary and secondary qualities of bodies, there are many other immediate objects of perception. Without pretending to a complete enumeration, I think they mostly fall under one or other of the following classes. 1st, Certain states or conditions of our own bodies. 2d, Mechanical powers or forces. 3d, Chemical powers. 4th, Medical powers or virtues. 5th, Vegetable and animal powers. [249]

That we perceive certain disorders in our own bodies by means of uneasy sensations, which nature hath conjoined with them, will not be disputed. Of this kind are toothache, headache, gout, and every distemper and hurt which we feel. The notions which our sense gives of these, have a strong analogy to our notions of secondary qualities. Both are similarly compounded, and may be similarly resolved, and they give light to each other.

In the toothache, for instance, there is, *first,* a painful feeling; and, *secondly,* a conception and belief of some disorder in the tooth, which is believed to be the cause of the uneasy feeling.* The first of these is a sensation, the second is perception; for it includes a conception and belief of an external object. But these two things, though of different natures, are so constantly conjoined in our experience and in our imagination, that we consider them as one. We give the same name to both; for the toothache is the proper name of the pain we feel; and it is the proper name of the disorder in the tooth which causes that pain. If it should be made a question whether the toothache be in the mind which feels it, or in the tooth that is affected, much might be said on both sides, while it is not observed that the word has two meanings.† But a little reflection satisfies us, that the pain is in the mind, and the disorder in the tooth. If some philosopher should pretend to have made the discovery that the toothache, the gout, the headache, are only sensations in the mind, and that it is a vulgar error to conceive that they are distempers of the body, he might defend his system in the same manner as those who affirm that there is no sound, nor colour, nor taste in bodies, defend that paradox. But both these systems, like most

paradoxes, will be found to be only an abuse of words.

We say that we *feel* the toothache, not that we perceive it. On the other hand, we say that we *perceive* the colour of a body, not that we feel it. Can any reason be given for this difference of phraseology? [250] In answer to this question, I apprehend that, both when we feel the toothache and when we see a coloured body, there is sensation and perception conjoined. But, in the toothache, the sensation being very painful, engrosses the attention; and therefore we speak of it as if it were felt only, and not perceived: whereas, in seeing a coloured body, the sensation is indifferent, and draws no attention. The quality in the body, which we call its colour, is the only object of attention; and therefore we speak of it as if it were perceived and not felt. Though all philosophers agree that, in seeing colour there is sensation, it is not easy to persuade the vulgar that, in seeing a coloured body, when the light is not too strong nor the eye inflamed, they have any sensation or feeling at all.

There are some sensations, which, though they are very often felt, are never attended to, nor reflected upon. We have no conception of them; and, therefore, in language there is neither any name for them, nor any form of speech that supposes their existence. Such are the sensations of colour, and of all primary qualities; and, therefore, those qualities are said to be perceived, but not to be felt. Taste and smell, and heat and cold, have sensations that are often agreeable or disagreeable, in such a degree as to draw our attention; and they are sometimes said to be felt, and sometimes to be perceived. When disorders of the body occasion very acute pain, the uneasy sensation engrosses the attention, and they are said to be felt, not to be perceived.*

There is another question relating to phraseology, which this subject suggests. A man says, he feels pain in such a particular part of his body; in his toe for instance. Now, reason assures us that pain being a sensation, can only be in the sentient being, as its subject—that is, in the mind. And, though philosophers have disputed much about the place of the mind; yet none of them ever placed it in the toe.†

---

* There is no such perception, *properly* so called. The cognition is merely an inference from the feeling; and its object, at least, only some hypothetical representation of a really *ignotum quid.* Here the subjective element preponderates so greatly as almost to extinguish the objective.—'.

† This is not correct. See above, p. 205, col. b note *, and Note D.—H.

---

* As already repeatedly observed, the objective element (perception) and the subjective element (feeling, sensation) are always in the inverse ratio of each other. This is a law of which Reid and the philosophers were not aware.—H.

† Not in the toe *exclusively.* But, both in ancient and modern times, the opinion has been held that the mind has as much a local presence in the toe as in the head. The doctrine, indeed, long generally maintained was, that, in relation to the body, *the soul is all in the whole, and all in every part.* On the question of the seat of the soul, which has been marvellously perplexed, I cannot enter. I shall only say, in general, that the first condition of the possibility of an

What shall we say then in this case? Do our senses really deceive us, and make us believe a thing which our reason determines to be impossible? [251] I answer, *first*, That, when a man says he has pain in his toe, he is perfectly understood, both by himself and those who hear him. This is all that he intends. He really feels what he and all men call a pain in the toe; and there is no deception in the matter. Whether, therefore, there be any impropriety in the phrase or not, is of no consequence in common life. It answers all the ends of speech, both to the speaker and the hearers.

In all languages there are phrases which have a distinct meaning; while, at the same time, there may be something in the structure of them that disagrees with the analogy of grammar or with the principles of philosophy. And the reason is, because language is not made either by grammarians or philosophers. Thus, we speak of feeling pain, as if pain was something distinct from the feeling of it. We speak of pain coming and going, and removing from one place to another. Such phrases are meant by those who use them in a sense that is neither obscure nor false. But the philosopher puts them into his alembic, reduces them to their first principles, draws out of them a sense that was never meant, and so imagines that he has discovered an error of the vulgar.

I observe, *secondly*, That, when we consider the sensation of pain by itself, without any respect to its cause, we cannot say with propriety, that the toe is either the place or the subject of it. But it ought to be remembered, that, when we speak of pain in the toe, the sensation is combined in our thought, with the cause of it, which really is in the toe. The cause and the effect are combined in one complex notion, and the same name serves for both. It is the business of the philosopher to analyse this complex notion, and to give different names to its different ingredients. He gives the name of *pain* to the sensation only, and the name of *disorder* to the unknown cause of it. Then it is evident that the disorder only is in the toe, and that it would be an error to think that the pain is in it.* But we ought not to ascribe this error to the vulgar, who never made the distinction, and who, under the name of pain, comprehend both the sensation and its cause.† [252]

Cases sometimes happen, which give occasion even to the vulgar to distinguish the painful sensation from the disorder which is the cause of it. A man who has had his leg cut off, many years after feels pain in a toe of that leg. The toe has now no existence; and he perceives easily, that the toe can neither be the place nor the subject of the pain which he feels; yet it is the same feeling he used to have from a hurt in the toe; and, if he did not know that his leg was cut off, it would give him the same immediate conviction of some hurt or disorder in the toe.*

The same phenomenon may lead the philosopher, in all cases, to distinguish sensation from perception. We say, that the man had a deceitful feeling, when he felt a pain in his toe after the leg was cut off; and we have a true meaning in saying so. But, if we will speak accurately, our sensations cannot be deceitful; they must be what we feel them to be, and can be nothing else. Where, then, lies the deceit? I answer, it lies not in the sensation, which is real, but in the seeming perception he had of a disorder in his toe. This perception, which Nature had conjoined with the sensation, was, in this instance, fallacious.

The same reasoning may be applied to every phenomenon that can, with propriety, be called a deception of sense. As when one who has the jaundice sees a body yellow, which is really white;† or when a man sees an object double, because his eyes are not both directed to it: in these, and other like cases, the sensations we have are real, and the deception is only in the perception which nature has annexed to them.

Nature has connected our perception of external objects with certain sensations. If the sensation is produced, the corresponding perception follows even when there is no object, and in that case is apt to deceive us. [253] In like manner, nature has connected our sensations with certain impressions that are made upon the nerves and brain; and, when the impression is made, from whatever cause, the corresponding sensation and perception immediately follow. Thus, in the man who feels pain in his toe after the leg is cut off, the nerve that went to the toe, part of which was cut off with the leg, had the same impression made upon the remaining part, which, in the natural state of his body, was caused

immediate, intuitive, or real perception of external things, which our consciousness assures that we possess, is the immediate connection of the cognitive principle with every part of the corporeal organism.—H.

* Only if the toe be considered as a mere material mass, and apart from an animating principle.—H.
† That the pain is where it is felt is, however, the doctrine of common sense. We only feel in as much as we have a body and a soul; we only feel pain in the toe in as much as we have such a member, and in

as much as the mind, or sentient principle, pervades it. We just as much feel in the toe as we think in the head. If (but only if) the latter be a *vitium subreptionis*, as Kant thinks, so is the former.—H.
* This illustration is Des Cartes'. If correct, it only shews that the connection of mind with organization extends from the centre to the circumference of the nervous system, and is not limited to any part.—H.
† The man does not see the white *body* at all—H.

by a hurt in the toe: and immediately this impression is followed by the sensation and perception which nature connected with it.*

In like manner, if the same impressions which are made at present upon my optic nerves by the objects before me, could be made in the dark, I apprehend that I should have the same sensations and see the same objects which I now see. The impressions and sensations would in such a case be real, and the perception only fallacious.*

Let us next consider the notions which our senses give us of those attributes of bodies called *powers*. This is the more necessary, because power seems to imply some activity; yet we consider body as a dead inactive thing, which does not act, but may be acted upon.

Of the mechanical powers ascribed to bodies, that which is called their *vis insita* or *inertia*, may first be considered. By this is meant, no more than that bodies never change their state of themselves, either from rest to motion, or from motion to rest, or from one degree of velocity or one direction to another. In order to produce any such change, there must be some force impressed upon them; and the change produced is precisely proportioned to the force impressed, and in the direction of that force.

That all bodies have this property, is a matter of fact, which we learn from daily observation, as well as from the most accurate experiments.. [254] Now, it seems plain, that this does not imply any activity in body, but rather the contrary. A power in body to change its state, would much rather imply activity than its continuing in the same state: so that, although this property of bodies is called their *vis insita*, or *vis inertiæ*, it implies no proper activity.

If we consider, next, the power of gravity, it is a fact that all the bodies of our planetary system gravitate towards each other. This has been fully proved by the great Newton. But this gravitation is not conceived by that philosopher to be a power inherent in bodies, which they exert of themselves, but a force impressed upon them, to which they must necessarily yield. Whether this be impressed by some subtile æther, or whether it be impressed by the power of the Supreme Being, or of some subordinate spiritual being, we do not know; but all sound natural philosophy, particularly that of Newton, supposes it to be an impressed force, and not inherent in bodies.†

So that, when bodies gravitate, they do not properly act, but are acted upon: they only yield to an impression that is made upon them. It is common in language to express, by active verbs, many changes in things wherein they are merely passive: and this way of speaking is used chiefly when the cause of the change is not obvious to sense. Thus we say that a ship sails, when every man of common sense knows that she has no inherent power of motion, and is only driven by wind and tide. In like manner, when we say that the planets gravitate towards the sun, we mean no more but that, by some unknown power, they are drawn or impelled in that direction.

What has been said of the power of gravitation may be applied to other mechanical powers, such as cohesion, magnetism, electricity; and no less to chemical and medical powers. By all these, certain effects are produced, upon the application of one body to another. [255] Our senses discover the effect; but the power is latent. We know there must be a cause of the effect, and we form a relative notion of it from its effect; and very often the same name is used to signify the unknown cause, and the known effect.

We ascribe to vegetables the powers of drawing nourishment, growing and multiplying their kind. Here likewise the effect is manifest, but the cause is latent to sense. These powers, therefore, as well as all the other powers we ascribe to bodies, are unknown causes of certain known effects. It is the business of philosophy to investigate the nature of those powers as far as we are able; but our senses leave us in the dark.

We may observe a great similarity in the notions which our senses give us of secondary qualities, of the disorders we feel in our own bodies, and of the various powers of bodies which we have enumerated. They are all obscure and relative notions, being a conception of some unknown cause of a known effect. Their names are, for the most part, common to the effect and to its cause; and they are a proper subject of philosophical disquisition. They might, therefore, I think, not improperly be called *occult* qualities.

This name, indeed, is fallen into disgrace since the time of Des Cartes. It is said to have been used by the Peripatetics to cloak their ignorance, and to stop all inquiry into the nature of those qualities called *occult*. Be it so. Let those answer for this abuse of the word who were guilty of it. To call a thing occult, if we attend to the meaning of the word, is rather modestly to confess ignorance, than to cloak it. It is to point it out as a proper subject for the investigation of philosophers, whose proper business it is to better the condition of humanity, by discovering what was before hid from human knowledge. [256]

---

* This is a doctrine which cannot be reconciled with that of an intuitive or objective perception. All here is subjective.—H.

† That all *activity* supposes an *immaterial* or *spiritual* agent, is an ancient doctrine. It is, however, only an hypothesis.—H.

Y

Were I therefore to make a division of the qualities of bodies as they appear to our senses, I would divide them first into those that are *manifest* and those that are *occult*. The manifest qualities are those which Mr Locke calls *primary;* such as Extension, Figure, Divisibility, Motion, Hardness, Softness, Fluidity. The nature of these is manifest even to sense ; and the business of the philosopher with regard to them, is not to find out their nature, which is well known, but to discover the effects produced by their various combinations ; and, with regard to those of them which are not essential to matter, to discover their causes as far as he is able.

The second class consists of occult qualities, which may be subdivided into various kinds : as, *first,* the secondary qualities ; *secondly,* the disorders we feel in our own bodies ; and, *thirdly,* all the qualities which we call powers of bodies, whether mechanical, chemical, medical, animal, or vegetable; or if there be any other powers not comprehended under these heads. Of all these the existence is manifest to sense, but the nature is occult ; and here the philosopher has an ample field.

What is necessary for the conduct of our animal life, the bountiful Author of Nature hath made manifest to all men. But there are many other choice secrets of Nature, the discovery of which enlarges the power and exalts the state of man. These are left to be discovered by the proper use of our rational powers. They are hid, not that they may be always concealed from human knowledge, but that we may be excited to search for them. This is the proper business of a philosopher, and it is the glory of a man, and the best reward of his labour, to discover what Nature has thus concealed. [257]

CHAPTER XIX.

OF MATTER AND OF SPACE.

THE objects of sense we have hitherto considered are qualities. But qualities must have a subject. We give the names of *matter, material substance,* and *body,* to the subject of sensible qualities ; and it may be asked what this *matter* is.

I perceive in a billiard ball, figure, colour, and motion ; but the ball is not figure, nor is it colour, nor motion, nor all these taken together ; it is something that has figure, and colour, and motion. This is a dictate of nature, and the belief of all mankind.

As to the nature of this something, I am afraid we can give little account of it, but that it has the qualities which our senses discover.

But how do we know that they are qualities, and cannot exist without a subject ? I confess I cannot explain how we know that they cannot exist without a subject, any more than I can explain how we know that they exist. We have the information of nature for their existence ; and I think we have the information of nature that they are qualities.

The belief that figure, motion, and colour are qualities, and require a subject, must either be a judgment of nature, or it must be discovered by reason, or it must be a prejudice that has no just foundation. There are philosophers who maintain that it is a mere prejudice ; that a body is nothing but a collection of what we call sensible qualities ; and that they neither have nor need any subject. This is the opinion of Bishop Berkeley and Mr Hume ; and they were led to it by finding that they had not in their minds any idea of substance. [258] It could neither be an idea of sensation nor of reflection.

But to me nothing seems more absurd than that there should be extension without anything extended, or motion without anything moved ; yet I cannot give reasons for my opinion, because it seems to me self-evident, and an immediate dictate of my nature.

And that it is the belief of all mankind, appears in the structure of all languages ; in which we find adjective nouns used to express sensible qualities. It is well known that every adjective in language must belong to some substantive expressed or understood—that is, every quality must belong to some subject.

Sensible qualities make so great a part of the furniture of our minds, their kinds are so many, and their number so great, that, if prejudice, and not nature, teach us to ascribe them all to a subject, it must have a great work to perform, which cannot be accomplished in a short time, nor carried on to the same pitch in every individual. We should find not individuals only, but nations and ages, differing from each other in the progress which this prejudice had made in their sentiments ; but we find no such difference among men. What one man accounts a quality, all men do, and ever did.

It seems, therefore, to be a judgment of nature, that the things immediately perceived are qualities, which must belong to a subject ; and all the information that our senses give us about this subject, is, that it is that to which such qualities belong. From this it is evident, that our notion of body or matter, as distinguished from its qualities, is a relative notion;* and I am

---

* That is,—our notion of *absolute* body is *relative.* This is incorrectly expressed. We can know, we can

afraid it must always be obscure until men have other faculties. [259]

The philosopher, in this, seems to have no advantage above the vulgar; for, as they perceive colour, and figure, and motion by their senses as well he does, and both are equally certain that there is a subject of those qualities, so the notions which both have of this subject are equally obscure. When the philosopher calls it a *substratum*, and a subject of inhesion, those learned words convey no meaning but what every man understands and expresses, by saying, in common language, that it is a thing extended, and solid, and movable.

The relation which sensible qualities bear to their subject—that is, to body—is not, however, so dark but that it is easily distinguished from all other relations. Every man can distinguish it from the relation of an effect to its cause; of a mean to its end; or of a sign to the thing signified by it.

I think it requires some ripeness of understanding to distinguish the qualities of a body from the body. Perhaps this distinction is not made by brutes, nor by infants; and if any one thinks that this distinction is not made by our senses, but by some other power of the mind, I will not dispute this point, provided it be granted that men, when their faculties are ripe, have a natural conviction that sensible qualities cannot exist by themselves without some subject to which they belong.

I think, indeed, that some of the determinations we form concerning matter cannot be deduced solely from the testimony of sense, but must be referred to some other source.

There seems to be nothing more evident than that all bodies must consist of parts; and that every part of a body is a body, and a distinct being, which may exist without the other parts; and yet I apprehend this conclusion is not deduced solely from the testimony of sense: for, besides that it is a necessary truth, and, therefore, no object of sense,* there is a limit beyond which we

cannot perceive any division of a body. The parts become too small to be perceived by our senses; but we cannot believe that it becomes then incapable of being farther divided, or that such division would make it not to be a body. [260]

We carry on the division and subdivision in our thought far beyond the reach of our senses, and we can find no end to it: nay, I think we plainly discern that there can be no limit beyond which the division cannot be carried.

For, if there be any limit to this division, one of two things must necessarily happen: either we have come by division to a body which is extended, but has no parts, and is absolutely indivisible; or this body is divisible, but, as soon as it is divided, it becomes no body. Both these positions seem to me absurd, and one or the other is the necessary consequence of supposing a limit to the divisibility of matter.

On the other hand, if it is admitted that the divisibility of matter has no limit, it will follow that no body can be called one individual substance. You may as well call it two, or twenty, or two hundred. For, when it is divided into parts, every part is a being or substance distinct from all the other parts, and was so even before the division. Any one part may continue to exist, though all the other parts were annihilated.

There is, indeed, a principle long received as an axiom in metaphysics, which I cannot reconcile to the divisibility of matter; it is, that every being is one, *omne ens est unum*. By which, I suppose, is meant, that everything that exists must either be one indivisible being, or composed of a determinate number of indivisible beings. Thus, an army may be divided into regiments, a regiment into companies, and a company into men. But here the division has its limit; for you cannot divide a man without destroying him, because he is an individual; and everything, according to this axiom, must be an individual, or made up of individuals. [261]

That this axiom will hold with regard to an army, and with regard to many other things, must be granted; but I require the evidence of its being applicable to all beings whatsoever.

Leibnitz, conceiving that all beings must have this metaphysical unity, was by this led to maintain that matter, and, indeed, the whole universe, is made up of monads—that is, simple and indivisible substances.

Perhaps the same apprehension might lead Boscovich into his hypothesis, which seems much more ingenious—to wit, that

conceive, only what is relative. Our knowledge of *qualities* or *phænomena* is necessarily relative; for these exist only as they exist *in relation to our faculties*. The knowledge, or even the conception, of a substance in itself, and apart from any qualities in relation to, and therefore cognisable or conceivable by, our minds, involves a contradiction. Of such we can form only a *negative* notion; that is, we can merely *conceive it as inconceivable*. But to call this negative notion a *relative notion*, is wrong; 1°, because all our (positive) notions are relative; and 2°, because this is itself a negative notion—*i. e.*, no notion at all—simply because there is no r lation. The same impropriate application of the term relative was also made by Reid when speaking of the secondary qualities.—H.

* It is creditable to Reid that he perceived that the quality of *necessity* is the criterion which distinguishes *native* from *adventitious* notions or judgments. He did not, however, always make the proper use of it. Leibnitz has the honour of first explicitly enouncing this criterion, and Kant of first fully applying it to the phænomena. In none has Kant been more successful than in this under consideration.—H.

matter is composed of a definite number of mathematical points, endowed with certain powers of attraction and repulsion.

The divisibility of matter without any limit, seems to me more tenable than either of these hypotheses; nor do I lay much stress upon the metaphysical axiom, considering its origin. Metaphysicians thought proper to make the attributes common to all beings the subject of a science. It must be a matter of some difficulty to find out such attributes; and, after racking their invention, they have specified three— to wit, Unity, Verity, and Goodness; and these, I suppose, have been invented to make a number, rather than from any clear evidence of their being universal.

There are other determinations concerning matter, which, I think, are not solely founded upon the testimony of sense : such as, that it is impossible that two bodies should occupy the same place at the same time ; or that the same body should be in different places at the same time ; or that a body can be moved from one place to another, without passing through the intermediate places, either in a straight course, or by some circuit. These appear to be necessary truths, and therefore cannot be conclusions of our senses; for our senses testify only what is, and not what must necessarily be.* [262]

We are next to consider our notion of *Space*. It may be observed that, although space be not perceived by any of our senses when all matter is removed, yet, when we perceive any of the primary qualities, space presents itself as a necessary concomitant ;† for there can neither be extension nor motion, nor figure nor division, nor cohesion of parts, without space.

There are only two of our senses by which the notion of space enters into the mind— to wit, touch and sight. If we suppose a man to have neither of these senses, I do not see how he could ever have any conception of space.‡ Supposing him to have both, until he sees or feels other objects, he can have no notion of space. It has neither colour nor figure to make it an object of sight : it has no tangible quality to make it an object of touch. But other objects of sight and touch carry the notion of space along with them ; and not the notion only, but the belief of it ; for a body could not exist if there was no space to contain it. It could not move if there was no space. Its situation, its distance, and every relation it has to other bodies, suppose space.

But, though the notion of space seems

not to enter, at first, into the mind, until it is introduced by the proper objects of sense, yet, being once introduced, it remains in our conception and belief, though the objects which introduced it be removed. We see no absurdity in supposing a body to be annihilated ; but the space that contained it remains ; and, to suppose that annihilated, seems to be absurd. It is so much allied to nothing or emptiness, that it seems incapable of annihilation or of creation.*

Space not only retains a firm hold of our belief, even when we suppose all the objects that introduced it to be annihilated, but it swells to immensity. We can set no limits to it, either of extent or of duration. Hence we call it immense, eternal, immovable, and indestructible. But it is only an immense, eternal, immovable, and indestructible void or emptiness. Perhaps we may apply to it what the Peripatetics said of their first matter, that, whatever it is, it is potentially only, not actually. [263]

When we consider parts of space that have measure and figure, there is nothing we understand better, nothing about which we can reason so clearly, and to so great extent. Extension and figure are circumscribed parts of space, and are the object of geometry, a science in which human reason has the most ample field, and can go deeper, and with more certainty, than in any other. But, when we attempt to comprehend the whole of space, and to trace it to its origin, we lose ourselves in the search. The profound speculations of ingenious men upon this subject differ so widely as may lead us to suspect that the line of human understanding is too short to reach the bottom of it.

Bishop Berkeley, I think, was the first who observed that the extension, figure, and space, of which we speak in common language, and of which geometry treats, are originally perceived by the sense of touch only ; but that there is a notion of extension, figure, and space, which may be got by sight, without any aid from touch. To distinguish these, he calls the first tangible extension, tangible figure, and tangible space. The last he calls visible.

As I think this distinction very important in the philosophy of our senses, I shall adopt the names used by the inventor to express it ; remembering what has been already observed—that space, whether tangible or visible, is not so properly an object of sense, as a necessary concomitant of the objects both of sight and touch.†

---

* See last note.—H.
† See above, p. 124, note † —H.
‡ *Vide supra*, p. 123, col. b, notes *, † ; and p. 126, col. b, note *.—H.

* His doctrine of space is an example of Reid's imperfect application of the criterion of necessity. See p. 123, note †. It seemingly required but little to rise to Kant's view of the conception of space, as an *a priori* or native form of thought.—H.
† See above, p. 124, note †.—H.

The reader may likewise be pleased to attend to this, that, when I use the names of tangible and visible space, I do not mean to adopt Bishop Berkeley's opinion, so far as to think that they are really different things, and altogether unlike. I take them to be different conceptions of the same thing; the one very partial, and the other more complete; but both distinct and just, as far as they reach. [264]

Thus, when I see a spire at a very great distance, it seems like the point of a bodkin; there appears no vane at the top, no angles. But, when I view the same object at a small distance, I see a huge pyramid of several angles, with a vane on the top. Neither of these appearances is fallacious. Each of them is what it ought to be, and what it must be, from such an object seen at such different distances. These different appearances of the same object may serve to illustrate the different conceptions of space, according as they are drawn from the information of sight alone, or as they are drawn from the additional information of touch.

Our sight alone, unaided by touch, gives a very partial notion of space, but yet a distinct one. When it is considered according to this partial notion, I call it visible space. The sense of touch gives a much more complete notion of space; and, when it is considered according to this notion, I call it tangible space. Perhaps there may be intelligent beings of a higher order, whose conceptions of space are much more complete than those we have from both senses. Another sense added to those of sight and touch, might, for what I know, give us conceptions of space as different from those we can now attain as tangible space is from visible, and might resolve many knotty points concerning it, which, from the imperfection of our faculties, we cannot, by any labour, untie.

Berkeley acknowledges that there is an exact correspondence between the visible figure and magnitude of objects, and the tangible; and that every modification of the one has a modification of the other corresponding. He acknowledges, likewise, that Nature has established such a connection between the visible figure and magnitude of an object, and the tangible, that we learn by experience to know the tangible figure and magnitude from the visible. And, having been accustomed to do so from infancy, we get the habit of doing it with such facility and quickness that we think we see the tangible figure, magnitude, and distance of bodies, when, in reality, we only collect those tangible qualities from the corresponding visible qualities, which are natural signs of them. [265]

The correspondence and connection which [264–266]

Berkeley shews to be between the visible figure and magnitude of objects, and their tangible figure and magnitude, is in some respects very similar to that which we have observed between our sensations and the primary qualities with which they are connected. No sooner is the sensation felt, than immediately we have the conception and belief of the corresponding quality. We give no attention to the sensation; it has not a name; and it is difficult to persuade us that there was any such thing.

In like manner, no sooner is the visible figure and magnitude of an object seen, than immediately we have the conception and belief of the corresponding tangible figure and magnitude. We give no attention to the visible figure and magnitude. It is immediately forgot, as if it had never been perceived; and it has no name in common language; and, indeed, until Berkeley pointed it out as a subject of speculation, and gave it a name, it had none among philosophers, excepting in one instance, relating to the heavenly bodies, which are beyond the reach of touch. With regard to them, what Berkeley calls visible magnitude was, by astronomers, called apparent magnitude.

There is surely an apparent magnitude, and an apparent figure of terrestrial objects, as well as of celestial; and this is what Berkeley calls their visible figure and magnitude. But this was never made an object of thought among philosophers, until that author gave it a name, and observed the correspondence and connection between it and tangible magnitude and figure, and how the mind gets the habit of passing so instantaneously from the visible figure as a sign to the tangible figure as the thing signified by it, that the first is perfectly forgot as if it had never been perceived. [266]

Visible figure, extension, and space, may be made a subject of mathematical speculation as well as the tangible. In the visible, we find two dimensions only; in the tangible, three. In the one, magnitude is measured by angles; in the other, by lines. Every part of visible space bears some proportion to the whole; but tangible space being immense, any part of it bears no proportion to the whole.

Such differences in their properties led Bishop Berkeley to think that visible and tangible magnitude and figure are things totally different and dissimilar, and cannot both belong to the same object.

And upon this dissimilitude is grounded one of the strongest arguments by which his system is supported. For it may be said, if there be external objects which have a real extension and figure, it must be either tangible extension and figure, or visible, or both.* The last appears absurd; nor was it ever maintained by any man, that the same object has two kinds of extension and figure totally dissimilar. There is then only one of the two really in the object; and the other must be ideal. But no reason can be assigned why the perceptions of one sense should be real, while those of another are only ideal; and he who is persuaded that the objects of sight are ideas only, has equal reason to believe so of the objects of touch.

This argument, however, loses all its force, if it be true, as was formerly hinted, that visible figure and extension are only a partial conception, and the tangible figure and extension a more complete conception of that figure and extension which is really in the object.† [267]

It has been proved very fully by Bishop Berkeley, that sight alone, without any aid from the informations of touch, gives us no perception, nor even conception of the distance of any object from the eye. But he was not aware that this very principle overturns the argument for his system, taken from the difference between visible and tangible extension and figure. For, supposing external objects to exist, and to have that tangible extension and figure which we perceive, it follows demonstrably, from the principle now mentioned, that their visible extension and figure must be just what we see it to be.

The rules of perspective, and of the projection of the sphere, which is a branch of perspective, are demonstrable. They suppose the existence of external objects, which have a tangible extension and figure; and, upon that supposition, they demonstrate what must be the visible extension and figure of such objects, when placed in such a position and at such a distance.

Hence, it is evident that the visible figure and extension of objects is so far from being incompatible with the tangible, that the first is a necessary consequence from the last in beings that see as we do. The correspondence between them is not arbitrary, like that between words and the thing they signify, as Berkeley thought; but it results necessarily from the nature of the two senses; and this correspondence being always found in experience to be exactly what the rules of perspective shew that it ought to be if the senses give true information, is an argument of the truth of both.

* Or neither. And this omitted supposition is the true. For neither sight nor touch give us *full* and *accurate* information in regard to the *real* extension and figure of objects. See above p. 126, notes *; and p. 303, col. b, note *.—H.
† If tangible figure and extension be only "*a more* complete conception,*" &c., it cannot be a cognition of real figure and extension.—H.

CHAPTER XX.

OF THE EVIDENCE OF SENSE, AND OF BELIEF IN GENERAL.

THE intention of nature in the powers which we call the external senses, is evident. They are intended to give us that information of external objects which the Supreme Being saw to be proper for us in our present state; and they give to all mankind the information necessary for life, without reasoning, without any art or investigation on our part. [268]

The most uninstructed peasant has as distinct a conception and as firm a belief of the immediate objects of his senses, as the greatest philosopher; and with this he rests satisfied, giving himself no concern how he came by this conception and belief. But the philosopher is impatient to know how his conception of external objects, and his belief of their existence, is produced. This, I am afraid, is hid in impenetrable darkness. But where there is no knowledge, there is the more room for conjecture, and of this, philosophers have always been very liberal.

The dark cave and shadows of Plato,* the species of Aristotle,† the films of Epicurus, and the ideas and impressions of modern philosophers,‡ are the productions of human fancy, successively invented to satisfy the eager desire of knowing how we perceive external objects; but they are all deficient in the two essential characters of a true and philosophical account of the phænomenon: for we neither have any evidence of their existence, nor, if they did exist, can it be shewn how they would produce perception.

It was before observed, that there are two ingredients in this operation of perception: *first*, the conception or notion of the object; and, *secondly*, the belief of its present existence. Both are unaccountable.

That we can assign no adequate cause of our first conceptions of things, I think, is now acknowledged by the most enlightened philosophers. We know that such is our constitution, that in certain circumstances we have certain conceptions; but how they are produced we know no more than how we ourselves were produced. [269]

When we have got the conception of external objects by our senses, we can analyse them in our thought into their simple ingredients; and we can compound those ingredients into various new forms, which the senses never presented. But it is

* See p. 262, col. b, note *.—H.
† See Note M.—H.
‡ By *ideas*, as repeatedly noticed, Reid under stands always certain representative entities distinct from the knowing mind.

beyond the power of human imagination to form any conception, whose simple ingredients have not been furnished by nature in a manner unaccountable to our understanding.

We have an immediate conception of the operations of our own minds, joined with a a belief of their existence; and this we call consciousness.* But this is only giving a name to this source of our knowledge. It is not a discovery of its cause. In like manner, we have, by our external senses, a conception of external objects, joined with a belief of their existence; and this we call perception. But this is only giving a name to another source of our knowledge, without discovering its cause.

We know that, when certain impressions are made upon our organs, nerves, and brain, certain corresponding sensations are felt, and certain objects are both conceived and believed to exist. But in this train of operations nature works in the dark. We can neither discover the cause of any one of them, nor any necessary connection of one with another; and, whether they are connected by any necessary tie, or only conjoined in our constitution by the will of heaven, we know not.†

That any kind of impression upon a body should be the efficient cause of sensation, appears very absurd. Nor can we perceive any necessary connection between sensation and the conception and belief of an external object. For anything we can discover, we might have been so framed as to have all the sensations we now have by our senses, without any impressions upon our organs, and without any conception of any external object. For anything we know, we might have been so made as to perceive external objects, without any impressions on bodily organs, and without any of those sensations which invariably accompany perception in our present frame. [270]

If our conception of external objects be unaccountable, the conviction and belief of their existence, which we get by our senses, is no less so.‡

* Here *consciousness* is made to consist in *conception.* But, as Reid could hardly mean that consciousness conceives (*i. e.,* represents) the operations about which it is conversant, and is not intuitively cognisant of them, it would seem that he occasionally employs conception for knowledge. This is of importance in explaining favourably Reid's use of the word Conception in relation to Perception. But then, how vague and vacillating is his language!—H.

† See p. 257, col. b, note *.—H.

‡ If an immediate knowledge of external things—that is, a consciousness of the qualities of the *non-ego*—be admitted, the belief of their existence follows of course. On this supposition, therefore, such a belief would not be unaccountable; for it would be accounted for by the fact of the knowledge in which it would necessarily be contained. Our belief, in this case, of the existence of external objects, would not be more inexplicable than our belief that 2+2=4. In both cases it would be sufficient to say, *we believe because we know;* for belief is only unaccountable when it is not the consequent or concomitant of

[270–271]

Belief, assent, conviction, are words which I do not think admit of logical definition, because the operation of mind signified by them is perfectly simple, and of its own kind. Nor do they need to be defined, because they are common words, and well understood.

Belief must have an object. For he that believes must believe something; and that which he believes, is called the object of his belief. Of this object of his belief, he must have some conception, clear or obscure; for, although there may be the most clear and distinct conception of an object without any belief of its existence, there can be no belief without conception.*

Belief is always expressed in language by a proposition, wherein something is affirmed or denied. This is the form of speech which in all languages is appropriated to that purpose, and without belief there could be neither affirmation nor denial, nor should we have any form of words to express either. Belief admits of all degrees, from the slightest suspicion to the fullest assurance. These things are so evident to every man that reflects, that it would be abusing the reader's patience to dwell upon them.

I proceed to observe that there are many operations of mind in which, when we analyse them as far as we are able, we find belief to be an essential ingredient. A man cannot be conscious of his own thoughts, without believing that he thinks. He cannot perceive an object of sense, without believing that it exists.† He cannot distinctly remember a past event, without believing that it did exist. Belief therefore is an ingredient in consciousness, in perception, and in remembrance. [271]

Not only in most of our intellectual operations, but in many of the active principles of the human mind, belief enters as an ingredient. Joy and sorrow, hope and fear, imply a belief of good or ill, either present or in expectation. Esteem, gratitude, pity, and resentment, imply a belief of certain qualities in their objects. In every action that is done for an end, there must be a belief of its tendency to that end. So large a share has belief in our intellectual

knowledge. By this, however, I do not, of course, mean to say that knowledge is not in itself marvellous and unaccountable. This statement of Reid again favours the opinion that his doctrine of perception is not really immediate.—H.

* Is *conception* here equivalent to *knowledge* or to *thought?*—H.

† Mr Stewart (*Elem.* I., ch. iii., p. 146, and *Essays,* II., ch. ii., p. 79, *sq.*) proposes a supplement to this doctrine of Reid, in order to explain why we believe in the existence of the qualities of external objects when they are not the objects of our perception. This belief he holds to be the result of *experience,* in combination with an original principle of our constitution, whereby we are *determined to believe in the permanence of the laws of nature.*—H

operations, in our active principles, and in our actions themselves, that, as faith in things divine is represented as the main spring in the life of a Christian, so belief in general is the main spring in the life of a man.

That men often believe what there is no just ground to believe, and thereby are led into hurtful errors, is too evident to be denied. And, on the other hand, that there are just grounds of belief can as little be doubted by any man who is not a perfect sceptic.

We give the name of evidence to whatever is a ground of belief. To believe without evidence is a weakness which every man is concerned to avoid, and which every man wishes to avoid. Nor is it in a man's power to believe anything longer than he thinks he has evidence.

What this evidence is, is more easily felt than described. Those who never reflected upon its nature, feel its influence in governing their belief. It is the business of the logician to explain its nature, and to distinguish its various kinds and degrees; but every man of understanding can judge of it, and commonly judges right, when the evidence is fairly laid before him, and his mind is free from prejudice. A man who knows nothing of the theory of vision may have a good eye; and a man who never speculated about evidence in the abstract may have a good judgment. [272]

The common occasions of life lead us to distinguish evidence into different kinds, to which we give names that are well understood; such as the evidence of sense, the evidence of memory, the evidence of consciousness, the evidence of testimony, the evidence of axioms, the evidence of reasoning. All men of common understanding agree that each of these kinds of evidence may afford just ground of belief, and they agree very generally in the circumstances that strengthen or weaken them.

Philosophers have endeavoured, by analysing the different sorts of evidence, to find out some common nature wherein they all agree, and thereby to reduce them all to one. This was the aim of the schoolmen in their intricate disputes about the criterion of truth. Des Cartes placed this criterion of truth in clear and distinct perception, and laid it down as a maxim, that whatever we clearly and distinctly perceive to be true, is true; but it is difficult to know what he understands by clear and distinct perception in this maxim. Mr Locke placed it in a perception of the agreement or disagreement of our ideas, which perception is immediate in intuitive knowledge, and by the intervention of other ideas in reasoning.

I confess that, although I have, as I think, a distinct notion of the different

kinds of evidence above-mentioned, and, perhaps, of some others, which it is unnecessary here to enumerate, yet I am not able to find any common nature to which they may all be reduced. They seem to me to agree only in this, that they are all fitted by Nature to produce belief in the human mind, some of them in the highest degree, which we call certainty, others in various degrees according to circumstances.

I shall take it for granted that the evidence of sense, when the proper circumstances concur, is good evidence, and a just ground of belief. My intention in this place is only to compare it with the other kinds that have been mentioned, that we may judge whether it be reducible to any of them, or of a nature peculiar to itself. [273]

First, It seems to be quite different from the evidence of reasoning. All good evidence is commonly called reasonable evidence, and very justly, because it ought to govern our belief as reasonable creatures. And, according to this meaning, I think the evidence of sense no less reasonable than that of demonstration.[*] If Nature give us information of things that concern us, by other means than by reasoning, reason itself will direct us to receive that information with thankfulness, and to make the best use of it.

But, when we speak of the evidence of reasoning as a particular kind of evidence, it means the evidence of propositions that are inferred by reasoning, from propositions already known and believed. Thus, the evidence of the fifth proposition of the first book of Euclid's Elements consists in this, That it is shewn to be the necessary consequence of the axioms, and of the preceding propositions. In all reasoning, there must be one or more premises, and a conclusion drawn from them. And the premises are called the reason why we must believe the conclusion which we see to follow from them.

That the evidence of sense is of a different kind, needs little proof. No man seeks a reason for believing what he sees or feels; and, if he did, it would be difficult to find one. But, though he can give no reason for believing his senses, his belief remains as firm as if it were grounded on demonstration.

Many eminent philosophers, thinking it unreasonable to believe when they could not shew a reason, have laboured to furnish us with reasons for believing our senses; but their reasons are very insufficient, and will not bear examination. Other philoso-

---

[*] Ζητεῖν λόγον ἀξιοῦντας τὴν αἴσθησιν, ἀββωσία τίς ἐσι διανοίας.—Ar' Iolle. Προσήχειν οὐ δεῖ πάντα τοῖς διὰ τῶν λόγων, ἀλλὰ πολλάκις μᾶλλον τοῖς φαινομένοις.—Id. Ἢ ἡ αἴσθησις μᾶλλον ἢ τῷ λόγῳ πιστευτέον καὶ τοῖς λόγοις, ἐὰν ὁμολογούμενα δεικνύωσι τοῖς φαινομένοις.—Id. Ἡ αἴσθησις πιστ'μης ἔχει δύναμιν.—Id.—H.

phers have shewn very clearly the fallacy of these reasons, and have, as they imagine, discovered invincible reasons against this belief; but they have never been able either to shake it in themselves, or to convince others. [274] The statesman continues to plod, the soldier to fight, and the merchant to export and import, without being in the least moved by the demonstrations that have been offered of the non-existence of those things about which they are so seriously employed. And a man may as soon, by reasoning, pull the moon out of her orbit, as destroy the belief of the objects of sense.

Shall we say, then, that the evidence of sense is the same with that of axioms, or self-evident truths? I answer, *First*, That, all modern philosophers seem to agree that the existence of the objects of sense is not self-evident, that some of them have endeavoured to prove it by subtle reasoning, others to refute it. Neither of these can consider it as self-evident.

Secondly, I would observe that the word *axiom* is taken by philosophers in such a sense as that the existence of the objects of sense cannot, with propriety, be called an axiom. They give the name of axiom only to self-evident truths, that are necessary, and are not limited to time and place, but must be true at all times and in all places. The truths attested by our senses are not of this kind; they are contingent, and limited to time and place.

Thus, that one is the half of two, is an axiom. It is equally true at all times and in all places. We perceive, by attending to the proposition itself, that it cannot but be true; and, therefore, it is called an eternal, necessary, and immutable truth. That there is at present a chair on my right hand, and another on my left, is a truth attested by my senses; but it is not necessary, nor eternal, nor immutable. It may not be true next minute; and, therefore, to call it an axiom would, I apprehend, be to deviate from the common use of the word. [275]

Thirdly, If the word axiom be put to signify every truth which is known immediately, without being deduced from any antecedent truth, then the existence of the objects of sense may be called an axiom; for my senses give me as immediate conviction of what they testify, as my understanding gives of what is commonly called an axiom.

There is, no doubt, an analogy between the evidence of sense and the evidence of testimony. Hence, we find, in all languages, the analogical expressions of the *testimony of sense*, of giving *credit* to our senses, and the like. But there is a real difference between the two, as well as a similitude. In believing upon testimony, we rely upon the authority of a person who

[274–276]

testifies; but we have no such authority for believing our senses.

Shall we say, then, that this belief is the inspiration of the Almighty? I think this may be said in a good sense; for I take it to be the immediate effect of our constitution, which is the work of the Almighty. But, if inspiration be understood to imply a persuasion of its coming from God, our belief of the objects of sense is not inspiration; for a man would believe his senses though he had no notion of a Deity. He who is persuaded that he is the workmanship of God, and that it is a part of his constitution to believe his senses, may think that a good reason to confirm his belief. But he had the belief before he could give this or any other reason for it.

If we compare the evidence of sense with that of memory, we find a great resemblance, but still some difference. I remember distinctly to have dined yesterday with such a company. What is the meaning of this? It is, that I have a distinct conception and firm belief of this past event; not by reasoning, not by testimony, but immediately from my constitution. And I give the name of memory to that part of my constitution by which I have this kind of conviction of past events. [276]

I see a chair on my right hand. What is the meaning of this? It is, that I have, by my constitution, a distinct conception and firm belief of the present existence of the chair in such a place and in such a position; and I give the name of seeing to that part of my constitution by which I have this immediate conviction. The two operations agree in the immediate conviction which they give. They agree in this also, that the things believed are not necessary, but contingent, and limited to time and place. But they differ in two respects:—*First*, That memory has something for its object that did exist in time past; but the object of sight, and of all the senses, must be something which exists at present;—and, *Secondly*, That I see by my eyes, and only when they are directed to the object, and when it is illuminated. But my memory is not limited by any bodily organ that I know, nor by light and darkness, though it has its limitations of another kind.[*]

These differences are obvious to all men, and very reasonably lead them to consider seeing and remembering as operations specifically different. But the nature of the evidence they give, has a great resemblance.

---

[*] There is a more important difference than these omitted. In memory, we cannot possibly be conscious or immediately cognisant of any object beyond the modifications of the *ego* itself. In perception, (if an *immediate perception* be allowed,) we must be conscious, or immediately cognisant, of some phænomenon of the *non-ego*.—H.

A like difference and a like resemblance there is between the evidence of sense and that of consciousness, which I leave the reader to trace.

As to the opinion that evidence consists in a perception of the agreement or disagreement of ideas, we may have occasion to consider it more particularly in another place. Here I only observe, that, when taken in the most favourable sense, it may be applied with propriety to the evidence of reasoning, and to the evidence of some axioms. But I cannot see how, in any sense, it can be applied to the evidence of consciousness, to the evidence of memory, or to that of sense.

When I compare the different kinds of evidence above-mentioned, I confess, after all, that the evidence of reasoning, and that of some necessary and self-evident truths, seems to be the least mysterious and the most perfectly comprehended; and therefore I do not think it strange that philosophers should have endeavoured to reduce all kinds of evidence to these. [277]

When I see a proposition to be self-evident and necessary, and that the subject is plainly included in the predicate, there seems to be nothing more that I can desire in order to understand why I believe it. And when I see a consequence that necessarily follows from one or more self-evident propositions, I want nothing more with regard to my belief of that consequence. The light of truth so fills my mind in these cases, that I can neither conceive nor desire anything more satisfying.

On the other hand, when I remember distinctly a past event, or see an object before my eyes, this commands my belief no less than an axiom. But when, as a philosopher, I reflect upon this belief, and want to trace it to its origin, I am not able to resolve it into necessary and self-evident axioms, or conclusions that are necessarily consequent upon them. I seem to want that evidence which I can best comprehend, and which gives perfect satisfaction to an inquisitive mind; yet it is ridiculous to doubt; and I find it is not in my power. An attempt to throw off this belief is like an attempt to fly, equally ridiculous and impracticable.

To a philosopher, who has been accustomed to think that the treasure of his knowledge is the acquisition of that reasoning power of which he boasts, it is no doubt humiliating to find that his reason can lay no claim to the greater part of it.

By his reason, he can discover certain abstract and necessary relations of things; but his knowledge of what really exists, or did exist, comes by another channel, which is open to those who cannot reason. He is led to it in the dark, and knows not how he came by it. [278]

It is no wonder that the pride of philosophy should lead some to invent vain theories in order to account for this knowledge; and others, who see this to be impracticable, to spurn at a knowledge they cannot account for, and vainly attempt to throw it off as a reproach to their understanding. But the wise and the humble will receive it as the gift of Heaven, and endeavour to make the best use of it.

CHAPTER XXI.

OF THE IMPROVEMENT OF THE SENSES.

Our senses may be considered in two views: *first*, As they afford us agreeable sensations, or subject us to such as are disagreeable; and, *secondly*, As they give us information of things that concern us.

In the *first* view, they neither require nor admit of improvement. Both the painful and the agreeable sensations of our external senses are given by nature for certain ends; and they are given in that degree which is the most proper for their end. By diminishing or increasing them, we should not mend, but mar the work of Nature.

Bodily pains are indications of some disorder or hurt of the body, and admonitions to use the best means in our power to prevent or remove their causes. As far as this can be done by temperance, exercise, regimen, or the skill of the physician, every man hath sufficient inducement to do it.

When pain cannot be prevented or removed, it is greatly alleviated by patience and fortitude of mind. While the mind is superior to pain, the man is not unhappy, though he may be exercised. It leaves no sting behind it, but rather matter of triumph and agreeable reflection, when borne properly, and in a good cause. [279] The Canadians have taught us that even savages may acquire a superiority to the most excruciating pains; and, in every region of the earth, instances will be found, where a sense of duty, of honour, or even of worldly interest, have triumphed over it.

It is evident that nature intended for man, in his present state, a life of labour and toil, wherein he may be occasionally exposed to pain and danger; and the happiest man is not he who has felt least of those evils, but he whose mind is fitted to bear them by real magnanimity.

Our active and perceptive powers are improved and perfected by use and exercise. This is the constitution of nature. But, with regard to the agreeable and disagreeable sensations we have by our senses, the very contrary is an established constitution of nature—the frequent repetition of them weakens their force. Sensations at first very disagreeable, by use become tolerable, and at last perfectly indifferent. And those that are at first very agreeable, by frequent repetition become insipid, and at last, perhaps, give disgust. Nature has set limits to the pleasures of sense, which we cannot pass; and all studied gratifications of them, as it is mean and unworthy of a man, so it is foolish and fruitless.

The man who, in eating and drinking, and in other gratifications of sense, obeys the calls of Nature, without affecting delicacies and refinements, has all the enjoyment that the senses can afford. If one could, by a soft and luxurious life, acquire a more delicate sensibility to pleasure, it must be at the expense of a like sensibility to pain, from which he can never promise exemption, and at the expense of cherishing many diseases which produce pain.

The improvement of our external senses, as they are the means of giving us information, is a subject more worthy of our attention; for, although they are not the noblest and most exalted powers of our nature, yet they are not the least useful. [280] All that we know, or can know, of the material world, must be grounded upon their information; and the philosopher, as well as the day-labourer, must be indebted to them for the largest part of his knowledge.

Some of our perceptions by the senses may be called original, because they require no previous experience or learning; but the far greatest part is acquired, and the fruit of experience.

Three of our senses—to wit, smell, taste, and hearing—originally give us only certain sensations, and a conviction that these sensations are occasioned by some external object. We give a name to that quality of the object by which it is fitted to produce such a sensation, and connect that quality with the object, and with its other qualities.

Thus we learn, that a certain sensation of smell is produced by a rose; and that quality in the rose, by which it is fitted to produce this sensation, we call the smell of the rose. Here it is evident that the sensation is original. The perception that the rose has that quality which we call its smell, is acquired. In like manner, we learn all those qualities in bodies which we call their smell, their taste, their sound. These are all secondary qualities, and we give the same name to them which we give to the sensations they produce; not from any similitude between the sensation and the quality of the same name, but because the quality is signified to us by the sensation as its sign, and because our senses give us no other knowledge of the quality but that it is fit to produce such a sensation.

By the other two senses, we have much more ample information. By sight, we

learn to distinguish objects by their colour, in the same manner as by their sound, taste, and smell. By this sense, we perceive visible objects to have extension in two dimensions, to have visible figure and magnitude, and a certain angular distance from one another. These, I conceive, are the original perceptions of sight.* [281]

By touch, we not only perceive the temperature of bodies as to heat and cold,† which are secondary qualities, but we perceive originally their three dimensions, their tangible figure and magnitude, their linear distance from one another, their hardness, softness, or fluidity. These qualities we originally perceive by touch only; but, by experience, we learn to perceive all or most of them by sight.

We learn to perceive, by one sense, what originally could have been perceived only by another, by finding a connection between the objects of the different senses. Hence the original perceptions, or the sensations of one sense become signs of whatever has always been found connected with them; and from the sign, the mind passes immediately to the conception and belief of the thing signified. And, although the connection in the mind between the sign and the thing signified by it, be the effect of custom, this custom becomes a second nature, and it is difficult to distinguish it from the original power of perception.

Thus, if a sphere of one uniform colour be set before me, I perceive evidently by my eye its spherical figure and its three dimensions. All the world will acknowledge that, by sight only, without touching it, I may be certain that it is a sphere; yet it is no less certain that, by the original power of sight, I could not perceive it to be a sphere, and to have three dimensions. The eye originally could only perceive two dimensions, and a gradual variation of colour on the different sides of the object.

It is experience that teaches me that the variation of colour is an effect of spherical convexity, and of the distribution of light and shade. But so rapid is the progress of the thought, from the effect to the cause, that we attend only to the last, and can hardly be persuaded that we do not immediately see the three dimensions of the sphere. [282]

Nay, it may be observed, that, in this case, the acquired perception in a manner effaces the original one; for the sphere is seen to be of one uniform colour, though originally there would have appeared a gradual variation of colour. But that ap-

---

* See above, p. 123, col. b, note †, and p. 185, col. a, note *.
† Whether heat, cold, &c., be objects of touch, or of a different sense, it is not here the place to inquire. —H.

parent variation we learn to interpret as the effect of light and shade falling upon a sphere of one uniform colour.

A sphere may be painted upon a plane, so exactly, as to be taken for a real sphere when the eye is at a proper distance and in the proper point of view. We say in this case, that the eye is deceived, that the appearance is fallacious. But there is no fallacy in the original perception, but only in that which is acquired by custom. The variation of colour, exhibited to the eye by the painter's art, is the same which nature exhibits by the different degrees of light falling upon the convex surface of a sphere.

In perception, whether original or acquired, there is something which may be called the sign, and something which is signified to us, or brought to our knowledge by that sign.

In original perception, the signs are the various sensations which are produced by the impressions made upon our organs. The things signified, are the objects perceived in consequence of those sensations, by the original constitution of our nature.

Thus, when I grasp an ivory ball in my hand, I have a certain sensation of touch. Although this sensation be in the mind and have no similitude to anything material, yet, by the laws of my constitution, it is immediately followed by the conception and belief, that there is in my hand a hard smooth body of a spherical figure, and about an inch and a half in diameter. . This belief is grounded neither upon reasoning, nor upon experience ; it is the immediate effect of my constitution, and this I call original perception.* [283]

In acquired perception, the sign may be either a sensation, or something originally perceived. The thing signified, is something which, by experience, has been found connected with that sign.

Thus, when the ivory ball is placed before my eye, I perceive by sight what I before perceived by touch, that the ball is smooth, spherical, of such a diameter, and at such a distance from the eye ; and to this is added the perception of its colour. All these things I perceive by sight, distinctly and with certainty. Yet it is certain from principles of philosophy, that, if I had not been accustomed to compare the informations of sight with those of touch, I should not have perceived these things by sight. I should have perceived a circular object, having its colour gradually more faint towards the shaded side. But I should not have perceived it to have three dimensions, to be spherical, to be of such a linear magnitude, and at such a distance from the eye. That these last mentioned are not

original perceptions of sight, but acquired by experience, is sufficiently evident from the principles of optics, and from the art of painters, in painting objects of three dimensions, upon a plane which has only two. And it has been put beyond all doubt, by observations recorded of several persons, who having, by cataracts in their eyes, been deprived of sight from their infancy, have been couched and made to see, after they came to years of understanding.*

Those who have had their eyesight from infancy, acquire such perceptions so early that they cannot recollect the time when they had them not, and therefore make no distinction between them and their original perceptions ; nor can they be easily persuaded that there is any just foundation for such a distinction. [284] In all languages men speak with equal assurance of their seeing objects to be spherical or cubical, as of their feeling them to be so ; nor do they ever dream that these perceptions of sight were not as early and original as the perceptions they have of the same objects by touch.

This power which we acquire of perceiving things by our senses, which originally we should not have perceived, is not the effect of any reasoning on our part : it is the result of our constitution, and of the situations in which we happen to be placed.

We are so made that, when two things are found to be conjoined in certain circumstances, we are prone to believe that they are connected by nature, and will always be found together in like circumstances. The belief which we are led into in such cases is not the effect of reasoning, nor does it arise from intuitive evidence in the thing believed ; it is, as I apprehend, the immediate effect of our constitution. Accordingly, it is strongest in infancy, before our reasoning power appears—before we are capable of drawing a conclusion from premises. A child who has once burnt his finger in a candle, from that single instance connects the pain of burning with putting his finger in the candle, and believes that these two things must go together. It is obvious that this part of our constitution is of very great use before we come to the use of reason, and guards us from a thousand mischiefs, which, without it, we would rush into ; it may sometimes lead us into error, but the good effects of it far overbalance the ill.

It is, no doubt, the perfection of a rational being to have no belief but what is grounded on intuitive evidence, or on just reasoning : but man, I apprehend, is not such a being ; nor is it the intention of nature that he should be such a being, in every period of his existence. We come into the world

---

* See above, p. 111, et alibi.—H.

* See above, p. 135, note †, and p. 182, note *.—H.

without the exercise of reason ; we are merely animal before we are rational creatures ; and it is necessary for our preservation, that we should believe many things before we can reason. How then is our belief to be regulated before we have reason to regulate it ? [285] Has nature left it to be regulated by chance ? By no means. It is regulated by certain principles; which are parts of our constitution ; whether they ought to be called animal principles, or instinctive principles, or what name we give to them, is of small moment ; but they are certainly different from the faculty of reason : they do the office of reason while it is in its infancy, and must, as it were, be carried in a nurse's arms, and they are leading-strings to it in its gradual progress.

From what has been said, I think it appears that our original powers of perceiving objects by our senses receive great improvement by use and habit ; and without this improvement, would be altogether insufficient for the purposes of life. The daily occurrences of life not only add to our stock of knowledge, but give additional perceptive powers to our senses ; and time gives us the use of our eyes and ears, as well as of our hands and legs.

This is the greatest and most important improvement of our external senses. It is to be found in all men come to years of understanding, but it is various in different persons according to their different occupations, and the different circumstances in which they are placed. Every artist requires an eye as well as a hand in his own profession ; his eye becomes skilled in perceiving, no less than his hand in executing, what belongs to his employment.

Besides this improvement of our senses, which nature produces without our intention, there are various ways in which they may be improved, or their defects remedied by art. As, *first*, by a due care of the organs of sense, that they be in a sound and natural state. This belongs to the department of the medical faculty.

Secondly, By accurate attention to the objects of sense. The effects of such attention in improving our senses, appear in every art. The artist, by giving more attention to certain objects than others do, by that means perceives many things in those objects which others do not. [286] Those who happen to be deprived of one sense, frequently supply that defect in a great degree, by giving more accurate attention to the objects of the senses they have. The blind have often been known to acquire uncommon acuteness in distinguishing things by feeling and hearing ; and the deaf are uncommonly quick in reading men's thoughts in their countenance.

A *third* way in which our senses admit of [285-287]

improvement, is, by additional organs, or instruments contrived by art. By the invention of optical glasses, and the gradual improvement of them, the natural power of vision is wonderfully improved, and a vast addition made to the stock of knowledge which we acquire by the eye. By speaking-trumpets and ear-trumpets some improvement has been made in the sense of hearing. Whether by similar inventions the other senses may be improved, seems uncertain.

A *fourth* method by which the information got by our senses may be improved, is, by discovering the connection which nature hath established between the sensible qualities of objects, and their more latent qualities.

By the sensible qualities of bodies, I understand those that are perceived immediately by the senses, such as their colour, figure, feeling, sound, taste, smell. The various modifications and various combinations of these, are innumerable ; so that there are hardly two individual bodies in Nature that may not be distinguished by their sensible qualities.

The latent qualities are such as are not immediately discovered by our senses ; but discovered sometimes by accident, sometimes by experiment or observation. The most important part of our knowledge of bodies is the knowledge of the latent qualities of the several species, by which they are adapted to certain purposes, either for food, or medicine, or agriculture, or for the materials or utensils of some art or manufacture. [287]

I am taught that certain species of bodies have certain latent qualities ; but how shall I know that this individual is of such a species ? This must be known by the sensible qualities which characterise the species. I must know that this is bread, and that wine, before I eat the one or drink the other. I must know that this is rhubarb, and that opium, before I use the one or the other for medicine.

It is one branch of human knowledge to know the names of the various species of natural and artificial bodies, and to know the sensible qualities by which they are ascertained to be of such a species, and by which they are distinguished from one another. It is another branch of knowledge to know the latent qualities of the several species, and the uses to which they are subservient.

The man who possesses both these branches is informed, by his senses, of innumerable things of real moment which are hid from those who possess only one, or neither. This is an improvement in the information got by our senses, which must keep pace with the improvements made in natural history, in natural philosophy, and in the arts.

It would be an improvement still higher if we were able to discover any connection between the sensible qualities of bodies and their latent qualities, without knowing the species, or what may have been discovered with regard to it.

Some philosophers, of the first rate, have made attempts towards this noble improvement, not without promising hopes of success. Thus, the celebrated Linnæus has attempted to point out certain sensible qualities by which a plant may very probably be concluded to be poisonous without knowing its name or species. He has given several other instances, wherein certain medical and economical virtues of plants are indicated by their external appearances. Sir Isaac Newton hath attempted to shew that, from the colours of bodies, we may form a probable conjecture of the size of their constituent parts, by which the rays of light are reflected. [288]

No man can pretend to set limits to the discoveries that may be made by human genius and industry, of such connections between the latent and the sensible qualities of bodies. A wide field here opens to our view, whose boundaries no man can ascertain, of improvements that may hereafter be made in the information conveyed to us by our senses.

CHAPTER XXII.

OF THE FALLACY OF THE SENSES.

COMPLAINTS of the fallacy of the senses have been very common in ancient and in modern times, especially among the philosophers. And, if we should take for granted all that they have said on this subject, the natural conclusion from it might seem to be, that the senses are given to us by some malignant demon on purpose to delude us, rather than that they are formed by the wise and beneficent Author of Nature, to give us true information of things necessary to our preservation and happiness.

The whole sect of atomists among the ancients, led by Democritus, and afterwards by Epicurus, maintained that all the qualities of bodies which the moderns call secondary qualities—to wit, smell, taste, sound, colour, heat, and cold—are mere illusions of sense, and have no real existence.* Plato maintained that we can attain no real knowledge of material things; and that eternal and immutable ideas are the only objects of real knowledge. The academics and sceptics anxiously sought for arguments to prove the fallaciousness of our senses, in order to support their favourite doctrine,

that even in things that seem most evident, we ought to withhold assent. [289]

Among the Peripatetics we find frequent complaints that the senses often deceive us, and that their testimony is to be suspected, when it is not confirmed by reason, by which the errors of sense may be corrected. This complaint they supported by many commonplace instances: such as, the crooked appearance of an oar in water; objects being magnified, and their distance mistaken, in a fog; the sun and moon appearing about a foot or two in diameter, while they are really thousands of miles; a square tower being taken at a distance to be round. These, and many similar appearances, they thought to be sufficiently accounted for from the fallacy of the senses: and thus the fallacy of the senses was used as a decent cover to conceal their ignorance of the real causes of such phænomena, and served the same purpose as their occult qualities and substantial forms.*

Des Cartes and his followers joined in the same complaint. Antony le Grand, a philosopher of that sect, in the first chapter of his Logic, expresses the sentiments of the sect as follows : " Since all our senses are fallacious, and we are frequently deceived by them, common reason advises that we should not put too much trust in them, nay, that we should suspect falsehood in everything they represent ; for it is imprudence and temerity to trust to those who have but once deceived us ; and, if they err at any time, they may be believed always to err. They are given by nature for this purpose only to warn us of what is useful and what is hurtful to us. The order of Nature is perverted when we put them to any other use, and apply them for the knowledge of truth."

When we consider that the active part of mankind, in all ages from the beginning of the world, have rested their most important concerns upon the testimony of sense, it will be very difficult to reconcile their conduct with the speculative opinion so generally entertained of the fallaciousness of the senses. [290] And it seems to be a very unfavourable account of the workmanship of the Supreme Being, to think that he has given us one faculty to deceive us—to wit, our senses ; and another faculty —to wit, our reason—to detect the fallacy.

It deserves, therefore, to be considered, whether the fallaciousness of our senses be not a common error, which men have been led into. from a desire to conceal their ignorance, or to apologize for their mistakes.

There are two powers which we owe to

---

* Not correctly stated. See above, p. 316, note §. The Epicureans denied the fallacy of Sense.—H.

* A very inaccurate representation of the Peripatetic doctrine touching this matter. In fact, the Aristotelian doctrine, and that of Reid himself, are almost the same.—H.

our external senses—sensation, and the perception of external objects.

It is impossible that there can be any fallacy in sensation : for we are conscious of all our sensations, and they can neither be any other in their nature, nor greater or less in their degree than we feel them. It is impossible that a man should be in pain, when he does not feel pain ; and when he feels pain, it is impossible that his pain should not be real, and in its degree what it is felt to be ; and the same thing may be said of every sensation whatsoever. An agreeable or an uneasy sensation may be forgot when it is past, but when it is present, it can be nothing but what we feel.

If, therefore, there be any fallacy in our senses, it must be in the perception of external objects, which we shall next consider.

And here I grant that we can conceive powers of perceiving external objects more perfect than ours, which, possibly, beings of a higher order may enjoy. We can perceive external objects only by means of bodily organs ; and these are liable to various disorders, which sometimes affect our powers of perception. The nerves and brain, which are interior organs of perception, are likewise liable to disorders, as every part of the human frame is. [291]

The imagination, the memory, the judging and reasoning powers, are all liable to be hurt, or even destroyed, by disorders of the body, as well as our powers of perception ; but we do not on this account call them fallacious.

Our senses, our memory, and our reason, are all limited and imperfect—this is the lot of humanity : but they are such as the Author of our being saw to be best fitted for us in our present state. Superior natures may have intellectual powers which we have not, or such as we have, in a more perfect degree, and less liable to accidental disorders ; but we have no reason to think that God has given fallacious powers to any of his creatures : this would be to think dishonourably of our Maker, and would lay a foundation for universal scepticism.

The appearances commonly imputed to the fallacy of the senses are many and of different kinds ; but I think they may be reduced to the four following classes.

First, Many things called deceptions of the senses are only conclusions rashly drawn from the testimony of the senses. In these cases the testimony of the senses is true, but we rashly draw a conclusion from it, which does not necessarily follow. We are disposed to impute our errors rather to false information than to inconclusive reasoning, and to blame our senses for the wrong conclusions we draw from their testimony.

Thus, when a man has taken a counter-
[291-293]

feit guinea for a true one, he says his senses deceived him ; but he lays the blame where it ought not to be laid : for we may ask him, Did your senses give a false testimony of the colour, or of the figure, or of the impression ? No. But this is all that they testified, and this they testified truly : From these premises you concluded that it was a true guinea, but this conclusion does not follow ; you erred, therefore, not by relying upon the testimony of sense, but by judging rashly from its testimony. [292] Not only are your senses innocent of this error, but it is only by their information that it can be discovered. If you consult them properly, they will inform you that what you took for a guinea is base metal, or is deficient in weight, and this can only be known by the testimony of sense.

I remember to have met with a man who thought the argument used by Protestants against the Popish doctrine of transubstantiation, from the testimony of our senses, inconclusive ; because, said he, instances may be given where several of our senses may deceive us : How do we know then that there may not be cases wherein they all deceive us, and no sense is left to detect the fallacy ? I begged of him to know an instance wherein several of our senses deceive us. I take, said he, a piece of soft turf ; I cut it into the shape of an apple ; with the essence of apples, I give it the smell of an apple ; and with paint, I can give it the skin and colour of an apple. Here then is a body, which, if you judge by your eye, by your touch, or by your smell, is an apple.

To this I would answer, that no one of our senses deceives us in this case. My sight and touch testify that it has the shape and colour of an apple : this is true. The sense of smelling testifies that it has the smell of an apple : this is likewise true, and is no deception. Where then lies the deception ? It is evident it lies in this—that because this body has some qualities belonging to an apple I conclude that it is an apple. This is a fallacy, not of the senses, but of inconclusive reasoning.

Many false judgments that are accounted deceptions of sense, arise from our mistaking relative motion for real or absolute motion. These can be no deceptions of sense, because by our senses we perceive only the relative motions of bodies ; and it is by reasoning that we infer the real from the relative which we perceive. A little reflection may satisfy us of this. [293]

It was before observed, that we perceive extension to be one sensible quality of bodies, and thence are necessarily led to conceive space, though space be of itself no object of sense. When a body is removed out of its place, the space which it filled remains empty till it is filled by some other body, and would remain if it should never be filled. Before any body existed, the space which bodies now occupy was empty space, capable of receiving bodies ; for no body can exist where there is no space to contain it. There is space therefore whereever bodies exist, or can exist.

Hence it is evident that space can have no limits. It is no less evident that it is immovable. Bodies placed in it are movable, but the place where they were cannot be moved ; and we can as easily conceive a thing to be moved from itself, as one part of space brought nearer to or removed farther from another.

The space, therefore, which is unlimited and immovable, is called by philosophers *absolute space*. Absolute or real motion is a change of place in absolute space.

Our senses do not testify the absolute motion or absolute rest of any body. When one body removes from another, this may be discerned by the senses ; but whether any body keeps the same part of absolute space, we do not perceive by our senses. When one body seems to remove from another, we can infer with certainty that there is absolute motion, but whether in the one or the other, or partly in both, is not discerned by sense.

Of all the prejudices which philosophy contradicts, I believe there is none so general as that the earth keeps its place unmoved. This opinion seems to be universal, till it is corrected by instruction or by philosophical speculation. Those who have any tincture of education are not now in danger of being held by it, but they find at first a reluctance to believe that there are antipodes ; that the earth is spherical, and turns round its axis every day, and round the sun every year : they can recollect the time when reason struggled with prejudice upon these points, and prevailed at length, but not without some effort. [294]

The cause of a prejudice so very general is not unworthy of investigation. But that is not our present business. It is sufficient to observe, that it cannot justly be called a fallacy of sense ; because our senses testify only the change of situation of one body in relation to other bodies, and not its change of situation in absolute space. It is only the relative motion of bodies that we perceive, and that we perceive truly. It is the province of reason and philosophy, from the relative motions which we perceive, to collect the real and absolute motions which produce them.

All motion must be estimated from some point or place which is supposed to be at rest. We perceive not the points of absolute space, from which real · and absolute motion must be reckoned : And there are obvious reasons that lead mankind in the

state of ignorance, to make the earth the fixed place from which they may estimate the various motions they perceive. The custom of doing this from infancy, and of using constantly a language which supposes the earth to be at rest, may perhaps be the cause of the general prejudice in favour of this opinion.

Thus it appears that, if we distinguish accurately between what our senses really and naturally testify, and the conclusions which we draw from their testimony by reasoning, we shall find many of the errors, called fallacies of the senses, to be no fallacy of the senses, but rash judgments, which are not to be imputed to our senses.

Secondly, Another class of errors imputed to the fallacy of the senses, are those which we are liable to in our acquired perceptions. Acquired perception is not properly the testimony of those senses which God hath given us, but a conclusion drawn from what the senses testify. [295] In our past experience, we have found certain things conjoined with what our senses testify. We are led by our constitution to expect this conjunction in time to come ; and when we have often found it in our experience to happen, we acquire a firm belief that the things which we have found thus conjoined, are connected in nature, and that one is a sign of the other. The appearance of the sign immediately produces the belief of its usual attendant, and we think we perceive the one as well as the other.

That such conclusions are formed even in infancy, no man can doubt : nor is it less certain that they are confounded with the natural and immediate perceptions of sense, and in all languages are called by the same name. We are therefore authorized by language to call them perception, and must often do so, or speak unintelligibly. But philosophy teaches us, in this, as in many other instances, to distinguish things which the vulgar confound. I have therefore given the name of acquired perception to such conclusions, to distinguish them from what is naturally, originally, and immediately testified by our senses. Whether this acquired perception is to be resolved into some process of reasoning, of which we have lost the remembrance, as some philosophers think, or whether it results from some part of our constitution distinct from reason, as I rather believe, does not concern the present subject. If the first of these opinions be true, the errors of acquired perception will fall under the first class before mentioned. If not, it makes a distinct class by itself. But whether the one or the other be true, it must be observed that the errors of acquired perception are not properly fallacies of our senses.

Thus, when a globe is set before me, I perceive by my eyes that it has three dimensions and a spherical figure. To say that this is not perception, would be to reject the authority of custom in the use of words, which no wise man will do: but that it is not the testimony of my sense of seeing, every philosopher knows. I see only a circular form, having the light and colour distributed in a certain way over it. [296] But, being accustomed to observe this distribution of light and colour only in a spherical body, I immediately, from what I see, believe the object to be spherical, and say that I see or perceive it to be spherical. When a painter, by an exact imitation of that distribution of light and colour which I have been accustomed to see only in a real sphere, deceives me, so as to make me take that to be a real sphere which is only a painted one, the testimony of my eye is true —the colour and visible figure of the object is truly what I see it to be: the error lies in the conclusion drawn from what I see— to wit, that the object has three dimensions and a spherical figure. The conclusion is false in this case; but, whatever be the origin of this conclusion, it is not properly the testimony of sense.

To this class we must refer the judgments we are apt to form of the distance and magnitude of the heavenly bodies, and of terrestrial objects seen on high. The mistakes we make of the magnitude and distance of objects seen through optical glasses, or through an atmosphere uncommonly clear or uncommonly foggy, belong likewise to this class.

The errors we are led into in acquired perception are very rarely hurtful to us in the conduct of life; they are gradually corrected by a more enlarged experience, and a more perfect knowledge of the laws of Nature: and the general laws of our constitution, by which we are sometimes led into them, are of the greatest utility.

We come into the world ignorant of everything, and by our ignorance exposed to many dangers and to many mistakes. The regular train of causes and effects, which divine wisdom has established, and which directs every step of our conduct in advanced life, is unknown, until it is gradually discovered by experience. [297]

We must learn much from experience before we can reason, and therefore must be liable to many errors. Indeed, I apprehend, that, in the first part of life, reason would do us much more hurt than good. Were we sensible of our condition in that period, and capable of reflecting upon it, we should be like a man in the dark, surrounded with dangers, where every step he takes may be into a pit. Reason would direct him to sit down, and wait till he could see about him.

In like manner, if we suppose an infant endowed with reason, it would direct him to do nothing, till he knew what could be done with safety. This he can only know by experiment, and experiments are dangerous. Reason directs, that experiments that are full of danger should not be made without a very urgent cause. It would therefore make the infant unhappy, and hinder his improvement by experience.

Nature has followed another plan. The child, unapprehensive of danger, is led by instinct to exert all his active powers, to try everything without the cautious admonitions of reason, and to believe everything that is told him. Sometimes he suffers by his rashness what reason would have prevented: but his suffering proves a salutary discipline, and makes him for the future avoid the cause of it. Sometimes he is imposed upon by his credulity; but it is of infinite benefit to him upon the whole. His activity and credulity are more useful qualities and better instructors than reason would be; they teach him more in a day than reason would do in a year; they furnish a stock of materials for reason to work upon; they make him easy and happy in a period of his existence when reason could only serve to suggest a thousand tormenting anxieties and fears: and he acts agreeably to the constitution and intention of nature even when he does and believes what reason would not justify. So that the wisdom and goodness of the Author of nature is no less conspicuous in withholding the exercise of our reason in this period, than in bestowing it when we are ripe for it. [298]

A third class of errors, ascribed to the fallacy of the senses, proceeds from ignorance of the laws of nature.

The laws of nature (I mean not moral but physical laws) are learned, either from our own experience, or the experience of others, who have had occasion to observe the course of nature.

Ignorance of those laws, or inattention to them, is apt to occasion false judgments with regard to the objects of sense, especially those of hearing and of sight; which false judgments are often, without good reason, called fallacies of sense.

Sounds affect the ear differently, according as the sounding body is before or behind us, on the right hand or on the left, near or at a great distance. We learn, by the manner in which the sound affects the ear, on what hand we are to look for the sounding body; and in most cases we judge right. But we are sometimes deceived by echoes, or by whispering galleries, or speaking trumpets, which return the sound, or alter its direction, or convey it to a distance without diminution.

The deception is still greater, because

z

more uncommon, which is said to be produced by Gastriloquists—that is, persons who have acquired the art of modifying their voice, so that it shall affect the ear of the hearers, as if it came from another person, or from the clouds, or from under the earth

I never had the fortune to be acquainted with any of these artists, and therefore cannot say to what degree of perfection the art may have been carried.

I apprehend it to be only such an imperfect imitation as may deceive those who are inattentive, or under a panic. For, if it could be carried to perfection, a Gastriloquist would be as dangerous a man in society as was the shepherd Gyges,* who, by turning a ring upon his finger, could make himself invisible, and, by that means, from being the king's shepherd, became King of Lydia. [299]

If the Gastriloquists have all been too good men to use their talent to the detriment of others, it might at least be expected that some of them should apply it to their own advantage. If it could be brought to any considerable degree of perfection, it seems to be as proper an engine for drawing money by the exhibition of it, as legerdemain or rope-dancing. But I have never heard of any exhibition of this kind, and therefore am apt to think that it is too coarse an imitation to bear exhibition, even to the vulgar.

Some are said to have the art of imitating the voice of another so exactly that in the dark they might be taken for the person whose voice they imitate. I am apt to think that this art also, in the relations made of it, is magnified beyond the truth, as wonderful relations are apt to be, and that an attentive ear would be able to distinguish the copy from the original.

It is indeed a wonderful instance of the accuracy as well as of the truth of our senses, in things that are of real use in life, that we are able to distinguish all our acquaintance by their countenance, by their voice, and by their handwriting, when, at the same time, we are often unable to say by what minute difference the distinction is made; and that we are so very rarely deceived in matters of this kind, when we give proper attention to the informations of sense.

However, if any case should happen, in which sounds produced by different causes are not distinguishable by the ear, this may prove that our senses are imperfect, but not that they are fallacious. The ear may not be able to draw the just conclusion, but it is only our ignorance of the laws of sound that leads us to a wrong conclusion. [300]

Deceptions of sight, arising from igno-

rance of the laws of nature, are more numerous and more remarkable than those of hearing.

The rays of light, which are the means of seeing, pass in right lines from the object to the eye, when they meet with no obstruction; and we are by nature led to conceive the visible object to be in the direction of the rays that come to the eye. But the rays may be reflected, refracted, or inflected in their passage from the object to the eye, according to certain fixed laws of nature, by which means their direction may be changed, and consequently the apparent place, figure, or magnitude of the object.

Thus, a child seeing himself in a mirror, thinks he sees another child behind the mirror, that imitates all his motions. But even a child soon gets the better of this deception, and knows that he sees himself only.

All the deceptions made by telescopes, microscopes, camera obscuras, magic lanthorns, are of the same kind, though not so familiar to the vulgar. The ignorant may be deceived by them; but to those who are acquainted with the principles of optics, they give just and true information; and the laws of nature by which they are produced, are of infinite benefit to mankind.

¶ There remains another class of errors, commonly called deceptions of sense, and the only one, as I apprehend, to which that name can be given with propriety: I mean such as proceed from some disorder or preternatural state, either of the external organ or of the nerves and brain, which are internal organs of perception.

In a delirium or in madness, perception, memory, imagination, and our reasoning powers, are strangely disordered and confounded. There are likewise disorders which affect some of our senses, while others are sound. Thus, a man may feel pain in his toes after the leg is cut off. He may feel a little ball double by crossing his fingers. [301] He may see an object double, by not directly both eyes properly to it. By pressing the ball of his eye, he may see colours that are not real. By the jaundice in his eyes, he may mistake colours. These are more properly deceptions of sense than any of the classes before mentioned.

We must acknowledge it to be the lot of human nature, that all the human faculties are liable, by accidental causes, to be hurt and unfitted for their natural functions, either wholly or in part: but as this imperfection is common to them all, it gives no just ground for accounting any of them fallacious.

Upon the whole, it seems to have been a common error of philosophers to account the senses fallacious. And to this error they have added another—that one use of reason is to detect the fallacies of sense.

[299–301]

---

* See Cicero, *De Officiis.* The story told by Herodotus is different.—H.

It appears, I think, from what has been said, that there is no more reason to account our senses fallacious, than our reason, our memory, or any other faculty of judging which nature hath given us. They are all limited and imperfect ; but wisely suited to the present condition of man. We are liable to error and wrong judgment in the use of them all ; but as little in the informations of sense as in the deductions of reasoning. And the errors we fall into with regard to objects of sense are not corrected by reason, but by more accurate attention to the informations we may receive by our senses themselves.

Perhaps the pride of philosophers may have given occasion to this error. Reason is the faculty wherein they assume a superiority to the unlearned. The informations of sense are common to the philosopher and to the most illiterate : they put all men upon a level ; and therefore are apt to be undervalued. We must, however, be beholden to the informations of sense for the greatest and most interesting part of our knowledge. [302] The wisdom of nature has made the most useful things most common, and they ought not to be despised on that account. Nature likewise forces our belief in those informations, and all the attempts of philosophy to weaken it are fruitless and vain.

I add only one observation to what has been said upon this subject. It is, that there seems to be a contradiction between what philosophers teach concerning ideas, and their doctrine of the fallaciousness of the senses. We are taught that the office of the senses is only to give us the ideas of external objects. If this be so, there can be no fallacy in the senses. Ideas can neither be true nor false. If the senses testify nothing, they cannot give false testimony. If they are not judging faculties, no judgment can be imputed to them, whether false or true. There is, therefore, a contradiction between the common doctrine concerning ideas and that of the fallaciousness of the senses. Both may be false, as I believe they are, but both cannot be true. [303]

ESSAY III.

OF MEMORY.

CHAPTER I.

THINGS OBVIOUS AND CERTAIN WITH REGARD TO MEMORY.

In the gradual progress of man, from infancy to maturity, there is a certain order in which his faculties are unfolded, and this seems to be the best order we can follow in treating of them.

The external senses appear first ; memory soon follows—which we are now to consider.

It is by memory that we have an immediate knowledge of things past.* The senses give us information of things only as they exist in the present moment ; and this information, if it were not preserved by memory, would vanish instantly, and leave us as ignorant as if it had never been.

Memory must have an object. Every man who remembers must remember something, and that which he remembers is called the object of his remembrance. In this, memory agrees with perception, but differs from sensation, which has no object but the feeling itself.* [304]

Every man can distinguish the thing remembered from the remembrance of it. We may remember anything which we have seen, or heard, or known, or done, or suffered ; but the remembrance of it is a particular act of the mind which now exists, and of which we are conscious. To confound these two is an absurdity, which a thinking man could not be led into, but by some false hypothesis which hinders him from reflecting upon the thing which he would explain by it.

In memory we do not find such a train of operations connected by our constitution as in perception. When we perceive an object by our senses, there is, first, some impression made by the object upon the organ of sense, either immediately, or by means of some medium. By this, an im-

---

* An *immediate* knowledge of a *past* thing is a contradiction. For we can only know a thing immediately, if we know it in itself, or as existing ; but what is past cannot be known in itself, for it is non-existent.—H.

* But have we only such a *mediate* knowledge of the real object in perception, as we have of the real object in memory ? On Reid's error, touching the object of memory, see, in general, Note B.—H.

pression is made upon the nerves and brain, in consequence of which we feel some sensation ; and that sensation is attended by that conception and belief of the external object which we call perception. These operations are so connected in our constitution, that it is difficult to disjoin them in our conceptions, and to attend to each without confounding it with the others. But, in the operations of memory, we are free from this embarrassment ; they are easily distinguished from all other acts of the mind, and the names which denote them are free from all ambiguity.

The object of memory, or thing remembered, must be something that is past ; as the object of perception and of consciousness must be something which is present. What now is, cannot be an object of memory ; neither can that which is past and gone be an object of perception or of consciousness.

Memory is always accompanied with the belief of that which we remember, as perception is accompanied with the belief of that which we perceive, and consciousness with the belief of that whereof we are conscious. Perhaps in infancy, or in a disorder of mind, things remembered may be confounded with those which are merely imagined ; but in mature years, and in a sound state of mind, every man feels that he must believe what he distinctly remembers, though he can give no other reason of his belief, but that he remembers the thing distinctly ; whereas, when he merely imagines a thing ever so distinctly, he has no belief of it upon that account. [305]

This belief, which we have from distinct memory, we account real knowledge, no less certain than if it was grounded on demonstration ; no man in his wits calls it in question, or will hear any argument against it.* The testimony of witnesses in causes of life and death depends upon it, and all the knowledge of mankind of past events is built on this foundation.

There are cases in which a man's memory is less distinct and determinate, and where he is ready to allow that it may have failed him ; but this does not in the least weaken its credit, when it is perfectly distinct.

Memory implies a conception and belief of past duration ; for it is impossible that a man should remember a thing distinctly, without believing some interval of duration, more or less, to have passed between the time it happened, and the present moment ; and I think it is impossible to shew how we could acquire a notion of duration if we had no memory. Things remembered must be things formerly perceived or

known. I remember the transit of Venus over the sun in the year 1769. I must therefore have perceived it at the time it happened, otherwise I could not now remember it. Our first acquaintance with any object of thought cannot be by remembrance. Memory can only produce a continuance or renewal of a former acquaintance with the thing remembered.

The remembrance of a past event is necessarily accompanied with the conviction of our own existence at the time the event happened. I cannot remember a thing that happened a year ago, without a conviction as strong as memory can give, that I, the same identical person who now remember that event, did then exist. [306]

What I have hitherto said concerning memory, I consider as principles which appear obvious and certain to every man who will take the pains to reflect upon the operations of his own mind. They are facts of which every man must judge by what he feels ; and they admit of no other proof but an appeal to every man's own reflection. I shall therefore take them for granted in what follows, and shall, first, draw some conclusions from them, and then examine the theories of philosophers concerning memory, and concerning duration, and our personal identity, of which we acquire the knowledge by memory.

CHAPTER II.

MEMORY AN ORIGINAL FACULTY.

FIRST, I think it appears, that memory is an original faculty, given us by the Author of our being, of which we can give no account, but that we are so made.

The knowledge which I have of things past, by my memory, seems to me as unaccountable as an immediate knowledge would be of things to come ;* and I can give no reason why I should have the one and not the other, but that such is the will of my Maker. I find in my mind a distinct conception, and a firm belief of a series of past events ; but how this is produced I know not. I call it memory, but this is only giving a name to it—it is not an account of its cause. I believe most firmly, what I distinctly remember ; but I can

---

* But see below, p. 362.—H.

* An *immediate* knowledge of *things to come*, is equally a contradiction as an *immediate* knowledge of *things past*. See the first note of last page. But if, as Reid himself allows, memory depend upon certain enduring affections of the brain, determined by past cognition, it seems a strange assertion, on this or on other accounts, that the possibility of a knowledge of the future is not more inconceivable than of a knowledge of the past. Maupertuis, however, has advanced a similar doctrine ; and some, also, of the advocates of animal magnetism.—H.

give no reason of this belief. It is the inspiration of the Almighty that gives me this understanding.* [307]

When I believe the truth of a mathematical axiom, or of a mathematical proposition, I see that it must be so: every man who has the same conception of it sees the same. There is a necessary and an evident connection between the subject and the predicate of the proposition; and I have all the evidence to support my belief which I can possibly conceive.

When I believe that I washed my hands and face this morning, there appears no necessity in the truth of this proposition. It might be, or it might not be. A man may distinctly conceive it without believing it at all. How then do I come to believe it? I remember it distinctly. This is all I can say. This remembrance is an act of my mind. Is it impossible that this act should be, if the event had not happened? I confess I do not see any necessary connection between the one and the other. If any man can shew such a necessary connection, then I think that belief which we have of what we remember will be fairly accounted for; but, if this cannot be done, that belief is unaccountable, and we can say no more but that it is the result of our constitution.

Perhaps it may be said, that the experience we have had of the fidelity of memory is a good reason for relying upon its testimony. I deny not that this may be a reason to those who have had this experience, and who reflect upon it. But I believe there are few who ever thought of this reason, or who found any need of it. It must be some very rare occasion that leads a man to have recourse to it; and in those who have done so, the testimony of memory was believed before the experience of its fidelity, and that belief could not be caused by the experience which came after it.

We know some abstract truths, by comparing the terms of the proposition which expresses them, and perceiving some necessary relation or agreement between them. It is thus I know that two and three make five; that the diameters of a circle are all equal. [308] Mr Locke having discovered this source of knowledge, too rashly concluded that all human knowledge might be derived from it; and in this he has been followed very generally—by Mr Hume in particular.

But I apprehend that our knowledge of the existence of things contingent can never be traced to this source. I know that such a thing exists, or did exist. This knowledge cannot be derived from the perception of a necessary agreement between existence and the thing that exists, because there is no such necessary agreement; and therefore no such agreement can be perceived either immediately or by a chain of reasoning. The thing does not exist necessarily, but by the will and power of him that made it; and there is no contradiction follows from supposing it not to exist.

Whence I think it follows, that our knowledge of the existence of our own thoughts, of the existence of all the material objects about us, and of all past contingencies, must be derived, not from a perception of necessary relations or agreements, but from some other source.

Our Maker has provided other means for giving us the knowledge of these things—means which perfectly answer their end, and produce the effect intended by them. But in what manner they do this, is, I fear, beyond our skill to explain. We know our own thoughts, and the operations of our minds, by a power which we call consciousness: but this is only giving a name to this part of our frame. It does not explain its fabric, nor how it produces in us an irresistible conviction of its informations. We perceive material objects and their sensible qualities by our senses; but how they give us this information, and how they produce our belief in it, we know not. We know many past events by memory; but how it gives this information, I believe, is inexplicable.

It is well known what subtile disputes were held through all the scholastic ages, and are still carried on about the prescience of the Deity. [309] Aristotle had taught that there can be no certain foreknowledge of things contingent; and in this he has been very generally followed, upon no other grounds, as I apprehend, but that we cannot conceive how such things should be foreknown, and therefore conclude it to be impossible. Hence has arisen an opposition and supposed inconsistency between divine prescience and human liberty. Some have given up the first in favour of the last, and others have given up the last in order to support the first.

It is remarkable that these disputants have never apprehended that there is any difficulty in reconciling with liberty the knowledge of what is past, but only of what is future. It is prescience only, and not memory, that is supposed to be hostile to liberty, and hardly reconcileable to it.

Yet I believe the difficulty is perfectly equal in the one case and in the other. I admit, that we cannot account for prescience of the actions of a free agent. But I maintain that we can as little account for memory of the past actions of a free agent. If any man thinks he can prove that the actions of a free agent cannot be foreknown,

---

* "The inspiration of the Almighty giveth them understanding."—Job.—H.

he will find the same arguments of equal force to prove that the past actions of a free agent cannot be remembered.* It is true, that what is past did certainly exist. It is no less true that what is future will certainly exist. I know no reasoning from the constitution of the agent, or from his circumstances, that has not equal strength, whether it be applied to his past or to his future actions. The past was, but now is not. The future will be, but now is not. The present is equally connected or unconnected with both.

The only reason why men have apprehended so great disparity in cases so perfectly like, I take to be this, That the faculty of memory in ourselves convinces us from fact, that it is not impossible that an intelligent being, even a finite being, should have certain knowledge of past actions of free agents, without tracing them from anything necessarily connected with them. [310] But having no prescience in ourselves corresponding to our memory of what is past, we find great difficulty in admitting it to be possible even in the Supreme Being.

A faculty which we possess in some degree, we easily admit that the Supreme Being may possess in a more perfect degree; but a faculty which has nothing corresponding to it in our constitution, we will hardly allow to be possible. We are so constituted as to have an intuitive knowledge of many things past; but we have no intuitive knowledge of the future.† We might perhaps have been so constituted as to have an intuitive knowledge of the future; but not of the past; nor would this constitution have been more unaccountable than the present, though it might be much more inconvenient. Had this been our constitution, we should have found no difficulty in admitting that the Deity may know all things future, but very much in admitting his knowledge of things that are past.

Our original faculties are all unaccountable. Of these memory is one. He only who made them, comprehends fully how they are made, and how they produce in us not only a conception, but a firm belief and assurance of things which it concerns us to know.

---

* This is a marvellous doctrine. The difficulty in the two cases is not the same. The *past, as past,* whether it has been the action of a free agent or not, is *now necessary ;* and, though we may be unable to understand how it can be remembered, the supposition of its remembrance involves no contradiction. On the contrary, the future action of a free agent is *ex hypothesi* not a necessary event. But an event cannot be now certainly foreseen, except it is· now certainly to be ; and to say that what is *certainly* to be is not *necessarily* to be, seems a contradiction.—H.

† If by *intuitive* be meant *immediate,* such a knowledge is impossible·in either case ; for we can know neither the ·*past* nor the *future*·in themselves, but only in the *present*—that is, mediately.—H.

CHAPTER III.

OF DURATION.

FROM the principles laid down in the first chapter of this Essay, I think it appears that our notion of duration, as well as our belief of it, is got by the faculty of memory.* It is essential to everything remembered that it be something which is past ; and we cannot conceive a thing to be past, without conceiving some duration, more or less, between it and the present. [311] As soon therefore as we remember anything, we must have both a notion and a belief of duration. It is necessarily suggested by every operation of our memory ; and to that faculty it ought to ·be ascribed. This is, therefore, a proper place to consider what is known concerning it.

Duration, Extension, and Number, are the measures of all things subject to mensuration. When we apply them to finite things which are measured by them, they seem of all things to be the most distinctly conceived, and most within the reach of human understanding.

Extension having three dimensions, has an endless variety of modifications, capable of being accurately defined ; and their various relations furnish the human mind with its most ample field of demonstrative reasoning. Duration having only one dimension, has fewer modifications ; but these are clearly understood—and their relations admit of measure, proportion, and demonstrative reasoning.

Number is called discrete quantity, because it is compounded of units, which are all equal and similar, and it can only be divided into units. This is true, in some sense, even of fractions of unity, to which we now commonly give the name of number. For, in every fractional number, the unit is supposed to be subdivided into a certain number of equal parts, which are the units of that denomination, and the fractions of that denomination are only divisible into units of the same denomination. Duration and extension are not discrete, but continued quantity. They consist of parts perfectly similar, but divisible without end.

In order to aid our conception of the magnitude and proportions of the various intervals of duration, we find it necessary to give a name to some known portion of it, such as an hour, a day, a year. These we consider as units, and, by the number of them contained in a larger interval, we form a distinct conception of its magnitude. [312] A similar expedient we find necessary to give

---

* Reid thus apparently makes *Time* an empirical or generalized notion.—H.

us a distinct conception of the magnitudes and proportions of things extended. Thus, number is found necessary, as a common measure of extension and duration. But this perhaps is owing to the weakness of our understanding. It has even been discovered, by the sagacity of mathematicians, that this expedient does not in all cases answer its intention. For there are proportions of continued quantity, which cannot be perfectly expressed by numbers; such as that between the diagonal and side of a square, and many others.

The parts of duration have to other parts of it the relations of prior and posterior, and to the present they have the relations of past and future. The notion of past is immediately suggested by memory, as has been before observed. And when we have got the notions of present and past, and of prior and posterior, we can from these frame a notion of the future; for the future is that which is posterior to the present. Nearness and distance are relations equally applicable to time and to place. Distance in time, and distance in place, are things so different in their nature and so like in their relation, that it is difficult to determine whether the name of distance is applied to both in the same, or an analogical sense.

The extension of bodies which we perceive by our senses, leads us necessarily to the conception and belief of a space which remains immoveable when the body is removed. And the duration of events which we remember leads us necessarily to the conception and belief of a duration which would have gone on uniformly though the event had never happened.*

Without space there can be nothing that is extended. And without time there can be nothing that hath duration. This I think undeniable; and yet we find that extension and duration are not more clear and intelligible than space and time are dark and difficult objects of contemplation. [313]

As there must be space wherever anything extended does or can exist, and time

---

when there is or can be anything that has duration, we can set no bounds to either, even in our imagination. They defy all limitation. The one swells in our conception to immensity, the other to eternity.

An eternity past is an object which we cannot comprehend; but a beginning of time, unless we take it in a figurative sense, is a contradiction. By a common figure of speech, we give the name of time to those motions and revolutions by which we measure it, such as days and years. We can conceive a beginning of these sensible measures of time, and say that there was a time when they were not, a time undistinguished by any motion or change; but to say that there was a time before all time, is a contradiction.

All limited duration is comprehended in time, and all limited extension in space. These, in their capacious womb, contain all finite existences, but are contained by none. Created things have their particular place in space, and their particular place in time; but time is everywhere, and space at all times. They embrace each the other, and have that mysterious union which the schoolmen conceived between soul and body. The whole of each is in every part of the other.

We are at a loss to what category or class of things we ought to refer them. They are not beings, but rather the receptacles of every created being, without which it could not have had the possibility of existence. Philosophers have endeavoured to reduce all the objects of human thought to these three classes, of substances, modes, and relations. To which of them shall we refer time, space, and number, the most common objects of thought? [314]

Sir Isaac Newton thought that the Deity, by existing everywhere and at all times, constitutes time and space, immensity and eternity. This probably suggested to his great friend, Dr Clarke, what he calls the argument *a priori* for the existence of an immense and eternal Being. Space and time, he thought, are only abstract or partial conceptions of an immensity and eternity which forces itself upon our belief. And as immensity and eternity are not substances, they must be the attributes of a Being who is necessarily immense and eternal. These are the speculations of men of superior genius. But whether they be as solid as they are sublime, or whether they be the wanderings of imagination in a region beyond the limits of human understanding, I am unable to determine.

The schoolmen made eternity to be a *nunc stans*—that is, a moment of time that stands still. This was to put a spoke into the wheel of time, and might give satisfaction to those who are to be satisfied by words without meaning. But I can as

---

* If *Space* and *Time* be *necessary generalizations* from experience, this is contrary to Reid's own doctrine, that experience can give us no *necessary* knowledge. If, again, they be *necessary-and original notions*, the account of their origin here given, is incorrect. It should have been said that experience is not the *source* of their existence, but only the *occasion* of their manifestation. On this subject, see, *instar omnium*, Cousin on Locke, in his "Cours de Philosophie," (t. ii., Leçons 17 and 18.) This admirable work has been well translated into English, by an American philosopher, Mr Henry; but the eloquence and precision of the author can only be properly appreciated by those who study the work in the original language. The reader may, however, consult likewise Stewart's "Philosophical Essays," (Essay ii., chap. 2,) and Royer Collard's "Fragments," (ix. and x.) These authors, from their more limited acquaintance with the speculations of the German philosophers, are, however, less on a level with the problem.—H.

easily believe a circle to be a square as time to stand still.

Such paradoxes and riddles, if I may so call them, men are involuntarily led into when they reason about time and space, and attempt to comprehend their nature. They are probably things of which the human faculties give an imperfect and inadequate conception. Hence difficulties arise which we in vain attempt to overcome, and doubts which we are unable to resolve. Perhaps some faculty which we possess not, is necessary to remove the darkness which hangs over them, and makes us so apt to bewilder ourselves when we reason about them. [315]

CHAPTER IV.

OF IDENTITY.

THE conviction which every man has of his Identity, as far back as his memory reaches, needs no aid of philosophy to strengthen it; and no philosophy can weaken it, without first producing some degree of insanity.

The philosopher, however, may very properly consider this conviction as a phænomenon of human nature worthy of his attention. If he can discover its cause, an addition is made to his stock of knowledge. If not, it must be held as a part of our original constitution, or an effect of that constitution produced in a manner unknown to us.

We may observe, first of all, that this conviction is indispensably necessary to all exercise of reason. The operations of reason, whether in action or in speculation, are made up of successive parts. The antecedent are the foundation of the consequent, and, without the conviction that the antecedent have been seen or done by me, I could have no reason to proceed to the consequent, in any speculation, or in any active project whatever.

There can be no memory of what is past without the conviction that we existed at the time remembered. There may be good arguments to convince me that I existed before the earliest thing I can remember; but to suppose that my memory reaches a moment farther back than my belief and conviction of my existence, is a contradiction.

The moment a man loses this conviction, as if he had drunk the water of Lethe, past things are done away; and, in his own belief, he then begins to exist. [316] Whatever was thought, or said, or done, or suffered before that period, may belong to some other person; but he can never impute it to himself, or take any subse-

quent step that supposes it to be his doing.

From this it is evident that we must have the conviction of our own continued existence and identity, as soon as we are capable of thinking or doing anything, on account of what we have thought, or done, or suffered before; that is, as soon as we are reasonable creatures.

That we may form as distinct a notion as we are able of this phenomenon of the human mind, it is proper to consider what is meant by identity in general, what by our own personal identity, and how we are led into that invincible belief and conviction which every man has of his own personal identity, as far as his memory reaches.

Identity in general, I take to be a relation between a thing which is known to exist at one time, and a thing which is known to have existed at another time.* If you ask whether they are one and the same, or two different things, every man of common sense understands the meaning of your question perfectly. Whence we may infer with certainty, that every man of common sense has a clear and distinct notion of identity.

If you ask a definition of identity, I confess I can give none; it is too simple a notion to admit of logical definition. I can say it is a relation; but I cannot find words to express the specific difference between this and other relations, though I am in no danger of confounding it with any other. I can say that diversity is a contrary relation, and that similitude and dissimilitude are another couple of contrary relations, which every man easily distinguishes in his conception from identity and diversity. [317]

I see evidently that identity supposes an uninterrupted continuance of existence. That which hath ceased to exist, cannot be the same with that which afterwards begins to exist; for this would be to suppose a being to exist after it ceased to exist, and to have had existence before it was produced, which are manifest contradictions. Continued uninterrupted existence is therefore necessarily implied in identity.

Hence we may infer that identity cannot, in its proper sense, be applied to our pains, our pleasures, our thoughts, or any operation of our minds. The pain felt this day is not the same individual pain which I felt yesterday, though they may be similar in kind and degree, and have the same cause. The same may be said of every feeling and of every operation of mind: they are all

---

* Identity is a relation between our cognitions of a thing, and not between_things themselves. It would, therefore, have been better in this sentence to have said, " a relation between a thing *as known* to exist at one time, and a thing *as known* to exist at another time."—H.

successive in their nature, like time itself, no two moments of which can be the same moment.

It is otherwise with the parts of absolute space. They always are, and were, and will be the same. So far, I think, we proceed upon clear ground in fixing the notion of identity in general.

It is, perhaps, more difficult to ascertain with precision the meaning of Personality; but it is not necessary in the present subject: it is sufficient for our purpose to observe, that all mankind place their personality in something that cannot be divided, or consist of parts. A part of a person is a manifest absurdity.

When a man loses his estate, his health, his strength, he is still the same person, and has lost nothing of his personality. If he has a leg or an arm cut off, he is the same person he was before. The amputated member is no part of his person, otherwise it would have a right to a part of his estate, and be liable for a part of his engagements; it would be entitled to a share of his merit and demerit—which is manifestly absurd. A person is something indivisible, and is what Leibnitz calls a *monad*. [318]

My personal identity, therefore, implies the continued existence of that indivisible thing which I call myself. Whatever this self may be, it is something which thinks, and deliberates, and resolves, and acts, and suffers. I am not thought, I am not action, I am not feeling; I am something that thinks, and acts, and suffers. My thoughts, and actions, and feelings, change every moment—they have no continued, but a successive existence; but that *self* or *I*, to which they belong, is permanent, and has the same relation to all the succeeding thoughts, actions, and feelings, which I call mine.

Such are the notions that I have of my personal identity. But perhaps it may be said, this may all be fancy without reality. How do you know?—what evidence have you, that there is such a permanent self which has a claim to all the thoughts, actions, and feelings, which you call yours?

To this I answer, that the proper evidence I have of all this is remembrance. I remember that, twenty years ago, I conversed with such a person; I remember several things that passed in that conversation; my memory testifies not only that this was done, but that it was done by me who now remember it. If it was done by me, I must have existed at that time, and continued to exist from that time to the present: if the identical person whom I call myself, had not a part in that conversation, my memory is fallacious—it gives a distinct and positive testimony of what is not true. Every man in his senses believes what he distinctly remembers, and everything he remembers

[318–320]

convinces him that he existed at the time remembered.

Although memory gives the most irresistible evidence of my being the identical person that did such a thing, at such a time, I may have other good evidence of things which befel me, and which I do not remember: I know who bare me and suckled me, but I do not remember these events. [319]

It may here be observed, (though the observation would have been unnecessary if some great philosophers had not contradicted it,) that it is not my remembering any action of mine that makes me to be the person who did it. This remembrance makes me to know assuredly that I did it; but I might have done it though I did not remember it. That relation to me, which is expressed by saying that I did it, would be the same though I had not the least remembrance of it. To say that my remembering that I did such a thing, or, as some choose to express it, my being conscious that I did it, makes me to have done it, appears to me as great an absurdity as it would be to say, that my belief that the world was created made it to be created.

When we pass judgment on the identity of other persons besides ourselves, we proceed upon other grounds, and determine from a variety of circumstances, which sometimes produce the firmest assurance, and sometimes leave room for doubt. The identity of persons has often furnished matter of serious litigation before tribunals of justice. But no man of a sound mind ever doubted of his own identity, as far as he distinctly remembered.

The identity of a person is a perfect identity; wherever it is real, it admits of no degrees; and it is impossible that a person should be in part the same, and in part different; because a person is a *monad*, and is not divisible into parts. The evidence of identity in other persons besides ourselves does indeed admit of all degrees, from what we account certainty to the least degree of probability. But still it is true that the same person is perfectly the same, and cannot be so in part, or in some degree only.

For this cause, I have first considered personal identity, as that which is perfect in its kind, and the natural measure of that which is imperfect. [320]

We probably at first derive our notion of identity from that natural conviction which every man has from the dawn of reason of his own identity and continued existence. The operations of our minds are all successive, and have no continued existence. But the thinking being has a continued existence; and we have an invincible belief that it remains the same when all its thoughts and operations change.

Our judgments of the identity of objects

of sense seem to be formed much upon the same grounds as our judgments of the identity of other persons besides ourselves.

Wherever we observe great similarity, we are apt to presume identity, if no reason appears to the contrary. Two objects ever so like, when they are perceived at the same time, cannot be the same; but, if they are presented to our senses at different times, we are apt to think them the same, merely from their similarity.

Whether this be a natural prejudice, or from whatever cause it proceeds, it certainly appears in children from infancy; and, when we grow up, it is confirmed in most instances by experience; for we rarely find two individuals of the same species that are not distinguishable by obvious differences.

A man challenges a thief whom he finds in possession of his horse or his watch, only on similarity. When the watchmaker swears that he sold this watch to such a person, his testimony is grounded on similarity. The testimony of witnesses to the identity of a person is commonly grounded on no other evidence.

Thus it appears that the evidence we have of our own identity, as far back as we remember, is totally of a different kind from the evidence we have of the identity of other persons, or of objects of sense. The first is grounded on memory, and gives undoubted certainty. The last is grounded on similarity, and on other circumstances, which in many cases are not so decisive as to leave no room for doubt. [321]

It may likewise be observed, that the identity of objects of sense is never perfect. All bodies, as they consist of innumerable parts that may be disjoined from them by a great variety of causes, are subject to continual changes of their substance, increasing, diminishing, changing insensibly. When such alterations are gradual, because language could not afford a different name for every different state of such a changeable being, it retains the same name, and is considered as the same thing. Thus we say of an old regiment that it did such a thing a century ago, though there now is not a man alive who then belonged to it. We say a tree is the same in the seed-bed and in the forest. A ship of war, which has successively changed her anchors, her tackle, her sails, her masts, her planks, and her timbers, while she keeps the same name, is the same.

The identity, therefore, which we ascribe to bodies, whether natural or artificial, is not perfect identity; it is rather something which, for the conveniency of speech, we call identity. It admits of a great change of the subject, providing the change be gradual, sometimes even of a total change. And the changes which in common language are made consistent with identity, differ from those that are thought to destroy it, not in kind, but in number and degree. It has no fixed nature when applied to bodies; and questions about the identity of a body are very often questions about words. But identity, when applied to persons, has no ambiguity, and admits not of degrees, or of more and less. It is the foundation of all rights and obligations, and of all accountableness; and the notion of it is fixed and precise. [322]

CHAPTER V.

MR LOCKE'S ACCOUNT OF THE ORIGIN OF OUR IDEAS, AND PARTICULARLY OF THE IDEA OF DURATION.

It was a very laudable attempt of Mr Locke " to inquire into the original of those ideas, notions, or whatever you please to call them, which a man observes, and is conscious to himself he has in his mind, and the ways whereby the understanding comes to be furnished with them." No man was better qualified for this investigation; and I believe no man ever engaged in it with a more sincere love of truth.

His success, though great, would, I apprehend, have been greater, if he had not too early formed a system or hypothesis upon this subject, without all the caution and patient induction, which is necessary in drawing general conclusions from facts.

The sum of his doctrine I take to be this—" That all our ideas or notions may be reduced to two classes, the simple and the complex: That the simple are purely the work of Nature, the understanding being merely passive in receiving them: That they are all suggested by two powers of the mind—to wit, *Sensation* and *Reflection;*[*] and that they are the materials of all our knowledge. That the other class of complex ideas are formed by the understanding itself, which, being once stored with simple ideas of sensation and reflection, has the power to repeat, to compare, and to combine them, even to an almost infinite variety, and so can make at pleasure new complex ideas: but that it is not in the power of the most exalted wit, or enlarged

---

* That Locke did not (as even Mr Stewart supposes) introduce Reflection, either name or thing, into the philosophy of mind, see Note I. Nor was he even the first explicitly to enunciate *Sense* and *Reflection* as the two sources of our knowledge; for I can shew that this had been done in a far more philosophical manner by some of the schoolmen; Reflection with them not being merely, as with Locke, a source of *adventitious, empirical,* or a *posteriori* knowledge, but the mean by which we disclose also the *native, pure,* or a *priori* cognitions which the intellect itself contains.—H.

understanding, by any quickness or variety of thought, to invent or frame one new simple idea in the mind, not taken in by the two ways before-mentioned. [323] That, as our power over the material world reaches only to the compounding, dividing, and putting together, in various forms, the matter which God has made, but reaches not to the production or annihilation of a single atom; so we may compound, compare, and abstract the original and simple ideas which Nature has given us; but are unable to fashion in our understanding any simple idea, not received in by our senses from external objects, or by reflection from the operations of our own mind about them."

This account of the origin of all our ideas is adopted by Bishop Berkeley and Mr Hume; but some very ingenious philosophers, who have a high esteem of Locke's Essay, are dissatisfied with it.

Dr Hutcheson of Glasgow, in his " Inquiry into the Ideas of Beauty and Virtue," has endeavoured to shew that these are original and simple ideas, furnished by original powers, which he calls the sense of beauty and the moral sense.

Dr Price, in his " Review of the Principal Questions and Difficulties in Morals," has observed, very justly, that, if we take the words *sensation* and *reflection*, as Mr Locke has defined them in the beginning of his excellent Essay, it will be impossible to derive some of the most important of our ideas from them; and that, by the understanding—that is by our judging and reasoning power—we are furnished with many simple and original notions.

Mr Locke says that, by reflection, he would be understood to mean " the notice which the mind takes of its own operations, and the manner of them." This, I think, we commonly call consciousness; from which, indeed, we derive all the notions we have of the operations of our own minds; and he often speaks of the operations of our own minds, as the only objects of reflection.

When reflection is taken in this confined sense, to say that all our ideas are ideas either of sensation or reflection, is to say that everything we can conceive is either some object of sense or some operation of our own minds, which is far from being true. [324]

But the word *reflection* is commonly used in a much more extensive sense; it is applied to many operations of the mind, with more propriety than to that of consciousness. We reflect, when we remember, or call to mind what is past, and survey it with attention. We reflect, when we define, when we distinguish, when we judge, when we reason, whether about things material or intellectual.

When reflection is taken in this sense, [323–325]

which is more common, and therefore more proper* than the sense which Mr Locke has put upon it, it may be justly said to be the only source of all our distinct and accurate notions of things. For, although our first notions of material things are got by the external senses, and our first notions of the operations of our own minds by consciousness, these first notions are neither simple nor clear. Our senses and our consciousness are continually shifting from one object to another; their operations are transient and momentary, and leave no distinct notion of their objects, until they are recalled by memory, examined with attention, and compared with other things.

This reflection is not one power of the mind; it comprehends many; such as recollection, attention, distinguishing, comparing, judging. By these powers our minds are furnished not only with many simple and original notions, but with all our notions, which are accurate and well defined, and which alone are the proper materials of reasoning. Many of these are neither notions of the objects of sense, nor of the operations of our own minds, and therefore neither ideas of sensation, nor of reflection, in the sense that Mr Locke gives to reflection. But, if any one chooses to call them ideas of reflection, taking the word in the more common and proper sense, I have no objection. [325]

Mr Locke seems to me to have used the word reflection sometimes in that limited sense which he has given to it in the definition before mentioned, and sometimes to have fallen unawares into the common sense of the word; and by this ambiguity his account of the origin of our ideas is darkened and perplexed.

Having premised these things in general of Mr Locke's theory of the origin of our ideas or notions, I proceed to some observations on his account of the idea of duration.

" Reflection," he says, " upon the train of ideas, which appear one after another in our minds, is that which furnishes us with the idea of succession; and the distance between any two parts of that succession, is that we call duration."

If it be meant that the idea of succession is prior to that of duration, either in time or in the order of nature, this, I think, is impossible, because succession, as Dr Price justly observes, presupposes duration, and can in no sense be prior to it; and there-

---

* This is not correct; and the employment of Reflection in another meaning than that of ἐπιστροφὴ πρὸς ἑαυτό—the reflex knowledge or consciousness which the mind has of its own affections—is wholly a secondary and less proper signification. See Note L. I may again notice, that Reid vacillates in the meaning he gives to the term *Reflection*. Compare above, p. 232, note *, and below, under p. 516.—H.

fore it would be more proper to derive the idea of succession from that of duration.

But how do we get the idea of succession? It is, says he, by reflecting upon the train of ideas which appear one after another in our minds.

Reflecting upon the train of ideas can be nothing but remembering it, and giving attention to what our memory testifies concerning it; for, if we did not remember it, we could not have a thought about it. So that it is evident that this reflection includes remembrance, without which there could be no reflection on what is past, and consequently no idea of succession. [326]

It may here be observed, that, if we speak strictly and philosophically, no kind of succession can be an object either of the senses or of consciousness; because the operations of both are confined to the present point of time, and there can be no succession in a point of time; and on that account the motion of a body, which is a successive change of place, could not be observed by the senses alone without the aid of memory.

As this observation seems to contradict the common sense and common language of mankind, when they affirm that they see a body move, and hold motion to be an object of the senses, it is proper to take notice, that this contradiction between the philosopher and the vulgar is apparent only, and not real. It arises from this, that philosophers an l the vulgar differ in the meaning they put upon what is called the *present* time, and are thereby led to make a different limit between sense and memory.

Philosophers give the name of the *present* to that indivisible point of time, which divides the future from the past: but the vulgar find it more convenient in the affairs of life, to give the name of *present* to a portion of time, which extends more or less, according to circumstances, into the past or the future. Hence we say, the present hour, the present year, the present century, though one point only of these periods can be present in the philosophical sense.

It has been observed by grammarians, that the present tense in verbs is not confined to an indivisible point of time, but is so far extended as to have a beginning, a middle, and an end; and that, in the most copious and accurate languages, these different parts of the present are distinguished by different forms of the verb.

As the purposes of conversation make it convenient to extend what is called the present, the same reason leads men to extend the province of sense, and to carry its limit as far back as they carry the present. Thus a man may say, I saw such a person just now: it would be ridiculous to find fault with this way of speaking, because it is authorized by custom, and has a distinct

meaning. [327] But, if we speak philosophically, the senses do not testify what we saw, but only what we see; what I saw last moment I consider as the testimony of sense, though it is now only the testimony of memory.

There is no necessity in common life of dividing accurately the provinces of sense and of memory; and, therefore, we assign to sense, not an indivisible point of time, but that small portion of time which we call the present, which has a beginning, a middle, and an end.

Hence, it is easy to see that, though, in common language, we speak with perfect propriety and truth, when we say that we see a body move, and that motion is an object of sense, yet when, as philosophers, we distinguish accurately the province of sense from that of memory, we can no more see what is past, though but a moment ago, than we can remember what is present; so that, speaking philosophically, it is only by the aid of memory that we discern motion, or any succession whatsoever. We see the present place of the body; we remember the successive advance it made to that place: the first can then only give us a conception of motion when joined to the last.

Having considered the account given by Mr Locke, of the idea of succession, we shall next consider how, from the idea of succession, he derives the idea of duration.

" The distance," he says, " between any parts of that succession, or between, the appearance of any two ideas in our minds, is that we call duration."

To conceive this the more distinctly, let us call the distance between an idea and that which immediately succeeds it, one element of duration; the distance between an idea, and the second that succeeds it, two elements, and so on: if ten such elements make duration, then one must make duration, otherwise duration must be made up of parts that have no duration, which is impossible. [328]

For, suppose a succession of as many ideas as you please, if none of these ideas have duration, nor any interval of duration be between one and another, then it is perfectly evident there can be no interval of duration between the first and the last, how great soever their number be. I conclude, therefore, that there must be duration in every single interval or element of which the whole duration is made up. Nothing indeed, is more certain, than that every elementary part of duration must have duration, as every elementary part of extension must have extension.

Now, it must be observed that, in these elements of duration, or single intervals of successive ideas, there is no succession of ideas; yet we must conceive them to have duration; whence we may conclude with certainty, that there is a conception of duration, where there is no succession of ideas in the mind.

We may measure duration by the succession of thoughts in the mind, as we measure length by inches or feet; but the notion or idea of duration must be antecedent to the mensuration of it, as the notion of length is antecedent to its being measured.

Mr Locke draws some conclusions from his account of the idea of duration, which may serve as a touchstone to discover how far it is genuine. One is, that, if it were possible for a waking man to keep only one idea in his mind without variation, or the succession of others, he would have no perception of duration at all; and the moment he began to have this idea, would seem to have no distance from the moment he ceased to have it.

Now, that one idea should seem to have no duration, and that a multiplication of that *no duration* should seem to have duration, appears to me as impossible as that the multiplication of nothing should produce something. [329]

Another conclusion which the author draws from this theory is, that the same period of duration appears long to us when the succession of ideas in our mind is quick, and short when the succession is slow.

There can be no doubt but the same length of duration appears in some circumstances much longer than in others; the time appears long when a man is impatient under any pain or distress, or when he is eager in the expectation of some happiness. On the other hand, when he is pleased and happy in agreeable conversation, or delighted with a variety of agreeable objects that strike his senses or his imagination, time flies away, and appears short.

According to Mr Locke's theory, in the first of these cases, the succession of ideas is very quick, and in the last very slow. I am rather inclined to think that the very contrary is the truth. When a man is racked with pain, or with expectation, he can hardly think of anything but his distress; and the more his mind is occupied by that sole object, the longer the time appears. On the other hand, when he is entertained with cheerful music, with lively conversation, and brisk sallies of wit, there seems to be the quickest succession of ideas, but the time appears shortest.

I have heard a military officer, a man of candour and observation, say, that the time he was engaged in hot action always appeared to him much shorter than it really was. Yet I think it cannot be supposed that the succession of ideas was then slower than usual.*

* In travelling, the time seems very short, while

If the idea of duration were got merely by the succession of ideas in our minds, that succession must, to ourselves, appear equally quick at all times, because the only measure of duration is the number of succeeding ideas; but I believe every man capable of reflection will be sensible, that at one time his thoughts come slowly and heavily, and at another time have a much quicker and livelier motion. [330]

I know of no ideas or notions that have a better claim to be accounted simple and original than those of Space and Time. It is essential both to space and time to be made up of parts; but every part is similar to the whole, and of the same nature. Different parts of space, as it has three dimensions, may differ both in figure and in magnitude; but time having only one dimension, its parts can differ only in magnitude; and, as it is one of the simplest objects of thought, the conception of it must be purely the effect of our constitution, and given us by some original power of the mind.

The sense of seeing, by itself, gives us the conception and belief of only two dimensions of extension, but the sense of touch discovers three; and reason, from the contemplation of finite extended things, leads us necessarily to the belief of an immensity that contains them.* In like manner, memory gives us the conception and belief of finite intervals of duration. From the contemplation of these, reason leads us necessarily to the belief of an eternity, which comprehends all things that have a beginning and end.* Our conceptions, both of space and time, are probably partial and inadequate,† and, therefore, we are apt to lose ourselves, and to be embarrassed in our reasonings about them.

Our understanding is no less puzzled when we consider the minutest parts of time and space than when we consider the whole. We are forced to acknowledge that in their nature they are divisible without end or limit; but there are limits beyond which our faculties can divide neither the one nor the other.

It may be determined by experiment, what is the least angle under which an object may be discerned by the eye, and what is the least interval of duration that may be discerned by the ear. I believe these may be different in different persons: But surely there is a limit which no man can exceed: and what our faculties can no longer divide is still divisible in it-

passing; very long in retrospect. The cause is obvious.—H.

* See above, p. 343, note *.—H.

† They are not *probably* but *necessarily* partial and inadequate. For we are unable positively to conceive Time or Space, either as infinite, (i. e., without limits,) or as not infinite (i. e., as limited.) —H.

self, and, by beings of superior perfection, may be divided into thousands of parts. [331]

I have reason to believe, that a good eye in the prime of life may see an object under an angle not exceeding half a minute of a degree, and I believe there are some human eyes still more perfect. But even this degree of perfection will appear great, if we consider how small a part of the retina of the eye it must be which subtends an angle of half a minute.

Supposing the distance between the centre of the eye and the retina to be six or seven tenths of an inch, the subtense of an angle of half a minute to that radius, or the breadth of the image of an object seen under that angle, will not be above the ten thousandth part of an inch. This shews such a wonderful degree of accuracy in the refracting power of a good eye, that a pencil of rays coming from one point of the object shall meet in one point of the retina, so as not to deviate from that point the ten thousandth part of an inch. It shews, likewise, that such a motion of an object as makes its image on the retina to move the ten thousandth part of an inch, is discernible by the mind.

In order to judge to what degree of accuracy we can measure short intervals of time, it may be observed that one who has given attention to the motion of a Second pendulum, will be able to beat seconds for a minute with a very small error. When he continues this exercise long, as for five or ten minutes, he is apt to err, more even than in proportion to the time—for this reason, as I apprehend, that it is difficult to attend long to the moments as they pass, without wandering after some other object of thought.

I have found, by some experiments, that a man may beat seconds for one minute, without erring above one second in the whole sixty; and I doubt not but by long practice he might do it still more accurately. From this I think it follows, that the sixtieth part of a second of time is discernible by the human mind. [332]

CHAPTER VI.

OF MR LOCKE'S ACCOUNT OF OUR PERSONAL IDENTITY.

IN a long chapter upon Identity and Diversity, Mr Locke has made many ingenious and just observations, and some which I think cannot be defended. I shall only take notice of the account he gives of our own *Personal Identity.* His doctrine upon this subject has been censured by Bishop Butler, in a short essay subjoined to

his "Analogy," with whose sentiments I perfectly agree.

Identity, as was observed, Chap. IV. of this Essay, supposes the continued existence of the being of which it is affirmed, and therefore can be applied only to things which have a continued existence. While any being continues to exist, it is the same being: but two beings which have a different beginning or a different ending of their existence, cannot possibly be the same. To this I think Mr Locke agrees.

He observes, very justly, that to know what is meant by the same person, we must consider what the word *person* stands for; and he defines a person to be an intelligent being, endowed with reason and with consciousness, which last he thinks inseparable from thought.

From this definition of a person, it must necessarily follow, that, while the intelligent being continues to exist and to be intelligent, it must be the same person. To say that the intelligent being is the person, and yet that the person ceases to exist, while the intelligent being continues, or that the person continues while the intelligent being ceases to exist, is to my apprehension a manifest contradiction. [333]

One would think that the definition of a person should perfectly ascertain the nature of personal identity, or wherein it consists, though it might still be a question how we come to know and be assured of our personal identity.

Mr Locke tells us, however, " that personal identity—that is, the sameness of a rational being—consists in consciousness alone, and, as far as this consciousness can be extended backwards to any past action or thought, so far reaches the identity of that person. So that, whatever hath the consciousness of present and past actions, is the same person to whom they belong."*

* See *Essay,* (Book ii. ch. 27, § 9.) The passage given as a quotation in the text, is the sum of Locke's doctrine, but not exactly in his words. Long before Butler, to whom the merit is usually ascribed, Locke's doctrine of Personal Identity had been attacked and refuted. This was done even by his earliest critic, John Sergeant, whose words, as he is an author wholly unknown to all historians of philosophy, and his works of the rarest, I shall quote. He thus argues:—" The former distinction forelaid, he (Locke) proceeds to make *personal identity in man to consist in the consciousness that we are the same thinking thing in different times and places.* He proves it, because consciousness is inseparable from thinking, and, as it seems to him, *essential* to it. Perhaps he may have had second thoughts, since he writ his 19th Chapter, where, § 4, he thought it probable that Thinking is but the action, and not the essence of the soul. His reason here is—' Because 'tis impossible for any to perceive, without perceiving that he does perceive,' which I have shewn above to be so far from impossible, that the contrary is such. But, to speak to the point : Consciousness of any action or other accident we have now, or have had, is nothing but our knowledge that it belonged to us; and, since we both agree that we have no innate knowledges, it follows, that all, both actual and habitual knowledges, which we have, are acquired or actual knowledges, which we have, are acquired or ac-

[331 333]

This doctrine hath some strange consequences, which the author was aware of, Such as, that, if the same consciousness can be transferred from one intelligent being to another, which he thinks we cannot shew to be impossible, then two or twenty intelligent beings may be the same person. And if the intelligent being may lose the consciousness of the actions done by him, which surely is possible, then he is not the person that did those actions ; so that one intelligent being may be two or twenty different persons, if he shall so often lose the consciousness of his former actions.

There is another consequence of this doctrine, which follows no less necessarily, though Mr Locke probably did not see it. It is, that a man may be, and at the same time not be, the person that did a particular action.

Suppose a brave officer to have been flogged when a boy at school, for robbing an orchard, to have taken a standard from the enemy in his first campaign, and to have been made a general in advanced life : Suppose also, which must be admitted to be possible, that, when he took the standard,

he was conscious of his having been flogged at school, and that when made a general he was conscious of his taking the standard, but had absolutely lost the consciousness ot his flogging. [334]

These things being supposed, it follows, from Mr Locke's doctrine, that he who was flogged at school is the same person who took the standard, and that he who took the standard is the same person who was made a general. Whence it follows, if there be any truth in logic, that the general is the same person with him who was flogged at school. But the general's consciousness does not reach so far back as his flogging—therefore, according to Mr Locke's doctrine, he is not the person who was flogged. Therefore, the general is, and at the same time is not the same person with him who was flogged at school.*

Leaving the consequences of this doctrine to those who have leisure to trace them, we may observe, with regard to the doctrine itself—

First, That Mr Locke attributes to consciousness the conviction we have of our past actions, as if a man may now be conscious of what he did twenty years ago. It is impossible to understand the meaning of this, unless by consciousness be meant memory, the only faculty by which we have an immediate knowledge of our past actions.†

Sometimes, in popular discourse, a man says he is conscious that he did such a thing, meaning that he distinctly remembers that he did it. It is unnecessary, in common discourse, to fix accurately the limits between consciousness and memory. This was formerly shewn to be the case with regard to sense and memory : and, therefore, distinct remembrance is sometimes called sense, sometimes consciousness, without any inconvenience.

But this ought to be avoided in philosophy, otherwise we confound the different powers of the mind, and ascribe to one what really belongs to another. If a man can be conscious of what he did twenty years or twenty minutes ago, there is no use for memory, nor ought we to allow that there is any such faculty. [335] The faculties of consciousness and memory are chiefly distinguished by this, that the first is an immediate knowledge of the present, the second an immediate knowledge of the past.‡

When, therefore, Mr Locke's notion of

cidental to the subject or knower. *Wherefore the man, or that thing, which is to be the knower, must have had individuality, or personality, from other principles, antecedently to this knowledge, called consciousness: and, consequently, he will retain his identity, or continue the same man, or (which is equivalent) the same person, as long as he has those individuating principles.* What those principles are which constitute this man, or this knowing *individuum,* I have shewn above, §§ 6, 7. It being then most evident, *that a man must be the same, ere he can know or be conscious that he is the same,* all his laborious descants and extravagant consequences which are built upon this supposition, that consciousness individuates the person, can need no farther refutation."

The same objection was also made by Leibnitz in his strictures on Locke's Essay. *Inter alia,* he says— " Pour ce qui est du *soi* il sera bon de le distinguer de l'*apparence du soi* et de la consciosite. Le *soi* fait l'*identité reelle* et physique, et l'apparence du soi, accompagnée de la verité, y joint l'identité personelle. Ainsi ne voulant point dire, que l'identité personelle ne s'étend pas plus loin que le souvenir, je dirois encore moins que le soi ou l'identité physique en dépend. L'identité reele et personelle se prouve le plus certainment qu'il se peut en matiére de fait, par la réflexion présente et immediate; elle se prouve suffisament pour l'ordinaire par notre souvenir d'intervalle ou par le temoignage conspirant des autres. Mais si Dieu changeoit extraordinairment l'identité reele, la personelle demeuroit, pourvu que l'homme conservât les apparences d'identité, tant les internes, (c'est-à-dire de la conscience,) que les externes, comme celles qui consistent dans ce qui paroit aux autres. Ainsi la conscience n'est pas le seul moyen de constituer l'identité personelle, et le rapport d'autrui ou même d'autres marques y peuvent suppléer. Mais il y a de la difficulté, s'il se trouve contradiction entre ces diverses apparences. La conscience se peut taire comme dans l'oubli ; mais si elle disoit bien clairment des choses, qui fussent contraires aux autres apparences, on seroit embarrassé dans la decision et comme suspendû quelques fois entre deux possibilités, celle de l'érreur du notre souvenir et celle de quelque deception dans les apparences externes."

For the best criticism of Locke's doctrine of Personal Identity, I may, however, refer the reader to M. Cousin's " *Cours de Philosophie,*" t. ii., Leçon xviii., p. 190-198.— H.

[334, 335]

* Compare Buffier's " *Traité des prémieres Vérités,*" *(Remarques sur Locke,* § 565,) who makes a similar criticism.—H.

† Locke, it. will be remembered, does not, like Reid, view consciousness as a co-ordinate faculty with memory ; but under consciousness he properly comprehends the various faculties as so many special modifications.—H.

‡ As already frequently stated, an *immediate* knowledge of the *past* is contradictory. This observation I cannot again repeat. See Note B.—H.

personal identity is properly expressed, it is that personal identity consists in distinct remembrance ; for, even in the popular sense, to say that I am conscious of a past action, means nothing else than that I distinctly remember that I did it.

Secondly, It may be observed, that, in this doctrine, not only is consciousness confounded with memory, but, which is still more strange, personal identity is confounded with the evidence which we have of our personal identity.

It is very true that my remembrance that I did such a thing is the evidence I have that I am the identical person who did it. And this, I am apt to think, Mr Locke meant. But, to say that my remembrance that I did such a thing, or my consciousness, makes me the person who did it, is, in my apprehension, an absurdity too gross to be entertained by any man who attends to the meaning of it ; for it is to attribute to memory or consciousness, a strange magical power of producing its object, though that object must have existed before the memory or consciousness which produced it.

Consciousness is the testimony of one faculty; memory is the testimony of another faculty. And, to say that the testimony is the cause of the thing testified, this surely is absurd, if anything be, and could not have been said by Mr Locke, if he had not confounded the testimony with the thing testified.

When a horse that was stolen is found and claimed by the owner, the only evidence he can have, or that a judge or witnesses can have that this is the very identical horse which was his property, is similitude. [336] But would it not be ridiculous from this to infer that the identity of a horse consists in similitude only ? The only evidence I have that I am the identical person who did such actions is, that I remember distinctly I did them ; or, as Mr Locke expresses it, I am conscious I did them. To infer from this, that personal identity consists in consciousness, is an argument which, if it had any force, would prove the identity of a stolen horse to consist solely in similitude.

Thirdly, Is it not strange that the sameness or identity of a person should consist in a thing which is continually changing, and is not any two minutes the same ?

Our consciousness, our memory, and every operation of the mind, are still flowing, like the water of a river, or like time itself. The consciousness I have this moment can no more be the same consciousness I had last moment, than this moment can be the last moment. Identity can only be affirmed of things which have a continued existence. Consciousness, and every kind of thought, is transient and momentary, and has no continued existence ; and, there-

fore, if personal identity consisted in consciousness, it would certainly follow that no man is the same person any two moments of his life ; and, as the right and justice of reward and punishment is founded on personal identity, no man could be responsible for his actions.

But, though I take this to be the unavoidable consequence of Mr Locke's doctrine concerning personal identity, and though some persons may have liked the doctrine the better on this account, I am far from imputing anything of this kind to Mr Locke. He was too good a man not to have rejected with abhorrence a doctrine which he believed to draw this consequence after it. [337]

Fourthly, There are many expressions used by Mr Locke, in speaking of personal identity, which, to me, are altogether unintelligible, unless we suppose that he confounded that sameness or identity which we ascribe to an individual, with the identity which, in common discourse, is often ascribed to many individuals of the same species.

When we say that pain and pleasure, consciousness and memory, are the same in all men, this sameness can only mean similarity, or sameness of kind ; but, that the pain of one man can be the same individual pain with that of another man, is no less impossible than that one man should be another man ; the pain felt by me yesterday can no more be the pain I feel to-day, than yesterday can be this day ; and the same thing may be said of every passion and of every operation of the mind. The same kind or species of operation may be in different men, or in the same man at different times ; but it is impossible that the same individual operation should be in different men, or in the same man at different times.

When Mr Locke, therefore, speaks of "the same consciousness being continued through a succession of different substances ;" when he speaks of " repeating the idea of a past action, with the same consciousness we had of it at the first," and of " the same consciousness extending to actions past and to come"—these expressions are to me unintelligible, unless he means not the same individual consciousness, but a consciousness that is similar, or of the same kind.

If our personal identity consists in consciousness, as this consciousness cannot be the same individually any two moments, but only of the same kind, it would follow that we are not for any two moments the same individual persons, but the same kind of persons.

As our consciousness sometimes ceases to exist, as in sound sleep, our personal identity must cease with it. Mr Locke allows, that the same thing cannot have two beginnings of existence; so that our identity would be irrecoverably gone every time we cease to think, if it was but for a a moment.* [338]

CHAPTER VII.

THEORIES CONCERNING MEMORY.

THE common theory of ideas—that is, of images in the brain or in the mind, of all the objects of thought—has been very generally applied to account for the faculties of memory and imagination, as well as that of perception by the senses.

The sentiments of the Peripatetics are expressed by Alexander Aphrodisiensis, one of the earliest Greek commentators on Aristotle, in these words, as they are translated by Mr Harris in his " Hermes :"— " Now, what Phancy or Imagination is, we may explain as follows :—We may conceive to be formed within us, from the operations of our senses about sensible objects, some Impression, as it were, or Picture, in our original Sensorium, being a relict of that motion caused within us by the external object ; a relict which, when the external object is no longer present, remains, and is still preserved, being, as it were, its Image,

and which, by being thus preserved, becomes the cause of our having Memory. Now, such a sort of relict, and, as it were, impression, they call Phancy or Imagination."*

Another passage from Alcinous *Of the Doctrines of Plato*, chap. 4, shews the agreement of the ancient Platonists and Peripatetics in this theory :—" When the form or type of things is imprinted on the mind by the organs of the senses, and so imprinted as not to be deleted by time, but preserved firm and lasting, its preservation is called Memory."* [339]

Upon this principle, Aristotle imputes the shortness of memory in children to this cause—that their brain is too moist and soft to retain impressions made upon it : and the defect of memory in old men he imputes, on the contrary, to the hardness and rigidity of the brain, which hinders its receiving any durable impression.†

This ancient theory of the cause of memory is defective in two respects : *First,* If the cause assigned did really exist, it by no means accounts for the phænomenon ; and, *secondly,* There is no evidence, nor even probability, that that cause exists.

It is probable that in perception some impression is made upon the brain as well as upon the organ and nerves, because all the nerves terminate in the brain, and because disorders and hurts of the brain are found to affect our powers of perception when the external organ and nerve are found ; but we are totally ignorant of the nature of this impression upon the brain : it can have no resemblance to the object perceived, nor does it in any degree account for that sensation and perception which are consequent upon it. These things have been argued in the second Essay, and shall now be taken for granted, to prevent repetition.

If the impression upon the brain be insufficient to account for the perception of objects that are present, it can as little account for the memory of those that are past.

So that, if it were certain that the impressions made on the brain in perception remain as long as there is any memory of the object, all that could be inferred from this, is, that, by the laws of Nature, there is a connection established between that impression, and the remembrance of that object. But how the impression contributes

---

* It is here proper to insert Reid's remarks on Personal Identity, as published by Lord Kames, in his " Essays on the Principles of Morality and Natural Religion," (third edition, p. 264.) These, perhaps, might have more appropriately found their place in the Correspondence of our Author.

" To return to our subject," says his Lordship, " Mr Locke, writing on personal identity, has fallen short of his usual accuracy. He inadvertently jumbles together the identity that is nature's work, with our knowledge of it. Nay, he expresses himself sometimes as if identity had no other foundation than that knowledge. I am favoured by Dr Reid with the following thoughts on personal identity :—

"' All men agree that personality is indivisible ; a part of a person is an absurdity. A man who loses his estate, his health, an arm, or a leg, continues still to be the same person. My personal identity, therefore, is the continued existence of that indivisible thing which I call myself. I am not thought ; I am not action ; I am not feeling ; but I think, and act, and feel. Thoughts, actions, feelings, change every moment ; but *self,* to which they belong, is permanent. If it be asked how I know that it is permanent, the answer is, that I know it from memory. Everything I remember to have seen, or heard, or done, or suffered, convinces me that I existed at the time remembered. But, though it is from memory that I have the knowledge of my personal identity, yet personal identity must exist in nature, independent of memory ; otherwise, I should only be the same person as far as my memory serves me ; and what would become of my existence during the intervals wherein my memory has failed me ? My remembrance of any of my actions does not make me to be the person who did the action, but only makes me know that I was the person who did it. And yet it was Mr Locke's opinion, that my remembrance of an action is what makes me to be the person who did it ; a pregnant instance that even men of the greatest genius may sometimes fall into an absurdity. Is it not an obvious corollary, from Mr Locke's opinion, that he never was born ? He could not remember his birth ; and, therefore, was not the person born at such a place and at such a time.' "—H.

[338, 339]

* The inference founded on these passages, is altogether erroneous. See Note K.—H.

† In this whole statement Reid is wrong. In the *first* place, Aristotle did not impute the defect of memory in children and old persons to any constitution of the *Brain ;* for, in his doctrine, the *Heart,* and not the Brain, is the primary sensorium in which the impression is made. In the *second* place, the term *impression* (τύπος), is used by Aristotle in an analogical, not in a literal signification. See Note K.—H.

2 A

to this remembrance, we should be quite ignorant; it being impossible to discover how thought of any kind should be produced, by an impression on the brain, or upon any part of the body. [340]

To say that this impression is memory, is absurd, if understood literally. If it is only meant that it is the cause of memory, it ought to be shewn how it produces this effect, otherwise memory remains as unaccountable as before.

If a philosopher should undertake to account for the force of gunpowder in the discharge of a musket, and then tell us gravely that the cause of this phænomenon is the drawing of the trigger, we should not be much wiser by this account. As little are we instructed in the cause of memory, by being told that it is caused by a certain impression on the brain. For, supposing that impression on the brain were as necessary to memory as the drawing of the trigger is to the discharge of the musket, we are still as ignorant as we were how memory is produced; so that, if the cause of memory, assigned by this theory, did really exist, it does not in any degree account for memory.

Another defect in this theory is, that there is no evidence nor probability that the cause assigned does exist; that is, that the impression made upon the brain in perception remains after the object is removed.

That impression, whatever be its nature, is caused by the impression made by the object upon the organ of sense, and upon the nerve. Philosophers suppose, without any evidence, that, when the object is removed, and the impression upon the organ and nerve ceases, the impression upon the brain continues, and is permanent; that is, that, when the cause is removed, the effect continues. The brain surely does not appear more fitted to retain an impression than the organ and nerve.

But, granting that the impression upon the brain continues after its cause is removed, its effects ought to continue while it continues; that is, the sensation and perception should be as permanent as the impression upon the brain, which is supposed to be their cause. But here again the philosopher makes a second supposition, with as little evidence, but of a contrary nature—to wit, that, while the cause remains—the effect ceases. [341]

If this should be granted also, a third must be made—That the same cause which at first produced sensation and perception, does afterwards produce memory—an operation essentially different, both from sensation and perception.

A fourth supposition must be made—That this cause, though it be permanent, does not produce its effect at all times; it must be like an inscription which is some-

times covered with rubbish, and on other occasions made legible; for the memory of things is often interrupted for a long time, and circumstances bring to our recollection what had been long forgot. After all, many things are remembered which were never perceived by the senses, being no objects of sense, and therefore which could make no impression upon the brain by means of the senses.

Thus, when philosophers have piled one supposition upon another, as the giants piled the mountains in order to scale the heavens, all is to no purpose—memory remains unaccountable; and we know as little how we remember things past, as how we are conscious of the present.

But here it is proper to observe, that, although impressions upon the brain give no aid in accounting for memory, yet it is very probable that, in the human frame, memory is dependent on some proper state or temperament of the brain.*

Although the furniture of our memory bears no resemblance to any temperament of brain whatsoever, as indeed it is impossible it should, yet nature may have subjected us to this law, that a certain constitution or state of the brain is necessary to memory. That this is really the case, many well-known facts lead us to conclude. [342]

It is possible that, by accurate observation, the proper means may be discovered of preserving that temperament of the brain which is favourable to memory, and of remedying the disorders of that temperament. This would be a very noble improvement of the medical art. But, if it should ever be attained, it would give no aid to understand how one state of the brain assists memory, and another hurts it.

I know certainly, that the impression made upon my hand by the prick of a pin occasions acute pain. But can any philosopher shew how this cause produces the effect? The nature of the impression is here perfectly known; but it gives no help to understand how that impression affects the mind; and, if we knew as distinctly that state of the brain which causes memory, we should still be as ignorant as before how that state contributes to memory. We might have been so constituted, for anything that I know, that the prick of a pin in the hand, instead of causing pain, should cause remembrance; nor would that constitution be more unaccountable than the present.

The body and mind operate on each other,

---

* Nothing more was meant by the philosopher in question, than that memory is, as Reid himself admits, dependent on a certain state of the brain, and on some unknown effect determined in it, to which they gave the metaphorical name—*impression, trace, type*, &c.—H.

according to fixed laws of nature ; and it is the business of a philosopher to discover those laws by observation and experiment : but, when he has discovered them, he must rest in them as facts whose cause is inscrutable to the human understanding.

Mr Locke, and those who have followed him, speak with more reserve than the ancients,* and only incidentally, of impressions on the brain as the cause of memory, and impute it rather to our retaining in our minds the ideas got either by sensation or reflection.

This, Mr Locke says, may be done two ways—"*First*, By keeping the idea for some time actually in view, which is called *contemplation ; Secondly*, By the power to revive again in our minds those ideas which, after imprinting, have disappeared, or have been, as it were, laid out of sight ; and this is memory, which is, as it were, the storehouse of our ideas." [343]

To explain this more distinctly, he immediately adds the following observation :— " But our ideas being nothing but actual perceptions in the mind, which cease to be anything when there is no perception of them, this laying up of our ideas in the repository of the memory signifies no more but this, that the mind has a power, in many cases, to revive perceptions which it once had, with this additional perception annexed to them, that it has had them before; and in this sense it is, that our ideas are said to be in our memories, when indeed they are actually nowhere; but only there is an ability in the mind, when it will, to revive them again, and, as it were, paint them anew upon itself, though some with more, some with less difficulty, some more lively, and others more obscurely."

In this account of memory, the repeated use of the phrase, *as it were*, leads one to judge that it is partly figurative ; we must therefore endeavour to distinguish the figurative part from the philosophical. The first, being addressed to the imagination, exhibits a picture of memory, which, to have its effect, must be viewed at a proper distance and from a particular point of view. The second, being addressed to the understanding, ought to bear a near inspection and a critical examination.

The analogy between memory and a repository, and between remembering and retaining, is obvious, and is to be found in all languages, it being very natural to express the operations of the mind by images taken from things material. But, in philosophy we ought to draw aside the veil of imagery, and to view them naked.

When, therefore, memory is said to be a repository or storehouse of ideas, where they are laid up when not perceived, and again brought forth as there is occasion, I take this to be popular and rhetorical. [344] For the author tells us, that when they are not perceived, they are nothing, and nowhere, and therefore can neither be laid up in a repository, nor drawn out of it.

But we are told, " That this laying up of our ideas in the repository of the memory signifies no more than this, that the mind has a power to revive perceptions, which it once had, with this additional perception annexed to them, that it has had them before." This, I think, must be understood literally and philosophically.

But it seems to me as difficult to revive things that have ceased to be anything, as to lay them up in a repository, or to bring them out of it. When a thing is once annihilated, the same thing cannot be again produced, though another thing similar to it may. Mr Locke, in another place, acknowledges that the same thing cannot have two beginnings of existence ; and that things that have different beginnings are not the same, but diverse. From this it follows, that an ability to revive our ideas or perceptions, after they have ceased to be, can signify no more but an ability to create new ideas or perceptions similar to those we had before.

They are said " to be revived, with this additional perception, that we have had them before." This surely would be a fallacious perception, since they could not have two beginnings of existence : nor could we believe them to have two beginnings of existence. We can only believe that we had formerly ideas or perceptions very like to them, though not identically the same. But whether we perceive them to be the same, or only like to those we had before, this perception, one would think, supposes a remembrance of those we had before, otherwise the similitude or identity could not be perceived.

Another phrase is used to explain this reviving of our perceptions—" The mind, as it were, paints them anew upon itself.' [345] There may be something figurative in this ; but, making due allowance for that, it must imply that the mind, which paints the things that have ceased to exist, must have the memory of what they were, since every painter must have a copy either before his eye, or in his imagination and memory.

These remarks upon Mr Locke's account of memory are intended to shew that his system of ideas gives no light to this faculty, but rather tends to darken it ; as little does it make us understand how we remember, and by that means have the certain knowledge of things past.

Every man knows what memory is, and has a distinct notion of it. But when Mr

---

* This is hardly correct. See Note K.—H.

Locke speaks of a power to revive in the mind those ideas which, after imprinting, have disappeared, or have been, as it were, laid out of sight, one would hardly know this to be memory, if he had not told us. There are other things which it seems to resemble at least as much. I see before me the picture of a friend. I shut my eyes, or turn them another way, and the picture disappears, or is, as it were, laid out of sight. I have a power to turn my eyes again towards the picture, and immediately the perception is revived. But is this memory? No surely; yet it answers the definition as well as memory itself can do.

We may observe, that the word perception is used by Mr Locke in too indefinite a way, as well as the word idea.

Perception, in the chapter upon that subject, is said to be the first faculty of the mind exercised about our ideas. Here we are told that·ideas are nothing but perceptions. Yet, I apprehend, it would sound oddly to say, that perception is the first faculty of the mind exercised about perception; and still more strangely to say, that ideas are the first faculty of the mind exercised about our ideas. But why should not ideas be a faculty as well as perception, if both are the same?† [346]

Memory is said to be a power to revive our perceptions. Will it not follow from this, that everything that can be remembered is a perception? If this be so, it will be difficult to find anything in nature but perceptions.‡

Our ideas, we are told, are nothing but actual perceptions; but, in many places of the Essay, ideas are said to be the objects of perception, and that the mind, in all its thoughts and reasonings, has no other immediate object which it does or can contemplate but its own ideas. Does it not appear from this, either that Mr Locke held the operations of the mind to·be the same thing with the objects of those operations,§ or that he used the word idea sometimes in one sense and sometimes in another, without any intimation, and probably without any apprehension of its ambiguity? It is an article of Mr Hume's philosophy, that there is no distinction between the operations of the mind and their objects.§ But I see no reason to impute this opinion to Mr Locke. I rather think that, notwith-

standing his great judgment and candour, his understanding was entangled by the ambiguity of the word idea, and that most of the imperfections of his Essay are owing to that cause.

Mr Hume saw farther into the consequences of the common system concerning ideas than any author had done before him. He saw the absurdity of making every object of thought double, and splitting it into a remote object, which has a separate and permanent existence, and an immediate object, called an idea or impression, which is an image of the former, and has no existence, but when we are conscious of it. According to this system, we have no intercourse with the external world, but by means of the internal world of ideas, which represents the other to the mind.

He saw it was necessary to reject one of these worlds as a fiction, and the question was, Which should be rejected?—whether all mankind, learned and unlearned, had feigned the existence of the external world without good reason; or whether philosophers had feigned the internal world of ideas, in order to account for the intercourse of the mind with the external? [347] Mr Hume adopted the first of these opinions, and employed his reason and eloquence in support of it.

Bishop Berkeley had gone so far in the same track as to reject the material world as fictitious; but it was left to Mr Hume to complete the system.

According to his system, therefore, impressions and ideas in his own mind are the only things a man can know or can conceive. Nor are these ideas representatives, as they were in the old system. There is nothing else in nature, or, at least, within the reach of our faculties, to be represented. What the vulgar call the perception of an external object, is nothing but a strong impression upon the mind. What we call the remembrance of a past event, is nothing but a present impression or idea, weaker than the former. And what we call imagination, is still a present idea, but weaker than that of memory.

That I may not do him injustice, these are his words in his "Treatise of Human Nature," [vol. I.] page 193.

"We find by experience that, when any impression has been present with the mind, it again makes its appearance there as an idea; and this it may do after two different ways, either when in its new appearance it retains a considerable degree of its first vivacity and is somewhat intermediate betwixt an impression and an·idea, or when it entirely loses that vivacity, and is a perfect idea. The faculty by which we repeat our impressions in the first manner, is called the memory, and the other the imagination."

---

* To some of the preceding strictures on Locke's account of memory, excuses might competently be pleaded.—H.

† This criticism only shews the propriety of the distinction of *perception* and *percept.* Locke and other·philosophers use the word *perception*, 1°, for the act or faculty of perceiving; 2°, for that which is perceived—the idea in their doctrine; and 3°, for either or both indifferently.—H.

‡ See above p. 222, b, note * ; p. 280, a. note *.—H.

§ The term object being then, used for the *immediate object*—viz., that of which we are conscious. —H

[346, 347]

Upon this account of memory and imagination, I shall make some remarks. [348] *First*, I wish to know what we are here to understand by experience? It is said, we find all this by experience; and I conceive nothing can be meant by this experience but memory—not that memory which our author defines, but memory in the common acceptation of the word. According to vulgar apprehension, memory is an immediate knowledge of something past. Our author does not admit that there is any such knowledge in the human mind. He maintains that memory is nothing but a present idea or impression. But, in defining what he takes memory to be, he takes for granted that kind of memory which he rejects. For, can we find by experience, that an impression, after its first appearance to the mind, makes a second and a third, with different degrees of strength and vivacity, if we have not so distinct a remembrance of its first appearance as enables us to know it upon its second and third, notwithstanding that, in the interval, it has undergone a very considerable change?*

All experience supposes memory; and there can be no such thing as experience, without trusting to our own memory, or that of others. So that it appears, from Mr Hume's account of this matter, that he found himself to have that kind of memory which he acknowledges and defines, by exercising that kind which he rejects.

Secondly, What is it we find by experience or memory? It is, "That, when an impression has been present with the mind, it again makes its appearance there as an idea, and that after two different ways."

If experience informs us of this, it certainly deceives us; for the thing is impossible, and the author shews it to be so. Impressions and ideas are fleeting, perishable things, which have no existence but when we are conscious of them. If an impression could make a second and a third appearance to the mind, it must have a continued existence during the interval of these appearances, which Mr Hume acknowledges to be a gross absurdity. [349] It seems, then, that we find, by experience, a thing which is impossible. We are imposed upon by our experience, and made to believe contradictions.

Perhaps it may be said, that these different appearances of the impression are not to be understood literally, but figuratively; that the impression is personified, and made to appear at different times and in different habits, when no more is meant but that an impression appears at one time; afterwards a thing of a middle nature, between an impression and an idea, which we call memory;

---

* See Note B.—H.

and, last of all, a perfect idea, which we call imagination: that this figurative meaning agrees best with the last sentence of the period, where we are told that memory and imagination are faculties, whereby we repeat our impresions in a more or less lively manner. To repeat an impression is a figurative way of speaking, which signifies making a new impression similar to the former.

If, to avoid the absurdity implied in the literal meaning, we understand the philosopher in this figurative one, then his definitions of memory and imagination, when stripped of the figurative dress, will amount to this, That memory is the faculty of making a weak impression, and imagination the faculty of making an impression still weaker, after a corresponding strong one. These definitions of memory and imagination labour under two defects: *First*, That they convey no notion of the thing defined; and, *Secondly*, That they may be applied to things of a quite different nature from those that are defined.

When we are said to have a faculty of making a weak impression after a corresponding strong one, it would not be easy to conjecture that this faculty is memory. Suppose a man strikes his head smartly against the wall, this is an impression; now, he has a faculty by which he can repeat this impression with less force, so as not to hurt him: this, by Mr Hume's account, must be memory. [350] He has a faculty by which he can just touch the wall with his head, so that the impression entirely loses its vivacity. This surely must be imagination; at least, it comes as near to the definition given of it by Mr Hume as anything I can conceive.

Thirdly, We may observe, that, when we are told that we have a faculty of repeating our impressions in a more or less lively manner, this implies that we are the efficient causes of our ideas of memory and imagination; but this contradicts what the author says a little before, where he proves, by what he calls a convincing argument, that impressions are the cause of their corresponding ideas. The argument that proves this had need, indeed, to be very convincing: whether we make the idea to be a second appearance of the impression, or a new impression similar to the former.

If the first be true, then the impression is the cause of itself. If the second, then the impression, after it is gone and has no existence, produces the idea. Such are the mysteries of Mr Hume's philosophy.

It may be observed, that the common system, that ideas are the only immediate objects of thought, leads to scepticism with regard to memory, as well as with regard to the objects of sense, whether those ideas are placed in the mind or in the brain.

Ideas are said to be things internal and present, which have no existence but during the moment they are in the mind. The objects of sense are things external, which have a continued existence. When it is maintained that all that we immediately perceive is only ideas or phantasms, how can we, from the existence of those phantasms, conclude the existence of an external world corresponding to them?

This difficult question seems not to have occurred to the Peripatetics.* Des Cartes saw the difficulty, and endeavoured to find out arguments by which, from the existence of our phantasms or ideas, we might infer the existence of external objects. [351] The same course was followed by Malebranche, Arnauld, and Locke; but Berkeley and Hume easily refuted all their arguments, and demonstrated that there is no strength in them.

The same difficulty with regard to memory naturally arises from the system of ideas; and the only reason why it was not observed by philosophers, is, because they give less attention to the memory than to the senses; for, since ideas are things present, how can we, from our having a certain idea presently in our mind, conclude that an event really happened ten or twenty years ago, corresponding to it?

There is the same need of arguments to prove, that the ideas of memory are pictures of things that really did happen, as that the ideas of sense are pictures of external objects which now exist. In both cases, it will be impossible to find any argument that has real weight. So that this hypothesis leads us to absolute scepticism, with regard to those things which we most distinctly remember, no less than with regard to the external objects of sense.

It does not appear to have occurred either to Locke or to Berkeley, that their system has the same tendency to overturn the testimony of memory as the testimony of the senses.

Mr Hume saw farther than both, and found this consequence of the system of ideas perfectly corresponding to his aim of establishing universal scepticism. His system is therefore more consistent than theirs, and the conclusions agree better with the premises.

But, if we should grant to Mr Hume that our ideas of memory afford no just ground to believe the past existence of things which we remember, it may still be asked, How it comes to pass that perception and memory are accompanied with belief, while bare imagination is not? Though this belief cannot be justified upon his system, it ought to be accounted for as a phænomenon of human nature. [352]

This he has done, by giving us a new theory of belief in general; a theory which suits very well with that of ideas, and seems to be a natural consequence of it, and which, at the same time, reconciles all the belief that we find in human nature to perfect scepticism.

What, then, is this belief? It must either be an idea, or some modification of an idea; we conceive many things which we do not believe. The idea of an object is the same whether we believe it to exist, or barely conceive it. The belief adds no new idea to the conception; it is, therefore, nothing but a modification of the idea of the thing believed, or a different manner of conceiving it. Hear himself:—

" All the perceptions of the mind are of two kinds, impressions and ideas, which differ from each other only in their different degrees of force and vivacity. Our ideas are copied from our impressions, and represent them in all their parts. When you would vary the idea of a particular object, you can only increase or diminish its force and vivacity. If you make any other change upon it, it represents a different object or impression. The case is the same as in colours. A particular shade of any colour may acquire a new degree of liveliness or brightness, without any other variation; but, when you produce any other variation, it is no longer the same shade or colour. So that, as belief does nothing but vary the manner in which we conceive any object, it can only bestow on our ideas an additional force and vivacity. An opinion, therefore, or belief, may be most accurately defined a lively idea, related to or associated with a present impression."

This theory of belief is very fruitful of consequences, which Mr Hume traces with his usual acuteness, and brings into the service of his system. [353] A great part of his system, indeed, is built upon it; and it is of itself sufficient to prove what he calls his hypothesis, " that belief is more properly an act of the sensitive than of the cogitative part of our natures."

It is very difficult to examine this account of belief with the same gravity with which it is proposed. It puts one in mind of the ingenious account given by Martinus Scriblerus of the power of syllogism, by making the *major* the male, and the *minor* the female, which, being coupled by the middle *term*, generate the conclusion. There is surely no science in which men of great parts and ingenuity have fallen into

* This is not correct. See above, p. 285, note †. To that note I may add, that *no orthodox Catholic could be an Idealist.* It was only the doctrine of transubstantiation that prevented Malebranche from pre-occupying the theory of Berkeley and Collier, which was in fact his own, with the transcendent reality of a material world left out, as a Protestant *hors d'œuvre.* This, it is curious, has never been observed. See Note P.—H.

such gross absurdities as in treating of the powers of the mind. I cannot help thinking that never anything more absurd was gravely maintained by any philosopher, than this account of the nature of belief, and of the distinction of perception, memory, and imagination.

The belief of a proposition is an operation of mind of which every man is conscious, and what it is he understands perfectly, though, on account of its simplicity, he cannot give a logical definition of it. If he compares it with strength or vivacity of his ideas, or with any modification of ideas, they are so far from appearing to be one and the same, that they have not the least similitude.

That a strong belief and a weak belief differ only in degree, I can easily comprehend; but that belief and no belief should differ only in degree, no man can believe who understands what he speaks. For this is, in reality, to say that something and nothing differ only in degree; or, that nothing is a degree of something.

Every proposition that may be the object of belief, has a contrary proposition that may be the object of a contrary belief. The ideas of both, according to Mr Hume, are the same, and differ only in degrees of vivacity—that is, contraries differ only in degree; and so pleasure may be a degree of pain, and hatred a degree of love. [354] But it is to no purpose to trace the absurdities that follow from this doctrine, for none of them can be more absurd than the doctrine itself.

Every man knows perfectly what it is to see an object with his eyes, what it is to remember a past event, and what it is to conceive a thing which has no existence. That these are quite different operations of his mind, he is as certain as that sound differs from colour, and both from taste; and I can as easily believe that sound, and colour, and taste differ only in degree, as that seeing, and remembering, and imagining, differ only in degree.

Mr Hume, in the third volume of his "Treatise of Human Nature," is sensible that his theory of belief is liable to strong objections, and seems, in some measure, to retract it; but in what measure, it is not easy to say. He seems still to think that belief is only a modification of the idea; but that vivacity is not a proper term to express that modification. Instead of it, he uses some analogical phrases, to explain that modification, such as "apprehending the idea more strongly, or taking faster hold of it."

There is nothing more meritorious in a philosopher than to retract an error upon conviction; but, in this instance, I humbly apprehend Mr Hume claims that merit [354—356]

upon too slight a ground. For I cannot perceive that the apprehending an idea more strongly, or taking faster hold of it, expresses any other modification of the idea than what was before expressed by its strength and vivacity, or even that it expresses the same modification more properly. Whatever modification of the idea he makes belief to be, whether its vivacity, or some other without a name, to make perception, memory, and imagination to be the different degrees of that modification, is chargeable with the absurdities we have mentioned.

Before we leave this subject of memory, it is proper to take notice of a distinction which Aristotle makes between memory and reminiscence, because the distinction has a real foundation in nature, though in our language, I think, we do not distinguish them by different names. [355]

Memory is a kind of habit which is not always in exercise with regard to things we remember, but is ready to suggest them when there is occasion. The most perfect degree of this habit is, when the thing presents itself to our remembrance spontaneously, and without labour, as often as there is occasion. A second degree is, when the thing is forgot for a longer or shorter time, even when there is occasion to remember it; yet, at last, some incident brings it to mind without any search. A third degree is, when we cast about and search for what we would remember, and so at last find it out. It is this last, I think, which Aristotle calls reminiscence, as distinguished from memory.

Reminiscence, therefore, includes a will to recollect something past, and a search for it. But here a difficulty occurs. It may be said, that what we will to remember we must conceive, as there can be no will without a conception of the thing willed. A will to remember a thing, therefore, seems to imply that we remember it already, and have no occasion to search for it. But this difficulty is easily removed. When we will to remember a thing, we must remember something relating to it, which gives us a relative conception of it; but we may, at the same time, have no conception what the thing is, but only what relation it bears to something else. Thus, I remember that a friend charged me with a commission to be executed at such a place; but I have forgot what the commission was. By applying my thought to what I remember concerning it, that it was given by such a person, upon such an occasion, in consequence of such a conversation, I am led, in a train of thought, to the very thing I had forgot, and recollect distinctly what the commission was. [356]

Aristotle says, that brutes have not reminiscence;* and this I think is probable; but, says he, they have memory. It cannot, indeed, be doubted but they have something very like to it, and, in some instances, in a very great degree. A dog knows his master after long absence. A horse will trace back a road he has once gone, as accurately as a man ; and this is the more strange, that the train of thought which he had in going must be reversed in his return. It is very like to some prodigious memories we read of, where a person, upon hearing an hundred names or unconnected words pronounced, can begin at the last, and go backwards to

the first, without losing or misplacing one. Brutes certainly may learn much from experience, which seems to imply memory.

Yet, I see no reason to think that brutes measure time as men do, by days, months, or years ; or that they have any distinct knowledge of the interval between things which they remember, or of their distance from the present moment If we could not record transactions according to their dates, human memory would be something very different from what it is, and, perhaps, resemble more the memory of brutes. [357]

ESSAY IV.

OF CONCEPTION.

CHAPTER I.

OF CONCEPTION, OR SIMPLE APPREHENSION IN GENERAL.

Conceiving, imagining,†apprehending, understanding, having a notion of a thing, are common words, used to express that operation of the understanding which the logicians call *simple apprehension.* The *having an idea of a thing,* is, in common language, used in the same sense, chiefly, I think, since Mr Locke's time.‡

Logicians define Simple Apprehension to be the bare conception of a thing without any judgment or belief about it. If this were intended for a strictly logical definition, it might be a just objection to it, that conception and apprehension are only synonymous words ; and that we may as well define conception by apprehension, as apprehension by conception ; but it ought to be

* This is a question which may be differently answered, according as we attribute a different meaning to the terms employed.—H.

† *Imagining* should not be confounded with *Conceiving,* &c. ; though some philosophers, as Gassendi, have not attended to the distinction. The words *Conception, Concept, Notion,* should be limited to the thought of what cannot be represented in the imagination, as the thought suggested by a general term. The Leibnitians call this *symbolical* in contrast to *intuitive* knowledge. This is the sense in which *conceptio* and *conceptus* have been usually and correctly employed. Mr Stewart, on the other hand, arbitrarily limits Conception to the reproduction, in imagination, of an object of sense as actually perceived. See Elements, vol. I., ch. iii. I cannot enter on a general criticism of Reid's nomenclature, though I may say something more of this in the sequel. See below, under pp. 371, 482.—H.

‡ *In this country* should be added. Locke only introduced into *English* philosophy the term *idea* in its Cartesian universality. Prior to him, the word was only used with us in its Platonic signification. *Before* Des Cartes, David Buchanan, a Scotch philosopher, who sojourned in France, had, however, employed *Idea* in an equal latitude. See Note G.— II.

remembered that the most simple operations of the mind cannot be logically defined. To have a distinct notion of them, we must attend to them as we feel them in our own minds. He that would have a distinct notion of a scarlet colour, will never attain it by a definition ; he must set it before his eye, attend to it, compare it with the colours that come nearest to it, and observe the specific difference, which he will in vain attempt to define.* [358]

Every man is conscious that he can conceive a thousand things, of which he believes nothing at all—as a horse with wings, a mountain of gold ; but, although conception may be without any degree of belief, even the smallest belief cannot be without conception. He that believes must have some conception of what he believes.

Without attempting a definition of this operation of the mind, I shall endeavour to explain some of its properties ; consider the theories about it ; and take notice of some mistakes of philosophers concerning it.

1. It may be observed that conception enters as an ingredient in every operation of the mind. Our senses cannot give us the belief of any object, without giving some conception of it at the same time. No man can either remember or reason about things of which he hath no conception. When we will to exert any of our active powers, there must be some conception of what we will to do. There can be no desire nor aversion, love nor hatred, without some conception of the object. We cannot feel pain without conceiving it, though we can conceive it without feeling it. These things are self-evident.

In every operation of the mind, there-

* We do not define the specific difference, but we define it by it.—H.

fore, in everything we call thought, there must be conception. When we analyse the various operations either of the understanding or of the will, we shall always find this at the bottom, like the *caput mortuum* of the chemists, or the *materia prima* of the Peripatetics ; but, though there is no operation of mind without conception, yet it may be found naked, detached from all others, and then it is called simple apprehension, or the bare conception of a thing.

As all the operations of our mind are expressed by language, every one knows that it is one thing to understand what is said, to conceive or apprehend its meaning, whether it be a word, a sentence, or a discourse ; it is another thing to judge of it, to assent or dissent, to be persuaded or moved. The first is simple apprehension, and may be without the last ; but the last cannot be without the first. ﹏ [359]

2. In bare conception there can neither be truth nor falsehood, because it neither affirms nor denies. Every judgment, and every proposition by which judgment is expressed, must be true or false ; and the qualities of true and false, in their proper sense, can belong to nothing but to judgments, or to propositions. which express judgment. In the bare conception of a thing there is no judgment, opinion, or belief included, and therefore it cannot be either true or false.

But it may be said, Is there anything more certain than that men may have true or false conceptions, true or false apprehensions, of things? I answer, that such ways of speaking are indeed so common, and so well authorized by custom, the arbiter of language, that it would be presumption to censure them. It is hardly possible to avoid using them. But we ought to be upon our guard that we be not misled by them, to confound things which, though often expressed by the same words, are really different. We must therefore remember what was before observed, Essay I. chap. 1—that all the words by which we signify the bare conception of a thing, are likewise used to signify our opinions, when we wish to express them with modesty and diffidence. And we shall always find, that, when we speak of true or false conceptions, we mean true or false opinions. An opinion, though ever so wavering, or ever so modestly expressed, must be either true or false ; but a bare conception, which expresses no opinion or judgment, can be neither.

If we analyse those speeches in which men attribute truth or falsehood to our conceptions of things, we shall find in every case, that there is some opinion or judgment implied in what they call conception. [360] A child conceives the moon to be flat, and a [359-361]

foot or two broad—that is, this is his opinion : and, when we say it is a false notion or a false conception, we mean that it is a false opinion. He conceives the city of London to be like his country village—that is, he believes it to be so, till he is better instructed. He conceives a lion to have horns ; that is, he believes that the animal which men call a lion, has horns. Such opinions language authorizes us to call conceptions ; and they may be true or false. But bare conception, or what the logicians call simple apprehension, implies no opinion, however slight, and therefore can neither be true nor false.

What Mr Locke says of ideas (by which word he very often means nothing but conceptions) is very just, when the word idea is so understood. Book II., chap. xxxii., § 1. " Though truth and falsehood belong in propriety of speech only to propositions, yet ideas are often termed true or false (as what words are there that are not used with great latitude, and with some deviation from their strict and proper signification ?) though I think that when ideas themselves are termed true or false, there is still some secret or tacit proposition, which is the foundation of that denomination : as we shall see, if we examine the particular occasions wherein they come to be called true or false ; in all which we shall find some kind of affirmation or negation, which is the reason of that denomination ; for our ideas, being nothing but bare appearances, or perceptions in our minds, cannot properly and simply in themselves be said to be true or false, no more than a simple name of anything can be said to be true or false."

It may be here observed, by the way, that, in this passage, as in many others, Mr Locke uses the word *perception*, as well as the word *idea*, to signify what I call conception, or simple apprehension. And in his chapter upon perception, Book II., chap. ix., he uses it in the same sense. Perception, he says, " as it is the first faculty of the mind, exercised about our ideas, so it is the first and simplest idea we have from reflection, and is by some called thinking in general. [361] It seems to be that which puts the distinction betwixt the animal kingdom and the inferior parts of nature. It is the first operation of all our faculties, and the inlet of all knowledge into our minds."

Mr Locke has followed the example given by Des Cartes, Gassendi, and other Cartesians,[*] in giving the name of *perception* to the bare conception of things : and he has been followed in this by Bishop Berkeley,

* Gassendi was not a Cartesian, but an *Anti-Cartesian*, though he adopted several points in his philosophy from Des Cartes—for example, the employment of the term *Idea* not in its Platonic limitation —H.

Mr Hume, and many late philosophers, when they treat of ideas. They have probably been led into this impropriety, by the common doctrine concerning ideas, which teaches us, that conception, perception by the senses, and memory, are only different ways of perceiving ideas in our own minds. * If that theory be well founded, it will indeed be very difficult to find any specific distinction between conception;and perception.† But there is reason to distrust any philosophical theory when it leads men to corrupt language, and to confound, under one name, operations of the mind which common sense and common language teach them to distinguish.

I grant that there are some states of the mind, wherein a man may confound his conceptions with what he perceives or remembers, and mistake the one for the other; as in the delirium of a fever, in some cases of lunacy and of madness, in dreaming, and perhaps in some momentary transports of devotion, or of other strong emotions, which cloud his intellectual faculties, and, for a time, carry a man out of himself, as we usually express it.

Even in a sober and sound state of mind, the memory of a thing may be so very weak that we may be in doubt whether we only dreamed or imagined it.

It may be doubted whether children, when their imagination first begins to work, can distinguish what they barely conceive from what they remember. [362] I have been told, by a man of knowledge and observation, that one of his sons, when he began to speak, very often told lies with great assurance, without any intention, as far as appeared, or any consciousness of guilt. From which the father concluded, that it is natural to some children to lie. I am rather inclined to think that the child had no intention to deceive, but mistook the rovings of his own fancy for things which he remembered.‡ This, however, I take to be very uncommon, after children can communicate their sentiments by language, though perhaps not so in a more early period.

Granting all this, if any man will affirm that they whose intellectual faculties are sound, and sober, and ripe, cannot with certainty distinguish what they perceive or remember, from what they barely conceive, when those operations have any degree of strength and distinctness, he may enjoy his opinion; I know not how to reason with him. Why should philosophers confound those operations in treating of ideas, when they would be ashamed to do it on other occasions? To distinguish the various powers of our minds, a certain degree of understanding is necessary. And if some, through a defect of understanding, natural or accidental, or from unripeness of understanding, may be apt to confound different powers, will it follow that others cannot clearly distinguish them?

To return from this digression—into which the abuse of the word perception, by philosophers, has led me—it appears evident that the bare conception of an object, which includes no opinion or judgment, can neither be true nor false. Those qualities, in their proper sense, are altogether inapplicable to this operation of the mind.

3. Of all the analogies between the operations of body and those of the mind, there is none so strong and so obvious to all mankind as that which there is between painting, or other plastic arts, and the power of conceiving objects in the mind. Hence, in all languages, the words by which this power of the mind and its various modifications are expressed, are analogical, and borrowed from those arts. [363] We consider this power of the mind as a plastic power, by which we form to ourselves images of the objects of thought.

In vain should we attempt to avoid this analogical language, for we have no other language upon the subject; yet it is dangerous, and apt to mislead. All analogical and figurative words have a double meaning; and, if we are not very much upon our guard, we slide insensibly from the borrowed and figurative meaning into the primitive. We are prone to carry the parallel between the things compared farther than it will hold, and thus very naturally to fall into error.

To avoid this as far as possible in the present subject, it is proper to attend to the dissimilitude between conceiving a thing in the mind, and painting it to the eye, as well as to their similitude. The similitude strikes and gives pleasure. The dissimilitude we are less disposed to observe; but the philosopher ought to attend to it, and to carry it always in mind, in his reasonings on this subject, as a monitor, to warn him against the errors into which the analogical language is apt to draw him.

When a man paints, there is some work done, which remains when his hand is taken off, and continues to exist though he should think no more of it. Every stroke of his pencil produces an effect, and this effect is different from his action in making it; for it remains and continues to exist when the action ceases. The action of painting is

* But see above, p. 280, a, note * et alibi.—H.

† Yet Reid himself defines Perception, a Conception (Imagination) accompanied with a belief in the existence of its object ; and Mr Stewart reduces the specific difference, at best only a concomitant, to an accidental circumstance, in holding that our imaginations are themselves conjoined with a temporary belief in their objective reality.—H.

‡ But compare above, p. 340, col. a.—H.

one thing; the picture produced is another thing. The first is the cause, the second is the effect.

Let us next consider what is done when he only conceives this picture. He must have conceived it before he painted it; for this is a maxim universally admitted, that every work of art must first be conceived in the mind of the operator. What is this conception? It is an act of the mind, a kind of thought. This cannot be denied. [364] But does it produce any effect besides the act itself? Surely common sense answers this question in the negative; for every one knows that it is one thing to conceive, another thing to bring forth into effect. It is one thing to project, another to execute. A man may think for a long time what he is to do, and after all do nothing. Conceiving, as well as projecting or resolving, are what the schoolmen called *immanent* acts of the mind, which produce nothing beyond themselves. But painting is a transitive act, which produces an effect distinct from the operation, and this effect is the picture. Let this, therefore, be always remembered, that what is commonly called the image of a thing in the mind, is no more than the act or operation of the mind in conceiving it.

That this is the common sense of men who are untutored by philosophy, appears from their language. If one ignorant of the language should ask, What is meant by conceiving a thing? we should very naturally answer, that it is having an image of it in the mind—and perhaps we could not explain the word better. This shews that conception, and the image of a thing in the mind, are synonymous expressions. The image in the mind, therefore, is not the object of conception, nor is it any effect produced by conception as a cause. It is conception itself. That very mode of thinking which we call conception, is by another name called an image in the mind. •

Nothing more readily gives the conception of a thing than the seeing an image of it. Hence, by a figure common in language, conception is called an image of the thing conceived. But to shew that it is not a real but a metaphorical image, it is called an image in the mind. We know nothing that is properly in the mind but thought; and, when anything else is said to be in the mind, the expression must be figurative, and signify some kind of thought. [365]

I know that philosophers very unanimously maintain, that in conception there

is a real image in the mind, which is the immediate object of conception, and distinct from the act of conceiving it. I beg the reader's indulgence to defer what may be said for or against this philosophical opinion to the next chapter; intending in this only to explain what appears to me to belong to this operation of mind, without considering the theories about it. I think it appears, from what has been said, that the common language of those who have not imbibed any philosophical opinion upon this subject, authorizes us to understand *the conception of a thing, and an image of it in the mind*, not as two different things, but as two different expressions, to signify one and the same thing; and I wish to use common words in their common acceptation.

4. Taking along with us what is said in the last article, to guard us against the seduction of the analogical language used on this subject, we may observe a very strong analogy, not only between conceiving and painting in general, but between the different kinds of our conceptions, and the different works of the painter. He either makes fancy pictures, or he copies from the painting of others, or he paints from the life; that is, from real objects of art or nature which he has seen. I think our conceptions admit of a division very similar.

First, There are conceptions which may be called fancy pictures. They are commonly called creatures of fancy, or of imagination. They are not the copies of any original that exists, but are originals themselves. Such was the conception which Swift formed of the island of Laputa, and of the country of the Lilliputians; Cervantes of Don Quixote and his Squire; Harrington of the Government of Oceana; and Sir Thomas More of that of Utopia. We can give names to such creatures of imagination, conceive them distinctly, and reason consequentially concerning them, though they never had an existence. They were conceived by their creators, and may be conceived by others, but they never existed. We do not ascribe the qualities of true or false to them, because they are not accompanied with any belief, nor do they imply any affirmation or negation. [366]

Setting aside those creatures of imagination, there are other conceptions, which may be called copies, because they have an original or archetype to which they refer, and with which they are believed to agree; and we call them true or false conceptions, according as they agree or disagree with the standard to which they are referred. These are of two kinds, which have different standards or originals.

The *first* kind is analogous to pictures taken from the life. We have conceptions of individual things that really exist, such

---

* We ought, however, to distinguish *Imagination* and *Image*, *Conception* and *Concept*. Imagination and Conception ought to be employed in speaking of the mental modification, one and indivisible, considered as an act; Image and Concept, in speaking of it, considered as a product or immediate object.—H.

as the city of London, or the government of Venice. Here the things conceived are the originals; and our conceptions are called true when they agree with the thing conceived. Thus, my conception of the city of London is true, when I conceive it to be what it really is.

Individual things which really exist, being the creatures of God, (though some of them may receive their outward form from man,) he only who made them knows their whole nature; we know them but in part, and therefore our conceptions of them must in all cases be imperfect and inadequate; yet they may be true and just, as far as they reach.

The *second* kind is analogous to the copies which the painter makes from pictures done before. Such I think are the conceptions we have of what the ancients called universals; that is, of things which belong or may belong to many individuals. These are kinds and species of things; such as man or elephant, which are species of substances; wisdom or courage, which are species of qualities; equality or similitude, which are species of relations.* It may be asked— From what original are these conceptions formed? And when are they said to be true or false? [367]

It appears to me, that the original from which they are copied—that is, the thing conceived—is the conception or meaning which other men, who understand the language, affix to the same words.

Things are parcelled into kinds and sorts, not by nature, but by men. The individual things we are connected with, are so many, that to give a proper name to every individual would be impossible. We could never attain the knowledge of them that is necessary, nor converse and reason about them, without sorting them according to their different attributes. Those that agree in certain attributes are thrown into one parcel, and have a general name given them, which belongs equally to every individual in that parcel. This common name must therefore signify those attributes which have been observed to be common to every individual in that parcel, and nothing else.

That such general words may answer their intention, all that is necessary is, that those who use them should affix the same meaning or notion—that is, the same conception to them. The common meaning is the standard by which such conceptions are formed, and they are said to be true or false according as they agree or disagree with it. Thus, my conception of felony is true and just, when it agrees with the meaning of that word in the laws relating to it, and in authors who understand the law. The meaning of the word is the thing conceived; and that meaning is the conception affixed to it by those who best understand the language.

An individual is expressed in language either by a proper name, or by a general word joined to such circumstances as distinguish that individual from all others; if it is unknown, it may, when an object of sense, and within reach, be pointed out to the senses; when beyond the reach of the senses, it may be ascertained by a description, which, though very imperfect, may be true, and sufficient to distinguish it from every other individual. Hence it is, that, in speaking of individuals, we are very little in danger of mistaking the object, or taking one individual for another. [368]

Yet, as was before observed, our conception of them is always inadequate and lame. They are the creatures of God, and there are many things belonging to them which we know not, and which cannot be deduced by reasoning from what we know. They have a real essence, or constitution of nature, from which all their qualities flow; but this essence our faculties do not comprehend. They are therefore incapable of definition; for a definition ought to comprehend the whole nature or essence of the thing defined.

Thus, Westminster Bridge is an individual object; though I had never seen or heard of it before, if I am only made to conceive that it is a bridge from Westminster over the Thames, this conception, however imperfect, is true, and is sufficient to make me distinguish it, when it is mentioned, from every other object that exists. The architect may have an adequate conception of its structure, which is the work of man; but of the materials, which are the work of God, no man has an adequate conception; and, therefore, though the object may be described, it cannot be defined.

Universals are always expressed by general words; and all the words of language, excepting proper names, are general words; they are the signs of general conceptions, or of some circumstance relating to them. These general conceptions are formed for the purpose of language and reasoning; and the object from which they are taken, and to which they are intended to agree, is the conception which other men join to the same words; they may, therefore, be adequate, and perfectly agree with the thing conceived. This implies no more than that men who speak the same language

[367. 368]

---

* Of all such we can have no adequate imagination. A universal, when represented in imagination, is no longer adequate, no longer a universal. We cannot have an *image* of Horse, but only of some individual of that species. We may, however, have a notion or conception of it. See below, p. 482.—H.

may perfectly agree in the meaning of many general words.

Thus mathematicians have conceived what they call a plane triangle. They have defined it accurately; and, when I conceive it to be a plane surface, bounded by three right lines, I have both a true and an adequate conception of it. [369] There is nothing belonging to a plane triangle which is not comprehended in this conception of it, or deducible from it by just reasoning. This definition expresses the whole essence of the thing defined, as every just definition ought to do; but this essence is only what Mr Locke very properly calls a nominal essence; it is a general conception formed by the mind, and joined to a general word as its sign.

If all the general words of a language had a precise meaning, and were perfectly understood, as mathematical terms are, all verbal disputes would be at an end, and men would never seem to differ in opinion, but when they differ in reality; but this is far from being the case. The meaning of most general words is not learned, like that of mathematical terms, by an accurate definition, but by the experience we happen to have, by hearing them used in conversation. From such experience, we collect their meaning by a kind of induction; and, as this induction is, for the most part, lame and imperfect, it happens that different persons join different conceptions to the same general word; and, though we intend to give them the meaning which use, the arbiter of language, has put upon them, this is difficult to find, and apt to be mistaken, even by the candid and attentive. Hence, in innumerable disputes, men do not really differ in their judgments, but in the way of expressing them.

Our conceptions, therefore, appear to be of *three* kinds. They are either the conceptions of individual things, the creatures of God; or they are conceptions of the meaning of general words; or they are the creatures of our own imagination: and these different kinds have different properties, which we have endeavoured to describe.

5. Our conception of things may be strong and lively, or it may be faint and languid in all degrees. These are qualities which properly belong to our conceptions, though we have no names for them but such as are analogical. Every man is conscious of such a difference in his conceptions, and finds his lively conceptions most agreeable, when the object is not of such a nature as to give pain. [370]

Those who have lively conceptions, commonly express them in a lively manner— that is, in such a manner as to raise lively conceptions and emotions in others. Such persons are the most agreeable companions [369–371]

in conversation, and the most acceptable in their writings.

The liveliness of our conceptions proceeds from different causes. Some objects, from their own nature, or from accidental associations, are apt to raise strong emotions in the mind. Joy and hope, ambition, zeal, and resentment, tend to enliven our conceptions; disappointment, disgrace, grief, and envy, tend rather to flatten them. Men of keen passions are commonly lively and agreeable in conversation; and dispassionate men often make dull companions. There is in some men a natural strength and vigour of mind which gives strength to their conceptions on all subjects, and in all the occasional variations of temper.

It seems easier to form a lively conception of objects that are familiar, than of those that are not; our conceptions of visible objects are commonly the most lively, when other circumstances are equal. Hence, poets not only delight in the description of visible objects, but find means, by metaphor, analogy, and allusion, to clothe every object they describe with visible qualities. The lively conception of these makes the object appear, as it were, before our eyes. Lord Kames, in his Elements of Criticism, has shewn of what importance it is in works of taste, to give to objects described, what he calls *ideal presence.** To produce this in the mind, is, indeed, the capital aim of poetical and rhetorical description. It carries the man, as it were, out of himself, and makes him a spectator of the scene described. This ideal presence seems to me, to be nothing else but a lively conception of the appearance which the object would make if really present to the eye. [371]

Abstract and general conceptions are never lively, though they may be distinct; and, therefore, however necessary in philosophy, seldom enter into poetical description without being particularised or clothed in some visible dress.†

It may be observed, however, that our conceptions of visible objects become more lively by giving them motion, and more still by giving them life and intellectual qualities. Hence, in poetry, the whole creation is animated, and endowed with sense and reflection.

Imagination, when it is distinguished from conception, seems to me to signify one species of conception—to wit, the con-

---

* The Ἐνάργεια, 'Τπστύπωσις, Φαντασία, Ὄψις, Εἰδωλοποιία, Visiones, of the ancient Rhetoricians.— H.

† They thus cease to be aught *abstract* and *general* and become merely individual *representations*. In precise language, they are no longer *νοήματα*, but φαντάσματα; no longer *Begriffe*, but *Anschauungen*; no longer *notions* or *concepts*, but *images*. The wor t "*particularised*" ought to have been *individualised* —H.

ception of visible objects. * Thus, in a mathematical proposition, I imagine the figure, and I conceive the demonstration; it would not, I think, be improper to say, I conceive both; but it would not be so proper to say, I imagine the demonstration.

6. Our conceptions of things may be clear, distinct, and steady; or they may be obscure, indistinct, and wavering. The liveliness of our conceptions gives pleasure, but it is their distinctness and steadiness that enables us to judge right, and to express our sentiments with perspicuity.

If we inquire into the cause, why, among persons speaking or writing on the same subject, we find in one so much darkness, in another so much perspicuity, I believe the chief cause will be found to be, that one had a distinct and steady conception of what he said and wrote, and the other had not. Men generally find means to express distinctly what they have conceived distinctly. Horace observes, that proper words spontaneously follow distinct conceptions—"*Verbaque provisam rem non invita sequuntur.*" But it is impossible that a man should distinctly express what he has not distinctly conceived. [372]

We are commonly taught that perspicuity depends upon a proper choice of words, a proper structure of sentences, and a proper order in the whole composition. All this is very true; but it supposes distinctness in our conceptions, without which there can be neither propriety in our words, nor in the structure of our sentences, nor in our method.

Nay, I apprehend that indistinct conceptions of things are, for the most part, the cause, not only of obscurity in writing and speaking, but of error in judging.

Must not they who conceive things in the same manner form the same judgment of their agreements and disagreements? Is it possible for two persons to differ with regard to the conclusion of a syllogism who have the same conception of the premises?

Some persons find it difficult to enter into a mathematical demonstration. I believe we shall always find the reason to be, that they do not distinctly apprehend it. A man cannot be convinced by what he does not understand. On the other hand, I think a man cannot understand a demonstration without seeing the force of it. I speak of such demonstrations as those of Euclid, where every step is set down, and nothing left to be supplied by the reader.

Sometimes one who has got through the first four books of Euclid's "Elements," and sees the force of the demonstrations, finds difficulty in the fifth. What is the reason of this? You may find, by a little conversation with him, that he has not a clear and steady conception of ratios, and of the terms relating to them. When the terms used in the fifth book have become familiar, and readily excite in his mind a clear and steady conception of their meaning, you may venture to affirm that he will be able to understand the demonstrations of that book, and to see the force of them. [373]

If this be really the case, as it seems to be, it leads us to think that men are very much upon a level with regard to mere judgment, when we take that faculty apart from the apprehension or conception of the things about which we judge; so that a sound judgment seems to be the inseparable companion of a clear and steady apprehension. And we ought not to consider these two as talents, of which the one may fall to the lot of one man, and the other to the lot of another, but as talents which always go together.

It may, however, be observed, that some of our conceptions may be more subservient to reasoning than others which are equally clear and distinct. It was before observed, that some of our conceptions are of individual things, others of things general and abstract. It may happen that a man who has very clear conceptions of things individually, is not so happy in those of things general and abstract. And this I take to be the reason why we find men who have good judgment in matters of common life, and perhaps good talents for poetical or rhetorical composition, who find it very difficult to enter into abstract reasoning.

That I may not appear singular in putting men so much upon a level in point of mere judgment, I beg leave to support this opinion by the authority of two very think ing men, Des Cartes and Cicero. The former, in his dissertation on Method, expresses himself to this purpose:—" Nothing is so equally distributed among men as judgment.* Wherefore, it seems reasonable to believe, that the power of distinguishing what is true from what is false, (which we properly call judgment or right reason,) is by nature equal in all men; and therefore that the diversity of our opinions does not arise from one person being endowed with a greater power of reason than another, but only from this, that we do not lead our

---

* It is to be regretted that Reid did not more fully develope 'he distinction of Imagination and Conception, on which he here and elsewhere inadequately touches. Imagination is not, though in conformity to the etymology of the term, to be limited to the representation of visible objects. See below, under p. 482. Neither ought the term *conceive* to be used in the extensive sense of *understand.*—H.

---

* " Judgment," *bona mens,* in the authentic Latin translation. I cannot, at the moment, lay hands on my copy of the French original; but, if I recollect aright, it is there *le bon sens.*—H.

thought in the same track, nor attend to the same things."

Cicero, in his third book "De Oratore," makes this observation—" It is wonderful when the learned and unlearned differ so much in art, how little they differ in judgment. For art being derived from Nature, is good for nothing, unless it move and delight Nature." [374]

From what has been said in this article, it follows, that it is so far in our power to write and speak perspicuously, and to reason justly, as it is in our power to form clear and distinct conceptions of the subject on which we speak or reason. And, though Nature hath put a wide difference between one man and another in this respect, yet that it is in a very considerable degree in our power to have clear and distinct apprehensions of things about which we think and reason, cannot be doubted.

7. It has been observed by many authors, that, when we barely conceive any object, the ingredients of that conception must either be things with which we were before acquainted by some other original power of the mind, or they must be parts or attributes of such things. Thus, a man cannot conceive colours if he never saw, nor sounds if he never heard. If a man had not a conscience, he could not conceive what is meant by moral obligation, or by right and wrong in conduct.

Fancy may combine things that never were combined in reality. It may enlarge or diminish, multiply or divide, compound and fashion the objects which nature presents; but it cannot, by the utmost effort of that creative power which we ascribe to it, bring any one simple ingredient into its productions which Nature has not framed and brought to our knowledge by some other faculty.

This Mr Locke has expressed as beautifully as justly. The dominion of man, in this little world of his own understanding, is much the same as in the great world of visible things; wherein his power, however managed by art and skill, reaches no farther than to compound and divide the materials that are made to his hand, but can do nothing towards making the least particle of matter, or destroying one atom that is already in being. [375] The same inability will every one find in himself, to fashion in his understanding any simple idea not received by the powers which God has given him.

I think all philosophers agree in this sentiment. Mr Hume, indeed, after acknowledging the truth of the principle in general, mentions what he thinks a single exception to it—That a man, who had seen all the shades of a particular colour except one, might frame in his mind a conception of that shade which he never saw. I think

[374-376]

this is not an exception; because a particular shade of a colour differs not specifically, but only in degree, from other shades of the same colour.

It is proper to observe, that our most simple conceptions are not those which nature immediately presents to us. When we come to years of understanding, we have the power of analysing the objects of nature, of distinguishing their several attributes and relations, of conceiving them one by one, and of giving a name to each, whose meaning extends only to that single attribute or relation : and thus our most simple conceptions are not those of any object in nature, but of some single attribute or relation of such objects.

Thus, nature presents to our senses bodies that are extended in three dimensions, and solid. By analysing the notion we have of body from our senses, we form to ourselves the conceptions of extension, solidity, space, a point, a line, a surface—all which are more simple conceptions than that of a body. But they are the elements, as it were, of which our conception of a body is made up, and into which it may be analysed. This power of analysing objects we propose to consider particularly in another place. It is only mentioned here, that what is said in this article may not be understood so as to be inconsistent with it. [376]

8. Though our conceptions must be confined to the ingredients mentioned in the last article, we are unconfined with regard to the arrangement of those ingredients. Here we may pick and choose, and form an endless variety of combinations and compositions, which we call creatures of the imagination. These may be clearly conceived, though they never existed: and, indeed, everything that is made, must have been conceived before it was made. Every work of human art, and every plan of conduct, whether in public or in private life, must have been conceived before it was brought to execution. And we cannot avoid thinking, that the Almighty, before he created the universe by his power, had a distinct conception of the whole and of every part, and saw it to be good, and agreeable to his intention.

It is the business of man, as a rational creature, to employ this unlimited power of conception, for planning his conduct and enlarging his knowledge. It seems to be peculiar to beings endowed with reason to act by a preconceived plan. Brute animals seem either to want this power, or to have it in a very low degree. They are moved by instinct, habit, appetite, or natural affection, according as these principles are stirred by the present occasion. But I see no reason to think that they can propose to themselves a connected plan of life, or form general rules of conduct Indeed, we see that many of the human species, to whom God has given this power, make little use of it. They act without a plan, as the passion or appetite which is strongest at the time leads them.

9. The last property I shall mention of this faculty, is that which essentially distinguishes it from every other power of the mind; and it is, that it is not employed solely about things which have existence. I can conceive a winged horse or a centaur, as easily and as distinctly as I can conceive a man whom I have seen. Nor does this distinct conception incline my judgment in the least to the belief that a winged horse or a centaur ever existed. [377]

It is not so with the other operations of our minds. They are employed about real existences, and carry with them the belief of their objects. When I feel pain, I am compelled to believe that the pain that I feel has a real existence. When I perceive any external object, my belief of the real existence of the object is irresistible. When I distinctly remember an event, though that event may not now exist, I can have no doubt but it did exist. That consciousness which we have of the operations of our own minds, implies a belief of the real existence of those operations.

Thus we see, that the powers of sensation, of perception, of memory, and of consciousness, are all employed solely about objects that do exist, or have existed. But conception is often employed about objects that neither do, nor did, nor will exist. This is the very nature of this faculty, that its object, though distinctly conceived, may have no existence. Such an object we call a creature of imagination; but this creature never was created.

That we may not impose upon ourselves in this matter, we must distinguish between that act or operation of the mind, which we call conceiving an object, and the object which we conceive. When we conceive anything, there is a real act or operation of the mind. Of this we are conscious, and can have no doubt of its existence. But every such act must have an object;* for he that conceives must conceive something. Suppose he conceives a centaur, he may have a distinct conception of this object, though no centaur ever existed.

I am afraid that, to those who are unacquainted with the doctrine of philosophers upon this subject, I shall appear in a very ridiculous light, for insisting upon a point so very evident as that men may barely conceive things that never existed. They will hardly believe that any man in his wits ever doubted of it. Indeed, I know no

* See below, p. 390, and Note P.—H.

truth more evident to the common sense and to the experience of mankind. But, if the authority of philosophy, ancient and modern, opposes it, as I think it does, I wish not to treat that authority so fastidiously as not to attend patiently to what may be said in support of it. [378]

CHAPTER II.

THEORIES CONCERNING CONCEPTION.

The theory of ideas has been applied to the conception of objects, as well as to perception and memory. Perhaps it will be irksome to the reader, as it is to the writer, to return to that subject, after so much has been said upon it; but its application to the conception of objects, which could not properly have been introduced before, gives a more comprehensive view of it, and of the prejudices which have led philosophers so unanimously into it.

There are two prejudices which seem to me to have given rise to the theory of ideas in all the various forms in which it has appeared in the course of above two thousand years; and, though they have no support from the natural dictates of our faculties, or from attentive reflection upon their operations, they are prejudices which those who speculate upon this subject are very apt to be led into by analogy.

The *first* is—That, in all the operations of the understanding, there must be some immediate intercourse between the mind and its object, so that the one may act upon the other. The *second*, That, in all the operations of understanding, there must be an object of thought, which really exists while we think of it; or, as some philosophers have expressed it, that which is not cannot be intelligible.

Had philosophers perceived that these are prejudices grounded only upon analogical reasoning, we had never heard of ideas in the philosophical sense of that word. [379]

The *first* of these principles has led philosophers to think that, as the external objects of sense are too remote to act upon the mind immediately, there must be some image or shadow of them that is present to the mind, and is the immediate object of perception. That there is such an immediate object of perception, distinct from the external object, has been very unanimously held by philosophers, though they have differed much about the name, the

* The reader will bear in mind what has been already said of the limited meaning attached by Reid to the term *Idea*, viz., something in, or present to the mind, but not a mere modification of the mind—and his error in supposing that all philosophers admitted this crude hypothesis. See Notes B, C, L, M, N, O, P, &c.—H.

nature, and the origin of those immediate objects.

We have considered what has been said in the support of this principle, Essay II. chap. 14, to which the reader is referred, to prevent repetition.

I shall only add to what is there said, That there appears no shadow of reason why the mind must have an object immediately present to it in its intellectual operations, any more than in its affections and passions. Philosophers have not said that ideas are the immediate objects of love or resentment, of esteem or disapprobation. It is, I think, acknowledged, that persons and not ideas, are the immediate objects of those affections; persons, who are as far from being immediately present to the mind as other external objects, and, sometimes, persons who have now no existence, in this world at least, and who can neither act upon the mind, nor be acted upon by it.

The *second* principle, which I conceive to be likewise a prejudice of philosophers, grounded upon analogy, is now to be considered.

It contradicts directly what was laid down in the last article of the preceding chapter —to wit, that we may have a distinct conception of things which never existed. This is undoubtedly the common belief of those who have not been instructed in philosophy; and they will think it as ridiculous to defend it by reasoning, as to oppose it. [380]

The philosopher says, Though there may be a remote object which does not exist, there must be an immediate object which really exists; for that which is not, cannot be an object of thought. The idea must be perceived by the mind, and, if it does not exist there, there can be no perception of it, no operation of the mind about it. *

This principle deserves the more to be examined, because the other before mentioned depends upon it; for, although the last may be true, even if the first was false, yet, if the last be not true, neither can the first. If we can conceive objects which have no existence, it follows that there may be objects of thought which neither act upon the mind, nor are acted upon by it; because that which has no existence can neither act nor be acted upon.

It is by these principles that philosophers have been led to think that, in every act of memory and of conception, as well as of perception, there are two objects—the one, the immediate object, the idea, the species, the form; the other, the mediate or external object. The vulgar know only

of one object, which, in perception, is something external that exists; in memory, something that did exist; and, in conception, may be something that never existed. * But the immediate object of the philosophers, the idea, is said to exist, and to be perceived in all these operations.

These principles have not only led philosophers to split objects into two, where others can find but one, but likewise have led them to reduce the three operations now mentioned to one, making memory and conception, as well as perception, to be the perception of ideas. But nothing appears more evident to the vulgar, than that what is only remembered, or only conceived, is not perceived; and, to speak of the perceptions of memory, appears to them as absurd as to speak of the hearing of sight. [381]

In a word, these two principles carry us into the whole philosophical theory of ideas, and furnish every argument that ever was used for their existence. If they are true, that system must be admitted with all its consequences. If they are only prejudices, grounded upon analogical reasoning, the whole system must fall to the ground with them.

It is, therefore, of importance to trace those principles, as far as we are able, to their origin, and to see, if possible, whether they have any just foundation in reason, or whether they are rash conclusions, drawn from a supposed analogy between matter and mind.

The unlearned, who are guided by the dictates of nature, and express what they are conscious of concerning the operations of their own mind, believe that the object which they distinctly perceive certainly exists; that the object which they distinctly remember certainly did exist, but now may not; but as to things that are barely conceived, they know that they can conceive a thousand things that never existed, and that the bare conception of a thing does not so much as afford a presumption of its existence. They give themselves no trouble to know how these operations are performed, or to account for them from general principles.

But philosophers, who wish to discover the causes of things, and to account for these operations of mind, observing that in other operations there must be not only an agent, but something to act upon, have been led by analogy to conclude that it must be so in the operations of the mind.

The relation between the mind and its conceptions bears a very strong and obvious analogy to the relation between a man and his work. Every scheme he forms, every discovery he makes by his reasoning powers, is very properly called the work of his mind. These works of the mind are sometimes

* In relation to this and what follows, see above, p. 282, b, note †; p. 279, a, note †; and Note B. H.

* See references in preceding note.—H.

2 B

great and important works, and draw the attention and admiration of men. [382]

It is the province of the philosopher to consider how such works of the mind are produced, and of what materials they are composed. He calls the materials ideas. There must therefore be ideas, which the mind can arrange and form into a regular structure. Everything that is produced, must be produced of something; and from nothing, nothing can be produced.

Some such reasoning as this seems to me to have given the first rise to the philosophical notions of ideas. Those notions were formed into a system by the Pythagoreans, two thousand years ago; and this system was adopted by Plato, and embellished with all the powers of a fine and lofty imagination. I shall, in compliance with custom, call it the Platonic system of ideas, though in reality it was the invention of the Pythagorean school.*

The most arduous question which employed the wits of men in the infancy of the Grecian philosophy was—What was the origin of the world?—from what principles and causes did it proceed? To this question very different answers were given in the different schools. Most of them appear to us very ridiculous. The Pythagoreans, however, judged, very rationally, from the order and beauty of the universe, that it must be the workmanship of an eternal, intelligent, and good being: and therefore they concluded the Deity to be one first principle or cause of the universe. But they conceived there must be more. The universe must be made of something. Every workman must have materials to work upon. That the world should be made out of nothing seemed to them absurd, because everything that is made must be made of something.

Nullam rem e nihilo gigni divinitus unquam.—LUCR.
De nibilo nibil, in nihilum nil posse reverti.—PERS.

This maxim never was brought into doubt: even in Cicero's time it continued to be held by all philosophers. [383] What natural philosopher (says that author in his second book of Divination) ever asserted that anything could take its rise from nothing, or be reduced to nothing? Because men must have materials to work upon, they concluded it must be so with the Deity. This was reasoning from analogy.

From this it followed, that an eternal uncreated matter was another first principle of the universe. But this matter they believed had no form nor quality. It was

the same with the *materia prima* or first matter of Aristotle, who borrowed this part of his philosophy from his predecessors.

To us it seems more rational to think that the Deity created matter with its qualities, than that the matter of the universe should be eternal and self-existent. But so strong was the prejudice of the ancient philosophers against what we call creation, that they rather chose to have recourse to this eternal and unintelligible matter, that the Deity might have materials to work upon.

The same analogy which led them to think that there must be an eternal matter of which the world was made, led them also to conclude that there must be an eternal pattern or model according to which it was made. Works of design and art must be distinctly conceived before they are made. The Deity, as an intelligent Being, about to execute a work of perfect beauty and regularity, must have had a distinct conception of his work before it was made. This appears very rational.

But this conception, being the work of the Divine intellect, something must have existed as its object. This could only be ideas, which are the proper and immediate object of intellect. [384]

From this investigation of the principles or causes of the universe, those philosophers concluded them to be three in number —to wit, an eternal matter as the material cause, eternal ideas as the model or exemplary cause, and an eternal intelligent mind as the efficient cause.

As to the nature of those eternal ideas, the philosophers of that sect ascribed to them the most magnificent attributes. They were immutable and uncreated;* the object of the Divine intellect before the world was made; and the only object of intellect and of science to all intelligent beings. As far as intellect is superior to sense, so far are ideas superior to all the objects of sense. The objects of sense being in a constant flux, cannot properly be said to exist. Ideas are the things which have a real and permanent existence. They are as various as the species of things, there being one idea of every species, but none of individuals. The idea is the essence of the species, and existed before any of the species was made. It is entire in every individual of the species, without being either divided or multiplied.

In our present state, we have but an imperfect conception of the eternal ideas; but it is the highest felicity and perfection of men to be able to contemplate them-

---

* Ideas in the Platonic, and Ideas in the modern signification, hold, as I have already shewn, little or no analogy to each other. See above, p. 204, a, notes † ‡; p. 225, b, note *; p. 262, b note *.—H.

* Whether, in the Platonic system, Ideas are, or are not, independent of the Deity, I have already stated, is, and always has been, a *vexata quæstio*.—H.

While we are in this prison of the body, sense, as a dead weight, bears us down from the contemplation of the intellectual objects; and it is only by a due purification of the soul, and abstraction from sense, that the intellectual eye is opened, and that we are enabled to mount upon the wings of intellect to the celestial world of ideas.

Such was the most ancient system concerning ideas, of which we have any account. And, however different from the modern, it appears to be built upon the prejudices we have mentioned—to wit, that in every operation there must be something to work upon; and that even in conception there must be an object which really exists. [385]

For, if those ancient philosophers had thought it possible that the Deity could operate without materials in the formation of the world, and that he could conceive the plan of it without a model, they could have seen no reason to make matter and ideas eternal and necessarily existent principles, as well as the Deity himself.

Whether they believed that the ideas were not only eternal, but eternally, and without a cause, arranged in that beautiful and perfect order which they ascribe to this intelligible world of ideas, I cannot say; but this seems to be a necessary consequence of the system : for, if the Deity could not conceive the plan of the world which he made, without a model which really existed, that model could not be his work, nor contrived by his wisdom ; for, if he made it, he must have conceived it before it was made ; it must therefore have existed in all its beauty and order independent of the Deity; and this I think they acknowledged, by making the model and the matter of this world, first principles, no less than the Deity.

If the Platonic system be thus understood, (and I do not see how it can hang together otherwise,) it leads to two consequences that are unfavourable to it.

First, Nothing is left to the Maker of this world but the skill to work after a model. The model had all the perfection and beauty that appears in the copy, and the Deity had only to copy after a pattern that existed independent of him. Indeed, the copy, if we believe those philosophers, falls very far short of the original ; but this they seem to have ascribed to the refractoriness of matter of which it was made.

Secondly, If the world of ideas, without being the work of a perfectly wise and good intelligent being, could have so much beauty and perfection, how can we infer from the beauty and order of this world, which is but an imperfect copy of the other, that it must have been made by a perfectly wise and good being ? [386] The force of this

reasoning, from the beauty and order of the universe, to its being the work of a wise being, which appears invincible to every candid mind, and appeared so to those ancient philosophers, is entirely destroyed by the supposition of the existence of a world of ideas, of greater perfection and beauty, which never was made. Or, if the reasoning be good, it will apply to the world of ideas, which must, of consequence, have been made by a wise and good intelligent being, and must have been conceived before it was made.

It may farther be observed, that all that is mysterious and unintelligible in the Platonic ideas, arises from attributing existence to them. Take away this one attribute, all the rest, however pompously expressed, are easily admitted and understood.

What is a Platonic idea? It is the essence of a species. It is the exemplar, the model, according to which all the individuals of that species are made. It is entire in every individual of the species, without being multiplied or divided. It was an object of the divine intellect from eternity, and is an object of contemplation and of science to every intelligent being. It is eternal, immutable, and uncreated ; and, to crown all, it not only exists, but has a more real and permanent existence than anything that ever God made.

Take this description altogether, and it would require an Œdipus to unriddle it. But take away the last part of it, and nothing is more easy. It is easy to find five hundred things which answer to every article in the description except the last.

Take, for an instance, the nature of a circle, as it is defined by Euclid—an object which every intelligent being may conceive distinctly, though no circle had ever existed; it is the exemplar, the model, according to which all the individual figures of that species that ever existed were made ; for they are all made according to the nature of a circle. [387] It is entire in every individual of the species, without being multiplied or divided. For every circle is an entire circle ; and all circles, in as far as they are circles, have one and the same nature. It was an object of the divine intellect from all eternity, and may be an object of contemplation and of science to every intelligent being. It is the essence of a species, and, like all other essences, it is eternal, immutable, and uncreated. This means no more but that a circle always was a circle, and can never be anything but a circle. It is the necessity of the thing, and not any act of creating power, that makes a circle to be a circle.

The nature of every species, whether of substance, of quality, or of relation, and in general everything which the ancients called an universal, answers to the description of a Platonic idea, if in that description you leave out the attribute of existence.

If we believe that no species of things could be conceived by the Almighty without a model that really existed, we must go back to the Platonic system, however mysterious. But, if it be true that the Deity could have a distinct conception of things which did not exist, and that other intelligent beings may conceive objects which do not exist, the system has no better foundation than this prejudice, that the operations of mind must be like those of the body.

Aristotle rejected the ideas of his master Plato as visionary; but he retained the prejudices that gave rise to them, and therefore substituted something in their place, but under a different name,* and of a different origin.

He called the objects of intellect, intelligible species; those of the memory and imagination, phantasms; and those of the senses, sensible species. This change of the name* was indeed very small; for the Greek word of Aristotle [ᵈᵉᵒˢ] which we translate *species* or *form*, is so near to the Greek word *idea*, both in its sound and signification, that, from their etymology, it would not be easy to give them different meanings. [388] Both are derived from the Greek word which signifies *to see*, and both may signify a vision or appearance to the eye. Cicero, who understood Greek well, often translates the Greek word *idea* by the Latin word *visio*. But both words being used as terms of art—one in the Platonic system, the other in the Peripatetic—the Latin writers generally borrowed the Greek word idea to express the Platonic notion, and translated Aristotle's word, by the words *species* or *forma*; and in this they have been followed in the modern languages.*

Those forms or species were called intelligible, to distinguish them from sensible species, which Aristotle held to be the immediate objects of sense.

He thought that the sensible species come from the external object, and defined a *sense* to be that which has the capacity to receive the form of sensible things without the matter; as wax receives the form of a seal without any of the matter of it. In like manner, he thought that the intellect receives the forms of things intelligible; and he calls it the place of forms.

I take it to have been the opinion of Aristotle, that the intelligible forms in the human intellect are derived from the sensible by abstraction, and other operations of the mind itself. As to the intelligible forms in the divine intellect, they must have had another origin; but I do not remember that he gives any opinion about them. He certainly maintained, however, that there is no intellection without intelligible species;* no memory or imagination without phantasms; no perception without sensible species. Treating of memory, he proposes a difficulty, and endeavours to resolve it—how a phantasm, that is a present object in the mind, should represent a thing that is past. [389]

Thus, I think, it appears that the Peripatetic system of species and phantasms, as well as the Platonic system of ideas, is grounded upon this principle, that in every kind of thought there must be some object that really exists; in every operation of the mind, something to work upon. Whether this immediate object be called an idea with Plato,† or a phantasm or species with Aristotle—whether it be eternal and uncreated, or produced by the impressions of external objects—is of no consequence in the present argument. In both systems, it was thought impossible that the Deity could make the world without matter to work upon; in both, it was thought impossible that an intelligent Being could conceive anything that did not exist, but by means of a model that really existed.

The philosophers of the Alexandrian school, commonly called the latter Platonists, conceived the eternal ideas of things to be in the Divine intellect, and thereby avoided the absurdity of making them a principle distinct from and independent of the Deity; but still they held them to exist really in the Divine mind as the objects of conception, and as the patterns and archetypes of things that are made.

Modern philosophers, still persuaded that of every thought there must be an immediate object that really exists, have not deemed it necessary to distinguish by different names the immediate objects of intellect, of imagination, and of the senses, but have given the common name of *idea* to them all.

Whether these ideas be in the sensorium, or in the mind, or partly in the one and partly in the other; whether they exist when they are not perceived, or only when

---

* Reid seems not aware that Plato, and Aristotle in relation to Plato, employed the terms ᵈᵉᵒˢ and ᵈᵉᵃ almost as convertible. In fact, the latter usually combats the ideal theory of the former by the name of ᵈᵉᵒˢ —e. g., τὰ εἴδη χωρίᵥ, τεγτίσματα γάρ ἐσι. M. Cousin, in a learned and ingenious paper of his " Nouveaux Fragments," has endeavoured to shew that Plato did not apply the two terms indifferently; and the same has been attempted by Richter. But so many exceptions must be admitted, that, apparently, no determinate rule can be established.—H.

* There is even less reason to attribute such a theory to Aristotle in relation to the intellect than in relation to sense and imagination. See even his oldest commentator, the Aphrodisian, Περὶ Ψυχῆς, f. 139, a. In fact, the greater number of those Peripatetics who admitted species in this crude form for the latter, rejected them for the former.—H.
† See above, p. 262, b, note *.—H.

they are perceived ; whether they are the workmanship of the Deity or of the mind itself, or of external natural causes—with regard to these points, different authors seem to have different opinions, and the same author sometimes to waver or be diffident ; but as to their existence, there seems to be great unanimity.* [390]

So much is this opinion fixed in the minds of philosophers, that I doubt not but it will appear to most a very strange paradox, or rather a contradiction, that men should think without ideas.

That it has the appearance of a contradiction, I confess. But this appearance arises from the ambiguity of the word idea. If the idea of a thing means only the thought of it, or the operation of the mind in thinking about it, which is the most common meaning of the word, to think without ideas, is to think without thought, which is undoubtedly a contradiction.

But an idea, according to the definition given of it by philosophers, is not thought, but an object of thought, which really exists and is perceived. Now, whether is it a contradiction to say, that a man may think of an object that does not exist ?

I acknowledge that a man cannot perceive an object that does not exist ; nor can he remember an object that did not exist ; but there appears to me no contradiction in his conceiving an object that neither does nor ever did exist.

Let us take an example. I conceive a centaur. This conception is an operation of the mind, of which I am conscious, and to which I can attend. The sole object of it is a centaur, an animal which, I believe, never existed. I can see no contradiction in this.†

The philosopher says, I cannot conceive a centaur without having an idea of it in my mind. I am at a loss to understand what he means. He surely does not mean that I cannot conceive it without conceiving it. This would make me no wiser. What then is this idea ? Is it an animal, half horse and half man ? No. Then I am certain it is not the thing I conceive. Perhaps he will say, that the idea is an image of the animal, and is the immediate object of my conception, and that the animal is the mediate or remote object.‡ [391]

To this I answer—*First*, I am certain there are not two objects of this conception, but one only ; and that one is as immediate an object of my conception as any can be.

Secondly, This one object which I conceive, is not the image of an animal—it is

an animal. I know what it is to conceive an image of an animal, and what it is to conceive an animal ; and I can distinguish the one of these from the other without any danger of mistake. The thing I conceive is a body of a certain figure and colour, having life and spontaneous motion. The philosopher says, that the idea is an image of the animal ; but that it has neither body, nor colour, nor life, nor spontaneous motion. This I am not able to comprehend.

Thirdly, I wish to know how this idea comes to be an object of my thought, when I cannot even conceive what it means ; and, if I did conceive it, this would be no evidence of its existence, any more than my conception of a centaur is of its existence. Philosophers sometimes say that we perceive ideas, sometimes that we are conscious of them. I can have no doubt of the existence of anything which I either perceive or of which I am conscious ;* but I cannot find that I either perceive ideas or am conscious of them.

Perception and consciousness are very different operations, and it is strange that philosophers have never determined by which of them ideas are discerned † This is as if a man should positively affirm that he perceived an object ; but whether by his eyes, or his ears, or his touch, he could not say.

But may not a man who conceives a centaur say, that he has a distinct image of it in his mind ? I think he may. And if he means by this way of speaking what the vulgar mean, who never heard of the philosophical theory of ideas, I find no fault with it. [392] By a distinct image in the mind, the vulgar mean a distinct conception ; and it is natural to call it so, on account of the analogy between an image of a thing and the conception of it. On account of this analogy, obvious to all mankind, this operation is called imagination, and an image in the mind is only a periphrasis for imagination. But to infer from this that there is really an image in the mind, distinct from the operation of conceiving the object, is to be misled by an analogical expression ; as if, from the phrases of deliberating and balancing things in the mind, we should infer that there is really a balance existing in the mind for weighing motives and arguments.

The analogical words and phrases used in all languages to express conception, do, no doubt, facilitate their being taken in a literal sense. But, if we only attend care-

---

* This, as already once and again stated, is not correct.—H.
† See above, p. 29?, b, note †, and Note B.—H.
‡ On this, and the subsequent reasoning in the present chapter, see Note B.—H.

* This is not the case, unless it be admitted that we are conscious of what we perceive—in other words, immediately cognitive of the *non-ego*.—H.
† But the philosophers did not, like Reid, make Consciousness one special faculty, and Perception another ; nor did they and Reid mean by Perception the same thing.—H.

fully to what we are conscious of in this operation, we shall find no more reason to think that images do really exist in our minds, than that balances and other mechanical engines do.

We know of nothing that is in the mind but by consciousness, and we are conscious of nothing but various modes of thinking; such as understanding, willing, affection, passion, doing, suffering. If philosophers choose to give the name of an idea to any mode of thinking of which we are conscious, I have no objection to the name, but that it introduces a foreign word into our language without necessity, and a word that is very ambiguous, and apt to mislead. But, if they give that name to images in the mind, which are not thought, but only objects of thought, I can see no reason to think that there are such things in nature. If they be, their existence and their nature must be more evident than anything else, because we know nothing but by their means. I may add, that, if they be, we can know nothing besides them. For, from the existence of images, we can never, by any just reasoning, infer the existence of anything else, unless perhaps the existence of an intelligent Author of them. In this, Bishop Berkeley reasoned right. [393]

In every work of design, the work must be conceived before it is executed—that is, before it exists. If a model, consisting of ideas, must exist in the mind, as the object of this conception, that model is a work of design no less than the other, of which it is the model; and therefore, as a work of design, it must have been conceived before it existed. In every work of design, therefore, the conception must go before the existence. This argument we applied before to the Platonic system of eternal and immutable ideas, and it may be applied with equal force to all the systems of ideas.

If now it should be asked, What is the idea of a circle? I answer, It is the conception of a circle. What is the immediate object of this conception? The immediate and the only object of it is a circle. But where is this circle? It is nowhere. If it was an individual, and had a real existence, it must have a place; but, being an universal, it has no existence, and therefore no place. Is it not in the mind of him that conceives it? The conception of it is in the mind, being an act of the mind; and in common language, a thing being in the mind, is a figurative expression, signifying that the thing is conceived or remembered.

It may be asked, Whether this conception is an image or resemblance of a circle? I answer, I have already accounted for its being, in a figurative sense, called the image of a circle in the mind. If the question is meant in the literal sense, we must observe, that the word conception has two meanings. Properly it signifies that operation of the mind which we have been endeavouring to explain; but sometimes it is put for the object of conception, or thing conceived.

Now, if the question be understood in the last of these senses, the object of this conception is not an image or resemblance of a circle; for it is a circle, and nothing can be an image of itself. [394]

If the question be—Whether the operation of mind in conceiving a circle be an image or resemblance of a circle? I think it is not; and that no two things can be more perfectly unlike, than a species of thought and a species of figure. Nor is it more strange that conception should have no resemblance to the object conceived, than that desire should have no resemblance to the object desired, or resentment to the object of resentment.

I can likewise conceive an individual object that really exists, such as St Paul's Church in London. I have an idea of it; that is, I conceive it. The immediate object of this conception is four hundred miles distant; and I have no reason to think that it acts upon me, or that I act upon it; but I can think of it notwithstanding. I can think of the first year or the last year of the Julian period.

If, after all, it should be thought that images in the mind serve to account for this faculty of conceiving things most distant in time and place, and even things which do not exist, which otherwise would be altogether inconceivable; to this I answer, that accounts of things, grounded upon conjecture, have been the bane of true philosophy in all ages. Experience may satisfy us that it is an hundred times more probable that they are false than that they are true.

This account of the faculty of conception, by images in the mind or in the brain, will deserve the regard of those who have a true taste in philosophy, when it is proved by solid arguments—First, That there are images in the mind, or in the brain, of the things we conceive. Secondly, That there is a faculty in the mind of perceiving such images. Thirdly, That the perception of such images produces the conception of things most distant, and even of things that have no existence. And, fourthly, That the perception of individual images in the mind, or in the brain, gives us the conception of universals, which are the attributes of many individuals. [395] Until this is done, the theory of images existing in the mind or in the brain, ought to be placed in the same category with the sensible species, materia prima of Aristotle, and the vortices of Des Cartes.

CHAPTER III.

MISTAKES CONCERNING CONCEPTION.

1. WRITERS on logic, after the example of Aristotle, divide the operations of the understanding into three : Simple Apprehension, (which is another word for Conception,) Judgment, and Reasoning. They teach us, that reasoning is expressed by a syllogism, judgment by a proposition, and simple apprehension by a term only—that is, by one or more words which do not make a full proposition, but only the subject or predicate of a proposition. If, by this they mean, as I think they do, that a proposition, or even a syllogism, may not be simply apprehended,* I believe this is a mistake.

In all judgment and in all reasoning, conception is included. We can neither judge of a proposition, nor reason about it, unless we conceive or apprehend it. We may distinctly conceive a proposition, without judging of it at all. We may have no evidence on one side or the other ; we may have no concern whether it be true or false. In these cases we commonly form no judgment about it, though we perfectly understand its meaning.†

A man may discourse, or plead, or write, for other ends than to find the truth. His learning, and wit, and invention may be employed, while his judgment is not at all, or very little. When it is not truth, but some other end he pursues, judgment would be an impediment, unless for discovering the means of attaining his end ; and, therefore, it is laid aside, or employed solely for that purpose. [396]

The business of an orator is said to be, to find out what is fit to persuade. This a man may do with much ingenuity, who never took the trouble to examine whether it ought to persuade or not. Let it not be thought, therefore, that a man judges of the truth of every proposition he utters, or hears uttered. In our commerce with the world, judgment is not the talent that bears the greatest price ; and, therefore, those who are not sincere lovers of truth, lay up this talent where it rusts and corrupts, while they carry others to market, for which there is greater demand.

2. The division commonly made by logicians, of simple apprehension, into Sensation, Imagination, and Pure Intellection, seems to me very improper in several respects.

First, Under the word sensation, they include not only what is properly so called, but the perception of external objects by the senses. These are very different operations of the mind ; and, although they are commonly conjoined by nature, ought to be carefully distinguished by philosophers.

Secondly, Neither sensation nor the perception of external objects, is simple apprehension. Both include judgment and belief, which are excluded from simple apprehension.*

Thirdly, They distinguish imagination from pure intellection by this, that, in imagination, the image is in the brain ;† in pure intellection, it is in the intellect. This is to ground a distinction upon an hypothesis. We have no evidence that there are images either in the brain or in the intellect. [397]

I take imagination, in its most proper sense, to signify a lively conception of objects of sight.‡ This is a talent of importance to poets and orators, and deserves a proper name, on account of its connection with those arts. According to this strict meaning of the word, imagination is distinguished from conception as a part from the whole. We conceive the objects of the other senses, but it is not so proper to say that we imagine them. We conceive judgment, reasoning, propositions, and arguments ; but it is rather improper to say that we imagine these things.

This distinction between imagination and conception, may be illustrated by an example, which Des Cartes uses to illustrate the distinction between imagination and pure intellection. We can imagine a triangle or a square so clearly as to distinguish them from every other figure. But we cannot imagine a figure of a thousand equal sides and angles so clearly. The best eye, by looking at it, could not distinguish it from every figure of more or fewer sides. And that conception of its appearance to the eye, which we properly call imagination, cannot be more distinct than the appearance itself ; yet we can conceive a figure of a thousand sides, and even can demonstrate the properties which distinguish it from all figures of more or fewer sides. It is not by the eye, but by a superior faculty, that we form the notion of a great

---

* Does Reid here mean, by apprehending *simply*, apprehending in one simple and indivisible act ?—H.

† There is no conception possible without a judgment affirming its (ideal) existence. There is no *consciousness,* in fact, possible without judgment. See above, p. 243, a, note *. It is to be observed, that Reid uses *conception* in the course of this chapter as convertible with *understanding* or *comprehension;* and, therefore, as we shall see, in a vaguer or more extensive meaning than the philosophers whose opinion he controverts.—H.

---

* See the last note.—H.

† But not the image, of which the mind is conscious. By image or idea in the brain, *species impressa, &c.,* was meant only the unknown corporeal antecedent of the known mental consequent, the image or idea in the mind, the *species express, &c.* Reid here refers principally to the Cartesian doctrine.—H.

‡ See above, p. 366, a, note * ; and, below, under p. 482.—H.

number, such as a thousand. And a distinct notion of this number of sides not being to be got by the eye, it is not imagined, but it is distinctly conceived, and easily distinguished from every other number. *

3. Simple apprehension is commonly represented as the first operation of the understanding; and judgment, as being a composition or combination of simple apprehensions.

This mistake has probably arisen from the taking sensation, and the perception of objects by the senses, to be nothing but simple apprehension. They are, very probably, the first operations of the mind; but they are not simple apprehensions.† [398]

It is generally allowed, that we cannot conceive sounds if we have never heard, nor colours if we have never seen; and the same thing may be said of the objects of the other senses. In like manner, we must have judged or reasoned before we have the conception or simple apprehension of judgment and of reasoning.

Simple apprehension, therefore, though it be the simplest, is not the first operation of the understanding; and, instead of saying that the more complex operations of the mind are formed by compounding simple apprehensions, we ought rather to say, that simple apprehensions are got by analysing more complex operations.

A similar mistake, which is carried through the whole of Mr Locke's Essay, may be here mentioned. It is, that our simplest ideas or conceptions are got immediately by the senses, or by consciousness, and the complex afterwards formed by compounding them. I apprehend it is far otherwise.

Nature presents no object to the senses, or to consciousness, that is not complex. Thus, by our senses we perceive bodies of various kinds; but every body is a complex object; it has length, breadth, and thickness; it has figure, and colour, and various other sensible qualities, which are blended together in the same subject; and I apprehend that brute animals, who have the same senses that we have, cannot separate the different qualities belonging to the same subject, and have only a complex and confused notion of the whole. Such also would be our notions of the objects of sense, if we had not superior powers of understanding, by which we can analyse the complex object, abstract every particular attribute from the rest, and form a distinct conception of it.

So that it is not by the senses imme-

diately, but rather by the powers of analysing and abstraction, that we get the most simple and the most distinct notions even of the objects of sense. This will be more fully explained in another place. [399]

4. There remains another mistake concerning conception, which deserves to be noticed. It is—That our conception of things is a test of their possibility, so that, what we can distinctly conceive, we may conclude to be possible; and of what is impossible, we can have no conception.

This opinion has been held by philosophers for more than an hundred years, without contradiction or dissent, as far as I know; and, if it be an error, it may be of some use to inquire into its origin, and the causes that it has been so generally received as a maxim whose truth could not be brought into doubt.

One of the fruitless questions agitated among the scholastic philosophers in the dark ages* was—What is the criterion of truth? as if men could have any other way to distinguish truth from error, but by the right use of that power of judging which God has given them.

Des Cartes endeavoured to put an end to this controversy, by making it a fundamental principle in his system, that whatever we clearly and distinctly perceive, is true.†

To understand this principle of Des Cartes, it must be observed, that he gave the name of perception to every power of the human understanding; and in explaining this very maxim, he tells us that sense, imagination, and pure intellection, are only different modes of perceiving, and, so the maxim was understood by all his followers.‡

The learned Dr Cudworth seems also to have adopted this principle:—"The criterion of true knowledge, says he, is only to be looked for in our knowledge and conceptions themselves: for the entity of all theoretical truth is nothing else but clear intelligibility, and whatever is clearly conceived is an entity and a truth; but that which is false, divine power itself cannot make it to be clearly and distinctly understood. [400] A falsehood can never be clearly conceived or apprehended to be true."—"Eternal and Immutable Morality," p. 172, &c.

This Cartesian maxim seems to me to have led the way to that now under consideration, which seems to have been adopted as the proper correction of the former. When the authority of Des Cartes declined, men began to see that we may clearly and distinctly conceive what is not true; but

---

* See above, p. 366, n, note *.—H.
† They are not *simple apprehensions*, in one sense—that is, the objects are not incomposite. But this was not the meaning in which the expression was used by the Logicians.—H.

* This was more a question with the Greek philosophers than with the schoolmen.—H.
† In this he proposed nothing new. –H.
‡ That is, in Des Cartes' signification of the word, different modes of being conscious. See above.—H.

thought, that our conception, though not in all cases a test of truth, might be a test of possibility.*

This indeed seems to be a necessary consequence of the received doctrine of ideas; it being evident that there can be no distinct image, either in the mind or anywhere else, of that which is impossible.† The ambiguity of the word *conceive*, which we observed, Essay I. chap. 1, and the common phraseology of saying *we cannot conceive such a thing*, when we would signify that we think it impossible, might likewise contribute to the reception of this doctrine.

But, whatever was the origin of this opinion, it seems to prevail universally, and to be received as a maxim.

" The bare having an idea of the proposition proves the thing not to be impossible ; for of an impossible proposition there can be no idea."—Dr SAMUEL CLARKE.

" Of that which neither does nor can exist we can have no idea."—LORD BOLINGBROKE.

" The measure of impossibility to us is inconceivableness, that of which we can have no idea, but that reflecting upon it, it appears to be nothing, we pronounce to be impossible."—ABERNETHY.　[401]

" In every idea is implied the possibility of the existence of its object, nothing being clearer than that there can be no idea of an impossibility, or conception of what cannot exist."—Dr PRICE.

" Impossibile est cujus nullam notionem formare possumus ; possibile e contra, cui aliqua respondet notio."—WOLFII ONTOLOGIA.‡

" It is an established maxim in metaphysics, that whatever the mind conceives, includes the idea of possible existence, or, in other words, that nothing we imagine is absolutely impossible."—D. HUME.

It were easy to muster up many other respectable authorities for this maxim, and I have never found one that called it in question.

If the maxim be true in the extent which

the famous Wolfius has given it in the passage above quoted, we shall have a short road to the determination of every question about the possibility or impossibility of things. We need only look into our own breast, and that, like the Urim and Thummim, will give an infallible answer. If we can conceive the thing, it is possible ; if not, it is impossible. And, surely, every man may know whether he can conceive what is affirmed or not.

Other philosophers have been satisfied with one half of the maxim of Wolfius. They say, that whatever we can conceive is possible ; but they do not say that whatever we cannot conceive is impossible.

I cannot help thinking even this to be a mistake, which philosophers have been unwarily led into, from the causes before mentioned. My reasons are these :—[402]

1. Whatever is said to be possible or impossible, is expressed by a proposition. Now, what is it to conceive a proposition ? I think it is no more than to understand distinctly its meaning.*　I know no more

---

* That is, of logical possibility—the absence of contradiction.—H.

† This is rather a strained inference.—H.

‡ These are not exactly Wolf's expressions. See "Ontologia," §§ 102, 103 ; " Philosophia Rationalis," §§ 522, 523. The same doctrine is held by Tschirnhausen and others. In so far, however, as it is said that *inconceivability* is the criterion of impossibility, it is manifestly erroneous. Of many contradictories, we are able to conceive neither ; but, by the law of thought, called that of Excluded Middle, one of two contradictories must be admitted—must be true. For example, we can neither conceive, on the one hand, an ultimate minimum of space or of time ; nor can we, on the other, conceive their infinite divisibility. In like manner, we cannot conceive the absolute commencement of time, or the utmost limit of space, and are yet equally unable to conceive them without any commencement or limit. The absurdity that would result from the assertion, that all that is inconceivable is impossible, is thus obvious ; and so far Reid's criticism is just, though not new.—H.

[401, 402]

---

* In this sense of the word Conception, I make bold to say that there is no philosopher who ever held an opinion different from that of our author. The whole dispute arises from Reid giving a wider signification to this term than that which it has generally received. In his view, it has two meanings ; in that of the philosophers whom he attacks, it has only one. To illustrate this, take the proposition—*a circle is square.* Here we easily *understand* the meaning of the affirmation, because what is necessary to an act of judgment is merely that the subject and predicate should be brought into a *unity of relation.* A judgment is therefore possible, even where the two terms are contradictory. But the philosophers never expressed, by the term conception, this understanding of the purport of a proposition. What they meant by conception was not the *unity of relation*, but the *unity of representation* ; and this unity of representation they made the criterion of logical possibility. To take the example already given : they did not say a circle may possibly be square, because we can understand the meaning of the proposition, a circle is square ; but, on the contrary, they said it is impossible that a circle can be square, and the proposition affirming this is necessarily false, because we cannot, in consciousness, bring to a *unity of representation* the repugnant notions, circle and square—that is, *conceive* the notion of *square circle.* Reid's mistake in this matter is so palpable that it is not more surprising that he should have committed it, than that so many should not only have followed him in the opinion, but even have lauded it as the refutation of an important error. To shew how completely Reid mistook the philosophers, it will be sufficient to quote a passage from Wolf's vernacular Logic, which I take from the English translation, (one, by the by, of the few tolerable versions we have of German philosophical works,) published in 1770:—

" It is carefully to be observed, that we have not always the notion of the thing present to us, or in view, when we speak or think of it ; but are satisfied when we imagine we sufficiently understand what we speak, if we think we recollect that we have had, at another time, the notion which is to be joined to this or the other word ;• and thus we represent to ourselves, as at a distance only, or obscurely, the thing denoted by the term.

" Hence, it usually happens that, when we combine words together, to each of which, apart, a meaning or notion answers, we imagine we understand what we utter, though that which is denoted by such combined words be impossible. and consequently can have no meaning. For that which is impossible is

that can be meant by simple apprehension or conception, when applied to a proposition. The axiom, therefore, amounts to this :—Every proposition, of which you understand the meaning distinctly, is possible. I am persuaded that I understand as distinctly the meaning of this proposition, *Any two sides of a triangle are together equal to the third*, as of this—*Any two sides of a triangle are together greater than the third* ; yet the first of these is impossible.

Perhaps it will be said, that, though you understand the meaning of the impossible proposition, you cannot suppose or conceive it to be true.

Here we are to examine the meaning of the phrases of *supposing* and *conceiving* a proposition to be true. I can certainly suppose it to be true, because I can draw consequences from it which I find to be impossible, as well as the proposition itself.

If, by conceiving it to be true, be meant giving some degree of assent to it, however small, this, I confess, I cannot do. But will it be said that every proposition to which I can give any degree of assent, is possible ? This contradicts experience, and, therefore, the maxim cannot be true in this sense.

Sometimes, when we say that *we cannot conceive a thing to be true*, we mean by that expression, that *we judge it to be impossible*. In this sense I cannot, indeed, conceive it to be true, that two sides of a triangle are equal to the third. I judge it to be impossible. If, then, we understand, in this sense, that maxim, that nothing we can conceive is impossible, the meaning will be, that nothing is impossible which we judge to be possible. But does it not often happen, that what one man judges to be possible, another man judges to be impossible ? The maxim, therefore, is not true in this sense. [403]

I am not able to find any other meaning of *conceiving a proposition*, or of *conceiving it to be true*, besides these I have mentioned. I know nothing that can be meant by having the idea of a proposition, but

either the understanding its meaning, or the judging of its truth. I can understand a proposition that is false or impossible, as well as one that is true or possible ; and I find that men have contradictory judgments about what is possible or impossible, as well as about other things. In what sense then can it be said, that the having an idea of a proposition gives certain evidence that it is possible ?

If it be said, that the idea of a proposition is an image of it in the mind, I think indeed there cannot be a distinct image, either in the mind or elsewhere, of that which is impossible ; but what is meant by the image of a proposition I am not able to comprehend, and I shall be glad to be informed.

2. Every proposition that is necessarily true stands opposed to a contradictory proposition that is impossible ; and he that conceives one conceives both. Thus a man who believes that two and three necessarily make five, must believe it to be impossible that two and three should not make five. He conceives both propositions when he believes one. Every proposition carries its contradictory in its bosom, and both are conceived at the same time. " It is confessed," says Mr Hume, " that, in all cases where we dissent from any person, we conceive both sides of the question ; but we can believe only one." From this, it certainly follows, that, when we dissent from any person about a necessary proposition, we conceive one that is impossible ; yet I know no philosopher who has made so much use of the maxim, that whatever we conceive is possible, as Mr Hume. A great part of his peculiar tenets is built upon it ; and, if it is true, they must be true. But he did not perceive that, in the passage now quoted, the truth of which is evident, he contradicts it himself. [404]

3. Mathematicians have, in many cases, proved some things to be possible, and others to be impossible, which, without demonstration, would not have been believed. Yet I have never found that any mathematician has attempted to prove a thing to be possible, because it can be conceived ; or impossible, because it cannot be conceived.[*] Why is not this maxim applied to determine whether it is possible to square the circle ? a point about which very eminent mathematicians have differed. It is easy to conceive that, in the infinite series of numbers, and intermediate fractions, some one number, integral or fractional, may bear the same ratio to another, as the side of a square bears to its diagonal ;[†] yet,

---

nothing at all, and of nothing there can be no idea. For instance, we have a notion of gold, as also of iron. But it is impossible that iron can at the same time be gold, consequently, neither can we have any notion of iron-gold ; and yet we understand what people mean when they mention iron-gold.

" In the instance alleged, it certainly strikes every one, at first, that the expression iron-gold is an empty sound ; but yet there are a thousand instances in which it does not so easily strike. For example, when I say a rectilineal two-lined figure, a figure contained under two right lines, I am equally well understood as when I say, a right-lined triangle, a figure c n-tained under three right lines. And it should seem we had a distinct notion of both figures. However, as we shew in Geometry that two right lines can never contain space, it is also impossible to form a notion of a rectilineal two-lined figure ; and consequently that expression is an empty sound."—P. 55.—H.

* All geometry is, in fact, founded on our intuitions of space—that is, in common language, on our conceptions of space and its relations.—H.

† We are able to conceive nothing infinite ; and we may *suppose*, but we cannot *conceive*, *represent*, or *imagine*, the possibility in question.—H.

however conceivable this may be, it may be demonstrated to be impossible.

4. Mathematicians often require us to conceive things that are impossible, in order to prove them to be so. This is the case in all their demonstrations *ad absurdum.* Conceive, says Euclid, a right line drawn from one point of the circumference of a circle to another, to fall without the circle :* I conceive this—I reason from it, until I come to a consequence that is manifestly absurd ; and from thence conclude that the thing which I conceived is impossible.

Having said so much to shew that our power of conceiving a proposition is no criterion of its possibility or impossibility, I shall add a few observations on the extent of our knowledge of this kind.

1. There are many propositions which, by the faculties God has given us, we judge to be necessary, as well as true. All mathematical propositions are of this kind, and many others. The contradictories of such propositions must be impossible. Our knowledge, therefore, of what is impossible, must, at least, be as extensive as our knowledge of necessary truth.

2. By our senses, by memory, by testimony, and by other means, we know many things to be true which do not appear to be necessary. But whatever is true is possible. Our knowledge, therefore, of what is possible must, at least, extend as far as our knowledge of truth. [405]

3. If a man pretends to determine the possibility or impossibility of things beyond these limits, let him bring proof. I do not say that no such proof can be brought. It has been brought in many cases, particularly in mathematics. But I say that his being able to conceive a thing, is no proof that it is possible.† Mathematics afford many instances of impossibilities in the nature of things, which no man would have believed if they had not been strictly demonstrated. Perhaps, if we were able to reason demonstratively in other subjects, to as great extent as in mathematics, we might find many things to be impossible, which we conclude without hesitation, to be possible.

It is possible, you say, that God might have made an universe of sensible and rational creatures, into which neither natural nor moral evil should ever enter. It may be so, for what I know. But how do you know that it is possible ? That you can conceive it, I grant ; but this is no proof.

I cannot admit, as an argument, or even as a pressing difficulty, what is grounded on the supposition that such a thing is possible, when there is no good evidence that it is possible, and, for anything we know, it may, in the nature of things, be impossible.

CHAPTER IV.

OF THE TRAIN OF THOUGHT IN THE MIND.

EVERY man is conscious of a succession of thoughts which pass in his mind while he is awake, even when they are not excited by external objects.   [406]

The mind, on this account, may be compared to liquor in the state of fermentation. When it is not in this state, being once at rest, it remains at rest, until it is moved by some external impulse. But, in the state of fermentation, it has some cause of motion in itself, which, even when there is no impulse from without, suffers it not to be at rest a moment, but produces a constant motion and ebullition, while it continues to ferment.

There is surely no similitude between motion and thought ; but there is an analogy, so obvious to all men, that the same words are often applied to both ; and many modifications of thought have no name but such as is borrowed from the modifications of motion. Many thoughts are excited by the senses. The causes or occasions of these may be considered as external. But, when such external causes do not operate upon us, we continue to think from some internal cause. From the constitution of the mind itself there is a constant ebullition of thought, a constant intestine motion ; not only of thoughts barely speculative, but of sentiments, passions, and affections, which attend them.

This continued succession of thought has, by modern philosophers, been called the *imagination.* I think it was formerly called the *fancy,* or the *phantasy.*† If the old name be laid aside, it were to be wished that it had got a name less ambiguous than that of imagination, a name which had two or three meanings besides.

It is often called the *train of ideas.* This may lead one to think that it is a train of bare conceptions ; but this would surely be a mistake. It is made up of many other operations of mind, as well as of conceptions, or ideas.

---

* Euclid does not require us to *conceive* or imagine any such impossibility. The proposition to which Reid must refer, is the second of the third Book of the Elements.—H.

† Not, certainly, that it is *really possible,* but that it is *problematically possible—i. e.,* involves no contradiction—violates no law of thought. This latter is that possibility alone in question.—H.

* By some only, and that improperly.—H.
† The Latin *Imaginatio,* with its modifications in the vulgar languages, was employed both in ancient and modern times to express what the Greeks denominated Φαντασία. *Phantasy,* of which *Phantsy* or *Fancy* is a corruption, and now employed in a more limited sense, was a common name for Imagination with the old English writers.—H.

Memory, judgment, reasoning. passions, affections, and purposes—in a word, every operation of the mind, excepting those of sense—is exerted occasionally in this train of thought, and has its share as an ingredient: so that we must take the word idea in a very extensive sense, if we make the train of our thoughts to be only a train of ideas. [407]

To pass from the name, and consider the thing, we may observe, that the trains of thought in the mind are of two kinds: they are either such as flow spontaneously, like water from a fountain, without any exertion of a governing principle to arrange them; or they are regulated and directed by an active effort of the mind, with some view and intention.

Before we consider these in their order, it is proper to premise that these two kinds, however distinct in their nature, are for the most part mixed, in persons.awake and come to years of understanding.

On the one hand, we are rarely so vacant of all project and design as to let our thoughts take their own course, without the least check or direction. Or if, at any time, we should be in this state, some object will present itself, which is too interesting not to engage the attention and rouse the active or contemplative powers that were at rest.

On the other hand, when a man is giving the most intense application to any speculation, or to any scheme of conduct, when he wills to exclude every thought that is foreign to his present purpose, such thoughts will often impertinently intrude upon him, in spite of his endeavours to the contrary, and occupy, by a kind of violence, some part of the time destined to another purpose. One man may have the command of his thoughts more than another man, and the same man more at one time than at another. But, I apprehend, in the best trained mind, the thoughts will sometimes be restive, sometimes capricious and self-willed, when we wish to have them most under command. [408]

It has been observed very justly, that we must not ascribe to the mind the power of calling up any thought at pleasure, because such a call or volition supposes that thought to be already in the mind; for, otherwise, how should it be the object of volition? As this must be granted on the one hand, so it is no less certain, on the other, that a man has a considerable power in regulating and disposing his own thoughts. Of this every man is conscious, and I can no more doubt of it than I can doubt whether I think at all.

We seem to treat the thoughts that present themselves to the fancy in crowds, as a great man treats those that attend his levee. They are all ambitious of his attention: he goes round the circle, bestowing a bow upon one, a smile upon another; asks a short question of a third; while a fourth is honoured with a particular conference; and the greater part have no particular mark of attention, but go as they came. It is true, he can give no mark of his attention to those who were not there but he has a sufficient number for making a choice and distinction.

In like manner, a number of thoughts present themselves to the fancy spontaneously; but, if we pay no attention to them, nor hold any conference with them, they pass with the crowd, and are immediately forgot, as if they had never appeared. But those to which we think proper to pay attention, may be stopped, examined, and arranged, for any particular purpose we have in view.

It may likewise be observed, that a train of thought, which was at first composed by application and judgment, when it has been often repeated, and becomes familiar, will present itself spontaneously. Thus, when a man has composed an air in music, so as to please his own ear, after he has played or sung it often, the notes will arrange themselves in just order, and it requires no effort to regulate their succession. [409]

Thus we see that the fancy is made up of trains of thinking—some of which are spontaneous, others studied and regulated, and the greater part are mixed of both kinds, and take their denomination from that which is most prevalent; and that a train of thought which at first was studied and composed, may, by habit, present itself spontaneously. Having premised these things, let us return to those trains of thought which are spontaneous, which must be first in the order of nature.

When the work of the day is over, and a man lies down to relax his body and mind, he cannot cease from thinking, though he desires it. Something occurs to his fancy; that is followed by another thing; and so his thoughts are carried on from one object to another, until sleep closes the scene.

In this operation* of the mind, it is not one faculty only that is employed; there are many that join together in its production. Sometimes the transactions of the day are brought upon the stage, and acted over again, as it were, upon this theatre of the imagination. In this case, memory surely acts the most considerable part, since the scenes exhibited are not fictions, but realities, which we remember; yet, in this case, the

---

* The word *process* might be here preferable. *Operation* would denote that the mind is active in associating the train of thought.—H.

memory does not act alone, other powers are employed, and attend upon their proper objects. The transactions remembered will be more or less interesting; and we cannot then review our own conduct, nor that of others, without passing some judgment upon it. This we approve, that we disapprove. This elevates, that humbles and depresses us. Persons that are not absolutely indifferent to us, can hardly appear, even to the imagination, without some friendly or unfriendly emotion. We judge and reason about things as well as persons in such reveries. We remember what a man said and did; from this we pass to his designs and to his general character, and frame some hypothesis to make the whole consistent. Such trains of thought we may call historical. [410]

There are others which we may call romantic, in which the plot is formed by the creative power of fancy, without any regard to what did or will happen. In these also, the powers of judgment, taste, moral sentiment, as well as the passions and affections, come in and take a share in the execution.

In these scenes, the man himself commonly acts a very distinguished part, and seldom does anything which he cannot approve. Here the miser will be generous, the coward brave, and the knave honest. Mr Addison, in the "Spectator," calls this play of the fancy, castle-building.

The young politician, who has turned his thoughts to the affairs of government, becomes, in his imagination, a minister of state. He examines every spring and wheel of the machine of government with the nicest eye and the most exact judgment. He finds a proper remedy for every disorder of the commonwealth, quickens trade and manufactures by salutary laws, encourages arts and sciences, and makes the nation happy at home and respected abroad. He feels the reward of his good administration, in that self-approbation which attends it, and is happy in acquiring, by his wise and patriotic conduct, the blessings of the present age, and the praises of those that are to come.

It is probable that, upon the stage of imagination, more great exploits have been performed in every age than have been upon the stage of life from the beginning of the world. An innate desire of self-approbation is undoubtedly a part of the human constitution. It is a powerful spur to worthy conduct, and is intended as such by the Author of our being. A man cannot be easy or happy, unless this desire be in some measure gratified. While he conceives himself worthless and base, he can relish no enjoyment. The humiliating, mortifying sentiment must be removed, and [410–412]

this natural desire of self-approbation will either produce a noble effort to acquire real worth, which is its proper direction, or it will lead into some of those arts of self-deceit, which create a false opinion of worth. [411]

A castle-builder, in the fictitious scenes of his fancy, will figure, not according to his real character, but according to the highest opinion he has been able to form of himself, and perhaps far beyond that opinion. For, in those imaginary conflicts, the passions easily yield to reason, and a man exerts the noblest efforts of virtue and magnanimity, with the same ease as, in his dreams, he flies through the air or plunges to the bottom of the ocean.

The romantic scenes of fancy are most commonly the occupation of young minds, not yet so deeply engaged in life as to have their thoughts taken up by its real cares and business.

Those active powers of the mind, which are most luxuriant by constitution, or have been most cherished by education, impatient to exert themselves, hurry the thought into scenes that give them play; and the boy commences in imagination, according to the bent of his mind, a general or a statesman, a poet or an orator.

When the fair ones become castle-builders, they use different materials; and, while the young soldier is carried into the field of Mars, where he pierces the thickest squadrons of the enemy, despising death in all its forms, the gay and lovely nymph, whose heart has never felt the tender passion, is transported into a brilliant assembly, where she draws the attention of every eye, and makes an impression on the noblest heart.

But no sooner has Cupid's arrow found its way into her own heart, than the whole scenery of her imagination is changed. Balls and assemblies have now no charms. Woods and groves, the flowery bank and the crystal fountain, are the scenes she frequents in imagination. She becomes an Arcadian shepherdess, feeding her flock beside that of her Strephon, and wants no more to complete her happiness. [412]

In a few years the love-sick maid is transformed into the solicitous mother. Her smiling offspring play around her. She views them with a parent's eye. Her imagination immediately raises them to manhood, and brings them forth upon the stage of life. One son makes a figure in the army, another shines at the bar; her daughters are happily disposed of in marriage, and bring new alliances to the family. Her children's children rise up before her, and venerate her grey hairs.

Thus the spontaneous sallies of fancy are as various as the cares and fears, the desires and hopes, of man.

Quicquid agunt homines, votum, timor, ira, voluptas,
Gaudia, discursus:

These fill up the scenes of fancy, as well as the page of the satirist. Whatever possesses the heart makes occasional excursions into the imagination, and acts such scenes upon that theatre as are agreeable to the prevailing passion. The man of traffic, who has committed a rich cargo to the inconstant ocean, follows it in his thought, and, according as his hopes or his fears prevail, he is haunted with storms, and rocks, and shipwreck; or he makes a happy and a lucrative voyage, and, before his vessel has lost sight of land, he has disposed of the profit which she is to bring at her return.

The poet is carried into the Elysian fields, where he converses with the ghosts of Homer and Orpheus. The philosopher makes a tour through the planetary system, or goes down to the centre of the earth, and examines its various strata. In the devout man likewise, the great objects that possess his heart often play in his imagination: sometimes he is transported to the regions of the blessed, from whence he looks down with pity upon the folly and the pageantry of human life; or he prostrates himself before the throne of the Most High with devout veneration; or he converses with celestial spirits about the natural and moral kingdom of God, which he now sees only by a faint light, but hopes hereafter to view with a steadier and brighter ray. [413]

In persons come to maturity, there is, even in these spontaneous sallies of fancy, some arrangement of thought; and I conceive that it will be readily allowed, that in those who have the greatest stock of knowledge, and the best natural parts, even the spontaneous movements of fancy will be the most regular and connected. They have an order, connection, and unity, by which they are no less distinguished from the dreams of one asleep, or the ravings of one delirious on the one hand, than from the finished productions of art on the other. How is this regular arrangement brought about? It has all the marks of judgment and reason, yet it seems to go before judgment, and to spring forth spontaneously.

Shall we believe with Leibnitz, that the mind was originally formed like a watch wound up; and that all its thoughts, purposes, passions, and actions, are effected by the gradual evolution of the original spring of the machine, and succeed each other in order, as necessarily as the motions and pulsations of a watch?

If a child of three or four years were put to account for the phænomena of a watch, he would conceive that there is a little man within the watch, or some other little animal, that beats continually, and produces the

motion. Whether the hypothesis of this young philosopher, in turning the watch-spring into a man, or that of the German philosopher, in turning a man into a watch-spring, be the most rational, seems hard to determine.*

To account for the regularity of our first thoughts, from motions of animal spirits, vibrations of nerves, attractions of ideas, or from any other unthinking cause, whether mechanical or contingent, seems equally irrational. [414]

If we be not able to distinguish the strongest marks of thought and design from the effects of mechanism or contingency, the consequence will be very melancholy; for it must necessarily follow, that we have no evidence of thought in any of our fellow men—nay, that we have no evidence of thought or design in the structure and government of the universe. If a good period or sentence was ever produced without having had any judgment previously employed about it, why not an Iliad or Æneid? They differ only in less and more; and we should do injustice to the philosopher of Laputa, in laughing at his project of making poems by the turning of a wheel, if a concurrence of unthinking causes may produce a rational train of thought.

It is, therefore, in itself highly probable to say no more, that whatsoever is regular and rational in a train of thought, which presents itself spontaneously to a man's fancy, without any study, is a copy of what had been before composed by his own rational powers, or those of some other person.

We certainly judge so in similar cases. Thus, in a book I find a train of thinking, which has the marks of knowledge and judgment. I ask how it was produced? It is printed in a book. This does not satisfy me, because the book has no knowledge nor reason. I am told that a printer printed it, and a compositor set the types. Neither does this satisfy me. These causes, perhaps, knew very little of the subject. There must be a prior cause of the composition. If was printed from a manuscript. True. But the manuscript is as ignorant as the printed book. The manuscript was written or dictated by a man of knowledge and judgment. This, and this only, will satisfy a man of common understanding; and it appears to him extremely ridiculous to believe that such a train of thinking could originally be produced by any cause that neither reasons nor thinks. [415]

Whether such a train of thinking be printed in a book, or printed, so to speak, in his mind, and issue spontaneously from his fancy, it must have been composed with

---

* The theory of our mental associations owes much to the philosophers of the Leibnitzian school.—H.

judgment by himself, or by some other rational being.

This, I think, will be confirmed by tracing the progress of the human fancy as far back as we are able.

We have not the means of knowing how the fancy is employed in infants. Their time is divided between the employment of their senses and sound sleep : so that there is little time left for imagination, and the materials it has to work upon are probably very scanty. A few days after they are born, sometimes a few hours, we see them smile in their sleep. But what they smile at is not easy to guess ; for they do not smile at anything they see, when awake, for some months after they are born. It is likewise common to see them move their lips in sleep, as if they were sucking.

These things seem to discover some working of the imagination ; but there is no reason to think that there is any regular train of thought in the mind of infants.

By a regular train of thought, I mean that which has a beginning, a middle, and an end, an arrangement of its parts, according to some rule, or with some intention. Thus, the conception of a design, and of the means of executing it ; the conception of a whole, and the number and order of the parts. These are instances of the most simple trains of thought that can be called regular.

Man has undoubtedly a power (whether we call it taste or judgment is not of any consequence in the present argument) whereby he distinguishes between a composition and a heap of materials ; between a house, for instance, and a heap of stones ; between a sentence and a heap of words ; between a picture and a heap of colours. [416] It does not appear to me that children have any regular trains of thought until this power begins to operate. Those who are born such idiots as never to shew any signs of this power, shew as little any signs of regularity of thought. It seems, therefore, that this power is connected with all regular trains of thought, and may be the cause of them.

Such trains of thought discover themselves in children about two years of age. They can then give attention to the operations of older children in making their little houses, and ships, and other such things, in imitation of the works of men. They are then capable of understanding a little of language, which shews both a regular train of thinking, and some degree of abstraction. I think we may perceive a distinction between the faculties of children of two or three years of age, and those of the most sagacious brutes. They can then perceive design and regularity in the works of others, especially of older children ; their

[416, 417]

little minds are fired with the discovery ; they are eager to imitate it, and never at rest till they can exhibit something of the same kind.

When a child first learns by imitation to do something that requires design, how does he exult ! Pythagoras was not more happy in the discovery of his famous theorem. He seems then first to reflect upon himself, and to swell with self-esteem. His eyes sparkle. He is impatient to shew his performance to all about him, and thinks himself entitled to their applause. He is applauded by all, and feels the same emotion from this applause, as a Roman Consul did from a triumph. He has now a consciousness of some worth in himself. He assumes a superiority over those who are not so wise, and pays respect to those who are wiser than himself. He attempts something else, and is every day reaping new laurels.

As children grow up, they are delighted with tales, with childish games, with designs and stratagems. Everything of this kind stores the fancy with a new regular train of thought, which becomes familiar by repetition, so that one part draws the whole after it in the imagination. [417]

The imagination of a child, like the hand of a painter, is long employed in copying the works of others, before it attempts any invention of its own.

The power of invention is not yet brought forth ; but it is coming forward, and, like the bud of a tree, is ready to burst its integuments, when some accident aids its eruption.

There is no power of the understanding that gives so much pleasure to the owner, as that of invention, whether it be employed in mechanics, in science, in the conduct of life, in poetry, in wit, or in the fine arts. One who is conscious of it, acquires thereby a worth and importance in his own eye which he had not before. He looks upon himself as one who formerly lived upon the bounty and gratuity of others, but who has now acquired some property of his own. When this power begins to be felt in the young mind, it has the grace of novelty added to its other charms, and, like the youngest child of the family, is caressed beyond all the rest.

We may be sure, therefore, that, as soon as children are conscious of this power, they will exercise it in such ways as are suited to their age, and to the objects they are employed about. This gives rise to innumerable new associations, and regular trains of thought, which make the deeper impression upon the mind, as they are its exclusive property.

I am aware that the power of invention is distributed among men more unequally than almost any other. When it is able to produce anything that is interesting to mankind we call it genius; a talent which is the lot of very few. But there is, perhaps, a lower kind or lower degree of invention that is more common. However this may be, it must be allowed that the power of invention in those who have it, will produce many new regular trains of thought; and these being expressed in works of art, in writing, or in discourse, will be copied by others. [418]

Thus, I conceive the minds of children, as soon as they have judgment to distinguish what is regular, orderly, and connected, from a mere medley of thought, are furnished with regular trains of thinking by these means.

First and chiefly, by copying what they see in the works and in the discourse of others. Man is the most imitative of all animals; he not only imitates with intention, and purposely, what he thinks has any grace or beauty, but even without intention, he is led, by a kind of instinct, which it is difficult to resist, into the modes of speaking, thinking, and acting, which he has been accustomed to see in his early years. The more children see of what is regular and beautiful in what is presented to them, the more they are led to observe and to imitate it.

This is the chief part of their stock, and descends to them by a kind of tradition from those who came before them; and we shall find that the fancy of most men is furnished from those they have conversed with, as well as their religion, language, and manners.

Secondly, By the additions or innovations that are properly their own, these will be greater or less, in proportion to their study and invention; but in the bulk of mankind are not very considerable.

Every profession and every rank in life, has a manner of thinking, and turn of fancy that is proper to it; by which it is characterised in comedies and works of humour. The bulk of men of the same nation, of the same rank, and of the same occupation, are cast, as it were, in the same mould. This mould itself changes gradually, but slowly, by new inventions, by intercourse with strangers, or by other accidents.* [419]

The condition of man requires a longer infancy and youth than that of other animals; for this reason, among others, that almost every station in civil society requires a multitude of regular trains of thought, to

be not only acquired, but to be made so familiar by frequent repetition, as to present themselves spontaneously when there is occasion for them.

The imagination even of men of good parts never serves them readily but in things wherein it has been much exercised. A minister of state holds a conference with a foreign ambassador with no greater emotion than a professor in a college prelects to his audience. The imagination of each presents to him what the occasion requires to be said, and how. Let them change places, and both would find themselves at a loss.

The habits which the human mind is capable of acquiring by exercise are wonderful in many instances; in none more wonderful than in that versatility of imagination which a well-bred man acquires by being much exercised in the various scenes of life. In the morning he visits a friend in affliction. Here his imagination brings forth from its store every topic of consolation; everything that is agreeable to the laws of friendship and sympathy, and nothing that is not so. From thence he drives to the minister's levee, where imagination readily suggests what is proper to be said or replied to every man, and in what manner, according to the degree of acquaintance or familiarity, of rank or dependence, of opposition or concurrence of interests, of confidence or distrust, that is between them. Nor does all this employment hinder him from carrying on some design with much artifice, and endeavouring to penetrate into the views of others through the closest disguises. From the levee he goes to the House of Commons, and speaks upon the affairs of the nation; from thence to a ball or assembly, and entertains the ladies. His imagination puts on the friend, the courtier, the patriot, the fine gentleman, with more ease than we put off one suit and put on another. [420]

This is the effect of training and exercise. For a man of equal parts and knowledge, but unaccustomed to those scenes of public life, is quite disconcerted when first brought into them. His thoughts are put to flight, and he cannot rally them.

There are feats of imagination to be learned by application and practice, as wonderful as the feats of balancers and ropedancers, and often as useless.

When a man can make a hundred verses standing on one foot, or play three or four games at chess at the same time without seeing the board, it is probable he hath spent his life in acquiring such a feat. However, such unusual phænomena shew what habits of imagination may be acquired.

When such habits are acquired and perfected, they are exercised without any labo-

---

* " * Non ad rationem sed ad similitudinem componimur," says Seneca; and Schiller—
" 'Man—he is aye an imitative creature,
And he who is the foremost leads the flock.''
There would be no end of quotations to the same effect.—H.

rious effort; like the habit of playing upon an instrument of music. There are innumerable motions of the fingers upon the stops or keys, which must be directed in one particular train or succession. There is only one arrangement of those motions that is right, while there are ten thousand that are wrong, and would spoil the music. The musician thinks not in the least of the arrangement of those motions; he has a distinct idea of the tune, and wills to play it. The motions of the fingers arrange themselves so as to answer his intention.

In like manner, when a man speaks upon a subject with which he is acquainted, there is a certain arrangement of his thoughts and words necessary to make his discourse sensible, pertinent, and grammatical. In every sentence there are more rules of grammar, logic, and rhetoric, that may be transgressed, than there are words and letters. He speaks without thinking of any of those rules, and yet observes them all, as if they were all in his eye. [421]

This is a habit so similar to that of a player on an instrument, that I think both must be got in the same way—that is, by much practice, and the power of habit.

When a man speaks well and methodically upon a subject without study and with perfect ease, I believe we may take it for granted that his thoughts run in a beaten track. There is a mould in his mind—which has been formed by much practice, or by study—for this very subject, or for some other so similar and analogous that his discourse falls into this mould with ease, and takes its form from it.

Hitherto we have considered the operations of fancy that are either spontaneous, or, at least, require no laborious effort to guide and direct them, and have endeavoured to account for that degree of regularity and arrangement which is found even in them. The natural powers of judgment and invention, the pleasure that always attends the exercise of those powers, the means we have of improving them by imitation of others, and the effect of practice and habits, seem to me sufficiently to account for this phænomenon, without supposing any unaccountable attractions of ideas by which they arrange themselves.

But we are able to direct our thoughts in a certain course, so as to perform a destined task.

Every work of art has its model framed in the imagination. Here the "Iliad" of Homer, the "Republic" of Plato, the "Principia" of Newton, were fabricated. Shall we believe that those works took the form in which they now appear of themselves?—that the sentiments, the manners, and the passions arranged themselves at once in the mind of Homer, so as to form

the "Iliad?" Was there no more effort in the composition than there is in telling a well-known tale, or singing a favourite song? This cannot be believed. [422]

Granting that some happy thought first suggested the design of singing the wrath of Achilles, yet, surely, it was a matter of judgment and choice where the narration should begin and where it should end.

Granting that the fertility of the poet's imagination suggested a variety of rich materials, was not judgment necessary to select what was proper, to reject what was improper, to arrange the materials into a just composition, and to adapt them to each other, and to the design of the whole?

No man can believe that Homer's ideas, merely by certain sympathies and antipathies, by certain attractions and repulsions inherent in their natures, arranged themselves according to the most perfect rules of epic poetry; and Newton's, according to the rules of mathematical composition.

I should sooner believe that the poet, after he invoked his muse, did nothing at all but listen to the song of the goddess. Poets, indeed, and other artists, must make their works appear natural; but nature is the perfection of art, and there can be no just imitation of nature without art. When the building is finished, the rubbish, the scaffolds, the tools and engines are carried out of sight; but we know it could not have been reared without them.

The train of thinking, therefore, is capable of being guided and directed, much in the same manner as the horse we ride. The horse has his strength, his agility, and his mettle in himself; he has been taught certain movements, and many useful habits, that make him more subservient to our purposes and obedient to our will; but to accomplish a journey, he must be directed by the rider.

In like manner, fancy has its original powers, which are very different in different persons; it has likewise more regular motions, to which it has been trained by a long course of discipline and exercise, and by which it may, *extempore*, and without much effort, produce things that have a considerable degree of beauty, regularity, and design. [423]

But the most perfect works of design are never extemporary. Our first thoughts are reviewed; we place them at a proper distance; examine every part, and take a complex view of the whole. By our critical faculties, we perceive this part to be redundant, that deficient; here is a want of nerves, there a want of delicacy; this is obscure, that too diffuse. Things are marshalled anew, according to a second and more deliberate judgment; what was deficient, is supplied; what was dislocated, is

put in joint ; redundances are lopped off,
and the whole polished.

Though poets, of all artists, make the
highest claim to inspiration ; yet, if we believe Horace, a competent judge, no production in that art can have merit which
has not cost such labour as this in the
birth.

> "Vos O!
> Pompilius sanguis, carmen reprehendite quod non
> Multa dies, et multa litura coercuit, atque
> Perfectum decies non castigavit ad unguem."

The conclusion I would draw from all
that has been said upon this subject is,
That everything that is regular in that
train of thought which we call fancy or
imagination, from the little designs and
reveries of children to the grandest productions of human genius, was originally
the offspring of judgment or taste, applied
with some effort greater or less. What
one person composed with art and judgment, is imitated by another with great
ease: What a man himself at first composed with pains, becomes by habit so
familiar as to offer itself spontaneously to
his fancy afterwards. But nothing that is
regular was ever at first conceived without
design, attention, and care. [424]

I shall now make a few reflections upon a
theory which has been applied to account
for this successive train of thought in the
mind. It was hinted by Mr Hobbes, but
has drawn more attention since it was distinctly explained by Mr Hume.

That author* thinks that the train of
thought in the mind is owing to a kind of
attraction which ideas have for other ideas
that bear certain relations to them. He
thinks the complex ideas—which are the
common subjects of our thoughts and reasoning—are owing to the same cause. The
relations which produce this attraction of
ideas, he thinks, are these three only—to
wit, causation, contiguity in time or place,
and similitude. He asserts that these are
the only general principles that unite ideas.
And having, in another place, occasion to
take notice of contrariety as a principle of
connection among ideas, in order to reconcile this to his system, he tells us gravely,
that contrariety may perhaps be considered
as a mixture of causation and resemblance.
That ideas which have any of these three
relations do mutually attract each other, so
that one of them being presented to the
fancy, the other is drawn along with it—
this he seems to think an original property
of the mind, or rather of the ideas, and
therefore inexplicable.†

First, I observe, with regard to this
theory, that, although it is true that the
thought of any object is apt to lead us to
the thought of its cause or effect, of things
contiguous to it in time or place, or of
things resembling it, yet this enumeration
of the relations of things which are apt to
lead us from one object to another, is very
inaccurate.

The enumeration is too large upon his
own principles ; but it is by far too scanty in
reality. Causation, according to his philosophy, implies nothing more than a constant conjunction observed between the
cause and the effect, and, therefore, contiguity must include causation, and his three
principles of attraction are reduced to two.
[425]

But when we take all the three, the enumeration is, in reality, very incomplete.
Every relation of things has a tendency,
more or less, to lead the thought, in a
thinking mind, from one to the other ; and
not only every relation, but every kind of
contrariety and opposition. What Mr
Hume says—that contrariety may perhaps
be considered as a mixture " of causation
and resemblance"—I can as little comprehend as if he had said that figure may perhaps be considered as a mixture of colour
and sound.

Our thoughts pass easily from the end
to the means ; from any truth to the evidence on which it is founded, the consequences that may be drawn from it, or the
use that may be made of it. From a part
we are easily led to think of the whole, from
a subject to its qualities, or from things
related to the relation. Such transitions in
thinking must have been made thousands
of times by every man who thinks and
reasons, and thereby become, as it were,
beaten tracks for the imagination.

Not only the relations of objects to each
other influence our train of thinking, but
the relation they bear to the present temper and disposition of the mind ; their relation to the habits we have acquired,
whether moral or intellectual ; to the company we have kept, and to the business in
which we have been chiefly employed. The
same event will suggest very different reflections to different persons, and to the
same person at different times, according
as he is in good or bad humour, as he is
lively or dull, angry or pleased, melancholy
or cheerful.

Lord Kames, in his " Elements of Criticism," and Dr Gerard, in his " Essay on
Genius," have given a much fuller and
juster enumeration of the causes that influence our train of thinking, and I have

---

* He should have said *this* author, for Hume is
referred to.—H.

† See above, p. 294, b, note †. The history of the
doctrine of Association has never yet been at all
adequately developed. Some of the most remarkable speculations on this matter are wholly unknown.
Of these I can, at present, say nothing.—H.   See
Notes D * *, D * * *.   [424, 425]

nothing to add to what they have said on this subject.

Secondly, Let us consider how far this attraction of ideas must be resolved into original qualities of human nature. [426] I believe the original principles of the mind, of which we can give no account but that such is our constitution, are more in number than is commonly thought. But we ought not to multiply them without necessity.

That trains of thinking, which, by frequent repetition, have become familiar, should spontaneously offer themselves to our fancy, seems to require no other original quality but the power of habit.*

In all rational thinking, and in all rational discourse, whether serious or facetious, the thought must have some relation to what went before. Every man, therefore, in all rational discourse, must have been accustomed to a train of related objects. These please the understanding, and, by custom, become like beaten tracks which invite the traveller.

As far as it is in our power to give a direction to our thoughts, which it is undoubtedly in a great degree, they will be directed by the active principles common to men—by our appetites, our passions, our affections, our reason, and conscience. And that the trains of thinking in our minds are chiefly governed by these, according as one or another prevails at the time, every man will find in his experience.

If the mind is at any time vacant from every passion and desire, there are still some objects that are more acceptable to us than others. The facetious man is pleased with surprising similitudes or contrasts ; the philosopher with the relations of things that are subservient to reasoning ; the merchant with what tends to profit ; and the politician with what may mend the state.

A good writer of comedy or romance can feign a train of thinking for any of the persons of his fable, which appears very natural, and is approved by the best judges. Now, what is it that entitles such a fiction to approbation ? Is it that the author has given a nice attention to the relations of causation, contiguity, and similitude in the ideas ? [427] This surely is the least part of its merit. But the chief part consists in this, that it corresponds perfectly with the general character, the rank, the habits, the present situation and passions of the person. If this be a just way of judging in criticism, it follows necessarily, that the circumstances last mentioned have the chief influence in suggesting our trains of thought.

It cannot be denied, that the state of the body has an influence upon our imagination. according as a man is sober or drunk, as he is fatigued or refreshed. Crudities and indigestion are said to give uneasy dreams, and have probably a like effect upon the waking thoughts. Opium gives to some persons pleasing dreams and pleasing imaginations when awake, and to others such as are horrible and distressing.

These influences of the body upon the mind can only be known by experience, and I believe we can give no account of them.

Nor can we, perhaps, give any reason why we must think without ceasing while we are awake. I believe we are likewise originally disposed, in imagination, to pass from any one object of thought to others that are contiguous to it in time or place. This, I think, may be observed in brutes and in idiots, as well as in children, before any habit can be acquired that might account for it. The sight of an object is apt to suggest to the imagination what has been seen or felt in conjunction with it, even when the memory of that conjunction is gone.

Such conjunctions of things influence not only the imagination, but the belief and the passions, especially in children and in brutes ; and perhaps all that we call memory in brutes is something of this kind.

They expect events in the same order and succession in which they happened before ; and by this expectation, their actions and passions, as well as their thoughts, are regulated. [428] A horse takes fright at the place where some object frighted him before. We are apt to conclude from this that he remembers the former accident. But perhaps there is only an association formed in his mind between the place and the passion of fear, without any distinct remembrance.

Mr Locke has given us a very good chapter upon the association of ideas ; and by the examples he has given to illustrate this doctrine, I think it appears that very strong associations may be formed at once— not of ideas to ideas only, but of ideas to passions and emotions ; and that strong associations are never formed at once, but when accompanied by some strong passion or emotion. I believe this must be resolved into the constitution of our nature.

Mr Hume's opinion—that the complex ideas, which are the common objects of discourse and reasoning, are formed by those original attractions of ideas to which he ascribes the train of thoughts in the mind— will come under consideration in another place.

To put an end to our remarks upon this theory of Mr Hume, I think he has real merit in bringing this curious subject under

---

* We can as well explain Habit by Association, as Association by Habit.—H.

the view of philosophers, and carrying it a certain length. But I see nothing in this theory that should hinder us to conclude, that everything in the trains of our thought, which bears the marks of judgment and reason, has been the product of judgment and reason previously exercised, either by the person himself, at that or some former time, or by some other person. The attraction of ideas will be the same in a man's second thoughts upon any subject as in his first. Or, if some change in his circumstances, or in the objects about him, should make any change in the attractions of his ideas, it is an equal chance whether the second be better than the first, or whether they be worse. But it is certain that every man of judgment and taste will, upon a review, correct that train of thought which first presented itself. If the attractions of ideas are the sole causes of the regular arrangement of thought in the fancy, there is no use for judgment or taste in any composition, nor indeed any room for their operation. [429]

There are other reflections, of a more practical nature and of higher importance, to which this subject leads.

I believe it will be allowed by every man, that our happiness or misery in life, that our improvement in any art or science which we profess, and that our improvement in real virtue and goodness, depend in a very great degree on the train of thinking that occupies the mind both in our vacant and in our more serious hours. As far, therefore, as the direction of our thoughts is in our power, (and that it is so in a great measure, cannot be doubted) it is of the last importance to give them that direction which is most subservient to those valuable purposes.

What employment can he have worthy of a man, whose imagination is occupied only about things low and base, and grovels in a narrow field of mean, unanimating, and uninteresting objects, insensible to those finer and more delicate sentiments, and blind to those more enlarged and nobler views which elevate the soul, and make it conscious of its dignity.

How different from him whose imagination, like an eagle in her flight, takes a wide prospect, and observes whatever it presents, that is new or beautiful, grand or important; whose rapid wing varies the scene every moment, carrying him sometimes through the fairy regions of wit and fancy, some-

times through the more regular and sober walks of science and philosophy!

The various objects which he surveys, according to their different degrees of beauty and dignity, raise in him the lively and agreeable emotions of taste. Illustrious human characters, as they pass in review, clothed with their moral qualities, touch his heart still more deeply. They not only awaken the sense of beauty, but excite the sentiment of approbation, and kindle the glow of virtue.

While he views what is truly great and glorious in human conduct, his soul catches the divine flame, and burns with desire to emulate what it admires. [430]

The human imagination is an ample theatre, upon which everything in human life, good or bad, great or mean, laudable or base, is acted.

In children, and in some frivolous minds, it is a mere toy-shop. And in some, who exercise their memory without their judgment, its furniture is made up of old scraps of knowledge, that are thread-bare and worn out.

In some, this theatre is often occupied by ghastly superstition, with all her train of *Gorgons, and Hydras, and Chimæras dire.* Sometimes it is haunted with all the infernal demons, and made the forge of plots, and rapine, and murder. Here everything that is black and detestable is first contrived, and a thousand wicked designs conceived that are never executed. Here, too, the furies act their part, taking a severe though secret vengeance upon the self-condemned criminal.

How happy is that mind in which the light of real knowledge dispels the phantoms of superstition; in which the belief and reverence of a perfect all-governing mind casts out all fear but the fear of acting wrong; in which serenity and cheerfulness, innocence, humanity, and candour, guard the imagination against the entrance of every unhallowed intruder, and invite more amiable and worthier guests to dwell!

There all the Muses, the Graces, and the Virtues fix their abode; for everything that is great and worthy in human conduct must have been conceived in the imagination before it was brought into act. And many great and good designs have been formed there, which, for want of power and opportunity, have proved abortive.

The man whose imagination is occupied by these guests, must be wise; he must be good; and he must be happy. [431]

ESSAY V.

OF ABSTRACTION.

CHAPTER I.

OF GENERAL WORDS.

THE words we use in language are either general words or proper names. Proper names are intended to signify one individual only. Such are the names of men, kingdoms, provinces, cities, rivers, and of every other creature of God, or work of man, which we choose to distinguish from all others of the kind, by a name appropriated to it. All the other words of language are general words, not appropriated to signify any one individual thing, but equally related to many.

Under general words, therefore, I comprehend not only those which logicians call general terms—that is, such general words as may make the subject or the predicate of a proposition, but likewise their auxiliaries or accessories, as the learned Mr Harris calls them ; such as prepositions, conjunctions, articles, which are•all general words, though they cannot properly be called general terms.

In every language, rude or polished, general words make the greatest part, and proper names the least. Grammarians have reduced all words to eight or nine classes, which are called parts of speech. Of these there is only one—to wit, that of *nouns*—wherein proper names are found. [432] All *pronouns, verbs, participles, adverbs, articles, prepositions, conjunctions,* and *interjections,* are general words. Of *nouns,* all *adjectives* are general words, and the greater part of *substantives.* Every substantive that has a plural number, is a general word ; for no proper name can have a plural number, because it signifies only one individual. In all the fifteen books of Euclid's Elements, there is not one word that is not general ; and the same may be said of many large volumes.

At the same time, it must be acknowledged, that all the objects we perceive are individuals. Every object of sense, of memory, or of consciousness, is an individual object. All the good things we enjoy or desire, and all the evils we feel or fear, must come from individuals ; and I think we may venture to say, that every creature which God has made, in the heavens above, or in the earth beneath, or in the waters under the earth, is an individual.*

How comes it to pass, then, that, in all languages, general words make the greatest part of the language, and proper names but a very small and inconsiderable part of it. This seemingly strange phænomenon may, I think, be easily accounted for by the following observations :—

First, Though there be a few individuals that are obvious to the notice of all men, and, therefore, have proper names in all languages—such as the sun and moon, the earth and sea—yet the greatest part of the things to which we think fit to give proper names, are .local ; known perhaps to a village or to a neighbourhood, but unknown to the greater part of those who speak the same language, and to all the rest of mankind. The names of such things being confined to a corner, and having no names answering to them in other languages, are not accounted a part of the language, any more than the customs of a particular hamlet are accounted part of the law of the nation. [433]

For this reason, there are but few proper names that belong to a language. It is next to be considered why there must be many general words in every language.

Secondly, It may be observed, that every individual object that falls within our view has various attributes ; and it is by them that it becomes useful or hurtful to us. We know not the essence of any individual object ; all the knowledge we can attain of it, is the knowledge of its attributes—its quantity, its various qualities, its various relations to other things, its place, its situation, and motions. It is by such attributes of things only that we can communicate our knowledge of them to others. By their attributes, our hopes or fears for them are regulated ; and it is only by attention to their attributes that we can make them subservient to our ends ; and therefore we give names to such attributes.

Now, all attributes must, from their nature, be expressed by general words, and are so expressed in all languages. In the ancient philosophy, attributes in general were called by two names which express

---

* This Boethius has well expressed :—" *Omne quod est, eo quod est, singulare est.*"—H.

their nature. They were called *universals*, because they might belong equally to many individuals, and are not confined to one. They were also called *predicables*, because whatever is predicated, that is, affirmed or denied of one subject, may be of more, and therefore is an universal, and expressed by a general word. A predicable therefore signifies the same thing as an attribute, with this difference only, that the first is Latin, the last English.* The attributes we find either in the creatures of God or in the works of men, are common to many individuals. We either find it to be so, or presume it may be so, and give them the same name in every subject to which they belong.

There are not only attributes belonging to individual subjects, but there are likewise attributes of attributes, which may be called secondary attributes. Most attributes are capable of different degrees and different modifications, which must be expressed by general words. [434]

Thus it is an attribute of many bodies to be moved; but motion may be in an endless variety of directions. It may be quick or slow, rectilineal or curvilineal; it may be equable, or accelerated, or retarded.

As all attributes, therefore, whether primary or secondary, are expressed by general words, it follows that, in every proposition we express in language, what is affirmed or denied of the subject of the proposition must be expressed by general words: and that the subject of the proposition may often be a general word, will appear from the next observation.

Thirdly, The same faculties by which we distinguish the different attributes belonging to the same subject, and give names to them, enable us likewise to observe, that many subjects agree in certain attributes while they differ in others. By this means we are enabled to reduce individuals which are infinite, to a limited number of classes, which are called kinds and sorts; and, in the scholastic language, *genera* and *species.*

Observing many individuals to agree in certain attributes, we refer them all to one class, and give a name to the class. This name comprehends in its signification not one attribute only, but all the attributes which distinguish that class; and by affirming this name of any individual, we affirm it to have all the attributes which characterise the class: thus men, dogs, horses, elephants, are so many different classes of animals. In like manner we marshal other substances, vegetable and inanimate, into classes.

Nor is it only substances that we thus form into classes. We do the same with regard to qualities, relations, actions, affections, passions, and all other things.

When a class is very large, it is divided into subordinate classes in the same manner. [435] The higher class is called a *genus* or kind: the lower a *species* or sort of the higher. Sometimes a species is still subdivided into subordinate species; and this subdivision is carried on as far as is found convenient for the purpose of language, or for the improvement of knowledge.

In this distribution of things into *genera* and *species*, it is evident that the name of the species comprehends more attributes than the name of the genus. The species comprehends all that is in the genus, and those attributes likewise which distinguish that species from others belonging to the same genus; and the more subdivisions we make, the names of the lower become still the more comprehensive in their signification, but the less extensive in their application to individuals.

Hence it is an axiom in logic—that the *more extensive* any general term is, it is the *less comprehensive*; and, on the contrary, the *more comprehensive*, the *less extensive.* Thus, in the following series of subordinate general terms— Animal— Man — Frenchman—Parisian, every subsequent term comprehends in its signification all that is in the preceding, and something more; and every antecedent term extends to more individuals than the subsequent.

Such divisions and subdivisions of things into *genera* and *species* with general names, are not confined to the learned and polished languages; they are found in those of the rudest tribes of mankind. From which we learn, that the invention and the use of general words, both to signify the attributes of things, and to signify the *genera* and *species* of things, is not a subtile invention of philosophers, but an operation which all men perform by the light of common sense. Philosophers may speculate about this operation, and reduce it to canons and aphorisms; but men of common understanding, without knowing anything of the philosophy of it, can put it in practice, in like manner as they can see objects, and make good use of their eyes, although they know nothing of the structure of the eye, or of the theory of vision. [436]

Every genus, and every species of things, may be either the subject or the predicate of a proposition—nay, of innumerable propositions; for every attribute common to the genus or species may be affirmed of it; and the genus may be affirmed of every species, and both genus and species of every individual to which it extends.

Thus, of man it may be affirmed, that he

* They are both Latin, or both English. The only difference is, that the one is of technical, the other of popular application, and that the former expresses as potential what the latter does as actual.—H.

is an animal made up of body and mind; that he is of few days, and full of trouble; that he is capable of various improvements in arts, in knowledge, and in virtue. In a word, everything common to the species may be affirmed of man; and of all such propositions, which are innumerable, man is the subject.

Again, of every nation and tribe, and of every individual of the human race that is, or was, or shall be, it may be affirmed that they are men. In all such propositions, which are innumerable, man is the predicate of the proposition.

We observed above an extension and a comprehension in general terms; and that, in any subdivision of things, the name of the lowest species is most comprehensive, and that of the highest genus most extensive. I would now observe, that, by means of such general terms, there is also an extension and comprehension of propositions, which is one of the noblest powers of language, and fits it for expressing, with great ease and expedition, the highest attainments in knowledge, of which the human understanding is capable.

When the predicate is a *genus* or a *species*, the proposition is more or less comprehensive, according as the predicate is. Thus, when I say that this seal is gold, by this single proposition I affirm of it all the properties which that metal is known to have. When I say of any man that he is a mathematician, this appellation comprehends all the attributes that belong to him as an animal, as a man, and as one who has studied mathematics. When I say that the orbit of the planet Mercury is an ellipsis, I thereby affirm of that orbit all the properties which Apollonius and other geometricians have discovered, or may discover, of that species of figure. [437]

Again, when the subject of a proposition is a *genus* or a *species*, the proposition is more or less extensive, according as the subject is. Thus, when I am taught that the three angles of a plane triangle are equal to two right angles, this properly extends to every species of plane triangle, and to every individual plane triangle that did, or does, or can exist.

It is by means of such extensive and comprehensive propositions, that human knowledge is condensed, as it were, into a size adapted to the capacity of the human mind, with great addition to its beauty, and without any diminution of its distinctness and perspicuity.

General propositions in science may be compared to the seed of a plant, which, according to some philosophers, has not only the whole future plant inclosed within it, but the seeds of that plant, and the plants [437–439]

that shall spring from them through all future generations.

But the similitude falls short in this respect, that time and accidents, not in our power, must concur to disclose the contents of the seed, and bring them into our view; whereas the contents of a general proposition may be brought forth, ripened, and exposed to view at our pleasure, and in an instant.

Thus the wisdom of ages, and the most sublime theorems of science, may be laid up, like an Iliad in a nut-shell, and transmitted to future generations. And this noble purpose of language can only be accomplished by means of general words annexed to the divisions and subdivisions of things. [438]

What has been said in this chapter, I think, is sufficient to shew that there can be no language, not so much as a single proposition, without general words; that they must make the greatest part of every language; and that it is by them only that language is fitted to express, with wonderful ease and expedition, all the treasures of human wisdom and knowledge.

CHAPTER II.

OF GENERAL CONCEPTIONS.

As general words are so necessary in language, it is natural to conclude that there must be general conceptions, of which they are the signs.

Words are empty sounds when they do not signify the thoughts of the speaker; and it is only from their signification that they are denominated general. Every word that is spoken, considered merely as a sound, is an individual sound. And it can only be called a general word, because that which it signifies is general. Now, that which it signifies, is conceived by the mind both of the speaker and hearer, if the word have a distinct meaning, and be distinctly understood. It is, therefore, impossible that words can have a general signification, unless there be conceptions in the mind of the speaker and of the hearer, of things that are general. It is to such that I give the name of general conceptions; and it ought to be observed, that they take this denomination, not from the act of the mind in conceiving, which is an individual act, but from the object or thing conceived, which is general.

We are, therefore, here to consider whether we have such general conceptions, and how they are formed. [439]

To begin with the conceptions expressed by general terms—that is, by such general words as may be the subject or the predicate of a proposition. They are either attributes of things, or they are *genera* or *species* of things.

It is evident, with respect to all the individuals we are acquainted with that we have a more clear and distinct conception of their attributes than of the subject to which those attributes belong.

Take, for instance, any individual body we have access to know—what conception do we form of it? Every man may know this from his consciousness. He will find that he conceives it as a thing that has length, breadth, and thickness, such a figure and such a colour; that it is hard, or soft, or fluid; that it has such qualities, and is fit for such purposes. If it is a vegetable, he may know where it grew, what is the form of its leaves, and flower, and seed. If an animal, what are its natural instincts, its manner of life, and of rearing its young. Of these attributes, belonging to this individual and numberless others, he may surely have a distinct conception; and he will find words in language by which he can clearly and distinctly express each of them.

If we consider, in like manner, the conception we form of any individual person of our acquaintance, we shall find it to be made up of various attributes, which we ascribe to him; such as, that he is the son of such a man, the brother of such another; that he has such an employment or office; has such a fortune; that he is tall or short, well or ill made, comely or ill favoured, young or old, married or unmarried; to this we may add his temper, his character, his abilities, and perhaps some anecdotes of his history.

Such is the conception we form of individual persons of our acquaintance. By such attributes we describe them to those who know them not; and by such attributes historians give us a conception of the personages of former times. Nor is it possible to do it in any other way. [440]

All the distinct knowledge we have or can attain of any individual is the knowledge of its attributes; for we know not the essence of any individual. This seems to be beyond the reach of the human faculties.

Now, every attribute is what the ancients called an universal. It is, or may be, common to various individuals. There is no attribute belonging to any creature of God which may not belong to others; and, on this account, attributes, in all languages, are expressed by general words.

It appears, likewise, from every man's experience, that he may have as clear and distinct a conception of such attributes as we have named, and of innumerable others, as he can have of any individual to which they belong.

Indeed, the attributes of individuals is all

that we distinctly conceive about them. It is true, we conceive a subject to which the attributes belong; but of this subject, when its attributes are set aside, we have but an obscure and relative[*] conception, whether it be body or mind.

This was before observed with regard to bodies, Essay II. chap. 19, [p. 322] to which we refer; and it is no less evident with regard to minds. What is it we call a mind? It is a thinking, intelligent, active being. Granting that thinking, intelligence, and activity, are attributes of mind, I want to know what the thing or being is to which these attributes belong? To this question I can find no satisfying answer. The attributes of mind, and particularly its operations, we know clearly; but of the thing itself we have only an obscure notion. [441]

Nature teaches us that thinking and reasoning are attributes, which cannot exist without a subject; but of that subject I believe the best notion we can form implies little more than that it is the subject of such attributes.

Whether other created beings may have the knowledge of the real essence of created things, so as to be able to deduce their attributes from their essence and constitution, or whether this be the prerogative of him who made them, we cannot tell; but it is a knowledge which seems to be quite beyond the reach of the human faculties.

We know the essence of a triangle, and from that essence can deduce its properties. It is an universal, and might have been conceived by the human mind though no individual triangle had ever existed. It has only what Mr Locke calls a nominal essence, which is expressed in its definition. But everything that exists has a real essence, which is above our comprehension; and, therefore, we cannot deduce its properties or attributes from its nature, as we do in the triangle. We must take a contrary road in the knowledge of God's works, and satisfy ourselves with their attributes as facts, and with the general conviction that there is a subject to which those attributes belong.

Enough, I think, has been said, to shew, not only that we may have clear and distinct conceptions of attributes, but that they are the only things, with regard to individuals, of which we have a clear and distinct conception.

The other class of general terms are those that signify the *genera* and *species* into which we divide and subdivide things. And, if we be able to form distinct conceptions of attributes, it cannot surely be denied that we may have distinct conceptions of *genera*

---

* See above, p. 322, note.—H.

and *species* ; because they are only collections of attributes which we conceive to exist in a subject, and to which we give a general name. [442] If the attributes comprehended under that general name be distinctly conceived, the thing meant by the name must be distinctly conceived. And the name may justly be attributed to every individual which has those attributes.

Thus, I conceive distinctly what it is to have wings, to be covered with feathers, to lay eggs. Suppose then that we give the name of *bird* to every animal that has these three attributes. Here undoubtedly my conception of a bird is as distinct as my notion of the attributes which are common to this species : and, if this be admitted to be the definition of a bird, there is nothing I conceive more distinctly. If I had never seen a bird, and can but be made to understand the definition, I can easily apply it to every individual of the species, without danger of mistake.

When things are divided and subdivided by men of science, and names given to the *genera* and *species*, those names are defined. Thus, the genera and species of plants, and of other natural bodies, are accurately defined by the writers in the various branches of natural history ; so that, to all future generations, the definition will convey a distinct notion of the genus or species defined.

There are, without doubt, many words signifying genera and species of things, which have a meaning somewhat vague and indistinct ; so that those who speak the same language do not always use them in the same sense. But, if we attend to the cause of this indistinctness, we shall find that it is not owing to their being general terms, but to this, that there is no definition of them that has authority. Their meaning, therefore, has not been learned by a definition, but by a kind of induction, by observing to what individuals they are applied by those who understand the language. We learn by habit to use them as we see others do, even when we have not a precise meaning annexed to them. A man may know that to certain individuals they may be applied with propriety ; but whether they can be applied to certain other individuals, he may be uncertain, either from want of good authorities, or from having contrary authorities, which leave him in doubt. [443]

Thus, a man may know that, when he applies the name of beast to a lion or a tiger, and the name of bird to an eagle or a turkey, he speaks properly. But whether a bat be a bird or a beast, he may be uncertain. If there was any accurate definition of a beast and of a bird, that was of sufficient authority, he could be at no loss.

It is said to have been sometimes a matter of dispute, with regard to a monstrous birth of a woman, whether it was a man or not. Although this be, in reality, a question about the meaning of a word, it may be of importance, on account of the privileges which laws have annexed to the human character. To make such laws perfectly precise, the definition of a man would be necessary, which I believe legislators have seldom or never thought fit to give. It is, indeed, very difficult to fix a definition of so common a word ; and the cases wherein it would be of any use so rarely occur, that perhaps it may be better, when they do occur, to leave them to the determination of a judge or of a jury, than to give a definition, which might be attended with unforeseen consequences.

A genus or species, being a collection of attributes conceived to exist in one subject, a definition is the only way to prevent any addition or diminution of its ingredients in the conception of different persons ; and when there is no definition that can be appealed to as a standard, the name will hardly retain the most perfect precision in its signification.

From what has been said, I conceive it is evident that the words which signify genera and species of things have often as precise and definite a signification as any words whatsoever ; and that, when it is otherwise, their want of precision is not owing to their being general words, but to other causes. [444]

Having shewn that we may have a perfectly clear and distinct conception of the meaning of general terms, we may, I think, take it for granted, that the same may be said of other general words, such as prepositions, conjunctions, articles. My design at present being only to shew that we have general conceptions no less clear and distinct than those of individuals, it is sufficient for this purpose, if this appears with regard to the conceptions expressed by general terms. To conceive the meaning of a general word, and to conceive that which it signifies, is the same thing. We conceive distinctly the meaning of general terms, therefore we conceive distinctly that which they signify. But such terms do not signify any individual, but what is common to many individuals ; therefore, we have a distinct conception of things common to many individuals—that is, we have distinct general conceptions.

We must here beware of the ambiguity of the word *conception*, which sometimes signifies the act of the mind in conceiving, sometimes the thing conceived, which is the object of that act.* If the word be taken

It is said to have been sometimes a matter

[442—444]

---

* "This last should be called *Concept*, which was a term in use with the old English philosophers.— H.

in the first sense, I acknowledge that every act of the mind is an individual act; the universality, therefore, is not in the act of the mind, but in the object or thing conceived. The thing conceived is an attribute common to many subjects, or it is a genus or species common to many individuals.

Suppose I conceive a triangle—that is, a plain figure, terminated by three right lines. He that understands this definition distinctly, has a distinct conception of a triangle. But a triangle is not an individual; it is a species. The act of my understanding in conceiving it is an individual act, and has a real existence; but the thing conceived is general, and cannot exist without other attributes, which are not included in the definition. [445] Every triangle that really exists must have a certain length of sides and measure of angles; it must have place and time. But the definition of a triangle includes neither existence nor any of those attributes; and, therefore, they are not included in the conception of a triangle, which cannot be accurate if it comprehend more than the definition.

Thus, I think, it appears to be evident, that we have general conceptions that are clear and distinct, both of attributes of things, and of genera and species of things.

CHAPTER III.

OF GENERAL CONCEPTIONS FORMED BY ANALYSING OBJECTS.

WE are next to consider the operations of the understanding, by which we are enabled to form general conceptions.

These appear to me to be three :—*First*, The resolving or analysing a subject into its known attributes, and giving a name to each attribute, which name shall signify that attribute, and nothing more.

Secondly, The observing one or more such attributes to be common to many subjects. The first is by philosophers called *abstraction;* the second may be called *generalising;* but both are commonly included under the name of *abstraction.*

It is difficult to say which of them goes first, or whether they are not so closely connected that neither can claim the precedence. For, on the one hand, to perceive an agreement between two or more objects in the same attribute, seems to require nothing more than to compare them together. [446] A savage, upon seeing snow and chalk, would find no difficulty in perceiving that they have the same colour. Yet, on the other hand, it seems impossible that he should observe this agreement without

abstraction—that is, distinguishing in his conception the colour, wherein those two objects agree, from the other qualities wherein they disagree.

It seems, therefore, that we cannot generalise without some degree of abstraction; but I apprehend we may abstract without generalising. For what hinders me from attending to the whiteness of the paper before me, without applying that colour to any other object. The whiteness of this individual object is an abstract conception, but not a general one, while applied to one individual only. These two operations, however, are subservient to each other; for the more attributes we observe and distinguish in any one individual, the more agreements we shall discover between it and other individuals.

A *third* operation of the understanding, by which we form abstract conceptions, is the combining into one whole a certain number of those attributes of which we have formed abstract notions, and giving a name to that combination. It is thus we form abstract notions of the genera and species of things. These three operations we shall consider in order.

With regard to abstraction, strictly so called, I can perceive nothing in it that is difficult either to be understood or practised. What can be more easy than to distinguish the different attributes which we know to belong to a subject? In a man, for instance, to distinguish his size, his complexion, his age, his fortune, his birth, his profession, and twenty other things that belong to him. To think and speak of these things with understanding, is surely within the reach of every man endowed with the human faculties. [447]

There may be distinctions that require nice discernment, or an acquaintance with the subject that is not common. Thus, a critic in painting may discern the style of Raphael or Titian, when another man could not. A lawyer may be acquainted with many distinctions in crimes, and contracts, and actions, which never occurred to a man who has not studied law. One man may excel another in the talent of distinguishing, as he may in memory or in reasoning; but there is a certain degree of this talent, without which a man would have no title to be considered as a reasonable creature.

It ought likewise to be observed, that attributes may, with perfect ease, be distinguished and disjoined in our conception, which cannot be actually separated in the subject. Thus, in a body, I can distinguish its solidity from its extension, and its weight from both. In extension I can distinguish length, breadth, and thickness; yet none of these can be separated from the body, or from one another. There may be attributes belonging to a subject, and inseparable from it, of which we have no knowledge, and consequently no conception; but this does not hinder our conceiving distinctly those of its attributes which we know.

Thus, all the properties of a circle are inseparable from the nature of a circle, and may be demonstrated from its definition; yet a man may have a perfectly distinct notion of a circle, who knows very few of those properties of it which mathematicians have demonstrated; and a circle probably has many properties which no mathematician ever dreamed of.

It is therefore certain that attributes, which in their nature are absolutely inseparable from their subject and from one another, may be disjoined in our conception; one cannot exist without the other, but one can be conceived without the other.

Having considered abstraction, strictly so called, let us next consider the operation of generalising, which is nothing but the observing one or more attributes to be common to many subjects. [448]

If any man can doubt whether there be attributes that are really common to many individuals, let him consider whether there be not many men that are above six feet high, and many below it; whether there be not many men that are rich, and many more that are poor; whether there be not many that were born in Britain, and many that were born in France. To multiply instances of this kind, would be to affront the reader's understanding. It is certain, therefore, that there are innumerable attributes that are really common to many individuals; and if this be what the schoolmen called *universale a parte rei*, we may affirm with certainty that there are such universals.

There are some attributes expressed by general words, of which this may seem more doubtful. Such are the qualities which are inherent in their several subjects. It may be said that every subject hath its own qualities, and that which is the quality of one subject cannot be the quality of another subject. Thus the whiteness of the sheet of paper upon which I write, cannot be the whiteness of another sheet, though both are called white. The weight of one guinea is not the weight of another guinea, though both are said to have the same weight.

To this I answer, that the whiteness of this sheet is one thing, whiteness is another; the conceptions signified by these two forms of speech are as different as the expressions. The first signifies an individual quality really existing, and is not a general conception, though it be an abstract one: the second signifies a general conception, which implies no existence, but may be predicated of everything that is white, and in the [448-450]

same sense. On this account, if one should say that the whiteness of this sheet is the whiteness of another sheet, every man perceives this to be absurd; but when he says both sheets are white, this is true and perfectly understood. The conception of whiteness implies no existence; it would remain the same though everything in the universe that is white were annihilated. [449]

It appears, therefore, that the general names of qualities, as well as of other attributes, are applicable to many individuals in the same sense, which cannot be if there be not general conceptions signified by such names.

If it should be asked, how early, or at what period of life men begin to form general conceptions? I answer, As soon as a child can say, with understanding, that he has two brothers or two sisters—as soon as he can use the plural number—he must have general conceptions; for no individual can have a plural number.

As there are not two individuals in nature that agree in everything, so there are very few that do not agree in some things. We take pleasure from very early years in observing such agreements. One great branch of what we call *wit*, which, when innocent, gives pleasure to every good-natured man, consists in discovering unexpected agreements in things. The author of Hudibras could discern a property common to the morning and a boiled lobster—that both turn from black to red. Swift could see something common to wit and an old cheese. Such unexpected agreements may shew wit; but there are innumerable agreements of things which cannot escape the notice of the lowest understanding; such as agreements in colour, magnitude, figure, features, time, place, age, and so forth. These agreements are the foundation of so many common attributes, which are found in the rudest languages.

The ancient philosophers called these universals, or predicables, and endeavoured to reduce them to five classes—to wit, Genus, Species, Specific Difference, Properties, and Accidents. Perhaps there may be more classes of universals or attributes—for enumerations, so very general, are seldom complete: but every attribute, common to several individuals, may be expressed by a general term, which is the sign of a general conception. [450]

How prone men are to form general conceptions we may see from the use of metaphor, and of the other figures of speech grounded on similitude. Similitude is nothing else than an agreement of the objects compared in one or more attributes, and if there be no attribute common to both, there can be no similitude.

The similitudes and analogies between

the various objects that nature presents to us, are infinite and inexhaustible. They not only please, when displayed by the poet or wit in works of taste, but they are highly useful in the ordinary communication of our thoughts and sentiments by language. In the rude languages of barbarous nations, similitudes and analogies supply the want of proper words to express men's sentiments, so much that in such languages there is hardly a sentence without a metaphor; and, if we examine the most copious and polished languages, we shall find that a great proportion of the words and phrases which are accounted the most proper, may be said to be the progeny of metaphor.

As foreigners, who settle in a nation as their home, come at last to be incorporated and lose the denomination of foreigners, so words and phrases, at first borrowed and figurative, by long use become denizens in the language, and lose the denomination of figures of speech. When we speak of the extent of knowledge, the steadiness of virtue, the tenderness of affection, the perspicuity of expression, no man conceives these to be metaphorical expressions; they are as proper as any in the language: yet it appears upon the very face of them, that they must have been metaphorical in those who used them first; and that it is by use and prescription that they have lost the denomination of figurative, and acquired a right to be considered as proper words. This observation will be found to extend to a great part, perhaps the greatest part of the words of the most perfect languages. Sometimes the name of an individual is given to a general conception, and thereby the individual in a manner generalised; as when the Jew Shylock, in Shakespeare, says— " A Daniel come to judgment; yea, a Daniel!" In this speech, " a Daniel" is an attribute, or an universal. The character of Daniel, as a man of singular wisdom, is abstracted from his person, and considered as capable of being attributed to other persons. [451]

Upon the whole, these two operations of abstracting and generalising appear common to all men that have understanding. The practice of them is, and must be, familiar to every man that uses language; but it is one thing to practise them, and another to explain how they are performed; as it is one thing to see, another to explain how we see. The first is the province of all men, and is the natural and easy operation of the faculties which God hath given us. The second is the province of philosophers, and, though a matter of no great difficulty in itself, has been much perplexed by the ambiguity of words, and still more by the hypotheses of philosophers.

Thus, when I consider a billiard ball, its colour is one attribute, which I signify by calling it white; its figure is another, which is signified by calling it spherical; the firm cohesion of its parts is signified by calling it hard; its recoiling, when it strikes a hard body, is signified by its being called elastic; its origin, as being part of the tooth of an elephant, is signified by calling it ivory; and its use by calling it a billiard ball.

The words by which each of those attributes is signified, have one distinct meaning, and in this meaning are applicable to many individuals. They signify not any individual thing, but attributes common to many individuals; nor is it beyond the capacity of a child to understand them perfectly, and to apply them properly to every individual in which they are found.

As it is by analysing a complex object into its several attributes that we acquire our simplest abstract conceptions, it may be proper to compare this analysis with that which a chemist makes of a compounded body into the ingredients which enter into its composition; for, although there be such an analogy between these two operations, that we give to both the name of analysis or resolution, there is, at the same time, so great a dissimilitude in some respects, that we may be led into error, by applying to one what belongs to the other. [452]

It is obvious that the chemical analysis is an operation of the hand upon matter, by various material instruments. The analysis we are now explaining, is purely an operation of the understanding, which requires no material instrument, nor produces any change upon any external thing; we shall, therefore, call it the intellectual or mental analysis.

In the chemical analysis, the compound body itself is the subject analysed. A subject so imperfectly known that it may be compounded of various ingredients, when to our senses it appears perfectly simple;* and even when we are able to analyse it into the different ingredients of which it is composed, we know not how or why the combination of those ingredients produces such a body.

Thus, pure sea-salt is a body, to appearance as simple as any in nature. Every the least particle of it, discernible by our senses, is perfectly similar to every other particle in all its qualities. The nicest taste, the quickest eye, can discern no mark of its being made up of different ingredients; yet, by the chemical art, it can be analysed into an acid and an alkali, and can be again produced by the combination of those two ingredients. But how this combination produces sea-salt, no man has been able to discover. The ingredients are both as unlike

---

* Something seems wanting in this clause.—H.

the compound as any bodies we know. No man could have guessed, before the thing was known, that sea-salt is compounded of those two ingredients; no man could have guessed that the union of those two ingredients should produce such a compound as sea-salt. Such, in many cases, are the phænomena of the chemical analysis of a compound body. [453]

If we consider the intellectual analysis of an object, it is evident that nothing of this kind can happen; because while the thing analysed is not an external object imperfectly known; it is a conception of the mind itself. And, to suppose that there can be anything in a conception that is not conceived, is a contradiction.

The reason of observing this difference between those two kinds of analysis is, that some philosophers, in order to support their systems, have maintained that a complex idea may have the appearance of the most perfect simplicity, and retain no similitude of any of the simple ideas of which it is compounded; just as a white colour may appear perfectly simple, and retain no similitude to any of the seven primary colours of which it is compounded; or as a chemical composition may appear perfectly simple, and retain no similitude to any of the ingredients.

From which those philosophers have drawn this important conclusion, that a cluster of the ideas of sense, properly combined, may make the idea of a mind; and that all the ideas which Mr Locke calls ideas of reflection, are only compositions of the ideas which we have by our five senses. From this the transition is easy, that, if a proper composition of the ideas of matter may make the idea of a mind, then a proper composition of matter itself may make a mind, and that man is only a piece of matter curiously formed.

In this curious system, the whole fabric rests upon this foundation, that a complex idea, which is made up of various simple ideas, may appear to be perfectly simple, and to have no marks of composition, because a compound body may appear to our senses to be perfectly simple.

Upon this fundamental proposition of this system I beg leave to make two remarks. [454]

1. Supposing it to be true, it affirms only what *may be*. We are, indeed, in most cases very imperfect judges of what may be. But this we know, that, were we ever so certain that a thing may be, this is no good reason for believing that it really is. A *may-be* is a mere hypothesis, which may furnish matter of investigation, but is not entitled to the least degree of belief. The transition from what may be to what really is, is familiar and easy to those who have a

[453–455]

predilection for a hypothesis; but to a man who seeks truth without prejudice or prepossession, it is a very wide and difficult step, and he will never pass from the one to the other, without evidence not only that the thing may be, but that it really is.

2. As far as I am able to judge, this, which it is said may be, cannot be. That a complex idea should be made up of simple ideas; so that to a ripe understanding reflecting upon that idea, there should be no appearance of composition, nothing similar to the simple ideas of which it is compounded, seems to me to involve a contradiction. The idea is a conception of the mind. If anything more than this is meant by the idea, I know not what it is; and I wish both to know what it is, and to have proof of its existence. Now, that there should be anything in the conception of an object which is not conceived, appears to me as manifest a contradiction as that there should be an existence which does not exist, or that a thing should be conceived and not conceived at the same time.

But, say these philosophers, a white colour is produced by the composition of the primary colours, and yet has no resemblance to any of them. I grant it. But what can be inferred from this with regard to the composition of ideas? To bring this argument home to the point, they must say, that because a white colour is compounded of the primary colours, therefore the idea of a white colour is compounded of the ideas of the primary colours. This reasoning, if it was admitted, would lead to innumerable absurdities. An opaque fluid may be compounded of two or more pellucid fluids. Hence, we might infer, with equal force, that the idea of an opaque fluid may be compounded of the idea of two or more pellucid fluids. [455]

Nature's way of compounding bodies, and our way of compounding ideas, are so different in many respects, that we cannot reason from the one to the other, unless it can be found that ideas are combined by fermentations and elective attractions, and may be analysed in a furnace by the force of fire and of menstruums. Until this discovery be made, we must hold those to be simple ideas, which, upon the most attentive reflection, have no appearance of composition; and those only to be the ingredients of complex ideas, which, by attentive reflection, can be perceived to be contained in them.

If the idea of mind and its operations, may be compounded of the ideas of matter and its qualities, why may not the idea of matter be compounded of the ideas of mind? There is the same evidence for the last *may-be* as for the first. And why may not the idea of sound be compounded of the ideas of colour; or the idea of colour of those of sound? Why may not the idea of wisdom be compounded of ideas of folly; or the idea of truth of ideas of absurdity? But we leave these mysterious *may-bes* to them that have faith to receive them.

CHAPTER IV.

OF GENERAL CONCEPTIONS FORMED BY COMBINATION.

As, by an intellectual analysis of objects, we form general conceptions of single attributes, (which, of all conceptions that enter into the human mind, are the most simple,) so, by combining several of these into one parcel, and giving a name to that combination, we form general conceptions that may be very complex, and, at the same time, very distinct. [456]

Thus, one who, by analysing extended objects, has got the simple notions of a point, a line, straight or curve, an angle, a surface, a solid, can easily conceive a plain surface, terminated by four equal straight lines, meeting in four points at right angles. To this species of figure he gives the name of a square. In like manner, he can conceive a solid terminated by six equal squares, and give it the name of a cube. A square, a cube, and every name of mathematical figure, is a general term, expressing a complex general conception, made by a certain combination of the simple elements into which we analyse extended bodies.

Every mathematical figure is accurately defined, by enumerating the simple elements of which it is formed, and the manner of their combination. The definition contains the whole essence of it. And every property that belongs to it may be deduced by demonstrative reasoning from its definition. It is not a thing that exists, for then it would be an individual; but it is a thing that is conceived without regard to existence.

A farm, a manor, a parish, a county, a kingdom, are complex general conceptions, formed by various combinations and modifications of inhabited territory, under certain forms of government.

Different combinations of military men form the notions of a company, a regiment, an army.

The several crimes which are the objects of criminal law, such as theft, murder, robbery, piracy, what are they but certain combinations of human actions and intentions, which are accurately defined in criminal law, and which it is found convenient to comprehend under one name, and consider as one thing?

When we observe that nature, in her animal, vegetable, and inanimate productions, has formed many individuals that agree in many of their qualities and attributes, we are led by natural instinct to expect their agreement in other qualities, which we have not had occasion to perceive. [457] Thus, a child who has once burnt his finger, by putting it in the flame of one candle, expects the same event if he puts it in the flame of another candle, or in any flame, and is thereby led to think that the quality of burning belongs to all flame. This instinctive induction is not justified by the rules of logic, and it sometimes leads men into harmless mistakes, which experience may afterwards correct; but it preserves us from destruction in innumerable dangers to which we are exposed.

The reason of taking notice of this principle in human nature in this place is, that the distribution of the productions of nature into *genera* and *species* becomes, on account of this principle, more generally useful.

The physician expects that the rhubarb which has never yet been tried will have like medical virtues with that which he has prescribed on former occasions. Two parcels of rhubarb agree in certain sensible qualities, from which agreement they are both called by the same general name *rhubarb*. Therefore it is expected that they will agree in their medical virtues. And, as experience has discovered certain virtues in one parcel, or in many parcels, we presume, without experience, that the same virtues belong to all parcels of rhubarb that shall be used.

If a traveller meets a horse, an ox, or a sheep, which he never saw before, he is under no apprehension, believing these animals to be of a species that is tame and inoffensive. But he dreads a lion or a tiger, because they are of a fierce and ravenous species.

We are capable of receiving innumerable advantages, and are exposed to innumerable dangers, from the various productions of nature, animal, vegetable, and inanimate. The life of man, if an hundred times longer than it is, would be insufficient to learn from experience the useful and hurtful qualities of every individual production of nature taken singly. [458] The Author of Nature hath made provision for our attaining that knowledge of his works which is necessary for our subsistence and preservation, partly by the constitution of the productions of nature, and partly by the constitution of the human mind.

For, *first*. In the productions of nature, great numbers of individuals are made so like to one another, both in their obvious and in their more occult qualities, that we are not only enabled, but invited, as it were,

[456—458]

to reduce them into classes, and to give a general name to a class; a name which is common to every individual of the class, because it comprehends in its signification those qualities or attributes only that are common to all the individuals of that class.

Secondly, The human mind is so framed, that, from the agreement of individuals in the more obvious qualities by which we reduce them into one class, we are naturally led to expect that they will be found to agree in their more latent qualities—and in this we are seldom disappointed.

We have, therefore, a strong and rational inducement, both to distribute natural substances into classes, *genera* and *species*, under general names, and to do this with all the accuracy and distinctness we are able. For the more accurate our divisions are made, and the more distinctly the several species are defined, the more securely we may rely that the qualities we find in one or in a few individuals will be found in all of the same species.

Every species of natural substances which has a name in language, is an attribute of many individuals, and is itself a combination of more simple attributes, which we observe to be common to those individuals. [459]

We shall find a great part of the words of every language—nay, I apprehend, the far greater part—to signify combinations of more simple general conceptions, which men have found proper to be bound up, as it were, in one parcel, by being designed by one name.

Some general conceptions there are, which may more properly be called *compositions* or *works* than mere combinations. Thus, one may conceive a machine which never existed. He may conceive an air in music, a poem, a plan of architecture, a plan of government, a plan of conduct in public or in private life, a sentence, a discourse, a treatise. Such compositions are things conceived in the mind of the author, not individuals that really exist; and the same general conception which the author had, may be communicated to others by language.

Thus, the "Oceana" of Harrington was conceived in the mind of its author. The materials of which it is composed are things conceived, not things that existed. His senate, his popular assembly, his magistrates, his elections, are all conceptions of his mind, and the whole is one complex conception. And the same may be said of every work of the human understanding.

Very different from these are the works of God, which we behold. They are works of creative power, not of understanding only. They have a real existence. Our best conceptions of them are partial and imperfect. But of the works of the human understanding our conception may be perfect and complete. They are nothing but what the author conceived, and what he can express by language, so as to convey his conception perfectly to men like himself.

Although such works are indeed complex general conceptions, they do not so properly belong to our present subject. They are more the objects of judgment and of taste, than of bare conception or simple apprehension. [460]

To return, therefore, to those complex conceptions which are formed merely by combining those that are more simple. Nature has given us the power of combining such simple attributes, and such a number of them as we find proper; and of giving one name to that combination, and considering it as one object of thought.

The simple attributes of things, which fall under our observation, are not so numerous but that they may all have names in a copious language. But to give names to all the combinations that can be made of two, three, or more of them, would be impossible. The most copious languages have names but for a very small part.

It may likewise be observed, that the combinations that have names are nearly though not perfectly, the same in the different languages of civilized nations that have intercourse with one another. Hence it is, that the Lexicographer, for the most part, can give words in one language answering perfectly, or very nearly, to those of another; and what is written in a simple style in one language, can be translated almost word for word into another *

From these observations we may conclude that there are either certain common principles of human nature, or certain common occurrences of human life, which dispose men, out of an infinite number that might be formed, to form certain combinations rather than others.

Mr Hume, in order to account for this phænomenon, has recourse to what he calls the associating qualities of ideas; to wit, *causation, contiguity in time and place, and similitude.* He conceives—"That one of the most remarkable effects of those associating qualities, is the complex ideas which are the common subjects of our thoughts. That this also is the cause why languages so nearly correspond to one another; Nature in a manner pointing out to every one those ideas which are most proper to be united into a complex one." [461]

I agree with this ingenious author, that Nature in a manner points out those simple ideas which are most proper to be united into a complex one : but Nature does this, not solely or chiefly by the relations between the simple ideas of contiguity, causation,

---

* This is only strictly true of the words relative to objects of sense.—H.

[459–461]

causation, and resemblance ; but rather by the fitness of the combinations we make, to aid our own conceptions, and to convey them to others by language easily and agreeably.

The end and use of language, without regard to the associating qualities of ideas, will lead men that have common understanding to form such complex notions as are proper for expressing their wants, their thoughts, and their desires : and in every language we shall find these to be the complex notions that have names.

In the rudest state of society, men must have occasion to form the general notions of man, woman, father, mother, son, daughter, sister, brother, neighbour, friend, enemy, and many others, to express the common relations of one person to another.

If they are employed in hunting, they must have general terms to express the various implements and operations of the chase. Their houses and clothing, however simple, will furnish another set of general terms, to express the materials, the workmanship, and the excellencies and defects of those fabrics. If they sail upon rivers or upon the sea, this will give occasion to a great number of general terms, which otherwise would never have occurred to their thoughts.

The same thing may be said of agriculture, of pasturage, of every art they practise, and of every branch of knowledge they attain. The necessity of general terms for communicating our sentiments is obvious ; and the invention of them, as far as we find them necessary, requires no other talent but that degree of understanding which is common to men. [462]

The notions of debtor and creditor, of profit and loss, of account, balance, stock on hand, and many others, are owing to commerce. The notions of latitude, longitude, course, distance, run, and those of ships, and of their various parts, furniture, and operations, are owing to navigation. The anatomist must have names for the various similar and dissimilar parts of the human body, and words to express their figure, position, structure, and use. The physician must have names for the various diseases of the body, their causes, symptoms, and means of cure.

The like may be said of the grammarian, the logician, the critic, the rhetorician, the moralist, the naturalist, the mechanic, and every man that professes any art or science.

When any discovery is made in art or in nature, which requires new combinations and new words to express it properly, the invention of these is easy to those who have a distinct notion of the thing to be expressed ; and such words will readily be adopted, and receive the public sanction.

If, on the other hand, any man of eminence, through vanity or want of judgment, should invent new words, to express combinations that have neither beauty nor utility, or which may as well be expressed in the current language, his authority may give them currency for a time with servile imitators or blind admirers ; but the judicious will laugh at them, and they will soon lose their credit. So true was the observation made by Pomponius Marcellus, an ancient grammarian, to Tiberius Cæsar :— " You, Cæsar, have power to make a man a denizen of Rome, but not to make a word a denizen of the Roman language."*

Among nations that are civilized, and have intercourse with one another, the most necessary and useful arts will be common ; the important parts of human knowledge will be common ; their several languages will be fitted to it, and consequently to one another.   [463]

New inventions of general use give an easy birth to new complex notions and new names, which spread as far as the invention does. How many new complex notions have been formed, and names for them invented in the languages of Europe, by the modern inventions of printing, of gunpowder, of the mariner's compass, of optical glasses ? The simple ideas combined in those complex notions, and the associating qualities of those ideas, are very ancient ; but they never produced those complex notions until there was use for them.

What is peculiar to a nation in its customs, manners, or laws, will give occasion to complex notions and words peculiar to the language of that nation. Hence it is easy to see why an impeachment, and an attainder, in the English language, and ostracism in the Greek language, have not names answering to them in other languages.

I apprehend, therefore, that it is utility, and not the associating qualities of the ideas, that has led men to form only certain combinations, and to give names to them in language, while they neglect an infinite number that might be formed.

The common occurrences of life, in the intercourse of men, and in their occupations, give occasion to many complex notions. We see an individual occurrence, which draws our attention more or less, and may be a subject of conversation. Other occurrences, similar to this in many respects, have been observed, or may be expected. It is convenient that we should be able to speak of what is common to them all, leaving out the unimportant cir-

---

* " Tu, Cæsar, civitatem dare potes hominibus, verbis non potes." See Suetonius *De Illust. Gram. mat.*, c. 22.—H.

cumstances of time, place, and persons. This we can do with great ease, by giving a name to what is common to all those individual occurrences. Such a name is a great aid to language, because it comprehends, in one word, a great number of simple notions, which it would be very tedious to express in detail. [464]

Thus, men have formed the complex notions of eating, drinking, sleeping, walking, riding, running, buying, selling, ploughing, sowing, a dance, a feast, war, a battle, victory, triumph ; and others, without number.

Such things must frequently be the subject of conversation ; and, if we had not a more compendious way of expressing them than by a détail of all the simple notions they comprehend, we should lose the benefit of speech.

The different talents, dispositions, and habits of men in society, being interesting to those who have to do with them, will in every language have general names—such as wise, foolish, knowing, ignorant, plain, cunning. In every operative art, the tools, instruments, materials, the work produced, and the various excellencies and defects of these, must have general names.

The various relations of persons, and of things which cannot escape the observation of men in society, lead us to many complex general notions ; such as father, brother, friend, enemy, master, servant, property, theft, rebellion.

The terms of art in the sciences make another class of general names of complex notions ; as in mathematics, axiom, definition, problem, theorem, demonstration.

I do not attempt a complete enumeration even of the classes of complex general conceptions. Those I have named as a specimen, I think, are mostly comprehended under what Mr Locke calls mixed modes and relations ; which, he justly observes, have names given them in language, in preference to innumerable others that might be formed ; for this reason only, that they are useful for the purpose of communicating our thoughts by language. [465]

In all the languages of mankind, not only the writings and discourses of the learned, but the conversation of the vulgar, is almost entirely made up of general words, which are the signs of general conceptions, either simple or complex. And in every language, we find the terms signifying complex notions to be such, and only such, as the use of language requires.

There remains a very large class of complex general terms, on which I shall make some observations ; I mean those by which we name the species, genera, and tribes of natural substances.

It is utility, indeed, that leads us to give

general names to the various species of natural substances ; but, in combining the attributes which are included under the specific name, we are more aided and directed by nature than in forming other combinations of mixed modes and relations. In the last, the ingredients are brought together in the occurrences of life, or in the actions or thoughts of men. But, in the first, the ingredients are united by nature in many individual substances which God has made. We form a general notion of those attributes wherein many individuals agree. We give a specific name to this combination, which name is common to all substances having those attributes, which either do or may exist. The specific name comprehends neither more nor fewer attributes than we find proper to put into its definition. It comprehends not time, nor place, nor even existence, although there can be no individual without these.

This work of the understanding is absolutely necessary for speaking intelligibly of the productions of nature, and for reaping the benefits we receive, and avoiding the dangers we are exposed to from them. The individuals are so many, that to give a proper name to each would be beyond the power of language. If a good or bad quality was observed in an individual, of how small use would this be, if there was not a species in which the same quality might be expected !   [466]

Without some general knowledge of the qualities of natural substances, human life could not be preserved. And there can be no general knowledge of this kind without reducing them to species under specific names. For this reason, among the rudest nations, we find names for fire, water, earth, air, mountains, fountains, rivers ; for the kinds of vegetables they use ; of animals they hunt or tame, or that are found useful or hurtful.

Each of those names signifies in general a substance having a certain combination of attributes. The name, therefore, must be common to all substances in which those attributes are found.

Such general names of substances being found in all vulgar languages, before philosophers began to make accurate divisions and less obvious distinctions, it is not to be expected that their meaning should be more precise than is necessary for the common purposes of life.

As the knowledge of nature advances, more species of natural substances are observed, and their useful qualities discovered. In order that this important part of human knowledge may be communicated, and handed down to future generations, it is not sufficient that the species have names. Such is the fluctuating state of language, that a general name will not always retain the same precise signification, unless it have a definition in which men are disposed to acquiesce.

There was undoubtedly a great fund of natural knowledge among the Greeks and Romans in the time of Pliny. There is a great fund in his Natural History; but much of it is lost to us—for this reason among others, that we know not what species of substance he means by such a name.

Nothing could have prevented this loss but an accurate definition of the name, by which the species might have been distinguished from all others as long as that name and its definition remained. [467]

To prevent such loss in future times, modern philosophers have very laudably attempted to give names and accurate definitions of all the known species of substances wherewith the bountiful Creator hath enriched our globe.

This is necessary, in order to form a copious and distinct language concerning them, and, consequently, to facilitate our knowledge of them, and to convey it to future generations.

Every species that is known to exist ought to have a name; and that name ought to be defined by such attributes as serve best to distinguish the species from all others.

Nature invites to this work, by having formed things so as to make it both easy and important.

For, *first*, We perceive numbers of individual substances so like in their obvious qualities, that the most unimproved tribes of men consider them as of one species, and give them one common name.

Secondly, The more latent qualities of substances are generally the same in all the individuals of a species; so that what, by observation or experiment, is found in a few individuals of a species, is presumed and commonly found to belong to the whole. By this we are enabled, from particular facts, to draw general conclusions. This kind of induction is, indeed, the master-key to the knowledge of Nature, without which we could form no general conclusions in that branch of philosophy.

And, *thirdly*, By the very constitution of our nature, we are led, without reasoning, to ascribe to the whole species what we have found to belong to the individuals. It is thus we come to know that fire burns and water drowns; that bodies gravitate and bread nourishes. [468]

The species of two of the kingdoms of Nature—to wit, the animal and the vegetable—seem to be fixed by Nature, by the power they have of producing their like. And, in these, men, in all ages and nations, have accounted the parent and the progeny of the same species. The differences among Naturalists, with regard to the species of these two kingdoms, are very inconsiderable, and may be occasioned by the changes produced by soil, climate, and culture, and sometimes by monstrous productions, which are comparatively rare.

In the inanimate kingdom we have not the same means of dividing things into species, and, therefore, the limits of species seem to be more arbitrary. But, from the progress already made, there is ground to hope that, even in this kingdom, as the knowledge of it advances, the various species may be so well distinguished and defined as to answer every valuable purpose.

When the species are so numerous as to burden the memory, it is greatly assisted by distributing them into *genera*, the *genera* into tribes, the tribes into orders, and the orders into classes.

Such a regular distribution of natural substances, by divisions and subdivisions, has got the name of a system.

It is not a system of truths, but a system of general terms, with their definitions; and it is not only a great help to memory, but facilitates very much the definition of the terms. For the definition of the genus is common to all the species of that genus, and so is understood in the definition of each species, without the trouble of repetition. In like manner, the definition of a tribe is understood in the definition of every genus, and every species of that tribe; and the same may be said of every superior division. [469]

The effect of such a systematical distribution of the productions of Nature is seen in our systems of zoology, botany, and mineralogy; in which a species is commonly defined accurately in a line or two, which, without the systematical arrangement, could hardly be defined in a page.

With regard to the utility of systems of this kind, men have gone into contrary extremes; some have treated them with contempt, as a mere dictionary of words; others, perhaps, rest in such systems as all that is worth knowing in the works of Nature.

On the one hand, it is not the intention of such systems to communicate all that is known of the natural productions which they describe. The properties most fit for defining and distinguishing the several species, are not always those that are most useful to be known. To discover and to communicate the uses of natural substances in life and in the arts, is, no doubt, that part of the business of a naturalist which is the most important; and the systematical arrangement of them is chiefly to be valued

[467–469]

for its subserviency to this end. This every judicious naturalist will grant.

But, on the other hand, the labour is not to be despised, by which the road to an useful and important branch of knowledge is made easy in all time to come; especially when this labour requires both extensive knowledge and great abilities.

The talent of arranging properly and defining accurately, is so rare, and at the same time so useful, that it may very justly be considered as a proof of real genius, and as entitled to a high degree of praise. There is an intrinsic beauty in arrangement, which captivates the mind, and gives pleasure, even abstracting from its utility ; as in most other things, so in this particularly, Nature has joined beauty with utility. The arrangement of an army in the day of battle is a grand spectacle. The same men crowded in a fair, have no such effect. It is not more strange, therefore, that some men spend their days in studying systems of Nature, than that other men employ their lives in the study of languages. The most important end of those systems, surely, is to form a copious and an unambiguous language concerning the productions of Nature, by which every useful discovery concerning them may be communicated to the present, and transmitted to all future generations, without danger of mistake. [470]

General terms, especially such as are complex in their signification, will never keep one precise meaning, without accurate definition ; and accurate definitions of such terms can in no way be formed so easily and advantageously as by reducing the things they signify into a regular system.

Very eminent men in the medical profession, in order to remove all ambiguity in the names of diseases, and to advance the healing art, have, of late, attempted to reduce into a systematical order the diseases of the human body, and to give distinct names and accurate definitions of the several species, *genera*, orders, and classes, into which they distribute them ; and I apprehend that, in every art and science, where the terms of the art have any ambiguity that obstructs its progress, this method will be found the easiest and most successful for the remedy of that evil.

It were even to be wished that the general terms which we find in common language, as well as those of the arts and sciences, could be reduced to a systematical arrangement, and defined so as that they might be free from ambiguity ; but, perhaps, the obstacles to this are insurmountable. I know no man who has attempted it but Bishop Wilkins in his Essay towards a real character and a philosophical language.*

The attempt was grand, and worthy of a man of genius.

The formation of such systems, therefore, of the various productions of Nature, instead of being despised, ought to be ranked among the valuable improvements of modern ages, and to be the more esteemed that its utility reaches to the most distant future times, and, like the invention of writing, serves to embalm a most important branch of human knowledge, and to preserve it from being corrupted or lost. [471]

CHAPTER V.

OBSERVATIONS CONCERNING THE NAMES GIVEN TO OUR GENERAL NOTIONS.

HAVING now explained, as well as I am able, those operations of the mind by which we analyse the objects which nature presents to our observation, into their simple attributes, giving a general name to each, and by which we combine any number of such attributes into one whole, and give a general name to that combination, I shall offer some observations relating to our general notions, whether simple or complex.

I apprehend that the names given to them by modern philosophers, have contributed to darken our speculations about them, and to render them difficult and abstruse.

We call them general notions, conceptions, ideas. The words notion and conception, in their proper and most common sense, signify the act or operation of the mind in conceiving an object. In a figurative sense, they are sometimes put for the object conceived. And I think they are rarely, if ever, used in this figurative sense, except when we speak of what we call general notions or general conceptions. The word idea, as it is used in modern times, has the same ambiguity.

Now, it is only in the last of these senses, and not in the first, that we can be said to have general notions or conceptions. The generality is in the object conceived, and not in the act of the mind by which it is conceived. Every act of the mind is an individual act, which does or did exist. [472] But we have power to conceive things which neither do nor ever did exist. We have power to conceive attributes without regard to their existence. The conception of such an attribute is a real and individual act of the mind ; but the attribute conceived is common to many individuals that do or may exist. We are too apt to confound an object of conception with the conception of

* In this attempt Wilkins was preceded by our countryman Dalgarno ; and from Dalgarno it is highly probable that Wilkins borrowed the idea. But even Dalgarno was not the first who conceived the project.—H.

that object. But the danger of doing this must be much greater when the object of conception is called a conception.

The Peripatetics gave to such objects of conception the names of universals, and of predicables. Those names had no ambiguity, and I think were much more fit to express what was meant by them than the names we use.

It is for this reason that I have so often used the word predicable, which has the same meaning with predicable. And, for the same reason, I have thought it necessary repeatedly to warn the reader, that when, in compliance with custom, I speak of general notions or general conceptions, I always mean things conceived, and not the act of the mind in conceiving them.

The Pythagoreans and Platonists gave the name of *ideas* to such general objects of conception, and to nothing else. As we borrowed the word idea from them, so that it is now familiar in all the languages of Europe, I think it would have been happy if we had also borrowed their meaning, and had used it only to signify what they meant by it. I apprehend we want an unambiguous word to distinguish things barely conceived from things that exist. If the word idea was used for this purpose only, it would be restored to its original meaning, and supply that want.

We may surely agree with the Platonists in the meaning of the word *idea*, without adopting their theory concerning ideas. We need not believe, with them, that ideas are eternal and self-existent, and that they have a more real existence than the things we see and feel. [473]

They were led to give existence to ideas, from the common prejudice that everything which is an object of conception must really exist; and, having once given existence to ideas, the rest of their mysterious system about ideas followed of course; for things merely conceived have neither beginning nor end, time nor place; they are subject to no change; they are the patterns and exemplars according to which the Deity made everything that he made; for the work must be conceived by the artificer before it is made.

These are undeniable attributes of the ideas of Plato; and, if we add to them that of real existence, we have the whole mysterious system of Platonic ideas. Take away the attribute of existence, and suppose them not to be things that exist, but things that are barely conceived, and all the mystery is removed; all that remains is level to the human understanding.

The word *essence* came to be much used among the schoolmen, and what the Platonists called the idea of a species, they called its essence. The word *essentia* is

said to have been made by Cicero; but even his authority could not give it currency, until long after his time. It came at last to be used, and the schoolmen fell into much the same opinions concerning essences, as the Platonists held concerning ideas. The essences of things were held to be uncreated, eternal, and immutable.

Mr Locke distinguishes two kinds of essence, the real and the nominal. By the real essence, he means the constitution of an individual, which makes it to be what it is. This essence must begin and end with the individual to which it belongs. It is not, therefore, a Platonic idea. But what Mr Locke calls the nominal essence, is the constitution of a species, or that which makes an individual to be of such a species; and this is nothing but that combination of attributes which is signified by the name of the species, and which we conceive without regard to existence. [474]

The essence of a species, therefore, is what the Platonists called the idea of the species.

If the word *idea* be restricted to the meaning which it bore among the Platonists and Pythagoreans, many things which Mr Locke has said with regard to ideas will be just and true, and others will not.

It will be true that most words (indeed all general words) are the signs of ideas; but proper names are not: they signify individual things, and not ideas. It will be true not only that there are general and abstract ideas, but that all ideas are general and abstract. It will be so far from the truth, that all our simple ideas are got immediately, either from sensation or from consciousness, that no simple idea is got by either, without the co-operation of other powers. The objects of sense, of memory, and of consciousness, are not ideas but individuals; they must be analysed by the understanding into their simple ingredients, before we can have simple ideas; and those simple ideas must be again combined by the understanding, in distinct parcels, with names annexed, in order to give us complex ideas. It will be probable not only that brutes have no abstract ideas, but that they have no ideas at all.

I shall only add that the learned author of the origin and progress of language, and, perhaps, his learned friend, Mr Harris, are the only modern authors I have met with who restrict the word *idea* to this meaning. Their acquaintance with ancient philosophy led them to this. What pity is it that a word which, in ancient philosophy, had a distinct meaning, and which, if kept to that meaning, would have been a real acquisition to our language, should be used by the moderns in so vague and ambiguous a manner, that it is more apt to perplex and darken our speculations, than to convey useful knowledge !

From all that has been said about abstract and general conceptions, I think we may draw the following conclusions concerning them. [475]

First, That it is by abstraction that the mind is furnished with all its most simple and most distinct notions. The simplest objects of sense appear both complex and indistinct, until by abstraction they are analysed into their more simple elements; and the same may be said of the objects of memory and of consciousness.

Secondly, Our most distinct complex notions are those that are formed by compounding the simple notions got by abstraction.

Thirdly, Without the powers of abstracting and generalising, it would be impossible to reduce things into any order and method, by dividing them into genera and species.

Fourthly, Without those powers there could be no definition; for definition can only be applied to universals, and no individual can be defined.

Fifthly, Without abstract and general notions there can neither be reasoning nor language.

Sixthly, As brute animals shew no signs of being able to distinguish the various attributes of the same subject; of being able to class things into genera and species; to define, to reason, or to communicate their thoughts by artificial signs, as men do—I must think, with Mr Locke, that they have not the powers of abstracting and generalising, and that, in this particular, nature has made a specific difference between them and the human species.

CHAPTER VI.

OPINIONS OF PHILOSOPHERS ABOUT UNIVERSALS.

In the ancient philosophy, the doctrine of universals—that is, of things which we express by general terms—makes a great figure. The ideas of the Pythagoreans and Platonists, of which so much has been already said, were universals. [476] All science is employed about universals as its object. It was thought that there can be no science, unless its object be something real and immutable; and therefore those who paid homage to truth and science, maintained that ideas or universals have a real and immutable existence.

The sceptics, on the contrary, (for there were sceptical philosophers in those early days,) maintained that all things are mutable and in a perpetual fluctuation; and, from this principle, inferred that there is [475–477]

no science, no truth; that all is uncertain opinion.

Plato, and his masters of the Pythagorean school, yielded this with regard to objects of sense, and acknowledged that there could be no science or certain knowledge concerning them. But they held that there are objects of intellect of a superior order and nature, which are permanent and immutable. These are ideas, or universal natures, of which the objects of sense are only the images and shadows.

To these ideas they ascribed, as I have already observed, the most magnificent attributes. Of man, of a rose, of a circle, and of every species of things, they believed that there is one idea or form, which existed from eternity, before any individual of the species was formed; that this idea is the exemplar or pattern, according to which the Deity formed the individuals of the species; that every individual of the species participates of this idea, which constitutes its essence; and that this idea is. likewise an object of the human intellect, when, by due abstraction, we discern it to be one in all the individuals of the species.

Thus the idea of every species, though one and immutable, might be considered in three different views or respects : *first*, As having an eternal existence before there was any individual of the species; *secondly*, As existing in every individual of that species, without division or multiplication, and making the essence of the species; and, *thirdly*, As an object of intellect and of science in man. [477]

Such I take to be the doctrine of Plato, as far as I am able to comprehend it. His disciple Aristotle rejected the first of these views of ideas as visionary, but differed little from his master with regard to the two last. He did not admit the existence of universal natures antecedent to the existence of individuals : but he held that every individual consists of matter and form; that the form (which I take to be what Plato calls the idea) is common to all the individuals of the species; and that the human intellect is fitted to receive the forms of things as objects of contemplation. Such profound speculations about the nature of universals, we find even in the first ages of philosophy.[*] I wish I could make them more intelligible to myself and to the reader.

The division of universals into five classes—to wit, genus, species, specific difference, properties, and accidents—is likewise very ancient, and I conceive was borrowed by the Peripatetics from the Pythagorean school.[†]

---

[*] Different philosophers have maintained that Aristotle was a Realist, a Conceptualist, and a Nominalist, in the strictest sense.—H.

[†] This proceeds on the supposition that the supposititious Pythagorean treatises are genuine.—H.

Porphyry has given us a very distinct treatise upon these, as an introduction to Aristotle's categories. But he has omitted the intricate metaphysical questions that were agitated about their nature: such as, whether genera and species do really exist in nature, or whether they are only conceptions of the human mind. If they exist in nature, whether they are corporeal or incorporeal; and whether they are inherent in the objects of sense, or disjoined from them. These questions, he tells us, for brevity's sake, he omits, because they are very profound, and require accurate discussion. It is probable that these questions exercised the wits of the philosophers till about the twelfth century. [478]

About that time, Roscelinus or Ruscelinus, the master of the famous Abelard, introduced a new doctrine—that there is nothing universal but words or names. For this, and other heresies, he was much persecuted. However, by his eloquence and abilities, and those of his disciple Abelard, the doctrine spread, and those who followed it were called Nominalists.[*] His antagonists, who held that there are things that are really universal, were called Realists. The scholastic philosophers, from the beginning of the twelfth century, were divided into these two sects. Some few took a middle road between the contending parties. That universality which the Realists held to be in things themselves, Nominalists in names only, they held to be neither in things nor in names only, but in our conceptions. On this account they were called Conceptualists: but, being exposed to the batteries of both the opposite parties, they made no great figure.[†]

When the sect of Nominalists was like to expire, it received new life and spirit from Occam, the disciple of Scotus, in the fourteenth century. Then the dispute about universals, a parte rei, was revived with the greatest animosity in the schools of Britain, France, and Germany, and carried on, not by arguments only, but by bitter reproaches, blows, and bloody affrays, until the doctrines of Luther and the other Reformers turned the attention of the learned world to more important subjects.

After the revival of learning, Mr Hobbes adopted the opinion of the Nominalists.[‡]

"Human Nature," chap 5, § 6—"It is plain, therefore," says he, "that there is nothing universal but names." And in his "Leviathan," part i. chap 4, "There being nothing universal but names, proper names bring to mind one thing only; universals recall any one of many."

Mr Locke, according to the division before mentioned, I think, may be accounted a Conceptualist. He does not maintain that there are things that are universal; but that we have general or universal ideas which we form by abstraction; and this power of forming abstract and general ideas, he conceives to be that which makes the chief distinction in point of understanding, between men and brutes. [479]

Mr Locke's doctrine about abstraction has been combated by two very powerful antagonists, Bishop Berkeley and Mr Hume, who have taken up the opinion of the Nominalists. The former thinks, "That the opinion that the mind hath a power of forming abstract ideas or notions of things, has had a chief part in rendering speculation intricate and perplexed, and has occasioned innumerable errors and difficulties in almost all parts of knowledge." That "abstract ideas are like a fine and subtile net, which has miserably perplexed and entangled the minds of men, with this peculiar circumstance, that by how much the finer and more curious was the wit of any man, by so much the deeper was he like to be ensnared, and faster held therein." That, "among all the false principles that have obtained in the world, there is none hath a more wide influence over the thoughts of speculative men, than this of abstract general ideas."

The good bishop, therefore, in twenty-four pages of the introduction to his "Principles of Human Knowledge," encounters this principle with a zeal proportioned to his apprehension of its malignant and extensive influence.

That the zeal of the sceptical philosopher against abstract ideas was almost equal to that of the bishop, appears from his words, "Treatise of Human Nature," Book I. part i. § 7:—"A very material question has been started concerning abstract or general ideas—whether they be general or particular, in the mind's conception of them. A great philosopher" (he means Dr Berkeley) "has disputed the received opinion in this particular, and has asserted that all general ideas are nothing but particular ones annexed to a certain term, which gives them a more extensive signification, and makes them recall, upon occasion, other individuals which are similar to them. As I look upon this to be one of the greatest and most valuable discoveries that have been made of late years in the republic of letters, I

[478, 479]

---

[*] Abelard was not a Nominalist like Roscelinus; but held a doctrine, intermediate between absolute Nominalism and Realism, corresponding to the opinion since called Conceptualism. A flood of light has been thrown upon Abelard's doctrines, by M. Cousin's introduction to his recent publication of the unedited works of that illustrious thinker.—H.

[†] The later Nominalists, of the school of Occam, were really Conceptualists in our sense of the term. —H.

[‡] Hobbes is justly said by Leibnitz to have been *ipsis Nominalibus nominalior. They were really Conceptualists.*—H

shall here endeavour to confirm it by some arguments, which, I hope, will put it beyond all doubt and controversy." [480]

I shall make an end of this subject, with some reflections on what has been said upon it by these two eminent philosophers.

1. *First*, I apprehend that we cannot, with propriety, be said to have abstract and general ideas, either in the popular or in the philosophical sense of that word. In the popular sense, an idea is a thought; it is the act of the mind in thinking, or in conceiving any object. This act of the mind is always an individual act, and, therefore, there can be no general idea in this sense. In the philosophical sense, an idea is an image in the mind, or in the brain, which, in Mr Locke's system, is the immediate object of thought; in the system of Berkeley and Hume, the only object of thought. I believe there are no ideas of this kind, and, therefore, no abstract general ideas. Indeed, if there were really such images in the mind or in the brain, they could not be general, because everything that really exists is an individual. Universals are neither acts of the mind, nor images in the mind.

As, therefore, there are no general ideas in either of the senses in which the word idea is used by the moderns, Berkeley and Hume have, in this question, an advantage over Mr Locke; and their arguments against him are good *ad hominem.* They saw farther than he did into the just consequences of the hypothesis concerning ideas, which was common to them and to him; and they reasoned justly from this hypothesis when they concluded from it, that there is neither a material world, nor any such power in the human mind as that of abstraction. [481]

A triangle, in general, or any other universal, might be called an idea by a Platonist; but, in the style of modern philosophy, it is not an idea, nor do we ever ascribe to ideas the properties of triangles. It is never said of any idea, that it has three sides and three angles. We do not speak of equilateral, isosceles, or scalene ideas, nor of right-angled, acute-angled, or obtuse-angled ideas. And, if these attributes do not belong to ideas, it follows, necessarily, that a triangle is not an idea. The same reasoning may be applied to every other universal.

Ideas are said to have a real existence in the mind, at least while we think of them; but universals have no real existence. When we ascribe existence to them, it is not an existence in time or place, but existence in some individual subject; and this existence means no more but that they are truly attributes of such a subject. Their existence is nothing but predicability, or the [480–482]

capacity of being attributed to a subject. The name of predicables, which was given them in ancient philosophy, is that which most properly expresses their nature.

2. I think it must be granted, in the *second* place, that universals cannot be the objects of imagination, when we take that word in its strict and proper sense. "I find," says Berkeley, "I have a faculty of imagining or representing to myself the ideas of those particular things I have perceived, and of variously compounding and dividing them. I can imagine a man with two heads, or the upper parts of a man joined to the body of a horse. I can imagine the hand, the eye, the nose, each by itself, abstracted or separated from the rest of the body. But then, whatever hand or eye I imagine, it must have some particular shape or colour. Likewise, the idea of a man that I frame to myself must be either of a white, or a black, or a tawny; a straight or a crooked; a tall, or a low, or a middle-sized man."

I believe every man will find in himself what this ingenious author found—that he cannot imagine a man without colour, or stature, or shape. [482]

Imagination, as we before observed, properly signifies a conception of the appearance an object would make to the eye if actually seen.* An universal is not an object of any external sense, and therefore cannot be imagined; but it may be distinctly conceived. When Mr Pope says, "The proper study of mankind is man," I conceive his meaning distinctly, though I neither imagine a black or a white, a crooked or a straight man. The distinction between conception and imagination is real, though it be too often overlooked, and the words taken to be synonymous. I can conceive a thing that is impossible,† but I cannot distinctly imagine a thing that is impossible. I can conceive a proposition or a demonstration, but I cannot imagine either. I can conceive understanding and will, virtue and vice, and other attributes of mind, but I cannot imagine them. In like manner, I can distinctly conceive universals, but I cannot imagine them.‡

As to the manner how we conceive universals, I confess my ignorance. I know not how I hear, or see, or remember, and as little do I know how I conceive things that have no existence. In all our original

---

* See above, p. 366, a, note.—H.
† See above, p. 377, b, note.—H.
‡ Imagination and Conception are distinguished, but the latter ought not to be used in the vague and extensive signification of Reid. The discrimination in question is best made in the German language of philosophy, where the terms *Begriffe* (Conceptions) are strongly contrasted with *Anschauungen* (Intuitions), *Bilden* (Images), &c. See above, p. 360, a, note † ; p. 365, b, note ‡. The reader may compare Stewart's "Elements," I. p. 196.—H.

faculties, the fabric and manner of operation is, I apprehend, beyond our comprehension, and perhaps is perfectly understood by him only who made them.

But we ought not to deny a fact of which we are conscious, though we know not how it is brought about. And I think we may be certain that universals are not conceived by means of images of them in our minds, because there can be no image of an universal.

3. It seems to me, that on this question Mr Locke and his two antagonists have divided the truth between them. He saw very clearly, that the power of forming abstract and general conceptions is one of the most distinguishing powers of the human mind, and puts a specific difference between man and the brute creation. But he did not see that this power is perfectly irreconcileable to his doctrine concerning ideas. [483]

His opponents saw this inconsistency; but, instead of rejecting the hypothesis of ideas, they explain away the power of abstraction, and leave no specific distinction between the human understanding and that of brutes.

4. Berkeley,[*] in his reasoning against abstract general ideas, seems unwillingly or unwarily to grant all that is necessary to support abstract and general conceptions.

"A man," he says, "may consider a figure merely as triangular, without attending to the particular qualities of the angles, or relations of the sides. So far he may abstract. But this will never prove that he can frame an abstract general inconsistent idea of a triangle."

If a man may consider a figure merely as triangular, he must have some conception of this object of his consideration; for no man can consider a thing which he does not conceive. He has a conception, therefore, of a triangular figure, merely as such. I know no more that is meant by an abstract general conception of a triangle.

He that considers a figure merely as triangular, must understand what is meant by the word triangular. If, to the conception he joins to this word, he adds any particular quality of angles or relation of sides, he misunderstands it, and does not consider the figure merely as triangular. Whence, I think, it is evident, that he who considers a figure merely as triangular must have the conception of a triangle, abstracting from any quality of angles or relation of sides.

The Bishop, in like manner, grants, "That we may consider Peter so far forth as man, or so far forth as animal, without

framing the forementioned abstract idea, in as much as all that is perceived is not considered." It may here be observed, that he who considers Peter so far forth as man, or so far forth as animal, must conceive the meaning of those abstract words *man* and *animal,* and he who conceives the meaning of them has an abstract general conception. [484]

From these concessions, one would be apt to conclude that the Bishop thinks that we can abstract, but that we cannot frame abstract ideas; and in this I should agree with him. But I cannot reconcile his concessions with the general principle he lays down before. "To be plain," says he, "I deny that I can abstract one from another, or conceive separately those qualities which it is impossible should exist so separated." This appears to me inconsistent with the concessions above mentioned, and inconsistent with experience.

If we can consider a figure merely as triangular, without attending to the particular quality of the angles or relation of the sides, this, I think, is conceiving separately things which cannot exist so separated: for surely a triangle cannot exist without a particular quality of angles and relation of sides. And it is well known, from experience, that a man may have a distinct conception of a triangle, without having any conception or knowledge of many of the properties without which a triangle cannot exist.

Let us next consider the Bishop's notion of generalising.[*] He does not absolutely deny that there are general ideas, but only that there are abstract general ideas. "An idea," he says, "which, considered in itself, is particular, becomes general, by being made to represent or stand for all other particular ideas of the same sort. To make this plain by an example: Suppose a geometrician is demonstrating the method of cutting a line in two equal parts. He draws, for instance, a black line, of an inch in length. This, which is in itself a particular line, is, nevertheless, with regard to its signification, general; since, as it is there used, it represents all particular lines whatsoever; so that what is demonstrated of it, is demonstrated of all lines, or, in other words, of a line in general. And as that particular line becomes general by being made a sign, so the name *line,* which, taken absolutely, is particular, by being a sign, is made general." [485]

Here I observe, that when a particular idea is made a sign to represent and stand for all of a sort, this supposes a distinction of things into sorts or species. To be of a sort implies having those attributes which

---

* On Reid's criticism of Berkeley, see Stewart, (*Elements,* II. p. 110, sq.)—H.

* See Stewart, (*Elements,* II. p. 125.)—H.

characterise the sort, and are common to all the individuals that belong to it. There cannot, therefore, be a sort without general attributes, nor can there be any conception of a sort without a conception of those general attributes which distinguish it. The conception of a sort, therefore, is an abstract general conception.

The particular idea cannot surely be made a sign of a thing of which we have no conception. I do not say that you must have an idea of the sort, but surely you ought to understand or conceive what it means, when you make a particular idea a representative of it; otherwise your particular idea represents, you know not what.

When I demonstrate any general property of a triangle, such as, that the three angles are equal to two right angles, I must understand or conceive distinctly what is common to all triangles. I must distinguish the common attributes of all triangles from those wherein particular triangles may differ. And, if I conceive distinctly what is common to all triangles, without confounding it with what is not so, this is to form a general conception of a triangle. And without this, it is impossible to know that the demonstration extends to all triangles.

The Bishop takes particular notice of this argument, and makes this answer to it :— " Though the idea I have in view, whilst I make the demonstration, be, for instance, that of an isosceles réctangular triangle, whose sides are of a determinate length, I may nevertheless be certain that it extends to all other rectilinear triangles, of what sort or bigness soever; and that because neither the right angle, nor the equality or determinate length of the sides, are at all concerned in the demonstration." [486]

But, if he do not, in the idea he has in view, clearly distinguish what is common to all triangles from what is not, it would be impossible to discern whether something that is not common be concerned in the demonstration or not. In order, therefore, to perceive that the demonstration extends to all triangles, it is necessary to have a distinct conception of what is common to all triangles, excluding from that conception all that is not common. And this is all I understand by an abstract general conception of a triangle.

Berkeley catches an advantage to his side of the question, from what Mr Locke expresses (too strongly indeed) of the difficulty of framing abstract general ideas, and the pains and skill necessary for that purpose. From which the Bishop infers, that a thing so difficult cannot be necessary for communication by language, which is so easy and familiar to all sorts of men.

There may be some abstract and general conceptions that are difficult, or even beyond the reach of persons of weak understanding; but there are innumerable which are not beyond the reach of children. It is impossible to learn language without acquiring general conceptions; for there cannot be a single sentence without them. I believe the forming these, and being able to articulate the sounds of language, make up the whole difficulty that children find in learning language at first.

But this difficulty, we see, they are able to overcome so early as not to remember the pains it cost them. They have the strongest inducement to exert all their labour and skill, in order to understand and to be understood; and they no doubt do so. [487]

The labour of forming abstract notions, is the labour of learning to speak, and to understand what is spoken. As the words of every language, excepting a few proper names, are general words, the minds of children are furnished with general conceptions, in proportion as they learn the meaning of general words. I believe most men have hardly any general notions but those which are expressed by the general words they hear and use in conversation. The meaning of some of these is learned by a definition, which at once conveys a distinct and accurate general conception. The meaning of other general words we collect, by a kind of induction, from the way in which we see them used on various occasions by those who understand the language. Of these our conception is often less distinct, and in different persons is perhaps not perfectly the same.

" Is it not a hard thing," says the Bishop, " that a couple of children cannot prate together of their sugar-plumbs and rattles, and the rest of their little trinkets, till they have first tacked together numberless inconsistencies, and so formed in their minds abstract general ideas, and annexed them to every common name they make use of ?"

However hard a thing it may be, it is an evident truth, that a couple of children, even about their sugar-plumbs and their rattles, cannot prate so as to understand and be understood, until they have learned to conceive the meaning of many general words—and this, I think, is to have general conceptions.

5. Having considered the sentiments of Bishop Berkeley on this subject, let us next attend to those of Mr Hume, as they are expressed Part I. § 7, " Treatise of Human Nature." He agrees perfectly with the Bishop, " That all general ideas are nothing but particular ones annexed to a certain term, which gives them a more extensive signification, and makes them recall, upon occasion, other individuals which are similar to them. [488] A particular

[486-488]

idea becomes general, by being annexed to a general term ; that is, to a term, which, from a customary conjunction, has a relation to many other particular ideas, and readily recalls them in the imagination. Abstract ideas are therefore in themselves individual, however they may become general in their representation. The image in the mind is only that of a particular object, though the application of it in our reasoning be the same as if it was universal."

Although Mr Hume looks upon this to be one of the greatest and most valuable discoveries that has been made of late years in the republic of letters, it appears to be no other than the opinion of the nominalists, about which so much dispute was held from the beginning of the twelfth century down to the Reformation, and which was afterwards supported by Mr Hobbes. I shall briefly consider the arguments by which Mr Hume hopes to have put it beyond all doubt and controversy.

First, He endeavours to prove, by three arguments, that it is utterly impossible to conceive any quantity or quality, without forming a precise notion of its degrees:

This is indeed a great undertaking ; but, if he could prove it, it is not sufficient for his purpose—for two reasons.

First, Because there are many attributes of things, besides quantity and quality ; and it is incumbent upon him to prove that it is impossible to conceive any attribute, without forming a precise notion of its degree. Each of the ten categories of Aristotle is a genus, and may be an attribute. And, if he should prove of two of them—to wit, quantity and quality—that there can be no general conception of them ; there remain eight behind, of which this must be proved. [489]

The other reason is, because, though it were impossible to conceive any quantity or quality, without forming a precise notion of its degree, it does not follow that it is impossible to have a general conception even of quantity and quality. The conception of a pound troy is the conception of a quantity, and of the precise degree of that quantity ; but it is an abstract general conception notwithstanding, because it may be the attribute of many individual bodies, and of many kinds of bodies. He ought, therefore, to have proved that we cannot conceive quantity or quality, or any other attribute, without joining it inseparably to some individual subject.

This remains to be proved, which will be found no easy matter. For instance, I conceive what is meant by a Japanese as distinctly as what is meant by an Englishman or a Frenchman. It is true, a Japanese is neither quantity nor quality, but it is an attribute common to every individual of a populous nation. I never saw an individual of that nation ; and, if I can trust my consciousness, the general term does not lead me to imagine one individual of the sort as a representative of all others.

Though Mr Hume, therefore, undertakes much, yet, if he could prove all he undertakes to prove, it would by no means be sufficient to shew that we have no abstract general conceptions.

Passing this, let us attend to his arguments for proving this extraordinary position, that it is impossible to conceive any quantity or quality, without forming a precise notion of its degree.

The first argument is, that it is impossible to distinguish things that are not actually separable. " The precise length of a line is not different or distinguishable from the line." [490]

I have before endeavoured to shew, that things inseparable in their nature may be distinguished in our conception. And we need go no farther to be convinced of this, than the instance here brought to prove the contrary. The precise length of a line, he says, is not distinguishable from the line. When I say, *This is a line,* I say and mean one thing. When I say, *It is a line of three inches,* I say and mean another thing. If this be not to distinguish the precise length of the line from the line, I know not what it is to distinguish.

Second argument.—" Every object of sense—that is, every impression—is an individual, having its determinate degrees of quantity and quality. But whatever is true of the impression is true of the idea, as they differ in nothing but their strength and vivacity."

The conclusion in this argument is, indeed, justly drawn from the premises. If it be true that ideas differ in nothing from objects of sense, but in strength and vivacity, as it must be granted that all the objects of sense are individuals, it will certainly follow that all ideas are individuals. Granting, therefore, the justness of this conclusion, I beg leave to draw two other conclusions from the same premises, which will follow no less necessarily.

First, If ideas differ from the objects of sense only in strength and vivacity, it will follow, that the idea of a lion is a lion of less strength and vivacity. And hence may arise a very important question, Whether the idea of a lion may not tear in pieces, and devour the ideas of sheep, oxen, and horses, and even of men, women, and children ?

Secondly, If ideas differ only in strength and vivacity from the objects of sense, it will follow that objects merely conceived, are not ideas ; for such objects differ from the objects of sense in respects of a very

[489, 490

different nature from strength and vivacity. [491] Every object of sense must have a real existence, and time and place. But things merely conceived may neither have existence, nor time nor place; and, therefore, though there should be no abstract ideas, it does not follow that things abstract and general may not be conceived.

The third argument is this:—"It is a principle generally received in philosophy, that everything in nature is individual; and that it is utterly absurd to suppose a triangle really existent which has no precise proportion of sides and angles. If this, therefore, be absurd in fact and reality, it must be absurd in idea, since nothing of which we can form a clear and distinct idea is absurd or impossible."

I acknowledge it to be impossible that a triangle should really exist which has no precise proportion of sides and angles; and impossible that any being should exist which is not an individual being; for, I think, a being and an individual being mean the same thing: but that there can be no attributes common to many individuals I do not acknowledge. Thus, to many figures that really exist it may be common that they are triangles; and to many bodies that exist it may be common that they are fluid. Triangle and fluid are not beings, they are attributes of beings.

As to the principle here assumed, that nothing of which we can form a clear and distinct idea is absurd or impossible, I refer to what was said upon it, chap. 3, Essay IV. It is evident that, in every mathematical demonstration, ad absurdum, of which kind almost one-half of mathematics consists, we are required to suppose, and, consequently, to conceive, a thing that is impossible. From that supposition we reason, until we come to a conclusion that is not only impossible but absurd. From this we infer that the proposition supposed at first is impossible, and, therefore, that its contradictory is true. [492]

As this is the nature of all demonstrations, ad absurdum, it is evident, (I do not say that we can have a clear and distinct idea,) but that we can clearly and distinctly conceive things impossible.

The rest of Mr Hume's discourse upon this subject is employed in explaining how an individual idea, annexed to a general term, may serve all the purposes in reasoning which have been ascribed to abstract general ideas—

"When we have found a resemblance among several objects that often occur to us, we apply the same name to all of them, whatever differences we may observe in the degrees of their quantity and quality, and whatever other differences may appear among them. After we have acquired a [491–493]

custom of this kind, the hearing of that name revives the idea of one of these objects, and makes the imagination conceive it, with all its circumstances and proportions." But, along with this idea, there is a readiness to survey any other of the individuals to which the name belongs, and to observe that no conclusion be formed contrary to any of them. If any such conclusion is formed, those individual ideas which contradict it immediately crowd in upon us, and make us perceive the falsehood of the proposition. If the mind suggests not always these ideas upon occasion, it proceeds from some imperfection in its faculties; and such a one as is often the source of false reasoning and sophistry.

This is, in substance, the way in which he accounts for what he calls "the foregoing paradox, that some ideas are particular in their nature, but general in their representation." Upon this account I shall make some remarks. [493]

1. He allows that we find a resemblance among several objects, and such a resemblance as leads us to apply the same name to all of them. This concession is sufficient to shew that we have general conceptions. There can be no resemblance in objects that have no common attribute; and, if there be attributes belonging in common to several objects, and in man a faculty to observe and conceive these, and to give names to them, this is to have general conceptions.

I believe, indeed, we may have an indistinct perception of resemblance without knowing wherein it lies. Thus, I may see a resemblance between one face and another, when I cannot distinctly say in what feature they resemble; but, by analysing the two faces, and comparing feature with feature, I may form a distinct notion of that which is common to both. A painter, being accustomed to an analysis of this kind, would have formed a distinct notion of this resemblance at first sight; to another man it may require some attention.

There is, therefore, an indistinct notion of resemblance when we compare the objects only in gross: and this I believe brute animals may have. There is also a distinct notion of resemblance when we analyse the objects into their different attributes, and perceive them to agree in some while they differ in others. It is in this case only that we give a name to the attributes wherein they agree, which must be a common name, because the thing signified by it is common. Thus, when I compare cubes of different matter, I perceive them to have this attribute in common, that they are comprehended under six equal squares, and this attribute only is signified by applying the name of cube to them all. When I com pare clean linen with snow, I perceive them to agree in colour ; and when I apply the name of white to both, this name signifies neither snow nor clean linen, but the attribute which is common to both.

2. The author says, that when we have found a resemblance among several objects, we apply the same name to all of them. [494]

It must here be observed, that there are two kinds of names which the author seems to confound, though they are very different in nature, and in the power they have in language. There are proper names, and there are common names or appellatives. The first are the names of individuals. The same proper name is never applied to several individuals on account of their similitude, because the very intention of a proper name is to distinguish one individual from all others ; and hence it is a maxim in grammar that proper names have no plural number. A proper name signifies nothing but the individual whose name it is ; and, when we apply it to the individual, we neither affirm nor deny anything concerning him.

A common name or appellative is not the name of any individual, but a general term, signifying something that is or may be common to several individuals. Common names, therefore, signify common attributes. Thus, when I apply the name of son or brother to several persons, this signifies and affirms that this attribute is common to all of them.

From this, it is evident that the applying the same name to several individuals on account of their resemblance, can, ·in consistence with grammar and common sense, mean nothing else than the expressing, by a general term, something that is common to those individuals, and which, therefore, may be truly affirmed of them all.

3. The author says, "It is certain that we form the idea of individuals whenever we use any general term. The word raises up an individual idea, and makes the imagination conceive it, with all its particular circumstances and proportions."

This fact he takes a great deal of pains to account for, from the effect of custom. [495]

But the fact should be ascertained before we take pains to account for it. I can see no reason to believe the fact ; and I think a farmer can talk of his sheep and his black cattle, without conceiving, in his imagination, one individual, with all its circumstances and proportions. If this be true, the whole of his theory of general ideas falls to the ground. To me it appears, that when a general term is well understood, it is only by accident if it suggest some individual of the kind ; but this effect is by no means constant.

I understand perfectly what mathematicians call a line of the fifth order ; yet I never conceived in my imagination any one of the kind in all its circumstances and proportions. Sir Isaac Newton first formed a distinct general conception of lines of the third order ; and afterwards, by great labour and deep penetration, found out and described the particular species comprehended under that general term. According to Mr Hume's theory, he must first have been acquainted with the particulars, and then have learned by custom to apply one general name to all of them.

The author observes, " That the idea of an equilateral triangle of an inch perpendicular, may serve us in talking of a figure, a rectilinear figure, a regular figure, a triangle, and an equilateral triangle."

I answer, the man that uses these general terms either understands their meaning, or he does not. If he does not understand their meaning, all his talk about them will be found only without sense, and the particular idea mentioned cannot enable him to speak of them with understanding. If he understands the meaning of the general terms, he will find no use for the particular idea.

4. He tells us gravely, " That in a globe of white marble the figure and the colour are undistinguishable, and are in effect the same." [496] How foolish have mankind been to give different names, in all ages and in all languages, to things undistinguishable, and in effect the same ? Henceforth, in all books of science and of entertainment, we may substitute figure for colour, and colour for figure. By this we shall make numberless curious discoveries, without danger of error.* [497]

---

* The whole controversy of Nominalism and Conceptualism is founded on the ambiguity of the terms employed. The opposite parti s are substantially at one. Had our British philosophers been aware of the Leibnitzian distinction of *Intuitive* and *Symbolical* knowledge ; and had we, like the Germans, different terms, like *Begriff* and *Anschauung*, to denote different kinds of thought, there would have been as little difference of opinion in regard to the nature of general n .tions in this country as in the Empire. With us, *Idea, Notion, Conception,* &c. are confounded, or applied by different philosophers in different senses. I must put the reader on his guard against Dr Thomas Brown's speculations on this subject. His own doctrine of universals, in so far as it is peculiar, is self-contradictory ; and nothing can be more erroneous than his statement of the doctrine held by others, especially by the Nominalists. —H.

ESSAY VI.

OF JUDGMENT

CHAPTER I.

OF JUDGMENT IN GENERAL.

JUDGING is an operation of the mind so familiar to every man who hath understanding, and its name is so common and so well understood, that it needs no definition.

As it is impossible by a definition to give a notion of colour to a man who never saw colours; so it is impossible by any definition to give a distinct notion of judgment to a man who has not often judged, and who is not capable of reflecting attentively upon this act of his mind. The best use of a definition is to prompt him to that reflection; and without it the best definition will be apt to mislead him.

The definition commonly given of judgment, by the more ancient writers in logic, was, that it is *an act of the mind, whereby one thing is affirmed or denied of another.* I believe this is as good a definition of it as can be given. Why I prefer it to some later definitions, will afterwards appear. Without pretending to give any other, I shall make two remarks upon it, and then offer some general observations on this subject. [498]

1. It is true that it is by affirmation or denial that we express our judgments; but there may be judgment which is not expressed. It is a solitary act of the mind, and the expression of it by affirmation or denial is not at all essential to it. It may be tacit, and not expressed. Nay, it is well known that men may judge contrary to what they affirm or deny; the definition therefore must be understood of mental affirmation or denial, which indeed is only another name for judgment.

2. Affirmation and denial is very often the expression of testimony, which is a different act of the mind, and ought to be distinguished from judgment.

A judge asks of a witness what he knows of such a matter to which he was an eye or ear-witness. He answers, by affirming or denying something　But his answer does not express his judgment; it is his testimony. Again, I ask a man his opinion in a matter of science or of criticism. His answer is not testimony; it is the expression of his judgment.

Testimony is a social act, and it is essen-

[498, 499]

tial to it to be expressed by words or signs. A tacit testimony is a contradiction : but there is no contradiction in a tacit judgment; it is complete without being expressed.

In testimony a man pledges his veracity for what he affirms; so that a false testimony is a lie: but a wrong judgment is not a lie; it is only an error.

I believe, in all languages, testimony and judgment are expressed by the same form of speech. A proposition affirmative or negative, with a verb in what is called the indicative mood, expresses both. To distinguish them by the form of speech, it would be necessary that verbs should have two indicative moods, one for testimony, and another to express judgment. [499] I know not that this is found in any language. And the reason is—not surely that the vulgar cannot distinguish the two, for every man knows the difference between a lie and an error of judgment—but that, from the matter and circumstances, we can easily see whether a man intends to give his testimony, or barely to express his judgment.

Although men must have judged in many cases before tribunals of justice were erected, yet it is very probable that there were tribunals before men began to speculate about judgment, and that the word may be borrowed from the practice of tribunals. As a judge, after taking the proper evidence, passes sentence in a cause, and that sentence is called his judgment, so the mind, with regard to whatever is true or false, passes sentence, or determines according to the evidence that appears. Some kinds of evidence leave no room for doubt. Sentence is passed immediately, without seeking or hearing any contrary evidence, because the thing is certain and notorious. In other cases, there is room for weighing evidence on both sides, before sentence is passed. The analogy between a tribunal of justice, and this inward tribunal of the mind, is too obvious to escape the notice of any man who ever appeared before a judge. And it is probable that the word *judgment*, as well as many other words we use in speaking of this operation of mind, are grounded on this analogy.

Having premised these things, that it may be clearly understood what I mean by judgment, I proceed to make some general observations concerning it.

First, Judgment is an act of the mind, specifically different from simple apprehension, or the bare conception of a thing.* It would be unnecessary to observe this, if some philosophers had not been led by their theories to a contrary opinion. [500]

Although there can be no judgment without a conception of the things about which we judge, yet conception may be without any judgment.† Judgment can be expressed by a proposition only, and a proposition is a complete sentence; but simple apprehension may be expressed by a word or words, which make no complete sentence. When simple apprehension is employed about a proposition, every man knows that it is one thing to apprehend a proposition—that is, to conceive what it means—but it is quite another thing to judge it to be true or false.

It is self-evident that every judgment must be either true or false; but simple apprehension, or conception, can neither be true nor false, as was shewn before.

One judgment may be contradictory to another; and it is impossible for a man to have two judgments at the same time, which he perceives to be contradictory. But contradictory propositions may be conceived‡ at the same time without any difficulty. That the sun is greater than the earth, and that the sun is not greater than the earth, are contradictory propositions. He that apprehends the meaning of one, apprehends the meaning of both. But it is impossible for him to judge both to be true at the same time. He knows that, if the one is true, the other must be false. For these reasons, I hold it to be certain that judgment and simple apprehension are acts of the mind specifically different.

Secondly, There are notions or ideas that ought to be referred to the faculty of judgment as their source; because, if we had not that faculty, they could not enter into our minds; and to those that have that faculty, and are capable of reflecting upon its operations, they are obvious and familiar.

Among these we may reckon the notion of judgment itself; the notions of a proposition—of its subject, predicate, and copula; of affirmation and negation, of true and false; of knowledge, belief, disbelief, opinion, assent, evidence. From no source could we acquire these notions, but from reflecting upon our judgments. Relations of things make one great class of our notions or ideas; and we cannot have the idea of any relation without some exercise of judgment, as will appear afterwards. [501]

Thirdly, In persons come to years of

understanding, judgment necessarily accompanies all sensation, perception by the senses, consciousness, and memory, but not conception.*

I restrict this to persons come to the years of understanding, because it may be a question, whether infants, in the first period of life, have any judgment or belief at all.* The same question may be put with regard to brutes and some idiots. This question is foreign to the present subject; and I say nothing here about it, but speak only of persons who have the exercise of judgment.

In them it is evident that a man who feels pain, judges and believes that he is really pained. The man who perceives an object, believes that it exists, and is what he distinctly perceives it to be; nor is it in his power to avoid such judgment. And the like may be said of memory, and of consciousness. Whether judgment ought to be called a necessary concomitant of these operations, or rather a part or ingredient of them, I do not dispute; but it is certain that all of them are accompanied with a determination that something is true or false, and a consequent belief. If this determination be not judgment, it is an operation that has got no name; for it is not simple apprehension, neither is it reasoning; it is a mental affirmation or negation; it may be expressed by a proposition affirmative or negative, and it is accompanied with the firmest belief. These are the characteristics of judgment; and I must call it judgment, till I can find another name to it.

The judgments we form are either of things necessary, or of things contingent. That three times three is nine, that the whole is greater than a part, are judgments about things necessary. [502] Our assent to such necessary propositions is not grounded upon any operation of sense, of memory, or of consciousness, nor does it require their concurrence; it is unaccompanied by any other operation but that of conception, which must accompany all judgment; we may therefore call this judgment of things necessary pure judgment. Our judgment of things contingent must always rest upon some other operation of the mind, such as sense, or memory, or consciousness, or credit in testimony, which is itself grounded upon judgment.

That I now write upon a table covered with green cloth, is a contingent event, which I judge to be most undoubtedly true. My judgment is grounded upon my perception, and is a necessary concomitant or ingredient of my perception. That I dined

---

* Which, however, implies a judgment affirming its subjective reality—an existential judgment.—H.

† See last note, and above, p. 243, a, note *, and p. 75, a, note †.—H.

‡ See above, p. 377, b, note.—H

---

* In so far as there can be Consciousness, there must be Judgment.—H.

with such a company yesterday, I judge to be true, because I remember it; and my judgment necessarily goes along with this remembrance, or makes a part of it.

There are many forms of speech in common language which shew that the senses, memory and consciousness, are considered as judging faculties. We say that a man judges of colours by his eye, of sounds by his ear. We speak of the evidence of sense, the evidence of memory, the evidence of consciousness. Evidence is the ground of judgment; and when we see evidence, it is impossible not to judge.

When we speak of seeing or remembering anything, we, indeed, hardly ever add that we judge it to be true. But the reason of this appears to be, that such an addition would be mere superfluity of speech, because every one knows that what I see or remember, I must judge to be true, and cannot do otherwise.

And, for the same reason, in speaking of anything that is self-evident or strictly demonstrated, we do not say that we judge it to be true. This would be superfluity of speech, because every man knows that we must judge that to be true which we hold self-evident or demonstrated. [503]

When you say you saw such a thing, or that you distinctly remember it, or when you say of any proposition that it is self-evident, or strictly demonstrated, it would be ridiculous after this to ask whether you judge it to be true; nor would it be less ridiculous in you to inform us that you do. It would be a superfluity of speech of the same kind as if, not content with saying that you saw such an object, you should add that you saw it with your eyes.

There is, therefore, good reason why, in speaking or writing, judgment should not be expressly mentioned, when all men know it to be necessarily implied; that is, when there can be no doubt. In such cases, we barely mention the evidence. But when the evidence mentioned leaves room for doubt, then, without any superfluity or tautology, we say we judge the thing to be so, because this is not implied in what was said before. A woman with child never says, that, going such a journey, she carried her child along with her. We know that, while it is in her womb, she must carry it along with her. There are some operations of mind that may be said to carry judgment in their womb, and can no more leave it behind them than the pregnant woman can leave her child. Therefore, in speaking of such operations, it is not expressed.

Perhaps this manner of speaking may have led philosophers into the opinion that, in perception by the senses, in memory, and in consciousness, there is no judgment at all. Because it is not mentioned in [503-505]

speaking of these faculties, they conclude that it does not accompany them; that they are only different modes of simple apprehension, or of acquiring ideas; and that it is no part of their office to judge. [504]

I apprehend the same cause has led Mr Locke into a notion of judgment which I take to be peculiar to him. He thinks that the mind has two faculties conversant about truth and falsehood. *First,* knowledge; and, *secondly,* judgment. In the first, the perception of the agreement or disagreement of the ideas is certain. In the second, it is not certain, but probable only.

According to this notion of judgment, it is not by judgment that I perceive that two and three make five; it is by the faculty of knowledge. I apprehend there can be no knowledge without judgment, though there may be judgment without that certainty which we commonly call knowledge.

Mr Locke, in another place of his Essay, tells us, " That the notice we have by our senses of the existence of things without us, though not altogether so certain as our intuitive knowledge, or the deductions of our reason about abstract ideas, yet is an assurance that deserves the name of knowledge." I think, by this account of it, and by his definitions before given of knowledge and judgment, it deserves as well the name of *judgment.*

That I may avoid disputes about the meaning of words, I wish the reader to understand, that I give the name of judgment to every determination of the mind concerning what is true or what is false. This, I think, is what logicians, from the days of Aristotle, have called judgment. Whether it be called one faculty, as I think it has always been, or whether a philosopher chooses to split it into two, seems not very material. And, if it be granted that, by our senses, our memory, and consciousness, we not only have ideas or simple apprehensions, but form determinations concerning what is true and what is false—whether these determinations ought to be called *knowledge* or *judgment,* is of small moment. [505]

The judgments grounded upon the evidence of sense, of memory, and of consciousness, put all men upon a level. The philosopher, with regard to these, has no prerogative above the illiterate, or even above the savage.

Their reliance upon the testimony of these faculties is as firm and as well grounded as his. His superiority is in judgments of another kind—in judgments about things abstract and necessary. And he is unwilling to give the name of judgment to that wherein the most ignorant and unimproved of the species are his equals.

But philosophers have never been able to give any definition of judgment which does not apply to the determinations of our senses, our memory, and consciousness, nor any definition of simple apprehension which can comprehend those determinations.

Our judgments of this kind are purely the gift of Nature, nor do they admit of improvement by culture. The memory of one man may be more tenacious than that of another; but both rely with equal assurance upon what they distinctly remember. One man's sight may be more acute, or his feeling more delicate, than that of another; but both give equal credit to the distinct testimony of their sight and touch.

And, as we have this belief by the constitution of our nature, without any effort of our own, so no effort of ours can overturn it.

The sceptic may perhaps persuade himself, in general, that he has no ground to believe his senses or his memory: but, in particular cases that are interesting, his disbelief vanishes, and he finds himself under a necessity of believing both. [506] These judgments may, in the strictest sense, be called *judgments of nature.* Nature has subjected us to them, whether we will or not. They are neither got, nor can they be lost by any use or abuse of our faculties; and it is evidently necessary for our preservation that it should be so. For, if belief in our senses and in our memory were to be learned by culture, the race of men would perish before they learned this lesson. It is necessary to all men for their being and preservation, and therefore is unconditionally given to all men by the Author of Nature.

I acknowledge that, if we were to rest in those judgments of Nature of which we now speak, without building others upon them, they would not entitle us to the denomination of reasonable beings. But yet they ought not to be despised, for they are the foundation upon which the grand superstructure of human knowledge must be raised. And, as in other superstructures the foundation is commonly overlooked, so it has been in this. The more sublime attainments of the human mind have attracted the attention of philosophers, while they have bestowed but a careless glance upon the humble foundation on which the whole fabric rests.

A fourth observation is, that some exercise of judgment is necessary in the formation of all abstract and general conceptions, whether more simple or more complex; in dividing, in defining, and, in general, in forming all clear and distinct conceptions of things, which are the only fit materials of reasoning.

These operations are allied to each other, and therefore I bring them under one observation. They are more allied to our rational nature than those mentioned in the last observation, and therefore are considered by themselves.

That I may not be mistaken, it may be observed that I do not say that abstract notions, or other accurate notions of things, after they have been formed, cannot be barely conceived without any exercise of judgment about them. I doubt not that they may: but what I say is, that, in their formation in the mind at first, there must be some exercise of judgment. [507]

It is impossible to distinguish the different attributes belonging to the same subject, without judging that they are really different and distinguishable, and that they have that relation to the subject which logicians express, by saying that they may be predicated of it. We cannot generalise, without judging that the same attribute does or may belong to many individuals. It has been shewn that our simplest general notions are formed by these two operations of distinguishing and generalising; judgment therefore is exercised in forming the simplest general notions.

In those that are more complex, and which have been shewn to be formed by combining the more simple, there is another act of the judgment required; for such combinations are not made at random, but for an end: and judgment is employed in fitting them to that end. We form complex general notions for conveniency of arranging our thoughts in discourse and reasoning; and, therefore, of an infinite number of combinations that might be formed, we choose only those that are useful and necessary.

That judgment must be employed in dividing as well as in distinguishing, appears evident. It is one thing to divide a subject properly, another to cut it in pieces. *Hoc·non est dividere, sed frangere rem*, said Cicero, when he censured an improper division of Epicurus. Reason has discovered rules of division, which have been known to logicians more than two thousand years.

There are rules likewise of definition of no less antiquity and authority. A man may no doubt divide or define properly without attending to the rules, or even without knowing them. But this can only be when he has judgment to perceive that to be right in a particular case, which the rule determines to be right in all cases.

I add in general, that, without some degree of judgment, we can form no accurate and distinct notions of things; so that one province of judgment is, to aid us in forming clear and distinct conceptions of things, which are the only fit materials for reasoning. [508]

This will probably appear to be a paradox to philosophers, who have always considered the formation of ideas of every kind as belonging to simple apprehension ; and that the sole province of judgment is to put them together in affirmative or negative propositions ; and therefore it requires some confirmation.

First, I think it necessarily follows, from what has been already said in this observation. For if, without some degree of judgment, a man can neither distinguish, nor divide, nor define, nor form any general notion, simple or complex, he surely, without some degree of judgment, cannot have in his mind the materials necessary to reasoning.

There cannot be any proposition in language which does not involve some general conception. The proposition, *that I exist,* which Des Cartes thought the first of all truths, and the foundation of all knowledge, cannot be conceived without the conception of existence, one of the most abstract general conceptions. A man cannot believe his own existence, or the existence of anything he sees or remembers, until he has so much judgment as to distinguish things that really exist from things which are only conceived. He sees a man six feet high ; he conceives a man sixty feet high : he judges the first object to exist, because he sees it ; the second he does not judge to exist, because he only conceives it. Now, I would ask, Whether he can attribute existence to the first object, and not to the second, without knowing what existence means ? It is impossible.

How early the notion of existence enters into the mind, I cannot determine ; but it must certainly be in the mind as soon as we can affirm of anything, with understanding, that it exists. [509]

In every other proposition, the predicate, at least, must be a general notion—a predicable and an universal being one and the same. Besides this, every proposition either affirms or denies. And no man can have a distinct conception of a proposition, who does not understand distinctly the meaning of affirming or denying. But these are very general conceptions, and, as was before observed, are derived from judgment, as their source and origin.

I am sensible that a strong objection may be made to this reasoning, and that it may seem to lead to an absurdity or a contradiction. It may be said, that every judgment is a mental affirmation or negation. If, therefore, some previous ·exercise of judgment be necessary to understand what is meant by affirmation or negation, the exercise of judgment must go before any judgment which is absurd.

In like manner, every judgment may be

expressed by a proposition, and a proposition must be conceived before we can judge of it. If, therefore, we cannot conceive the meaning of a proposition without a previous exercise of judgment, it follows that judgment must be previous to the conception of any proposition, and at the same time that the conception of a proposition must be previous to all judgment, which is a contradiction.

The reader may please to observe, that I have limited what I have said to distinct conception, and some degree of judgment ; and it is by this means I hope to avoid this labyrinth of absurdity and contradiction. The faculties of conception and judgment have an infancy and a maturity as man has. What I have said is limited to their mature state. I believe in their infant state they are very weak and indistinct ; and that, by imperceptible degrees, they grow to maturity, each giving aid to the other, and receiving aid from it. But which of them first began this friendly intercourse, is beyond my ability to determine. It is like the question concerning the bird and the egg. [510]

In the present state of things, it is true that every bird comes from an egg, and every egg from a bird ; and each may be said to be previous to the other. But, if we go back to the origin of things, there must have been some bird that did not come from any egg, or some egg that did not come from any bird.

In like manner, in the mature state of man, distinct conception of a proposition supposes some previous exercise of judgment, and distinct judgment supposes distinct conception. Each may truly be said to come from the other, as the bird from the egg, and the egg from the bird. But, if we trace back this succession to its origin —that is, to the first proposition that was ever conceived by the man, and the first judgment he ever formed—I determine nothing about them, nor do I know in what order, or how, they were produced, any more than how the bones grow in the womb of her that is with child.

The first exercise of these faculties of conception and judgment is hid, like the sources of the Nile, in an unknown region.

The necessity of some degree of judgment to clear and distinct conceptions of things, may, I think, be illustrated by this similitude.

An artist, suppose a carpenter, cannot work in his art without tools, and these tools must be made by art. The exercise of the art, therefore, is necessary to make the tools, and the tools are necessary to the exercise of the art. There is the same appearance of contradiction, as in what I have advanced concerning the necessity of

2 E

some degree of judgment, in order to form clear and distinct conceptions of things. These are the tools we must use in judging and in reasoning, and without them must make very bungling work; yet these tools cannot be made without some exercise of judgment. [511]

The necessity of some degree of judgment in forming accurate and distinct notions of things will farther appear, if we consider attentively what notions we can form, without any aid of judgment, of the objects of sense, of the operations of our own minds, or of the relations of things.

To begin with the objects of sense. It is acknowledged, on all hands, that the first notions we have of sensible objects are got by the external senses only, and probably before judgment is brought forth; but these first notions are neither simple, nor are they accurate and distinct: they are gross and indistinct, and, like the *chaos*, a *rudis indigestaque moles*. Before we can have any distinct notion of this mass, it must be analysed; the heterogeneous parts must be separated in our conception, and the simple elements, which before lay hid in the common mass, must first be distinguished, and then put together into one whole.

In this way it is that we form distinct notions even of the objects of sense; but this process of analysis and composition, by habit, becomes so easy, and is performed so readily, that we are apt to overlook it, and to impute the distinct notion we have formed of the object to the senses alone; and this we are the more prone to do because, when once we have distinguished the sensible qualities of the object from one another, the sense gives testimony to each of them.

You perceive, for instance, an object white, round, and a foot in diameter. I grant that you perceive all these attributes of the object by sense; but, if you had not been able to distinguish the colour from the figure, and both from the magnitude, your senses would only have given you one complex and confused notion of all these mingled together.

A man who is able to say with understanding, or to determine in his own mind, that this object is white, must have distinguished whiteness from other attributes. If he has not made this distinction, he does not understand what he says. [512]

Suppose a cube of brass to be presented at the same time to a child of a year old and to a man. The regularity of the figure will attract the attention of both. Both have the senses of sight and of touch in equal perfection; and, therefore, if anything be discovered in this object by the man, which cannot be discovered by the child, it must be owing, not to the senses, but to some other faculty which the child has not yet attained.

First, then, the man can easily distinguish the body from the surface which terminates it; this the child cannot do. *Secondly,* The man can perceive that this surface is made up of six planes of the same figure and magnitude; the child cannot discover this. *Thirdly,* The man perceives that each of these planes has four equal sides and four equal angles; and that the opposite sides of each plane and the opposite planes are parallel.

It will surely be allowed, that a man of ordinary judgment may observe all this in a cube which he makes an object of contemplation, and takes time to consider; that he may give the name of a square to a plane terminated by four equal sides and four equal angles; and the name of a cube to a solid terminated by six equal squares: all this is nothing else but analysing the figure of the object presented to his senses into its simplest elements, and again compounding it of those elements.

By this analysis and composition two effects are produced. *First,* From the one complex object which his senses presented, though one of the most simple the senses can present, he educes many simple and distinct notions of right lines, angles, plain surface, solid, equality, parallelism; notions which the child has not yet faculties to attain. *Secondly,* When he considers the cube as compounded of these elements, put together in a certain order, he has then, and not before, a distinct and scientific notion of a cube. The child neither conceives those elements, nor in what order they must be put together in order to make a cube; and, therefore, has no accurate notion of a cube which can make it a subject of reasoning. [513]

Whence I think we may conclude, that the notion which we have from the senses alone, even of the simplest objects of sense, is indistinct and incapable of being either described or reasoned upon, until it is analysed into its simple elements, and considered as compounded of those elements.

If we should apply this reasoning to more complex objects of sense, the conclusion would be still more evident. A dog may be taught to turn a jack, but he can never be taught to have a distinct notion of a jack. He sees every part as well as a man; but the relation of the parts to one another and to the whole, he has not judgment to comprehend.

A distinct notion of an object, even of sense, is never got in an instant; but the sense performs its office in an instant. Time is not required to see it better, but to analyse it, to distinguish the different parts, and their relation to one another and to the whole.

Hence it is that, when any vehement passion or emotion hinders the cool application of judgment, we get no distinct notion of an object, even though the sense be long directed to it. A man who is put into a panic, by thinking he sees a ghost, may stare at it long without having any distinct notion of it ; it is his understanding, and not his sense, that is disturbed by his horror. If he can lay that aside, judgment immediately enters upon its office, and examines the length and breadth, the colour, and figure, and distance of the object. Of these, while his panic lasted, he had no distinct notion, though his eyes were open all the time.

When the eye of sense is open, but that of judgment shut by a panic, or any violent emotion that engrosses the mind, we see things confusedly, and probably much in the same manner that brutes and perfect idiots do, and infants before the use of judgment. [514]

There are, therefore, notions of the objects of sense which are gross and indistinct, and there are others that are distinct and scientific. The former may be got from the senses alone, but the latter cannot be obtained without some degree of judgment.

The clear and accurate notions which geometry presents to us of a point, a right line, an angle, a square, a circle, of ratios direct and inverse, and others of that kind, can find no admittance into a mind that has not some degree of judgment. They are not properly ideas of the senses, nor are they got by compounding ideas of the senses, but by analysing the ideas or notions we get by the senses into their simplest elements, and again combining these elements into various accurate and elegant forms, which the senses never did nor can exhibit.

Had Mr Hume attended duly to this, it ought to have prevented a very bold attempt, which he has prosecuted through fourteen pages of his " Treatise of Human Nature," to prove that geometry is founded upon ideas that are not exact, and axioms that are not precisely true.

A mathematician might be tempted to think that the man who seriously undertakes this has no great acquaintance with geometry ; but I apprehend it is to be imputed to another cause, to a zeal for his own system. We see that even men of genius may be drawn into strange paradoxes, by an attachment to a favourite idol of the understanding, when it demands so costly a sacrifice.

We Protestants think that the devotees of the Roman Church pay no small tribute to her authority when they renounce their five senses in obedience to her decrees. Mr Hume's devotion to his system carries him [514–516]

even to trample upon mathematical demonstration. [515]

The fundamental articles of his system are, that all the perceptions of the human mind are either impressions or ideas, and that ideas are only faint copies of impressions. The idea of a right line, therefore, is only a faint copy of some line that has been seen, or felt by touch ; and the faint copy cannot be more perfect than the original. Now of such right lines, it is evident that the axioms of geometry are not precisely true ; for two lines that are straight to our sight or touch may include a space, or they may meet in more points than one. If, therefore, we cannot form any notion of a straight line more accurate than that which we have from the senses of sight and touch, geometry has no solid foundation. If, on the other hand, the geometrical axioms are precisely true, the idea of a right line is not copied from any impression of sight or touch, but must have a different origin and a more perfect standard.

As the geometrician, by reflecting only upon the extension and figure of matter, forms a set of notions more accurate and scientific than any which the senses exhibit, so the natural philosopher, reflecting upon other attributes of matter, forms another set, such as those of density, quantity of matter, velocity, momentum, fluidity, elasticity, centres of gravity, and of oscillation. These notions are accurate and scientific ; but they cannot enter into a mind that has not some degree of judgment, nor can we make them intelligible to children, until they have some ripeness of understanding.

In navigation, the notions of latitude, longitude, course, leeway, cannot be made intelligible to children ; and so it is with regard to the terms of every science, and of every art about which we can reason. They have had their five senses as perfect as men for years before they are capable of distinguishing, comparing, and perceiving the relations of things, so as to be able to form such notions. They acquire the intellectual powers by a slow progress, and by imperceptible degrees ; and by means of them, learn to form distinct and accurate notions of things, which the senses could never have imparted. [516]

Having said so much of the notions we get from the senses alone of the objects of sense, let us next consider what notions we can have from consciousness alone of the operations of our minds.

Mr Locke very properly calls consciousness an internal sense. It gives the like immediate knowledge of things in the mind— that is, of our own thoughts and feelings— as the senses give us of things external. There is this difference, however, that an

2 E 2

external object may be at rest, and the sense may be employed about it for some time. But the objects of consciousness are never at rest: the stream of thought flows like a river, without stopping a moment; the whole train of thought passes in succession under the eye of consciousness, which is always employed about the present. But is it consciousness that analyses complex operations, distinguishes their different ingredients, and combines them in distinct parcels under general names? This surely is not the work of consciousness, nor can it be performed without reflection,* recollecting and judging of what we were conscious of, and distinctly remember. This reflection does not appear in children. Of all the powers of the mind, it seems to be of the latest growth, whereas consciousness is coeval with the earliest.†

Consciousness, being a kind of internal sense, can no more give us distinct and accurate notions of the operations of our minds, than the external senses can give of external objects. Reflection upon the operations of our minds is the same kind of operation with that by which we form distinct notions of external objects. They differ not in their nature, but in this only, that one is employed about external, and the other about internal objects; and both may, with equal propriety, be called reflection. [517]

Mr Locke has restricted the word reflec-

tion to that which is employed about the operations of our minds, without any authority, as I think, from custom, the arbiter of language. For, surely, I may reflect upon what I have seen or heard, as well as upon what I have thought.* The word, in its proper and common meaning, is equally applicable to objects of sense, and to objects of consciousness.† He has likewise confounded reflection with consciousness, and seems not to have been aware that they are different powers, and appear at very different periods of life ‡

If that eminent philosopher had been aware of these mistakes about the meaning of the word reflection, he would, I think, have seen that, as it is by reflection upon the operations of our own minds that we can form any distinct and accurate notions of them, and not by consciousness without reflection, so it is by reflection upon the objects of sense, and not by the senses without reflection, that we can form distinct notions of them. Reflection upon anything, whether external or internal, makes it an object of our intellectual powers, by which we survey it on all sides, and form such judgments about it as appear to be just and true.

I proposed, in the *third* place, to consider our notions of the relations of things: and here I think, that, without judgment, we cannot have any notion of relations.

There are two ways in which we get the notion of relations. The first is, by comparing the related objects, when we have before had the conception of both. By this comparison, we perceive the relation, either immediately, or by a process of reasoning. That my foot is longer than my finger, I perceive immediately; and that three is the half of six. This immediate perception is immediate and intuitive judgment. That the angles at the base of an isosceles triangle are equal, I perceive by a process of reasoning, in which it will be acknowledged there is judgment.

Another way in which we get the notion of relations (which seems not to have occurred to Mr Locke) is, when, by attention to one of the related objects, we perceive or judge that it must, from its nature, have a certain relation to something else, which before, perhaps, we never thought of; and thus our attention to one of the related ob-

---

* See above, p. 2½2, a, note *.—H.

† See above, p. 239, b.—As a corollary of this truth, Mr Stewart makes the following observations, in which he is supported by every competent authority in education. The two northern universities have long withdrawn themselves from the reproach of placing Physics last in their curriculum of arts. In that of Edinburgh, no order is prescribed; but in St Andrew's and Glasgow, the class of Physics still stands after those of Mental Philosophy. This absurdity is, it is to be observed, altogether of a modern introduction For, when our Scottish universities were founded, and long after, the philosophy of mind was taught by the Professor of Physics. " I apprehend," says Mr Stewart, " that the study of the mind should form the last branch of the education of youth; an order which nature herself seems to point out, by what I have already remarked with respect to the development of our faculties. After the understanding is well stored with particular facts, and has been conversant with particular scientific pursuits, it will be enabled to speculate concerning its own powers with additional advantage, and will run no hazard in indulging too far in such inquiries. Nothing can be more absurd, on this as well as on many other accounts, than the common practice which is followed in our universities, [in some only,] of beginning a course of philosophical education with the study of Logic. If this order were completely reversed; and if the study of Logic were delayed till after the mind of the student was well stored with particular facts in Physics, in Chemistry, in Natural and Civil History, his attention might be led with the most important advantage, and without any danger to his power of observation, to an examination of his own faculties, which, besides opening to him a new and pleasing field of speculation, would enable him to form an estimate of his own powers, of the acquisitions he has made, of the habits he has formed, and of the farther improvements of which his mind is susceptible."—H.

---

* See note before last, and note at p. 347, b.—H.

† Mr Stewart makes a curious mistatement of the meaning attached by Reid to the word Reflection, if this passage and others are taken into account.—See *Elements*, I. p. 106, note †.—H.

‡ Consciousness and Reflection cannot be analysed into different powers. Reflection is only, in Locke's meaning of the word, (and this is the more correct,) Consciousness, concentrated by an act of Will on the phænomena of mind—i. e., internal Attention; in Reid's, what is it but Attention in general?—H.

jects produces the notion of a correlate, and of a certain relation between them. [518]

Thus, when I attend to colour, figure, weight, I cannot help judging these to be qualities which cannot exist without a subject; that is, something which is coloured, figured, heavy. If I had not perceived such things to be qualities, I should never have had any notion of their subject, or of their relation to it.

By attending to the operations of thinking, memory, reasoning, we perceive or judge that there must be something which thinks, remembers, and reasons, which we call the mind. When we attend to any change that happens in Nature, judgment informs us that there must be a cause of this change, which had power to produce it; and thus we get the notions of cause and effect, and of the relation between them. When we attend to body, we perceive that it cannot exist without space; hence we get the notion of space, (which is neither an object of sense nor of consciousness,) and of the relation which bodies have to a certain portion of unlimited space, as their place.

I apprehend, therefore, that all our notions of relations may more properly be ascribed to judgment as their source and origin, than to any other power of the mind. We must first perceive relations by our judgment, before we can conceive them without judging of them; as we must first perceive colours by sight, before we can conceive them without seeing them. I think Mr Locke, when he comes to speak of the ideas of relations, does not say that they are ideas of sensation or reflection, but only that they terminate in, and are concerned about, ideas of sensation or reflection. [519]

The notions of unity and number are so abstract, that it is impossible they should enter into the mind until it has some degree of judgment. We see with what difficulty, and how slowly, children learn to use, with understanding, the names even of small numbers, and how they exult in this acquisition when they have attained it. Every number is conceived by the relation which it bears to unity, or to known combinations of units; and upon that account, as well as on account of its abstract nature, all distinct notions of it require some degree of judgment.

In its proper place, I shall have occasion to shew that judgment is an ingredient in all determinations of taste, in all moral determinations, and in many of our passions and affections. So that this operation, after we come to have any exercise of judgment, mixes with most of the operations of our minds, and, in analysing them, cannot be overlooked without confusion and error.

[518—520]

CHAPTER II.

OF COMMON SENSE.

THE word *sense*, in common language, seems to have a different meaning from that which it has in the writings of philosophers; and those different meanings are apt to be confounded, and to occasion embarrassment and error.

Not to go back to ancient philosophy upon this point, modern philosophers consider sense as a power that has nothing to do with judgment. Sense they consider as the power by which we receive certain ideas or impressions from objects; and judgment as the power by which we compare those ideas, and perceive their necessary agreements and disagreements. [520]

The external senses give us the idea of colour, figure, sound, and other qualities of body, primary or secondary. Mr Locke gave the name of an internal sense to consciousness, because by it we have the ideas of thought, memory, reasoning, and other operations of our own minds. Dr Hutcheson of Glasgow, conceiving that we have simple and original ideas which cannot be imputed either to the external senses or to consciousness, introduced other internal senses; such as the sense of harmony, the sense of beauty, and the moral sense. Ancient philosophers also spake of internal senses, of which memory was accounted one.

But all these senses, whether external or internal, have been represented by philosophers as the means of furnishing our minds with ideas, without including any kind of judgment. Dr Hutcheson defines a sense to be a determination of the mind to receive any idea from the presence of an object independent on our will.

"By this term (sense) philosophers, in general, have denominated those faculties in consequence of which we are liable to feelings relative to ourselves only, and from which they have not pretended to draw any conclusions concerning the nature of things; whereas truth is not relative, but absolute and real.—(Dr Priestly's "Examination of Dr Reid," &c., p. 123.)

On the contrary, in common language, sense always implies judgment. A man of sense is a man of judgment. Good sense is good judgment. Nonsense is what is evidently contrary to right judgment. Common sense is that degree of judgment which is common to men with whom we can converse and transact business.

Seeing and hearing, by philosophers, are called senses, because we have ideas by

* On *Common Sense*, name and thing, see Note A. —H.

them ; by the vulgar they are called senses, because we judge by them. We judge of colours by the eye; of sounds by the ear ; of beauty and deformity by taste ; of right and wrong in conduct, by our moral sense or conscience. [521]

Sometimes philosophers, who represent it as the sole province of sense to furnish us with ideas, fall unawares into the popular opinion that they are judging faculties. Thus Locke, Book IV. chap. 2 :—" And of this, (that the quality or accident of colour doth really exist, and hath a being without me,) the greatest assurance I can possibly have, and to which my faculties can attain, is the testimony of my eyes, which are the proper and sole judges of this thing."

This popular meaning of the word *sense* is not peculiar to the English language. The corresponding words in Greek, Latin, and, I believe, in all the European languages, have the same latitude. The Latin words *sentire, sententia, sensa,** *sensus,* from the last of which the English word *sense* is borrowed, express judgment or opinion, and are applied indifferently to objects of external sense, of taste, of morals, and of the understanding.

I cannot pretend to assign the reason why a word, which is no term of art, which is familiar in common conversation, should have so different a meaning in philosophical writings. I shall only observe, that the philosophical meaning corresponds perfectly with the account which Mr Locke and other modern philosophers give of judgment. For, if the sole province of the senses, external and internal, be to furnish the mind with the ideas about which we judge and reason, it seems to be a natural consequence, that the sole province of judgment should be to compare those ideas, and to perceive their necessary relations.

These two opinions seem to be so connected, that one may have been the cause of the other. I apprehend, however, that, if both be true, there is no room for any knowledge or judgment, either of the real existence of contingent things, or of their contingent relations.

To return to the popular meaning of the word sense. I believe it would be much more difficult to find good authors who never use it in that meaning, than to find such as do. [522]

We may take Mr Pope as good authority for the meaning of an English word. He uses it often, and, in his "Epistle to the Earl of Burlington," has made a little descant upon it.

* What does *sensa* mean ? Is it an erratum, or does he refer to *sensa,* once only. I believe, employed by Cicero, and interpreted by Nonius Marcellus, as *quæ sentiuntur ?"—H.

" Oft have you hinted to your brother Peer,
A certain truth, which many buy too dear:
Something there is more needful than expense,
And something previous ev'n to taste—'tis sense.
Good sense, which only is the gift of heaven,
And, though no science, fairly worth the seven;
A light which in yourself you must perceive,
Jones and Le Notre have it not to give."

This inward light or sense is given by heaven to different persons in different degrees. There is a certain degree of it which is necessary to our being subjects of law and government, capable of managing our own affairs, and answerable for our conduct towards others : this is called common sense, because it is common to all men with whom we can transact business, or call to account for their conduct.

The laws of all civilised nations distinguish those who have this gift of heaven, from those who have it not. The last may have rights which ought not to be violated, but, having no understanding in themselves to direct their actions, the laws appoint them to be guided by the understanding of others. It is easily discerned by its effects in men's actions, in their speeches, and even in their looks ; and when it is made a question whether a man has this natural gift or not, a judge or a jury, upon a short conversation with him, can, for the most part, determine the question with great assurance.

The same degree of understanding which makes a man capable of acting with common prudence in the conduct of life, makes him capable of discovering what is true and what is false in matters that are self-evident, and which he distinctly apprehends. [523]

All knowledge, and all science, must be built upon principles that are self-evident ; and of such principles every man who has common sense is a competent judge, when he conceives them distinctly. Hence it is, that disputes very often terminate in an appeal to common sense.

While the parties are in the first principles on which their arguments are grounded, there is room for reasoning ; but when one denies what to the other appears too evident to need or to admit of proof, reasoning seems to be at an end ; an appeal is made to common sense, and each party is left to enjoy his own opinion.

There seems to be no remedy for this, nor any way left to discuss such appeals, unless the decisions of common sense can be brought into a code in which all reasonable men shall acquiesce. This, indeed, if it be possible, would be very desirable, and would supply a desideratum in logic ; and why should it be thought impossible that reasonable men should agree in things that are self-evident ?

All that is intended in this chapter is to explain the meaning of common sense, that it may not be treated, as it has been by some, as a new principle, or as a word with-

[521–523]

out any meaning. I have endeavoured to shew that sense, in its most common, and therefore its most proper meaning, signifies judgment, though philosophers often use it in another meaning. From this it is natural to think that common sense should mean common judgment; and so it really does.

What the precise limits are which divide common judgment from what is beyond it on the one hand, and from what falls short of it on the other, may be difficult to determine; and men may agree in the meaning of the word who have different opinions about those limits, or who even never thought of fixing them. This is as intelligible as, that all Englishmen should mean the same thing by the county of York, though perhaps not a hundredth part of them can point out its precise limits. [524]

Indeed, it seems to me, that common sense is as unambiguous a word and as well understood as the county of York. We find it in innumerable places in good writers; we hear it on innumerable occasions in conversation; and, as far as I am able to judge, always in the same meaning. And this is probably the reason why it is so seldom defined or explained.

Dr Johnson, in the authorities he gives, to shew that the word *sense* signifies understanding, soundness of faculties, strength of natural reason, quotes Dr Bentley for what may be called a definition of common sense, though probably not intended for that purpose, but mentioned accidentally: "God hath endowed mankind with power and abilities, which we call natural light and reason, and common sense."

It is true that common sense is a popular and not a scholastic word; and by most of those who have treated systematically of the powers of the understanding, it is only occasionally mentioned, as it is by other writers. But I recollect two philosophical writers, who are exceptions to this remark. One is Buffier, who treated largely of common sense, as a principle of knowledge, above fifty years ago. The other is Bishop Berkeley, who, I think, has laid as much stress upon common sense, in opposition to the doctrines of philosophers, as any philosopher that has come after him. If the reader chooses to look back to Essay II. chap. 10, he will be satisfied of this, from the quotations there made for another purpose, which it is unnecessary here to repeat.

Men rarely ask what common sense is; because every man believes himself possessed of it, and would take it for an imputation upon his understanding to be thought unacquainted with it. Yet I remember two very eminent authors who have put this question; and it is not improper to hear their sentiments upon a subject so frequently mentioned, and so rarely canvassed. [525]

It is well known that Lord Shaftesbury gave to one of his Treatises the title of "Sensus Communis; an Essay on the Freedom of Wit and Humour, in a Letter to a Friend;" in which he puts his friend in mind of a free conversation with some of their friends on the subjects of morality and religion. Amidst the different opinions started and maintained with great life and ingenuity, one or other would, every now and then, take the liberty to appeal to common sense. Every one allowed the appeal; no one would offer to call the authority of the court in question, till a gentleman whose good understanding was never yet brought in doubt, desired the company, very gravely, that they would tell him what common sense was.

"If," said he, "by the word *sense*, we were to understand opinion and judgment, and by the word *common*, the generality or any considerable part of mankind, it would be hard to discover where the subject of common sense could lie; for that which was according to the sense of one part of mankind, was against the sense of another. And if the majority were to determine common sense, it would change as often as men changed. That in religion, common sense was as hard to determine as *catholic* or *orthodox*. What to one was absurdity, to another was demonstration.

"In policy, if plain British or Dutch sense were right, Turkish and French must certainly be wrong. And as mere nonsense as passive obedience seemed, we found it to be the common sense of a great party amongst ourselves, a greater party in Europe, and perhaps the greatest part of all the world besides. As for morals, the difference was still wider; for even the philosophers could never agree in one and the same system. And some even of our most admired modern philosophers had fairly told us that virtue and vice had no other law or measure than mere fashion and vogue." [526]

This is the substance of the gentleman's speech, which, I apprehend, explains the meaning of the word perfectly, and contains all that has been said or can be said against the authority of common sense, and the propriety of appeals to it.

As there is no mention of any answer immediately made to this speech, we might be apt to conclude that the noble author adopted the sentiments of the intelligent gentleman whose speech he recites. But the contrary is manifest, from the title of *Sensus Communis* given to his Essay, from his frequent use of the word, and from the whole tenor of the Essay.

The author appears to have a double intention in that Essay, corresponding to the double title prefixed to it. One intention is, to justify the use of wit, humour, and ridicule, in discussing among friends the gravest subjects. " I can very well suppose," says he, " men may be frighted out of their wits; but I have no apprehension they should be laughed out of them. I can hardly imagine that, in a pleasant way, they should ever be talked out of their love for society, or reasoned out of humanity and common sense."

The other intention, signified by the title *Sensus Communis*, is carried on hand in hand with the first, and is to shew that common sense is not so vague and uncertain a thing as it is represented to be in the sceptical speech before recited. " I will try," says he, " what certain knowledge or assurance of things may be recovered in that very way, (to wit, of humour,) by which all certainty, you thought, was lost, and an endless scepticism introduced." [527]

He gives some criticisms upon the word *sensus communis* in Juvenal, Horace, and Seneca ; and, after shewing, in a facetious way throughout the treatise, that the fundamental principles of morals, of politics, of criticism, and of every branch of knowledge, are the dictates of common sense, he sums up the whole in these words :—" That some moral and philosophical truths there are so evident in themselves that it would be easier to imagine half mankind run mad, and joined precisely in the same species of folly, than to admit anything as truth which should be advanced against such natural knowledge, fundamental reason, and common sense." And, on taking leave, he adds :—" And now, my friend, should you find I had moralised in any tolerable manner, according to common sense, and without canting, I should be satisfied with my performance."

Another eminent writer who has put the question what common sense is, is Fenelon, the famous Archbishop of Cambray.

That ingenious and pious author, having had an early prepossession in favour of the Cartesian philosophy, made an attempt to establish, on a sure foundation, the metaphysical arguments which Des Cartes had invented to prove the being of the Deity. For this purpose, he begins with the Cartesian doubt. He proceeds to find out the truth of his own existence, and then to examine wherein the evidence and certainty of this and other such primary truths consisted. This, according to Cartesian principles, he places in the clearness and distinctness of the ideas. On the contrary, he places the absurdity of the contrary propositions, in their being repugnant to his clear and distinct ideas.

To illustrate this; he gives various examples of questions manifestly absurd and ridiculous, which every man of common understanding would, at first sight, perceive to be so ; and then goes on to this purpose.

" What is it that makes these questions ridiculous ? Wherein does this ridicule precisely consist ? It will, perhaps, be replied, that it consists in this, that they shock common sense. But what is this same common sense ? It is not the first notions that all men have equally of the same things. [528] This common sense, which is always and in all places the same ; which prevents inquiry ; which makes inquiry in some cases ridiculous ; which, instead of inquiring, makes a man laugh whether he will or not ; which puts it out of a man's power to doubt : this sense, which only waits to be consulted—which shews itself at the first glance, and immediately discovers the evidence or the absurdity of a question—is not this the same that I call my ideas ?

" Behold, then, those ideas or general notions, which it is not in my power either to contradict or examine, and by which I examine and decide in every case, insomuch that I laugh instead of answering, as often as anything is proposed to me, which is evidently contrary to what these immutable ideas represent."

I shall only observe upon this passage, that the interpretation it gives of Des Cartes' criterion of truth, whether just or not, is the most intelligible and the most favourable I have met with.

I beg leave to mention one passage from Cicero, and to add two or three from late writers, which shew that this word is not become obsolete, nor has changed its meaning.

" De Oratore," lib. 3.—" Omnes enim tacito quodam · sensu, sine ulla arte aut ratione, in artibus ac rationibus, recta ac prava dijudicant. Idque cum faciant in picturis, et in signis, et in aliis operibus, ad quorum intelligentiam a natura minus habent instrumenti, tum multo ostendunt magis in verborum, numerorum, vocumque judicio ; quod ea sint in communibus infixa sensibus ; neque earum rerum quemquam funditus natura voluit expertem."

" Hume's " Essays and Treatises," vol. I. p. 5.—" But a philosopher who proposes only to represent the common sense of mankind in more beautiful and more engaging colours, if by accident he commits a mistake, goes no farther, but, renewing his appeal to common sense, and the natural sentiments of the mind, returns into the right path, and secures himself from any dangerous illusion." [529]

Hume's " Enquiry concerning the Principles of Morals," p. 2.—" Those who have refused the reality of moral distinctions may be ranked among the disingenuous' disputants. The only way of converting an antagonist of this kind is to leave him to himself: for, finding that nobody keeps up the controversy with him, it is probable he will at last, of himself, from mere weariness, come over to the side of common sense and reason."

Priestley's "Institutes," Preliminary Essay, vol. i. p. 27—"Because common sense is a sufficient guard against many errors in religion, it seems to have been taken for granted that that common sense is a sufficient instructor also, whereas in fact, without positive instruction, men would naturally have been mere savages with respect to religion; as, without similar instruction, they would be savages with respect to the arts of life and the sciences. Common sense can only be compared to a judge; but what can a judge do without evidence and proper materials from which to form a judgment?"

Priestley's "Examination of Dr Reid," &c. page 127.—"But should we, out of complaisance, admit that what has hitherto been called judgment may be called sense, it is making too free with the established signification of words to call it common sense, which, in common acceptation, has long been appropriated to a very different thing—viz., to that capacity for judging of common things that persons of middling capacities are capable of." Page 129.—"I should, therefore, expect that, if a man was so totally deprived of common sense as not to be able to distinguish truth from falsehood in one case, he would be equally incapable of distinguishing it in another."

[530]

From this cloud of testimonies, to which hundreds might be added, I apprehend, that whatever censure is thrown upon those who have spoke of common sense as a principle of knowledge, or who have appealed to it in matters that are self-evident, will fall light, when there are so many to share in it. Indeed, the authority of this tribunal is too sacred and venerable, and has prescription too long in its favour to be now *wisely* called in question. Those who are disposed to do so, may remember the shrewd saying of Mr Hobbes—"When reason is against a man, a man will be against reason." This is equally applicable to common sense.

From the account I have given of the meaning of this term, it is easy to judge both of the proper use and of the abuse of it.

It is absurd to conceive that there can be any opposition between reason and common sense.* It is indeed the first-born of Reason; and, as they are commonly joined

together in speech and in writing, they are inseparable in their nature.

We ascribe to reason two offices, or two degrees. The first is to judge of things self-evident; the second to draw conclusions that are not self-evident from those that are. The first of these is the province, and the sole province, of common sense; and, therefore, it coincides with reason in its whole extent, and is only another name for one branch or one degree of reason. Perhaps it may be said, Why then should you give it a particular name, since it is acknowledged to be only a degree of reason? It would be a sufficient answer to this, Why do you abolish a name which is to be found in the language of all civilized nations, and has acquired a right by prescription? Such an attempt is equally foolish and ineffectual. Every wise man will be apt to think that a name which is found in all languages as far back as we can trace them, is not without some use. [531]

But there is an obvious reason why this degree of reason should have a name appropriated to it; and that is, that, in the greatest part of mankind, no other degree of reason is to be found. It is this degree that entitles them to the denomination of reasonable creatures. It is this degree of reason, and this only, that makes a man capable of managing his own affairs, and answerable for his conduct towards others. There is therefore the best reason why it should have a name appropriated to it.

These two degrees of reason differ in other respects, which would be sufficient to entitle them to distinct names.

The first is purely the gift of Heaven. And where Heaven has not given it, no education can supply the want. The second is learned by practice and rules, when the first is not wanting. A man who has common sense may be taught to reason. But, if he has not that gift, no teaching will make him able either to judge of first principles or to reason from them.

I have only this farther to observe, that the province of common sense is more extensive in refutation than in confirmation. A conclusion drawn by a train of just reasoning from true principles cannot possibly contradict any decision of common sense, because truth will always be consistent with itself. Neither can such a conclusion receive any confirmation from common sense, because it is not within its jurisdiction.

But it is possible that, by setting out from false principles, or by an error in reasoning, a man may be led to a conclusion that contradicts the decisions of common sense. In this case, the conclusion is within the jurisdiction of common sense, though the reasoning on which it was

---

* See above, p. 100, b, note †; and Mr Stewart's "Elements," II. p. 92.—H.

grounded be not; and a man of common sense may fairly reject the conclusion without being able to shew the error of the reasoning that led to it. [532]

Thus, if a mathematician, by a process of intricate demonstration, in which some false step was made, should be brought to this conclusion, that two quantities, which are both equal to a third, are not equal to each other, a man of common sense, without pretending to be a judge of the demonstration, is well entitled to reject the conclusion, and to pronounce it absurd.

CHAPTER III.

SENTIMENTS OF PHILOSOPHERS CONCERNING JUDGMENT.

A DIFFERENCE about the meaning of a word ought not to occasion disputes among philosophers; but it is often very proper to take notice of such differences, in order to prevent verbal disputes. There are, indeed, no words in language more liable to ambiguity than those by which we express the operations of the mind; and the most candid and judicious may sometimes be led into different opinions about their precise meaning.

I hinted before what I take to be a peculiarity in Mr Locke with regard to the meaning of the word judgment, and mentioned what, I apprehend, may have led him into it. But let us hear himself, Essay, book iv. chap. 14 :—" The faculty which God has given to man to supply the want of clear and certain knowledge, where that cannot be had, is judgment; whereby the mind takes its ideas to agree or disagree; or, which is the same, any proposition to be true or false, without perceiving a demonstrative evidence in the proofs. Thus the mind has two faculties conversant about truth and falsehood. *First,* Knowledge, whereby it certainly perceives, and is undoubtedly satisfied of, the agreement or disagreement of any ideas. *Secondly,* Judgment, which is the putting ideas together, or separating them from one another in the mind, when their certain agreement or disagreement is not perceived, but presumed to be so." [533]

Knowledge, I think, sometimes signifies things known; sometimes that act of the mind by which we know them. And in like manner opinion sometimes signifies things believed; sometimes the act of the mind by which we believe them. But judgment is the faculty which is exercised in both these acts of the mind. In knowledge, we judge without doubting; in opinion, with some mixture of doubt. But I know no authority, besides that of Mr Locke, for

calling knowledge a faculty, any more than for calling opinion a faculty.

Neither do I think that knowledge is confined within the narrow limits which Mr Locke assigns to it; because the far greatest part of what all men call human knowledge, is in things which neither admit of intuitive nor of demonstrative proof.

I have all along used the word *judgment* in a more extended sense than Mr Locke does in the passage above-mentioned. I understand by it that operation of mind by which we determine, concerning anything that may be expressed by a proposition, whether it be true or false. Every proposition is either true or false; so is every judgment. A proposition may be simply conceived without judging of it. But when there is not only a conception of the proposition, but a mental affirmation or negation, an assent or dissent of the understanding, whether weak or strong, that is judgment.

I think that, since the days of Aristotle, logicians have taken the word in that sense, and other writers, for the most part, though there are other meanings, which there is no danger of confounding with this. [534]

We may take the authority of Dr Isaac Watts, as a logician, as a man who understood English, and who had a just esteem of Mr Locke's Essay. Logic. Introd. page 5—" Judgment is that operation of the mind, wherein we join two or more ideas together by one affirmation or negation; that is, we either affirm or deny *this* to be *that.* So: *this tree is high ; that horse is not swift ; the mind of man is a thinking being; mere matter has no thought belonging to it; God is just; good men are often miserable in this world ; a righteous governor will make a difference betwixt the evil and the good;* which sentences are the effect of judgment, and are called propositions." And, Part II. chap. ii. § 9—" The evidence of sense is, when we frame a proposition according to the dictate of any of our senses. So we judge *that grass is green ; that a trumpet gives a pleasant sound ; that fire burns wood; water is soft ; and iron hard.*"

In this meaning, judgment extends to every kind of evidence, probable or certain and to every degree of assent or dissent. It extends to all knowledge as well as to all opinion; with this difference only, that in knowledge it is more firm and steady, like a house founded upon a rock. In opinion it stands upon a weaker foundation, and is more liable to be shaken and overturned.

These differences about the meaning of words are not mentioned as if truth was on one side and error on the other, but as an apology for deviating, in this instance, from the phraseology of Mr Locke, which is, for the most part, accurate and distinct; and because attention to the different meanings that are put upon words by different authors, is the best way to prevent our mistaking verbal differences for real differences of opinion.

The common theory concerning ideas naturally leads to a theory concerning judgment, which may be a proper test of its truth; for, as they are necessarily connected, they must stand or fall together. Their connection is thus expressed by Mr Locke, Book IV. chap. 1.—" Since the mind, in all its thoughts and reasonings, hath no other immediate object but its own ideas, which it alone does or can contemplate, it is evident that our knowledge is only conversant about them. Knowledge then seems to me to be nothing but the *perception of the connection and agreement, or disagreement and repugnancy, of any of our ideas. In this alone it consists.*" [535]

There can only be one objection to the justice of this inference; and that is, that the antecedent proposition from which it is inferred seems to have some ambiguity; for, in the first clause of that proposition, the mind is said to have no other *immediate* object but its own ideas; in the second, that it has no other object at all; that it does or can contemplate ideas alone.*

If the word *immediate* in the first clause be a mere expletive, and be not intended to limit the generality of the proposition, then the two clauses will be perfectly consistent, the second being only a repetition or explication of the first; and the inference that our knowledge is only conversant about ideas will be perfectly just and logical.

But, if the word *immediate* in the first clause be intended to limit the general proposition, and to imply that the mind has other objects besides its own ideas, though no other immediate objects, then it will not be true that it does or can contemplate ideas alone; nor will the inference be justly drawn that our knowledge is only conversant about ideas.

Mr Locke must either have meant his antecedent proposition, without any limitation by the word *immediate*, or he must have meant to limit it by that word, and to signify that there are objects of the mind which are not ideas.

The first of these suppositions appears to me most probable, for several reasons. [536]

First, Because, when he purposely defines the word *idea*, in the introduction to the Essay, he says it is whatsoever is the object of the understanding when a man thinks, or whatever the mind can be employed about in thinking. Here there is no room left for objects of the mind that are not ideas. The same definition is often repeated throughout the Essay. Sometimes, indeed, the word *immediate* is added, as in the passage now under consideration; but there is no intimation made that it ought to be understood when it is not expressed. Now, if it had really been his opinion that there are objects of thought which are not ideas, this definition, which is the groundwork of the whole Essay, would have been very improper, and apt to mislead his reader.

Secondly, He has never attempted to shew how there can be objects of thought which are not immediate objects; and, indeed, this seems impossible. For, whatever the object be, the man either thinks of it, or he does not. There is no medium between these. If he thinks of it, it is an immediate object of thought while he thinks of it. If he does not think of it, it is no object of thought at all. Every object of thought, therefore, is an immediate object of thought, and the word *immediate*, joined to objects of thought, seems to be a mere expletive.

Thirdly, Though Malebranche and Bishop Berkeley believed that we have no ideas of minds, or of the operations of minds, and that we may think and reason about them without ideas, this was not the opinion of Mr Locke. He thought that there are ideas of minds, and of their operations, as well as of the objects of sense; that the mind perceives nothing but its own ideas, and that all words are the signs of ideas.

A *fourth* reason is, That to suppose that he intended to limit the antecedent proposition by the word *immediate*, is to impute to him a blunder in reasoning, which I do not think Mr Locke could have committed; for what can be a more glaring paralogism than to infer that, since ideas are partly, though not solely, the objects of thought, it is evident that all our knowledge is only conversant about them. If, on the contrary, he meant that ideas are the only objects of thought, then the conclusion drawn is perfectly just and obvious; and he might very well say, *that, since it is ideas only that the mind does or can contemplate, it is evident that our knowledge is only conversant about them.* [537]

As to the conclusion itself, I have only to observe, that, though he extends it only to what he calls knowledge, and not to what he calls judgment, there is the same reason for extending it to both.

It is true of judgment, as well as of knowledge, that it can only be conversant about objects of the mind, or about things

* In reference to the polemic that follows, see, for a solution, what has been said above in regard to the ambiguity of the term *object*, and Note B. In regard to the doctrine of *Ideas*, as held by the philosophers, see above, and Note C, &c.—H.

which the mind can contemplate. Judgment, as well as knowledge, supposes the conception of the object about which we judge ; and to judge of objects that never were nor can be objects of the mind, is evidently impossible.

This, therefore, we may take for granted, that, if knowledge be conversant about ideas only, because there is no other object of the mind, it must be no less certain that judgment is conversant about ideas only, for the same reason.

Mr Locke adds, as the result of his reasoning, " Knowledge, then, seems to me to be nothing but the perception of the connection and agreement, or disagreement and repugnancy, of any of our ideas. In this alone it consists."

This is a very important point, not only on its own account, but on account of its necessary connection with his system concerning ideas, which is such as that both must stand or fall together ; for, if there is any part of human knowledge which does not consist in the perception of the agreement or disagreement of ideas, it must follow that there are objects of thought and of contemplation which are not ideas. [538]

This point, therefore, deserves to be carefully examined. With this view, let us first attend to its meaning, which, I think, can hardly be mistaken, though it may need some explication.

Every point of knowledge, and every judgment, is expressed by a proposition, wherein something is affirmed or denied of the subject of the proposition.

By perceiving the connection or agreement of two ideas, I conceive, is meant perceiving the truth of an affirmative proposition, of which the subject and predicate are ideas. In like manner, by perceiving the disagreement and repugnancy of any two ideas, I conceive is meant perceiving the truth of a negative proposition, of which both subject and predicate are ideas. This I take to be the only meaning the words can bear, and it is confirmed by what Mr Locke says in a passage already quoted in this chapter, that " the mind, taking its ideas to agree or disagree, is the same as taking any proposition to be true or false." Therefore, if the definition of knowledge given by Mr Locke be a just one, the subject, as well as the predicate of every proposition, by which any point of knowledge is expressed, must be an idea, and can be nothing else ; and the same must hold of every proposition by which judgment is expressed, as has been shewn above.

Having ascertained the meaning of this definition of human knowledge, we are next to consider how far it is just.

First, I would observe that, if the word

idea be taken in the meaning which it had at first among the Pythagoreans and Platonists, and if by knowledge be meant only abstract and general knowledge, (which I believe Mr Locke had chiefly in his view,) I think the proposition is true, that such knowledge consists solely in perceiving the truth of propositions whose subject and predicate are ideas. [539]

By ideas here I mean things conceived abstractly, without regard to their existence. We commonly call them abstract notions, abstract conceptions, abstract ideas—the Peripatetics called them universals ; and the Platonists, who knew no other ideas, called them ideas without addition.

Such ideas are both subject and predicate in every proposition which expresses abstract knowledge.

The whole body of pure mathematics is an abstract science ; and in every mathematical proposition, both subject and predicate are ideas, in the sense above explained. Thus, when I say the side of a square is not commensurable to its diagonal—in this proposition *the side and the diagonal of a square* are the subjects, (for, being a relative proposition, it must have two subjects.) A square, its side, and its diagonal, are ideas, or universals ; they are not individuals, but things predicable of many individuals. Existence is not included in their definition, nor in the conception we form of them. The predicate of the proposition is *commensurable*, which must be an universal, as the predicate of every proposition is so. In other branches of knowledge, many abstract truths may be found, but, for the most part, mixed with others that are not abstract.

I add, that I apprehend that what is strictly called demonstrative evidence, is to be found in abstract knowledge only. This was the opinion of Aristotle, of Plato, and, I think, of all the ancient philosophers ; and I believe in this they judged right. It is true, we often meet with demonstration in astromony, in mechanics, and in other branches of natural philosophy ; but, I believe, we shall always find that such demonstrations are grounded upon principles of suppositions, which have neither intuitive nor demonstrative evidence. [540]

Thus, when we demonstrate that the path of a projectile *in vacuo* is a parabola, we suppose that it is acted upon with the same force and in the same direction through its whole path by gravity. This is not intuitively known, nor is it demonstrable ; and, in the demonstration, we reason from the laws of motion, which are principles not capable of demonstration, but grounded on a different kind of evidence.

Ideas, in the sense above explained, are creatures of the mind ; they are fabricated by its rational powers ; we know their nature and their essence—for they are nothing more than they are conceived to be;—and, because they are perfectly known, we can reason about them with the highest degree of evidence.

And, as they are not things that exist, but things conceived, they neither have place nor time, nor are they liable to change.

When we say that they are in the mind, this can mean no more but that they are conceived by the mind, or that they are objects of thought. The act of conceiving them is, no doubt, in the mind ; the things conceived have no place, because they have not existence. Thus, a circle, considered abstractly, is said figuratively to be in the mind of him that conceives it ; but in no other sense than the city of London or the kingdom of France is said to be in his mind when he thinks of those objects.

Place and time belong to finite things that exist, but not to things that are barely conceived. They may be objects of conception to intelligent beings in every place and at all times. Hence the Pythagoreans and Platonists were led to think that they are eternal and omnipresent. If they had existence, they must be so ; for they have no relation to any one place or time, which they have not to every place and to every time.

The natural prejudice of mankind, that what we conceive must have existence, led those ancient philosophers to attribute existence to ideas ; and by this they were led into all the extravagant and mysterious parts of their system. When it is purged of these, I apprehend it to be the only intelligible and rational system concerning ideas. [541]

I agree with them, therefore, that ideas are immutably the same in all times and places ; for this means no more but that a circle is always a circle, and a square always a square.

I agree with them that ideas are the patterns or exemplars by which everything was made that had a beginning : for an intelligent artificer must conceive his work before it is made ; he makes it according to that conception ; and the thing conceived, before it exists, can only be an idea.

I agree with them that every species of things, considered abstractly, is an idea ; and that the idea of the species is in every individual of the species, without division or multiplication. This, indeed, is expressed somewhat mysteriously, according to the manner of the sect ; but it may easily be explained.

Every idea is an attribute ; and it is a common way of speaking to say, that the attribute is in every subject of which it may

541–543]

truly be affirmed. Thus, *to be above fifty years of age* is an attribute or idea. This attribute may be in, or affirmed of, fifty different individuals, and be the same in all, without division or multiplication.

I think that not only every species, but every genus, higher or lower, and every attribute considered abstractly, is an idea. These are things conceived without regard to existence ; they are universals, and, therefore, ideas, according to the ancient meaning of that word. [542]

It is true that, after the Platonists entered into disputes with the Peripatetics, in order to defend the existence of eternal ideas, they found it prudent to contract the line of defence, and maintained only that there is an idea of every species of natural things, but not of the genera, nor of things artificial. They were unwilling to multiply beings beyond what was necessary ; but in this, I think, they departed from the genuine principles of their system.

The definition of a species is nothing but the definition of the genus, with the addition of a specific difference ; and the division of things into species is the work of the mind, as well as their division into genera and classes. A species, a genus, an order, a class, is only a combination of attributes made by the mind, and called by one name. There is, therefore, the same reason for giving the name of idea to every attribute, and to every species and genus, whether higher or lower : these are only more complex attributes, or combinations of the more simple. And, though it might be improper, without necessity, to multiply beings which they believed to have a real existence, yet, had they seen that ideas are not things that exist, but things that are conceived, they would have apprehended no danger nor expense from their number.

Simple attributes, species and genera, lower or higher, are all things conceived without regard to existence ; they are universals ; they are expressed by general words ; and have an equal title to be called by the name of *ideas*.

I likewise agree with those ancient philosophers that ideas are the object, and the sole object, of science, strictly so called—that is, of demonstrative reasoning.

And, as ideas are immutable, so their agreements and disagreements, and all their relations and attributes, are immutable. All mathematical truths are immutably true. Like the ideas about which they are conversant, they have no relation to time or place, no dependence upon existence or change. That the angles of a plane triangle are equal to two right angles always was, and always will be, true, though no triangle had ever existed. [543]

The same may be said of all abstract truths : on that account they have often been called eternal truths ; and, for the same reason, the Pythagoreans ascribed eternity to the ideas about which they are conversant. They may very properly be called necessary truths ; because it is impossible they should not be true at all times and in all places.

Such is the nature of all truth that can be discovered, by perceiving the agreements and disagreements of *ideas*, when we take that word in its primitive sense. And that Mr Locke, in his definition of knowledge, had chiefly in his view abstract truths, we may be led to think from the examples he gives to illustrate it.

But there is another great class of truths, which are not abstract and necessary, and, therefore, cannot be perceived in the agreements and disagreements of ideas. These are all the truths we know concerning the real existence of things—the truth of our own existence—of the existence of other things, inanimate, animal, and rational, and of their various attributes and relations.

These truths may be called contingent truths. I except only .the existence and attributes of the Supreme Being, which is the only necessary truth I know regarding existence.

All other beings that exist depend for their existence, and all that belongs to it, upon the will and power of the first cause ; therefore, neither their existence, nor their nature, nor anything that befalls them, is necessary, but contingent.

But, although the existence of the Deity be necessary, I apprehend we can only deduce it from contingent truths. The only arguments for the existence of a Deity which I am able to comprehend, are grounded upon the knowledge of my own existence, and the existence of other finite beings. But these are contingent truths.   [544]

I believe, therefore, that by perceiving agreements and disagreements of ideas, no contingent truth whatsoever can be known, nor the real existence of anything, not even our own existence, nor the existence of a Deity, which is a necessary truth. Thus I have endeavoured to shew what knowledge may, and what cannot be attained, by perceiving the agreements and disagreements of ideas, when we take that word in its primitive sense.

We are, in the *next* place, to consider, whether knowledge consists in perceiving the agreement or disagreement of ideas, taking *ideas* in any of the senses in which the word is used by Mr Locke and other modern philosophers.

1. Very often the word *idea* is used so, that to have the idea of anything is a *periphrasis* for conceiving it. In this sense, an idea is not an object of thought, it is thought itself. It is the act of the mind by which we conceive any object. And it is evident that this could not be the meaning which Mr Locke had in view in his definition of knowledge.

2. A second meaning of the word *idea* is that which Mr Locke gives in the introduction to his Essay, when he is making an apology for the frequent use of it :—"It being that term, I think, which serves best to stand for whatsoever is the object of the understanding when a man thinks, or whatever it is which a man can be employed about in thinking."

By this definition, indeed, everything that can be the object of thought is an idea. The objects of our thoughts may, I think, be reduced to two classes.

The first class comprehends all those objects which we not only can think of, but which we believe to have a real existence : such as the Creator of all things, and all his creatures that fall within our notice. [545] I can think of the sun and moon, the earth and sea, and of the various animal, vegetable, and inanimate productions with which it hath pleased the bountiful Creator to enrich our globe. I can think of myself,ʼ of my friends and acquaintance. I think of the author of the Essay with high esteem. These, and such as these, are objects of the understanding which we believe to have real existence.

A second class of objects of the understanding which a man may be employed about in thinking, are things which we either believe never to have existed, or which we think of without regard to their existence.

Thus, I can think of Don Quixote, of the Island of Laputa, of Oceana, and of Utopia, which I believe never to have existed. Every attribute, every species, and every genus of things, considered abstractly, without any regard to their existence or non-existence, may be an object of the understanding.

To this second class of objects of the understanding, the name of idea does very properly belong, according to the primitive sense of the word, and I have already considered what knowledge does and what does not consist in perceiving the agreements and disagreements of such ideas.

But, if we take the word idea in so extensive a sense as to comprehend, not only the second, but also the first class of objects of the understanding, it will undoubtedly be true that all knowledge consists in perceiving the agreements and disagreements of ideas : for it is impossible that there can be any knowledge, any judgment, any opinion, true or false, which is not employed about the objects of the understanding. But whatsoever is an object of the understanding is an idea, according to this second meaning of the word.

Yet I am persuaded that Mr Locke, in his definition of knowledge, did not mean that the word idea should extend to all those things which we commonly consider as objects of the understanding. [546]

Though Bishop Berkeley believed that sun, moon, and stars, and all material things, are ideas, and nothing but ideas, Mr Locke nowhere professes this opinion. He believed that we have ideas of bodies, but not that bodies are ideas. In like manner, he believed that we have ideas of minds, but not that minds are ideas. When he inquired so carefully into the origin of all our ideas, he did not surely mean to find the origin of whatsoever may be the object of the understanding, nor to resolve the origin of everything that may be an object of understanding into sensation and reflection.

3. Setting aside, therefore, the two meanings of the word idea, before mentioned, as meanings which Mr Locke could not have in his view in the definition he gives of knowledge, the only meaning that could be intended in this place is that which I before called the philosophical meaning of the word idea, which hath a reference to the theory commonly received about the manner in which the mind perceives external objects, and in which it remembers and conceives objects that are not present to it. It is a very ancient opinion, and has been very generally received among philosophers, that we cannot perceive or think of such objects immediately, but by the medium of certain images or representatives of them really existing in the mind at the time.

To those images the ancients gave the name of species and phantasms. Modern philosophers have given them the name of ideas. "'Tis evident," says Mr Locke, book iv., chap. 4, "the mind knows not things immediately, but only by the intervention of the ideas it has of them." And in the same paragraph he puts this question: "How shall the mind, when it perceives nothing but its own ideas, know that they agree with things themselves?" [547]

This theory I have already considered, in treating of perception, of memory, and of conception. The reader will there find the reasons that lead me to think that it has no solid foundation in reason, or in attentive reflection upon those operations of our minds; that it contradicts the immediate dictates of our natural faculties, which are of higher authority than any theory; that it has taken its rise from the same prejudices which led all the ancient philosophers to think that the Deity could not make this world without some eternal matter to work upon, and which led the [546-548]

Pythagoreans and Platonists to think that he could not conceive the plan of the world he was to make without eternal ideas really existing as patterns to work by; and that this theory, when its necessary consequences are fairly pursued, leads to absolute scepticism, though those consequences were not seen by most of the philosophers who have adopted it.

I have no intention to repeat what has before been said upon those points; but only, taking ideas in this sense, to make some observations upon the definition which Mr Locke gives of knowledge.

First, If all knowledge consists in perceiving the agreements and disagreements of ideas—that is, of representative images of things existing in the mind—it obviously follows that, if there be no such ideas, there can be no knowledge. So that, if there should be found good reason for giving up this philosophical hypothesis, all knowledge must go along with it.

I hope, however, it is not so: and that, though this hypothesis, like many others, should totter and fall to the ground, knowledge will continue to stand firm upon a more permanent basis. [548]

The cycles and epicycles of the ancient astronomers were for a thousand years thought absolutely necessary to explain the motions of the heavenly bodies. Yet now, when all men believe them to have been mere fictions, astronomy has not fallen with them, but stands upon a more rational foundation than before. Ideas, or images of things existing in the mind, have, for a longer time, been thought necessary for explaining the operations of the understanding. If they should likewise at last be found to be fictions, human knowledge and judgment would suffer nothing by being disengaged from an unwieldy hypothesis. Mr Locke surely did not look upon the existence of ideas as a philosophical hypothesis. He thought that we are conscious of their existence, otherwise he would not have made the existence of all our knowledge to depend upon the existence of ideas.

Secondly, Supposing this hypothesis to be true, I agree with Mr Locke that it is an evident and necessary consequence that our knowledge can be conversant about ideas only, and must consist in perceiving their attributes and relations. For nothing can be more evident than this, that all knowledge, and all judgment and opinion, must be about things which are or may be immediate objects of our thought. What cannot be the object of thought, or the object of the mind in thinking, cannot be the object of knowledge or of opinion.

Everything we can know of any object, must be either some attribute of the object, or some relation it bears to some other object or objects. By the agreements and disagreements of objects, I apprehend Mr Locke intended to express both their attributes and their relations. If ideas then be the only objects of thought, the consequence is necessary, that they must be the only objects of knowledge, and all knowledge must consist in perceiving their agreements and disagreements—that is, their attributes and relations.

The use I would make of this consequence, is to shew that the hypothesis must be false, from which it necessarily follows. For if we have any knowledge of things that are not ideas, it will follow no less evidently, that ideas are not the only objects of our thoughts. [549]

Mr Locke has pointed out the extent and limits of human knowledge, in his fourth book, with more accuracy and judgment than any philosopher had done before; but he has not confined it to the agreements and disagreements of ideas. And I cannot help thinking that a great part of that book is an evident refutation of the principles laid down in the beginning of it.

Mr Locke did not believe that he himself was an idea; that his friends and acquaintance were ideas; that the Supreme Being, to speak with reverence, is an idea; or that the sun and moon, the earth and the sea, and other external objects of sense, are ideas. He believed that he had some certain knowledge of all those objects. His knowledge, therefore, did not consist solely in perceiving the agreements and disagreements of his ideas; for, surely, to perceive the existence, the attributes, and relations of things, which are not ideas, is not to perceive the agreements and disagreements of ideas. And, if things which are not ideas be objects of knowledge, they must be objects of thought. On the contrary, if ideas be the only objects of thought, there can be no knowledge, either of our own existence, or of the existence of external objects, or of the existence of a Deity.

This consequence, as far as concerns the existence of external objects of sense, was afterwards deduced from the theory of ideas by Bishop Berkeley with the clearest evidence; and that author chose rather to adopt the consequence than to reject the theory on which it was grounded. But, with regard to the existence of our own minds, of other minds, and of a Supreme Mind, the Bishop, that he might avoid the consequence, rejected a part of the theory, and maintained that we can think of minds, of their attributes and relations, without ideas. [550]

Mr Hume saw very clearly the consequences of this theory, and adopted them in his speculative moments; but candidly acknowledges that, in the common busi-

ness of life, he found himself under a necessity of believing with the vulgar. His "Treatise of Human Nature" is the only system to which the theory of ideas leads; and, in my apprehension, is, in all its parts, the necessary consequence of that theory.

Mr Locke, however, did not see all the consequences of that theory; he adopted it without doubt or examination, carried along by the stream of philosophers that went before him; and his judgment and good sense have led him to say many things, and to believe many things, that cannot be reconciled to it.

He not only believed his own existence, the existence of external things, and the existence of a Deity; but he has shewn very justly how we come by the knowledge of these existences.

It might here be expected that he should have pointed out the agreements and disagreements of ideas from which these existences are deduced; but this is impossible, and he has not even attempted it.

Our own existence, he observes, *we know intuitively;* but this intuition is not a perception of the agreement or disagreement of ideas; for the subject of the proposition, *I exist,* is not an idea, but a person.

The knowledge of external objects of sense, he observes, *we can have only by sensation. This sensation* he afterwards expresses more clearly by *the testimony of our senses, which are the proper and sole judges of this thing;* whose testimony is *the greatest assurance we can possibly have, and to which our faculties can attain.* This is perfectly agreeable to the common sense of mankind, and is perfectly understood by those who never heard of the theory of ideas. Our senses testify immediately the existence, and many of the attributes and relations of external material beings; and, by our constitution, we rely with assurance upon their testimony, without seeking a reason for doing so. This assurance, Mr Locke acknowledges, deserves the name of knowledge. But those external things are not ideas, nor are their attributes and relations the agreements and disagreements of ideas, but the agreements and disagreements of things which are not ideas. [551]

To reconcile this to the theory of ideas, Mr Locke says, *That it is the actual receiving of ideas from without that gives us notice of the existence of those external things.*

This, if understood literally, would lead us back to the doctrine of Aristotle, that our ideas or species come from without from the external objects, and are the image or form of those objects. But Mr Locke; I believe, meant no more by it, but that our ideas of sense must have a cause, and that we are not the cause of them ourselves.

Bishop Berkeley acknowledges all this, and shews very clearly that it does not afford the least shadow of reason for the belief of any material object—nay, that there can be nothing external that has any resemblance to our ideas but the ideas of other minds.

It is evident, therefore, that the agreements and disagreements of ideas can give us no knowledge of the existence of any material thing. If any knowledge can be attained of things which are not ideas, that knowledge is a perception of agreements and disagreements; not of ideas, but of things that are not ideas.

As to the existence of a deity, though Mr Locke was aware that Des Cartes, and many after him, had attempted to prove it merely from the agreements and disagreements of ideas; yet "he thought it an ill way of establishing that truth, and silencing Atheists, to lay the whole stress of so important a point upon that sole foundation." And, therefore, he proves this point, with great strength and solidity, from our own existence, and the existence of the sensible parts of the universe. [552] By memory, Mr Locke says, we have the knowledge of the past existence of several things. But all conception of past existence, as well as of external existence, is irreconcileable to the theory of ideas; because it supposes that there may be immediate objects of thought, which are not ideas presently existing in the mind.

I conclude, therefore, that, if we have any knowledge of our own existence, or of the existence of what we see about us, or of the existence of a Supreme Being, or if we have any knowledge of things past by memory, that knowledge cannot consist in perceiving the agreements and disagreements of ideas.

This conclusion, indeed, is evident of itself. For, if knowledge consists solely in the perception of the agreement or disagreement of ideas, there can be no knowledge of any proposition, which does not express some agreement or disagreement of ideas; consequently, there can be no knowledge of any proposition, which expresses either the existence, or the attributes or relations of things, which are not ideas. If, therefore, the theory of ideas be true, there can be no knowledge of anything but of ideas. And, on the other hand, if we have any knowledge of anything besides ideas, that theory must be false.

There can be no knowledge, no judgment or opinion about things which are not immediate objects of thought. This I take to be self-evident. If, therefore, ideas be the only immediate objects of thought, they must be the only things in nature of which we can have any knowledge, and about

which we can have any judgment or opinion.

This necessary consequence of the common doctrine of ideas Mr Hume saw, and has made evident in his "Treatise of Human Nature;" but the use he made of it was not to overturn the theory with which it is necessarily connected, but to overturn all knowledge, and to leave no ground to believe anything whatsoever. If Mr Locke had seen this consequence, there is reason to think that he would have made another use of it. [553]

That a man of Mr Locke's judgment and penetration did not perceive a consequence so evident, seems indeed very strange; and I know no other account that can be given of it but this—that the ambiguity of the word idea has misled him in this, as in several other instances. Having at first defined ideas to be whatsoever is the object of the understanding when we think, he takes it very often in that unlimited sense; and so everything that can be an object of thought is an idea. At other times, he uses the word to signify certain representative images of things in the mind, which philosophers have supposed to be immediate objects of thought. At other times, things conceived abstractly, without regard to their existence, are called ideas. Philosophy is much indebted to Mr Locke for his observations on the abuse of words. It is pity he did not apply these observations to the word idea, the ambiguity and abuse of which has very much hurt his excellent Essay.

There are some other opinions of philosophers concerning judgment, of which I think it unnecessary to say much.

Mr Hume sometimes adopts Mr Locke's opinion, that it is the perception of the agreement or disagreement of our ideas; sometimes he maintains that judgment and reasoning resolve themselves into conception, and are nothing but particular ways of conceiving objects; and he says, that an opinion or belief may most accurately be defined, *a lively idea related to or associated with a present impression.*—Treatise of Human Nature, vol. I. page 172.

I have endeavoured before, in the first chapter of this Essay, to shew that judgment is an operation of mind specifically distinct from the bare conception of an object. I have also considered his notion of belief, in treating of the theories concerning memory. [554].

Dr Hartley says—"That assent and dissent must come under the notion of ideas, being only those very complex internal feelings which adhere by association to such clusters of words as are called propositions in general, or affirmations and negations in particular."

This, if I understand its meaning, agrees with the opinion of Mr Hume, above men-

2 F

tioned, and has therefore been before considered.

Dr Priestley has given another definition of judgment:—" It is nothing more than the perception of the universal concurrence, or the perfect coincidence of two ideas; or the want of that concurrence or coincidence." This, I think, coincides with Mr Locke's definition, and therefore has been already considered.

There are many particulars which deserve to be known, and which might very properly be considered in this Essay on judgment; concerning the various kinds of propositions by which our judgments are expressed; their subjects and predicates; their conversions and oppositions: but as these are to be found in every system of logic, from Aristotle down to the present age, I think it unnecessary to swell this Essay with the repetition of what has been said so often. The remarks which have occurred to me upon what is commonly said on these points, as well as upon the art of syllogism; the utility of the school logic, and the improvements that may be made in it, may be found in a "Short Account of Aristotle's Logic, with Remarks," which Lord Kames has honoured with a place in his " Sketches of the History of Man." [555]

CHAPTER IV.

OF FIRST PRINCIPLES IN GENERAL.

ONE of the most important distinctions of our judgments is, that some of them are intuitive, others grounded on argument.

It is not in our power to judge as we will. The judgment is carried along necessarily by the evidence, real or seeming, which appears to us at the time. But, in propositions that are submitted to our judgment, there is this great difference—some are of such a nature that a man of ripe understanding may apprehend them distinctly, and perfectly understand their meaning, without finding himself under any necessity of believing them to be true or false, probable or improbable. The judgment remains in suspense, until it is inclined to one side or another by reasons or arguments.

But there are other propositions which are no sooner understood than they are believed. The judgment follows the apprehension of them necessarily, and both are equally the work of nature, and the result of our original powers. There is no searching for evidence, no weighing of arguments; the proposition is not deduced or inferred from another; it has the light of truth in itself, and has no occasion to borrow it from another.

Propositions of the last kind, when they are used in matters of science, have commonly been called *axioms*; and on whatever occasion they are used, are called *first principles*, *principles of common sense*, *common notions*, *self-evident truths*. Cicero calls them *naturæ judicia*, *judicia communibus hominum sensibus infixa*. Lord Shaftesbury expresses them by the words, *natural knowledge*, *fundamental reason*, and *common sense*. [556]

What has been said, I think, is sufficient to distinguish first principles, or intuitive judgments, from those which may be ascribed to the power of reasoning; nor is it a just objection against this distinction, that there may be some judgments concerning which we may be dubious to which class they ought to be referred. There is a real distinction between persons within the house, and those that are without; yet it may be dubious to which the man belongs that stands upon the threshold.

The power of reasoning—that is, of drawing a conclusion from a chain of premises—may with some propriety be called an art. " All reasoning," says Mr Locke, " is search and casting about, and requires pains and application." It resembles the power of walking, which is acquired by use and exercise. Nature prompts to it, and has given the power of acquiring it; but must be aided by frequent exercise before we are able to walk. After repeated efforts, much stumbling, and many falls, we learn to walk; and it is in a similar manner that we learn to reason.

But the power of judging in self-evident propositions, which are clearly understood, may be compared to the power of swallowing our food. It is purely natural, and therefore common to the learned and the unlearned, to the trained and the untrained. It requires ripeness of understanding, and freedom from prejudice, but nothing else.

I take it for granted that there are self-evident principles. Nobody, I think, denies it. And if any man were so sceptical as to deny that there is any proposition that is self-evident, I see not how it would be possible to convince him by reasoning.

But yet there seems to be great difference of opinions among philosophers about first principles. What one takes to be self-evident, another labours to prove by arguments, and a third denies altogether. [557]

Thus, before the time of Des Cartes, it was taken for a first principle, that there is a sun and a moon, an earth and sea, which really exist, whether we think of them or not. Des Cartes thought that the existence of those things ought to be proved by argument; and in this he has been followed by Malebranche, Arnauld, and Locke. They have all laboured to prove, by very weak reasoning, the existence of external objects of sense; and Berkeley and Hume, sensible of the weakness of their arguments, have been led to deny their existence altogether.

The ancient philosophers granted, that all knowledge must be grounded on first principles, and that there is no reasoning without them. The Peripatetic philosophy was redundant rather than deficient in first principles. Perhaps the abuse of them in that ancient system may have brought them into discredit in modern times; for, as the best things may be abused, so that abuse is apt to give a disgust to the thing itself; and as one extreme often leads into the opposite, this seems to have been the case in the respect paid to first principles in ancient and modern times.

Des Cartes thought one principle, expressed in one word, *cogito*, a sufficient foundation for his whole system, and asked no more.

Mr Locke seems to think first principles of very small use. Knowledge consisting, according to him, in the perception of the agreement or disagreement of our ideas; when we have clear ideas, and are able to compare them together, we may always fabricate first principles as often as we have occasion for them. Such differences we find among philosophers about first principles.

It is likewise a question of some moment, whether the differences among men about first principles can be brought to any issue? When in disputes one man maintains that to be a first principle which another denies, commonly both parties appeal to common sense, and so the matter rests. Now, is there no way of discussing this appeal? Is there no mark or criterion, whereby first principles that are truly such, may be distinguished from those that assume the character without a just title? I shall humbly offer in the following propositions what appears to me to be agreeable to truth in these matters, always ready to change my opinion upon conviction. [558]

1. *First*, I hold it to be certain. and even demonstrable, that all knowledge got by reasoning must be built upon first principles.*

This is as certain as that every house must have a foundation. The power of reasoning, in this respect, resembles the mechanical powers or engines; it must have a fixed point to rest upon, otherwise it spends its force in the air, and produces no effect.

When we examine, in the way of analysis, the evidence of any proposition, either we find it self-evident, or it rests upon one or more propositions that support it. The same thing may be said of the propositions

that support it, and of those that support them, as far back as we can go. But we cannot go back in this track to infinity. Where then must this analysis stop? It is evident that it must stop only when we come to propositions which support all that are built upon them, but are themselves supported by none—that is, to self-evident propositions.

Let us again consider a synthetical proof of any kind, where we begin with the premises, and pursue a train of consequences, until we come to the last conclusion or thing to be proved. Here we must begin, either with self-evident propositions or with such as have been already proved. When the last is the case, the proof of the propositions, thus assumed, is a part of our proof; and the proof is deficient without it. Suppose then the deficiency supplied, and the proof completed, is it not evident that it must set out with self-evident propositions, and that the whole evidence must rest upon them? So that it appears to be demonstrable that, without first principles, analytical reasoning could have no end, and synthetical reasoning could have no beginning; and that every conclusion got by reasoning must rest with its whole weight upon first principles, as the building does upon its foundation. [559]

2. A *second* proposition is, That some first principles yield conclusions that are certain, others such as are probable, in various degrees, from the highest probability to the lowest.

In just reasoning, the strength or weakness of the conclusion will always correspond to that of the principles on which it is grounded.

In a matter of testimony, it is self-evident that the testimony of two is better than that of one, supposing them equal in character, and in their means of knowledge; yet the simple testimony may be true, and that which is preferred to it may be false.

When an experiment has succeeded in several trials, and the circumstances have been marked with care, there is a self-evident probability of its succeeding in a new trial; but there is no certainty. The probability, in some cases, is much greater than in others; because, in some cases, it is much easier to observe all the circumstances that may have influence upon the event than in others. And it is possible that, after many experiments made with care, our expectation may be frustrated in a succeeding one, by the variation of some circumstance that has not, or perhaps could not be observed.

Sir Isaac Newton has laid it down as a first principle in natural philosophy, that a property which has been found in all bodies upon which we have had access to make

---

* So Aristotle, *plurics*.—H.

experiments, and which has always been found in its quantity to be in exact proportion the quantity of matter in every body, is to be held as an universal property of matter. [560]

This principle, as far as I know, has never been called in question. The evidence we have, that all matter is divisible, movable, solid, and inert, is resolvable into this principle; and, if it be not true, we cannot have any rational conviction that all matter has those properties. From the same principle that great man has shewn that we have reason to conclude that all bodies gravitate towards each other.

This principle, however, has not that kind of evidence which mathematical axioms have. It is not a necessary truth, whose contrary is impossible; nor did Sir Isaac ever conceive it to be such. And, if it should ever be found, by just experiments, that there is any part in the composition of some bodies which has not gravity, the fact, if duly ascertained, must be admitted as an exception to the general law of gravitation.

In games of chance, it is a first principle that every side of a die has an equal chance to be turned up; and that, in a lottery, every ticket has an equal chance of being drawn out. From such first principles as these, which are the best we can have in such matters, we may deduce, by demonstrative reasoning, the precise degree of probability of every event in such games.

But the principles of all this accurate and profound reasoning can never yield a certain conclusion, it being impossible to supply a defect in the first principles by any accuracy in the reasoning that is grounded upon them. As water, by its gravity, can rise no higher in its course than the fountain, however artfully it be conducted; so no conclusion of reasoning can have a greater degree of evidence than the first principles from which it is drawn.

From these instances, it is evident that, as there are some first principles that yield conclusions of absolute certainty, so there are others that can only yield probable conclusions; and that the lowest degree of probability must be grounded on first principles as well as absolute certainty.[*] [561]

3. A *third* proposition is, That it would contribute greatly to the stability of human knowledge, and consequently to the improvement of it, if the first principles upon which the various parts of it are grounded were pointed out and ascertained.

We have ground to think so, both from facts, and from the nature of the thing.

There are two branches of human knowledge in which this method has been followed—to wit, mathematics and natural philosophy; in mathematics, as far back as we have books. It is in this science only, that, for more than two thousand years since it began to be cultivated, we find no sects, no contrary systems, and hardly any disputes; or, if there have been disputes, they have ended as soon as the animosity of parties subsided, and have never been again revived. The science, once firmly established upon the foundation of a few axioms and definitions, as upon a rock, has grown from age so age, so as to become the loftiest and the most solid fabric that human reason can boast.[*]

Natural philosophy, till less than two hundred years ago, remained in the same fluctuating state with the other sciences. Every new system pulled up the old by the roots. The system-builders, indeed, were always willing to accept of the aid of first principles, when they were of their side; but, finding them insufficient to support the fabric which their imagination had raised, they were only brought in as auxiliaries, and so intermixed with conjectures, and with lame inductions, that their systems were like Nebuchadnezzar's image, whose feet were partly of iron and partly of clay.

Lord Bacon first delineated the only solid foundation on which natural philosophy can be built; and Sir Isaac Newton reduced the principles laid down by Bacon into three or four axioms, which he calls *regulæ philosophandi*. From these, together with the phenomena observed by the senses, which he likewise lays down as first principles, he deduces, by strict reasoning, the propositions contained in the third book of his "Principia," and in his "Optics;" and by this means has raised a fabric in those two branches of natural philosophy, which is not liable to be shaken by doubtful disputation, but stands immovable upon the basis of self-evident principles. [562]

This fabric has been carried on by the accession of new discoveries; but is no more subject to revolutions.

The disputes about *materia prima*, substantial forms, Nature's abhorring a vacuum, and bodies having no gravitation in their proper place, are now no more. The builders in this work are not put to the necessity of holding a weapon in one hand while they build with the other; their whole employment is to carry on the work.

Yet it seems to be very probable, that, if natural philosophy had not been reared upon this solid foundation of self-evident principles, it would have been to this day a field

* Compare Stewart's "Elements," ii. p. 38.—H.   * See Stewart's "Elements," ii. p. 42.—H.

[560, 562]

of battle, wherein every inch of ground would have been disputed, and nothing fixed and determined.

I acknowledge that mathematics and natural philosophy, especially the former, have this advantage of most other sciences, that it is less difficult to form distinct and determinate conceptions of the objects about which they are employed; but, as this difficulty is not insuperable, it affords a good reason, indeed, why other sciences should have a longer infancy; but no reason at all why they may not at last arrive at maturity, by the same steps as those of quicker growth.

The facts I have mentioned may therefore lead us to conclude, that, if in other branches of philosophy the first principles were laid down, as has been done in mathematics and natural philosophy, and the subsequent conclusions grounded upon them, this would make it much more easy to distinguish what is solid and well supported from the vain fictions of human fancy. [563]

But, laying aside facts, the nature of the thing leads to the same conclusion.

For, when any system is grounded upon first principles, and deduced regularly from them, we have a thread to lead us through the labyrinth. The judgment has a distinct and determinate object. The heterogeneous parts being separated, can be examined each by itself.

The whole system is reduced to axioms, definitions, and deductions. These are materials of very different nature, and to be measured by a very different standard; and it is much more easy to judge of each, taken by itself, than to judge of a mass wherein they are kneaded together without distinction. Let us consider how we judge of each of them.

First, As to definitions, the matter is very easy. They relate only to words, and differences about them may produce different ways of speaking, but can never produce different ways of thinking, while every man keeps to his own definitions.

But, as there is not a more plentiful source of fallacies in reasoning than men's using the same word sometimes in one sense and at other times in another, the best means of preventing such fallacies, or of detecting them when they are committed, is definitions of words as accurate as can be given.

Secondly, As to deductions drawn from principles granted on both sides, I do not see how they can long be a matter of dispute among men who are not blinded by prejudice or partiality; for the rules of reasoning by which inferences may be drawn from premises have been for two thousand years fixed with great unanimity. No man pretends to dispute the rules of reasoning

laid down by Aristotle and repeated by every writer in dialectics. [564]

And we may observe by the way, that the reason why logicians have been so unanimous in determining the rules of reasoning, from Aristotle down to this day, seems to be, that they were by that great genius raised, in a scientific manner, from a few definitions and axioms. It may farther be observed, that, when men differ about a deduction, whether it follows from certain premises, this I think is always owing to their differing about some first principle. I shall explain this by an example.

Suppose that, from a thing having begun to exist, one man infers that it must have had a cause; another man does not admit the inference. Here it is evident, that the first takes it for a self-evident principle, that everything which begins to exist must have a cause. The other does not allow this to be self-evident. Let them settle this point, and the dispute will be at an end.

Thus, I think, it appears, that, in matters of science, if the terms be properly explained, the first principles upon which the reasoning is grounded be laid down and exposed to examination, and the conclusions regularly deduced from them, it might be expected that men of candour and capacity, who love truth, and have patience to examine things coolly, might come to unanimity with regard to the force of the deductions, and that their differences might be reduced to those they may have about first principles.

4. A *fourth* proposition is, That Nature hath not left us destitute of means whereby the candid and honest part of mankind may be brought to unanimity when they happen to differ about first principles. [565]

When men differ about things that are taken to be first principles or self-evident truths, reasoning seems to be at an end. Each party appeals to common sense. When one man's common sense gives one determination, another man's a contrary determination, there seems to be no remedy but to leave every man to enjoy his own opinion. This is a common observation, and, I believe, a just one, if it be rightly understood.

It is in vain to reason with a man who denies the first principles on which the reasoning is grounded. Thus, it would be in vain to attempt the proof of a proposition in Euclid to a man who denies the axioms. Indeed, we ought never to reason with men who deny first principles from obstinacy and unwillingness to yield to reason.

But is it not possible, that men who really love truth, and are open to conviction, may differ about first principles?

I think it is possible, and that it cannot, without great want of charity, be denied to be possible.

When this happens, every man who believes that there is a real distinction between truth and error, and that the faculties which God has given us are not in their nature fallacious, must be convinced that there is a defect or a perversion of judgment on the one side or the other.

A man of candour and humility will, in such a case, very naturally suspect his own judgment, so far as to be desirous to enter into a serious examination, even of what he has long held as a first principle. He will think it not impossible, that, although his heart be upright, his judgment may have been perverted, by education, by authority, by party zeal, or by some other of the common causes of error, from the influence of which neither parts nor integrity exempt the human understanding. [566]

In such a state of mind, so amiable, and so becoming every good man, has Nature left him destitute of any rational means by which he may be enabled, either to correct his judgment if it be wrong, or to confirm it if it be right ?

I hope it is not so. I hope that, by the means which nature has furnished, controversies about first principles may be brought to an issue, and that the real lovers of truth may come to unanimity with regard to them.

It is true that, in other controversies, the process by which the truth of a proposition is discovered, or its falsehood detected, is, by shewing its necessary connection with first principles, or its repugnancy to them. It is true, likewise, that, when the controversy is, whether a proposition be itself a first principle, this process cannot be applied. The truth, therefore, in controversies of this kind, labours under a peculiar disadvantage. But it has advantantages of another kind to compensate this.

1. For, in the *first* place, in such controversies, every man is a competent judge; and therefore it is difficult to impose upon mankind.

To judge of first principles, requires no more than a sound mind free from prejudice, and a distinct conception of the question. The learned and the unlearned, the philosopher and the day-labourer, are upon a level, and will pass the same judgment, when they are not misled by some bias, or taught to renounce their understanding from some mistaken religious principle.

In matters beyond the reach of common understanding, the many are led by the few, and willingly yield to their authority. But, in matters of common sense, the few must yield to the many, when local and temporary prejudices are removed. No man is now moved by the subtle arguments of Zeno against motion, though, perhaps, he knows not how to answer them. [567]

The ancient sceptical system furnishes a remarkable instance of this truth. That system, of which Pyrrho° was reputed the father, was carried down, through a succession of ages, by very able and acute philosophers, who taught men to believe nothing at all, and esteemed it the highest pitch of human wisdom to withhold assent from every proposition whatsoever. It was supported with very great subtilty and learning, as we see from the writings of Sextus Empiricus, the only author of that sect whose writings have come down to our age. The assault of the sceptics against all science seems to have been managed with more art and address than the defence of the dogmatists.

Yet, as this system was an insult upon the common sense of mankind, it died away of itself; and it would be in vain to attempt to revive it. The modern scepticism is very different from the ancient, otherwise it would not have been allowed a hearing; and, when it has lost the grace of novelty, it will die away also, though it should never be refuted.

The modern scepticism, I mean that of Mr Hume, is built upon principles which were very generally maintained by philosophers, though they did not see that they led to scepticism. Mr Hume, by tracing, with great acuteness and ingenuity, the consequences of principles commonly received, has shewn that they overturn all knowledge, and at last overturn themselves, and leave the mind in perfect suspense.

2. *Secondly*, We may observe that opinions which contradict first principles, are distinguished, from other errors, by this :— That they are not only false but absurd ; and, to discountenance absurdity, Nature hath given us a particular emotion—to wit, that of ridicule—which seems intended for this very purpose of putting out of countenance what is absurd, either in opinion or practice. [568]

This weapon, when properly applied, cuts with as keen an edge as argument. Nature hath furnished us with the first to expose absurdity ; as with the last to refute error. Both are well fitted for their several offices, and are equally friendly to truth when properly used.

Both may be abused *to* serve the cause of error ; but the same degree of judgment which serves to detect the abuse of argument in false reasoning, serves to detect the abuse of ridicule when it is wrong directed.

Some have, from nature, a happier talent for ridicule than others ; and the same thing holds with regard to the talent of reasoning. Indeed, I conceive there is hardly any absurdity, which, when touched with the pencil of a Lucian, a Swift, or a Voltaire, would not be put out of countenance, when there is not some religious panic, or very powerful prejudice, to blind the understanding.

But it must be acknowledged that the emotion of ridicule, even when most natural, may be stifled by an emotion of a contrary nature, and cannot operate till that is removed.

Thus, if the notion of sanctity is annexed to an object, it is no longer a laughable matter; and this visor must be pulled off before it appears ridiculous. Hence we see, that notions which appear most ridiculous to all who consider them coolly and indifferently, have no such appearance to those who never thought of them but under the impression of religious awe and dread.

Even where religion is not concerned, the novelty of an opinion to those who are too fond of novelties ; the gravity and solemnity with which it is introduced ; the opinion we have entertained of the author ; its apparent connection with principles already embraced, or subserviency to interests which we have at heart ; and, above all, its being fixed in our minds at that time of life when we receive implicitly what we are taught—may cover its absurdity, and fascinate the understanding for a time. [569]

But, if ever we are able to view it naked, and stripped of those adventitious circumstances from which it borrowed its importance and authority, the natural emotion of ridicule will exert its force. An absurdity can be entertained by men of sense no longer than it wears a mask. When any man is found who has the skill or the boldness to pull off the mask, it can no longer bear the light ; it slinks into dark corners for a while, and then is no more heard of, but as an object of ridicule.

Thus I conceive, that first principles, which are really the dictates of common sense, and directly opposed to absurdities in opinion, will always, from the constitution of human nature, support themselves, and gain rather than lose ground among mankind.

3. *Thirdly*, It may be observed, that, although it is contrary to the nature of first principles to admit of direct or *apodictical* proof; yet there are certain ways of reasoning even about them, by which those that are just and solid may be confirmed, and those that are false may be detected. It may here be proper to mention some of the topics from which we may reason in matters of this kind.

First, It is a good argument *ad hominem*, if it can be shewn that a first principle which a man rejects, stands upon the same footing with others which he admits : for, when this is the case, he must be guilty of an inconsistency who holds the one and rejects the other.

[569–571]

Thus the faculties of consciousness, of memory, of external sense, and of reason, are all equally the gifts of nature. No good reason can be assigned for receiving the testimony of one of them, which is not of equal force with regard to the others. The greatest sceptics admit the testimony of consciousness, and allow that what it testifies is to be held as a first principle. If, therefore, they reject the immediate testimony of sense or of memory, they are guilty of an inconsistency. [570]

Secondly, A first principle may admit of a proof *ad absurdum*.

In this kind of proof, which is very common in mathematics, we suppose the contradictory proposition to be true. We trace the consequences of that supposition in a train of reasoning ; and, if we find any of its necessary consequences to be manifestly absurd, we conclude the supposition from which it followed to be false ; and, therefore its contradictory to be true.

There is hardly any proposition, especially of those that may claim the character of first principles, that stands alone and unconnected. It draws many others along with it in a chain that cannot be broken. He that takes it up must bear the burden of all its consequences ; and, if that is too heavy for him to bear, he must not pretend to take it up.

Thirdly, I conceive that the consent of ages and nations, of the learned and unlearned, ought to have great authority with regard to first principles, where every man is a competent judge.

Our ordinary conduct in life is built upon first principles, as well as our speculations in philosophy ; and every motive to action supposes some belief. When we find a general agreement among men, in principles that concern human life, this must have great authority with every sober mind that loves truth.

It is pleasant to observe the fruitless pains which Bishop Berkeley takes to shew that his system of the non-existence of a material world did not contradict the sentiments of the vulgar, but those only of the philosophers.

With good reason he dreaded more to oppose the authority of vulgar opinion in a matter of this kind, than all the schools of philosophers. [571]

Here, perhaps, it will be said, What has authority to do in matters of opinion ? Is truth to be determined by most votes ? Or is authority to be again raised out of its grave to tyrannise over mankind ?

I am aware that, in this age, an advocate for authority has a very unfavourable plea ; but I wish to give no more to authority than is its due.

Most justly do we honour the names of

those benefactors to mankind who have contributed more or less to break the yoke of that authority which deprives men of the natural, the unalienable right of judging for themselves; but, while we indulge a just animosity against this authority, and against all who would subject us to its tyranny, let us remember how common the folly is, of going from one faulty extreme into the opposite.

Authority, though a very tyrannical mistress to private judgment, may yet, on some occasions, be a useful handmaid. This is all she is entitled to, and this is all I plead in her behalf.

The justice of this plea will appear by putting a case in a science, in which, of all sciences, authority is acknowledged to have least weight.

Suppose a mathematician has made a discovery in that science which he thinks important; that he has put his demonstration in just order; and, after examining it with an attentive eye, has found no flaw in it, I would ask, Will there not be still in his breast some diffidence, some jealousy, lest the ardour of invention may have made him overlook some false step? This must be granted. [572]

He commits his demonstration to the examination of a mathematical friend, whom he esteems a competent judge, and waits with impatience the issue of his judgment. Here I would ask again, Whether the verdict of his friend, according as it is favourable or unfavourable, will not greatly increase or diminish his confidence in his own judgment? Most certainly it will, and it ought.

If the judgment of his friend agree with his own, especially if it be confirmed by two or three able judges, he rests secure of his discovery without farther examination; but, if it be unfavourable, he is brought back into a kind of suspense, until the part that is suspected undergoes a new and a more rigorous examination.

I hope what is supposed in this case is agreeable to nature, and to the experience of candid and modest men on such occasions; yet here we see a man's judgment, even in a mathematical demonstration, conscious of some feebleness in itself, seeking the aid of authority to support it, greatly strengthened by that authority, and hardly able to stand erect against it, without some new aid.

Society in judgment, of those who are esteemed fair and competent judges, has effects very similar to those of civil society: it gives strength and courage to every individual; it removes that timidity which is as naturally the companion of solitary judgment, as of a solitary man in the state of nature.

Let us judge for ourselves, therefore; but

let us not disdain to take that aid from the authority of other competent judges, which a mathematician thinks it necessary to take in that science which, of all sciences, has least to do with authority.

In a matter of common sense, every man is no less a competent judge than a mathematician is in a mathematical demonstration; and there must be a great presumption that the judgment of mankind, in such a matter, is the natural issue of those faculties which God hath given them. Such a judgment can be erroneous only when there is some cause of the error, as general as the error is. When this can be shewn to be the case, I acknowledge it ought to have its due weight. But, to suppose a general deviation from truth among mankind in things self-evident, of which no cause can be assigned, is highly unreasonable. [573]

Perhaps it may be thought impossible to collect the general opinion of men upon any point whatsoever; and, therefore, that this authority can serve us in no stead in examining first principles. But I apprehend that, in many cases, this is neither impossible nor difficult.

Who can doubt whether men have universally believed the existence of a material world? Who can doubt whether men have universally believed that every change that happens in nature must have a cause? Who can doubt whether men have universally believed, that there is a right and a wrong in human conduct; some things that merit blame, and others that are entitled to approbation?

The universality of these opinions, and of many such that might be named, is sufficiently evident, from the whole tenor of human conduct, as far as our acquaintance reaches, and from the history of all ages and nations of which we have any records.

There are other opinions that appear to be universal, from what is common in the structure of all languages.

Language is the express image and picture of human thoughts; and from the picture we may draw some certain conclusions concerning the original.

We find in all languages the same parts of speech; we find nouns, substantive and adjective; verbs, active and passive, in their various tenses, numbers, and moods. Some rules of syntax are the same in all languages.

Now, what is common in the structure of languages, indicates an uniformity of opinion in those things upon which that structure is grounded. [574]

The distinction between substances, and the qualities belonging to them; between thought and the being that thinks; between thought and the objects of thought; is to be found in the structure of all languages. And, therefore, systems of philosophy, which abolish those distinctions, wage war with the common sense of mankind.

We are apt to imagine that those who formed languages were no metaphysicians; but the first principles of all sciences are the dictates of common sense, and lie open to all men; and every man who has considered the structure of language in a philosophical light, will find infallible proofs that those who have framed it, and those who use it with understanding have the power of making accurate distinctions, and of forming general conceptions, as well as philosophers. Nature has given those powers to all men, and they can use them when occasions require it, but they leave it to the philosophers to give names to them, and to descant upon their nature. In like manner, nature has given eyes to all men, and they can make good use of them; but the structure of the eye, and the theory of vision, is the business of philosophers.

Fourthly, Opinions that appear so early in the minds of men that they cannot be the effect of education or of false reasoning, have a good claim to be considered as first principles. Thus, the belief we have, that the persons about us are living and intelligent beings, is a belief for which, perhaps, we can give some reason, when we are able to reason; but we had this belief before we could reason, and before we could learn it by instruction. It seems, therefore, to be an immediate effect of our constitution.

The *last* topic I shall mention is, when an opinion is so necessary in the conduct of life, that, without the belief of it, a man must be led into a thousand absurdities in practice, such an opinion, when we can give no other reason for it, may safely be taken for a first principle. [575]

Thus I have endeavoured to shew, that, although first principles are not capable of direct proof, yet differences, that may happen with regard to them among men of candour, are not without remedy; that Nature has not left us destitute of means by which we may discover errors of this kind; and that there are ways of reasoning, with regard to first principles, by which those that are truly such may be distinguished from vulgar errors or prejudices.

CHAPTER V.

THE FIRST PRINCIPLES OF CONTINGENT TRUTHS.

"SURELY," says Bishop Berkeley, "it is a work well deserving our pains to make a strict inquiry concerning the first principles of knowledge; to sift and examine [575, 576]

them on all sides." What was said in the last chapter is intended both to shew the importance of this inquiry, and to make it more easy.

But, in order that such an inquiry may be actually made, it is necessary that the first principles of knowledge be distinguished from other truths, and presented to view, that they may be sifted and examined on all sides. In order to this end, I shall attempt a detail of those I take to be such. and of the reasons why I think them entitled to that character. [576]

If the enumeration should appear to some redundant, to others deficient, and to others both—if things which I conceive to be first principles, should to others appear to be vulgar errors, or to be truths which derive their evidence from other truths, and therefore not first principles – in these things every man must judge for himself. I shall rejoice to see an enumeration more perfect in any or in all of those respects; being persuaded that the agreement of men of judgment and candour in first principles would be of no less consequence to the advancement of knowledge in general, than the agreement of mathematicians in the axioms of geometry has been to the advancement of that science.

The truths that fall within the compass of human knowledge, whether they be self-evident, or deduced from those that are self-evident, may be reduced to two classes. They are either necessary and immutable truths, whose contrary is impossible; or they are contingent and mutable, depending upon some effect of will and power, which had a beginning, and may have an end.

That a cone is the third part of a cylinder of the same base and the same altitude, is a necessary truth. It depends not upon the will and power of any being. It is immutably true, and the contrary impossible. That the sun is the centre about which the earth, and the other planets of our system, perform their revolutions, is a truth; but it is not a necessary truth. It depends upon the power and will of that Being who made the sun and all the planets, and who gave them those motions that seemed best to him.

If all truths were necessary truths, there would be no occasion for different tenses in the verbs by which they are expressed. What is true in the present time, would be true in the past and future; and there would be no change or variation of anything in nature.

We use the present tense in expressing necessary truths; but it is only because there is no flexion of the verb which includes all times. When I say that three is the half of six, I use the present tense only; but I mean to express not only what now is, but what always was, and always will be; and so every proposition is to be understood by which we mean to express a necessary truth. Contingent truths are of another nature. As they are mutable, they may be true at one time, and not at another; and, therefore, the expression of them must include some point or period of time. [577]

If language had been a contrivance of philosophers, they would probably have given some flexion to the indicative mood of verbs, which extended to all times past, present, and future; for such a flexion only would be fit to express necessary propositions, which have no relation to time. But there is no language, as far as I know, in which such a flexion of verbs is to be found. Because the thoughts and discourse of men are seldom employed about necessary truths, but commonly about such as are contingent, languages are fitted to express the last rather than the first.

The distinction commonly made between abstract truths, and those that express matters of fact, or real existences, coincides in a great measure, but not altogether, with that between necessary and contingent truths. The necessary truths that fall within our knowledge are, for the most part, abstract truths. We must except the existence and nature of the Supreme Being, which is necessary. Other existences are the effects of will and power. They had a beginning, and are mutable. Their nature is such as the Supreme Being was pleased to give them. Their attributes and relations must depend upon the nature God has given them, the powers with which he has endowed them, and the situation in which he hath placed them.

The conclusions deduced by reasoning from first principles, will commonly be necessary or contingent, according as the principles are from which they are drawn. On the one hand, I take it to be certain, that whatever can, by just reasoning, be inferred from a principle that is necessary, must be a necessary truth, and that no contingent truth can be inferred from principles that are necessary.* [578]

Thus, as the axioms in mathematics are all necessary truths, so are all the conclusions drawn from them; that is, the whole body of that science. But from no mathematical truth can we deduce the existence of anything; not even of the objects of the science.

On the other hand, I apprehend there are very few cases in which we can, from principles that are contingent, deduce truths that are necessary. I can only recollect

one instance of this kind—namely—that, from the existence of things contingent and mutable, we can infer the existence of an immutable and eternal cause of them.

As the minds of men are occupied much more about truths that are contingent than about those that are necessary, I shall first endeavour to point out the principles of the former kind.

1. *First*, then, I hold, as a first principle, the existence of everything of which I am conscious.

Consciousness is an operation of the understanding of its own kind, and cannot be logically defined. The objects of it are our present pains, our pleasures, our hopes, our fears, our desires, our doubts, our thoughts of every kind; in a word, all the passions, and all the actions and operations of our own minds, while they are present. We may remember them when they are past; but we are conscious of them only while they are present.

When a man is conscious of pain, he is certain of its existence; when he is conscious that he doubts or believes, he is certain of the existence of those operations.

But the irresistible conviction he has of the reality of those operations is not the effect of reasoning; it is immediate and intuitive. The existence therefore of those passions and operations of our minds, of which we are conscious, is a first principle, which nature requires us to believe upon her authority. [579]

If I am asked to prove that I cannot be deceived by consciousness—to prove that it is not a fallacious sense—I can find no proof. I cannot find any antecedent truth from which it is deduced, or upon which its evidence depends. It seems to disdain any such derived authority, and to claim my assent in its own right.

If any man could be found so frantic as to deny that he thinks, while he is conscious of it, I may wonder, I may laugh, or I may pity him, but I cannot reason the matter with him. We have no common principles from which we may reason, and therefore can never join issue in an argument.

This, I think, is the only principle of common sense that has never directly been called in question.* It seems to be so firmly rooted in the minds of men, as to retain its authority with the greatest sceptics. Mr Hume, after annihilating body and mind, time and space, action and causation, and even his own mind, acknowledges the reality of the thoughts, sensations, and passions of which he is conscious.

---

* See Stewart's "Elements," ii. p. 38

* It could not possibly be called in question. For, in doubting the fact of his consciousness, the sceptic must at least affirm the fact of his doubt; but to affirm a doubt is to affirm the *consciousness* of it; the doubt would, therefore, be self-contradictory—i. e. annihilate itself.—H.

No philosopher has attempted, by any hypothesis, to account for this consciousness of our own thoughts, and the certain knowledge of their real existence which accompanies it. By this they seem to acknowledge that this at least is an original power of the mind; a power by which we not only have ideas, but original judgments, and the knowledge of real existence.

I cannot reconcile this immediate knowledge of the operations of our own minds with Mr Locke's theory, that all knowledge consists in perceiving the agreement and disagreement of ideas. What are the ideas, from whose comparison the knowledge of our own thoughts results? Or what are the agreements or disagreements which convince a man that he is in pain when he feels it? [580]

Neither can I reconcile it with Mr Hume's theory, that to believe the existence of anything, is nothing else than to have a strong and lively conception of it; or, at most, that belief is only some modification of the idea which is the object of belief. For, not to mention that propositions, not ideas, are the object of belief, in all that variety of thoughts and passions of which we are conscious we believe the existence of the weak as well as of the strong, the faint as well as the lively. No modification of the operations of our minds disposes us to the least doubt of their real existence.

As, therefore, the real existence of our thoughts, and of all the operations and feelings of our own minds, is believed by all men—as we find ourselves incapable of doubting it, and as incapable of offering any proof of it—it may justly be considered as a first principle, or dictate of common sense.

But, although this principle rests upon no other, a very considerable and important branch of human knowledge rests upon it,

For from this source of consciousness is derived all that we know, and indeed all that we can know, of the structure and of the powers of our own minds; from which we may conclude, that there is no branch of knowledge that stands upon a firmer foundation; for surely no kind of evidence can go beyond that of consciousness.

How does it come to pass, then, that in this branch of knowledge there are so many and so contrary systems? so many subtile controversies that are never brought to an issue? and so little fixed and determined? Is it possible that philosophers should differ most where they have the surest means of agreement—where everything is built upon a species of evidence which all men acquiesce in, and hold to be the most certain? [581]

This strange phænomenon may, I think, be accounted for, if we distinguish between [580–582]

consciousness and reflection, which are ofter improperly confounded *

The first is common to all men at all times; but is insufficient of itself to give us clear and distinct notions of the operations of which we are conscious, and of their mutual relations and minute distinctions. The second—to wit, attentive reflection upon those operations, making them objects of thought, surveying them attentively, and examining them on all sides—is so far from being common to all men, that it is the lot of very few. The greatest part of men, either through want of capacity, or from other causes, never reflect attentively upon the operations of their own minds. The habit of this reflection, even in those whom nature has fitted for it, is not to be attained without much pains and practice.

We can know nothing of the immediate objects of sight, but by the testimony of our eyes; and I apprehend that, if mankind had found as great difficulty in giving attention to the objects of sight, as they find in attentive reflection upon the operations of their own minds, our knowledge of the first might have been in as backward a state as our knowledge of the last.

But this darkness will not last for ever. Light will arise upon this benighted part of the intellectual globe. When any man is so happy as to delineate the powers of the human mind as they really are in nature, men that are free from prejudice, and capable of reflection, will recognise their own features in the picture; and then the wonder will be, how things so obvious could be so long wrapped up in mystery and darkness; how men could be carried away by false theories and conjectures, when the truth was to be found in their own breasts if they had but attended to it.

2. Another first principle, I think, is, *That the thoughts of which I am conscious, are the thoughts of a being which I call* MYSELF, *my* MIND, *my* PERSON. [582]

The thoughts and feelings of which we are conscious are continually changing, and the thought of this moment is not the thought of the last; but something which I call myself, remains under this change of thought. This self has the same relation to all the successive thoughts I am conscious of—they are all my thoughts; and every thought which is not my thought, must be the thought of some other person.

If any man asks a proof of this, I confess I can give none; there is an evidence in the proposition itself which I am unable to resist. Shall I think that thought can stand by itself without a thinking being? or that ideas can feel pleasure or pain? My nature dictates to me that it is impossible.

---

* Compare above, pp. 239, b, 258, a.—H.

And that nature has dictated the same to all men, appears from the structure of all languages : for in all languages men have expressed thinking, reasoning, willing, loving, hating, by personal verbs, which, from their nature, require a person who thinks, reasons, wills, loves, or hates. From which it appears, that men have been taught by nature to believe that thought requires a thinker, reason a reasoner, and love a lover.

Here we must leave Mr Hume, who conceives it to be a vulgar error, that, besides the thoughts we are conscious of, there is a mind which is the subject of those thoughts. If the mind be anything else than impressions and ideas, it must be a word without a meaning. The mind, therefore, according to this philosopher, is a word which signifies a bundle of perceptions ; or, when he defines it more accurately—" It is that succession of related ideas and impressions, of which we have an intimate memory and consciousness."

I am, therefore, that succession of related ideas and impressions of which I have the intimate memory and consciousness.

But who is the *I* that has this memory and consciousness of a succession of ideas and impressions ? Why, it is nothing but that succession itself. [583]

Hence, I learn, that this succession of ideas and impressions intimately remembers, and is conscious of itself. I would wish to be farther instructed, whether the impressions remember and are conscious of the ideas, or the ideas remember and are conscious of the impressions, or if both remember and are conscious of both ? and whether the ideas remember those that come after them, as well as those that were before them ? These are questions naturally arising from this system, that have not yet been explained.

This, however, is clear, that this succession of ideas and impressions, not only remembers and is conscious, but that it judges, reasons, affirms, denies—nay, that it eats and drinks, and is sometimes merry and sometimes sad.

If these things can be ascribed to a succession of ideas and impressions, in a consistency with common sense, I should be very glad to know what is nonsense.

The scholastic philosophers have been wittily ridiculed, by representing them as disputing upon this question—*Num chimæra bombinans in vacuo possit comedere secundas intentiones ?* and I believe the wit of man cannot invent a more ridiculous question. But, if Mr Hume's philosophy be admitted, this question deserves to be treated more gravely : for if, as we learn from this philosophy, a succession of ideas and impressions may eat, and drink, and be merry, I see no good reason why a chimera, which, if not the same is of kin to

an idea, may not chew the cud upon that kind of food which the schoolmen call second intentions.*

3. Another first principle I take to be— *That those things did really happen which I distinctly remember.* [584]

This has one of the surest marks of a first principle ; for no man ever pretended to prove it, and yet no man in his wits calls it in question : the testimony of memory, like that of consciousness, is immediate ; it claims our assent upon its own authority.†

Suppose that a learned counsel, in defence of a client against the concurring testimony of witnesses of credit, should insist upon a new topic to invalidate the testimony. " Admitting," says he, " the integrity of the witnesses, and that they distinctly remember what they have given in evidence— it does not follow that the prisoner is guilty. It has never been proved that the most distinct memory may not be fallacious. Shew me any necessary connection between that act of the mind which we call memory, and the past existence of the event remembered. No man has ever offered a shadow of argument to prove such a connection ; yet this is one link of the chain of proof against the prisoner ; and, if it have no strength, the whole proof falls to the ground : until this, therefore, be made evident—until it can be proved that we may safely rest upon the testimony of memory for the truth of past events—no judge or jury can justly take away the life of a citizen upon so doubtful a point."

I believe we may take it for granted, that this argument from a learned counsel would have no other effect upon the judge or jury, than to convince them that he was disordered in his judgment. Counsel is allowed to plead everything for a client that is fit to persuade or to move ; yet I believe no counsel ever had the boldness to plead this topic. And for what reason ? For no other reason, surely, but because it is absurd. Now, what is absurd at the bar, is so in the philosopher's chair. What would be ridiculous, if delivered to a jury of honest sensible citizens, is no less so when delivered gravely in a philosophical dissertation.

Mr Hume has not, as far as I remember, directly called in question the testimony of

---

* All this criticism of Hume proceeds upon the erroneous hypothesis that he was a *Dogmatist.* He was a *Sceptic*—that is, he *accepted* the principles asserted by the prevalent Dogmatism ; and only shewed that such and such conclusions were, on these principles, inevitable. The absurdity was not Hume's, but Locke's. This is the kind of criticism, however, with which Hume is generally assailed.—H.

† The datum of *Memory* does not stand upon the same ground as the datum of simple Consciousness. In so far as memory is consciousness, it cannot be denied. We cannot, without contradiction, deny the fact of memory as a present consciousness ; but we may, without contradiction, suppose that the past given therein, is only an illusion of the present.—H.

memory; but he has laid down the premises by which its authority is overturned, leaving it to his reader to draw the conclusion. [585]

He labours to shew that the belief or assent which always attends the memory and senses is nothing but the vivacity of those perceptions which they present. He shews very clearly, that this vivacity gives no ground to believe the existence of external objects. And it is obvious that it can give as little ground to believe the past existence of the objects of memory.

Indeed the theory concerning ideas, so generally received by philosophers, destroys all the authority of memory, as well as the authority of the senses. Des Cartes, Malebranche, and Locke, were aware that this theory made it necessary for them to find out arguments to prove the existence of external objects, which the vulgar believe upon the bare authority of their senses; but those philosophers were not aware that this theory made it equally necessary for them to find arguments to prove the existence of things past, which we remember, and to support the authority of memory.

All the arguments they advanced to support the authority of our senses, were easily refuted by Bishop Berkeley and Mr Hume, being indeed very weak and inconclusive. And it would have been as easy to answer every argument they could have brought, consistent with their theory, to support the authority of memory.

For, according to that theory, the immediate object of memory, as well as of every other operation of the understanding, is an idea present in the mind. And, from the present existence of this idea of memory I am left to infer, by reasoning, that, six months or six years ago, there did exist an object similar to this idea. [586]

But what is there in the idea that can lead me to this conclusion? What mark does it bear of the date of its archetype? Or what evidence have I that it had an archetype, and that it is not the first of its kind?

Perhaps it will be said, that this idea or image in the mind must have had a cause.

I admit that, if there is such an image in the mind, it must have had a cause, and a cause able to produce the effect; but what can we infer from its having a cause? Does it follow that the effect is a type, an image, a copy of its cause? Then it will follow, that a picture is an image of the painter, and a coach of the coachmaker.

A past event may be known by reasoning; but that is not remembering it. When I remember a thing distinctly, I disdain equally to hear reasons for it or against it. And so I think does every man in his senses.

[585–587]

4. Another first principle is, *Our own personal identity and continued existence, as far back as we remember any thing distinctly.*

This we know immediately, and not by reasoning. It seems, indeed, to be a part of the testimony of memory. Everything we remember has such a relation to ourselves as to imply necessarily our existence at the time remembered. And there cannot be a more palpable absurdity than that a man should remember what happened before he existed. He must therefore have existed as far back as he remembers anything distinctly, if his memory be not fallacious. This principle, therefore, is so connected with the last mentioned, that it may be doubtful whether both ought not to be included in one. Let every one judge of this as he sees reason. The proper notion of identity, and the sentiments of Mr Locke on this subject, have been considered before, under the head of Memory. [587]

5. Another first principle is, *That those things do really exist which we distinctly perceive by our senses, and are what we perceive them to be.*

It is too evident to need proof, that all men are by nature led to give implicit faith to the distinct testimony of their senses, long before they are capable of any bias from prejudices of education or of philosophy.

How came we at first to know that there are certain beings about us whom we call father, and mother, and sisters, and brothers, and nurse? Was it not by the testimony of our senses? How did these persons convey to us any information or instruction? Was it not by means of our senses?

It is evident we can have no communication, no correspondence or society with any created being, but by means of our senses. And, until we rely upon their testimony, we must consider ourselves as being alone in the universe, without any fellow-creature, living or inanimate, and be left to converse with our own thoughts.

Bishop Berkeley surely did not duly consider that it is by means of the material world that we have any correspondence with thinking beings, or any knowledge of their existence; and that, by depriving us of the material world, he deprived us, at the same time, of family, friends, country, and every human creature; of every object of affection, esteem, or concern, except ourselves.

The good Bishop surely never intended this. He was too warm a friend, too zealous a patriot, and too good a Christian to be capable of such a thought. He was not aware of the consequences of his system, and therefore they ought not to be imputed to him ; but we must impute them to the system itself. It stifles every generous and social principle. [588]

When I consider myself as speaking to men who hear me, and can judge of what I say, I feel that respect which is due to such an audience. I feel an enjoyment in a reciprocal communication of sentiments with candid and ingenious friends ; and my soul blesses the Author of my being, who has made me capable of this manly and rational entertainment.

But the Bishop shews me, that this is all a dream ; that I see not a human face ; that all the objects I see, and hear, and handle, are only the ideas of my own mind ; ideas are my only companions. Cold company, indeed ! Every social affection freezes at the thought !

But, my Lord Bishop, are there no minds left in the universe but my own ? Yes, indeed ; it is only the material world that is annihilated ; everything else remains as it was.

This seems to promise some comfort in my forlorn solitude. But do I see those minds ? No. Do I see their ideas ? No. Nor do they see me or my ideas. They are, then, no more to me than the inhabitants of Solomon's isles, or of the moon ; and my melancholy solitude returns. Every social tie is broken, and every social affection is stifled.

This dismal system, which, if it could be believed, would deprive men of every social comfort, a very good Bishop, by strict and accurate reasoning, deduced from the principles commonly received by philosophers concerning ideas. The fault is not in the reasoning, but in the principles from which it is drawn.

All the arguments urged by Berkeley and Hume, against the existence of a material world, are grounded upon this principle—that we do not perceive external objects themselves, but certain images or ideas in our own minds.* But this is no dictate of common sense, but directly contrary to the sense of all who have not been taught it by philosophy. [589]

We have before examined the reasons given by philosophers to prove that ideas, and not external objects, are the immediate objects of perception, and the instances given to prove the senses fallacious. Without repeating what has before been said upon those points, we shall only here observe, that, if external objects are perceived immediately, we have the same reason to

believe their existence as philosophers have to believe the existence of ideas, while they hold them to be the immediate objects of perception.*

6. Another first principle, I think, is, *That we have some degree of power over our actions, and the determinations of our will.*

All power must be derived from the fountain of power, and of every good gift. Upon His good pleasure its continuance depends, and it is always subject to his control.

Beings to whom God has given any degree of power, and understanding to direct them to the proper use of it, must be accountable to their Maker. But those who are intrusted with no power can have no account to make ; for all good conduct consists in the right use of power ; all bad conduct in the abuse of it.

To call to account a being who never was intrusted with any degree of power, is an absurdity no less than it would be to call to account an inanimate being. We are sure, therefore, if we have any account to make to the Author of our being, that we must have some degree of power, which, as far as it is properly used, entitles us to his approbation ; and, when abused, renders us obnoxious to his displeasure. [590]

It is not easy to say in what way we first get the notion or idea of *power.* It is neither an object of sense nor of consciousness. We see events, one succeeding another ; but we see not the power by which they are produced. We are conscious of the operations of our minds ; but power is not an operation of mind. If we had no notions but such as are furnished by the external senses, and by consciousness, it seems to be impossible that we should ever have any conception of power. Accordingly, Mr Hume, who has reasoned the most accurately upon this hypothesis, denies that we have any idea of power, and clearly refutes the account given by Mr Locke of the origin of this idea.

But it is in vain to reason from a hypothesis against a fact, the truth of which every man may see by attending to his own thoughts. It is evident that all men, very early in life, not only have an idea of power, but a conviction that they have some degree of it in themselves ; for this conviction is necessarily implied in many operations of mind, which are familiar to every man, and without which no man can act the part of a reasonable being.

First, It is implied in every act of volition. " Volition, it is plain," says Mr Locke, " is an act of the mind, knowingly

---

*   * Idealism, as already noticed, rests equally well, if not better, on the hypothesis that what we perceive (or are conscious of in perception) is only a modification of mind, as on the hypothesis that, in perception, we are conscious of a representative entity distinct from mind as from the external reality.—H.

    * Philosophers admitted that we are *conscious* of these: does Reid admit this of external objects ?—H.

exerting that dominion which it takes itself to have over any part of the man, by employing it in, or withholding it from any particular action." Every volition, therefore, implies a conviction of power to do the action willed. A man may desire to make a visit to the moon, or to the planet Jupiter; but nothing but insanity could make him will to do so. And, if even insanity produced this effect, it must be by making him think it to be in his power.

Secondly, This conviction is implied in all deliberation; for no man in his wits deliberates whether he shall do what he believes not to be in his power. *Thirdly,* The same conviction is implied in every resolution or purpose formed in consequence of deliberation. A man may as well form a resolution to pull the moon out of her sphere, as to do the most insignificant action which he believes not to be in his power. The same thing may be said of every promise or contract wherein a man plights his faith; for he is not an honest man who promises what he does not believe he has power to perform. [591]

As these operations imply a belief of some degree of power in ourselves; so there are others equally common and familiar, which imply a like belief with regard to others.

When we impute to a man any action or omission, as a ground of approbation or of blame, we must believe he had power to do otherwise. The same is implied in all advice, exhortation, command, and rebuke, and in every case in which we rely upon his fidelity in performing any engagement or executing any trust.

It is not more evident that mankind have a conviction of the exis ence of a material world, than that they have the conviction of some degree of power in themselves and in others; every one over his own actions, and the determinations of his will—a conviction so early, so general, and so interwoven with the whole of human conduct, that it must be the natural effect of our constitution, and intended by the Author of our being to guide our actions.

It resembles our conviction of the existence of a material world in this respect also, that even those who reject it in speculation, find themselves under a necessity of being governed by it in their practice; and thus it will always happen when philosophy contradicts first principles.

7. Another first principle is—*That the natural faculties, by which we distinguish truth from error, are not fallacious.* If any man should demand a proof of this, it is impossible to satisfy him. For, suppose it should be mathematically demonstrated, this would signify nothing in this case; because, to judge of a demonstration, a man [591–593]

must trust his faculties, and take for granted the very thing in question. [592]

If a man's honesty were called in question, it would be ridiculous to refer it to the man's own word, whether he be honest or not. The same absurdity there is in attempting to prove, by any kind of reasoning, probable or demonstrative, that our reason is not fallacious, since the very point in question is, whether reasoning may be trusted.

If a sceptic should build his scepticism upon this foundation, that all our reasoning and judging powers are fallacious in their nature, or should resolve at least to withhold assent until it be proved that they are not, it would be impossible by argument to beat him out of this stronghold; and he must even be left to enjoy his scepticism.

Des Cartes certainly made a false step in this matter, for having suggested this doubt among others—that whatever evidence he might have from his consciousness, his senses, his memory, or his reason, yet possibly some malignant being had given him those faculties on purpose to impose upon him; and, therefore, that they are not to be trusted without a proper voucher. To remove this doubt, he endeavours to prove the being of a Deity who is no deceiver; whence he concludes, that the faculties he had given him are true and worthy to be trusted.

It is strange that so acute a reasoner did not perceive that in this reasoning there is evidently a begging of the question.

For, if our faculties be fallacious, why may they not deceive us in this reasoning as well as in others? And, if they are not to be trusted in this instance without a voucher, why not in others? [593]

Every kind of reasoning for the veracity of our faculties, amounts to no more than taking their own testimony for their veracity; and this we must do implicitly, until God give us new faculties to sit in judgment upon the old; and the reason why Des Cartes satisfied himself with so weak an argument for the truth of his faculties, most probably was, that he never seriously doubted of it.

If any truth can be said to be prior to all others in the order of nature, this seems to have the best claim; because, in every instance of assent, whether upon intuitive, demonstrative, or probable evidence, the truth of our faculties is taken for granted, and is, as it were, one of the premises on which our assent is grounded. [*]

How then come we to be assured of this

---

[*] There is a presumption in favour of the veracity of the primary data of consciousness. This can only be rebutted by shewing that these facts are contradictory. Scepticism attempts to shew this on the principles which Dogmatism postulates.—H.

fundamental truth on which all others rest? Perhaps evidence, as in many other respects it resembles light, so in this also—that, as light, which is the discoverer of all visible objects, discovers itself at the same time, so evidence, which is the voucher for all truth, vouches for itself at the same time.

This, however, is certain, that such is the constitution of the human mind, that evidence discerned by us, forces a corresponding degree of assent. And a man who perfectly understood a just syllogism, without believing that the conclusion follows from the premises, would be a greater monster than a man born without hands or feet.

We are born under a necessity of trusting to our reasoning and judging powers; and a real belief of their being fallacious cannot be maintained for any considerable time by the greatest sceptic, because it is doing violence to our constitution. It is like a man's walking upon his hands, a feat which some men upon occasion can exhibit; but no man ever made a long journey in this manner. Cease to admire his dexterity, and he will, like other men, betake himself to his legs.   [594]

We may here take notice of a property of the principle under consideration, that seems to be common to it with many other first principles, and which can hardly be found in any principle that is built solely upon reasoning; and that is, that in most men it produces its effect without ever being attended to, or made an object of thought. No man ever thinks of this principle, unless when he considers the grounds of scepticism; yet it invariably governs his opinions. When a man in the common course of life gives credit to the testimony of his senses, his memory, or his reason, he does not put the question to himself, whether these faculties may deceive him; yet the trust he reposes in them supposes an inward conviction, that, in that instance at least, they do not deceive him.

It is another property of this and of many first principles, that they force assent in particular instances, more powerfully than when they are turned into a general proposition. Many sceptics have denied every general principle of science, excepting perhaps the existence of our present thoughts; yet these men reason, and refute, and prove, they assent and dissent in particular cases. They use reasoning to overturn all reasoning, and judge that they ought to have no judgment, and see clearly that they are blind. Many have in general maintained that the senses are fallacious, yet there never was found a man so sceptical as not to trust his senses in particular instances when his safety required it; and it may be observed of those who have professed scep-

ticism, that their scepticism lies in generals, while in particulars they are no less dogmatical than others.

8. Another first principle relating to existence, is, *That there is life and intelligence in our fellow-men with whom we converse.*

As soon as children are capable of asking a question, or of answering a question, as soon as they shew the signs of love, of resentment, or of any other affection, they must be convinced that those with whom they have this intercourse are intelligent beings.   [595]

It is evident they are capable of such intercourse long before they can reason. Every one knows that there is a social intercourse between the nurse and the child before it is a year old. It can, at that age, understand many things that are said to it.

It can by signs ask and refuse, threaten and supplicate. It clings to its nurse in danger, enters into her grief and joy, is happy in her soothing and caresses, and unhappy in her displeasure. That these things cannot be without a conviction in the child that the nurse is an intelligent being, I think must be granted.

Now, I would ask how a child of a year old comes by this conviction? Not by reasoning surely, for children do not reason at that age. Nor is it by external senses, for life and intelligence are not objects of the external senses.

By what means, or upon what occasions, Nature first gives this information to the infant mind is not easy to determine. We are not capable of reflecting upon our own thoughts at that period of life; and before we attain this capacity, we have quite forgot how or on what occasion we first had this belief; we perceive it in those who are born blind, and in others who are born deaf; and therefore Nature has not connected it solely either with any object of sight, or with any object of hearing. When we grow up to the years of reason and reflection, this belief remains. No man thinks of asking himself what reason he has to believe that his neighbour is a living creature. He would be not a little surprised if another person should ask him so absurd a question; and perhaps could not give any reason which would not equally prove a watch or a puppet to be a living creature.

But, though you should satisfy him of the weakness of the reasons he gives for his belief, you cannot make him in the least doubtful. This belief stands upon another foundation than that of reasoning; and therefore, whether a man can give good reasons for it or not, it is not in his power to shake it off.   [596]

Setting aside this natural conviction, I believe the best reason we can give, to prove that other men are living and intelligent, is, that their words and actions indicate like powers of understanding as we are conscious of in ourselves. The very same argument applied to the works of nature, leads us to conclude that there is an intelligent Author of nature, and appears equally strong and obvious in the last case as in the first; so that it may be doubted whether men, by the mere exercise of reasoning. might not as soon discover the existence of a Deity, as that other men have life and intelligence.

The knowledge of the last is absolutely necessary to our receiving any improvement by means of instruction and example; and, without these means of improvement, there is no ground to think that we should ever be able to acquire the use of our reasoning powers. This knowledge, therefore, must be antecedent to reasoning, and therefore must be a first principle.

It cannot be said that the judgments we form concerning life and intelligence in other beings are at first free from error. But the errors of children in this matter lie on the safe side; they are prone to attribute intelligence to things inanimate. These errors are of small consequence, and are gradually corrected by experience and ripe judgment. But the belief of life and intelligence in other men, is absolutely necessary for us before we are capable of reasoning; and therefore the Author of our being hath given us this belief antecedently to all reasoning.

9. Another first principle I take to be, *That certain features of the countenance, sounds of the voice, and gestures of the body, indicate certain thoughts and dispositions of mind.* [597]

That many operations of the mind have their natural signs in the countenance, voice, and gesture, I suppose every man will admit. *Omnis enim motus animi,* says Cicero, *suum quemdam habet a natura vultum, et vocem et gestum.* The only question is, whether we understand the signification of those signs, by the constitution of our nature, by a kind of natural perception similar to the perceptions of sense; or whether we gradually learn the signification of such signs from experience, as we learn that smoke is a sign of fire, or that the freezing of water is a sign of cold? I take the first to be the truth.

It seems to me incredible, that the notions men have of the expression of features, voice, and gesture, are entirely the fruit of experience. Children, almost as soon as born, may be frighted, and thrown into fits by a threatening or angry tone of voice. I knew a man who could make an infant cry, by whistling a melancholy tune in the same or in the next room; and again, by altering his key, and the strain of his music,

could make the child leap and dance for joy.

It is not by experience surely that we learn the expression of music; for its operation is commonly strongest the first time we hear it. One air expresses mirth and festivity—so that, when we hear it, it is with difficulty we can forbear to dance; another is sorrowful and solemn. One inspires with tenderness and love; another with rage and fury.

"Hear how Timotheus varied lays surprise,
And bid alternate passions fall and rise;
While at each change, the son of Lybian Jove
Now burns with glory, and then melts with love.
Now his fierce eyes with sparkling fury glow,
Now sighs steal out, and tears begin to flow.
Persians and Greeks, like turns of Nature, found,
And the world's victor stood subdu'd by sound."

It is not necessary that a man have studied either music or the passions, in order to his feeling these effects. The most ignorant and unimproved, to whom Nature has given a good ear, feel them as strongly as the most knowing. [598]

The countenance and gesture have an expression no less strong and natural than the voice. The first time one sees a stern and fierce look, a contracted brow, and a menacing posture, he concludes that the person is inflamed with anger. Shall we say, that, previous to experience, the most hostile countenance has as agreeable an appearance as the most gentle and benign? This surely would contradict all experience: for we know that an angry countenance will fright a child in the cradle. Who has not observed that children, very early, are able to distinguish what is said to them in jest from what is said in earnest, by the tone of the voice, and the features of the face? They judge by these natural signs, even when they seem to contradict the artificial.

If it were by experience that we learn the meaning of features, and sound, and gesture, it might be expected that we should recollect the time when we first learned those lessons, or, at least, some of such a multitude.

Those who give attention to the operations of children, can easily discover the time when they have their earliest notices from experience—such as that flame will burn, or that knives will cut. But no man is able to recollect in himself, or to observe in others, the time when the expression of the face, voice, and gesture, were learned.

Nay, I apprehend that it is impossible that this should be learned from experience.

When we see the sign, and see the thing signified always conjoined with it, experience may be the instructor, and teach us how that sign is to be interpreted. But

2 G

how shall experience instruct us when we see the sign only, when the thing signified is invisible? Now, this is the case here: the thoughts and passions of the mind, as well as the mind itself, are invisible, and therefore their connection with any sensible sign cannot be first discovered by experience: there must be some earlier source of this knowledge. [599]

Nature seems to have given to men a faculty or sense, by which this connection is perceived. And the operation of this sense is very analogous to that of the external senses.

When I grasp an ivory ball in my hand, I feel a certain sensation of touch. In the sensation there is nothing external, nothing corporeal. The sensation is neither round nor hard; it is an act of feeling of the mind, from which I cannot, by reasoning, infer the existence of any body. But, by the constitution of my nature, the sensation carries along with it the conception and belief of a round hard body really existing in my hand.

In like manner, when I see the features of an expressive face, I see only figure and colour variously modified. But, by the constitution of my nature, the visible object brings along with it the conception and belief of a certain passion or sentiment in the mind of the person.

In the former case, a sensation of touch is the sign. and the hardness and roundness of the body I grasp is signified by that sensation. In the latter case, the features of the person is the sign, and the passion or sentiment is signified by it.

The power of natural signs, to signify the sentiments and passions of the mind, is seen in the signs of dumb persons, who can make themselves to be understood in a considerable degree, even by those who are wholly inexperienced in that language.

It is seen in the traffic which has been frequently carried on between people that have no common acquired language. They can buy and sell, and ask and refuse, and shew a friendly or hostile disposition by natural signs. [600]

It was seen still more in the actors among the ancients who performed the gesticulation upon the stage, while others recited the words. To such a pitch was this art carried, that we are told Cicero and Roscius used to contend whether the orator could express anything by words, which the actor could not express in dumb show by gesticulation; and whether the same sentence or thought could not be acted in all the variety of ways in which the orator could express it in words.

But the most surprising exhibition of this kind, was that of the pantomimes among the Romans, who acted plays, or scenes of plays, without any recitation, and yet could be perfectly understood.

And here it deserves our notice, that, although it required much study and practice in the pantomimes to excel in their art, yet it required neither study nor practice in the spectators to understand them. It was a natural language, and therefore understood by all men, whether Romans, Greeks, or barbarians, by the learned and the unlearned.

Lucian relates, that a king, whose dominions bordered upon the Euxine Sea, happening to be at Rome in the reign of Nero, and having seen a pantomime act, begged him of Nero, that he might use him in his intercourse with all the nations in his neighbourhood; for, said he, I am obliged to employ I don't know how many interpreters, in order to keep a correspondence with neighbours who speak many languages, and do not understand mine; but this fellow will make them all understand him.

For these reasons, I conceive, it must be granted, not only that there is a connection established by Nature between certain signs in the countenance, voice, and gesture, and the thoughts and passions of the mind; but also, that, by our constitution, we understand the meaning of those signs, and from the sign conclude the existence of the thing signified. [601]

10. Another first principle appears to me to be—*That there is a certain regard due to human testimony in matters of fact, and even to human authority in matters of opinion.*

Before we are capable of reasoning about testimony or authority, there are many things which it concerns us to know, for which we can have no other evidence. The wise Author of nature hath planted in the human mind a propensity to rely upon this evidence before we can give a reason for doing so. This, indeed, puts our judgment almost entirely in the power of those who are about us in the first period of life; but this is necessary both to our preservation and to our improvement. If children were so framed as to pay no regard to testimony or to authority, they must, in the literal sense, perish for lack of knowledge. It is not more necessary that they should be fed before they can feed themselves, than that they should be instructed in many things before they can discover them by their own judgment.

But, when our faculties ripen, we find reason to check that propensity to yield to testimony and to authority, which was so necessary and so natural in the first period of life. We learn to reason about the regard due to them, and see it to be a childish weakness to lay more stress upon them than than reason justifies. Yet, I believe, to the end of life, most men are more apt to go into this extreme than into the contrary; and the natural propensity still retains some force.

The natural principles, by which our judgments and opinions are regulated before we come to the use of reason, seem to be no less necessary to such a being as man, than those natural instincts which the Author of nature hath given us to regulate our actions during that period. [602]

11. *There are many events depending upon the will of man, in which there is a self-evident probability, greater or less, according to circumstances.*

There may be in some individuals such a degree of frenzy and madness, that no man can say what they may or may not do. Such persons we find it necessary to put under restraint, that as far as possible they may be kept from doing harm to themselves or to others. They are not considered as reasonable creatures, or members of society. But, as to men who have a sound mind, we depend upon a certain degree of regularity in their conduct; and could put a thousand different cases, wherein we could venture, ten to one, that they will act in such a way, and not in the contrary.

If we had no confidence in our fellow-men that they will act such a part in such circumstances, it would be impossible to live in society with them. For that which makes men capable of living in society, and uniting in a political body under government, is, that their actions will always be regulated, in a great measure, by the common principles of human nature.

It may always be expected that they will regard their own interest and reputation, and that of their families and friends; that they will repel injuries, and have some sense of good offices; and that they will have some regard to truth and justice, so far at least as not to swerve from them without temptation.

It is upon such principles as these, that all political reasoning is grounded. Such reasoning is never demonstrative; but it may have a very great degree of probability, especially when applied to great bodies of men. [603]

12. The last principle of contingent truths I mention is, *That, in the phænomena of nature, what is to be, will probably be like to what has been in similar circumstances.*

We must have this conviction as soon as we are capable of learning anything from experience; for all experience is grounded upon a belief that the future will be like the past. Take away this principle, and the experience of an hundred years makes

us no wiser with regard to what is to come.

This is one of those principles which, when we grow up and observe the course of nature, we can confirm by reasoning. We perceive that Nature is governed by fixed laws, and that, if it were not so, there could be no such thing as prudence in human conduct; there would be no fitness in any means to promote an end; and what, on one occasion, promoted it, might as probably, on another occasion, obstruct it.

But the principle is necessary for us before we are able to discover it by reasoning, and therefore is made a part of our constitution, and produces its effects before the use of reason.

This principle remains in all its force when we come to the use of reason; but we learn to be more cautious in the application of it. We observe more carefully the circumstances on which the past event depended, and learn to distinguish them from those which were accidentally conjoined with it.

In order to this, a number of experiments, varied in their circumstances, is often necessary. Sometimes a single experiment is thought sufficient to establish a general conclusion. Thus, when it was once found, that, in a certain degree of cold, quicksilver became a hard and malleable metal, there was good reason to think that the same degree of cold will always produce this effect to the end of the world. [604]

I need hardly mention, that the whole fabric of natural philosophy is built upon this principle, and, if it be taken away, must tumble down to the foundation.

Therefore the great Newton lays it down as an axiom, or as one of his laws of philosophising, in these words, *Effectuum naturalium ejusdem generis easdem esse causas.* This is what every man assents to, as soon as he understands it, and no man asks a reason for it. It has, therefore, the most genuine marks of a first principle.

It is very remarkable, that, although all our expectation of what is to happen in the course of nature is derived from the belief of this principle, yet no man thinks of asking what is the ground of this belief.

Mr Hume, I think, was the first* who put this question; and he has shewn clearly and invincibly, that it is neither grounded upon reasoning, nor has that kind of intuitive evidence which mathematical axioms have. It is not a necessary truth.

He has endeavoured to account for it upon his own principles. It is not my business, at present, to examine the account he has given of this universal belief of man-

* Compare above, " Inquiry," c. vi. § 24. Stewart's "Elements", i. p. 205. " Philosophical Essays," p. 74, sq.—H.

[602–604]

* Hume was not the first: but on the various opinions touching the ground of this expectancy, I cannot touch.—H.

kind; because, whether his account of it be just or not, (and I think it is not,) yet, as this belief is universal among mankind, and is not grounded upon any antecedent reasoning, but upon the constitution of the mind itself, it must be acknowledged to be a first principle, in the sense in which I use that word.

I do not at all affirm, that those I have mentioned are all the first principles from which we may reason concerning contingent truths. Such enumerations, even when made after much reflection, are seldom perfect. [605]

CHAPTER VI.

FIRST PRINCIPLES OF NECESSARY TRUTHS.

ABOUT most of the first principles of necessary truths there has been no dispute, and therefore it is the less necessary to dwell upon them. It will be sufficient to divide them into different classes; to mention some, by way of specimen, in each class; and to make some remarks on those of which the truth has been called in question.

They may, I think, most properly be divided according to the sciences to which they belong.

1. There are some first principles that may be called *grammatical*. such as, *That every adjective in a sentence must belong to some substantive expressed or understood ; That every complete sentence must have a verb.*

Those who have attended to the structure of language, and formed distinct notions of the nature and use of the various parts of speech, perceive, without reasoning, that these, and many other such principles, are necessarily true.

2. There are *logical* axioms : such as, *That any contexture of words which does not make a proposition, is neither true nor false ; That·every proposition is either true or false ; That no proposition can be both true and false at the same time ; That reasoning in a circle proves nothing ; That whatever may be truly affirmed of a genus, may be truly affirmed of all the species, and all the individuals belonging to that genus.* [606]

3. Every one knows there are *mathematical* axioms.* Mathematicians have, from the days of Euclid, very wisely laid down the axioms or first principles on which they reason. And the effect which this appears to have had upon the stability and happy progress of this science, gives no small encouragement to attempt to lay the foundation of other sciences in a similar manner, as far as we are able.

* See Stewart's " Elements," ii. p. 38, sq.--H.

Mr Hume hath discovered, as he apprehends, a weak side, even in mathematical axioms ;· and thinks that it is not strictly true, for instance, that two right lines can cut one another in one point only.

The principle·he reasons from is, That every simple idea is a copy of a preceding impression ; and therefore in its precision and accuracy, can never go beyond its original. From which he reasons in this manner : No man ever saw or felt a line so straight that it might not cut another, equally straight, in two or more points. Therefore, there can be no idea of such a line.

The ideas that are most essential to geometry—such as those of equality, of a straight line, and of a square surface, are far, he says, from being distinct and determinate ; and the definitions destroy the pretended demonstrations. Thus, mathematical demonstration is found to be a rope of sand.

I agree with this acute author, that, if we could form no notion of points, lines, and surfaces, more accurate than those we see and handle, there could be no mathematical demonstration.

But every man that has understanding, by analysing, by abstracting, and compounding the rude materials exhibited by his senses, can fabricate, in his own mind, those elegant and accurate forms of mathematical lines, surfaces, and solids. [607]

If a man finds himself incapable of forming a precise and determinate notion of the figure which mathematicians call a cube, he not only is no mathematician, but is incapable of being one. But, if he has a precise and determinate notion of that figure, he must perceive that it is terminated by six mathematical surfaces, perfectly square and perfectly equal. He must perceive that these surfaces are terminated by twelve mathematical lines, perfectly straight and perfectly equal, and that those lines are terminated by eight mathematical points.

When a man is conscious of having these conceptions distinct and determinate, as every mathematician is, it is in vain to bring metaphysical arguments to convince him that they are not distinct. You may as well bring arguments to convince a man racked with pain that he feels no pain.

Every theory that is inconsistent with our having accurate notions of mathematical lines, surfaces, and solids, must be false. Therefore it follows, that they are not copies of our impressions.

The Medicean Venus is not a copy of the block of marble from which it was made. It is true, that the elegant statue was formed out of the rude block, and that, too, by a manual operation, which, in a literal sense, we may call abstraction. Mathematical notions are formed in the understanding by an abstraction of another kind, out of the rude perceptions of our senses.

As the truths of natural philosophy are not necessary truths, but contingent, depending upon the will of the Maker of the world, the principles from which they are deduced must be of the same nature, and, therefore, belong not to this class. [608]

4. I think there are axioms, even in matters of *taste*. Notwithstanding the variety found among men, in taste, there are, I apprehend, some common principles, even in matters of this kind. I never heard of any man who thought it a beauty in a human face to want a nose, or an eye, or to have the mouth on one side. How many ages have passed since the days of Homer! Yet, in this long tract of ages, there never was found a man who took Thersites for a beauty.

The *fine arts* are very properly called the *arts of taste*, because the principles of both are the same; and, in the fine arts, we find no less agreement among those who practise them than among other artists.

No work of taste can be either relished or understood by those who do not agree with the author in the principles of taste.

Homer and Virgil, and Shakspeare and Milton, had the same taste; and all men who have been acquainted with their writings, and agree in the admiration of them, must have the same taste.

The fundamental rules of poetry and music, and painting, and dramatic action and eloquence, have been always the same, and will be so to the end of the world.

The variety we find among men in matters of taste, is easily accounted for, consistently with what we have advanced.

There is a taste that is acquired, and a taste that is natural. This holds with respect both to the external sense of taste and the internal. Habit and fashion have a powerful influence upon both.

Of tastes that are natural, there are some that may be called rational, others that are merely animal.

Children are delighted with brilliant and gaudy colours, with romping and noisy mirth, with feats of agility, strength, or cunning; and savages have much the same taste as children. [609]

But there are tastes that are more intellectual. It is the dictate of our rational nature, that love and admiration are misplaced when there is no intrinsic worth in the object.

In those operations of taste which are rational, we judge of the real worth and excellence of the object, and our love or admiration is guided by that judgment. In such operations there is judgment as well as feeling, and the feeling depends upon the judgment we form of the object.

[608—610]

I do not maintain that taste, so far as it is acquired, or so far as it is merely animal, can be reduced to principles. But, as far as it is founded on judgment, it certainly may.

The virtues, the graces, the muses, have a beauty that is intrinsic. It lies not in the feelings of the spectator, but in the real excellence of the object. If we do not perceive their beauty, it is owing to the defect or to the perversion of our faculties.

And, as there is an original beauty in certain moral and intellectual qualities, so there is a borrowed and derived beauty in the natural signs and expressions of such qualities.

The features of the human face, the modulations of the voice, and the proportions, attitudes, and gesture of the body, are all natural expressions of good or bad qualities of the person, and derive a beauty or a deformity from the qualities which they express.

Works of art express some quality of the artist, and often derive an additional beauty from their utility or fitness for their end.

Of such things there are some that ought to please, and others that ought to displease. If they do not, it is owing to some defect in the spectator. But what has real excellence will always please those who have a correct judgment and a sound heart. [610]

The sum of what has been said upon this subject is, that, setting aside the tastes which men acquire by habit and fashion, there is a natural taste, which is partly animal, and partly rational. With regard to the first, all we can say is, that the Author of nature, for wise reasons, has formed us so as to receive pleasure from the contemplation of certain objects, and disgust from others, before we are capable of perceiving any real excellence in one or defect in the other. But that taste which we may call rational, is that part of our constitution by which we are made to receive pleasure from the contemplation of what we conceive to be excellent in its kind, the pleasure being annexed to this judgment, and regulated by it. This taste may be true or false, according as it is founded on a true or false judgment. And, if it may be true or false, it must have first principles.

5. There are also first principles in *morals*.

That an unjust action has more demerit than an ungenerous one: That a generous action has more merit than a merely just one: That no man ought to be blamed for what it was not in his power to hinder: That we ought not to do to others what we would think unjust or unfair to be done to us in like circumstances. These are moral axioms, and many others might be named which appear to me to have no less evidence than those of mathematics.

Some perhaps may think that our determinations, either in matters of taste or in morals, ought not to be accounted necessary truths : That they are grounded upon the constitution of that faculty which we call taste, and of that which we call the moral sense or conscience; which faculties might have been so constituted as to have given determinations different, or even contrary to those they now give : That, as there is nothing sweet or bitter in itself, but according as it agrees or disagrees with the external sense called taste ; so there is nothing beautiful or ugly in itself, but according as it agrees or disagrees with the internal sense, which we also call taste ; and nothing morally good or ill in itself, but according as it agrees or disagrees with our moral sense. [611]

This indeed is a system, with regard to morals and taste, which hath been supported in modern times by great authorities. And if this system be true, the consequence must be, that there can be no principles, either of taste or of morals, that are necessary truths. For, according to this system, all our determinations, both with regard to matters of taste, and with regard to morals, are reduced to matters of fact—I mean to such as these, that by our constitution we have on such occasions certain agreeable feelings, and on other occasions certain disagreeable feelings.

But I cannot help being of a contrary opinion, being persuaded that a man who determined that polite behaviour has great deformity, and that there is great beauty in rudeness and ill-breeding, would judge wrong, whatever his feelings were.

In like manner, I cannot help thinking that a man who determined that there is more moral worth in cruelty, perfidy, and injustice, than in generosity, justice, prudence, and temperance, would judge wrong, whatever his constitution was.

And, if it be true that there is judgment in our determinations of taste and of morals, it must be granted that what is true or false in morals, or in matters of taste, is necessarily so. For this reason, I have ranked the first principles of morals and of taste under the class of necessary truths.

6. The last class of first principles I shall mention, we may call *metaphysical.*

I shall particularly consider three of these, because they have been called in question by Mr Hume. [612]

The *first* is, *That the qualities which we perceive by our senses must have a subject, which we call body, and that the thoughts we are conscious of must have a subject, which we call mind.*

It is not more evident that two and two make four, than it is that figure cannot exist, unless there be something that is figured, nor motion without something that is moved. I not only perceive figure and motion, but I perceive them to be qualities. They have a necessary relation to something in which they exist as their subject. The difficulty which some philosophers have found in admitting this, is entirely owing to the theory of ideas. A subject of the sensible qualities which we perceive by our senses, is not an idea either of sensation or of consciousness; therefore say they, we have no such idea. Or, in the style of Mr Hume, from what impression is the idea of substance derived ? It is not a copy of any impression; therefore there is no such idea.

The distinction between sensible qualities, and the substance to which they belong, and between thought and the mind that thinks, is not the invention of philosophers ; it is found in the structure of all languages, and therefore must be common to all men who speak with understanding. And I believe no man, however sceptical he may be in speculation, can talk on the common affairs of life for half an hour, without saying things that imply his belief of the reality of these distinctions.

Mr Locke acknowledges, " That we cannot conceive how simple ideas of sensible qualities should subsist alone ; and therefore we suppose them to exist in, and to be supported by, some common subject." In his Essay, indeed, some of his expressions seem to leave it dubious whether this belief, that sensible qualities must have a subject, be a true judgment or a vulgar prejudice. [613] But in his first letter to the Bishop of Worcester, he removes this doubt, and quotes many passages of his Essay, to shew that he neither denied nor doubted of the existence of substances, both thinking and material ; and that he believed their existence on the same ground the Bishop did—to wit, " on the repugnancy to our conceptions, that modes and accidents should subsist by themselves." He offers no proof of this repugnancy ; nor, I think, can any proof of it be given, because it is a first principle.

It were to be wished that Mr Locke, who inquired so accurately and so laudably into the origin, certainty, and extent of human knowledge, had turned his attention more particularly to the origin of these two opinions which he firmly believed ; to wit, that sensible qualities must have a subject which we call body, and that thought must have a subject which we call mind. A due attention to these two opinions which govern the belief of all men, even of sceptics in the practice of life, would probably have led him to perceive, that sensation and consciousness are not the only sources of human knowledge; and that there are principles of belief in human nature, of which we can give no other account but that they necessarily result from the constitution of our faculties; and that, if it were in our power to throw off their influence upon our practice and conduct, we could neither speak nor act like reasonable men.

We cannot give a reason why we believe even our sensations to be real and not fallacious; why we believe what we are conscious of; why we trust any of our natural faculties. We say, it must be so, it cannot be otherwise. This expresses only a strong belief, which is indeed the voice of nature, and which therefore in vain we attempt to resist. But if, in spite of nature, we resolve to go deeper, and not to trust our faculties, without a reason to shew that they cannot be fallacious, I am afraid, that, seeking to become wise, and to be as gods, we shall become foolish, and, being unsatisfied with the lot of humanity, we shall throw off common sense.

The *second* metaphysical principle I mention is—*That whatever begins to exist, must have a cause which produced it.*[*] [614]

Philosophy is indebted to Mr Hume in this respect among others, that, by calling in question many of the first principles of human knowledge, he hath put speculative men upon inquiring more carefully than was done before into the nature of the evidence upon which they rest. Truth can never suffer by a fair inquiry; it can bear to be seen naked and in the fullest light; and the strictest examination will always turn out in the issue to its advantage. I believe Mr Hume was the first who ever called in question whether things that begin to exist must have a cause.

With regard to this point, we must hold one of these three things, either that it is an opinion for which we have no evidence, and which men have foolishly taken up without ground; or, *secondly,* That it is capable of direct proof by argument; or, *thirdly,* That it is self-evident, and needs no proof, but ought to be received as an axiom, which cannot, by reasonable men, be called in question.

The first of these suppositions would put an end to all philosophy, to all religion, to all reasoning that would carry us beyond the objects of sense, and to all prudence in the conduct of life.

As to the second supposition, that this principle may be proved by direct reasoning, I am afraid we shall find the proof extremely difficult, if not altogether impossible.

I know only of three or four arguments

that have been urged by philosophers, in the way of abstract reasoning, to prove that things which begin to exist must have a cause.

One is offered by Mr Hobbes, another by Dr Samuel Clarke, another by Mr Locke. Mr Hume, in his "Treatise of Human Nature," has examined them all;[*] and, in my opinion, has shewn that they take for granted the thing to be proved; a kind of false reasoning, which men are very apt to fall into when they attempt to prove what is self-evident. [615]

It has been thought, that, although this principle does not admit of proof from abstract reasoning, it may be proved from experience, and may be justly drawn by induction, from instances that fall within our observation.

I conceive this method of proof will leave us in great uncertainty, for these three reasons:

1*st,* Because the proposition to be proved is not a contingent but a *necessary* proposition. It is not that things which begin to exist commonly have a cause, or even that they always in fact have a cause; but that they must have a cause, and cannot begin to exist without a cause.

Propositions of this kind, from their nature, are incapable of proof by induction. Experience informs us only of what *is* or *has been,* not of what *must be;* and the conclusion must be of the same nature with the premises.[†]

For this reason, no mathematical proposition can be proved by induction. Though it should be found by experience in a thousand cases, that the area of a plane triangle is equal to the rectangle under the altitude and half the base, this would not prove that it must be so in all cases, and cannot be otherwise; which is what the mathematician affirms.[‡]

In like manner, though we had the most ample experimental proof that things which have begun to exist had a cause, this would not prove that they must have a cause. Experience may shew us what is the established course of nature, but can never shew what connections of things are in their nature necessary.

2*dly,* General maxims, grounded on experience, have only a degree of probability proportioned to the extent of our experience, and ought always to be understood so as to leave room for exceptions, if future experience shall discover any such. [616]

The law of gravitation has as full a proof from experience and induction as any principle can be supposed to have. Yet, if any philosopher should, by clear experiment,

* Vol. i. p. 144-145.—H.
† See below, p. 627; and " Active Powers," p. 31, and above, p. 323, a, note *.—H.
‡ So Aristotle.—H.

shew that there is a kind of matter in some bodies which does not gravitate, the law of gravitation ought to be limited by that exception.

Now it is evident that men have never considered the principle of the necessity of causes, as a truth of this kind which may admit of limitation or exception ; and therefore it has not been received upon this kind of evidence.

3*dly*, I do not see that experience could satisfy us that every change in nature actually has a cause.

In the far greatest part of the changes in nature that fall within our observation, the causes are unknown ; and, therefore, from experience, we cannot know whether they have causes or not.

Causation is not an object of sense. The only experience we can have of it, is in the consciousness we have of exerting some power in ordering our thoughts and actions. But this experience is surely too narrow a foundation for a general conclusion, that all things that have had or shall have a beginning, must have a cause.

For these reasons, this principle cannot be drawn from experience, any more than from abstract reasoning.

The *third* supposition is—That it is to be admitted as a first or self-evident principle. Two reasons may be urged for this.

1. The universal consent of mankind, not of philosophers only, but of the rude and unlearned vulgar.

Mr Hume, as far as I know, was the first that ever expressed any doubt of this principle.* And when we consider that he has rejected every principle of human knowledge, excepting that of consciousness, and has not even spared the axioms of mathematics, his authority is of small weight. [617]

Indeed, with regard to first principles, there is no reason why the opinion of a philosopher should have more authority than that of another man of common sense, who has been accustomed to judge in such cases. The illiterate vulgar are competent judges ; and the philosopher has no prerogative in matters of this kind ; but he is more liable than they to be misled by a favourite system, especially if it is his own.

Setting aside the authority of Mr Hume, what has philosophy been employed in since men first began to philosophise, but in the investigation of the causes of things ? This it has always professed, when we trace it to its cradle. It never entered into any man's thought, before the philosopher we have mentioned, to put the previous question, whether things have a cause or not ? Had it been thought possible that they might not, it may be presumed that, in the

variety of absurd and contradictory causes assigned, some one would have had recourse to this hypothesis.

They could conceive the world to arise from an egg, from a struggle between love and strife, between moisture and drought, between heat and cold ; but they never supposed that it had no cause. We know not any atheistic sect that ever had recourse to this topic, though by it, they might have evaded every argument that could be brought against them, and answered all objections to their system.

But rather than adopt such an absurdity, they contrived some imaginary cause—such as chance, a concourse of atoms, or necessity—as the cause of the universe. [618]

The accounts which philosophers have given of particular phænomena, as well as of the universe in general, proceed upon the same principle. That every phænomenon must have a cause, was always taken for granted. *Nil turpius physico*, says Cicero, *quam fieri causa quicquam dicere*. Though an Academic, he was dogmatical in this. And Plato, the father of the Academy, was no less so. " Πάντι γὰρ ἀδύνατον χωρὶς αἰτίου γίνεσιν ἰχῦν : it is impossible that anything should have its origin without a cause."—TIMÆUS.

I believe Mr Hume was the first who ever held the contrary.* This, indeed, he avows, and assumes the honour of the discovery. " It is," says he, " a maxim in philosophy, that whatever begins to exist, must have a cause of existence. This is commonly taken for granted in all reasonings, without any proof given or demanded. It is supposed to be founded on intuition, and to be one of those maxims which, though they may be denied with the lips, it is impossible for men in their hearts really to doubt of. But, if we examine this maxim by the idea of knowledge above explained, we shall discover in it no mark of such intuitive certainty." The meaning of this seems to be, that it did not suit with his theory of intuitive certainty, and, therefore, he excludes it from that privilege.

The vulgar adhere to this maxim as firmly and universally as the philosophers. Their superstitions have the same origin as the systems of philosophers—to wit, a desire to know the causes of things. *Felix qui potuit rerum cognoscere causas*, is the universal sense of men ; but to say that anything can happen without a cause, shocks the common sense of a savage.

This universal belief of mankind is easily accounted for, if we allow that the necessity of a cause of every event is obvious to the rational powers of a man. But it is impossible to account for it otherwise. It

---

* Hume was not the first.—H.   * See last note.—H.

cannot be ascribed to education, to systems of philosophy, or to priestcraft. One would think that a philosopher who takes it to be a general delusion or prejudice, would endeavour to shew from what causes in human nature such a general error may take its rise. But I forget that Mr Hume might answer upon his own principles, that since things may happen without a cause—this error and delusion of men may be universal without any cause. [619]

2. A second reason why I conceive this to be a first principle, is, That mankind not only assent to it in speculation, but that the practice of life is grounded upon it in the most important matters, even in cases where experience leaves us doubtful; and it is impossible to act with common prudence if we set it aside.

In great families, there are so many bad things done by a certain personage, called *Nobody*, that it is proverbial that there is a Nobody about every house who does a great deal of mischief; and even where there is the exactest inspection and government, many events will happen of which no other author can be found; so that, if we trust merely to experience in this matter, Nobody will be found to be a very active person, and to have no inconsiderable share in the management of affairs. But whatever countenance this system may have from experience, it is too shocking to common sense to impose upon the most ignorant. A child knows that, when his top, or any of his playthings, are taken away, it must be done by somebody. Perhaps it would not be difficult to persuade him that it was done by some invisible being, but that it should be done by nobody he cannot believe.

Suppose a man's house to be broke open, his money and jewels taken away. Such things have happened times innumerable without any apparent cause; and were he only to reason from experience in such a case, how must he behave? He must put in one scale the instances wherein a cause was found of such an event, and in the other scale the instances where no cause was found, and the preponderant scale must determine whether it be most probable that there was a cause of this event, or that there was none. Would any man of common understanding have recourse to such an expedient to direct his judgment? [620]

Suppose a man to be found dead on the highway, his skull fractured, his body pierced with deadly wounds, his watch and money carried off. The coroner's jury sits upon the body; and the question is put, What was the cause of this man's death?—was it accident, or *felo de se*, or murder by persons unknown? Let us suppose an adept in Mr Hume's philosophy to make one of the jury, and that he insists upon the

previous question, whether there was any cause of the event, and whether it happened without a cause.

Surely, upon Mr Hume's principles, a great deal might be said upon this point; and, if the matter is to be determined by past experience, it is dubious on which side the weight of argument might stand. But we may venture to say, that, if Mr Hume had been of such a jury, he would have laid aside his philosophical principles, and acted according to the dictates of common prudence.

Many passages might be produced, even in Mr Hume's philosophical writings, in which he, unawares, betrays the same inward conviction of the necessity of causes which is common to other men. I shall mention only one, in the "Treatise of Human Nature," and in that part of it where he combats this very principle:—"As to those impressions," says he, "which arise from the senses, their ultimate cause is, in my opinion, perfectly inexplicable by human reason; and it will always be impossible to decide with certainty whether they arise immediately from the object, or are produced by the creative power of the mind, or are derived from the Author of our being."

Among these alternatives, he never thought of their not arising from any cause.* [621]

The arguments which Mr Hume offers to prove that this is not a self-evident principle, are three. *First,* That all certainty arises from a comparison of ideas, and a discovery of their unalterable relations, none of which relations imply this proposition, That whatever has a beginning must have a cause of existence. This theory of certainty has been examined before.

The *second* argument is, That whatever we can conceive is possible. This has likewise been examined.

The *third* argument is, That what we call a cause, is only something antecedent to, and always conjoined with, the effect. This is also one of Mr Hume's peculiar doctrines, which we may have occasion to consider afterwards. It is sufficient here to observe, that we may learn from it that night is the cause of day, and day the cause of night: for no two things have more constantly followed each other since the beginning of the world.

The [*third* and] *last* metaphysical principle I mention, which is opposed by the same author, is, *That design and intelligence in the cause may be inferred, with certainty, from marks or signs of it in the effect.*

---

* See above, p. 444, note *. It is the triumph of scepticism to shew that *speculation* and *practice* are irreconcilable.—H.

Intelligence, design, and skill, are not objects of the external senses, nor can we be conscious of them in any person but ourselves. Even in ourselves, we cannot, with propriety, be said to be conscious of the natural or acquired talents we possess. We are conscious only of the operations of mind in which they are exerted. Indeed, a man comes to know his own mental abilities, just as he knows another man's, by the effects they produce, when there is occasion to put them to exercise.

A man's wisdom is known to us only by the signs of it in his conduct; his eloquence by the signs of it in his speech. In the same manner, we judge of his virtue, of his fortitude, and of all his talents and virtues. [622]

Yet it is to be observed, that we judge of men's talents with as little doubt or hesitation as we judge of the immediate objects of sense.

One person, we are sure, is a perfect idiot; another, who feigns idiocy to screen himself from punishment, is found, upon trial, to have the understanding of a man, and to be accountable for his conduct. We perceive one man to be open, another cunning; one to be ignorant, another very knowing; one to be slow of understanding, another quick. Every man forms such judgments of those he converses with; and the common affairs of life depend upon such judgments. We can as little avoid seeing what is before our eyes.

From this it appears, that it is no less a part of the human constitution, to judge of men's characters, and of their intellectual powers, from the signs of them in their actions and discourse, than to judge of corporeal objects by our senses; that such judgments are common to the whole human race that are endowed with understanding; and that they are absolutely necessary in the conduct of life.

Now, every judgment of this kind we form, is only a particular application of the general principle, that intelligence, wisdom, and other mental qualities in the cause, may be inferred from their marks or signs in the effect.

The actions and discourses of men are effects, of which the actors and speakers are the causes. The effects are perceived by our senses; but the causes are behind the scene. We only conclude their existence and their degrees from our observation of the effects.

From wise conduct, we infer wisdom in the cause; from brave actions, we infer courage; and so in other cases.   [623]

This inference is made with perfect security by all men. We cannot avoid it; it is necessary in the ordinary conduct of life; it has therefore the strongest marks of being a first principle.

Perhaps some may think that this principle may be learned either by reasoning or by experience, and therefore that there is no ground to think it a first principle.

If it can be shewn to be got by reasoning, by all, or the greater part of those who are governed by it, I shall very readily acknowledge that it ought not to be esteemed a first principle. But I apprehend the contrary appears from very convincing arguments.

First, The principle is too universal to be the effect of reasoning. It is common to philosophers and to the vulgar; to the learned and to the most illiterate; to the civilized and to the savage. And of those who are governed by it, not one in ten thousand can give a reason for it.

Secondly, We find philosophers, ancient and modern, who can reason excellently in subjects that admit of reasoning, when they have occasion to defend this principle, not offering reasons for it, or any *medium* of proof, but appealing to the common sense of mankind; mentioning particular instances, to make the absurdity of the contrary opinion more apparent, and sometimes using the weapons of wit and ridicule, which are very proper weapons for refuting absurdities, but altogether improper in points that are to be determined by reasoning.

To confirm this observation, I shall quote two authors, an ancient and a modern, who have more expressly undertaken the defence of this principle than any others I remember to have met with, and whose good sense and ability to reason, where reasoning is proper, will not be doubted.   [624]

The first is Cicero, whose words, (*l.b.* l. cap. 13. *De Divinatione*,) may be thus translated.

"Can anything done by chance have all the marks of design? Four dice may by chance turn up four aces; but do you think that four hundred dice, thrown by chance, will turn up four hundred aces? Colours thrown upon canvas without design may have some similitude to a human face; but do you think they might make as beautiful a picture as that of the Coan Venus? A hog turning up the ground with his nose may make something of the form of the letter A; but do you think that a hog might describe on the ground the Andromache of Ennius? Carneades imagined that, in the stone quarries at Chios, he found, in a stone that was split, a representation of the head of a little Pan, or sylvan deity. I believe he might find a figure not unlike; but surely not such a one as you would say had been formed by an excellent sculptor like Scopas. For so, verily, the case is, that chance never perfectly imitates design." Thus Cicero.*

* See also Cicero "*De Natura Deorum*," L ii. c. 37.—H.

Now, in all this discourse, I see very good sense, and what is apt to convince every unprejudiced mind; but I see not in the whole a single step of reasoning. It is barely an appeal to every man's common sense.

Let us next see how the same point is handled by the excellent Archbishop Tillotson. (1st Sermon, vol. i.)

"For I appeal to any man of reason, whether anything can be more unreasonable than to impute an effect to chance which carries in the face of it all the arguments and characters of design? Was ever any considerable work, in which there was required a great variety of parts, and an orderly and regular adjustment of these parts, done by chance? Will chance fit means to ends, and that in ten thousand instances, and not fail in any one? [625] How often might a man, after he had jumbled a set of letters in a bag, fling them out upon the ground before they would fall into an exact poem, yea, or so much as make a good discourse in prose? And may not a little book be as easily made as this great volume of the world? How long might a man sprinkle colours upon canvass with a careless hand, before they would make the exact picture of a man? And is a man easier made by chance than his picture? How long might twenty thousand blind men, which should be sent out from the remote parts of England, wander up and down before they would all meet upon Salisbury plains, and fall into rank and file in the exact order of an army? And yet this is much more easy to be imagined than how the innumerable blind parts of matter should rendezvous themselves into a word. A man that sees Henry VII.'s chapel at Westminster might, with as good reason, maintain, (yea, and much better, considering the vast difference between that little structure and the huge fabric of the world,) that it was never contrived or built by any man, but that the stones did by chance grow into those curious figures into which we see them to have been cut and graven; and that, upon a time, (as tales usually begin,) the materials of that building—the stone, mortar, timber, iron, lead, and glass—happily met together, and very fortunately ranged themselves into that delicate order in which we see them now, so close compacted that it must be a very great chance that parts them again. What would the world think of a man that should advance such an opinion as this, and write a book for it? If they would do him right, they ought to look upon him as mad. But yet he might maintain this opinion with a little more reason than any man can have to say that the world was made by chance, or that the first men grew out of the earth, as plants do now; for, can

[625–627]

anything be more ridiculous and against all reason, than to ascribe the production of men to the first fruitfulness of the earth, without so much as one instance or experiment in any age or history to countenance so monstrous a supposition? The thing is at first sight so gross and palpable, that no discourse about it can make it more apparent. And yet these shameful beggars of principles, who give this precarious account of the original of things, assume to themselves to be the men of reason, the great wits of the world, the only cautious and wary persons, who hate to be imposed upon, that must have convincing evidence for everything, and can admit nothing without a clear demonstration for it." [626]

In this passage, the excellent author takes what I conceive to be the proper method of refuting an absurdity, by exposing it in different lights, in which every man of common understanding conceives it to be ridiculous. And, although there is much good sense, as well as wit, in the passage I have quoted, I cannot find one *medium* of proof in the whole.

I have met with one or two respectable authors who draw an argument from the doctrine of chances, to shew how improbable it is that a regular arrangement of parts should be the effect of chance, or that it should not be the effect of design.

I do not object to this reasoning; but I would observe that the doctrine of chances is a branch of mathematics little more than an hundred years old. But the conclusion drawn from it has been held by all men from the beginning of the world. It cannot, therefore, be thought that men have been led to this conclusion by that reasoning. Indeed, it may be doubted whether the first principle upon which all the mathematical reasoning about chances is grounded, is more self-evident than this conclusion drawn from it, or whether it is not a particular instance of that general conclusion.

We are next to consider whether we may not learn this truth from experience, That effects which have all the marks and tokens of design, must proceed from a designing cause. [627]

I apprehend that we cannot learn this truth from experience for two reasons.

First, Because it is a necessary truth, not a contingent one. It agrees with the experience of mankind since the beginning of the world, that the area of a triangle is equal to half the rectangle under its base and perpendicular. It agrees no less with experience, that the sun rises in the east and sets in the west. So far as experience goes, these truths are upon an equal footing. But every man perceives this distinction between them—that the first is a necessary truth, and that it is impossible it should not be true; but the last is not necessary, but contingent, depending upon the will of Him who made the world. As we cannot learn from experience that twice three must necessarily make six, so neither can we learn from experience that certain effects must proceed from a designing and intelligent cause. Experience informs us only of what has been, but never of what must be.*

Secondly, It may be observed, that experience can shew a connection between a sign and the thing signified by it, in those cases only where both the sign and thing signified are perceived and have always been perceived in conjunction. But, if there be any case where the sign only is perceived, experience can never shew its connection with the thing signified. Thus, for example, thought is a sign of a thinking principle or mind. But how do we know that thought cannot be without a mind ? If any man should say that he knows this by experience, he deceives himself. It is impossible he can have any experience of this; because, though we have an immediate knowledge of the existence of thought in ourselves by consciousness, yet we have no immediate knowledge of a mind. The mind is not an immediate object either of sense or of consciousness. We may, therefore, justly conclude, that the necessary connection between thought and a mind, or thinking being, is not learned from experience. [628]

The same reasoning may be applied to the connection between a work excellently fitted for some purpose, and design in the author or cause of that work. One of these —to wit, the work—may be an immediate object of perception. But the design and purpose of the author cannot be an immediate object of perception; and, therefore, experience can never inform us of any connection between the one and the other, far less of a necessary connection.

Thus, I think, it appears, that the principle we have been considering—to wit, that from certain signs or indications in the effect, we may infer that there must have been intelligence, wisdom, or other intellectual or moral qualities in the cause, is a principle which we get, neither by reasoning nor by experience; and, therefore, if it be a true principle, it must be a first principle. There is in the human understanding a light, by which we see immediately the evidence of it, when there is occasion to apply it.

Of how great importance this principle is in common life, we have already observed. And I need hardly mention its importance in natural theology.

The clear marks and signatures of wis-

dom, power, and goodness, in the constitution and government of the world, is, of all arguments that have been advanced for the being and providence of the Deity, that which in all ages has made the strongest impression upon candid and thinking minds; an argument, which has this peculiar advantage, that it gathers strength as human knowledge advances, and is more convincing at present than it was some centuries ago.

King Alphonsus might say, that he could contrive a better planetary system than that which astronomers held in his day.* That system was not the work of God, but the fiction of men. [629]

But since the true system of the sun, moon, and planets, has been discovered, no man, however atheistically disposed, has pretended to shew how a better could be contrived.

When we attend to the marks of good contrivance which appear in the works of God, every discovery we make in the constitution of the material or intellectual system becomes a hymn of praise to the great Creator and Governor of the world. And a man who is possessed of the genuine spirit of philosophy will think it impiety to contaminate the divine workmanship, by mixing it with those fictions of human fancy, called theories and hypotheses, which will always bear the signatures of human folly, no less than the other does of divine wisdom.

I know of no person who ever called in question the principle now under our consideration, when it is applied to the actions and discourses of men. For this would be to deny that we have any means of discerning a wise man from an idiot, or a man that is illiterate in the highest degree from a man of knowledge and learning, which no man has the effrontery to deny.

But, in all ages, those who have been unfriendly to the principles of religion, have made attempts to weaken the force of the argument for the existence and perfections of the Deity, which is founded on this principle. That argument has got the name of the argument from final causes; and as the meaning of this name is well understood, we shall use it.

The argument from final causes, when reduced to a syllogism, has these two premises: —*First,* That design and intelligence in the cause, may, with certainty, be inferred from marks or signs of it in the effect. This is the principle we have been considering, and

---

* See above p. 455; and " Active Powers,"p. 31.—H.

* Alphonso X. of Castile. He flourished in the thirteenth century—a great mathematician and astronomer. To him we owe the Alphonsine Tables. His saying was not so pious and philosophical as Reid states; but that, " Had he been present with God at the creation, he could have supplied some useful hints towards the better ordering of the universe." —H

we may call it the *maj.r* proposition of the argument. The *secon·l*, which we call the *minor* proposition, is, That there are in fact the clearest marks of design and wisdom in the works of nature; and the *conclusion* is, That the works of nature are the effects of a wise and intelligent Cause. One must either assent to the conclusion, or deny one or other of the premises. [630]

Those among the ancients who denied a God or a Providence, seem to me to have yielded the major proposition, and to have denied the minor; conceiving that there are not in the constitution of things such marks of wise contrivance as are sufficient to put the conclusion beyond doubt. This, I think, we may learn, from the reasoning of Cotta the academic, in the third book of Cicero, of the Nature of the Gods. The gradual advancement made in the knowledge of nature, hath put this opinion quite out of countenance.

When the structure of the human body was much less known than it is now, the famous Galen saw such evident marks of wise contrivance in it, that, though he had been educated an Epicurean, he renounced that system, and wrote his book of the use of the parts of the human body, on purpose to convince others of what appeared so clear to himself, that it was impossible that such admirable contrivance should be the effect of chance.

Those, therefore, of later times, who are dissatisfied with this argument from final causes, have quitted the stronghold of the ancient atheists, which had become untenable, and have chosen rather to make a defence against the major proposition.

Des Cartes seems to have led the way in this, though he was no atheist. But, having invented some new arguments for the being of God, he was, perhaps, led to disparage those that had been used before, that he might bring more credit to his own. Or perhaps he was offended with the Peripatetics, because they often mixed final causes with physical, in order to account for the phænomena of nature. [631] He maintained, therefore, that physical causes only should be assigned for phænomena; that the philosopher has nothing to do with final causes; and that it is presumption in us to pretend to determine for what end any work of nature is framed. Some of those who were great admirers of Des Cartes, and followed him in many points, differed from him in this, particularly Dr Henry More and the pious Archbishop Fenelon : but others, after the example of Des Cartes, have shewn a contempt of all reasoning from final causes. Among these, I think, we may reckon Maupertuis and Buffon. But the most direct attack has been made upon this principle by Mr [630–632]

Hume, who puts an argument in the mouth of an Epicurean, on which he seems to lay great stress.

The argument is, That the universe is a singular effect, and, therefore, we can draw no conclusion from it, whether it may have been made by wisdom or not.*

If I understand the force of this argument, it amounts to this, That, if we had been accustomed to see worlds produced, some by wisdom and others without it, and had observed that such a world as this which we inhabit was always the effect of wisdom, we might then, from past experience, conclude that this world was made by wisdom; but, having no such experience, we have no means of forming any conclusion about it.

That this is the strength of the argument appears, because, if the marks of wisdom seen in one world be no evidence of wisdom, the like marks seen in ten thousand will give as little evidence, unless, in time past, we perceived wisdom itself conjoined with the tokens of it; and, from their perceived conjunction in time past, conclude that, although, in the present world, we see only one of the two, the other must accompany it. [632]

Whence it appears that this reasoning of Mr Hume is built on the supposition that our inferring design from the strongest marks of it, is entirely owing to our past experience of having always found these two things conjoined. But I hope I have made it evident that this is not the case. And, indeed, it is evident that, according to this reasoning, we can have no evidence of mind or design in any of our fellowmen.

How do I know that any man of my acquaintance has understanding? I never saw his understanding. I see only certain effects, which my judgment leads me to conclude to be marks and tokens of it.

But, says the sceptical philosopher, you can conclude nothing from these tokens, unless past experience has informed you that such tokens are always joined with understanding. Alas! sir, it is impossible I can ever have this experience. The understanding of another man is no immediate object of sight, or of any other faculty which God hath given me; and unless I can conclude its existence from tokens that are visible, I have no evidence that there is understanding in any man.

It seems, then, that the man who maintains that there is no force in the argument from final causes, must, if he will be consistent, see no evidence of the existence of any intelligent being but himself.

* See Stewart's " Elements," ii. p 579.—H.

CHAPTER VII.

OPINIONS, ANCIENT AND MODERN, ABOUT
FIRST PRINCIPLES.

I KNOW no writer who has treated expressly of first principles before Aristotle; but it is probable that, in the ancient Pythagorean school, from which both Plato and Aristotle borrowed much, this subject had not been left untouched. [633]

Before the time of Aristotle, considerable progress had been made in the mathematical sciences, particularly in geometry. The discovery of the forty-seventh proposition of the first book of Euclid, and of the five regular solids, is, by antiquity, ascribed to Pythagoras himself; and it is impossible he could have made those discoveries without knowing many other propositions in mathematics. Aristotle mentions the incommensurability of the diagonal of a square to its side, and gives a hint of the manner in which it was demonstrated. We find likewise some of the axioms of geometry mentioned by Aristotle as axioms, and as indemonstrable principles of mathematical reasoning.

It is probable, therefore, that, before the time of Aristotle, there were elementary treatises of geometry, which are now lost; and that in them the axioms were distinguished from the propositions which require proof.

To suppose that so perfect a system as that of Euclid's "Elements" was produced by one man, without any preceding model or materials, would be to suppose Euclid more than a man. We ascribe to him as much as the weakness of human understanding will permit, if we suppose that the inventions in geometry, which had been made in a tract of preceding ages, were by him not only carried much farther, but digested into so admirable a system that his work obscured all that went before it, and made them be forgot and lost.

Perhaps, in like manner, the writings of Aristotle with regard to first principles, and with regard to many other abstract subjects, may have occasioned the loss of what had been written upon those subjects by more ancient philosophers. [634]

Whatever may be in this, in his second book upon demonstration, he has treated very fully of first principles; and, though he has not attempted any enumeration of them, he shews very clearly that all demonstration must be built upon truths which are evident of themselves, but cannot be demonstrated. His whole doctrine of syllogisms is grounded upon a few axioms, from which he endeavours to demonstrate the rules of syllogism in a mathematical way;

and in his topics he points out many of the first principles of probable reasoning.

As long as the philosophy of Aristotle prevailed, it was held as a fixed point, that all proof must be drawn from principles already known and granted.

We must observe, however, that, in that philosophy, many things were assumed as first principles, which have no just claim to that character: such as, that the earth is at rest; that nature abhors a vacuum; that there is no change in the heavens above the sphere of the moon; that the heavenly bodies move in circles, that being the most perfect figure; that bodies do not gravitate in their proper place; and many others.

The Peripatetic philosophy, therefore, instead of being deficient in first principles, was redundant; instead of rejecting those that are truly such, it adopted, as first principles, many vulgar prejudices and rash judgments: and this seems in general to have been the spirit of ancient philosophy.*

It is true, there were among the ancients sceptical philosophers, who professed to have no principles, and held it to be the greatest virtue in a philosopher to withhold assent, and keep his judgment in a perfect equilibrium between contradictory opinions. But, though this sect was defended by some persons of great erudition and acuteness, it died of itself, and the dogmatic philosophy of Aristotle obtained a complete triumph over it. [635]

What Mr Hume says of those who are sceptical with regard to moral distinctions seems to have had its accomplishment in the ancient sect of Sceptics. "The only way," says he, "of converting antagonists of this kind is to leave them to themselves; for, finding that nobody keeps up the controversy with them, it is probable they will at last of themselves, from mere weariness, come over to the side of common sense and reason."

Setting aside this small sect of the Sceptics, which was extinct many ages before the authority of Aristotle declined, I know of no opposition made to first principles among the ancients. The disposition was, as has been observed, not to oppose, but to multiply them beyond measure.

Men have always been prone, when they leave one extreme, to run into the opposite; and this spirit, in the ancient philosophy, to multiply first principles beyond reason, was a strong presage that, when the authority of the Peripatetic system was at an end,

---

* The Peripatetic philosophy did not assume any such principles as original and self-evident; but professed to establish them all upon induction and generalization. In practice its induction of instances might be imperfect, and its generalization from particulars rash; but in theory, at least, it was correct. —H.

the next reigning system would diminish their number beyond reason.

This, accordingly, happened in that great revolution of the philosophical republic brought about by Des Cartes. That truly great reformer in philosophy, cautious to avoid the snare in which Aristotle was taken, of admitting things as first principles too rashly, resolved to doubt of everything, and to withhold his assent, until it was forced by the clearest evidence.*

Thus Des Cartes brought himself into that very state of suspense which the ancient Sceptics recommended as the highest perfection of a wise man, and the only road to tranquillity of mind. But he did not remain long in this state; his doubt did not arise from despair of finding the truth, but from caution, that he might not be imposed upon, and embrace a cloud instead of a goddess. [636]

His very doubting convinced him of his own existence; for that which does not exist can neither doubt, nor believe, nor reason. Thus he emerged from universal scepticism by this short enthymeme, *Cogito, ergo sum.*

This enthymeme consists of an antecedent proposition, *I think*, and a conclusion drawn from it, *therefore I exist.*

If it should be asked how Des Cartes came to be certain of the antecedent proposition, it is evident that for this he trusted to the testimony of consciousness. He was conscious that he thought, and needed no other argument.

So that the first principle which he adopts in this famous enthymeme is this, That those doubts, and thoughts, and reasonings, of which he was conscious, did certainly exist, and that his consciousness put their existence beyond all doubt.

It might have been objected to this first principle of Des Cartes, How do you know that your consciousness cannot deceive you? You have supposed that all you see, and hear, and handle, may be an illusion. Why, therefore, should the power of consciousness have this prerogative, to be believed implicitly, when all our other powers are supposed fallacious?

To this objection I know no other answer that can be made but that we find it impossible to doubt of things of which we are conscious. The constitution of our nature forces this belief upon us irresistibly.

This is true, and is sufficient to justify Des Cartes in assuming, as a first principle, the existence of thought, of which he was conscious. [637]

He ought, however, to have gone farther in this track; and to have considered whether there may not be other first principles

which ought to be adopted for the same reason. But he did not see this to be necessary, conceiving that, upon this one first principle, he could support the whole fabric of human knowledge.

To proceed to the conclusion of Des Cartes's enthymeme. From the existence of his thought he infers his own existence. Here he assumes another first principle, not a contingent, but a necessary one; to wit, that, where there is thought, there must be a thinking being or mind.

Having thus established his own existence, he proceeds to prove the existence of a supreme and infinitely perfect Being; and, from the perfection of the Deity, he infers that his senses, his memory, and the other faculties which God had given him, are not fallacious.

Whereas other men, from the beginning of the world, had taken for granted, as a first principle, the truth and reality of what they perceive by their senses, and from thence inferred the existence of a Supreme Author and Maker of the world, Des Cartes took a contrary course, conceiving that the testimony of our senses, and of all our faculties, excepting that of consciousness, ought not to be taken for granted, but to be proved by argument.

Perhaps some may think that Des Cartes meant only to admit no other first principle of contingent truths besides that of consciousness; but that he allowed the axioms of mathematics, and of other necessary truths, to be received without proof. [638]

But I apprehend this was not his intention; for the truth of mathematical axioms must depend upon the truth of the faculty by which we judge of them. If the faculty be fallacious, we may be deceived by trusting to it. Therefore, as he supposes that all our faculties, excepting consciousness, may be fallacious, and attempts to prove by argument that they are not, it follows that, according to his principles, even mathematical axioms require proof. Neither did he allow that there are any necessary truths, but maintained, that the truths which are commonly so called, depend upon the will of God. And we find his followers, who may be supposed to understand his principles, agree in maintaining, that the knowledge of our own existence is the first and fundamental principle from which all knowledge must be deduced by one who proceeds regularly in philosophy.

There is, no doubt, a beauty in raising a large fabric of knowledge upon a few first principles. The stately fabric of mathematical knowledge, raised upon the foundation of a few axioms and definitions, charms every beholder. Des Cartes, who was well acquainted with this beauty in the mathematical sciences, seems to have been am-

---

* On the Cartesian doubt, see Note R.—H.

bitious to give the same beautiful simplicity to his system of philosophy; and therefore sought only one first principle as the foundation of all our knowledge, at least of contingent truths.

And so far has his authority prevailed, that those who came after him have almost universally followed him in this track. This, therefore, may be considered as the spirit of modern philosophy, to allow of no first principles of contingent truths but this one, that the thoughts and operations of our own minds, of which we are conscious, are self-evidently real and true; but that everything else that is contingent is to be proved by argument.

The existence of a material world, and of what we perceive by our senses, is not self-evident, according to this philosophy. Des Cartes founded it upon this argument, that God, who hath given us our senses, and all our faculties, is no deceiver, and therefore they are not fallacious. [639]

I endeavoured to shew that, if it be not admitted as a first principle, that our faculties are not fallacious, nothing else can be admitted; and that it is impossible to prove this by argument, unless God should give us new faculties to sit in judgment upon the old.

Father Malebranche agreed with Des Cartes, that the existence of a material world requires proof; but, being dissatisfied with Des Cartes's argument from the perfection of the Deity, thought that the only solid proof is from divine revelation.

Arnauld, who was engaged in controversy with Malebranche, approves of his antagonist in offering an argument to prove the existence of the material world, but objects to the solidity of his argument, and offers other arguments of his own.

Mr Norris, a great admirer of Des Cartes and of Malebranche, seems to have thought all the arguments offered by them and by Arnauld to be weak, and confesses that we have, at best, only probable evidence of the existence of the material world.

Mr Locke acknowledges that the evidence we have of this point is neither intuitive nor demonstrative; yet he thinks it may be called knowledge, and distinguishes it by the name of sensitive knowledge; and, as the ground of this sensitive knowledge, he offers some weak arguments, which would rather tempt one to doubt than to believe.

At last, Bishop Berkeley and Arthur Collier, without any knowledge of each other, as far as appears by their writings, undertook to prove, that there neither is nor can be a material world. The excellent style and elegant composition of the former have made his writings to be known and read, and this system to be attributed to him only, as if Collier had never existed. [640]

Both, indeed, owe so much to Malebranche, that, if we take out of his system the peculiarities of our seeing all things in God, and our learning the existence of an external world from divine revelation, what remains is just the system of Bishop Berkeley. · I make this observation, by the way, in justice to a foreign author, to whom British authors seem not to have allowed all that is due. *

Mr Hume hath adopted Bishop Berkeley's arguments against the existence of matter, and thinks them unanswerable.

We may observe, that this great metaphysician, though in general he declares in favour of universal scepticism, and therefore may seem to have no first principles at all, yet, with Des Cartes, he always acknowledges the reality of those thoughts and operations of mind of which we are conscious.† So that he yields the antecedent of Des Cartes's enthymeme *cogito*, but denies the conclusion *ergo sum*, the mind being, according to him, nothing but that train of impressions and ideas of which we are conscious.

Thus, we see that the modern philosophy, of which Des Cartes may justly be accounted the founder, being built upon the ruins of the Peripatetic, has a spirit quite opposite, and runs into a contrary extreme. The Peripatetic not only adopted as first principles those which mankind have always rested upon in their most important transactions, but, along with them, many vulgar prejudices; so that this system was founded upon a wide bottom, but in many parts unsound. The modern system has narrowed the foundation so much, that every superstructure raised upon it appears top-heavy.

From the single principle of the existence of our thoughts, very little, if any thing, can be deduced by just reasoning, especially if we suppose that all our other faculties may be fallacious.

Accordingly, we find that Mr Hume was not the first that was led into scepticism by the want of first principles. For, soon after Des Cartes, there arose a sect in France called *Egoists*, who maintained that we have no evidence of the existence of anything but ourselves.‡ [641]

Whether these egoists, like Mr Hume,

---

* If I recollect aright, (I write this note at a distance from books,) Locke explicitly anticipates the Berkeleian idealism in his " Examination of Father Malebranche's Opinion." This was also done by Bayle. In fact, Malebranche, and many others before him, would inevitably have become Idealists, had they not been Catholics. But an Idealist, as I have already observed, no consistent Catholic could be. See above, p. 255, note †, and p. 358, note *. —H.

† See above, p. 442, b, note.—H.

‡ See above p. 269, a, note § ; and p. 293, b, note *.—H.

believed themselves to be nothing but a train of ideas and impressions, or to have a more permanent existence, I have not learned, having never seen any of their writings; nor do I know whether any of this sect did write in support of their principles. One would think they who did not believe that there was any person to read, could have little inducement to write, unless they were prompted by that inward monitor which Persius makes to be the source of genius and the teacher of arts. There can be no doubt, however, of the existence of such a sect, as they are mentioned by many authors, and refuted by some, particularly by Buffier, in his treatise of first principles.

Those Egoists and Mr Hume seem to me to have reasoned more consequentially from Des Cartes' principle than he did himself; and, indeed, I cannot help thinking, that all who have followed Des Cartes' method, of requiring proof by argument of everything except the existence of their own thoughts, have escaped the abyss of scepticism by the help of weak reasoning and strong faith more than by any other means. And they seem to me to act more consistently, who, having rejected the first principles on which belief must be grounded, have no belief, than they, who, like the others, rejecting first principles, must yet have a system of belief, without any solid foundation on which it may stand.

The philosophers I have hitherto mentioned, after the time of Des Cartes, have all followed his method, in resting upon the truth of their own thoughts as a first principle, but requiring arguments for the proof of every other truth of a contingent nature; but none of them, excepting Mr Locke, has expressly treated of first principles, or given any opinion of their utility or inutility. We only collect their opinion from their following Des Cartes in requiring proof, or pretending to offer proof of the existence of a material world, which surely ought to be received as a first principle, if anything be, beyond what we are conscious of. [642]

I proceed, therefore, to consider what Mr Locke has said on the subject of first principles or maxims.

I have not the least doubt of this author's candour in what he somewhere says, that his essay was mostly spun out of his own thoughts. Yet, it is certain, that, in many of the notions which we are wont to ascribe to him, others were before him, particularly Des Cartes, Gassendi, and Hobbes. Nor is it at all to be thought strange, that ingenious men, when they are got into the same track, should hit upon the same things.

But, in the definition which he gives of knowledge in general, and in his notions [642, 643]

concerning axioms or first principles, I know none that went before him, though he has been very generally followed in both.

His definition of knowledge, that it consists solely in the perception of the agreement or disagreement of our ideas, has been already considered. But supposing it to be just, still it would be true, that some agreements and disagreements of ideas must be immediately perceived; and such agreements or disagreements, when they are expressed by affirmative or negative propositions, are first principles, because their truth is immediately discerned as soon as they are understood.

This, I think, is granted by Mr Locke, book 4, chap. 2. "There is a part of our knowledge," says he, "which we may call intuitive. In this the mind is at no pains of proving or examining, but perceives the truth as the eye does light, only by being directed toward it. And this kind of knowledge is the clearest and most certain that human frailty is capable of. This part of knowledge is irresistible, and, like bright sunshine, forces itself immediately to be perceived, as soon as ever the mind turns its view that way." [643]

He farther observes—"That this intuitive knowledge is necessary to connect all the steps of a demonstration."[*]

From this, I think, it necessarily follows, that, in every branch of knowledge, we must make use of truths that are intuitively known, in order to deduce from them such as require proof.

But I cannot reconcile this with what he says, § 8, of the same chapter:—"The necessity of this intuitive knowledge in every step of scientifical or demonstrative reasoning gave occasion, I imagine, to that mistaken axiom, that all reasoning was *ex praecognitis et praeconcessis*, which, how far it is mistaken, I shall have occasion to shew more at large, when I come to consider propositions, and particularly those propositions which are called maxims, and to shew that it is by a mistake that they are supposed to be the foundation of all our knowledge and reasonings."

I have carefully considered the chapter on maxims, which Mr Locke here refers to; and, though one would expect, from the quotation last made, that it should run contrary to what I have before delivered concerning first principles, I find only two or three sentences in it, and those chiefly incidental, to which I do not assent; and I am always happy in agreeing with a philosopher whom I so highly respect.

He endeavours to shew that axioms or intuitive truths are not innate.[†]

---

[*] See Stewart's "Elements," ii. p. 49.—H.
[†] He does more. He attempts to shew that they are all generalizations from experience; whereas ex-

To this I agree. I maintain only, that when the understanding is ripe, and when we distinctly apprehend such truths, we immediately assent to them. [644]

He observes, that self-evidence is not peculiar to those propositions which pass under the name of axioms, and have the dignity of axioms ascribed to them. '

I grant that there are innumerable self-evident propositions, which have neither dignity nor utility, and, therefore, deserve not the name of axioms, as that name is commonly understood to imply not only self-evidence, but some degree of dignity or utility. That a man is a man, and that a man is not a horse, are self-evident propositions ; but they are, as Mr Locke very justly calls them, trifling propositions. Til-lotson very wittily says of such propositions, that they are so surfeited with truth, that they are good for nothing ; and as they deserve not the name of axioms, so neither do they deserve the name of knowledge.

He observes, that such trifling self-evident propositions as we have named are not derived from axioms, and therefore that all our knowledge is not derived from axioms.

I grant that they are not derived from axioms, because they are themselves self-evident. But it is an abuse of words to call them knowledge, as it is, to call them axioms ; for no man can be said to be the wiser or more knowing for having millions of them in store.

He observes, that the particular propositions contained under a general axiom are no less self-evident than the general axiom, and that they are sooner known and understood. Thus, it is as evident that my hand is less than my body, as that a part is less than the whole ; and I know the truth of the particular proposition sooner than that of the general.

This is true. A man cannot perceive the truth of a general axiom, such as, that a part is less than the whole, until he has the general notions of a part and a whole formed in his mind ; and, before he has these general notions, he may perceive that his hand is less than his body. [645]

A great part of this chapter on maxims is levelled against a notion, which, it seems, some have entertained, that all our knowledge is derived from these two maxims— to wit, *whatever is, is ;* and *it is impossible for the same thing to be, and not to be.*[*]

This I take to be a ridiculous notion, justly deserving the treatment which Mr

Locke has given it, if it at all merited his notice. These are identical propositions ; they are trifling, and surfeited with truth. No knowledge can be derived from them.

Having mentioned how far I agree with Mr Locke concerning maxims or first principles, I shall next take notice of two or three things, wherein I cannot agree with him.

In the seventh section of this chapter, he says, That, concerning the real existence of all other beings, besides ourselves and a first cause, there are no maxims.

I have endeavoured to shew that there are maxims, or first principles, with regard to other existences. Mr Locke acknowledges that we have a knowledge of such existences, which, he says, is neither intuitive nor demonstrative, and which, therefore, he calls sensitive knowledge. It is demonstrable, and was long ago demonstrated by Aristotle, that every proposition to which we give a rational assent, must either have its evidence in itself, or derive it from some antecedent proposition. And the same thing may be said of the antecedent proposition. As, therefore, we cannot go back to antecedent propositions without end, the evidence must at last rest upon propositions, one or more, which have their evidence in themselves—that is, upon first principles.

As to the evidence of our own existence, and of the existence of a first cause, Mr Locke does not say whether it rests upon first principles or not. But it is manifest, from what he has said upon both, that it does. [646]

With regard to our own existence, says he, we perceive it so plainly and so certainly that it neither needs nor is capable of any proof. This is as much as to say that our own existence is a first principle ; for it is applying to this truth the very definition of a first principle.

He adds, that, if I doubt, that very doubt makes me perceive my own existence, and will not suffer me to doubt of that. If I feel pain, I have as certain perception of my existence as of the pain I feel.

Here we have two first principles plainly implied—*First*, That my feeling pain, or being conscious of pain, is a certain evidence of the real existence of that pain ; and, *secondly*, That pain cannot exist without a mind or being that is pained. That these are first principles, and incapable of proof, Mr Locke acknowledges. And it is certain, that, if they are not true, we can have no evidence of our own existence ; for, if we may feel pain when no pain really exists, or if pain may exist without any being that is pained, then it is certain that our feeling pain can give us no evidence of our existence.

Thus, it appears that the evidence of our

perience only affords the occasions on which the *native* (not innate) or *a priori* cognitions, virtually possessed by the mind, actually manifest their existence.—H.

[*] These are called, the principle of *Identity,* and the principle of *Contradiction,* or, more properly, *Non-contradiction.*—H.

own existence, according to the view that Mr Locke gives of it, is grounded upon two of those first principles which we had occasion to mention.

If we consider the argument he has given for the existence of a first intelligent cause, it is no less evident that it is grounded upon other two of them. The first, That what begins to exist must have a cause of its existence; and the second, That an unintelligent and unthinking being cannot be the cause of beings that are thinking and intelligent. Upon these two principles, he argues, very convincingly, for the existence of a first intelligent cause of things. And, if these principles are not true, we can have no proof of the existence of a first cause, either from our own existence, or from the existence of other things that fall within our view. [647]

Another thing advanced by Mr Locke upon this subject is, that no science is or hath been built upon maxims.

Surely Mr Locke was not ignorant of geometry, which hath been built upon maxims prefixed to the elements, as far back as we are able to trace it.* But, though they had not been prefixed, which was a matter of utility rather than necessity, yet it must be granted that every demonstration in geometry is grounded either upon propositions formerly demonstrated, or upon self-evident principles.

Mr Locke farther says, that maxims are not of use to help men forward in the advancement of the sciences, or new discoveries of yet unknown truths; that Newton, in the discoveries he has made in his never-enough-to-be-admired book, has not been assisted by the general maxims—whatever is, is; or, the whole is greater than a part; or the like.

I answer, the first of these is, as was before observed, an identical trifling proposition, of no use in mathematics, or in any other science. The second is often used by Newton, and by all mathematicians, and many demonstrations rest upon it. In general, Newton, as well as all other mathematicians, grounds his demonstrations of mathematical propositions upon the axioms laid down by Euclid, or upon propositions which have been before demonstrated by help of those axioms. [648]

But it deserves to be particularly observed, that Newton, intending, in the third book of his " Principia," to give a more scientific form to the physical part of astronomy, which he had at first composed in a popular form, thought proper to follow the example of Euclid, and to lay down first, in what he

calls " *Regulæ Philosophandi*," and in his " *Phænomena*," the first principles which he assumes in his reasoning.

Nothing, therefore, could have been more unluckily adduced by Mr Locke to support his aversion to first principles, than the example of Sir Isaac Newton, who, by laying down the first principles upon which he reasons in those parts of natural philosophy which he cultivated, has given a stability to that science which it never had before, and which it will retain to the end of the world.

I am now to give some account of a philosopher, who wrote expressly on the subject of first principles, after Mr Locke.

Pere Buffier, a French Jesuit, first published his " *Traite des premiers Veritez, et de la Source de nos Jugemens*," in 8vo, if I mistake not, in the year 1724. It was afterwards published in folio, as a part of his " *Cours des-Sciences.*" Paris, 1732.

He defines first principles to be propositions so clear that they can neither be proved nor combated by those that are more clear.

The first source of first principles he mentions, is, that intimate conviction which every man has of his own existence, and of what passes in his own mind. Some philosophers, he observes, admitted these as first principles, who were unwilling to admit any others; and he shews the strange consequences that follow from this system.

A second source of first principles he makes to be common sense; which, he observes, philosophers have not been wont to consider. He defines it to be the disposition which Nature has planted in all men, or the far greater part, which leads them, when they come to the use of reason, to form a common and uniform judgment upon objects which are not objects of consciousness, nor are founded on any antecedent judgment. [649]

He mentions, not as a full enumeration, but as a specimen, the following principles of common sense.

1. That there are other beings and other men in the universe, besides myself.

2. That there is in them something that is called truth, wisdom, prudence; and that these things are not purely arbitrary.

3. That there is something in me which I call intelligence, and something which is not that intelligence, which I call my body; and that these things have different properties.

4. That all men are not in a conspiracy to deceive me and impose upon my credulity.

5. That what has not intelligence cannot produce the effects of intelligence, nor can pieces of matter thrown together by chance form any regular work, such as a clock or watch.

---

* Compare Stewart's " Elements," ii. pp. 38, 43, 19C. On this subject, " satius est silere quam parum dicere."—H.

He explains very particularly the several parts of his definition of common sense, and shews how the dictates of common sense may be distinguished from common prejudices; and then enters into a particular consideration of the primary truths that concern being in general; the truths that concern thinking beings; those that concern body; and those on which the various branches of human knowledge are grounded. I shall not enter into a detail of his sentiments on these subjects. I think there is more which I take to be original in this treatise than in most books of the metaphysical kind I have met with; that many of his notions are solid; and that others, which I cannot altogether approve, are ingenious. [650]

The other writers I have mentioned, after Des Cartes, may, I think, without impropriety, be called Cartesians. For, though they differ from Des Cartes in some things, and contradict him in others, yet they set-out from the same principles, and follow the same method, admitting no other first principle with regard to the existence of things but their own existence, and the existence of those operations of mind of which they are conscious, and requiring that the existence of a material world, and the existence of other men and things, should be proved by argument.

This method of philosophising is common to Des Cartes, Malebranche, Arnauld, Locke, Norris, Collier, Berkeley, and Hume; and, as it was introduced by Des Cartes, I call it the Cartesian system, and those who follow it Cartesians, not intending any disrespect by this term, but to signify a particular method of philosophising common to them all, and begun by Des Cartes.

Some of these have gone the utmost length in scepticism, leaving no existence in nature but that of ideas and impressions. Some have endeavoured to throw off the belief of a material world only, and to leave us ideas and spirits. All of them have fallen into very gross paradoxes, which can never sit easy upon the human understanding, and which, though adopted in the closet, men find themselves under a necessity of throwing off and disclaiming when they enter into society.

Indeed, in my judgment, those who have reasoned most acutely and consequentially upon this system, are they that have gone deepest into scepticism.

Father Buffier, however, is no Cartesian in this sense. He seems to have perceived the defects of the Cartesian system while it was in the meridian of its glory, and to have been aware that a ridiculous scepticism is the natural issue of it, and therefore nobly attempted to lay a broader foundation for human knowledge, and has the honour of being the first, as far as I know, after Aristotle, who has given the world a just treatise upon first principles. [651]

Some late writers, particularly Dr Oswald, Dr Beattie, and Dr Campbell, have been led into a way of thinking somewhat similar to that of Buffier; the two former, as I have reason to believe, without any intercourse with one another, or any knowledge of what Buffier had wrote on the subject. Indeed, a man who thinks, and who is acquainted with the philosophy of Mr Hume, will very naturally be led to apprehend, that, to support the fabric of human knowledge, some other principles are necessary than those of Des Cartes and Mr Locke. Buffier must·be acknowledged to have the merit of having discovered this, before the consequences of the Cartesian system were so fully displayed as they have been by Mr Hume. But I am apt to think that the man who does not see this now, must have but a superficial knowledge of these subjects.*

The three writers above mentioned have my high esteem and affection as men; but I intend to say nothing of them as writers upon this subject, that I may not incur the censure of partiality. Two of them have been joined so closely with me in the animadversions of a celebrated writer,† that we may be thought too near of kin to give our testimony of one another.

CHAPTER VIII.

OUR intellectual powers are wisely fitted by the Author of our nature for the discovery of truth, as far as suits our present state. Error is not their natural issue, any more than disease is of the natural structure of the body. Yet, as we are liable to various diseases of body from accidental causes, external and internal; so we are, from like causes, liable to wrong judgments. [652]

Medical writers have endeavoured to enumerate the diseases of the body, and to reduce them to a system, under the name of nosology; and it were to be wished that we had also a nosology of the human understanding.

When we know a disorder of the body, we are often at a loss to find the proper remedy; but in most cases the disorders of the understanding point out their remedies so plainly, that he who knows the one must know the other.

Many authors have furnished useful materials for this purpose, and some have endeavoured to reduce them to a system. I

---

* See Note A.—H.   † Priestley.—H.

like best the general division given of them by Lord Bacon, in his fifth book " *De Augmentis Scientiarum,*" and more fully treated in his " *Novum Organum.*" He divides them into four classes—*idola tribus, idola specus, idola fori,* and *idola theatri.* The names are perhaps fanciful ; but I think the division judicious, like most of the productions of that wonderful genius. And as this division was first made by him, he may be indulged the privilege of giving names to its several members.

I propose in this chapter to explain the several members of this division, according to the meaning of the author, and to give instances of each, without confining myself to those which Lord Bacon has given, and without pretending to a complete enumeration.

To every bias of the understanding, by which a man may be misled in judging, or drawn into error, Lord Bacon gives the name of an idol. The understanding, in its natural and best state, pays its homage to truth only. The causes of error are considered by him as so many false deities, who receive the homage which is due only to truth. [653]

A. The first class are the *idola tribus. These are such as beset the whole human species ; so that every man is in danger from them.* They arise from principles of the human constitution, which are highly useful and necessary in our present state ; but, by their excess or defect, or wrong direction, may lead us into error.

As the active principles of the human frame are wisely contrived by the Author of our being for the direction of our actions, and yet, without proper regulation and restraint, are apt to lead us wrong, so it is also with regard to those parts of our constitution that have influence upon our opinions. Of this we may take the following instances :—

1. First,—*Men are prone to be led too much by authority in their opinions.*

In the first part of life, we have no other guide ; and, without a disposition to receive implicitly what we are taught, we should be incapable of instruction, and incapable of improvement.

When judgment is ripe, there are many things in which we are incompetent judges. In such matters, it is most reasonable to rely upon the judgment of those whom we believe to be competent and disinterested. The highest court of judicature in the nation relies upon the authority of lawyers and physicians in matters belonging to their respective professions.

Even in matters which we have access to know, authority always will have, and ought to have, more or less weight, in proportion to the evidence on which our own

[653-655]

judgment rests, and the opinion we have of the judgment and candour of those who differ from us, or agree with us. The modest man, conscious of his own fallibility in judging, is in danger of giving too much to authority ; the arrogant of giving too little. [654]

In all matters belonging to our cognizance, every man must be determined by his own final judgment, otherwise he does not act the part of a rational being. Authority may add weight to one scale ; but the man holds the balance, and judges what weight he ought to allow to authority. If a man should even claim infallibility, we must judge of his title to that prerogative. If a man pretend to be an ambassador from heaven, we must judge of his credentials. No claim can deprive us of this right, or excuse us for neglecting to exercise it.

As, therefore, our regard to authority may be either too great or too small, the bias of human nature seems to lean to the first of these extremes ; and I believe it is good for men in general that it should do so.

When this bias concurs with an indifference about truth, its operation will be the more powerful.

The love of truth is natural to man, and strong in every well-disposed mind. But it may be overborne by party zeal, by vanity, by the desire of victory, or even by laziness. When it is superior to these, it is a manly virtue, and requires the exercise of industry, fortitude, self-denial, candour, and openness to conviction.

As there are persons in the world of so mean and abject a spirit that they rather choose to owe their subsistence to the charity of others, than by industry to acquire some property of their own ; so there are many more who may be called mere beggars with regard to their opinions. Through laziness and indifference about truth, they leave to others the drudgery of digging for this commodity ; they can have enough at second hand to serve their occasions. Their concern is not to know what is true, but what is said and thought on such subjects ; and their understanding, like their clothes, is cut according to the fashion. [655]

This distemper of the understanding has taken so deep root in a great part of mankind, that it can hardly be said that they use their own judgment in things that do not concern their temporal interest. Nor is it peculiar to the ignorant ; it infects all ranks. We may guess their opinions when we know where they were born, of what parents, how educated, and what company they have kept. These circumstances determine their opinions in religion, in politics, and in philosophy.

2. A *second* general prejudice arises from *a disposition to measure things less known and less familiar, by those that are better known and more familiar.*

This is the foundation of analogical reasoning, to which we have a great proneness by nature, and to it indeed we owe a great part of our knowledge. It would be absurd to lay aside this kind of reasoning altogether, and it is difficult to judge how far we may venture upon it. The bias of human nature is to judge from too slight analogies.

The objects of sense engross our thoughts in the first part of life, and are most familiar through the whole of it. Hence, in all ages men have been prone to attribute the human figure and human passions and frailties to superior intelligences, and even to the Supreme Being.

There is a disposition in men to materialize everything, if I may be allowed the expression ; that is, to apply the notions we have of material objects to things of another nature. Thought is considered as analogous to motion in a body ; and as bodies are put in motion by impulses, and by impressions made upon them by contiguous objects, we are apt to conclude that the mind is made to think by impressions made upon it, and that there must be some kind of contiguity between it and the objects of thought. Hence the theories of ideas and impressions have so generally prevailed. [656]

Because the most perfect works of human artists are made after a model, and of materials that before existed, the ancient philosophers universally believed that the world was made of a pre-existent uncreated matter ; and many of them, that there were eternal and uncreated models of every species of things which God made.

The mistakes in common life, which are owing to this prejudice, are innumerable, and cannot escape the slightest observation. Men judge of other men by themselves, or by the small circle of their acquaintance. The selfish man thinks all pretences to benevolence and public spirit to be mere hypocrisy or self-deceit. The generous and open-hearted believe fair pretences too easily, and are apt to think men better than they really are. The abandoned and profligate can hardly be persuaded that there is any such thing as real virtue in the world. The rustic forms his notions of the manners and characters of men from those of his country village, and is easily duped when he comes into a great city.

It is commonly taken for granted, that this narrow way of judging of men is to be cured only by an extensive intercourse with men of different ranks, professions, and nations ; and that the man whose acquaintance has been confined within a narrow circle, must have many prejudices and nar-

row notions, which a more extensive intercourse would have cured.

3. Men are often led into error by *the love of simplicity, which disposes us to reduce things to few principles, and to conceive a greater simplicity in nature than there really is.* [657]

To love simplicity, and to be pleased with it wherever we find it, is no imperfection, but the contrary. It is the result of good taste. We cannot but be pleased to observe, that all the changes of motion produced by the collision of bodies, hard, soft, or elastic, are reducible to three simple laws of motion, which the industry of philosophers has discovered.

When we consider what a prodigious variety of effects depend upon the law of gravitation ; how many phænomena in the earth, sea, and air, which, in all preceding ages, had tortured the wits of philosophers, and occasioned a thousand vain theories, are shewn to be the necessary consequences of this one law ; how the whole system of sun, moon, planets, primary and secondary, and comets, are kept in order by it, and their seeming irregularities accounted for and reduced to accurate measure—the simplicity of the cause, and the beauty and variety of the effects, must give pleasure to every contemplative mind. By this noble discovery, we are taken, as it were, behind the scene in this great drama of nature, and made to behold some part of the art of the divine Author of this system, which, before this discovery, eye had not seen, nor ear heard, nor had it entered into the heart of man to conceive.

There is, without doubt, in every work of nature, all the beautiful simplicity that is consistent with the end for which it was made. But, if we hope to discover how nature brings about its ends, merely from this principle, that it operates in the simplest and best way, we deceive ourselves, and forget that the wisdom of nature is more above the wisdom of man, than man's wisdom is above that of a child.

If a child should sit down to contrive how a city is to be fortified, or an army arranged in the day of battle, he would, no doubt, conjecture what, to his understanding, appeared the simplest and best way. But could he ever hit upon the true way ? No surely. When he learns from fact how these effects are produced, he will then see how foolish his childish conjectures were. [658]

We may learn something of the way in which nature operates from fact and observation ; but, if we conclude that it operates in such a manner, only because to our

---

* See " Inquiry," ch. vii. § 3, above, p. 206, sqq —H.

understanding that appears to be the best and simplest manner, we shall always go wrong.

It was believed, for many ages, that all the variety of concrete bodies we find on this globe is reducible to four elements, of which they are compounded, and into which they may be resolved. It was the simplicity of this theory, and not any evidence from fact, that made it to be so generally received; for the more it is examined, we find the less ground to believe it.

The Pythagoreans and Platonists were carried farther by the same love of simplicity. Pythagoras, by his skill in mathematics, discovered, that there can be no more than five regular solid figures, terminated by plain surfaces, which are all similar and equal; to wit, the tetrahedron, the cube, the octahedron, the dodecahedron, and the eicosihedron. As nature works in the most simple and regular way, he thought that all the elementary bodies must have one or other of those regular figures; and that the discovery of the properties and relations of the regular solids would be a key to open the mysteries of nature.

This notion of the Pythagoreans and Platonists has undoubtedly great beauty and simplicity. Accordingly it prevailed, at least, to the time of Euclid. He was a Platonic philosopher, and is said to have wrote all the books of his "Elements" in order to discover the properties and relations of the five regular solids. This ancient tradition of the intention of Euclid in writing his "Elements," is countenanced by the work itself. For the last books of the "Elements" treat of the regular solids, and all the preceding are subservient to the last. [659]

So that this most ancient mathematical work, which, for its admirable composition, has served as a model to all succeeding writers in mathematics, seems, like the two first books of Newton's "Principia," to have been intended by its author to exhibit the mathematical principles of natural philosophy.

It was long believed, that all the qualities of bodies,[*] and all their medical virtues, were reducible to four—moisture and dryness, heat and cold; and that there are only four temperaments of the human body—the sanguine, the melancholy, the bilious, and the phlegmatic. The chemical system, of reducing all bodies to salt, sulphur, and mercury, was of the same kind. For how many ages did men believe, that the division of all the objects of thought into ten categories, and of all that can be affirmed or denied of anything, into five universals or predicables, were perfect enumerations?

The evidence from reason that could bo produced for those systems was next to nothing, and bore no proportion to the ground they gained in the belief of men; but they were simple and regular, and reduced things to a few principles; and this supplied their want of evidence.

Of all the systems we know, that of Des Cartes was most remarkable for its simplicity.[*] Upon one proposition, *I think*, he builds the whole fabric of human knowledge. And from mere matter, with a certain quantity of motion given it at first, he accounts for all the phænomena of the material world.

The physical part of this system was mere hypothesis. It had nothing to recommend it but its simplicity; yet it had force enough to overturn the system of Aristotle, after that system had prevailed for more than a thousand years.

The principle of gravitation, and other attracting and repelling forces, after Sir Isaac Newton had given the strongest evidence of their real existence in nature, were rejected by the greatest part of Europe for half a century, because they could not be accounted for by matter and motion. So much were men enamoured with the simplicity of the Cartesian system. [660]

Nay, I apprehend, it was this love of simplicity, more than real evidence, that led Newton himself to say, in the preface to his "Principia," speaking of the phænomena of the material world—"Nam multa me movent ut nonnihil suspicer, ea omnia ex viribus quibusdam pendere posse, quibus corporum particulæ, per causas nondum cognitas, vel in se mutuo impelluntur, et secundum figuras regulares cohæerent, vel ab invicem fugantur et recedunt." For certainly we have no evidence from fact, that all the phænomena of the material world are produced by attracting or repelling forces.

With his usual modesty, he proposes it only as a slight suspicion; and the ground of this suspicion could only be, that he saw that many of the phænomena of nature depended upon causes of this kind; and therefore was disposed, from the simplicity of nature, to think that all do.

When a real cause is discovered, the same love of simplicity leads men to attribute effects to it which are beyond its province.

A medicine that is found to be of great use in one distemper, commonly has its virtues multiplied, till it becomes a *panacea*. Those who have lived long, can recollect many instances of this. In other branches of knowledge, the same thing often happens. When the attention of men is turned to any

* See above, p. 206, b, note †.—H.

particular cause, by discovering it to have remarkable effects, they are in great danger of extending its influence, upon slight evidence, to things with which it has no connection. Such prejudices arise from the natural desire of simplifying natural causes, and of accounting for many phænomena from the same principle. [661]

4. One of the most copious sources of error in philosophy is *the misapplication of our noblest intellectual power to purposes for which it is incompetent.*

Of all the intellectual powers of man, that of *invention* bears the highest price. It resembles most the power of creation, and is honoured with that name.

We admire the man who shews a superiority in the talent of finding the means of accomplishing an end; who can, by a happy combination, produce an effect, or make a discovery beyond the reach of other men; who can draw important conclusions from circumstances that commonly pass unobserved; who judges with the greatest sagacity of the designs of other men, and the consequences of his own actions. To this superiority of understanding we give the name of genius, and look up with admiration to everything that bears the marks of it.

Yet this power, so highly valuable in itself, and so useful in the conduct of life, may be misapplied; and men of genius, in all ages, have been prone to apply it to purposes for which it is altogether incompetent.

The works of men and the works of Nature are not of the same order. The force of genius may enable a man perfectly to comprehend the former, and see them to the bottom. What is contrived and executed by one man may be perfectly understood by another man. With great probability, he may from a part conjecture the whole, or from the effects may conjecture the causes; because they are effects of a wisdom not superior to his own. [662]

But the works of Nature are contrived and executed by a wisdom and power infinitely superior to that of man; and when men attempt, by the force of genius, to discover the causes of the phænomena of Nature, they have only the chance of going wrong more ingeniously. Their conjectures may appear very probable to beings no wiser than themselves; but they have no chance to hit the truth. They are like the conjectures of a child how a ship of war is built, and how it is managed at sea.

Let the man of genius try to make an animal, even the meanest; to make a plant, or even a single leaf of a plant, or a feather of a bird; he will find that all his wisdom and sagacity can bear no comparison with the wisdom of Nature, nor his power with the power of Nature.

The experience of all ages shews how prone ingenious men have been to invent hypotheses to explain the phænomena of Nature; how fond, by a kind of anticipation, to discover her secrets. Instead of a slow and gradual ascent in the scale of natural causes, by a just and copious induction, they would shorten the work, and, by a flight of genius, get to the top at once. This gratifies the pride of human understanding; but it is an attempt beyond our force, like that of Phaeton to guide the chariot of the sun.

When a man has laid out all his ingenuity in fabricating a system, he views it with the eye of a parent; he strains phænomena to make them tally with it, and make it look like the work of Nature.

The slow and patient method of induction, the only way to attain any knowledge of Nature's work, was little understood until it was delineated by Lord Bacon, and has been little followed since. It humbles the pride of man, and puts him constantly in mind that his most ingenious conjectures with regard to the works of God are pitiful and childish. [663]

There is no room here for the favourite talent of invention. In the humble method of information, from the great volume of Nature we must receive all our knowledge of Nature. Whatever is beyond a just interpretation of that volume is the work of man; and the work of God ought not to be contaminated by any mixture with it.

To a man of genius, self-denial is a difficult lesson in philosophy as well as in religion. To bring his fine imaginations and most ingenious conjectures to the fiery trial of experiment and induction, by which the greater part, if not the whole, will be found to be dross, is a humiliating task. This is to condemn him to dig in a mine, when he would fly with the wings of an eagle.

In all the fine arts, whose end is to please, genius is deservedly supreme. In the conduct of human affairs, it often does wonders; but in all inquiries into the constitution of Nature, it must act a subordinate part, ill-suited to the superiority it boasts. It may combine, but it must not fabricate. It may collect evidence, but must not supply the want of it by conjecture. It may display its powers by putting Nature to the question in well-contrived experiments, but it must add nothing to her answers.

5. *In avoiding one extreme, men are very apt to rush into the opposite.*

Thus, in rude ages, men, unaccustomed to search for natural causes, ascribe every uncommon appearance to the immediate interposition of invisible beings; but when philosophy has discovered natural causes of many events, which, in the days of ignorance, were ascribed to the immediate operation of gods or dæmons, they are apt to think that all the phænomena of Nature may be accounted for in the same way and that there is no need of an invisible Maker and Governor of the world. [664]

Rude men are, at first, disposed to ascribe intelligence and active power to everything they see move or undergo any change. "Savages," says the Abbé Raynal, "wherever they see motion which they cannot account for, there they suppose a soul." When they come to be convinced of the folly of this extreme, they are apt to run into the opposite, and to think that everything moves only as it is moved, and acts as it is acted upon.

Thus, from the extreme of superstition, the transition is easy to that of atheism; and from the extreme of ascribing activity to every part of Nature, to that of excluding it altogether, and making even the determinations of intelligent beings, the links of one fatal chain, or the wheels of one great machine.

The abuse of occult qualities in the Peripatetic philosophy led Des Cartes and his followers to reject all occult qualities, to pretend to explain all the phænomena of Nature by mere matter and motion, and even to fix disgrace upon the name of occult quality.

6. Men's judgments are often perverted by their affections and passions. This is so commonly observed, and so universally acknowledged, that it needs no proof nor illustration.

B. The second class of idols in Lord Bacon's division are the *idola specus.*

These are prejudices which have their origin, not from the constitution of human nature, but from something peculiar to the individual.

As in a cave objects vary in their appearance according to the form of the cave and the manner in which it receives the light, Lord Bacon conceives the mind of every man to resemble a cave, which has its particular form, and its particular manner of being enlightened; and, from these circumstances, often gives false colours and a delusive appearance to objects seen in it.* [665]

For this reason he gives the name of *idola specus* to those prejudices which arise from the particular way in which a man has been trained, from his being addicted to some particular profession, or from something particular in the turn of his mind.

A man whose thoughts have been confined to a certain track by his profession or manner of life, is very apt to judge wrong when he ventures out of that track. He is apt to draw everything within the sphere of his profession, and to judge by its maxims of things that have no relation to it.

The mere mathematician is apt to apply measure and calculation to things which do not admit of it. Direct and inverse ratios have been applied by an ingenious author to measure human affections, and the moral worth of actions. An eminent mathematician* attempted to ascertain by calculation the ratio in which the evidence of facts must decrease in the course of time, and fixed the period when the evidence of the facts on which Christianity is founded shall become evanescent, and when in consequence no faith shall be found on the earth. I have seen a philosophical dissertation, published by a very good mathematician, wherein, in opposition to the ancient division of things into ten categories, he maintains that there are no more, and can be no more than two categories, to wit, *data* and *quæsita.*†

The ancient chemists were wont to explain all the mysteries of Nature, and even of religion, by salt, sulphur, and mercury.

Mr Locke, I think, mentions an eminent musician, who believed that God created the world in six days, and rested the seventh, because there are but seven notes in music. I knew one of that profession, who thought that there could be only three parts in harmony—to wit, bass, tenor, and treble —because there are but three persons in the Trinity. [666]

The learned and ingenious Dr Henry More having very elaborately and methodically compiled his "*Enchiridium Metaphysicum,*" and "*Enchiridium Ethicum,*" found all the divisions and subdivisions of both to be allegorically taught in the first chapter of Genesis. Thus even very ingenious men are apt to make a ridiculous figure, by drawing into the track in which their thoughts have long run, things altogether foreign to it.‡

Different persons, either from temper or from education, have different tendencies of understanding, which, by their excess, are unfavourable to sound judgment.

Some have an undue admiration of antiquity, and contempt of whatever is modern; others go as far into the contrary extreme. It may be judged, that the former are per-

---

* If Bacon took his simile of the cave from Plato, he has perverted it from its proper meaning; for, in the Platonic signification, the *idola specus* should denote the prejudices of the species, and not of the individual—that is, express what Bacon denominates by *idola tribus.*—H.

[664–666]

---

* Craig.—H.

† Reid refers to his uncle, James Gregory, Professor of Mathematics in St Andrew's and Edinburgh. See above, p. 68, b. .—H.

‡ "Musicians think our souls are harmonies;
Physicians hold that they complexions be
Epicures make them swarms of atomies,
Which do by chance into the body flee.
Sir John Davies, in the first and second lines, alludes to Aristoxenus and Galen.—H.

sons who value themselves upon their acquaintance with ancient authors, and the latter such as have little knowledge of this kind.

Some are afraid to venture a step out of the beaten track, and think it safest to go with the multitude ; others are fond of singularities, and of everything that has the air of paradox.

Some are desultory and changeable in their opinions ; others unduly tenacious. Most men have a predilection for the tenets of their sect or party, and still more for their own inventions.

C. The *idola fori* are the *fallacies arising from the imperfections and the abuse of language*, which is an instrument of thought as well as of the communication of our thoughts. [667]

Whether it be the effect of constitution or of habit, I will not take upon me to determine; but, .from one or both of these causes, it happens that no man can pursue a train of thought or reasoning without the use of language. Words are the signs of our thoughts; and the sign is so associated with the thing signified, that the last can hardly present itself to the imagination, without drawing the other along with it.

A man who would compose in any language must think in that language. If he thinks in one language what he would express in another, he thereby doubles his labour ; and, after all, his expressions will have more the air of a translation than of an original.

This shews that our thoughts take their colour in some degree from the language we use ; and that, although language ought always to be subservient to thought, yet thought must be, at some times and in some degree, subservient to language.

As a servant that is extremely useful and necessary to his master, by degrees acquires an authority over him, so that the master must often yield to the servant, such is the case with regard to language. Its intention is to be a servant to the understanding ; but it is so useful and so necessary that we cannot avoid being sometimes led by it when it ought to follow. We cannot shake off this impediment—we must drag it along with us ; and, therefore, must direct our course, and regulate our pace, as it permits.

Language must have many imperfections when applied to philosophy, because it was not made for that use. In the early periods of society, rude and ignorant men use certain forms of speech, to express their wants, their desires, and their transactions with one another. Their language can reach no farther than their speculations and notions ; and, if their notions be vague and ill-defined, the words by which they express them must be so likewise.

It was a grand and noble project of Bishop Wilkins* to invent a philosophical language, which should be free from the imperfections of vulgar languages. Whether this attempt will ever succeed, so far as to be generally useful, I shall not pretend to determine. The great pains taken by that excellent man in this design have hitherto produced no effect. Very few have ever entered minutely into his views ; far less have his philosophical language and his real character been brought into use. [668]

He founds his philosophical language and real character upon a systematical division and subdivision of all the things which may be expressed by language ; and, instead of the ancient division into ten categories, has made forty categories, or *summa genera*. But whether this division, though made by a very comprehensive mind, will always suit the various systems that may be introduced, and all the real improvements that may be made in human knowledge, may be doubted. The difficulty is still greater in the subdivisions ; so that it is to be feared that this noble attempt of a great genius will prove abortive, until philosophers have the same opinions and the same systems in the various branches of human knowledge.

There is more reason to hope that the languages used by philosophers may be gradually improved in copiousness and in distinctness ; and that improvements in knowledge and in language may go hand in hand and facilitate each other. But I fear the imperfections of language can never be perfectly remedied while our knowledge ·is imperfect.

However this may be, it is evident that the imperfections of language, and much more the abuse of it, are the occasion of many errors ; and that in many disputes which have engaged learned men, the difference has been partly, and in some wholly, about the meaning of words.

Mr Locke found it necessary to employ a fourth part of his " Essay on Human Understanding" about words, their various kinds, their imperfection and abuse, and the remedies of both ; and has made many observations upon these subjects well worthy of attentive perusal. [669]

D. The fourth class of prejudices are the *idola theatri*, by which are meant *prejudices arising from the systems or sects in which we have been trained, or which we have adopted.*

A false system once fixed in the mind, becomes, as it were, the medium through which we see objects : they receive a tincture from it, and appear of another colour than when seen by a pure light.

Upon the same subject, a Platonist, a

Peripatetic, and an Epicurean, will think differently, not only in matters connected with his peculiar tenets, but even in things remote from them.

A judicious history of the different sects of philosophers, and the different methods of philosophising, which have obtained among mankind, would be of no small use to direct men in the search of truth. In such a history, what would be of the greatest moment is not so much a minute detail of the *dogmata* of each sect, as a just delineation of the spirit of the sect, and of that point of view in which things appeared to its founder. This was perfectly understood, and, as far as concerns the theories of morals, is executed with great judgment and candour by Dr Smith in his theory of moral sentiments.

As there are certain temperaments of the body that dispose a man more to one class of diseases than to another, and, on the other hand, diseases of that kind, when they happen by accident, are apt to induce the temperament that is suited to them—there is something analogous to this in the diseases of the understanding. [670]

A certain complexion of understanding may dispose a man to one system of opinions more than to another; and, on the other hand, a system of opinions, fixed in the mind by education or otherwise, gives that complexion to the understanding which is suited to them.

It were to be wished, that the different systems that have prevailed could be classed according to their spirit, as well as named from their founders. Lord Bacon has distinguished false philosophy into the sophistical, the empirical, and the superstitious, and has made judicious observations upon each of these kinds. But I apprehend this subject deserves to be treated more fully by such a hand, if such a hand can be found. [671]

ESSAY VII.

OF REASONING.

CHAPTER I.

OF REASONING IN GENERAL, AND OF DEMONSTRATION.

THE power of reasoning is very nearly allied to that of judging; and it is of little consequence in the common affairs of life to distinguish them nicely. On this account, the same name is often given to both. We include both under the name of reason.* The assent we give to a proposition is called judgment, whether the proposition be self-evident, or derive its evidence by reasoning from other propositions.

Yet there is a distinction between reasoning and judging. Reasoning is the process by which we pass from one judgment to another, which is the consequence of it. Accordingly our judgments are distinguished into intuitive, which are not grounded upon any preceding judgment, and discursive, which are deduced from some preceding judgment by reasoning.

In all reasoning, therefore, there must be a proposition inferred, and one or more from which it is inferred. And this power of inferring, or drawing a conclusion, is only another name for reasoning; the proposition inferred being called the *conclusion*, and the proposition or propositions from which it is inferred, the *premises*. [672]

Reasoning may consist of many steps; the first conclusion being a premise to a second, that to a third, and so on, till we come to the last conclusion. A process consisting of many steps of this kind, is so easily distinguished from judgment, that it is never called by that name. But when there is only a single step to the conclusion, the distinction is less obvious, and the process is sometimes called judgment, sometimes reasoning.

It is not strange that, in common discourse, judgment and reasoning should not be very nicely distinguished, since they are in some cases confounded even by logicians. We are taught in logic, that judgment is expressed by one proposition, but that reasoning requires two or three. But so various are the modes of speech, that what in one mode is expressed by two or three propositions, may, in another mode, be expressed by one. Thus I may say, *God is good; therefore good men shall be happy.* This is reasoning, of that kind which logicians call an enthymeme, consisting of an antecedent proposition, and a conclusion drawn from it.* But this reasoning may

---

* See Stewart's "Elements," ii. p. 12.—H.

* The enthymeme is a mere abbreviation of expression; in the mental process there is no ellipsis. By

be expressed by one proposition, thus:—
*Because God is good, good men shall be
happy.* This is what they call a causal
proposition, and therefore expresses judgment; yet the enthymeme, which is reasoning, expresses no more.

Reasoning, as well as judgment, must be
true or false : both are grounded upon evidence which may be probable or demonstrative, and both are accompanied with assent
or belief. [673]

The power of reasoning is justly accounted
one of the prerogatives of human nature ;
because by it many important truths have
been and may be discovered, which without it would be beyond our reach ; yet it
seems to be only a kind of crutch to a
limited understanding. We can conceive
an understanding, superior to human, to
which that truth appears intuitively, which
we can only discover by reasoning. For
this cause, though we must ascribe judgment to the Almighty, we do not ascribe
reasoning to him, because it implies some
defect or limitation of understanding. Even
among men, to use reasoning in things that
are self-evident, is trifling ; like a man
going upon crutches when he can walk
upon his legs.

What reasoning is, can be understood
only by a man who has reasoned, and who
is capable of reflecting upon this operation
of his own mind. We can define it only by
synonymous words or phrases, such as inferring, drawing a conclusion, and the like.
The very notion of reasoning, therefore, can
enter into the mind by no other channel
than that of reflecting upon the operation
of reasoning in our own minds ; and the
notions of premises and conclusion, of a
syllogism and all its constituent parts, of
an enthymeme, sorites, demonstration, paralogism, and many others, have the same
origin.

It is nature, undoubtedly, that gives us
the capacity of reasoning. When this is
wanting, no art nor education can supply it.
But this capacity may be dormant through
life, like the seed of a plant, which, for want
of heat and moisture, never vegetates. This
is probably the case of some savages.

Although the capacity be purely the gift
of nature, and probably given in very different degrees to different persons ; yet the
power of reasoning seems to be got by habit,
as much as the power of walking or running.
Its first exertions we are not able to recollect in ourselves, or clearly to discern in
others. They are very feeble, and need to
be led by example, and supported by authority. By degrees it acquires strength,
chiefly by means of imitation and exercise. [674]

enthymeme, Aristotle also meant something very different from what is vulgarly supposed.—H.

The exercise of reasoning on various subjects not only strengthens the faculty, but
furnishes the mind with a store of materials.
Every train of reasoning, which is familiar,
becomes a beaten track in the way to many
others. It removes many obstacles which
lay in our way, and smooths many roads
which we may have occasion to travel in
future disquisitions.

When men of equal natural parts apply
their reasoning power to any subject, the
man who has reasoned much on the same
or on similar subjects, has a like advantage
over him who has not, as the mechanic
who has store of tools for his work, has of
him who has his tools to make, or even to
invent.

In a train of reasoning, the evidence of
every step, where nothing is left to be supplied by the reader or hearer, must be immediately discernible to every man of ripe
understanding who has a distinct comprehension of the premises and conclusion, and
who compares them together. To be able
to comprehend, in one view, a combination
of steps of this kind, is more difficult, and
seems to require a superior natural ability.
In all, it may be much improved by habit.

But the highest talent in reasoning is the
invention of proofs; by which, truths remote from the premises are brought to light.
In all works of understanding, invention
has the highest praise : it requires an extensive view of what relates to the subject,
and a quickness in discerning those affinities
and relations which may be subservient to
the purpose.

In all invention there must be some end
in view : and sagacity in finding out the
road that leads to this end, is, I think, what
we call invention. In this chiefly, as I apprehend, and in clear and distinct conceptions, consists that superiority of understanding which we call *genius.* [675]

In every chain of reasoning, the evidence
of the last conclusion can be no greater than
that of the weakest link of the chain, whatever may be the strength of the rest.

The most remarkable distinction of reasonings is, that some are probable, others
demonstrative.

In every step of demonstrative reasoning, the inference is necessary, and we perceive it to be impossible that the conclusion
should not follow from the premises. In
probable reasoning, the connection between
the premises and the conclusion is not necessary, nor do we perceive it to be impossible
that the first should be true while the last
is false.

Hence, demonstrative reasoning has no
degrees, nor can one demonstration be
stronger than another, though, in relation
to our faculties, one may be more easily
comprehended than another. Every demonstration [673–675]

monstration gives equal strength to the conclusion, and leaves no possibility of its being false.

It was, I think, the opinion of all the ancients, that demonstrative reasoning can be applied only to truths that are necessary, and not to those that are contingent. In this, I believe, they judged right. Of all created things, the existence, the attributes, and, consequently, the relations resulting from those attributes, are contingent. They depend upon the will and power of Him who made them. These are matters of fact, and admit not of demonstration.

The field of demonstrative reasoning, therefore, is the various relations of things abstract, that is, of things which we conceive, without regard to their existence. Of these, as they are conceived by the mind, and are nothing but what they are conceived to be, we may have a clear and adequate comprehension. Their relations and attributes are necessary and immutable. They are the things to which the Pythagoreans and Platonists gave the name of ideas. I would beg leave to borrow this meaning of the word *idea* from those ancient philosophers, and then I must agree with them, that ideas are the only objects about which we can reason demonstratively. [676]

There are many even of our ideas about which we can carry on no considerable train of reasoning. Though they be ever so well defined and perfectly comprehended, yet their agreements and disagreements are few, and these are discerned at once. We may go a step or two in forming a conclusion with regard to such objects, but can go no farther. There are others, about which we may, by a long train of demonstrative reasoning, arrive at conclusions very remote and unexpected.

The reasonings I have met with that can be called strictly demonstrative, may, I think, be reduced to two classes. They are either metaphysical, or they are mathematical.

In metaphysical reasoning, the process is always short. The conclusion is but a step or two, seldom more, from the first principle or axiom on which it is grounded, and the different conclusions depend not one upon another.

It is otherwise in mathematical reasoning. Here the field has no limits. One proposition leads on to another, that to a third, and so on without end.

If it should be asked, why demonstrative reasoning has so wide a field in mathematics, while, in other abstract subjects, it is confined within very narrow limits, I conceive this is chiefly owing to the nature of quantity, the object of mathematics.

Every quantity, as it has magnitude, and is divisible into parts without end, so, in

[676–678]

respect of its magnitude, it has a certain ratio to every quantity of the kind. The ratios of quantities are innumerable, such as, a half, a third, a tenth, double, triple. [677] All the powers of number are insufficient to express the variety of ratios. For there are innumerable ratios which cannot be perfectly expressed by numbers, such as, the ratio of the side to the diagonal of a square, or of the circumference of a circle to the diameter. Of this infinite variety of ratios, every one may be clearly conceived and distinctly expressed, so as to be in no danger of being mistaken for any other.

Extended quantities, such as lines, surfaces, solids, besides the variety of relations they have in respect of magnitude, have no less variety in respect of figure; and every mathematical figure may be accurately defined, so as to distinguish it from all others.

There is nothing of this kind in other objects of abstract reasoning. Some of them have various degrees; but these are not capable of measure, nor can be said to have an assignable ratio to others of the kind. They are either simple, or compounded of a few indivisible parts; and therefore, if we may be allowed the expression, can touch only in few points. But mathematical quantities being made up of parts without number, can touch in innumerable points, and be compared in innumerable different ways.

There have been attempts made to measure the merit of actions by the ratios of the affections and principles of action from which they proceed. This may perhaps, in the way of analogy, serve to illustrate what was before known; but I do not think any truth can be discovered in this way. There are, no doubt, degrees of benevolence, self-love, and other affections; but, when we apply ratios to them, I apprehend we have no distinct meaning.

Some demonstrations are called direct, others indirect. The first kind leads directly to the conclusion to be proved. Of the indirect, some are called demonstrations *ad absurdum*. In these, the proposition contradictory to that which is to be proved is demonstrated to be false, or to lead to an absurdity; whence it follows, that its contradictory—that is, the proposition to be proved—is true. This inference is grounded upon an axiom in logic, that of two contradictory propositions, if one be false, the other must be true.* [678]

Another kind of indirect demonstration proceeds by enumerating all the suppositions that can possibly be made concerning the proposition to be proved, and then

---

* This is called the *principle of Extended Hiadus*—viz., between two contradictories—H

demonstrating that all of them, excepting that which is to be proved, are false; whence it follows, that the excepted supposition is true. Thus, one line is proved to be equal to another, by proving first that it cannot be greater, and then that it cannot be less : for it must be either greater, or less, or equal; and two of these suppositions being demonstrated to be false, the third must be true.

All these kinds of demonstration are used in mathematics, and perhaps some others. They have all equal strength. The direct demonstration is preferred where it can be had, for this reason only, as I apprehend, because it is the shortest road to the conclusion. The nature of the evidence, and its strength, is the same in all : only we are conducted to it by different roads.

CHAPTER II.

WHETHER MORALITY BE CAPABLE OF DEMONSTRATION.

What has been said of demonstrative reasoning, may help us to judge of an opinion of Mr Locke, advanced in several places of his Essay—to wit, "That morality is capable of demonstration as well as mathematics."

In book III., chap. 11, having observed that mixed modes, especially those belonging to morality, being such combinations of ideas as the mind puts together of its own choice, the signification of their names may be perfectly and exactly defined, he adds—[679]

Sect. 16. " Upon this ground it is that I am bold to think that morality is capable of demonstration as well as mathematics; since the precise real essence of the things moral words stand for may be perfectly known, and so the congruity or incongruity of the things themselves be certainly discovered, in which consists perfect knowledge. Nor let any one object, That the names of substances are often to be made use of in morality, as well as those of modes, from which will arise obscurity; for, as to substances, when concerned in moral discourses, their divers natures are not so much inquired into as supposed : v. g. When we say that man is subject to law, we mean nothing by man but a corporeal rational creature : what the real essence or other qualities of that creature are, in this case, is no way considered."

Again, in book IV., ch. iii., § 18:—" The idea of a Supreme Being, whose workmanship we are, and the idea of ourselves, being such as are clear in us, would, I suppose, if duly considered and pursued, afford such foundation of our duty and rules of action as might place morality among the sciences

capable of demonstration. The relation of other modes may certainly be perceived, as well as those of number and extension ; and I cannot see why they should not be capable of demonstration, if due methods were thought on to examine or pursue their agreement or disagreement."

He afterwards gives, as instances, two propositions, as moral propositions of which we may be as certain as of any in mathematics ; and considers at large what may have given the advantage to the ideas of quantity, and made them be thought more capable of certainty and demonstration.[680]

Again, in the 12th chapter of the same book, § 7, 8 :—" This, I think, I may say, that, if other ideas that are the real as well as nominal essences of their several species were pursued in the way familiar to mathematicians, they would carry our thoughts farther, and with greater evidence and clearness, than possibly we are apt to imagine. This gave me the confidence to advance that conjecture which I suggest, chap iii.—viz., That morality is capable of demonstration as well as mathematics."

From these passages, it appears that this opinion was not a transient thought, but what he had revolved in his mind on different occasions. He offers his reasons for it, illustrates it by examples, and considers at length the causes that have led men to think mathematics more capable of demonstration than the principles of morals.

Some of his learned correspondents, particularly his friend Mr Molyneux, urged and importuned him to compose a system of morals according to the idea he had advanced in his Essay ; and, in his answer to these solicitations, he only pleads other occupations, without suggesting any change of his opinion, or any great difficulty in the execution of what was desired.

The reason he gives for this opinion is ingenious ; and his regard for virtue, the highest prerogative of the human species, made him fond of an opinion which seemed to be favourable to virtue. and to have a just foundation in reason.

We need not, however, be afraid that the interest of virtue may suffer by a free and candid examination of this question, or indeed of any question whatever. For the interests of truth and of virtue can never be found in opposition. Darkness and error may befriend vice, but can never be favourable to virtue. [681]

Those philosophers who think that our determinations in morals are not real judgments—that right and wrong in human conduct are only certain feelings or sensations in the person who contemplates th action —must reject Mr Locke's opinion without examination For, if the principles of morals be not a matter of judgment, but of feeling only, there can be no demonstration of them ; nor can any other reason be given for them, but that men are so constituted by the Author of their being as to contemplate with pleasure the actions we call virtuous, and with disgust those we call vicious.

It is not, therefore, to be expected that the philosophers of this class should think this opinion of Mr Locke worthy of examination, since it is founded upon what they think a false hypothesis. But if our determinations in morality be real judgments, and, like all other judgments, be either true or false, it is not unimportant to understand upon what kind of evidence those judgments rest.

The argument offered by Mr Locke, to shew that morality is capable of demonstration, is, " That the precise real essence of the things moral words stand for, may be perfectly known, and so the congruity or incongruity of the things themselves be perfectly discovered, in which consists perfect knowledge."

It is true, that the field of demonstration is the various relations of things conceived abstractly, of which we may have perfect and adequate conceptions. And Mr Locke, taking all the things which moral words stand for to be of this kind, concluded that morality is as capable of demonstration as mathematics.

I acknowledge that the names of the virtues and vices, of right and obligation, of liberty and property, stand for things abstract, which may be accurately defined, or, at least, conceived as distinctly and adequately as mathematical quantities. And thence, indeed, it follows, that their mutual relations may be perceived as clearly and certainly as mathematical truths. [682]

Of this Mr Locke gives two pertinent examples. The first—" Where there is no property, there is no injustice, is," says he, " a proposition as certain as any demonstration in Euclid."

When injustice is defined to be a violation of property, it is as necessary a truth, that there can be no injustice where there is no property, as that you cannot take from a man that which he has not.

The second example is, " That no government allows absolute liberty." This is a truth no less certain and necessary.

Such abstract truths I would call metaphysical rather than moral. We give the name of mathematical to truths that express the relations of quantities considered abstractly ; all other abstract truths may be called metaphysical. But if those mentioned by Mr Locke are to be called moral truths, I agree with him that there are many such that are necessarily true, and that have all the evidence that mathematical truths can have.

[682, 683]

It ought, however, to be remembered, that, as was before observed, the relations of things abstract, perceivable by us, excepting those of mathematical quantities, are few, and, for the most part, immediately discerned, so as not to require that train of reasoning which we call demonstration. Their evidence resembles more that of mathematical axioms than mathematical propositions.

This appears in the two propositions given as examples by Mr Locke. The first follows immediately from the definition of injustice ; the second from the definition of government. Their evidence may more properly be called intuitive than demonstrative. And this I apprehend to be the case, or nearly the case, of all abstract truths that are not mathematical, for the reason given in the last chapter. [683]

The propositions which I think are properly called moral, are those that affirm some moral obligation to be, or not to be incumbent on one or more individual persons. To such propositions, Mr Locke's reasoning does not apply, because the subjects of the proposition are not things whose real essence may be perfectly known. They are the creatures of God ; their obligation results from the constitution which God hath given them, and the circumstances in which he hath placed them. That an individual hath such a constitution, and is placed in such circumstances, is not an abstract and necessary, but a contingent truth. It is a matter of fact, and, therefore, not capable of demonstrative evidence, which belongs only to necessary truths.

The evidence which every man hath of his own existence, though it be irresistible, is not demonstrative. And the same thing may be said of the evidence which every man hath, that he is a moral agent, and under certain moral obligations. In like manner, the evidence we have of the existence of other men, is not demonstrative ; nor is the evidence we have of their being endowed with those faculties which make them moral and accountable agents.

If man had not the faculty given him by God of perceiving certain things in conduct to be right, and others to be wrong, and of perceiving his obligation to do what is right, and not to do what is wrong, he would not be a moral and accountable being.

If man be endowed with such a faculty, there must be some things which, by this faculty, are immediately discerned to be right, and others to be wrong ; and, therefore, there must be in morals, as in other sciences, first principles which do not derive their evidence from any antecedent principles, but may be said to be intuitively discerned.

Moral truths, therefore, may be divided

iuto two classes—to wit, such as are self-evident to every man whose understanding and moral faculty are ripe, and such as are deduced by reasoning from those that are self-evident. If the first be not discerned without reasoning, the last never can be so by any reasoning. [684]

If any man could say, with sincerity, that he is conscious of no obligation to consult his own present and future happiness ; to be faithful to his engagements ; to obey his Maker ; to injure no man ; I know not what reasoning, either probable or demonstrative, I could use to convince him of any moral duty. As you cannot reason in mathematics with a man who denies the axioms, as little can you reason with a man in morals who denies the first principles of morals. The man who does not, by the light of his own mind, perceive some things in conduct to be right, and others to be wrong, is as incapable of reasoning about morals as a blind man is about colours. Such a man, if any such man ever was, would be no moral agent, nor capable of any moral obligation.

Some first principles of morals must be immediately discerned, otherwise we have no foundation on which others can rest, or from which we can reason.

Every man knows certainly, that, what he approves in other men, he ought to do in like circumstances, and that he ought not to do what he condemns in other men. Every man knows that he ought, with candour, to use the best means of knowing his duty. To every man who has a conscience, these things are self-evident. They are immediate dictates of our moral faculty, which is a part of the human constitution ; and every man condemns himself, whether he will or not, when he knowingly acts contrary to them. The evidence of these fundamental principles of morals, and of others that might be named, appears, therefore, to me to be intuitive rather than demonstrative.

The man who acts according to the dictates of his conscience, and takes due pains to be rightly informed of his duty, is a perfect man with regard to morals, and merits no blame, whatever may be the imperfections or errors of his understanding. He who knowingly acts contrary to them, is conscious of guilt, and self-condemned. Every particular action that falls evidently within the fundamental rules of morals, is evidently his duty ; and it requires no reasoning to convince him that it is so. [685]

Thus, I think it appears, that every man of common understanding knows certainly, and without reasoning, the ultimate ends he ought to pursue, and that reasoning is necessary only to discover the most proper means of attaining them ; and in this, indeed, a good man may often be in doubt.

Thus, a magistrate knows that it is his duty to promote the good of the community which hath intrusted him with authority ; and to offer to prove this to him by reasoning, would be to affront him. But whether such a scheme of conduct in his office, or another, may best serve that end, he may in many cases be doubtful. I believe, in such cases, he can very rarely have demonstrative evidence. His conscience determines the end he ought to pursue, and he has intuitive evidence that his end is good ; but prudence must determine the means of attaining that end ; and prudence can very rarely use demonstrative reasoning, but must rest in what appears most   obable.

I apprehend, that, in every kind of duty we owe to God or man, the case is similar—that is, ⌐that the obligation of the most general rules of duty is self-evident ; that the application of those rules to particular actions is often no less evident ; and that, when it is not evident, but requires reasoning, that reasoning can very rarely be of the demonstrative, but must be of the probable kind. ⌐ Sometimes it depends upon the temper, and talents, and circumstances of the man himself ; sometimes upon the character and circumstances of others ; sometimes upon both ; and these are things which admit not of demonstration. [686]

Every man is bound to employ the talents which God hath given him to the best purpose : but if, through accidents which he could not foresee, or ignorance which was invincible, they be less usefully employed than they might have been, this will not be imputed to him by his righteous Judge.

It is a common and a just observation, that the man of virtue plays a surer game in order to obtain his end than the man of the world. It is not, however, because he reasons better concerning the means of attaining his end ; for the children of this world are often wiser in their generation than the children of light. But the reason of the observation is, that involuntary errors, unforeseen accidents, and invincible ignorance, which affect deeply all the concerns of the present world, have no effect upon virtue or its reward.

In the common occurrences of life, a man of integrity, who hath exercised his moral faculty in judging what is right and what is wrong, sees his duty without reasoning, as he sees the highway. The cases that require reasoning are few, compared with those that require none ; and a man may be very honest and virtuous who cannot reason, and who knows not what demonstration means.

The power of reasoning, in those that have it, may be abused in morals, as in other matters. To a man who uses it with un upright heart, and a single eye to find what is his duty, it will be of great use; but when it is used to justify what a man has a strong inclination to do, it will only serve to deceive himself and others. When a man can reason, his passions will reason, and they are the most cunning sophists we meet with.

If the rules of virtue were left to be discovered by demonstrative reasoning, or by reasoning of any kind, sad would be the condition of the far greater part of men, who have not the means of cultivating the power of reasoning. As virtue is the business of all men, the first principles of it are written in their hearts, in characters so legible that no man can pretend ignorance of them, or of his obligation to practise them. [687]

Some knowledge of duty and of moral obligation is necessary to all men. Without it they could not be moral and accountable creatures, nor capable of being members of civil society. It may, therefore, be presumed that Nature has put this knowledge within the reach of all men. Reasoning and demonstration are weapons which the greatest part of mankind never was able to wield. The knowledge that is necessary to all, must be attainable by all. We see it is so in what pertains to the natural life of man.

Some knowledge of things that are useful and things that are hurtful, is so necessary to all men, that without it the species would soon perish. But it is not by reasoning that this knowledge is got, far less by demonstrative reasoning. It is by our senses, by memory, by experience, by information; means of knowledge that are open to all men, and put the learned and the unlearned, those who can reason and those who cannot, upon a level.

It may, therefore, be expected, from the analogy of nature, that such a knowledge of morals as is necessary to all men should be had by means more suited to the abilities of all men than demonstrative reasoning is.

This, I apprehend, is in fact the case. When men's faculties are ripe, the first principles of morals, into which all moral reasoning may be resolved, are perceived intuitively, and in a manner more analogous to the perceptions of sense than to the conclusions of demonstrative reasoning. [688]

Upon the whole, I agree with Mr Locke, that propositions expressing the congruities and incongruities of things abstract, which moral words stand for, may have all the evidence of mathematical truths. But this is not peculiar to things which moral words stand for. It is common to abstract propositions of every kind. For instance, you cannot take from a man what he has not.

A man cannot be bound and perfectly free at the same time. I think no man will call these moral truths; but they are necessary truths, and as evident as any in mathematics. Indeed, they are very nearly allied to the two which Mr Locke gives us instances of moral propositions capable of demonstration. Of such abstract propositions, I think it may more properly be said that they have the evidence of mathematical axioms, than that they are capable of demonstration.

There are propositions of another kind, which alone deserve the name of moral propositions. They are such as affirm something to be the duty of persons that really exist. These are not abstract propositions; and, therefore, Mr Locke's reasoning does not apply to them. The truth of all such propositions depends upon the constitution and circumstances of the persons to whom they are applied.

Of such propositions, there are some that are self-evident to every man that has a conscience; and these are the principles from which all moral reasoning must be drawn. They may be called the axioms of morals. But our reasoning from these axioms to any duty that is not self-evident can very rarely be demonstrative. Nor is this any detriment to the cause of virtue, because to act against what appears most probable in a matter of duty, is as real a trespass against the first principles of morality, as to act against demonstration; and, because he who has but one talent in reasoning, and makes the proper use of it, shall be accepted, as well as he to whom God has given ten. [689]

CHAPTER III.

OF PROBABLE REASONING.

THE field of demonstration, as has been observed, is necessary truth: the field of probable reasoning is contingent truth—not what necessarily must be at all times, but what is, or was, or shall be.

No contingent truth is capable of strict demonstration; but necessary truths may sometimes have probable evidence.

Dr Wallis discovered many important mathematical truths, by that kind of induction which draws a general conclusion from particular premises. This is not strict demonstration, but, in some cases, gives as full conviction as demonstration itself; and a man may be certain, that a truth is demonstrable before it ever has been demonstrated. In other cases, a mathematical proposition may have such probable evidence from induction or analogy as encourages the mathematician to investigate

2 I

its demonstration. But still the reasoning, proper to mathematical and other necessary truths, is demonstration; and that which is proper to contingent truths, is probable reasoning.

These two kinds of reasoning differ in other respects. In demonstrative reasoning, one argument is as good as a thousand. One demonstration may be more elegant than another; it may be more easily comprehended, or it may be more subservient to some purpose beyond the present. On any of these accounts it may deserve a preference: but then it is sufficient by itself; it needs no aid from another; it can receive none. To add more demonstrations of the same conclusion, would be a kind of tautology in reasoning; because one demonstration, clearly comprehended, gives all the evidence we are capable of receiving. [690]

The strength of probable reasoning, for the most part, depends not upon any one argument, but upon many, which unite their force, and lead to the same conclusion. Any one of them by itself would be insufficient to convince; but the whole taken together may have a force that is irresistible, so that to desire more evidence would be absurd. Would any man seek new arguments to prove that there were such persons as King Charles I. or Oliver Cromwell?

Such evidence may be compared to a rope made up of many slender filaments twisted together. The rope has strength more than sufficient to bear the stress laid upon it, though no one of the filaments of which it is composed would be sufficient for that purpose.

It is a common observation, that it is unreasonable to require demonstration for things which do not admit of it. It is no less unreasonable to require reasoning of any kind for things which are known without reasoning. All reasoning must be grounded upon truths which are known without reasoning. In every branch of real knowledge there must be first principles whose truth is known intuitively, without reasoning, either probable or demonstrative. They are not grounded on reasoning, but all reasoning is grounded on them. It has been shewn, that there are first principles of necessary truths, and first principles of contingent truths. Demonstrative reasoning is grounded upon the former, and probable reasoning upon the latter.

That we may not be embarrassed by the ambiguity of words, it is proper to observe, that there is a popular meaning of *probable evidence*, which ought not to be confounded with the philosophical meaning, above explained. [691]

In common language, probable evidence is considered as an inferior degree of evidence, and is opposed to certainty: so that what is certain is more than probable, and what is only probable is not certain. Philosophers consider probable evidence, not as a degree, but as a species of evidence, which is opposed, not to certainty, but to another species of evidence, called demonstration.

Demonstrative evidence has no degrees; but probable evidence, taken in the philosophical sense, has all degrees, from the very least to the greatest, which we call certainty.

That there is such a city as Rome, I am as certain as of any proposition in Euclid; but the evidence is not demonstrative, but of that kind which philosophers call probable. Yet, in common language, it would sound oddly to say, it is probable there is such a city as Rome, because it would imply some degree of doubt or uncertainty.

Taking probable evidence, therefore, in the philosophical sense, as it is opposed to demonstrative, it may have any degrees of evidence, from the least to the greatest.

I think, in most cases, we measure the degrees of evidence by the effect they have upon a sound understanding, when comprehended clearly and without prejudice. Every degree of evidence perceived by the mind, produces a proportioned degree of assent or belief. The judgment may be in perfect suspense between two contradictory opinions, when there is no evidence for either, or equal evidence for both. The least preponderancy on one side inclines the judgment in proportion. Belief is mixed with doubt, more or less, until we come to the highest degree of evidence, when all doubt vanishes, and the belief is firm and immovable. This degree of evidence, the highest the human faculties can attain, we call certainty. [692]

Probable evidence not only differs in kind from demonstrative, but is itself of different kinds. The chief of these I shall mention, without pretending to make a complete enumeration.

The first kind is that of human testimony, upon which the greatest part of human knowledge is built.

The faith of history depends upon it, as well as the judgment of solemn tribunals, with regard to men's acquired rights, and with regard to their guilt or innocence, when they are charged with crimes. A great part of the business of the judge, of counsel at the bar, of the historian, the critic, and the antiquarian, is to canvass and weigh this kind of evidence; and no man can act with common prudence in the ordinary occurrences of life, who has not some competent judgment of it.

The belief we give to testimony, in many cases, is not solely grounded upon the vera-
[690–692]

city of the testi.er. In a single testimony, we consider the motives a man might have to falsify. If there be no appearance of any such motive, much ore if there be motives on the other side, his testimony has weight independent of his moral character. If the testimony be circumstantial, we consider how far the circumstances agree together, and with things that are known. It is so very difficult to fabricate a story which cannot be detected by a judicious examination of the circumstances, that it acquires evidence by being able to bear such a trial. There is an art in detecting false evidence in judicial proceedings, well known to able judges and barristers; so that I believe few false witnesses leave the bar without suspicion of their guilt.

When there is an agreement of many witnesses, in a great variety of circumstances, without the possibility of a previous concert, the evidence may be equal to that of demonstration. [693]

A second kind of probable evidence, is the authority of those who are good judges of the point in question. The supreme court of judicature of the British nation, is often determined by the opinion of lawyers in a point of law, of physicians in a point of medicine, and of other artists, in what relates to their several professions. And, in the common affairs of life, we frequently rely upon the judgment of others, in points of which we are not proper judges ourselves.

A third kind of probable evidence, is that by which we recognise the identity of things and persons of our acquaintance. That two swords, two horses, or two persons, may be so perfectly alike as not to be distinguishable by those to whom they are best known, cannot be shewn to be impossible. But we learn either from nature, or from experience, that it never happens; or so very rarely, that a person or thing, well known to us, is immediately recognised without any doubt, when we perceive the marks or signs by which we were in use to distinguish it from all other individuals of the kind.

This evidence we rely upon in the most important affairs of life; and, by this evidence, the identity, both of things and of persons, is determined in courts of judicature.

A fourth kind of probable evidence, is that which we have of men's future actions and conduct, from the general principles of action in man, or from our knowledge of the individuals.

Notwithstanding the folly and vice that are to be found among men, there is a certain degree of prudence and probity which we rely upon in every man that is not insane. If it were not so, no man would be safe in the company of another, and there could be

[693—695]

no society among mankind. If men were as much disposed to hurt as to do good, to lie as to speak truth, they could not live together; they would keep at as great distance from one another as possible, and the race would soon perish. [694]

We expect that men will take some care of themselves, of their family, friends, and reputation; that they will not injure others without some temptation; that they will have some gratitude for good offices, and some resentment of injuries.

Such maxims with regard to human conduct, are the foundation of all political reasoning, and of common prudence in the conduct of life. Hardly can a man form any project in public or in private life, which does not depend upon the conduct of other men, as well as his own, and which does not go upon the supposition that men will act such a part in such circumstances. This evidence may be probable in a very high degree; but can never be demonstrative. The best concerted project may fail, and wise counsels may be frustrated, because some individual acted a part which it would have been against all reason to expect.

Another kind of probable evidence, the counterpart of the last, is that by which we collect men's characters and designs from their actions, speech, and other external signs.

We see not men's hearts, nor the principles by which they are actuated; but there are external signs of their principles and dispositions, which, though not certain, may sometimes be more trusted than their professions; and it is from external signs that we must draw all the knowledge we can attain of men's characters.

The next kind of probable evidence I mention, is that which mathematicians call the probability of chances.

We attribute some events to chance, because we know only the remote cause which must produce some one event of a number; but know not the more immediate cause which determines a particular event of that number in preference to the others. [695]

I think all the chances about which we reason in mathematics are of this kind. Thus, in throwing a just die upon a table, we say it is an equal chance which of the six sides shall be turned up; because neither the person who throws, nor the bystanders, know the precise measure of force and direction necessary to turn up any one side rather than another. There are here, therefore six events, one of which must happen; and as all are supposed to have equal probability, the probability of any one side being turned up, the ace, for instance, is as one to the remaining number, five.

The probability of turning up two aces

2 I 2

with two dice is as one to thirty-five; because here there are thirty-six events, each of which has equal probability.

Upon such principles as these, the doctrine of chances has furnished a field of demonstrative reasoning of great extent, although the events about which this reasoning is employed be not necessary, but contingent, and be not certain, but probable.

This may seem to contradict a principle before advanced, that contingent truths are not capable of demonstration: but it does not: for, in the mathematical reasonings about chance, the conclusion demonstrated, is not, that such an event shall happen, but that the probability of its happening bears such a ratio to the probability of its failing; and this conclusion is necessary upon the suppositions on which it is grounded.

The last kind of probable evidence I shall mention, is that by which the known laws of Nature have been discovered, and the effects which have been produced by them in former ages, or which may be expected in time to come.

The laws of Nature are the rules by which the Supreme Being governs the world. We deduce them only from facts that fall within our own observation, or are properly attested by those who have observed them. [696]

The knowledge of some of the laws of nature is necessary to all men in the conduct of life. These are soon discovered even by savages. They know that fire burns, that water drowns, that bodies gravitate towards the earth. They know that day and night, summer and winter, regularly succeed each other. As far back as their experience and information reach, they know that these have happened regularly; and, upon this ground, they are led, by the constitution of human nature, to expect that they will happen in time to come, in like circumstances.

The knowledge which the philosopher attains of the laws of Nature differs from that of the vulgar, not in the first principles on which it is grounded, but in its extent and accuracy. He collects with care the phænomena that lead to the same conclusion, and compares them with those that seem to contradict or to limit it. He observes the circumstances on which every phænomenon depends, and distinguishes them carefully from those that are accidentally conjoined with it. He puts natural bodies in various situations, and applies them to one another in various ways, on purpose to observe the effect; and thus acquires from his senses a more extensive knowledge of the course of Nature in a short time, than could be collected by casual observation in many ages.

But what is the result of his laborious researches? It is, that, as far as he has been able to observe, such things have always happened in such circumstances, and such bodies have always been found to have such properties. These are matters of fact, attested by sense, memory, and testimony, just as the few facts which the vulgar know are attested to them.

And what conclusions does the philosopher draw from the facts he has collected? They are, that like events have happened in former times in like circumstances, and will happen in time to come; and these conclusions are built on the very same ground on which the simple rustic concludes that the sun will rise to-morrow. [697]

Facts reduced to general rules, and the consequences of those general rules, are all that we really know of the material world. And the evidence that such general rules have no exceptions, as well as the evidence that they will be the same in time to come as they have been in time past, can never be demonstrative. It is only that species of evidence which philosophers call probable. General rules may have exceptions or limitations which no man ever had occasion to observe. The laws of nature may be changed by him who established them. But we are led by our constitution to rely upon their continuance with as little doubt as if it was demonstrable.

I pretend not to have made a complete enumeration of all the kinds of probable evidence; but those I have mentioned are sufficient to shew, that the far greatest part, and the most interesting part of our knowledge, must rest upon evidence of this kind; and that many things are certain for which we have only that kind of evidence which philosophers call probable.

CHAPTER IV.

OF MR HUME'S SCEPTICISM WITH REGARD TO REASON.

IN the "Treatise of Human Nature," book I. part iv. § 1, the author undertakes to prove two points:—First, That all that is called human knowledge (meaning demonstrative knowledge) is only probability; and, secondly, That this probability, when duly examined, evanishes by degrees, and leaves at last no evidence at all: so that, in the issue, there is no ground to believe any one proposition rather than its contrary; and "all those are certainly fools who reason or believe anything." [698]

According to this account, reason, that boasted prerogative of man, and the light of his mind, is an *ignis fatuus*, which misleads the wandering traveller, and leaves him at last in absolute darkness.

How unhappy is the condition of man,

born under a necessity of believing contradictions, and of trusting to a guide who confesses herself to be a false one!

It is some comfort, that this doctrine can never be seriously adopted by any man in his senses. And after this author had shewn that "all the rules of logic require a total extinction of all belief and evidence," he himself, and all men that are not insane, must have believed many things, and yielded assent to the evidence which he had extinguished.

This, indeed, he is so candid as to acknowledge. "He finds himself absolutely and necessarily determined, to live and talk and act like other people in the common affairs of life. And since reason is incapable of dispelling these clouds, most fortunately it happens, that nature herself suffices to that purpose, and cures him of this philosophical melancholy and delirium." See § 7.

This was surely a very kind and friendly interposition of nature; for the effects of this philosophical delirium, if carried into life, must have been very melancholy.

But what pity is it, that nature, (whatever is meant by that personage,) so kind in curing this delirium, should be so cruel as to cause it. Doth the same fountain send forth sweet waters and bitter? Is it not more probable, that, if the cure was the work of nature, the disease came from another hand, and was the work of the philosopher? [699]

To pretend to prove by reasoning that there is no force in reason, does indeed look like a philosophical delirium. It is like a man's pretending to see clearly, that he himself and all other men are blind.

A common symptom of delirium is, to think that all other men are fools or mad. This appears to have been the case of this author, who concluded, "That all those are certainly fools who reason or believe anything."

Whatever was the cause of this delirium, it must be granted that, if it was real and not feigned, it was not to be cured by reasoning; for what can be more absurd than to attempt to convince a man by reasoning who disowns the authority of reason. It was, therefore, very fortunate that Nature found other means of curing it.

It may, however, not be improper to inquire, whether, as the author thinks, it was produced by a just application of the rules of logic, or, as others may be apt to think, by the misapplication and abuse of them.

First, Because we are fallible, the author infers that all knowledge degenerates into probability.

That man, and probably every created being, is fallible; and that a fallible being cannot have that perfect comprehension

[699-701]

and assurance of truth which an infallible being has—I think ought to be granted. It becomes a fallible being to be modest, open to new light, and sensible that, by some false bias, or by rash judging, he may be misled. If this be called a degree of scepticism, I cannot help approving of it, being persuaded that the man who makes the best use he can of the faculties which God has given him, without thinking them more perfect than they really are, may have all the belief that is necessary in the conduct of life, and all that is necessary to his acceptance with his Maker. [700]

It is granted, then, that human judgments ought always to be formed with an humble sense of our fallibility in judging.

This is all that can be inferred by the rules of logic from our being fallible. And if this be all that is meant by our knowledge degenerating into probability, I know no person of a different opinion.

But it may be observed, that the author here uses the word probability in a sense for which I know no authority but his own. Philosophers understand probability as opposed to demonstration; the vulgar as opposed to certainty; but this author understands it as opposed to infallibility, which no man claims.

One who believes himself *to* be fallible may still hold it to be certain that two and two make four, and that two contradictory propositions cannot both be true. He may believe some things to be probable only, and other things to be demonstrable, without making any pretence to infallibility.

If we use words in their proper meaning, it is impossible that demonstration should degenerate into probability from the imperfection of our faculties. Our judgment cannot change the nature of the things about which we judge. What is really demonstration, will still be so, whatever judgment we form concerning it. It may, likewise, be observed, that, when we mistake that for demonstration which really is not, the consequence of this mistake is, not that demonstration degenerates into probability, but that what we took to be demonstration is no proof at all; for one false step in ·a demonstration destroys the whole, but cannot turn it into another kind of proof. [701]

Upon the whole, then, this first conclusion of our author, That the fallibility of human judgment turns all knowledge into probability, if understood literally, is absurd; but, if it be only a figure of speech, and means no more but that, in all our judgments, we ought *to* be sensible of our fallibility, and ought to hold our opinions with that modesty that becomes fallible creatures—which I take to be what the author meant—this, I think, nobody denies, nor was it necessary to enter into a laborious proof of it.

One is never in greater danger of transgressing against the rules of logic than in attempting to prove what needs no proof. Of this we have an instance in this very case; for the author begins his proof, that all human judgments are fallible, with affirming that some are infallible.

" In all demonstrative sciences," says he, " the rules are certain and infallible; but when we apply them, our fallible and uncertain faculties are very apt to depart from them, and fall into error."

He had forgot, surely, that the rules of demonstrative sciences are discovered by our fallible and uncertain facult'es, and have no authority but that of human judgment. If they be infallible, some human judgments are infallible; and there are many in various branches of human knowledge which have as good a claim to infallibility as the rules of the demonstrative sciences.

We have reason here to find fault with our author for not being sceptical enough, as well as for a mistake in reasoning, when he claims infallibility to certain decisions of the human faculties, in order to prove that all their decisions are fallible.

The second point which he attempts to prove is, That this probability, when duly examined, suffers a continual diminution, and at last a total extinction.

The obvious consequence of this is, that no fallible being can have good reason to believe anything at all; but let us hear the proof. [702]

" In every judgment, we ought to correct the first judgment derived from the nature of the object, by another judgment derived from the nature of the understanding. . Beside the original uncertainty inherent in the subject, there arises another, derived from the weakness of the faculty which judges. Having adjusted these two uncertainties together, we are obliged, by our reason, to add a new uncertainty, derived from the possibility of error in the estimation we make of the truth and fidelity of our faculties. This is a doubt of which, if we would closely pursue our reasoning, we cannot avoid giving a decision. But this decision, though it should be favourable to our preceding judgment, being founded only on probability, must weaken still farther our first evidence. The third uncertainty must, in like manner be criticised by a fourth, and so on without end.

" Now, as every one of these uncertainties takes away a part of the original evidence, it must at last be reduced to nothing. Let our first belief be ever so strong, it must infallibly perish, by passing through so many examinations, each of which carries off somewhat of its force and vigour. No finite

object can subsist under a decrease repeated *in infinitum.*

" When I reflect on the natural fallibility of my judgment, I have less confidence in my opinions than when I only consider the objects concerning which I reason. And when I proceed still farther, to turn the scrutiny against every successive estimation I make of my faculties, all the rules of logic require a continual diminution, and at last a total extinction of belief and evidence."

This is the author's Achillean argument against the evidence of reason, from which he concludes, that a man who would govern his belief by reason must believe nothing at all, and that belief is an act, not of the cogitative, but of the sensitive part of our nature. [703]

If there be any such thing as motion, (said an ancient Sceptic,[*]) the swift-footed Achilles could never overtake an old man in a journey. For, suppose the old man to set out a thousand paces before Achilles, and that, while Achilles has travelled the thousand paces, the old man has gone five hundred; when Achilles has gone the five hundred, the old man has gone two hundred and fifty; and when Achilles has gone the two hundred and fifty, the old man is still one hundred and twenty-five before him. Repeat these estimations *in infinitum,* and you will still find the old man foremost; therefore Achilles can never overtake him; therefore there can be no such thing as motion.

The reasoning of the modern Sceptic against reason is equally ingenious, and equally convincing. Indeed, they have a great similarity.

If we trace the journey of Achilles two thousand paces, we shall find the very point where the old man is overtaken. But this short journey, by dividing it into an infinite number of stages, with corresponding estimations, is made to appear infinite. In like manner, our author, subjecting every judgment to an infinite number of successive probable estimations, reduces the evidence to nothing.

To return then to the argument of the modern Sceptic. I examine the proof of a theorem of Euclid. It appears to me to be strict demonstration. But I may have overlooked some fallacy; therefore I examine it again and again, but can find no flaw in it. I find all that have examined it agree with me. I have now that evidence of the truth of the proposition which I and all men call demonstration, and that belief of it which we call certainty. [704]

Here my sceptical friend interposes, and assures me, that the rules of logic reduce

---

* Zeno Eleates. He is improperly called, *simpliciter, Sceptic.*—H.

this demonstration to no evidence at all. I am willing to hear what step in it he thinks fallacious, and why. He makes no objection to any part of the demonstration, but pleads my fallibility in judging. I have made the proper allowance for this already, by being open to conviction. But, says he, there are two uncertainties, the first inherent in the subject, which I have already shewn to have only probable evidence ; the second arising from the weakness of the faculty that judges. I answer, it is the weakness of the faculty only that reduces this demonstration to what you call probability. You must not therefore make it a second uncertainty ; for it is the same with the first. To take credit twice in an account for the same article is not agreeable to the rules of logic. Hitherto, therefore, there is but one uncertainty—to wit, my fallibility in judging.

But, says my friend, you are obliged by reason to add a new uncertainty, derived from the possibility of error in the estimation you make of the truth and fidelity of your faculties. I answer—

This estimation is ambiguously expressed ; it may either mean an estimation of my liableness to err by the misapplication and abuse of my faculties ; or it may mean an estimation of my liableness to err by conceiving my faculties to be true and faithful, while they may be false and fallacious in themselves, even when applied in the best manner. I shall consider this estimation in each of these senses.

If the first be the estimation meant, it is true that reason directs us, as fallible creatures, to carry along with us, in all our judgments, a sense of our fallibility. It is true also, that we are in greater danger of erring in some cases, and less in others ; and that this danger of erring may, according to the circumstances of the case, admit of an estimation, which we ought likewise to carry along with us in every judgment we form. [705]

When a demonstration is short and plain ; when the point to be proved does not touch our interest or our passions ; when the faculty of judging, in such cases, has acquired strength by much exercise—there is less danger of erring ; when the contrary circumstances take place, there is more.

In the present case, every circumstance is favourable to the judgment I have formed. There cannot be less danger of erring in any case, excepting, perhaps, when I judge of a self-evident axiom.

The Sceptic farther urges, that this decision, though favourable to my first judgment, being founded only on probability, must still weaken the evidence of that judgment.

Here I cannot help being of a quite contrary opinion ; nor can I imagine how an ingenious author could impose upon himself so grossly ; for surely he did not intend to impose upon his reader.

After repeated examination of a proposition of Euclid, I judge it to be strictly demonstrated ; this is my first judgment. But, as I am liable to err from various causes, I consider how far I may have been misled by any of these causes in this judgment. My decision upon this second point is favourable to my first judgment, and therefore, as I apprehend, must strengthen it. To say that this decision, because it is only probable, must weaken the first evidence, seems to me contrary to all rules of logic, and to common sense.

The first judgment may be compared to the testimony of a credible witness ; the second, after a scrutiny into the character of the witness, wipes off every objection that can be made to it, and therefore surely must confirm and not weaken his testimony. [706]

But let us suppose, that, in another case, I examine my first judgment upon some point, and find that it was attended with unfavourable circumstances, what, in reason, and according to the rules of logic, ought to be the effect of this discovery ?

The effect surely will be, and ought to be, to make me less confident in my first judgment, until I examine the point anew in more favourable circumstances. If it be a matter of importance, I return to weigh the evidence of my first judgment. If it was precipitate before, it must now be deliberate in every point. If, at first, I was in passion, I must now be cool. If I had an interest in the decision, I must place the interest on the other side.

It is evident that this review of the subject may confirm my first judgment, notwithstanding the suspicious circumstances that attended it. Though the judge was biassed or corrupted, it does not follow that the sentence was unjust. The rectitude of the decision does not depend upon the character of the judge, but upon the nature of the case. From that only, it must be determined whether the decision be just. The circumstances that rendered it suspicious are mere presumptions, which have no force against direct evidence.

Thus, I have considered the effect of this estimation of our liableness to err in our first judgment, and have allowed to it all the effect that reason and the rules of logic permit. In the case I first supposed, and in every case where we can discover no cause of error, it affords a presumption in favour of the first judgment. In other cases, it may afford a presumption against it. But the rules of logic require, that we should not judge by presumptions, where we have direct evidence. The effect of an unfavourable presumption should only be, to make us examine the evidence with the greater care. [707]

The sceptic urges, in the last place, that this estimation must be subjected to another estimation, that to another, and so on, *in infini um ;* and as every new estimation takes away from the evidence of the first judgment, it must at last be totally annihilated.

I answer, *first,* It has been shewn above, that the first estimation, supposing it unfavourable, can only afford a presumption against the first judgment; the second, upon the same supposition, will be only the presumption of a presumption; and the third, the presumption that there is a presumption of a presumption. This infinite series of presumptions resembles an infinite series of quantities, decreasing in geometrical proportion, which amounts only to a finite sum. The infinite series of stages of Achilles's journey after the old man, amounts only to two thousand paces; nor can this infinite series of presumptions outweigh one solid argument in favour of the first judgment, supposing them all to be unfavourable to it.

Secondly, I have shewn, that the estimation of our first judgment may strengthen it ; and the same thing may be said of all the subsequent estimations. It would, therefore, be as reasonable to conclude, that the first judgment will be brought to infallible certainty when this series of estimations is wholly in its favour, as that its evidence will be brought to nothing by such a series supposed to be wholly unfavourable to it. But, in reality, one serious and cool re-examination of the evidence by which our first judgment is supported, has, and in reason ought to have more force to strengthen or weaken it, than an infinite series of such estimations as our author requires.

Thirdly, I know no reason nor rule in logic, that requires that such a series of estimations should follow every particular judgment. [708]

A wise man, who has practised reasoning, knows that he is fallible, and carries this conviction along with him in every judgment he forms. He knows likewise that he is more liable to err in some cases than in others. He has a scale in his mind, by which he estimates his liableness to err, and by this he regulates the degree of his assent in his first judgment upon any point.

The author's reasoning supposes, that a man, when he forms his first judgment, conceives himself to be infallible ; that by a second and subsequent judgment, he discovers that he is not infallible ; and that by a third judgment, subsequent to the second, he estimates his liableness to err in such a case as the present.

If the man proceed in this order. I grant, that his second judgment will, with good reason, bring down the first from supposed infallibility to fallibility ; and that his third judgment will, in some degree, either strengthen or weaken the first, as it is corrected by the second.

But every man of understanding proceeds in a contrary order. When about to judge in any particular point, he knows already that he is not infallible. He knows what are the cases in which he is most or least liable to err. The conviction of these things is always present to his mind, and influences the degree of his assent in his first judgment, as far as to him appears reasonable.

If he should afterwards find reason to suspect his first judgment, and desires to have all the satisfaction his faculties can give, reason will direct him not to form such a series of estimations upon estimations, as this author requires, but to examine the evidence of his first judgment carefully and coolly; and this review may very reasonably, according to its result, either strengthen or weaken, or totally overturn his first judgment. [709]

This infinite series of estimations, therefore, is not the method that reason directs, in order to form our judgment in any case. It is introduced without necessity, without any use but to puzzle the understanding, and to make us think, that to judge, even in the simplest and plainest cases, is a matter of insurmountable difficulty and endless labour; just as the ancient Sceptic, to make a journey of two thousand paces appear endless, divided it into an infinite number of stages.

But we observed, that the estimation which our author requires, may admit of another meaning, which, indeed, is more agreeable to the expression, but inconsistent with what he advanced before.

By the possibility of error in the estimation of the truth and fidelity of our faculties, may be meant, that we may err by esteeming our faculties true and faithful, while they may be false and fallacious, even when used according to the rules of reason and logic.

If this be meant, I answer, *first,* That the truth and fidelity of our faculty of judging is, and must be taken for granted in every judgment and in every estimation.

If the sceptic can seriously doubt of the truth and fidelity of his faculty of judging when properly used, and suspend his judgment upon that point till he finds proof, his scepticism admits of no cure by reasoning, and he must even continue in it until he have new faculties given him, which shall have authority to sit in judgment upon the old. Nor is there any need of an endless succession of doubts upon this subject ; for the first puts an end to all judgment and

⌐707–709⌐

reasoning, and to the possibility of conviction by that means. The sceptic has here got possession of a stronghold, which is impregnable to reasoning, and we must leave him in possession of it till Nature, by other means, makes him give it up. [710]

Secondly, I observe, that this ground of scepticism, from the supposed infidelity of our faculties, contradicts what the author before advanced in this very argument—to wit, that "the rules of the demonstrative sciences are certain and infallible, and that truth is the natural effect of reason, and that error arises from the irruption of other causes."

But, perhaps, he made these concessions unwarily. He is, therefore, at liberty to retract them, and to rest his scepticism upon this sole foundation, That no reasoning can prove the truth and fidelity of our faculties. Here he stands upon firm ground; for it is evident that every argument offered to prove the truth and fidelity of our faculties, takes for granted the thing in question, and is, therefore, that kind of sophism which logicians call *petitio principii.*

All we would ask of this kind of sceptic is, that he would be uniform and consistent, and that his practice in life do not belie his profession of scepticism, with regard to the fidelity of his faculties; for the want of faith, as well as faith itself, is best shewn by works. If a sceptic avoid the fire as much as those who believe it dangerous to go into it, we can hardly avoid thinking his scepticism to be feigned, and not real.

Our author, indeed, was aware, that neither his scepticism nor that of any other person, was able to endure this trial, and, therefore, enters a caveat against it. "Neither I," says he, "nor any other person was ever sincerely and constantly of that opinion. Nature, by an absolute and uncontrollable necessity, has determined us to judge, as well as to breathe and feel. My intention, therefore," says he, "in displaying so carefully the arguments of that fantastic sect, is only to make the reader sensible of the truth of my hypothesis, that all our reasonings concerning causes and effects, are derived from nothing but custom, and that belief is more properly an act of the [710–713]

sensitive than of the cogitative part of our nature." [711]

We have before considered the first part of this hypothesis, Whether our reasoning about causes be derived only from custom?

The other part of the author's hypothesis here mentioned is darkly expressed, though the expression seems to be studied, as it is put in Italics. It cannot, surely, mean that belief is not an act of thinking. It is not, therefore, the power of thinking that he calls the cogitative part of our nature. Neither can it be the power of judging, for all belief implies judgment; and to believe a proposition means the same thing as to judge it to be true. It seems, therefore, to be the power of reasoning that he calls the cogitative part of our nature.

If this be the meaning, I agree to it in part. The belief of first principles is not an act of the reasoning power; for all reasoning must be grounded upon them. We judge them to be true, and believe them without reasoning. But why this power of judging of first principles should be called the sensitive part of our nature, I do not understand.

As our belief of first principles is an act of pure judgment without reasoning; so our belief of the conclusions drawn by reasoning from first principles, may, I think, be called an act of the reasoning faculty. [712]

Upon the whole, I see only two conclusions that can be fairly drawn from this profound and intricate reasoning against reason. The first is, That we are fallible in all our judgments and in all our reasonings. The second, That the truth and fidelity of our faculties can never be proved by reasoning; and, therefore, our belief of it cannot be founded on reasoning. If the last be what the author calls his hypothesis, I subscribe to it, and think it not an hypothesis, but a manifest truth; though I conceive it to be very improperly expressed, by saying that belief is more properly an act of the sensitive than of the cogitative part of our nature.* [713]

---

* In the preceding strictures, the Sceptic is again too often assailed as a Dogmatist. See above, p. 441 note *.—H.

ESSAY VIII.

OF TASTE.

CHAPTER I.

OF TASTE IN GENERAL.

THAT power of the mind by which we are capable of discerning and relishing the beauties of Nature, and whatever is excellent in the fine arts, is called *taste*.

The external sense of taste, by which we distinguish and relish the various kinds of food, has given occasion to a metaphorical application of its name to this internal power of the mind, by which we perceive what is beautiful and what is deformed or defective in the various objects that we contemplate.

Like the taste of the palate, it relishes some things, is disgusted with others ; with regard to many, is indifferent or dubious ; and is considerably influenced by habit, by associations, and by opinion. These obvious analogies between external and internal taste, have led men, in all ages, and in all or most polished languages,* to give the name of the external sense to this power of discerning what is beautiful and what is ugly and faulty in its kind with disgust. [714]

In treating of this as an intellectual power of the mind, I intend only to make some observations, first on its nature, and then on its objects.

1. In the external sense of taste, we are led by reason and reflection to distinguish between the agreeable sensation we feel, and the quality in the object which occasions it. Both have the same name, and on that account are apt to be confounded by the vulgar, and even by philosophers. The sensation I feel when I taste any sapid body is in my mind ; but there is a real quality in the body which is the cause of this sensation. These two things have the same name in language, not from any similitude in their nature, but because the one is the sign of the other, and because there is little occasion in common life to distinguish them.

This was fully explained in treating of the secondary qualities of bodies. The reason of taking notice of it now is, that the internal power of taste bears a great analogy in this respect to the external.

When a beautiful object is before us, we may distinguish the agreeable emotion it produces in us, from the quality of the object which causes that emotion. When I hear an air in music that pleases me, I say, it is fine, it is excellent. This excellence is not in me ; it is in the music. But the pleasure it gives is not in the music ; it is in me. Perhaps I cannot say what it is in the tune that pleases my ear, as I cannot say what it is in a sapid body that pleases my palate ; but there is a quality in the sapid body which pleases my palate, and I call it a delicious taste ; and there is a quality in the tune that pleases my taste, and I call it a fine or an excellent air.

This ought the rather to be observed, because it is become a fashion among modern philosophers, to resolve all our perceptions into mere feelings or sensations in the person that perceives, without any thing corresponding to those feelings in the external object. [715] According to those philosophers, there is no heat in the fire, no taste in a sapid body ; the taste and the heat being only in the person that feels them.* In like manner, there is no beauty in any object whatsoever ; it is only a sensation or feeling in the person that perceives it.

The language and the common sense of mankind contradict this theory. Even those who hold it, find themselves obliged to use a language that contradicts it. I had occasion to shew, that there is no solid foundation for it when applied to the secondary qualities of body ; and the same arguments shew equally, that it has no solid foundation when applied to the beauty of objects, or to any of those qualities that are perceived by a good taste.

But, though some of the qualities that please a good taste resemble the secondary qualities of body, and therefore may be called occult qualities, as we only feel their effect, and have no more knowledge of the cause, but that it is something which is adapted by nature to produce that effect— this is not always the case.

Our judgment of beauty is in many cases more enlightened. A work of art may appear beautiful to the most ignorant, even to a child. It pleases, but he knows not

---

* This is hardly correct.—H.

* But see, above, p. 205, b, note *, and p. 310, b, note †.—H.

why. To one who understands it perfectly, and perceives how every part is fitted with exact judgment to its end, the beauty is not mysterious; it is perfectly comprehended; and he knows wherein it consists, as well as how it affects him.

2. We may observe, that, though all the tastes we perceive by the palate are either agreeable or disagreeable, or indifferent; yet, among those that are agreeable, there is great diversity, not in degree only, but in kind. And, as we have not general names for all the different kinds of taste, we distinguish them by the bodies in which they are found. [716]

In like manner, all the objects of our internal taste are either beautiful, or disagreeable, or indifferent; yet of beauty there is a great diversity, not only of degree, but of kind. The beauty of a demonstration, the beauty of a poem, the beauty of a palace, the beauty of a piece of music, the beauty of a fine woman, and many more that might be named, are different kinds of beauty; and we have no names to distinguish them but the names of the different objects to which they belong.

As there is such diversity in the kinds of beauty as well as in the degrees, we need not think it strange that philosophers have gone into different systems in analysing it, and enumerating its simple ingredients. They have made many just observations on the subject; but, from the love of simplicity, have reduced it to fewer principles than the nature of the thing will permit, having had in their eye some particular kinds of beauty, while they overlooked others.

There are moral beauties as well as natural; beauties in the objects of sense, and in intellectual objects; in the works of men, and in the works of God; in things inanimate, in brute animals, and in rational beings; in the constitution of the body of man, and in the constitution of his mind. There is no real excellence which has not its beauty to a discerning eye, when placed in a proper point of view; and it is as difficult to enumerate the ingredients of beauty as the ingredients of real excellence.

3. The taste of the palate may be accounted most just and perfect, when we relish the things that are fit for the nourishment of the body, and are disgusted with things of a contrary nature. The manifest intention of nature in giving us this sense, is, that we may discern what it is fit for us to eat and to drink, and what it is not. Brute animals are directed in the choice of their food merely by their taste. [717] Led by this guide, they choose the food that nature intended for them, and seldom make mistakes, unless they be pinched by hunger, or deceived by artificial compositions. In infants likewise the taste is commonly sound

⌈716-718⌉

and uncorrupted, and of the simple productions of nature they relish the things that are most wholesome.

In like manner, our internal taste ought to be accounted most just and perfect, when we are pleased with things that are most excellent in their kind, and displeased with the contrary. The intention of nature is no less evident in this internal taste than in the external. Every excellence has a real beauty and charm that makes it an agreeable object to those who have the faculty of discerning its beauty; and this faculty is what we call a good taste.

A man who, by any disorder in his mental powers, or by bad habits, has contracted a relish for what has no real excellence, or what is deformed and defective, has a depraved taste, like one who finds a more agreeable relish in ashes or cinders than in the most wholesome food. As we must acknowledge the taste of the palate to be depraved in this case, there is the same reason to think the taste of the mind depraved in the other.

There is therefore a just and rational taste, and there is a depraved and corrupted taste. For it is too evident, that, by bad education, bad habits, and wrong associations, men may acquire a relish for nastiness, for rudeness, and ill-breeding, and for many other deformities. To say that such a taste is not vitiated, is no less absurd than to say, that the sickly girl who delights in eating charcoal and tobacco-pipes, has as just and natural a taste as when she is in perfect health.

4. The force of custom, of fancy, and of casual associations, is very great both upon the external and internal taste. An Eskimaux can regale himself with a draught of whale-oil, and a Canadian can feast upon a dog. A Kamschatkadale lives upon putrid fish, and is sometimes reduced to eat the bark of trees. The taste of rum, or of green tea, is at first as nauseous as that of ipecacuan, to some persons, who may be brought by use to relish what they once found so disagreeable. [718]

When we see such varieties in the taste of the palate produced by custom and associations, and some, perhaps, by constitution, we may be the less surprised that the same causes should produce like varieties in the taste of beauty; that the African should esteem thick lips and a flat nose; that other nations should draw out their ears, till they hang over their shoulders; that in one nation ladies should paint their faces, and in another should make them shine with grease.

5. Those who conceive that there is no standard in nature by which taste may be regulated, and that the common proverb, "That there ought to be no dispute about

taste," is to be taken in the utmost latitude, go upon slender and insufficient ground. The same arguments might be used with equal force against any standard of truth.

Whole nations by the force of prejudice are brought to believe the grossest absurdities ; and why should it be thought that the taste is less capable of being perverted than the judgment ? It must indeed be acknowledged, that men differ more in the faculty of taste than in what we commonly call judgment ; and therefore it may be expected that they should be more liable to have their taste corrupted in matters of beauty and deformity, than their judgment in matters of truth and error.

If we make due allowance for this, we shall see that it is as easy to account for the variety of tastes, though there be in nature a standard of true beauty, and consequently of good taste, as it is to account for the variety and contrariety of opinions, though there be in nature a standard of of truth, and, consequently, of right judgment. [719]

6. Nay, if we speak accurately and strictly, we shall find that, in every operation of taste, there is judgment implied.

When a man pronounces a poem or a palace to be beautiful, he affirms something of that poem or that palace ; and every affirmation or denial expresses judgment. For we cannot better define judgment, than by saying that it is an affirmation or denial of one thing concerning another. I had occasion to shew, when treating of judgment, that it is implied in every perception of our external senses. There is an immediate conviction and belief of the existence of the quality perceived, whether it be colour, or sound, or figure ; and the same thing holds in the perception of beauty or deformity.

If it be said that the perception of beauty is merely a feeling in the mind that perceives, without any belief of excellence in the object, the necessary consequence of this opinion is, that when I say Virgil's " Georgics" is a beautiful poem, I mean not to say anything of the poem, but only something concerning myself and my feelings. Why should I use a language that expresses the contrary of what I mean ?

My language, according to the necessary rules of construction, can bear no other meaning but this, that there is something in the poem, and not in me, which I call beauty. Even those who hold beauty to be merely a feeling in the person that perceives it, find themselves under a necessity of expressing themselves as if beauty were solely a quality of the object, and not of the percipient.

No reason can be given why all mankind should express themselves thus, but that they believe what they say. It is therefore contrary to the universal sense of mankind, expressed by their language, that beauty is not really in the object, but is merely a feeling in the person who is said to perceive it. Philosophers should be very cautious in opposing the common sense of mankind ; for, when they do, they rarely miss going wrong. [720]

Our judgment of beauty is not indeed a dry and unaffecting judgment, like that of a mathematical or metaphysical truth. By the constitution of our nature, it is accompanied with an agreeable feeling or emotion, for which we have no other name but the sense of beauty. This sense of beauty, like the perceptions of our other senses, implies not only a feeling, but an opinion of some quality in the object which occasions that feeling.

In objects that please the taste, we always judge that there is some real excellence, some superiority to those that do not please. In some cases, that superior excellence is distinctly perceived, and can be pointed out ; in other cases, we have only a general notion of some excellence which we cannot describe. Beauties of the former kind may be compared to the primary qualities perceived by the external senses ; those of the latter kind, to the secondary.

7. Beauty or deformity in an object, results from its nature or structure. To perceive the beauty, we must perceive the nature or structure from which it results. In this the internal sense differs from the external. Our external senses may discover qualities which do not depend upon any antecedent perception. Thus, I can hear the sound of a bell, though I never perceived anything else belonging to it. But it is impossible to perceive the beauty of an object without perceiving the object, or, at least, conceiving it. On this account, Dr Hutcheson called the senses of beauty and harmony reflex or secondary senses ; because the beauty cannot be perceived unless the object be perceived by some other power of the mind. Thus, the sense of harmony and melody in sounds supposes the external sense of hearing, and is a kind of secondary to it. A man born deaf may be a good judge of beauties of another kind, but can have no notion of melody or harmony. The like may be said of beauties in colouring and in figure, which can never be perceived without the senses by which colour and figure are perceived. [721]

CHAPTER II.

OF THE OBJECTS OF TASTE; AND, FIRST, OF
NOVELTY.

A PHILOSOPHICAL analysis of the objects of taste is like applying the anatomical knife to a fine face. The design of the philosopher, as well as of the anatomist, is not to gratify taste, but to improve knowledge. The reader ought to be aware of this, that he may not entertain an expectation in which he will be disappointed.

By the objects of taste, I mean those qualities or attributes of th'ngs which are, by Nature, adapted to please a good taste. Mr Addison, and Dr Akenside after him, have reduced them to three—to wit, *novelty, grandeur,* and *beauty.* This division is sufficient for all I intend to say upon the subject, and therefore I shall adopt it—observing only, that beauty is often taken in so extensive a sense as ·to comprehend all the objects of taste; yet all the authors I have met with, who have given a division of the objects of taste, make beauty one species.

I take the reason of this to be, that we have specific names for some of the qualities that please the taste, but not for all; and therefore all those fall under the general name of beauty, for which there is no specific name in the division.

There are, indeed, so many species of beauty, that it would be as difficult to enumerate them perfectly, as to enumerate all the tastes we perceive by the palate. Nor does there appear to me sufficient reason for making, as some very ingenious authors have done, as many different internal senses as there are different species of beauty or deformity. [722]

The division of our external senses is taken from the organs of perception, and not from the qualities perceived. We have not the same means of dividing the internal; because, though some kinds of beauty belong only to objects of the eye, and others to objects of the ear, there are many which we cannot refer to any bodily organ; and therefore I conceive every division that has been made of our internal senses to be in some degree arbitrary. They may be made more or fewer, according as we have distinct names for the various kinds of beauty and deformity; and I suspect the most copious languages have not names for them all.

Novelty is not properly a quality of the thing to which we attribute it, far less is it a sensation in the mind to which it is new; it is a relation which the thing has to the knowledge of the person. What is new to one man, may not be so to another; [722, 723]

what is new this moment, may be familiar to the same person some time hence. When an object is first brought to our knowledge, it is new, whether it be agreeable or not.

It is evident, therefore, with regard to novelty, (whatever may be said of other objects of taste,) that it is not merely a sensation in the mind of him to whom the thing is new ; it is a real relation which the thing has to his knowledge at that time.

But we are so constituted, that what is new to us commonly gives pleasure upon that account, if it be not in itself disagreeable. It rouses our attention, and occasions an agreeable exertion of our faculties.

The pleasure we receive from novelty in objects has so great influence in human life, that it well deserves the attention of philosophers; and several ingenious authors —particularly Dr Gerard, in his " Essay on Taste"—have, I think, successfully accounted for it, from the principles of the human constitution. [723]

We can perhaps conceive a being so made, that his happiness consists in a continuance of the same unvaried sensations or feelings, without any active exertion on his part. Whether this be possible or not, it is evident that man is not such a being; his good consists in the vigorous exertion of his active and intellective powers upon their proper objects ; he is made for action and progress, and cannot be happy without it ; his enjoyments seem to be given by Nature, not so much for their own sake, as to encourage the exercise of his various powers. That tranquillity of soul in which some place human happiness, is not a dead rest, but a regular progressive motion.

Such is the constitution of man by the appointment of Nature. This constitution is perhaps a part of the imperfection of our nature ; but it is wisely adapted to our state, which is not intended to be stationary, but progressive. The eye is not satiated with seeing, nor the ear with hearing; something is always wanted. Desire and hope never cease, but remain to spur us on to something yet to be acquired ; and, if they could cease, human happiness must end with them. That our desire and hope be properly directed, is our part ; that they can never be extinguished, is the work of Nature.

It is this that makes human life so busy a scene. Man must be doing something, good or bad, trifling or important ; and he must vary the employment of his faculties, or their exercise will become languid, and the pleasure that attends it sicken of course.

The notions of enjoyment, and of activity,

considered abstractly, are no doubt very
different, and we cannot perceive a necessary connection between them. But, in our
constitution, they are so connected by the
wisdom of Nature, that they must go hand
in hand ; and the first must be led and
supported by the last. [724]

An object at first, perhaps, gave much
pleasure, while attention was directed to it
with vigour. But attention cannot be long
confined to one unvaried object, nor can it
be carried round in the same narrow circle.
Curiosity is a capital principle in the human
constitution, and its food must be what is
in some respect new. What is said of the
Athenians may, in some degree, be applied
to all mankind, That their time is spent
in hearing, or telling, or doing some new
thing.

Into this part of the human constitution,
I think, we may resolve the pleasure we
have from novelty in objects.

Curiosity is commonly strongest in children and in young persons, and accordingly
novelty pleases them most. In all ages, in
proportion as novelty gratifies curiosity, and
occasions a vigorous exertion of any of our
mental powers in attending to the new object, in the same proportion it gives pleasure. In advanced life, the indolent and
inactive have the strongest passion for news,
as a relief from a painful vacuity of thought.

But the pleasure derived from new objects,
in many cases, is not owing solely or chiefly
to their being new, but to some other circumstance that gives them value. The new
fashion in dress, furniture, equipage, and
other accommodations of life, gives pleasure, not so much, as I apprehend, because
it is new, as because it is a sign of rank,
and distinguishes a man from the vulgar.

In some things novelty is due, and the
want of it a real imperfection. Thus, if an
author adds to the number of books with
which the public is already overloaded, we
expect from him something new; and, if he
says nothing but what has been said before
in as agreeable a manner, we are justly
disgusted. [725]

When novelty is altogether separated
from the conception of worth and utility, it
makes but a slight impression upon a truly
correct taste. Every discovery in nature,
in the arts, and in the sciences, has a real
value, and gives a rational pleasure to a
good taste. But things that have nothing
to recommend them but novelty, are fit
only to entertain children, or those who are
distressed from a vacuity of thought. This
quality of objects may therefore be compared to the cypher in arithmetic, which
adds greatly to the value of significant
figures; but, when put by itself, signifies
nothing at all.

CHAPTER III.

OF GRANDEUR.

THE qualities which please the taste are
not more various in themselves than are
the emotions and feelings with which they
affect our minds.

Things new and uncommon affect us with
a pleasing surprise, which rouses and invi-
gorates our attention to the object. But
this emotion soon flags, if there is nothing
but novelty to give it continuance, and
leaves no effect upon the mind.

The emotion raised by grand objects is
awful, solemn, and serious.

Of all objects of contemplation, the Supreme Being, is the most grand. His
eternity, his immensity, his irresistible power,
his infinite knowledge and unerring wisdom,
his inflexible justice and rectitude, his supreme government, conducting all the
movements of this vast universe to the noblest ends and in the wisest manner—are
objects which fill the utmost capacity of the
soul, and reach far beyond its comprehension.

The emotion which this grandest of all
objects raises in the human mind, is what
we call devotion ; a serious recollected temper, which inspires magnanimity, and disposes to the most heroic acts of virtue. [726]

The emotion produced by other objects
which may be called grand, though in an
inferior degree, is, in its nature and in its
effects, similar to that of devotion. It disposes to seriousness, elevates the mind
above its usual state, to a kind of enthusiasm, and inspires magnanimity, and a contempt of what is mean.

Such, I conceive, is the emotion which
the contemplation of grand objects raises in
us. We are next to consider what this
grandeur in objects is.

To me it seems to be nothing else but
such a degree of excellence, in one kind or
another, as merits our admiration.

There are some attributes of mind which
have a real and intrinsic excellence, compared with their contraries, and which, in
every degree, are the natural objects of
esteem, but, in an uncommon degree, are objects of admiration. We put a value upon
them because they are intrinsically valuable
and excellent.

The spirit of modern philosophy would
indeed lead us to think, that the worth and
value we put upon things is only a sensation
in our minds, and not anything inherent in
the object ; and that we might have been so
constituted as to put the highest value upon
the things which we now despise, and to
despise the qualities which we now highly
esteem.

It gives me pleasure to observe, that Dr Price, in his "Review of the Questions concerning Morals," strenuously opposes this opinion, as well as that which resolves moral right and wrong into a sensation in the mind of the spectator. That judicious author saw the consequences which these opinions draw after them, and has traced them to their source—to wit, the account given by Mr Locke, and adopted by the generality of modern philosophers, of the origin of all our ideas, which account he shews to be very defective. [727]

This proneness to resolve everything into feelings and sensations, is an extreme into which we have been led by the desire of avoiding an opposite extreme, as common in the ancient philosophy.

At first, men are prone by nature and by habit to give all their attention to things external. Their notions of the mind, and its operations, are formed from some analogy they bear to objects of sense ; and an external existence is ascribed to things which are only conceptions or feelings of the mind.

This spirit prevailed much in the philosophy both of Plato and of Aristotle, and produced the mysterious notions of eternal and self-existent ideas, of *materia prima*, of substantial forms, and others of the like nature.

From the time of Des Cartes, philosophy took a contrary turn. That great man discovered, that many things supposed to have an external existence, were only conceptions or feelings of the mind. This track has been pursued by his successors to such an extreme as to resolve everything into sensations, feelings, and ideas in the mind, and to leave nothing external at all.

The Peripatetics thought that heat and cold which we feel to be qualities of external objects. The moderns make heat and cold to be sensations only, and allow no real quality of body to be called by that name : and the same judgment they have formed with regard to all secondary qualities.

So far Des Cartes and Mr Locke went. Their successors being put into this track of converting into feelings things that were believed to have an external existence, found that extension, solidity, figure, and all the primary qualities of body, are sensations or feelings of the mind ; and that the material world is a phænomenon only, and has no existence but in our mind. [728]

It was then a very natural progress to conceive, that beauty, harmony, and grandeur, the objects of taste, as well as right and wrong, the objects of the moral faculty, are nothing but feelings of the mind.

Those who are acquainted with the writings of modern philosophers, can easily trace this doctrine of feelings, from Des [727-729]

Cartes down to Mr Hume, who put the finishing stroke to it, by making truth and error to be feelings of the mind, and belief to be an operation of the sensitive part of our nature.

To return to our subject, if we hearken to the dictates of common sense, we must be convinced that there is real excellence in some things, whatever our feelings or our constitution be.

It depends no doubt upon our constitution, whether we do or do not perceive excellence where it really is : but the object has its excellence from its own constitution, and not from ours.

The common judgment of mankind in this matter sufficiently appears in the language of all nations, which uniformly ascribes excellence, grandeur, and beauty to the object, and not to the mind that perceives it. And I believe in this, as in most other things, we shall find the common judgment of mankind and true philosophy not to be at variance.

Is not power in its nature more excellent than weakness ; knowledge than ignorance ; wisdom than folly ; fortitude than pusillanimity ?

Is there no intrinsic excellence in self-command, in generosity, in public spirit ? Is not friendship a better affection of mind than hatred, a noble emulation than envy ? [729]

Let us suppose, if possible, a being so constituted as to have a high respect for ignorance, weakness, and folly ; to venerate cowardice, malice, and envy, and to hold the contrary qualities in contempt ; to have an esteem for lying and falsehood ; and to love most those who imposed upon him, and used him worst. Could we believe such a constitution to be anything else than madness and delirium ? It is impossible. We can as easily conceive a constitution, by which one should perceive two and three to make fifteen, or a part to be greater than the whole.

Every one who attends to the operations of his own mind will find it to be certainly true, as it is the common belief of mankind, that esteem is led by opinion, and that every person draws our esteem, as far only as he appears either to reason or fancy to be amiable and worthy.

There is therefore a real intrinsic excellence in some qualities of mind, as in power, knowledge, wisdom, virtue, magnanimity. These, in every degree, merit esteem ; but in an uncommon degree they merit admiration ; and that which merits admiration we call grand.

In the contemplation of uncommon excellence, the mind feels a noble enthusiasm, which disposes it to the imitation of what it admires.

When we contemplate the character of Cato—his greatness of soul, his superiority to pleasure, to toil, and to danger; his ardent zeal for the liberty of his country; when we see him standing unmoved in misfortunes, the last pillar of the liberty of Rome, and falling nobly in his country's ruin—who would not wish to be Cato rather than Cæsar in all his triumph ? [730]

Such a spectacle of a great soul struggling with misfortune, Seneca thought not unworthy of the attention of Jupiter himself, " Ecce spectaculum Deo dignum, ad quod respiciat Jupiter suo operi intentus, vir fortis cum mala fortuna compositus."

As the Deity is, of all objects of thought, the most grand, the descriptions given in holy writ of his attributes and works, even when clothed in simple expression, are acknowledged to be sublime.   The expression of Moses, " And God said, Let there be light, and there was light,"* has not escaped the notice of Longinus, a Heathen critic, as an example of the sublime.

What we call sublime in description, or in speech of any kind, is a proper expression of the admiration and enthusiasm which the subject produces in the mind of the speaker.   If this admiration and enthusiasm appears to be just, it carries the hearer along with it involuntarily, and by a kind of violence rather than by cool conviction : for no passions are so infectious as those which hold of enthusiasm.

But, on the other hand, if the passion of the speaker appears to be in no degree justified by the subject or the occasion, it produces in the judicious hearer no other emotion but ridicule and contempt.

The true sublime cannot be produced solely by art in the composition ; it must take its rise from grandeur in the subject, and a corresponding emotion raised in the mind of the speaker.   A proper exhibition of these, though it should be artless, is irresistible, like fire thrown into the midst of combustible matter.   [731]

When we contemplate the earth, the sea, the planetary system, the universe, these are vast objects ; it requires a stretch of imagination to grasp them in our minds. But they appear truly grand, and merit the highest admiration, when we consider them as the work of God, who, in the simple style of scripture, stretched out the heavens, and laid the foundation of the earth ; or, in the poetical language of Milton—

> " In his hand
> He took the golden compasses, prepar'd
> In God's eternal store, to circumscribe
> This universe and all created things.
> One foot he centr'd, and the other turn'd
> Round thro' the vast profundity obscure ;

---

* Better translated—" Be there light, and light there was "—H.

And said, Thus far extend, thus far thy bounds
This be thy just circumference, O world."

When we contemplate the world of Epicurus, and conceive the universe to be a fortuitous jumble of atoms, there is nothing grand in this idea.   The clashing of atoms by blind chance has nothing in it fit to raise our conceptions, or to elevate the mind. But the regular structure of a vast system of beings, produced by creating power, and governed by the best laws which perfect wisdom and goodness could contrive, is a spectacle which elevates the understanding, and fills the soul with devout admiration.

A great work is a work of great power, great wisdom, and great goodness, well contrived for some important end.   But power, wisdom, and goodness, are properly the attributes of mind only.   They are ascribed to the work figuratively, but are really inherent in the author : and by the same figure, the grandeur is ascribed to the work, but is properly inherent in the mind that made it.

Some figures of speech are so natural and so common in all languages, that we are led to think them literal and proper expressions. Thus an action is called brave, virtuous, generous ; but it is evident, that valour, virtue, generosity, are the attributes of persons only, and not of actions.   In the action considered abstractly, there is neither valour, nor virtue, nor generosity.   The same action done from a different motive may deserve none of those epithets.   [732] The change in this case is not in the action, but in the agent ; yet, in all languages, generosity and other moral qualities are ascribed to actions.   By a figure, we assign to the effect a quality which is inherent only in the cause.

By the same figure, we ascribe to a work that grandeur which properly is inherent in the mind of the author.

When we consider the " Iliad " as the work of the poet, its sublimity was really in the mind of Homer.   He conceived great characters, great actions, and great events, in a manner suitable to their nature, and with those emotions which they are naturally fitted to produce ; and he conveys his conceptions and his emotions by the most proper signs.   The grandeur of his thoughts is reflected on our eye by his work, and, therefore, it is justly called a grand work.

When we consider the things presented to our mind in the " Iliad " without regard to the poet, the grandeur is properly in Hector and Achilles, and the other great personages, human and divine, brought upon the stage.

Next to the Deity and his works, we admire great talents and heroic virtue in men, whether represented in history or in fiction. The virtues of Cato, Aristides, Socrates,

Marcus Aurelius, are truly grand. Extraordinary talents and genius, whether in poets, orators, philosophers, or lawgivers, are objects of admiration, and therefore grand. We find writers of taste seized with a kind of enthusiasm in the description of such personages.

What a grand idea does Virgil give of the power of eloquence, when he compares the tempest of the sea, suddenly calmed by the command of Neptune, to a furious sedition in a great city, quelled at once by a man of authority and eloquence. [733]

" Sic ait, ac dicto citius tumida æquora placat :
Ac veluti magno in populo, si forte coorta est
Seditio, sævitque animis ignobile vulgus ;
Jamque faces et saxa volant, furor arma ministrat ;
Tum pietate gravem, et meritis, si forte virum quem
Conspexere, silent, arrectisque auribus adstant.
Ille regit dictis animos, et pectora mulcet.
Sic cunctus pelagi cecidit fragor."

The wonderful genius of Sir Isaac Newton, and his sagacity in discovering the laws of Nature, is admirably expressed in that short but sublime epitaph by Pope :—

" Nature and Nature's laws lay hid in night ;
God said, Let Newton be—and all was light."

Hitherto we have found grandeur only in qualities of mind ; but, it may be asked, Is there no real grandeur in material objects ?

It will, perhaps, appear extravagant to deny that there is ; yet it deserves to be considered, whether all the grandeur we ascribe to objects of sense be not derived from something intellectual, of which they are the effects or signs, or to which they bear some relation or analogy.

Besides the relations of effect and cause, of sign and thing signified, there are innumerable similitudes and analogies between things of very different nature, which lead us to connect them in our imagination, and to ascribe to the one what properly belongs to the other.

Every metaphor in language is an instance of this ; and it must be remembered, that a very great part of language, which we now account proper, was originally metaphorical ; for the metaphorical meaning becomes the proper, as soon as it becomes the most usual ; much more, when that which was at first the proper meaning falls into disuse. [734]

The poverty of language, no doubt, contributes in part to the use of metaphor ; and, therefore, we find the most barren and uncultivated languages the most metaphorical. But the most copious language may be called barren, compared with the fertility of human conceptions, and can never, without the use of figures, keep pace with the variety of their delicate modifications.

But another cause of the use of metaphor is, that we find pleasure in discovering relations, similitudes, analogies, and even contrasts, that are not obvious to every eye.

[733–735]

All figurative speech presents something of this kind ; and the beauty of poetical language seems to be derived in a great measure from this source.

Of all figurative language, that is the most common, the most natural, and the most agreeable, which either gives a body, if we may so speak, to things intellectual, and clothes them with visible qualities; or which, on the other hand, gives intellectual qualities to the objects of sense.

To beings of more exalted faculties, intellectual objects may, perhaps, appear to most advantage in their naked simplicity. But we can hardly conceive them but by means of some analogy they bear to the objects of sense. The names we give them are almost all metaphorical or analogical.

Thus, the names of grand and sublime, as well as their opposites, mean and low, are evidently borrowed from the dimensions of body ; yet, it must be acknowledged, that many things are truly grand and sublime, to which we cannot ascribe the dimensions of height and extension.

Some analogy there is, without doubt, between greatness of dimension, which is an object of external sense, and that grandeur which is an object of taste. On account of this analogy, the last borrows its name from the first ; and, the name being common, leads us to conceive that there is something common in the nature of the things. [735]

But we shall find many qualities of mind, denoted by names taken from some quality of body to which they have some analogy, without anything common in their nature.

Sweetness and austerity, simplicity and duplicity, rectitude and crookedness, are names common to certain qualities of mind, and to qualities of body to which they have some analogy ; yet he would err greatly who ascribed to a body that sweetness or that simplicity which are the qualities of mind. In like manner, greatness and meanness are names common to qualities perceived by the external sense, and to qualities perceived by taste ; yet he may be in an error, who ascribes to the objects of sense that greatness or that meanness which is only an object of taste.

As intellectual objects are made more level to our apprehension by giving them a visible form ; so the objects of sense are dignified and made more august, by ascribing to them intellectual qualities which have some analogy to those they really possess. The sea rages, the sky lowers, the meadows smile, the rivulets murmur, the breezes whisper, the soil is grateful or ungrateful—such expressions are so familiar in common language, that they are scarcely accounted poetical or figurative ; but they give a kind of dignity to inanimate objects, and make our conception of them more agreeable.

2 K

When we consider matter as an inert, extended, divisible, and movable substance, there seems to be nothing in these qualities which we can call grand; and when we ascribe grandeur to any portion of matter, however modified, may it not borrow this quality from something intellectual, of which it is the effect, or sign, or instrument, or to which it bears some analogy? or, perhaps, because it produces in the mind an emotion that has some resemblance to that admiration which truly grand objects raise? [736]

A very elegant writer on the sublime and beautiful,* makes everything grand or sublime that is terrible. Might he not be led to this by the similarity between dread and admiration? Both are grave and solemn passions; both make a strong impression upon the mind; and both are very infectious. But they differ specifically, in this respect, that admiration supposes some uncommon excellence in its object, which dread does not. We may admire what we see no reason to dread; and we may dread what we do not admire. In dread, there is nothing of that enthusiasm which naturally accompanies admiration, and is a chief ingredient of the emotion raised by what is truly grand or sublime.

Upon the whole, I humbly apprehend that true grandeur is such a degree of excellence as is fit to raise an enthusiastical admiration; that this grandeur is found, originally and properly, in qualities of mind; that it is discerned, in objects of sense, only by reflection, as the light we perceive in the moon and planets is truly the light of the sun; and that those who look for grandeur in mere matter, seek the living among the dead.

If this be a mistake, it ought, at least, to be granted, that the grandeur which we perceive in qualities of mind, ought to have a different name from that which belongs properly to the objects of sense, as they are very different in their nature, and produce very different emotions in the mind of the spectator. [737]

CHAPTER IV.

OF BEAUTY.

BEAUTY is found in things so various and so very different in nature, that it is difficult to say wherein it consists, or what there can be common to all the objects in which it is found.

Of the objects of sense, we find beauty in colour, in sound, in form, in motion. There are beauties of speech, and beauties of thought; beauties in the arts, and in the sciences; beauties in actions, in affections, and in characters.

In things so different and so unlike is there any quality, the same in all, which we may call by the name of beauty? What can it be that is common to the thought of a mind and the form of a piece of matter, to an abstract theorem and a stroke of wit?

I am indeed unable to conceive any quality in all the different things that are called beautiful, that is the same in them all. There seems to be no identity, nor even similarity, between the beauty of a theorem and the beauty of a piece of music, though both may be beautiful. The kinds of beauty seem to be as various as the objects to which it is ascribed.

But why should things so different be called by the same name? This cannot be without a reason. If there be nothing common in the things themselves, they must have some common relation to us, or to something else, which leads us to give them the same name. [738]

All the objects we call beautiful agree in two things, which seem to concur in our sense of beauty. *First,* When they are perceived, or even imagined, they produce a certain agreeable emotion or feeling in the mind; and, *secondly,* This agreeable emotion is accompanied with an opinion or belief of their having some perfection or excellence belonging to them.

Whether the pleasure we feel in contemplating beautiful objects may have any necessary connection with the belief of their excellence, or whether that pleasure be conjoined with this belief, by the good pleasure only of our Maker, I will not determine. The reader may see Dr Price's sentiments upon this subject, which merit consideration, in the second chapter of his "Review of the Questions concerning Morals."

Though we may be able to conceive these two ingredients of our sense of beauty disjoined, this affords no evidence that they have no necessary connection. It has indeed been maintained, that whatever we can conceive, is possible: but I endeavoured, in treating of conception, to shew, that this opinion, though very common, is a mistake. There may be, and probably are, many necessary connections of things in nature, which we are too dim-sighted to discover.

The emotion produced by beautiful objects is gay and pleasant. It sweetens and humanises the temper, is friendly to every benevolent affection, and tends to allay sullen and angry passions. It enlivens the mind, and disposes it to other agreeable emotions, such as those of love, hope, and joy. It gives a value to the object, abstracted from its utility.

In things that may be possessed as property, beauty greatly enhances the price.

* Burke.—H.

A beautiful dog or horse, a beautiful coach or house, a beautiful picture or prospect, is valued by its owner and by others, not only for its utility, but for its beauty. [739]

If the beautiful object be a person, his company and conversation are, on that account, the more agreeable, and we are disposed to love and esteem him. Even in a perfect stranger, it is a powerful recommendation, and disposes us to favour and think well of him, if of our own sex, and still more if of the other.

"There is nothing," says Mr Addison, "that makes its way more directly to the soul than beauty, which immediately diffuses a secret satisfaction and complacence through the imagination, and gives a finishing to anything that is great and uncommon. The very first discovery of it strikes the mind with an inward joy, and spreads a cheerfulness and delight through all its faculties."

As we ascribe beauty, not only to persons, but to inanimate things, we give the name of love or liking to the emotion, which beauty, in both these kinds of objects, produces. It is evident, however, that liking to a person is a very different affection of mind from liking to an inanimate thing. The first always implies benevolence; but what is inanimate cannot be the object of benevolence. The two affections, however different, have a resemblance in some respects; and, on account of that resemblance, have the same name. And perhaps beauty, in these two different kinds of objects, though it has one name, may be as different in its nature as the emotions which it produces in us.

Besides the agreeable emotion which beautiful objects produce in the mind of the spectator, they produce also an opinion or judgment of some perfection or excellence in the object. This I take to be a second ingredient in our sense of beauty, though it seems not to be admitted by modern philosophers. [740]

The ingenious Dr Hutcheson, who perceived some of the defects of Mr Locke's system, and made very important improvements upon it, seems to have been carried away by it, in his notion of beauty. In his " Inquiry concerning Beauty," § I, "Let it be observed," says he, "that in the following papers, the word beauty is taken for the idea raised in us, and the sense of beauty for our power of receiving that idea." And again—"Only let it be observed, that, by absolute or original beauty, is not understood any quality supposed to be in the object which should, of itself, be beautiful, without relation to any mind which perceives it: for beauty, like other names of sensible ideas, properly denotes the perception of some mind; so cold, hot, sweet, [739–741]

bitter, denote the sensations in our minds, to which, perhaps, there is no resemblance in the objects which excite these ideas in us; however, we generally imagine otherwise. Were there no mind, with a sense of beauty, to contemplate objects, I see not how they could be called beautiful."

There is no doubt an analogy between the external senses of touch and taste, and the internal sense of beauty. This analogy led Dr Hutcheson, and other modern philosophers, to apply to beauty what Des Cartes and Locke had taught concerning the secondary qualities perceived by the external senses.

Mr Locke's doctrine concerning the secondary qualities of body, is not so much an error in judgment as an abuse of words. He distinguished very properly between the sensations we have of heat and cold, and that quality or structure in the body which is adapted by Nature to produce those sensations in us. He observed very justly, that there can be no similitude between one of these and the other. They have the relation of an effect to its cause, but no similitude. This was a very just and proper correction of the doctrine of the Peripatetics, who taught, that all our sensations are the very form and image of the quality in the object by which they are produced. [741]

What remained to be determined was, whether the words, heat and cold, in common language, signify the sensations we feel, or the qualities of the object which are the cause of these sensations. Mr Locke made heat and cold to signify only the sensations we feel, and not the qualities which are the cause of them. And in this, I apprehend, lay his mistake. For it is evident, from the use of language, that hot and cold, sweet and bitter, are attributes of external objects, and not of the person who perceives them. Hence, it appears a monstrous paradox to say, there is no heat in the fire, no sweetness in sugar; but, when explained according to Mr Locke's meaning, it is only, like most other paradoxes, an abuse of words.*

The sense of beauty may be analysed in a manner very similar to the sense of sweetness. It is an agreeable feeling or emotion, accompanied with an opinion or judgment of some excellence in the object, which is fitted by Nature to produce that feeling.

The feeling is, no doubt, in the mind, and so also is the judgment we form of the object: but this judgment, like all others, must be true or false. If it be a true judgment, there is some real excellence in the object. And the use of all languages shews that the name of beauty belongs to this ex-

---

rellence of the object, and not to the feelings of the spectator.

To say that there is, in reality, no beauty in those objects in which all men perceive beauty, is to attribute to man fallacious senses. But we have no ground to think so disrespectfully of the Author of our being; the faculties he hath given us are not fallacious; nor is that beauty which he hath so liberally diffused over all the works of his hands, a mere fancy in us, but a real excellence in his works, which express the perfection of their Divine Author.

We have reason to believe, not only that the beauties we see in nature are real, and not fanciful, but that there are thousands which our faculties are too dull to perceive. We see many beauties, both of human and divine art, which the brute animals are incapable of perceiving; and superior beings may excel us as far in their discernment of true beauty as we excel the brutes. [742]

The man who is skilled in painting or statuary sees more of the beauty of a fine picture or statue than a common spectator. The same thing holds in all the fine arts. The most perfect works of art have a beauty that strikes even the rude and ignorant; but they see only a small part of that beauty which is seen in such works by those who understand them perfectly, and can produce them.

This may be applied, with no less justice, to the works of Nature. They have a beauty that strikes even the ignorant and inattentive. But the more we discover of their structure, of their mutual relations, and of the laws by which they are governed, the greater beauty, and the more delightful marks of art, wisdom, and goodness, we discern.

Thus the expert anatomist sees numberless beautiful contrivances in the structure of the human body, which are unknown to the ignorant.

Although the vulgar eye sees much beauty in the face of the heavens, and in the various motions and changes of the heavenly bodies, the expert astronomer, who knows their order and distances, their periods, the orbits they describe in the vast regions of space, and the simple and beautiful laws by which their motions are governed, and all the appearances of their stations, progressions, and retrogradations, their eclipses, occultations, and transits are produced—sees a beauty, order, and harmony reign through the whole planetary system, which delights the mind. The eclipses of the sun and moon, and the blazing tails of comets, which strike terror into barbarous nations, furnish the most pleasing entertainment to his eye, and a feast to his understanding. [743]

In every part of Nature's works, there

are numberless beauties, which, on account of our ignorance, we are unable to perceive. Superior beings may see more than we; but He only who made them, and, upon a review, pronounced them all to be very good, can see all their beauty.

Our determinations with regard to the beauty of objects, may, I think, be distinguished into two kinds; the first we may call instinctive, the other rational.

Some objects strike us at once, and appear beautiful at first sight, without any reflection, without our being able to say why we call them beautiful, or being able to specify any perfection which justifies our judgment. Something of this kind there seems to be in brute animals, and in children before the use of reason; nor does it end with infancy, but continues through life.

In the plumage of birds and of butterflies, in the colours and form of flowers, of shells, and of many other objects, we perceive a beauty that delights; but cannot say what it is in the object that should produce that emotion.

The beauty of the object may in such cases be called an occult quality. We know well how it affects our senses; but what it is in itself we know not. But this, as well as other occult qualities, is a proper subject of philosophical disquisition; and, by a careful examination of the objects to which Nature hath given this amiable quality, we may perhaps discover some real excellence in the object, or, at least, some valuable purpose that is served by the effect which it produces upon us.

This instinctive sense of beauty, in different species of animals, may differ as much as the external sense of taste, and in each species be adapted to its manner of life. By this perhaps the various tribes are led to associate with their kind, to dwell among certain objects rather than others, and to construct their habitation in a particular manner. [744]

There seem likewise to be varieties in the sense of beauty in the individuals of the same species, by which they are directed in the choice of a mate, and in the love and care of their offspring.

"We see," says Mr Addison, "that every different species of sensible creatures has its different notions of beauty, and that each of them is most affected with the beauties of its own kind. This is nowhere more remarkable than in birds of the same shape and proportion, where we often see the mate determined in his courtship by the single grain or tincture of a feather, and never discovering any charms but in the colour of its own species."

" Scit thalamo servare fidem, sanctasque veretur
Connubii leges; non illum in pectore candor
Sollicitat niveus; neque pravum accendit amorem

Splendida lanugo, vel honesta in vertice crista ;
Purpureusve nitor pennarum ; ast armina late
Fœminea explorat cautus, maculasque requirit
Cognatas, paribusque interlita e rpora guttis :
Ni faceret, pictis sylvam circum undique mons.
                tris
Confusam aspiceres vulgo, partusque biformes,
Et genus ambiguum, et veneris monumenta ne.
fandæ.

" Hinc merula in nigro se oblectat nigra marito;
Hinc socium lasciva petit philomela canorum,
Agnoscitque pares sonitus ; hinc noctua tetram
Canitiem alarum, et glaucos miratur ocellos.
Nempe sibi semper constat, crescitqu· quotannis
Lucida progenies, castos confessa parentes :
Vere novo exultat, plumasque decora juventus
Explicat ad solem, patriisque coloribus ardet."

In the human kind there are varieties in the taste of beauty, of which we can no more assign a reason than of the variety of their features, though it is easy to perceive that very important ends are answered by both. These varieties are most observable in the judgments we form of the features of the other sex ; and in this the intention of nature is most apparent. [745]

As far as our determinations of the comparative beauty of objects are instinctive, they are no subject of reasoning or of criticism ; they are purely the gift of nature, and we have no standard by which they may be measured.

But there are judgments of beauty that may be called rational, being grounded on some agreeable quality of the object which is distinctly conceived, and may be specified.

This distinction between a rational judgment of beauty and that which is instinctive, may be illustrated by an instance.

In a heap of pebbles, one that is remarkable for brilliancy of colour and regularity of figure, will be picked out of the heap by a child. He perceives a beauty in it, puts a value upon it, and is fond of the property of it. For this preference, no reason can be given, but that children are, by their constitution, fond of brilliant colours, and of regular figures.

Suppose again that an expert mechanic views a well constructed machine. He sees all its parts to be made of the fittest materials, and of the most proper form ; nothing superfluous, nothing deficient ; every part adapted to its use, and the whole fitted in the most perfect manner to the end for which it is intended. He pronounces it to be a beautiful machine. He views it with the same agreeable emotion as the child viewed the pebble ; but he can give a reason for his judgment, and point out the particular perfections of the object on which it is grounded. [746]

Although the instinctive and the rational sense of beauty may be perfectly distinguished in speculation, yet, in passing judgment upon particular objects, they are often so mixed and confounded, that it is difficult to assign to each its own province. Nay, it

[745-747]

may often happen, that a judgment of the beauty of an object, which was at first merely instinctive, shall afterwards become rational, when we discover some latent perfection of which that beauty in the object is a sign.

As the sense of beauty may be distinguished into instinctive and rational ; so I think beauty itself may be distinguished into original and derived.

As some objects shine by their own light, and many more by light that is borrowed and reflected ; so I conceive the lustre of beauty in some objects is inherent and original, and in many others is borrowed and reflected.

There is nothing more common in the sentiments of all mankind, and in the language of all nations, than what may be called a communication of attributes ; that is, transferring an attribute, from the subject to which it properly belongs, to some related or resembling subject.

The various objects which nature presents to our view, even those that are most different in kind, have innumerable similitudes, relations, and analogies, which we contemplate with pleasure, and which lead us naturally to borrow words and attributes from one object to express what belongs to another. The greatest part of every language under heaven is made up of words borrowed from one thing, and applied to something supposed to have some relation or analogy to their first signification. [747]

The attributes of body we ascribe to mind, and the attributes of mind to material objects. To inanimate things we ascribe life, and even intellectual and moral qualities. And, although the qualities that are thus made common belong to one of the subjects in the proper sense, and to the other metaphorically, these different senses are often so mixed in our imagination, as to produce the same sentiment with regard to both.

It is therefore natural, and agreeable to the strain of human sentiments and of human language, that in many cases the beauty which originally and properly is in the thing signified, should be transferred to the sign ; that which is in the cause to the effect ; that which is in the end to the means ; and that which is in the agent to the instrument.

If what was said in the last chapter of the distinction between the grandeur which we ascribe to qualities of mind, and that which we ascribe to material objects, be well founded, this distinction of the beauty of objects will easily be admitted as perfectly analagous to it. I shall therefore only illustrate it by an example.

There is nothing in the exterior of a man more lovely and more attractive than perfect good breeding. But what is this good breeding? It consists of all the external signs of due respect to our superiors, condescension to our inferiors, politeness to all with whom we converse or have to do, joined in the fair sex with that delicacy of outward behaviour which becomes them. And how comes it to have such charms in the eyes of all mankind; for this reason only, as I apprehend, that it is a natural sign of that temper, and those affections and sentiments with regard to others, and with regard to ourselves, which are in themselves truly amiable and beautiful.

This is the original, of which good breeding is the picture; and it is the beauty of the original that is reflected to our sense by the picture. The beauty of good breeding, therefore, is not originally in the external behaviour in which it consists, but is derived from the qualities of mind which it expresses. And though there may be good breeding without the amiable qualities of mind, its beauty is still derived from what it naturally expresses. [748]

Having explained these distinctions of our sense of beauty into instinctive and rational, and of beauty itself into original and derived, I would now proceed to give a general view of those qualities in objects, to which we may justly and rationally ascribe beauty, whether original or derived.

But here some embarrassment arises from the vague meaning of the word beauty, which I had occasion before to observe.

Sometimes it is extended, so as to include everything that pleases a good taste, and so comprehends grandeur and novelty, as well as what in a more restricted sense is called beauty. At other times, it is even by good writers confined to the objects of sight, when they are either seen, or remembered, or imagined. Yet it is admitted by all men, that there are beauties in music; that there is beauty as well as sublimity in composition, both in verse and in prose; that there is beauty in characters, in affections, and in actions. These are not objects of sight; and a man may be a good judge of beauty of various kinds, who has not the faculty of sight.

To give a determinate meaning to a word so variously extended and restricted, I know no better way than what is suggested by the common division of the objects of taste into novelty, grandeur, and beauty. Novelty, it is plain, is no quality of the new object, but merely a relation which it has to the knowledge of the person to whom it is new. Therefore, if this general division be just, every quality in an object that pleases a good taste, must, in one degree or another, have either grandeur or beauty. It may still be difficult to fix the precise limit betwixt grandeur and beauty; but they must together comprehend everything fitted by its nature to please a good taste— that is, every real perfection and excellence in the objects we contemplate. [749]

In a poem, in a picture, in a piece of music, it is real excellence that pleases a good taste. In a person, every perfection of the mind, moral or intellectual, and every perfection of the body, gives pleasure to the spectator, as well as to the owner, when there is no envy nor malignity to destroy that pleasure.

It is, therefore, in the scale of perfection and real excellence that we must look for what is either grand or beautiful in objects. What is the proper object of admiration is grand, and what is the proper object of love and esteem is beautiful.

This, I think, is the only notion of beauty that corresponds with the division of the objects of taste which has been generally received by philosophers. And this connection of beauty with real perfection, was a capital doctrine of the Socratic school. It is often ascribed to Socrates, in the dialogues of Plato and of Xenophon.

We may, therefore, take a view, first, of those qualities of mind to which we may justly and rationally ascribe beauty, and then of the beauty we perceive in the objects of sense. We shall find, if I mistake not, that, in the first, original beauty is to be found, and that the beauties of the second class are derived from some relation they bear to mind, as the signs or expressions of some amiable mental quality, or as the effects of design, art, and wise contrivance.

As grandeur naturally produces admiration, beauty naturally produces love. We may, therefore, justly ascribe beauty to those qualities which are the natural objects of love and kind affection.

Of this kind chiefly are some of the moral virtues, which, in a peculiar manner, constitute a lovely character. Innocence, gentleness, condescension, humanity, natural affection, public spirit, and the whole train of the soft and gentle virtues: these qualities are amiable from their very nature, and on account of their intrinsic worth. [750]

There are other virtues that raise admiration, and are, therefore, grand; such as magnanimity, fortitude, self-command, superiority to pain and labour, superiority to pleasure, and to the smiles of Fortune as well as to her frowns.

These awful virtues constitute what is most grand in the human character; the gentle virtues, what is most beautiful and lovely. As they are virtues, they draw the approbation of our moral faculty; as they are becoming and amiable, they affect our sense of beauty.

Next to the amiable moral virtues, there are many intellectual talents which have an intrinsic value, and draw our love and esteem to those who possess them. Such are, knowledge, good sense, wit, humour, cheerfulness, good taste, excellence in any of the fine arts, in eloquence, in dramatic action ; and, we may add, excellence in every art of peace or war that is useful in society.

There are likewise talents which we refer to the body, which have an original beauty and comeliness ; such as health, strength, and agility, the usual attendants of youth ; skill in bodily exercises, and skill in the mechanic arts. These are real perfections of the man, as they increase his power, and render the body a fit instrument for the mind.

I apprehend, therefore, that it is in the moral and intellectual perfections of mind, and in its active powers, that beauty originally dwells ; and that from this as the fountain, all the beauty which we perceive in the visible world is derived. [751]

This, I think, was the opinion of the ancient philosophers before-named ; and it has been adopted by Lord Shaftesbury and Dr Akenside among the moderns.

" Mind, mind alone, bear witness, earth and heav'n! The living fountains in itself contains Of beauteous and sublime. Here hand in hand Sit paramount the graces. Here enthron'd, Celestial Venus, with divinest airs, Invites the soul to never-fading joy."—*Akenside.*

But neither mind, nor any of its qualities or powers, is an immediate object of perception to man. We are, indeed, immediately conscious of the operations of our own mind ; and every degree of perfection in them gives the purest pleasure, with a proportional degree of self-esteem, so flattering to self-love, that the great difficulty is to keep it within just bounds, so that we may not think of ourselves above what we ought to think.

Other minds we perceive only through the medium of material objects, on which their signatures are impressed. It is through this medium that we perceive life, activity, wisdom, and every moral and intellectual quality in other beings. The signs of those qualities are immediately perceived by the senses ; by them the qualities themselves are reflected to our understanding ; and we are very apt to attribute to the sign the beauty or the grandeur which is properly and originally in the things signified.

The invisible Creator, the Fountain of all perfection, hath stamped upon all his works signatures of his divine wisdom, power, and benignity, which are visible to all men. The works of men in science, in the arts of taste, and in the mechanical arts, bear the signatures of those qualities of mind which were employed in their production. Their external behaviour and conduct in life expresses the good or bad qualities of their mind. [752]

[751–758]

In every species of animals, we perceive by visible signs their instincts, their appetites, their affections, their sagacity. Even in the inanimate world, there are many things analogous to the qualities of mind ; so that there is hardly anything belonging to mind which may not be represented by images taken from the objects of sense ; and, on the other hand, every object of sense is beautified, by borrowing attire from the attributes of mind.

Thus, the beauties of mind, though invisible in themselves, are perceived in the objects of sense, on which their image is impressed.

If we consider, on the other hand, the qualities in sensible objects to which we ascribe beauty, I apprehend we shall find in all of them some relation to mind, and the greatest in those that are most beautiful.

When we consider inanimate matter abstractly, as a substance endowed with the qualities of extension, solidity, divisibility, and mobility, there seems to be nothing in these qualities that affects our sense of beauty. But when we contemplate the globe which we inhabit, as fitted by its form, by its motions, and by its furniture, for the habitation and support of an infinity of various orders of living creatures, from the lowest reptile up to man, we have a glorious spectacle indeed ! with which the grandest and the most beautiful structures of human art can bear no comparison.

The only perfection of dead matter is its being, by its various forms and qualities, so admirably fitted for the purposes of animal life, and chiefly that of man. It furnishes the materials of every art that tends to the support or the embellishment of human life. By the Supreme Artist, it is organized in the various tribes of the vegetable kingdom, and endowed with a kind of life ; a work which human art cannot imitate, nor human understanding comprehend. [753]

In the bodies and various organs of the animal tribes, there is a composition of matter still more wonderful and more mysterious, though we see it to be admirably adapted to the purposes and manner of life of every species. But in every form, unorganized, vegetable, or animal, it derives its beauty from the purposes to which it is subservient, or from the signs of wisdom or of other mental qualities which it exhibits.

The qualities of inanimate matter, in which we perceive beauty, are—sound, colour, form, and motion ; the first an object of hearing, the other three of sight ; which we may consider in order.

In a single note, sounded by a very fine

voice, there is a beauty which we do not perceive in the same note, sounded by a bad voice or an imperfect instrument. I need not attempt to enumerate the perfections in a single note, which give beauty to it. Some of them have names in the science of music, and there perhaps are others which have no names. But I think it will be allowed, that every quality which gives beauty to a single note, is a sign of some perfection, either in the organ, whether it be the human voice or an instrument, or in the execution. The beauty of the sound is both the sign and the effect of this perfection; and the perfection of the cause is the only reason we can assign for the beauty of the effect.

In a composition of sounds, or a piece of music, the beauty is either in the harmony, the melody, or the expression. The beauty of expression must be derived, either from the beauty of the thing expressed, or from the art and skill employed in expressing it properly.

In harmony, the very names of concord and discord are metaphorical, and suppose some analogy between the relations of sound, to which they are figuratively applied, and the relations of minds and affections, which they originally and properly signify. [754]

As far as I can judge by my ear, when two or more persons, of a good voice and ear, converse together in amity and friendship, the tones of their different voices are concordant, but become discordant when they give vent to angry passions; so that, without hearing what is said, one may know by the tones of the different voices, whether they quarrel or converse amicably. This, indeed, is not so easily perceived in those who have been taught, by good-breeding, to suppress angry tones of voice, even when they are angry, as in the lowest rank, who express their angry passions without any restraint.

When discord arises occasionally in conversation, but soon terminates in perfect amity, we receive more pleasure than from perfect unanimity. In like manner, in the harmony of music, discordant sounds are occasionally introduced, but it is always in order to give a relish to the most perfect concord that follows.

Whether these analogies, between the harmony of a piece of music, and harmony in the intercourse of minds, be merely fanciful, or have any real foundation in fact, I submit to those who have a nicer ear, and have applied it to observations of this kind. If they have any just foundation, as they seem to me to have, they serve to account for the metaphorical application of the names of concord and discord to the relations of sounds; to account for the pleasure we have from harmony in music; and to

shew, that the beauty of harmony is derived from the relation it has to agreeable affections of mind.

With regard to melody, I leave it to the adepts in the science of music, to determine whether music, composed according to the established rules of harmony and melody, can be altogether void of expression; and whether music that has no expression can have any beauty. To me it seems, that every strain in melody that is agreeable, is an imitation of the tones of the human voice in the expression of some sentiment or passion, or an imitation of some other object in nature; and that music, as well as poetry, is an imitative art. [755]

The sense of beauty in the colours, and in the motions of inanimate objects, is, I believe, in some cases instinctive. We see that children and savages are pleased with brilliant colours and sprightly motions. In persons of an improved and rational taste, there are many sources from which colours and motions may derive their beauty. They, as well as the forms of objects, admit of regularity and variety. The motions produced by machinery, indicate the perfection or imperfection of the mechanism, and may be better or worse adapted to their end, and from that derive their beauty or deformity. The colours of natural objects, are commonly signs of some good or bad quality in the object; or they may suggest to the imagination something agreeable or disagreeable.

In dress and furniture, fashion has a considerable influence on the preference we give to one colour above another.

A number of clouds of different and ever-changing hue, seen on the ground of a serene azure sky, at the going down of the sun, present to the eye of every man a glorious spectacle. It is hard to say, whether we should call it grand or beautiful. It is both in a high degree. Clouds towering above clouds, variously tinged, according as they approach nearer to the direct rays of the sun, enlarge our conceptions of the regions above us. They give us a view of the furniture of those regions, which, in an unclouded air, seem to be a perfect void; but are now seen to contain the stores of wind and rain, bound up for the present, but to be poured down upon the earth in due season. Even the simple rustic does not look upon this beautiful sky, merely as a show to please the eye, but as a happy omen of fine weather to come.

The proper arrangement of colour, and of light and shade, is one of the chief beauties of painting; but this beauty is greatest, when that arrangement gives the most distinct, the most natural, and the most agreeable image of that which the painter intended to represent. [756]

If we consider, in the last place, the beauty of form or figure in inanimate objects, this, according to Dr Hutcheson, results from regularity, mixed with variety. Here, it ought to be observed, that regularity, in all cases, expresses design and art: for nothing regular was ever the work of chance; and where regularity is joined with variety, it expresses design more strongly. Besides, it has been justly observed, that regular figures are more easily and more perfectly comprehended by the mind than the irregular, of which we can never form an adequate conception.

Although straight lines and plain surfaces have a beauty from their regularity, they admit of no variety, and, therefore, are beauties of the lowest order. Curve lines and surfaces admit of infinite variety, joined with every degree of regularity; and, therefore, in many cases, excel in beauty those that are straight.

But the beauty arising from regularity and variety, must always yield to that which arises from the fitness of the form for the end intended. In everything made for an end, the form must be adapted to that end; and everything in the form that suits the end, is a beauty; everything that unfits it for its end, is a deformity.

The forms of a pillar, of a sword, and of a balance are very different. Each may have great beauty; but that beauty is derived from the fitness of the form and of the matter for the purpose intended. [757]

Were we to consider the form of the earth itself, and the various furniture it contains, of the inanimate kind; its distribution into land and sea, mountains and valleys, rivers and springs of water, the variety of soils that cover its surface, and of mineral and metallic substances laid up within it, the air that surrounds it, the vicissitudes of day and night, and of the seasons: the beauty of all these, which indeed is superlative, consists in this, that they bear the most lively and striking impression of the wisdom and goodness of their Author, in contriving them so admirably for the use of man, and of their other inhabitants.

The beauties of the vegetable kingdom are far superior to those of inanimate matter, in any form which human art can give it. Hence, in all ages, men have been fond to adorn their persons and their habitations with the vegetable productions of nature.

The beauties of the field, of the forest, and of the flower-garden, strike a child long before he can reason. He is delighted with what he sees; but he knows not why. This is instinct, but it is not confined to childhood; it continues through all the stages of life. It leads the florist, the botanist, the philosopher, to examine and compare the objects which Nature, by this powerful instinct, recommends to his attention. By degrees, he becomes a critic in beauties of this kind, and can give a reason why he prefers one to another. In every species, he sees the greatest beauty in the plants or flowers that are most perfect in their kind—which have neither suffered from unkindly soil nor inclement weather; which have not been robbed of their nourishment by other plants, nor hurt by any accident. When he examines the internal structure of those productions of Nature, and traces them from their embryo state in the seed to their maturity, he sees a thousand beautiful contrivances of Nature, which feast his understanding more than their external form delighted his eye.

Thus, every beauty in the vegetable creation, of which he has formed any rational judgment, expresses some perfection in the object, or some wise contrivance in its Author. [758]

In the animal kingdom, we perceive still greater beauties than in the vegetable. Here we observe life, and sense, and activity, various instincts and affections, and, in many cases, great sagacity. These are attributes of mind, and have an original beauty.

As we allow to brute animals a thinking principle or mind, though far inferior to that which is in man; and as, in many of their intellectual and active powers, they very much resemble the human species, their actions, their motions, and even their looks, derive a beauty from the powers of thought which they express.

There is a wonderful variety in their manner of life; and we find the powers they possess, their outward form, and their inward structure, exactly adapted to it. In every species, the more perfectly any individual is fitted for its end and manner of life, the greater is its beauty.

In a race-horse, everything that expresses agility, ardour, and emulation, gives beauty to the animal. In a pointer, acuteness of scent, eagerness on the game, and tractableness, are the beauties of the species. A sheep derives its beauty from the fineness and quantity of its fleece; and in the wild animals, every beauty is a sign of their perfection in their kind.

It is an observation of the celebrated Linnæus, that, in the vegetable kingdom, the poisonous plants have commonly a lurid and disagreeable appearance to the eye, of which he gives many instances. I apprehend the observation may be extended to the animal kingdom, in which we commonly see something shocking to the eye in the noxious and poisonous animals.

The beauties which anatomists and physiologists describe in the internal structure of the various tribes of animals; in the organs of sense, of nutrition, and of motion, are expressive of wise design and contrivance, in fitting them for the various kinds of life for which they are intended. [759]

Thus, I think, it appears that the beauty which we perceive in the inferior animals, is expressive, either of such perfections as their several natures may receive, or expressive of wise design in Him who made them, and that their beauty is derived from the perfections which it expresses.

But of all the objects of sense, the most striking and attractive beauty is perceived in the human species, and particularly in the fair sex.

Milton represents Satan himself, in surveying the furniture of this globe, as struck with the beauty of the first happy pair.

" Two of far nobler shape, erect and tall,
Godlike erect! with native honour clad
In naked majesty, seem'd lords of all.
And worthy seem'd, for in their looks divine,
The image of their glorious Maker, shone
Truth, wisdom, sanctitude severe and pure;
Severe, but in true filial freedom plac'd,
Whence true authority in man : though both
Not equal, as their sex not equal seem'd,
For contemplation he, and valour form'd,
For softness she, and sweet attractive grace."

In this well-known passage of Milton, we see that this great poet derives the beauty of the first pair in Paradise from those expressions of moral and intellectual qualities which appeared in their outward form and demeanour.

The most minute and systematical account of beauty in the human species, and particularly in the fair sex, I have met with, is in " Crito; or, a Dialogue on Beauty," said to be written by the author of " Polymetis,"* and republished by Dodsley in his collection of fugitive pieces. [760]

I shall borrow from that author some observations, which, I think, tend to shew that the beauty of the human body is derived from the signs it exhibits of some perfection of the mind or person.

All that can be called beauty in the human species may be reduced to these four heads : colour, form, expression, and grace. The two former may be called the body, the two latter the soul of beauty.

The beauty of colour is not owing solely to the natural liveliness of flesh-colour and red, nor to the much greater charms they receive from being properly blended together; but is also owing, in some degree, to the idea they carry with them of good health, without which all beauty grows languid and less engaging, and with which it always recovers an additional strength and lustre. This is supported by the authority of Cicero. *Venustas et pulchritudo corporis secerni non potest a valetudine.*

* Spence, under the name of Sir Harry Beaumont.—H.

Here I observe, that, as the colour of the body is very different in different climates, every nation preferring the colour of its climate, and as, among us, one man prefers a fair beauty, another a brunette, without being able to give any reason for this preference; this diversity of taste has no standard in the common principles of human nature, but must arise from something that is different in different nations, and in different individuals of the same nation.

I observed before, that fashion, habit, associations, and perhaps some peculiarity of constitution, may have great influence upon this internal sense, as well as upon the external. Setting aside the judgments arising from such causes, there seems to remain nothing that, according to the common judgment of mankind, can be called beauty in the colour of the species, but what expresses perfect health and liveliness, and in the fair sex softness and delicacy; and nothing that can be called deformity but what indicates disease and decline. And if this be so, it follows, that the beauty of colour is derived from the perfections which it expresses. This, however, of all the ingredients of beauty, is the least. [761]

The next in order is form, or proportion of parts. The most beautiful form, as the author thinks, is that which indicates delicacy and softness in the fair sex, and in the male either strength or agility. The beauty of form, therefore, lies all in expression.

The third ingredient, which has more power than either colour or form, he calls expression, and observes, that it is only the expression of the tender and kind passions that gives beauty; that all the cruel and unkind ones add to deformity; and that, on this account, good nature may very justly be said to be the best feature, even in the finest face. Modesty, sensibility, and sweetness, blended together, so as either to enliven or to correct each other, give almost as much attraction as the passions are capable of adding to a very pretty face.

It is owing, says the author, to the great force of pleasingness which attends all the kinder passions, that lovers not only seem, but really are, more beautiful to each other than they are to the rest of the world; because, when they are together, the most pleasing passions are more frequently exerted in each of their faces than they are in either before the rest of the world. There is then, as a French author very well expresses it, a soul upon their countenances, which does not appear when they are absent from one another, or even in company that lays a restraint upon their features.

There is a great difference in the same face, according as the person is in a better or a worse humour, or more or less lively. The best complexion, the finest features, and the exactest shape, without anything of the mind expressed in the face, is insipid and unmoving. The finest eyes in the world, with an excess of malice or rage in them, will grow shocking. The passions can give beauty without the assistance of colour or form, and take it away where these have united most strongly to give it; and therefore this part of beauty is greatly superior to the other two. [762]

The last and noblest part of beauty is grace, which the author thinks undefinable.

Nothing causes love so generally and irresistibly as grace. Therefore, in the mythology of the Greeks and Romans, the Graces were the constant attendants of Venus the goddess of love. Grace is like the cestus of the same goddess, which was supposed to comprehend everything that was winning and engaging, and to create love by a secret and inexplicable force, like that of some magical charm.

There are two kinds of grace—the majestic and the familiar; the first more commanding, the last more delightful and engaging. The Grecian painters and sculptors used to express the former most strongly in the looks and attitudes of their Minervas, and the latter in those of Venus. This distinction is marked in the description of the personages of Virtue and Pleasure in the ancient fable of the Choice of Hercules.

" Graceful, but each with different grace they move,
This striking sacred awe, that softer winning love."

In the persons of Adam and Eve in Paradise, Milton has made the same distinction—

" For contemplation he, and valour formed,
For softness she, and sweet attractive grace."[763]

Though grace be so difficult to be defined, there are two things that hold universally with relation to it. *First*, There is no grace without motion; some genteel or pleasing motion, either of the whole body or of some limb, or at least some feature. Hence, in the face, grace appears only on those features that are moveable, and change with the various emotions and sentiments of the mind, such as the eyes and eyebrows, the mouth and parts adjacent. When Venus appeared to her son Æneas in disguise, and, after some conversation with him, retired, it was by the grace of her motion in retiring that he discovered her to be truly a goddess.

" Dixit, et avertens rosea cervice refulsit,
Ambrosiæque comæ divinum vertice odorem
Spiravere; pedes vestis defluxit ad imos;
Et vera incessu patuit dea. Ille, ubi matrem
Agnovit," &c.

A *second* observation is, That there can be no grace with impropriety, or that nothing can be graceful that is not adapted to the character and situation of the person.

From these observations, which appear [726-765.]

to me to be just, we may, I think, conclude, that grace, as far as it is visible, consists of those motions, either of the whole body, or of a part or feature, which express the most perfect propriety of conduct and sentiment in an amiable character.

Those motions must be different in different characters; they must vary with every variation of emotion and sentiment; they may express either dignity or respect, confidence or reserve, love or just resentment, esteem or indignation, zeal or indifference. Every passion, sentiment, or emotion, that in its nature and degree is just and proper, and corresponds perfectly with the character of the person, and with the occasion, is what may we call the soul of grace. The body or visible part consists of those emotions and features which give the true and unaffected expression of this soul. [764]

Thus, I think, all the ingredients of human beauty, as they are enumerated and described by this ingenious author, terminate in expression: they either express some perfection of the body, as a part of the man, and an instrument of the mind, or some amiable quality or attribute of the mind itself.

It cannot, indeed, be denied, that the expression of a fine countenance may be unnaturally disjoined from the amiable qualities which it naturally expresses: but we presume the contrary till we have clear evidence; and even then we pay homage to the expression, as we do to the throne when it happens to be unworthily filled.

Whether what I have offered to shew, that all the beauty of the objects of sense is borrowed, and derived from the beauties of mind which it expresses or s ggests to the imagination, be well-founded or not, I hope this terrestrial Venus will not be deemed less worthy of the homage which has always been paid to her, by being conceived more nearly allied to the celestial than she has commonly been represented.

To make an end of this subject, taste seems to be progressive as man is. Children, when refreshed by sleep, and at ease from pain and hunger, are disposed to attend to the objects about them; they are pleased with brilliant colours, gaudy ornaments, regular forms, cheerful countenances, noisy mirth and glee. Such is the taste of childhood, which we must conclude to be given for wise purposes. A great part of the happiness of that period of life is derived from it; and, therefore, it ought to be indulged. It leads them to attend to objects which they may afterwards find worthy of their attention. It puts them upon exerting their infant faculties of body and mind, which, by such exertions, are daily strengthened and improved. [765]

As they advance in years and in understanding, other beauties attract their attention, which, by their novelty or superiority, throw a shade upon those they formerly admired. They delight in feats of agility, strength, and art; they love those that excel in them, and strive to equal them. In the tales and fables they hear, they begin to discern beauties of mind. Some characters and actions appear lovely, others give disgust. The intellectual and moral powers begin to open, and, if cherished by favourable circumstances, advance gradually in strength, till they arrive at that degree of perfection to which human nature, in its present state, is limited.

In our progress from infancy to maturity, our faculties open in a regular order appointed by Nature; the meanest first, those of more dignity in succession, until the moral and rational powers finish the man. Every faculty furnishes new notions, brings new beauties into view, and enlarges the province of taste; so that we may say, there is a taste of childhood, a taste of youth, and a manly taste. Each is beautiful in its season; but not so much so, when carried beyond its season. Not that the man ought to dislike the things that please the child or the youth, but to put less value upon them, compared with other beauties, with which he ought to be acquainted.

Our moral and rational powers justly claim dominion over the whole man. Even taste is not exempted from their authority; it must be subject to that authority in every case wherein we pretend to reason or dispute about matters of taste; it is the voice of reason that our love or our admiration

ought to be proportioned to the merit of the object. When it is not grounded on real worth, it must be the effect of constitution, or of some habit, or casual association. A fond mother may see a beauty in her darling child, or a fond author in his work, to which the rest of the world are blind. In such cases, the affection is pre-engaged, and, as it were, bribes the judgment, to make the object worthy of that affection. For the mind cannot be easy in putting a value upon an object beyond what it conceives to be due. When affection is not carried away by some natural or acquired bias, it naturally is and ought to be led by the judgment.   [766]

As, in the division which I have followed of our intellectual powers, I mentioned Moral Perception and Consciousness, the reader may expect that some reason should be given, why they are not treated of in this place.

As to Consciousness, what I think necessary to be said upon it has been already said, Essay vi., chap. 5. As to the faculty of moral perception, it is indeed a most important part of human understanding, and well worthy of the most attentive consideration, since without it we could have no conception of right and wrong, of duty and moral obligation, and since the first principles of morals, upon which all moral reasoning must be grounded, are its immediate dictates; but, as it is an active as well as an intellectual power, and has an immediate relation to the other active powers of the mind, I apprehend that it is proper to defer the consideration of it till these be explained.

24578428R00299

Printed in Great Britain
by Amazon